THE GODDESSESS

LOVE UNDERGROUND

Persephone's Tale

❧

Alicia Fields

A SIGNET ECLIPSE BOOK

Persephone laughed, and he looked hurt. "You don't want to be a hero, either. They made you. They burnt some offering and made a lot of smoke, and old Hesperia went into a trance and said the first thing that came into her head. And it was you, because you'd been braggy. I know you."

"You do," he conceded. "That's why I have to marry you. Someone who didn't know me would never put up with me."

"And you think that's an enticement? Nobody will marry you if that's the way you propose."

"I am not proposing," he said. He moved a step closer, pressing her against the wall. "You have been given to me, which is the proper way to do it. Girls don't get to pick their husbands. They are chosen for them, and your mother chose me."

"Well, I chose someone else!" She pushed him, hard, and he staggered back a bit. He lunged at her, gripping her arm, and she sank her teeth into his shoulder.

"Ow! You she-cat!" His hand closed tighter on her arm. She struggled, and her fist connected with his nose. It felt satisfactory, the way she remembered feeling when she had rolled him in the mud for stealing eggs from Demeter's hens when they were seven, and blaming it on her.

Hermes stumbled away from her. "You had better come with me," he said, panting, "and have that baby born in the upper air. If you don't it's likely to be a monster." His nose was bloody, and he put a hand to it. "It may be a monster anyway. You're lucky I'm still willing to have you."

"You've wanted me since we were eight and you got me to let you look under my dress," Persephone said. "You just didn't want to marry me."

"Well, I do now. And anyway I can't go home without you. Your mother will make it rain forever."

"Mother will be fine now." Persephone knew that, too, in some mysterious way. Her mother's garden was growing again and things were coming out of it, and that would be all right. Persephone was surprised by the things that she knew now. How very odd to have learned about the people of the upper air by living underground. Hermes looked at her doggedly. She didn't think he had learned anything and probably wouldn't because he already knew too much. "Oh, Hermes, stop and think about it," she said. "You know you don't want to get married. You'll make an awful husband, and your wife will be just like Bopis, scurrying around after you, trying to keep you home."

"And that monster will make you a better one?" Hermes's pride was stung.

"Don't be an idiot. He isn't a monster." But she thought of the Minotaur for a moment, the monster of King Minos's caverns. His wife had mated with a bull and borne that. No. Her hand brushed against her belly protectively.

Hermes saw it. "See? You *are* afraid. Come out of here with me now. If it's a monster we'll expose it, and no one will have to know."

My child? If it's a monster I will nurse it at my breast as Pasiphaë did. "No," she said. "I will stay, and what will happen will happen. Now, go away."

Hermes was silent a moment, thinking. "All right. Show me the door."

"It's just ahead."

"I can't see it. I'm afraid of this place, and I don't

trust *him*. Guide me to the entrance if you want me to leave."

"Very well," she said stiffly. "Come this way."

He walked silently behind her down the sloping corridor, while the stone travelers flowed in the other direction. For a moment he thought they made room for him on the wall. Beckoning hands invited him in. He turned his head from them quickly lest he fall into the stone.

"There," Persephone said. She halted at the wide mouth of the cavern entrance.

"It will still be high tide," Hermes said.

"Look." Persephone stepped a few paces through the entrance. The light outside was clear and golden, and the floor was dry, littered with shrunken patches of seaweed and half-buried shells. His lost hat lay upside down on the sand.

"It must be illusion," Hermes said stubbornly. "He is trying to drown us. It was high tide an hour ago."

"It isn't now," Persephone said. "Time is odd here. Now, go."

He hesitated a moment, shifting from foot to foot, apparently watching the light outside. A gull squawked in the air above the cavern mouth. Persephone moved to stand beside him.

"Go," she said. "Go and tell Mother I am content here."

His hand shot out, grasping her wrist, and his other arm came about her waist. He lifted her half off her feet.

"Let me go!"

"You'll feel differently when you are out of this place," he panted, struggling with her.

"Hades *will* kill you!" she gasped. "Let me go!"

"I am sent by Zeus," Hermes said stubbornly. "Zeus commands even him. Be still!"

She bit his ear, tasting blood.

"Stop that!" His hand covered her face as he tried to get her over his shoulder, and she writhed in his grip as she had writhed in Hades's. Hermes wasn't as big. She pounded his back with her fists and swung her knee into his groin. She sank her teeth in his shoulder again. He howled, but he didn't drop her.

She flailed at him, cursing him and shrieking. Someone would hear her. She wasn't going to go with him. Where was Cerberus?

"I will curse you!" she shouted into his bloody ear. His nose was bleeding badly, too. "I will make it wither and fall off. Mother could do it, and I can do it, too, and I will!"

Hermes didn't say anything, just staggered on toward the open air while she writhed and beat at him with her fists. The two sentinel stones stopped him. He couldn't pass between them with her hanging on his back. He set her down and began dragging her through by her wrists.

She fought him, but he was stronger than she had thought. "You'll never carry me up that cliff!" she gasped at him.

"We'll see." Hermes jerked her between the stones, and their momentum flung them out under the overhanging roof of rock. He pulled her from under it into the sunlight before she could dig her heels in.

Demeter sat up in the bed, her wild hair tangled about her head. Before Triptolemus could ask where

she was going, she had flung on her gown and
pulled her mantle about her shoulders.

He followed her to the door.

"I heard her!"

"Heard who?"

She didn't answer him. She just ran barefoot
through the garden, her feet making urgent prints in
the soft earth of the cabbage bed. She splashed across
the brook and set out at a run across the headland,
toward the cliff.

Triptolemus stood scratching his head in the doorway. He ought, he supposed, to follow her. He
doubted it would change whatever was going to happen, but it seemed like a gesture that had to be made.
He reached for his tunic.

The sunlight struck Persephone's face in a shower
of light, like warm luminescent water. She turned
toward it, gasping, breathing in the scent of salt and
flowers and hay.

"See?" Hermes said. He was shaking, as if he had
run for miles. "It calls to you."

Why hadn't it called to her when she had explored
the beach? When she had sailed across the sea? Why
now and not then?

Something huge and silent surged past her, nearly
bowling her over, and leaped on Hermes.

"Call him off!" Hermes shouted, staring into Cerberus's enormous mouth. The dog's lips were drawn
back and he growled, a deep rumble that Hermes
could feel clear through the paws pinning him to
the sand.

"Cerberus! Come!" The dog backed away reluc-

tantly. "Leave him be." Hermes had grown paler, his face drawn.

"Guard!" a voice said. It was not Persephone's voice; it was Hades's, and Hermes saw him standing on the sand behind Persephone as if he had materialized out of the stone. Cerberus froze. "He will kill you if I tell him to," Hades said amiably.

Hermes sat up, his white face smeared with blood. "Zeus commands you to release her," he said. His tongue felt thick in his mouth.

"He commands nothing of the sort. And if he did, I have no reason to obey."

Hermes stood with an effort, straightening his blood-smeared tunic. He eyed Cerberus nervously. Cerberus gave him a fanged smile. Persephone watched them. This was not over. Something more would happen. She knew both of them well enough to know that. And something was wrong with Hermes. His arms looked like bones. The smell of the air overwhelmed her, thick with grapes and rosemary and the dusty scent of daisies.

There was a flash of light, and she saw the knife in Hermes's hand. He had had it hidden in his tunic. He lunged at Hades, and Hades's arm shot out to close around his wrist. They grappled with each other on the sand. Hermes was smaller, but he was strong and wiry and he had the knife. Cerberus, growling, followed the men with his dark gaze.

They broke apart and circled each other, seeking the advantage. Hermes's red hair was plastered to his head with sweat and blood, and his green eyes were sunken and sullen. He had started this; he would not back down now and be made a fool of. The sun that blazed off the water and the sand

flashed on the knife again. Hermes leaped at Hades, and a line of red opened along Hades's left arm.

The knowledge that one was bound to kill the other over her made her desperate. Persephone flung herself at them, and the knife flashed by her ear. "Enough!"

Hermes froze, staring at the knife in terror. Hades didn't back away until she faced him and said between her teeth, "This was about choice. You are not the one with the choice to make." She spun and pointed a finger at Hermes. "And nor are you!" Then she turned slowly, staring at the path down the cliff face. "And nor are you, Mother," she said and set out toward the steps. Demeter was nearly at the bottom by the time she reached them.

"Oh my girl!" Demeter held out her arms, and Persephone went into them.

"Mother!" She clung to Demeter. Her mother smelled of the garden, a scent compounded of beans and figs and green wheat. She breathed it in, like drinking wine too fast, and staggered against Demeter.

"I've come to take you home."

That was why. Because now was the time to choose, not on Hades's ship or in the storm that Triptolemus had come out of. Now, when her mother stood in her arms, and it was all so achingly clear how much she loved her, and the smells of the earth. She turned to look at Hades, standing stock-still on the sand. He wasn't even watching Hermes anymore. He was watching her.

"No." It was barely a whisper, but she could feel the word growing louder. "No."

Demeter couldn't hear it. "He has put some en-

chantment over you," she said. She marched toward Hades, and a wind whipped up around her feet, thrashing her skirts in its fingers. "Thief!" she spat the word at him.

He bowed his head in a wary gesture of respect. "What I stole is free to go." His voice was sad.

"Set her free."

"I do." He looked gravely at Persephone. He had seen her growing drunk on the air that shone around her like a veil.

Hermes, ignored, glanced from Persephone to the cliff face and back. He sidled toward her, reaching for her arm.

"No." Hades hadn't appeared to see him, but now he bent and plucked a piece of wood from the sand. It might once have been a traveler's staff. Persephone could have sworn it had not been there before. He balanced it in both hands. "I believe this may be yours. You must have lost it on the way in. That happens. People come here burdened with too many things, and they lose them. There's your hat, too."

Hermes looked as if he were going to lunge at Hades again.

"I am very tired of you," Hades said. His eyes flashed with anger, and he pushed Hermes hard with the staff until Hermes staggered. Then he bent over him and said something Persephone couldn't hear. When he was through, he turned back to Demeter, paying Hermes no more attention.

A hand fell on Hermes's shoulder. "You should come back with me now," Triptolemus told him. "You don't know how long you've been gone."

Hermes felt his stomach cramping. His vision

smeared oddly across the sky and water. "What do you mean?"

"Time is odd here. I was underground a few weeks, and a whole season had come and gone when I came out."

"I didn't eat," Hermes said. That seemed now as if it might have been bad advice. He held his hands out in front of him. They were clawlike, the skin stretched on bones.

"That would be it then," Triptolemus said. "You've been gone a month, lad." Hermes was weaving on his feet now. Triptolemus picked him up and slung him over his shoulder. "It's a long way up the cliff, lad. Best to set out now before they start in. It'll spoil the weather for sure."

"What did you do to him?" Demeter demanded of Hades.

"Nothing he didn't do to himself. People are like that, I find."

"Give me back my child." Her expression alternated between pleading and anger, and the wind swirled around her head, making her hair fly with sparks.

"I have. I saw her with you. She longs for you."

"You are wise," Demeter said grimly.

"No." Persephone's voice was barely a whisper, but they both heard it this time. It grew out of the earth under her feet and the cold salt air. It was almost visible, and it had a scent like roses. It stilled Demeter's wind. "No. Mother, forgive me. I love you, but I don't want your life."

Demeter's eyes widened. Hades looked a little startled, too. Persephone tested this newfound power.

She spoke again, and the words floated on a summer breeze. "I will choose, because I am not yours, and not his. I am mine." *Mine.* It was a very satisfactory word.

Demeter's eyes teared. "I can't bear to lose you. How am I to bring you home, then?"

"By inviting me," Persephone said. "I'll bring your grandchild."

Demeter's mouth tightened for a moment, and then she closed her eyes. The rest of her wind fell into stillness.

"Look." Persephone pointed to the figures halfway up the cliff path. "That is a good man. I'm glad you didn't kill him. I'll come to see you both, with the baby."

"Is that a promise?"

"Always. And tell Hermes I forgive him, but being a hero doesn't suit him." She held her arms out, and Demeter clung to her.

Slowly, after a long while, Demeter pulled away. "As soon as the baby comes. Promise me."

"I promise, Mother."

Demeter set out for the cliff path then, and a gentle breeze followed her, smelling of roses.

Persephone looked at Hades. "What did you say to Hermes?" she asked him quietly.

"I told him I would give him to the bones that sleep in the cellars," Hades said. "I meant it, and he believed me."

"Why? He was already half-dead of hunger." His flesh had fallen away slowly as she watched him, the moment they had come out into the sun.

Hades closed his eyes for a moment with a look

of infinite pain. "I thought I had lost you," he whispered. "I was angry. I had to put it somewhere."

Persephone took his arm. "No, you'll have me forever now. I hope you don't change your mind. I don't think this is a choice I can unmake."

"Never." He looked at her solemnly. She stood on tiptoe to kiss him, startling him. His eyes flashed with elation and relief, and she felt his hand tremble as he took her elbow and led her back into the cavern. Cerberus padded at their heels. "You are a mess," he said finally. "I hope that is not your blood."

"No, it's all Hermes's." She looked at his arm a long time but didn't say anything.

"You are wondering about my blood," Hades said. "I do have some, as you can see," he said, turning the words to a small joke.

"Hermes said . . ." She bit her lip.

"Hermes said you have married a monster unwittingly. I know; I was listening."

"Did you hear everything?"

"Enough to see your doubts about the child."

Persephone put her hand over her belly again. "I thought of the story you told me of Minos's monster, about Pasiphaë. That was her child, no matter how she got it. What did she think when her husband chained it up?"

"Well, it was reputed to be violent."

"It was her child."

"It's a story."

"Stories are powerful. That's something I learned here."

Hades smiled then. "Ours is not going to be a

monster. You may examine my head for horns if you wish."

"Narcissa is dead. Did you know?"

"I did." Hades put his arm around her shoulders. "I dislike knowing things like that, but we take the knowledge that comes to us. It is always better than ignorance."

"Are you sure?" They passed by the corridor that led to the kitchen garden, and she turned down it. He followed her.

"If she was dead and you didn't know it, you still wouldn't have her."

Scylla beamed at them as they came through the kitchen. "The young hero gone off home, I see."

"Yes, he couldn't stay longer," Hades said, "but he'll get a hero's welcome up above all the same. He's been gone a month."

"I told him time was strange here," Persephone said. "I don't understand it myself."

"Think of it as circular," Hades said. "I do. It makes things simpler."

Persephone thought that sounded doubtful, but it didn't matter. It was what it was. She went into the garden and sat down on a bench under Pomona's pomegranate tree. The pomegranates were just beginning to form at the blossom ends, round little fruits like marbles. She picked one and balanced it in her hand. "The stubborn fool never would eat the whole time he was here."

"Just as well," Hades said. "I have found there is some truth to that rumor. One can leave, of course, but one will come back."

Everyone has to come back, Persephone thought. She laughed. "So when I go to visit Mother, I will have

to come back?" That might be useful. You couldn't argue with fated things.

"True. But she can visit you, too, for that matter. As you can see, the living come here fairly often."

"When the baby comes," Persephone said. She rubbed her fingers over her stomach, feeling the possibilities inside.

Everyone knew she was trouble from the start. Even Zeus knew it the minute he saw her. For one thing, she didn't have that look that newborn babies always had—slightly squashed and slit-eyed as if they weren't quite awake yet. This one's eyes were wide open and she looked like someone who had arrived to take charge. *I am here,* that look said. *Watch out.* And she was beautiful, which newborn babies also rarely are. Her eyes were the color of lapis lazuli, not the slate blue of normal newborns, and her hair was a cloud of rose gold curls just as long as the first joint of his finger. Like everyone else, he fell in love.

The farm he brought her home to was in Argolis, on the fertile plain that lay below the hill fort village of Tiryns. There his family raised cattle, goats, and olives and were a power in the world. The rest of the household took one look at her and knew trouble when they saw it, too. To begin with, Zeus claimed he had found her on a fishing trip off Cythera. He said, casually, that she had been lying in the surf, an exposed baby left to die, as surplus girl children often were.

"And why exactly do we need another one?" Hera inquired. She fixed the baby with steely gray eyes,

looking from the child to Zeus and back again, perhaps measuring their features against each other. "We have a daughter."

"A playmate for Hebe," Zeus said jovially.

Hebe looked up from her dolls and smiled at Mama and Papa. Hebe was a biddable child.

"This house doesn't need another mouth to feed," old Rhea said, stumping into the nursery on her two canes.

"Let me worry about that, Mother," Zeus said. His mouth compressed slightly and a tic started under his left eye, the tic that his mother always produced in him.

"Always bringing home your bastard brats." Rhea mouthed the remaining stumps of her teeth. "You'll be putting your poor mother out into the snow next, to make room for them."

"It hardly ever snows, Mother."

"It might as well," old Cronos said, joining her. "Death song for this farm. Going to go under soon the way you and your brothers run it. I might as well die now."

Zeus looked at his father with exasperation. Cronos was nearly as bent as Rhea, they were like two malevolent bears, half crouched over their canes. Hera stood with her arms crossed, tapping her long fingers on the folds of her gown. This was between her and Zeus. Stubbornly, she refused to take advantage of his parents' opinions on the child. Shortly after her marriage Hera had found herself drawn into the ongoing war in which Zeus, his siblings and his parents continually engaged, and from which no one ever escaped.

"If you'd married a woman with some fire to her you wouldn't be out rutting with servingmaids in a hay barn every night," Cronos said, reminding her why.

"I told you, Father. I found the child," Zeus said between his teeth. "In the surf. She was wet and cold."

"No need for another girl," Cronos said. "Waste of resources."

"Should have exposed the last one," Rhea said.

Hebe, playing with her dolls on the nursery floor

beside her brothers, pretended she hadn't heard that. Hebe was seven, quite old enough to understand things. That particular thing she had been hearing all her life, so that she hardly took notice anymore.

"That other one, too," Rhea said. "The deformed one. Ill luck to keep that one. I said so." She pointed a wavering finger at Hephaestus, who sat with his brother and Hebe, pounding a wooden block with his wooden hammer.

"That will do!" Hera turned on her mother-in-law with fire in her eye. "Get out!" She flapped her mantle at Rhea as if she were shooing chickens. "Out! Get out or I *will* put you outside. I'll put your bed in the barn!"

"Zeus! Are you going to let her talk to me that way? She's wicked! She'll freeze me to death! Save your poor old mother!" Rhea sucked her teeth at Hera with a malign glare, tottering on her canes. She sifted both of them to one hand and crossed her fingers against the evil eye with the other, nearly toppling herself over.

"This isn't your business, Mother."

"Ungrateful children come to a bad end, always," Cronos grumbled. He had been tall in his youth, but was bent so nearly double with age that he had to cock his head to look up at Zeus with a mad eye.

"Or yours." Zeus put a hand on each. "Now go and sit down and rest, or I'll call a servant and have you carried."

"It's come to this," Cronos said, stumping along on his cane, closer to his son. "All my children betray me."

"Heracles!" Zeus shouted, and a muscular servant appeared. "Take my parents to their sitting room, please."

"Yes, lord." Heracles scooped up Cronos in his arms and carried him off while Cronos beat at him with his cane. In a few moments he came back, slightly battered, for Rhea.

Zeus let out a deep breath. "Patricide begins to look a more acceptable option, daily."

"You won't, though," Hera said. "You're still afraid of him."

"True, alas." Zeus ran a hand through his coppery

hair, as if combing his father out of it. "Now . . ." He peered into the rush basket where he had laid the baby, and tickled her. She cooed at him. "Abut the child . . . I thought, a playmate for Hebe."

"Hebe has her brothers," Hera said. She and Zeus were united in their opposition to his parents, but only in that. The two boys on the nursery floor eyed them watchfully, with considerably more attention than they had given their grandparents. When Mama used that tone, someone was often sorry quite soon. Hephaestus went on pounding his hammer on his blocks, his odd twisted feet stuck straight out in front of him, but Ares got up from his toy soldiers and trotted over to peer into the rush basket at the baby.

"Pretty," he said. "Can we keep her?" The shrieks of two more little boys outside the window claimed his attention, and he darted out the door, abandoning the baby for them. In a moment they heard louder shrieking.

"We need another girl," Zeus said cajolingly. "With all these boys."

Hera's mouth flattened out. The two boys outside, Dionysus and Hermes, were Zeus's, but they weren't hers. Their mothers were servants on the farm, among the many who had received his attentions.

"Always room for one more. That's my sweet." Zeus slid an arm around her.

"That's generally been your theory," Hera said. She eyed the baby again. "You've been overpopulating the farm for years." She had milky skin and shimmering hair the color of chestnuts. She was the most beautiful woman in the village, maybe even in the city of Tiryns, but the simmering anger she directed at her husband made it a fearsome loveliness, like the statue of some dangerous goddess, that only Zeus had the nerve to approach.

Hebe and Hephaestus watched in silence. When their parents struck sparks, things caught on fire, and it was better not to be in the direct path of the flames.

"What would you like?" Zeus asked. "Some splendid present for being such a good wife? For putting up with troublesome old Zeus?"

"I'll think of something," Hera said between her teeth, because she knew he was going to keep this baby no matter what she said. "I put up with a lot, so it had better be extremely splendid." She swept from the nursery, leaving Zeus with the baby, who began to howl. He shouted for the nursemaid.

So she stayed. Zeus claimed she wasn't his, but he never had a good answer for why he had brought her home. He had never been the best of fathers to the children he had already, male or female, calling them to him to pet them like puppies and dismissing them carelessly when they bored him, and sometimes seeming to forget their names. But he named this one himself. He called her Aphrodite, meaning "Wave Born."

The farm he brought her to was on land that had first been worked by the ancestors of his clan, and handed down over the years to Cronos and Rhea. The rocky hillside supported olive groves and the lower land pastured cattle and goats or was tilled for grain. A terraced vineyard climbed the slope in between. Of Cronos it was rumored that he *had* killed his father for control of the land. The old couple were now too feeble to run the farm themselves, but still able to tell their children when they were doing it wrong. They terrified Aphrodite as she grew, sitting in their armchairs at the center of the great hall like spiders. They appeared to unnerve her aunts and uncles as well. There were four of them besides Zeus—Poseidon and Hades, and the sisters Demeter and Hestia, plus Poseidon's wife Amphitrite—and they all avoided the grandparents' scolding tongues when they could manage it, sending the unfortunate farm servants to care for them, and gritting their teeth through dinner as Cronos expounded on the numerous errors Poseidon made in his training of the young horses, and Rhea complained of Hera's supervision of the kitchen and Amphitrite's lack of children.

Zeus and Hera's children, who ate in the nursery with Zeus's other sons, got most of their information

on family matters from eavesdropping on these conversations.

"When I am grown," Ares said, "I will lock them up in a tower, if Father hasn't done it already by then."

"He would have," Hephaestus said, 'but Grandfather threatened to curse him, and Father thinks he can."

"Always another mouth to feed," Rhea's voice came querulously through the wall. "And in these hard times. Likely your poor old parents will starve, for you feeding your bastards all our food."

"What hard times?" Hermes asked. He had never noticed any. His mother was a maid here, but he was petted and spoiled by Zeus.

"Grandmother says it's hard times," Hebe said. She was the oldest, at nine. "She caught me in the garden yesterday and told me I'd never have a dowry, and I'd have to go on the streets."

"Spiteful old witch," Dionysus said.

"She's always saying I should have been exposed. She thinks poor little Aphrodite should too."

"She's afraid because she's old," Hephaestus said. He was well aware of what his grandmother had always said about him. He was eight and Ares seven. Hermes and Dionysus were five and six.

"Lots of people are old," Hebe said, "and they don't tear at each other like jackals."

"Our family does."

Hermes pointed at the baby, now two, banging her spoon on the table. "Maybe Father brought us that one to give them something new to complain about. Keep them off his back."

"Didn't work," Ares said.

"Baby, don't do that." Hebe took the spoon away from Aphrodite before she could smack her cup with it. "Before this one they complained about you," she said to Hermes.

"Do you think she's Father's?" Dionysus asked.

"No!" Ares said. "He found her. He said so."

Hephaestus snorted. "There are enough of Father's children to go around the village twice."

"This one is different," Ares said stubbornly.

Hebe sighed. The only time Ares ever stopped fighting with his brothers or the village boys, or lining up armies of bugs and trying to make them fight each other, was when Aphrodite toddled into the yard to find him. Hebe knew that even at two, Aphrodite was dangerously beautiful. Her beauty wasn't just in the eyes, it was a presence, a force like an overpowering scent. There might be other girl children as beautiful, or maybe even more so, if you painted her picture and showed it to people and asked them to vote on the prettiest. But no one who saw her in person ever saw anyone else to match her. She was going to be more beautiful than Mother, Hebe thought, and that was going to make more trouble yet.

Aphrodite wasn't sure when she had figured out for herself that she was beautiful. She had simply always known it. Wherever she went people looked at her, and they would do things for her without being asked. If she asked, they would do nearly everything. Or the men would. Hera told her not to get above herself, and Hebe told her to be careful. The shepherd boys made her wreaths of daisies when she came out to play with the new lambs, and Heracles carved her a little wooden horse on wheels. Ares pulled her around in his goat cart and uncle Poseidon gave her rides on his shoulders. Animals liked her, too. The goats and Hera's chickens followed her everywhere she went.

When Aphrodite was five years old, a woman who ran a very high class house of hetairae in Mycenae tried to buy her. (Hera would have sold her if Zeus hadn't been there.) Aphrodite wasn't sure what the woman had wanted, but she had promised her beautiful dresses and to teach her to play the lyre, and Aphrodite had wanted to go with her.

"You wouldn't have liked it," Hephaestus said solemnly. But he thought she might have.

When she was seven, two twelve-year-old boys in the village outside Tiryns fought over her and one

pushed the other off a wall and broke both his legs. Aphrodite watched them with interest, twining one rose-gold curl around her finger. She yearned for those boys, for both of them, they were so wonderful and strong, and she liked the way they moved inside their skin, like young horses. They gave her an explosive sense of power, rolling in the dirt like that, pummeling each other for her sake.

"You come home!" Ares said, grabbing her by the arm. "You belong to us!"

"Ow! You're hurting me!"

Ares loosened his grip. "Sorry. But you stay away from those louts."

"Why?" Aphrodite demanded. "They gave me a sweet. One of them did."

"You can't take sweets from strange boys," Hephaestus said, hobbling beside her.

Aphrodite looked at him thoughtfully. He always seemed to know things. The boys in the village teased him because of his feet and threw rocks at him because they knew he couldn't catch them. When Ares was with him, Ares caught them instead and beat their heads together. Aphrodite knew Hephaestus didn't like that when it happened, but she didn't understand why. Who would want rocks thrown at them? "Why can't I have the sweet?" she asked.

"Because they will want something for it," Hephaestus said.

"Because you're ours," Ares said.

When she was ten, a group of mothers from Tiryns came to the farm to complain to Hera that Aphrodite had been in a cattle shed kissing boys, each in turn, in exchange for a silver bead or a bronze bracelet, or whatever he could offer her. She was wearing the offending bracelets when Hera turned her over her knee.

"Disgraceful!" Hera's hand came down wielding an ivory hairbrush.

"Ow!" Aphrodite thrashed on her lap as Hera got a good grip on her hair with her other hand.

The brush came down again. "No child of my

household will behave like a trollop! In a shed! With seven boys!"

"Ow! Stop!" Aphrodite wailed, kicking her feet, her face slick with tears.

"Stay! Away! From boys!" The brush came down with each word.

Hebe stood to one side, worried. Hebe was seventeen and she would not until now have thought of kissing a boy until her parents presented her with a suitable husband; then she would kiss him *after* the wedding.

"There!" Hera grabbed Aphrodite by the shoulders and stood her on her feet again. "You are not to go into the village alone again! Do you understand me?"

Aphrodite sniffled, rubbing her backside. Hera's anger sparked out of her gray eyes like lightning but Aphrodite still didn't comprehend why. "Yes, Mother," she said, because it was easier to say that than to argue. But it had been fun, kissing those boys. It had felt very nice in places that Aphrodite hadn't noticed before. She looked sorrowfully at her bare wrists. Hera had taken the bracelets.

"You need work to do," her Aunt Hestia said, taking her by the ear and leading her to the kitchen, where she washed dishes for a ten-day until her hands were raw, snuffling at her misfortune to the household snake, who came out of his basket and wrapped a sympathetic coil about her ankle, his flat head resting on her foot. After that her Aunt Demeter took her into the kitchen garden, where she set out bean seedlings until all the nails on her reddened hands were broken to the quick. The Aunts were not unkind, and said they had her best interests at heart, but dishwater and beans didn't make her stop liking boys.

Hephaestus was sixteen then, old enough to know danger when he saw it, but he couldn't help feeling sorry for her as she mourned her confiscated bracelets. He had begun to take over the forge on the farm by then, sitting on a stool he had built, his lame feet dangling, hammering out bridle bits and sheaths for

wagon wheels, spear points for hunting and cauldrons for the kitchen. Sometimes Aphrodite would sit and watch him, her tame hen in her lap, or one of the other farm animals who always came to her hand. Today it was a goat, its knobby head resting on her knees. She looked so sad that on impulse, he said, "If *I* made you something, Mother would let you keep it."

Aphrodite's face brightened. "Would you? What would you make me?"

"I have a little gold. I could make you a girdle to wear with your good gown. Not all gold, bronze mostly, but I could put gold ornaments on it. What do you like?"

Aphrodite's eyes shone. "I like doves. They make such a sweet sound. There's one that sits on my windowsill every morning. Could I have doves on it?"

"Doves it shall be," Hephaestus said.

Aphrodite beamed at him. A ten-day later, when it was finished, she fastened it around her slim hips to admire herself. The girdle was forged of delicate, spiraling links of bronze, with gold rosettes between the links, and the buckle, as promised, was a pair of gold doves, facing each other.

"I made it so you can move the buckle when you get bigger, and you won't outgrow it," he said.

Aphrodite sighed with delight and danced across the yard. "I'm going to go look at myself in the pool!" she called to him. Hera possessed a silver mirror, but just now Aphrodite felt it might be unwise to borrow it. She ran along the wagon road that sloped down from the farmyard into a grove of trees. From the road, the path to the sacred spring branched off and she darted along it.

It was cool and mysterious in the woods by the spring where the Goddess lived. In the heart of the woods an olive tree stood guard over a spring-fed pool and a stone altar, all three so old they had been there in the time of Erebus, the first of Cronos's clan, so Mother had said. Beside the altar sat the omphalos, a round stone shaped by an ancient hand, and nearly as

tall as Aphrodite. The omphalos was the navel of the world, older even than the altar and the tree. Aphrodite thought that the Goddess talked to her here sometimes, but she had never said so to anyone. She suspected she would have been spanked for impertinence, as it was common knowledge that the Goddess spoke only to her priestesses in her temple. But Aphrodite had heard her.

This morning she knelt beside the pool and looked into its black water. Her pale face shimmered back at her and around her waist shone the magical, marvelous girdle that Hephaestus had made for her. Aphrodite held her breath, staring at her reflection. The girdle glowed, it sang, it felt warm against her hips and waist.

On impulse she unbuckled it and dipped it in the water. "Make everyone love me," she asked the Goddess. Its bronze spirals flashed like golden fish in the depths. Ares had begun to run after older girls and leave her behind. "Make him love *me*," she told the water and the golden belt.

Be careful what you wish for, the water whispered back.

Aphrodite cocked her head, trying to decide if she had really heard that.

No other sound came back t o her except the liquid *plop!* of a frog at the far end of the pool. Aphrodite shrugged and put her marvelous girdle back on, feeling its still-warm links imprint themselves on her waist. What could be wrong with being loved?

"Let me go." Persephone tugged at the grip of whoever, or whatever, it was. The grip didn't loosen.

She writhed in his arms and pummeled him with her fists. Persephone was a country girl, used to working in her mother's garden and catching wild goats for amusement. She was nearly as strong as any boy in the village.

Her mind filled with pale wraiths brushing by her as they passed, ghostly fingers tearing at her cloak; and that seemed worse than seeing where she was going. The air was dank this far below the sun. Her arms and legs ached like fire.

They passed no one else in the cold corridors and Persephone began to weep silently. She would never find her way out of this maze. And the pale, dark-bearded man who was plainly Hades himself would rape her or eat her or suck her soul away or all three, and she would never see her mother again. She burst into a despairing howl just as the sheeplike servants stopped at a doorway with a wooden door in it instead of a tapestry. The door had a large bronze bolt on the outside.

The largest sheep servant patted her shoulder clumsily. "No one will hurt you."

"Then what does he want with me?" Persephone demanded, sniffling.

The servant opened the heavy door. "Marry you, I think," he said, and pushed her inside.

"*Marry me?*" The door closed behind her and she heard the click of the bolt. Their footsteps padded away outside it. . . .

SIGNET ECLIPSE
Published by New American Library, a division of
Penguin Group (USA) Inc., 375 Hudson Street,
New York, New York 10014, USA
Penguin Group (Canada), 90 Eglinton Avenue East, Suite 700, Toronto,
Ontario M4P 2Y3, Canada (a division of Pearson Penguin Canada Inc.)
Penguin Books Ltd., 80 Strand, London WC2R 0RL, England
Penguin Ireland, 25 St. Stephen's Green, Dublin 2,
Ireland (a division of Penguin Books Ltd.)
Penguin Group (Australia), 250 Camberwell Road, Camberwell, Victoria 3124,
Australia (a division of Pearson Australia Group Pty. Ltd.)
Penguin Books India Pvt. Ltd., 11 Community Centre, Panchsheel Park,
New Delhi - 110 017, India
Penguin Group (NZ), cnr Airborne and Rosedale Roads, Albany,
Auckland 1310, New Zealand (a division of Pearson New Zealand Ltd.)
Penguin Books (South Africa) (Pty.) Ltd., 24 Sturdee Avenue,
Rosebank, Johannesburg 2196, South Africa

Penguin Books Ltd., Registered Offices:
80 Strand, London WC2R 0RL, England

First published by Signet Eclipse, an imprint of New American Library,
a division of Penguin Group (USA) Inc.

First Printing, July 2005
10 9 8 7 6 5 4 3 2 1

PUBLISHER'S NOTE
This is a work of fiction. Names, characters, places, and incidents either are
the product of the author's imagination or are used fictitiously, and any
resemblance to actual persons, living or dead, business establishments,
events, or locales is entirely coincidental.

   The publisher does not have any control over and does not assume any
responsibility for author or third-party Web sites or their content.

AUTHOR'S NOTE

The country of myth is not the world that we inhabit, but an older place, next door to the land of fairy tale. Like fairy tales, myth is peopled with the stuff of legend; however, while fairy tales tell the small domestic legend—the wicked stepmother, the younger brother who finds his fortune—myth tells the wider story—how fire came to mankind, why the winds blow, how the crops and animals were tamed for our use. All these great steps toward civilization took centuries, with small discovery after small discovery. Myth compresses that history into story, which is always more powerful and memorable.

In Greece, in between the grandeur of the Minoan civilization of Crete and that of the Mycenaeans of the mainland, from about 1600 B.C. to 1200 B.C., and the age of recorded history, which began in about 750 B.C., there was a Dark Age, a long period of wars and invasions during which those older worlds crumbled. Technology and knowledge were lost, and many of the refugees of those wars scattered to the islands of the Aegean. Such are the dark times when myth is born, when we yearn for the adventures of heroes in a greater, brighter time. That is the time into which I have put this tale of Persephone and Demeter and Hades.

As well as its own time, myth has its own landscape, and so this story, which is halfway between the tale as the Greek bards told it, and the account that history and anthropology would give us, is set in that Dark Age, when old skills were lost and later regained, on an unnamed island of the Greek archipelago.

I

Stepping Across the Border

When Persephone was small, her mother taught her how to plant seed in the ground and wait patiently, absolutely not digging it up to see how it was coming along, for it to sprout. The process was beautiful: First, two fat leaves would appear, then green tendrils promising beans, or the curly leaves of cabbage, or the slender shoots that would grow to tall bristly heads of wheat. She took her first steps in Demeter's garden, following her mother down the rows while Demeter hoed the weeds away with a pointed stick and cut stray branches from the fig tree with her small bronze pruning knife.

Persephone thought of her mother as a melon, her head topped with a leafy crown, her green body rounded at the hips like the statues of Earth Mother, which women kept in their houses to bring babies. She padded through the garden at Demeter's heels, talking to the bees, and the mantises with their cocked triangular heads and bulging eyes. As she

grew older, she took to the woods with her cousin
Hermes, bringing back armfuls of flowers and clay
jars containing toads and newts for further study in
the brook that ran behind the garden. Persephone
was aware, without quite knowing why, that most
people in the village were a little afraid of her
mother. That offered a certain immunity when she
stole honey from someone's hives or lay on her back
in the sunny grass and sucked the milk from someone's goat, but it did not keep Demeter from smack-
ing her. No one else was allowed to except for Great-
Grandfather Aristippus, who was the high priest of
Zeus and therefore in direct communication with
the gods.

The girls of her age, Echo and Narcissa, who were
her particular friends and somewhat more strictly su-
pervised, could be counted on to take part in her
tamer adventures. Only Hermes, however, would take
risks with her, as when they climbed to the top of
Aristippus's goat shed to spy on Great-Grandfather,
who liked to hide in there with girls while his wife,
Bopis, was looking for him. Only Hermes would help
her set a snare for a wild goat and then try to tame
it with offerings of cabbage from Demeter's garden.
Like all island children, they took to the water early.
It was Hermes who tried to make a boat of her goat
cart, and set them adrift so that they had to swim
back when the goat cart sank.

It was also Hermes who convinced her when they
were eight to show him what she looked like naked.

"Only if you do, too," Persephone said. She was
curious. She had caught a glimpse of Great-
Grandfather once, and of course she knew what male
goats looked like, but it was hard to picture, all the

same. She was unimpressed with Hermes and said so.

"It gets bigger when you get older," he said indignantly.

"Will mine?" She peered down.

"I don't think so. I've never heard of that happening. Let me look. Hmmm . . .

At that point Demeter had caught them. She came in from the garden, where they had thought she was planting beans, and chased Hermes from the house with a rake. He took to his heels naked and laughing, while Persephone pulled her dress back on, and fled into the woods.

"You stay away from that boy!" Demeter yelled at her daughter. "You stay away from all boys! They will give you nothing but grief."

Persephone learned to be more wary of Hermes as they grew older. He was precocious and, she discovered, he made things up. Even though he was fun, you couldn't ever quite trust what he told you.

By her sixteenth summer, Persephone knew a few things about her world: The earth was flat. At its center was Hellas, comprising the island on which she lived, and a surrounding archipelago of other islands large and small. The River Ocean flowed around the world, and through its middle ran the Sea where Hellas stood with its roots in the bottom of the world. In the North lived the Hyperboreans, a perpetually happy race who existed in inaccessible bliss behind the mountains. Their icy winds brought winter to Hellas. In the South lived a legendarily virtuous people called the Aethiopians, whose behavior was generally cited to Persephone as an example when she teased the goats or made a dam in the brook and flooded the beans. In the West lay the Elysian Fields where those favored by the gods went to share their immortality without dying first. No one seemed to know what was in the East. Persephone guessed the Sun's house was there, as each morning the Sun drove his fiery chariot out of the Ocean, across the sky, and down into the waters in the West. Great-Grandfather said at night the Sun traveled around the back side in a winged boat.

When Demeter was Persephone's age she had gone away somewhere, but no one knew whether it was to the happy Hyperboreans or the virtuous Aethiopians, or maybe even inside the borders of the Elysian Fields. She was gone for several years and was presumed to have been eaten by lions, until she reappeared with a child on her hip and the knowledge of how to tame the plants that grew wild on the island. She knew how to grow them for her own rather than just pick them where she could find them. Teaching this to the people of her village, mainly goat herders, had given Demeter her reputation. They decided that wisdom had to come from the gods, in whom they believed implicitly, although no one had actually seen one, but there was no other accepted explanation.

Persephone had asked her mother several times who her father had been, but Demeter would never say. No one else had the nerve to ask, and all Demeter told Persephone was, "Watch out."

"Watch out for what?" Persephone had asked her when she was eight.

"For strangers," Demeter had answered.

"What kind of strangers?" Persephone had asked her when she was twelve.

"Men," Demeter had said and wouldn't say anything else.

It was clear to Persephone at sixteen that her mother's order was not going to be difficult to obey. All the boys in the village were too afraid of Demeter to court Persephone. The exception was Hermes, who still wasn't afraid of anything because he didn't have enough sense to be. Hermes had thought he could ride old Leucippus's big ram, and it had tipped him off and butted him into the river. This did not stop Hermes from bragging about it afterward. He had convinced the smaller boys to climb a wild bee tree and bring him down the comb. When they were stung, he had advised them to run for the village rather than the river with a cloud of bees behind them. Hermes liked to stir things up just to see what would happen. He courted all the girls indiscriminately, and he was not the faithful sort.

Persephone and her friends would see him hiding in the rushes while they bathed in the river. They would throw stones at him for spying on them, but Hermes would just laugh and run away. An hour later he would be back, his pointed face peering at them from between the gray leaves of an olive tree.

"Go away! You nasty boy!" Echo shook one small fist at him and pitched a rock from the pool's bottom into the branches with the other.

Hermes slid down the tree, his red hair a flash like a russet fox among the olive leaves, and then he was gone, bounding over the hillocky bank and into the woods, leaving his cackling laugh hanging behind him in the still, hot summer air.

"Ooh! And I saw him with Clytie just yesterday, crawling all over her, the slut, after he asked *me* to go walking last full-of-the-moon!" Echo balled both fists up and pounded them on the water.

"And you trusted him?" Narcissa shook her head solemnly, wet dark hair dripping over bare shoulders.

"Echo, you know he always lies." Persephone paddled in the slow water where the stream widened into a bathing pool. Her chin skimmed just above the surface, and her long hair floated around her like gold seaweed.

Echo pouted. "Well, of course I do, but this was different. He *said* it was different. And anyway, what was he doing with a cow like Clytie? Honestly, that girl will go with anyone, so I don't see that she really counts. Except of course, she does count because he *promised me*. Anyway—"

Echo was the shortest of the girls, and she was standing on a rock embedded in the bottom of the pool so that her breasts just bobbed on the surface. They reminded Persephone of figs and she watched them idly to see if they were going to sprout leaves and split open while Echo nattered on. They didn't, so she lay back in the cool water, paddling with her fingers just enough to keep her from drifting downstream. Their shucked dresses lay on the bank. No boy except Hermes would have the nerve to come near the pool after seeing those dresses. If Demeter didn't curse him so that his penis withered like an uprooted stalk (it was rumored that she could do so), the girls would heave rocks at him and tell his mother. Girls in Persephone's village didn't lie down with boys when they didn't want to. Persephone was not aware, and nor were they, that this was not the case elsewhere. There was something in Demeter's garden that protected women.

"So anyway, Harmonia wanted to go out after the spring bonfires with Tros, and her mother wouldn't let her because his people are so poor. . . ." Echo had taken a new tack.

Narcissa grinned at Persephone and lay back in the water, too. They watched a dragonfly skim over the pool. It was blue with emerald wingtips. Echo liked to talk even when you weren't listening. Sometimes you found out something interesting from her, such as the fact that Glaucus, who was as old as dirt, was finally dying, and his daughters were fighting over who would inherit his house and his sixty goats, and one of them had tried to cut another one's fingers off with a cheese knife. Or that Dryope, Glaucus's third wife, had run away and was hiding from the daughters, because she was afraid they would come after her next. What the daughters didn't know was that Dryope had all of Glaucus's gold.

"Glaucus has gold?" Narcissa sat up in the water, paddling with both hands.

"Yes, and no one knows where he got it. His daughters don't even know he has it. I heard it all from Dryope because I gave her a cake and some milk when she came to our house. Mother wouldn't let her stay; she's afraid of those old women." Glaucus's daughters were nearly as old as he was.

No one in the village had any gold to speak of, except for those few who had been off the island. There was no reason to leave. Anything you might want was right here, which made gold fairly useless, although coveted just the same. Demeter had said once, darkly, that people were not rational when it came to gold.

"Well, where is she staying?" Persephone asked.

"I don't know," Echo said regretfully. "She wouldn't tell me where she was going when she left."

"She probably wished she hadn't told you about the gold," Narcissa said. "You can't keep a secret."

"I can so!" Echo looked indignant, her freckled face squinched in outrage.

"Oh, you can't," Persephone said lazily. "You know you can't. You told Tros when I said that Harmonia could do better than him."

Narcissa pointed a finger at Echo. "Then you told her mother she didn't come home all night after the equinox bonfires, when her mother thought she was in bed."

"I didn't mean to!" Echo clapped her hand to her mouth.

"And then you told *my* mother that Arachne finished my weaving for me. You know I hate weaving, and she made me make two whole blankets as punishment."

"I didn't mean to!" Echo wailed. "It just slipped out!"

Persephone grinned. "Everything slips out. Echo, you cannot keep a secret. You had better try to keep your mouth shut about Glaucus and Dryope and any gold, or everyone in the village will be in a buzz over it, and someone will come after *you* with a cheese knife."

Echo pouted, arms folded across her breasts. "Well, if you're going to be like that, I just won't say anything else."

"You've already said it," Narcissa said.

"Don't be cross, Echo," Persephone said, ducking under the water. She surfaced just behind the shorter girl, spouting river water at the back of her head.

Echo turned and dove at Persephone's legs, pulling her under. They wrestled, shrieking, while Narcissa watched primly. When Echo, who was stronger than she looked, had ducked Persephone three times, they paddled to the riverbank and lay panting in the shallows.

"Something's going on," Narcissa said. "You two were making too much noise to hear it, bellowing like cows. Listen!"

They cocked their heads toward the path that ran away over the tree-dotted hillocks toward the village. The sound of wailing and the shrill of pipes hung in the air.

"Glaucus has died," Persephone said. She heaved herself out of the shallows and picked up her dress.

"Maybe it's pirates!" Echo said.

"Then *everyone* would be screaming," Narcissa pointed out. "That's mourning. We'd better go. It's not respectful to be lolling here in the pool." Glaucus was older than Persephone's great-grandfather and so was due some honor, even if he had been nearly as unpleasant as his daughters.

"Do you suppose Dryope can hear it?" Echo said.

"Probably," Persephone said, her head muffled by the folds of her dress. She pulled it down and pinned the right shoulder. "Sound carries up into the hills."

"I bet she doesn't come down," Echo said, drying her feet with her hem. "If I were Dryope I'd be looking for a nice boat on the other side of the island. One with a handsome captain."

"He was her husband," Narcissa said. "She owes him something even if he was an evil old toad."

"Well, I think she paid her debt," Persephone said, tying her sash. "Living with him all those years. Ugh. Would you marry someone like that just because he had sixty goats?"

Persephone was in her sixteenth summer, the eldest of the three, and even fourteen-year-old Echo was of marriageable age. It was a topic they discussed at some length almost daily, while floating in the pool, or cursing their weaving in the flat courtyard in front of Narcissa's mother's house.

"You wouldn't have to," Narcissa said. Persephone was by far the most beautiful girl on the island, and Demeter had no need to marry off her daughter for goats.

"I'll be lucky if I get married at all," Persephone sighed. "Mother says men aren't worth the trouble."

"Glaucus had all that gold, too," Echo pointed out.

"Even gold wouldn't be enough to marry him." Persephone shuddered pointedly. "And anyway, no one knew that. Unless he told Dryope's parents, to convince them to let him have her."

"No, he didn't," Echo said. "She found it in a trunk. It was locked, and she broke the lock off with a rock."

They set off up the stony path to the village, contemplating Dryope's ingenuity. It was the most interesting turn of events that had happened locally in a long time, and they were gratified by the idea that they knew more than anyone else.

"She must have had some reason for marrying him," Persephone said. "He was awful."

"Her family was very poor," Narcissa said, "and

he wasn't, even without the gold. Sometimes that's all it takes."

"Oh, poor thing. Well, I hope she gets away."

They crested the last hill and came down into the village through the olive grove that Demeter had planted fifteen years before. Just in the last year the trees were beginning to hang heavy with fruit. Olives gave the people of Hellas light, food, and soap, and they took a long time to mature. The wild ones were jealously guarded from outsiders. Beyond them lay Demeter's vineyard, another ingathering of the wild, with the grapevines arranged in neat rows and pruned to bear the most fruit.

They could hear the pipes and the wailing clearly now, with the high notes of a lyre in between. As they came through the vineyard, a procession wound out from among the mud houses and into the agora, the dirt courtyard that was the heart of the village. At its center grew a single ancient olive tree, and the ground around it was packed as hard as stone from decades of feet. The agora was the daily marketplace, where anyone with something to say stood and harangued the village, where marriages were solemnized and deaths mourned, and where the village elders, all men, sat in the evening and drank wine and discussed matters of great importance.

Glaucus's daughters, draped in black, were howling and pulling at their veils, while Glaucus lay on a litter, wrapped like a cocoon in his shroud. Great-Grandfather Aristippus was there, leaning on his staff, nearly as old as Glaucus had been, his white shock of hair standing up as if on fire in the late afternoon sunlight. His wife, Bopis, was there, too; she narrowed her eyes when she saw Persephone.

Bopis didn't like Demeter or Persephone because Demeter's mother was a daughter of Aristippus whom he had got with another woman. Persephone saw her mother and scooted through the crowd to her, pulling the folds of her mantle up over her wet hair in respect. Great-Grandfather Aristippus was invoking the gods, asking them to take Glaucus down the river of the dead into the land of spirits and look on him kindly there. Hades, the deity who ruled the Underworld, lived in a cave at the foot of the cliffs that lined the island's southern shore. Beneath the shroud there would be two copper pennies on Glaucus's eyes, to pay the invisible boatman who would row his ghost downriver to Hades's dark realm.

Demeter put an arm around her daughter. "You're wet," she whispered. "You were supposed to be pruning the grapes."

"It was hot," Persephone said. "We went swimming."

"We?"

"Echo and Narcissa and me. Hermes was there, hiding in a tree. We threw rocks at him."

Demeter snorted.

"He gives himself airs because he's my cousin."

"Second cousin," Demeter said. "My cousin Maia never did have any sense, and that boy is proof of it. She claimed he was fathered by Zeus."

"Right. And Zeus wore a shepherd's cloak and snuck into her bed at night disguised." Persephone chuckled. She knew things, even if she wasn't married. Any country girl did. Demeter herself had never made any claims about Persephone's father, but Persephone privately thought that if anyone had had an affair with a god, it was more likely to be her mother than Cousin Maia, who had buck teeth and was nearly bald from a rash.

"Well, you're not going to marry him."

"Mother!" Persephone whispered, indignant. "I wouldn't want to!"

"You'll want somebody. I know girls," Demeter said sharply. "You're too pretty."

Persephone shrugged. So far she hadn't seen any boy she would be willing to marry.

Demeter poked her. "Now, be quiet. People are looking at us."

Persephone shrugged again. Her mother had been both a scandal and a minor deity herself since her return with the gift of gardening from wherever she had been. Persephone was used to people looking at them. She turned to watch the procession, with Great-Grandfather Aristippus, Bopis, and the wailing daughters at its head, snaking its way along the edge of the goat pasture toward the rocky cliff that rose behind the pasture's western edge. It mirrored the one that dropped down to the sea on the southern shore. Here the village dead were laid to rest, in chambers carved out of the rock, with things beside them they might need for their journey. Glaucus had been provided with a jug of good wine, a slab of goat cheese, and a loaf of bread. His best knife lay beside him, along with a herd of small clay goats. Two of the daughters had wanted to give him the best cookpot, as well, but they had been overruled by the third daughter with the cheese knife.

The passage to Glaucus's family tomb sloped downward into the mountainside, a stone-lined corridor wide enough for only one at a time. Most of the village

waited respectfully outside, but Demeter and Persephone followed the wailing daughters, Phaedon the
doctor, Aristippus, the priestess of Hestia, so old she
had to be carried chair-fashion by two young men, and
others who represented power in the village.

Glaucus's young wife was nowhere to be seen, a
circumstance that was commented upon in a low
murmur throughout the funeral.

"She was a slut anyway," the youngest daughter
said.

"No worse than some," the middle daughter muttered, nursing bandaged fingers and casting a baleful
glare at her elder sister.

The eldest turned on her, and they fussed among
themselves like a trio of weathered black crows, eyes
beady beneath their black veils, voices rising until Aristippus stomped his staff hard on the rocks and
coughed, and they settled down again, rattling feathers.

Persephone giggled, and Demeter tweaked her ear.

They stood in the tomb's antechamber while Glaucus and his grave goods were laid in the round rock-
cut tomb at the end of the passage. Two smaller
chambers held his first two wives, and Persephone
privately thought that Dryope was better off wherever she was. Despite his wealth, Glaucus had
worked his first wives to death, and only his final
demise had prevented the same thing happening
again.

Now the boatman would come for Glaucus and
demand his pennies, with which Persephone imagined he would be reluctant to part; then he would
leave his body behind, and the boatman would row
the ghost of Glaucus down the rivers that ran inside
the earth and deposit him in the realm of Death.

By the time the proper prayers had been said, the stone tomb had begun to close in on Persephone, or seemed to. She felt as if the bones of those wives might rise and pull her into their chambers with them. She was relieved when they turned around and filed up into the light again. As she reached the passage's mouth, she gasped and took deep breaths of the sunlit air.

The men of the village filled in the passageway's opening with rocks, and the procession wound its way back to the village. No one heard any more of Dryope, and Persephone imagined her sailing away in a boat with a red sail, her arms glittering with gold bracelets. She thought no more of death until the next week when Narcissa's father, Echemus, capsized his boat while fishing for tunny and was brought home nearly drowned.

At first it was thought he would live. He had retched up seawater and then more seawater and blood, but he was breathing; however, his breathing grew labored, and there was a pain in his chest that would not subside, so that each breath cut him like a knife. He was laid on a bed where Narcissa's mother hovered over him. The village doctor boiled herbs in a cauldron and had him breathe the vapors. Bopis offered advice about the dangers of seawater and the evil eye. Apollo was prayed to, and Narcissa's mother sacrificed a kid, but Echemus only grew worse. His breathing sounded dark, as if it came whistling laboriously from inside a cave. Narcissa clung to Persephone and Echo and cried, while her mother sat stoically by the bedside, losing hope.

Persephone always associated a terrible or a great

event with the smell of cooking meat. Meat was scarce—if you ate your goats and sheep they couldn't give you milk and wool—and animals were almost always killed only to give some meat to the gods. After that, however, someone had to dispose of the actual meat, since the gods ate only the vapors rising from it, its essence, its other self which traveled to their world. You didn't waste things, not in Persephone's village, where there was very little to waste, so the living people ate the meat that stayed behind in this world.

Persephone kept watch with the rest in Narcissa's house, gnawing a rib bone with one hand, the other arm around Narcissa's shoulders. Narcissa wept quietly, her share untouched, while Bopis bustled about, organizing things.

"I said that was a bad day to sail," Bopis said, carrying an armful of soiled bed linens. "And with a red sky. Father always warned me, and of course I listened, not like the folk today. The young ones are the worst, but that Echemus didn't even stop to listen to me when I told him his boat needed caulking. Of course it didn't actually leak. I believe it capsized, but these things go together. Careless is as careless does, and now poor Irene . . ."

"Eat," Echo said on Narcissa's other side. "You don't want the gods to think we don't appreciate what they give us back."

"I can't." Narcissa looked at the collop of meat in her bowl with revulsion. "It looks like the inside of something."

"It *is* the inside of something," Echo said. "It was inside the goat."

"He's going to die. Mother talked to Aristippus

this morning about sending him down to . . . down to the shore."

The other girls drew in their breath. Persephone felt the fine gold hairs on her arms rise. "To—to *him*?"

Narcissa nodded miserably. "Mother doesn't want to. She's afraid. But Aristippus says sometimes people with what he has have lived."

Echo's eyes grew wide. People sent to the shore either came back living or didn't come back at all. Their bodies went into the house of the dead with their souls. And you never knew, you just never knew what had happened.

"Sometimes he gives them back," Persephone said, trying to comfort Narcissa. She laid her gnawed rib across the edge of her bowl and wiped her hands with some water from the clay jug that stood among the cookpots. The goat smell still drifted from the hearth in the Temple of Apollo across the agora.

Echemus was a well-off man, not so well-off as Glaucus had been, but enough to have a stone floor to his house and a bed apiece for his family. He lay behind a hanging woven by Narcissa and her mother, while Aristippus talked softly and insistently with his wife. Narcissa buried her face in her hands.

Sometimes when a villager was wounded too badly to recover, or in unbearable pain, or near death from disease, the village gave the person to the dark shade at the foot of the cliffs. Once in a while, the person would return healed, possessing only dim, dreamlike memories of the Underworld; most often, however, that person was never seen again. It was there that Aristippus proposed to take Echemus and give him to Hades alive.

Narcissa's mother came wailing from behind the curtain, and all three girls stood up.

"Irene"—Aristippus put a hand on her shoulder—"Be quiet now. We are asking a great gift of him."

"He will take him!" Irene wailed.

"Hush! He will have him anyway soon enough," Bopis said. "I've seen that look in his eyes before. Do you remember that child who drowned on the other side of the headland?"

Phaedon, the doctor, emerged from behind the curtain, as well, scrubbing his hands on the hem of his robe. "He has a fever in his lungs from the seawater," he said. "My diagnosis is definite." He held up one finger for emphasis.

"I don't want you to tell me what he has!" Irene turned on him. "I want you to heal him!"

Phaedon regarded her haughtily, a mere woman. Irene returned a furious glare. "Proper diagnosis is the heart of medicine," Phaedon informed her. "Only then do we know how a cure may be effected."

"Then effect one!"

"In this case, there is none," Phaedon retorted.

Aristippus took her by the arm and steered her away from Phaedon. The doctor picked the biggest piece of goat meat out of those still left in the big bowl by the hearth and departed.

Aristippus turned to Narcissa. "Help your mother get him on a litter." Narcissa whimpered. He looked at Persephone. "Go ask Demeter to come and help."

Bopis snorted, but she didn't offer to help get Echemus on the litter herself. Death was catching; everybody knew that.

Persephone gave Narcissa a squeeze and darted out the door. The whole idea of handing someone over still alive to the dark presence at the foot of the cliff, sacrificed like the goat, made her skin crawl. She took a deep breath of fresh air as she came out of the house, but the smell of goat meat still hung in it. She could see the smoke rising from the temple where the bones were burning. The temple complex was a small collection of huts at the east end of the village, with separate altars to Apollo; to Hestia, the keeper of the hearth; and to Zeus who ruled the gods on their mountaintop. Great-Grandfather oversaw the Temple of Zeus and Apollo; Hesperia, who was a crone so old that no one remembered her being a child, or even a young woman, tended the Temple of Hestia where the sacred fire of the village burned. Persephone darted past the temples, making a quick bow of respect at Hesperia, who frightened her, and who was sitting nodding in the sun outside her door.

Hermes watched her go from his perch in the olive tree in the agora. After a moment he slid down and followed her. She jumped when he popped up in front of her on the path.

"You scared me. Don't pop out at people like that!"

"Old Echemus is dying, isn't he?"

"Yes, they're going to give him to . . . you know. Great-Grandfather says people with what he has sometimes live."

"Great-Grandfather ought to know. He's older than that olive tree." Aristippus was Hermes's family patriarch, as well. His mother, Maia, was the granddaughter of Aristippus and Bopis. "Where are you off to?"

"To fetch Mother. Irene needs her."

"Aha." Hermes grinned at her conspiratorially. His eyes were interested, gray green and slightly slanted under a shock of unruly hair. "They'll all be wailing and carrying on at the cliff. Never miss us."

"I'm not going anywhere with you," Persephone said severely.

"I'm more fun than a trip to the land of the dead!"

"Barely," Persephone said, but she chuckled in spite of herself. Hermes was maddening, but sometimes he made her laugh.

He slid an arm about her waist as they walked, and she pushed him away.

"What we ought to do is get married," Hermes said seriously. "Then I wouldn't have to try to lure you off into the woods."

Persephone thought maybe he really meant it, but he couldn't keep his hands off the other girls, and that wouldn't change if she married him. She wasn't going to have that; she wasn't going to be Bopis.

He slid his arm around her waist again and nuzzled her neck. A shiver of pleasure ran through her, and she pushed him away again, harder. "No! Now go and annoy some other girl! I have to find Mother." She began to run, and he dropped behind.

"You'll be sorry!" he called after her. "When you're an old lady, married to some lout, you'll think to yourself, 'Ah! I could have had Hermes!'"

"Mother!"

Demeter was cutting the first of the wheat to ripen, her bronze sickle in one hand, the other wrapped around a sheaf of waving stalks. She straightened at Persephone's footsteps.

"Mother! They're going to take Echemus down to

the coast—you know, to *him*." No one liked to call Hades by his right name, lest they summon him by mistake. "And Great-Grandfather wants you to come and help. Irene and Narcissa are frightened." Persephone was frightened, too, but Demeter nodded briskly and tucked her sickle in her sash.

"Very well. I'll come. You stay here. I don't like you going near that place."

Persephone didn't want to go, either, but she thought of Narcissa's pale miserable face and frightened eyes. "Mother, I have to come. I promised Narcissa." Everyone was looking out for Irene. No one would pay any attention to the daughter.

Since her return to the village with a child, Demeter had not known what it was like to have friends, as her daughter had. Women who had been girls of her age now gave her nervous respect but not friendship. Still, she could remember a time when they had, and so she nodded again. "But you must stay well back, with Narcissa. Irene and Grandfather and I will take him to the cave mouth. You are not to go near it. Understood?"

"Yes, Mother."

They had already loaded Echemus on a litter when Persephone and Demeter arrived. He was pale and sweating, and his breath rasped like a saw. His eyes were open, and Persephone could tell by the panic shown in them that he knew where they were taking him. She put her hand to her mouth. She wondered if the goat had known, too.

The little procession wound through the village much as Glaucus's funeral had, but this time it ran to the south where a path followed the river toward the coast. At the cliffs it zigzagged down along steps

that had been cut in the rock, through the sea spray
that blew up around them. Gulls squawked overhead
in the blue, and Persephone could see boats like
small dark toys on the sea beyond the harbor. Along
the cliff top above them, poppies grew, blooming a
deep blood scarlet, their heads nodding in the sea
breeze.

Hermes trailed them at a distance, waiting to see
what would happen next. He liked it best when upheaval was in the air. It made life interesting. Persephone's hips swayed as she walked, her arm about
Narcissa, and he grinned as he felt himself stiffen,
watching her. Eventually he would have her. All the
girls gave in eventually. Persephone was the most
important of them, and so he could afford to wait.

It was slow going, carrying a litter down the steep
trail, and Persephone held her breath as Irene stumbled. Demeter, at the head of the litter beside her,
righted it swiftly, helped by Aristippus, who carried
both poles at the other end. There were younger,
stronger men than he in the village, and certainly
stronger than Irene (Demeter was another matter),
but it was important who brought a patient to the
god of Death. If the sick soul didn't seem to matter
much to its bearers, then he might not be so inclined
to give it back.

At its foot they crunched over sand and small
stones, and bits of dried seaweed left from the high
tide. The gulls circled overhead, interested, to see if
there was something to eat. When it became clear
that there was not, they squawked and flew toward
the harbor.

Demeter and Irene set the litter down beneath the
slanted stone that overhung the cave mouth. Perse-

phone could see that the cave ran deep into the cliff, dark and mysterious, its floor also littered with the scraps of the last tide. She wondered if anyone would watch to be sure that someone came for Echemus before the water rose again. But maybe he wouldn't come if there were watchers. Maybe you just had to trust him. The thought lifted the hair on her arms again.

Aristippus raised his staff. "Lord!" he called in a booming voice that echoed back at them out of the cave mouth. "Lord! We have laid a soul at your doorstep."

Nothing stirred inside the cave, but Aristippus motioned to Demeter and Irene to come away and leave the litter there. Behind them on the sand, the men of the village had gathered, and now Persephone saw that one of them carried a black sheep on his shoulders. She turned her head away as they cut its throat. Of course, there would be a gift for this god, too.

Irene wailed one more time, stuffing her black veil into her mouth with her fist, as if Echemus were already dead. Demeter took her by the hand and pulled her away. They started up the cliff path again, no one looking back. That was another of the rules. If you looked back, it was said, he might keep you, too. By the time the last villager reached the top to stand amid the blowing poppies, Echemus and the sheep were both gone from the sand below.

The sea brings things to those who live along its shore: small bits of smooth glass rounded from broken bottles sunk leagues away; the outer husks of creatures unimaginably strange; wood from what was once a boat; drowned sailors. All were collected,

taken in, as were the offerings left by the living in
the village on the headland.

Two shadows came out from the cave mouth,
smoky forms scuttling crabwise along the sand, lifting the litter by its poles. They disappeared into the
depths. A moment later two more, or perhaps the
same ones, emerged again, and hoisted the sheep by
its feet.

Hades watched the procession of the living climb
the cliffs, knowing they would not dare look back at
him. He stared into the bright mist that blew around
the cliff, squinting his eyes at the light. The girl with
gold hair was at the end of the line, arm around her
weeping friend. She looked like a piece of floating
light, the corporeal embodiment of the scent of flowers. Gold hair was rare in her village. Hades had
noticed her before, picking flowers and playing like
a child in the river. She was past marriageable age,
but he thought her mother had something to do with
that. Demeter had the kind of power that you could
feel at a distance. Now he watched the daughter until
she passed from his sight. When she was gone he
could still see her outline, bright against the poppies.

II

Under the Earth

Echemus did not come back. Narcissa and Irene haunted the top of the cliff path as if sheer will could make him materialize. By late in the month of Gamelion, they knew he would not come, and men began to court Irene, a widow with a fine house and sheep and goats.

"Two have come from over the mountain," Narcissa said with disgust, "and wanted to marry me and Mother both. They said they didn't care who married which—we could choose."

"Oh, you don't want to marry someone from the north island," Echo said. "He'll take you away there, and they eat their meat raw and keep their women in cages. I've heard that."

"They do not," said Persephone. "They're just like us. Mother said. And anyway you've been to the big market there. You bought red sandals."

"That doesn't mean it wasn't all for show," Echo

said darkly. "Don't you do it, Narcissa. I heard once
of a girl who went there to marry and—"

"I'm not going to," Narcissa said. "They're both
ugly."

"Imagine marrying someone who didn't care
which one he got," Persephone said, but she knew
that Narcissa was bound to marry someone soon.
And then Echo. And she would be alone. The other
two were hiding from their mothers, for whom they
were supposed to be weaving and making cheese,
respectively, to pick flowers in the meadow on the
headland with Persephone. The flowers weren't for
anything in particular, not for a festival, or a wreath
for the statue of Hestia. They were picked solely for
their loveliness, so the girls could put them in a jar
at home until they faded. A woman couldn't do such
a thing when she married. She couldn't run away
from a husband and babies and wash and weaving
to pick flowers like a child. The older women in the
village told Persephone this often, shaking their
heads. Bopis, Great-Grandfather's wife, in particular
predicted ruin. Persephone privately thought that
Bopis wouldn't be so sour if Great-Grandfather
wasn't *still* chasing after other women. Sometimes
they even let him catch them.

Persephone gathered her armful of white daisies
against her chest and breathed in their summery
tang. The iris and jonquils that bloomed in spring
had better scent, but Persephone loved the flowers
of summer with their sharp dusty smell. In a corner
of her mantle was a handful of pale pink peroukas.
At the edge of the meadow the poppies that grew
on the headland waved their bloodred heads. Persephone bent to add them to her gleanings.

"You know those won't keep," Narcissa said.

Persephone smiled. "They'll last a little while. Till evening anyway. There are so many of them." Enough to waste, she thought, pulling them into her arms. Their scarlet heads made the daisies blaze whiter than ever. The sky above was the deep hot blue of midsummer. The sunlight, dusty white, bounced off the limestone walls of the village and off the bright, glassy surface of the sea below. Tiny black boats, like dots, marked the fishing fleet. Above them in the tawny hills, they could hear the baaing of sheep and the bleating of goats. The whir of insects in the meadow grass was a hot, sleepy lullaby.

Persephone sat down in the grass, her flowers in her lap, and yawned. She unslung the goatskin wine bag from her shoulder. Echo produced a half loaf of bread and a piece of cheese wrapped in cloth from the folds of her mantle, and Narcissa a handful of dried figs. They shared them between them, sighing in contentment.

"Bopis is coming to see Mother again tonight, with some horrible old man she's found," Narcissa said. "With Father dead, everyone thinks we need marrying off right away."

"Make her find you a handsome one," Echo said sleepily.

Persephone plugged the wineskin and lay back in the grass with her hands behind her head. "Tell her to find one for me," she murmured.

"You know you don't mean that," Narcissa said. "Your mother hates men."

"I know," Persephone murmured. "So she isn't going to find me one, is she?" Lately it had begun to seem to her that running wild wouldn't be quite so much fun once she found herself doing it alone. But she wasn't sure she had really meant what she said. When she thought of Echo's older sister, with a baby on her hip and one at her heels, her figure and three teeth gone already, the alternative didn't look all that enticing, either.

They awoke to the sound of footsteps, and Persephone's shrieks. There were dark shapes everywhere, their shadows black across the wildflowers as if they had emerged suddenly from the ground. They made muffled grunts but spoke no words, and their footsteps made the earth thunder. One of them had Persephone in his arms, her gold hair flying around her as she struggled, her spilled flowers a red and white carpet at her feet.

"Let her go!" Echo leaped at him, and one of the black shadows sent her flying back with a blow from its fist. Narcissa stood clutching her mantle to her chest, frozen, her face as pale as ice. A shadow came toward her, too, but a shout from the one holding Persephone called it back. They started toward the cliff's edge with her.

Echo sat up among the trampled flowers, her head spinning. The dark, terrifying shapes wheeled in her vision and dropped out of sight. She staggered to her feet. "Run!" Echo grabbed Narcissa by the wrist and yanked. They turned and raced across the meadow for home.

"He came up out of the ground!" Echo said. "With black horses and a black chariot! The ground just opened! We saw it!" She looked at them, wild-eyed, while Narcissa sat shaking on a bench under the olive tree.

"Who came out of the ground? Calm down, child." Irene took Echo by the shoulders. She looked around her at the crowd. "Someone go and fetch Demeter."

"I always said it was a mistake to let that girl run wild," Bopis said. "Mark my words, I said."

"I'm here," Demeter said quietly behind her. No one ever knew quite how she did that. "Who has taken my child?"

"I don't know!" Echo said. "He was black, and he drove enormous black horses, and they had teeth like fangs! He came out of the ground!"

"Oh, indeed?" Hermes shook his russet head scornfully. He could be counted on to appear wherever there was any trouble brewing, Echo thought. "And I suppose the ground closed up again after him? Or did you fall in the hole?"

"Be quiet!" Demeter snapped at him. "Narcissa?"

"They must have. They were just there all of a sudden, and Persephone was screaming, and they had her."

"Where did they take her?" Demeter's jaw was clenched so tightly no one was sure how the words came out.

"Over the cliff!" Narcissa said, trembling.

Bopis made the sign against the evil eye, and everyone else did, too.

"In a chariot?" Hermes raised an eyebrow.

"They flew!" Echo said. "I saw them! They went over the path to the caves."

Irene drew her breath in. She looked despairingly at Demeter. "We should never have let them go down there. Never have let him see them!"

"We don't know it's him yet." Phaedon, the doctor, held up a finger. "We have not yet ascertained the full facts."

"Who else could it be?" The villagers asked themselves the question and argued the evidence.

"In a chariot?" Despite Hermes's skepticism, they were all willing to believe in the chariot; the ground opened all the time—this was earthquake country.

No one in the village drove a chariot; horses were expensive to keep up. A chariot was a rich man's conveyance. And one that could go down a cliff? Well, that settled it.

"It was only to be expected," Bopis pronounced.

Irene began to weep, clutching her daughter to her.

Aristippus spoke for the first time. "If *he* has taken her, she won't come back." He looked at Demeter.

Demeter's feet were planted wide apart, as if she braced herself for some struggle. The village watched her uneasily. "I will find her," she said and turned on her heel. The implication that someone would be sorry hung in the air.

"Let me go!" Persephone struggled in the grip of whoever, or whatever, it was. The grip didn't loosen. She could feel him staggering a bit under her weight, and she swung her head around and sank her teeth into the arm that gripped her. It was enveloped in a dark material that left a taste of salt in her mouth.

"Ow! Stop that!" He staggered a bit, and she felt them both tipping. "Do you want to go down the cliff on your head?" He righted himself, and they kept going down. Persephone's mantle was tangled around her face, and she shook her head to free it.

The cliff face swung into view and bobbed in her vision as they staggered down the narrow steps. She caught a flash of blue sky, a gull's interested face, the pale pink blossoms of peroukas growing between the steps. She began kicking her feet, hoping to hit something tender. The voice was male.

More dark forms clambered down the cliff below and above her. They moved with the agility of mountain sheep. Her captor seemed equally sure-footed, but he said, as she struggled, "If I drop you, you'll break your head."

"Let me go!" She writhed in his arms and pummeled him with her fists. Persephone was a country girl, used to working in her mother's garden and catching wild goats for amusement. She was nearly as strong as any boy in the village.

He stumbled on one of the steps, but he didn't loosen his grip. "There's no point in your going on saying that; I'm not going to." The voice was panting a little, however.

Persephone began to kick again. The grip around her waist made her frantic, until she didn't care if she fell, if she could just make him let her go. Her captor lost his footing, and they began to slide, bumping over the steps in a fashion that was probably more painful for him than for her. At any rate, she hoped so. He kept his arms locked tightly around her, and they slid in a heap to the bottom.

"Take her," he said, gasping, and two of his dark servants appeared and gripped her by the arms and feet. The grasp around her middle loosened, and they hefted her like a freshly killed deer. She thrashed her arms and legs.

"Quit it, or I'll have them tie you up," her captor

said ominously from behind her. "And I ache like Typhon, you witch."

Persephone's last glimpse of him as she hung upside down caught him rubbing his backside ruefully. He was tall, with curling dark hair and a dark beard, his skin milky pale as befitted someone who lived underground. His tunic was of dark wool that she could tell was good cloth even at a distance, and his cloak the same, although just now ragged with their descent and studded with burrs and dry twigs. He inspected his shins and glared at her as they dragged her into the cave.

The roof was low and the initial opening merely a slanted outcropping of rock that looked as if its shade might provide shelter for some weary traveler. The sand on the floor was damp, and a tidal pool scent rose from it. She wondered desperately how far the water traveled at high tide. If everyone was dead here it might not matter. The floor was strewn with huge boulders as if some god had flung a handful of marbles, and she saw that the cave's depth was deceptive. Persephone's captors wound among the rocks and squeezed through a narrow gap, banging her head against the stone as they went. She heard him yell "Watch it!" behind her, and the servants made apologetic noises. His voice boomed and echoed in the rock. They turned abruptly, dodging another outcrop, and she saw the real cave mouth, a dark opening in the earth wide enough to drive cattle through, four abreast.

"No!" she said pleadingly, and then she screamed, "No!" but they paid her no heed. They ducked their heads and plunged into the mountain.

Persephone closed her eyes in terror, still screaming "No!" but her mind filled with pale wraiths brushing by her as they passed, ghostly fingers tearing at her cloak, and that seemed worse than seeing where she was going. She opened them again. There was no one to be seen but her bearers, and the passage walls made her blink in surprise.

The passageway went into the earth as Glaucus's tomb had done, but seemed to wander up as often as down, its walls lined with smooth dressed stone and lit with oil lamps set in niches. Off it branched other passageways whose windings she could just glimpse as they passed. In the pools of light the walls were carved with images she could barely make out. She stared at them as they passed, and sometimes a carved face stared back. The air was dank this far below the sun. Her arms and legs ached like fire.

"Put me down and I'll walk," she said finally.

They stopped, apparently considering this. "Might run off," one of them said at last, startling her. She hadn't been sure they could speak.

"How could I, with both of you here?" She tried to sound dignified, despite her terror and the stone walls closing around her the way they had in Glaucus's tomb. Their voices were deep and sepulchral. They considered her request, while she hung from their grip like a deer.

Finally the one at her head said, "Arms. One each," and they set her upright. A huge hand closed around each arm.

Persephone rubbed her wrists and eyed them warily. They were tall, as tall as her captor had been, and like him, dressed all in black. The hands on her arms looked human. Their faces were human too, probably—long and mournful and vaguely sheeplike.

They made her think uneasily of the black rams sacrificed at the cave mouth.

"This way," one of them said, prodding her with his free hand, and they set off down the passage. Now that she was upright, she could see that the stonework here was indeed much finer than Glaucus's tomb, where the rough stones had jutted from the passage walls and snagged her mantle. Here the stones were cut flat and dressed so that the joinery was almost invisible. The carved faces were of people all hurrying along, walking endlessly toward the same destination, some with servants behind, some with a child by the hand. The lamps that sat in the niches along the walls were of fine pottery painted with sea creatures, shells, and waves. An octopus goggled at her, round-eyed, as they passed. More passages branched off the main one, and they took first one and then another. Persephone tried desperately to fix the way in her head, but they all looked alike, and she lost count of the doorways as they went. She thought of the tales of heroes and heroines who had found their way out of labyrinths with a ball of string, and wondered if they habitually carried string here, just in case.

They came into a large room and she stopped, goggling at it, before they hurried her through. Around the raised hearth in the center, tiles gleamed blue and yellow, making a pattern like waves all around the base. It was lit, warming the dank air, and smoke rose from it into a vent in the stone roof, going somewhere. Around the walls were couches and benches covered in embroidered fabric, interspersed with life-size statues in marble and bronze—youths with a spear or discus, maidens virtuously spinning. Persephone thought suddenly of the souls who came here. Was that where they went? Into bronze and stone? The dark sheeplike servants hustled her across a smooth stone floor covered with thick weavings laid down on top, and out a door at the far end. She tried to look back at the great room as the hanging in the doorway brushed her head, but they tugged her onward.

They passed no one else in the cold corridors, and Persephone began to weep silently. She would never find her way out of this maze. The pale, dark-bearded man who was plainly Hades himself would rape her or eat her or suck her soul away or all three, and she would never see her mother again. She burst into a despairing howl just as the sheeplike servants stopped at a doorway with a wooden door in it instead of a tapestry. The door had a large bronze bolt on the outside.

The largest sheep servant patted her shoulder clumsily. "No one will hurt you."

"Then what does he want with me?" Persephone demanded, sniffling.

The servant opened the heavy door. "Marry you, I think," he said, and pushed her inside.

"*Marry me?*" The door closed behind her, and she heard the click of the bolt. Their footsteps padded away outside it.

Marry her?

The room was larger than she expected, with a tiled hearth like the one in the great room. Its warmth was inviting, and she sat on its edge, pulling her mantle around her. As in the great hall, the smoke went up through a vent into somewhere she couldn't see. There were two couches, an armchair, and two of the small backless benches most Hellenes used when they wanted to sit down, these with luxuriously padded seats. A loom and a basket with raw wool, a spindle, and a distaff stood in opposite corners, and on a three-legged table near the hearth was an array of food: wine and water in silver pitchers, a silver goblet, a plate of figs and cheese, a loaf of bread, a cruet of olive oil, a bowl of pastries, and another of mutton in a mint sauce. Persephone looked at the mutton and her stomach flipped over.

She got up and banged on the door, but no one came; she hadn't really expected them to. She was plainly being left to think things over and appreciate the luxury he was offering. She glared at the loom and the basket.

There was another door at the other side of the chamber, this one hung with only a tapestry. She explored, pushing the tapestry aside, and found a second chamber behind it, dominated by a huge bed hung with red curtains. Persephone stared at it, and in spite of herself, pressed the mattress down with one palm. It was soft, as if it was stuffed with down. Her bed at home was stuffed with straw. She sat on it gingerly, and leaped up again. Oh no, he wasn't going to entice her into bed with goose feathers!

She prowled about the rest of the room, discovering a vanity table laden with a seemingly endless array of pots of bronze and alabaster and painted clay, holding creams and unguents and rouges enough to paint an entire brothel. Persephone poked indignantly at a pot of rouge with one finger.

Another door opened off this room, too, and she followed it to find a plastered chamber painted yellow and containing a five-foot terracotta tub with bottom and sides adorned with leaping dolphins. For some reason the dolphins made her want to weep. They looked joyful, as if they had no idea they were painted here on the bottom of a tub inside a mountain, not frolicking in the waters off the headland. Persephone had never seen a bathing tub before, but she had heard of them. They were such things as rich men had, richer than Glaucus, men who lived on the other side of the mountain. A three-legged stool held a flask of oil, a bowl of sponges, and a strigil for scraping oneself clean. An open chest beside it offered piles of folded clothes. She turned from the chest and found herself face-to-face with a marble servant holding a towel over his arm. She shrieked and clapped her hand over her mouth. Behind the marble servant an arch opened onto yet another chamber, this one nearly entirely filled with a pool of water tiled in more blue and yellow, with a painted squid at its bottom. Hangings depicting sea nymphs splashing in a cove covered the walls. At the pool's center was a bronze drain, and at its end a clay pipe dribbled a musical stream of fresh water. Persephone put a toe in the water and jerked it back again. It was hot, as if it came out of the boiling heart of the earth.

Beyond the pool was yet another arch, this one with a discreet tapestry across it. She peered into a small stone room and found a stone seat with a hole in it. The sound of flowing water came from somewhere, and a ewer of water sat beside the seat. She sniffed cautiously, and her eyes widened. Hades was so rich his guests need not even leave his halls to shit.

Persephone backed out of the little room and sat

down by the pool to think. After a few minutes she got up and came back with the tray of food. She set it on the pool's edge, took her sandals off, and put her feet in the water. The pool had steps at this end, and she rested them on the highest one. The warm water bubbled around her ankles. She ate a fig and thought.

Item one: She wasn't dead, so far as she could tell.

Item two: She hadn't seen any dead people, except maybe for those carved into the walls.

Item three: Unless you counted the statues.

Persephone ate a pastry and licked the honey and fine flakes of dough from her fingers. It was important to be logical. Hellenes valued logic. It was what made them civilized, so Aristippus said. He had told her this when she was small, when the sun was in her eyes and she had demanded petulantly that he move it. The sun went one way, he said, because that was how Apollo drove his chariot. No one had the power to make him move it for their own ends, and if he did it would likely set the world on fire, so there was no use asking for things you couldn't have. Ask instead for what you might get. He had said that with a nudge and a wink at her mother taking bread from the oven in the courtyard, and Demeter had given her a piece of it hot with a bowl of olive oil to dip it in. There, said Aristippus. See?

Persephone wasn't certain how to apply this logic to her current situation, but at any rate (see item one) she wasn't dead. She ate another pastry, filled with crushed nuts and honey, the kind that were so tedious to make that they were kept for weddings and feasts. Hades (she named him firmly to herself) must be rich enough to have a kitchen full of cooks. He

probably had a hunchback or a wall-eye, she thought
moodily, some excellent reason why he would have
to kidnap a wife. Unless of course he really was
Death, in which case she could see that courting
would be difficult. She ate an olive and another
pastry.

Item four: There was no sunlight here. How did
anyone live without sunlight? Even with enough
money to afford to keep lamps lit all day and all
night.

Item five: How did you tell whether it was day
or night?

Persephone was running out of numbers that she
knew, and couldn't feel that she was any farther
along with her problem.

Item six: If you eat in someone's house you bind
yourself to them. That idea came to her, and she put
down the bowl of olives. Mother had said that, and
so had Aristippus. Food was what kept everyone
alive, so naturally sharing it with someone meant
something. Did it count if no one knew? Did it count
if the other person didn't need food because he was
Death? She rearranged the pastries in the bowl to
look as untouched as possible and took the tray back
to the central chamber, her wet feet leaving footprints
on the cold stone. She thought with longing of the
carpets she had seen in the great hall and went back
for her sandals. While she sat on the goose-down bed
tying them, she heard the bolt rattle in the chamber
outside. She got to her feet, faced the doorway, and
braced for whatever was going to happen to her.

A sheeplike face poked its long nose through the
far wall instead, around a curtain she hadn't noticed
before, and she screamed.

"Master sent you a present." He held out a folded carpet of the sort she had seen in the great hall, laid across his arms like the statue with the towel. "Master forgets that the floors are cold for young ladies from the upper air."

"How did you get in here?" Persephone backed away.

"Chamber is a spiral, madam. Like a seashell. Many doors." He laid the carpet on the bed and lifted the hanging he had come through with one hand. Persephone could see that the unnoticed door opened on the chamber with the pool. She had not thought to look behind the hangings on its walls, but she could see now that the pool was the chamber's true heart. All doors except the one to the outside world opened onto it.

The servant hefted the carpet again and disappeared back into the wall. She heard movement in the outer chamber and lifted the hanging to see him laying the carpet on the floor beside the hearth. He bowed toward Persephone. "I will bring more. Master says not but one of us at a time, so as not to frighten the young lady." He bowed again, backing through the door into the corridor, and slapped it shut briskly. She heard the bolt slide.

A few minutes later he was back, with another carpet. He laid it on the other side of the hearth and bustled out, returning with a third. All the carpets were blue, woven with shells and tritons riding fish. Persephone began to feel as if she were drowning in so many fish. The octopi would inhabit her dreams, driving out the ghosts she feared, only to replace them with bulbous heads and goggling eyes, tentacles plucking at her bedclothes.

"No more fish," she said when he came back a fourth time.

He looked disappointed. "Master is very fond of fish."

"Well, I'm not. And I'm not fond of your master either." Persephone stamped her foot and pointed at the tray of food. "And take that away. I won't eat it and you can tell him so."

"Very good food," the servant said hopefully. "No fish."

"Take it away!"

The servant sighed and hefted the tray. This time he was gone a long time. When he reappeared he bore a red carpet, rolled up on his shoulder. He took it into the bedchamber and unrolled it with a flourish. "No fish!" he announced.

There was a restrained design of waves around the edges, but as he said, no fish.

"Thank you."

The servant bowed. "One more thing." He popped out the door and back in with quick snicks of the bolt. He was stooped and elderly, but surprisingly agile. Persephone suspected that if she raced him for the unbolted door, she would never make it. He unfolded a cloth package and shook it out. It was a gown, already pinned at the shoulders with pearls. The cloth was pale blue and finer than anything Persephone had seen. He draped it across the bed, gesturing to it enticingly like a salesman selling goods. He laid a mantle of deeper blue beside it, with an ebony box containing six more pearl pins. "Finest quality. From my master." He looked hopeful. When Persephone didn't answer him, he said, still hopeful,

"Young ladies like these things." Finally he sighed and bowed himself out.

When she was sure he had gone, Persephone touched the cloth gingerly. It felt like milk beneath her fingers, cool and slippery and with a faint sheen. The edges of the mantle were embroidered in gold thread. Persephone's own gown, which had been her second best, was covered in mud and burrs and stained with grass on the backside. Persephone sighed and pulled it over her head. She turned it to the other side, refolded and repinned it with her own bronze pins. Both women's gowns and men's tunics were made from a single sheet of cloth folded over the top and wrapped around the body. One pinned it at the shoulders and open side, and arranged the folds with a girdle tied at the waist. If one was wealthy, embroidery might decorate the hem. The pins that held the shoulders might be made of precious stones or artful twists of bronze. Village fops like Hermes spent hours achieving the perfect fold. The pearls in the ebony box were worth a fortune. Persephone snapped it closed.

Item seven: honor before greed.

No one came back for hours, until she had slept her way in the goose-down bed into what she thought must be the next day. She awoke, burrowed into the soft folds of a mountain of blanket, which had not served to keep out the dank cold or the dreams of pale ghosts riding the wind that blew into the cave mouth and down the long corridors. No octopi, but the sound of the sea was all around her, not quite heard, like the whushing in a shell. The oil lamps had been freshly filled. She got up and used the room with the stone seat, wondering where it *went*.

Her skin felt gritty and itched, and she oiled it and scraped herself down with the strigil. Someone had filled the bathtub while she slept (she thought uneasily of a parade of soft-footed sheep servants trotting past her with ewers) so she got in it and sank to her chin. The water was still warm—it must have come from the pool—and soothed the bruises she was just beginning to feel from yesterday's fall.

She got out of the bath, wrapping herself in one of the soft towels from the chest (she couldn't bring herself to take the one the statue held out to her). When she walked into the bedroom the sheep servant was standing there. Persephone screamed, and he winced.

"Madam need not make that noise every time," he said reproachfully.

"Then don't keep sneaking in!" Persephone said, teeth chattering with the cold.

"Master sends something to break the fast." She could see a tray of wine and water and figs on the table by the bed.

"Take it away!"

"Madam will grow thin."

"Good. Then he won't want me."

The sheep servant shook his head. "Oh, I don't think so. Master is in love. He said madam is 'like a piece of sunlight.' He sent madam a present."

Persephone snatched the ebony box, twin to the first one, from the tray and threw it against the wall. A spill of polished stones and gold fell out and lay winking in the lamplight. "Get out!"

The sheep servant bowed himself out, and she sat down weeping on the bed, her face in her hands.

Persephone was not a girl who spent much time crying, even as a child. Generally, after having a good howl, she had trotted off and done something. It was not always something anyone liked very much, but she had taken action. When Hermes had painted mustaches on all her dolls, she had lain in wait for him in the branches of an oak tree and dropped a bag of sheep manure on his head. When her mother had refused her the wherewithal to buy a pair of green sandals with red embroidery from a peddler, she had traded him Demeter's best copper pot for them. When Bopis had complained that Persephone was allowed to run wild like a savage and set other, well-behaved children a bad example, she had danced through the agora, wearing nothing but a wreath of grape leaves, and stuck her tongue out at her. All three instances had brought swift punishment from Demeter—the first because she had ruined Hermes's tunic, the second for stealing, and the third for disrespect—but Persephone had considered them all well worth the paddling.

Now she remembered the jackal pup she had wanted to keep for a pet. Demeter had told her that it would not be happy, and Great-Grandfather had told her it would eat their chickens. Everyone else had told her it would bite her. All three had proved true, and she had set it loose again near the den where she had stolen it. So now she sat up after a middling cry, and tried to think what would annoy her captor the most.

*   *   *

Hades himself came to see her on the third day. Perhaps the old sheep servant had told him that he was getting nowhere with his gifts when Persephone dropped the gold and aquamarine necklace and matching earrings down the hole in the stone seat and sent something unsavory after them.

He found her sitting on the edge of the hearth in her old gown, now more repulsive than ever, her hair a tangle of snarls and mats.

"I did give you a comb," he said mildly.

Persephone inspected him from slitted eyes, like a cat. He looked to be her mother's age, or maybe younger. It was very hard to tell. His pale skin was nearly unlined. His nails and heavy beard were neatly trimmed, and the dark curling hair on his head was held in place with a silver fillet. Dark eyebrows slanted over startlingly blue eyes. He wore a brown tunic embroidered with pale acanthus leaves around the borders and a mantle dyed with the dark purple that came from sea snails. This dye was so costly that even Glaucus had had only a band of it around the hem of his best tunic. Hades's sandals were soft dark leather with bronze buckles. He was tall. His head nearly bumped the ceiling.

When Persephone didn't say anything, he drew up a stool and sat down. "I brought you some food." He gestured at the tray he had set on a table.

Persephone pressed her lips together.

"You must be hungry."

The smell of an omelette of eggs and cheese drifted from under the cover on the tray. She ignored it resolutely.

"You know I won't hurt you."

Persephone sniffed.

"You look a mess."

"I'm not going to get better looking."

"You could get cleaner."

"But I won't."

Hades sighed. "It's a shame. They say that filth affects the mind. Pretty soon a person goes raving mad. Then they're seen running on all fours and grunting like a pig. I've seen it happen."

"Then no one marries them," Persephone pointed out.

"Oh, I have a great tolerance for that sort of thing," Hades said. "Living down here as I do."

"With dead people." Persephone shuddered.

"Very few of them are dead," Hades said.

"Then where is Echemus?"

Hades sighed. "He *is* dead, I am afraid. They don't understand what sort of ailments to send me. There is not much I can do for pneumonia."

"Great-Grandfather said that sometimes people with what he had have lived," Persephone countered, interested in spite of herself.

"Indeed. But not through my agency. In those cases, the body heals itself, or it does not. All I can do is give it rest, and hope. Or ease the passing," he added.

"Where is he then?"

"Dead, as I told you. I buried him."

"Where is his spirit?"

"Gone, I suppose, on its own errands." He saw Persephone's perplexed expression, and said, "You think they all live with me, don't you? Maybe they do. Sometimes I think some of them are still here."

Persephone looked around her as if something had brushed her hair.

"I have given my servants instructions not to let any spirits in here with you," he assured her solemnly. "However"— he took the cover off the plate—"if you don't eat, you're likely to be one yourself."

Persephone leaped from her seat on the hearth and snatched the plate. He looked gratified for a moment until she flung it at him.

Hades sat very still for a long while, while Persephone considered that she might have overdone it. Finally he brushed the omelette from his beard and said carefully, "Don't you think that I might grow on you?"

"No!"

He stood. "In that case, I shall go and have a bath." He eyed her appraisingly. "You might do the same."

III

Fire and Rain

When Demeter was angry someone was generally sorry afterward. Now that she was angry at Death no one knew quite what she might do. At first she had climbed down the steps from the headland to stand outside the caves and shout for Persephone. When there was no answer she had shouted his name instead and blundered about the dank stone chamber while the sea washed her ankles, trying to find the way in. Whatever way he had taken was sealed, or hidden by magic. She had stayed there all night, pleading with him, but no living thing had come out.

Now she stalked up and down the rows of her garden, her white gown a flash in the sunlight like an angry heron. The village watched her at a respectful distance.

"No good is going to come of this," her cousin Maia said, pulling her mantle around her head and shoulders as if whatever was going to happen might drop out of the wild blue sky on her. "That child was allowed to run around like a wild goat, and now look."

"We all said so," Bopis said with satisfaction.

"I feel responsible." Irene sighed. "I let the girls go down there with poor Echemus. And all for nothing anyway. I haven't even a body to bury." She sniffed loudly at all of it.

"It was Persephone he took," Maia said. "Narcissa and Echo were with her, and nothing ran off with *them*."

"Persephone's prettier," Hermes said. "I would have run off with her if it was me. Echo has freckles, and Narcissa's nose is nearly as big as Echemus's was."

"It is not!" Irene rounded on him. "Narcissa has an elegant profile, just like a painting on a vase!"

Maia took her son by the arm. "This is women's talk. Go and see to the goats. Two of them were in the vineyard yesterday. I told you to keep better watch on them."

"Yes, Mother." He bowed low at her and ran off, chuckling.

Doris, Echo's mother, glared after him.

The sun burned down on them like a bowl full of brass, and only Hermes, bathing in the river, was cool.

Demeter knew they were watching her. How on earth did you talk to women who had never been out of the village and tell them all the things there were on the earth that could swallow you whole? The gaping jaws of Death and Mischance and Vengeance? They had no idea. She had been Persephone's age when she had fallen off the edge of the world.

That had been chance, too. She had gone down to the beach alone, to a rocky cove where no one ever came, to see what the tide had brought in. That particular morning it had brought a young man mending his boat. He was from Eleusis on the mainland, which no one Demeter knew had ever seen. They had talked all morning about the things that lay over the horizon, and when he sailed in the afternoon she had sailed with him.

It hadn't been a kidnapping exactly. Village life was dull, and so were the men courting her, presented by Grandfather who had raised her and wanted her well situated, and Bopis, who hated her and just wanted her out of the house. Triptolemus, on the other hand, had been handsome, with a head of gold curls, merry blue eyes, and muscular shoulders. She had gone with him willingly, lured by tales of wonders. He spoke of five-storied houses with painted walls big enough to hold her village, ships with hundreds of oars, chariots with silver wheels, and tamed trees arranged in rows.

It hadn't been quite like that. The wonderful cities were dead, torn apart by wars and rebellions. The silver chariot wheels he had stolen out of an ancient grave. And the peaceful hills he had described—a sailor's homesick vision—were infested with bandits. They arrived for the funeral of his brother.

Demophon had been alive the first time Demeter saw him and in flames the next. He had welcomed Triptolemus home with a brotherly arm about his shoulders and an appreciative glance at Demeter, although the parents had been less pleased and the two sisters looked at her with suspicion. But there had been a feast all the same, with a great deal of wine, watered less and less as the evening wore on, and much singing and boasting. By the end of it, the men could barely walk, and Demeter's head was spinning, too. Triptolemus's father, Celeus, was nodding on his couch, and his mother, Metanira, and her daughters had gone to bed. Demeter wanted to go to bed, too, but didn't know where she was to go.

"That's a fine piece of sea glass you picked up," Demophon said, slapping his brother's shoulder. "Give her to me, and I'll give you my best ram."

Triptolemus laughed. "She's worth more than that, you young fool."

"My best ram and four jars of oil."

Demeter's eyes widened. "I am not a slave!" She looked at Triptolemus, horrified.

Triptolemus nodded drunkenly. "You're my woman. Worth more than that anyway."

"My best ram, four jars of oil, and an ox. How about that?" Demophon flopped on the bench beside Demeter. "You'd like me, wouldn't you? I'm handsomer than Triptolemus anyway." He tried to kiss her, his breath heavy with wine and garlic, and she shoved him away.

Demophon lurched and lost his balance. He toppled, slowly, like a tree being felled, while she watched, and he landed in the hearth. It was sheer evil chance that his fall swept a clay lamp off the table and into the fire with him, where it broke on the coals. His oil-soaked mantle had tangled around his right arm where it lay in the flames, and as he struggled, a gout of flame shot up from the hem of his tunic. He tried to stagger to his feet but fell again with his face in the heart of the fire, and his hair caught.

"Get him up!" Triptolemus leaped from his couch, and Demeter helped him tug Demophon from the flames.

"Father!"

Celeus jerked awake, rubbing sleep and wine from his eyes. They rolled Demophon in his mantle and doused the flames, but he was horribly burned. Celeus shouted for Metanira, who came screaming from their bedchamber.

Metanira and her daughters cut away the charred cloth and rubbed his burned skin with unguents. They sent for the village doctor, who gave them a poultice of herbs and shook his gray head despairingly. Everyone knew that no one that badly burned ever healed. Metanira had Demophon taken to his chamber, and she and her daughters sat with him through three days. Demophon's skin peeled away in horrible strips, and the red raw flesh underneath it oozed yellow fluid. Gradually it hardened and turned black. His breathing grew labored, and the burned flesh on his lips and mouth fell away.

When Demeter tried to bring them food, Metanira's eyes flashed and she shrieked at Demeter, "Get out! This is your doing! Get out of my sight!"

Demeter hid, weeping, while Demophon died. Triptolemus told her it wasn't her fault, but he, too, spent most of his time at his brother's bedside. By the time they buried Demophon, Demeter felt like a ghost in the house herself, and hid most of the day in the olive orchard.

The tame trees Triptolemus had told her of were actually there. Triptolemus had laughed at her on their arrival when she had run into the olive grove and stared in wonder at the trees, dozens of them lined up in straight rows like game pieces.

"You are an ignorant islander," he had said, shaking his head.

"Teach me to plant trees," she told him the day after the funeral.

"That isn't women's work," Celeus said.

"Let the whore plant trees," Metanira said. "I don't want her in my house."

Demeter had known then she couldn't stay. She wasn't even sure why she had come, other than impulse, and the fact that Triptolemus was so handsome; but it was clear to her now that he would go only so far against his parents' wishes, and that he would not marry her. Maybe he never would have. She was reasonably sure that he would not have sold her to Demophon, but she was increasingly aware that he could probably do what he wanted to with her in this foreign country.

While Metanira glowered at her from her chamber window, spindle and distaff in hand, Demeter followed Faunus, Celeus's gardener, who practiced a skill she had never heard of before. On her home island, the men and boys went into the hills at the start of winter and beat the nearly ripe olives out of the trees with flails. The women gathered grain in May from wild wheat that grew on the hillsides and valley floor, and figs in summer and grapes in autumn. Here in Eleusis, Demeter followed the plow that Faunus drove behind an ox, and sowed the wheat in rows. She helped him prune the grapes, and he showed her how to take cuttings from the vines. Together they planted beans and cabbages in neat rows and tied the trailing pea vines to trellises. He was a slave and treated her as if she must be one, too, although at night she slept with Triptolemus and ate with his family, while Celeus, despite his sorrow, tried jovially to be kind, and Metanira and the daughters shot her poisoned looks. Demeter bit by bit stole seeds from the gardener's store and hid them in a little jar in a hole she dug behind the goat shed.

Demeter lived with Triptolemus in Eleusis through the cycle of one year. Midway through she knew she was pregnant. While the garden grew, she grew, and Metanira announced that she had known the girl was a whore. Triptolemus was pleased, when he was not hunting or fishing or taking the wheat crop to market in his boat, and had time to think about her. For the sake of what they were sure would be Triptolemus's son, the sisters grew somewhat kinder.

The baby was born in the spring, a year to the day after Demophon's death. Metanira, prepared to forgive all if it was a boy, held up a small squalling girl by the feet and dropped her in Demeter's bloody lap.

"It looks sickly. It ought to be exposed," she said vindictively, while Demeter looked pleadingly at Triptolemus.

"No need to talk of that tonight," Triptolemus said cheerfully, ushering his mother out of the chamber. "Give her one night with the babe, can't you? We'll talk tomorrow."

"The child is an ill omen."

Triptolemus didn't sleep with her that night, and before daylight Demeter got out of the bed, washed herself and the baby with water from the pitcher in their chamber, and dressed. She packed the clothes that Triptolemus had given her into a sack and stole the gardener's pruning knife from the potting shed. By moonlight she cut shoots from the best grapevines and unearthed her jar of seeds, digging into the dirt behind the goat shed like a dog, while the baby watched her, eyes bright as silver coins under the moon. Demeter scooped up baby, cuttings, seeds, and sack and stole Triptolemus's best boat.

How could she have explained all that to Persephone? Told her how her mother had sailed away with a young man just because his hair was gold and his eyes were blue? She had never told even Aristippus what had happened, but Demeter had come home armed with new knowledge and planted her garden. When the village had seen what she grew, they had asked no more questions for fear that she would take it all away again.

And what did it all matter to her now if her child was gone? And who could go down into the earth and get her back? Demeter went into her house and closed the door behind her.

The sun blazed just a shade brighter, as if in sympathy with her anger. It had been a hot summer, and the sky was the deep clear blue of a bird's egg. Its heat shimmered on the sea and on the white limestone walls of Demeter's house. When she emerged it was only to pace wildly up and down the headland, shouting at him, calling for Persephone. Nothing ever answered her but the white gulls wheeling in the sky overhead. Summer in Hellas is always hot, but now it seemed as if Apollo had halted his chariot stock-still in the noon sky. The irrigation channels that

brought water from the river to the garden cracked
and dried out, and Demeter didn't come out to tend
them. The bean vines withered, and their leaves
turned brown. The cabbages, even under their shade-
cloth, wilted and then desiccated so that there was
left only a ragged spiral of transparent green leaf that
crumbled when touched.

The grass turned brown underfoot, and the poppies on the headland withered, leaving only their tall
brown stalks and urn-shaped seedpods rattling in
the wind.

The sheep and goats foraged farther and farther
up the mountain for graze. The village boys scam-
pered after them, with what food could be spared,
half a loaf of bread and a bag of dried fish to see
them through. More often than not they slept in the
hills with the flocks. The river ran lower, and the
water in the well came up muddy. When the breeze
blew, the agora disappeared in a cloud of dust.

"It's her!" Phaedon, the doctor, said coughing, his
mantle to his mouth. He pointed at Demeter's house,
sitting silently in the heat. "Look at her garden!"

The brown bean vines rattled to dust on their
trellises.

"It's the heat," Maia said.

"She brought it," Bopis said.

"We've had hot spells before," Phaedon said.
"She's let those channels she dug go dry."

"Do you suppose it's cursed the whole island?"
Hermes asked.

"Well, of course it has, boy! You can't have a place
like that"— he nodded at the garden—"and not have
it spill over."

Magic leaks. Everyone knew that. When you lived

near a place of magic, near anything touched by the gods, you felt its vibrations in your skin. When there was upheaval there, it was mirrored in the world outside and around it. That only stood to reason. Demeter's garden was dying, and it was taking the island with it.

"The whole village is suffering." Aristippus thumped his staff on the tiles, but Demeter didn't look up. She sat with her face to the window, staring out at the sea off the headland. "Pay attention to me!"

"They managed before."

"That would be very true if the whole island were not drying up like a slug in the sun." Aristippus thumped his staff again. "You changed things with all your new ways. They can't go back to the old ones. The island can't."

"I don't care. I want my child back." Demeter's pale brown hair was unkempt, and she hadn't bothered in a moon to wash her clothes in the river that now was sluggish and dark as mud anyway.

"Sulking won't bring her back."

"It gives me pleasure."

"It does not." Aristippus got between her and the window. "He will give her back or he won't. Won't, most likely, since he stole her." He glowered at Demeter. "She would have married sometime. Gone away."

"She would not."

"Maybe you should have let her," he said.

For three months Demeter did not go into her garden, and no one saw her except as a wild form pacing on the headland. Weeds, which do not mind drought, overran the garden, swallowing up the dried husks of her vegetables. The bug people, unmolested, came out and ate the rest. The wheatfields, harvested in the month of Maimakterion, were tinder dry, and a spark from the temple hearth caught them on fire. The men of the village fought it through the night with jugs of water, shovels, and blankets, but the fire ate the whole field and singed the olive grove before they stopped it. A stray spark ran along the grapevines, and a whole row blazed and crackled into cinders. The glow of the flames lit the night sky.

Demeter, watching from her window, thought of Demophon.

At the start of the month of Elaphebolion the village scoured out the wine vats with boiling seawater and harvested what was left of the grapes.

"You will come to the agora for the pressing," Aristippus said to Demeter, and this time she nodded listlessly. She had combed her hair and put on a clean gown, but it was like watching a walking corpse, to see her coming softly along the path from her house to the agora where the winepresses had been set up. Scrubbed and dried, they held promise each year of a new vintage, but this year the festival had lost its heart. Everyone was just slightly hungry, and half the grapes had gone bad on the vines for reasons that no one could explain.

The islanders had dragged benches out of their houses into the open for the old people to sit on and watch the pressing. Demeter sat down on one, listlessly as if she had been dropped there accidentally by someone who was carrying her somewhere.

The old men on either side of her edged away, but Demeter didn't seem to notice.

Hermes danced past her, playing his flute, a jaunty tune to accompany the grapepickers coming single file down the path from the vineyard in the morning sun, baskets on their shoulders. Demeter should have been at the procession's head, but she didn't look up.

The harvesters dumped the grapes into the biggest vats, where it was the job of the young people to dance the wine out of them. Three or four boys set the tempo with their flutes, and the rest climbed into the vat, laughing and pushing each other, dancing for the attention of the girls who had hiked their skirts over their knees to dance beside them.

The pressed juice ran in a red stream out a spout at the bottom of the vat, into a smaller tub where it would be left to ferment until spring. Through the morning the men brought the grapes in baskets and dumped them beneath the dancers' feet. Under Bopis's supervision, the women carried plates of dried fish and cheese and cups of last year's vintage, well watered, and handed them around. The dancers leaned over the edges of the vat to grab a cup and drain it.

"Hey ho, Echo." Hermes flicked a piece of grape pulp at her. "Want to watch the moon come up with me tonight?"

Echo considered him, remembering their last moonlit walk. He was handsome—something about him made you want to abandon caution and dance through the field with him—but completely unreliable. The number of girls who had thought he would marry them could not be counted on both her hands. "Mother says I am not to," she said primly, and

sought refuge next to Harmonia and Tros, who were
dancing hand in hand while Harmonia's mother
glared at them. They would be married soon, despite
Tros's lack of wealth. He had almost earned enough
for the bride price that her father had set, in the
assumption that it would be beyond him. Tros was
a faithful sort—Harmonia wasn't even more than
passably good-looking.

What made love? Echo wondered. Bopis was a
sour old busybody just because Aristippus wouldn't
leave other women alone, although to give him his
due, he didn't chase young girls anymore. Widows
were his specialty, and no wonder Bopis wanted to
marry Irene off. And look at poor Persephone,
snatched up in the arms of a fearful being, not even
human. He probably loved her. Persephone, so far
as Echo knew, had never loved anyone, but Echo
thought she had wanted to. It was the one indul-
gence that her mother had denied her. Persephone
could have had anything else—freedom to roam the
hills playing with the wild goats, to spend her days
picking flowers and romping in the stream, pleasures
that her friends had to filch time for from their other
duties. But not love. No young men. No old men,
for that matter. Demeter hadn't even dedicated her
to Hestia, or to Artemis, the goddess who roamed the
countryside hunting and indulging in other sports
reserved for men, always virgin and untouched;
however, there had been no men allowed to come
courting and offer a bride price. After the first one or
two, no one had even tried. It was as if Persephone's
virginity was Demeter's offering to avert from her
whatever fate had befallen Demeter so long ago.

Echo wondered what that had been. It must have

been a man, that stood to reason, or she wouldn't have had Persephone. She had gone somewhere over mountain, over sea, who knew, to the gods, people said, and been given gifts. Apparently a child had been one of them. The gods were like that, just ask Maia, although Echo didn't think Hermes was a god's son, despite Hermes's insistence that he was. "A child of the god" was a euphemism for a baby got in unorthodox ways: in the hayfield on solstice night, for instance.

But something else had been given to Demeter, along with the child. It had been impossible to tell Demeter from her garden. When you saw her in it, it seemed as if her feet went into the earth and her fingers ended in sprouts of green leaves. She was the garden. No wonder that a child who had grown up in it would appeal to a man who lived down in the darkness; but child and garden and mother had all been one in some way, Echo thought. When she saw Demeter sitting lifelessly now while life danced around her to the flute song, she thought of bean pods stripped of their seed or wheat chaff when the grain has been threshed out of it. There was something gone out of Demeter now, and the absence made Echo want to cry.

They danced in the vats until the noon sun tilted and slid down the western sky. The air was hot and sticky with juice. Insects buzzed around them, and the vintner's boys fished them out of the vats with a scoop. Dogs trotted between the legs of the watchers, seeing if anyone had dropped anything to eat. A cat, unnoticed, slunk along the windowsill of Narcissa's house and began licking a cheese on the table, the gift of Narcissa's mother's suitor, another from the north island. She would have this one, Narcissa had told Echo, and he had a younger brother also in the market for a wife. This was the last year she would dance in the vintage with Narcissa, Echo suspected.

The sun dropped farther, burnishing the water to copper in the west. Echo's legs ached. Her dress was splashed with juice from hem to shoulders. It was the old one that she always wore for the vintage, splotched with wine of other years. She could trace the history of her girlhood in the faded stains. The pale one at the hem, bleached with much subsequent washing, was from the first year she had been allowed to dance in the vats. She had been so short she had sunk into the grapes up to her waist. Persephone and Narcissa had each taken one of her hands and held her upright until she got her footing. Persephone should be here now, dancing beside her. Echo felt a hole in the air between herself and Narcissa.

"Hey ho, Echo." Hermes was there again, cavorting beside her in the vat.

"Go and dance somewhere else," she said irritably.

Hermes's mouth was red with wine stains, and he handed a clay cup to her. "Here. Keep your strength up."

Echo took it and drank. It was the last of the wine from four years ago, just on the edge of going bad. She swallowed and handed him back the cup. Hermes handed it to Narcissa, and Echo knitted her brows to see Hermes in Persephone's place.

Hermes seemed to catch her thought from the air; he had an unsettling way of doing that. "I could bring her back," he said, grinning as he danced.

"Go down there?" Echo snorted.

"You would pee all over yourself just thinking about going into that cave," Narcissa said.

Hermes looked offended. "I go down there all the time. He's old. I will wrestle him for her and pin him on the first try!"

"He'll feed you to his dog," Arachne said from the other side of the vat. She was a slender girl with long dark ringlets. She swayed gracefully as she danced, like a stalk of grass, never seeming out of breath while everyone else huffed and puffed.

"What dog?"

"Haven't you seen it? Since you go down there all the time?"

"No, I haven't." Hermes narrowed his eyes at her, as if trying to decide whether she was making that up.

"Just at dusk," Arachne said dreamily. "I've seen it twice. It comes out to play in the surf. It has three heads," she added.

Hermes looked unnerved.

Echo giggled. "Great big heads." She snapped her teeth at him.

"With green foam," Narcissa said knowingly. "We've seen it, too."

"No foam," Arachne said. "Just teeth. I made a weaving of it. I'll show you."

Narcissa sighed. Arachne's weavings were magical. It was as if she just painted things on the loom. Narcissa's mother was always asking her why she couldn't weave like Arachne, which was a silly question because no one could.

"Never mind," Hermes said. "You'll change your tune when I go down there and bring her back."

"Then why haven't you?" Echo asked him.

"Demeter has to promise her to me. I'm not going to go fight a dog with three heads just to be kind."

"And you just asked me to watch the moon come up with you!" Echo threw a handful of grapes at him. "Faithless! Faithless!"

They all started shouting "Faithless!" at him and threw more grapes. Hermes vaulted over the side of the vat in a shower of juice.

"Be careful, you cursed goat!" The vintner shook his paddle at him.

Hermes dodged between the vats and climbed into another one.

"That one won't do anything," Arachne said with a sniff.

"No, but somebody had better," Echo said, watching Demeter. She hadn't moved since the morning. She sat on the bench as if she were a pile of laundry.

When the last juice had been run into the tubs, Demeter stood finally and looked around her as if she had been asleep. She walked back to her house, leaving the village to dance out the rest of the evening on the packed dirt of the agora. Aristippus saw her go and knew there would be no more to be got from her tonight, so he gave his attention to dancing in the wine, which was a matter of some importance. He joined the end of the line as the dancers flew by him, taking the hand of Irene, still a passably attractive widow, while the onlookers clapped out a rhythm to flute and lyre. Nearly everyone in the village played one instrument or the other, although the lyre was considered somewhat more respectable. In their midst Bopis stood stiffly, watching Aristippus to be sure he didn't disappear with Irene as the moon rose.

The vintner's boys dumped the juice into the press
and hung on the end of the heavy beam until the
juice flowed into the storage vats and left the pulp
behind. The dregs of the old vintage were handed
round. The fermentation process never really
stopped, and it spoiled if you left it too long. Four
years was elderly, so it needed to be drunk.

"I'm elderly," Phaedon said with satisfaction, pulling on his cup. "I need to be drunk, too."

"Get up and dance, you old goat," Echo's mother
Doris said, prodding him with her sandal. They were
brother and sister, and she felt entitled.

"Bah, woman. Dance yourself." Phaedon settled
back on his bench. Doris grinned and sat down next
to him. "I paid good money in my youth to study
with a man who studied with a man who once studied with Asclepius. I have no need to cavort like a
ram in spring. It is undignified."

"You mean your bones ache," Doris said. "Mine
too. There is a bad winter coming."

Phaedon sniffed and flicked a small grasshopper
out of his beard. "No one but gods and soothsayers
know what the weather will be," he said. That was
a proverb, but the truth was that everyone generally
knew what the weather would be: hot and sunny in
the summer, mild and sunny in the winter, occasionally with a bit of rain.

"This will be different," Doris said. "You mark
my words."

The dancers snaked past them, feet skipping to the
flutes, clothes flying, bare feet stained red to the
knees. Some of the girls, despite Bopis's orders, still
had their gowns hitched up, as if they just hadn't
remembered to let them down.

"Shameless," Doris muttered.

Phaedon took the knot of hair on the back of her neck in his hand and gave it a shake back and forth. "Old women forget things. Men have much better memories. I, for instance, remember quite clearly pulling you out of the dance at the vintage when you were sixteen, on Mother's orders, because your skirt was up to your backside."

"Nonsense," Doris said primly. "I don't remember anything like that at all."

"All the men of that year do," Phaedon said, chortling.

Doris ignored him, watching the sky.

Phaedon elbowed her, to see if she had got the joke, and saw what she was watching.

To the west, where the sun was sinking in the water, dark clouds were boiling up, lit from below by the sun, like fire in a forge. As they watched, the clouds rose like a dreadful being climbing out of the sea. The sun dropped below the horizon and the air darkened suddenly about them as if a door had shut. The dancers hopped uncertainly on one foot and stopped while the flutes and lyres jangled into silence. The sky rumbled, and they saw a distant flash of lightning on the water.

Before the tubs of new wine could be sealed and rolled away to the cellars where they were left to age, the sky opened. Water poured down on them as if out of a bucket, and the agora filled with mud. The vintner's boys slipped and slid as they rolled the tubs away. Echo pulled her mantle over her head and took her mother by the hand.

"Get out of this! You'll catch your death!" She could feel the cold rain plastering her mantle to her hair, and the sticky hem of her gown to her shins. Her sandals, retrieved from under a bench, were sodden with mud.

They ran for home, tugging the benches they had brought from their house and sliding in the mud.

When the storm stopped, the wind and rain had knocked down half the unripe olives and had broken whole branches from the trees. The storm had also torn a hole in the thatch roof of the Temple of Hestia and put out her fire. The whole village stood wailing outside the temple. The fire on Hestia's hearth was the heart of the village, daughter of the sacred fire of the ruined city on the mainland from which the ancestors of these villagers had fled generations ago, carrying their hearth fire in a clay pot. To allow the fire to go out was sacrilege. Hesperia, Hestia's ancient priestess, stood wavering in the temple courtyard, her thin arms shaking as if a sea breeze might blow her over.

"What are we to do?" Phaedon asked her. He attempted to look businesslike, but his eyes were uneasy. Bopis, quiet for once, shivered in her wet mantle.

Hesperia mumbled something no one could understand.

"The goddess must tell us," Aristippus said. "The priestess will go into a trance, and the goddess will speak." He seemed to be talking to Hesperia more than to anyone else. She nodded, her chin trembling, and shuffled back into the temple.

Echo clung to her mother's arm. This was bad. It was bad to let your own hearth fire go out, your own little offering to Hestia. To let the village fire go out . . . well, who knew what might happen if the goddess was not placated. The hearth fire was where anyone could go for refuge, where no one could kill you without sacrilege if you sought its asylum. Without it the village itself was naked, unprotected by any power.

Phaedon and Nicias, Irene's new suitor, brought a young goat and killed it in the temple doorway, cutting its throat and letting the blood pour into a bronze bowl. They put the bowl on the altar and the bones in the cold hearth. Over them they laid all the dry tinder that could be found, liberally sprinkled with oil and herbs, and set a torch to it. Old Hesperia came forth, leaning on Aristippus, and stood in the smoke, arms outstretched.

At first Echo thought she would choke. She began to cough, and Aristippus thumped her back. Her eyes bulged, and Echo looked uneasily at Phaedon, the doctor. If they killed the priestess of Hestia trying to get a divination from her, surely that would not be good.

Hesperia coughed again and stepped back from the smoke. She looked wild-eyed, like a sheep caught in briars. "There is worse to come," she said, which was not what anyone wanted to hear. "The sky will freeze."

"What must we do?" Aristippus asked her.

"Take back that which is lost." Hesperia sounded puzzled, as if that wasn't what she had thought she was going to say.

A murmur rose from the crowd. Demeter was not among them. Demeter was sitting in her house, where the rain had washed mud all over the floors, and she hadn't even cleaned it up. Doris knew that;

she had been to see her, to make sure she wasn't drowned. Echo thought privately that Demeter was the cause of the storm, and not likely to be its victim, but that was not a thought she wished to speak aloud. She did wonder, if mother and daughter and garden were all one, what effect that was having on the man who ruled the caves underground and had stolen the daughter.

"Take her back, lest the sky freeze," Hesperia said again. She began to shuffle away. "And sacrifice two more goats," she added, over her shoulder. She disappeared behind the hangings at the back of the temple.

The goats were not a problem, although there was some discussion over the question of *whose* goats. But the taking back of that which was lost—that was another matter. Hermes rather abruptly stopped boasting that he was the man for the job in case that someone decided he might be, Echo thought. Demeter said nothing. Irene told her of the divination, but Demeter only nodded, as if waiting for them to do it. The village waited, too, torn between anger at Demeter whose grief, they were sure, was the cause of theirs, and fear of provoking her further.

In Thargelion, the month of the olive harvest, it snowed. In all of Hellas snow fell in any strength only in the mountains. The sea moderated the climate, and the valleys might get only a dusting of frost, or a thin blanket of white, no more than would hold a footprint, in a cold year. Now the sea itself seemed to have frozen and fallen from the air, breaking more olive boughs and filling the agora up to men's calves. The olives still left on the trees were spotted and half gone bad. The houses, built to keep cool in a warm climate, were chambers of ice, badly lit by coals in bronze braziers set in every room by those who could afford them. Those who could not huddled together and froze. Glaucus's daughters, who were rich enough to actually own a slave, were too afraid to take him into the house with them, and he was found dead among the goats.

Tros and Harmonia's wedding was stopped in midbanquet because a snake fleeing the snow was found like an evil omen coiled among the wedding cakes. Harmonia went home weeping with her mother while a delegation of the village elders conferred. At the end of their conference they set out grimly for the cold, silent house where Demeter lived.

IV

❧

Souls in Jars

"Madam must be very uncomfortable like that. Lack of hygiene causes rashes of the skin." The old servant peered down his nose at Persephone.

"Madam is," Persephone said grumpily, sitting on the edge of her bed and resolutely ignoring the freshly filled tub of water just beyond the hanging. She had lived underground for a week now. "But *he* won't like me this way."

"He will not wish to make love to you perhaps," the servant said, considering that, "but he appears to like you in any condition." He sighed.

"Why?" Persephone demanded.

"Madam, who knows? What makes love?"

"He can't love me. He doesn't even know me. I throw things at him."

"Ah, yes. He hopes that will pass."

"Then he is crazy. I'm not going to marry Death."

"Oh, it isn't as bad as all that," the servant said.

"And what are you? And those others? Where do you come from?"

"I am Lycippus. I am from Thrace."

"Then you're not . . ." Persephone looked uneasily at the roast mutton with rosemary on her tray.

"Perhaps madam should eat," Lycippus said. "Madam can't go on like this."

Persephone knew she couldn't. She hadn't eaten in six days. Her head was swimming, and she was never sure if she really saw the things that floated past her peripheral vision, or the pale wraiths that seemed to hang in the corridor outside when Lycippus opened the door.

"If madam wishes to try this nice dish of squid with fig sauce . . ." Lycippus appeared to notice her aversion to the mutton. "Or we have a nice pheasant pie." He bent down toward her with an avuncular expression. "If madam wishes to eat just a bit, I shan't tell him."

The pheasant pie was hot, and its odor circled her head. Starving herself was probably a bad idea. If she died, she would have to stay here, anyway.

"Just a bite," Lycippus said, cajoling her as if she were a wayward child.

"If I eat will you let me out?" she asked craftily.

"Oh, that would be a very bad idea. Madam would get lost in the caves."

"I wouldn't go anywhere."

"Well, perhaps we might take a stroll. If madam eats a bit. And stays with me."

Persephone grabbed the pheasant pie, just big enough to fit in her hand, and sank her teeth into it. It was wonderful, savory and delicate, baked in a light crust with onions and peas. She would have just one bite. Maybe two. She gobbled it down, and Lycippus patted her on the head.

"Madam will feel much better now."

Persephone wiped her fingers on her grimy gown. "Now we'll take a walk. You promised."

"If madam will be careful . . ." Lycippus opened the door, and Persephone darted through it. "Madam, wait!"

Persephone fled down the corridor and dodged through the first doorway she saw. It opened into another corridor that slanted upward a bit, so she took it. She could hear Lycippus puffing and calling behind her. His voice grew fainter as she ran, taking any turn that led upward. The walls were lit by oil lamps in their niches (he must be wealthy beyond belief, or else it was magic oil that never burned up) making intermittent pools of light on the gray stone. She couldn't hear Lycippus any longer, but she thought she heard voices raised somewhere, shouting back and forth to each other. Her corridor ended and branched three ways, all going down. She stopped, gasping for breath, and took a frantic step into each one. She hadn't realized how weak she had grown in just a few days. her head was spinning. She leaned against the stone wall. There were no carvings here, just blank stone. Behind her she could hear more shouting. She fled down the middle corridor.

The walls grew rougher, the stone unfinished, and the lamps were farther apart. She stumbled over the uneven floor, and something scuttled past her feet. She ran from it. This had been the wrong way. It was going down. She took another opening on her left that went up again, but the path was still rough, plainly not the way they had come in. She saw a dimly lit room filled with dusty wine jars. Farther on there were bones, a white tumble on a bier. Persephone fled back the way she had come.

Her heart was hammering in her chest so loudly she grew frightened and stopped. She crumpled onto the rough stone, weeping, her head buried against her knees. Lycippus had warned her. She would never find her way out, and they would never find her here, either. She had run too fast for the old servant to keep up. She thought they could search for weeks in these corridors and not come upon her.

She was cold in the dank passageway and thirsty, her tongue dry in her mouth. After a while she pushed herself to her feet and tried to find the room with the wine jars. It wasn't where she thought it had been, nor could she find the chamber with the bones again. She sank down on the stone and closed her eyes.

A rat went over her feet, and she sat up shrieking. Her voice echoed in the stone corridor under the earth, and nothing answered her. She wondered how long it would take her to starve to death. Surely she was halfway there already. Wispy shades appeared to flutter around her head, ready to take her hand. She closed her eyes despairingly, and then opened them again when she heard more rats. Could she follow the rats? Surely they were going somewhere. If anyone could find food, it was a rat. She got to her feet and propped herself against the wall until she was sure she wasn't going to faint. She would wait here until a rat went by and then she would follow it.

Something was coming. She could hear movement

in the corridor. She flattened herself against the wall and stood perfectly still so as not to frighten the rat back the other way. The corridor made a bend where a lamp sat in its niche, and the thing she had heard came around it. Persephone stuck her fist in her mouth to stifle a scream when she saw it, her heart pounding against her breastbone. It wasn't a rat.

It was a huge beast, as black as the depths of the cave. The light caught its eyes, and they glowed green, like a lamp under seawater. Its mouth was open, and she could see the saliva hanging in ropes from its jaws. She stood frozen. There was no point in fleeing from it. Its huge paws would run her down in seconds. She whimpered and waited for it to leap at her throat.

It padded closer, tongue lolling, and gave a deep sonorous bark. Then it sat down on her foot and leaned its huge, hideous head against her.

Persephone shuddered. It drooled, dripping saliva on her foot.

"Good boy!"

His voice rang in the stone corridor, and Hades came around the bend behind the dog. When he reached them, he patted the dog's monstrous head and regarded her with curiosity. "What made you do a foolish thing like that? If Cerberus hadn't tracked you, you could have died down here. It's happened."

She didn't have any answer. Her leg muscles quivered with the effort of standing.

"You're done in," he said. He scooped her up before she could protest and carried her down the corridor. She tried to struggle, but she was too tired. And there was the dog looking up at her, jaws agape. If Hades dropped her, the dog would probably swallow her. She tried to pull her feet up out of its reach.

"He doesn't bite people unless I ask him to," Hades said.

He carried her to her chamber by a route that she was fairly sure was not the one she had taken in her flight, and set her down. "Please don't do that again. It's very hard not to get lost down here. It takes a long time to train servants when I hire new ones."

"You hire them?" She saw Lycippus peering out at her from the bath, a jug in his hand.

"Did you think they were ghosts?"

"Of course not," she said uncertainly, because he sounded so amused.

"I don't buy slaves, either. I prefer people who are motivated to stay by me. They don't get lost in the caverns, for instance."

"Then why did you kidnap me?" she demanded.

He raised dark eyebrows. "Frankly, it never occurred to me that you would come willingly."

"I wouldn't."

"There. You see?" He put his hand on the door. "I'll stop locking this if you'll promise not to do that again." He closed the door behind him, but she didn't hear the bolt slide.

"Perhaps now madam would like to bathe," Lycippus said.

"Why couldn't I get out?" she demanded. "I went up every time the corridor branched."

"We are inside the cliff, madam. Many corridors go up. To go out you must go down. Up a little, too. Sideways a bit."

"Oh." In spite of herself, Persephone looked longingly at the bath.

"The dog has soiled your gown, madam," Lycippus said tactfully. "There are clean ones in the bathchamber."

"Is the master certain that it was wise not to lock the door?" Lycippus poured a silver goblet a third full of wine and added water to fill it. The master was a man of moderate habits, despite his reputation. Stealing that girl from the upper air was the worst thing Lycippus had known him to do. Of course she was probably going to cause more trouble than she was worth.

"She knows she can't get out now," Hades said. "She won't try it again. She's a fast learner."

Lycippus thought that she would more likely try something else, possibly even more ill-advised. "Perhaps the master is not taking the right approach," he offered.

"Indeed? And in your vast experience of courtship, what would you suggest?"

Lycippus sighed. "It is possible to buy a bride. It is also possible to court a woman before taking her home with you."

"And how close do you think she would have let me get to her, to start courting?"

Lycippus sighed again. "I was thinking of women in other places, Lord. Areas less . . . primitive. Master has traveled widely."

Hades reclined on his couch. The dog, who had been sprawled on the floor by the hearth, came and put its head into his hand. He scratched its ears. "This is the one I wanted," he informed Lycippus. "So if you are going to be helpful, concentrate on that."

"If master will permit," Lycippus said, "Master will have to let the lady get used to him." He tutted. "These people are not widely educated. One must give her time. Bring her presents, perhaps."

"I sent her an extremely valuable aquamarine necklace," Hades observed, "and she threw it down the commode."

"Ah, exactly. Master *sent* it. Perhaps master should try bringing his gifts himself."

Hades eyed him consideringly. "If you will recall, I took that advice two days back, and she threw eggs on me."

"One must be persistent in wooing." Lycippus bustled about, tidying the hall. "These things require time," he offered, a pair of wax tablets tucked under his arm, and Hades's stylus in one hand. He balanced a draughts board and a bag of game pieces in the other.

Hades stood up and paced, wine cup in hand, while Lycippus sprinkled sand and dried herbs on the rugs and swept it up again with a broom, dodging around the master's feet. The huge dog paced after him.

"Go and sit down!" Lycippus said to the dog and he flopped on the floor again in the pile of sand and sweepings. "Tsk! Take the dog to see her. Women like dogs."

"She didn't appear to."

"She doesn't know him well." Lycippus prodded the dog with his foot. "Move!"

"Do you think I should take her the same necklace again, or another one?"

Lycippus paused in his sweeping. "The first neck-lace is in the drains."

"Well, I'm not going to leave it there. I thought I mentioned that. Get it out."

"I shall delegate the task," Lycippus said gravely.

"Wise man."

"And I should take her another one, if I were you. That one will have associations difficult to remove."

Hades smiled. "Then we shall sell it, when next you take ship for the mainland. Give me that." He held out his hand for the draughts board. "I shall teach her to play."

"A happy thought, Lord."

"Indeed. And the pieces are small enough not to hurt, should she throw them at me."

The door swung open. Persephone, who had been driven by boredom to begin spinning the wool in the basket, dropped it lest anyone think she was going to do that sort of thing here. Without turning her head, she slewed her eyes around to see who it was: Hades, bearing a tray of food and wine. The dog paced at his heel.

"I am told you enjoyed the pheasant pie," he re-marked, setting the tray on the three-legged table next to her seat.

"It was passable," she said icily, but her eyes dropped to the tray.

"You might as well eat. If you don't, Cerberus will be into it as soon as you turn your back. He's very badly trained, I'm afraid."

"You said he only bit people when you told him to," Persephone retorted, eyeing the dog warily. It waved a plumed tail and sighed at her.

"He loves you, too," Hades observed.

"He is drooling. He wants my dinner. And you don't love me."

Hades sat down on a bench opposite her. "I do. I find it very odd."

There didn't seem to be a good answer to that, since she found it extremely odd herself. If Death was in love with you, what on earth did that mean? She gave in and reached for the tray. If you ate in someone's house you couldn't kill them, but she doubted that being dead would have much effect on Death. On the other hand, they couldn't kill you. That might be important, since she wasn't sure what a marriage ceremony with Death involved. And there were honey and nutmeat sweets on the tray.

"I brought you a gift," he said. "I don't think it will fit down the commode."

Persephone looked up at him, her mouth full of nuts and honey. He held out a silver mirror, polished to a high shine. Persephone stopped chewing and stared. She had never seen herself in a good mirror before. Her mother owned a bronze one, rather elderly and scratched, and her only other reflection had been in the pool or the still surface of a basin of water. This one had a stand to hold it upright, cast with silver deer supporting it with their hooves on each side. Hades set it on the table before her. She put the sweet down and licked her fingers, and the girl in the mirror did the same. Her hair was pale, like ripe wheat, and her eyes, seen clearly, were a blue green like the sea in shallow water. Her face was triangular, wide at the forehead and narrow at the chin, with arching brows and thick pale lashes. There was a mole just at the corner of her left eye.

It was pale and flat, and she hadn't even known it was there. She put a finger to it, and then to her mouth and small, curled ears.

"You are very beautiful, you know," Hades said.

Persephone turned away from the mirror. "I might be a shrew, you know."

"You are," he agreed.

"Then what do you want with me?"

"You bring me light," he said. "It's dark down here."

Persephone thought about that over the next weeks, trying to discern what it was that he thought she could give him. He came regularly to bring her meals and left the door unbolted behind him, but she didn't leave. She knew now she wouldn't find her way out of the caverns, and to go to him in the great hall, where Lycippus had offered to escort her, smacked of giving in. Instead, she waited for him to come to her, and spun the wool to keep herself from screaming, although she hid it in the basket whenever she heard footsteps.

While she spun, she thought of what was happening in the upper air, about the wine making in the fall, and the olive harvest at the start of winter, and whether Narcissa or her mother, Irene, was married by now. She lost track of time, with no way to mark the days as they came and went, and no way to be sure when a day had gone by in the first place, except by the appearance of Lycippus or her captor with her meals. She imagined Echo and Narcissa dancing the vintage out of the grapes without her, the sun hot on the rocks by the headland. In her mind she saw the olives, dark greenish black, tumbling from the heavy branches as the boys beat them with their flails, and the littlest ones climbed to the highest branches to pelt the others. There would be singing and dancing and much foolishness at the pressing as the men, five of them at a time, took turns working the lever that squeezed the oil from the olives.

The summer solstice must be long gone by, she thought, the season turning toward the equinox when night and day stood balanced. Then came the long cool slide toward the winter solstice, when the sun shone for the shortest, heart-stopping day in the sky, and you were never really sure that this year it would turn around and creep northward again into the lengthening days of another spring. All that was happening in the air above her, but like the shades of the dead who lived here, she had no way to know it.

"What are you thinking?"

His voice startled her out of her reverie, and she looked up quickly, stuffing the skein of spun wool behind her and sticking herself on the spindle.

"I hate spinning," she said.

"Really? Some women find it soothing."

Persephone looked at it with loathing. "It's only something to do."

"Well then, I have brought you something more interesting to do." He set the draughts board on a table. "Only you have to do it with me." He shook the bag of men into his hand.

Persephone watched him suspiciously as he laid them out on the board. They were carved in the shape of owls and made of onyx and some green stone she didn't recognize.

"Do you know how to play?"

"I have played with Mother." Persephone eyed him thoughtfully. "She is going to be most awfully angry, you know."

"I'm sure she'll get over it," Hades said, arranging the draughtsmen. "I will be an admirable son-in-law." But Persephone thought he looked just a little uneasy, as if Demeter was something he hadn't considered—or had thought of and decided to ignore.

"Mother makes things happen," Persephone said.

"Women do." Hades moved one of his black owls toward her green ones.

"She made Glaucus get boils all over his backside once, when he beat his wife," Persephone offered.

"I shan't beat you."

"They were large boils, filled with pus."

"I'm sure they were a coincidence."

"Nothing of the sort."

"So far my backside is intact."

"Just wait," Persephone said darkly.

Hades smiled. "I don't think you're afraid of me anymore."

Persephone pushed a green owl toward his. "That doesn't mean I am going to marry you."

"Noooo," Hades said, considering his next move, "but you have figured out I'm not going to rape you. That seems an admirable beginning."

"If you did that, it would fall off," Persephone informed him. "Mother can do that, even down here." She wasn't entirely certain of that, but she wouldn't have been surprised.

"I thought, actually, that it didn't seem the foundation for a happy marriage," Hades remarked.

"I'm not going to marry you."

"What are your plans, then?"

Persephone narrowed her eyes at him. "I'm going to wait until you get bored with me."

Hades pushed an owl forward and deftly removed one of hers from the board. "I am a patient man. And you look very nice in that gown."

"My old one was spoiled by your dog." Persephone pushed the dog's head from the lap of the new gown and smoothed the shining folds. They rippled and shimmered like blue water. "What is this made of?"

"It is called silk," Hades said. "No one knows where the fiber comes from. They make it in another world."

"In the Underworld?" What else did he have here, where she had never been? The idea of exploring his kingdom was intriguing and terrifying.

"No, in the East. A long way east."

"There is nothing in the East but the Ocean."

"With all due respect, you are an ignorant child." He glared at her as she captured one of his black owls. "A good draughts player, however. There is a whole world beyond what you know of here in Hellas. There are things you never imagined."

"Tell me some of them." She put her chin in her hand, bored with the draughts already.

"Elephants."

"What are elephants?"

"Animals as big as your house, with ears like monstrous fig leaves and a nose like a snake which he blows through like a flute."

"I don't believe that. Where do these miraculous elephants live?"

"To the south," Hades said. "Among the Aethiopians."

"Have you seen one?" Persephone asked him suspiciously. They sounded like gorgons or chimaeras, which everyone was fairly certain didn't exist, or had died out.

"I have." Hades twisted a bracelet off his wrist and handed it to her. It was made of silver embossed with strange animals. One appeared to be an elephant.

She turned it over in her hand. Like all his possessions, it was richly made, of fine workmanship and finer materials, and just a little odd. His clothes, for instance—the fabric of his tunic was embroidered with a border of scarlet poppies against a golden background. They shimmered so, it must be made of the strange otherworldly silk. His cloak was black wool (she thought of the sheep again) caught at the shoulder with a heavy gold pin shaped like a pomegranate. The fillet that bound his dark hair was a golden snake that clenched its own tail in its mouth.

The world contained more than she had imagined. "Tell me more," she said to him.

"About what?"

"About the world. About things like elephants that live outside of Hellas."

"There were miraculous things inside Hellas, too, but they are gone now for a while," he said. "Whole cities crumbled to dust and bits of painted clay. The palace of King Minos at Knossos where they danced with bulls."

"How could you dance with a bull?"

"Very carefully. It was dangerous. They were a sacrifice to their gods."

Persephone had never known of any sacrifice but the goat kids they gave to Apollo and Zeus, and to Hestia in her temple, and of course the black ram they gave to Hades when they took someone to him. "What happens to them?" she asked.

"The dancers? They used to die when they grew too big to flip between the horns."

"No, the sheep we bring you. That my village brings you."

"We eat them. What do you do with all the other sacrifices your people make?"

"We eat them," she said, "but the gods don't. They eat the smell of the burning bones."

"We are usually hungrier than that, down here."

She studied him across the draughts board. He didn't look like a god, who she had always imagined would have fiery hair or burning eyes or smoke issuing from the mouth, or some other indication of divine status. Hades—no one at home liked to call him by his actual name, but she found that she had got used to it—merely looked like a human man of somewhat indeterminate age. Up close she could see fine lines around his eyes and the corners of his mouth. His hair and beard were dark brown, not the blue black she had at first thought they were, and they curled, so that he looked a bit like a faun— something else she had never seen, but everyone knew what they looked like. The woods were full of them.

"How many of you are there? Down here, eating sheep?" There must be more. Someone was doing the cooking and the laundry. Her soiled clothes disappeared and came back clean.

"Quite a few, actually. I haven't sent anyone else to you because I didn't want to frighten you."

"That might have suggested to you that it wasn't a good idea to grab me and leap off a cliff with me," she retorted.

Hades smiled. "I couldn't see a way around that." He inspected a plate of fresh fish on her tray. "This is very good. The cook simmers it with olive oil and leeks." He picked up a piece between thumb and forefinger and offered it to her.

"Thank you. I can feed myself." She took a bite of fish in her fingers and glared at him.

Hades popped his bite into his own mouth.

"How do you know all these things?" she asked him. Persephone had always thought that her mother and her great-grandfather between them knew all there was to be known. Clearly she had been mistaken.

"I have been places," he said. "Not all places are Hellas."

"Tell me about them," she demanded.

Hades considered, eating fish as he thought. "In Mycenae there was a palace where they buried their dead wrapped in gold. They worshiped a scared snake and lived by the thousands in a city with houses five stories tall."

"What happened to them?" Persephone tried to imagine people like that. How had they made those houses stay up?

"They liked to make war. They besieged Ilium for ten years over a woman, and the war ruined them. War has a way of doing that. You who live in these islands and on the mainland now are their heirs."

"I've heard that story," Persephone said. "They must have been very stupid in that city. Who would believe that a giant wooden horse big enough to hide an army was a goodwill gift from an enemy?"

"People stupid enough to kidnap a king's wife and fight over her for ten years. They sacrificed their children after it was ended, to seal the peace. A thing like that lays a shadow on a land."

"What happened to all their gold?" Persephone wanted to know.

"It lies buried in the ground with their dead."

"Is that where you get yours?" No wonder the god of Death was rich, if people buried themselves wrapped in gold.

Hades looked indignant. "I am not a grave robber."

"Well then," Persephone said, plainly waiting for an answer.

"I have ships that go out to places you haven't seen. To India, for instance, where there are big cats, like lions, that are striped red and black. And monkeys."

"What are monkeys?" she wanted to know, distracted from the subject of gold.

He chuckled. "They are much like people. Like little hairy people, with tails. They have hands, and they throw things at each other."

"You should bring one back." Persephone wanted one immediately.

"I did. It got into the kitchen and opened all of Cook's stores and strewed flour everywhere, and ate the mussels he was keeping for dinner. Then it caught its tail on fire in a lamp and set the hangings alight before Lycippus dunked it in the pool in this chamber."

Persephone laughed, clapping her hand over her mouth. "Oh, I want to see it!"

"You can't. I sold it to a man who had sold me bad wine. For all I know the beast sank his ship."

She laughed again, and he thought he saw light pour from her face. It turned his heart over.

"Get me another," she said. She thought with glee of turning it loose in Bopis's kitchen. It would annoy her worse than Great-Grandfather chasing women.

"There are some creatures who should not live in houses," Hades said.

"I tried to keep a jackal pup once," she said.

"There. You see. I will get you anything else that you want."

Persephone thought for a long moment, more somber now. "I don't know what I want," she said finally. "I thought I did."

"And what did you think you wanted?"

"Just to go on as I had been. Playing in the woods. Running after my friends. But all my friends will get married."

"Aha."

She regarded him darkly. "I didn't say *I* wanted to." She breathed deeply, a long breath of the dank air, not quite dried by the fire in the hearth, not quite scented enough to mask the faint smell of mold. "But I miss the sun."

"I will give you all the lamps you want," Hades offered.

"Lamps are not the sun."

"What if you went back to the upper air," he said, "and nothing was the same? What if time slows here in these caves, and not in the upper air? What then?"

"Does it?" Fear ran down her back. What if her mother and everyone she knew were dead already?

"I don't know," he said finally. "It is different here. I know that. And I know this: Once when the world was young, everything was different sizes. Dogs as big as horses. Horses as small as cats. Their skeletons are buried in the earth. It happens sometimes that someone digs them up. I have seen them. If the animals can change, then anything can shift."

"Where are all those animals now? Do animal souls come here?" If her mother and her friends were dead, wouldn't she have seen *them* here? Was he hiding them? "Where do you keep the human souls?"

"I don't keep souls; it's not like putting them in jars. I don't know where souls go," Hades said. "That is as truthful an answer as I can give you."

"They must go somewhere."

"The Aegyptians actually do put theirs in jars, or they think they do," he said.

That didn't seem helpful as an answer, but the notion intrigued her. "Who are the Aegyptians?"

"They live to the east of here, not as far east as the people who make silk. They embalm their dead with spices so the bodies will never decay and store their internal organs in jars. One of their gods is a jackal, and one of their goddesses is a cat."

"How much of this are you making up?" Persephone demanded. It sounded like the nursery tales that Bopis used to tell her to frighten her as a child.

"Practically none." Hades smiled. "You have no idea how odd the world really is."

"What's in the West?" Persephone demanded.

"A great ocean. I have heard that there is another

land on the other side of it, but I have never had the courage to try to cross it."

What kind of ocean would halt Death? Persephone put out two careful fingers and laid them on the back of his hand.

"Seeing if I am alive?"

She jerked them back. He was much too able to read her thoughts. She returned her attention to the draughts board and extracted one of his men with a move that hadn't occurred to him.

Hades chuckled. "You seem to have won." He sounded appreciative. "Would you like to see the rest of my kingdom? I promise you I shan't let you get lost."

She stood up and looked him in the eye. "Are you really Death?" His hand had been quite warm.

"Your people think so."

Persephone considered that. "Not everything they think is true. That's what *I* think. About Mother, for instance—I think most of the things they think she can do happen because they think she can. Not all," she admitted.

Hades grinned at her conspiratorially. It was a nice smile, rather like the dog's, toothy but friendly. "I'm sure the falling-off part is among the ones that are true."

"No doubt," Persephone said. "Some things are." She looked up, as if she could see through the stone roof to the upper air, smell what was in the wind. "I don't quite understand how."

"No one does," Hades said. He was serious now, dark brows solemn. "It's all part of the dance. That's what they call it where the monkeys live. The dance of life, and death. It's all a great circle. It . . . carries things with it sometimes, from one world to another.''

Persephone thought about that, thought that here beneath the earth they were in a different world from that of the air above them. The thought, circling around on the wheel he had spoken of, came to her, quite clearly: *Something is wrong up there.*

V

❧

Bridal Feast

Narcissa stood on a stool while Bopis and her mother arranged the yards and yards of pale veiling in which they were going to envelop and deliver her, a moth in a cocoon, to her husband. Echo thought she looked stunned, like a goat that someone had knocked in the head. Outside, torches went back and forth in the falling snow as guests gathered for the wedding.

"He's very rich," Bopis said, tweaking folds into place. "Such a good match, I told you, Irene, and how nice for the two of you to be married and live so close by, especially when Narcissa starts to have her babies. Of course *you're* too old for such a thing. Such a blessing Nicias already has children from his first wife, poor girl, and won't want more, but Narcissa has good big hips. She'll have easy babies—not like the trial I had when I was young. It was dreadful, but then I've always been so small. . . ."

Echo caught Narcissa's eye and winked at her, but

Narcissa didn't blink. Weaving the crown of olive
leaves for Narcissa's head, Echo thought, *I'm not
going to let any of the old biddies in the house with me
when I'm about to get married. They're enough to scare
anyone.* She wrinkled her nose at Bopis. Bopis's big
cow eyes were damp with the emotion of the moment, or with relief at getting Irene married off, too,
the next day. Bopis spent her life in a constant frenzy
to run everything in the village and to keep Aristippus from straying. Echo had seen the old man with
Clytie in the woods, just past the lower goat pasture.
She had been feeding him grapes, the two of them
bundled in one cloak. Clytie would go with anyone.

Echo was beginning to think that maybe being a
slut was not such a bad idea. No one expected Clytie
to get married. She could feed grapes to old men
behind their wives' backs if she felt like it, and not
if she didn't, which wasn't the case if you were married to the old man. Narcissa looked as if this was
dawning on her, although at least Nicias's brother
Phitias was young, no more than five-and-twenty.

Echo could hear flutes now, escorting Phitias
through the gently falling snow to his bride. The
snow really was beautiful, even if it was bad for the
trees. Echo had heard that people in the mountains
of the mainland, when caught in storms, often felt
very warm and happy just before they died. Maybe
this was like that. After the disaster of Tros and Harmonia's wedding—finally held after an extra sacrifice
had been made to Hestia because of the snakes—
everyone with an opinion on the matter had gone to
talk to Demeter in her cold house, where she sat
beside the unlit hearth looking as if she were made
of snow herself.

Of course Echo hadn't been allowed to come—she was much too young and unimportant—but she had eavesdropped and watched from outside the window, nose plastered against the limestone sill. Demeter had offered no help, but had just huddled into herself, pouring her grief into the weather while lightning crackled over the gray water. Echo thought she had been out on the headland again; her hair was dark with rainwater.

"No good will come of it. I said so at the time!" Bopis's voice was shrill and vengeful.

"We were happy enough here before *you* came with that child and no father." That was Glaucus's eldest daughter.

"Hush!" Irene said, shocked.

"Things like this didn't happen then," Glaucus's daughter sniffed. "Strange weather coming from Hestia knows where."

"Hestia was quite clear about it," Aristippus said. "We are to retrieve that which is lost. And Demeter must make up her mind to help us."

"If Demeter wanted the girl back, she'd have had her by now, if you want my opinion," Bopis sniffed.

"No one does!" Demeter spun around on her seat, and they all gasped. She hadn't moved since they had come in. She narrowed her eyes at Bopis. "If I knew how to get her back, I'd have her by now, *Grandmother*."

"That's what we have come here to take counsel on," Aristippus said, stepping between Demeter and Bopis.

Echo thought for a moment that Demeter was going to launch herself at Bopis. She looked like a wildcat ready to spring. "It was *your* idea to send Echemus down there," Demeter said to Aristippus. "*Your* idea," she said to Bopis, "and my girl went with us, and he saw her! *You* tell me how to get her back. *You* go down the cliff and knock on Death's door."

"Oooh yes, send Bopis!" Hermes said, crouching under the window beside Echo. "Please!"

"What are you doing here?" Echo hissed.

"Same thing you're doing—eavesdropping. But old Cow Eyes is right—this sort of thing never happened before *she* came back."

"And how would you know?" Echo asked him scornfully. "You were a baby."

"Mother remembers," Hermes said.

"I say she ought to leave," Bopis said from inside the house. Her voice carried an awful satisfaction. "My own granddaughter—I never thought I would be forced to such a choice, but it's for the good of all. If Demeter can't control the consequences of her emotions, and everyone knows how vengeful a woman's rage is"— She glared at Aristippus—"Well then, we have the children to think of."

There was a murmuring of cautious agreement inside. "Harmonia may be pregnant already. What if something should mark the baby?"

"My aunt's cousin saw a snake once, and her baby's teeth came in like fangs. They had to file them down."

"I heard of a woman once who had a child with three arms. She had eaten squid."

"*I* ate squid," Irene retorted, flapping her arms at them. "My children are all normal. Have you lost your minds? Demeter, they are fools, but you *must* stop grieving so."

"Then bring me back my child," Demeter said softly.

Aristippus knelt in front of her, his white-bearded face near hers. In spite of his age, and lascivious nature, he was still the most powerful figure in the village. Any other old man would be a laughing-stock, Echo thought, but somehow women *wanted* to go with Aristippus. He bent close to Demeter, blue eyes grave under bushy white brows. "How, child? That's what we need to know."

Demeter's tears filled her eyes and spilled over onto her hands. "I don't know," she whispered. "Who can give orders to Death?"

"See now," Hermes said outside the window, in Echo's ear. "That's just the problem. No one knows how to get in there and out again. In is the easy part. It's the out, you know, that's hard. Better to send her on her way and let it be someone else's trouble."

Echo crouched under the window, glaring at him. "Then tell me, Most Clever, if Demeter is causing this awful weather, what will happen, do you think, if you *do* drive her out of the village? Do you really think it will just go and snow someplace else, wher-ever she goes? *I* think we'll have an earthquake if she gets any madder or sadder, and it won't be some-where else."

Hermes sniffed, adjusting the folds of his mantle where it had trailed in the mud and snow. "What a lot of worry over a girl who probably ran off with the man of her own accord," he said sulkily. "That one wasn't any better than she had to be. Any of the boys can tell you that."

Echo leaped on him, rolling him in the mud. "Take

it back! Yah, you coward! You said *you* could go and get her if you wanted to. I heard you!"

Hermes writhed in her grasp. His red hair was splotched with mud, and he spit dirt out of his mouth. "I did not. I said it would be a hero's task."

"And you said *you* were the hero! I heard you. At the grape pressing. So did Narcissa and Arachne! You said you would go and get her if Demeter would promise her to you! You goat's backside!" She took him by the ears and tried to pound his head in the snow.

"Ow!" Hermes howled and shoved her off him, twisting her wrist.

"You aren't any hero, you lying, braggy goat's prick! Go stick it in a knothole!" She swung at him and connected her fist with his ear.

Hermes howled and smacked her in the nose.

Multiple heads popped out of the window, with Aristippus at the center. "Silence! You are a disgrace!" He pointed at Hermes. "What are you doing?"

Hermes rubbed his ear. "She hit me."

Echo glared at him, her nose bleeding. "He's a liar! He bragged at the wine pressing that he could get Persephone back, and now he won't admit it."

"Are you five years old?" Echo's mother Doris pushed her head through the window next to Aristippus. "Fighting with boys?"

Aristippus raised an eyebrow at Hermes. "*Did* you say that?"

Hermes lied with agility and abandon to everyone else, but he found it hard, for some reason, to lie to Aristippus. "Well, sort of, Grandfather. Not exactly."

"Yes or no?"

"Well, in a way. Maybe. I said I thought it could be done."

"You said you would do it if Demeter promised you Persephone," Echo interrupted. "You thought you were safe, because you knew Persephone wouldn't have a braggy little prick like you if you were the last man on the island!"

"Echo!" Aristippus pointed his finger at her now. "Be quiet."

Echo subsided and packed a handful of snow against her bleeding nose. The argument inside seemed to have quieted, as well.

"Demeter has asked the proper question," Aristippus said when they were silent. "Who can give orders to Death? That is a question we must ask the gods, I think. And since it is Hestia who has told us we must seek our lost one, then we must also ask her how to do it. Demeter will ask, because it is her child." He looked her way, ignoring the two in the snow outside.

Echo crept to the window again and saw Demeter nod her head.

"And you will light a fire in here," he ordered.

"It won't do any good," Demeter whispered. "I have tried."

"Tchah!" Bopis sucked on a tooth and sent someone for a torch and dry kindling, but Demeter was right; it wouldn't light.

Aristippus scratched his head.

"Demeter." Irene knelt down by her. "You must let the fire kindle."

"It won't." Demeter shook her head. She was wrapped in furs in that icy house. "It never lights."

Echo wondered what it would be like to have that

kind of power, for things to happen just because you felt them. Blood from her nose dripped into the snow, making splotches like poppies. Maybe it wouldn't be a good thing. Who knew what would grow from your blood, for instance, if you were a person like that.

While Echo was thinking, her mother emerged from the house and took her by the arm, rolling her eyes. Doris dragged her away, and Echo stuck her tongue out at Hermes as they passed.

"Tomorrow," Doris said, "tomorrow, Demeter will go to ask the goddess what to do next, and there is no telling *what* she will say. You know how priestesses are when they're in a trance. Half the time you can't figure out what they mean; it's all riddles. Then there are two weddings to get ready for, if we don't all freeze, and you've spoiled your mantle with blood. Why did I have children?"

"To be a comfort in your old age," Echo said, and Doris snorted.

The next day Demeter went in the dawn light through the snow to the Temple of Hestia and offered a goat kid, cutting its throat herself in a spray of blood that showered over her feet. The temple was old, the oldest thing in the village, and dim and smoky with age and the fires of many sacrifices. Only the new thatch on the roof was clean. Hesperia shuffled up out of the chair in which she usually sat propped, and rolled her eyes back in her head.

They waited, breath held. Finally Hesperia opened her mouth. "You have asked an unlucky question," she told Demeter. "You must ask it again on an auspicious day. At the next dark of the moon you may ask."

That was all she would say, no matter how many

further questions they put to her. Echo privately suspected that the goddess—or Hesperia—wanted time to think about the matter. But the snow lessened then from a steady sleeting downpour to a light falling dust, which everyone decided was a good omen. The village turned its immediate attention to the weddings of Narcissa and her mother.

"Echo, I can't do it." Narcissa looked out at Echo from the leaves of the olive tree where they had hidden from Narcissa's mother in the blue dusk. The faint veil of snow drifted and caught in the leaves, powdering them white.

"We could run away to sea and be pirates," Echo said. It was their childhood game. Persephone had been the captain, Echo the first mate, and Narcissa the rich merchant sailing to the mainland to buy gold and fine clothes for his daughters at home. The pirates captured the merchant and sold him into slavery until he escaped, or ransomed himself with wine and figs.

"I would if I could," Narcissa said. "If I had known, I would have asked Dryope to take me with her. I could have been her servant and companion, and we could have had adventures." She sniffed dolefully. That had been their other game, in which they slew monsters and rescued lost heirs, who often proved to be themselves.

"Oh, Narcissa," Echo said miserably, "I'll come visit."

"If your husband will let you," Narcissa said. "Persephone's gone, and in a year they'll make you marry, too; then I'll never see either of you anymore."

Echo wrapped her mantle more tightly around her shoulders. It was cold in the snowy branches of the olive tree. She could hear Narcissa's mother calling. When the three of them had talked about getting married this summer, it hadn't seemed real—just something to speculate about in the meadow while the bees buzzed around their heads in the sun. Now Narcissa was actually going to be taken off by a man to his house. Echo was a country girl; she knew what would happen next. For herself, Echo thought that didn't sound so dreadful as long as you liked the man—the dogs and the goats obviously enjoyed it, and it must be fun or Clytie wouldn't do it—but she thought Narcissa was terrified.

"I can't do it," Narcissa said again. "I have nightmares about it. He puts his hands on me and he turns into a snake, or it's bigger than my arm, or something awful. I've thought about hiding a knife in my gown."

"No!" Echo said. "Narcissa, it won't be that bad. You can't!"

"It will be that bad," Narcissa said with conviction. "If I could just stay with you, maybe Persephone would come back, and it would be just the three of us again."

Echo blinked at her. "Narcissa, it doesn't work like that. Life doesn't."

"I asked Mother to give me to the goddess, so I wouldn't have to, but she said it's too late. I'm already betrothed, and we can't insult Phitias or Nicias, not if Mother is going to marry Nicias."

"Give you to the goddess?" She knew Narcissa meant Hestia; there wasn't any temple to Artemis on the island. Irene would need Narcissa's bride price, and a temple paid that when it took in a new virgin. "Oh, Narcissa, no. Look at poor old Hesperia. She's never been allowed to do anything in her life but sit in that temple while her joints stiffen."

"She's fed," Narcissa said. "She's respected. She doesn't have to go with men."

"Oh, darling, it won't be that bad." Echo scooted a bit down her branch and put her arms around Narcissa. "It won't be, and you'll have babies to take care of you when you're old."

Narcissa buried her face in Echo's shoulder and howled.

Now Echo watched Narcissa being made ready for her wedding and wondered if maybe it was going to be that bad, after all. The snow was still falling in a thin veil, and Narcissa's friends ducked in and out through it all morning, bringing presents: a mantle of deep scarlet wool woven with pale green acanthus leaves from Arachne; a bronze mirror with poppies around the edge from Echo; a bronze fillet for her hair from Demeter in Persephone's name. Clytie brought a painted clay box of dried figs and sweets, and Harmonia a carved wooden box holding a painted distaff and spindle. Irene gave her a cameo ring that had been her grandmother's, and Phitias sent a necklace of pearls. Everything that could be worn, she put on dutifully, looking like an advertisement at a merchant's stall. Bopis and Irene took the scarlet mantle and bronze fillet off again ("Another day, dear, they'll be lovely"), painted her lips and cheeks with rouge, and pronounced her ready.

Narcissa stepped down off her stool with Bopis holding the folds of her veil so that they kept their careful arrangement. Beyond the hanging that shielded Narcissa's preparations from the wedding guests, Phitias waited by the hearth with his brother. Echo could feel him there, and she thought Narcissa could, too. Narcissa's hands shook, but the rest of her was perfectly still.

"Come, dear." Bopis prodded her gently between the shoulder blades. Narcissa threw a stricken look at her mother and Echo.

"You look beautiful, darling. Everyone is waiting for you." Irene took her hand and led her into the outer room while Bopis held the hanging to one side. On the threshold, Irene gave over Narcissa's hand to Nicias, who as her own betrothed constituted the family's only male relative. Nicias smiled and patted Narcissa's fingers. Narcissa didn't move. He tugged at her hand a bit. Narcissa took three steps to the hearth where Phitias waited for her.

Phitias wasn't bad-looking, Echo thought, with a handsome nose and stocky, muscular body. His hands were nice, too, long-fingered and shapely. He smiled at Narcissa who looked as if she couldn't see him. She looked through the crowd of guests as if they weren't there, either, as if she had just come to stand by the hearth for no particular reason. A fire blazed at its center, and coals glowed in bronze braziers in the corners of the room. Irene's house was crowded with well-wishers. Nearly everyone in the village was there, those who couldn't fit into the house standing patiently under a canopy outside the open door. Echo saw Hermes leaning against the doorpost, and she made a rude gesture at him when she thought her mother wasn't looking.

Doris was looking and cuffed her gently behind the ear. "Do you want to bring bad luck to your friend's marriage?"

"I don't think I could make it worse," Echo whispered to her mother. "She doesn't want to do it. She told me last night she'd rather go to the goddess."

"She'll come around," Doris said with conviction. "Girls don't know what they want. Look at me. I wanted to marry a pig boy. Luckily for me, my parents had sense enough to give me to your father."

"We never see Father," Echo protested. "He's always on the other side of the island, selling goats." And drinking in the tavern there, but she didn't say that, since her mother already knew it.

"Well, then, see? We have a fine house and a good life here."

Echo wondered if her mother counted her father's absence as a factor in that equation. Probably. Maybe Phitias would go away and sell goats, and Narcissa would be able to breathe. Right now she looked as if she were suffocating.

"Hush now; they're starting," Doris said.

Nicias had killed a fine ram in honor of the occasion. He and Phitias laid the thigh bone on the hearth, and the elders asked for Hestia's blessing on the match.

Nicias said, "Grant to Phitias love and tenderness toward this young bride, that he may instruct her with understanding and kindness, and train her to be the guardian of his house and the mother of his children."

Irene said, "Give to Phitias and his bride long life and contentment in each other's company." For either sex, marriage was as inevitable as being born and dying. There wasn't anything you could do about it, so you had best hope for contentment.

Phitias said, "I pledge to you dominion over all my household and all my goods."

Narcissa said nothing. No one expected her to.

The wedding guests exploded in whoops and cheers. Irene, Doris, and Bopis brought out plates of sesame cakes and pitchers of bridal wine. Demeter was not there, but they hadn't expected her to be, and were all rather relieved that she wasn't. Bopis poured a few drops of wine into a cup and spilled them on the floor for the gods, then Nicias superintended the mixing of the wine with water in silver ewers (borrowed for the occasion from all households who possessed them), and cups were handed round. Hermes took a tray of them outside to the well-wishers waiting in the snow, and Echo followed him with a plate of cakes.

"Yes, it was a lovely ceremony," he was saying to Glaucus's youngest daughter. Funny how all three were still called "Glaucus's daughters," Echo thought. They were all older than dirt and widows who were so cross no one would marry them, but still they had to take their identity from a man. Echo shrugged. It was the way it was. She threaded her way through the fading afternoon light with cakes and smiled and nodded while everyone told her how happy Narcissa was going to be. She was afraid to go back inside and see Narcissa herself with her frozen smile and blank eyes.

Nicias emerged and set pine-knot torches, kindled from the bride's family hearth, into stands outside the house, while accepting congratulations on his own upcoming marriage. Inside, cakes and wine were consumed, and Irene and Bopis were getting Narcissa ready.

When they came out, Phitias had her arm linked firmly through his and was smiling proudly, unaware that his bride could have been carved out of wood for all the expression she showed. The village lined up behind them in procession, bearing the pine-flares, and, singing, set out for the house which Phitias had borrowed for the night. In the morning they would attend Nicias's wedding to Narcissa's mother, and the four of them would set out for Nicias's village on the other side of the mountain.

The procession halted outside the door, and the maidens of the village clustered around the bridal pair.

"Long life and many babies to Phitias and Narcissa," they sang, their voices blending sweetly in the smoky dusk. "Grow old together, keep each other safe."

Then Phitias opened the door, and they disappeared inside. Echo caught one last glimpse of Narcissa's pale face, her eyes blank.

In the morning they began the ritual all over again for Irene to wed Nicias. Narcissa stayed inside until afternoon, as befitted a bride married only the night before, but Echo paced in the square outside Phitias's door, hoping for a glimpse of her.

"She won't come out this morning," Hermes said, leering. "Got other things to do."

"You don't understand," Echo said, not even bothering to be angry at him.

Clytie giggled. "Narcissa likes girls," she said to Hermes.

"What?" Echo spun around to face her, fists balled.

"I'm not saying she ever *did* anything," Clytie said slyly. "But you know she never wanted to marry."

"Fine talk from you—you've done plenty," Echo said, "and you like *anything*!"

Hermes hooted. "Narcissa wanted to marry little freckled Echo, not Phitias. Phitias is too big and hairy for her!"

Echo turned on him. "If you say one more word about that, I will kill you while you are sleeping," she told him.

"Hold on! It was just a joke!" Hermes held his hands up. "No need to take offense."

"I mean it," Echo said. "Now, you go away from her house now, and don't get near her or her husband or his brother before they leave, do you hear me?" She stood as close to him as she could get, staring up at his surprised face, her jaw set.

After a moment, he backed away. "All right, you cat." He turned on his heel.

Echo turned to Clytie. "You, too."

"I didn't mean any harm," Clytie said.

"No, you're just stupid. Stupid and a slut!" Echo retorted, and stomped off, immediately ashamed of herself for having called Clytie names.

Narcissa emerged from the house in time for her mother's marriage. Her hair was pinned up like a married woman's, and her grave dark face oddly serene, as if she were somewhere quite unreachable behind it. Echo tried to talk to her. "How is it, being married?" she asked, because that was the question girls asked each other.

"He's kind," Narcissa said.

Echo let her breath out. "Then it's all right?"

"No. He's just kind."

"Harmonia says it gets better after a few weeks," Echo offered.

"Harmonia *wanted* Tros," Narcissa said. "That makes all the difference, I expect." She pulled her mantle over her head and went into her mother's house, leaving Echo in the street.

Irene was married to Nicias, in much the same fashion that Narcissa had been wed to Phitias. The torchlit procession sang them to Nicias's quarters, with somewhat less ceremony, and Narcissa disappeared back into Phitias's house. In the morning they all packed up their belongings and left for Nicias's village on the other side of the mountain, driving Irene's goats ahead of them. The house was rented out.

The weather stayed as contrary as a wild goat. At the dark of the moon just past the solstice in Skirophorion, on a day that Aristippus said Zeus had pronounced auspicious, he took Demeter to the Temple of Hestia again to consult the goddess.

The village went with them, trailing through the agora in a murmuring band, shivering in the cold wind that blew from the north. Echo and Doris bundled up and went, escorted by Echo's uncle Phaedon. The limestone and mud brick temple was icy, and the dark smoky walls smelled of old fires and wet ash. A stone statue of the goddess, blackened with smoke, stood at the rear beside her altar. The face, carved by the island's first refugees, was impenetrable. Hestia was both guardian mother of all households and virgin goddess, procreative power held in check and so doubly potent. The fire in the hearth, never allowed to go out, gave off a sullen red glow, the only light in the temple. Aristippus called out to Hesperia, and the old priestess, wrapped in fur rugs, emerged from her lair at the back. Echo, standing on tiptoe to see past Phaedon's shoulder, thought she looked like an insect, waving her thin arms at him.

"We have come to ask the goddess again the question we brought to her a month ago," Aristippus said respectfully, when the sacrifice had been made. Hestia's fire blazed brighter with the oily bones and the aromatic herbs that Bopis, elbowing Aristippus aside, strewed on it.

"Then let a woman ask it," Hesperia said. Her voice was a thin croak. "This is woman's business."

Demeter fell to her knees in front of the altar. She looked nearly as thin as Hesperia, her face stretched taut against her skull, as if the outer part of her was disappearing and soon all that would be left was her bones. "Mother, tell me how I may bring back my child." Her voice was a pleading whisper.

Hesperia sucked in her breath, making a low hum at the back of her throat. Her eyes rolled up. The smoke rose around her and the kneeling form of Demeter. She rocked back and forth on her heels until Echo thought she would fall over. Bopis seemed to think so, too—she stood with arms outstretched as if to catch her if she toppled.

"Hnnnn-nnnnh!" Hesperia opened her eyes wide. "The messenger shall be sent in the spring, to open the earth. Zeus will command it, and send him." Her eyes snapped up again, only the whites showing.

"What messenger, Mother?" Demeter asked her.

"He has already spoken," Hesperia rasped. "He has named his journey and his price." The whites of her eyes glistened, and her mouth opened and closed silently several more times. She crumpled abruptly, and Bopis just managed to catch her as she fell.

"Who has spoken?" Bopis asked her, but she didn't answer. A long snore came from her lips.

Echo slewed her head around, scanning the crowd. She knew who.

Demeter did, too. She rose slowly and pointed a finger at Hermes. He stood beside one of the limestone columns that held the temple roof, looking as if he rather wished he were inside it instead. "You," Demeter said, finger still pointing, "you will go and fetch my daughter."

"Why? Why am I to go?" Alarmed, Hermes swiveled his head around, as if seeking someone more suitable.

Because you bragged you could, and you caught the gods' eye, Echo thought. The gods' attention was never something you wanted.

"Because it is your task."

"Down there? With three-headed dogs?"

"You bear a message from Zeus," Aristippus said. "The dog will not hurt the messenger of the gods."

"I would feel better if the dog told me that," Hermes said. "You're the priest of Zeus. Why are you not to take the message?"

"I am old," Aristippus said.

"Aristippus is needed here," Bopis announced. The corollary was plain: *And we can do without you.* She laid Hesperia on a rug and beckoned Echo forward to fan her face.

"And how am I to make him give her back?" Hermes demanded.

"You are to tell him that Zeus commands it. He

will not refuse an order from Zeus when Zeus sends his own son to bring it."

Hermes looked as if he were willing now to argue his mother's version of his origins, but Aristippus held up a hand. "The gods have spoken. Zeus and the Great Mother have laid this on you. It is your fate."

Hermes looked at the new roof thatch, already beginning to darken, as if he might find some escape there, another hole perhaps, blown by Demeter's storm.

"You will be famous," Bopis told him, smiling proudly at her great-grandson. "Zeus will guide you." Maia, who had been silent until now, wailed suddenly and threw her mantle over her head. "Hush," Bopis said.

Hermes had gone white, but no one argued with the gods, and this pronouncement had been less ambiguous than most. He narrowed his eyes angrily at Demeter. "If you hadn't allowed her to run wild like a she-goat this wouldn't have happened. She should have been married two years ago to someone who could control her."

His voice was bitter, and Echo thought about how fine the line was between love and anger. Hermes might be faithless, but he had wanted Persephone since they were children. If he had her, he would still be faithless, but he would still want her. (She thought of Aristippus, who had fought four other men for Bopis in their youth, so it was said.) She knelt on the rug, waving the fan over Hesperia's face, and rubbed her hands. They were almost fleshless, like chicken feet. Behind her she could hear Demeter's angry voice, and Aristippus's soothing one.

"There was a price!" Hermes spat. "You needn't think I'm going to go down there without that."

"She is not going to marry," Demeter said flatly. "Not him, not you."

"Then there is no bargain. You heard the old woman. I named my journey and my price. No price, no journey."

"The gods have spoken, Demeter," Aristippus said.

Bopis nodded. "Indeed, and we must not ignore the gods when they speak, or be begrudging with the things they ask of us. Agamemnon gave his daughter Iphigenia to the gods when they asked it of him."

"That is a *story*!" Demeter spat.

Bopis looked horrified. "You will bring all their anger on us. Best that Hermes fetches her home and marries her. Then we'll have no more trouble with her."

Echo, patting Hesperia's cold hands, thought that unlikely. Persephone was trouble from the start, just like her mother. Some were victims of fate, like Narcissa, she thought. Some were the force that drove fate; that was Persephone. Some, like herself, just trundled along, making things suit them as best they could. Others, like Hermes, poked fate with a stick to see if it would bite them.

"I will make this bargain with you," she heard Demeter say to Hermes. "You shall have my daughter if you can find her and bring her home unscathed."

VI

❧

The Bull Dancers

"Something is the matter." Persephone said it again, insistently, as the thought coalesced in her head. Something above them, in the upper air, had gone wrong. They were walking down a corridor into Hades's mountain. Somehow she discovered that she had taken his arm. Cerberus paced beside them, drooling. "Something is the matter."

"What would you like? Anything within my command."

"No, something is wrong up there. On the earth. Where I come from."

Hades patted her hand. "Something is always wrong up there. That's why I find it so pleasant down here."

"No, something bad is the matter, and don't treat me as if I were six. Not if you plan to marry me."

"Then you are considering it?"

"I am not considering it. I am giving you advice on courtship. In case you abduct someone else."

"I doubt I shall try. Lycippus has convinced me that it was ill-advised, so I won't make a habit of it."

"Has Lycippus convinced you to let me go?"

"No."

She was beginning to think that he would, in a while, if she insisted on it. Knowing that made it easier to stay. Now that she was no longer afraid of him, every time she thought about leaving, she thought of all the things here that she hadn't seen, things she might not even know existed, or know about, like the monkey, if she left without seeing them. She ran her fingertips along the hurrying people carved into the walls, moving silently beside them. "Who made these?" she asked him, distracted from her own quest by theirs.

"A stone carver who stayed with me for a while, a very long time ago. His boat was wrecked on the shore here."

"Where did he go?"

"I don't know. He died, and we buried him."

Persephone thought of pursuing that story but she suspected she would get nowhere. Every time she asked Hades directly if he was Death, or ruled the dead, or had power over them somehow, he side-stepped. She didn't know what to make of his refusal to either reassure her or display his true nature. He seemed to be waiting for her to reach some conclusion of her own.

They came to a fork in the corridor, and he stopped. "I promised to show you my kingdom. What would you like to see?" he asked her.

"I want to see the chamber I found when I tried to run away. There were bones in it." She didn't know why she had asked to see that. The bones were the first things that had come into her head.

"Very well," he said, as if she had requested a tour of the kitchen or his storehouses.

They turned down corridor after branching corridor, and the walls grew rough, as they had in her earlier flight. Cerberus leaned against her thigh as they went, in what she thought he took to be a reassuring gesture. It was like being leaned into by a cow. She had given up refusing Hades's garments and had even allowed Lycippus to throw her own away. (He had bundled them into a neat pile with just his fingertips and whisked them away, to some fire, she suspected.) The silk gown rustled around her feet, over new sandals of deep sea blue leather. The mantle around her shoulders was wool against the chill of the caves, but so finely woven that it could have passed through a finger ring. A pattern like waves was woven into its borders.

The oil lamps in their niches grew farther apart, and Hades plucked one out and carried it to give them more light. The painted octopus on its base looked in the flicker as if it had coiled about his hand.

"I believe this is the chamber of which you spoke," he said quietly, stopping abruptly opposite a door she hadn't expected. She must have approached it from the opposite direction in her flight. The chamber was small, low-roofed in rough stone, and the bones lay on a bier of stones and clay. Persephone could just see faint traces of red paint on the clay where age and dampness had not quite rotted it away. The bones were those of a woman, she thought from the shape of the hips, and she murmured a quick prayer to the goddess for her. The head and foot of the bier were coated with a dusting of powder, and some dark liquid had dripped to the floor below. Among the scattered bones she could see the glint of gold—a twisted collar, a finger ring slipped from separated phalanges.

"Who was she?" she whispered.

"I don't know," Hades answered her, and she thought he was telling the truth. "She has always been here."

"She is older than you?"

"Apparently so. She frightens Lycippus. He brings her offerings of meal and oil."

"Are there more?"

"No, she is alone. There were more chambers, but no one lived in them but her."

You are Death, Persephone thought. No one but Death would take up residence in a tomb. Again the feeling that something was wrong seeped through the stone to her from the earth above. A faint breath of air stirred, and she looked at the chamber ceiling and saw a shaft rising through the rock. There was no light, but she could feel the earth breathing through it.

She waited until they were out of the burial chamber before she asked him, "What is wrong up there? I know something is."

Hades took her arm again and tucked it into his, as if they were out for a stroll through the agora. "They are looking for you, I expect."

"Do you think it's Mother?"

"I wouldn't be surprised. Mother and whoever has been touched by her anger."

"What will they do?" Why was she asking him that? Did she *want* him to be prepared for a rescue?

"They will come after you," Hades said. "They will send a hero, I expect. It's traditional."

Persephone hadn't thought of that. She had assumed that Mother would come. If they sent a hero, then they would expect her to marry the hero. Rescued maidens always did. "Mother won't agree to that," she said firmly.

Hades chuckled. "Perhaps you should make your own plans, then."

When had anyone given her a chance to make her own plans? Mother had let her run wild, but forbidden her to marry. How long could you amuse yourself playing with wild animals and stringing daisy chains? But what did she want instead? To yearn like Harmonia over a village lad with rough hands and not much more between his ears than his goats had between theirs? To give herself to the goddess and grow old like Hesperia, alone with no one to talk to but the gods, who didn't speak often and made little conversation? To live like her mother, tending the garden and sleeping alone in a narrow bed, growing everything but children? None of those prospects seemed satisfactory. And in any case, if she chose Harmonia's life, where would she find her Tros? All the boys in her village, with the exception of Hermes, were afraid of her. Hermes really did want to marry her, she suspected darkly, and suspected also that no good would come of it. He was like fire in thatch, as greedy and unpredictable.

The thought flickered through her mind that here there was someone who knew things, who had plainly been across the world before he had settled, for reasons of his own fate, into these caves. Who owned wonders she hadn't even discovered yet.

Would Hades allow her to stay here if she wouldn't marry him? Would he settle for companionship, and leave her free to go to the upper earth and breathe when she felt the need?

He had an uncanny way of catching her thoughts out of the air. Now he said, "I have always felt sorry for her—the woman who lies on that bier—alone like that forever. I hope she didn't lie by herself in life."

"Show me where you live," Persephone said abruptly. A wave of loneliness seemed to wash from the burial chamber into the corridor and lap at her ankles. "Show me what you do all day."

"Really?" Hades smiled. She thought he was pleased.

They retraced their steps, with Cerberus padding beside them, branched at Hades's direction into a new corridor, and came to the central hall through which she had been dragged when she had first come. Braziers burned cheerfully in each corner, sending out gold pools of warmth. Cerberus flopped happily beside one, nearly tumbling it over. Among the bronze and marble statues, Persephone took note now of a desk littered with tablets of wax and clay, a stand in which rested a cithara whose frame was inlaid with bits of ivory, and elaborate silver lamps suspended from chains secured in the stone ceiling. The walls were dressed stone, hung with alternating painted panels and tapestries of the sea creatures of which her captor seemed so enamored—huge squid with beady eyes, bulbous-headed octopi, a school of dolphins. On the other hand, the wooden panels depicted scenes of the upper air—youths and maidens gamboling in the forest, a herd of fauns romping with a nymph, a field of flowers bright with the scarlet heads of poppies. Persephone didn't remember these. She went to them, staring, as if she could breathe in the scent of the flowers.

"I hope you like them," he said. "I had them done so you'd have a taste of home."

Had them done? Did he keep an artist on his staff? Along with the cook, the gardener, and who knew how many maids to clean? "How many people are here?" she asked him.

Hades looked a little embarrassed. "I don't quite know." He brightened. "Lycippus would," he offered.

Was he offering to make her mistress of a kingdom with so many servants he couldn't count them? What on earth would she do with them? Demeter had never kept so much as a maid. No one in the village except Glaucus's daughters did. It was considered the wife's job to do the work.

"Where do you get your food?" she demanded. "You can't live on the sheep people bring you."

"Well, one doesn't want to waste a good sheep."

"Someone fishes."

"True. I am fond of fish. I have always lived by the sea, one place or another."

There was always the faint scent of the sea in his caves, just as there was on her island above them. Hellas was born of the sea. But she had never seen work like the creatures that adorned nearly every piece of clay in his halls, from the lamp in his hand to her bathtub. "Is it one of your servants who paints these?" she asked him.

"No, these are old. They come from that place I told you of where they danced with bulls."

"You lived there?"

"For a little."

"And took much with you."

His lip twitched. "I have ships that sail out to trade with the world. There is a lot of the world, and many people's treasures are for sale in it."

Persephone sat down on a couch, which was spread with a woolen cloth and a fur blanket. "Tell me," she demanded. She pulled the fur over her feet and curled into the cushions.

"Tell you what? Tell you what is for sale?"

"Everything is for sale, I expect," she said. "Tell me about the world."

He sat on the end of her couch. "Is that what you want? Is that the thing that would make you stay? Not jewelry or silk dresses?"

"Maybe." Maybe it was. "Maybe I would just want to go and see these things myself."

"Maybe they are overrated."

"Not to someone who has never seen them. I should like to see those people dance with bulls."

"They are long gone. You can see pictures of them, painted on their walls."

Persephone's eyes roved over the room, looking for something to query him about. "Those." She pointed at the desk. "What are those?"

He rose and came back with a wax tablet and a stylus from the jumble on the desk. "For keeping records. So many jars of oil, so many bushels of wheat. See. . . . This is ten jars . . . and this is four oxen."

She watched while he inscribed a series of marks in the wax with the stylus, and she knew instantly that this was brilliant and important, a turning point, a new pattern in what he had called the dance of the world. At home people put stones in a bag to keep track of things. This would make all the difference. An idea like this could have been what made him rich.

"When you want to use it again," he said, "you melt the wax." He held the tablet over the lamp and smoothed the softened surface with the stylus. His marks disappeared, sinking rippleless into the wax.

"Let me try," Persephone demanded. "How did you think to do this?" This was an idea as magical as what her mother knew about the tree inside the seed.

"It isn't my personal invention," Hades said, handing her the tablet and stylus. "They used it at Knossos where they danced with bulls, and at Mycenae."

"Why do we not know about it?" Persephone made three squiggly scratches in the wax. "What does that mean?"

"Nothing. You have to learn the symbols first. That's why this way works better than just making a mark for each one when you have three thousand thirty-one cows."

"No one has that many cows."

"That was an example. Say you are a king and you do have all those cows. This means 'cow.' " He made a mark. "And this means 'three thousand thirty-one.' "

"And people have forgotten how to do this?" She remembered his saying that those cities had fallen to wars and pirates.

"In Hellas they have forgotten. Not elsewhere. There are many ways to write things down. This is just one of them."

She took the tablet back and copied his marks in the wax.

"If you want to keep a permanent record," he continued, since she seemed so interested, "you write it in soft clay and fire it. Then it will last."

"Teach me to do this." Was this how Mother had gained her knowledge? From a man who wanted to keep her? Was that why she was so determined that Persephone not marry? Had the price been too high? Persephone yearned to learn this anyway. This was power, the kind of power Mother had.

"All right," Hades said. "What do you want to keep track of?"

"I don't know. How many servants you have. And don't say you have to ask Lycippus."

"Very well. Fifty-one."

"Fifty-one servants." She handed him the tablet and stylus.

Hades made the marks, and she copied them.

Cerberus, bored, came away from his brazier and laid his huge head on her knee. "One dog."

"One dog." Hades inscribed him on the tablet.

Persephone copied it. She looked about the room. "Four braziers. Six marble boys with no clothes. One cithara."

Hades dutifully wrote them down. "This means 'none'" he said solemnly, "and this means 'clothes.'"

Persephone copied the marks. "One woman. One . . . What *are* you?" Maybe if she asked him, this time he would tell her.

"One woman," Hades said, incising the wax. "One man."

"Does that mean human man?"

"Are there other kinds?"

"Well, there are gods. My second cousin Hermes says *his* father is Zeus. Although we all think if he was, it must have been dark. Aunt Maia is no beauty."

"Oh, well, Zeus. He'll lie down with anyone. That's no test."

Persephone cocked her head to one side, to indicate that she was thinking that over. "If someone was a god—the god of Death, for instance—why would he need to steal women? Wouldn't there be lots of women just waiting to go off with him and have little godlets?"

"One would think so," Hades said.

"On the other hand, my aunt Maia insisted that Zeus met her in the woods in the form of a black bull and ravished her against her will. That's what Mother says she said."

"And was Mother ravished against her will, too?"

"I am beginning to suspect not," Persephone admitted. "I don't think anyone could manage it."

"I don't imagine so, if she can make it fall off afterward."

"I hadn't thought of that before, really," Persephone said. "It seems more complicated than I had expected." She poked at the wax with the stylus, making little circles with the tip.

"What does?"

"Being ravished. Or not ravished. Or seduced. Or however you want to look at it."

Hades took the tablet and stylus and set them on the floor. He propped himself on the other end of the couch, leaning on one elbow, hand in his dark hair. "Personally I have always found it unnervingly complicated. There is a deeply uncomfortable wisdom to be gained from one's forays into that realm."

"And are you wise?"

"Not yet. Perhaps I should have said knowledge, not wisdom."

She looked at him carefully. His eyes were friendly, the deep startling blue of seawater. She could see the dark shadow on his pale cheeks where he shaped his beard into a fashionable line. Dark hair curled over his forehead, twining around the silver fillet. He put his hand on her foot, fingers curling lightly around the instep. Her skin tingled. She wondered if it was possible to be seduced by your own body, rather than by someone else's; if simple longing for human contact was most of it. He was human, she was absolutely certain of that. Maybe something else, as well, in the same way that Maia's Zeus might have been a god and at the same time merely a red-haired man she felt disinclined to name.

"Come. I want to show you something." He stood and held out his hand, and on impulse she gave him hers. They went out through the door by which they had entered, accompanied by the dog, and took an unfamiliar corridor that sloped downward. At its end were two steps down and the smell of baking bread. There were no travelers carved on these walls, but instead the outlines of people kneading dough, measuring oil, frying fish, and a woman with a cleaver chasing a chicken.

A woman in a bloody apron (perhaps the model for the one on the wall) ducked out of a doorway, and seeing them, snatched the apron off and stuffed it behind her back.

"Good evening, Lord."

"Good evening, Scylla. We are on our way to see the gardens."

"Pomona will just be out watering, Lord."

"Where do you grow gardens?" Persephone demanded.

"You will see." Hades smiled, and seemed pleased with himself. Scylla stood at respectful attention, the bloody apron still bundled behind her back, as he led Persephone through the kitchens.

The other servants ceased their work and bowed their heads respectfully. A whisper followed their footsteps. *Master's young lady. Look at that hair! Will she stay? I heard she threw his necklace in the drain! She did; Lycippus sent Apis to fish it out again.* Persephone saw the dog poke his huge head into a bowl of meal. A girl in a flour-daubed tunic whacked him on the nose with a wooden spoon.

An elderly man with his head halfway into a clay oven popped it out again, bearing a loaf on a wooden paddle. "Would madam like to try a bite? Fresh from the oven." He tore off a piece and dipped it into a bowl of olive oil.

Persephone took it, holding it over her other hand so it wouldn't drip. It was hot and wonderful, the oil fresh and full of the scent of the olive groves her mother had planted. "This is fresh oil. You can't have olive trees down here!" she said to Hades.

"Wait," he said, smiling. He led her through the far end of the kitchen where a boy was cleaning squid, turning their long tubular bodies inside out with a practiced flick of his wrist. He tossed a head to the dog who caught it with a *clomp!* of jaws. Drying herbs hung from racks bolted to the ceiling, and a live chicken fussed on the floor underfoot, pecking at spilled grain.

"Get her back in the henhouse, please," Hades said as they passed.

Beyond the kitchen a door opened onto a courtyard bigger than Hades's great hall. To Persephone's amazement, light rained down on it, the brilliant blue white sun of the upper air, not the flickering yellow of oil lamps. At its center an ancient olive tree lifted limbs to the light, which she now saw came down a shaft in the rock. If she craned her head, she could see sky.

A woman with a watering can bustled around a raised bed of onions with a basket in her other hand. "It's been a mess, Lord," she said to Hades when she saw him. "Very peculiar weather up there, and snow of all things. I've had to tent all the vegetables, even down here."

"I'm afraid we're responsible for that," Hades said. "We are working on the problem."

"The fruit trees don't like it. You know the soil doesn't go very deep here, and they won't stand the stress."

Hades turned to Persephone. "My dear, this is Pomona. She oversees the garden."

Persephone almost informed him tartly that she wasn't his dear, but it didn't seem civilized. Pomona had a nice face, broad and friendly. Her slightly froggy mouth stretched into a smile at the sight of Persephone. "I know your mother, of course," she said. "Or I know *of* her—she's done some excellent work with beans. We grow most of what we eat right here," she told Persephone. "We buy wheat, of course, and wine, and extra oil. But as you can see, we have persuaded the apples, and the figs and pomegranates to bear very nicely."

Persephone gawked about the courtyard, feeling like the country cousin come to town for the fair to see her first pig. Autumn vegetables grew in raised beds—onions and garlic and purpley bronze cabbage and yellow squash. The pomegranate tree was studded with round scarlet fruit, and two boys were picking apples, piling them into baskets.

"I thought perhaps you might like to come here," Hades said to her. "Perhaps it will assuage your yearning for the upper air. I'll make sure you know the way."

Persephone breathed in the apple smell, tinted with garlic and onions from the basket in Pomona's hand. Hades broke off a ripe pomegranate from the tree and cracked it with his fingers, spilling a crescent of ruby seeds, still embedded like jewels in their membrane, into his palm. He pried a few from it and ate them, and handed the rest of the piece to Persephone. She picked six seeds delicately from the membrane and put them in her mouth, staining fingers and lips. They were tart and sweet, and the tiny seeds under the ruby flesh crunched between her teeth.

Pomona, who had been watering cabbage seedlings, took her basket and can into the kitchen, leaving them alone, except for the hen who had escaped the roost and now flew up into the branches of the olive tree.

Hades offered the rest of the pomegranate to Persephone.

"I would give you anything you asked for, if you would stay with me," he said quietly.

Persephone looked around the garden. She could come here to smell the air and the apples any time she wanted to; he had said so. Why did that seem no less and no more interesting to her now than returning to her village? She took the split pomegranate and studied its chambered interior.

"Would you take me to see those pictures of the people who danced with bulls?" she asked him. "Would you take me there?"

"Away from here?"

"Yes," she said firmly. "Into the upper air, away from here. I won't try to run home. If I did I would never see anyone dance with bulls."

Hades leaned against the rough gray bark of the olive tree, apparently thinking. The tree was old and gnarled, far older than Demeter's grove. Persephone wondered if it was as old as the woman whose bones lay on the bier below them. She watched its leaves stir in the faint wind, the breath of the caves that whispered in the shaft, and waited to see what he would say.

He looked up finally. "The sea is rough this time of year."

"You said you would give me anything I asked for."

"Very well, then."

The boat was dark. It nearly disappeared against the night and the sea. Persephone watched as Lycippus, muttering, and six sailors loaded it with jars of water and boxes of provisions. Cerberus sat beside her on the sand, head against her knee. She was almost used to him now. His warm breath blew against her shins. The tide ran little strings of white foam along the dark rollers that rumbled in from the west.

She wasn't sure where on the island they were, or even if they were still on her island. Hades's caverns might be deep and long enough to reach under the sea to some other island for all she knew. The wind blew chill, in long whining gusts, and she wrapped herself in the heavy woolen mantle he had given her.

"Ready?" He was at her shoulder. "Are you still sure? It's a long voyage."

"I'm ready."

He took her arm and helped her into the boat, and the sailors pushed it out into the tide. Cerberus splashed after them and heaved himself over the bow. The tide was turning, and they set the mast and raised the sail, a dark splotch against the dark sky. The helmsman looked over his shoulder at Hades, and Hades nodded.

There was a shelter in the stern, enclosed on three sides and laid with carpets, hides, and pillows, which Persephone knew must be for her, but she sat on deck as long as she could stay awake, watching the dark water slip past the bow, and the slow wheel of the stars overhead. Just as for her mother, boats and the sea held no terrors for her. Hades stood in the stern, the wind whipping his beard and hair into damp wisps. She thought he was watching the water, but for what she didn't know. Once, as they slid past the last of the breakers rolling inland, he threw a handful of meal onto the water. The moon, a waxing half circle of silver like a cat's eye, slid into the water ahead of them, and the dark sail bellied full of wind.

There was something odd about Hades's boat. It seemed to cut straight through the water no matter which quarter the wind came from. When Persephone woke in the morning, stretching and yawning under the shelter of the deckhouse in the stern, they were out of sight of any coastline, plowing through blue water toward a blank horizon. Her eyes widened, but she didn't say anything. Nearly all the shipping in Hellas hugged the coastlines, clinging to the safety of known landfalls. She saw Charon, the helmsman, drop a lead line and inspect the sand that stuck to the wax embedded in its bottom core, when he had hauled it up again. What it signified, he didn't say, but he seemed satisfied and turned the tiller to angle the boat a bit more to the south.

Hades knelt beside her with a cup in his hand. "You are an admirable sailor," he commented.

"You said the sea would be rough," she said.

"It may yet, but perhaps certain quarters favor us. I've done my best to placate them." He handed her the cup of watered wine, and she drank. Two of the crew were cooking cakes in a pan over a charcoal brazier, and when they were done he brought her one. She ate it, hot and sticky with honey, with her fingers, and licked them clean. Hades presented her with a clay pot, and he and the crew politely turned their backs while she used it and flung the contents overboard. It occurred to her, not for the first time, how usefully men were constructed for such things as sea voyages. With any luck, she thought, counting fingers, she would not begin to bleed on this journey. In the caverns, Lycippus had tactfully presented her with a basket of clean rags and taken the soiled ones away to be washed.

The sun bounced a bright gray white winter light off the water, making her squint her eyes. "How far have we come?"

"With luck we'll make land tomorrow night," Hades said. He stood beside her, watching the horizon to the southwest.

"Storm coming, Lord," Charon said abruptly and they turned.

Lycippus, who was packing the kitchen gear, looked up to the northeast, the way they had come, and swore. There was just the faintest smudge along the horizon, but it darkened as they watched, and the wind picked up.

"Mother?" Persephone whispered.

"Maybe," Hades said. "But it's the time of year for it. We'll try to outrun it."

The sailors scurried to tie down the kitchen gear and everything else, stuffing Persephone's bedding of hides and cushions into boxes and roping them to the deck. (She wondered, watching them, where Hades had slept.) The dark clouds grew nearer, and the chop of the sea increased. She whispered, "Mother, leave us be. I'll come back, I promise," but the wind didn't abate.

"Come belowdecks." Hades took her arm and led her to the stairs that descended three steps to the lower deck. She had to crouch to duck beneath the low ceiling, and he motioned her to a bench where he wrapped her in more warm hides and braced her against the pitching of the ship. Cerberus thumped down the stairs after them and lay at her feet. It was dim, the only light coming from the stairs and the gaps between the planking of the upper deck. Above them she could hear the shouting of the crew and Lycippus cursing. He came belowdecks, too, abruptly, and sat looking furious, on the bench opposite them. Persephone thought Charon had ordered him below.

Hades stood, tucking the hides around her, and said to Lycippus, "Look after the lady." He climbed back up the stairs. Cerberus started to follow him, but he said, "Sit," in a voice that brooked no argument. Cerberus sat. The sky darkened quickly, throwing the chamber belowdecks into a charcoal gloom. Cerberus whined and stuck his head in Persephone's lap. She stroked his ears as the ship heaved from side to side.

They heard more shouting above deck, Hades's voice above the rest. The wind howled, and water spat through the gaps in the decking and sloshed down the stairs.

"Mother, don't!" Persephone said desperately, but she didn't think it was Demeter. There was a crack of thunder and a flash of light, then a downpour of rain. Someone above them slammed the trap down over the stairs, plunging them into near total darkness.

The boat plunged on through the storm, running before it, but it was like trying to flee from an oncoming arrow. They walloped from side to side in the waves while the wind howled around them. She heard Hades shout to the crew to take down the sail before it capsized them. What if he were washed overboard, she thought suddenly, desperately. She would be alone with these men of his who would blame her. She was sure they already thought she was responsible for the storm—she was half afraid herself that she was. She could hear Hades on deck bellowing at someone, or something, promising it something if it called off the storm. She couldn't make out all the words. Lycippus moaned and put his head in his hands.

Persephone tried again to talk to the sea. "Be still. I asked to take this voyage. I can't go back to Mother if you drown me. Or him. Be still."

Nothing outside heard her, or was willing to bargain if it did. The wind roared again, and she felt the ship shudder against its force. The trap slammed open, and Hades blundered down the steps, water streaming from his cloak. He grabbed her hand. "Tell it you come willingly!"

"I tried!" she gasped, staggering as he pulled her to her feet.

"Up here where it can see you. Up where the storm can see us!"

The trap banged shut behind them, and she followed him, slipping in the water that foamed across the deck, bending into the wind. A wave slapped them, and they both staggered. Hades gripped her more tightly. The deck dropped from under their feet, and they fell thrashing on the sloping planks. Hades pulled her upright, and they leaned together as they fought their way through the wind to the stern. Persephone leaned against the stern rail, gripping it tightly as the storm pulled at her and whipped her hair about her face.

"Tell it!" Hades shouted over the wind's roar. "Tell the sea!" His own hair was plastered to his head, and water sheeted from his beard.

"Let us be!" Persephone shouted into the storm. "This was my choice! Let us be! I swear I'll come home again!"

"You heard her!" Hades bellowed into the wind.

The wind seemed to circle them as if it was listening. It roared around the two of them on the deck while the helmsman and crew struggled with the tiller and the boat lurched in the waves. Hades gripped her to him tightly, hands clenched around her waist, feet braced against the heaving deck. She leaned into him, struggling to stay upright.

"She *chose!*" Hades shouted into the wind again.

Imperceptibly at first, the gale lessened. The ship righted slightly. "I *chose!*" Persephone shouted, echoing him.

The wind dropped further, and the black sky paled. The rain fell in a fine mist and then vanished entirely as the sun broke from the black clouds. The clouds retreated, leaving the sun to draw them westward.

For the rest of the voyage the sun shone and the sky was clear as obsidian at night, the stars winking bright against it. Persephone spread her rugs and furs out on the open deck where she could see in all directions and reclined, watching the stars. At the back of her mind was the knowledge that she had made a promise, maybe two contradictory promises, but she would worry about them later. For now the voyage filled her, and the anticipation of seeing what she thought of as "the world" excited her. Hades dragged his own sleeping gear from wherever he had been the night before and lay beside her, but never touched her. He just lay and watched the stars with her and listened to the murmur of the water parting beneath the keel and the creaking of the hemp ropes that stayed the sail. In the morning they sighted land.

"Crete," Hades said, leaning on the rail and pointing to the low hump that rose from the western horizon.

"Is that where they danced with the bulls?"

"Yes."

As they neared the coast, she could see huts along the shore, the antlike figures of people, and the dark curves of beached boats.

"We'll skirt the coast a bit," Hades said, "and make land a bit farther along. We may not be welcome if they know we come over seas."

Persephone hadn't thought of that. She had pictured a ruined palace empty of people, inhabited maybe by the scurryings of mice and rats, the bull dancers solemn and solitary in their paint. "There are people there?"

"They are ghosts of an old civilization," Hades said. "No place ever entirely empties. They live on the edge of what they once were, and camp in its ruins."

He brought the boat to shore around the curve of a headland where the sea washed onto a rocky inlet. The sailors dragged it up on the sand into the scrub that grew above the tideline and covered it over with cut brush. They left two to guard it, and the rest followed Hades and Persephone, with Lycippus in attendance. They were a little cavalcade of retainers escorting a merchant and his lady, so Hades said. Privately, Persephone thought his presence carried an aura that would unnerve any bandit enough to keep them safe. It wasn't anything she could put her finger on, no corpselike tinge of the Underworld seemed to follow him, and yet somehow he was a personage one would think twice about annoying. With that observation came the realization of the privileged place she occupied. After all, she had put his gifts down the drain and thrown an omelette at him.

The landscape was much like that of her island. The sky above them was a bright clear blue now, bouncing off the blue green of the sea and the white foam of the breakers that slid onto the rocky coast and rolled away again endlessly. They took a path up from the beach, which seemed unmarked and of which Hades seemed quite certain. On the headland above they found a road, a rough track rutted by wheels and the hooves of cattle. They followed it for a ways and then turned inland on a narrower, less used track. The way was rocky, and Persephone stumbled on the stones.

"Shall I find you a mount?" Hades asked her. "It isn't very far, but I can buy you something to ride in a village, I expect."

She shook her head. "I asked to come here. I can walk."

"As you wish." He didn't seem inclined to argue with her or to cosset her if she didn't demand it.

They stopped to eat in the shade of a plane tree, where a stream burbled by to provide them with water for the wine. Demeter's anger-fueled weather did not seem to have reached this far, and the hills were the normal verdant green of winter in Hellas. The day was mild and Persephone shed her woolen mantle and stretched her arms to the sun. When they had eaten, the servants packed up the bags and boxes of dried fruit and fish, bread and olives, and flasks of unwatered wine, and strapped them to their backs. They set out once more. At dusk they came to the ruins.

Seen from a distance, Knossos might have been the enchanted land of her nursery tales, Mt. Olympus where the gods had gone to live. What had been a single building covered more ground than her village twice over. Persephone gaped at the stone walls and tumbled stairways, now leading nowhere, that must once have reached the sky. "Men built this," she said, assuring herself that it must have been so.

"And men destroyed it," Hades added. "In the morning I will show you the bull-leapers, but you must stay close by me. It isn't entirely safe."

They camped for the night in a tent which Lycippus produced from somewhere in the baggage and pitched in the shadow of the ruins. Cerberus, Lycippus, and the crew slept outside under the stars, and Persephone didn't protest when Hades lay down beside her. As before, he made no move to touch her, but merely bundled himself in his rugs and began, she thought, to snore. She woke to a bright cool dawn and the sound of birdsong in the plane trees and the tamarisk branches.

"How can you live in caves when there is this to sleep under?" she asked Hades as he woke.

She hadn't really expected him to answer her, but after a long silence he said, "Men."

She raised her eyebrows at him, mocking his habitual gesture, and he laughed. "No one enters *my* domain who hasn't been invited." He stood and stretched. "Come. You wanted to see people dance with bulls."

When they had eaten, he led her toward a crumbled stair. A shadowy figure scuttled out of their way and vanished into a doorway. Persephone turned to follow its flight and noted that Lycippus was just behind them with a large sword in his hand. Cerberus, pacing beside them, bared his teeth.

"All ruins have their rats," Hades said. "You are

not to go gawking and get separated from me. The stones are unstable in places, as well."

The stair led upward to a wide hallway, its roof supported with red pillars. Many had cracks running down their length, and Hades walked carefully. He whistled Cerberus away from his investigation of a fallen cornice. The walls were painted with the sort of sea creatures that she had seen on lamps and pottery in his house. In the room beyond there were scenes of women dancing. The women's dresses left their breasts bare, and their wild black hair curled down their backs in ringlets. Their skirts were made in pleated tiers, one above the other, and even more startling, they carried snakes in their hands.

"They dance for the goddess," Hades said.

Persephone thought that looked considerably more interesting a form of worship than the rituals practiced by Hesperia in Hestia's temple. They went cautiously through a sagging doorway into yet another chamber. The walls here were also cracked, and she could see where ornaments and gilding had been pried from the pillars and the stone benches that lined one wall.

"There is nothing left but the paintings on the walls," Hades said. "No doubt they also would have been stolen if anyone could figure out how to do it."

Persephone raised her eyebrows at him, since that had worked the last time, and he laughed. A great many things in Hades's domain had come from here, she realized. The lord of Death, it seemed, gathered in dead civilizations as well.

"Here," he said. He led her past a row of red pillars, and there they were, leaping on the wall, the people who danced with bulls. Before her a red and white bull bent his head, huge horns pointing forward, and a pale girl caught them in her hands. You could see the way she was going to go, flipping heels over head, up over the horns to land on the bull's back, where a red-skinned boy danced on his hands. Behind the bull, another girl stood waiting to catch him.

What would that be like, Persephone wondered. To fly over the bull's horns, courting death, and land on his broad back. How wonderful a thing to be able to do, but why?

"For the gods," Hades said, as she stood gaping. "Or maybe just for sport. It's hard to say. Sometimes a thing is both."

She spent the rest of the day wandering wide-eyed through the palace of Knossos while Hades told her the legend of King Minos who had kept his court here, and of his miraculous monster, half-man, half-bull. The Minotaur was the child of his wife who had fallen in love with a bull, and he kept it chained in the labyrinthine corridors below them.

"Was it real?" she wanted to know. "Was there really such a thing?" It seemed possible after hearing of elephants and monkeys.

"I have never seen one," Hades said.

There were stories of gods taking animal form to court mortal maidens, but Persephone had always only half believed them, and in any case the resulting children were always human. Still, in a place like this, you never knew. She craned her neck, peering into the shadowy depths of the roof, where birds had begun to nest. As they passed a broken stairway, she saw the glint of water below them in a sunken pool, and a snake slithered past her feet.

"Soon they will own it," Hades said. "When man moves out, the creatures of the wild move in. They reclaim a place. It doesn't take very long."

On one wall a woman in a barebreasted dress stood crowned with a diadem and holding two snakes aloft, as if she offered this place to them. Persephone wouldn't have been surprised to see them slither from her fingers. The shadows lengthened, and she began to hurry, scrambling to see all that there was to be seen before the darkness fell. Hades had warned her that they would spend only a day here; to stay longer would attract undue attention from the watchers she already felt in the shadows. She and Hades had taken nothing away, which so far had given them free passage, but it wouldn't last. "Looters are quite territorial," he said, "and there are tombs beneath this place that have not yet been robbed, I imagine."

When they left, they passed through the chamber of the bull-leapers again. In the dusk the dancers moved on the walls as if alive in the flicker of Lycippus's torch. Persephone held her breath, watching them. She could feel how you would do it. The waiting for just the right moment in the bull's stride, balancing on the balls of the feet. The running start, no going back after that, the horns in your grip, the flip, the broad hot back under your palms, just for an instant, and then the flip down to the waiting catcher on the floor, the turn to catch the dancer coming after you. The sense of it ran through her like the spark off a cat's fur.

"What happened to them if they missed?"

They were sitting on a flat stone in the darkness,

watching as the moon washed the ruined walls. That thought had been in her mind.

"They died," Hades said. "Most likely. I think part of the dance was the risk of death."

Behind them the servants were putting away the kitchen gear, and chasing Cerberus out of the dirty pots. Lycippus busied himself fluffing blankets and pillows in their tent. Their homely bustle made a comforting counterpoint to the great bulk of the ruined castle and the vastness of the sky overhead. Persephone thought of the Minotaur, the wild cursed offspring of King Minos and his love-besotted wife, Pasiphaë, who had lusted after a bull. The arc of love was very wide, she thought, and as often as not it lay down in darkness.

She could feel Hades's warmth at her side, the slow intake and exhale of his breath. Whatever he was, he was alive, and her skin began to yearn toward his as the bull dancers had yearned toward the bull. There was some dark knowledge to be gained from him, and not just the awakening that came with binding your body to another's. It occurred to her that she had a knowledge he wanted, too, something he might have possessed once and lost in his caves after so many years. Might that make a man desperate enough to steal it? She put her hand on his, and she felt him freeze, as if he feared movement would frighten her off.

"Why did you steal me?" she asked him. "Truly?"

He was silent a long time. "I don't know," he said at length. "I thought I did. You were so beautiful; you have no idea. Like a little ball of light. I thought you would light the caverns."

"And did I?"

She thought maybe he smiled. "In your way. But you didn't want anything I could give you, and I didn't know you the way I thought I would. You were just some angry girl I had stolen, and I didn't know what to do with you. You weren't the woman I made up for myself when I watched you up on the headland."

"And now?"

"Now if you go away the caves will be darker than they were before you came."

"You could get a monkey," she suggested, and he laughed. His right hand closed over her fingers where they lay on his left. Her skin felt warm, cheeks flushed so that the cool air stung, and when he stood, she rose with him, hand in hand still, and went with him into the tent.

Hades closed the tent flap and stood waiting, she thought, to see what she would do. Persephone unpinned her gown at one shoulder and let it slide, thinking of the dancers who bared their breasts to dance for the goddess. Whatever it was she was doing, it was a dance of its own sort, a dance with the heart or some more insistent organ, the dance her mother had tried to shield her from. Had the mothers of those leaping figures told them not to dance with bulls? Had Pasiphaë's? She lay down on the blankets and the piled pillows, and when he lay down beside her he was naked, too.

"Are you sure?" he whispered. If she changed her mind, he would stop. She knew that. Hermes wouldn't have, but this man would.

"I'm sure." She hadn't known it until just that moment, but she was. All the mothers' warnings, all the fear of whatever ghosts followed him, even—for now—her yearning for the sun, rolled away on the murmur of the distant waves. The moonlight outside was bright enough to sift through the tent walls, and she could see him, a pale outline in the bed beside her. His skin was always milky, and now the moonlight tinted it with silver so that he looked like one of his statues.

He stroked his fingers down her throat to her breast. She turned to him, and they danced a very old dance, indeed.

VII

Poppies and Centaurs

"The change in master is quite astounding." Lycippus beamed at Persephone in a congratulatory manner, and apparently waited for her to blush, which she declined to do. Hades stood whistling in the bow of the boat. The weather seemed to have taken on his mood, and the air was golden and balmy for midwinter. Persephone favored Lycippus with a grin and a snort of amusement.

"Is there anything which I may bring madam?" Lycippus inquired primly. Clearly he wasn't going to make any clearer reference to the goings-on in the tent the night before, and just as clearly he had been in full earshot. Persephone was under the impression that they had not been quiet.

"No, thank you," she said sweetly. *A magical messenger to explain things to my mother*, she thought. Mother hadn't mentioned to her that it was so much fun. Maybe that was why Mother had been so adamant that Persephone never marry, or even lie down with a man—Mother knew how much fun it was, and that had cost her something. Persephone still wondered what the price of her joy had been.

She joined Hades in the bow, and he broke off his whistling in midnote. "Are we going to sail into another storm?" she asked him. She wasn't sure what Mother was aware of by now, but she was fairly certain it was more than Persephone would care for.

"Oddly enough, I don't think so," Hades said. "Your mother will try other things, no doubt, but you made a free choice. She'll have to respect that."

"Why?" Persephone wasn't at all certain of that.

"It's the rules," Hades said, but he didn't elaborate.

The rules for what? For minor deities having congress with mortal girls? Or girls who slipped their mother's leash?

"We will invite your mother to visit us. That may soothe her feelings," Hades said.

Persephone swallowed. She had known this was going to come up. "I didn't say I would marry you," she said carefully.

"You slept with me!" he blurted, startled.

"I chose to. As you pointed out. It happens all the time in the upper air; I'm sure it must be the same everywhere."

He was standing next to her, and she felt his muscles tense, as if he had flinched, or braced himself for something. She thought, frightened, her stomach suddenly queasy, that he might actually love her, that he might have meant everything he had said.

"I will stay awhile," she said carefully, because anything else seemed cruel. It seemed to her that now she had the upper hand.

"I was about to say that I would have a door cut between your quarters and mine," he said. His voice was matter-of-fact; he might have been discussing buying grain with the cook. "The design of the inner chambers is a spiral. They are actually next to each other."

Persephone slipped her arm through his. "I would like that," she told him.

"Then you will stay?" He sounded puzzled.

"I will stay for a while," she told him. "I will yearn for the upper air eventually; you know that. And the kitchen garden won't be enough."

"I see."

"You don't see," she said, suddenly irritated. "I don't see, either. I don't know what I want, but I've never had the chance to decide for myself before." She didn't say that when you married someone, then you were stuck with them no matter what, as Dryope had been. Only death had freed Dryope, and she had had to launch herself on an unfamiliar wind to make her escape even so. Narcissa and Harmonia would doubtless be married by now. Could she go back to the upper air and ask them how it was? If they were sorry; if it had been worth it? How on earth did you know?

"How do *you* know?" she demanded of him. "How do *you* know you want me forever?"

"I am older than you," he said. "By rather a lot, I'm afraid."

That was normal in Persephone's world, and she said so.

"Not the best system, perhaps," he admitted. "Perhaps a couple ought to be wild and young together."

"And then when they discover they hate each

other, they're both unhappy," Persephone said darkly. "For longer, because he's young."

Hades laughed. She could feel his bunched muscles relax like a loosened bowstring. "You're a pessimist," he said, chuckling.

There was no question of locked doors now. Hades gave Cerberus some mysterious command, and the dog appeared at her doorway whenever she opened it, and padded silently at her side wherever she went. If she got lost she told him so, and he led her to familiar territory—usually the kitchens.

"That one has enough appetite for three heads," Scylla said, giving him the shank bone of something, which he retired into a corner to gnaw. They heard crunching sounds as he worried it.

"Do *you* know your way around everywhere down here?" Persephone asked, hoisting herself onto a stool to watch Scylla knead bread. She had got lost again and found herself, abruptly and unappetizingly, where the drains emptied into the sea.

"Mostly," Scylla said, slapping at the dough. "I've been here two years come this next equinox."

"How did you come here?" Surely he didn't have to kidnap his staff, as well. But where did he find them? Did he send a crier around the agora? *Come and work for the lord of the Dead. Excellent wages, quiet neighbors.*

"I was running away from my husband, the old swine," Scylla said. "He used to beat me and one day I couldn't take it anymore. I knocked him on the head with a stone quern and ran. Lycippus met me on the road. I don't know where *he* came from, or why he was on that road. I've never asked."

"Did you come by boat?"

"Oh yes, the strangest thing. We saw storm clouds in the distance, but whatever way the helmsman turned the tiller, the clouds just moved over somewhere else. We had a fair wind and no breath of bad weather the whole way."

No wonder people thought of the weather as a god, Persephone decided. It probably was.

In the next months she explored the whole of Hades's caverns, with Cerberus as her lifeline. He followed her anywhere, as she poked her nose into storerooms full of oil jars and sacks of meal, into chambers of ice where Hades apparently stored meat—the haunch of something huge hung from a hook in the ceiling—and into a little room where a man she had never seen before sat on a high stool before a table, tallying something. His table and the floor about him were stacked with wax tablets and sheets of soft clay in wooden frames. A shelf behind him held clay tablets already fired, their information frozen in them forever. Persephone could see nothing to count in the chamber with him. When she stopped in the doorway he looked at her over his tablet, stylus in hand, but didn't speak. She was afraid to ask him what he counted, for fear it would be souls, and fled.

After a while the corridor before her began to slant downward abruptly, and she could smell the sea. Cerberus woofed happily, following the brine scent. A set of stone steps went farther down, and she followed them. Cerberus was running before her now. At the foot he stopped and waited for her, tail wagging. The stone floor was damp now, and puddled with seawater past the steps. Persephone wondered if it flooded at high tide. There were no lamps, but a faint pale light shimmered on the stone. When the corridor bent abruptly she found its source: a bright flare of daylight and the sound of gulls squawking in the air outside. The opening was low, just high enough for the dog to squeeze through, and Persephone followed him, bending to wriggle through. Outside, the light was so bright she had to close her eyes. Cerberus barked again and darted forward to splash in the tide pool just beyond the cave mouth. Persephone waded into it after him and turned to look at the cliff. This entrance was so small no one would notice it, and it was clearly underwater at high tide. She could see the waterline and the seaweed that had caught on the jagged rocks just above the opening.

She played happily in the tide pool with the dog until the sun began to sink, and they retreated back into the caverns. She was sure Hades knew where she had been—she and the dog both stank of seaweed at dinner—but he didn't question her.

Another day, down a different passage she found a shaft opening to the surface above them. It lit a courtyard where a garden was planted with the same poppies that grew on the headland. The leaves had gone brown and flat, but the seedpods rustled in the air that whispered down the shaft. Hades himself was tending them, and he smiled when he saw her.

"If you like, I will teach you to use these," he said.

"What are they for?" She had always thought them useless except for their ephemeral beauty that withered by dusk when you picked them.

"Something your mother doesn't know. Another lost art, the art of sleep." He cupped the pod left at the stalk's end when the scarlet petals had fallen. The pod had been slit in several places, and he inspected the gummy juice that ran from the cuts. He smelled it and tasted it on the tip of his finger. "Not quite."

Hades knew so many things that Persephone had never heard of that she wondered sometimes if he made them up to keep her there. By day, or at least when the servants, who seemed to know, told her it was day, she explored the caverns. The only path she never tried to find now was the one that led to the beach where she had entered. If she found that, she would have to decide what to do about it. At night, in the chamber that now opened off Hades's own, she lay propped on one elbow in the feather bed and listened to his stories of other worlds where half-human creatures like centaurs roamed and faithful wives were turned into birds.

"Tell me a real story!" she said, annoyed at so many magical beings, and he laughed.

"Very well," he said, "I have seen your friend Narcissa whom you told me of."

"Narcissa! Where?" Persephone put her hand to her mouth. Was Narcissa dead? A horrible vision of Narcissa with a knife to her breast filled her mind, although she didn't know why.

"No. I am sorry if I frightened you. No, she is living with her husband on the north island—she married the younger brother of her mother's new husband." Persephone had told him stories in return for his, of her village. He had seemed as interested in their homely doings as she was in his tales of wonders.

"Why were you there?"

He was silent a moment. "I thought that if you

knew what was happening above, then you might not want so desperately to go there yourself. It is not a lovely place."

"Is she happy?"

"No."

"And you thought that a good tale to tell me?"

"No, I thought it truthful. Would you go back there and be the same?"

"I am not Narcissa."

"True enough. Your mother has promised you to your cousin Hermes if he can rescue you from me." His lip curled as if he didn't expect Hermes to offer him any trouble.

"*What?*"

"Indeed. I was there. The goddess spoke, and your mother acquiesced."

Persephone sat up in bed. "And you were there? They would have speared you on sight."

"As well they didn't get sight of me, then." Hades poured wine from a silver ewer into his cup and added a splash of water. He poured another for Persephone. "Shall we drink confusion to your cousin Hermes?"

Persephone drank indignantly. "I can't believe Mother agreed to that."

"Your mother wants you back. She loves you dearly."

"All mothers love their daughters," Persephone said rebelliously. "Then they marry them off. Mine was different."

"Perhaps your cousin seems the more palatable of two unpleasant choices," Hades said gently.

"And *you* are arguing her case for her?"

Hades chuckled. "No, I am considering the odds."

"Of what?"

"Of sending your cousin Hermes away with a flea in his ear without actually killing him, which would anger certain quarters."

Persephone folded her arms across her chest. "It wouldn't anger me. Mother! How could she agree to that?"

Hades blew out the lamp. "Think about it in the morning."

He was persuasive, or her body was easily persuaded; it amounted to much the same thing. Persephone gave herself over to new-found pleasures and refused to contemplate either Hermes or Demeter until daybreak. Narcissa, however, troubled her dreams when she finally slept.

In the morning she whistled up Cerberus, although she was fairly sure she didn't need him still, and went to sit among the poppies and think. He barked cheerfully as they set out, apparently hoping they would end in the kitchens again; when she came to the poppy garden he lay down to sleep on the cool stone that marked the paths between the rows, disappearing from sight in a rustle of drying poppy heads. Persephone sat on the bench in the middle of the garden, where Hades had laid his cutting knife while he told her what poppy juice could do. It had seemed to Persephone at first to be kin to death and had frightened her, but she had come to see that it gave a shorter sleep and the rest that let bodies heal, and she began to see what had happened to the people who had been brought to him living. She wondered if poppies offered the same balm to a restless mind, and Hades had said they did, but at a price. Now she accorded them a wary respect, but their beds were a place where she could sit and catch a breath of the upper air without the bustle and busyness of the kitchen.

Spring was coming up there. She could feel it by day, a green yearning in her veins, nearly as strong as the one that drew her to Hades by night. She thought she could hear her mother's voice on that current, a whisper of air down the shaft, saying, *You cannot stay. Come away. You cannot stay.* And Narcissa's whispering, *Go back; go back. I am lost; I am lost.* Persephone didn't know what to make of that; it was fainter than her mother's voice, and thin with some sadness Persephone didn't recognize. But her mother's voice grew stronger. If she stayed and Hermes came for her, she would have to marry him, which would be worse than marrying Hades. If she went back of her own will, she wouldn't have to have Hermes. It mattered when you chose something instead of letting it come for you. Hades had said so. Why should she have thought that she could keep this man and her freedom, too? Was that the lesson her mother had learned?

Persephone watched Hades as he slept that night, sleepless herself. Narcissa's voice had faded into a faint sad whisper, as her mother's grew louder and more insistent. *You cannot keep him,* her mother said. *You can never keep them. I know. Come away. Come away before Hermes finds you. I had to promise him.*

"Why did you have to promise him?" Persephone whispered urgently to the empty air.

Promise him, the whisper said. *Had to.*

"Mother!" Persephone crept from the bed and wrapped herself in her mantle. She wasn't sure whether she was actually talking to Demeter or to some ghost that moved through her chambers on the breath of the caverns. Nothing answered her. She paced the chamber while Hades slept, apparently oblivious for once. Her bare feet made no sound on the rugs, and she could hear Cerberus snoring in the next room. Lately she had had to whistle him up if she wanted his escort. If she slipped out now, she thought he wouldn't wake and come with her. She shed her mantle and pulled her gown over her head, pinning it with the old bronze pins she had worn when she came here. If she was leaving she would not take with her any of Hades's gifts besides the clothing she wore.

Persephone slid from the chamber into Hades's rooms next door. He had easily opened the wall between them, and she thought that doorway must always have been there, waiting for her to come through it. His chambers were dimly lit by a single oil lamp, as hers were, and she took this light, lest the absence of hers wake him. The walls in his chamber were painted black, and on one poppies grew, some in full bloom, some gone to seed, their crowned pods waving on slender stalks. Above them stars pricked the blackness so that the poppies seemed to have opened in the moonlight. On the opposite wall a silver river flowed through a dark valley, dark trees bending over it. A boat lay on the near shore as if it waited for a passenger.

Persephone padded silently past the poppies and the boat, her sandals in her hand, until she was in the corridor outside. She closed the door in a silent whisper, almost as faint as her mother's voice, and set out along it, pausing only to buckle her sandals. She knew the way now, she was nearly sure, and she became certain when she reached the journeyers on the walls. They hurried along in the opposite direction, set faces fixed on something Persephone couldn't see. One of them bore Echemus's face, Narcissa's father, or a visage very like his. Had he been there before? She began to hurry, half-afraid she would see someone else she knew, someone who should have been alive.

As she got closer to the cave mouth she became surer that she was going in the right direction. The scent of the sea came to her as it had in the corridor near the tide pool entrance. When she had first come she had smelled the sea everywhere in the caverns, but she had grown used to it over the months. Now only the sharp scent near the cave's entrances was noticeable. It was cold here, too, colder than it had been deeper inside where Hades kept braziers burning. A high thin wail, like a keening child, came to her ears, and a little cold wind stirred around her ankles. She began to wish she had brought her woolen mantle with her after all, but it was a long climb up to the headland, and easier without its enveloping folds.

The keening grew louder, and she knew it was the wind outside. A storm was brewing. She hurried along before she changed her mind, racing for the faint spill of daylight she could now see coming from the entrance. It must be just after dawn. The passage was wet at its lowest point, the water nearly to her ankles as she splashed through the opening, and the wind was wild even in the shelter of the overhang. It whistled and howled between the great boulders that littered the cave mouth, stirring the incoming tide to a froth.

"Mother! Stop it!" she hissed, but the wind paid no heed. Maybe it wasn't Mother this time. The water was cold around her ankles, and she pulled the hem of her gown up and tucked it in her sash. A little later, she thought, and she would have had to swim. She squeezed through the gap between the sentinel stones that guarded the caverns' true entrance and splashed into the oncoming tide, buffeted by the wind that threw her against the boulders. Spray rose from the breakers and blew in her face, stinging her eyes and half blinding her. She slipped, turning her ankle on a stone. The wind abated for a moment and she saw, crouching on hands and knees in the surf, the low rolling clouds that hid the sky and a wild white light between them.

Persephone staggered to her feet, wondering if she could climb the cliff in this wind. She couldn't go back. If she went back, she would not leave again. She wasn't sure why she knew this, but she was certain of it. Hermes would come for her, and he would be killed for his effort; the chain of blood debt his death would forge would link them all forever. She knew that, too. It had something to do with choices freely made or surrender forced. Whatever she did now would have repercussions, echoes that bounced back and forth through the caverns, and ripples that ran out across the surface of the sea forever.

She struggled through the rising surf, limping on her bad ankle. There was a crack of lightning over the sea and an answering boom of thunder. The rain sheeted down. She struggled clear of the cave mouth and turned to see the stunted trees on the headland above her bent nearly double in the wind. She could barely make out the path up the cliff. She ran for it, and another crack of lightning spun her around in her tracks. Beyond the wall of surf the sea roared, tossing something in its hand. Persephone halted, shading her eyes with her palm, shielding them from the stinging rain. A ship heaved on the water just beyond the inlet that guarded the cave mouth. It had no business here—there was no safe harbor to be found outside Hades's caverns. The bay where the fishing boats anchored was to the east, around the rocky shoulder of the island. This one was a stranger, or one of their own blown off course, but no fisherman of her village would have ventured out in a squall that must have been blowing up since before dawn. It had to be a stranger, come to trade with the village, making for shore to take on water, or lost, driven before the storm from some other place. Persephone struggled through the surf, pulling off her wet gown. She waved it over her head like a flag and shouted, trying to turn them back. The ship came on, driven before the wind. It would founder on the rocks in another moment if it had not already. This inlet was treacherous, fanged at high tide with sharp stones just below the waterline. While she watched, the ship shuddered on the rocks, and she saw the mast tilt as it snapped in two. She abandoned the sodden gown and dove into the surf.

VIII

The Men from the Sea

The water was cold and wild, but Persephone had grown up swimming in the waters off her island, in rough seas and calm. Demeter had taught her, saying only that one day she might need to know the way to speak to the waves. Persephone had never swum in seas as rough as this, but she knew the currents off this coast, and the sailors on that boat clearly did not. Sailors, oddly, often were not good swimmers because they had too much respect for the sea, as Echemus had said before he drowned, to meddle with it so intimately.

Persephone shivered as the wild water slapped her face and filled her mouth, but she kept swimming. All she could think was that those were her people, people of the upper air, and what good was her escape from the halls of the dead if she watched them go down into those icy caverns under the sea? She did stop to wonder if Poseidon, the sea god, who was held to be kin to Hades, had sent this storm.

Storms like this were thought to be his doing, when he felt inclined to exact tribute from the mortals who sailed on top of his waters. If so, there might be no saving them—what Poseidon wanted, he took. A wave rolled her under and spat her out again, coughing and gagging. She drew in enough air to shout "Stop it!" into the waves, in case it was Poseidon, his anger stirred by Hades's loss. There was no slackening of the wind or the current. She fought the water, keeping her eyes on the boat, half-hidden behind the sheeting rain and the tumbling breakers.

The wind blew something past her head, skimming the water, and she saw that it was a bird, a gull caught in the wind's fist, tumbling beak over tail. She could hear voices now, faint in the roar of the storm, shouting from the ship. She tried to call back to them, but the wind blew her own voice away and the sea filled her mouth with water.

The waves fought her as she swam, and the wind pulled and tossed her, driving her westward from the ship. She angled back through the roaring water and saw the ship's mast fall away entirely and the bow disappear in the storm. Only the stern, snagged on the fanged rocks, was visible now. Faintly she saw heads bobbing in the water, appearing and disappearing in the curtain of rain and blowing spray. She struggled toward them, her lungs burning. She could feel her feet beginning to numb in the icy sea. The waves caught her like a huge hand, shoving her down into the depths. She broke free and struggled upward again.

"Let me go!" she told it fiercely, gasping. Before her voyage with Hades it would never have occurred to her to speak to the storm or that it might listen;

but lately she had begun to think that it might all be one, weather and people and sea and earth, all breathing with one slow deep breath like the air that stirred in the caverns. "Let me have them!" she said to it, aloud, and a wave smacked her in the face and rolled her under again. She surfaced, spitting and furious. "They aren't yours!"

She had fought her way nearly to the ship. A face and arm broke from a wave before her, choking and flailing, eyes wide with terror. Persephone grabbed the arm around the wrist and hung on. The man thrashed in the water, fighting her or the storm, or both.

"Be still!" she screamed at him over the wind. "Lie still!" She caught him around the throat and began to take him with her, back through the waves. He flailed and thrashed in her grip and then when she shouted again in his ear, went still.

It was easier going back to the shore, even with the current pulling her westward, but she was gasping for breath when she felt sand under her feet. She tried to set the sailor upright, but his knees buckled and he began to slide away in the surf. She grabbed him by both arms and pulled him farther in, to where the water splashed around her calves. He was too heavy to lift, and so she dragged him by both arms to a rock, itself by now a third submerged, and pushed him up onto it. She turned him facedown so that the water in him would run out, and looked back at the surf. Another body struggled in the gray water just where the inlet's bottom dropped off into deeper seas. She glanced at the man on the rock. She thought he was breathing, barely. She set her shoulders and turned to the surf again.

Too far, a voice said in her head. *Too far, too cold. Too cold.* She ignored it, wading deeper into the surf and then diving through the waves that battered the shore. Even the stern of the ship was gone now. She scanned the sea for the face she had seen and found him again. The waves tossed him up and drew him under; she dove for the place she had seen him.

They surfaced together, face-to-face. He shrieked when she reached for him, as the other one had, as if she were a creature of the storm, come to pull him downward. She shouted at him, grabbed him by the hair, and tried to get her arm around his neck. He fought her and the waves thrust her downward. When she clawed her way to the surface her lungs burned and she struggled to draw breath. She couldn't see him. Another wave pushed her down, and she collided with something cold as a fish: a foot. She reached for it and pulled them both to the surface.

This time she got a grip on him and began to tow him to shore. She knew she was almost done. Her arms and legs felt like lead; her lungs hurt with every breath, and her feet and hands were numb. The shore seemed to recede as she swam toward it.

"You've taken the rest," she gasped. "Give me these!"

The storm seemed to slacken as if thinking about that. Then it redoubled its anger, slamming her down into the freezing water, pulling at her captive, trying to wrest him from her. The sailor began to fight her again, too, disoriented, certain that some creature of the depths had him in its toils.

"Stop!" she shouted at him. "Stop it! I'm trying to get you to shore!"

He wailed something that she thought might be a prayer. It was hard to say to whom. His accent was strange, but she thought the words were her own language.

Her right arm felt as if bone rubbed on bone when she lifted it, and her legs would barely kick. The shore and the entrance to the caverns looked ever more distant. She knew she was too numb to feel the cold when she thought that it would be so easy to stop now and to let the sea take them both. So easy just to float on the storm, light as a bird's feather. . . .

She saw herself in the surf with her mother. Demeter held Persephone under the arms, letting her find her place on the sea's breast. The water rolled under her, easy as a cow's gait. *Speak to the sea with respect,* Demeter said. *Don't fight it, and it will take you where you want to go.*

The shore was even farther away, she thought, sliding away from them as she swam. Speak to it. How did you speak to the sea except with your body? She swam on, pulling the drowned sailor with her. The shore was a high cliff of white stone with red flowers blooming at its top. It was a dark tumble of boulders where the octopus hid and reached out his long tentacles for wayfarers. It was a silver beach where a black river ran into the ground and a boat waited for them on its shore. The arm that stroked through the surf was all bones; she could see the separate finger bones like the bones of the woman on the bier. They were too thin to catch the water. She stroked again and kicked, and her face ran aground on the sand.

She lay with her head in the water, chin on the sand and the sea wrack buried and unearthed by the storm, until she took a breath and choked on seawater. She lifted herself and saw the headland before her veiled in rain, and the sailor facedown on his rock. The water lapped at his feet, higher now. The one she had brought in with her floated on the waves beside her, her fingers tangled in his hair. She struggled to her feet, swaying as the wind buffeted her and the current battered her legs. She lifted the second man from the water, heaving him up under his arms, and pulled him to the rock. The cave mouth was filling fast with the tide, and she knew this rock to be underwater when the full tide was in. There might be time to get the man she held through the rising water and into the caverns, before the other drowned. There probably wasn't, though. Nevertheless, she pulled the man to her again and began to half drag, half float him through the swirling current. He was inert now, and cold as ice. She wasn't even sure he was alive.

Getting him through the narrow gap was hard. The current tried to pull him from her grip, and his shredded clothing snagged on the stones. Her numbed fingers refused to close tightly, and he kept slipping from their grasp. She tugged at him furiously, unwilling to lose her prize at this juncture, while the storm wind howling in the cave mouth whipped her wet hair into her eyes and battered her bare skin with blowing sand.

"Persephone!"

She heard her name shouted above the wind and looked up to see Hades wading toward her from the cavern. A wave buffeted her, trying to drag her out into the sea, and he gripped her by the arms. "You've gone mad! Come inside. You can run away from me some other time!"

"Help me with him!"

"Leave him! The water will fill the entrance in a few minutes!"

"No! And there is another on the rocks out there. Their ship went down in the inlet."

"And you went out to get them?" He took stock of her, naked and shivering, the drowned sailor still in her grasp, and his eyes widened with respect.

"Help me get them inside."

"They are the sea's," he shouted at her over the wind. "It won't let you have them. And I won't lose you in trying."

"They are mine," Persephone said flatly.

"And you are mine." He glared at her, the blowing spray soaking his hair and beard. "Even if you won't stay with me." He was still wearing the tunic he had slept in. It was soaked and plastered to his body. "I'm not going to lose you. Leave them!"

"No!" Persephone wrested the man free of the rocks and struggled to carry him past Hades's bulk, which guarded the narrow passage. The water was up to her waist now, and only Hades's grip kept them both from being pulled under by the current. A spar from the drowned ship tumbled by them, borne on the roaring current.

"Leave them before you drown!"

"I won't!"

"Leave them. This is the land of the dead, isn't it?"

She stopped struggling with the sailor and looked him in the eye. "Not if I am going to live here."

He paused. They eyed each other for a long moment, considering, and then he nodded. Persephone still clutched the inert sailor with frozen hands. Hades took him from her grip. "Lift his feet."

Persephone grabbed the man's feet as Hades's servants had once carried her, and they struggled through the rising water with him. It was waist high going through the wide entrance, and the lower passage was flooded, as well. The stone journeyers rose from the lapping water as if they were swimming. The two fought their way through and up the first sloping corridor until the floor was visible. The drowned man weighed more with every step.

"Here! Stop here!" Hades gasped. "The water never comes past here even in a storm."

They set the man down on the stone floor and Hades turned him on his face and began to press on his back. Water ran from the open mouth, but he didn't move. "Go and fetch Lycippus," Hades said. "Send him to me and get yourself dry and warm."

"There is another out there!" Persephone said urgently. "We have to get him."

Hades sighed. "The water will have taken him by now."

"No, it won't," she said stubbornly.

"Then this man may die if I leave him now. It is always a trade, and there is always a price. You decide."

"I'm going back for the one outside." She turned and started back through the lapping water in the corridor and he leaped up and followed her.

"I will get him. Go back."

"No. It will take both of us."

"You are the most aggravating woman I ever met. Who are these sailors to you?"

She shivered, wrapping bare arms against wet skin. "People from my world. And if I'm so aggravating what do you want with me?"

"I ask myself that." He turned and plunged through the water, which was rising rapidly.

She followed him. By the time they got to the entrance, they were swimming. The water was nearly to the roof. He looked at her, shaking the water from his eyes, held out his hand, and she took it. They dived through the opening and slipped underwater between the stones that narrowed the passage. Persephone followed Hades blindly. He seemed to know where he was going and she wondered, with the half of her mind at leisure to contemplate stray thoughts, if he had gone in and out this way at high tide before. Outside the cavern mouth they surfaced sputtering and saw the sailor miraculously still on his rock. The water licked his face, and the cold spray blew over him.

"If he isn't drowned now, he will be by the time we take him back through that," Hades said, pointing an arm above the water to the swells that rose and fell inside the cavern mouth. "And so will we."

"I want him," Persephone said stubbornly.

"Consider him a wedding present," Hades said, floating beside her. A strand of seaweed clung to his head. He heaved the man off his rock and into the water, keeping the head aloft as well as he could. "You take one arm," he said to Persephone. "We'll have to separate to get him past the rocks. When we get there, I'll go first, then turn and pull him through. You follow. Keep your hand on the rock so you remember which way you're going, and which way is up. I'll catch you as soon as you come through."

She nodded, and said to the silent sailor, "We're going under the water," unsure whether he could hear her at all. She had seen his chest rise and fall faintly when Hades had picked him up. "Hold your breath," she told him in case he could.

They each took an arm and dove, Persephone following Hades's lead through the boulders that guarded the entrance, mysterious and distorted under the water. The salt stung her eyes, and her bones felt like ice. At the narrow gap, she clung to the rocks while Hades went ahead. The man stuck between them, and she shoved at him desperately. His knees were bunched under his chin, pinned by the rocks. Her lungs started to burn. Hades motioned for her to go back and surface outside the cave, but she shook her head. He yanked violently at the man, putting his foot against the folded knees. They buckled and he floated through. Persephone felt her way after him and felt Hades's hand close around her wrist. He put the man's other hand in hers, and they swam for the entrance.

The water was all the way to the cavern roof now and had completely flooded the lower passage. It was as black as night inside the water-filled corridor. She tried to surface and bumped her head on the stone. The memory of Glaucus's grave passage filled her mind. She felt Hades's hand close over hers and pry loose her grip on the sailor's wrist. He had the sailor in one hand and her in the other, she thought, or at least she hoped he did, and she followed blindly. The freezing black water surrounded them and she knew she would be lost, drowned before she could feel her way to the surface, if she let go of

Hades's hand. The dark flooded passage was more terrifying than the open ocean had been.

She began to see things again in the darkness, white shimmery lights that she knew didn't exist, the headland oddly rising in the distance, a cow floating in the water ahead of them. Hades yanked hard on her wrist and she surfaced into the dim glow of the lamplit passage. She gasped, sucking in air.

The stone figures swam beside her, gradually rising from the black water. The sailor floated at the end of Hades's other arm, hair drifting like weeds around his face, gray as the stone people's. She paddled until she could stand on the floor of the corridor, and together they pulled the sailor from the water.

"Madam!" Lycippus bustled down the corridor from above and wrapped her in a blanket. He must have heard the commotion, or Cerberus had. The dog sniffed suspiciously at the inert forms on the corridor floor. "Madam will take her death from cold." Lycippus added another blanket, this one wrapped about her head so that she could barely see out. More servants pattered after him down the corridor. "Madam needs a hot bath," he said firmly. She was sure that the unspoken comment just beneath was that Madam needed to get her clothes on. She shivered violently, teeth chattering, thinking longingly of the bath, but she knelt to look at the sailors first. She wasn't sure either was breathing.

"Go away and get warm," Hades said, bending over them. "I'll throw them back in the water unless you do."

"Master knows what to do for them," Lycippus

said, tugging at her arm. She saw Scylla from the
kitchen standing amid the crowd, a flour-streaked
apron wrapped around her middle, and turned
toward a known face. Scylla held out her arms, and
Persephone went to her.

"Oh, you poor thing, you're cold as ice." Scylla
put a floury hand on Persephone's and looked
shocked. "We must get you warm right away.
Come along."

Persephone let Scylla lead her up the corridor to
her chamber, with a detour at the kitchen where
Scylla shouted for help. Four or five people came—
Persephone lost count—carrying buckets from the
hot pool to pour into her tub. When it was filled,
Scylla shooed them all out again, unwound Persephone from her blankets, and ordered her into it.
Scylla dumped a basket of some kind of herbs in
after her. The hot water felt blissful against her
clammy skin, but her teeth kept chattering.

"Whatever were you doing out in that storm?"
Scylla demanded. She wrapped a towel around her
hand and dragged a bronze brazier across the floor
from the bedchamber so that Persephone could feel
the heat from its coals.

"I was leaving," Persephone said.

"Leaving the master?"

"I thought I'd better." Persephone sighed. "They
are sending a hero after me."

"Oh dear, that's always bad," Scylla said.

"I know," Persephone said miserably. "Hades will
kill him, and then dreadful things will happen."

"Who is this hero?"

"My cousin Hermes."

"Oh dear," Scylla said again.

Persephone sank down in the tub so that only her eyes and nose showed, like a frog. The hot water made her sleepy. She would think about the hero later. Scylla sat with her until the water cooled and Persephone began to shiver again. Scylla held out a towel, and Persephone hauled herself from the tub into its folds. Scylla put a hand to her forehead. "You feel warm enough now. I'll make you some hot broth, though, to clear your lungs."

"I want to see them," Persephone said.

"Who, dear?"

"The men we brought back. Their ship broke up in the storm. On the rocks in the inlet."

"And you and the master went out after them?"

"I saw them when I was leaving."

"*You* went out after them? Alone?" Scylla's eyes widened.

"I only got two of them," Persephone said. "There were more, but the storm was bad." Her eyes closed. She was sleepy.

"Mercy!" Scylla eyed her shrewdly. "No wonder. . . . Well, then, you go and see them, they'll be in the infirmary. I'll have some broth sent along up there for you. Then I'll just get on with my baking." She bustled off, muttering, and Persephone thought regretfully that now the story would be all over the caverns by nightfall, no doubt embellished with fanciful detail.

By the time she got to the infirmary it was clear that the tale had made its rounds without waiting. The servants stepped aside for her as if she had been Hades.

Lamps lit the walls of the dim chamber where the sick of Hades's kingdom were treated, and where, she had learned, he took those left at his gates. The shreds of the drowned men's wet clothing had been stripped off and they lay wrapped in blankets, their beds circled by braziers for warmth. She could hear a faint rattling breath from one, the younger of the two, an olive-skinned, dark-haired boy who looked not much older than she was. She could see that the other one, older, had pale hair, nearly colorless now that it was dry, and his skin looked as though it should have been pink. Just now it was ashen. They were foreign, she thought, from the way their beards were trimmed, but oddly matched as ships' crews often were.

"Where are they from?" she whispered to Hades, who sat on a stool between the beds.

"North of here, I think. Neither of them is right in the head." He looked at her. "Are you warm? Does your chest hurt? Are you still shaking?"

"No, and no, and no," she said. She yawned.

He looked relieved. "If you begin to cough, you must tell me."

She drew up another stool and sat beside him.

"You won't make them better by watching them," he told her.

"Tell me what you have done with them." She felt proprietary about them somehow. They were hers.

"Very well. We have held them upside down and beat them on the back and drained as much water from them as we could. We have put them to bed in warm sheets. We have boiled mullein and propped them up to inhale the vapors. We have given them both a dose of poppy syrup to bring sleep and ease their pain."

"Will they live?"

"That I do not know. You can pray for them if you think it makes a difference."

Persephone wasn't certain who might answer her prayer. Hestia had apparently ordered her brought home, and Great-Grandfather Aristippus was a priest of Zeus, and so must certainly have that god's ear. And what would the sun god Apollo care for pleas from someone living beneath the earth where his light never came?

"They will heal themselves or they will not," Hades said. "That has been my experience." He looked weary. He too was bundled in dry clothes, an extra cloak about his shoulders.

"But you help them heal somehow. Isn't that why people bring their desperate ones to you?"

"I only offer them sleep and what little knowledge of healing we possess. We are ignorant, my dear."

If Hades considered himself ignorant, she wondered if anything could be known for certain. Maybe that didn't matter. Maybe things could be believed into being. She looked at the younger man, whose breath rattled in his chest. His lips were blistered from the salt water and he had sores around his mouth. "We don't know their names," she said. "How can I pray for them if they have no names?"

"Name them, then," Hades said. "They are yours."

She hadn't thought of that. Maybe naming them would bind them to her, keep them living. "Then I will call him Ceyx," she said, for the drowned husband of Hades's tale, who with his wife had become a bird nesting on the open sea.

"And the other?" Hades looked indulgent, as if she were naming puppies.

"Oceanus," she said.

"Excellent choice. And what will you do with them if they live?"

"Set them free, I suppose. My village will take them in."

Hades raised an eyebrow. "All that trouble and you don't plan to keep them?"

"You have no slaves here. You said so."

"True. And I should be grateful to them, since they brought you to me again."

Lycippus and the other servants moved a tactful distance away. Persephone looked at her hands, folded in her lap, the fingers twisting at her gown. "I have lost the silk gown you gave me," she said.

"There are more."

"And the blue sandals."

"The sea nymphs will like them." He smiled and took her hand. "We will go out in a boat someday and see them combing their hair in the waves, wearing your clothes."

"I didn't really want to leave you," she whispered, "but if they've sent Hermes for me, he will make dreadful trouble."

"Heroes always do," he said.

"Hermes is worse. I don't know how to explain it. Things happen when he's around. Balls fly into hornets' nests. Soup boils over and scalds someone. If you kill him—"

"I have no intention of killing him. Inconveniencing him, perhaps."

"I'm not sure that will be enough," she said sleepily. "People like Hermes seem to need . . ."

"Forceful measures?"

She nodded, yawning. Suddenly she was as sleepy now as if he had fed her poppy syrup, as well.

Hades snapped his fingers for Lycippus. "Escort madam to her chamber," he said. He helped her to her feet. "Go, my dear. You are worn out and you will take sick if you don't sleep."

"What about Hermes?"

"Hermes is nowhere about at the moment, unless he has been washed out to sea, a development earnestly to be wished."

Persephone nodded sleepily. The water would keep him out for a while. Long enough to sleep. She was so sleepy. She let Lycippus take her elbow and guide her down the corridors to her chamber. She yawned again and fell into the bed she had left that morning. The blankets were in a heap on the floor as if Hades had put them off all at once when he saw she was gone. Lycippus drew them up over her and blew out all but one lamp, in a high niche where its flame made a little pool of gold on the wall, its light blowing through painted anemones. Persephone wasn't certain where those had come from. They had just appeared one day, after their return from Knossos, the colors still wet. Hades had a way of thinking of things she might like and providing them. She had considered asking him for bull dancers on her wall, but had thought better of it. The bull dance had been some kind of offering, and it still held power. It wasn't just something to decorate your house. She would be content with anemones, and with his other small gifts from the outer world— sailors for instance.

She slept deeply and when she woke, there was a tray of fruit and cold fish beside the bed, with a pitcher of sweet wine. Persephone sat up, rubbing her eyes. They stung and her hair was sticky with salt. She stood, yawning, rotating her arms to ease the stiffness from them. At her first step, a small maidservant popped in from the outer chamber and a moment later another parade passed her, bound for the bathchamber with more buckets.

"Scylla said madam would want to wash her hair," the maidservant said. "Shall I help?"

"No," Persephone yawned. "No, I will be all right by myself, but tell Scylla thank you."

I could have a lady's maid, she thought as she bent over the tub, drowning her hair in warm water. *Someone to dress my hair and buckle my sandals and bring me things. I could be utterly useless. I mustn't let him do that.* She worked soap into the stiff strands, and thought, *And if I stay here, what will I do instead? Besides be his wife?* She couldn't imagine. Hades's wife had no work to do. The distaff and the loom had been only for her amusement, to play at work, should she wish to. She poured a pitcher of clean water over her hair. *And if I went home, what would I do?* She saw herself there—endlessly a child, frolicking on the headland, braiding anemones into garlands to wear in her graying hair—and shivered.

She toweled her hair dry and pinned it into a knot at the back of her neck with the silver pins that had just appeared one morning on her dressing table. *I will ask him for something practical now*, she thought firmly. *Before he brings me a troop of jugglers or a dancing sheep.*

He was still in the infirmary, brewing some kind of potion in a clay beaker that sat on bronze legs over one of the braziers. He tasted it carefully with the tip of the stick he had used to stir it.

"Ah!" He put the stick back in the beaker when

he saw her and came to meet her. "Are you better, my dear?"

She smiled at him. "I am awake at all events. Have you been here this whole time? Are they better?"

"Yes, and no," he said, turning to the beds. "Your Oceanus is breathing somewhat more easily, but Ceyx is feverish."

"And is there nothing to be done for that?"

"Willow, which I have tried."

She looked down at them dubiously. "I have never tried to heal anything but sick goats. Will you teach me?"

"It's much the same in some ways. Except that goats rarely fall in the water." He sat down on the stool beside Ceyx and motioned her forward.

She dragged another up beside his and sat. "I am beginning to think I shouldn't have called him for a drowned man," she whispered. "Maybe he wouldn't like being a bird. I don't suppose he will turn to one, either, if he dies."

"If he dies, it won't be because of his name."

"Names are powerful." They both knew that. When you named a thing you called it, in one way or another. Bound it, perhaps to some fate that you didn't know about, but the name did.

Ceyx's breath came harshly from his throat with a thin whine behind it that was the air trying to get out through too narrow a passage. Persephone took one of his hands in hers, while Hades watched her gravely.

"He's young," he said. "Have you fallen in love?"

Persephone shook her head. "No." She turned to Hades. "Not with him."

"Then why do you weep for him?" Her cheeks were wet with tears.

"Because I can't make him stay with me. I felt the same about the jackal pup."

Hades nodded. "I will teach you about the poppies. They don't always work, but when they don't, they ease the passing. This one"—he gestured at Ceyx—"will reach the crisis soon. Do you want to stay?"

"I will stay." If she was going to live in Death's kingdom, best she become acquainted with it.

Ceyx died on the breath of the morning tide—so said Lycippus; Persephone had no way to see outside—so perhaps he was well named after all. She imagined his spirit as a small feathered bird, borne aloft on the coast wind. Was there a mate waiting for him somewhere, by the hearth on some other island? And what would she think when the brown bird landed on her sill?

They wrapped his body in the sheet, and Lycippus and another took him away to the realm of the woman on the red bier. Persephone saw that Lycippus carried oil and a bag of meal.

In the other bed, Oceanus lay quietly, his breath a whisper, but his color was better; he looked less as if he had been sculpted of white marble. He had a deep wound in one thigh, ripped into his flesh by his dying ship, no doubt. Awake, it would have pained him greatly, but he slept on under his blanket of poppies. Hades and Lycippus had dressed the wound with honey, and she could see that it was less inflamed than before.

Hades stood, stretching. "After sickroom air, it is a good thing to breathe fresh. Come and I will show you how to use the poppies."

He took her first to the garden. Before they had

reached the courtyard where the poppies grew she could smell the clean air that whistled down the shaft, and the faint scent of salt hanging in it. Daylight spilled through the arched door that opened on the poppy beds, white and clean as sea foam. She took a deep breath and heard Hades do the same.

Even this far down the shaft, the new leaves were wet with dew. There were no flowers yet, only the bristly young green of the new season, and the occasional dry stalk of last year's stems. The poppy heads of last year had all been gathered. Hades knelt and brushed his fingers against soft, hairy leaves beginning to push from the soil. "These will bloom in a month," he said, "just like the ones that grow wild above. That's where I dug the ancestors of these."

She nodded, kneeling beside him.

"When the petals fall, the seedpods form, and they are what make the poppy juice. You saw me in the winter tending them. You make small slits in the pods and the juice runs from them and thickens. That is what makes the drug. I'll show you how that's done." He took her arm, and they wound their way back through the corridors to the infirmary.

Hades had his apothecary in a room adjoining the sickbeds. One wall was lined with shelves laden with clay pots and beakers, and spoons for measuring. On the opposite one, another field of poppies bloomed. They bent their heads seductively in an invisible breeze. A large brazier heated the room, and a smaller one sat on a table for heating potions. Persephone stood gazing about the chamber, wondering what was in each jar and pot. There were too many to count.

-"The tricky part," Hades was saying, "is that each

year's crop is different. One must guess at the strength, and too much is dangerous. If you give them too much they never wake at all."

Persephone left off contemplating the pots as a new thought occurred to her. "Have you ever done that?"

"Done what?"

She thought he was deliberately misunderstanding her. "Given someone too much?"

He was silent for a moment. "A hopeless case, you mean?"

"Yes."

He was silent again. Finally, he said, "No."

So he had done that. Mercy on the wings of sleep.

Hades turned toward the sickroom. "Let us look at your remaining jackal pup."

Oceanus's eyes opened at their footsteps. He saw Hades first and breathed through parched lips, "Water." His accent was odd but understandable.

Persephone fetched a cup and poured it full from the ewer on the table against the wall. She bent over him and he screamed. The cup flew from her hands as she retreated.

"The Nereid!"

Persephone picked up the shards of the broken cup. "I am not a nereid," she said to him shortly.

"Don't let her take me!" he implored Hades. His eyes were wild with fear.

"I will protect you," Hades said solemnly, and Persephone glared at him as she filled another cup. Nereids were sea nymphs, who lived in the depths and rode the waves on dolphins. They were often kind to sailors, but took the drowned ones to their underwater kingdom to live. Apparently this one went in fear of such a briny courtship.

"She came for me, in the storm," he whispered. "I felt her take me by the hair."

"Then how do you know you aren't underwater already?" Persephone asked him crossly as she held the cup to his trembling lips.

Oceanus wailed and tried to bat the cup away.

"Be still! You aren't underwater, and I am not a Nereid. Look—no fins!" She held her sandaled foot out for him to inspect.

"Look for seaweed in her hair," Hades suggested solemnly. "It's a sure sign."

Persephone caught his eye and burst into laughter. Oceanus looked dubiously from one to the other.

"We found you in the storm, sailor," Hades said. "My wife braved the waves to rescue you."

"Am I the only one?" he whispered.

"The only one who lived."

He closed his eyes. "This island was always cursed."

Persephone studied him curiously. "Where are you from?"

"Eleusis." When he opened his eyes, they were a bright pale blue. They fixed on her with apprehension. "The other one came from here," he said.

"What other one?"

"The witch."

Persephone carefully set down the cup, from which he had finally been persuaded to drink. "The witch?" she asked him.

"I found a witch on these shores once. I was mending my boat and she came up out of the surf and threw an enchantment over me so that I took her away with me."

"Oh?" There was a quiet, thoughtful silence as Persephone busied herself with straightening his blanket and fluffing the pillow behind his head. "Sit up a bit for me—just so—there, that's better. What happened then, when you took her home with you?"

"She set an ill spell on my brother with her wiles, and he burned to death. Then she bore me a child, a useless girl. I was going to expose it, but she fled in the night and took the child with her. She stole my best boat," he added, aggrieved.

Mother! Persephone thought. It must be. "Men like that," Mother had always said dismissively. Men with a practiced explanation for everything that befell them, none of it their own fault. How often had a man like that found a woman somewhere and molded her in his head to his own liking, only to find that she was nothing like that in reality? Persephone slipped a glance at Hades. Hades had done that and seen the folly in it. That might be rare. More to the point now, how often had a woman done the same, and found herself trapped? Persephone could tell that this one had been handsome in his youth. His pale hair looked as if it has once been bright as hers. She could still see glints of gold among the white strands. Had Demeter yearned, as Persephone had, for knowledge beyond her own shores, and had the misfortune to look for it in this sailor? Persephone was conscious of Hades watching her astutely. She patted Oceanus benevolently on his forehead. "There, you'll need to rest now. I'll send someone with broth for you to drink."

"You know something your jackal cub does not," Hades said when they had left the sickroom.

"Maybe." Persephone was reluctant to say it aloud.

"I could hazard a guess," Hades offered.

Of course he would have heard the old gossip. He seemed uncannily able to come and go about the village unseen. "I am not certain of it," she said, but she was.

"What will you do with him now?" he asked.

"Give him to Mother." Persephone had just decided that. She had heard in Oceanus's bitterness the bones of a tale told often, over and over to himself, to explain why things had happened as they had. It held the echo of her mother's explanations. She supposed that always happened; you had to have some story to tell yourself about why you had done what you had done. "I'll send him up to the village when he's well."

Hades chuckled. "It may have been pointless to rescue him in that case. I doubt she'll be glad to see him."

"Or he her. But they have business that is not finished. When it is, things may be easier for us here." And maybe neither of them would have to spend their lives in endless bitter justification, explaining to themselves again why they had left a man they loved.

Hades looked mournful. "If he doesn't want a bride price."

Persephone gave a hoot of laughter. "You can give him those aquamarines."

IX

❧

Demeter's Garden

But it wouldn't be that simple to stay here, Persephone knew that. Nothing to do with the heart
was ever that simple. Her childhood had been filled
with Demeter's warnings—veiled allusions to "men
like that," admonitions to be wary of strangers, not
to be seduced by promises lightly spoken. Not to
marry, to leave men alone. Now that she had done
all that she had been warned not to, she could feel
her mother's fingers on her wrist, tugging her toward
the upper air, Demeter's voice whispering that "men
like that" were never reliable, would bring you to
grief, that it was much better to stay mateless and
safe.

And on her other side stood not Hades, but her
grown-up self, the self that knew what it wanted, the
self that had seen the bull dancers and felt the leap
in her blood, and the joy and terror of the dance.
Had her mother felt that with Triptolemus? Persephone had learned from him his true name, and had

asked him the witch's name; now she knew for certain that names held power. She had not told him what she knew, but she studied him so intently as he grew well that he became suspicious and pleaded with Lycippus not to allow her to carry him off to the sea.

"No one is going to take you under the sea, you crazy man," Lycippus said briskly, shaving him. He had propped Triptolemus up against a pillow.

"I don't like the way she looks at me. There's something about her eyes."

"The mistress has very nice eyes," Lycippus said primly.

"They glow," Triptolemus said fretfully.

"Nonsense." Hades had failed to confide in Lycippus that this sailor might be the mistress's father, but attentive servants had ways of knowing these things. The man was very nearly well now, well enough to be sent on up the stairs to the village where he had been assured that the local folk would take him in. If that didn't cause a change in the weather, Lycippus would be very much surprised.

They sent Triptolemus on his way on a balmy spring day when little patches of cloud drifted over the island like tufts of wool and the poppies on the headland bloomed. Hades gave him a woolen tunic and cloak and new sandals, and bade him tell the village folk that the lord and lady of the lower caverns had fished him from the sea and healed him.

Persephone hoped that news of her contentment might sway Demeter to her side. On the other hand, it was entirely possible that Demeter would take one look at Triptolemus and allow him no chance to say anything at all. *That is my father,* Persephone thought, watching him climb the cliff. It was an odd sensation. Persephone and Hades stood side by side at the cave mouth, just visible beneath the overhanging lip of the cavern, and waved jauntily. Hades's arm was about her waist, as if they were gracious hosts and he a guest setting out along his road home. That seemed to worry Triptolemus, too. She thought regretfully that he wasn't very astute. When he had realized that Hades's domain was under the ground, they had had to convince him all over again that not only was he not drowned, but he was not dead on land, either. Now he looked back at them every so often, his brow furrowed with worry. The sea breeze blew his new cloak clumsily about him.

Triptolemus climbed the last step and pulled himself up onto the headland to stand for a moment among the blooming poppies. The wind stiffened; he wrapped the cloak about himself and headed toward the village, following the path through the meadow until he could see the lime-washed walls of the island's houses and the Temple of Zeus and Apollo gleaming in the white sun. The air was dusty with pollen and the smell of goats.

A boy with red hair and a traveler's hat and staff was loading a pack under the olive tree in the agora when Triptolemus reached it, but there was no one else to be seen.

The boy put his pack down. "Who are you?"

"A stranger seeking shelter. I was wrecked off your coast." He was aware that his clothes were new, and that that looked odd.

"Wrecked? There hasn't been a storm in weeks."

"Someone took me in—in the caverns below the headland." It was difficult to explain because Triptolemus wasn't exactly sure where he had been.

The boy's red brows rose under his hat. "Someone took you in," he said carefully, but his voice was friendly. "What sort of a someone?"

"A lady. I thought she was a Nereid . . . I still do . . . she swam out and took me by the hair, and they bore me away into a cavern where a man with a dark beard gave me a potion. He must have been Poseidon. It's all very strange now. . . ." Triptolemus's voice trailed off. He wasn't sure he remembered it very well.

More people began to appear in the agora, drawn by the voices.

A woman with thin dark hair pinned to the top of her head like a bird's nest said to the boy, "Hermes! You were to have set out by now!"

"Mother! This sailor—"

The boy was interrupted by an old man with a long white beard and an authoritative look. "We welcome the stranger at our shores," he told Triptolemus, "but you come at an ill time."

"Well, we are always glad to welcome a traveler. We are famous here on the island for our hospitality, and no doubt he'll be happy to repay us in some fashion, so . . ." That was an old woman with a water jug. She looked nearly as authoritative as the old man and went on talking while the rest talked over her.

"Mother! Great-Grandfather! He says he's been in the caverns!"

"What of your boat, fellow? Anything left of it?"

"Why have you not set out to rescue my daughter?"

Triptolemus turned to see who it was who had spoken last.

"What is your name, man?" the white-bearded ancient asked, and Triptolemus told him.

That was when the sky exploded. A thunderbolt came out of a dark cloud that hadn't been there two minutes before. The bolt cracked across the agora and sizzled on the ground where the stranger stood. It tossed him into the air, where it hung him in the olive tree. The rest of the village fled indoors, cowering while Demeter stood beneath the tree, her eyes blazing like the lightning. Rain poured down in sheets, and the wind blew up until Triptolemus thought he was at sea again and wailed despairingly, clinging to his branch.

By the time Hermes and young Tros had retrieved him, under Aristippus's direction, Triptolemus knew whose village he had come to.

They carried him to Demeter's house, through the storm and her desolate garden. "I think he's fainted," Tros said. He sloshed through a mud puddle, gripping Triptolemus under the arms.

"Wouldn't you?" Hermes said. He shifted his hands for a better grip on Triptolemus's feet.

Demeter walked beside them, appearing not to notice the sheeting rain. Hermes thought maybe she didn't feel it, since it was her rain.

They put Triptolemus in Demeter's bed, at her direction. He opened his eyes once, saw Demeter's face looming above him, and closed them again with a whimper.

Tros left in a hurry, but Hermes stood shivering by the fire. "I'll stay a moment if I may," he said to

Demeter. "He says he's been in the caverns, so maybe he can . . . and after all, if he's really . . ." The latter was territory he was reluctant to tread on.

"Go and fetch my daughter!" Demeter spun around, eyes blazing, and pointed her finger at him. Hermes swore he could see lightning coming from it.

"Of course." He backed up a bit. "I'll just have to repack my things. The storm has ruined all of it," he added pointedly.

Demeter narrowed her eyes at him. He could see the lightning dance in the pupils. "You don't need anything but a spear. You are to rescue my daughter, not recite a poem." A muscle ticked just under her eye, as if something were working its way out. Hermes left without seeing what.

Triptolemus woke in Demeter's bed. Rain was still pouring down outside, and the sky was nearly black. Inside, the house was warm and smelled of broth. Triptolemus buried his head in the pillow. He should have let the Nereid keep him. It might not be so bad at the bottom of the sea. Sea nymphs were said to be ethereally beautiful and amorous, besides. It had just been that he was so afraid of the water. He heard footsteps and groaned.

"So my daughter has sent you back to me, from the realm of the Dead. Does she know who you are?" Demeter stood over him with a bowl in her hands.

Triptolemus shook his head. "I don't know." He sat up. "Is that my daughter? She is beautiful," he said hopefully, as if Demeter might give him credit for his part in that.

"The one you were going to expose? That daughter?"

"That was my mother," Triptolemus said sulkily.

"Don't lie to me. You are too stupid to get away with it."

Triptolemus sighed. "I know. Demophon was the smart one. He could always figure things out."

"Was that why your mother was going to kill my child? Because hers had died?"

"Demophon was her favorite."

"You're like me then," Demeter said with a snort of anger. "You've never been anyone's favorite."

"No." That was the way it had been; she was right.

"Drink this." She handed him the bowl. He regarded it suspiciously. "If I was going to kill you I would have just cut off your head while you slept. Poison is too much trouble. Drink it."

Triptolemus drank. It was warm and faintly sweet as if it had honey in it, but it didn't have the aftertaste of the potions they had given him in the caverns, so he went on drinking. He didn't want to fall asleep in Demeter's bed again with Demeter awake.

"Is it true my daughter has married that man?"

Triptolemus put the bowl down. "I don't know. He called her his wife."

"He may call her a sea snail and it won't make her so."

"How did our daughter come to that place? And why are you angry about it? She seems very well-off."

"I never said she was *your* daughter." Demeter glared at him.

Triptolemus sighed. "She is, though, isn't she? She's the right age. And she has a look of me, now that I think about it. She looked familiar."

"She looked familiar because she looks like *me*," Demeter said, exasperated.

"I don't know." Triptolemus tried to figure it out. "Maybe she looks like us both?" he suggested.

"Maybe *you* should go and fetch her back to me then."

"She sent me up here. I don't think she wants to come back."

"She must come back." Demeter looked out the window at the sheeting rain. Lightning cracked again in the storm's heart. "It won't stop until she does."

"Did you do that?" Triptolemus looked even more unnerved.

"I think so," Demeter said. "It just happens when I want it to. It doesn't matter if I try not to want it. It happens anyway."

Triptolemus eyed her uneasily, wondering what else she might want. "And what will you do with me?"

"I don't know," Demeter said.

Triptolemus shuddered. He could think of several unpleasant possibilities.

"You can start by digging the garden while I think about it."

Triptolemus didn't object. He had been half-afraid she would want to feed it with his blood. She disappeared and left him in her bed, and it was a long time before he fell asleep.

In the morning the two of them went out to look at the sodden ruin that was Demeter's garden. She had planted nothing this spring, and all that grew was weeds and what had come up from plants left

to rot in the fall: stray rambling squashes and pea
vines, leeks and overwintered parsley. The rain had
stopped, but the sky was sullen, matching Demeter's mood.

Triptolemus tried to think what had come over her.
He had never been afraid of her when she had lived
with him at Eleusis. His mother and sisters had bullied
her, he remembered, and she had spent all her time
in the garden with old Faunus, his mother's slave, who
was older than the stones in the earth. She seemed to
have acquired some dangerous abilities since then. She
didn't look any older, either, although if you saw her
next to Persephone you would know which was the
mother and which the daughter. Persephone was lithe
and oddly regal, while Demeter's body was generous,
sensual, like the fruit of her apple trees. He watched
her round hips shift as she bent to pull a thistle from
the mud beside her doorway, where crocuses were
blooming white and purple in the muck, and felt himself hardening in spite of himself.

"You can start by cleaning up the mess," Demeter
told him, interrupting this meditation, and the urge
vanished, to his relief.

He found Demeter's plow in a shed, half-broken
and dull, and set it to rights, whistling between his
teeth. This, at least, he knew how to do, having
served an apprenticeship of his own with old Faunus
in his youth, before he began to sail on the sea, before
Demeter, before Demophon. He had been the favorite
then, the only son.

When the plow was mended, Demeter sent him to
Aristippus to fetch the village's ox, used to till the
wheatfields in the spring.

"Staying awhile, are you?" Aristippus asked him.

The plow bit into the mud and turned the sodden weeds over. Demeter watched him from her house, pausing in the window as she cleaned the muddy floors and shook out the bedclothes. She took a basket of laundry to the stream, and came back with a garland of red poppies about her head.

The village watched this development with uncertainty.

"Do you think she's going to *keep* him?" Harmonia asked Tros over a breakfast of figs and cheese. She patted her rounded belly and smiled when she felt the child kick back at her hand.

"Ill luck to speculate about that, I expect," Tros grunted. "I'd as soon put it in a beehive, if you were to ask me."

"I remember when we were girls," Doris said to Echo as they milked the goats. "She was never happy with any of the village boys. She wanted I don't know what, but it wasn't here. And *that* is what she found? The gods help us all; you might as well stay at home." The doe turned her head to mouth a strand of Doris's hair, soft nose rubbing her cheek. "Stop that!"

"Who knows *where* he's come from?" Glaucus's daughters said. "He could be anybody, and I don't believe he's that girl's father. How could you know after all this time? We all think so. She ought to send him about his business before he robs somebody or worse." They nodded their heads firmly, like a row of crows.

"You have a responsibility to see that he marries her," Bopis told Aristippus. "Living with that man without any proper ceremony, it doesn't set the girls a good example."

"A misalignment of the humors," Phaedon said to the vintner, whose boil he was lancing. "Too much black bile makes a man melancholic. He should come to me."

"Do you suppose he'll stay here?" the vintner asked. "Ow! With her? Ow, you ham-fisted ox!"

"Now, your problem is yellow bile that causes eruptions of the skin. It is to be hoped he stays. She needs a man. It's not natural the way she's lived. Sexual intercourse opens the entrance to the womb, and allows blood to flow out so it doesn't back up into the heart and lungs, causing licentiousness and dangerous hallucinations." Phaedon applied the needle again to the other side of the boil. "The womb may close up again when a woman is widowed; I've seen it happen. Then it begins to wander, moves about the body, and causes all manner of trouble. She'll do well to take him."

The vintner nodded. "Just goes to show. Look at all this weather. Ow! Didn't even have the decency to dedicate herself to the goddess if she didn't want a man. Nobody worries about priestesses; they're all crazy anyway."

Hesperia pottered among the bones and ashes behind the altar in the Temple of Hestia. They would mate and bring forth children; she had seen it in the smoke. Or maybe they already had. But whether they would be monsters or blessed ones, she couldn't tell, or even which couple she was watching. Sometimes she thought they were the same people.

"What am I to you?" Persephone asked Hades. She sat in a chair, playing for her own amusement with the distaff and wool, while he stretched on a couch like a comfortable cat and watched her.

"My queen, my heart." He smiled in the firelight.

"How flattering. Oh, I've snarled it again, bother!" She struggled with the recalcitrant threads. "It's a mercy I won't have to wear this. No, I meant something else. Mother wants me back; I can still feel it. Every time I go near any of the entrances, or into the gardens, the hair stands up on my arms and the back of my neck prickles. I want to get married."

"And you think that will keep your mother away? I had considered that we *were* married."

"You didn't grow up in my village."

"No. Regrettably."

Persephone snorted. "My dear, I am not even yet entirely sure you're human, and my village most certainly isn't. If you don't want Mother to take me back, you will have to marry me properly, in the human fashion."

Hades chuckled. "You put my bride price down the drains."

"Will you be serious?"

• His face darkened. "I am. I came here to live because I saw little good in the affairs of people like those of your village."

"That doesn't matter," Persephone said with certainty. "It's the choice that matters. You said that yourself. It's making the free choice. If you don't want Mother to take me back, you will have to make *your* choice, before witnesses."

"If it's a free choice, why before witnesses?" he inquired.

Persephone set the distaff spinning again, and the

thread lengthened from her fingers. "Because what you won't say before witnesses, you don't mean. Then I am no more than poor Cousin Maia who claims she slept with Zeus and got my cousin Hermes."

Hades looked thoughtful.

"Now it's your choice," Persephone said.

She stood fidgeting on a stool while Scylla and Pomona tugged and fiddled with her gown. How many brides had stood thus, Persephone mused, wondering what the man they were going to wed would be like. Some would not have seen him at all, or very rarely, just a face glimpsed by lamplight, in conversation with her father, with talk of oxen and goats and jars of oil, flowing over watered wine and sweetmeats that weren't offered to her. Some, the ones who weren't wealthy, whose marriage and bedding made no difference to anyone, might have picked him out themselves, tested him out, too, in the hayfield on a warm midsummer night, and be already swelling with the first child. But they wouldn't know him, either. Not really. Did anyone ever?

"You're lovely," Pomona said. "It's lighter in these caverns already for your presence. The master's a different man."

"Who is he?" Persephone whispered.

"He'll make you a fine, faithful husband, not like some." Pomona stood back to admire her veil, crowned with scarlet pomegranate blossoms.

"That's not what I asked you," Persephone said, pursuing it.

"Well, we don't know," Scylla said, "but no one

who comes here wants to leave, so that's a good sign."

Triptolemus had, Persephone thought, but he had had unfinished business elsewhere. Maybe no one knew more of her prospective husband than the fates had revealed to her. Scylla held up the silver mirror that had been Hades's gift to her, and she looked at her reflection in its watery surface. Her wheat-colored hair fell down her back in waves, and the veil, sheer as gossamer, floated out over it, anchored by the wreath of pomegranate.

"Lovely," Scylla sighed. She gave Persephone her hand to help her down from the stool, and, Pomona carrying the ends of the veil to keep them from the floor, they set out solemnly for the great hall where Hades was waiting for her.

He was there, beside the hearth, with Lycippus in attendance. Odd, Persephone thought fleetingly, to be taken to your marriage by servants; no friends, no family, unless you counted Cerberus, stretched beside the hearth, panting. His fangs glinted milky white in his mouth, but it was a cheerful expression, a wolfy smile of goodwill.

Hades wore a black tunic stitched with white and scarlet poppies, and Persephone thought as she walked across the hall to him, how alike the poppies and the pomegranates were when they had made their fruit. Each bore on its head the little crown that had been the pod of the blossom. *I will be queen here,* she thought. *Queen over the flowers of sleep and the fruit with the seed at its heart, and the shades of those who have eaten both.*

Hades took her hand and with his other, strewed meal on the stones of the floor for whatever gods he prayed to. If he did. Sometimes she thought he spoke directly to them. He filled a cup of wine and dipped his fingers in, flicking a spatter onto the floor. The ruby drops shone against the meal like pomegranate seeds; then he held the cup to her. She took it and drank, the silver of the bowl cool in her fingers. She could see their faces in it, wavy and distorted like looking into a pond with ripples. His face, dark and smiling, shimmered beside hers, and she thought she saw people behind him, faces she didn't know, but when she turned there was no one there.

The wine was thick and sweet, almost unwatered, and it made her head spin. He took the cup and drank after her; then he bent his head to kiss her. "You are chosen," he said. "I am chosen. We are each freely chosen of the other."

It seemed an odd wedding ceremony. Usually you asked the gods for prosperity and children, and the grace to get along with each other. But their needs were different, and these seemed the right words. "Chosen," she repeated after him.

There was something in the air over the island just then. It hung below the clouds like a face, curious, watching, transparent yet visible. It saw the handfasting between Hades and his bride, and it saw the two in the garden, pulling weeds—turning the earth, upending the warm soil, slipping in the seed. It saw the two below again, standing among the vegetable beds now where the bright air drifted down through rock to touch their hair. Hades had ordered wine and sesame cake for all his servants, and they crowded the gardens, drinking to the lord's and lady's health.

Whatever was in the air drank, too. Its breath was sweet with the scent of wine and cake when it drifted over Demeter's garden. Demeter stopped pulling thistles and lifted her head. She stretched her neck like a cat's, following the air. Triptolemus eyed her warily.

In Hades's garden the servants were getting drunk. Lycippus leaned against an apple tree, clay cup cradled in both hands. His bushy brows looked to Scylla like hairy caterpillars, and she giggled as they went up and down while he spoke to her. The kitchen boys and the girls from the laundry were dancing in a line, spiraling hand in hand around the raised beds, while the baker played the flute and an old woman who swept the floors kept time, beating a saucepan on her knee with a spoon. A man Persephone recognized as Charon, the helmsman of Hades's boat, played the lyre, and the dancers danced faster and faster around them. Cerberus ran behind, barking joyfully, tongue flapping, and upended a small maidservant.

When all the wine had been drunk, and Hades was reasonably certain that no one was sober enough to find more, they took their leave, and slipped away to bed to seal the marriage in the usual way. They could still hear Scylla and Lycippus, of all people, singing behind them, and Charon bellowing a sea chantey over it all.

"They'll all have a bad head in the morning," Persephone said.

Hades chuckled. "No one feels that they have properly celebrated a wedding without a bad head."

Persephone slipped a hand into his. At the end of

the corridor, he pushed open the door of his chamber and drew her inside, "Come in with me—wife." His eyes gleamed, and he bent to kiss her.

She smiled, and the longing for him ran clear down her body when his beard brushed her chin. His hands fiddled with the pins at her shoulders and tangled themselves in the billowing veil. "This is a dreadful thing," he muttered, half laughing. "Take it off."

"I don't think I can. Scylla pinned it in my hair with wire, I think. Or glue."

"Come into the light." He led her to the glow of a pottery lamp, its surface painted with one of the sinuous, bug-eyed octopi he was so fond of. It appeared to be smiling at her, or maybe that was just the wine. She tugged at the veil and its pomegranate crown. It didn't budge.

"Hold still while I untangle you." She could feel his fingers in her hair, fishing for hairpins. "Aha!" A pin like a bronze fishhook skittered across the floor. "That woman is wasted in the kitchen. She could build military defenses."

Persephone stood obediently while he dismantled her headdress, turning around when he told her to, and giggling when he swore at it. Finally he lifted it from her head and set it on a table. She shook her head, and the last tresses fell loose.

"Oh, my dear, you are so beautiful." His voice was low and soft.

"More beautiful than yesterday?"

"Infinitely." The gown, too, slid from her shoulders. He put the pins on the table with the crown and veil, all her finery now just a little pile of cloth, and the real bride in his arms. He ran his hands through the cascade of her hair. She leaned against him for a moment, listening to the steady thud of his heart, before he lifted her in his arms and took her to the bed.

The plowed earth in the garden was thick with worms, wriggling indignantly as the blade turned them over to the light. Triptolemus held a clod of earth in his hand and watched the worms, pink squirming ribbons seeking blindly. What did worms look for? he wondered. Refuge, he supposed. He scratched his head. Triptolemus was not given to pondering matters. Thinking things over was foreign to him, and he had never thought of himself as a man whose ideas were clever. The worms were a good sign, though. This dirt had been well tended. He put his hand to the plow again and hee-yup'd at the ox, who switched its ropey tail and began to lumber reluctantly down the row. The feel of the plow came back to him, familiar as the pull of a tiller in his hand. Why had he quit working the earth and gone to sea? He couldn't remember now. It had had something to do with Demophon, who had somehow claimed his mother's land as his, without anyone ever saying so, even though he was the younger. So Triptolemus had gone to sea, and sold the grain and olive oil that Demophon raised, and brought back wondrous things from far away, and still his mother preferred Demophon.

Triptolemus turned the ox at the end of the row, coming around behind it, holding the blade's path smooth, its feel satisfying in his hand. Demeter followed behind him, sowing seed from a fold of her apron. Triptolemus was conscious of her there, like being stalked by some large beast. She had seemed better tempered this morning and had even cooked him a breakfast of cheese and eggs from the hens that scratched in the turned earth for bugs. He had slept in her bed again last night, and she had slept he did not know where, but he had lain awake for most of it, half wishing and half fearing that she would get in beside him.

Hermes saw them as he made his way out of the village toward the headland and the path down the cliff. He had put the journey off as long as he could, hoping that Persephone might come home on her own or Demeter might change her mind and the weather improve, now that she had a man in her bed. Hermes assumed the old sailor was in her bed. What on earth would she want with him otherwise? The earth felt unsteady under his boots, as if it were getting ready to buckle. Hellas was a jumpy country; they were used to having the dishes rattled suddenly off their shelves and the wine jars overturned. But something in the air felt different. Something in the world was realigning itself, settling into some new pattern. He had wanted Persephone for years, he thought grumpily. Since they were fourteen, at least. If he had had her then, they wouldn't have all this trouble now. He would probably be tired of her by now, and glad enough to let another man have her. It was her mother's fault, that was what came of living without a man. Old Phaedon was right—the womb closed up and mysterious forces built up inside. Although if that were the case, Hermes wondered uneasily what would happen if Demeter set hers loose again.

He began to cross the meadow, thumping his staff
on the ground to scare snakes. There had been more
of them than usual this year, driven from their bur-
rows by the rain and found hiding in cookpots and
empty jars, or hanging coiled like a rope from the
rafters under the thatch. His footsteps seemed to fall
into rhythm with whatever was happening in the
earth as behind him Demeter and Triptolemus finished plowing the garden and went into her house.
Below, Hades and Persephone slipped away from the
revelry among the fruit trees. The ground shuddered
slightly. The skies opened, and a warm, soft, drench-
ing rain began to fall, slicking the steps that zigzagged down the cliff face and soaking his hat so
that the brim turned downward and he might as well
have had his head in a kettle. Hermes swore, and
pulled his traveling cloak about him, his pack bumping against his back. His plan was to come to the
caverns as if he were a traveler who had lost his
way, and insinuate himself inside. That shouldn't be
hard to do. Triptolemus had spoken of servants. No
doubt they would answer the door, so to speak, not
the master himself . . . *him* . . . Hades. Hermes allowed his name into his head with some trepidation.
Best not to use a name like that too often. If you
spoke their name, they heard you, and knew you
were coming.

The rain was coming harder now; he stumbled on
a loose stone and bumped down three steps on his
backside until he could grab a sapling that clung to
the cliffside beside the stairs. It rubbed his hand raw
along the palm, but he got his footing back. He went
more cautiously after that, clinging to whatever grew
beside the steps while the rain poured off his hat.

Out to sea he could see blue sky and the gold glint of sun dancing on the water. Apparently it was only raining on this island. He slithered to the bottom of the stairs and saw what the rain had blinded him to—the tide was coming in. He hadn't thought of that, and neither had anyone else, he thought. They were all so anxious to send him on his errand. His foot slipped on the last stair, and he landed with a splash in water a hand's span deep. He righted himself, wrung the water from his hat, and rolled the brim back up, rather unsuccessfully. It slowly unrolled again as he splashed his way toward the cavern mouth.

The tide licked his ankles, and suddenly it was deeper than it had been, deeper than it had any right to be, as if it had begun to hurry. The wind picked up, knocking him sideways, so that he struggled to keep his footing. Something knew he was here, he thought. He bent low into the wind and forced his way through the rising water. The tide was foaming about his waist now, and he could feel the current as it ran out again, sucking at his knees, trying to pull him under, take him out to sea with it.

Ahead he could see the cavern mouth, nearly filled with seawater. The tide lapped against the stones, colder than the rain. There was an entrance here, he knew. Hermes had hidden on the headland and watched when Echemus and two others had been left. He had seen the old servants with the long faces come out and carry them into the darkness under the overhanging lip of rock, and not appear again. Lately he had seen the dog, too, the one that Arachne saw, come out and play in the surf. It was huge, he recalled uneasily, although he thought she had been fanciful about the number of heads. With a dog that big, it didn't matter. One head was plenty. So there was an entrance here, hidden at high tide. Like all the island's children, Hermes could swim, and had explored other caverns that ate into the shoreline around its edge. He was angry at Persephone for putting him to this trouble, and at Hades for thinking he could have what Hermes wanted. He shed his pack with some reluctance, and his hat and staff, setting them on the top of a half-submerged boulder, in the hope that the tide might not rise that high. He floundered deeper into the cavern mouth, seeking the way in that he knew was there. He was swimming now, his head nearly bumping the stone roof above. A wave came in, and rolled him under the surf. It smacked him against a submerged rock, and the rough stone scraped his face raw. He surfaced, sputtering and cursing, and hit his head on the cavern roof.

Hermes took a gulp of air before there was no air to be had, then dived, feeling his way between the boulders, trying to keep his orientation. It would be so easy to turn back or even upside down without knowing it. The waves tried to roll him head over heels, and he floundered, feeling only a wall of stone before him. Finally his fingers found the gap between the two pillars that guarded Hades's kingdom, and he pulled himself through. The lord of the caverns was no match for him, he thought with satisfaction, swimming. But he was getting very short of air. He tried to surface, and hit his head again.

This was someone's fault, and it wasn't his. Hermes plowed ahead through the dark water. The swell of the tide buffeted him, and the salt stung his

eyes. It was dark as a hole in the water here. He
blundered on, lungs burning, thrashing with growing
anxiety in the darkness. Something seized him by
the throat, and he expelled the last of his air in an
involuntary scream. Seawater ran into his mouth. He
fought desperately with whatever it was: something
huge with powerful jaws that gripped the back of
his neck. It pulled him down into the depths, and
his lungs filled with seawater.

Hermes awoke on a stone floor, facedown. His
chest burned with each breath. He lifted his head,
and a monstrous wet dog looked back at him, a
hand's span from his nose. It lay on the floor, drooling, paws crossed one over the other. Hermes lowered his head again, groaning.

"The master doesn't care for unexpected visitors,"
a voice above him said. "That was most ill advised.
And at high tide, too." The voice tutted and sucked
at a tooth disapprovingly. "You are lucky Cerberus
went to get you."

Hermes raised his head again, and this time
propped himself on his elbows. His head ached
nearly as badly as his lungs. "That's a fine way to
keep your front door," he said testily. "Full of
water."

"Allow me to help you up," the voice said, and a
pair of hands gripped him under his arms.

Hermes staggered to his feet and turned to find
himself with one of the old servants he had watched
take Echemus in. "It started to rain," he said. "It
never rains this time of year. And the tide doesn't
come in that fast, either."

"The weather has been odd lately," the old servant

said. "I am Lycippus. Permit me to take you to my master. He'll be the one you're wanting to see, I expect."

Hermes wasn't at all sure of that. "I am a traveler," he said, recalling his story. "Lost in the storm."

"Odd," Lycippus said. "We don't get many of those here."

"I imagine not," Hermes said. "Perhaps I might beg a warm corner from your mistress. No need to trouble the master."

"I shall inform them both of your presence," Lycippus said. He beckoned Hermes down the corridor.

Hermes followed him, shivering, keeping one eye on the dog and the other on the carved journeyers on the wall. It might not be a good idea, he decided, to stay here any longer than necessary.

Lycippus led him through a series of passages until Hermes began to worry that he would not be able to find his way out again if he wanted to. Escorted to a large room filled with marble and bronze statues, he was left dripping by the hearth. The dog sat down next to him and began to give off the warm odor of wet dog in the heat from the fire.

Hermes pulled a chair to the hearth and sat next to the dog. "Thank you," he said to it, in case it could talk, because it paid to ingratiate oneself with the servants of those one wished to put something over on.

The dog didn't answer, but a furious voice from the door said, "What are you doing here?"

X

The Hero

It was Persephone, dressed in a purple gown that made Hermes's eyes bulge at the thought of its probable cost. Her golden hair was crowned with a fillet of gold set with gold poppies, and she wore a necklace of deep green stones. He blinked again. The maid who had run wild in the woods was gone. This girl was regal, and he could tell by her expression that she knew things she hadn't known when she left.

"I came to fetch you home," he said, hoping she was in a receptive mood. By the look of her clothing she might not be. "Zeus commands it," he added for good measure.

"Bah!" she said. "You are dripping on a good carpet."

"You might have offered me dry clothes," Hermes said.

"I might have."

"I nearly drowned getting here," he said. "There was a storm and the tide was coming in, and I was attacked by the dog."

"The dog has good instincts."

"That is an ungrateful way to treat the one who has come to rescue you," Hermes said, aggrieved. He was surprised by how much he wanted her now. Wet and cold as he was, it made him stiffen just to look at her.

"I don't need to be rescued."

"Of course you do. You're in the toils of a monster. He'll likely kill you soon."

"You're an idiot. I don't want a hero. Heroes only make trouble."

"Well, if you had married me when you should have, you wouldn't need a hero," Hermes retorted.

"You didn't want to marry me. You wanted to lie in the hayfield with me. Me and a dozen other girls!" She glared at him. "Faithless goat."

"What if I had wanted to marry you?" Hermes asked her. "What then?"

She thought about that for a minute. If he hadn't been faithless . . . but faithlessness was his essence, his core. Hermes would always look for something new. "You're like Great-Grandfather. You'll lie with anyone. Your wife will run herself ragged trying to keep you out of other girls' beds."

"That didn't mean I didn't want to marry you," Hermes protested.

Persephone chuckled. She sat down in a chair. "You would have been sorry, the first time you did it with another girl. Go marry someone who won't cut it off with a carving knife some night while you're asleep."

"I can't," Hermes said gloomily. The prospect sounded all too likely. "I have to rescue you, and if I rescue you, your mother will give you to me."

"Nobody can give me to anybody now."

"You have to marry the hero who saves you," Hermes said. "It's the rules." He turned with his back to the hearth, trying to dry his other side. It was dank in the caverns, and his nose felt blue. Persephone, he noted, had an elegant woolen mantle about her shoulders. "I'm cold," he told her.

"Maybe you'll die," she said without much sympathy, but she clapped her hands and a servant who must have been lurking in the corridor appeared immediately. "Bring our guest something dry to wear, please. And something to eat."

"Oh, no," Hermes said, "oh, no. You won't trick me that way."

Persephone ignored him. She rose from her chair and took her wool and spindle from its basket. She began to draw out a line of thread, considering him silently as she twisted it between her fingers.

Hermes edged away, eyeing the twirling spindle at the end of the strand. She looked a bit too much like the Fates who spun the thread of life and clipped it off at its other end. Perhaps it had not been the best idea to demand her for a wife, but that wasn't the sort of thing you could go back on. And he had enjoyed thinking of himself in the hero's role. The hero always married the maiden when he had saved her. Otherwise, what was the point in saving her? One might as well let the sea monster have her. "I did want to marry you," he said crossly. "You're the only one I could ever be faithful to."

Persephone snorted.

Lycippus appeared with an armful of dry clothes and a tray bearing a bowl of fruit and savory pies.

The other servant came behind him with a jug of wine and two goblets.

"With the master's compliments," Lycippus said as he handed the clothes to Hermes. Hermes looked about him uneasily. "The master is occupied at the moment," Lycippus said blandly. "But he bids you welcome." He set the tray on a table and looked firmly at Cerberus, who pretended he wasn't interested in it.

Persephone gathered up her wool and spindle. "I'll just leave you for a moment while you change into something dry." She left him with the two servants.

"You've caught a nasty cold," Lycippus remarked as he pulled Hermes's wet tunic over his head. "I've seen cases like this before, very dangerous."

Hermes sneezed.

"Reckless to stand around in wet clothes all this time."

"You didn't bring me any dry ones!" Hermes said.

"Ah! An oversight." He removed Hermes's loincloth and toweled the visitor off briskly, ignoring Hermes's protests that he could dry himself. "Perhaps a cup of wine to warm the blood." Lycippus whipped the towel away and helped Hermes into a loincloth that appeared to have been made for a horse, and a tunic that was three sizes too large and came halfway down his shins. "The master's best," he said. "He wishes you to feel welcome." He scooped Hermes's wet clothes up in his arm.

Persephone reappeared as Lycippus and the other servant left. She snorted again when she saw the tunic, and Hermes glared at her.

"You need a cup of wine," she said, laying aside her wool. "Let me pour you some."

Hermes watched her suspiciously. She handed him the cup and began to peel a pomegranate from the fruit bowl, her nails biting into the smooth shiny skin just under the crown.

"Don't eat that!" He lunged to take it away from her.

"Don't be silly." She held her hand away from his reach. "They keep very well down here, in the cold cellar. They remind me of Mother's garden."

"That's the last you'll see of your mother's garden if you eat that," Hermes said urgently. "If you eat in a place, you bind yourself to it. We mustn't eat here."

Persephone put the pomegranate down carefully in the bowl—the juice stained anything it touched a bright red purple—and stared at him, as if a fish had begun to talk to her.

"Hermes, I have been here since last summer. I've been eating since I got here. How do you think I survived?"

"The dead don't need food." He tried to move the fruit bowl out of her reach.

"Well, I'm not dead!"

"How do you know? We must be careful taking you home again. I'm not allowed to look back, I think." He frowned. "Or maybe that's for fighting gorgons. I don't remember." He rubbed his head as if it hurt.

Persephone put down the wine cup as well as the fruit. "Hermes, who sent you here?" she asked him gently.

"Your mother. I said I could save you if she would give you to me. Maybe I bragged a little. Then Hestia's priestess said to get you back because your mother was making it snow—it's been dreadful weather ever since you were taken: snow and rain and windstorms. It's a wonder we didn't have a volcano explode somewhere. And she said to send me because I said I could save you, and she told your mother to give you to me if I did."

"And you thought I would go with you?"

"When you save a maiden, she doesn't have to help you," Hermes said with dignity. "Most of them faint with fear, I believe."

"And how are you planning to save me?" Persephone inquired. "Just for the sake of argument."

Hermes rubbed his head again. It ached with a dull throbbing roar that he could almost hear. "I believe if we just wait for low tide, then we walk out together—I'm almost sure it's gorgons you aren't supposed to look at—then if you really are still alive you probably won't fall into a pile of bones at the entrance."

She looked at him suspiciously and decided he was only half joking. He really thought she might. It would serve him right if she did. She wondered if she could manage it. She suspected that imagination could conjure whatever image it expected and toyed with the idea of a basket of bones over a doorway before discarding it as ignoble. It would amuse Hades, though.

Hermes was sitting still now, his slightly slanted gray green eyes alert, waiting to see what she would do. And on the other hand, Hermes had done something quite dangerous for her sake.

"It's not your world down here," he said quietly. "You belong to the upper air. You're what makes the trees grow." He sounded serious.

Persephone contemplated him thoughtfully, dis-

tracted by the clear memory of his lips nuzzling her
neck and the shiver that had run through her when
he did it. He was like a goat, playful and charming,
alarmingly sexual, with a knowing eye and with a
goat's morals. Fine for a fling in the vineyard under
a solstice moon, if you could be sure you wouldn't
fall in love and pine for him while he was off on the
next chase. Persephone had always been pretty sure
she wouldn't, but not sure enough.

And why was she thinking of that? She glared at
him. He smelled of the upper air, she realized suddenly. Even in Hades's tunic, his hair drenched with
seawater and the dank tinge of the caverns that never
quite went away, he smelled like sunlight and grapevines and olives on the tree. He would talk her into
going with him if she wasn't careful.

"It's dark here," Hermes said. "Don't you long for
the light?"

"It's light enough. There is a garden I go sit in.
There are shafts that open to the sky."

"It will call to you. If you don't come home, it will
call to you all your life."

That might be true. "Hermes, listen to me." She
leaned forward and put her hand on his, because he
had been willing to come for her. Great-Grandfather
might have ordered it, but Hermes could have lied
and said there was no way in, that the door was
sealed. He hadn't, though. "The world is full of wonders. Every place I have been will call to me afterward. But I will live here."

"Always? In the dark? With your only light from
a shaft in the rock?"

"I have been places, outside these caverns. I am
not a prisoner. I have seen the people dance with

bulls on the palace walls at Knossos. He took me there because I asked him to. I have seen things you can't imagine. Go and see them for yourself, but don't try to take me with you. I have seen what I need to."

He turned his hand palm up and gripped hers. "Not everything. I could show you things you haven't seen."

She tried to pull her hand back, but he wouldn't let her. "Those I don't need to see."

Green eyes, the color of the shallows around the island, held hers. "Let me show them to you before you decide."

Goat eyes, and something dancing goat-footed in the grass. Flute song. It was the same dance he proposed that the bull dancers danced. *I have danced that with someone else. Not with you. Too late for you.* "All you can offer me is the attraction of your body," she said, knowing that that was substantial. He breathed the scent of the upper air through his skin; she could taste it. "Hades is more complicated. I'll take the complication. I'll keep my bargain."

"With him?"

"No, with myself." She didn't think he understood, but when she twisted her hand gently in his, his fingers loosened.

"Ah!" said Hades from the doorway. "I see you have welcomed our guest."

Persephone snatched her hand away from Hermes's. Hermes stood, tucking the monstrous tunic into its sash to shorten it. She thought he was annoyed by the joke, but except for a twitch of his mouth, he gave no sign of it.

Hades wore a tunic of black silk stitched with

green leaves, which fit him perfectly. He took the pomegranate from the bowl and broke it the rest of the way open. "Just come in on the tide?" he inquired pleasantly.

"In a manner of speaking," Hermes said.

"I see you've met my wife."

"We are old acquaintances." Hermes stood his ground. He was a good head shorter than Hades.

"Cousins," Persephone said firmly. *Not old lovers. We could have been, but we weren't.*

"All my wife's relatives are welcome here," Hades said. He picked a few blood-colored seeds from the pomegranate and ate them. Persephone wasn't sure whether she imagined it or not, but she thought there was a touch of something sinister in his voice. Maybe it was just the way he put it.

"Kind of you," Hermes said.

Hades smiled. He had very white teeth, and Persephone thought suddenly that teeth were the only part of people's bones that showed outside their skin. Hades had a way of making people think of things like that when he was so inclined. "I have asked the kitchen to send us some dinner," he said.

"I don't want to put you to any trouble." Hermes edged closer to Persephone. He eyed the doorway suggestively, and she shook her head at him.

"He thinks if he eats here, he won't be able to leave," Persephone said.

"We'll make sure he can leave," Hades said. He looked closely at Hermes, whose russet hair was beginning to dry but whose nose and eyes were red. "A sustaining broth first, perhaps." He set the pieces of the pomegranate back in the bowl, where they gleamed like living rubies. Lycippus and two others entered, bearing trays, and he motioned them to the small tables that populated the room. The servants drew three couches up to the hearth beneath the gaze of a marble boy with shepherd's pipes, and arranged the tables handily with plates of dried, spiced fish; a dish of lentils and mutton, olives, figs and onion; and an omelette of eggs and oysters.

Hermes saw Persephone stretch herself along one of the couches to dine as a man would do. She saw him watching her and said very quietly, "I am queen here. You don't understand that."

"And is being queen better than being free?" he asked her softly.

Hades smiled at him with a little more tooth than was really necessary. Persephone thought he looked like Cerberus. "There are many definitions of free, my friend. The dead are free. The stupid are free of knowledge. How free would you hope to be?"

"Free to wander the upper air," Hermes said. He glanced at the painted panels on the wall. "To breathe that in without the smell of paint to tell me it is false. To live a true life, not one of visions conjured from smoke."

"There are no visions here!" Persephone said angrily.

"How do you know?" Hermes demanded. "How do you know all you have seen here has not been visions in your head, born of sorcery?"

Persephone thought of the ghosts she had seen when she first came. She looked uneasily at Lycippus. He looked more like a sheep than ever.

Hades speared a fish from the platter with his knife. The marble boy looked over his shoulder, motionless in his music. "For all you know," he said, "your own world might be illusion. How will you prove differently?"

Hermes looked hungrily at the fish but he didn't eat.

"If that's an illusory fish, it shouldn't hurt you to eat it," Hades commented.

Hermes sat on the edge of his couch as if he thought it might swallow him if he reclined. "Zeus commands that you return her to the upper air. I am sent to fetch her."

"That is her choice," Hades said. "Tell that to Zeus when you see him."

Persephone looked at Hades. She thought he meant that, despite her promise to stay with him if he would save two lost sailors from their own sea. The air stirred in the chamber, drifting down the series of shafts and connecting tunnels that Hades—or whoever had come before him—had devised. It carried the scent of apples, or maybe that was Hermes, sitting beside her. *Mother?* She let the thought float out onto the air current, but nothing answered her. If she just knew that things were well with Mother, she could be easy. "What of the upper air?" she asked Hermes. "What of my world? What happens in it now?"

"The weather is bad," Hermes said. "It is likely we will starve."

"What of Mother and the sailor?"

"Your estimable father? He is living with her and goes in terror of her, I think. That and some other urge."

Persephone smiled.

"Don't think she has forgotten you, though," Hermes said. He sneezed. "I wish everyone's emotions didn't come out in the weather. I suppose you know you spoiled the vintage," he added. "It's a dire state of affairs when the town can't drink its sorrows away."

The vision of her village, white and dusty against the gray green hills, came into her head. She wondered if this was what always happened when the gods gave you what you wanted. You had to give up something in exchange, and that was the price. "Tell me more. What else is happening?"

"Narcissa and her mother are both married. I wouldn't ask more about *that* if I were you. Tros and Harmonia have a son. Bopis caught Great-Grandfather with Clytie in a goat shed."

Persephone clapped her hand over her mouth to stifle a snort of laughter. "Oh, no!"

"We all knew they were in there. It was like watching a rock overbalance from a cliff. You couldn't do anything to stop it; you just watched it fall."

"But what did she do?"

"She chased Clytie out with a threshing flail. Clytie climbed a tree and Bopis danced around under it, shrieking imprecations and waving the flail while Great-Grandfather took refuge in the Temple of Zeus and Apollo. Bopis was afraid to go in there after him, so she waited outside, sitting on a bucket, for most of the day until he came out; then they went home together."

"Oh, I wish I had seen that!" A wave of longing for village doings washed over her until she caught Hades watching her and sobered. "What about Echo?"

"She misses you. If you came home you could see her. You could see Narcissa. It might save her."

"It won't," Hades said. "I have seen Narcissa. Unless you want to kill her husband and promise she will never have to wed again, you can't save her. It's very often like that, in your world."

Hermes looked at him a moment, considering. "And yours is better."

"It's another choice. That's all."

Persephone turned to him. "Could I really not save Narcissa? If I went there and then came back?"

"Even if you did not come back, my darling. No."

"Why should she have a dreadful life? It isn't fair. That was her father they brought to you last year, the one who died."

"I never promised he wouldn't," Hades said.

"That's just it," Hermes said. "You hold out false hope. Take him to the lord of Death and he may give him back. Bah!"

"Life holds out false hope."

"Better to be dead?" Hermes leaned forward, green eyes intent. "To forgo the smell of new grass in spring? The feel of water on your skin, the taste of wine, of ripe figs in your mouth?"

"All of that you may have here."

"What about the new kids in the spring, the lambs kicking in the field? What about the linnet's song or the sweep of the shearwater's wings over the sea? What about the moon? Let alone the sun and the gold warmth that lies like a blanket on the earth? The smell of new wheat, and the scent of the threshing floor? Have you seen the way the moon shines on limestone walls when it rises? Have you watched the sun go down in the water like a puddle of fire, with your arm around a girl?" Hermes's voice was impassioned. "Have you danced knee-deep in the grapes at the vintage? Have you done any of those things? Will you let *her*?"

Persephone yearned toward him in spite of herself. He made it all sound so real.

"I have done all those things," Hades said quietly, "and found them wanting. And have *you* watched one army roll toward another, spears flashing, banners waving, determined to kill, to bloody their path, and slaughter the widows and orphans afterward? Have you seen a city topple and all its wonders lost from sheer blind spite and ignorance? What about pestilence? Have you watched that black cloud sweep over a land because its inhabitants were too stupid to keep themselves clean?"

"That's just life," Hermes said sulkily. "You take the good with the bad."

"Precisely. All part of the dance. Even us down here. We are the other side of the wheel, my friend. There is no difference."

"There must be," Hermes said.

"No."

Hermes glared angrily about the room, at the fish and sinuous octopi, whose style Persephone now recognized from the walls of Knossos, and the painted panels of the Upperworld where the sun shone unendingly on ever-blowing poppies. His eyes fell on the statues, the bronze and marble youths and the lovely maidens resting white arms eternally on empty air. Their cold beauty made him wonder, as Persephone had once, if they might be all that was left of someone. Someone with nothing but beauty to leave behind. The warmth in the chamber came not so much from the hearth, he thought, as from Persephone on her couch, blond hair spilling over one shoulder where it had loosened from its pins, pale hands playing with a fig. Her skin had been golden once; now it was white as milk. It didn't matter. She exuded an aureole of light, just visible to the eye. No wonder Hades had wanted her. She brought the Upperworld into this one, kept the wheel from stopping in the darkness.

Hades stood up. He looked at Persephone thoughtfully. "I believe I will leave you to show your cousin our domain here, if he is interested. I shall be in our chambers, my dear." He bent, kissed her cheek, and departed, whistling Cerberus after him.

Hermes stared. "It's a trick," he said quietly.

"No." No, he was giving her the chance to go with Hermes if she wanted to. Persephone sat up. "He wants you to see his kingdom. You may find something to tell Mother that will ease her mind."

"He is attempting to lure me into his lair." Hermes folded his arms.

"Well, you might as well come, because you'll never find your way out without me to show you." He hesitated and she said, "Come *on*. You should be glad I'm willing to talk to you after the way you've behaved." Maybe he would tell her some more about the village and Mother before he left. There was no harm in asking him that.

Hermes rose and followed her into the corridor, looking uneasily over his shoulder for whatever ghosts or monsters might be lurking. She led him with no apparent uncertainty through a maze of passageways, some of which displayed the journeyers he had seen earlier carved into their walls, some plain, some ancient and roughly hewn like the chambers of a tomb.

"This is what makes the people who are left with him here live or die," she said, showing him the garden of poppies, now bright again with scarlet blooms. "They are the secret of sleep. Take that back to Mother as my gift to her. Tell her to slit the pods and let the juice that runs out thicken."

"Poppies are poison."

"Too much, yes. Like too much wine. It's all a circle that comes back again, Hermes. You know that. You knew it before I did." He had, too. It was what made girls go lie with him when they knew he was unfaithful.

He thought that she knew an uncomfortable amount now. It would not make her easy to be married to.

She drew him down the corridor into the oldest caves. "This is the storeroom. I think we could live a long time on just what is put by here."

He peered into the dusty recesses at row after row of clay jars, the farthest ones thick with dust and cobwebs, their necks incised with strange markings.

"He has ships that sail places you have never heard of."

"So he says."

She thought of taking him to see the woman on the bier, but it seemed disrespectful, and Persephone felt protective of her. Hermes would act as if he were seeing a dancing bear. She took him to see the pool instead, assuming, rightly, that it would impress him.

Hermes did his best not to let that show. She had led him in through the door from her sitting room, avoiding the suggestion that might be implied by taking him through the bedchamber. The marble servant with the towels hung over one arm was just visible in the bathchamber doorway, and Hermes jumped when he saw it. He glared at the pool and the painted squid on the bottom as he had glared at everything else in Hades's domain.

"Put your toe in," Persephone suggested.

"Very likely something will pull me under."

"Bah! Don't be a baby," she said scornfully, as if they were ten again and she was daring him, or he her, to try to ride a wild ram. She knew he wanted to. He was like a ferret; he would investigate anything.

He bent and stuck a cautious finger in the water. "It's hot!"

"It comes from a spring below the island," she said, knowledgeable now. "Where the earth is hot. And look at this!" She pulled aside the hanging from the doorway beyond to display the stone seat.

As she had expected, the seat and its drains caught his attention. He left the pool and peered down the hole, not even wrinkling his nose, trying to see where it went. "Even old Glaucus didn't have anything like this," he said, marveling.

"Dryope!" Persephone said, tugging at his arm. "That's what I wanted to ask you. Get your head out of that; it isn't sanitary. Has anyone heard of Dryope?"

"No," Hermes said, emerging reluctantly.

"She can't have just vanished."

"Of course she can. People just vanish all the time. Probably taken down here," he added ominously.

"Don't be ridiculous." If Dryope were dead, would she have seen her? Would her face appear suddenly among the journeyers on the wall?

"I did hear," Hermes said, "that a man from the north island was paid in gold to take a woman nobody knew to somewhere he was forbidden to mention. It was all so mysterious that even the gossips couldn't get a grip on it. There are four versions circulating now. One of them holds her to have been Athena in disguise. A rival faction has decided she was a queen from the East, fulfilling a vow. Nobody seems to think she was just a happy widow who looted her husband's treasury."

"That wouldn't make such a good story," Persephone said, relieved. "Do you think it was Dryope?"

"I could think it was a sea turtle or Apollo in a dress and it wouldn't make any difference. It was or it wasn't."

"You are the most exasperating person! It makes a difference to *me*. You know things. I don't know how you do, but you do, and you're usually right."

"All right then, I think it was Dryope."

"Good."

"That doesn't mean it was, though."

"Stop that! Come along, and I'll show you the garden and the kitchens."

"Who needs food here?" Hermes asked suspiciously. "The dead don't eat."

"There are fifty-one servants who aren't dead, and they eat. I eat. My husband eats. You watched us."

"Illusion," Hermes retorted.

"You are maddening. Come along."

"And then will you come away with me like a sensible girl before that monster gets you?"

"If you are referring to my husband," she said haughtily, "you had better be more respectful." If she told him she absolutely wasn't coming with him, he would probably leave, and she was enjoying the novelty of a visitor, even if it was Hermes. "Come on." She motioned him through the outer chamber and into the corridor. She was almost certain that Hades was in his own chamber, well within earshot. As he had told her, the rooms in their quarters spiraled around each other like a nautilus.

In the corridor they found several servants, just passing by with arms full of linen, or trimming lamp wicks. Hades was not as careless as he had seemed. Hermes took note of them, too. "We are being watched," he hissed to Persephone. "Be on your guard."

Persephone didn't respond. She was certain now that Hades would let her go if she wanted to leave, and also that he would know about it instantly.

They found Scylla bustling in the kitchen, chopping cabbage. "Ah! It's the hero!" she said when she saw Hermes. "We heard one was coming. It must have been wet getting in; you look half-drowned. I'll fix you some hot wine."

Hermes eyed her suspiciously.

"Baker has just made some lovely bread, too."

"Oh, I want some." Persephone looked for it. "Hot bread is the best thing."

"Well, sit yourselves down, and I'll fetch you something nice." Scylla shooed them toward stools in the corner of the kitchen, as if they were children.

Hermes looked annoyed. This was not how heroes were supposed to be greeted. He was either supposed to fight his way through armies of supernatural soldiers, or be greeted by a grateful populace, joyful at their liberation. Possibly both. He was definitely not supposed to be sat down in the kitchen and fed bread as if he were a playmate come to visit.

He looked grumpy, and Persephone noticed it.

"There's no point in giving yourself airs with Scylla," she said.

"Here we are." Scylla trotted back with a basket of small hot loaves and a clay pitcher of heated wine. The smell was wondrous. Persephone inhaled a deep breath. "I just ate, and I'm starving already. This is so good."

"Now, I've watered the wine a bit more than usual because you can't be too careful." Scylla held out the pitcher, and Persephone, puzzled, rose to take it. Did Scylla think she was going to get tipsy and be kidnapped again by her hero? As she stood, Hermes saw her outlined against the light that spilled through the door from the garden. His brows rose.

Persephone tore off a piece of bread and dipped it in the little bowl of olive oil that Scylla had brought. "This is wonderful. Hermes, don't be such a fool. Nobody *wants* you to stay here forever, believe me, so you might as well eat. I've been eating since I got here."

"Apparently," Hermes said slowly. He thought. This changed things. Maybe. He wasn't sure. Maybe it didn't. They had sent him to fetch her. And this development might give him some advantages. "I'll take you home anyway," he said, appearing to come to a decision. His expression was magnanimous. "Not every man would, but I'm an understanding fellow. Things can happen."

Persephone looked perplexed.

"Nonsense!" Scylla said briskly. "You can't take the mistress anywhere in her condition. This hero business is all very well, but now she has other matters to think of."

XI

Love Is Dangerous

Persephone stared at them both, and very quietly a new piece of knowledge clicked into place with complete certainty. This was a development she had not anticipated. She put her hands to her waist. Scylla had known. Did Hades know? Maybe everyone had known but herself. She counted backward in her head and then on her fingers. It was so hard to tell what time of day it was down here, much less what month, and her flow had been odd since she had come. Scylla said they all were, that it was because they never saw the moon. Persephone saw Scylla beaming at her now.

"Your mother will be greatly distressed," Hermes said sternly.

Persephone burst into laughter. That was an understatement, she felt sure, and certainly an excellent reason not to see Mother for a while yet. "Hermes, I can't go anywhere with you. If you think I'm going home to Mother in this condition—"

"Well, it would just upset the good lady, I'm sure," Scylla said. "She'll come round when she sees the babe; they always do. The same thing happened to my sister, but it was all for the best. She married the boy—he had no prospects; that was why our mother didn't like him—and they were happy, you know. Not like me. My man had prospects, but he was an old beast."

Persephone, thinking, listened to her with half an ear. It appeared that life existed very happily in the land of the Dead, and that there were always more choices than two. Hades had said that, she thought, but she hadn't known what he meant. Now she did. She would have bargaining power with him, too, once this child was born, because half of it would belong to the upper air.

"Hermes," she said, noticing him standing with arms folded, scowling, "go home."

Echo watched Demeter in her garden from a distance. No one liked to get too close to Demeter these days. The weather swerved like a runaway cart, brightening to sun when she smiled, boiling into storm when she grew annoyed. When she looked at Triptolemus, the earth burst with new shoots, indiscriminately growing vegetables and weeds, a hand's span's growth in a night. Sometimes when the two of them went into Demeter's house the sun blazed with a sudden heat as if it were falling to earth, or the warm rain started, soaking everything, only to dry off in a hot mist in an hour.

If the loss of Persephone had set the weather to swinging, then the reappearance of Triptolemus had made it more giddy yet, if somewhat more moderate.

There was no more snow, and the rain kept the hot sun from cooking the land as it had the year before, but it was a nervous, unsteady life with weather like this.

"How can anyone make any plans when it's just as likely to pour as to bake?" Doris complained, taking her laundry off the line for the third time in a day.

It didn't seem to be that way on the north island, as if Demeter's reach was narrowing, using itself up in a burst of wild energy. Echo had pestered Doris unrelentingly until she had said they might go visit Narcissa and Irene, and see how they were getting on, pointing out that at least there they wouldn't need a rain hat and a fan in the same day. Echo was afraid of how Narcissa was getting on, but she had to see. All her friends were disappearing. She suspected that Doris had some such idea in mind for her, too. Doris had consulted Bopis before they left, in a low-voiced conversation that reviewed the merits of several candidates, as well as their disadvantages, ranging from baldness and a goiter to a possibly insane grandmother. The only one Echo found promising was the last, a pleasant-faced boy named Salmoneus, an orphan with a herd of goats to tend on his own. The possibly insane grandmother was long dead, and she thought she was willing to take her chances in preference to the aged miller with the goiter, Bopis's candidate of choice. Matchmaking was Bopis's main occupation. She was related to half the people on the island and could be counted on to know when someone was in need of a wife, or could be persuaded that he was. She arranged passage for Doris and Echo with a potter driving an oxcart of

jugs to the north island to sell, and sent them off with
a lunch of dried fish and bread, and encouraging last-
minute advice.

"Now, be sure to talk seriously with Irene. She's
made a very good match, and she'll be in a position
to help you present Echo to some suitable men."

Echo was doubtful as to the benefits of suitability.
No one could have called *him*—Hades, she said
firmly, naming him in her head—no one could have
thought him suitable, but from what Triptolemus had
said, Persephone was happy down there. Echo would
like to visit her, she thought wistfully, wondering if
she had the courage, if the prospect wasn't so fright-
ening. The prospect of seeing Narcissa was almost
worse, but at least no more mortal danger than the
jolting of the oxcart accompanied it. Maybe, Echo
thought hopefully, Narcissa would be happier in her
marriage now. Bopis had assured her that nice girls
were always frightened when they married, but they
got over it. Nice girls being girls who hadn't already
tried things out in a hayfield, Echo gathered. Maybe
she would try out Salmoneus before she made up
her mind.

The weather turned from sun to rain to high wind
and back to cloudless sun by the time the cart had
crossed the first ridge. On the other side of the ridge
it settled down. Clearly Demeter's reach had grown
shorter. Echo and Doris, sitting on the seat beside the
driver, took off their traveling cloaks and hats and
tucked them into a marginally clean corner of the
cart. The clay jars rattled gently in their straw beds,
and the ox snorted and switched his tail at the swarm
of flies that accompanied them. Behind them, on the
southern side of the ridge, a dark cloud blew over

the place where the village stood, rained like a maid pouring out a bucket, and then vanished like mist.

Doris tutted. "She doesn't know what she wants; that's the trouble. If she doesn't settle down and figure it out, we'll never get anything planted."

"Strangest thing *I* ever saw," the potter said, flicking the reins. "Hee-yup. I don't hold with messing around with the supernatural, myself. No good ever comes of it. We ought to give the gods their sacrifice every so often, keep 'em happy, and leave 'em alone otherwise. It started with sending that fellow down the cliff. Stands to reason if you've got somebody like *that* living below you, you don't want to call yourself to his attention, if you know what I mean."

"Sometimes he heals them," Doris said.

"Yes, but at what cost? That's what I want to know. Carrying off maidens and all. I don't hold with it."

Doris abandoned the conversation, and Echo thought about the potter's words as they jolted along. The supernatural was all around you. How could you not have doings with it? Some people just had a more direct connection to it than others. For Demeter it was like a fabric that she could fold any way she wanted. For the potter, Echo suspected it was a pitch-black pit that he preferred not to look into. She didn't voice this train of thought, though. The only person she knew who liked talking about things like that was Hermes.

They spent the night under a pine tree, wrapped in their cloaks, listening to the potter snore. In the morning they woke, smelling of pine needles, and washed and watered the ox in the stream that trickled past the cart track. By midday they were in the north island village where Phitias and Nicias had taken their brides.

Irene heard the rumble of the cart in the square and rushed out to see who it was. The north island village did not appear to be much more interesting than the southern one, and anyone in a cart was a diversion. She gave a shriek of recognition as they tumbled off the seat, and embraced Doris.

"It's Echo," Doris said. "She would see Narcissa, and she plagued me until I agreed to bring her."

"Well, of course, and such a nice surprise." Irene hustled the two of them into her house, a much larger one than her old one, and right in the center of the village. "Nicias will be pleased, and it will do Narcissa good."

"How is she?" Doris asked. "Not pregnant already?"

"No, though I know Phitias is hoping. No, she just seems to be in the doldrums. She tells me she is fine, but . . . Well! I know Phitias is a kind husband; it's not that. . . ." Irene trailed off. "I don't know quite what it is. But she'll be glad to see Echo."

"Where is she?" Echo asked.

"Phitias has built her the loveliest house," Irene said. "Just around the corner, next to the Temple of Hestia. I was hoping that might, but it doesn't seem . . ." She trailed off again. Echo thought Irene wasn't really sure what it was she was trying to say. Narcissa seemed to be a thought that eluded her.

What Echo saw immediately was that Narcissa was thin. Not just slender as she had always been, but skeletal. Her eyes were huge and her wrists like sticks where they protruded from her mantle. She kept its folds wrapped about her, the end bundled over her head as if she wanted to hide.

"Narcissa!" Echo stood in her doorway gaping.

Narcissa peered at her.

"It's Echo, you silly girl," Irene said, bustling them all into Narcissa's house. "Come all the way up from the South to see you. Now isn't that nice?"

Narcissa followed them into her house, where Irene bustled more in the pantry, saying, "Well, aren't you going to offer us something to eat, dear? And have something yourself; it will do you good."

Narcissa let her mother fix them a bowl of dried figs and a dish of cold eels and set it all out on a table, but she didn't eat.

"We're going to take a walk," Echo said when she saw that. She scooped the figs into a fold of her mantle. "We'll just take these with us. I want to explore. Narcissa, have you a wineskin?"

Narcissa nodded, but she didn't move.

"Ha!" Echo said. "There it is. We'll steal a bit of this nice wine, too." She upended the pitcher Irene had brought, and poured half of it into the skin. Irene and Doris watched them indulgently, but Echo could tell Doris was shocked by Narcissa, too.

"What have you been doing to yourself?" she demanded as soon as they left the house.

Narcissa was silent.

Echo looked around her at the town, as if it were at fault, and swallowed newcomers. It was bigger than her own, but the air had the same bright, dusty sheen. The sun bounced off the limestone walls in a blue-white flare. People passed them in the streets, bound on the usual errands, carrying jugs or baskets or driving goats. An old woman passed them, clutching by its feet a chicken that clucked in apparent contentment. On the hill Echo could see vineyards. The north island had learned from the south. "Come on." She led Narcissa that way, up a goat track that wound through scraggly grass and a burst of purple anemones. At the top of the hill she sat her down under a grapevine and uncorked the wineskin. She tipped a few drops on the grass for whatever deities might be lurking. "*What* is the matter with you?"

Narcissa was still, hands folded in her lap, lost in her voluminous mantle. Finally she spoke. "I told you I couldn't do it," she whispered.

"Eat this." Echo handed her a fig. "How bad is it?"

Narcissa looked at the fig with revulsion. "I can't. It will make me ill."

"You're ill because you haven't been eating. You're thin as a stick."

"No, it makes me feel like I want to throw up. I'm all right, I just can't eat."

"And that is 'all right'?" Echo demanded. "What is your husband thinking of? Has he had the doctor to see you?"

"He wanted to. I couldn't bear him to touch me."

"The doctor? Or your husband?"

"Both," she whispered.

"Well, you can come home with us," Echo announced.

Narcissa shook her head. "You know I can't."

Echo did know. It was all very well to make wild talk, sitting under a grapevine drinking wine, but no one was going to let Narcissa leave a nice man who had built her such a nice house.

"Are you pregnant? Maybe that's why you feel sick."

"No!" Narcissa shook her head vehemently.

"When was your last flow?"

"I don't remember. But I am *not* pregnant!"

Echo didn't think she was either. Girls who were pregnant had a kind of bloom on them, even if they got thin at first from being sick. That was how the village busybodies always knew. Narcissa looked like someone who was starving.

"Tell me about Persephone," Narcissa whispered. "Has she come back?"

"Not exactly, but the strangest thing—her father is here, living with Demeter! She hit him with a lightning bolt and knocked him into the olive tree in the agora. Then she took him *home* with her!"

"Persephone's *father*?"

"You know, we were never really sure she *had* one. Well, he appeared in the agora last week as if he had just fallen out of the sky like a bird's egg, and said that he'd been shipwrecked and the lord and lady who lived in the caverns had saved him. He said the lady swam out to fetch him in a raging storm, stark naked. He thought she was a Nereid."

"That sounds like Persephone," Narcissa said with a small smile.

"It was, and as far as I'm concerned it's clear no one is holding her against her will; but Demeter still wants her back, and they've sent Hermes off to fetch her! And the weather is stranger than ever since her father moved in with Demeter. It's just like living in a ballad."

"What about you?" Narcissa looked at her wistfully.

Echo surveyed the vineyard. At the far end a boy was pruning the vines. She could hear a faint hum of bees in the air. "It would be nice to be somewhere the weather isn't so chancy. But Bopis has found Mother some prospects for me, and I think I'm going to take young Salmoneus. Do you remember him? His parents both died last winter, and he has all those goats to manage alone—and I'm good with goats."

Narcissa was silent. Echo chattered on, her voice soothing in the warm sun. After a while Narcissa reached for the figs in Echo's lap and ate one. Echo handed her the wine. "He's not so much older than I am. He doesn't talk much, but he doesn't seem to mind when I do—not like Father who's always shushing me. I don't think men like to talk; I don't know why. The only one I know who'll talk about anything but how the plowing's coming or whose goat is sick is Hermes. Demeter says he can marry Persephone if he can fetch her back, but I don't think he can."

"Marry her or fetch her back?" Narcissa asked. She tipped the wineskin up and drank.

"There you go; that'll do you good. Both, I should think. It doesn't sound to me as if Persephone wants to leave—Triptolemus, that's her father, says it's a palace down there, like a whole city underground. And if she did want to leave, you know she wouldn't marry Hermes."

"I always thought she secretly liked him," Narcissa said pensively.

"Love's an odd thing," Echo said. "I always did, too, but he's so flighty, and you could never make him be faithful. Persephone wouldn't put up with that. And personally, I think he might be sorry if he got her. Look at her mother—that old man looks as if someone's put a spell on him. I saw him plowing her garden, and he looked as tired as the ox. Love is dangerous."

"I know that," Narcissa said. She tipped up the wineskin again. She looked fragile to Echo, as if she might crumble into bones at any moment under the folds of her mantle, but her eyes were bright. They glittered like water, and she began to laugh.

"Don't you think you could learn to care for him?" Echo asked her hesitantly. "He doesn't mistreat you, does he?"

"No." Narcissa let out a long breath. "I don't want to talk about it. Just for this afternoon, let's not talk about it."

"All right," Echo said. "We'll be pirates instead. We'll go and salvage the wreckage of Triptolemus's ship and be rich and the terror of the seas. Here." She reached out her hand for the wineskin and lifted it, tipping back her chin.

Narcissa laughed shakily. "That sounds better. We'll kidnap Bopis and sell her for ransom."

"He might not buy her back," Echo said, "and nobody else would! Then we'd have to keep her."

"Horrors. But we could make her do the washing."

Echo snorted. "What we really ought to do is kidnap Aristippus and keep him till he promises not to chase girls. Bopis wouldn't be nearly so bad if she wasn't mad at him all the time."

"That's the thing," Narcissa said, taking back the wineskin. "Like you said, love is dangerous." She upended it and drank the last. "Dangerous."

*　　*　　*

When they came back to Narcissa's house they were just a little unsteady, and Doris and Irene eyed them suspiciously. "Well! Did you girls have a good time?" Irene asked.

"Yes, Mother." Narcissa kissed the top of her head. "I am going to go and lie down now. I feel a little faint. Echo thinks I might be pregnant."

Irene's eyes lit up. "Oh, yes, do lie down. Take a nice nap, and we'll look in on you later before Phitias comes home. Won't he be excited!"

She swept Doris and Echo up with her and bustled them out again, back down the street to her house. "There is such a lovely courtyard in the back," Irene said to Doris and Echo. "We can sit out there and talk. Oh my, I am so glad you came, such good news. Echo, did she eat?"

"She ate a fig," Echo said dubiously.

"Wonderful. She'll be on the mend soon, I'm sure, I was always taken that way myself in the first few months." Irene took them through her house and proudly showed them the walled courtyard, which Nicias had built for his first wife.

They settled in chairs there, and Echo tilted her head to the sun and closed her eyes, drowsy with the wine, listening to them talk, like the high distant chatter of birds in the trees. The names of the suitors Bopis had proposed for her circled her head like flies, and she batted them away. Irene knew a "nice young man" no more than thirty, with a little vineyard of his own. Nicias had a second cousin. The next-door neighbor was a recent widower with seven children. *I will marry Salmoneus*, Echo thought drowsily. *I would rather have goats.* He would let her come north and visit Narcissa, she thought. Maybe Persephone would come, too, and the three of them could sit in the vineyard the way she and Narcissa had today, and it would be like old times. Echo decided that if Hermes came back in one piece, she would ask him to take her to see Persephone. Maybe everything would be fine. She drowsed in the sun, warmed by the wine they had drunk, listening to the bees and her heartbeat in her head. She didn't wake until she began to snore and her mother pinched her.

Echo fumbled with her mantle, which had fallen on her feet.

"Disgraceful!" Doris said, laughing.

"I'll just go see if Narcissa is awake yet," Echo said with dignity.

"That's fine, dear," Irene said. "You go along, and we'll come in just a bit. Nicias and Phitias will be here soon, and we'll all have a meal together."

Echo yawned and straightened her gown. She noted that she had spilled wine on the front and arranged the mantle to cover it.

Doris shook her head, still laughing.

Echo knew they were pleased because she had got Narcissa to eat. She kissed her mother and bobbed her head respectfully at Irene and let herself back into Irene's house, which was very splendid, with bronze braziers in all the corners and lamps hanging from the heavy roof beams under fresh thatch. Echo trailed her hand along the fine weavings that covered the walls and the painted plaster leaves that encircled the outer door. She slipped into the agora and made her way along the street to Narcissa's house.

No one answered when she tapped her fist on the door. Echo peered through the crack between the door and the wall and could see no light. Narcissa must be still asleep. She pushed at the latch and poked her head inside. The house was dark, with only the low afternoon sun falling in a broad band from the window. She didn't see Narcissa at first in the dim light and then as her eyes grew accustomed, she saw her clearly.

Narcissa hung from the rafters just above the cold hearth, on which she had piled a stool on top of a chair. The stool lay on its side among the ashes, and Narcissa's body swayed just barely in the breath of air from the open door.

Echo screamed and righted the stool. She teetered on it and wrenched at the knotted rope, but it wouldn't give. She ran to the kitchen, spilling the stool in the ashes again, and found a knife. She sawed desperately with it at the rope, not looking at Narcissa's horrible face. When the rope gave, she fell, with Narcissa, into the ashes. Echo tore the noose from her neck and began to sob.

Love is dangerous. The words came back to her. She stood up slowly and went to the door, to meet Irene and Doris, with Nicias and Narcissa's husband, on the threshold.

"Hermes, I don't love you." Persephone shivered even though she sat next to the cook fire.

"Yes, you do," Hermes said dubiously. "You used to." He looked uncertain.

"No, I didn't. And something awful is wrong. I can't talk about this with you now."

"What? What's wrong?" Hermes looked argumentative. But he felt it too, some slow cold wind down the back of his neck.

"I don't know. Something has happened in the upper air."

"Probably your mother cooking up a hailstorm."

"No. It isn't Mother." She stood up. "Scylla, what is it?"

"Someone coming, maybe," Scylla said. "I don't know. Sometimes we feel them, down here."

"Feel whom?"

"Travelers. The restless ones. The ones who don't know where they belong." She busied herself with the cabbage.

Persephone pulled her mantle about her. "Hermes, I'm going to show you the way out."

"Take some of that nice bread before you go," Scylla said. "It's a cold climb up that cliff."

"I'm not going," Hermes said.

"Well, then eat something and don't be tiresome!" Persephone snapped at him. "I can hear your stomach growling."

"Maybe that's just your ghost coming," Hermes said sulkily.

Persephone slapped him, and he gaped at her. "Be careful I don't keep you here," she hissed. "I could, you know."

Hermes stared. "All right. Show me the way out."

She led him through the maze of corridors, stalking along in front of him, not waiting to see if he followed her. At the entrance, he thought, he would grab her and they would go. When she was in the upper air, whatever spell the caverns had laid on her would dissipate. Probably. "You don't know what's good for you," he said cajolingly. "If you stay here any longer you'll never get out. You'll be like them."

He waved his hand at the journeyers on the passage wall.

She didn't answer, and she didn't look back at him.

Beside him, they almost seemed to be moving. Out of the corner of his eye he saw the flutter of a cloak and caught the faint tap of a staff on the edge of his hearing. They shifted, their pattern realigned, as if they made room for another.

Demeter felt it in the wind that blew over the island, some breath of warning and danger. "Do you long for Eleusis?" she asked Triptolemus abruptly. She had moved back into her bed and kept him in it with her. Now she sat with the sheet wrapped around her waist and studied him as if he were a new sort of plant among her beans.

"I don't know." He was breathing hard, his chest slick with sweat. Whether he did or not, his body responded to hers. "Does it matter?"

She hesitated. What did the body know of what the heart wanted? "I begin to think it is dangerous to keep you caged like this."

"No doubt as dangerous as when I kept you."

She blinked at him, surprised.

"I have thought about it since I came here." He ran his fingers through his pale hair. There were still faint glints of gold in it, but he was no longer beautiful. He was growing old, and his bones ached. "I am not a fool. The winds do not blow a man into the same waves twice in a lifetime without some meaning. I was very young that first time. I didn't know who you were."

Demeter thought of the two of them on his boat,

after he had mended it, asleep on the deck wrapped
in the same cloak. The stars had looked like spangles
of ice in a warm black sky, puddles reflected in a
black sea. They flickered as she watched, and the
flicker had bubbled in their blood while the sea rolled
under them. "I was just a girl then. It was the baby.
And Faunus's garden. That was where the knowledge came from. After that things began to grow
when I told them to."

"And now our daughter has married the lord of
Death, to whom she would have gone too young to
marry if you had stayed. You were right. Mother
would have made me expose her."

"And you would have listened."

He nodded. "I owed it to her. I owed her everything, because we killed Demophon."

Demeter laid a hand on his arm for a moment.
Gestures of affection from her were rare. Mostly she
made love to him silently, savagely, consumingly.
"Take that grief and throw it on the sea, Triptolemus." Her voice was low and vehement. "Demophon had an ill nature and a grasping heart. Your
mother was a fool."

"The world is mysterious that way," he said. "I
never understand half of it."

"Do you want to go back, then?"

"To Eleusis?"

"Yes, to Eleusis."

"Alone?"

"Are your mother and sisters still there?"

"Yes."

"Then alone."

"My mother is still there mourning Demophon. If

I go back I will have to be Demophon for her again. It's hard to do, and painful."

Love is dangerous. Something whispered that in her ear. "Am I like that?" she asked him abruptly.

He smiled at her now, rueful. "A little."

"Go back if you will, then," she said quietly, "or stay here if you will." She spread her fingers out. She would open her hand and wait for the rush of wings.

"If I stay of my own will," he said, propping himself on one elbow, "I will not be Demeter's pet." He might not understand things, but he could understand that.

"No." She looked at her open hand. "Nor I Triptolemus's doxy."

"And do you think we may both be easy in that bargain?" He looked hopeful.

"No." Demeter lay down again beside him. "Love is uneasy. Look what my love for my daughter has done to the world, but life is very plain without it." He reached for her, and she knew with a wistful certainty that if you didn't allow the danger in, there was no hope of joy. She knew also that not everybody won.

"This is Chickpea," Salmoneus said. He stroked the goat's pale brown head while it watched him with yellow eyes and black barred pupils. "And this is Pomegranate, and Ivy, and Violet."

Echo brushed her hand down Ivy's back. Ivy swayed a little and closed her eyes. The two bleating kids that had been following her stuck their heads under her belly and began to suck.

"That's Hawthorn." He pointed to the buck who

stood guarding his little flock, beard wagging. "He's a little cranky, but just with other buck goats. He likes me. He'll like you, too."

Echo considered that. Salmoneus had a pleasant face and sandy hair somewhere between tan and brown, like his goats. He smelled a little like them, too. But he was sweet-natured, and she wouldn't have a mother-in-law. That seemed promising. She knelt and scratched the nursing kids behind their ears and they waggled their tails.

"Those two are Acanthus and Anemone." Salmoneus looked doubtful. "I don't have anything for a bride price but goats."

"I like goats," Echo said. Violet butted her knees gently. She sat in the meadow grass and let Violet put her head on her lap.

Salmoneus sat down beside her. "Bopis says your father turned down two other suitors," he said.

"Because I wouldn't have them," Echo said. Technically, he could have made her have one of them, but Doris had convinced him that it would be cruel, after Narcissa. As Narcissa's gift, Echo was to be given her choice.

Salmoneus looked admiringly at this display of will. "Would you have me?" he whispered.

His breath was warm on her neck. Echo thought she could hear the thin sound of pipes. Something just out of sight danced on goats' hooves through the grass, and her blood hummed after it.

Aristippus felt it, too, like the rustle of autumn leaves outside the one high window of the goat shed. These days amorous dalliance was a chancy thing, but Clytie didn't seem to mind whether anything much came of it. She was content to cuddle with him and wait to see if something was going to happen, feed him with her fingers, and play with his hair. He had given up pursuing young girls years ago, settling for the more sedate company of lonely widows, but Clytie had danced across his horizon and winked at him, and Aristippus had found himself younger than he had thought. He wasn't so vain as to think Clytie loved him. He gave her presents, and Clytie liked presents. But she was a happy girl despite the whole village thinking she was a slut. Sluthood suited Clytie just fine.

"I wouldn't be married," she confided to him, "and have some man own me and order me about." She tapped him on the nose. "And like as not be after other women all the time as soon as I lost my looks."

"A man needs cheerful company," Aristippus said. "It wears a man down, all that glowering and nagging."

"Well, why did you marry her, then?" Clytie had been trying to figure that out. All the couples of her acquaintance seemed to grate on each other's nerves, to have developed little ruts that their wagon wheels ran through endlessly, digging them ever deeper.

"She was beautiful," Aristippus said fondly.

"See, that's all it is. Just beauty. Me, I'm putting things by, so that when I'm old and funny looking I won't need faithless old men. Hah!" She tickled his beard.

"It wasn't just beauty," he said. "Every man on the island wanted her. That is always stimulative."

"Every man on the island wants me," Clytie said cheerfully.

"They don't want to marry you, you wicked girl.

Bopis was standoffish. She made herself look like a challenge." Aristippus smiled reminiscently.

"Bopis is respectable." Clytie stuck her nose in the air and pursed her lips together. "Respectability is overrated. When *I* am old and ugly, I will still have my sheep and a nice house, and I *won't* have an old ugly husband telling me to make his supper and wash his smelly tunic."

Aristippus laughed. "If you married, you would be just as bad as Bopis."

"That's why I won't." Clytie tossed her head of dark curls. "I saw how my mother lived. When she died, I said I wouldn't be like her." Clytie's father had worked her mother to death while Clytie stayed out of the house and slept in the hayfield half the nights. By the time he died, her mother was so tired she had just lain down and died, too. "In fact, I told the goddess so," Clytie said, "and she didn't strike me dead."

"It's not always like that," Aristippus said.

"It's like that often enough. Harmonia *would* have that Tros, and I heard her just yesterday at the well complaining that he never comes home at night now."

"Watch out or she'll be blaming you."

"Tros is dull as a ditch full of water. He's just hiding because Harmonia is too tired to dance attendance on him." Clytie had stood where Harmonia couldn't see her, just in case, though. Respectable women were quick to blame Clytie for their husbands' failings.

"He'll be wanting some loving," Aristippus said. "Women with babies give it all to the baby."

"At least the baby appreciates them." Clytie snuggled closer to Aristippus and played with his beard. "That's another thing I shall remember not to do," Clytie informed him. "No babies."

"Well, you can't predict that." Aristippus slapped her on the bottom.

Clytie snorted. Men were ignorant. Much better not to have babies than let some man who couldn't be bothered with girls expose them on a hillside. The four daughters born after Clytie had been silent, half-blue things, even before her father had ordered them exposed. Her mother was so tired all the time she couldn't make a boy baby, or even a healthy girl. Clytie remembered Bopis now, coming to see her mother after the last one, and driving her father out of the house for the afternoon. Bopis had spoken in whispers, holding her mother's thin hand and stroking her bruised arms. She had left a pouch of something beside the bed, and her mother had got up and hidden it in the clothes chest when Bopis left. After that there had been no more babies, and her mother had shown Clytie where to pick the herbs that had been in Bopis's pouch.

"Bopis knows," Clytie said. "Bopis knows more than you think."

Bopis knew where Aristippus was. He hadn't dared take the little trollop into their own shed again, and so he had gone to ground in someone else's. Bopis had come to speak with young Salmoneus about the betrothal arrangements. Echo was determined to have him, and her parents (so ill-advised, but there was no talking to some people) were going to let her make her own choice. Bopis was clicking her tongue over the folly of that when she saw the scrap of green wool caught on a thorn bush. It had a brown border, and she knew that scrap. It was the one that she had seen dangling from Aristippus's hem this morning. She had told him to take the tunic off and let her mend it, but he had pushed her away and said he had important matters to attend to, more important than darning a tunic.

Bopis narrowed her eyes. Someone had crossed through the tall grass beside the goat track here not long ago. She turned off the path to Salmoneus's cottage and headed for his goat shed, cutting through the meadow to come around by the back. She pricked her ears for incriminating sounds as she went. The low bleating of a goat and the tinkle of a bell came from the hillside as she slunk cautiously through the dry grass, the incriminating scrap of wool clutched in her fist. Aristippus was going to be sorry he hadn't let her mend it.

The goat bleated again as Bopis swiveled her head, trying to see if Salmoneus was about. A faint giggle danced along the air, and she froze, trying to pinpoint the sound. There were just the goats' low-voiced conversation and a bee humming past her ear, bent on its own errands. Bopis's mouth tightened. She had been beautiful once, and he had sat at her feet and recited poetry to her. That had been before she married him. She heard the giggle again, some female who would frolic like a trollop in goat sheds, and Bopis knew who it was. She marched purposefully toward the shed now, her mantle flapping behind her like a sail. "I know you are in there!" She thumped her walking staff on the ground as she went, vengeance in her eyes.

She heard a faint shriek, and it seemed now not to be in the shed. Bopis veered toward the oak trees.

There was a rustle among the long grass and last year's leaves. "Aha!" She ducked under a low-hanging branch and came face-to-face with Salmoneus. Behind him Echo was pulling her dress over her head.

"You!" Bopis and Salmoneus stared at each other, red-faced. Echo yanked her dress down and stood, brushing thistles from the hem.

"Oh. I. Er . . ." Salmoneus cast about for the proper thing to say while Echo hid her face in her hands. When it became clear that he wasn't going to think of anything, she lowered them.

"We're very sorry," Echo said. "And we won't do it again."

"Don't be ridiculous!" Bopis snapped. "Of course you'll do it again. Men have no restraint."

"I'm sorry," Salmoneus managed. "It—it was the goats, I think . . . and the grass . . . and . . ."

"Be quiet! Echo, your mother is going to be severely disappointed."

"Do you have to tell her?" Echo twisted one bare toe in the dirt. Her sandals, Bopis noted, were in the tree. "We *are* going to get married."

"Out in the woods in front of anyone who comes along! You could at least have had the decency to go inside."

"Oh. I suppose we could have." Salmoneus lived alone.

"I'm surprised you didn't use the goat shed!" Bopis said, suddenly narrowing her eyes. "Since it's so handy."

"Isn't very clean in there," Salmoneus said hastily.

"Spiders," Echo said. "Big ones."

Bopis slid another suspicious glance at the goat shed, its roof just visible through the oak leaves.

"Please don't tell Mother." Echo sidled up to her, making shooing motions at Salmoneus. "It was just that I was so lonely, and I do like Salmoneus. He'll be a good husband, and I wanted to please him, and . . ."

"There will be plenty of time for that," Bopis said severely. "You will have a duty to do after your marriage."

"I was frightened," Echo said, seizing inspiration. "I thought at least I would know what it was like, you know." She moved farther into the trees, where there was a rotten stump, and sat down on it, making room for Bopis, and looked hopeful. "If I just had someone older to talk to. Mother is so busy, with the wedding and everything. . . ."

"Poor child." Bopis appeared to weaken. She sat next to Echo and patted her hand. "This isn't the way to go about things. You'll get a reputation, you know."

"I know," Echo said sorrowfully. She saw that Salmoneus had disappeared.

"That's important. Men have latitude that we women are not allowed. And wouldn't want," she added firmly. "Whatever a man may do, it is of the utmost importance that his wife be known for her virtue."

Echo thought that sounded unfair, but she didn't say so. You didn't argue about things like that with Bopis. But she did wonder, too, whether Bopis had ever found that rule unfair, considering everything.

She cocked her head cautiously, but no sound came from the distant goat shed.

"How did you come to forget yourself so?" Bopis demanded sternly. "And don't blather at me about grass and goats like that young scoundrel."

It had been the goats, though, Echo thought. There was something old and knowing about goats. You looked in their yellow eyes and things looked back at you, old things, things that had to do with the dark of the moon and new grass in the stubble of a mowed field and some song you couldn't quite hear. She didn't think she could explain that to Bopis. "It just . . . it just seemed to happen," she said helplessly. "Even if I was afraid."

"A girl who will let herself be overcome by her physical sensations is headed on the road to ruin," Bopis informed her. "Women do not have the same sensations that men do, and if a girl gets to imagining that she does, no good ever comes of it. Our function is to make babies, to give birth to the next generation, that is what the Mother wants."

"Uncle Phaedon says intercourse opens the entrance to the womb, and lets the blood flow out so it doesn't back up and cause licentiousness and hallucinations," Echo said.

Bopis said, "Tchah!"

"He says it will travel about in your body if you aren't careful to do it often enough," Echo said.

"How did you come to hear such an unsuitable conversation?" Bopis demanded. "That is talk for a girl on her wedding night, not before."

"Uncle Phaedon explained it to Mother when Father complained that she wouldn't let him in her bed but once a month."

"Men always think they know more than women,"
Bopis said darkly, "particularly when it comes to
knowing things about women."

"Well, how are *we* supposed to know anything,"
Echo said, "if no one ever tells us?"

"There is a time to be told things," Bopis said severely, "and experimentation on your own is a bad
idea. What would you do now if young Salmoneus
decided not to go through with the betrothal? Suppose he didn't like you?"

Echo hadn't thought of that, not with the goat song
running in her blood. "I think he did, though."

"Well, that is doubly disgraceful," Bopis said severely. "It is not nice at all to enjoy yourself the
first time."

"If nobody had a good time, they wouldn't do it,"
Echo said rebelliously. She had thought about that,
and thought about Clytie, just moments ago lying in
Salmoneus's goat shed with Bopis's husband. At least
Echo hoped they weren't still there. She was sure
Salmoneus had gone to warn them. He knew they
were in there; he and Echo had heard them, and
fallen to giggling so helplessly that they had rolled
around in the grass, and then one thing had led to
another. She couldn't tell Bopis that, either.

"A lady has standards to maintain," Bopis said.
"You must understand that. Even if you are so
thoughtless of your own future as to marry this
young man, and I do not think he was the best
choice, but what's done is done, we all make our bed
and then must lie in it, just look at what I have suffered at that man's hands, all for being young and
foolish, but that is another story and the Mother
knows I do not complain of it." She stopped to un-

wind the thread of the conversation and pounced again on the beginning of it. "You must never make it easy for them. Men think what is easy is not valuable; nor is it."

Echo kicked her foot against the base of the stump. "I'll remember that, Aunt Bopis." "Aunt" was a courtesy title for any village busybody to whom you were not related.

"If you do, my child, you'll be better off." Bopis stood, shaking leaves off the hem of her mantle. The goats bleated somewhere deeper in the woods, and they heard the crunch of brush underfoot. Through the branches Bopis caught a glimpse of a green tunic. She swung her head around to Echo with sudden suspicion. "Who was that?"

"Who, Aunt?"

"Someone else in the woods, you wicked child. Have you been keeping me here while he got away?"

"Oh, no. Absolutely not." There was no need to ask who. Bopis spent most of her time vengefully tracking her errant husband. Echo considered that it would serve Clytie right if they were caught, but she didn't want to think about what Bopis would do to Salmoneus for having them in his goat shed. Not that they had asked. No one would tell Aristippus, the priest of Zeus, no to anything. Echo didn't think she could bear it if Bopis changed her father's mind about letting her marry Salmoneus. "I saw him going toward Uncle Phaedon's house just an hour ago," she offered. Uncle Phaedon lived in the opposite direction, and fortuitously, near the cottage where Clytie lived.

Bopis looked at the scrap of wool, still clutched in her hand. "How odd," she said icily. Echo did her best to look innocent. "You talk entirely too much, my girl," Bopis told her. "One of these days that tongue of yours will get you in trouble."

She stalked off, betrothal negotiations forgotten, the wool balled in her fist. Salmoneus emerged from the trees. "The old harpy," he said. "I'm scared to death of her."

"That makes two of us," Echo said. "Do you suppose we could make our marriage not be like theirs?"

"I'm counting on it."

Or like Narcissa's, or like Persephone's, either, for that matter. Echo looked up at Salmoneus's friendly face. He had a smattering of freckles like hers across his nose. "Love is dangerous," she told him.

"Then we'll face it together," he said. "Just us and the goats."

Ivy and Hawthorn appeared, picking their way daintily through the little clearing. They butted their heads against Echo's legs, and she scratched them between their horns.

face as emaciated as if she were bones already. The carver had caught her in midstride, one foot with its toes to the floor, heel lifted, hurrying on. Her feet and the hands clutching her mantle were skeletal, too.

"We had better hurry," Hermes said. "He'll be after us soon."

Persephone looked at Narcissa's face on the passage wall and began to weep.

Hermes took her by the arm. "He has enchanted you. The outside air will break the spell."

Persephone pointed a finger at the wall.

Hermes peered at it. The flicker of the lamps in their niches made the figure seem to move. "That's Narcissa! Do you see what he is now? How can you stay with a monster like that?"

"They come to him," Persephone said, weeping.

"He doesn't take them."

"Of course he takes them. He's Death! Can't you understand that?"

"Death isn't a person," Persephone traced Narcissa's gaunt face with her fingertip. "Death is . . . circumstance, maybe. Marriage was her death," she said, knowing that suddenly. Why hadn't her mother and Bopis and all the rest seen that, and not sent her off to this?

"Don't be stupid," Hermes said. "Am I going to have to carry you off over my shoulder? I can do it."

He eyed her consideringly.

"You can't." Persephone pushed him away, but he didn't move far. She could feel the wall against her back. "Hermes, you don't want to marry me anyway."

"Well, I have to. That's what being a hero is about. You marry the girl. You save her, and then you marry her."

XII

❧

Pomegranate Seed

Persephone saw the travelers realign themselves on the corridor wall. She had seen it before, and never mentioned it to Hades. They never did it if you looked right at them, but when you turned your head half away, out of the corner of your eye you saw the movement. When you looked back, you were almost certain there was someone new among them. There were so many it was hard to be sure, but she knew she had seen Echemus, Narcissa's father. He wasn't there now, where she had first seen him, and she had thought yesterday she had seen him near the great hall. She thought they moved, walked on along the corridor wall until they came to wherever they were going. Where the carvings ended, there was a boat carved on the wall, waiting to sail into the stone.

Now she stopped in her march to the cavern entrance, her fingers to her mouth. Narcissa was there on the wall, her mantle drawn over her head, her

CHILTON BOOK COMPANY

REPAIR MANUAL

TOYOTA Corolla, Tercel and MR2 1984-90
Covers all models

President GARY INGERSOLL
Senior Vice President, Book Publishing and Research RONALD A. HOXTER
Publisher KERRY A. FREEMAN, S.A.E.
Editor-In-Chief DEAN F. MORGANTINI, S.A.E.
Senior Editor RICHARD J. RIVELE, S.A.E.
Editor ANTHONY TORTORICI, S.A.E.

CHILTON BOOK COMPANY
Radnor, Pennsylvania
19089

CONTENTS

GENERAL INFORMATION and MAINTENANCE

1 How to use this book
2 Tools and Equipment
6 Routine Maintenance

ENGINE PERFORMANCE and TUNE-UP

57 Tune-Up Procedures
58 Tune-Up Specifications

ENGINE and ENGINE OVERHAUL

81 Engine Electrical System
98 Engine Service
101 Engine Specifications

EMISSION CONTROLS

199 Emission Controls System and Service
223 Electronic Engine Controls

FUEL SYSTEM

293 Carbureted Fuel System
310 Gasoline Fuel Injection System
326 Diesel Fuel System

CHASSIS ELECTRICAL

341 Heating and Air Conditioning
352 Accessory Service
355 Instruments and Switches
367 Lighting
371 Circuit Protection

DRIVE TRAIN

381 Manual Transmission
428 Clutch
433 Automatic Transmission

SUSPENSION and STEERING

451 Front Suspension
473 Rear Suspension
488 Steering

BRAKES

536 Brake Systems
527 Front Disc Brakes
536 Rear Disc Brakes
533 Rear Drum Brakes

BODY

545 Exterior
548 Interior

MECHANIC'S DATA

561 Mechanic's Data
563 Glossary
569 Abbreviations
571 Index

**317 Chilton's Fuel Economy
and Tune-Up Tips**

557 Chilton's Body Repair Tips

SAFETY NOTICE

Proper service and repair procedures are vital to the safe, reliable operation of all motor vehicles, as well as the safety of those performing repairs. This book outlines procedures for serviceing and repairing vehicles using safe effective methods. The procedures contain many NOTES, CAUTIONS and WARNINGS which should be followed along with standard safety procedures to eliminate the possibility of personal injury or improper service which could damage the vehicle or compromise its safety.

It is important to note that repair procedures and techniques, tools and parts for servicing motor vehicles, as well as the skill and experience of the individual performing the work vary widely. It is not possible to anticipate all of the conceivable ways or conditions under which vehicles may be serviced, or to provide cautions as to all of the possible hazards that may result. Standard and accepted safety precautions and equipment should be used during cutting, grinding, chiseling, prying,or any other process that can cause material removal or projectiles.

Some procedures require the use of tools specially designed for a specific purpose. Before substituting another tool or procedure, you ust be com-pletely satisfied that neither your personal safety, nor the performance of the vehicle will be endangered.

Although the information in this guide is based on industry sources and is as complete as possible at the time of publication, the possibility exists that the manufacturer made later changes which could not be included here. While striving for total accuracy, Chilton Book Company cannot assume responsibilty for any errors, changes, or omissions that may occur in the compilation of this data.

PART NUMBERS

Part numbers listed in the reference are not recommendations by Chilton for any product by brand name. They are references that can be used with interchange manuals and aftermarket supplier catalogs to locate each brand supplier's discrete part number.

SPECIAL TOOLS

Special tools are recommended by the vehicle manufacturer to perform their specific job. Use has been kept to a minimum, but where absolutely neccesary, they are referred to in the text by the part number of the tool manufacturer. These tools can be purchased, under the appropiate part number, from Toyota dealers or Toyota Motor Sales, U.S.A. (address below) or an equivalent tool can be purchased locally from a tool supplier or parts outlet. Before substituting any tool for the one recommended, read the SAFETY NOTICE at the top of this page.

ACKNOWLEDGEMENTS

The Chilton Book Company expresses appreciation to Toyota Motor Sales, U.S.A., Inc.2055 W. 190th Street, Torrance California 90504 , for their generous assistance

Chilton's Repair Manual: Toyota Corolla, Tercel and MR2 1984–90

General Information and Maintenance

HOW TO USE THIS BOOK

Chilton's Repair Manual for the Toyota Corolla, Tercel and MR2 vehicles is intended to teach you more about the inner workings of your automobile and save you money on its upkeep. Chapters 1 and 2 will probably be the most frequently used in the book. The first chapter contains all the information that may be required at a moment's notice. Aside from giving the location of various serial numbers and the proper towing instructions, it also contains all the information on basic day-to-day maintenance that you will need to ensure good performance and long vehicle component life. Chapter 2 contains the necessary tune-up procedures to assist you not only in keeping the engine running properly and at peak performance levels, but also in restoring some of the more delicate vehicle components to operating condition in the event of a failure. Chapters 3 through 10 cover repairs (rather than maintenance) for various portions of your car.

When using the Table of Contents, refer to the bold listings for the subject of the chapter and the smaller listings (or the index) for information on a particular component.

In general, there are some things a proficient mechanic has which must be allowed for when a non-professional does work on his/her car. These are:

1. A sound knowledge of the construction of the parts he is working with; their order of assembly, etc.

2. A knowledge of potentially hazardous situations; particularly how to prevent them.

3. Manual dexterity and common sense.

This book provides step-by-step instructions and illustrations whenever possible. Use them carefully and wisely — don't just jump headlong into disassembly (review the complete service procedure first!). When there is doubt about being able to readily reassemble something, make a careful drawing (mark vacuum hoses etc. or matchmark components such as a driveshaft to rear flange) of the component before taking it apart. Assembly always looks simple when everything is still assembled.

Always replace cotter pins, gaskets, O-rings and oil seals etc. with new ones. Non-reusable parts are indicated in the component illustrations by a diamond symbol.

CAUTIONS WARNINGS, AND NOTES will be provided where appropriate to help prevent you from injuring yourself or damaging your car. Consequently, you should always read through the entire procedure before beginning the work so as to familiarize yourself with any special problems which may occur during the given procedure. Since no number of warnings could cover every possible situation, you should work slowly and try to envision what is going to happen in each operation ahead of time.

When it comes to tightening things, there is generally a slim area between too loose to properly seal or resist vibration and so tight as to risk damage or warping. When dealing with major engine parts, or with any aluminum component, it pays to buy a torque wrench and go by the recommended figures.

When reference is made in this book to the right side or the left side of the car, it should be understood that the positions are always to be viewed from the front seat. This means that the LEFT SIDE of the car is the DRIVER'S SIDE and RIGHT SIDE is the PASSENGER'S SIDE. This will hold true throughout the book, regardless of how you might be looking at the car at the time.

Always be conscious of the need for safety in your work. Never get under a car unless it is firmly supported by jackstands or ramps. Never smoke near, or allow flame to get near the battery or the fuel system. Keep your clothing, hands and hair clear of the fan and pulleys when working near the engine if it is running. Most importantly, try to be patient; even in the midst of an argument with a stubborn bolt, reaching for the largest hammer in the garage is usually a cause for later regret and more extensive repair. As you gain confidence and experience, working on your car will become a source of pride and satisfaction.

TOOLS AND EQUIPMENT

NOTE: *Special tools are occasionally necessary to perform a specific job or are recommended to make a job easier. Their use has been kept to a minimum. When a special tool is indicated, it will be referred to by the manufacturer's designation. Toyota designates these as SST (Special Shop Tools), followed by the part number. Where possible, an illustration will be provided. Some special tools are unique to the vehicle, others are the manufacturer's version of common repair tools. These tools can usually be purchased from your local Toyota dealer or from an automotive parts store.*

The service procedures in this book pre–suppose a familiarity with hand tools and their proper use. However, it is possible that you may have a limited amount of experience with the sort of equipment needed to work on an automobile. This section is designed to help you assemble a basic set of tools that will handle most of the jobs you may undertake.

In addition to the normal assortment of screwdrivers and pliers, automotive service work requires an investment in wrenches, sockets (and the handles needed to drive them), and various measuring tools such as a torque wrench and feeler gauges.

You will find that virtually every nut and bolt on your Toyota is metric. Therefore, despite a few close size similarities, standard inch size tools will not fit and MUST NOT be used. You will need a set of metric wrenches as your most basic tool kit, ranging from about 6mm to 17mm in size. High quality forged wrenches are available in three styles: open end, box end, and combination open/box end. The combination tools are generally the most desirable as a starter set; the wrenches shown in the accompanying illustration are of the combination type. If you plan to do any work on the hydraulic system, a set of line wrenches (sometimes called flare nut wrenches) is highly recommended.

The other set of tools inevitably required is a ratchet handle and socket set. This set should have the same size range as your wrench set.

The ratchet, extension, and flex drives for the sockets are available in many sizes; it is advisable to choose a $^3/_8$ in. drive set initially. One break in the inch/metric sizing war is that metric sized sockets sold in the U.S. have inch sized drive ($^1/_4$ in., $^3/_8$ in., $^1/_2$ in., etc.). Thus, if you already have an inch sized socket set, you need only buy new metric sockets in the sizes needed. Sockets are available in 6-and 12-point versions; 6-point types are stronger and are a good choice for a first set. The choice of a drive handle for the sockets should be made with some care.

If this is your first set, take the plunge and invest in a flex–head ratchet; it will get into many places otherwise accessible only through a long chain of universal joints, extensions, and adapters. An alternative is a flex handle, which lacks the ratcheting feature but has a head which pivots 180°; such a tool is shown below the ratchet handle in the illustration. In addition to the range of sockets mentioned, a rubber lined spark plug socket should be purchased with the set. Since spark plug size varies, know (or ask) which size is appropriate for your car.

The most important thing to consider when purchasing hand tools is quality. Don't be misled by the low cost of "bargain tools". Forged wrenches, tempered screwdriver blades, and fine tooth ratchets are much better investments than their less expensive counterparts. The skinned knuckles and frustration inflicted by poor quality tools make any job an unhappy chore. Another consideration is that quality hand tools come with an unbeatable replacement guarantee: if the tool breaks, you get a new one, no questions asked.

Most jobs can be accomplished using the tools on the accompanying lists. There will be an occasional need for a special tool, such as snap ring pliers; that need will be mentioned in the text. It would not be wise to buy a large assortment of tools on the theory that someday they will be needed. Instead, the tools should be acquired one or two at a time, each for a specific job. This will avoid unnecessary expense and help insure that you have the right tool for the job at hand.

The tools needed for basic maintenance jobs, in addition to the wrenches and sockets mentioned, include:

1. A floor jack, with a lifting capacity at least equal to the weight of the car. Capacity of $1^1/_2$ times the weight is better.
2. Jackstands, for support
3. Oil filter wrench
4. Oil filler spout or funnel
5. Grease gun
6. Battery post and clamp cleaner

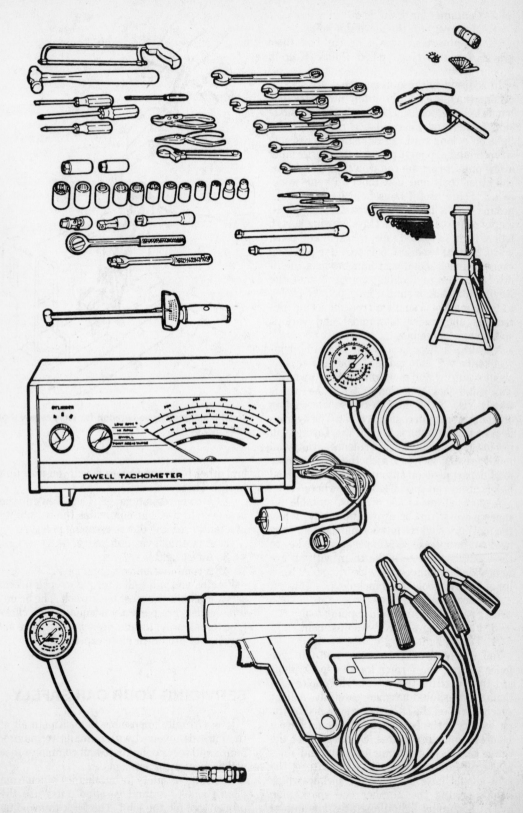

You need only a basic assortment of hand tools for most maintenance and repair jobs

7. Container for draining oil

8. Many rags for the inevitable spills

9. Oil absorbent gravel or cat box filler gravel, for absorbing spilled fluids. Keep a broom handy.

In addition to these items there are several others which are not absolutely necessary, but handy to have around. These include a transmission funnel and filler tube, a drop (trouble) light on a long cord, an adjustable (crescent) wrench, and slip joint pliers. After performing a few projects on the car, you'll be amazed at the other tools and non–tools on your workbench. Some useful household items to have around are: a large turkey baster or siphon, empty coffee cans and ice trays (storing parts), ball of twine, assorted tape, markers and pens, whisk broom, tweezers, golf tees (for plugging vacuum lines), metal coat hangers or a roll of mechanics's wire (holding things out of the way), dental pick or similar long, pointed probe, a strong magnet, a small mirror (for seeing into recesses and under manifolds) and various small pieces of lumber.

A hydraulic floor jack is one of the best investments you can make if you are serious about repairing and maintaining your own car. The small jack that comes with the car is simply NOT SAFE enough to use when doing anything more than changing a flat. The hydraulic floor jack ($1\frac{1}{2}$ ton is fine for the Toyota) will pay for itself quickly in convenience, utility and much greater safety. Watch the ads for your local department or automotive store. A good jack is always on special sale somewhere.

A more advanced list of tools, suitable for tune-up work, can be drawn up easily. While the tools are slightly more sophisticated, they need not be outrageously expensive. The key to these purchases is to make them with an eye towards adaptability and wide range. A basic list of tune-up tools could include:

1. Tachometer/dwell meter

2. Spark plug gauge and gapping tool

3. Feeler gauges for valve adjustment

4. Timing light.

You will need both wire type and flat type feeler gauges, the former for the spark plugs and the latter for the valves. The choice of a timing light should be made carefully. A light which works on the DC current supplied by the car battery is the best choice; it should have a xenon tube for brightness. Since many of the newer cars have electronic ignition, and since nearly all cars will have it in the future, the light should have an inductive pickup which clamps around the number one spark plug cable (the timing light illustrated has one of these pickups).

In addition to these basic tools, there are sev-

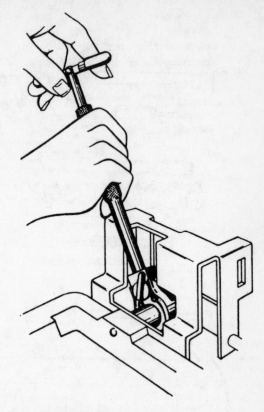

Newly designed speedwrench for easy removal of nuts and bolts

eral other tools and gauges which you may find useful. These include:

1. A compression gauge. The screw-in type is slower to use, but eliminates the possibility of a faulty reading due to escaping pressure.

2. A manifold vacuum gauge.

3. A test light.

4. A combination volt/ohmmeter.

Finally, you will find a torque wrench necessary for all but the most basic work. The beam-type models are perfectly adequate. The click-type (breakaway) torque wrenches are more accurate, but are much more expensive.

SERVICING YOUR CAR SAFELY

It is virtually impossible to anticipate all of the hazards involved with automotive maintenance and service, but care and common sense will prevent most accidents.

The rules of safety for mechanics range from "don't smoke around gasoline", to "use the proper tool for the job". The trick to avoiding injuries is to develop safe work habits and take every possible precaution.

Dos

• Do keep a fire extinguisher and first aid kit within easy reach.

• Do wear safety glasses or goggles when cutting, drilling, grinding or prying, even if you have 20–20 vision. If you wear glasses for the sake of vision, they should be made of hardened glass that can serve also as safety glasses, or wear safety goggles over your regular glasses.

• Do shield your eyes whenever you work around the battery. Batteries contain sulfuric acid. In case of contact with the eyes or skin, flush the area with water or a mixture of water and baking soda and get medical attention immediately.

• Do use safety stands for any under car service. Jacks are for raising vehicles; safety stands are for making sure the vehicle stays raised until you want it to come down. Whenever the car is raised, block the wheels remaining on the ground and set the parking brake.

• Do use adequate ventilation when working with any chemicals or hazardous materials. Like carbon monoxide, the asbestos dust resulting from brake lining wear can be poisonous in sufficient quantities.

• Do disconnect the negative battery cable when working on the electrical system. The secondary ignition system can contain up to 40,000 volts.

• Do follow manufacturer's directions whenever working with potentially hazardous materials. Both brake fluid and antifreeze are poisonous if taken internally.

• Do properly maintain your tools Loose hammerheads, mushroomed punches and chisels, frayed or poorly grounded electrical cords, excessively worn screwdrivers, spread wrenches (open end), cracked sockets, slipping ratchets, or faulty droplight sockets can cause accidents.

• Do use the proper size and type of tool for the job being done.

• Do when possible, pull on a wrench handle rather than push on it, and adjust your stance to prevent a fall.

Always support the car securely with jackstands; never use cinder blocks, tire changing jacks or the like

• Do be sure that adjustable wrenches are tightly closed on the nut or bolt and pulled so that the face is on the side of the fixed jaw.

• Do select a wrench or socket that fits the nut or bolt. The wrench or socket should be straight, not cocked.

• Do set the parking brake and block the drive wheels if the work requires the engine running.

Don'ts

• Don't run an engine in a garage or anywhere else without proper ventilation — EVER! Carbon monoxide is poisonous; it takes a long time to leave the human body and you can build up a deadly supply of it in your system by simply breathing in a little every day. You may not realize you are slowly poisoning yourself. Always use power vents, windows, fans or open the garage doors.

• Don't work around moving parts while wearing a necktie or other loose clothing. Short sleeves are much safer than long, loose sleeves; hard-toed shoes with neoprene soles protect your toes and give a better grip on slippery surfaces. Jewelry such as watches, fancy belt buckles, beads or body adornment of any kind is not safe working around a car. Long hair should be hidden under a hat or cap.

• Don't use pockets for toolboxes. A fall or bump can drive a screwdriver deep into your body. Even a wiping cloth hanging from the back pocket can wrap around a spinning shaft or fan.

• Don't smoke when working around gasoline, cleaning solvent or other flammable material.

• Don't smoke when working around the battery. When the battery is being charged, it gives off explosive hydrogen gas.

• Don't use gasoline to wash your hands; there are excellent soaps available. Gasoline may contain lead, and lead can enter the body through a cut, accumulating in the body until you are very ill. Gasoline also removes all the natural oils from the skin so that bone dry hands will suck up oil and grease.

• Don't service the air conditioning system unless you are equipped with the necessary tools and training. The refrigerant, R-12, is extremely cold when compressed, and when released into the air will instantly freeze any surface it contacts, including your eyes. Although the refrigerant is normally non-toxic; R-12 becomes a deadly poisonous gas in the presence of an open flame. One good whiff of the vapors from burning refrigerant can be fatal.

• Don't use screwdrivers for anything other than driving screws! A screwdriver used as a

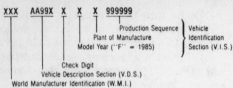

Production Sequence
Plant of Manufacture
Model Year ("F" = 1985)
Check Digit
Vehicle Description Section (V.D.S.)
World Manufacturer Identification (W.M.I.)

Vehicle
Identification
Section (V.I.S.)

FORMAT: X = Alphabetic or Numeric Characters
A = Alphabetic Characters only
9 = Numeric Characters only

17 digit VIN used on all models

The sections of the V.I.N. have been separated for description purposes; however, the actual V.I.N. on the vehicles will not have any spaces between the sections.

The 17 digit V.I.N. is displayed in three separate locations on each vehicle.

- Name plate within engine compartment. (MR2 — front compartment)
- V.I.N. plate on top left dashboard.
- Certification plate on left door or door post.

The section of the V.I.N. used to translate to the Series Prefix/Japan Model Code is the vehicle description section identified under the column heading V.D.S.

prying tool or chisel can snap when least expected, causing bodily harm. Besides, you ruin a good tool when it is used for purposes other than those intended.

• Don't use a bumper jack (that little scissors or pantograph jack that comes with the car) for anything other than changing a flat tire! If you are serious about repairing and maintaining your own car, then one of the best investments you can make is in a hydraulic floor jack of at least 1¹/₂ ton capacity.

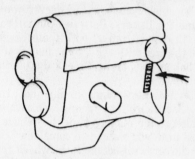

Engine serial number location

SERIAL NUMBER IDENTIFICATION

Vehicle

The serial number on all models consists of a 17 digit format. All models have the vehicle identification number (VIN) stamped on a plate which is attached to the left side of the instrument panel or dashboard (the 17 digit VIN is displayed in three separate locations on each vehicle). This plate is visible through the windshield.

The VIN is also stamped on a name plate in the engine compartment which is usually located on the firewall. On the MR2 vehicles, it is located in the front compartment.

The VIN is also stamped on the certification plate on the left door or door post.

Engine

The engine serial number consists of an engine series identification number, followed by a 7-digit production number. The serial number is stamped on the left side of the engine.

Transmission/Transaxle

The manual and automatic transmission/transaxle identification numbers are stamped on the housing or on an identification tag which is attached to the unit.

The VIN plate on later model Toyotas can be found in three different locations

ROUTINE MAINTENANCE

Air Cleaner

All of the dirt and dust present in the air is kept out of the engine by means of the air cleaner filter element. Proper maintenance is vital, as a clogged element not only restricts the air flow and thus the power, but can also cause premature engine wear.

The filter element should be cleaned/inspected every 6 months or 7,500–10,000 miles (12,000–16,000km) or more often if the car is driven under dry, dusty conditions. Remove the filter element and using low pressure compressed air, blow the dirt out.

NOTE: *The filter element used on Toyota vehicles is of the dry, disposable type. It should never be washed, soaked or oiled.*

The filter element must be replaced at 30,000 mile (48,000km) intervals or more often under dry, dusty conditions. Be sure to use the correct one; all Toyota elements are of the same type but they come in a variety of sizes.

Engine Identification Chart

Model	Years	Engine Displacement cu. in. (cc)	Engine Series Identification	No. of Cylinders/Liters	Engine Type	No. Valves Per Engine
Corolla	1984–88	96.8 (1587)	4A-C	4-1.6L	SOHC	8
Corolla (Diesel)	1984–85	112.2 (1839)	1C	4-1.8L	SOHC	8
Corolla	1985–90	96.8 (1587)	4A-GE	4-1.6L	DOHC	16
Corolla	1989–90	96.8 (1587)	4A-F, 4A-FE	4-1.6L	DOHC	16
Tercel	1984–88	88.6 (1452)	3A-C, 3A	4-1.5L	SOHC	8
Tercel	1987–90	88.9 (1457)	3E, 3E-E	4-1.5L	SOHC	12
MR2	1985–89	96.8 (1587)	4A-GE	4-1.6L	DOHC	16
MR2	1988–89	96.8 (1587)	4A-GZE ①	4-1.6L	DOHC	16

SOHC—Single overhead camshaft
DOHC—Double overhead camshaft
① Supercharged

Sometimes the air filter can be cleaned with low pressure compressed air

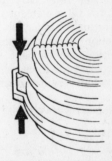

Installing air filter element in the correct position

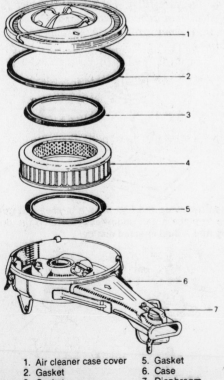

1. Air cleaner case cover
2. Gasket
3. Gasket
4. Cleaner element
5. Gasket
6. Case
7. Diaphragm

Air cleaner assembly

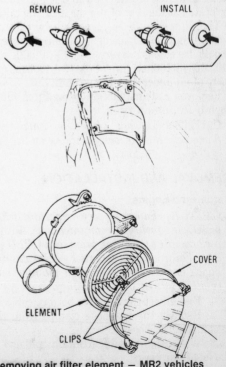

REMOVE   INSTALL

COVER

ELEMENT

CLIPS

Removing air filter element — MR2 vehicles

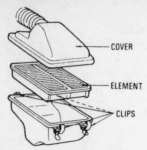

Corollas with a diesel engine use a slightly different air filter than other models. cleaning procedures are still the same

REMOVAL AND INSTALLATION

1. Unfasten the wing nut and/or clips that retain the air filter element cover. Remove the cover and air filter element. On MR2 vehicles it is necessary to remove the rear luggage side trim panel.

2. Clean out the filter case (air cleaner) with a rag. Fit the filter element into the air cleaner. Make certain (filter usually marked for correct installation) it is not upside down. Double check that the element is properly seated; if it is crooked, the cover won't seat and air leaks will admit unfiltered air into the motor.

3. Installation is the reverse of the removal procedures.

Fuel Filter

The replaceable fuel filter is in the fuel line, either mounted on the firewall under the hood or located at the rear of the car near the tank.

The filter should be inspected for external damage and/or leakage at least once a year; it should be changed every 25,000–30,000 mile (40,200–48,200km) intervals (24 months) or more often under dry, dusty conditions.

Removal and installation procedures differ slightly for certain years.

CAUTION: *Do not smoke or have open flame near the car when working on the fuel system.*

REMOVAL AND INSTALLATION

Carbureted Engine

CAUTION: *Safety is very important when preforming fuel system maintenance. Always perform this service operation on a COLD engine. Failure to conduct fuel system maintenance and repairs in a safe manner may result in serious personal injury.*

1. Disconnect the negative battery cable.
2. Remove the gas hose clamps from the inlet and outlet hoses.
3. Work the hoses off (contain spillage) of the fuel filter necks.

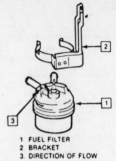

1. FUEL FILTER
2. BRACKET
3. DIRECTION OF FLOW

Fuel filter and mounting bracket — carbureted engine

4. Snap the filter out of its bracket and replace it with a new one. Replace the gas line hose or clamps as necessary.

NOTE: *The arrow on the fuel filter MUST always point toward the carburetor.*

5. Installation of the remaining components is in the reverse order of removal. Run the engine for a few minutes and check the fuel filter for any leaks.

Fuel Injected Engine

CAUTION: *Safety is very important when preforming fuel system maintenance. Always perform this service operation on a COLD engine. The fuel system is under pressure — fuel pressure must be released before removing the fuel filter. Failure to conduct fuel system maintenance and repairs in a safe manner may result in serious personal injury.*

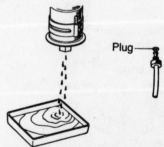

Plug

When removing the fuel lines it is always a good idea to place a pan underneath to catch the dripping fuel — fuel injected engine

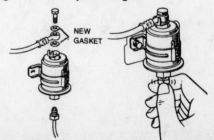

NEW GASKET

Hand tighten the fuel inlet line — fuel injected engine

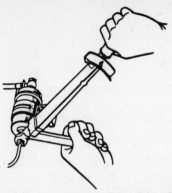

A torque wrench is essential when tightening the fuel lines to the fuel filter — fuel injected engine

1. Disconnect the negative battery cable. Unbolt the retaining screws and remove the protective shield for the fuel filter (if so equipped).

2. Place a pan under the delivery pipe (large connection) to catch the dripping fuel and SLOWLY loosen the union bolt to bleed off the fuel pressure.

3. Remove the union bolt and drain the remaining fuel.

4. Disconnect and plug the inlet line.

5. Unbolt and remove the fuel filter.

NOTE: *When tightening the fuel line bolts to the fuel filter, you must use a torque wrench. The tightening torque is very important, as under or over tightening may cause fuel leakage. Insure that there is no fuel line interference and that there is sufficient clearance between it and any other parts.*

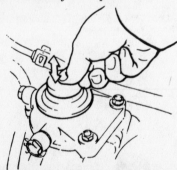

When replacing the diesel fuel filter, always use the priming pump to fill the filter with fuel before starting the engine

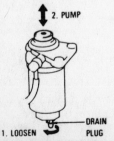

2. PUMP

1. LOOSEN   DRAIN PLUG

When draining water from the diesel fuel filter, turn the drain plug counterclockwise

6. Coat the flare nut, union nut and bolt threads with engine oil.

7. Hand tighten the inlet line to the fuel filter.

8. Install the fuel filter and then tighten the inlet bolt to 23–33 ft. lbs.

9. Reconnect the delivery pipe using new gaskets and then tighten the union bolt to 18–25 ft. lbs.

10. Run the engine for a few minutes and check for any fuel leaks.

11. Install the protective shield (if so equipped).

Diesel Engine

CAUTION: *Safety is very important when preforming fuel system maintenance. Failure to conduct fuel system maintenance and repairs in a safe manner may result in serious personal injury. Review the complete service procedure before starting this repair.*

1. Disconnect the negative battery cable. Disconnect the fuel level warning switch connector at the lower end of the filter.

2. Drain the fuel from the filter, loosen the two mounting bolts and remove the filter assembly from the vehicle.

3. Remove the water level warning switch from the filter housing and then unscrew the filter from the housing. An oil filter strap wrench may come in handy when removing the filter.

4. Install the water level warning switch using a new O-ring.

5. Coat the filter gasket lightly with diesel fuel and then screw it in hand tight. DO NOT use a wrench to tighten the fuel filter.

6. Mount the filter assembly, tighten the bolts and connect the warning switch.

7. Using the priming pump on top of the filter, fill the filter with fuel and check for leaks.

DRAINING DIESEL FUEL FILTER SYSTEM

NOTE: *When the fuel filter warning light or buzzer comes on, the water in the fuel filter must be drained immediately.*

1. Raise the hood and position a small pan or jar underneath the drain plug to catch the water about to be released.

2. Reach under the fuel filter and turn the drain plug counterclockwise about 2–2$\frac{1}{2}$ turns.

NOTE: *Loosening the drain plug more than the suggested amount will cause water to ooze from around the threads of the plug.*

3. Depress the priming pump on top of the filter housing until fuel is the only substance being forced out.

4. Retighten the drain plug by hand only, do not use a wrench.

PCV Valve

SERVICING, REMOVAL AND INSTALLATION

Gasoline Engines Only

The PCV valve regulates crankcase ventilation during various engine operating conditions. Inspect the PCV valve system every 60,000 miles (96,500km) or as needed. At high vacuum (idle speed and partial load range) it will open slightly and at low vacuum (full throttle) it will open fully. This causes vapor to be removed from the crankcase by the engine vacuum and then sucked into the combustion chamber where it is dissipated.

1. Check the ventilation hoses for leaks or clogging. Clean or replace as necessary.

2. Locate the PCV valve in the cylinder head cover or in the manifold-to-crankcase line. Remove it.

3. Blow into the crankcase end of the valve. There should be a free passage of air through the valve.

4. Blow into the intake manifold end of the valve. There should be little or no passage of air through the valve.

5. If the PCV valve failed either of the preceding two checks, it will require replacement.

6. Installation is in the reverse order of removal procedure.

NOTE: *On some models with fuel injection there is no PCV valve. The vapor passage in the ventilation lines is controlled by two orifices.*

To check the PCV system on these models, inspect the hoses for cracks, leaks or other damage. Blow through the orifices to make sure they are not blocked. Replace all components as necessary.

Evaporative Canister and System

SERVICING, REMOVAL AND INSTALLATION

Gasoline Engines Only

Inspect the charcoal canister assembly every 60,000 miles (96,500km) or as needed. Check the fuel and vapor lines and the vacuum hoses for proper connections and correct routing, as well as condition. Replace clogged, damaged or deteriorated parts as necessary.

If the charcoal canister is clogged, (check for clogged filter or stuck check valve) it may be cleaned using low pressure compressed air. When cleaning air should flow through (out the bottom) freely and no charcoal should come out.

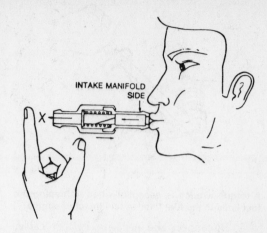

Air should not pass through the PCV valve when blowing through the intake manifold side

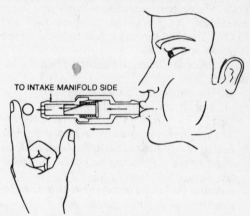

Air should pass through the PCV valve when blowing into the crankcase side

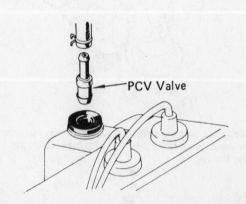

Removing the PCV valve

The canister is removed by unfastening the various hoses form the canister (mark all hoses for correct installation), and removing the mounting bolts from the mounting bracket or loosening the mounting clamp and removing

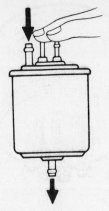

Cleaning the charcoal canister

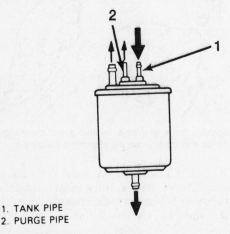

1. TANK PIPE
2. PURGE PIPE

Checking the charcoal canister

the canister. Installation is in the reverse order of removal.

Battery

SPECIFIC GRAVITY TEST (EXCEPT MAINTENANCE FREE BATTERIES)

At least once a year, check the specific gravity of the battery. It should be between 1.20 and 1.26 in.Hg at room temperature.

The specific gravity can be checked with the use of an hydrometer, an inexpensive instrument available from many sources, including auto parts stores. The hydrometer has squeeze bulb at one end and a nozzle at the other. Battery electrolyte is sucked into the hydrometer until the float is lifted from its seat. The specific gravity is then read by noting the position of the float. Generally, if after charging, the specific gravity between any two cells varies more than 50 points (0.050), the battery is bad and should be replaced.

It is not possible to check the specific gravity in this manner on sealed (maintenance free) bat-

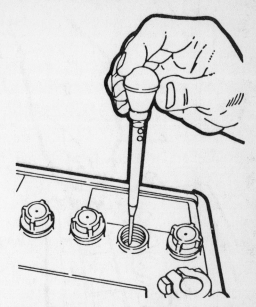

The specific gravity of the battery can be checked with a simple float-type hydrometer

teries. Instead, the indicator built into the top of the case must be relied on to display any signs of battery deterioration. If the indicator is dark, the battery can be assumed to be OK. If the indicator is light, the specific gravity is low, and the battery should be charged or replaced.

SERVICING CABLES AND CLAMPS

Once a year (or as necessary), the battery terminals and the cable clamps should be cleaned. Loosen the clamps and remove the cables, negative cable first. On batteries with posts on top, the use of a puller specially made for the purpose is recommended. These are inexpensive,

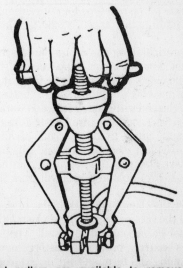

Special pullers are available to remove cable clamps

Clean the battery posts with a wire brush, or the special tool shown

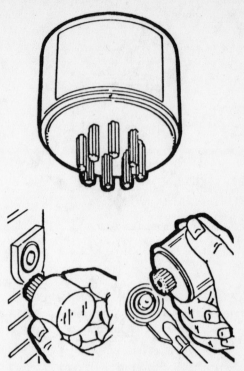

Special tools are also available for cleaning the posts and clamps on side terminal batteries

and available in auto parts stores. Side terminal battery cables are secured with a bolt.

Clean the cable clamps and the battery terminal with a wire brush, until all corrosion, grease, etc., is removed and the metal is shiny. It is especially important to clean the inside of the clamp (use old knife or equivalent) thoroughly, since a small deposit of foreign material or oxidation there will prevent a sound electrical connection and inhibit either starting or charging. Special tools are available for cleaning these parts, one type for conventional batteries and another type for side terminal batteries.

Before installing the cables, loosen the battery holddown clamp or strap, remove the battery and check the battery tray. Clear it of any debris, and check it for soundness (battery tray can be cleaned with baking soda and water solution). Rust should be wire brushed away, and the metal given a couple coats of anti-rust paint. Replace the battery and tighten the holddown clamp or strap securely, but be careful not to over tighten, which will crack the battery case.

After the clamps and terminals are clean, re-install the cables, negative cable last; DO NOT hammer on the clamps to install. Tighten the clamps securely, but do not distort them. Give the clamps and terminals a thin external coat of grease or equivalent after installation, to retard corrosion.

Check the cables at the same time that the terminals are cleaned. If the cable insulation is cracked or broken, or if the ends are frayed, the cable should be replaced with a new cable of the same length and gauge.

NOTE: *Keep flame or sparks away from the battery; it gives off explosive hydrogen gas. Battery electrolyte contains sulfuric acid. If you should splash any on your skin or in your eyes, flush the affected area with plenty of clear water; if it lands in your eyes, get medical help immediately.*

CHECKING FLUID LEVEL

Check the battery electrolyte level at least once a month, or more often in hot weather or during periods of extended car operation. The level can be checked through the case on translucent batteries; the cell caps must be removed on other models. The caps must be removed on other models. The electrolyte level in each cell should be kept filled to the split ring inside, or the line marked on the outside of the case.

If the level is low, add only distilled water, or colorless, odorless drinking water, through the opening until the level is correct. Each cell is completely separate from the others, so each must be checked and filled individually.

If water is added in freezing weather, the car should be driven several miles to allow the

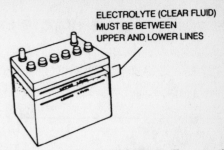

ELECTROLYTE (CLEAR FLUID)
MUST BE BETWEEN
UPPER AND LOWER LINES

Some batteries have level indicator lines on the side

Clean the inside of the clamps with a wire brush, or the special tool

water to mix with the electrolyte. Otherwise, the battery could freeze.

REPLACEMENT

When it becomes necessary to replace the battery, select a battery with a rating equal to or greater than the battery originally installed. Deterioration and just plain aging of the battery cables, starter motor, and associated wires makes the battery's job harder in successive years. The slow increase in electrical resistance over time makes it prudent to install a new battery with a greater capacity than the old. Details on battery removal and installation are covered in Chapter 3.

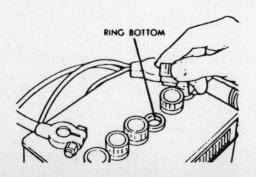

RING BOTTOM

Fill each battery cell to the bottom of the split ring with water

Belts

INSPECTION

Check the condition of the drive belts and check and adjust the belt tension every 10,000–15,000 miles (16,000–24,000km) or 1 year.

1. Inspect the belts for signs of glazing or cracking. A glazed belt will be perfectly smooth from slippage, while a good belt will have a slight texture of fabric visible. Cracks will usually start at the inner edge of the belt and run outward. Replace the belt at the first sign of cracking or if the glazing is severe.

2. By placing your thumb midway between the two pulleys, it should be possible to depress the belt about 1/4–1/2 inch (6–13mm). It is best to use a drive belt tension gauge to check belt tension. If any of the belts can be depressed more than this, or cannot be depressed this much, adjust the tension. Inadequate tension will result in slippage and wear, while excessive tension will damage bearings and cause belts to fray and crack.

3. All drive belts should be replaced every 60,000 miles (96,500km) or as necessary. Drive belts should be replaced for preventive maintenance. It is always best to replace all drive belts at one time during this service operation.

ADJUSTING

Alternator

To adjust the tension of the alternator drive belt on all models, loosen the pivot and mounting bolts on the alternator. Using a wooden hammer handle, a broomstick or your hand, move the alternator one way or the other until the proper tension is achieved. Do not use a screwdriver or any other metal device such as a pry bar, as a lever. Tighten the mounting bolts securely, run the engine about minute, stop the engine then recheck the belt tension.

Air Conditioning Compressor

A/C compressor (always use caution when working near the A/C compressor) belt tension can be adjusted by turning the tension adjusting bolt which is located on the compressor ten-

HOW TO SPOT WORN V-BELTS

V-Belts are vital to efficient engine operation—they drive the fan, water pump and other accessories. They require little maintenance (occasional tightening) but they will not last forever. Slipping or failure of the V-belt will lead to overheating. If your V-belt looks like any of these, it should be replaced.

Cracking or weathering

This belt has deep cracks, which cause it to flex. Too much flexing leads to heat build-up and premature failure. These cracks can be caused by using the belt on a pulley that is too small. Notched belts are available for small diameter pulleys.

Softening (grease and oil)

Oil and grease on a belt can cause the belt's rubber compounds to soften and separate from the reinforcing cords that hold the belt together. The belt will first slip, then finally fail altogether.

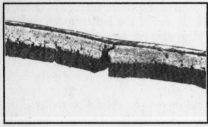

Glazing

Glazing is caused by a belt that is slipping. A slipping belt can cause a run-down battery, erratic power steering, overheating or poor accessory performance. The more the belt slips, the more glazing will be built up on the surface of the belt. The more the belt is glazed, the more it will slip. If the glazing is light, tighten the belt.

Worn cover

The cover of this belt is worn off and is peeling away. The reinforcing cords will begin to wear and the belt will shortly break. When the belt cover wears in spots or has a rough jagged appearance, check the pulley grooves for roughness.

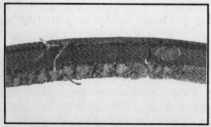

Separation

This belt is on the verge of breaking and leaving you stranded. The layers of the belt are separating and the reinforcing cords are exposed. It's just a matter of time before it breaks completely.

sioner bracket. Turn the bolt clockwise to tighten the belt and counterclockwise to loosen it.

Air Pump

To adjust the tension of the air pump drive belt, loosen the adjusting lever bolt and the pivot bolt. Move the pump in or out until the desired tension is felt.

NOTE: *The tension should be checked between the air pump and the crankshaft pulley on cars without air conditioning. On cars with A/C the tension should be checked between the A/C compressor and the crankshaft pulley.*

Power Steering Pump

Tension on the power steering belt is adjusted by means of an idler pulley (some models may use just a lower adjusting bracket setup — similar to alternator adjustment service procedure). Loosen the lock bolt and turn the adjusting bolt on the idler pulley until the desired tension is felt and then tighten the lock bolt.

REMOVAL AND INSTALLATION

If a belt must be replaced, the driven unit must be loosened and moved to its extreme loosest position, generally by moving it toward the center of the motor. After removing the old

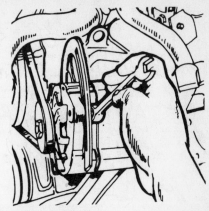

Loosen the pivot bolt

belt, check the pulleys for dirt or built-up material which could affect belt contact. Carefully install the new belt, remembering that it is new and unused — it may appear to be just a little too small to fit over the pulley flanges. Fit the belt over the largest pulley (usually the crankshaft pulley at the bottom center of the motor) first, then work on the smaller one(s). Gentle pressure in the direction of rotation is helpful. Some belts run around a third or idler pulley, which acts as an additional pivot in the belt's path. It may be possible to loosen the idler

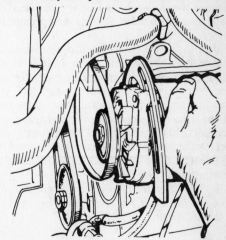

Push the component inwards

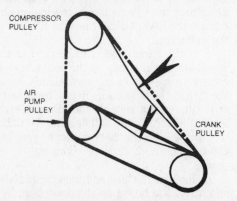

Air pump drive belt tension checking locations with and without A/C

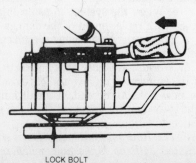

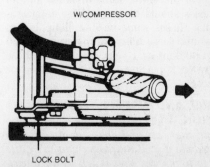

Moving the air pump to tension the drive belt with and without A/C

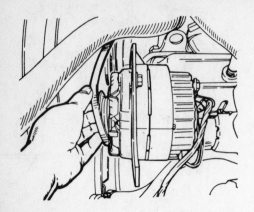

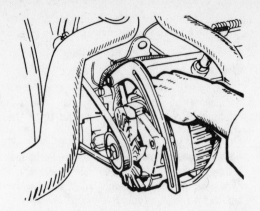

Slip the old belt off and the new one on

Pull outwards to tension the belt

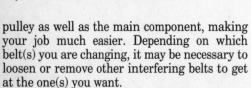

pulley as well as the main component, making your job much easier. Depending on which belt(s) you are changing, it may be necessary to loosen or remove other interfering belts to get at the one(s) you want.

When buying replacement belts, remember that the fit is critical according to the length of the belt, the width of the belt, the depth of the belt and the angle or profile of the V shape (always match up old belt with new belt if possible). The belt shape should exactly match the shape of the pulley; belts that are not an exact match can cause noise, slippage and premature failure.

After the new belt is installed, draw tension on it by moving the driven unit away from the motor and tighten its mounting bolts. This is sometimes a three- or four-handed job; you may find an assistant helpful. Make sure that all the bolts you loosened are retightened and that any other loosened belts also have the correct tension. A new belt can be expected to stretch a bit after installation so be prepared to re-adjust your new belt.

NOTE: *After installing a new belt, run the engine for about 5 minutes and then recheck the belt tension.*

Hoses

The upper and lower radiator hoses and all heater hoses should be checked for deterioration, leaks (hoses sometime swell up before breaking) and loose hose clamps every 15,000 miles (24,000km) or 1 year. Replace the hose clamps when replacing the radiator hose or heater hose.

REMOVAL AND INSTALLATION

CAUTION: *When draining the coolant, keep in mind that cats and dogs are attracted by the ethylene glycol antifreeze, and are quite likely to drink any that is left in an uncovered container or in puddles on the ground.*

This will prove fatal in sufficient quantity. Always drain the coolant into a sealable container. Coolant should be reused unless it is contaminated or several years old.

1. Drain the cooling system. This is always done with the motor COLD. Follow this service procedure:

    a. Remove the radiator cap.

    b. Position the drain pan under the drain cock on the bottom of the radiator. Additionally, some engines have a drain cock on the side of the engine block, near the oil filter. This may be opened to aid in draining the cooling system. If for some reason the radiator drain cock can't be used, you can loosen and remove the lower radiator hose at its joint to the radiator.

    c. If the lower hose is to be used as the drain, loosen the clamp on the hose and slide it back so it's out of the way. Gently break the grip of the hose on its fitting by twisting or prying with a suitable tool. Do not exert too much force or you will damage the radiator fitting. As the hose loosens, you can expect a gush of fluid to come out — be ready!

    d. Remove the hose end from the radiator and direct the hose into the drain pan. You now have fluid running from both the hose and the radiator.

    e. When the system stops draining, proceed with replacement of the damaged hose.

2. Loosen the hose clamps at each end of the hose to be removed.

3. Working the hose back and forth, slide it off its connection remove the old hose. Install the new hose as needed. A small amount of light grease on the inside of the hose end will ease installation.

NOTE: *Radiator and heater hoses should be routed with no kinks and, when installed, should be in the same position as the original. If other than specified hose is used,*

HOW TO SPOT BAD HOSES

Both the upper and lower radiator hoses are called upon to perform difficult jobs in an inhospitable environment. They are subject to nearly 18 psi at under hood temperatures often over 280°F., and must circulate nearly 7500 gallons of coolant an hour—3 good reasons to have good hoses.

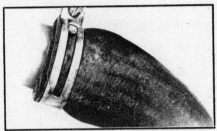

Swollen hose

A good test for any hose is to feel it for soft or spongy spots. Frequently these will appear as swollen areas of the hose. The most likely cause is oil soaking. This hose could burst at any time, when hot or under pressure.

Cracked hose

Cracked hoses can usually be seen but feel the hoses to be sure they have not hardened; a prime cause of cracking. This hose has cracked down to the reinforcing cords and could split at any of the cracks.

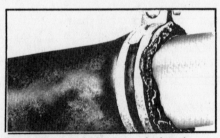

Frayed hose end (due to weak clamp)

Weakened clamps frequently are the cause of hose and cooling system failure. The connection between the pipe and hose has deteriorated enough to allow coolant to escape when the engine is hot.

Debris in cooling system

Debris, rust and scale in the cooling system can cause the inside of a hose to weaken. This can usually be felt on the outside of the hose as soft or thinner areas.

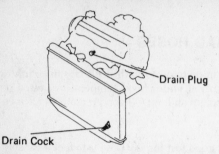

Location of draincocks of the cooling system. never drain hot coolant — wait for the engine to cool

make sure it does not rub against either the engine or the frame while the engine is running, as this may wear a hole in the hose. Contact points may be insulated with a piece of sponge or foam; plastic wire ties are particularly handy for this job.

4. Position the new hose clamps at least 6mm ($1/4$ in.) or more from the end of the hose and tighten them. Make sure that the hose clamps are beyond the bead and placed in the center of the clamping surface before tightening them.

5. Fill the system with coolant. Toyota strongly recommends the coolant mixture be a 50–50 mix of antifreeze and water. This mixture gives best combination of antifreeze and anti-boil characteristics for year-round driving.

6. Install and tighten the radiator cap. Start the engine and check visually for leaks. Allow the engine to warm up fully and continue to check your work for signs of leakage. A very small leak may not be noticed until the system develops internal pressure. Leaks at hose ends are generally clamp related and can be cured by snugging the clamp. Larger leaks may require removing the hose again – to do this you MUST WAIT UNTIL THE ENGINE HAS COOLED DOWN. NEVER UNCAP A HOT RADIATOR. After all leaks are cured, check the coolant level in the radiator (with the engine cold) and fill the coolant level as necessary.

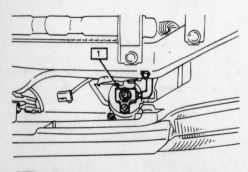

1 SIGHT GLASS

Location of receiver-dryer and sight glass

Air Conditioning System

NOTE: *This book contains simple service procedures for your air conditioning system. More comprehensive testing, diagnosis and service procedures may be found n CHILTON'S GUIDE TO AIR CONDITIONING SERVICE AND REPAIR, available from your local retailer.*

SAFETY PRECAUTIONS

There are two particular hazards associated with air conditioning systems and they both relate to refrigerant gas.

The refrigerant (generic designation: R-12, trade name: Freon, a registered trademark of the DuPont Co.) is an extremely cold substance. When exposed to air, it will instantly freeze any surface it comes in contact with, including your eyes.

The other hazard relates to fire. Although normally non-toxic, refrigerant gas becomes highly poisonous in the presence of an open flame. One good whiff of the vapor formed by refrigerant can be fatal. Keep all forms of fire (including cigarettes) well clear of the air conditioning system.

Further, it is being established that the chemicals in R-12 (dichlorodifluoromethane) contribute to the damage occurring in the upper atmosphere. The time may soon come when sophisticated recovery equipment will be necessary to prevent the release of this gas when working on an air conditioning system.

Most repair work other than servicing (discharge, evacuate and charge) the A/C system, should be left to a professional mechanic (ASE certified) with the proper equipment and related training.

SYSTEM CHECKS

A lot of A/C problems can be avoided by simply running the air conditioner at least once a week, regardless of the season. simply let the system run for at least 5 minutes a week (even in the winter), and you'll keep the internal parts lubricated as well as preventing the hoses from hardening.

Checking For A/C Oil Leaks

Refrigerant leaks show up only as oily areas on the various components because the compressor oil is transported around the entire system along with the refrigerant. Look for oily spots on all the hoses and lines, and especially on the hose and tube connections. If there are oily deposits, the system may have a leak, and you should have it checked by a qualified mechanic.

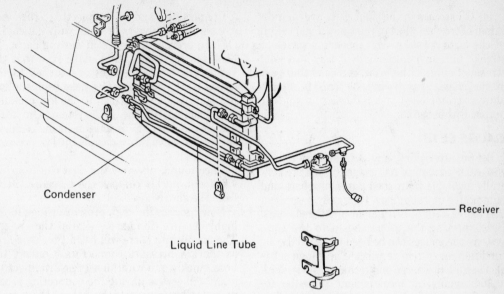

Condenser

Liquid Line Tube

Receiver

Sight glass for checking refrigerant level

Check the A/C Compressor Belt

The compressor drive belt should be checked frequently for tension and condition. Refer to the section in this chapter on "Belts".

Keep the A/C Condenser Clear

The condenser is mounted in front of the radiator (and is often mistaken for the radiator). It serves to remove heat from the air conditioning system and cool the refrigerant. Proper air flow through the condenser is critical to the operation of the system.

Periodically inspect the front of the condenser for bent fins or foreign material (dirt, bugs, leaves, etc.). If any cooling fins are bent, straighten them carefully with needle nose

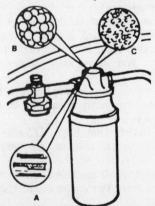

Oil streaks (A), constant bubbles (B) or foam (C) indicate there is not enough refrigerant in the system. Occasional bubbles during initial operation is normal. A clear sight glass indicates a proper charge of refrigerant or no refrigerant at all, which can be determined by the presence of cold air at the outlets in the car

pliers. You can remove any debris with a stiff bristle brush or hose.

A/C Refrigerant Level Check

Factory installed Toyota air conditioners have a sight glass for checking the refrigerant charge. The sight glass is on top of the receiver/drier which is located in the front of the engine compartment, on the right or left side of the condenser assembly (some models are in front of the condenser/some models are located on side of engine compartment) depending upon the vehicle.

NOTE: *If your car is equipped with an aftermarket air conditioner, the following system check may not apply. Contact the manufacturer of the unit for instructions on system checks.*

1. With the engine and the air conditioning system running, look for the flow of refrigerant through the sight glass. If the air conditioner is working properly, you'll be able to see a continuous flow of clear refrigerant through the sight glass, with perhaps an occasional bubble at very high temperatures.

2. Cycle the air conditioner ON and OFF to make sure what you are seeing is refrigerant. Since the refrigerant is clear, it is possible to mistake a completely discharged system for one that is fully charged. Turn the system off and watch the sight glass. If there is refrigerant in the system, you'll see bubbles during the off cycle. If you observe no bubbles when the system is running and the air flow from the unit in the car is delivering cold air, everything is OK.

3. If you observe bubbles in the sight glass while the system is operating, the system is low on refrigerant.

4. Oil streaks in the sight glass are an indication of trouble. Most of the time, if you see oil in the sight glass, it will appear as series of streaks, although occasionally it may be a solid stream of oil. In either case, it means that part of the charge has been lost. This is almost always accompanied by a reduction in cold air output within the car.

GAUGE SETS

Before attempting any A/C service repair, you will need a set of A/C gauges. These are generally available from good parts suppliers and automotive tool suppliers. Generally described, this tool is a set of two gauges and three hoses. By connecting the proper hoses to the car's system, the gauges can be used to "see" the air conditioning system at work. The gauge set is also used to discharge and recharge the system.

Additionally, if a component must be removed from the system, a vacuum pump will be needed to evacuate (draw vacuum) within the system to eliminate any moisture which has entered during repairs. These pumps can be purchased outright; many find it easier to rent one from a supplier on an as-needed basis.

Small cans of refrigerant will be needed; make sure you purchase enough to meet the capacity of the A/C system.

DISCHARGING THE SYSTEM

CAUTION: *Always wear protective goggles and gloves before proceeding with this service procedure.*

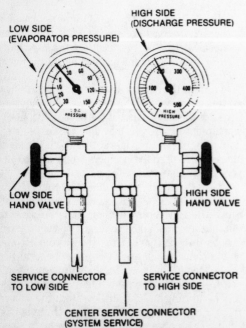

Manifold gauges for the air conditioning system

Connecting and disconnecting the A/C gauges should always be done with the engine OFF to prevent injury from moving parts. To hook up the gauges, first make sure that the valves on the A/C gauges are turned to the closed (OFF) position. The hose from the low pressure gauge will attach to the low pressure side (suction) of the A/C system. On latter models the letter "S" is mark near the compressor service valve this indicates the low pressure side.

Once found, unscrew the dust cap from the valve and quickly connect the threaded fitting from the gauge hose.

Now connect the high pressure gauge to the high pressure (discharge) side of the system. The connecting ports will be in the same area as the low pressure connectors. Connect the hose quickly and carefully. Pressurized refrigerant will escape during the connecting procedure. On latter models the letter "D" is mark near the compressor service valve this indicates the high pressure side.

To discharge the air conditioning system install the A/C gauge set and follow this service procedure as follows:

1. Place the center hose of the gauge set into a container.

2. Slowly open the valve on the low pressure gauge to allow refrigerant to flow into the container. You should just hear a light hissing, indicating a slow discharge from the system. If you empty the system too quickly you will drain the lubricating oil as well. This oil is critical to the system's well being and replacing it is not within the scope of this book. If no discharge occurs, first check for proper hose hookup. If all checks of your hook-up are OK, you may be attempting to discharge an already empty system.

3. Close the gauge valve when the gauge indicates zero pressure in the system. There should be very little, if any, oil in your drainage container. You have now discharged the system.

If you wish to thoroughly evacuate the system (vacuum pump needed), follow the lettered steps below.

a. Confirm that high "D" side and low "S" side pressure hoses are correctly attached and secure on their fittings. Confirm that gauge valves are closed. Connect the center hose from the gauge set to the vacuum pump.

b. Start the vacuum pump, then open both gauge valves slowly and at the same time.

c. Run the pump until the low pressure gauge shows 28 in. Hg of vacuum. Note the time that 28 in. Hg is reached; if the temper-

Troubleshooting Basic Air Conditioning Problems

Problem	Cause	Solution
There's little or no air coming from the vents (and you're sure it's on)	• The A/C fuse is blown • Broken or loose wires or connections • The on/off switch is defective	• Check and/or replace fuse • Check and/or repair connections • Replace switch
The air coming from the vents is not cool enough	• Windows and air vent wings open • The compressor belt is slipping • Heater is on • Condenser is clogged with debris • Refrigerant has escaped through a leak in the system • Receiver/drier is plugged	• Close windows and vent wings • Tighten or replace compressor belt • Shut heater off • Clean the condenser • Check system • Service system
The air has an odor	• Vacuum system is disrupted • Odor producing substances on the evaporator case • Condensation has collected in the bottom of the evaporator housing	• Have the system checked/repaired • Clean the evaporator case • Clean the evaporator housing drains
System is noisy or vibrating	• Compressor belt or mountings loose • Air in the system	• Tighten or replace belt; tighten mounting bolts • Have the system serviced

Sight glass condition
  Constant bubbles, foam or oil streaks
  Clear sight glass, but no cold air
  Clear sight glass, but air is cold
  Clouded with milky fluid
	
	• Undercharged system
	
	• No refrigerant at all
	• System is OK
	• Receiver drier is leaking dessicant
		
		• Charge the system
		
		• Check and charge the system
		
		• Have system checked

Large difference in temperature of lines	• System undercharged	• Charge and leak test the system
Compressor noise	• Broken valves • Overcharged • Incorrect oil level • Piston slap • Broken rings • Drive belt pulley bolts are loose	• Replace the valve plate • Discharge, evacuate and install the correct charge • Isolate the compressor and check the oil level. Correct as necessary. • Replace the compressor • Replace the compressor • Tighten with the correct torque specification
Excessive vibration	• Incorrect belt tension • Clutch loose • Overcharged • Pulley is misaligned	• Adjust the belt tension • Tighten the clutch • Discharge, evacuate and install the correct charge • Align the pulley
Condensation dripping in the passenger compartment	• Drain hose plugged or improperly positioned • Insulation removed or improperly installed	• Clean the drain hose and check for proper installation • Replace the insulation on the expansion valve and hoses
Frozen evaporator coil	• Faulty thermostat • Thermostat capillary tube improperly installed • Thermostat not adjusted properly	• Replace the thermostat • Install the capillary tube correctly • Adjust the thermostat
Low side low—high side low	• System refrigerant is low • Expansion valve is restricted	• Evacuate, leak test and charge the system • Replace the expansion valve
Low side high—high side low	• Internal leak in the compressor—worn	• Remove the compressor cylinder head and inspect the compressor. Replace the valve plate assembly if necessary. If the compressor pistons, rings or

Troubleshooting Basic Air Conditioning Problems (cont.)

Problem	Cause	Solution
Low side high—high side low (cont.)		cylinders are excessively worn or scored replace the compressor
	• Cylinder head gasket is leaking	• Install a replacement cylinder head gasket
	• Expansion valve is defective	• Replace the expansion valve
	• Drive belt slipping	• Adjust the belt tension
Low side high—high side high	• Condenser fins obstructed	• Clean the condenser fins
	• Air in the system	• Evacuate, leak test and charge the system
	• Expansion valve is defective	• Replace the expansion valve
	• Loose or worn fan belts	• Adjust or replace the belts as necessary
Low side low—high side high	• Expansion valve is defective	• Replace the expansion valve
	• Restriction in the refrigerant hose	• Check the hose for kinks—replace if necessary
	• Restriction in the receiver/drier	• Replace the receiver/drier
	• Restriction in the condenser	• Replace the condenser
Low side and high side normal (inadequate cooling)	• Air in the system	• Evacuate, leak test and charge the system
	• Moisture in the system	• Evacuate, leak test and charge the system

ature is above 85°F (29°C), run the pump another 30 minutes. If the temperature is below 85°F (29°C), run the pump another 50 minutes. The target value of 28 in. Hg of vacuum is valid at or close to sea level. For every 1000 feet (305m) of altitude in your area, reduce the expected reading by 1 in. Hg of vacuum. Example: At 2000 feet (610m) above sea level, you would expect a reading of 26 in. Hg of vacuum.

d. When the pump has been run for the proper period of time, and the proper gauge readings have been maintained, close both gauge valves and shut off the pump. Disconnect the hose from the vacuum pump. The air conditioning system has now been evacuated and sealed. A system which is not leaking should hold this vacuum with the pump off.

CHARGING THE SYSTEM

NOTE: *The refrigerant capacities are 1.3–1.7 lbs. for Corolla, Tercel and MR2 vehicles. Always look on the top of the A/C compressor for a service label that has the refrigerant capacity — use that amount listed if different than above.*

1. Confirm that the high "D" side and low "S" side pressure hoses are correctly connected and secure on their fittings. Confirm that the gauge valves are closed.

2. Attach the center hose to the R-12 refrigerant source, usually a 16 oz. (473mL) can.

Make sure the control valve for the can is closed before connecting.

3. Hang or position the can so that it stays upright during the remaining procedures. DO NOT turn the can upside down or on its side during charging. Severe damage to the system can occur.

4. Open the low pressure valve; make sure the high pressure valve is firmly closed.

5. Start the engine, and set the blower fan on top speed with the air conditioning controls ON and set for maximum cooling. Run the engine at 1000 rpm and begin filling the system. Determine the total weight (in pounds or ounces) delivered into the A/C system. DO NOT exceed the specified charge weight. The refrigerant charge weight is 1.3–1.7 lbs. for Corolla, Tercel and MR2 vehicles.

6. Change cans as necessary to achieve the correct total. Remember to shut off the can control valve before changing the can. When the correct weight has been delivered into the system, shut off the can control valve. Run the engine for an additional 30 seconds to clear the lines and gauges.

7. With the engine running, disconnect the low pressure "S" side hose from the connecting port. Then disconnect the high pressure "D" side; hold the fitting down and unscrew it rapidly to avoid loss of refrigerant.

CAUTION: *Never disconnect any gauge hose at any fitting except the connecting port. Sudden loss of refrigerant could result!*

8. Replace the protective dust caps on the line fittings and shut off the engine.

Windshield Wipers

For maximum effectiveness and longest element life, the windshield and wiper blades should be kept clean. Dirt, tree sap, road tar and so on will cause streaking, smearing and blade deterioration if left on the glass. It is advisable to wash the windshield carefully with a commercial glass cleaner at least once a month. Wipe off the rubber blades with the wet rag afterwards. Do not attempt to move the wipers back and forth by hand; damage to the motor and drive mechanism will result.

If the blades are found to be cracked, broken or torn, they should be replaced immediately. Replacement intervals will vary with usage, although deterioration usually limits blade life to about one year. If the wiper pattern is smeared or streaked, or if the blade chatters across the glass, the blades should be replaced. It is easiest and most sensible to replace them in pairs.

There are basically three different types of wiper blade refills, which differ in their method of replacement. One type has two release buttons, approximately $1/3$ of the way up from the ends of the blade frame. Pushing the buttons down releases a lock and allows the rubber blade to be removed from the frame. The new blade slides back into the frame and locks into place.

The second type of refill has two metal tabs which are unlocked by squeezing them together. The rubber blade can then be withdrawn from the frame jaws. A new one is installed by inserting it into the front frame jaws and sliding it rearward to engage the remaining frame jaws. There are usually four jaws; when installing, be certain that the refill is engaged in all of them. At the end of its travel, the tabs

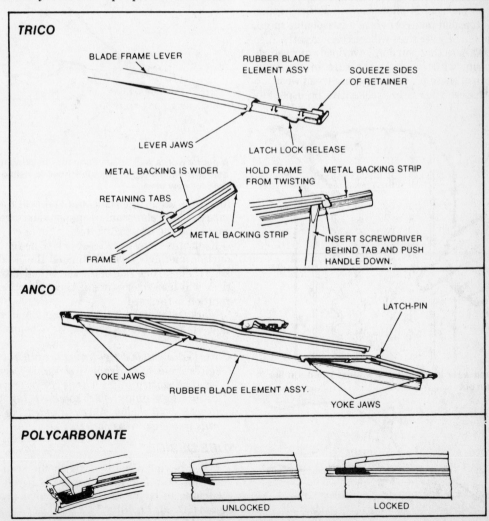

The three types of wiper element retention

will lock into place on the front jaws of the wiper blade frame.

The third type is a refill made from polycarbonate. The refill has a simple locking device at one end which flexes downward out of the groove into which the jaws of the holder fit, allowing easy release. By sliding the new refill through all the jaws and pushing through the slight resistance when it reaches the end of its travel, the refill will lock into position.

Regardless of the type of refill used, make sure that all of the frame jaws are engaged as the refill is pushed into place and locked. The metal blade holder and frame will scratch the glass if allowed to touch it.

Tires and Wheels

Common sense and good driving habits will afford maximum tire life. Fast starts, sudden stops and hard cornering are hard on tires and will shorten their useful life span. If you start at normal speeds, allow yourself sufficient time to stop, and take corners at a reasonable speed, the life of your tires will increase greatly. Also make sure that you don't overload your vehicle or run with incorrect pressure in the tires. Both of these practices increase tread wear.

Inspect your tires frequently. Be especially

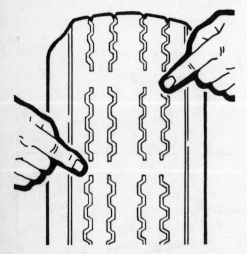

Tread wear indicators will appear when the tire is worn out

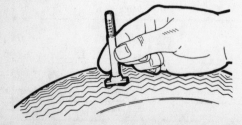

Tread depth can also be checked with an inexpensive gauge

careful to watch for bubbles in the tread or side wall, deep cuts, or under inflation. Remove any tires with bubbles. If the cuts are so deep that they penetrate to the cords, discard the tire. Any cut in the sidewall of a radial tire renders it unsafe. Also look for uneven tread wear patterns that indicate that the front end is out of alignment or that the tires are out of balance.

Store the tires at the proper inflation pressure if they are mounted on wheels. Keep them is a cool dry place, laid on their sides. If the tires are stored in the garage or basement, do not let them stand on a concrete floor; set them on strips of wood.

TIRE ROTATION

So that the tires wear more uniformly, it is recommended that the tires be rotated every 7,500 miles (12,000km) — NEVER USE COMPACT SPARE TIRE OTHER THAN FOR TEMPORARY USE! This can only be done when all

A penny works well as anything for checking tread depth; when the top of Lincoln's head is visible, it's time for new tires

four tires are of the same size and load rating capacity. Any abnormal wear should be investigated and the cause corrected.

Radial tires may be cross-switched; newer production methods have eliminated the need to keep them on one side of the car. Studded snow tires will lose their studs if their direction of rotation is reversed.

Mark the wheel position or direction of rotation on radial studded snow tires before removal.

NOTE: *Avoid overtightening the lug nuts or the brake disc or drum may become permanently distorted. Alloy wheels can be cracked by overtightening. The specified lug nut torque is 76 ft. lbs. Always tighten the lug nuts in a criss-cross pattern.*

TIRE DESIGN

When buying new tires, you should keep the following points in mind, especially if you are switching to larger tires or a different profile series (50, 60, 70, 78):

1. All four tires should be of the same construction type. Radial, bias, or bias-belted tires

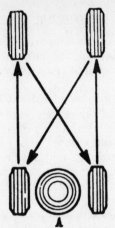 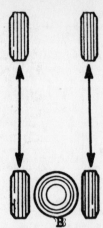

Tire rotation patterns "A" is recommended "B" is acceptable. Note that the spare tire is not used in the rotation

should NOT BE MIXED. Radial tires are highly recommended for their excellent handling and fuel mileage characteristics.

2. The wheels must be the correct width for the tire. Tire dealers have charts of tire and wheel compatibility. A mismatch can cause sloppy handling and rapid tread wear. The tread width should match the rim width (inside bead to inside bead) within 25mm (1 in.). For radial tires the rim width should be 80% or less of the tire (not tread) width. The illustration gives an example of a tire size designation number.

3. The height (mounted diameter) of the new tires can change speedometer accuracy, engine speed per given road speed, fuel mileage, acceleration, and ground clearance.

4. Most models use a space-saving spare tire mounted on a special wheel. This wheel and tire is for EMERGENCY USE ONLY. Never try to mount a regular tire on a special spare wheel.

5. There shouldn't be any body interference when the car is loaded, on bumps or in turning through maximum range.

TIRE INFLATION

The importance of proper tire inflation cannot be overemphasized. A tire employs air under pressure as part of its structure. It is designed around the supporting strength of air at a specified pressure. For this reason, improper inflation drastically reduces the tire's ability to perform as it was intended. A tire will lose some air in day-to-day use; having to add a few pounds of air periodically is not necessarily a sign of a leaking tire.

Tire pressures should be checked regularly with a reliable pressure gauge. Too often the gauge on the end of the air hose at your corner garage or service station is not accurate enough because it suffers too much abuse. Always check tire pressure when the tires are cold, as pressure increases with temperature. If you

METRIC TIRE SIZES

P 155   80 R 13

TIRE TYPE
P - PASSENGER
T - TEMPORARY
C - COMMERCIAL

ASPECT RATIO
$\frac{(SECTION\ HEIGHT)}{(SECTION\ WIDTH)} \times 100$
70
75
80

RIM DIAMETER
(INCHES)
12
13
14

SECTION WIDTH
(MILLIMETERS)
145
155
ETC.

CONSTRUCTION TYPE
R - RADIAL
B - BIAS-BELTED
D - DIAGONAL (BIAS)

SECTION
WIDTH

SECTION
HEIGHT

Common (P-Metric) tire coding. A performance code such as H or V may appear before the R; the designation M+S may appear at the end of the code to indicate a snow or all season tire

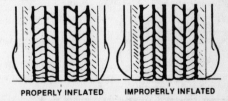

PROPERLY INFLATED   IMPROPERLY INFLATED

RADIAL TIRE

Radial tires have a characteristic sidewall bulge; don't try to measure the air pressure by looking at the tire. Always use a quality air gauge

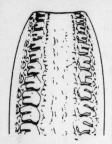

• DRIVE WHEEL HEAVY
  ACCELERATION
• OVERINFLATION

• HARD CORNERING
• UNDERINFLATION
• LACK OF ROTATION

Examples of inflation-related tire wear patterns. As little as two pounds under the specification can induce premature wear

must move the vehicle to check the tire inflation, do not drive more than 1 mile (1.6km) before checking. A cold tire is one that has not been driven for a period of couple hours.

Never exceed the maximum tire pressure embossed on the tire! This maximum pressure is rarely the correct pressure for everyday driving. Consult your owners' manual for the proper tire pressures for your vehicle.

P-metric radial tires – e.g., **P**175R-13 – are designed to be run at maximum inflation pressure at all times. Check the maximum pressure embossed on the tire sidewall.

CARE OF SPECIAL WHEELS

If you have invested money in magnesium, aluminum alloy or sport wheels, special precautions should be taken to make sure your investment is not wasted and that your special wheels look good for the lifetime of the car.

Special wheels are easily scratched and/or damaged. Occasionally check the rims for cracking, impact damage or air leaks. If any of these are found, replace the wheel. In order to prevent this type of damage, and the costly replacement of a special wheel, observe the following precautions:

• Use extra care not to damage the wheels during removal, installation, balancing, etc. After removal of the wheels from the car, place them on a mat or other protective surface. If they are to be stored for any length of time, support them on strips of wood. Never store tires upright – the tread will develop flat spots.

• While driving, watch for sharp obstacles.

• When washing, use a mild detergent and water. Avoid cleansers with abrasives or the use of hard brushes. There are many cleaners and polishes for special wheels. Use them.

• If possible, remove your special wheels from the car during the winter months. Salt

Troubleshooting Basic Wheel Problems

Problem	Cause	Solution
The car's front end vibrates at high speed	• The wheels are out of balance • Wheels are out of alignment	• Have wheels balanced • Have wheel alignment checked/adjusted
Car pulls to either side	• Wheels are out of alignment • Unequal tire pressure • Different size tires or wheels	• Have wheel alignment checked/adjusted • Check/adjust tire pressure • Change tires or wheels to same size
The car's wheel(s) wobbles	• Loose wheel lug nuts • Wheels out of balance • Damaged wheel • Wheels are out of alignment • Worn or damaged ball joint • Excessive play in the steering linkage (usually due to worn parts) • Defective shock absorber	• Tighten wheel lug nuts • Have tires balanced • Raise car and spin the wheel. If the wheel is bent, it should be replaced • Have wheel alignment checked/adjusted • Check ball joints • Check steering linkage • Check shock absorbers
Tires wear unevenly or prematurely	• Incorrect wheel size • Wheels are out of balance • Wheels are out of alignment	• Check if wheel and tire size are compatible • Have wheels balanced • Have wheel alignment checked/adjusted

Tire Size Comparison Chart

"60 Series"	"70 Series"	"78 Series"	1965–77	"60 Series"	"70 Series"	"80 Series"
"Letter" sizes			**Inch Sizes**	**Metric-inch Sizes**		
		Y78-12	5.50-12, 5.60-12 6.00-12	165/60-12	165/70-12	155-12
		W78-13	5.20-13	165/60-13	145/70-13	135-13
		Y78-13	5.60-13	175/60-13	155/70-13	145-13
			6.15-13	185/60-13	165/70-13	155-13, P155/80-13
A60-13	A70-13	A78-13	6.40-13	195/60-13	175/70-13	165-13
B60-13	B70-13	B78-13	6.70-13 6.90-13	205/60-13	185/70-13	175-13
C60-13	C70-13	C78-13	7.00-13	215/60-13	195/70-13	185-13
D60-13	D70-13	D78-13	7.25-13			
E60-13	E70-13	E78-13	7.75-13			195-13
			5.20-14	165/60-14	145/70-14	135-14
			5.60-14	175/60-14	155/70-14	145-14
			5.90-14			
A60-14	A70-14	A78-14	6.15-14	185/60-14	165/70-14	155-14
	B70-14	B78-14	6.45-14	195/60-14	175/70-14	165-14
	C70-14	C78-14	6.95-14	205/60-14	185/70-14	175-14
D60-14	D70-14	D78-14				
E60-14	E70-14	E78-14	7.35-14	215/60-14	195/70-14	185-14
F60-14	F70-14	F78-14, F83-14	7.75-14	225/60-14	200/70-14	195-14
G60-14	G70-14	G77-14, G78-14	8.25-14	235/60-14	205/70-14	205-14
H60-14	H70-14	H78-14	8.55-14	245/60-14	215/70-14	215-14
J60-14	J70-14	J78-14	8.85-14	255/60-14	225/70-14	225-14
L60-14	L70-14		9.15-14	265/60-14	235/70-14	
	A70-15	A78-15	5.60-15	185/60-15	165/70-15	155-15
B60-15	B70-15	B78-15	6.35-15	195/60-15	175/70-15	165-15
C60-15	C70-15	C78-15	6.85-15	205/60-15	185/70-15	175-15
	D70-15	D78-15				
E60-15	E70-15	E78-15	7.35-15	215/60-15	195/70-15	185-15
F60-15	F70-15	F78-15	7.75-15	225/60-15	205/70-15	195-15
G60-15	G70-15	G78-15	8.15-15/8.25-15	235/60-15	215/70-15	205-15
H60-15	H70-15	H78-15	8.45-15/8.55-15	245/60-15	225/70-15	215-15
J60-15	J70-15	J78-15	8.85-15/8.90-15	255/60-15	235/70-15	225-15
	K70-15		9.00-15	265/60-15	245/70-15	230-15
L60-15	L70-15	L78-15, L84-15	9.15-15			235-15
	M70-15	M78-15				255-15
		N78-15				

Note: Every size tire is not listed and many size comparisons are approximate, based on load ratings. Wider tires than those supplied new with the vehicle, should always be checked for clearance.

Troubleshooting Basic Tire Problems

Problem	Cause	Solution
The car's front end vibrates at high speeds and the steering wheel shakes	• Wheels out of balance • Front end needs aligning	• Have wheels balanced • Have front end alignment checked
The car pulls to one side while cruising	• Unequal tire pressure (car will usually pull to the low side) • Mismatched tires • Front end needs aligning	• Check/adjust tire pressure • Be sure tires are of the same type and size • Have front end alignment checked
Abnormal, excessive or uneven tire wear See "How to Read Tire Wear"	• Infrequent tire rotation • Improper tire pressure • Sudden stops/starts or high speed on curves	• Rotate tires more frequently to equalize wear • Check/adjust pressure • Correct driving habits
Tire squeals	• Improper tire pressure • Front end needs aligning	• Check/adjust tire pressure • Have front end alignment checked

and sand used for snow removal can severely damage the finish.

• Make sure that the recommended lug nut torque is never exceeded or the wheel may crack. Never use snow chains on special wheels; severe scratching will occur.

FLUIDS AND LUBRICANTS

Oil and Fuel Recommendations

OIL

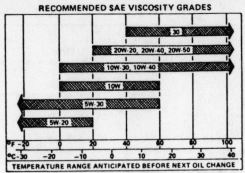

RECOMMENDED SAE VISCOSITY GRADES

TEMPERATURE RANGE ANTICIPATED BEFORE NEXT OIL CHANGE

NOTICE: Do not use SAE 5W-20 oils for continuous high-speed driving.

Oil viscosity chart

The SAE (Society of Automotive Engineers) grade number indicates the viscosity of the engine oil and thus its ability to lubricate at a given temperature. The lower the SAE grade number, the lighter the oil; the lower the viscosity, the easier it is to crank the engine in cold weather.

Oil viscosities should be chosen from those oils recommended for the lowest anticipated temperatures during the oil change interval.

Multi-viscosity oils (10W–30, 20W–50, etc.) offer the important advantage of being adaptable to temperature extremes. They allow easy starting at low temperatures, yet they give good protection at high speeds and engine temperatures. This is a decided advantage in changeable climates or in long distance touring.

The API (American Petroleum Institute) designation indicates the classification of engine oil used under certain given operating conditions. Only oils designated for use "Service SG" should be used. Oils of the SG type perform a variety of functions inside the engine in

addition to their basic functions inside the engine in addition to their basic function as a lubricant. Through a balanced system of metallic detergents and polymeric dispersions, the oil prevents the formation of high and low temperature deposits and also keeps sludge and particles of dirt in suspension. Acids, particularly sulfuric acid, as well as other by-products of combustion, are neutralized. Both the SAE grade number and the API designation can be found on top of the oil can.

Diesel engines also require SG engine oil. In addition, the oil must qualify for a CC rating. The API has a number of different diesel engine ratings, including CB, CC, and CD. Any of these other oils are fine as long as the designation CC appears on the can along with them. Do not use oil labeled only SG or only CC. Both designations must always appear together.

For recommended oil viscosities, refer to the

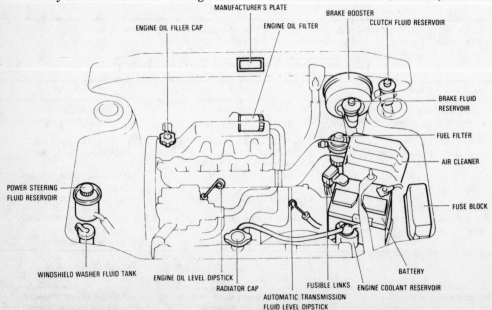

Engine compartment locations — Corolla FWD with diesel engine

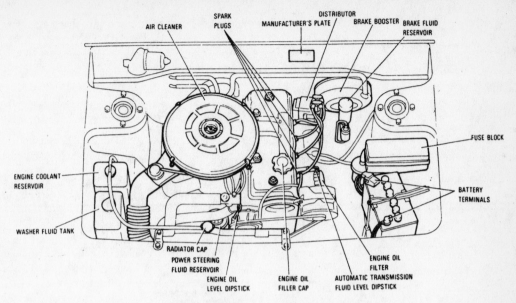

Engine compartment locations — Tercel

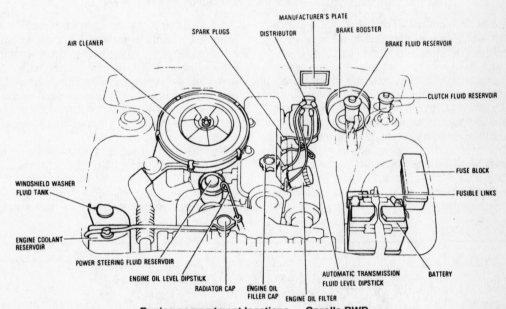

Engine compartment locations — Corolla RWD

chart. Note that 10W–30 and 10W–40 grade oils are not recommended for sustained high speed driving when the temperature rises above the indicated limit.

NOTE: *Non-detergent or straight mineral oils should not be used in your car.*

SYNTHETIC OIL

There are many excellent synthetic and fuel-efficient oils currently available that can provide better gas mileage, longer service life, and in some cases better engine protection. These benefits do not come without a few hitches, however, the main one being the price of synthetic

oils, which is three or four times the price per quart of conventional oil.

Synthetic oil is not for every car and ever type of driving, so you should consider your engine's condition and your type of driving. Also, check your car's warranty conditions regarding the use of synthetic oils.

Both brand new engines and older, high mileage engines are the wrong candidates for synthetic oil. The synthetic oils are so slippery that they can prevent the proper break-in of new engines; most manufacturer's recommend that you wait until the engine is properly broken in — 5,000 miles (8,046km) — before using synthetic oil. Older engines with wear have a dif-

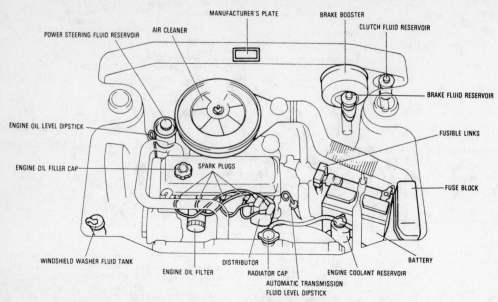

Engine compartment locations — Corolla FWD with gasoline engine

ferent problem with synthetics: they use consume during operation) more oil as they age. Slippery synthetic oils get past these worn parts easily. If your engine is using conventional oil, it will use synthetics much faster. If your car is leaking oil past old seals you'll have a much greater leak problem with synthetics.

Consider your type of driving. If most of your accumulated mileage is high speed, highway type driving, the more expensive synthetic oils may be of benefit. Extended highway driving gives the engine chance to warm up, accumulating less acids in the oil and putting less stress on the engine over the long run. Under

these conditions, the oil change interval can be extended (as long as your oil filter can last the extended life of the oil) up to the advertised mileage claims of the synthetics. Cars with synthetic oils may show increased fuel economy in highway driving, due to less internal friction. However, many automotive experts agree that 50,000 miles (80,465km) is too long to keep any oil in your engine.

Cars used under harder circumstances, such as stop-and-go, city type driving, short trips, or extended idling, should be serviced more frequently. For the engines in these cars, the much greater cost of synthetic or fuel-efficient

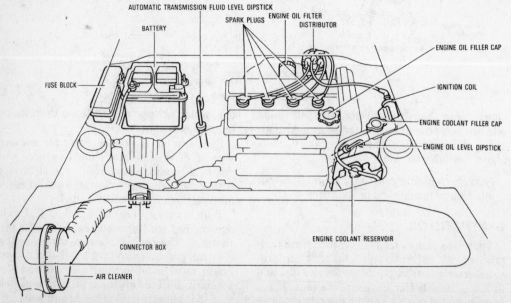

Engine compartment locations — MR2

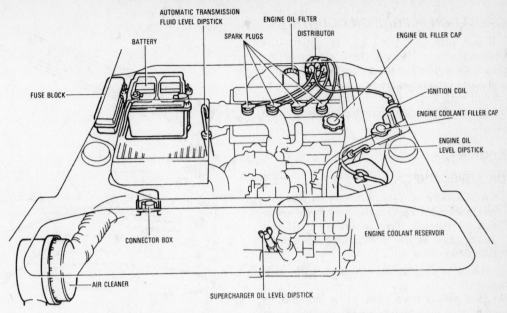

Engine compartment locations — MR2 with supercharged engine

oils may not be worth the investment. Internal wear increases much quicker on these cars, causing greater oil consumption and leakage.

NOTE: *The mixing of conventional and synthetic oils is NOT recommended. If you are using synthetic oil, it might be wise to carry 2 or 3 quarts with you no matter where you drive, as not all service stations carry this type of lubricant.*

FUEL

All Corolla, Tercel and MR2 vehicles (except Corolla diesel) are designed to run on unleaded fuel. The use of leaded fuel in a car requiring unleaded fuel will plug the catalytic converter (NEVER USE LEADED FUEL IN UNLEAD VEHICLE), rendering it inoperative and will increase exhaust back-pressure to the point where engine output will be severely reduced. In all cases, the minimum octane rating of the fuel used must be at least Research Octane No. 91 (octane rating 87) or higher. All unleaded fuels sold in the U.S. are required to meet this minimum octane rating.

The use of a fuel too low in octane (a measurement of anti-knock quality) will result in spark knock. Since many factors affect operating efficiency, such as altitude, terrain, air temperature and humidity, knocking may result even though the recommended fuel is being used. If persistent knocking occurs, it may be necessary to switch to a higher grade of fuel. Continuous or heavy knocking may result in engine damage.

NOTE: *Your engine's fuel requirement can change with time, mainly due to carbon buildup, which changes the compression ratio. If your engine pings, knocks or runs on, switch to a higher grade of fuel. Sometimes just changing brands will cure the problem. If it becomes necessary to retard the timing from specifications, don't change it more than a few degrees. Retarded timing will reduce power output and fuel mileage and will increase the engine temperature.*

Corolla Diesels require the use of diesel fuel. At no time should gasoline be substituted. Two grades of diesel fuel are manufactured, #1 and #2, although #2 grade is generally more available. Better fuel economy results from the use of #2 grade fuel. In some northern parts of the U.S. and in most parts of Canada, #1 grade fuel is available in the winter or a winterized blend of #2 grade is supplied in winter months. When the temperature falls below 20°F (−7°C), #1 grade or winterized #2 grade fuel are the only fuels that can be used. Cold temperatures cause unwinterized #2 to thicken (it actually gels), blocking the fuel lines and preventing the engine from running.

DIESEL CAUTIONS:
• Do not use home heating oil in your car.
• Do not use ether or starting assist fluids in your car.
• Do not use any fuel additives recommended for use in gasoline engines.

It is normal that the engine noise level is louder during the warm-up period in winter. It is also normal that whitish-blue smoke may be emitted from the exhaust after starting and during warm-up. The amount of smoke depends upon the outside temperature.

OPERATION IN FOREIGN COUNTRIES

If you plan to drive your car outside the United States or Canada, there is a possibility that fuels will be too low in anti-knock quality and could produce engine damage. It is wise to consult with local authorities upon arrival in a foreign country to determine the best fuels available.

Engine

OIL LEVEL CHECK

CAUTION: *Prolonged and repeated skin contact with used engine oil, with no effort to remove the oil, may be harmful. Always follow these simple precautions when handling used motor oil.*

• Avoid prolonged skin contact with used motor oil.

• Remove oil from skin by washing thoroughly with soap and water or waterless hand cleaner. Do not use gasoline, thinners or other solvents.

• Avoid prolonged skin contact with oil-soaked clothing. Every time you stop for fuel, check the engine oil as follows:

1. Park the car on level ground.

2. When checking the oil level it is best for the engine to be at operating temperature, although checking the oil immediately after stopping will lead to a false reading. Wait a few minutes after turning off the engine to allow the oil to drain back into the crankcase.

3. Open the hood and locate the dipstick. Pull the dipstick from its tube, wipe it clean and reinsert it.

4. Pull the dipstick out again and, holding is horizontally, read the oil level. The oil should be between the **F** and **L** or high and low marks on the dipstick. If the oil is below the **L** or low mark, add oil of the proper viscosity through the capped opening on the top of the cylinder head cover. See the "Oil and Fuel Recommendations" chart in this chapter for the proper viscosity and rating of oil to use.

5. Replace the dipstick and check the oil level again after adding any oil. Be careful not to overfill the crankcase. Approximately 1 quart (0.9L) of oil will raise the level from the **L** or low mark to the **F** or high mark. Excess oil will generally be consumed at an accelerated rate.

OIL AND FILTER CHANGE

CAUTION: *Prolonged and repeated skin contact with used engine oil, with no effort to remove the oil, may be harmful. Always follow these simple precautions when handling used motor oil:*

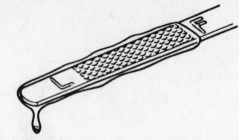

Oil dipstick

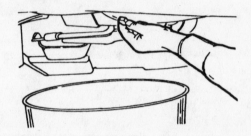

By keeping an inward pressure on the drain plug as you unscrew it, the oil won't escape past the threads

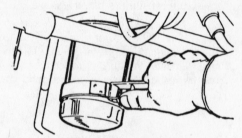

Remove the oil filter with a strap wrench

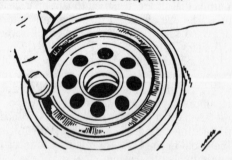

Lubricate the gasket on the new filter with clean engine oil. A dry gasket may not make a good seal and will allow the filter to leak.

• Avoid prolonged skin contact with used motor oil.

• Remove oil from skin by washing thoroughly with soap and water or waterless hand cleaner. Do not use gasoline, thinners or other solvents.

• Avoid prolonged skin contact with oil-soaked clothing.

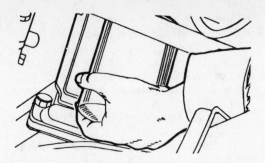

Install the new oil filter by hand

Add oil through the cylinder head cover only

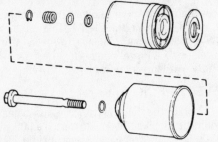

Exploded view of the oil filter used on California diesel engines

Gasoline Engines

NOTE: *All Corolla, Tercel and MR2 vehicles should have the oil changed every 7,500–10,000 miles (12,000–16,000km) or 1 year. Always replace the oil filter when changing the engine oil in the vehicle.*

The oil drain plug is located on the bottom, rear of the oil pan (bottom of the engine, underneath the car — some models are on the side of oil pan).

The mileage figures given are the Toyota recommended intervals assuming normal driving and conditions. If your car is being used under dusty, polluted or off-road conditions (severe driving conditions), change the oil and filter more frequently than specified. The same goes for cars driven in stop-and-go traffic or only for short distances. Always drain the oil after the engine has been running long enough to bring it to normal operating temperature. Hot oil will flow easier and more contaminants will be re-

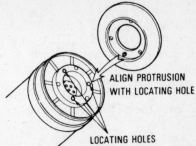

On California diesel engines, always make sure that the protrusion on the new gasket aligns with one of the locating holes on the filter

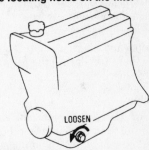

Oil drain plug location

moved along with the oil than if it were drained cold. To change the oil and filter:

1. Run the engine until it reaches normal operating temperature.

2. Jack up the front of the car and support on safety stands.

3. Slide a drain pan of at least 6 quart (5.7L) capacity under the oil pan.

4. Loosen the drain plug. Turn the plug out by hand. By keeping an inward pressure on the plug as you unscrew it, oil won't escape past the threads and you can remove it without being burned by hot oil. The engine oil will be hot. Keep your arms, face and hands away from the oil as it drains out.

5. Allow the oil to drain completely and then install the drain plug. Don't overtighten the plug, or you'll be buying a new pan or a replacement plug for stripped threads.

6. Using a strap wrench, remove the oil filter. Keep in mind that it's holding about 1 quart (0.9L) of dirty, hot oil.

7. Empty the old filter into the drain pan and dispose of the filter.

NOTE: *Please dispose of used motor oil properly. Do not throw it in the trash or pour it on the ground. Take it to your dealer or local service station for recycling.*

8. Using a clean rag, wipe off the filter adaptor on the engine block. Be sure that the rag doesn't leave any lint which could clog an oil passage.

9. Coat the rubber gasket on the filter with fresh oil. Spin it onto the engine by hand; when the gasket touches the adaptor surface give it

another 1/2–3/4 turn. No more, or you'll squash the gasket and it will leak (some oil filters have installation directions about how tight to make the oil filter – follow the directions as necessary).

10. Refill the engine with the correct amount of fresh oil. See the Capacities Chart.

11. Check the oil level on the dipstick. It is normal for the level to be a bit above the full mark. Start the engine and allow it to idle for a few minutes.

NOTE: *Do not run the engine above idle speed until it has built up oil pressure, indicated when the oil light goes out.*

12. Shut off the engine, allow the oil to drain for a minute, and check the oil level. Check around the filter and drain plug for any leaks, and correct as necessary.

Diesel Engine

NOTE: *All Corolla diesel vehicles should have the oil changed every 5,000 miles (8,046km) or 4 months. The mileage figures given are the Toyota recommended intervals assuming normal driving and conditions. If your car is being used under severe driving conditions, change the oil and filter more frequently than specified. Always replace the oil filter when changing the engine oil in the vehicle.*

1. Run the engine until it reaches normal operating temperature.

2. Jack up the front of the car and support on safety stands.

3. Slide a drain pan of at least 6 quart (5.7L) capacity under the oil pan.

4. Loosen the drain plug. Turn the plug out by hand. By keeping an inward pressure on the plug as you unscrew it, oil won't escape past the threads and you can remove it without being burned by hot oil. The engine oil will be hot. Keep your arms, face and hands away from the oil as it drains out.

5. Allow the oil to drain completely and then install the drain plug. Don't overtighten the plug, or you'll be buying a new pan or a replacement plug for stripped threads.

6. Loosen the retaining bolt and pull it out. Remove the oil filter case.

7. Lift off the rubber gasket and then take out the filter element.

NOTE: *Be careful not to lose the rubber washer, washer spring, snap ring and O-ring from inside the oil filter case when removing the filter element.*

8. Using a new rubber gasket, position it on the oil filter element so that the gasket tab aligns with the hole in the element.

9. Install the snapring washer and new

rubber washer into the filter case and then install the new filter element and gasket.

10. Coat the rubber gasket with clean engine oil and install the entire oil filter assembly onto the engine block.

11. Refill the engine with the correct amount of fresh oil. See the Capacities Chart.

12. Check the oil level on the dipstick. It is normal for the level to be a bit above the full mark. Start the engine and allow it to idle for a few minutes.

NOTE: *Do not run the engine above idle speed until it has built up oil pressure, indicated when the oil light goes out.*

13. Shut off the engine, allow the oil to drain for a minute, and check the oil level. Check around the filter and drain plug for any leaks, and correct as necessary.

NOTE: *Please dispose of used diesel motor oil properly. Do not throw it in the trash or pour it on the ground. Take it to your dealer or local service station for recycling.*

Manual Transmission/Transaxle

FLUID RECOMMENDATIONS

All manual transmission/transaxles use API GL-4 or GL-5 (oil grade) SAE 75W–90 or SAE 80W–90 (viscosity). Some 1984–85 Corolla models with a diesel engine use Dexron®II automatic transmission fluid.

LEVEL CHECK

The oil in the manual transmission/transaxle should be checked at least every 15,000 miles (24,000km) and replaced every 25,000–30,000 miles (40,200–48,200km) if necessary.

1. With the car parked on a level surface, remove the filler plug from the side of the transmission/transaxle housing.

2. If the lubricant begins to trickle out of the hole, there is enough. Otherwise, carefully insert your finger (watch out for sharp threads) and check to see if the oil is up to the edge of the hole.

3. If not, add oil through the hole until the level is at the edge of the hole. Most gear lubricants come in a plastic squeeze bottle with a nozzle, making additions simple. You can also use a common everyday kitchen baster.

4. Replace the filler plug.

DRAIN AND REFILL

1. Raise and safely support the vehicle as necessary. The oil must be hot before it is drained. If the car is driven until the engine is at normal operating temperature, the oil should be hot enough.

2. Remove the filler plug to provide a vent.

3. The drain plug is on the bottom of the

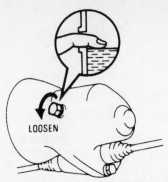

Checking the oil level with your finger — manual transaxle

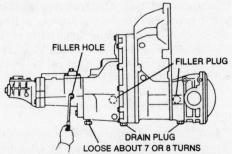

Drain plug and filler plug locations on the 4WD transaxle

transmission/transaxle. Place large container underneath the transmission and remove the plug.

4. Allow the oil to drain completely. Clean off the plug and replace it. Tighten it until it is just snug.

5. Fill the transmission/transaxle with SAE 80 or SAE 80W/90 gear oil (the transaxle on Corollas with a diesel engine uses Dexron®II automatic transmission fluid). This usually comes in a plastic squeeze bulb or use a kitchen baster to squirt the oil in. Refer to the Capacities Chart for the proper amount of oil to put in.

6. The oil level should come up to the top of the filler hole.

7. Replace the filler plug, drive the car for a few minutes, stop, and check for any leaks.

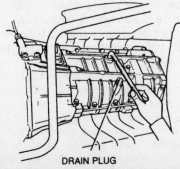

Manual transmission drain plug and filler plug locations

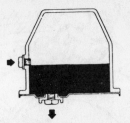

The manual transmission oil level should be up to the bottom of the filler (upper) plug hole

NOTE: *Please dispose of used oil properly. Do not throw it in the trash or pour it on the ground. Take it to your dealer or local service station for recycling.*

Automatic Transmission/ Transaxle

FLUID RECOMMENDATIONS

All automatic transmission/transaxles use ATF Type Dexron®II automatic transmission fluid.

LEVEL CHECK

Check the automatic transmission/transaxle fluid level at least every 15,000 miles (24,000km) (more if possible — check once a month). The dipstick is in the rear of the engine compartment.

The fluid level should be checked only when the transmission is HOT (normal operating temperature). The transmission/transaxle is considered hot after about 20 miles (32km) of highway driving.

1. Park the car on a level surface with the engine idling. Shift the transmission/transaxle into **N** or **P** and set the parking brake.

2. Remove the dipstick, wipe it clean and reinsert it firmly. Be sure that it has been pushed all the way in. Remove the dipstick and check the fluid level while holding it horizontally. With the engine running, the fluid level should be between the second and third notches on the dipstick.

3. If the fluid level is below the second

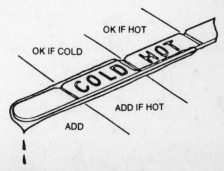

Automatic transmission dipstick

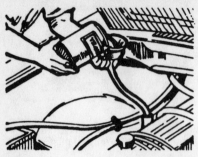

Add automatic transmission fluid through the dipstick tube

notch, add the required type of transmission fluid until the proper level is reached. This is easily done with the aid of a funnel. Check the level often as you are filling the transmission/transaxle. Be extremely careful not to overfill it. Overfilling will cause slippage, seal damage and overheating. Approximately one pint (0.47L) of transmission fluid will raise the level from one notch to the other.

The fluid on the dipstick should always be a bright red color. If it is discolored (brown or black), or smells burnt, serious transmission troubles, probably due to overheating, should be suspected. The transmission should be inspected by a qualified service (ASE certified) technician to locate the cause of the burnt fluid.

DRAIN AND REFILL

The automatic transmission/transaxle fluid should be changed at least every 25,000–30,000 miles (40,200–48,200km). If the car is normally used in severe service, such as stop-and-go driving, trailer towing or the like, the interval should be halve or as necessary. The fluid should be hot before it is drained; a 20 minute drive will accomplish this.

Toyota automatic transmission/transaxles have a drain plug in them so you can remove the plug, drain the fluid, replace the plug and then refill the transmission/transaxle.

1. Raise and safely support the vehicle as necessary. Remove the plug and drain the fluid into a large pan.

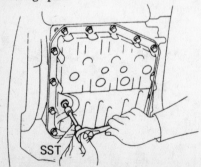

Drain plug location — automatic transaxle vehicle

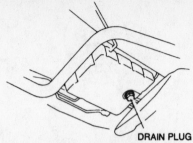

DRAIN PLUG

Drain plug location — automatic transmission vehicle

2. Install the drain plug.
3. It is a good idea to measure the amount of fluid drained from the transmission/transaxle to determine the correct amount of fresh fluid to add. This is because some parts of the transmission may not drain completely and using the dry refill amount specified in the Capacities Chart could lead to overfilling. Fluid is added only through the dipstick tube. Always use the proper type automatic transmission fluid.
4. Add ATF Type Dexron®II automatic transmission fluid (vehicle must be on a level surface when refilling) to the correct level.
5. Replace the dipstick after filling. Start the engine and allow it to idle. DO NOT race the engine.
6. After the engine has idled for a few minutes, shift the transmission slowly through the gears (always hold you foot on the brake pedal) and then return it to Park. With the engine still idling, check the fluid level on the dipstick. If necessary, add more fluid to raise the level to where it is supposed to be.
7. Check the drain plug for transmission fluid leakage. Dispose of used transmission oil properly. Do not throw it in the trash or pour it on the ground. Take it to your dealer or local service station for recycling.

PAN AND FILTER SERVICE

The automatic transmission/transaxle filter should be changed every time the transmission fluid is change. Always replace the transmission/transaxle pan gasket when oil pan is removed. Note location of all transmission/transaxle oil filter (strainer) retaining bolts. Always torque all transmission/transaxle oil pan retaining bolts in progressive steps.

NOTE: *This service operation should be performed with the engine and transmission/transaxle COLD.*

1. Raise and safely support the vehicle as necessary. Remove the plug and drain the fluid. When the fluid stops coming out of the drain hole, loosen the pan retaining screws until the pan can be pulled down at one corner. If the pan is stuck, tap the edges lightly with a plastic

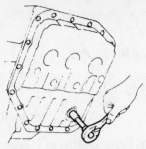

Drain plug location — automatic transaxle vehicle

Oil Strainer
Removing oil filter automatic transaxle vehicle

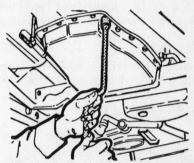

Removing the oil pan on the automatic transmission — automatic transaxle similar

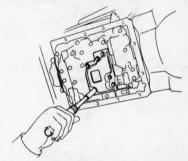

Removing oil filter automatic transmission vehicle

mallet to loosen it; DON't pry it or wedge a screwdriver into the seam. Lower the corner of the pan and allow the remaining fluid to drain out.

2. After the pan has drained completely, remove the pan retaining screws and then remove the pan and gasket.

3. Clean the pan thoroughly and allow it to air dry. If you wipe it out with a rag you run the risk of leaving bits of lint in the pan which will clog the tiny hydraulic passages in the transmission/transaxle.

4. With the pan removed, on most models the transmission/transaxle filter is visible. The filter should be changed any time the transmission oil is drained. Remove the bolts (automatic transmission vehicle have 6 retaining bolts; automatic transaxle vehicles have 3 retaining bolts) holding the filter and remove the filter and gasket if so equipped.

NOTE: *On some models filter retaining bolts are different lengths and MUST BE reinstalled in their correct locations. Take great care not to interchange them.*

5. Clean the mating surfaces for the oil pan and the filter; make sure all traces of the old gasket material is removed.

6. Install the new filter assembly (some models use a gasket under the oil filter). Install the 3 retaining bolts in their correct locations and tighten only to 7 ft. lbs. on automatic transaxle vehicles. On vehicles with a automatic transmission torque 6 retaining bolts to about 48 inch lbs.

7. Install the pan (magnets in the correct

location in oil pan) using a new gasket and torque retaining bolts in progressive steps to about 60 inch lbs.

8. Install the drain plug.

9. It is a good idea to measure the amount of fluid drained from the transmission/transaxle to determine the correct amount of fresh fluid to the be added. This is because some parts of the transmission/transaxle may not drain completely. Do not overfill the transmission/transaxle assembly.

10. With the engine off, add new Dexron® II fluid through the dipstick tube to the correct level. Refer to the Capacities Chart at the end of Chapter 1 as necessary.

11. Start the engine (always hold your foot on the brake) and shift the gear selector into all positions from P through L, allowing each gear to engage momentarily. Shift into P. DO NOT race the engine!

12. With the engine idling, check the fluid

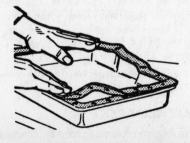

Always replace the gasket when installing the oil pan

level. Add fluid up to correct level on the dipstick.

13. Check the transmission/transaxle oil pan and drain plug for oil leakage. Dispose of used oil properly. Do not throw it in the trash or pour it on the ground. Take it to your dealer or local service station for recycling.

Drive Axle

FLUID RECOMMENDATIONS

All rear wheel drive vehicles and the rear differential on the 4-wheel drive Tercel use API GL–5 hypoid type gear oil, SAE 80W–90.

LEVEL CHECK

The oil in the differential should be checked at least every 15,000 miles (24,000km) and replaced every 25,000–30,000 miles (40,200–48,200km).

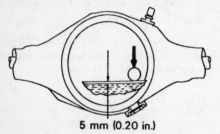

5 mm (0.20 in.)

The fluid level in the differential should be up to the edge of the filler hole (large arrow)

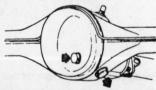

Filler (upper) plug and drain (lower) plug locations on the rear differential — rear wheel drive and 4WD only

1. With the car parked on a level surface, remove the filler plug from the back of the differential assembly. The plug on the bottom of the differential assembly is the drain plug.

2. If the oil begins to trickle out of the hole, there is enough. Otherwise, carefully insert your finger (watch for sharp threads) into the hole and check to see if the oil is up to the bottom edge of the filler hole.

3. If not, add oil through the hole until the level is at the edge of the hole. Most gear oils come in a plastic squeeze bottle with a nozzle, making additions simple. You can also use a common everyday kitchen baster. Use standard GL–5 hypoid type gear oil, SAE 90W or SAE 80W, if you live in a particularly cold area.

4. Replace the filler plug and run the

engine for a while. Turn off the engine and check for leaks.

DRAIN AND REFILL

The gear oil in the differential should be changed at least every 25,000–30,000 miles (40,200–48,200km).

To drain and fill the differential, proceed as follows:

1. Park the vehicle on a level surface. Set the parking brake.

2. Remove the filler (upper) plug. Place a container which is large enough to catch all of the differential oil, under the drain plug.

3. Remove the drain (lower) plug and gasket, if so equipped. Allow all of the oil to drain into the container.

4. Install the drain plug. Tighten it so that it will not leak, but do not over tighten.

5. Refill with the proper grade and viscosity of axle lubricant. Be sure that the level reaches the bottom of the filler plug.

6. Install the filler plug and check for leakage.

Cooling System

FLUID RECOMMENDATIONS

The correct coolant for the Corolla, Tercel and MR2 vehicles is any permanent, high quality ethylene glycol antifreeze mixed in a 50–50 concentration with water. This mixture gives the best combination of antifreeze and anti-boil characteristics within the engine.

LEVEL CHECK

CAUTION: *Always allow the car to sit and cool for an hour or so (longer is better) before removing the radiator cap. To avoid injury when working on a warm engine, cover the radiator cap with a thick cloth and turn it slowly counterclockwise until the pressure begins to escape. After the pressure is completely removed, remove the cap. Never remove the cap until the pressure is gone.*

It's best to check the coolant level when the engine is COLD. The radiator coolant level should be between the LOW and the FULL lines on the expansion tank when the engine is cold. If low, check for leakage and add coolant up to the FULL line but do not overfill it.

NOTE: *Check the freeze protection rating of the antifreeze at least once a year or as necessary with a suitable antifreeze tester.*

DRAIN AND REFILL

The engine coolant should be changed every 30,000 miles (48,200km) or 2 years, whichever comes first. Replacing the coolant is necessary

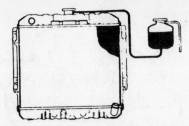

Always check the level in the expansion tank; do not remove the cap if there is any heat in the system

to remove the scale, rust and chemical by-products which build up in the system.

1. Draining the cooling system is always done with the motor **COLD**.

2. Remove the radiator cap.

3. Position the drain pan under the drain cock on the bottom of the radiator. Additionally, some engines have a drain cock on the side of the engine block, near the oil filter. This should be opened to aid in draining the cooling system completely. If for some reason the radiator drain cock can't be used, you can loosen and remove the lower radiator hose at its joint to the radiator.

CAUTION: *When draining the coolant, keep in mind that cats and dogs are attracted by the ethylene glycol antifreeze, and are quite likely to drink any that is left in an uncovered container or in puddles on the ground. This will prove fatal in sufficient quantity. Always drain the coolant into a sealable container. Coolant should be reused unless it is contaminated or several years old.*

4. If the lower hose is to be used as the drain, loosen the clamp on the hose and slide it back so it's out of the way. Gently break the grip of the hose on its fitting by twisting or prying with a suitable tool. Do not exert too much force or you will damage the radiator fitting. Remove the hose end from the radiator

and direct the hose into the drain pan. You now have fluid running from both the hose and the radiator.

5. When the system stops draining, close both drain cocks as necessary.

6. Using a funnel if necessary, fill the radiator with 50–50 solution of antifreeze and water. Allow time for the fluid to run through the hoses and into the engine.

7. Fill the radiator to just below the neck. With the radiator cap off, start the engine and let it idle; this will circulate the coolant and begin to eliminate air in the system. Top up the radiator as the level drops.

8. When the level is reasonably stable, shut the engine off, and replace the radiator cap. Fill the expansion tank to a level halfway between the LOW and FULL lines and cap the expansion tank.

9. Drive the car for 10 or 15 minutes; the temperature gauge should be fully within the normal operating range. It is helpful to set the heater to its hottest setting while driving – this circulates the coolant throughout the entire system and helps eliminate air bubbles.

10. After the engine has cooled (2–3 hours), check the level in the radiator and the expansion tank adding coolant as necessary.

CLEANING AND FLUSHING THE COOLING SYSTEM

Proceed with draining the system as outlined above. When the system has drained, reconnect any hoses close the radiator drain cock. Move the temperature control for the heater to its hottest position; this allows the heater core to be flushed as well. Using a garden hose or bucket, fill the radiator and allow the water to run out the engine drain cock. Continue until the water

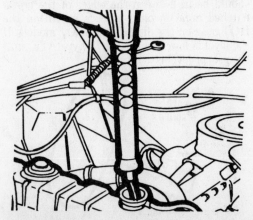

The freezing protection rating can be checked with an antifreeze tester

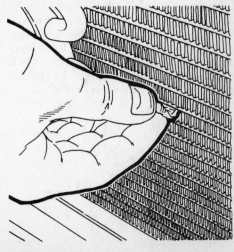

Clean the radiator fins of any debris which impedes air flow

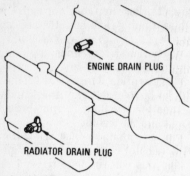

Drain plug locations

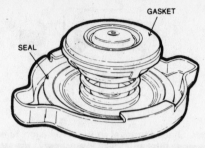

Check the radiator cap seal and gasket condition

runs clear. Be sure to clean the expansion tank as well.

If the system is badly contaminated with rust or scale, you can use a commercial flushing solution to clean it out. Follow the manufacturer's instructions. Some causes of rust are air in the system, failure to change the coolant regularly, use of excessively hard or soft water, and/or failure to use the correct mix of antifreeze and water.

After the system has been flushed, continue with the refill procedures outlined above. Check the condition of the radiator cap and its gasket, replacing the radiator cap as necessary.

Brake and Clutch Master Cylinders

FLUID RECOMMENDATIONS

All Corolla, Tercel and MR2 vehicles use DOT 3 or SAE J1703 brake fluid. The brake and clutch master cylinders use the same type brake fluid.

LEVEL CHECK

The brake and clutch master cylinders are located under the hood, in the left rear section of the engine compartment. They are made of translucent plastic so that the levels may be checked without removing the tops. The fluid level in both reservoirs should be checked at least every 15,000 miles (24,000km) or 1 year.

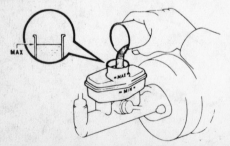

Always fill the master cylinder slowly so as not to create air bubbles in the system

The fluid level should be maintained at the upper most mark on the side of the reservoir. Any sudden decrease in the level indicates a possible leaks in the system and should be checked out immediately.

When making additions of brake fluid, use only fresh, uncontaminated brake fluid meeting or exceeding DOT 3 standards. Be careful not to spill any brake fluid on painted surfaces, as it eats the paint. Do not allow the brake fluid container or the master cylinder reservoir to remain open any longer than necessary; brake fluid absorbs moisture from the air, reducing its effectiveness and causing corrosion in the lines.

Power Steering Pump

FLUID RECOMMENDATIONS

All Corolla, Tercel and MR2 vehicles use ATF Dexron®II transmission fluid.

LEVEL CHECK

The fluid level in the power steering reservoir should be checked at least every 15,000 miles (24,000km) or 1 year. The vehicle should be parked on level ground, with the engine warm and running at normal idle. Remove the filler cap and check the level on the dipstick; it should be in between the edges of the cross-hatched area on older models or within the **HOT** area on the dipstick on newer models. If the level is low, add Dexron®II type ATF until the proper level is achieved.

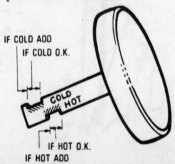

Power steering pump dipstick on newer models

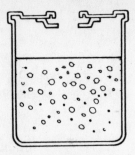

Foaming indicates air in the system

Chassis Greasing

Chassis lubrication for some models is limited to greasing the ball joint assemblies every 25,000–30,000 miles (40,200–48,200km) or 1 year.

1. Remove the screw plug from the ball joint. Install a grease nipple.
2. Using a hand-operated grease gun, lubricate the ball joint with NLGI #1 or NLGI #2 molybdenum-disulphide lithium-based grease.
3. Remove the nipped and reinstall the screw plug.
4. Repeat for the other ball joint(s).

Body Lubrication

There is no set period recommended by Toyota for body lubrication. However, it is a good idea to lubricate the following body points at least once a year, especially in the fall before cold weather.

Lubricate with engine oil:
- Door lock latches
- Door lock rollers
- Door, hood and hinge pivots **Lubricate with Lubriplate:**
- Trunk lid latch and hinge
- Glove box door latch
- Front seat slides **Lubricate with silicone spray:**
- All rubber weather stripping
- Hood stops

When finished lubricating a body part, be sure that all the excess lubricant has been wiped off, especially in the areas of the car which may come in contact with clothing.

Wheel Bearings

REMOVAL, PACKING AND INSTALLATION

Rear Wheel Drive Models

The front wheel bearings (inner and outer bearings) should be cleaned, inspected and repacked every 40,000 miles (64,300km) or every 4 years. These bearings should be inspected and serviced more frequently in areas of heavy road salt use or extremely rainy areas. To ser-

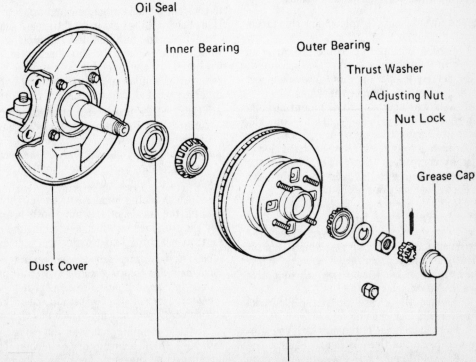

Front wheel bearing assembly installation — rear wheel drive vehicles

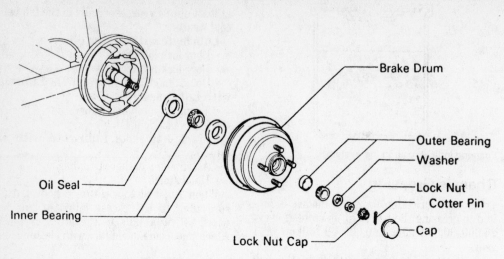

Brake Drum

Outer Bearing

Washer

Lock Nut

Cotter Pin

Cap

Oil Seal

Inner Bearing

Lock Nut Cap

Rear wheel bearing assembly installation — front wheel drive vehicles

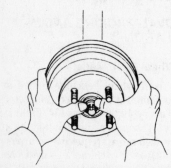

Removing wheel bearings from the vehicle

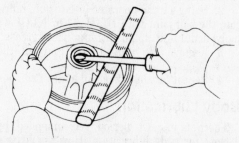

Removing oil seal from hub/drum — disc/rotor similar procedure

vice the front wheel bearings follow this procedure:

1. Loosen the lug nuts while the car is on the ground. Raise the car and place jackstands at the correct support points (always support the vehicle safely). Remove the wheel.

2. Remove the brake caliper mounting bolts and remove the caliper from the knuckle. (Refer to Chapter 9 as necessary). Support the caliper from a piece of stiff wire or string tied to a nearby component. Do NOT disconnect the fluid hose running to the caliper; simply move the entire assembly out of the way.

CAUTION: *Some brake pads and shoes contain asbestos, which has been determined to be a cancer causing agent. Never clean the brake surfaces with compressed air! Avoid inhaling any dust from brake surfaces! When cleaning brakes, use commercially available brake cleaning fluids.*

3. Remove the grease cap (don't distort it) the cotter pin, lock cap and nut.

4. Hold the outside of the hub with your fingers and place the thumbs lightly against the inner edge of the hub. Pull outward gently; the whole assembly will slide off and your thumbs will keep the outer wheel bearing from falling

to the ground. The inner bearing (on the other side of the hub) is held in by the grease seal.

5. Place the hub and disc assembly on the work bench. Remove the outer bearing and flat washer. Turn the assembly over and use a seal remover or similar suitable tool to pry out the inner grease seal. Remove the inner bearing.

NOTE: *Since this is a maintenance procedure, DO NOT attempt to remove the bearing races from the inside of the hub and disc. The races should be removed only in the event of bearing replacement, refer to Chapter 8 as necessary.*

6. Clean all the components thoroughly, including the inside of the hub, both bearings and the stub axle on which everything mounts. All traces of the old grease must be removed.

NOTE: *Use only proper commercial parts cleaners. Do not use gasoline or similar products for cleaning parts. A stiff–bristled parts cleaning brush or even an old, clean paint brush is very handy for cleaning bearings.*

7. After cleaning, allow all the parts to air dry. Never blow bearings dry with compressed air. Inspect all the parts. Look carefully for any signs of imperfect surfaces, cracking, bluing or looseness. Check the matching surface on

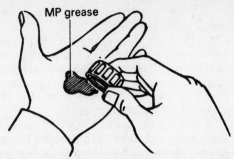

MP grease

Packing wheel bearings with multi-purpose grease

which the bearing run; the races should be virtually perfect and free of damage.

8. Repack the wheel bearings using high quality multi–purpose (MP) grease. Each bearing must be fully packed. The use of a bearing packer is highly recommended but the job can be done by hand. To repack the front wheel bearings follow this procedure:

a. Place a golf ball–sized lump of MP grease in the palm of your hand.

b. Hold the bearing in your other hand and force the wide side of the bearing into the grease. Use a pushing and scraping motion to force the grease up into the rollers. Continue this until grease oozes out the small side of the bearing.

c. Change the position by which you hold the bearing and repeat the procedure, forcing grease into an untreated area of the bearing.

d. Continue around the bearing until all the rollers are packed solid with grease.

e. Place the bearing on a clean, lint–free rag or towel while greasing other components.

9. Coat the inside of the hub with a liberal layer of grease. Remember that the stub axle comes through here; don't pack it solid.

10. Fill the grease cup about 1/2 full of MP grease.

11. Install the inner bearing into the disc. Use a new grease seal and install it with a seal installer such as SST 09550–00050 or equiva-

lent. Do not attempt to use a hammer or drift; the seal may be damaged. Coat the lip of the seal lightly with a bit of MP grease.

12. Fit the outer bearing loosely into place and put the large flat washer over it. Again holding the washer and bearing in place with your thumbs, fit the assembly onto the stub axle. Make sure the small tooth on the inside of the bearing washer aligns with the groove in the stub axle.

13. Install the outer bearing and thrust washer.

ADJUST THE BEARING PRELOAD AS FOLLOWS:

a. Install the adjusting nut onto the axle. Use the torque wrench and set the adjusting nut to 21 ft. lbs.

b. Turn the hub right and left two or three times each way; this will allow the bearings to seat in the correct position.

c. Retighten the adjusting nut to 21 ft. lbs.

d. Loosen the adjusting nut until it can be turned by hand. Confirm that there is absolutely no brake drag.

e. Measure and make note of the rotation frictional force of the oil seal.

f. Tighten the adjusting nut until the preload is within specification. The preload specification is 0–2.3 lbs. in addition to rotation friction force of the oil seal. Insure that the hub rotates smoothly.

g. Measure the hub axial play. The limit for axial play is 0.05mm (0.0020 in.).

NOTE: *A front wheel bearing either too loose or too tight will wear prematurely and possibly affect the behavior of the wheel.*

14. Install the lock cap, a new cotter pin (always!) and the grease cap. If the cotter pin hole does not line up, first try turning the lock cap to a different position. If this is ineffective, tighten the nut by the smallest possible amount.

15. Install the brake caliper. Tighten the mounting bolts 47 ft. lbs.

16. Reinstall the wheel and lower the vehicle

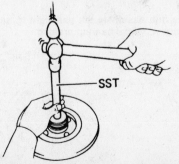

SST

Installing oil seal from rotor/disc — hub/drum similar procedure

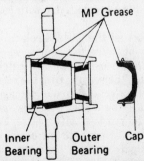

MP Grease

Inner Bearing Outer Bearing Cap

Multi-purpose grease should be in all shaded areas of hub assembly

to the ground. Final tighten the lug nuts when the car is on the ground.

Front Wheel Drive Models

The rear wheel bearings (inner and outer bearings) should be cleaned, inspected and re-packed every 30,000 miles (48,200km) or every 4 years. These bearings should be inspected and serviced more frequently in areas of heavy road salt use or extremely rainy areas. To service the rear wheel bearings follow this procedure:

1. Raise and safely support the vehicle. Remove the rear tire/wheel assembly.

2. Remove the grease cap (don't distort it) the cotter pin, lock cap and nut.

3. Hold the outside of the hub/drum with your fingers and place the thumbs lightly against the inner edge of the hub/drum. Pull outward gently; the whole assembly will slide off and your thumbs will keep the outer wheel bearing from falling to the ground. The inner bearing (on the other side of the hub/drum) is held in by the grease seal.

4. Place the hub/drum assembly on the work bench. Remove the outer bearing and flat washer. Turn the assembly over and use a seal remover or similar suitable tool to pry out the inner grease seal. Remove the inner bearing.

NOTE: *Since this is a maintenance procedure, DO NOT attempt to remove the bearing races from the inside of the hub/drum. The races should be removed only in the event of bearing replacement, refer to Chapter 8 as necessary.*

5. Clean all the components thoroughly, including the inside of the hub/drum, both bearings and the stub axle on which everything mounts. All traces of the old grease must be removed.

NOTE: *Use only proper commercial parts cleaners. Do not use gasoline or similar products for cleaning parts. A stiff-bristled parts cleaning brush or even an old, clean paint brush is very handy for cleaning bearings.*

6. After cleaning, allow all the parts to air dry. Never blow bearings dry with compressed air.

7. Inspect all the parts. Look carefully for any signs of imperfect surfaces, cracking, bluing or looseness. Check the matching surface on which the bearing run; the races should be virtually perfect and free of damage.

8. Repack the wheel bearings using high quality multi-purpose (MP) grease. Each bearing must be fully packed. The use of a bearing packer is highly recommended but the job can be done by hand.

To repack the rear wheel bearings follow this procedure:

a. Place a golf ball–sized lump of MP grease in the palm of your hand.

b. Hold the bearing in your other hand and force the wide side of the bearing into the grease. Use a pushing and scraping motion to force the grease up into the rollers. Continue this until grease oozes out the small side of the bearing.

c. Change the position by which you hold the bearing and repeat the procedure, forcing grease into an untreated area of the bearing.

d. Continue around the bearing until all the rollers are packed solid with grease.

e. Place the bearing on a clean, lint–free rag or towel while greasing other components.

9. Coat the inside of the hub/drum with a liberal layer of grease. Remember that the stub axle comes through here; don't pack it solid.

10. Fill the grease cup about $1/2$ full of MP grease.

11. Install the inner bearing into the hub/drum. Use a new grease seal and install it with a seal installer or equivalent. Do not attempt to use a hammer or drift; the seal may be damaged. Coat the lip of the seal lightly with a bit of MP grease.

12. Fit the outer bearing loosely into place and put the large flat washer over it. Again holding the washer and bearing in place with your thumbs, fit the hub/drum assembly onto the stub axle. Make sure the small tooth on the inside of the bearing washer aligns with the groove in the stub axle.

13. Install the outer bearing and thrust washer.

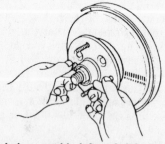

Rotate hub assembly left and right to seat wheel bearings — wheel bearing preload

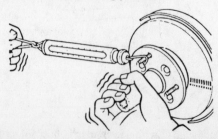

Final adjustment procedure — wheel bearing preload

Use torque wrench to set adjusting nut — wheel bearing preload

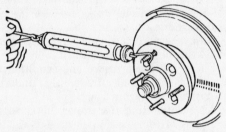

Use a spring scale tool to measure rotating force — wheel bearing preload

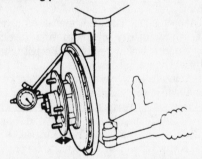

Measure hub axial play — wheel bearing preload

ADJUST THE BEARING PRELOAD AS FOLLOWS:

a. Install the adjusting nut onto the axle. Use the torque wrench and set the adjusting nut to 22 ft. lbs.

b. Turn the hub/drum right and left two or three times each way; this will allow the bearings to seat in the correct position.

c. Loosen the adjusting nut until it can be turned by hand. Confirm that there is absolutely no brake drag.

d. Measure and make note of the rotation frictional force of the oil seal.

e. Tighten the adjusting nut until the preload is within specification. The preload specification is 0.9–2.2 lbs. in addition to rotation friction force of the oil seal. Insure that the hub rotates smoothly.

14. Install the lock cap, a new cotter pin (always!) and the grease cap. If the cotter pin hole does not line up, first try turning the lock cap to a different position. If this is ineffective, tightening the nut by the smallest possible amount.

15. Check rear brake shoe adjustment. Install the tire/wheel assembly.

TRAILER TOWING

NOTE: *Always consult with your Toyota Dealer about trailer weight and special equipment. Some vehicles are not recommended to tow a trailer; some vehicles have different weight limits between manual and automatic transmission/transaxle types. Toyota All-Trac vehicles require a hitch with a special protector. Please consult your local Toyota dealer for specific advice regarding this hitch assembly. Towing a trailer qualifies as severe duty for the tow vehicle. Maintenance must be performed more frequently.*

General Recommendations

Your vehicle was primarily designed to carry passengers and cargo. It is important to remember that towing a trailer will place additional loads on your vehicle's engine, drive train, steering, braking and other systems. However, if you find it necessary to tow a trailer, using the proper equipment is a must.

Local laws may require specific equipment such as trailer brakes or fender mounted mirrors. Check your local laws.

$$\frac{\text{TONGUE LOAD}}{\text{TOTAL TRAILER WEIGHT}} \times 100 = 9 \text{ to } 11\ \%$$

The trailer cargo load should be distributed so that the tongue load is 9 to 11% of the total trailer weight, not exceeding the maximum of the 150 lbs.

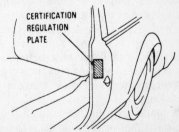

The gross vehicle weight must not exceed the Gross Vehicle Weight Rating (GVWR) indicated on the Certification Regulation Plate. The gross vehicle weight is the sum of weights of the unloaded vehicle, driver, passengers, luggage, hitch and trailer tongue load. It also includes the weight of any special equipment installed on your vehicle.

The trailer hitch assembly should conform to all applicable laws and be sufficient for the maximum trailer load.

Almost all trailers now come equipped with a rear and side lighting. A wiring harness must be installed to connect the automotive lighting and brake light systems to the trailer. Any reputable hitch installer can perform this installation. You can also install the harnesses, but great care must be paid to matching the correct wires during the installation. Each circuit must be wired individually for taillights, brake lights, right and left turn signals and in many cases, reverse lights. If the trailer is equipped with electric brakes, the wiring for this circuit should be installed at the same time as the lighting harness. Remember that the additional lighting may exceed the present fuse rating in the car's fuse box; upgrading the fuse may be necessary.

Cooling System

One of the most common, if not the most common, problems associated with trailer towing is engine overheating.

The cooling system should be checked frequently and maintained in top notch condition. If the engine temperature gauge indicates overheating, particularly on long grades, immediately turn off the air conditioner (if in use), pull off the road and stop in a safe location. Do not attempt to "limp in" with a hot motor!

Transmission

The increased load of a trailer causes an increase in the temperature of the automatic transmission fluid. Heat is the worst enemy of an automatic transmission. As the temperature of the fluid increases, the life of the fluid decreases.

It is essential, therefore, that you install an automatic transmission cooler or supplement the one already present.

The cooler, which consists of a multi-tube, finned heat exchanger, is usually installed in front of the radiator or air conditioning compressor, and hooked inline with the transmission cooler tank inlet line. Follow the cooler manufacturer's installation instructions.

Select a cooler of at least adequate capacity, based upon the combined gross weights of the car and trailer.

Cooler manufacturers recommend that you use an aftermarket cooler in addition to the present cooling tank in your radiator.

NOTE: *A transmission cooler can sometimes cause slow or harsh shifting in the transmission during cold weather, until the fluid has a chance to come up to normal operating temperature. Some coolers can be purchased with or retrofitted with a temperature bypass valve which will allow fluid flow through the cooler only when the fluid has reached operating temperature or above.*

Handling A Trailer

Towing a trailer with ease and safety requires a certain amount of skill that can only be gained through experience. Many trailer accidents occur because the driver – however skilled – forgot some of the basics.

• When loading the trailer, keep about 60% of the weight forward of the axle. This will prevent the trailer from trying to pass the car during cornering.

• Always perform a walk-around check of all the lighting before pulling out.

• Check the tire pressure and condition on both the car and trailer frequently. Underinflated tires are a hazard.

• After connecting the trailer, observe the car for any extreme nose-up or nose-down attitudes. If the car is not approximately level with the trailer connected, rebalance the load in the trailer.

• Stopping distances are increased dramatically. Allow plenty of room and anticipate stops. Sudden braking may jackknife the trailer or throw the car into a skid.

• Accelerate slowly and smoothly. Jerky driving will cause increased wear on the drive line.

• Avoid sharp turns. The trailer will always turn "inside" the car; allow plenty of room.

• Crosswinds and rough roads increase instability. Know when you're about to be passed by a large vehicle and prepare for it.

• If swaying begins, grip the steering wheel firmly and hold the vehicle straight ahead. Reduce speed gradually without using the brake. If you make NO extreme corrections in brakes, throttle or steering, the car and trailer will stabilize quickly.

• Passing requires much greater distances for acceleration. Plan ahead. Remember to allow for the length of the trailer when pulling back in.

• Use a lower gear to descend long grades. Slow down before down shifting.

• Avoid riding the brake. This will overheat the brakes and reduce their efficiency.

• When parking the combination, always apply the parking brake and place blocks under the trailer wheels. A heavy trailer may literally drag the car down a grade. Don't forget to remove the chocks before leaving.

• Backing up with a trailer is a skill to be practiced before it is needed. Find a large open area (get permission if necessary) and spend at least an hour learning how to do it.

PUSHING AND TOWING

Pushing Starting Vehicle

Push starting or "kick starting" the Corolla, Tercel and MR2 vehicles is not recommended.

It is possible to push start a manual transmission/transaxle vehicle as an emergency, no–alternative measure. To push start the car; turn the ignition switch to the ON position, push in the clutch pedal, put the gear shift lever in second or third gear and depress the gas pedal just a bit. As the car begins to pick up momentum while being pushed, release the clutch pedal. Immediately as the engine catches, push the clutch pedal in and apply sufficient throttle to keep the engine running. NEVER attempt to push start the car while it is in REVERSE.

The Corolla, Tercel and MR2 vehicles equipped with an automatic transmission can NOT be push started no matter how far or how fast they are pushed.

Towing the Vehicle

The absolute best way to have the car towed or transported is on a flat–bed or rollback transporter. These units are becoming more common and are very useful for moving disabled vehicles quickly. Most vehicles have lower body work and undertrays which can be easily damaged by the sling of a conventional tow truck; an operator unfamiliar with your particu-

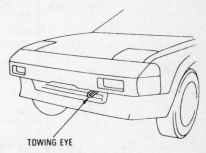

TIE-DOWN TABS

Tie down tabs location on all vehicles except MR2

TOWING EYE

Tie down location MR2 vehicle

lar model can cause severe damage to the suspension or drive line by hooking up chains and J–hooks incorrectly.

If a flatbed is not available (your should specifically request one), the car may be towed by a hoist or conventional tow vehicle. Front wheel drive cars with automatic transmission must be towed with the drive wheels off the ground. FWD cars with a manual transmission can be towed with either end up in the air or with all four wheels on the ground. You need only remember that the transmission must be in Neutral, the parking brake must be off and the ignition switch must be in the **ACC** position. The steering column lock is not strong enough to hold the front wheels straight under towing.

Rear wheel drive cars should also be towed with the drive wheels off the ground if possible. If the rear is elevated, the ignition should be in the **ACC** position to release the steering column. If a RWD car must be towed with the rear wheels on the ground, release the parking brake and put the transmission in **N** or neutral. Manual transmission RWD cars then may be towed. Automatic transmission RWD cars should not be towed faster than 30 mph (56 kmh) or farther than 50 miles (80km). (Although the car is in neutral, parts of the automatic transmission still turn with the wheels. Damage can result from towing farther or faster than recommended.) If the car must be towed farther or faster, the driveshaft must be disconnected at the differential to avoid damage.

On 4-wheel drive vehicles with manual trans-

FWD towing procedure

PRECAUTIONS WHEN TOWING FULL-TIME 4WD VEHICLES

1. Use one of the methods shown below to tow the vehicle.

2. When there is trouble with the chassis and drivetrain, use method ① (flat bed truck) or method ② (sling type toe truck with dollies)

3. Recommended Methods: No. ① , ② or ③
   Emergency Method: No. ④

Type of Transaxle / Towing Method	Manual Transaxle			Automatic Transaxle			
	Parking Brake	T/M Shift Lever Position	Center Diff.	Parking Brake	T/M Shift Lever Position	Center Diff. Control Switch	Mode Select Lever on Transaxle
① Flat Bed Truck ② Sling-Type Tow Truck with Dollies	Applied	1st Gear	Free or Lock (Center Differential Control Switch "ON" or "OFF")	Applied	"P" range	"AUTO" or "OFF"	Free (Normal Driving) (No Special Operation Necessary)
③ Sling-Type Two Truck (Front wheels must be able to rotate freely)	Released	Neutral	Free (Center Differential Control Switch "OFF")	Release	"N" range	"OFF"	↑
④ Towing with a Rope	Released	Neutral	Free (Center Differential Control Switch "OFF")	Released	"N" range	"OFF"	↑ NOTE: Do not tow the vehicle at a speed faster than 18 mph (30 km/h) or a distance greater than 50 miles (80 km).

NOTE: **Do not use any towing methods other than those shown above.**
For example, the towing method shown below is dangerous, so do not use it.

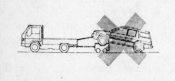

During towing with this towing method, there is a danger of the drivetrain heating up and causing breakdown, or of the front wheels flying off the dolly.

JUMP STARTING A DEAD BATTERY

The chemical reaction in a battery produces explosive hydrogen gas. This is the safe way to jump start a dead battery, reducing the chances of an accidental spark that could cause an explosion.

Jump Starting Precautions

1. Be sure both batteries are of the same voltage.
2. Be sure both batteries are of the same polarity (have the same grounded terminal).
3. Be sure the vehicles are not touching.
4. Be sure the vent cap holes are not obstructed.
5. Do not smoke or allow sparks around the battery.
6. In cold weather, check for frozen electrolyte in the battery. Do not jump start a frozen battery.
7. Do not allow electrolyte on your skin or clothing.
8. Be sure the electrolyte is not frozen.

CAUTION: *Make certain that the ignition key, in the vehicle with the dead battery, is in the OFF position. Connecting cables to vehicles with on-board computers will result in computer destruction if the key is not in the OFF position.*

Jump Starting Procedure

1. Determine voltages of the two batteries; they must be the same.
2. Bring the starting vehicle close (they must not touch) so that the batteries can be reached easily.
3. Turn off all accessories and both engines. Put both cars in Neutral or Park and set the handbrake.
4. Cover the cell caps with a rag—do not cover terminals.
5. If the terminals on the run-down battery are heavily corroded, clean them.
6. Identify the positive and negative posts on both batteries and connect the cables in the order shown.
7. Start the engine of the starting vehicle and run it at fast idle. Try to start the car with the dead battery. Crank it for no more than 10 seconds at a time and let it cool off for 20 seconds in between tries.
8. If it doesn't start in 3 tries, there is something else wrong.
9. Disconnect the cables in the reverse order.
10. Replace the cell covers and dispose of the rags.

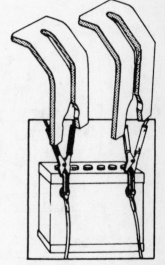

Side terminal batteries occasionally pose a problem when connecting jumper cables. There frequently isn't enough room to clamp the cables without touching sheet metal. Side terminal adaptors are available to alleviate this problem and should be removed after use.

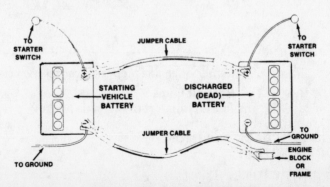

Make sure vehicles do not touch

This hook–up for negative ground cars only

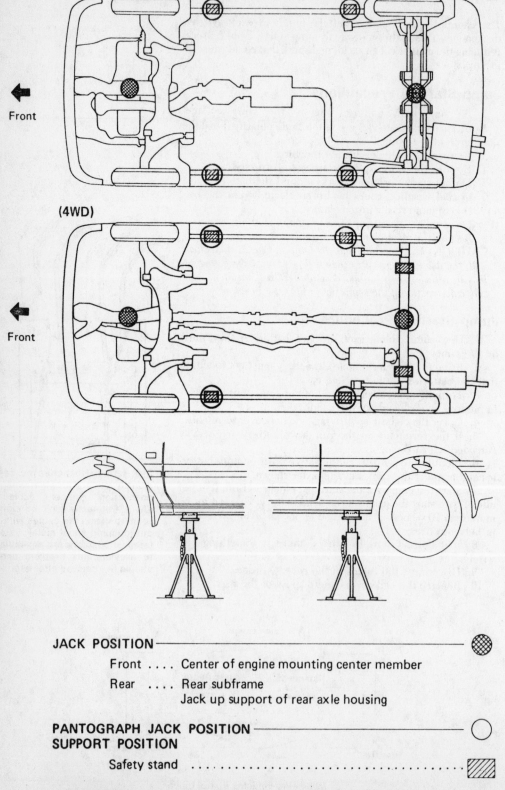

Front

(4WD)

Front

JACK POSITION ⬤

 Front .... Center of engine mounting center member
 Rear .... Rear subframe
     Jack up support of rear axle housing

PANTOGRAPH JACK POSITION ○
SUPPORT POSITION

 Safety stand .... ▨

Vehicle lift and support locations — Corolla FWD and Corolla All-Trac

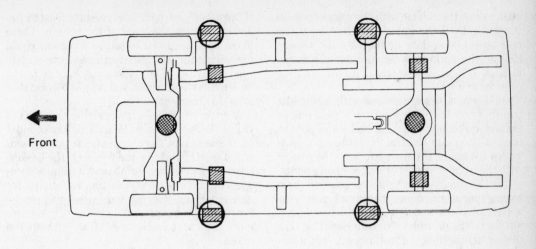

Front

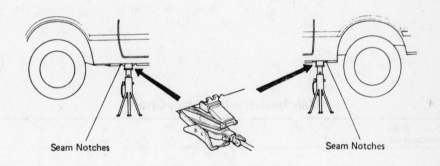

Seam Notches   Seam Notches

JACK POSITION ─────────────────────⬤

    Front . . . . Center of front suspension crossmember
    Rear . . . . Center of rear axle housing

PANTOGRAPH JACK POSITION ──────────────◯
SUPPORT POSITION

    Safety stand . . . . ▨

Vehicle lift and support locations — Corolla RWD

mission tow the vehicle with the rear wheels on the ground. (If the vehicle is lifted from the rear use a towing dolly under the front wheels) Release the parking brake and put the transmission in Neutral. The rear drive control lever must be in FWD.

On 4-wheel drive vehicles with automatic transmission tow with the rear wheels on the ground. Release the parking brake and put the transmission into Neutral. Never tow a vehicle with a automatic transmission from the rear or with the front wheels (drive wheels) on ground.

The Corolla All–Trac vehicle presents its own towing problems. Since the front and rear wheels are connected through the drive system, all four wheels must be considered in the towing arrangement. If a flatbed is not available, the All–Trac should be towed with the front end elevated. As the rear wheels roll on ground, the front wheels will turn. They must be clear of the hoist and sling equipment. If the vehicle cannot be towed front–end–up, both ends must be elevated, using a set of dolly wheels.

Most vehicles have conveniently located tie-down hooks at the front of the vehicle. These make ideal locations to secure a rope or chain for towing the car or extracting it from an off–road excursion. The vehicle may only be towed on hard surfaced roads and only in a normal or forward direction.

A driver must be in the towed vehicle to control it. Before towing, the parking brake must be released and the transmission put in neutral. Do NOT flat tow the vehicle if the brakes, steering, axles, suspension or drive line is damaged. If the engine is not running, the power assists for the steering and brakes will not be operating. Steering and braking will require more time and much more effort without the assist.

JACKING

There are certain safety precautions which should be observed when jacking the vehicle.

Maintenance Intervals Chart

Miles × 1000 or months of age	10 12	20 24	30 36	40 48	50 60	60 72
Engine oil and filter	R	R	R	R	R	R
Body lubrication	•	I	•	I	•	I
Engine idle speed	I	•	I	•	•	I
Engine coolant	•	•	I	•	•	R
Spark plugs	•	•	I	•	•	R
Air filter	I	•	R	•	•	R
Valve clearance	•	•	•	•	•	A
Engine drive belts	•	I	•	I	•	I
Charcoal canister	•	•	•	•	•	I
Fuel lines and connections	•	•	I	•	•	I
Fuel filter cap gasket	•	•	I	•	•	R
Exhaust system	•	I	•	I	•	I
Engine timing belt	•	•	I	•	•	R
Wheels and tires	I	I	I	I	I	I
Brakes	•	I	•	I	•	I
Fluid levels check	I	I	I	I	I	I
Transmission fluid	I	I	I	I	I	I

R: Replace
I: Inspect and clean, adjust, repair, service or replace as necessary
REMINDER: These are maximum intervals, not to be exceeded. More frequent maintenance and inspection may be required depending on usage of the vehicle. See service maintenance interval chart in your owner's manual.
NOTE: This chart is to be used as a maintenance service guide only. All years, models and diesel engines may differ. Consult your owner's manual as necessary.

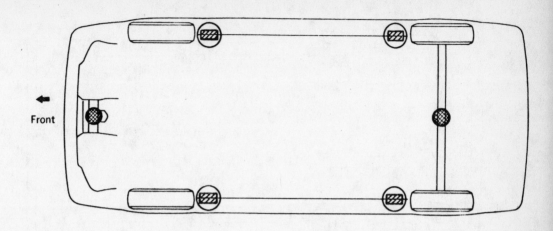

Front

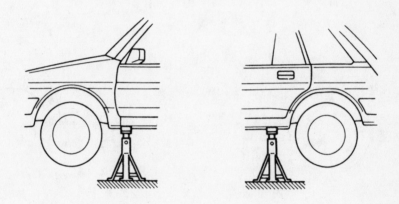

JACK POSITION ⬤

    Front .... Front crossmember
    Rear .... Rear axle beam

    CAUTION: When jack-up the rear and front, make sure the car
              is not carrying any extra weight.

PANTOGRAPH JACK POSITION ◯
SUPPORT POSITION

    Safety stand .... ▧

Vehicle lift and support locations — Tercel FWD

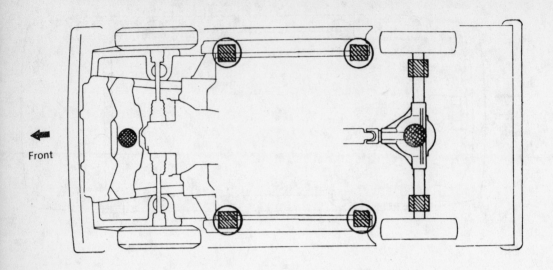

Front

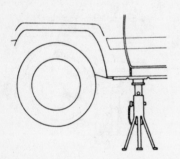
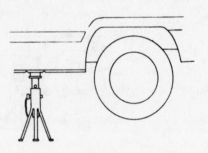

JACK POSITION _____ ⬙

    Front .... Center of crossmember
    Rear .... Center of rear axle housing

PANTOGRAPH JACK POSITION _____ ○
SUPPORT POSITION
    Safety stand .... ▨

Vehicle lift and support locations — Tercel 4WD

They are as follows:

1. Always jack the car on a level surface.

2. Set the parking brake, and block the rear wheels, if the front wheels are to be raised. This will keep the car from rolling backward off the jack.

3. If the rear wheels are to be raised, block off the front wheels to keep the car from rolling forward.

4. Block the wheel diagonally opposite the one which is being raised.

NOTE: *The tool kit which is supplied with most Toyota passenger cars includes a wheel block.*

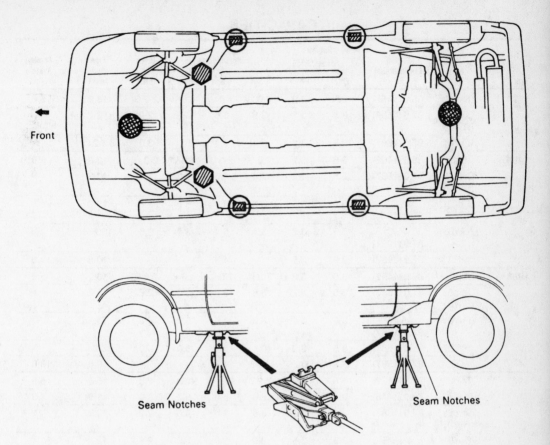

JACK POSITION ⬡

Front .... Jack up support of front luggage pan
Rear .... Rear engine mounting

PANTOGRAPH JACK POSITION ◯

SUPPORT POSITION

Safety stand .... ▨

NOTE: If the arms of the swing arm lift cannot be positioned as shown by the rectangles above, position them under the floor pan reinforcements shown by the hexagons.

Vehicle lift and support locations — MR2

5. If the vehicle is being raised in order to work underneath it, support it with jackstands. Do not place the jackstands against the sheet metal panels beneath the car or they will become distorted.

CAUTION: *Do not work beneath a vehicle supported only by a tire changing jack.*

6. Do not use a bumper jack to raise the vehicle; the bumpers are not designed for this purpose.

CAPACITIES

Year	Model	Engine Displacement cu. in. (cc)	Engine Crankcase with Filter	Engine Crankcase without Filter	Transmission (pts.) 4-Spd	Transmission (pts.) 5-Spd	Transmission (pts.) Auto.	Drive Axle (pts.)	Fuel Tank (gal.)	Cooling System (qts.)
1984	Tercel	88.6 (1452)	3.5	3.2	7.0 ①	7.0 ①	4.6 ②	2.0 ③	13.2	5.6
	Corolla (RWD)	97.0 (1587)	3.5	3.2	3.6	3.6	5.0	2.2	13.2	⑤
	(FWD)	97.0 (1587)	3.5	3.2	5.4	5.4	5.0	3.0	13.2 ④	⑤
1985	Tercel	88.6 (1452)	3.5	3.2	7.0 ①	7.0 ①	4.6 ②	2.0 ③	13.2	5.6
	Corolla (RWD)	97.0 (1587)	3.5	3.2	3.6	3.6	5.0	2.2	13.2	⑤
	(FWD)	4A-GE 97.0 (1587)	3.9	3.5	3.6	3.6	5.0	2.8	13.2	⑤
	(FWD)	4A-C 97.0 (1587)	3.5	3.2	5.4	5.4	5.0	3.0	13.2 ④	⑤
	MR2	97.0 (1587)	3.9	3.5	—	4.8	—	—	10.8	13.6
1986	Tercel	88.6 (1452)	3.5	3.2	7.0 ①	7.0 ①	4.6 ②	2.0 ③	13.2	5.6
	Corolla (RWD)	97.0 (1587)	3.5	3.2	3.6	3.6	5.0	2.2	13.2	⑤
	(RWD)	4A-GE 97.0 (1587)	3.9	3.5	3.6	3.6	5.0	2.8	13.2	⑤
	(FWD)	97.0 (1587)	3.5	3.2	5.4	5.4	5.0	3.0	13.2 ④	⑤
	MR2	97.0 (1587)	3.9	3.5	—	4.8	—	—	10.8	13.6
1987	Tercel	88.6 (1452)	3.5	3.2	7.2 ①	7.2 ①	4.6 ②	2.0	13.2	5.6
		88.9 (1456)	3.4	3.1	5.0	5.0	5.2	3.0	11.9	4.9
	Corolla (RWD)	97.0 (1587)	3.5	3.2	3.6	3.6	5.0	2.2	13.2	⑤
	(RWD)	4A-GE 97.0 (1587)	3.9	3.5	3.6	3.6	5.0	2.8	13.2	⑤
	(FWD)	97.0 (1587)	3.5	3.2	5.4	5.4	5.0	3.0	13.2 ④	6.3
	MR2	97.0 (1587)	3.9	3.5	—	4.8	—	—	10.8	13.6
1988	Tercel	88.6 (1452)	3.5	3.2	8.2	8.2	8.8	2.2	13.2	5.6
		88.9 (1456)	3.4	3.1	5.0	5.0	4.6	3.0	11.9	5.3
	Corolla	4A-LC 97.0 (1587)	3.5	3.2	5.4	5.4	⑥	3.0	13.2 ④	6.4
		4A-F 97.0 (1587)	3.3	3.2	5.4	5.4	⑥	3.0	13.2	6.3
		4A-GE 97.0 (1587)	3.9	3.5	5.4	5.4	⑥	3.0	13.2	6.3
	MR2	97.0 (1587)	3.5	3.2	—	⑦	6.6	—	10.8	⑧
1989–90	Tercel	88.9 (1456)	3.4	3.1	5.0	5.0	4.6	3.0	11.9	5.5
	Corolla	4A-F, 4A-FE 97.0 (1587)	3.4	3.2	5.4	5.4	⑥	3.0	13.2	5.9
		4A-GE 97.0 (1587)	3.9	3.6	5.4	5.4	⑥	3.0	13.2	6.3
	MR2	97.0 (1587)	3.5	3.2	—	⑦	6.6	—	10.8	⑧

① 4wd: 8.2
② 4wd: 8.8
③ 4wd: 2.2
④ Station wagon: 12.4
⑤ 1984: MT—5.7, AT—6.6
　1985-87: FWD—6.3; RWD MT—5.9, AT—5.8

⑥ A240E, A241H: 6.6
　A131L: 5.2
⑦ C52: 5.4; E51: 8.8
⑧ MT: 12.9
　AT: 13.6

Engine Performance and Tune-Up

2

TUNE-UP PROCEDURES

In order to extract the full measure of performance and economy from your engine it is essential that it be properly tuned at regular intervals. A regular tune-up will keep your Toyota's engine running smoothly and will prevent the annoying minor breakdowns and poor performance associated with an untuned engine.

A complete tune-up (replace spark plugs, air filter, make necessary adjustments etc.) should be performed every 30,000 miles or 36 months, whichever comes first. This interval time or mileage should be halved or adjusted as necessary if the car is operated under severe conditions, such as trailer towing, prolonged idling, continual stop and start driving, or if starting or running problems are noticed. It is assumed that the routine maintenance (described in Chapter 1) has been kept up, as this will have a decided effect on the results of a tune-up.

If the specifications on the tune-up sticker in the engine compartment of your Toyota disagree with the Tune-Up Specifications chart in this chapter, the figures on the sticker MUST BE USED. The sticker often reflects changes made during the production run.

NOTE: *On some models (Corolla GT-S, FX-16 and MR2) platinum spark plugs may be used, the recommended mile change interval is 60,000 miles.*

Spark Plugs

Spark plugs ignite the air and fuel mixture in the cylinder as the piston reaches the top of the compression stroke. The controlled explosion that results forces the piston down, turning the crankshaft and the rest of the drive train.

The average life of a normal, spark plug (platinum plugs 60,000 mile change interval) is about 15,000–20,000 miles, although manufac-

turers are now claiming spark plug lives of up to 30,000 miles or more. This is, however, dependent on a number of factors: the mechanical condition of the engine; the type of fuel; the driving conditions; and the driver.

Manufacturers are now required to certify that the spark plugs in their engines will meet emission specifications for 30,000 miles if all maintenance is performed properly. Certain types of plugs can be certified even beyond this point.

When you remove the spark plugs, check their condition. They are a good indicator of the condition of the engine. Refer to the color insert "Chilton's Fuel Economy & Tune-Up Tips" section Spark Plug Diagnosis.

When a regular spark plug is functioning normally or, more accurately, when the plug is installed in an engine that is functioning properly, the plugs can be taken out, cleaned, gapped, and reinstalled without doing the engine any harm.

NOTE: *On platinum spark plugs applications DO NOT use a wire brush for cleaning spark plugs. NEVER attempt to adjust gap/clean used platinum spark plug. Platinum spark plugs should be replaced every 60,000 miles.*

When, and if, a spark plug fouls and being to misfire, you will have to investigate, correct the cause of the fouling, and either clean or replace the plug.

There are several reasons why a spark plug will foul and you can learn which is at fault by just looking at the plug. A few of the most common reasons for plug fouling, and a description of the fouled plug's appearance, are listed in the Color Insert, which also offers solutions to the problems.

Spark plugs suitable for use in your Toyota's engine are offered in a number of different heat ranges. The amount of heat which the plug ab-

Gasoline Engine Tune-Up Specifications Chart

Year	Engine Designation	Model	Engine Displacement cu. in. (cc)	Spark Plugs Type	Gap (in.)	Ignition Timing (deg.) MT	AT	Compression Pressure (psi)	Fuel Pump (psi)	Idle Speed (rpm) MT	AT	Valve Clearance In.	Ex.
1984	3A	Tercel	88.6 (1452)	BPR5EY	0.031	5B	5B	178	2.6–3.5	①	①	0.008	0.012
	3A-C	Tercel	88.6 (1452)	BPR5EY-11	0.043	5B	5B	178	2.6–3.5	①	①	0.008	0.012
	4A-C	Corolla	97.0 (1587)	BRP5EY-11	0.043	5B	5B	178	2.6–3.5	①	①	0.008	0.012
1985	3A	Tercel	88.6 (1452)	BPR5EY	0.031	5B	5B	178	2.6–3.5	①	①	0.008	0.012
	3A-C	Tercel	88.6 (1452)	BPR5EY-11(14)	0.043	5B	5B	178	2.6–3.5	①	①	0.008	0.012
	4A-C	Corolla	97.0 (1587)	BPR5EY-11(15)	0.043	5B	5B	178	2.5–3.5	①	①	0.008	0.012
	4A-GE	Corolla	97.0 (1587)	BCPR5EP-11	0.043	10B	—	179	33–39	800	—	0.008	0.012
	4A-GE	MR2	97.0 (1587)	BCPR5EP-11	0.043	10B	①	179	33–39	800	①	0.008	0.012
1986	3A	Tercel	88.6 (1452)	BPR5EY	0.031	5B	5B	178	2.6–3.5	①	①	0.008	0.012
	3A-C	Tercel	88.6 (1452)	BPR5EY-11	0.043	5B	5B	178	2.6–3.5	①	①	0.008	0.012
	4A-C	Corolla	97.0 (1587)	BPR5EY-11	0.043	5B	5B	178	2.5–3.5	①	①	0.008	0.012
	4A-GE	Corolla	97.0 (1587)	BCPR5EP-11	0.043	10B	10B	179	33–38	800	800	0.008	0.012
	4A-GE	MR2	97.0 (1587)	BCPR5EP-11	0.043	10B	①	179	33–39	800	①	0.008	0.012
1987	3A-C	Tercel	88.6 (1452)	BPR5EY-11(14)	0.043	5B	5B	178	2.6–3.5	①	①	0.008	0.012
	3E	Tercel	88.9 (1457)	BPR5EY-11	0.043	3B	3B	184	2.6–3.5	①	①	0.008	0.008
	4A-C	Corolla	97.0 (1587)	BPR5EY-11	0.043	5B	5B	163	2.5–3.5	①	①	0.008	0.012
	4A-GE	Corolla	97.0 (1587)	BCPR5EP-11	0.043	10B	10B	179	33–38	①	①	0.008	0.012
	4A-GE	MR2	97.0 (1597)	BCPR5EP-11	0.043	10B	①	179	33–39	800	①	0.008	0.012
1988	3A-C	Tercel	88.6 (1452)	BPR5EY-11	0.043	5B	5B	178	2.6–3.5	①	①	0.008	0.012
	3E	Tercel	88.9 (1457)	BPR5EY-11	0.043	3B	3B	184	2.6–3.5	①	①	0.008	0.008
	4A-C	Corolla	97.0 (1587)	BRP5EY-11	0.043	5B	5B	163	2.5–3.5	①	①	0.008	0.012
	4A-GE	Corolla	97.0 (1587)	BCPR5EP-11	0.043	10B	10B	179	33–38	①	①	0.008	0.010
	4A-GE	MR2	97.0 (1587)	BCPR5EP-11	0.043	10B	①	179	33–38	800	①	0.008	0.010
	4A-GZE	MR2	97.0 (1587)	BCPR6EP-11	0.043	10B	①	156	33–38	800	800	0.008	0.010
1989	3E	Tercel	88.9 (1457)	BPR5EY-11	0.043	3B	3B	184	2.6–3.5	700	900	0.008	0.008
	4A-FE	Corolla	97.0 (1587)	BCPR5EY	0.031	10B	10B	191	38–44	800	800	0.008	0.010
	4A-F	Corolla	97.0 (1587)	BCPR5EY-11	0.043	5B	5B	191	2.5–3.5	650	750	0.008	0.010
	4A-GE	Corolla	97.0 (1587)	BCPR5EP-11	0.043	10B	10B	179	38–44	800	800	0.008	0.010
	4A-GE	MR2	97.0 (1587)	BCPR5EP-11	0.043	10B	10B	179	33–38	800	800	0.008	0.010
	4A-GZE	MR2	97.0 (1587)	BCPR6EP-11	0.043	10B	10B	156	33–38	800	800	0.008	0.010
1990	3E	Tercel	88.9 (1457)	BPR5EY-11	0.043	3B	3B	184	2.6–3.5	700	900	0.008	0.008
	3E-E	Tercel	88.9 (1457)	BPR5EY-11	0.043	3B	3B	184	38–44	800	①	0.008	0.008
	4A-FE	Corolla	97.0 (1587)	BCPR5EY	0.031	10B	10B	191	38–44	800	800	0.008	0.010
	4A-GE	MR2	97.0 (1587)	BCPR5EP-11	0.043	10B	10B	179	38–44	800	800	0.008	0.010

Note: On California and Canada vehicles always refer to underhood emission sticker as specifications are based on USA vehicles. On all vehicles, if specifications differ from emission sticker, always use specifications on emission sticker.
① See underhood emission sticker
② Always refer to service procedure "Ignition Timing" in Chapter 2.

Diesel Engine Tune-Up Specifications Chart

Model	Year	Engine Type	Warm Valve Clearance (in.)		Intake Valve Opens (deg.)	Injection Pump Setting (deg.)	Injection Nozzle Pressure (psi)		Idle Speed (rpm)	Compression Pressure (psi)
			In.	Ex.			New	Used		
Corolla	1984–85	1C-L	0.008–0.012	0.010–0.014	NA	25–30B	2062–2205	2062–2205	700	356–427

sorbs is determined by the length of the lower insulator. The longer the insulator, the hotter the plug will operate; the shorter the insulator, the cooler it will operate. A spark plug that absorbs (or retains) little heat and remains too cool will accumulate deposits of lead, oil, and carbon, because it is not hot enough to burn them off. This leads to fouling and consequent misfiring. A spark plug that absorbs too much heat will have no deposits, but the electrodes will burn away quickly and, in some cases, pre-ignition may result. Pre-ignition occurs when the spark plug tips get so hot that they ignite the fuel/air mixture before the actual spark fires. This premature ignition will usually cause a pinging sound under conditions of low speed and heavy load. In severe cases, the heat may become high enough to start the fuel/air mixture burning throughout the combustion chamber rather than just to the front of the

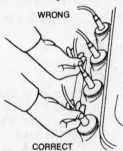

When removing the spark plug wire, always remove it by the rubber boot

plug. In this case, the resultant explosion will be strong enough to damage pistons, rings, and valves.

In most cases the factory recommended heat range is correct; it is chosen to perform well under a wide range of operating conditions. However, if most of your driving is long distance, high speed travel, you may want to install a spark plug one step colder than standard. If most of your driving is of the short trip variety, when the engine may not always reach operating temperature, a hotter plug may help burn off the deposits normally accumulated under those conditions.

REMOVAL, INSPECTION AND INSTALLATION

1. Number the spark plug wires (mark at the end of plug wire or boot) so that you won't cross them when you replace them.

2. Remove the wire from the end of the spark plug by grasping the wire by the rubber boot. If the boot sticks to the plug, remove it by twisting and pulling at the same time. Do not pull the wire itself or you will damage the core.

3. Use the correct size spark plug socket (spark plug sockets come in two sizes 5/8 and 13/16 in. − use the correct size socket for the spark plug) to loosen all of the plugs about two turns.

NOTE: *On most engines the cylinder head is cast from aluminum. Remove the spark*

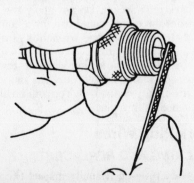

Regular spark plugs in good condition can be filed and re-used

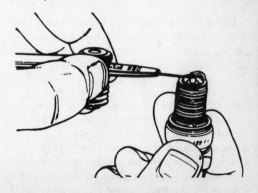

Always use a wire gauge to check the plug gap

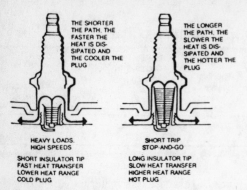

THE SHORTER THE PATH, THE FASTER THE HEAT IS DISSIPATED AND THE COOLER THE PLUG

THE LONGER THE PATH, THE SLOWER THE HEAT IS DISSIPATED AND THE HOTTER THE PLUG

HEAVY LOADS, HIGH SPEEDS

SHORT TRIP STOP-AND-GO

SHORT INSULATOR TIP
FAST HEAT TRANSFER
LOWER HEAT RANGE
COLD PLUG

LONG INSULATOR TIP
SLOW HEAT TRANSFER
HIGHER HEAT RANGE
HOT PLUG

Spark plug heat range

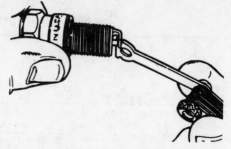

Adjust the spark plug gap by bending the side electrode

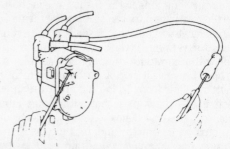

Checking the spark plug cable resistance

plugs when the engine is cold, if possible, to prevent damage to the threads.

If removal of the plugs is difficult, apply a few drops of penetrating oil or silicone spray to the area around the base of the plug, and allow it a few minutes to work.

4. If compressed air is available, apply it to the area around the spark plug holes. Otherwise, use a rag or a brush to clean the area. Be careful not to allow any foreign material to drop into the spark plug holes.

5. Remove the plugs by unscrewing them the rest of the way from the engine.

INSPECTION

Check the spark plugs for deposits and wear. If they are not going to be replaced, clean the plugs thoroughly (never clean platinum plugs – just replace the platinum plugs). Remember that any kind of deposit will decrease the efficiency of the plug. Regular spark plugs can be cleaned on a spark plug cleaning machine, which can sometimes be found in service stations, or you can do an acceptable job of cleaning with a stiff brush. If the plugs are cleaned, the electrodes must be filed flat. Use an ignition point file, not an emery board or the like, which will leave deposits. The electrodes must be filed perfectly flat with sharp edges; rounded edges reduce the spark plug voltage by as much as 50%.

Check spark plug gap before installation. The ground electrode (the L-shaped one connected to the body of the plug) must be parallel to the center electrode and the specified size wire gauge (see Tune-Up Specifications) should pass through the gap with a slight drag.

NOTE: *Never adjust the gap (or try to clean spark plug – just replace spark plug) on a used platinum tipped spark plug.*

Always check the gap on new regular spark plugs, too; they are not always set correctly at the factor. Do not use a flat feeler gauge when measuring the gap, because the reading will be inaccurate. Wire gapping tools usually have a

bending tool attached, use that to adjust the side electrode until the proper distance is obtained. Absolutely never bend the center electrode. Also, be careful not to bend the side electrode too far or too often; it may weaken and break off within the engine, causing serious damage.

NOTE: *On most platinum spark plugs applications the spark plug gap is preset at the manufacturer.*

INSTALLATION

1. Lubricate the threads of the spark plugs with a drop of oil. Install the plugs and tighten them hand tight (a long piece of vacuum hose attached to the top of the spark plug will help you start the spark plug by hand). Take care not to cross-thread them.

2. Tighten the spark plugs with the correct size spark plug socket. Do not apply the same amount of force you would use for a bolt; just snug them in. If a torque wrench is available, tighten to 13–15 ft. lbs.

3. Install the spark plug wires on their respective spark plugs. Make sure the spark plug wires are firmly connected. You will be able to feel them click into place.

Spark Plug Wires

CHECKING AND REPLACING

At every tune-up, visually inspect the spark plug cables for burns, cuts, or breaks in the insulation. Check the boots and the nipples on the distributor cap and coil. Replace any damaged wiring.

Every 30,000 miles or so, the resistance of the wires may be checked with an ohmmeter. Wires with excessive resistance will cause misfiring, and may make the engine difficult to start in damp weather. Generally the useful life of the cables is 30,000–50,000 miles.

To check resistance, remove the distributor cap, leaving the wires attached. Connect one lead of an ohmmeter to an electrode within the cap; connect the other lead to the corresponding spark plug terminal (remove it from the plug for this test). Replace any wire which shows a resistance over 25,000Ω. Test the high tension lead from the coil by connecting the ohmmeter between the center contact in the distributor cap and either of the primary terminals of the coil. If resistance is more than 25,000Ω, remove the cable from the coil and check the resistance of the cable alone. Anything over 15,000Ω is cause for replacement. It should be remembered that resistance is also a function of length; the longer the cable, the greater the resistance. Thus, if the cables on your car are longer than the factory originals, resistance will be higher, quite possibly outside these limits.

When installing new spark plug wires (cables), replace them ONE AT A TIME to avoid mixups. Start by replacing the longest one first. Install the boot firmly over the spark plug. Route the wire over the same path as the original. Insert the nipple firmly into the tower on the cap or the coil.

FIRING ORDERS

NOTE: *To avoid confusion, spark plug wires should be replaced one at a time. The distributor terminal position and distributor rotation may differ slightly from that which is illustrated due to lack of factory service information available at the time of this publication. The firing order for all 4 cylinder en-*

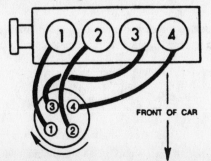

4A-FE engine firing order — other engines similar/ rotation and terminal position may differ.

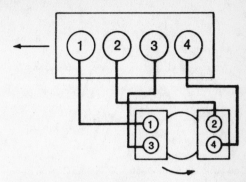

1A-C, 3A, 3A-C, and 4A-C engines — firing order (1984 shown, others similar)

gines is 1–3–4–2. The No. 1 spark plug is always located closes to the front of the engine (water pump or timing belt assembly). The distributor tower terminal cap usually is marked for the No. 1 location.

ELECTRONIC IGNITION

Electronic ignition systems offer many advances over the conventional breaker point ignition system. By eliminating the points, maintenance requirements are greatly reduced. An electronic ignition system is capable of producing much higher voltage, which in turn aids in starting, reduces spark fouling and provides better emission control.

NOTE: *This book contains simple testing procedures for your Corolla , Tercel and MR2 electronic ignition system. More comprehensive testing on this system and other electronic control systems on your car can be found in CHILTON'S ELECTRONIC ENGINE CONTROLS MANUAL, available at your local retailer.*

The electronic ignition system consists of a distributor with a signal generator, an ignition coil and an electronic igniter. The signal generator is used to activate the electronic components of the ignition. It is located in the distributor and consists of three main components; the signal rotor, the pick-up coil and the permanent magnet. The signal rotor (not to be confused with the normal rotor) revolves with the distributor shaft, while the pickup coil and the permanent magnet are stationary. As the signal rotor spins, the teeth on it pass a projection leading from the pickup coil. As they pass, voltage is allowed to flow through the system, firing the spark plugs. There is no physical contact and no electrical arcing, hence no need to replace burnt or worn parts.

Service consists of inspection of the distributor cap, rotor and the ignition wires, replacing

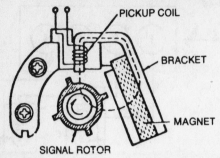

Components of an electronic ignition signal generator

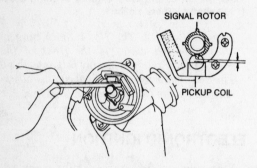

Checking the air gap on electronic ignition system

them as necessary. In addition, the air gap between the signal rotor and the projection on the pickup coil should be checked periodically.

CHECKING THE AIR GAP ADJUSTMENT

Carbureted Engines

1. Remove the distributor cap. Inspect the cap for cracks, carbon tracks or a worn center contact. Cracks in the cap can be very hard to see. They are usually hairline thin and run in odd directions within the cap.

Replace the cap if necessary, transferring the wires one at a time from the old cap to the new one.

2. Pull the ignition rotor (not the signal rotor) straight up and remove it. Replace it if the contacts are worn, burned or pitted. Do not file the contacts.

3. Turn the engine over (you may use a socket wrench on the front pulley bolt to do this) until the projection on the pickup coil is directly opposite the signal rotor tooth.

4. Get a non-ferrous (paper, brass, or plastic) feeler gauge of 0.3mm (0.012 in.), and insert it into the pick-up air gap. DO NOT use an ordinary metal feeler gauge! The gauge should just touch either side of the gap. The permissible range is 0.20–0.40mm (0.008–0.016 in.).

NOTE: *The air gap is not adjustable. If the gap is not within specifications, the pick-up coil assembly must be replaced.*

Fuel Injected Engines

These electronically controlled fuel injection systems rely on the Electronic Control Module (ECM) for proper operation. Because the ECM needs to receive information from the distributor (and to control its function), there are two pickup coils in the distributor. Make sure you measure the gap to each coil.

1. Remove the distributor cap. Inspect the cap for cracks, carbon tracks or a worn center contact. Cracks in the cap can be very hard to see. They are usually hairline thin and run in odd directions within the cap.

Replace the cap if necessary, transferring the wires one at a time from the old cap to the new one.

2. Pull the ignition rotor (not the signal rotor) straight up and remove it. Replace it if the contacts are worn, burned or pitted. Do not file the contacts.

3. Turn the engine over (you may use a socket wrench on the front pulley bolt to do this) until the projection on the pickup coil is directly opposite a signal rotor tooth.

4. Get a non-ferrous (paper, brass, or plastic) feeler gauge of 0.3mm (0.012 in.), and insert it into the air gaps between the signal rotor and the pickup coil projections on each side. DO NOT use an ordinary metal feeler gauge! The gauge should just touch either side of the gap. The permissible range is 0.2–0.4mm (0.008–0.016 in.).

5. The air gap is totally non-adjustable. Should it be out of specification, the entire distributor must be replaced.

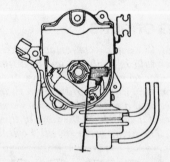

Checking the air gap on electronic ignition system

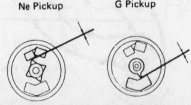

Measuring the air gap on 4A-GE engine — the Ne pickup is the rpm sensor and the G pickup is the crankshaft angle (engine position) sensor

PARTS REPLACEMENT

The two most commonly replaced parts in the distributor (aside from the cap and rotor as maintenance) will be the signal generator and the igniter. Replacement of any internal piece usually requires removal of the distributor from the engine.

NOTE: *The distributor on some engine contains no replaceable parts except the ignition coil. Any other failed item in the distributor requires replacement of the complete unit.*

Distributor Removal

WARNING: *Once the distributor is removed, the engine should not be turned or moved out of position. Should this occur, please refer to the Distributor section of Chapter 3.*

3A, 3E, 3A-C and 4A-C Engines

1. Disconnect the negative battery cable.
2. Disconnect the distributor wire at its connector.
3. Label and disconnect the vacuum hoses running to the vacuum advance unit on the side of the distributor.
4. Remove the distributor cap (leave the spark plug wires connected) and swing it out of the way.
5. Carefully note the position of the distributor rotor relative to the distributor housing; a mark made on the casing will be helpful during

reassembly. Use a marker or tape so the mark doesn't rub off during the handling of the case.
6. Remove the distributor holddown bolts.
7. Carefully pull the distributor out from the engine.
8. If the engine has not been moved out of position, align the rotor with the mark you made earlier and reinstall the distributor. Position it carefully and make sure the drive gear engages properly within the engine. Complete the installation by following Steps 1–6 above in reverse order.
9. Check and reset the engine timing. Please refer to the Ignition Timing section later in this Chapter.

3E-E, 4A-GE and 4A-GZE Engines

1. Label and disconnect the coil and spark plug wiring at the distributor cap.
2. Disconnect the distributor wire at its connector.
3. Remove the distributor holddown bolts. Before moving or disturbing the distributor, mark the position of the distributor relative to the engine. Use a marker or tape so the mark doesn't rub off during the handling of the case.
4. Remove the distributor from the engine.
5. Remove the O-ring from the distributor shaft.
6. If the engine has not been moved out of position, align the rotor with the mark you made earlier and reinstall the distributor. Posi-

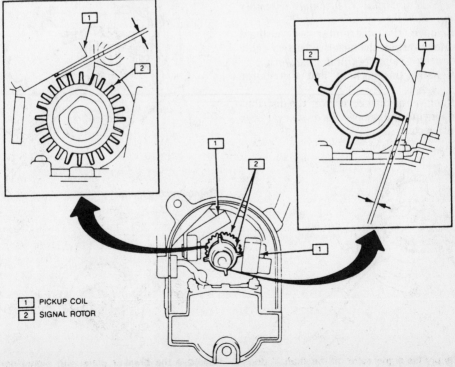

| 1 | PICKUP COIL |
| 2 | SIGNAL ROTOR |

Checking the air gap on 4A-FE engine

tion it carefully and make sure the drive gear engages properly within the engine. Complete the installation by following Steps 1–5 above in reverse order. For complete reinstallation instructions, refer to the Distributor section in Chapter 3.

4A-FE Engine

1. Disconnect the negative battery cable.
2. Disconnect all electrical connections at the distributor, including the plug wires.
3. Remove the distributor cap.
4. Mark the position of the distributor case relative to the engine. Use a marker or tape so the mark doesn't rub off during the handling of the case. Also mark the position of the distributor rotor relative to the case.
5. Remove the distributor mounting bolts.
6. Remove the distributor from the engine and remove the O-ring from the distributor shaft.
7. If the engine has not been moved out of position, align the rotor with the mark you made earlier and reinstall the distributor. Position it carefully and make sure the drive gear engages properly within the engine. Complete the installation by following Steps 1–6 above in reverse order.

Coil, Igniter, Signal Generator Assembly (Integrated Ignition Assembly) Replacement

NOTE: *Review the complete service procedure before this repair. Note position and routing of all internal distributor assembly wiring.*

1. Remove the distributor as outlined above. Make certain the negative battery cable is disconnected before beginning the work.
2. Remove the packing and distributor rotor.
3. Remove the dust cover over the distributor components and remove the dust cover over the ignition coil.

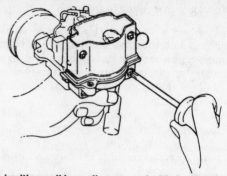

The ignition coil is easily removed with the distributor of the car

4. Remove the nuts and disconnect the wiring from the ignition coil.
5. Remove the four screws and remove the ignition coil from the distributor.
6. At the igniter terminals, disconnect the wiring from the connecting points.
7. Loosen and remove the two screws holding the igniter and remove it from the distributor.
8. If the signal rotor is to be replaced, use a screwdriver and CAREFULLY pry the rotor and spring up and off the shaft. When replacing the rotor, use a small bearing driver or long socket to fit over the shaft on top of the signal rotor. Tap gently; the force will be equally dis-

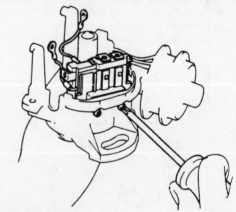

Removing the igniter

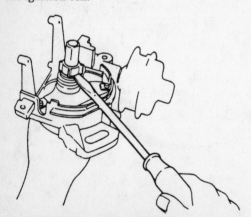

Carefully pry the signal rotor off the shaft — don't damage the shaft or distributor housing

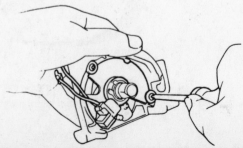

Remove the breaker plate with signal generator (pickup coil)

tributed and the rotor will slide evenly into place.

NOTE: *At this point of the service procedure, the breaker plate with the signal generator (pick-up coil) can be removed from the distributor housing by removing the retaining screws.*

9. Install the igniter and connect its wiring. Pay particular attention to the correct routing of the wiring within the housing. There is one correct position only; any other wiring placements risk damage.

10. Install the ignition coil and secure its wiring. Again, watch the wiring positions.

11. Reinstall the dust covers, the packing and distributor rotor.

12. Reinstall the distributor and set the engine timing.

IGNITION TIMING

Ignition timing is the measurement (in degrees) of crankshaft position at the instant the spark plug fires. Ignition timing is adjusted by loosening the distributor locking device and turning the distributor in the engine.

It takes a fraction of a second for the spark from the plug to completely ignite the mixture in the cylinder. Because of this, the spark plug must fire before the piston reaches TDC (top dead center, the highest point in its travel), if the mixture is to be completely ignited as the piston passes TDC. This measurement is given in degrees (of crankshaft rotation) before the piston reaches top dead center (BTDC). If the ignition timing setting for your engine is 7° BTDC, this means that the spark plug must fire at a time when the piston for that cylinder is 7° before top dead center of its compression stroke. However, this only holds true while your engine is at idle speed.

As you accelerate from idle, the speed of your engine (rpm) increases. The increase in rpm means that the pistons are now traveling up and down much faster. Because of this, the spark plugs will have to fire even sooner if the mixture is to be completely ignited as the piston passes TDC. To accomplish this, the distributor incorporates means to advance the timing of the spark as the engine speed increases.

The distributor in your carbureted vehicle (Corolla and Tercel) has two means of advancing the ignition timing. One is called centrifugal advance and is actuated by weights in the distributor. The other is called vacuum advance and is controlled by the larger circular housing on the side of the distributor.

In addition, some distributors have a vacuum-retard mechanism which is contained in the same housing on the side of the distributor as the vacuum advance. The function of this mechanism is to retard the timing of the ignition spark under certain engine conditions. The causes more complete burning of the air/fuel mixture in the cylinder and consequently lowers exhaust emissions.

Because these mechanisms change ignition timing, it is necessary to disconnect and plug the vacuum lines from the distributor when setting the basic ignition timing.

The fuel injected vehicles (Corolla, Tercel and MR2) have neither a centrifugal advance nor a vacuum unit. All the timing changes are controlled electronically by the ECM. This solid state "brain" receives data from many sensors (including the distributor), and commands changes in spark timing (and other functions) based on immediate driving conditions. This instant response allows the engine to be kept at peak performance and economy throughout the driving cycle. Basic timing can still be checked and adjusted on these motors.

If the ignition timing is set too far advanced (BTDC), the ignition and expansion of the air/fuel mixture in the cylinder will try to force the piston down while it is still traveling upward. This causes engine ping, a sound which resembles marbles being dropped into an empty tin can. If the ignition timing is too far retarded (after, or ATDC), the piston will have already started down on the power stroke when the air/fuel mixture ignites and expands. This will cause the piston to be forced down only a portion of its travel. This results in poor engine performance and lack of power.

Ignition timing adjustment is checked with a timing light. This instrument is connected to the number one (No. 1) spark plug of the engine. The timing light flashes every time an electrical current is sent from the distributor through the no. 1 spark plug wire to the spark plug. The crankshaft pulley and the front cover of the engine are marked with a timing pointer and a timing scale.

When the timing pointer is aligned with the 0 mark on the timing scale, the piston in the No. 1 cylinder is at TDC of it compression stroke. With the engine running, and the timing light aimed at the timing pointer and timing scale, the stroboscopic (periodic) flashes from the timing light will allow you to check the ignition timing setting of the engine. The timing light flashes every time the spark plug in the No. 1 cylinder of the engine fires. Since the flash from the timing light makes the crankshaft pulley seem to stand still for a moment, you will be able to read the exact position of the piston in the No. 1 cylinder on the timing scale on the front of the engine.

If you're buying a timing light, make sure the unit you select is rated for electronic or solid-state ignitions. Generally, these lights have two wires which connect to the battery with alligator clips and a third wire which connects to no. 1 plug wire. The best lights have an inductive pick-up on the third wire; this allows you to simply clip the small box over the wire. Older lights may require the removal of the plug wire and the installation of an inline adapter. Since the spark plugs in the twin-cam engines (4A-GE and 4A-FE) are in deep wells, rigging the adapter can be difficult. Buy quality the first time and the tool will give lasting results and ease of use.

CHECKING AND ADJUSTMENT

All Carbureted Engines

These engine requires a special tachometer hook-up to the service connector wire coming out of the distributor. As many tachometers are not compatible with this hook-up, we recommend that you consult with the manufacturer or salesman before purchasing a certain type.

NOTE: *NEVER allow the ignition coil terminal to become grounded; severe and expensive damage can occur to the coil and/or igniter.*

1. Warm the engine to normal operating temperature. Do not attempt to check timing or idle speed on a cold motor — all the readings will be different. Connect a tachometer and check the engine idle speed to be sure it is within the specification given in the Tune-Up Specifications chart or underhood emission sticker. Adjust the idle if needed and shut the engine off.

2. If the timing marks are difficult to see, use a dab of paint or chalk to make them more visible.

3. Connect a timing light according to the manufacturer's instructions.

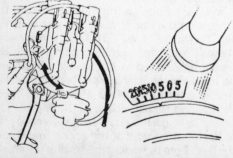

Timing marks 3A-C and 4A-C engines (note the disconnected vacuum hose)

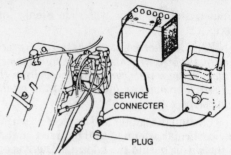

Tachometer installation — note special tachometer hook-up

4. Label and disconnect the vacuum line(s) from the distributor vacuum unit. Plug it (them) with a pencil or golf tee(s).

5. Be sure that the timing light wires are clear of the fan and start the engine.

6. Allow the engine to run at the specified idle speed with the gear shift in correct position. Refer to the underhood emission sticker as necessary.

CAUTION: *Be sure that the parking brake is set and the wheels are blocked to prevent the car from rolling in either direction.*

7. Point the timing light at the marks on the tab alongside the crank pulley. With the engine at idle, timing should be at the specification given on the Tune-Up Specification Chart at the beginning of the chapter or refer to the underhood emission sticker as necessary.

8. If the timing is not at the specification, loosen the bolts at the base of the distributor just enough so that the distributor can be turned. Turn the distributor to advance or retard the timing as required. Once the proper marks are seen to align with the timing light, timing is correct.

9. Stop the engine and tighten the bolts. Start the engine and recheck the timing and idle speed (adjust as necessary). Stop the engine; disconnect the tachometer and the timing light. Connect the vacuum line(s) to the distributor vacuum unit.

All Fuel Injected Engine

NOTE: *This is a general service procedure for setting base ignition timing. Refer to underhood emission sticker for correct specifications and any additional service procedures steps.*

These engines requires a special tachometer hook-up to the service connector wire coming out of the distributor or to the diagnostic connector. As many tachometers are not compatible with this hook-up, we recommend that you consult with the manufacturer or salesman before purchasing a certain type.

NOTE: *NEVER allow the ignition coil terminal (tachometer terminal) to become*

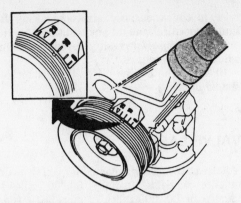

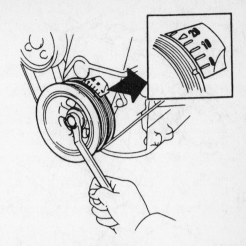

Ignition timing marks, 4A-GE engine — note the small notch on the pulley this is the mark to align with the degree scale

Timing marks 4A-FE engine

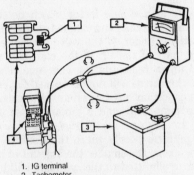

1. IG terminal
2. Tachometer
3. Battery
4. Diagnostic connector

Correct tachometer hook-up 4A-FE engine

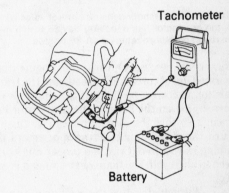

Tachometer

Battery

Tachometer

Battery

Correct tachometer hook-up 3E-E engine

grounded; severe and expensive damage can occur to the coil and/or igniter.

1. Warm the engine to normal operating temperature. Turn off all electrical accessories. Do not attempt to check timing specification or idle speed on a cold motor — all the readings will be different.

2. Connect a tachometer and check the engine idle speed to be sure it is within the specification given in the Tune-Up Specifications chart or underhood emission sticker.

3. Using a small jumper wire, short both terminals of the Check Engine connector located near the wiper motor. On some engines remove the cap on the diagnostic connector. Using a small jumper wire, short terminals E1 and T together. Adjust idle speed as necessary.

4. If the timing marks are difficult to see, shut engine off use a dab of paint or chalk to make them more visible.

5. Connect a timing light according to the manufacturer's instructions.

6. Start the engine and use the timing light to observe the timing marks. With the jumper wire in the connector the timing should be to specifications (refer to underhood emission

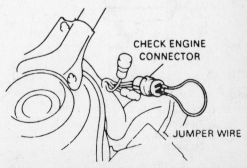

CHECK ENGINE CONNECTOR

JUMPER WIRE

Jumper wire must be installed to check timing (4A-GE engine)

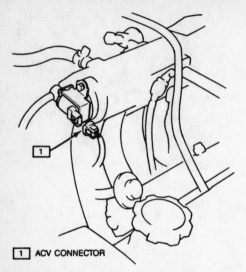

| 1 | ACV CONNECTOR |

Use care when handling the air control valve wiring — the connector has a locking device which must be released before removal 4A-FE engine

sticker as necessary) with the engine fully warmed up (at correct idle speed) and the transmission in correct position. If the timing is not correct, loosen the bolts at the distributor just enough so that the distributor can be turned. Turn the distributor to advance or retard the timing as required. Once the proper marks are seen to align with the timing light, timing is correct.

7. Without changing the position of the distributor, tighten the distributor bolt(s) and double check the timing with the light (check idle speed as necessary).

8. Disconnect the jumper wire at the Check Engine connector or Diagnostic connector.

9. Check the timing again with the light (4A-FE engine disconnect the ACV connector)

refer to the underhood emission sticker for timing specification and any additional service procedure steps. If necessary, repeat the timing adjustment procedure.

10. Shut the engine off and disconnect all test equipment.

VALVE LASH

Refer to the owner's manual for vehicle maintenance schedule (usually 30,000 miles/48 months or 60, 000 miles/72 months — some 1984 vehicles 15,000 miles/12 months) for valve clearance adjustment (lash) as all years and model engines have different mile and time intervals.

Valve lash is one factor which determines how far the intake and exhaust valves will open into the cylinder. If the valve clearance is too large, part of the lift of the camshaft will be used up in removing the excessive clearance, thus the valves will not be opened far enough. This condition has two effects, the valve train components will emit a tapping noise as they take up the excessive clearance, and the engine will perform poorly, since the less the intake valve opens, the smaller the amount of air/fuel mixture admitted to the cylinders will be. The less the exhaust valves open, the greater the back-pressure in the cylinder which prevents the proper air/fuel mixture from entering the cylinder.

If the valve clearance is too small, the intake and exhaust valves will not fully seat on the cylinder head when they close. When a valve seats on the cylinder head it does two things, it seals the combustion chamber so none of the gases

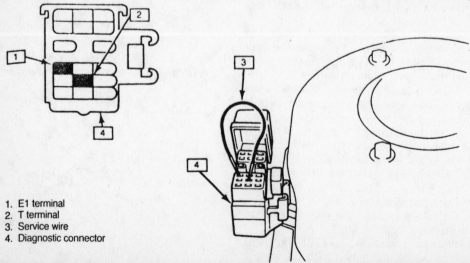

1. E1 terminal
2. T terminal
3. Service wire
4. Diagnostic connector

Checking the timing requires shorting the E_1 and T terminals at the diagnostic connector — see text for details

in the cylinder can escape and it cools itself by transferring some of the heat it absorbed from the combustion process through the cylinder head and into the engine cooling system. Therefore, if the valve clearance is too small, the engine will run poorly (due to gases escaping from the combustion chamber), and the valves will overheat and warp (since they cannot transfer heat unless they are touching the seat in the cylinder head).

NOTE: *While all valve adjustments must be as accurate as possible, it is better to have the valve adjustment slightly loose than slightly tight, as burnt valves may result form overly tight adjustments.*

ADJUSTMENT

3A, 3A-C and 4A-C Engines (8 Valves)
3E and 3E-E Engines (12 Valves)

1. Start the engine and run it until it reaches normal operating temperature.

2. Stop the engine. Remove the air cleaner assembly. Remove the valve cover.

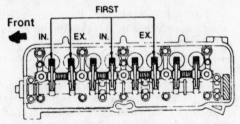

Adjust these valves FIRST on 3A, 3A-C and 4A-C engines

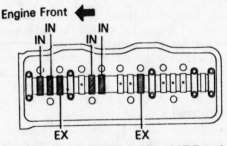

Adjust these valves FIRST on 3E and 3E-E engines

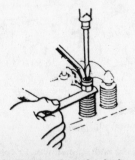

Checking and adjusting the valve lash

CAUTION: *Be careful when removing components; the engine will be hot.*

3. Turn the crankshaft until the pointer or notch on the pulley aligns with the **O** or the **T** mark on the timing scale. This will ensure that the engine is at TDC. Turning the engine (with a wrench on the crankshaft bolt) is much easier if the spark plugs are removed.

NOTE: *Check that the rocker arms on the No. 1 cylinder are loose and those on the No. 4 cylinder are tight. If not, turn the crankshaft one complete revolution (360°).*

4. Using a feeler gauge, check the clearance between the bottom of the rocker arm and the top of the valve stem. This measurement should correspond to the one given in the Tune-Up Specifications Chart in this chapter. Check only the valves listed under First in the accompanying illustrations for your engine.

5. If the clearance is not within specifications, the valves will require adjustment. Loosen the locknut on the rocker arm and, still holding the nut with an open end wrench, turn the adjustment screw to achieve the correct clearance. This is a detail-oriented job; work for exact clearance.

6. Once the correct clearance is achieved, keep the adjustment screw from turning with your screwdriver, and then tighten the locknut. Recheck the valve clearance. If it's proper, proceed to the next valve as shown on the diagram.

7. After the correct four valves have been adjusted, turn the engine one complete revolution (360°) and adjust the remaining valves. Follow Steps 4–6 and use the valve arrangement illustration marked Second.

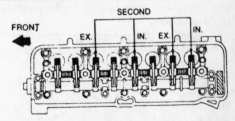

Adjust these valves SECOND on 3A, 3A-C and 4A-C engines

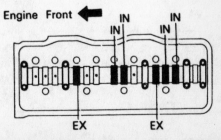

Adjust these valves SECOND on 3E and 3E-E engines

8. Use a new gasket and then install the valve cover. Install any other components which were removed for access to the cover.

9. Start the engine. Listen for any excessive tapping (indicating a loosened rocker) and check the valve cover for any signs of oil leaks.

1C Diesel Engine

1. Start the engine and run it until it reaches normal operating temperature. Stop the engine. Remove the air cleaner assembly. Remove any other hoses, cables, etc. which are attached to, or in the way of, the cylinder head cover. Remove the cylinder head cover.

CAUTION: *Be careful when removing components as the engine will be hot.*

2. Use a wrench and turn the crankshaft until the notch in the pulley aligns with the timing pointer in the front cover. This will insure that the engine is at TDC.

NOTE: *Check that the valve lifters on the No. 1 cylinder are loose and that those on the No. 4 cylinder are tight. If not, turn the crankshaft one complete revolution (360°) and then realign the marks.*

3. Using a flat feeler gauge, measure the clearance between the camshaft lobe and the valve lifter. This measurement should correspond to the one given in the Tune-Up chart. Check only the valves listed under **First** in the accompanying valve arrangement illustrations for your particular engine.

NOTE: *If the measurement is within specifications, go on to the next step. If not, record the measurement taken for each individual valve.*

4. Turn the crankshaft one complete revolution and realign the timing marks as previously described.

5. Measure the clearance of the valves shown in the valve arrangement illustration marked **Second**.

NOTE: *If the measurement for this set of valves (and also the previous one) is within specifications, you need go no further, the procedure is finished. If not, record the measurements and proceed to Step 6.*

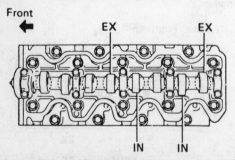

Adjust these valve SECOND on 1C-L diesel engine

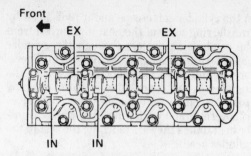

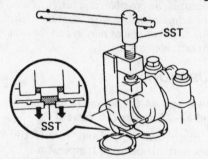

Adjust these valves FIRST on 1C-L diesel engine

Installing the special tool to depress the valve lifters — diesel engine

6. Turn the crankshaft to position the intake camshaft lobe of the cylinder to be adjusted, upward.

7. Using a small screwdriver, turn the valve lifter so that the notch is easily accessible.

8. Install SST #09248-64010 or equivalent between the two camshaft lobes and then turn the handle so that the tool presses down both (intake and exhaust) valve lifters evenly.

9. Using a small screwdriver and a magnet, remove the valve shims.

10. Measure the thickness of the old shim with a micrometer. Locate that particular measurement in the Installed Shim Thickness column of the accompanying chart, then locate the already recorded measurement for that valve in the Measured Clearance column of the chart. Index the two columns to arrive at the proper replacement shim thickness.

NOTE: *On Diesel engines, replacement shims are available in 25 sizes, in increments*

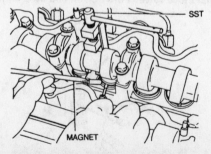

Use a magnet and screwdriver to remove the old valve shims — diesel engine

SHIM SELECTION CHART

Exhaust

Measured Clearance (mm)	Installed Shim Thickness (mm)																																																
	2.200	2.225	2.250	2.275	2.300	2.325	2.350	2.375	2.400	2.425	2.450	2.475	2.500	2.525	2.550	2.575	2.600	2.625	2.650	2.675	2.700	2.725	2.750	2.775	2.800	2.825	2.850	2.875	2.900	2.925	2.950	2.975	3.000	3.025	3.050	3.075	3.100	3.125	3.150	3.175	3.200	3.225	3.250	3.275	3.300	3.325	3.350	3.375	3.400
0.000-0.025											01	01	01	03	03	05	05	07	07	09	09	11	11	13	13	15	15	17	17	19	19	21	21	23	23	25	25	27	27	29	29	31	31	33	33	35	35	37	37
0.026-0.050										01	01	01	03	03	05	05	07	07	09	09	11	11	13	13	15	15	17	17	19	19	21	21	23	23	25	25	27	27	29	29	31	31	33	33	35	35	37	37	39
0.051-0.075									01	01	01	03	03	05	05	07	07	09	09	11	11	13	13	15	15	17	17	19	19	21	21	23	23	25	25	27	27	29	29	31	31	33	33	35	35	37	37	39	39
0.076-0.100								01	01	01	03	03	05	05	07	07	09	09	11	11	13	13	15	15	17	17	19	19	21	21	23	23	25	25	27	27	29	29	31	31	33	33	35	35	37	37	39	39	41
0.101-0.125							01	01	01	03	03	05	05	07	07	09	09	11	11	13	13	15	15	17	17	19	19	21	21	23	23	25	25	27	27	29	29	31	31	33	33	35	35	37	37	39	39	41	41
0.126-0.150						01	01	01	03	03	05	05	07	07	09	09	11	11	13	13	15	15	17	17	19	19	21	21	23	23	25	25	27	27	29	29	31	31	33	33	35	35	37	37	39	39	41	41	43
0.151-0.175					01	01	01	03	03	05	05	07	07	09	09	11	11	13	13	15	15	17	17	19	19	21	21	23	23	25	25	27	27	29	29	31	31	33	33	35	35	37	37	39	39	41	41	43	43
0.176-0.200				01	01	01	03	03	05	05	07	07	09	09	11	11	13	13	15	15	17	17	19	19	21	21	23	23	25	25	27	27	29	29	31	31	33	33	35	35	37	37	39	39	41	41	43	43	45
0.201-0.225			01	01	01	03	03	05	05	07	07	09	09	11	11	13	13	15	15	17	17	19	19	21	21	23	23	25	25	27	27	29	29	31	31	33	33	35	35	37	37	39	39	41	41	43	43	45	45
0.226-0.249		01	01	01	03	03	05	05	07	07	09	09	11	11	13	13	15	15	17	17	19	19	21	21	23	23	25	25	27	27	29	29	31	31	33	33	35	35	37	37	39	39	41	41	43	43	45	45	47
0.250-0.350																																																	
0.351-0.375	03	05	05	07	07	09	09	11	11	13	13	15	15	17	17	19	19	21	21	23	23	25	25	27	27	29	29	31	31	33	33	35	35	37	37	39	39	41	41	43	43	45	45	47	47	49	49	49	
0.376-0.400	05	05	07	07	09	09	11	11	13	13	15	15	17	17	19	19	21	21	23	23	25	25	27	27	29	29	31	31	33	33	35	35	37	37	39	39	41	41	43	43	45	45	47	47	49	49	49		
0.401-0.425	05	07	07	09	09	11	11	13	13	15	15	17	17	19	19	21	21	23	23	25	25	27	27	29	29	31	31	33	33	35	35	37	37	39	39	41	41	43	43	45	45	47	47	49	49	49			
0.426-0.450	07	07	09	09	11	11	13	13	15	15	17	17	19	19	21	21	23	23	25	25	27	27	29	29	31	31	33	33	35	35	37	37	39	39	41	41	43	43	45	45	47	47	49	49	49				
0.451-0.475	07	09	09	11	11	13	13	15	15	17	17	19	19	21	21	23	23	25	25	27	27	29	29	31	31	33	33	35	35	37	37	39	39	41	41	43	43	45	45	47	47	49	49	49					
0.476-0.500	09	09	11	11	13	13	15	15	17	17	19	19	21	21	23	23	25	25	27	27	29	29	31	31	33	33	35	35	37	37	39	39	41	41	43	43	45	45	47	47	49	49	49						
0.501-0.525	09	11	11	13	13	15	15	17	17	19	19	21	21	23	23	25	25	27	27	29	29	31	31	33	33	35	35	37	37	39	39	41	41	43	43	45	45	47	47	49	49	49							
0.526-0.550	11	11	13	13	15	15	17	17	19	19	21	21	23	23	25	25	27	27	29	29	31	31	33	33	35	35	37	37	39	39	41	41	43	43	45	45	47	47	49	49	49								
0.551-0.575	11	13	13	15	15	17	17	19	19	21	21	23	23	25	25	27	27	29	29	31	31	33	33	35	35	37	37	39	39	41	41	43	43	45	45	47	47	49	49	49									
0.576-0.600	13	13	15	15	17	17	19	19	21	21	23	23	25	25	27	27	29	29	31	31	33	33	35	35	37	37	39	39	41	41	43	43	45	45	47	47	49	49	49										
0.601-0.625	13	15	15	17	17	19	19	21	21	23	23	25	25	27	27	29	29	31	31	33	33	35	35	37	37	39	39	41	41	43	43	45	45	47	47	49	49	49											
0.626-0.650	15	15	17	17	19	19	21	21	23	23	25	25	27	27	29	29	31	31	33	33	35	35	37	37	39	39	41	41	43	43	45	45	47	47	49	49	49												
0.651-0.675	15	17	17	19	19	21	21	23	23	25	25	27	27	29	29	31	31	33	33	35	35	37	37	39	39	41	41	43	43	45	45	47	47	49	49	49													
0.676-0.701	17	17	19	19	21	21	23	23	25	25	27	27	29	29	31	31	33	33	35	35	37	37	39	39	41	41	43	43	45	45	47	47	49	49	49														
0.701-0.725	17	19	19	21	21	23	23	25	25	27	27	29	29	31	31	33	33	35	35	37	37	39	39	41	41	43	43	45	45	47	47	49	49	49															
0.726-0.750	19	19	21	21	23	23	25	25	27	27	29	29	31	31	33	33	35	35	37	37	39	39	41	41	43	43	45	45	47	47	49	49	49																
0.751-0.775	19	21	21	23	23	25	25	27	27	29	29	31	31	33	33	35	35	37	37	39	39	41	41	43	43	45	45	47	47	49	49	49																	
0.776-0.800	21	21	23	23	25	25	27	27	29	29	31	31	33	33	35	35	37	37	39	39	41	41	43	43	45	45	47	47	49	49	49																		
0.801-0.825	21	23	23	25	25	27	27	29	29	31	31	33	33	35	35	37	37	39	39	41	41	43	43	45	45	47	47	49	49	49																			
0.826-0.850	23	23	25	25	27	27	29	29	31	31	33	33	35	35	37	37	39	39	41	41	43	43	45	45	47	47	49	49	49																				
0.851-0.875	23	25	25	27	27	29	29	31	31	33	33	35	35	37	37	39	39	41	41	43	43	45	45	47	47	49	49	49																					
0.876-0.900	25	25	27	27	29	29	31	31	33	33	35	35	37	37	39	39	41	41	43	43	45	45	47	47	49	49	49																						
0.901-0.925	25	27	27	29	29	31	31	33	33	35	35	37	37	39	39	41	41	43	43	45	45	47	47	49	49	49																							
0.926-0.950	27	27	29	29	31	31	33	33	35	35	37	37	39	39	41	41	43	43	45	45	47	47	49	49	49																								
0.951-0.975	27	29	29	31	31	33	33	35	35	37	37	39	39	41	41	43	43	45	45	47	47	49	49	49																									
0.976-1.000	29	29	31	31	33	33	35	35	37	37	39	39	41	41	43	43	45	45	47	47	49	49	49																										
1.001-1.025	29	31	31	33	33	35	35	37	37	39	39	41	41	43	43	45	45	47	47	49	49	49																											
1.026-1.050	31	31	33	33	35	35	37	37	39	39	41	41	43	43	45	45	47	47	49	49	49																												
1.051-1.075	31	33	33	35	35	37	37	39	39	41	41	43	43	45	45	47	47	49	49	49																													
1.076-1.100	33	33	35	35	37	37	39	39	41	41	43	43	45	45	47	47	49	49	49																														
1.101-1.125	33	35	35	37	37	39	39	41	41	43	43	45	45	47	47	49	49	49																															
1.126-1.150	35	35	37	37	39	39	41	41	43	43	45	45	47	47	49	49	49																																
1.151-1.175	35	37	37	39	39	41	41	43	43	45	45	47	47	49	49	49																																	
1.176-1.200	37	37	39	39	41	41	43	43	45	45	47	47	49	49	49																																		
1.201-1.225	37	39	39	41	41	43	43	45	45	47	47	49	49	49																																			
1.226-1.250	39	39	41	41	43	43	45	45	47	47	49	49	49																																				
1.251-1.275	39	41	41	43	43	45	45	47	47	49	49	49																																					
1.276-1.300	41	41	43	43	45	45	47	47	49	49	49																																						
1.301-1.325	41	43	43	45	45	47	47	49	49	49																																							
1.326-1.350	43	43	45	45	47	47	49	49	49																																								
1.351-1.375	43	45	45	47	47	49	49	49																																									
1.376-1.400	45	45	47	47	49	49	49																																										
1.401-1.425	45	47	47	49	49	49																																											
1.426-1.450	47	47	49	49	49																																												
1.451-1.475	47	49	49	49																																													
1.476-1.500	49	49	49																																														
1.501-1.525	49	49																																															
1.526-1.550	49																																																

Exhaust Valve Clearance (cold): 0.25 – 0.35 mm (0.0010 – 0.014 in.)

Example: 2.700 mm (0.1063 in.) shim installed
Measured clearance is 0.450 mm (0.0177 in.).
Replace 2.700 mm (0.1063 in.) shim with shim No. 27.

Shim Thickness

Shim No.	Thickness mm (in.)	Shim No.	Thickness mm (in.)
01	2.20 (0.0866)	27	2.85 (0.1122)
03	2.25 (0.0886)	29	2.90 (0.1142)
05	2.30 (0.0906)	31	2.95 (0.1161)
07	2.35 (0.0925)	33	3.00 (0.1181)
09	2.40 (0.0945)	35	3.05 (0.1201)
11	2.45 (0.0965)	37	3.10 (0.1220)
13	2.50 (0.0984)	39	3.15 (0.1240)
15	2.55 (0.1004)	41	3.20 (0.1260)
17	2.60 (0.1024)	43	3.25 (0.1280)
19	2.65 (0.1043)	45	3.30 (0.1299)
21	2.70 (0.1063)	47	3.35 (0.1319)
23	2.75 (0.1083)	49	3.40 (0.1339)
25	2.80 (0.1102)		

SHIM SELECTION CHART

Intake

Installed Shim Thickness (mm)

(Large triangular shim-selection matrix cross-referencing "Measured Clearance (mm)" rows — from 0.000–0.025 down to 1.476–1.500 — against "Installed Shim Thickness (mm)" columns from 2.200 to 3.400 in 0.025 increments. The intersecting cells give the replacement shim number, e.g. 01, 03, 05, 07 … 49.)

Shim No.	Thickness mm (in.)	Shim No.	Thickness mm (in.)
01	2.20 (0.0866)	27	2.85 (0.1122)
03	2.25 (0.0886)	29	2.90 (0.1142)
05	2.30 (0.0906)	31	2.95 (0.1161)
07	2.35 (0.0925)	33	3.00 (0.1181)
09	2.40 (0.0945)	35	3.05 (0.1201)
11	2.45 (0.0965)	37	3.10 (0.1220)
13	2.50 (0.0984)	39	3.15 (0.1240)
15	2.55 (0.1004)	41	3.20 (0.1260)
17	2.60 (0.1024)	43	3.25 (0.1280)
19	2.65 (0.1043)	45	3.30 (0.1299)
21	2.70 (0.1063)	47	3.35 (0.1319)
23	2.75 (0.1083)	49	3.40 (0.1339)
25	2.80 (0.1102)		

Shim Thickness

Intake Valve Clearance (cold): 0.20 – 0.30 mm (0.008" – 0.012 in.)

Example: 2.700 mm (0.1063 in.) shim installed Measured clearance is 0.350 mm (0.0138 in.). Replace 2.700 mm (0.1063 in.) shim with shim No. 25.

of 0.050mm, from 2.200mm to 3.400mm.

11. Install the new shim, remove the special tool and then recheck the valve clearance.

12. Installation of the remaining components is in the reverse order of removal. Check and adjust (if necessary), both the injection timing and the idle speed.

4A-GE and 4A-GZE Engines (16 valve) 4A-F 4A-FE Engines (16 valves)

NOTE: *The use of the correct special tools or their equivalent is REQUIRED for this procedure. The valve adjustment requires removal of the adjusting shims (Tool kit J–37141 available from Kent-Moore Tool or a Toyota equivalent) and accurate measurement of the shims with a micrometer. A selection of replacement shims (refer to parts department of your Toyota dealer) is also required. Do not attempt this procedure if you are not equipped with the proper tools. Valves on this motor are adjusted with the motor cold. Do not attempt adjustment if the engine has been run within the previous 4 hours. An overnight cooling period is recommended.*

1. Remove the valve cover following procedures discussed in Chapter 3.

2. Turn the crankshaft to align the groove

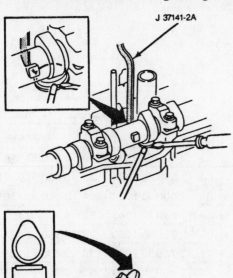

Carefully remove the shim to be replaced (above) with a small screwdriver and magnetic tools — clean and dry the shim before measuring with a micrometer (below)

in the crankshaft pulley with the **0** mark on the timing belt cover. Removing the spark plugs makes this easier, but is not required.

3. Check that the lifters on No.1 cylinder are loose and those on No.4 are tight. If not, turn the crankshaft pulley one full revolution (360°).

4. Using the feeler gauge, measure the clearance on the four valves shown in the diagram labeled First Pass. Make a WRITTEN record of any measurements which are not within specification.

5. Rotate the crankshaft pulley one full turn (360°) and check the clearance on the other four valves. These are shown on the diagram labeled Second Pass. Any measurements not within specification should be added to your WRITTEN record.

6. For ANY given valve needing adjustment:

   a. Turn the crankshaft pulley until the camshaft lobe points upward over the valve. This takes the tension off the valve and spring.

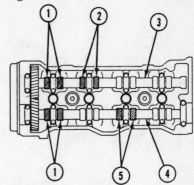

1. Valves—number 1 cylinder
2. Valves—number 2 cylinder
3. Intake camshaft
4. Exhaust camshaft
5. Valves—number 3 cylinder

FIRST PASS when checking valve clearance on twin cam engines

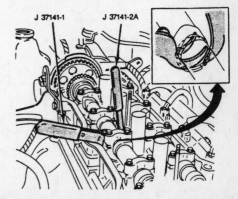

Use the correct tools to depress and hold down the valve lifter

Intake

Installed Shim Thickness (mm)

Measured Clearance (mm) columns correspond to installed shim thicknesses: 2.500, 2.525, 2.550, 2.575, 2.600, 2.620, 2.640, 2.650, 2.660, 2.680, 2.700, 2.720, 2.740, 2.750, 2.760, 2.780, 2.800, 2.820, 2.840, 2.850, 2.860, 2.880, 2.900, 2.920, 2.940, 2.950, 2.960, 2.980, 3.000, 3.020, 3.040, 3.050, 3.060, 3.080, 3.100, 3.120, 3.140, 3.150, 3.160, 3.180, 3.200, 3.225, 3.250, 3.275, 3.300

Measured Clearance (mm)
0.000 – 0.009
0.010 – 0.025
0.026 – 0.029
0.030 – 0.040
0.041 – 0.050
0.051 – 0.070
0.071 – 0.075
0.076 – 0.090
0.091 – 0.100
0.101 – 0.120
0.121 – 0.125
0.126 – 0.140
0.141 – 0.149
0.150 – 0.250
0.251 – 0.270
0.271 – 0.275
0.276 – 0.290
0.291 – 0.300
0.301 – 0.320
0.321 – 0.325
0.326 – 0.340
0.341 – 0.350
0.351 – 0.370
0.371 – 0.375
0.376 – 0.390
0.391 – 0.400
0.401 – 0.420
0.421 – 0.425
0.426 – 0.440
0.441 – 0.450
0.451 – 0.470
0.471 – 0.475
0.476 – 0.490
0.491 – 0.500
0.501 – 0.520
0.521 – 0.525
0.526 – 0.540
0.541 – 0.550
0.551 – 0.570
0.571 – 0.575
0.576 – 0.590
0.591 – 0.600
0.601 – 0.620
0.621 – 0.625
0.626 – 0.640
0.641 – 0.650
0.651 – 0.670
0.671 – 0.675
0.676 – 0.690
0.691 – 0.700
0.701 – 0.720
0.721 – 0.725
0.726 – 0.740
0.741 – 0.750
0.751 – 0.770
0.771 – 0.775
0.776 – 0.790
0.791 – 0.800
0.801 – 0.820
0.821 – 0.825
0.826 – 0.840
0.841 – 0.850
0.851 – 0.870
0.871 – 0.875
0.876 – 0.890
0.891 – 0.900
0.901 – 0.925
0.926 – 0.950
0.951 – 0.975
0.976 – 1.000
1.001 – 1.025

The body of the chart contains shim number values (02, 04, 06, 08, 10, 12, 14, 16, 18, 20, 22, 24, 26, 28, 30, 32, 34) arranged diagonally across the matrix indicating the replacement shim number for each combination of measured clearance and installed shim thickness.

Shim thickness — mm (in.)

Shim No.	Thickness	Shim No.	Thickness
02	2.500 (0.0984)	20	2.950 (0.1161)
04	2.550 (0.1004)	22	3.000 (0.1181)
06	2.600 (0.1024)	24	3.050 (0.1201)
08	2.650 (0.1043)	26	3.100 (0.1220)
10	2.700 (0.1063)	28	3.150 (0.1240)
12	2.750 (0.1083)	30	3.200 (0.1260)
14	2.800 (0.1102)	32	3.250 (0.1280)
16	2.850 (0.1122)	34	3.300 (0.1299)
18	2.900 (0.1142)		

Intake valve clearance (cold):
    0.15 – 0.25 mm (0.006 – 0.010 in.)

Example: A 2.800 mm shim is installed
    and the measured clearance
    is 0.450 mm.
    Replace the 2.800 mm shim
    with shim No. 24 (3.050 mm).
    Shim selection chart

Exhaust

Measured Clearance (mm)	Installed Shim Thickness (mm)																																												
	2.500	2.525	2.550	2.575	2.600	2.620	2.640	2.650	2.660	2.680	2.700	2.720	2.740	2.750	2.760	2.780	2.800	2.820	2.840	2.850	2.860	2.880	2.900	2.920	2.940	2.950	2.960	2.980	3.000	3.020	3.040	3.050	3.060	3.080	3.100	3.120	3.140	3.150	3.160	3.180	3.200	3.225	3.250	3.275	3.300
0.000 - 0.009												02	02	02	02	04	04	06	06	06	06	08	08	10	10	10	10	12	12	14	14	14	14	16	16	18	18	18	18	20	20	22	22	24	24
0.010 - 0.025												02	02	02	04	04	06	06	06	06	08	08	10	10	10	10	12	12	14	14	14	14	16	16	18	18	18	18	20	20	22	22	22	24	26
0.026 - 0.040											02	02	02	04	04	04	06	06	06	08	08	08	10	10	10	12	12	12	14	14	14	16	16	16	18	18	18	20	20	20	22	22	24	24	26
0.041 - 0.050										02	02	02	04	04	04	06	06	06	08	08	08	10	10	10	12	12	12	14	14	14	16	16	16	18	18	18	20	20	20	22	22	22	24	24	26
0.051 - 0.070										02	02	04	04	04	04	06	06	08	08	08	08	10	10	12	12	12	12	14	14	16	16	16	16	18	18	20	20	20	20	22	22	24	24	26	26
0.071 - 0.090								02	02	02	04	04	04	06	06	06	08	08	08	10	10	10	12	12	12	14	14	14	16	16	16	18	18	18	20	20	20	22	22	22	24	24	26	26	28
0.091 - 0.100							02	02	02	04	04	04	06	06	06	08	08	08	10	10	10	12	12	12	14	14	14	16	16	16	18	18	18	20	20	20	22	22	22	24	24	24	26	26	28
0.101 - 0.120						02	02	02	02	04	04	06	06	06	06	08	08	10	10	10	10	12	12	14	14	14	14	16	16	18	18	18	18	20	20	22	22	22	22	24	24	26	26	28	28
0.121 - 0.140					02	02	02	04	04	04	06	06	06	08	08	08	10	10	10	12	12	12	14	14	14	16	16	16	18	18	18	20	20	20	22	22	22	24	24	24	26	26	28	28	30
0.141 - 0.150					02	02	04	04	04	06	06	06	08	08	08	10	10	10	12	12	12	14	14	14	16	16	16	18	18	18	20	20	20	22	22	22	24	24	24	26	26	26	28	28	30
0.151 - 0.170				02	02	04	04	04	04	06	06	08	08	08	08	10	10	12	12	12	12	14	14	16	16	16	16	18	18	20	20	20	20	22	22	24	24	24	24	26	26	28	28	30	30
0.171 - 0.190			02	02	04	04	04	06	06	06	08	08	08	10	10	10	12	12	12	14	14	14	16	16	16	18	18	18	20	20	20	22	22	22	24	24	24	26	26	26	28	28	30	30	32
0.191 - 0.199			02	02	04	04	06	06	06	08	08	08	10	10	10	12	12	12	14	14	14	16	16	16	18	18	18	20	20	20	22	22	22	24	24	24	26	26	26	28	28	28	30	30	32
0.200 - 0.300																																													
0.301 - 0.320	04	06	06	08	08	10	10	10	10	12	12	14	14	14	14	16	16	18	18	18	18	20	20	22	22	22	22	24	24	26	26	26	26	28	28	30	30	30	30	32	32	34	34		
0.321 - 0.325	04	06	06	08	08	10	10	10	12	12	12	14	14	14	16	16	16	18	18	18	20	20	20	22	22	22	24	24	24	26	26	26	28	28	28	30	30	30	32	32	32	34	34		
0.326 - 0.340	06	06	08	08	10	10	10	12	12	12	14	14	14	16	16	16	18	18	18	20	20	20	22	22	22	24	24	24	26	26	26	28	28	28	30	30	30	32	32	32	34	34			
0.341 - 0.350	06	06	08	08	10	10	12	12	12	12	14	14	16	16	16	16	18	18	20	20	20	20	22	22	24	24	24	24	26	26	28	28	28	28	30	30	32	32	32	32	34	34			
0.351 - 0.370	06	08	08	10	10	12	12	12	12	14	14	16	16	16	16	18	18	20	20	20	20	22	22	24	24	24	24	26	26	28	28	28	28	30	30	32	32	32	32	34	34				
0.371 - 0.375	06	08	08	10	10	12	12	12	14	14	14	16	16	16	18	18	18	20	20	20	22	22	22	24	24	24	26	26	26	28	28	28	30	30	30	32	32	32	34	34	34				
0.376 - 0.390	08	08	10	10	12	12	12	14	14	14	16	16	16	18	18	18	20	20	20	22	22	22	24	24	24	26	26	26	28	28	28	30	30	30	32	32	32	34	34	34					
0.391 - 0.400	08	08	10	10	12	12	14	14	14	14	16	16	18	18	18	18	20	20	22	22	22	22	24	24	26	26	26	26	28	28	30	30	30	30	32	32	34	34	34	34					
0.401 - 0.420	08	10	10	12	12	14	14	14	14	16	16	18	18	18	18	20	20	22	22	22	22	24	24	26	26	26	26	28	28	30	30	30	30	32	32	34	34	34	34						
0.421 - 0.425	08	10	10	12	12	14	14	14	16	16	16	18	18	18	20	20	20	22	22	22	24	24	24	26	26	26	28	28	28	30	30	30	32	32	32	34	34	34							
0.426 - 0.440	10	10	12	12	14	14	14	16	16	16	18	18	18	20	20	20	22	22	22	24	24	24	26	26	26	28	28	28	30	30	30	32	32	32	34	34	34								
0.441 - 0.450	10	10	12	12	14	14	16	16	16	16	18	18	20	20	20	20	22	22	24	24	24	24	26	26	28	28	28	28	30	30	32	32	32	32	34	34									
0.451 - 0.470	10	12	12	14	14	16	16	16	16	18	18	20	20	20	20	22	22	24	24	24	24	26	26	28	28	28	28	30	30	32	32	32	32	34	34										
0.471 - 0.475	10	12	12	14	14	16	16	16	18	18	18	20	20	20	22	22	22	24	24	24	26	26	26	28	28	28	30	30	30	32	32	32	34	34	34										
0.476 - 0.490	12	12	14	14	16	16	16	18	18	18	20	20	20	22	22	22	24	24	24	26	26	26	28	28	28	30	30	30	32	32	32	34	34	34											
0.491 - 0.500	12	12	14	14	16	16	18	18	18	18	20	20	22	22	22	22	24	24	26	26	26	26	28	28	30	30	30	30	32	32	34	34	34	34											
0.501 - 0.520	12	14	14	16	16	18	18	18	18	20	20	22	22	22	22	24	24	26	26	26	26	28	28	30	30	30	30	32	32	34	34	34	34												
0.521 - 0.525	12	14	14	16	16	18	18	18	20	20	20	22	22	22	24	24	24	26	26	26	28	28	28	30	30	30	32	32	32	34	34	34													
0.526 - 0.540	14	14	16	16	18	18	18	20	20	20	22	22	22	24	24	24	26	26	26	28	28	28	30	30	30	32	32	32	34	34	34														
0.541 - 0.550	14	14	16	16	18	18	20	20	20	20	22	22	24	24	24	24	26	26	28	28	28	28	30	30	32	32	32	32	34	34															
0.551 - 0.570	14	16	16	18	18	20	20	20	20	22	22	24	24	24	24	26	26	28	28	28	28	30	30	32	32	32	32	34	34																
0.571 - 0.575	14	16	16	18	18	20	20	20	22	22	22	24	24	24	26	26	26	28	28	28	30	30	30	32	32	32	34	34	34																
0.576 - 0.590	16	16	18	18	20	20	20	22	22	22	24	24	24	26	26	26	28	28	28	30	30	30	32	32	32	34	34	34																	
0.591 - 0.600	16	16	18	18	20	20	22	22	22	22	24	24	26	26	26	26	28	28	30	30	30	30	32	32	34	34	34	34																	
0.601 - 0.620	16	18	18	20	20	22	22	22	22	24	24	26	26	26	26	28	28	30	30	30	30	32	32	34	34	34	34																		
0.621 - 0.625	16	18	18	20	20	22	22	22	24	24	24	26	26	26	28	28	28	30	30	30	32	32	32	34	34	34																			
0.626 - 0.640	18	18	20	20	22	22	22	24	24	24	26	26	26	28	28	28	30	30	30	32	32	32	34	34	34																				
0.641 - 0.650	18	18	20	20	22	22	24	24	24	24	26	26	28	28	28	28	30	30	32	32	32	32	34	34																					
0.651 - 0.670	18	20	20	22	22	24	24	24	24	26	26	28	28	28	28	30	30	32	32	32	32	34	34																						
0.671 - 0.675	18	20	20	22	22	24	24	24	26	26	26	28	28	28	30	30	30	32	32	32	34	34	34																						
0.676 - 0.690	20	20	22	22	24	24	24	26	26	26	28	28	28	30	30	30	32	32	32	34	34	34																							
0.691 - 0.700	20	20	22	22	24	24	26	26	26	26	28	28	30	30	30	30	32	32	34	34	34	34																							
0.701 - 0.720	20	22	22	24	24	26	26	26	26	28	28	30	30	30	30	32	32	34	34	34	34																								
0.721 - 0.725	20	22	22	24	24	26	26	26	28	28	28	30	30	30	32	32	32	34	34	34																									
0.726 - 0.740	22	22	24	24	26	26	26	28	28	28	30	30	30	32	32	32	34	34	34																										
0.741 - 0.750	22	22	24	24	26	26	28	28	28	28	30	30	32	32	32	32	34	34																											
0.751 - 0.770	22	24	24	26	26	28	28	28	28	30	30	32	32	32	32	34	34																												
0.771 - 0.775	22	24	24	26	26	28	28	28	30	30	30	32	32	32	34	34	34																												
0.776 - 0.790	24	24	26	26	28	28	28	30	30	30	32	32	32	34	34	34																													
0.791 - 0.800	24	24	26	26	28	28	30	30	30	30	32	32	34	34	34	34																													
0.801 - 0.820	24	26	26	28	28	30	30	30	30	32	32	34	34	34	34																														
0.821 - 0.825	24	26	26	28	28	30	30	30	32	32	32	34	34	34																															
0.826 - 0.840	26	26	28	28	30	30	30	32	32	32	34	34	34																																
0.841 - 0.850	26	26	28	28	30	30	32	32	32	32	34	34																																	
0.851 - 0.870	26	28	28	30	30	32	32	32	32	34	34																																		
0.871 - 0.875	26	28	28	30	30	32	32	32	34	34	34																																		
0.876 - 0.890	28	28	30	30	32	32	32	34	34	34																																			
0.891 - 0.900	28	28	30	30	32	32	34	34	34	34																																			
0.901 - 0.925	28	30	30	32	32	34	34	34																																					
0.926 - 0.950	30	30	32	32	34	34																																							
0.951 - 0.975	30	32	32	34	34																																								
0.976 - 1.000	32	32	34	34																																									
1.001 - 1.025	32	34	34																																										
1.026 - 1.050	34	34																																											
1.051 - 1.075	34																																												

Shim thickness mm (in.)

Shim No.	Thickness	Shim No.	Thickness
02	2.500 (0.0984)	20	2.950 (0.1161)
04	2.550 (0.1004)	22	3.000 (0.1181)
06	2.600 (0.1024)	24	3.050 (0.1201)
08	2.650 (0.1043)	26	3.100 (0.1220)
10	2.700 (0.1063)	28	3.150 (0.1240)
12	2.750 (0.1083)	30	3.200 (0.1260)
14	2.800 (0.1102)	32	3.250 (0.1280)
16	2.850 (0.1122)	34	3.300 (0.1299)
18	2.900 (0.1142)		

Exhaust valve clearance (cold):
0.20 – 0.30 mm (0.008 – 0.012 in.)

Example: **A 2.800 mm shim is installed and the measured clearance is 0.450 mm. Replace the 2.800 mm shim with shim No. 22 (3.000 mm).**

Shim selection chart

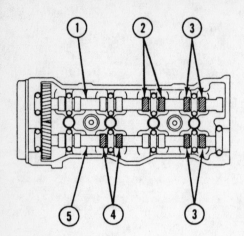

1. Intake camshaft
2. Valves—number 3 cylinder
3. Valves—number 4 cylinder
4. Valves—number 2 cylinder
5. Exhaust camshaft

SECOND PASS when checking valve clearance on twin cam engines — requires the crankshaft to be rotated 360⁰

b. Using the forked tool, press the valve lifter downward and hold it there. Some tool kits require a second tool for holding the lifter in place, allowing the first to be removed.

c. Using small magnetic tools, remove the adjusting shim from the top of the lifter.

d. Use the micrometer and measure the thickness of the shim removed. Determine the thickness of the new shim using the formula below or the selection charts. For the purposes of the following formula, T = Thickness of the old shim; A = Valve clearance measured; N = Thickness of the new shim

• For the intake side (camshaft nearest to the intake manifold): $N = T + (A - 0.20mm)$

• For the exhaust side (camshaft nearest to the exhaust manifold): $N = T + (A - 0.25mm)$

e. Select a shim closest to the calculated thickness. Use the lifter depressor tool to press down the lifter and install the shim. Shims are available in 17 sizes from 2.50mm to 3.30mm. The standard increment is 0.05mm.

f. Repeat Steps a through e for each valve needing adjustment.

7. Reinstall the valve cover, following the procedures outlined in Chapter 3.

8. Check and adjust the timing and idle speed, following the procedures outlined in this Chapter.

IDLE SPEED AND MIXTURE ADJUSTMENT

CARBURETED ENGINES

This section contains only adjustments as they normally apply to engine tune-up. Descriptions of the carburetor and fuel systems and complete adjustment procedures can be found in Chapter 5.

When the engine in your Toyota is running, air/fuel mixture from the carburetor is being drawn into the engine by a partial vacuum created by the downward movement of the pistons. The amount of air/fuel mixture that enters the engine is controlled by the throttle plates in the bottom of the carburetor. When the engine is not running, the throttle plates are closed, completely blocking off the bottom of the carburetor from the inside of the engine.

The throttle plates are connected, through the throttle linkage, to the gas pedal inside the car. What you actually are doing when you depress the gas pedal is opening the throttle plate in the carburetor to admit more air/fuel mixture to the engine. The further you open the throttle plates in the carburetor, the higher the engine speed becomes.

To keep the engine is idling, it is necessary to open the throttle plates slightly. To prevent having to keep your foot on the gas pedal when the engine is idling, an idle speed adjusting screw is included on the carburetor. This screw has the same effect as keeping your foot on the gas pedal — it holds the throttle plate open just a bit. When the screw is turned in, it opens the throttle, raising the idle speed of the engine. This screw is called the curb idle adjusting screw, and the procedures in this section will tell you how to adjust it.

When you first start the car after an overnight period, the cold motor requires a different air-fuel mixture to run properly. Because of the different mixture, the idle speed must be higher during cold engine operation. This High Idle (sometimes called cold idle or fast idle) speed is also adjustable and should be checked periodically. If the high idle is too low, the car will bog and stall until it warms up. If the high idle is set too high, the engine is wasting fuel and suffering increased and premature wear.

Before performing any carburetor adjustments, ALL of the following conditions must be met:

• All accessories are switched off
• Ignition timing is set correctly and all vacuum lines are connected
• Transmission/transaxle in Neutral and engine warmed up to normal operating temperature

- Choke opened fully
- Fuel level in carburetor sight glass at the correct level. If the level is too high or low, adjust the float level as explained in Chapter 5.
- Tachometer installed with the + connector running to the service connector. Refer to the Ignition Timing section of Chapter 2 for further illustrations of tachometer installation.

Curb Idle Speed Adjustment

Once all the above conditions are met, the curb idle can be adjusted by turning the adjusting screw (knob) at the rear of the carburetor. It has a knurled plastic head that may be gripped with the fingers (no screwdriver required) but may be hard to get at under the air cleaner housing. Turn the knob clockwise to raise the idle and counterclockwise to lower it. Keep a close eye on the tachometer while turning the knob; sometimes a small change in the adjustor causes a big change in the idle speed. Adjust the idle speed to the rpm shown in the Tune-Up Specifications chart at the beginning of this chapter.

Idle Mixture Adjustment

To conform with Federal regulations, the idle mixture adjusting screw is adjusted at the factory and plugged with a steel plug by the manufacturer. Under normal conditions there should be no need to remove this plug.

When troubleshooting rough idle, check all other possible causes before attempting to adjust the idle mixture. Only if no other factors are found to be at fault should the idle mixture

be adjusted. Since this repair involves removal of the carburetor, it is recommended that the car be thoroughly checked on an exhaust emissions analyzer as part of the diagnostic procedure before committing to the repair. If you perform this repair incorrectly or if the idle mixture is not the cause of your problem, you may cause the car to become uncertifiable under Federal and State or Provincial emission laws.

1. Following the procedures given in Chapter 5, remove the carburetor.

2. Using the following procedure remove the Mixture Adjusting Screw plug (MAS plug).

    a. Plug all of the carburetor ports to prevent the entry of steel particles when drilling.

    b. Mark the center of the plug with a punch.

    c. Drill a 6mm hole in the center of the plug. As there is only 1mm clearance between the plug and the screw below it, drill carefully and slowly to avoid drilling onto the screw. The drill may force the plug off at any time.

    d. Through the hole in the plug, fully screw in the mixture adjusting screw with a screwdriver.

NOTE: *Be careful not to damage the screw tip by tightening the screw too tightly.*

    e. Use a 7mm drill to force the plug off.

3. Inspect the mixture adjusting screw as follows:

    a. Blow off any steel particles with compressed air.

    b. Remove the screw and inspect it. If the drill has gnawed into the screw top or if the

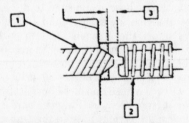

Drilling the mixture adjusting screw plug

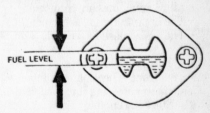

FUEL LEVEL

Check the fuel level in the float bowl

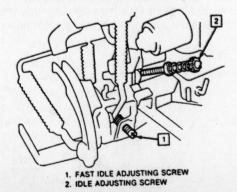

1. FAST IDLE ADJUSTING SCREW
2. IDLE ADJUSTING SCREW

Curb idle and fast idle adjusting screws

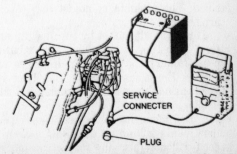

SERVICE CONNECTER

PLUG

Special service connector required for tachometer hook-up

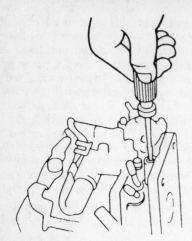

Seating the adjusting screw

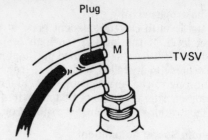

Plugging M port on TVSV valve — high idle adjustment

tapered portion is damaged, replace the screw.

4. Reinstall the mixture adjusting screw. Fully seat the idle mixture adjusting screw and then back it out 3^1/4 turns.

NOTE: *Be careful not to damage the screw tip by tightening the screw too tight.*

5. Reinstall the carburetor on the engine. Reconnect the vacuum hoses to their proper locations.

6. Reinstall the air cleaner.

7. Adjust the idle speed and mixture as follows:

   a. Check the following initial conditions:
- The air cleaner is installed
- The engine is at normal operating temperature
- The choke is fully open
- All accessories are switch off
- All vacuum lines are connected
- The ignition timing is correct
- The transmission/transaxle is in neutral (N)
- The float level is correct
- The front wheels are pointed straight ahead (power steering equipped vehicles)

   b. Start the engine

   c. Turn the mixture adjustment screw slowly until the maximum idle speed is obtained. The preliminary adjustment of 3^1/4 turn should be fairly close.

   d. Set the idle speed by turning the idle speed adjusting screw. The idle mixture speed should be as shown on either the underhood Emissions Label or the Tune-Up Specifications chart at the beginning of this Chapter.

   e. Before moving to the next step, repeat adjustments (c) and (d) until the maximum speed will not raise any further no matter how much the idle mixture adjusting screw is adjusted.

   f. Final adjust to 650 rpm by turning the mixture adjusting screw.

   g. Final adjust the idle speed to specification by turning the idle adjusting screw.

8. Reinstall the mixture adjusting screw plugs. Remove the air cleaner and the EGR vacuum modulator bracket. With the tapered end of the plug facing inward, tap in the plug until it is even with the carburetor surface.

9. Reinstall the EGR vacuum modulator bracket and the air cleaner.

High Idle Adjustment

1. Stop the engine and remove the air cleaner and its housing.

2. Plug the hot idle compensator hose. It's the hose that runs from the lower front part of the carburetor body to a small valve on the air cleaner housing. If not plugged, it will create a vacuum leak causing either a rough idle or stalling.

3. On the left side of the engine, between the block and the firewall, find the vacuum valve with five hoses connected to it. One hose will be in a separate position and four will be in line. This is the thermo vacuum switching valve (TVSV). Of the four hoses in line, one will be labeled **M**; it's usually the second one from the upper or outer end of the valve.

4. Give the hose on the **M** port ^{1}/2 turn and remove it from the port. Plug the port (not the hose) with an airtight plug to prevent vacuum leaks.

5. Hold the throttle plate open slightly (you can move the linkage with your fingers or pull

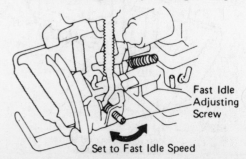

Fast Idle Adjusting Screw

Set to Fast Idle Speed

Fast idle speed adjustment

gently on the accelerator cable) and move the choke plate to its fully closed position. Hold the choke closed as you release the throttle cable.

6. Start the engine but DO NOT move the gas pedal or the accelerator cable. The engine has been fooled into thinking it's cold – the choke is set and the high idle is engaged. If you move the accelerator, you'll undo everything set up in the previous five steps.

7. Adjust the high idle by turning the Fast Idle adjusting screw; it's located just to the left and below the curb idle adjusting screw. You'll need a short, narrow screwdriver to adjust the screw. Set the fast idle to 3000 rpm.

CAUTION: *The engine is running at high speed. Beware of moving parts and hot surfaces.*

8. When the fast idle is set correctly, shut the engine off. Remove the plug from the M port of the TVSV and reconnect its hose. Remove the plug from the hot idle compensator hose.

9. Reinstall the air cleaner housing and the filter; connect the hose.

FUEL INJECTED ENGINES

Idle Speed Adjustment

One of the merits of electronic fuel injection is that it requires so little adjustment. The computer (ECM) does most of the work in compensating for changes in climate, engine temperature, electrical load and driving conditions. The curb idle on the fuel injected engines should be checked periodically but not adjusted unless off specifications by more than 50 rpm.

The idle speed adjusting screw is located on the side of the throttle body. You can find the throttle body by following the accelerator cable to its end. The adjusting screw may have a cap over it. If so, pop the cap off with a small screwdriver.

With the engine fully warmed up, properly connect a tachometer. Make sure that all the electrical accessories (cooling fan off) on the car are turned off and remove the cap over the adjustor screw, if there is one. Start the engine

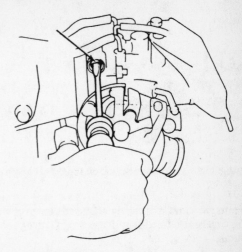

Idle speed adjusting location – fuel injected late model

(race the engine at 2,500 rpm for about 2 minutes) and use a screwdriver to turn the screw. The idle speed should be as shown on the underhood Emissions Label or in the Tune-Up Specifications chart at the beginning of this chapter.

If for any reason the idle cannot be brought into specification by this adjustment, return the screw to its original setting and follow other diagnostic procedures to find the real cause of the problem. Do not try to cure other problems with this adjustment.

Mixture Adjustment

The air/fuel ratio burned within the engine is controlled by the ECM, based on information delivered by the various sensors on the engine. It is not adjustable as a routine maintenance item. The easiest way to check the air/fuel mixture is to put the car through a tailpipe emissions test. Whether or not this is required in your area, it's a good way of putting numbers on the combustion efficiency of the engine. The engine can only burn so much fuel; if too much is being delivered, it will show up on the test as unburned hydrocarbons (HC).

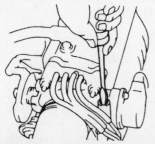

Idle speed adjusting location – fuel injected early model

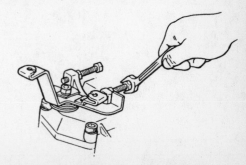

Adjusting the idle speed on the diesel engine

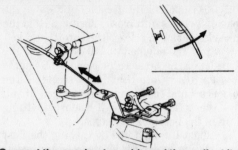

Adjusting the maximum speed on the diesel engine

Connect the accelerator cable and then adjust it so there is no slack on diesel engine

Putting the car through this test once a year from the time it is newly acquired can provide an excellent baseline for diagnosing future problems.

DIESEL ENGINE

Idle And Maximum Speed Adjustment

1. Run the engine until it reaches normal operating temperature.

NOTE: *The air cleaner should be in place, all accessories should be turned off and the transmission should be in Neutral.*

2. Install a tachometer that is compatible with diesel engines.

3. Disconnect the accelerator cable from the injection pump and then check that the idle speed is within specifications. If not, adjust it with the adjustment screw on the injection pump.

4. With the tachometer still connected, check the engine maximum speed by fully depressing the adjusting lever on the injection pump. Maximum speed should be approximately 5,100 rpm.

5. If maximum speed is not within specifications, turn the adjusting screw until it is.

6. Connect the accelerator cable and adjust it so that there is no slack.

7. Check to see that the adjusting lever is stopped by the maximum speed adjusting screw when the accelerator pedal is depressed all the way to the floor.

Engine and Engine Overhaul

3

ENGINE ELECTRICAL

For any electrical system to operate, it must make a complete circuit. This simply means that the power flow from the battery must make a complete circle. When an electrical component is operating, power flows from the battery to the components, passes through the component (load) causing it to function, and returns to the battery through the ground path of the circuit. This ground may be either another wire or the actual metal part of the car upon which the component is mounted.

Perhaps the easiest way to visualize this is to think of connecting a light bulb with two wires attached to it to the battery. If one of the two wires was attached to the negative (–) post of the battery and the other wire to the positive (+) post, the light bulb would light and the circuit would be complete. Electricity could follow a path from the battery to the bulb and back to the battery. Its not hard to see that with longer wires on our light bulb, it could be mounted anywhere on the car. Further, one wire could be fitted with a switch so that the light could be turned on and off at will. Various other items could be added to our primitive circuit to make the light flash, become brighter or dimmer under certain conditions or advise the user that it's burned out.

Some automotive components don't use a wire to battery--they ground to the metal of the car through their mounting points. The electrical current runs through the chassis of the vehicle and returns to the battery through the ground (–) cable; if you look, you'll see that the battery ground cable connects between the battery and the body of the car.

Every complete circuit must include a load--something to use the electricity coming from the source. If you were to connect a wire between the two terminals of the battery (DON'T

do this) without the light bulb, the battery would attempt to deliver its entire power supply from one pole to another almost instantly. This is a short circuit. The electricity is taking a short-cut to get to ground and is not being used by any load in the circuit. This sudden and uncontrolled electrical flow can cause great damage to other components in the circuit and can develop a tremendous amount of heat. A short in an automotive wiring harness can develop sufficient heat to melt the insulation on all the surrounding wires and reduce a multi-wire cable to one sad lump of plastic and copper. Two common causes of shorts are broken insulation (thereby exposing the wire to contact with surrounding metal surfaces) or a failed switch (the pins inside the switch come out of place, touch each other and reroute the electricity).

Some electrical components which require a large amount of current to operate also have a relay in their circuit. Since these circuits carry a large amount of current (amperage or amps), the thickness of the wire in the circuit (wire gauge) is also greater. If this large wire were connected from the load to the control switch on the dash, the switch would have to carry the high amperage load and the dash would be twice as large to accommodate wiring harnesses as thick as your wrist. To prevent these problems, a relay is used. The large wires in the circuit are connected from the battery to one side of the relay and from the opposite side of the relay to the load. The relay is normally open, preventing current from passing through the circuit. An additional, smaller wire is connected from the relay to the control switch for the circuit. When the control switch is turned on, it grounds the smaller wire to the relay and completes its circuit. The main switch inside the relay close, sending power to the component without routing the main power through the inside of the car. Some common circuits which may use relays are the horn, headlights, starter and rear window defogger systems.

It is possible for larger surges of current to pass through the electrical system of your car. If this surge of current were to reach the load in the circuit, it could burn it out or severely damage it. To prevent this, fuse and/or circuit breakers and/or fusible links are connected into the supply wires of the electrical system. These items are nothing more than a built-in weak spot in the system. It's much easier to go to a known location (the fuse box) to see why a circuit is inoperative than to dissect 15 feet of wiring under the dashboard, looking for what happened.

When an electrical current of excessive power passes through the fuse, the fuse blows and breaks the circuit, preventing the passage of current and protecting the components.

A circuit breaker is basically a self-repairing fuse. It will open the circuit in the same fashion as a fuse, but when either the short is removed or the surge subsides, the circuit breaker resets itself and does not need replacement.

A fuse link (fusible link or main link) is a wire that acts as a fuse. It is normally connected between the starter relay and the main wiring harness under the hood. Since the starter is the highest electrical draw on the car, an internal short during starter use could direct about 130 amps into the wrong places. Consider the damage potential of introducing this current into a system whose wiring is rated at 15 amps and you'll understand the need for protection. Since this link is very early in the electrical path, it's the first place to look if nothing on the car works but the battery seems to be charged and is properly connected.

Electrical problems generally fall into one of three areas:

1. The component that is not functioning is not receiving current.

2. The component is receiving power but not using it or using it incorrectly (component failure).

3. The component is improperly grounded.

The circuit can be can be checked with a test light and a jumper wire. The test light is a device that looks like a pointed screwdriver with a wire on one end and a bulb in its handle. A jumper wire is simply a piece of wire with alligator clips on each end. If a component is not working, you must follow a systematic plan to determine which of the three causes is the villain.

1. Turn on the switch that controls the item not working.

NOTE: *Some items only work when the ignition switch is turned on.*

2. Disconnect the power supply wire from the component.

3. Attach the ground wire on the test light to a good metal ground.

4. Touch the end probe of the test light to the power wire; if there is current in the wire, the light in the test light will come on. You have now established that current is getting to the component.

5. Turn the ignition or dash switch off and reconnect the wire to the component.

If the test light does not go on, then the problem is between the battery and the component. This includes all the switches, fuses, relays and the battery itself. Next place to look is the fuse box; check carefully either by eye or by using the test light across the fuse clips. The easiest way to check is to simply replace the fuse. If the fuse is blown, and upon replacement, immediately blows again, there is a short between the fuse and the component. This is generally (not always) a sign of an internal short in the component. Disconnect the power wire at the component again and replace the fuse; if the fuse holds, the component is the problem.

If all the fuses are good and the component is not receiving power, find the switch for the circuit. Bypass the switch with the jumper wire. This is done by connecting one end of the jumper to the power wire coming into the switch and the other end to the wire leaving the switch. If the component comes to life, the switch has failed.

WARNING: *Never substitute the jumper for the component. The circuit needs the electrical load of the component. If you bypass it, you cause a short circuit.*

Checking the ground for any circuit can mean tracing wires to the body, cleaning connections or tightening mounting bolts for the component itself. If the jumper wire can be connected to the case of the component or the ground connector, you can ground the other end to a piece of clean, solid metal on the car. Again, if the component starts working, you've found the problem.

It should be noted that generally the last place to look for an electrical problem is in the wiring itself. Unless the car has undergone unusual circumstances (major body work, flood damage, improper repairs, etc.) the wiring is not likely to change its condition. A systematic search through the fuse, the connectors and switches and the component itself will almost always yield an answer. Loose and/or corroded connectors--particularly in ground circuits--are becoming a larger problem in modern cars. The computers and on-board electronic (solid state) systems are highly sensitive to improper grounds and will change their function drastically if one occurs.

Remember that for any electrical circuit to work, ALL the connections must be clean and tight.

BATTERY AND STARTING SYSTEM

Basic Operating Principles

The battery is the first link in the chain of mechanisms which work together to provide cranking of the automobile engine. In most modern cars, the battery is a lead/acid electrochemical device consisting of six 2v subsections (cells) connected in series so the unit is capable of producing approximately 12v of electrical pressure. Each subsection consists of a series of positive and negative plates held a short distance apart in a solution of sulfuric acid and water.

The two types of plates are of dissimilar metals. This causes a chemical reaction to be set up, and it is this reaction which produces current flow from the battery when its positive and negative terminals are connected to an electrical appliance such as a lamp or motor. The continued transfer of electrons would eventually convert the sulfuric acid to water, and make the two plates identical in chemical composition. As electrical energy is removed from the battery, its voltage output tends to drop. Thus, measuring battery voltage and battery electrolyte composition are two ways of checking the ability of the unit to supply power. During the starting of the engine, electrical energy is removed from the battery. However, if the charging circuit is in good condition and the operating conditions are normal, the power removed from the battery will be replaced by the generator (or alternator) which will force electrons back through the battery, reversing the normal flow, and restoring the battery to its original chemical state.

The battery and starting motor are linked by very heavy electrical cables designed to minimize resistance to the flow of current. Generally, the major power supply cable that leaves the battery goes directly to the starter, while other electrical system needs are supplied by a smaller cable. During starter operation, power flows from the battery to the starter and is grounded through the car's frame and the battery's negative ground strap.

The starting motor is a specially designed, direct current electric motor capable of producing a very great amount of power for its size. One thing that allows the motor to produce a great deal of power is its tremendous rotating speed. It drives the engine through a tiny pinion gear (attached to the starter's arma-

ture), which drives the very large flywheel ring gear at a greatly reduced speed. Another factor allowing it to produce so much power is that only intermittent operation is required of it. Thus, little allowance for air circulation is required, and the windings can be built into a very small space.

The starter solenoid is a magnetic device which employs the small current supplied by the start circuit of the ignition switch. This magnetic action moves a plunger which mechanically engages the starter and closes the heavy switch connecting it to the battery. The starting switch circuit consists of the starting switch contained within the ignition switch, a transmission neutral safety switch or clutch pedal switch, and the wiring necessary to connect these in series with the starter solenoid or relay.

The pinion, a small gear, is mounted to a one-way drive clutch. This clutch is splined to the starter armature shaft. When the ignition switch is moved to the **start** position, the solenoid plunger slides the pinion toward the flywheel ring gear via a collar and spring. If the teeth on the pinion and flywheel match properly, the pinion will engage the flywheel immediately. If the gear teeth butt one another, the spring will be compressed and will force the gears to mesh as soon as the starter turns far enough to allow them to do so. As the solenoid plunger reaches the end of its travel, it closes the contacts that connect the battery and starter and then the engine is cranked.

As soon as the engine starts, the flywheel ring gear begins turning fast enough to drive the pinion at an extremely high rate of speed. At this point, the one-way clutch begins allowing the pinion to spin faster than the starter shaft so that the starter will not operate at excessive speed. When the ignition switch is released from the starter position, the solenoid is de-energized, and a spring pulls the gear out of mesh interrupting the current flow to the starter.

Some starters employ a separate relay, mounted away from the starter, to switch the motor and solenoid current on and off. The relay replaces the solenoid electrical switch, but does not eliminate the need for a solenoid mounted on the starter used to mechanically engage the starter drive gears. The relay is used to reduce the amount of current the starting switch must carry.

THE CHARGING SYSTEM

Basic Operating Principles

The automobile charging system provides electrical power for operation of the vehicle's ignition and starting systems and all the electrical accessories. The battery services as an electrical surge or storage tank, storing (in chemical form) the energy originally produced by the engine driven generator. The system also provides a means of regulating generator output to protect the battery from being overcharged and to avoid excessive voltage to the accessories.

The storage battery is a chemical device incorporating parallel lead plates in a tank containing a sulfuric acid/water solution. Adjacent plates are slightly dissimilar, and the chemical reaction of the two dissimilar plates produces electrical energy when the battery is connected to a load such as the starter motor. The chemical reaction is reversible, so that when the generator is producing a voltage (electrical pressure) greater than that produced by the battery, electricity is forced into the battery, and the battery is returned to its fully charged state.

The vehicle's generator is driven mechanically, through V-belts, by the engine crankshaft. It consists of two coils of fine wire, one stationary (the stator), and one movable (the rotor). The rotor may also be known as the armature, and consists of fine wire wrapped around an iron core which is mounted on a shaft. The electricity which flows through the two coils of wire (provided initially by the battery in some cases) creates an intense magnetic field around both rotor and stator, and the interaction between the two fields creates voltage, allowing the generator to power the accessories and charge the battery.

There are two types of generators: the earlier is the direct current (DC) type. The current produced by the DC generator is generated in the armature and carried off the spinning armature by stationary brushes contacting the commutator. The commutator is a series of smooth metal contact plates on the end of the armature. The commutator plates, which are separated from one another by a very short gap, are connected to the armature circuits so that current will flow in one direction only in the wires carrying the generator output. The generator stator consists of two stationary coils of wire which draw some of the output current from the generator to form a powerful magnetic field and create the interaction of fields which generates the voltage. The generator field is wired in series with the regulator.

Newer automobiles use alternating current generators or alternators, because they are more efficient, can be rotated at higher speeds, and have fewer brush problems. In an alternator, the field rotates while all the current produced passes only through the stator winding. The brushes bear against continuous slip rings

rather than a commutator. This causes the current produced to periodically reverse the direction of its flow. Diodes (electrical one-way valves) block the flow of current from traveling in the wrong direction. A series of diodes is wired together to permit the alternating flow of the stator to be rectified back to 12 volts DC for use by the vehicles's electrical system.

The regulator consists of several circuits. Each circuit has a core, or magnetic coil of wire, which operates a switch. Each switch is connected to ground through one or more resistors. The coil of wire responds directly to system voltage. When the voltage reaches the required level, the magnetic field created by the winding of wire closes the switch and inserts a resistance into the generator field circuit, thus reducing the output. The contacts of the switch cycle open and close many times each second to precisely control voltage. On many newer cars, the regulating function is performed by solid-state (rather than mechanical) components. The regulator is often built in to the alternator; this system is termed an integrated or internal regulator.

While alternators are self-limiting as far as maximum current is concerned, DC generators employ a current regulating circuit which responds directly to the total amount of current flowing through the generator circuit rather than to the output voltage. The current regulator is similar to the voltage regulator except that all system current must flow through the energizing coil on its way to the various accessories.

ENGINE ELECTRICAL

Ignition Coil

TESTING/PRIMARY RESISTANCE CHECK

NOTE: *This test requires the use of an ohmmeter. When using this tool, make sure the scale is set properly for the range of resistance you expect to encounter during the test.*

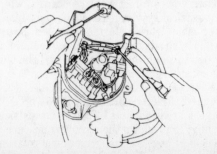

Checking the coil secondary resistance — internal coil

Always perform these tests with the ignition OFF. The specifications may differ (use these specifications as a range-if assembly is shorted it will be way out of the specification range) due to production changes and emission standards.

In order to check the coil primary resistance, you must first disconnect all wires from the ignition coil terminals. Using an ohmmeter, check the resistance between the positive and the negative terminals on the coil. The resistance should be:

• 1984 and later 3A-C (exc. Canada 4-Wheel Drive wagon), USA 4A-C: 0.4–0.5Ω.
• 1984 and later Canada 4-Wheel Drive wagon and Canadian, 4A-C: 1.2–1.5Ω.
• 1984 and later 3K-C w/o igniter: 1.2–1.5Ω; w/igniter: 1.3–1.6Ω.
• 1985 and later 4A-GE, 4A-GZE: 0.5–0.7Ω.
• 1987 and later 3E, 3E-E: 0.4–0.5Ω.
• 1989 and later 4A-F, 4A-FE: 1.3–1.6Ω

If the resistance is not within these tolerances (range), the coil will require replacement.

TESTING/SECONDARY RESISTANCE CHECK

NOTE: *This test requires the use of an ohmmeter. When using this tool, make sure the scale is set properly for the range of resistance you expect to encounter during the test. Always perform these tests with the ignition*

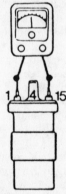

Checking the coil primary resistance — external coil

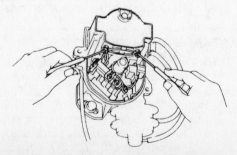

Checking the coil primary resistance — internal coil

Checking the coil secondary resistance — external coil

OFF. The specifications may differ (use these specifications as a range-if assembly is shorted it will be way out of the specification range) due to production changes and emission standards.

In order to check the coil secondary resistance, you must first disconnect all wires from the ignition coil terminals. Using an ohmmeter, check the resistance between the positive terminal and the coil wire terminal. The resistance should be:

• 1984 and later 3A-C and 4A-C: 7,700–10,400Ω.
• 1984 and later 3K-C w/o igniter: 8,000–12,000Ω; w/igniter: 10,000–15,000Ω.
• 1985 and later 4A-GE and 4A-GZE: 11,000–16,000Ω.
• 1987 and later 3E, 3E-E: 10,200–13,800Ω.
• 1989 and later 4A-F, 4A-FE: 10,400–14,000Ω

If the resistance is not within these tolerances (range), the coil will require replacement.

REMOVAL AND INSTALLATION

External coils (coils which are not built into the distributor) are easily replaced by the following service procedure:

1. Make certain the ignition is OFF and the key is removed. Disconnect the negative battery cable.
2. Disconnect the high tension wire (running between the coil and the distributor) from the coil.
3. Label and disconnect the low tension wires from the coil.
4. Loosen the coil bracket and remove the coil. Install the new coil and tighten the bracket.
5. Attach the low tension wires first, then the coil wire. Reconnect the battery cable.

The internal coils found within the distributor can be changed without removing the distributor. A selection of various short screwdrivers may be required for access to the screws.

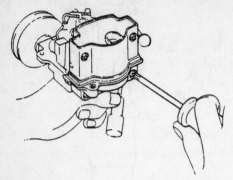

The internal coil is easily removed with the distributor of the car

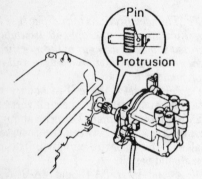

Distributor alignment

1. Disconnect the negative battery cable.
2. Remove the distributor cap with the wires attached and set it aside.
3. Remove the rotor and the dust cover(s).
4. Remove the nuts and disconnect the wires from the terminals on the coil.
5. Remove the four retaining screws and remove the coil. Note that later cars have a gasket below the coil--remove it carefully to avoid damage.
6. Install the coil, paying close attention to the gasket and its placement.
7. Connect the wiring to the coil and be careful of the routing of the wires.
8. Install the dust cover(s), the rotor and the cap.
9. Reconnect the battery.

Distributor

REMOVAL AND INSTALLATION

WARNING: *Once the distributor is removed, the engine should NOT be turned or moved out of position. Should this occur, please refer to the end of this section to set initial timing see INSTALLATION-TIMING LOST. This service procedure is for all models/engines modify steps as necessary.*

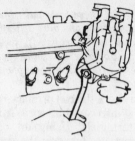

Loosen the pinch bolt and then pull the distributor straight out

1. Disconnect the negative battery cable.
2. Disconnect the distributor wire(s) at its connector.
3. Label and disconnect the vacuum hoses running to the vacuum advance unit on the side of the distributor if so equipped.
4. Remove the distributor cap (leave the spark plug wires connected) and swing it out of the way. If necessary, label and disconnect the coil and spark plug wiring at the distributor cap.
5. Carefully note the position of the distributor rotor relative to the distributor housing (also note position of distributor to the engine assembly); a mark made on the casing/housing will be necessary during reassembly. Use a marker or tape so the mark doesn't rub off during handling of the case/housing.
6. Remove the distributor hold-down bolts.
7. Carefully pull the distributor from the engine assembly. Remove the O-ring from the distributor shaft if so equipped.
8. If the engine has not been moved out of position, align the rotor with the mark you made earlier and reinstall the distributor (align mark made for distributor housing to engine assembly-install new O-ring if so equipped). Position it carefully and make sure the drive gear engages properly within the engine. Install the holding bolts.
9. Install the distributor cap and re-attach the vacuum lines to their correct ports if so equipped.
10. Install the wiring to the distributor, and connect the battery cable.
11. Check and adjust the timing as necessary.

INSTALLATION – TIMING LOST

If the engine has been cranked, dismantled or the timing otherwise lost while the distributor was out, proceed as follows:
1. Remove the No. 1 spark plug.
2. Place your finger over the spark plug hole and rotate the crankshaft clockwise to TDC (Top Dead Center). Watch the timing marks on the pulley; as they approach the ZERO point, you should feel pressure (compres-

sion) on your finger. If not, turn the crankshaft another full rotation and line up the timing marks-align the timing marks to the specifications.

NOTE: *The spark plugs on some engines are in deep wells; use a screwdriver or equivalent to fill the hole and feel the compression.*

3. Temporarily install the rotor in the distributor without the dust cover. Turn the distributor shaft so that the rotor is pointing toward the No. 1 terminal in the distributor cap. On some engines align the drilled mark on the driven gear with the cavity of the housing.

4. Align the matchmarks on the distributor body and the block which were made during the removal. Install the distributor in the block by rotating it slightly (no more than one gear tooth in either direction) until the driven gear (lubricate drive gear with clean engine oil) meshes with the drive.

5. If necessary rotate the distributor, once it is installed, so that the projection on the pickup coil is almost opposite the signal rotor tooth. Temporarily tighten the pinch bolt.

6. Remove the rotor and install the dust cover. Replace the rotor and the distributor cap.

7. Install the primary wire and the vacuum line(s) if so equipped.

8. Install the No. 1 spark plug. Connect the

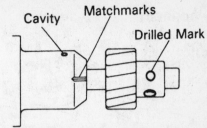

On some engines align the drilled mark on the driven gear with the cavity of the housing

cables to the spark plugs in the proper order by using the marks made during removal. Install the high tension lead if it was removed.

9. Start the engine. Adjust the idle speed and ignition timing as necessary.

Igniter (Ignition Module)

REMOVAL AND INSTALLATION

NOTE: *The distributor on the 4A-FE engine contains no replaceable parts except the ignition coil. Any other failed item in the distributor requires replacement of the complete unit.*

1. Remove the distributor as outlined above. Make certain the negative battery cable is disconnected before beginning the work.

2. Remove the packing and distributor rotor.

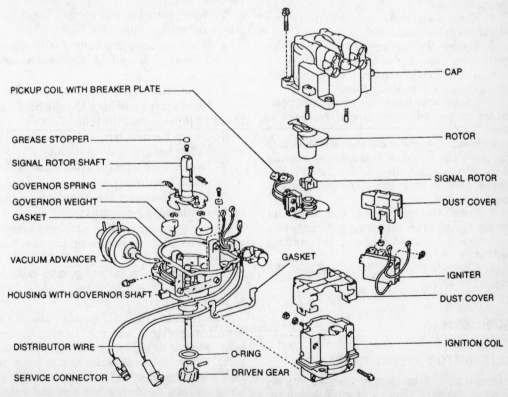

Exploded view of electronic distributor

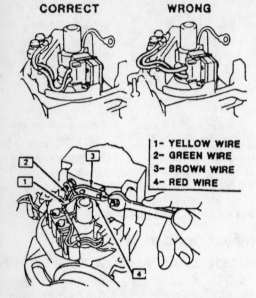

CORRECT WRONG

1- YELLOW WIRE
2- GREEN WIRE
3- BROWN WIRE
4- RED WIRE

Correct wiring placement is required during reassembly. The spinning rotor can cut a wire. Above: wiring path for igniter assembly; below: typical color code and placement for ignition coil wiring — some color of wiring may be different on some models

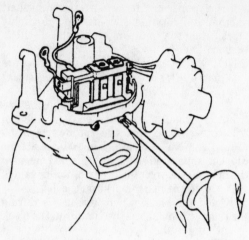

Remove the igniter

3. Remove the dust cover over the distributor components and remove the dust cover over the ignition coil.

4. Remove the nuts and disconnect the wiring from the ignition coil.

5. Remove the four screws and remove the ignition coil from the distributor.

6. At the igniter terminals, disconnect the wiring from the connecting points.

7. Loosen and remove the two screws holding the igniter and remove it from the distributor.

8. Install the igniter and connect its wiring. Pay particular attention to the correct routing of the wiring within the housing. There is one correct position only; any other wiring placements risk damage.

9. Install the ignition coil and secure its wiring. Again, watch the wiring positions.

10. Reinstall the dust covers, the packing and distributor rotor.

11. Reinstall the distributor and set the engine timing.

Alternator

ALTERNATOR PRECAUTIONS

Several precautions must be observed with alternator equipped vehicles to avoid damaging the unit. They are as follows:

1. If the battery is removed or disconnected for any reason, make sure that it is reconnected with the correct polarity. Reversing the battery connections may result in damage to the one-way rectifiers.

2. When utilizing a booster battery as a starting aid, always connect it as follows: positive to positive, and negative (booster battery) to a good ground on the engine of the car being started.

3. Never use a fast charger as a booster to start a car with an alternator.

4. When servicing the battery with a fast charger, always disconnect the car battery cables.

5. Never attempt to polarize an alternator.

6. Never apply more than 12 volts when attempting to jump start the vehicle.

7. Do not use test lamps of more than 12 volts (V) for checking diode continuity.

8. Do not short across or ground any of the terminals on the alternator.

9. Never disconnect the alternator or the battery with the engine running.

10. Always disconnect the battery terminals when performing any service on the electrical system.

11. Disconnect the battery ground cable if arc welding (such as body repair) is to be done on any part of the car.

Noise from an alternator may be caused by a loose drive pulley, a loose belt, loose mounting bolts, worn or dirty bearings or worn internal parts. A high frequency whine that is heard at high engine speed or full alternator output is acceptable and should not be considered a sign of alternator failure.

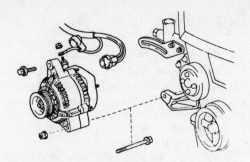

Alternator removal and installation

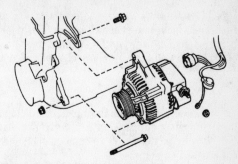

Alternator removal and installation

REMOVAL AND INSTALLATION

All Models/Engines

1. Disconnect the negative battery cable.

NOTE: *Failure to disconnect the battery can cause personal injury and damage to the car. If a tool is accidentally shorted at the alternator, it can become hot enough to cause a serious burn. On some models the alternator* is mounted very low on the engine. On these models it may be necessary to remove the gravel shield and work from underneath the car in order to gain access to the alternator retaining bolts.

2. Disconnect the large connector from the alternator.

3. Remove the nut and the single wire from the alternator.

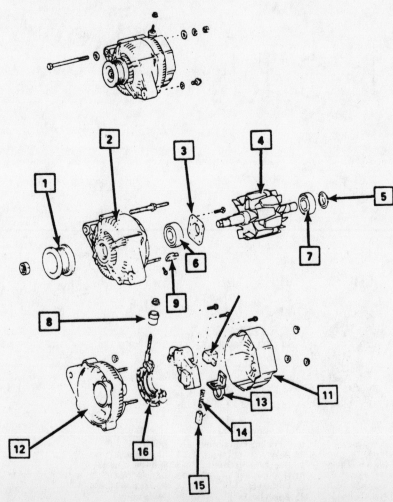

1. Pulley
2. Drive end frame
3. Retainer
4. Rotor
5. Bearing cover
6. Front bearing
7. Rear bearing
8. Terminal insulator
9. Rubber insulator
   IC regulator
10. Brush holder
11. Rear end cover
12. Rear end frame
13. Cover
14. Spring
15. Brush
16. Rectifier holder

Exploded view of the early model alternator

NOTE: *Diesel engine alternators are equipped with a vacuum pump. Before removal, two oil lines and a vacuum hose must first be disconnected-reconnect upon installation.*

4. Loosen the adjusting lock bolt (lower bolt) and pivot (upper) bolt. Remove the drive belt. It may be necessary to remove other belts for access.

5. Remove the lower bolt first, support the alternator and remove the upper pivot bolt. Remove the alternator from the car.

6. Installation is reverse of the above procedure. When reinstalling, remember to leave the bolts finger tight so that the belt may be adjusted to the correct tension.

7. Make sure that the electrical plugs and connectors are properly seated and secure in their mounts.

Regulator

REMOVAL AND INSTALLATION

The voltage regulator is contained within the alternator. It is called an IC type (Integrated Circuit). The alternator must be removed to replace the regulator.

1. Disconnect the negative battery cable.
2. Remove the alternator.
3. Support the alternator on a workbench, pulley end down but not resting on the pulley.
4. At the side of the alternator, remove the nut and the plastic terminal insulator.
5. Remove the three nuts and remove the end cover.
6. Remove the five screws and carefully remove the brush holder and then the IC regulator. Be careful to keep track of various small parts (washers, etc.)--they will be needed during reassembly.

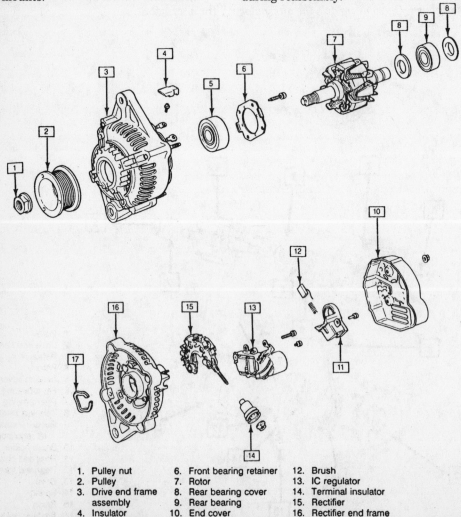

1. Pulley nut	6. Front bearing retainer	12. Brush
2. Pulley	7. Rotor	13. IC regulator
3. Drive end frame assembly	8. Rear bearing cover	14. Terminal insulator
4. Insulator	9. Rear bearing	15. Rectifier
5. Front bearing	10. End cover	16. Rectifier end frame
	11. Brush holder	17. Wave washer

Exploded view of the late model alternator

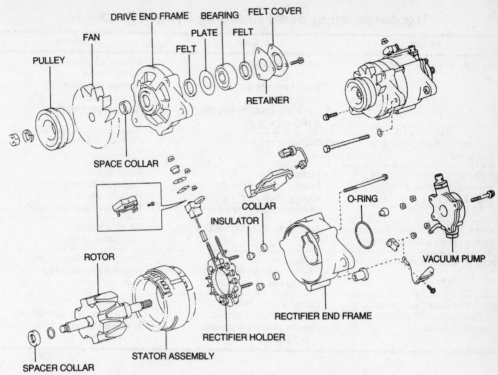

Exploded view of the alternator used on diesel engine

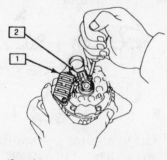

1. IC regulator
2. Brush holder

Removing the IC regulator from the alternator

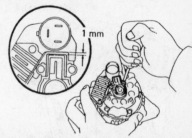

Maintain the minimum clearance between the brush holder and the connector when reassembling. 1mm = 0.004 in.

7. When reinstalling, place the cover over the brush holder. Install the regulator and the brush holder onto the alternator and secure them with the five screws. Make sure the brush holder's cover doesn't slip to one side during installation.

8. Before reinstalling the rear cover, check that the gap between the bush holder and the connector is at least 1mm. After confirming this gap, install the rear alternator cover and its three nuts.

9. Install the terminal insulator and its nut. Hold the alternator horizontally and spin the pulley by hand. Make sure everything turns smoothly and there is no sign of noise or binding.

Battery

REMOVAL AND INSTALLATION

1. Disconnect the negative battery cable (special pullers are available to remove the clamps).

CAUTION: *Spilled acid can be neutralized with a baking soda and water solution. If you somehow get acid into your eyes, flush it out with lots of clean water and get to a doctor as quickly as possible.*

2. Disconnect the positive battery cable.

3. On early models, remove the bolt holding the battery retainer and remove the retainer. On later models, remove the front retainer bolt first, then the rear retainer bolt and the retainer.

4. Remove the battery. You are reminded

Troubleshooting Basic Charging System Problems

Problem	Cause	Solution
Noisy alternator	• Loose mountings • Loose drive pulley • Worn bearings • Brush noise • Internal circuits shorted (High pitched whine)	• Tighten mounting bolts • Tighten pulley • Replace alternator • Replace alternator • Replace alternator
Squeal when starting engine or accelerating	• Glazed or loose belt	• Replace or adjust belt
Indicator light remains on or ammeter indicates discharge (engine running)	• Broken fan belt • Broken or disconnected wires • Internal alternator problems • Defective voltage regulator	• Install belt • Repair or connect wiring • Replace alternator • Replace voltage regulator
Car light bulbs continually burn out— battery needs water continually	• Alternator/regulator overcharging	• Replace voltage regulator/alternator
Car lights flare on acceleration	• Battery low • Internal alternator/regulator problems	• Charge or replace battery • Replace alternator/regulator
Low voltage output (alternator light flickers continually or ammeter needle wanders)	• Loose or worn belt • Dirty or corroded connections • Internal alternator/regulator problems	• Replace or adjust belt • Clean or replace connections • Replace alternator or regulator

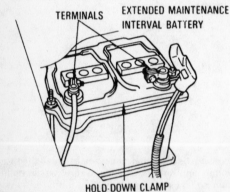

TERMINALS   EXTENDED MAINTENANCE INTERVAL BATTERY

HOLD-DOWN CLAMP

Battery hold down clamp installation

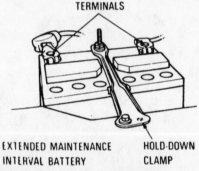

TERMINALS

EXTENDED MAINTENANCE INTERVAL BATTERY   HOLD-DOWN CLAMP

Battery hold down clamp installation

that the battery is a fairly heavy item. Use care in lifting it out of the car.

5. Clean the battery posts thoroughly before reinstalling or when installing a new one.

6. Clean the cable clamps, using the special tools or a wire brush, both inside and out.

7. The new battery is installed in the reverse order of removal. Make certain that the retainer is correctly placed and its bolts are tight. Connect the positive cable first, then the negative cable. Do not hammer them into place. The terminals should be coated with grease to prevent corrosion.

NOTE: *Removing the battery may require resetting various digital equipment such as radio memory and the clock.*

Starter

REMOVAL AND INSTALLATION

1. Disconnect the negative battery cable.

2. Disconnect all the wiring from the starter terminals.

3. On early models, remove the transaxle cable and bracket from the transaxle.

4. Remove the starter mounting bolts (some models remove the heat insulator).

5. Remove the starter.

6. Installation is the reverse of the removal procedure.

OVERHAUL AND SOLENOID REPLACEMENT

The starter solenoid (magnetic switch) is an integral part of the Reduction Type starter as-

Alternator Specifications

		Alternator		
Year	Engine (cc)	Field Current @ 12v (amps)	Output (amps)	Regulated Volts @ 75°F
1984	ALL	10	30	13.9–15.1
1985	ALL	10	30	13.9–15.1
1986	ALL	10	30	13.9–15.1
1987	ALL	10	30	13.9–15.1
1988	ALL	10	30	13.9–15.1
1989	ALL	10	60	13.5–14.8
1990	ALL	10	60	13.5–14.8

NOTE: The maximum output of the Alternator should be in the Regulated Volts Range.

sembly on most late models vehicles. It cannot be replaced without complete disassembly. On Conventional Type starter assembly the starter solenoid (magnetic switch) can be replaced without complete disassembly-follow this service procedure as a guide modify any service steps as necessary.

1. Remove the starter from the car.

2. Disconnect the wire lead from the magnetic switch terminal.

3. Remove the two long, through bolts holding the field frame to the magnetic switch. Pull out the field frame with the armature from the magnetic switch.

4. On 1.0kw (1000 watt) starters, remove

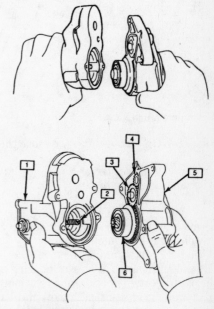

1. Starter solenoid assembly
2. Spring
3. Idler gear
4. Pinion gear
5. Drive housing
6. Clutch and drive assembly

Disassembly of the magnetic switch (solenoid) from the drive housing

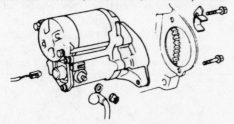

Starter assembly removal

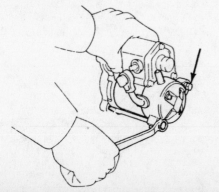

Separate the starter components by removing the two through bolts

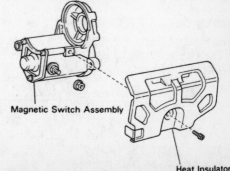

Magnetic Switch Assembly

Heat Insulator

Removing heat insulator from the starter assembly

Starter Specifications

Year	Lock Test		No-Load Test			Brush Tension (lbs.)
	Amps	Volts	Amps	Volts	RPM	
1984 ①	NOT RECOMMENDED		50A	11V	5,000	2.2–3.0
1984–88	NOT RECOMMENDED		90	11.5	3,500+	3.9–5.3
1989–90	NOT RECOMMENDED		90	11.5	5,800+	4.0–5.5

① Conventional type starter

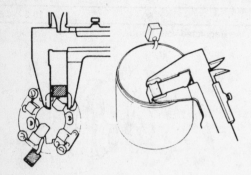

Checking the brush length

the felt seal. On 1.4kw starters, remove the O-ring.

5. To remove the starter housing from the magnetic switch assembly:

    a. For 1.0 kw starters, remove the two screws and remove the starter housing with the idler gear and clutch assembly.

    b. For 1.4kw units, remove the two screws and remove the starter housing with the pinion gear, idler and clutch assembly.

6. Using a magnetic tool, remove the spring and steel ball from the clutch shaft hole.

7. Remove the end cover from the field frame.

8. On 1.4kw units, remove the O-ring.

9. Use a small screwdriver or steel wire to separate the brush springs and remove the brushes from the holder.

10. Pull the brush holder off the field frame.

11. Remove the armature from the field frame.

12. Perform testing and repairs as necessary:

    a. Measure the length of the brushes. If they are less than the acceptable minimum length, replace them with new brushes.

Standard Length:
- 1.0kw – 13mm
- 1.4kw – 15mm
- 0.8kw – 16mm

Minimum Length:
- 1.0kw – 8.5mm
- 1.4kw – 10mm
- 0.8kw – 10.5mm

    b. Check the magnetic switch by performing the pull-in coil open circuit test. Using an ohmmeter, check for continuity between terminal 50 and terminal C. If there is no continuity, replace the magnetic switch.

    c. Check the hold in coil of the magnetic switch. Use the ohmmeter to check for continuity between terminal 50 and the body

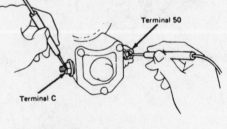

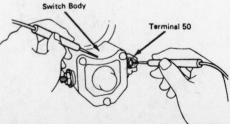

Performing the pull-in test (upper) and the hold-in test (below) will check the function of the solenoid

1.0 kW Type   **1.4 kW Type**

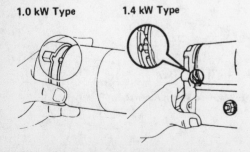

Match the field frame protrusion during reassembly

(case) of the unit. If there is no continuity, replace the switch.

13. To reassemble the starter, apply high-temperature grease to the armature bearings and insert the armature into the field frame.

14. Use a screwdriver or a steel wire to hold the brush spring back and install the brushes into the holder(s).

NOTE: *Make certain the positive wires to the brushes are not grounded or touching surrounding parts.*

15. For 1.4kw starters, install the O-ring on the field frame.

16. Install the end cover on the field frame.

17. Apply grease to the ball and spring and insert them into the clutch shaft hole.

18. Install the gears and clutch assembly to the starter housing. Apply grease to the gear and clutch assemblies and:

a. For 1.0kw starters, place the clutch assembly, idler gear and bearing in the starter housing.

b. For 1.4kw starters, place the clutch assembly, idler gear, bearing and pinion gear in the starter housing.

19. Insert the spring into the clutch shaft hole and place the starter housing onto the magnetic switch. Install the two screws.

20. On 1.0kw units, install the felt seal on the armature shaft. On 1.4kw units, install the O-ring on the field frame.

21. Install the field frame with armature onto

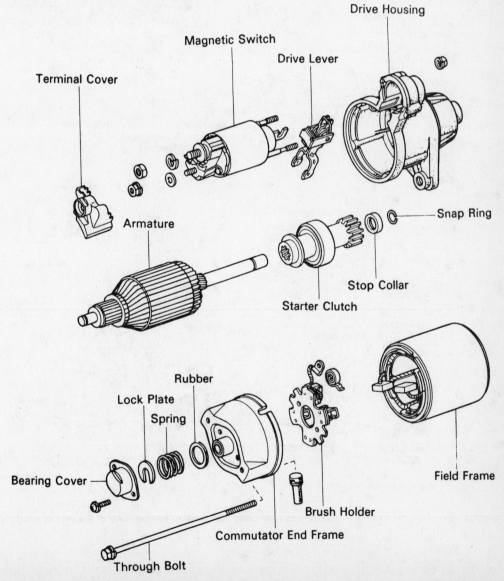

Exploded view of starter motor — starter solenoid (magnetic switch) external part of the starter assembly

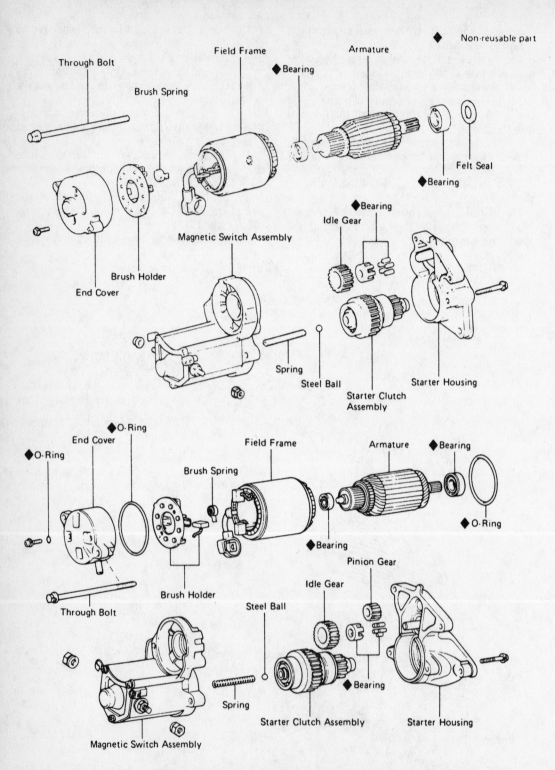

Exploded view of starter motors — starter solenoid (magnetic switch) integral part of the starter assembly

Troubleshooting Basic Starting System Problems

Problem	Cause	Solution
Starter motor rotates engine slowly	• Battery charge low or battery defective	• Charge or replace battery
	• Defective circuit between battery and starter motor	• Clean and tighten, or replace cables
	• Low load current	• Bench-test starter motor. Inspect for worn brushes and weak brush springs.
	• High load current	• Bench-test starter motor. Check engine for friction, drag or coolant in cylinders. Check ring gear-to-pinion gear clearance.
Starter motor will not rotate engine	• Battery charge low or battery defective	• Charge or replace battery
	• Faulty solenoid	• Check solenoid ground. Repair or replace as necessary.
	• Damage drive pinion gear or ring gear	• Replace damaged gear(s)
	• Starter motor engagement weak	• Bench-test starter motor
	• Starter motor rotates slowly with high load current	• Inspect drive yoke pull-down and point gap, check for worn end bushings, check ring gear clearance
	• Engine seized	• Repair engine
Starter motor drive will not engage (solenoid known to be good)	• Defective contact point assembly	• Repair or replace contact point assembly
	• Inadequate contact point assembly ground	• Repair connection at ground screw
	• Defective hold-in coil	• Replace field winding assembly
Starter motor drive will not disengage	• Starter motor loose on flywheel housing	• Tighten mounting bolts
	• Worn drive end busing	• Replace bushing
	• Damaged ring gear teeth	• Replace ring gear or driveplate
	• Drive yoke return spring broken or missing	• Replace spring
Starter motor drive disengages prematurely	• Weak drive assembly thrust spring	• Replace drive mechanism
	• Hold-in coil defective	• Replace field winding assembly
Low load current	• Worn brushes	• Replace brushes
	• Weak brush springs	• Replace springs

the magnetic switch assembly and install the two through bolts.

NOTE: *There is a protrusion or tab on each part; make sure you line them up correctly.*

22. Connect the wire to the terminal on the magnetic switch.

23. Reinstall the starter on the vehicle. starter chart see rich, was not with other charts!

ENGINE MECHANICAL

Understanding the Engine

The piston engine is a metal block containing a series of round chambers or cylinders. The upper part of the engine block is usually an iron or aluminum- alloy casting. The casting forms outer walls around the cylinders with hollow areas in between, through which coolant circulates. The lower block provides a number of rigid mounting points for the crankshaft and its bearings. The lower block is referred to as the crankcase.

The crankshaft is a long, steel shaft mounted at the bottom of the engine and free to turn in its mounts. The mounting points (generally four to seven) and the bearings for the crankshaft are called main bearings. The crankshaft is the shaft which is made to turn through the function of the engine; this motion is then passed into the transmission/transaxle and on to the drive wheels.

Attached to the crankshaft are the connecting rods which run up to the pistons within the cylinders. As the air/fuel mixture explodes within the tightly sealed cylinder, the piston is forced downward. This motion is transferred through the connecting rod to the crankshaft and the shaft turns. As one piston finishes its power stroke, its next upward journey forces the burnt gasses out of the cylinder through the now-open exhaust valve. By the top of the stroke, the exhaust valve has closed and the intake valve has begun to open, allowing the fresh air/fuel charge to be sucked into the cylinder by the downward stroke of the piston. The intake valve closes, the piston once again comes back up and compresses the charge in the closed cylinder. At the top (approximately) of this stroke the spark plug fires, the charge explodes and another power stroke takes place. If you count the piston motions in between power strokes, you'll see why most automotive engines are called four-stroke or four-cycle engines.

While one cylinder is performing this cycle, all the others are also contributing; but in different timing. Obviously, all the cylinders cannot fire at once or the power flow would not be steady. As any one cylinder is on its power stroke, another is on its exhaust stroke, another on intake and another on compression. These constant power pulses keep the crank turning; a large round flywheel attached to the end of the crankshaft provides a stable mass to smooth out the rotation.

At the top of the engine, the cylinder head(s) provide tight covers for the cylinders. They contain machined chambers into which the fuel charge is forced as the piston reaches the top of its travel. These combustion chambers contain at least one intake and one exhaust valve which are opened and closed through the action of the camshaft. The spark plugs are screwed into the cylinder head so that the tips of the plugs protrude into the chamber.

Since the timing of the valve action (opening and closing) is critical to the combustion process, the camshaft is driven by the crankshaft via a belt or chain. The valves are operated either by pushrods (called overhead valves--the valves are above the cam) or by the direct action of the cam pushing on the valves (overhead cam).

Lubricating oil is stored in a pan or sump at the bottom of the engine. It is force fed to all the parts of the engine by the oil pump which may be driven off wither the crank or the cam shaft. The oil lubricates the entire engine by travelling through passages in the block and head. Additionally, the circulation of the oil provides 25–40% of the engine cooling.

If all this seems very complicated, keep in mind that the sole purpose of any motor--gas, diesel, electric, solar, etc.--is to turn a shaft. The motion of the shaft is then harnessed to perform a task such as pumping water, moving the car, etc. Accomplishing this shaft-turning in an automotive engine requires many supporting systems such as fuel delivery, exhaust handling, lubrication, cooling, starting, etc. Operation of these systems involve principles of mechanics, vacuum, electronics, etc. Being able to identify a problem by what system is involved will allow you to begin accurate diagnosis of the symptoms and causes.

Engine Overhaul Tips

Most engine overhaul procedures are fairly standard. In addition to specific parts replacement procedures and complete specifications for your individual engine, this chapter also is a guide to accepted rebuilding procedures. Examples of standard rebuilding practice are shown and should be used along with specific details concerning your particular engine.

Competent and accurate machine shop services will ensure maximum performance, reliability and engine life.

In most instances it is more profitable for the do-it-yourself mechanic to remove, clean and inspect the component, buy the necessary parts and deliver these to a shop for actual machine work.

On the other hand, much of the rebuilding work (crankshaft, block, bearings, piston rods, and other components) is well within the scope of the do-it-yourself mechanic. Patience, proper tools, and common sense coupled a basic understanding of the motor can yield satisfying and economical results.

TOOLS

The tools required for an engine overhaul or parts replacement will depend on the depth of your involvement. With a few exceptions, they will be the tools found in a mechanic's tool kit (see Chapter 1). More in-depth work will require any or all of the following:
• A dial indicator (reading in thousandths) mounted on a universal base
• Micrometers and telescope gauges
• Jaw and screw-type pullers
• Gasket scrapers
• Valve spring compressor
• Ring groove cleaner
• Piston ring expander and compressor
• Ridge reamer
• Cylinder hone or glaze breaker
• Plastigage®
• Engine stand

The use of most of these tools is illustrated in this Chapter. Many can be rented for a one-time use from a local parts jobber or tool supply house specializing in automotive work.

Occasionally, the use of special tools is called for. See the information on Special Tools and

Safety Notice in the front of this book before substituting another tool.

INSPECTION TECHNIQUES

Procedures and specifications are given in this chapter for inspecting, cleaning and assessing the wear limits of most major components. Other procedures such as Magnaflux® and Zyglo® can be used to locate material flaws and stress cracks. Magnaflux® is a magnetic process applicable only to ferrous (iron and steel) materials. The Zyglo® process coats the material with a fluorescent dye penetrant and can be used on any material. Checks for suspected surface cracks can be more readily made using spot check dye. The dye is sprayed onto the suspected area, wiped off and the area sprayed with a developer. Cracks will show up brightly.

OVERHAUL TIPS

Aluminum has become extremely popular for use in engines, due to its low weight. Observe the following precautions when handling aluminum parts:
• Never hot tank aluminum parts (the caustic hot tank solution will eat the aluminum.)
• Remove all aluminum parts (identification tag, etc.) from engine parts prior to the tanking.
• Always coat threads lightly with engine oil or anti-seize compounds before installation to prevent seizure.
• Never over tighten bolts or spark plugs especially in aluminum threads.

Stripped threads in any component can be repaired using any of several commercial repair kits (Heli-Coil®, Microdot®, Keenserts®, etc.).

When assembling the engine, any parts that will be in frictional contact must be prelubed to provide lubrication at initial start-up. Any product specifically formulated for this purpose can be used, but engine oil is not recommended as a prelube.

When semi-permanent (locked, but removable) installation of bolts or nuts is desired, threads should be cleaned and coated with Loctite® or other similar, commercial non-hardening sealant.

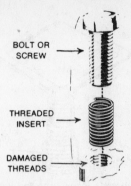

Damaged bolt holes can be repaired with thread repair inserts

Drill out the damaged threads with specified drill. Drill completely through the hole or to the bottom of a blind hole

REPAIRING DAMAGED THREADS

Several methods of repairing damaged threads are available. Heli-Coil® (shown here), Keenserts® and Microdot® are among the most widely used. All involve basically the same principle--drilling out stripped threads, tapping the hole and installing a prewound insert--making welding, plugging and oversize fasteners unnecessary.

Two types of thread repair inserts are usually supplied: a standard type for most Inch Coarse, Inch Fine, Metric Course and Metric Fine thread sizes and a spark plug type to fit most spark plug port sizes. Consult the individual manufacturer's catalog to determine exact applications. Typical thread repair kits will contain a selection of prewound threaded inserts, a tap (corresponding to the outside diameter threads of the insert) and an installation tool. Spark plug inserts usually differ because they

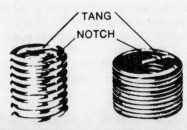

Standard thread repair insert (left) and spark plug thread insert (right)

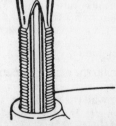

With the tap supplied, tap the hole to receive the thread insert. Keep the tap well oiled and back it out frequently to avoid clogging the threads

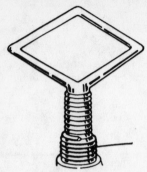

Screw the threads insert onto the installation tool until the tang engages the bolt. Screw the insert into the tapped hole until it is 1/4–1/2 turn below the top surface. After installation break off the tang with a hammer and punch

require a tap equipped with pilot threads and a combined reamer/tap section. Most manufacturers also supply blister-packed thread repair inserts separately in addition to a master kit containing a variety of taps and inserts plus installation tools.

Before effecting a repair to a threaded hole, remove any snapped, broken or damaged bolts or studs. Penetrating oil can be used to free frozen threads. The offending item can be removed with locking pliers or with a screw or stud extractor. After the hole is clear, the thread can be repaired, as shown in the series of accompanying illustrations.

Checking Engine Compression

A noticeable lack of engine power, excessive oil consumption and/or poor fuel mileage measured over an extended period are all indicators of internal engine wear. Worn piston rings, scored or worn cylinder bores, leaking head gaskets, sticking or burnt valves and worn valve seats are all possible culprits here. A check of each cylinder's compression will help you locate the problems.

As mentioned in the Tools and Equipment section of Chapter 1, a screw-in type compression gauge is more accurate that the type you simply hold against the spark plug hole, although it takes slightly longer to use. It's worth it to obtain a more accurate reading. Follow the procedures below.

Gasoline Engines

1. Warm up the engine to normal operating temperature.
2. Remove all the spark plugs.
3. Disconnect the high tension lead from the ignition coil.
4. Fully open the throttle either by operating the carburetor throttle linkage by hand or

by having an assistant floor the accelerator pedal.

5. Screw the compression gauge into the No.1 spark plug hole until the fitting is snug.

NOTE: *Be careful not to crossthread the plug hole. On aluminum cylinder heads use extra care, as the threads in these heads are easily ruined.*

6. Ask an assistant to depress the accelerator pedal fully on both carbureted and fuel injected vehicles. Then, while you read the compression gauge, ask the assistant to crank the engine two or three times in short bursts using the ignition switch.

7. Read the compression gauge at the end of each series of cranks, and record the highest of these readings. Repeat this procedure for each of the engine's cylinders.

As a general rule, new motors will have compression on the order of 150–170 pounds per square inch (psi). This number will decrease with age and wear. The number of pounds of pressure that your test shows is not as important as the evenness between all the cylinders. Many cars run very well with all cylinders at 105 psi. The lower number simply shows a general deterioration internally. This car probably burns a little oil and may be a bit harder to start, but based on these numbers doesn't warrant an engine tear-down yet.

Compare the highest reading of all the cylinders. Any variation of more than 10% should be considered a sign of potential trouble. For example, if your compression readings for cylinders 1 through 4 were: 135 psi, 125 psi, 90 psi and 125 psi, it would be fair to say that cylinder number three is not working efficiently and is almost certainly the cause of your oil burning, rough idle or poor fuel mileage.

8. If a cylinder is unusually low, pour a tablespoon of clean engine oil into the cylinder through the spark plug hole and repeat the compression test. If the compression comes up after adding the oil, it appears that the cylinder's piston rings or bore are damaged or worn. If the pressure remains low, the valves may not be seating properly (a valve job is needed), or the head gasket may be blown near that cylinder. If compression in any two adjacent cylinders is low, and if the addition of oil doesn't help the compression, there is leakage past the head gasket. Cil and coolant in the combustion chamber can result from this problem. There may be evidence of water droplets on the engine dipstick when a head gasket has blown.

Diesel Engine

NOTE: *When using diesel compression test for diagnosis of internal engine problems-refer to diesel specialist or a diesel engine ser-*

vice publication for additional service procedures as necessary.

1. Warm the engine up to operating temperature.

2. Disconnect the fuel-cut solenoid wire.

3. Remove all four glow plugs on diesel engine.

4. Screw the compression gauge into the No. 1 glow plug hole until the fitting is snug. Be very careful not to cross-thread the hole.

5. Ask your assistant to crank the engine a few times using the ignition switch.

6. Record the highest reading on the gauge, and compare it to the compression specifications in the Tune-Up Specifications Chart in this Chapter.

7. Repeat the procedure for the remaining cylinders, recording each cylinder's compres-sion. If a cylinder is unusually low, pour a tablespoon of clear engine oil into the cylinder through the glow plug hole and repeat the compression test. If the compression comes up after adding the oil, it appears that cylinder's piston rings or bore are damaged or worn. If the pressure remains low, the valves may not be seating properly (a valve job is needed) or the head gasket may be blown near that cylinder.

Engine

REMOVAL AND INSTALLATION

NOTE: *On all engine removal and installation procedures modify service steps as necessary. On all fuel injected engines relieve fuel pressure before starting this repair. Use the removal and installation service procedures*

Torque Specifications 1984–87
All Readings in ft. lbs.

Engine Type	Cylinder Head Bolts	Rod Bearing Bolts	Main Bearing Bolts	Crankshaft Pulley Bolt	Flywheel-to-Crankshaft Bolts	Manifold Intake	Manifold Exhaust
3A, 3A-C, 4A-C	40–47	26–32 ①	40–47	55–61	55–61	15–21	15–21
1C	60–65	45–50	75–78	70–75	63–68	10–15	32–36
3E	See Text	27–31	40–47	105–117	60–70	11–17	33–42
4A-LC	40–47	32–40	40–47	80–94	55–61	15–21	15–21
4A-GE	40–47	32–40	40–47	100–110	50–58	15–21	15–21

① Connecting rods purchased after 2/15/84: 34–39

Torque Specifications 1988–90
All Readings in ft. lbs.

Engine Type	Cylinder Head Bolts	Rod Bearing Bolts	Main Bearing Bolts	Crankshaft Pulley Bolt	Flywheel-to-Crankshaft Bolts	Manifold Intake	Manifold Exhaust
4A-C	40–47	32–40	40–47	80–94	55–61	15–21	15–21
4A-GE	See Text	32–40	40–47	100–110	50–58	15–21	27–31
3E	See Text	27–31	40–47	105–117	60–70	11–17	27–33
3A-C	40–47	34–39	40–47	80–94	55–61	15–21	15–21
4A-GZE	See Text	32–40	40–47	100–110	50–58	15–21	27–31
4A-F	40–47	32–40	40–47	80–94	55–61	11–17	15–21
4A-FE	40–47	32–40	40–47	80–94	55–61	11–17	15–21
3E-E	See Text	29	42	112	88	14	38

NOTE: On all engine torque procedures refer to necessary text for any additional service procedure or specification change.

Piston and Ring Specifications

All measurements in inches

Engine Type	Piston Clearance	Ring Gap			Ring Side Clearance		
		Top Compression	Bottom Compression	Oil Control	Top Compression	Bottom Compression	Oil Control
3A, 3A-C	0.0039–0.0047	0.0079–0.0157 ①	0.0059–0.0138 ②	0.0039–0.0236 ③	0.0016–0.0031	0.0012–0.0028	snug
4A-C	0.0039–0.0047	④	⑤	⑥	0.0016–0.0031 ⑦	0.0012–0.0028 ⑧	snug
1C	0.0016–0.0024	0.0098–0.0193	0.0079–0.0173	0.0079–0.0193	0.0079–0.0081	0.0079–0.0081	snug
3E	0.0028–0.0035	0.0102–0.0142	0.0118–0.0177	0.0059–0.0157	0.0016–0.0031	0.0012–0.0028	snug
4A-LC	0.0035–0.0043	0.0098–0.0138	0.0059–0.0165	0.0078–0.0276	0.0016–0.0031	0.0012–0.0028	snug
4A-GEC, 4A-GELC	0.0039–0.0047	0.0098–0.0138	0.0078–0.0118	0.0078–0.0276	0.0016–0.0031	0.0012–0.0028	snug
4A-F	0.0024–0.0031	0.0098–0.0138	0.0059–0.0118	0.0039–0.0236	0.0016–0.0031	0.0012–0.0028	snug
4A-FE	0.0024–0.0031	0.0098–0.0138	0.0059–0.0118	0.0039–0.0236	0.0020–0.0031	0.0012–0.0028	snug
3E-E	0.0028–0.0035	0.0102–0.0189	0.0118–0.0224	0.0059–0.0205	0.0016–0.0031	0.0012–0.0028	snug

① TP—0.0079–0.0193
  Riken—0.0079–0.0173
② TP—0.0059–0.0173
  Riken—0.0059–0.0154
③ TP—0.0039–0.0272
  Riken—0.0118–0.0390
④ FWD:
  TP—0.0098–0.0138
  Riken—0.0079–0.0138
  RWD:
  0.0098–0.0185

⑤ FWD:
  0.0059–0.0118
  RWD:
  0.0059–0.0165
⑥ FWD:
  TP—0.0079–0.0276
  Ripkin—0.0118–0.0354
  RWD:
  0.0118–0.0390

⑦ FWD:
  0.0012–0.0028
⑧ FWD:
  0.0008–0.0024

Camshaft Specifications

All measurements in inches

Engine	Journal Diameter				Bearing Clearance	Camshaft End Play
	1	2	3	4		
3A, 3A-C, 4A-C, 1C-L	1.1015–1.1022	1.1015–1.1022	1.1015–1.1022	1.1015–1.1022	0.0015–0.0029	0.0031–0.0071
3E	1.0622–1.0628	0.0622–1.0628	0.0622–1.0628	0.0622–1.0628	0.0015–0.0029	0.0031–0.0071
4A-LC	1.1015–1.1022	0.1015–1.1022	0.1015–1.1022	0.1015–1.1022	0.0015–0.0029	0.0031–0.0071
4A-GEC, 4A-GELC	1.0610–1.0616	1.0610–1.0616	1.0610–1.0616	1.0610–1.0616	0.0014–0.0028	0.0031–0.0075
4A-F	1.9035–1.9041 ①	1.9035–1.9041	1.9035–1.9041	1.9035–1.9041	0.0015–0.0028	②
4A-FE	1.9035–1.9041 ①	1.9035–1.9041	1.9035–1.9041	1.9035–1.9041	0.0015–0.0028	②
3E-E	1.0622–1.0628	0.0622–1.0628	0.0622–1.0628	0.0622–1.0628	0.0015–0.0029	0.0031–0.0071

① Exhaust No. 1: 0.9822–0.9829
② Intake Camshaft: 0.0012–0.0033
  Exhaust Camshaft: 0.0014–0.0035

Valve Specifications

Engine Type	Seat Angle (deg.)	Face Angle (deg.)	Spring Pressure (lbs.)	Spring Installed Height (in.)	Stem-To-Guide Clearance (in.)		Stem Diameter (in.)	
					Intake	Exhaust	Intake	Exhaust
3A, 3A-C, 4A-C	45	44.5	52.0	1.520	0.0010–0.0024	0.0012–0.0026	0.2744–0.2750	0.2742–0.2748
1C	45	44.5	53.0	1.587	0.0008–0.0022	0.0014–0.0028	0.3140–0.3146	0.3134–0.3140
3E	45	44.5	35.1	1.384	0.0010–0.0024	0.0012–0.0026	0.2350–0.2356	0.2348–0.2354
4A-LC	45	44.5	52.0	1.520	0.0010–0.0024	0.0012–0.0026	0.2744–0.2750	0.2742–0.2748
4A-GEC, 4A-GELC	45	44.5	35.9	1.366	0.0010–0.0024	0.0012–0.0026	0.2350–0.2356	0.2348–0.2354
4A-F	45	44.5	34.8	1.366	0.0010–0.0024	0.0012–0.0026	0.2350–0.2356	0.2348–0.2354
4A-FE	45	45.5	34.8	1.366	0.0010–0.0024	0.0012–0.0026	0.2350–0.2356	0.2348–0.2354
3E-E	45	45.5	35.1	1.384	0.0010–0.0024	0.0012–0.0026	0.2350–0.2356	0.2348–0.2354

Crankshaft and Connecting Rod Specifications

All measurements in inches

Engine Type	Crankshaft				Connecting Rod		
	Main Brg. Journal Dia.	Main Brg. Oil Clearance	Shaft End-Play	Thrust on No.	Journal Diameter	Oil Clearance	Side Clearance
3A, 3A-C, 4A-C	1.8892–1.8898	0.0005–0.0019 ①	0.0008–0.0073	3	1.5742–1.5748	0.0008–0.0020	0.0059–0.0098
1C	2.2435–2.2441	0.0013–0.0026	0.0016–0.0094	3	1.9877–1.9882	0.0014–0.0025	0.0031–0.0118
3E	1.9683–1.9685	0.0006–0.0014	0.0008–0.0087	3	1.8110–1.8113	0.0006–0.0019	0.0059–0.0138
4A-LC	1.8891–1.8898	0.0006–0.0013	0.0008–0.0087	3	1.5742–1.5748	0.0008–0.0020	0.0059–0.0098
4A-GEC, 4A-GELC	1.8891–1.8898	0.0005–0.0015	0.0008–0.0087	3	1.5742–1.5748	0.0008–0.0020	0.0059–0.0098
4A-F	1.8891–1.8898	0.0006–0.0013	0.0008–0.0087	3	1.5742–1.5748	0.0008–0.0020	0.0059–0.0098
4A-FE	1.8891–1.8898	0.0006–0.0013	0.0008–0.0087	3	1.5742–1.5748	0.0008–0.0020	0.0059–0.0098
3E-E	1.9683–1.9685	0.0006–0.0014	0.0008–0.0087	3	1.8110–1.8113	0.0006–0.0019	0.0059–0.0138

① 3A-C: 0.0012–0.0026

General Engine Identification Chart

Model	Year	Engine Type	Engine Displacement Cu. In. (cc)	Fuel System Type	Horsepower (@ rpm)	Torque @ rpm (ft. lbs.)	Bore × Stroke (in.)	Compression Ratio
Corolla	1984–88	4A-C	97 (1587)	CARB.	70 @ 4800	85 @ 2800	3.94 × 3.03	9.0:1
	1984–85	1C-L	112.2 (1839)	DFI	56 @ 4500	76 @ 3000	3.27 × 3.35	22.5:1
	1985–90	4A-GE	97 (1587)	EFI	112 @ 6600	97 @ 4800	3.19 × 3.03	9.4:1
	1986–88	4A-C	97 (1587)	CARB.	74 @ 5200	86 @ 2800	3.19 × 3.03	9.0:1
	1989	4A-F	97 (1587)	CARB.	90 @ 6000	95 @ 3600	3.20 × 3.00	9.5:1
	1989–90	4A-FE	97 (1587)	EFI	102 @ 5800	101 @ 4800	3.19 × 3.03	9.5:1
Tercel	1984	1A-C, 3A	88.6 (1452)	CARB.	60 @ 4800	72 @ 2800	3.05 × 3.03	8.7:1
	1984–89	3A-C	88.6 (1452)	CARB.	62 @ 5200	75 @ 2800	3.05 × 3.03	9.0:1
	1987–90	3E	88.9 (1456)	CARB.	78 @ 6000	87 @ 4000	2.87 × 3.54	9.3:1 ①
	1990	3E-E	88.9 (1456)	EFI	82 @ 5200	89 @ 4400	2.87 × 3.43	9.3:1
MR2	1985–89	4A-GE	97 (1587)	EFI	115 @ 6600	100 @ 4800	3.19 × 3.03	9.4:1
	1988–89	4A-GZE	97 (1587)	EFI ②	145 @ 6400	140 @ 4000	3.19 × 3.03	8.0:1

CARB. Carburetor
DFI Diesel Fuel Injection
EFI Electronic Fuel Injection
① Calif.: 90 @ 2600
② Supercharged Engine

as guide as some years and models may differ slightly. All wires, hoses and necessary components should be marked before removal for correct installation. Review the complete service procedure before starting this repair.

Corolla Rear Wheel Drive 4A-C Engine

1. Drain the radiator, cooling system, transmission, and engine oil.

CAUTION: *When draining the coolant, keep in mind that cats and dogs are attracted by the ethylene glycol antifreeze, and are quite likely to drink any that is left in an uncovered container or in puddles on the ground. This will prove fatal in sufficient quantity. Always drain the coolant into a sealable container. Coolant should be reused unless it is contaminated or several years old.*

2. Disconnect the battery-to-starter cable at the positive battery terminal after first disconnecting the negative cable.

3. Scribe marks on the hood and its hinges to aid in alignment during installation.

4. Remove the hood supports from the body. Remove the hood. Do not remove the supports from the hood.

5. Unfasten the headlight bezel retaining screws and remove the bezels. Remove the radiator grille attachment screws and remove the grille.

6. Remove the hood lock assembly-detach hood cable as necessary. Remove wiring from the horns then remove the horn assembly.

7. Detach both the upper and lower hoses from the radiator. On cars with automatic transmissions, disconnect and plug the lines from the oil cooler. Remove the radiator.

8. Unfasten the clamps and remove the heater and by-pass hoses from the engine. Remove the heater control cable from the water valve.

9. Remove the wiring from the coolant temperature and oil pressure sending units.

10. Remove the air cleaner from its bracket, complete with its attendant hoses.

11. Unfasten the accelerator torque rod from the carburetor. On models equipped with automatic transmissions, remove the transmission linkage as well.

12. Remove the emission control system hoses and wiring, as necessary (mark them to aid in installation).

13. Remove the clutch hydraulic line support bracket.

14. Unfasten the high tension and primary wires from the coil.

15. Mark the spark plug cables and remove them from the distributor.

16. Detach the right hand front engine mount.

17. Remove the fuel line at the pump.

18. Detach the downpipe from the exhaust manifold.

19. Detach the left hand front engine mount.

20. Disconnect all of the wiring harness multi-connectors.

21. On cars equipped with manual transmissions, remove the shift lever boot and the shift lever cap boot.

22. Unfasten the four gear selector lever cap retaining screws, remove the gasket and withdraw the gear selector lever assembly from the top of the transmission.

NOTE: *On all Corolla 5-speed models, the floor console must be removed first.*

23. Lift the rear wheels of the car off the ground and support the car with jackstands.

CAUTION: *Be sure that the car is securely supported!*

24. On cars equipped with automatic transmissions, disconnect the gear selector control rod.

25. Detach the exhaust pipe support bracket.

26. Disconnect the driveshaft from the rear of the transmission.

27. Unfasten the speedometer cable from the transmission. Disconnect the wiring from the back-up light switch and the neutral safety switch (automatic only).

28. Detach the clutch release cylinder assembly, complete with hydraulic lines. Do not disconnect the lines.

29. Unbolt the rear support member mounting insulators.

30. Support the transmission and detach the rear support member retaining bolts. Withdraw the support member from under the car.

31. Install lifting hooks on the engine lifting brackets. Attach a suitable hoist to the engine.

32. Remove the jack from under the transmission.

33. Raise the engine and move it toward the front of the car. Use care to avoid damaging the components which remain on the car.

34. Support the engine on a workstand.

35. Install the engine using a suitable hoist in the correct position in the vehicle. Raise and lower the vehicle as necessary to perform each service operation.

36. Support the transmission and install the rear support member/insulators.

37. Install the clutch release cylinder assembly.

38. Connect the speedometer cable to the transmission. Reconnect the wiring to the back-up light switch and the neutral safety switch (automatic only).

39. Reconnect the driveshaft to the rear of the transmission.

40. Install the exhaust pipe support bracket.

On cars equipped with automatic transmissions, reconnect the gear selector control rod.

41. Install the gear selector lever, lever boot (manual transmission) assembly floor console as necessary.

42. Reconnect all of the wiring harness multi-connectors. Install the left and right engine mount.

43. Install the complete exhaust system. Reconnect the fuel line at the pump.

44. Install the spark plug wires, clutch line support bracket and all emission control system hoses/wiring.

45. Fasten the accelerator torque rod to the carburetor. On models equipped with automatic transmissions, install the transmission linkage.

46. Install the air cleaner and all hoses, electrical wiring to the coolant temperature and oil pressure sending units.

47. Install the heater control cable and all heater hoses.

48. Install the radiator. Install the upper and lower hoses to the radiator. On cars with automatic transmissions, reconnect the lines to the oil cooler.

49. Install the headlight bezel with retaining screws. Install the grille assembly.

50. Install the hood lock assembly with hood cable. Install horns and electrical wiring to the horns.

51. Install the hood assembly in the correct location. Reconnect the battery cable.

52. Refill all fluid levels with the correct fluid to the proper level. Bleed systems as necessary. Make all necessary adjustments. Start the engine. Check for any fluid leaks, roadtest the vehicle for proper operation.

Corolla Rear Wheel Drive 4A-GE Engine

1. Disconnect the battery cables (negative cable first) and then remove the battery.

2. Remove the hood (mark hood hinges for correct installation) and the engine undercover splash shield.

3. Remove the No. 2 air cleaner hose. Disconnect the actuator and accelerator cables from their bracket on the cylinder head.

4. From inside the vehicle; remove the center console, lift up the shift boot and remove the shifter.

5. Drain the engine oil and transmission fluid. On automatic transmission equipped vehicles, disconnect the two cooler lines from the radiator.

CAUTION: *The EPA warns that prolonged contact with used engine oil may cause a number of skin disorders, including cancer! You should make every effort to minimize your exposure to used engine oil. Protective gloves should be worn when changing the oil. Wash your hands and any other exposed skin areas as soon as possible after exposure to used engine oil. Soap and water, or waterless hand cleaner should be used.*

6. Drain the radiator and engine coolant. Remove the radiator hoses and then remove the radiator and shroud.

CAUTION: *When draining the coolant, keep in mind that cats and dogs are attracted by the ethylene glycol antifreeze, and are quite likely to drink any that is left in an uncovered container or in puddles on the ground. This will prove fatal in sufficient quantity. Always drain the coolant into a sealable container. Coolant should be reused unless it is contaminated or several years old.*

7. Remove the air cleaner assembly.

8. Remove the power steering pump and the pump mounting bracket.

9. Loosen the water pump pulley set nuts, remove the drive belt adjusting bolt and remove the drive belt.

10. Remove the set nuts and remove the fluid coupling with the fan and water pump pulley.

11. Remove the air conditioning compressor and its mounting bracket. DO NOT DISCONNECT THE TWO HOSES. Position the compressor (with the hoses connected) to the side and out of the way. Wire the compressor to the frame so it can not slip, and so there is no tension on the hoses.

12. Remove the spark plug wires from the plugs and cover mounting brackets. Disconnect the coil wire. Remove the distributor.

13. Remove the exhaust pipe bracket from the pipe and clutch housing.

14. Disconnect, and separate, the exhaust pipe from the exhaust manifold.

15. Disconnect the starter wire harness.

16. Relieve the fuel pressure. Remove the fuel hose from the pulsation damper and pressure regulator

17. Remove the cold start injector pipe. Remove the PCV hose from the intake manifold.

18. Tag and disconnect all related vacuum hoses: Brake booster hose; Charcoal canister hose from the intake manifold; VSV hose from the air valve; Two air valve hoses from the vacuum pipe; and the Vacuum sensing hose from the pressure regulator.

19. Remove the wiring harness and the vacuum pipe from the No.3 timing cover.

20. Tag and disconnect all the related wires: Two igniter connections; Oil pressure sender gauge connector; Noise filter connector; Relay block connector; Ground strap (between the oil filter retainer and the body); Ground strap connector; Solenoid resistor connector; Four injector connectors; Ground strap from the intake manifold; Ground strap (between the cylinder head and body); Water temperature sender gauge connector; VSV connector; and the Throttle position sensor connector. Position the harness to one side without disconnecting it from the engine.

21. Raise and safely support the front of the vehicle.

22. Remove the engine mounting bolts on either side of the engine.

23. Unbolt the clutch release cylinder (if so equipped) without disconnecting the hydraulic line and position it out of the way.

24. Disconnect the driveshaft. Tag and disconnect the speedometer cable and the back-up switch connector. Remove the O-ring.

25. Disconnect any cables from the clutch and extension housings. Lower the vehicle.

26. Attach a suitable engine sling and hoist to the lift bracket on the engine. Support the engine rear mounting on a jack. Remove the rear mounting bolts. Carefully raise the engine and transmission and remove from the vehicle.

27. Remove the starter, the two stiffener plates and then remove the transmission from the engine.

28. Install the engine and transmission in the reverse order of removal. Raise and lower the vehicle as necessary to perform each service operation.

29. Attach a suitable engine sling and hoist to the lift bracket on the engine. Support the engine rear mounting on a jack. Carefully raise the engine and transmission and install it in the vehicle. Install the rear mounting bolts.

30. Install the driveshaft. Reconnect the speedometer cable and the back-up switch connector.

31. Install all engine mounting bolts in the correct location.

32. Install the clutch release cylinder if so equipped.

33. Reconnect and route in the correct location all related wiring, ground strap, electrical harness, vacuum pipe and vacuum hoses.

34. Install the cold start injector pipe. Install the PCV hose to the intake manifold. Install or reconnect all fuel line connections.

35. Reconnect the starter wire harness. Install the exhaust pipe to the exhaust manifold.

36. Install the distributor and all ignition wires.

37. Install or reconnect the air conditioning compressor, fan/water pump pulley, power steering pump/bracket. Install and adjust all drive belts.

38. Install the radiator and shroud, air cleaner assembly, radiator hoses, heater hoses.

On automatic transmission equipped vehicles, connect the two cooler lines to the radiator.

39. Install shifter assembly. Install any necessary cables or hoses that were removed during this service procedure.

40. Install the undercovers and hood assembly. Reconnect the battery.

41. Refill all fluid levels with the correct fluid to the proper level. Bleed systems as necessary. Make all necessary adjustments. Start the engine. Check for any fluid leaks, roadtest the vehicle for proper operation.

MR2 4A-GE and 4A-GZE Engines

1. Disconnect the negative battery cable. Relieve the fuel pressure.

2. Remove the hood (mark for correct installation).

3. Raise and support the vehicle safely.

4. Remove the engine under covers.

5. Drain the cooling system, engine oil and transaxle fluid.

CAUTION: *When draining the coolant, keep in mind that cats and dogs are attracted by the ethylene glycol antifreeze, and are quite likely to drink any that is left in an uncovered container or in puddles on the ground. This will prove fatal in sufficient quantity. Always drain the coolant into a sealable container. Coolant should be reused unless it is contaminated or several years old.*

The EPA warns that prolonged contact with used engine oil may cause a number of skin disorders, including cancer! You should make every effort to minimize your exposure to used engine oil. Protective gloves should be worn when changing the oil. Wash your hands and any other exposed skin areas as soon as possible after exposure to used engine oil. Soap and water, or waterless hand cleaner should be used.

6. Remove the suspension upper brace that criss-crosses from the struts to the fire wall.

7. Remove the air cleaner assembly.

8. Remove both air connector tubes.

9. Disconnect the accelerator cable from the throttle body.

10. If equipped with cruise control, disconnect the wiring and remove the cruise control actuator and accelerator linkage assemblies.

11. Disconnect the brake booster vacuum hose.

12. Disconnect the ground strap connector.

13. Remove the check connector and supercharger pressure sensor if so equipped.

14. Remove the injector solenoid resistor, fuel pump relay, fuel pump resistor and the air conditioning vacuum switching valve.

15. Disconnect the filler and overflow hoses from the water filler connection. Remove the water filler from the engine.

16. Remove the engine relay box. Disconnect the wires and connectors from the box.

17. Remove the ignition coil and igniter.

18. From inside the luggage compartment, disconnect the wiring harnesses for the ECU, starter relay, cooling fan and engine wires.

19. Disconnect the starter wiring.

20. Disconnect the radiator hose from the water inlet.

21. Disconnect and plug the fuel inlet and return hoses.

22. Disconnect the radiator hoses from the water outlet housing.

23. Disconnect the heater hoses.

24. Disconnect the control cables from the transaxle.

25. Remove the tailpipe and front exhaust pipe.

26. Remove the engine compartment cooling fan.

27. Remove the idler pulley bracket and unbolt the air conditioning compressor. Move the compressor off to the side and out of the way. Leave the refrigerant lines connected.

28. Remove the intercooler if so equipped.

29. Remove the rear engine mounting insulator.

30. Disconnect the speedometer cable from the transaxle.

31. Disconnect the stabilizer link from the shock absorber.

32. Remove the wire clamp bolt and remove the ABS speed sensor.

33. Remove the lower suspension arms.

34. Remove the driveshafts.

35. Remove the 4 bolts and remove the lower crossmember.

36. Remove the front engine mounting insulator.

37. Remove the nut and bolt attaching the clutch release cylinder to the transaxle. Remove the mounting bracket bolts and remove the clutch release cylinder without disconnecting the hydraulic tube.

38. Remove the right and left hand engine mounting stays.

39. Remove the lateral control rod and air cleaner case bracket.

40. Connect a suitable lifting device to the engine hanger brackets. Tension the lifting device to support the weight of the engine, then remove the left and right hand mounting insulator fasteners; 2 bolts and 3 nuts for each insulator.

41. Carefully lower then raise the engine from the vehicle.

42. Install the engine assembly in the vehi-

cle. During installation, observe the following torque specifications:

a. When installing the rear engine mount insulator, tighten the 10mm bolts to 38 ft. lbs.; tighten the 12mm bolts to 58 ft. lbs.

b. Install the front engine mount insulator to the body and tighten the inner bolt to 38 ft. lbs., tighten the outer bolts to 54 ft. lbs.

c. Connect the mounting bracket to the insulator and install the through-bolt. Bounce the engine several times and tighten the through-bolt to 58 ft. lbs.

43. Install the lower crossmember. Install the driveshafts to the transaxle.

44. Install the lower suspension arms and stabilizer link.

45. Reconnect the speedometer cable to the transaxle. Install the intercooler assembly if so equipped.

46. Install the engine compartment cooling fan, control cables to the transaxle.

47. Install the exhaust system, ignition coil and igniter.

48. Install the suspension upper brace that criss-crosses from the struts to the fire wall.

49. Install the check connector, pressure sensor if so equipped and air cleaner assembly.

50. Install any necessary components, cables, ground straps, vacuum hoses that were removed during this service procedure.

51. Install the hood assembly. Reconnect the battery.

52. Refill all fluid levels with the correct fluid to the proper level. Bleed systems as necessary. Make all necessary adjustments. Start the engine. Check for any fluid leaks, roadtest the vehicle for proper operation.

Corolla Front Wheel Drive 4A-C Engine
Tercel Front Wheel Drive/4-Wheel Drive 3A, 3A-C,
3E and 3E-E Engines

1. Disconnect the negative battery cable.

2. Drain the cooling system and save the coolant for reuse.

CAUTION: *When draining the coolant, keep in mind that cats and dogs are attracted by the ethylene glycol antifreeze, and are quite likely to drink any that is left in an uncovered container or in puddles on the ground. This will prove fatal in sufficient quantity. Always drain the coolant into a sealable container. Coolant should be reused unless it is contaminated or several years old.*

3. Drain the engine oil and the transmission oil.

CAUTION: *Used motor oil may cause skin cancer if repeatedly left in contact with the skin for prolonged periods. Although this is unlikely unless you handle oil on a daily basis, it is wise to thoroughly wash your hands with soap and water immediately after handling used motor oil.*

4. With the help of an assistant, remove the hood (mark hood hinges for correct installation) from the car. Be careful not to damage the paint finish.

5. Remove the air cleaner assembly from the carburetor.

6. Disconnect the upper radiator hose from the engine and remove the overflow hose.

7. Remove the coolant hose at the cylinder head rear coolant pipe and remove the coolant hose at the thermostat housing.

NOTE: *On Tercel 3E-E engine the fuel system is under pressure. Release pressure slowly and contain spillage. Observe no smoking/no open flame precautions. Have a Class B-C (dry powder) fire extinguisher within arm's reach at all times.*

8. Remove the fuel hoses from the fuel pump.

9. Loosen the adjustor(s) and remove the alternator belt, the power steering and/or air conditioning drive belts depending on equipment.

10. Label and remove all wiring running to the motor. Be careful when unhooking wiring connectors; many have locking devices which must be released.

11. Label and disconnect vacuum hoses. Make sure your labels contain accurate information for reconnecting both ends of the hose. Make sure the labels will stay put on the hoses.

12. Disconnect the wiring at the transaxle.

13. Disconnect the speedometer cable at the transaxle.

14. Safely elevate and support the vehicle on jackstands.

15. Disconnect the exhaust pipe from the manifold. Be ready to deal with rusty hardware.

16. Disconnect the air hose at the converter pipe, if so equipped.

17. Loosen and remove the transaxle cooler lines at the radiator.

18. Remove the left and right undercovers (splash shields) under the car.

19. If so equipped, remove the power steering pump from its mounts and lay it aside. Leave the hoses attached. The pump may be hung on a piece of stiff wire to be kept out of the way.

20. If so equipped, remove the air conditioning compressor from its mounts and position out of the way. DO NOT loosen any hoses or fittings--simply move the compressor out of the way. It may be hung from a piece of stiff wire to be kept out of the way.

21. Disconnect the cable and bracket from the transaxle.

22. Disconnect the steering knuckles at the lower control arms.

23. Have an assistant step on the brake pedal while you loosen the nuts and bolts holding the driveshafts to the transaxle. Let the disconnected shafts hang down clear of the transaxle. Remove the driveshaft assembly to the rear differential on 4-Wheel Drive vehicles.

24. Remove the flywheel cover. If equipped with an automatic transmission, remove the flexplate-to-torque converter bolts.

25. Disconnect the front and rear mounts at the crossmember by first removing the two bolt covers and removing the two bolts at each mount. Remove the center crossmember under the engine.

26. Remove the clip and washer holding the shift cable; disconnect the cable at the outer shift lever or outer selector lever.

27. Lower the vehicle to the ground. Remove the radiator and fan assembly.

28. Install the engine hoist to the lifting bracket on the engine. Keep the wiring harness in front of the chain. Draw tension on the hoist enough to support the engine but no more. Double check the hoist attachments before proceeding.

29. Remove the through bolt to the right side engine mount.

30. Remove the left side transaxle mount bolt and remove the mount.

31. Lift the engine and transaxle assembly out of the engine compartment, proceeding slowly and watching for any interference. Pay particular attention to not damaging the right side engine mount, the power steering housing and the neutral safety switch. Make sure wiring, hoses and cables are clear of the engine.

32. Support the engine assembly on a suitable stand; do not allow it to remain on the hoist for any length of time.

33. To install lower the engine and transaxle into the car, paying attention to clearance and proper position. Raise and lower the vehicle as necessary to perform each service operation.

34. Install the left side transaxle mount and its bolt.

35. Install and tighten the right side through bolt for the motor mount.

36. When the engine is securely mounted within the car, the lifting devices may be removed. Replace the radiator and fan assembly.

37. Safely elevate and support the vehicle on jackstands.

38. Install the center crossmember and connect the shift cable.

39. Connect the front and rear mountings for the crossmember and reinstall the bolt covers.

40. Install the flywheel-to-torque converter bolts. Tighten them to the final specification in steps.

41. Replace the flywheel cover.

42. Connect the driveshafts to the transaxle. Install the driveshaft assembly to the rear differential on 4-Wheel Drive vehicles.

43. Reconnect the steering knuckles to the lower control arms.

44. Reattach the cable and bracket to the transaxle.

45. Depending on equipment, reinstall the power steering pump and/or the air conditioning compressor. Tighten the mounting bolts enough to hold the unit in place but no more; the belts will be installed later.

46. Install the left and right splash shields (under covers).

47. Reconnect the transmission cooler lines to the radiator and connect the air hose at the converter pipe.

48. Connect the exhaust pipe to the manifold.

49. Lower the vehicle to the ground; reconnect the speedometer cable at the transaxle.

50. Paying close attention to proper routing and labeling, connect the wiring and vacuum hoses to the engine.

51. Install the drive belts (alternator, power steering and air conditioning) and make sure the belts are properly seated on the pulleys. Adjust the belts to the correct tension and tighten the bolts.

52. Connect the fuel hoses at the fuel pump. Use new clamps if necessary.

53. Attach the coolant hoses: at the thermostat housing, at the cylinder head rear pipe, at the overflow, and at the outlet for the upper hose. Insure that the hoses are firmly over the ports; use new clamps wherever needed.

54. Install the air cleaner assembly onto the carburetor.

55. Have an assistant help reinstall the hood. Make sure its is properly adjusted and secure.

56. Refill the transmission with the proper fluid.

57. Refill the engine oil to the proper level.

58. Refill the engine coolant with the proper amount of fluid.

59. Double check all installation items, paying particular attention to loose hoses or hanging wires, untightened nuts, poor routing of hoses and wires (too tight or rubbing) and tools left in the engine area.

60. Check all fluid levels. Bleed systems as necessary. Make all necessary adjustments. Start the engine. Check for any fluid leaks, roadtest the vehicle for proper operation.

Corolla Front Wheel Drive 4A-GE Engine

1. Disconnect the negative battery cable.

2. With a helper remove the hood (mark hood hinges for correct installation) from the car. Use care not to damage the paint finish on the vehicle.

3. Drain the engine oil.

CAUTION: *Used motor oil may cause skin cancer if repeatedly left in contact with the skin for prolonged periods. Although this is unlikely unless you handle oil on a daily basis, it is wise to thoroughly wash your hands with soap and water immediately after handling used motor oil.*

4. Drain the cooling system. Save the coolant for reuse.

CAUTION: *When draining the coolant, keep in mind that cats and dogs are attracted by the ethylene glycol antifreeze, and are quite likely to drink any that is left in an uncovered container or in puddles on the ground. This will prove fatal in sufficient quantity. Always drain the coolant into a sealable container. Coolant should be reused unless it is contaminated or several years old.*

5. Drain the transaxle oil.

6. Remove the air cleaner assembly.

7. Remove the coolant reservoir tank and remove the PCV hose.

8. Remove the heater hoses from the water inlet housing.

9. Disconnect the fuel inlet hose from the fuel filter.

NOTE: *On fuel injected engine the fuel system is under pressure. Release pressure slowly and contain spillage. Observe no smoking/no open flame precautions. Have a Class B-C (dry powder) fire extinguisher within arm's reach at all times.*

10. Disconnect the heater and air hoses from the air valve.

11. Remove the fuel return hose from the pressure regulator.

12. If equipped with a manual transaxle, remove the slave cylinder from the housing.

Loosen the mounting bolts and move the cylinder out of the way but do not loosen or remove the fluid hose running to the cylinder.

13. Disconnect the vacuum hose running to the charcoal canister.

14. Disconnect the shift control cable, the speedometer cable (at the trans.) and the accelerator cable (at the throttle body).

15. If the car has cruise control, disconnect the cables. Remove the cruise control actuator by:

    a. Disconnecting the vacuum hose,

    b. Removing the cover and the three bolts,

    c. Disconnecting the actuator connector and removing the actuator.

16. Remove the ignition coil.

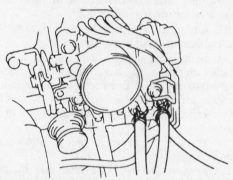

Disconnect the heater and air hoses from the air valve — Corolla FWD 4A-GE engine

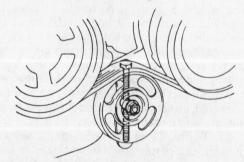

The idler pulley adjuster is behind the pulley — Corolla FWD 4A-GE engine

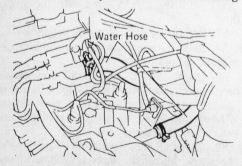

Location of the hoses at the water inlet housing — Corolla FWD 4A-GE engine

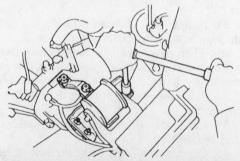

Removing the left side engine mount at the transaxle — Corolla FWD 4A-GE engine

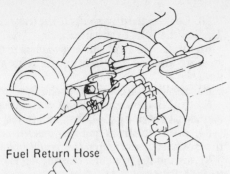

Fuel Return Hose

Location of the fuel return hose at the pressure regulator — Corolla FWD 4A-GE engine

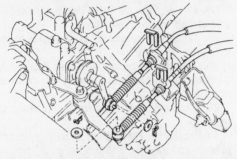

Removing the control cables at the transaxle — Corolla FWD 4A-GE engine

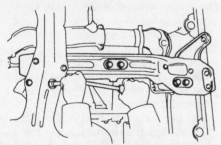

Removing the engine mounts from the crossmember — Corolla FWD 4A-GE engine

17. Remove the main engine wiring harness in the following steps:

a. Inside the car, remove the right side cowl (kick) panel.

b. Disconnect the connectors at junction block 4.

c. Remove the cover over the Electronic Control Module (ECM) and carefully disconnect the ECM plugs.

d. Pull the main wiring harness into the engine compartment.

18. Disconnect the wiring at the number 2 junction block in the engine compartment.

19. Remove the engine and transaxle ground straps.

20. Disconnect the washer change valve connector.

21. Remove the wiring at the cruise control vacuum pump connector and the vacuum switch connector.

22. Remove the hose from the brake vacuum booster.

23. Depending on equipment, remove the air conditioning compressor and/or the power steering pump. Note that the units are to be removed from their mounts and placed out of the way--hoses and lines DO NOT disconnect from the units.

a. Remove the power steering pump pulley nut.

b. Loosen the idler pulley adjusting bolt and pulley bolt.

c. Remove the four compressor mounting bolts.

d. Move the compressor aside and suspend it from stiff wire out of the way.

e. Loosen the compressor bracket bolts.

f. Disconnect the oil pressure connector.

g. Loosen the power steering pump lock bolts and pivot bolts.

h. Remove the pump and its bracket; suspend it out of the way with a piece of stiff wire.

24. Safely elevate the vehicle and support on jackstands. Double check the stands and make sure the vehicle is solidly supported.

25. Remove the splash shields under the car.

26. Disconnect the oil cooler hoses.

27. Disconnect the exhaust pipe from the exhaust manifold.

28. Carefully disconnect the wiring from the oxygen sensor.

29. Remove the cover under the flywheel.

30. Remove the front and rear motor mounts from the center crossmember.

31. Remove the center crossmember.

32. Disconnect the right side control arm at the steering knuckle.

33. Disconnect the driveshafts from the transaxle.

34. Lower the vehicle to the ground. Install the engine hoist to the lifting bracket on the engine. Hang the engine wires and hoses on the lift chain. Take tension on the hoist sufficient to support the motor; double check all hoist attaching points.

35. Disconnect the right side engine mount by removing the bolt.

36. Disconnect the left side motor mount from the transaxle bracket.

37. Lift the engine and transaxle from the vehicle. Be careful to avoid hitting the steering box and the throttle position sensor.

38. Support the engine assembly on a suitable stand; do not allow it to remain on the hoist for any length of time.

39. Disconnect the radiator fan temperature switch connector.

40. Disconnect the start injector time switch.

41. Remove the vacuum hoses from the Bi-metal Vacuum Switching Valves (BVSV).

42. Remove the hoses from the water bypass valves and remove the water inlet housing assembly.

43. Label and remove the wiring connectors from the reverse switch, the water temperature sensor, and the water temperature switch. On cars with automatic transmissions remove the wiring to the neutral safety switch and the transaxle solenoid.

44. If equipped with automatic transmission, remove the six torque converter- to-flexplate bolts.

45. Remove the starter along with its cable and connector.

46. Support the transaxle, remove the retaining bolts in the case and remove the transaxle from the engine. Pull the unit straight off the engine; do not allow it to hang partially removed on the shaft. Keep the automatic transaxle level; if it tilts forward the converter may fall off.

47. Before reinstalling the engine in the car, several components must be reattached or connected. Install the transaxle to the engine; tighten the 12mm bolts to 47 ft. lbs and the 10mm bolts to 34 ft. lbs

48. Install the starter, its cable and connector. Tighten the mounting bolts to 29 ft. lbs.

50. Install the six torque converter-to-flexplate bolts on automatic transaxles. Tighten the bolts to specification.

51. Attach the wiring to the reverse light switch, the water temperature sensor and the water temperature switch.

52. Connect the hoses to the water bypass pipes and the wiring to the start injector time switch and the radiator fan temperature switch.

53. On automatic transaxle vehicles, connect the wiring to the neutral safety switch and the transmission solenoid.

54. Reinstall the water inlet housing assembly and connect the vacuum hoses to the BVSVs.

55. Attach the lifting mechanism to the engine; drape the hoses and wires on the chain.

56. Lower the engine and transaxle into place in the vehicle. Be careful not to hit the power steering gear housing or the throttle position sensor.

57. Install the right motor mount and through bolt; tighten it to 58 ft. lbs.

58. Install the left mount and attach it to the transaxle bracket. When the engine is securely mounted in the car, the lifting equipment may be removed.

59. Safely elevate and support the vehicle on jackstands.

60. Connect the driveshafts to the transaxle. Tighten the bolts to specifications.

61. Attach the right side control arm to the steering knuckle and tighten the bolts and nuts.

62. Replace the cover under the flywheel.

63. Install the engine mount center crossmember, tightening the bolts to 29 ft. lbs.

64. Install the front and rear mounts onto the crossmember. Tighten the mount bolts to 35 ft. lbs and the front and rear through bolts to 58 ft. lbs.

65. Using new gaskets and nuts, connect the exhaust pipe to the exhaust manifold.

66. Connect the wiring to the oxygen sensor and attach the oil cooler lines.

67. Lower the vehicle from its stands to the ground.

68. Install the power steering pump and pulley with its bracket. Tighten the lock bolt and the pivot bolt.

69. Connect the wiring to the oil pressure unit.

70. Install the compressor bracket, the compressor and the belt. Tighten the pulley bolt on the power steering pump to 28 ft. lbs.

71. Install the drive belts and adjust them to the proper tension. Make certain each belt is properly fitted on its pulleys.

72. Connect the vacuum hose to the brake booster.

73. Install the wiring to the No.2 junction block. Connect the cable from the starter to the positive battery terminal and connect the engine and transaxle ground straps. DO NOT connect the negative battery cable at this time.

74. Attach the connectors for the washer change valve, and, if equipped, the cruise control vacuum pump and vacuum switch.

75. Connect the main engine wiring harness by:

    a. Feeding the two connectors from the engine compartment back into the passenger compartment,

    b. Connecting the ECM connector(s) and replacing the cover,

    c. Connecting the wiring to the No.4 junction block and

    d. Replacing the right side kick panel.

76. Reinstall the ignition coil.

77. If so, equipped install the cruise control actuator.

78. Connect or reinstall the cables for the accelerator, the cruise control, the speedometer and the shifter.

79. Install the vacuum hose to charcoal canister.

80. On cars with manual transaxles, attach the clutch slave cylinder to the bell housing.

81. Attach the fuel return hose to the pres-

sure regulator, the heater and air hoses to the air valve and the fuel hose to the fuel filter.

82. Connect the heater hoses to the water inlet housing.

83. Reinstall the PCV hose, the coolant reservoir and the air cleaner assembly.

84. Fill the transaxle with the correct amount of oil, and fill the engine with oil.

85. Fill the cooling system with the proper amount of fluid.

86. Double check all installation items, paying particular attention to loose hoses or hanging wires, untightened nuts, poor routing of hoses and wires (too tight or rubbing) and tools left in the engine area.

87. Connect the negative battery cable.

88. Start the engine and allow it to approach normal operating temperature. Check carefully for leaks. Shut the engine off.

89. Elevate the front end of the car, support on jackstands and install the splash shields below the car.

90. Lower the car to the ground. With your helper, install the hood and adjust it for proper fit and latching. Road test the vehicle for proper operation.

Corolla Front Wheel Drive 4A-F and 4A-FE Engines

1. Remove the hood (mark the hood hinges for correct installation). Have a helper assist you and be careful not to damage the painted body work.

2. Disconnect the negative battery cable, then the positive battery cable and remove the battery.

3. Raise the vehicle and safely support it on jackstands.

4. Remove the left and right splash shields.

5. Drain the engine oil and the transmission oil.

CAUTION: *Used motor oil may cause skin cancer if repeatedly left in contact with the skin for prolonged periods. Although this is unlikely unless you handle oil on a daily basis, it is wise to thoroughly wash your*

Disconnect the fuel line — Corolla FWD 4A-FE engine

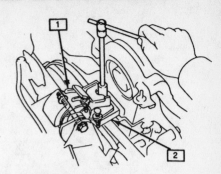

1. Engine mount
2. Engine mount bracket

Removing the engine mount to bracket bolt — Corolla FWD 4A-FE engine

hands with soap and water immediately after handling used motor oil.

6. Drain the engine coolant and save it in closed containers for reuse.

CAUTION: *When draining the coolant, keep in mind that cats and dogs are attracted by the ethylene glycol antifreeze, and are quite likely to drink any that is left in an uncovered container or in puddles on the ground. This will prove fatal in sufficient quantity. Always drain the coolant into a sealable container. Coolant should be reused unless it is contaminated or several years old.*

7. Remove the air cleaner hose and the air cleaner assembly.

8. Remove the coolant reservoir. Remove the radiator and fan assembly.

9. Disconnect the accelerator cable and if equipped with automatic transaxle, the throttle cable.

10. Disconnect and remove the cruise control actuator.

11. Label and disconnect the main engine wiring harness from its related sensors and switches.

12. Remove the ground strap connector and its bolt. Disconnect the wiring to the vacuum sensor, the oxygen sensor and the air conditioning compressor.

13. Label and disconnect the brake booster vacuum hose, the power steering vacuum hose, the charcoal canister vacuum hose and the vacuum switch vacuum hose.

14. Carefully disconnect the fuel inlet and return lines.

NOTE: *On the 4A-FE engine the fuel system is under pressure. Release pressure slowly and contain spillage. Observe no smoking/no open flame precautions. Have a Class B-C (dry powder) fire extinguisher within arm's reach at all times.*

15. Disconnect the heater hoses.

16. Loosen the power steering pump mounting bolt and through bolt. Remove the drive belt.

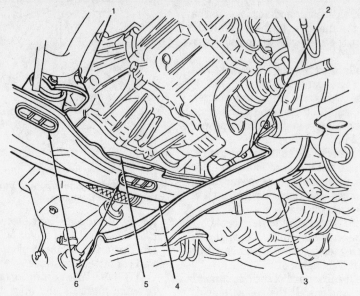

1. Front transaxle mount
2. Rear transaxle mount
3. Main crossmember
4. Center support
5. Center transaxle mount
6. Mount bolt shields

Detail of the crossmember and center support — Corolla FWD 4A-FE engine

17. Remove the four bolts holding the air conditioner compressor and remove the compressor. DO NOT loosen or remove any lines or hoses. Move the compressor out of the way and hang it from a piece of stiff wire.

18. Disconnect the speedometer cable from the transaxle.

19. On cars with manual transmissions, unbolt the clutch slave cylinder from the bell housing and move the cylinder out of the way. Don't disconnect any lines or hoses. Disconnect the shift control cables by removing the two clips, the washers and retainers.

20. On cars with automatic transmissions, remove the clip and retainer and separate the control cable from the shift lever.

21. Elevate the car and support it safely on jackstands.

22. Remove the two bolts from the exhaust pipe flange and separate the pipe from the exhaust manifold.

23. Remove the nuts and bolts and separate the driveshafts from the transaxle.

24. Remove the through bolt from the rear transaxle mount.

25. Remove the nuts from the center transaxle mount and the rear mount.

26. Lower the vehicle to the ground and attach the lifting equipment to the brackets on the engine. Take tension on the hoist line or chain just enough to support the motor but no more. Hang the engine wires and hoses on the chain or cable.

27. Remove the three exhaust hanger bracket nuts and the hanger. Remove the two center crossmember-to-main crossmember bolts. Remove the three center crossmember-to-radiator support bolts.

CAUTION: *Support the crossmembers with a jack or jackstands when loosening the bolts. The pieces are heavy and could fall on you.*

28. Remove the eight crossmember-to-body bolts, then remove the two bolts holding the control arm brackets to the underbody. Remove the two center mount-to-transaxle bolts and remove the mount. Carefully lower the center mount and crossmember and remove from under the car.

29. At the left engine mount, remove the three bolts and the bracket, then remove the bolt, two nuts, through bolt and mounting. Remove the three bolts and the air cleaner bracket.

30. Loosen and remove the five bolts and disconnect the mounting bracket from the transaxle bracket. Remove the through bolt and mounting.

31. Carefully and slowly raise the engine and transaxle assembly out of the car. Tilt the transaxle down to clear the right engine mount. Be careful not to hit the steering gear housing. Make sure the engine is clear of all wiring, lines and hoses.

32. Support the engine assembly on a suitable stand; do not allow it to remain on the hoist for any length of time.

33. With the engine properly supported, disconnect the reverse light switch and the neutral safety switch (automatic tans.).

34. Remove the rear end cover plate.

35. For automatic transaxles, remove the six torque converter mounting bolts.

36. Remove the starter.

37. Support the transaxle, remove the retaining bolts in the case and remove the transaxle from the engine. Pull the unit straight off the engine; do not allow it to hang partially removed on the shaft. Keep the automatic transaxle level; if it tilts forward the converter may fall off.

38. Before reinstalling the engine in the car, several components must be reattached or connected. Install the transaxle to the engine; tighten the 12mm bolts to 47 ft. lbs and the 10mm bolts to 34 ft. lbs

39. Install the starter, its cable and connector. Tighten the mounting bolts to 29 ft. lbs.

40. Install the six torque converter-to-flexplate bolts on automatic transaxles. Tighten the bolts to specification.

41. Install the rear cover plate and connect the wiring to the reverse light switch and the neutral safety switch (automatic trans.).

42. Attach the chain hoist or lift apparatus to the engine and lower it into the engine compartment. Before it is completely in position, attach the power steering pump and its through bolt to the motor.

NOTE: *Tilt the transaxle downward and lower the engine to clear the left motor mount. As before, be careful not to hit the power steering housing (rack) or the throttle position sensor.*

43. Level the engine and align each mount with its bracket.

44. Install the right mounting insulator (bushing) to the engine bracket with the two nuts and bolt. Tighten the bolt temporarily.

45. Align the right insulator with the body bracket and install the through bolt and nut. Temporarily tighten the nut and bolt.

46. Align the left mounting insulator with the transaxle case bracket. Temporarily install the three bracket bolts.

47. With the engine held in place by these mounts, repeat Steps 44, 45 and 46, tightening the bolts to the following tightness. Step 44: 38 ft. lbs.; Step 45: 64 ft. lbs.; Step 46: 35 ft. lbs.

48. Install the left side mounting support with its two bolts; tighten them to 15 ft. lbs.

49. With the engine securely mounted in the car, the lifting equipment may be removed. Elevate the car and support it on jackstands.

50. Install the center mount to the transaxle with its two bolts and tighten them to 45 ft. lbs.

51. Position the center mount over the front and rear studs and start two nuts on the center mount only. Loosely install the three center support-to-radiator support bolts.

52. Loosely install the two front mount bolts. Raise the main crossmember into place over the rear studs and align all the underbody bolts.

53. Install the two rear mount nuts; leave them loose.

54. Loosely install the eight underbody bolts, the lower control arm bracket bolts, the two center support-to-crossmember bolts and the exhaust hanger bracket and nuts.

55. With everything loose, but in place, make a second pass over all the nuts and bolts tightening them to the following specifications:
- Crossmember-to-underbody bolts: 152 ft. lbs
- Lower control arm bracket-to-underbody bolts: 94 ft. lbs.
- Center support-to-radiator support: 45 ft. lbs
- Center support-to-crossmember: 45 ft. lbs.
- Front, center and rear mount bolts: 45 ft. lbs.

56. Install the rear transaxle mount and tighten its bolt to 64 ft. lbs

57. Install the nuts on the center transaxle mount and tighten them to 45 ft. lbs

58. Reconnect the driveshafts to the transaxle.

59. Using a new gasket, connect the exhaust pipe to the manifold and install the exhaust pipe bolts.

60. Lower the vehicle to the ground.

61. Either connect the control cables to the shift outer lever and selector lever and attach the control cables to manual transaxles or reconnect the control cable to the shift lever and install the clip and retainer on automatic transaxles. If equipped with manual transaxle, reattach the clutch slave cylinder to its mount.

62. Attach the speedometer cable to the transaxle.

63. Install the air conditioning compressor and drive belt if so equipped.

64. Install the power steering pump, pivot bolt and drive belt if so equipped. Adjust the belts to the correct tension.

65. Install the fuel inlet and outlet lines.

66. Connect the heater hoses. Make sure they are in the correct positions and that the clamps are in sound condition.

67. Connect the vacuum hoses to the vacuum switch, the charcoal canister, the vacuum sensor, the power steering and the brake booster.

68. Connect the wiring to the air conditioning, the oxygen sensor and the vacuum sensor.

69. Observing the labels made at the time of disassembly, reconnect the main engine harness to its sensors and switches. Work carefully

and make sure each connector is properly matched and firmly seated.

70. Install the ground strap connector and its bolt; connect the wiring at the No.2 junction block in the engine compartment.

71. Install the cruise control actuator if so equipped.

72. Connect the accelerator cable and throttle cable (automatic) to their brackets.

73. Install the radiator and cooling fan assembly. Install the overflow reservoir.

74. Install the air cleaner assembly and the air intake hose.

75. Install the battery. Connect the positive cable to the starter terminal, then to the battery. DO NOT connect the negative battery cable at this time.

76. Fill the transmission with the correct amount of fluid.

77. Refill the engine coolant.

78. Fill the engine with the correct amount of oil.

79. Double check all installation items, paying particular attention to loose hoses or hanging wires, untightened nuts, poor routing of hoses and wires (too tight or rubbing) and tools left in the engine area.

80. Connect the negative battery cable. Start the engine and allow it to idle. As the engine warms up, shift the automatic transmission into each gear range allowing it to engage momentarily. After each gear has been selected, put the shifter in PARK and check the transmission fluid level.

81. Shut the engine off and check the engine area carefully for leaks, particularly around any line or hose which was disconnected during removal.

82. Elevate and support the front end of the car on jackstands. Replace the left and right splash shields and lower the vehicle.

83. With the help of an assistant, reinstall the hood. Adjust the hood for proper fit and latching. Roadtest the vehicle for proper operation.

Corolla Front Wheel Drive 1C-L Diesel Engine

1. Drain the engine coolant.

CAUTION: *When draining the coolant, keep in mind that cats and dogs are attracted by the ethylene glycol antifreeze, and are quite likely to drink any that is left in an uncovered container or in puddles on the ground. This will prove fatal in sufficient quantity. Always drain the coolant into a sealable container. Coolant should be reused unless it is contaminated or several years old.*

2. Remove the hood (mark the hood hinges for correct installation).

3. Remove the battery.

4. Disconnect and tag all cables attached to various engine parts.

5. Disconnect and tag all electrical wires attached to various engine parts.

6. Disconnect and tag all vacuum liens connected to various engine parts.

7. Remove the cruise control actuator and bracket.

8. Disconnect the radiator and heater hoses.

9. Disconnect the automatic transmission cooler lines at the radiator.

10. Unbolt the two radiator supports and lift out the radiator.

11. Remove the air cleaner assembly.

12. Disconnect all wiring and linkage at the transmission.

13. Pull out the injection system wiring harness and secure to the right side fender apron.

14. Disconnect the fuel lines at the fuel filter and return pipes.

15. Disconnect the speedometer cable at the transmission.

16. Remove the clutch release cylinder without disconnect the fluid line.

17. Unbolt the air conditioning compressor and secure it out of the way.

18. Raise and support the car on jackstands.

19. Drain the transaxle fluid.

20. While someone holds the brake pedal depressed, unbolt both axle shafts. It's a good idea to wrap the boots with shop towels to prevent grease loss.

21. Unbolt the power steering pump and secure it out of the way.

22. Disconnect the exhaust pipe from the manifold.

23. Disconnect the front and rear engine mounts at the frame member.

24. Lower the vehicle.

25. Attach an engine crane at the lifting eyes.

26. Take up the engine weight with the crane and remove the right and left side engine mounts.

27. Slowly and carefully, remove the engine and transaxle assembly.

28. Install the engine/transaxle assembly in the vehicle. Torque the engine mount bolts to 29 ft. lbs. Raise and lower the vehicle as necessary for each step of this service procedure.

29. Connect the front and rear engine mounts at the frame member. Install the exhaust pipe to the manifold.

30. Install both axle shafts to the transaxle assembly.

31. Install the speedometer cable and clutch release cylinder if so equipped.

32. Reconnect and route in the correct loca-

tion all related electrical wiring, injection wiring, linkage and vacuum hoses.

33. Install cruise control actuator/bracket and power steering pump. Install and adjust all drive belts.

34. Install the radiator and shroud, air cleaner assembly, radiator hoses, heater hoses. On automatic transmission equipped vehicles, connect the two cooler lines to the radiator.

35. Install any necessary cables, linkage or hoses that were removed during this service procedure.

36. Install the hood assembly. Reconnect the battery.

37. Refill all fluid levels with the correct fluid to the proper level. Bleed systems as necessary. Make all necessary adjustments. Start the engine. Check for any fluid leaks, roadtest the vehicle for proper operation.

Valve Cover (Cam Cover or Rocker Arm Cover)

REMOVAL AND INSTALLATION

1C-L Diesel Engine, 3A-C, 3A, 3E and 3E-E Engines

1. Disconnect the negative battery cable. Remove the air cleaner and its assorted hoses and lines.

2. Tag and disconnect any wires, hoses or lines which might interfere with the cylinder head cover removal.

3. Unscrew the retaining screws/bolts and then lift off the cylinder head cover.

NOTE: *If the cylinder head cover is stuck, tap it lightly with a rubber mallet to loosen it. DO NOT attempt to pry it off.*

4. Using a new gasket and silicone sealant, replace the cylinder head cover and tighten the bolts down until they are snug—not too tight!

5. Installation of the remaining components is in the reverse order of removal.

4A-C Engine

1. Disconnect the negative battery cable.
2. Remove the air cleaner assembly.
3. Disconnect the PCV hose.
4. Disconnect the accelerator cable.
5. Disconnect the wire harness.
6. Remove the upper timing belt cover bolts and the cover. Remove the two valve cover bolts.
7. Remove the valve cover and its gasket.

NOTE: *If the cover is stuck in place, tap a corner with a plastic or rubber mallet. Don't pry the cover up; it will deform and leak.*

8. Clean the mating surfaces on the head and the cover; install a new gasket.
9. Place the cover and gasket in position on the head. Make sure the cover is straight and that the rubber bushings are on the studs.

10. Install the cover nuts and the upper belt cover with its bolts. Tighten the cover nuts to 15 ft. lbs.

11. Connect the wiring harness, the accelerator cable and the PCV hose.

12. Install the air cleaner assembly and connect the negative battery cable.

13. Start the engine and check for leaks after the engine has warmed up. Minor leaks may be cured by slightly snugging the cover bolts and the timing belt cover bolts. Any leak that is still present after about a $^1/_4$ turn CANNOT be cured by further tightening. Remove the cover again and either reposition or replace the gasket.

4A-GE and 4A-GZE Engines

1. Disconnect the negative battery cable.
2. Disconnect or remove the PCV valve, the accelerator cable and the wiring harness.
3. Disconnect (mark or label) the spark plug wires at the plugs and disconnect the wiring to the noise filter.
4. Disconnect the oil pressure sender wire and, if equipped with air conditioning, the wire to the compressor.

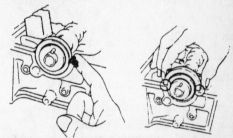

Apply sealant to these points before reinstalling the valve cover — 4A-C, 4A-GE and 4A-GZE engines

5. Remove the center cover (between the cam covers) and its gasket.
6. Remove the cap nuts, the rubber seals and remove the valve covers.

NOTE: *If the cover is stuck in place, tap a corner with a plastic or rubber mallet. Don't pry the cover up; it will deform and leak.*

7. Clean the mating surfaces of the head and the covers.
8. Apply RTV sealant to the cylinder head before reassembly. This step is REQUIRED to prevent oil leakage.
9. Install the covers with new gaskets. Install the seals and the cap nut, making sure everything is properly seated. tighten the cap nuts to 15 ft. lbs.
10. Install the center cover with its gasket.
11. Connect the wiring to the oil pressure

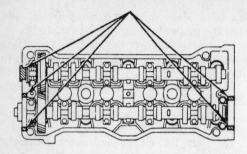

Apply sealant to these points before reinstalling the valve cover — 4A-F and 4A-FE engines

sender and the compressor, if equipped.

12. Connect the wiring to the noise filter and install the spark plug wires.

13. Connect, in this order, the wiring harness, the accelerator cable, the PCV valve and the negative battery cable.

14. Start the engine and check for leaks after the engine has warmed up. Minor leaks may be cured by slightly snugging the cover bolts. Any leak that is still present after about a ¼ turn CANNOT be cured by further tightening. Remove the cover again and either reposition or replace the gasket.

4A-F and 4A-FE Engines

1. Disconnect the negative battery cable.

2. Disconnect the PCV and the vacuum hose.

3. Loosen the engine wiring harness running over the upper timing belt cover for easier access to the valve cover.

4. Remove the spark plug wires (mark or label) from the spark plugs.

5. Remove the three cap nuts, the seals below them and remove the valve cover.

6. Clean the mating surfaces of the head and the cover. Install a new gasket before installing the valve cover.

7. Apply RTV sealant to the cylinder head before reassembly. This step is REQUIRED to prevent oil leakage.

8. Install the covers with new gaskets. Install the seals and the cap nut, making sure everything is properly seated. Tighten the cap nuts to 15 ft. lbs.

9. Reconnect the spark plug wires and reposition the wiring harness over the timing belt cover.

10. Connect the vacuum hose, the PCV and the negative battery cable.

11. Start the engine and check for leaks after the engine has warmed up. Minor leaks may be cured by slightly snugging the cover bolts. Any leak that is still present after about a ¼ turn CANNOT be cured by further tightening. Remove the cover again and either reposition or replace the gasket.

Rocker Arms

REMOVAL AND INSTALLATION

3A, 3A-C and 4A-C Engines

1. Remove the valve cover as described previously.

2. Loosen each rocker support bolt little-by-little, in three steps, in the proper sequence.

3. Remove the bolts and remove the rocker assembly from the head. Inspect the valve contacting surfaces for wear. Inspect the rocker-to-shaft clearance by wiggling the rocker on the shaft. Play should be virtually none; any noticeable motion requires replacement of the rocker arms and/or the shaft.

4. Disassemble the rockers from the shaft. Check the contact surfaces for signs of visible wear or scoring.

5. Using either an inside micrometer or a dial indicator, measure the inside diameter of the rocker arm. Using a regular micrometer, measure the diameter of the shaft. Maximum allowable difference (oil clearance) between the two measurements is 0.06mm.

6. After replacing any needed parts, loosen the adjusting screw lock nuts.

7. The rocker shaft has oil holes in it. When assembling the rockers onto the shaft, make sure the holes point to the left, the right and down. (Said another way, when viewed from the end of the shaft, the oil holes are at 3, 6 and 9 o'clock.)

NOTE: *Failure to observe this positioning will cause the rockers to starve for oil, causing expensive and premature wear.*

8. Install the rocker assembly on the head. Tighten the retaining bolts in three steps and in the correct sequence. Torque the bolts to 18 ft. lbs on the third pass.

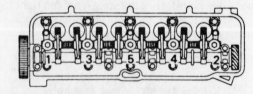

Rocker arm support bolt loosening sequence — 3A, 3A-C and 4A-C engines

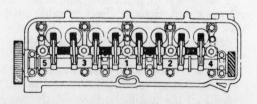

Tighten the rocker arm support bolts in this sequence — 3A, 3A-C and 4A-C engines

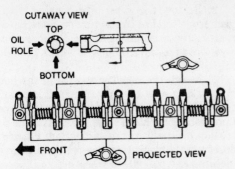

Oil hole positioning — 3A, 3A-C and 4A-C engines

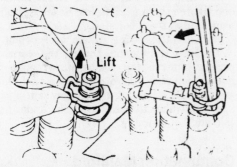

Rocker arm spring clip removal — 3E and 3E-E engines

9. Set the motor to TDC and adjust the valves, using the procedures discussed in Chapter 2.

3E and 3E-E Engines

1. Remove the camshaft.
2. Loosen the rocker arm adjusting screw locknuts.
3. Pull up on the top of the spring while prying the spring with a suitable tool.
4. Remove the rocker arms and arrange them in order. Check the contact surface for any signs of pitting or wear.
5. Check that the adjusting screw is as shown and install a new spring to the rocker arm.
6. Press the bottom lip of the spring until it fits into the groove on the rocker arm pivot.

NOTE: *Put the valve adjusting screw in the rocker arm pivot.*

7. Pry the rocker spring clip onto the pivot. Pull the rocker arm up and down to check that there is spring tension and that the rocker does not rattle. Adjust the valves as necessary.

4A-GE, 4A-GZE, 4A-F and 4A-FE Engines

The twin camshaft motors (one cam for the intake valves and one for the exhaust valves) use direct-acting cams; that is, the lobes of the camshaft act directly on the valve mechanism. These engines do not have rocker arms.

1C-L Diesel Engine

The diesel engine uses no rocker arms or rocker shaft as the valves are operated directly off of the camshaft.

Thermostat

REMOVAL AND INSTALLATION

All Models

The thermostat is installed on the inlet side of the water pump. Its purpose is to prevent overheating of the coolant by controlling the flow into the engine from the radiator. During warm up, the thermostat remains closed so that the coolant within the engine heats quickly and aids the warming up process.

As the coolant temperature increases, the thermostat gradually opens, allowing a supply of lower temperature coolant (from the radiator) to enter the water pump and circulate through the engine.

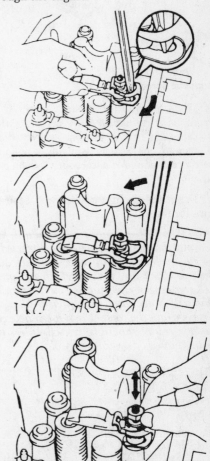

Rocker arm spring clip installation — 3E and 3E-E engines

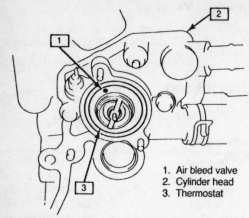

1. Air bleed valve
2. Cylinder head
3. Thermostat

Correct placement of the air bleed valve during thermostat replacement

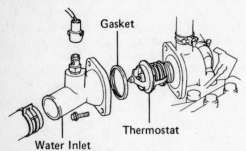

Gasket

Thermostat

Water Inlet

Thermostat assembly

NOTE: *A thermostat should never be removed as a countermeasure to overheating problem. The vehicle cooling system should be serviced, necessary components replaced, correct coolant added and cooling system pressurized.*

1. Drain the cooling system and save the coolant for reuse.

CAUTION: *When draining the coolant, keep in mind that cats and dogs are attracted by the ethylene glycol antifreeze, and are quite likely to drink any that is left in an uncovered container or in puddles on the ground. This will prove fatal in sufficient quantity. Always drain the coolant into a sealable container. Coolant should be reused unless it is contaminated or several years old.*

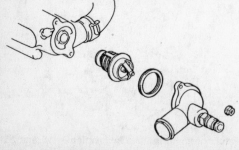

Thermostat assembly

2. Remove the water inlet housing (disconnect any electrical connection on housing) and remove the thermostat. Carefully observe the positioning of the thermostat within the housing.

3. Install the new thermostat in the housing, making sure it is in correctly. It is possible to install it backwards. Additionally, make certain that the air bleed valve aligns with the protrusion on the water inlet housing. Failure to observe this placement can result in poor air bleeding and possible overheating.

4. Install the water inlet housing cover with a new gasket. Install the two hold down bolts and tighten them to 20 ft. lbs. (in steps) Do not over tighten these bolts!

5. Refill the cooling system with coolant.

6. Start the engine. During the warm up period, observe the temperature gauge for normal behavior. Also during this period, check the water inlet housing area for any sign of leakage. Remember to check for leaks under both cold and hot conditions.

Combination Manifold

REMOVAL AND INSTALLATION

3A, 3A-C 4A-C Engines

The intake and exhaust manifolds on these engines are a one-piece or combination design. They can not be separated from each other or serviced individually. Refer to Cylinder Head Removal and Installation service procedure for illustrations.

1. Disconnect the negative battery cable.
2. Remove the air cleaner assembly.
3. Label and disconnect all vacuum hoses at the carburetor.
4. Disconnect the accelerator cable and, for automatic transmissions, the throttle cable.
5. Label and disconnect the electrical connections at the carburetor.
6. Disconnect the fuel line at the fuel pump.
7. Carefully loosen and remove the carburetor mounting bolts and remove the carburetor.

CAUTION: *The carburetor bowls contain gasoline which may spill or leak during removal. Observe no smoking/no open flame precautions. Have a Class B-C (dry powder) fire extinguisher within arm's reach at all times.*
NOTE: *Keep the carburetor level (do not tilt) during removal and handling. As soon as it is off the car, wrap or cover it with a clean towel to keep dirt out.*

8. Remove the Early Fuel Evaporation (EFE) gasket.
9. Remove the vacuum line and dashpot bracket.

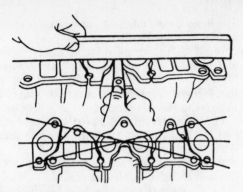

Measuring the manifold for warpage

10. Carefully remove the heat shields on the manifold; don't break the bolts.

11. Safely elevate and support the vehicle on jackstands.

12. Disconnect the exhaust pipe at the manifold and exhaust bracket at the engine.

13. Remove the hose at the converter pipe.

14. Lower the car to the ground and remove or disconnect the vacuum hose to the brake booster.

15. Remove the bracket for the accelerator and throttle cables.

16. Evenly loosen and then remove the bolts and nuts holding the manifold to the engine. Remove the manifold and its gaskets.

17. Using a precision straight edge and a feeler gauge, check the mating surfaces of the manifold for warpage. If the warpage is greater than the maximum allowable specification, replace the manifold. Maximum permitted warpage: Intake 0.2mm; Exhaust 0.3mm

18. When reinstalling, always use new gaskets and make sure they are properly positioned. Place the manifold in position and loosely install the nuts and bolts until all are just snug. Double check the placement of the manifold and in two passes tighten the retaining nuts and bolts to 18 ft. lbs.

19. Reinstall the bracket for the accelerator and throttle cables and connect the vacuum hose to the brake vacuum booster.

20. Elevate and safely support the car on jackstands.

21. Reconnect the hose at the converter pipe. Install the exhaust bracket at the engine and, using new gaskets, connect the exhaust pipe to the manifold.

22. Lower the vehicle to the ground. Install the heat shield onto the manifold.

23. Reinstall the vacuum line and the dashpot bracket.

24. Install the EFE gasket.

25. Reinstall the carburetor. Slowly and evenly tighten the mounting nuts and bolts to 8–10 ft. lbs. Connect the electrical connectors to the carburetor.

26. Connect and secure the fuel line to the fuel pump.

27. Attach the accelerator cable and throttle valve cable (automatic trans.).

28. Observing the labels made earlier, install the vacuum lines. Be careful of the routing and make sure that each line fits snugly on its port. double check each line for crimps or twists.

29. Install the air cleaner assembly and connect the negative battery cable.

30. Start the engine, check for leaks and roadtest for proper operation.

Intake Manifold

REMOVAL AND INSTALLATION

4A-GE and 4A-GZE Engines

NOTE: *Refer to Cylinder Head Removal and Installation service procedure for illustrations. On 4A-GZE engine refer to Supercharger Removal and Installation procedure as necessary. Modify this service procedure as necessary.*

1. Disconnect the negative battery cable.

2. Drain the cooling system. Relieve the fuel pressure.

CAUTION: *When draining the coolant, keep in mind that cats and dogs are attracted by the ethylene glycol antifreeze, and are quite likely to drink any that is left in an uncovered container or in puddles on the ground.*

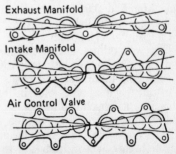

Removing the fuel rail and injectors on the 4A-GE engine

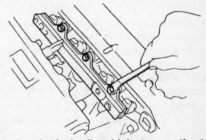

Check for warpage in three positions on the 4A-GE engine manifolds and air control valve

This will prove fatal in sufficient quantity. Always drain the coolant into a sealable container. Coolant should be reused unless it is contaminated or several years old.

3. Remove the air cleaner assembly. Remove all air ducts, hoses, cables and components to supercharger assembly as necessary.

4. Remove the upper radiator hose at the engine.

5. Disconnect the accelerator cable and, on automatic transmissions, the throttle valve cable.

6. Label and disconnect vacuum hoses at the manifolds.

7. Disconnect and remove the fuel delivery pipe (fuel rail) and remove the injectors. During removal, be careful not to drop the injectors.

CAUTION: *The fuel system is under pressure. Release pressure slowly and contain spillage. Observe no smoking/no open flame precautions. Have a Class B-C (dry powder) fire extinguisher within arm's reach at all times.*

8. Disconnect the vacuum hose to the brake booster and remove the heat shield(s) from the manifold(s).

9. Safely raise the car and support it on jackstands.

10. Disconnect the wire for the water temperature sensor and remove the water outlet housing (thermostat housing) and the bypass pipe.

11. Remove the exhaust bracket and disconnect the exhaust pipe at the manifold. Remove the support bracket for the intake manifold.

12. Lower the vehicle to the ground.

13. Remove the intake manifold with the air control valve and gaskets and/or remove the exhaust manifold with its gaskets.

14. Using a precision straight edge and a feeler gauge, check the mating surfaces of the manifolds for warpage. If the warpage is greater than the maximum allowable specification, replace the manifold.

Maximum allowable warpage:
• Intake Manifold: 0.05mm
• Exhaust Manifold: 0.3mm
• Air Control Valve: 0.05mm.

15. When reinstalling, always use new gaskets and make sure they are properly positioned. Place the manifold(s) in position and loosely install the nuts and bolts until all are just snug. Double check the placement of the manifold(s) and in two passes tighten the retaining nuts and bolts. The exhaust manifold retaining bolts should be tightened to 18 ft. lbs. and the intake manifold bolts should be tightened to 20 ft. lbs. (refer to Torque Specification Chart for specification change as necessary).

The bolts for the intake support bracket should also be tightened to 20 ft. lbs

16. With the manifold(s) in place, elevate and support the vehicle; install the support bracket for the intake manifold and connect the exhaust pipe to the exhaust manifold. Attach the exhaust bracket.

17. Install the bypass pipe, the water outlet housing and connect the wiring to the water temperature sensor.

18. Lower the car to the ground and install the heat shield(s) on the manifolds.

19. Connect the vacuum hose for the brake vacuum booster.

20. Install the fuel delivery pipe and the injectors. Tighten the mounting bolts to 13 ft. lbs.

21. Observing the labels made earlier, install the vacuum lines. Be careful of the routing and make sure that each line fits snugly on its port.

22. Double check each line for crimps or twists.

23. Connect the accelerator cable and throttle valve cable (automatic trans.)

24. Reconnect the upper radiator hose.

25. Install the air cleaner assembly. Install all air ducts, hoses, cables and components to supercharger assembly as necessary.

26. Refill the coolant.

27. Connect the negative battery cable. Start the engine, check for leaks and roadtest for proper operation.

4A-F and 4A-FE Engines

NOTE: *This Removal and Installation procedure is for both engines modify service steps as necessary. Refer to Cylinder Head Removal and Installation service procedure for illustrations.*

1. Disconnect the negative battery cable. On the 4A-FE engine relieve the fuel pressure.

2. Drain the cooling system.

CAUTION: *When draining the coolant, keep in mind that cats and dogs are attracted by the ethylene glycol antifreeze, and are quite likely to drink any that is left in an un-*

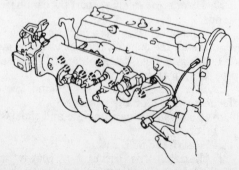

Removing the intake manifold assembly — 4A-FE engine

covered container or in puddles on the ground. This will prove fatal in sufficient quantity. Always drain the coolant into a sealable container. Coolant should be reused unless it is contaminated or several years old.

3. Remove the air cleaner assembly.

4. Label and disconnect the vacuum hoses at the manifold.

5. Label and disconnect the wiring to the throttle position sensor, the cold start injector, the injector connectors, the air control valve and the vacuum sensor.

6. Disconnect the cold start injector pipe. On the 4A-F engine disconnect all connections at carburetor assembly.

CAUTION: *The fuel system is under pressure. Release pressure slowly and contain spillage. Observe no smoking/no open flame precautions. Have a Class B-C (dry powder) fire extinguisher within arm's reach at all times.*

7. Disconnect the water hose from the air valve.

8. Raise and safely support the car on jackstands.

9. Remove the intake manifold support bracket. Lower the car to the ground.

10. Remove the seven bolts, two nuts and the ground cable. Remove the intake manifold and its gaskets.

11. Measure the intake manifold mating surface with a precision straight edge and a feeler gauge. If the warpage exceeds 0.2mm, the manifold must be replaced.

12. To reassemble, install the manifold with new gaskets in position. Attach the seven bolts, two nuts and the ground cable connector.

13. Raise and safely support the car; install the manifold support bracket and its bolts. Lower the car to the ground.

14. Tighten the manifold mounting nuts and bolts evenly to 14 ft. lbs. (work from the center to ends in steps).

15. Connect the water hose to the air valve.

16. Connect the fuel line to the cold-start in-

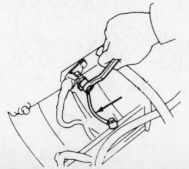

Removing the cold start injector line at the 4A-FE engine intake manifold

jector. On the 4A-F engine reconnect all connections to the carburetor assembly.

17. Connect the wiring to the throttle position sensor, the cold start injector, the injector connectors, the air control valve and the vacuum sensor.

18. Observing the labels made earlier, install the vacuum lines. Be careful of the routing and make sure that each line fits snugly on its port. Double check each line for crimps or twists.

19. Connect the accelerator and throttle valve (automatic trans.) cables to their brackets.

20. Refill the coolant.

21. Install the air cleaner assembly and connect the negative battery cable.

22. Start the engine, check for leaks and roadtest for proper operation.

3E and 3E-E Engines

NOTE: *This Removal and Installation procedure is for both engines modify service steps as necessary. Refer to Cylinder Head Removal and Installation service procedure for illustrations.*

1. Disconnect the negative battery cable. On the 3E-E engine relieve the fuel pressure.

2. Drain the cooling system. Remove the air cleaner assembly.

CAUTION: *When draining the coolant, keep in mind that cats and dogs are attracted by the ethylene glycol antifreeze, and are quite likely to drink any that is left in an uncovered container or in puddles on the ground. This will prove fatal in sufficient quantity. Always drain the coolant into a sealable container. Coolant should be reused unless it is contaminated or several years old.*

3. Tag and disconnect all wires, hoses or cables that interfere with intake manifold removal.

4. Remove the necessary components in order to gain access to the intake manifold retaining bolts.

5. Remove the carburetor or throttle body.

6. Disconnect the intake manifold water hoses.

7. Remove the intake manifold retaining bolts. Remove the intake manifold from the vehicle.

8. Installation is the reverse of the removal procedure. Use new gaskets, as required. Tighten to 14 ft. lbs. working from the center to the ends in steps. Start the engine, check for leaks and roadtest for proper operation.

1C-L Diesel Engine

NOTE: *Refer to Cylinder Head Removal and Installation service procedure for illustrations. For engine injection pump and* lines service procedures refer to Chapter 5 as necessary.

1. Disconnect the negative battery cable.
2. Drain the coolant.

CAUTION: *When draining the coolant, keep in mind that cats and dogs are attracted by the ethylene glycol antifreeze, and are quite likely to drink any that is left in an uncovered container or in puddles on the ground. This will prove fatal in sufficient quantity. Always drain the coolant into a sealable container. Coolant should be reused unless it is contaminated or several years old.*

3. Remove the air cleaner.
4. Tag and disconnect all wires, hoses and cables which are in the way of manifold removal.
5. Remove the coolant bypass pipe.
6. Unbolt and remove the manifold.
7. Installation is in the reverse order of removal. Torque intake manifold retaining bolts to 13 ft. lbs. working from the center to the ends in steps. Start the engine, check for leaks and roadtest for proper operation.

Exhaust Manifold

REMOVAL AND INSTALLATION

4A-GE and 4A-GZE Engines

NOTE: *Refer to Cylinder Head Removal and Installation service procedure for illustrations. On 4A-GZE engine refer to Supercharger Removal and Installation procedure as necessary. Modify this service procedure as necessary.*

1. Disconnect the negative battery cable.
2. Drain the cooling system. Relieve the fuel pressure if necessary.

CAUTION: *When draining the coolant, keep in mind that cats and dogs are attracted by the ethylene glycol antifreeze, and are quite likely to drink any that is left in an uncov-*

ered container or in puddles on the ground. This will prove fatal in sufficient quantity. Always drain the coolant into a sealable container. Coolant should be reused unless it is contaminated or several years old.

3. Remove the air cleaner assembly. Remove all air ducts, hoses, cables and components to supercharger assembly as necessary.
4. Remove the upper radiator hose at the engine.
5. Disconnect the accelerator cable and, on automatic transmissions, the throttle valve cable.
6. Label and disconnect vacuum hoses at the manifolds.
7. Disconnect and remove the fuel delivery pipe (fuel rail) and remove the injectors. During removal, be careful not to drop the injectors.

CAUTION: *The fuel system is under pressure. Release pressure slowly and contain spillage. Observe no smoking/no open flame precautions. Have a Class B-C (dry powder) fire extinguisher within arm's reach at all times.*

8. Disconnect the vacuum hose to the brake booster and remove the heat shield(s) from the manifold(s).
9. Safely raise the car and support it on jackstands.
10. Disconnect the wire for the water temperature sensor and remove the water outlet housing (thermostat housing) and the bypass pipe.
11. Remove the exhaust bracket and disconnect the exhaust pipe at the manifold. Remove the support bracket for the intake manifold.
12. Lower the vehicle to the ground.
13. Remove the intake manifold with the air control valve and gaskets and/or remove the exhaust manifold with its gaskets.
14. Using a precision straight edge and a feeler gauge, check the mating surfaces of the manifolds for warpage. If the warpage is

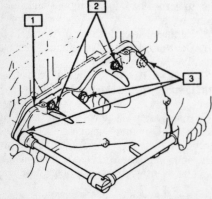

1. Exhaust manifold
2. Nut
3. Bolt

Location of retaining bolts, 4A-FE exhuast manifold

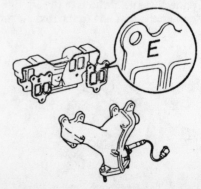

Exhaust manifold gasket installation — 3E and 3E-E engines

greater than the maximum allowable specification, replace the manifold.

Maximum allowable warpage:
- Intake Manifold: 0.05mm
- Exhaust Manifold: 0.3mm
- Air Control Valve: 0.05mm.

15. When reinstalling, always use new gaskets and make sure they are properly positioned. Place the manifold(s) in position and loosely install the nuts and bolts until all are just snug. Double check the placement of the manifold(s) and in two passes tighten the retaining nuts and bolts. The exhaust manifold retaining bolts should be tightened to 18 ft. lbs. and the intake manifold bolts should be tightened to 20 ft. lbs. (refer to Torque Specification Chart for specification change as necessary). The bolts for the intake support bracket should also be tightened to 20 ft. lbs

16. With the manifold(s) in place, elevate and support the vehicle; install the support bracket for the intake manifold and connect the exhaust pipe to the exhaust manifold. Attach the exhaust bracket.

17. Install the bypass pipe, the water outlet housing and connect the wiring to the water temperature sensor.

18. Lower the car to the ground and install the heat shield(s) on the manifolds.

19. Connect the vacuum hose for the brake vacuum booster.

20. Install the fuel delivery pipe and the injectors. Tighten the mounting bolts to 13 ft. lbs.

21. Observing the labels made earlier, install the vacuum lines. Be careful of the routing and make sure that each line fits snugly on its port.

22. Double check each line for crimps or twists.

23. Connect the accelerator cable and throttle valve cable (automatic trans.)

24. Reconnect the upper radiator hose.

25. Install the air cleaner assembly. Install all air ducts, hoses, cables and components to supercharger assembly as necessary.

26. Refill the coolant.

27. Connect the negative battery cable. Start the engine, check for leaks and roadtest for proper operation.

4A-F and 4A-FE Engines

NOTE: *Refer to Cylinder Head Removal and Installation service procedure for illustrations.*

1. Disconnect the negative battery cable.

2. Remove the five bolts and remove the upper heat shield (insulator) from the manifold.

3. Raise and safely support the vehicle on jackstands.

4. Disconnect the exhaust pipe from the exhaust manifold and remove the manifold support and its two bolts.

5. Lower the vehicle to the ground. Disconnect the oxygen sensor wire.

6. Remove the two nuts and three bolts holding the manifold to the engine. Remove the manifold and its gaskets. When the manifold is clear of the car, remove the lower heat shield.

7. Measure the exhaust manifold mating surface with a precision straight edge and a feeler gauge. If the warpage exceeds 0.28mm, the manifold must be replaced.

8. Before reinstalling, attach the lower heat shield to the manifold with the three bolts. Tighten the bolts to 18 ft. lbs.

9. Install the manifold with new gaskets and tighten (working from the center to the ends in steps) its bolts and nuts to 18 ft. lbs.

10. Raise the car and safely support in on jackstands. Install the manifold support and tighten the bolts to 18 ft. lbs.

11. Connect the exhaust pipe to the manifold with new gaskets and tighten the bolts.

12. Lower the car to the ground. Install the upper heat shield on the manifold and tighten its five bolts to 18 ft. lbs.

13. Connect the wiring to the oxygen sensors.

14. Connect the negative battery cable.

3E and 3E-E Engines

NOTE: *Refer to Cylinder Head Removal and Installation service procedure for illustrations.*

1. Disconnect the negative battery cable. Remove the exhaust manifold heat insulator shield assembly.

2. Remove the necessary components in order to gain access to the exhaust manifold retaining bolts.

3. Disconnect the exhaust manifold bolts at the exhaust pipe. Disconnect the oxygen sensor electrical wire. It may be necessary to raise and support the vehicle safely before removing these bolts.

4. Remove the exhaust manifold retaining bolts. Remove the exhaust manifold from the vehicle.

5. Installation is the reverse of the removal procedure. During installation, the **E** mark on the gasket must face outward. Tighten the exhaust manifold retaining bolts to specifications (refer to Torque Specification Chart as necessary).

1C-L Diesel Engine

NOTE: *Refer to Cylinder Head Removal and Installation service procedure for illustrations.*

1. Disconnect the negative battery cable.
2. Raise and support the vehicle on jack-stands.
3. Remove the gravel shield from underneath the engine.
4. Remove the downpipe support bracket.
5. Unscrew the bolts from the exhaust flange and then detach the downpipe from the manifold.
6. Loosen the manifold retaining bolts. Always remove and tighten the manifold bolts in two or three stages, starting from the inside and working out.
7. Installation is in the reverse order of removal. Always use a new gasket and tighten the retaining bolts to the proper specifications (refer to Torque Specification Chart as necessary).

Supercharger

REMOVAL AND INSTALLATION

MR2 4A-GZE Engine

1. Disconnect the negative cable at the battery. Drain the cooling system and remove the radiator reservoir tank.
CAUTION: *When draining the coolant, keep in mind that cats and dogs are attracted by the ethylene glycol antifreeze, and are quite likely to drink any that is left in an uncovered container or in puddles on the ground. This will prove fatal in sufficient quantity. Always drain the coolant into a sealable container. Coolant should be reused unless it is contaminated or several years old.*
2. Remove the vacuum switching valve (VSV) and the intercooler assembly.
3. Remove the air flow meter with the No. 3 air cleaner hose. Disconnect the accelerator cable (rod) and throttle cable.
4. Disconnect the PCV, brake booster, ACV, A/C idle-up and emission control vacuum hoses.
5. Remove the No. 1 intake air connector pipe and its air hose.

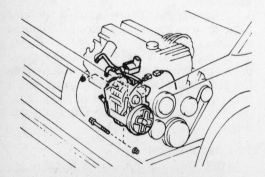

Removal of supercharger assembly — MR2

6. Loosen the idler pulley locknut and adjusting bolt and remove the supercharger drive belt.
7. Disconnect the No. 2 and 3 water by-pass hoses. Loosen the air hose clamp.
8. Remove the air inlet duct stay. Remove the throttle body.
9. Disconnect the ACV and supercharger connectors and the 2 ACV hoses. Remove the 2 nuts and the ACV. Remove the pivot bolt and nut, remove the 2 stud bolts and then rotate the assembly so the hub is facing upward; remove the supercharger.
10. Installation is the reverse of the removal procedure. Tighten the 2 stud bolts to 25 ft. lbs. and pivot bolt side to 47 ft. lbs. Refill the engine coolant and intercooler assembly.

Air Conditioning Compressor

REMOVAL AND INSTALLATION

All Models

NOTE: *Please refer to the Air Conditioning Section in Chapter 1 so that the system may be discharged properly. Always wear eye protection and gloves when discharging the system. Observe no smoking/no open flame rules.*

1. Disconnect the negative battery cable.
2. Remove the electrical connector to the compressor.
3. Safely discharge the system.
4. Remove the two hoses from the compressor fittings. Immediately cap the compressor ports and the hose ends to prevent dirt from entering.
5. Loosen or remove the compressor drive belt.
6. To remove the air conditioning assembly from the bottom of the vehicle raise and safely support the vehicle on jackstands. Remove the splash shield under the engine. On some models it may be necessary to remove the air conditioning compressor from the top of the engine compartment.
7. Remove the compressor mounting bolts and remove the compressor from the engine (top or bottom of engine compartment).
8. When reinstalling, support the compressor in place and install the retaining bolts.
9. With the vehicle safely supported by jackstands, reinstall the splash shields as necessary.
10. Lower the vehicle if necessary and install the drive belt. Adjust it to the proper tension.
11. Always use new O-rings in the hose ends and connect the hoses to the compressor. tighten both lines to 18 ft. lbs.
12. Install the wiring to the compressor. Connect the negative battery cable.

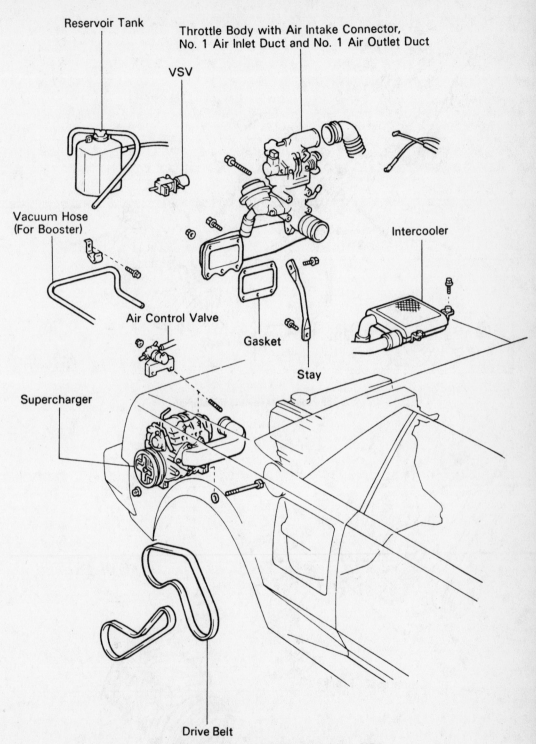

Reservoir Tank

Throttle Body with Air Intake Connector,
No. 1 Air Inlet Duct and No. 1 Air Outlet Duct

VSV

Vacuum Hose
(For Booster)

Intercooler

Air Control Valve

Gasket

Stay

Supercharger

Drive Belt

Exploded view supercharger assembly — MR2

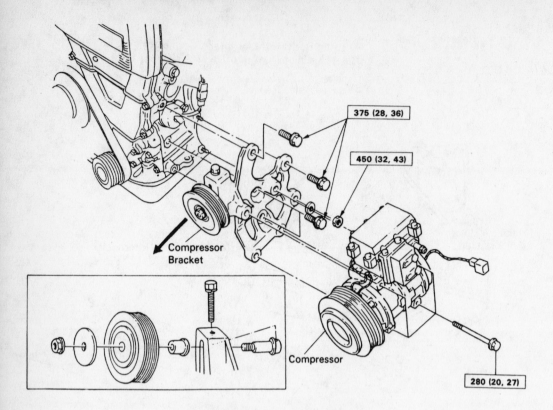

375 (28, 36)

450 (32, 43)

Compressor
Bracket

Compressor

280 (20, 27)

A/C compressor assembly installation

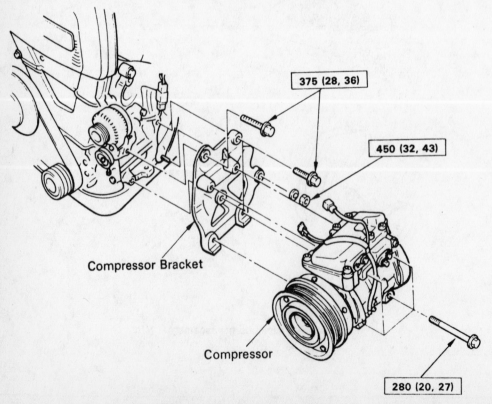

375 (28, 36)

450 (32, 43)

Compressor Bracket

Compressor

280 (20, 27)

A/C compressor assembly installation

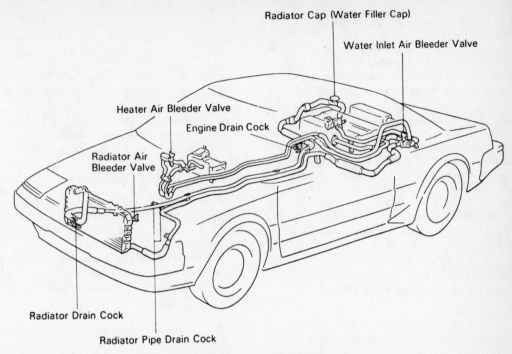

Radiator Cap (Water Filler Cap)

Water Inlet Air Bleeder Valve

Heater Air Bleeder Valve

Engine Drain Cock

Radiator Air
Bleeder Valve

Radiator Drain Cock

Radiator Pipe Drain Cock

Cooling circuit — MR2 vehicle

13. Evacuate/recharge the air conditioning system as explained in Chapter 1.

Radiator

REMOVAL AND INSTALLATION

All Models

1. Drain the cooling system. On the MR2 vehicle refer to cooling circuit illustration for drain cock locations.

CAUTION: *When draining the coolant, keep in mind that cats and dogs are attracted by the ethylene glycol antifreeze, and are quite likely to drink any that is left in an uncovered container or in puddles on the ground. This will prove fatal in sufficient quantity. Always drain the coolant into a sealable container. Coolant should be reused unless it is contaminated or several years old.*

2. Unfasten the clamps and remove the radiator upper and lower hoses. If equipped with an automatic transmission, remove the oil cooler lines (always use a line wrench).

3. Detach the hood lock cable and remove the hood lock from the radiator upper support as necessary.

NOTE: *On some older models it may be necessary to remove the grille in order to gain access to the hood lock/radiator support assembly.*

4. Remove the fan shroud (any electrical cooling fan connection), if so equipped.

5. On models equipped with a coolant recovery system, disconnect the hose from the thermal expansion tank from its bracket.

6. Unbolt and remove the radiator upper support.

7. Unfasten the bolts and remove the radia-

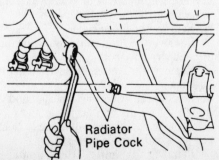

Radiator
Pipe Cock

Radiator drain cock — MR2

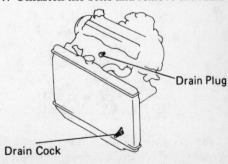

Drain Plug

Drain Cock

Radiator drain cock

tor. Use care not to damage the radiator fins on the cooling fan.

8. Installation is performed in the reverse order of removal. Remember to check the transmission fluid level on cars with automatic transmissions. Fill the radiator to the specified level.

9. Certain models are equipped with an electric, rather than a belt-driven, cooling fan. Using a radiator-mounted thermoswitch, the fan operates when the coolant temperatures reaches about 203°F (95°C) and stops when it lowers to about 190°F (88°C). It is attached to the radiator by the four radiator retaining bolts. Radiator removal is the same for this engine as all others, except for disconnecting the wiring harness and thermoswitch connector.

Condenser

REMOVAL AND INSTALLATION

All Models

NOTE: *Please refer to the Air Conditioning Section in Chapter 1 so that the system may be discharged properly. Always wear eye protection and gloves when discharging the system. Observe no smoking/no open flame rules.*

1. Disconnect the negative battery cable. Safely discharge the air conditioning system.

2. Remove the grille (as necessary) and the hood lock brace. On some models the front bumper, horn, oil cooler and condenser fan may have to be removed.

3. Disconnect the flexible discharge hose from the condenser inlet fitting. Use (one wrench should be a line or flare nut wrench-use this on fitting) two wrenches, one to counterhold the fitting and one to turn. Failure to counterhold the fitting may result in damage to the lines.

4. Disconnect the liquid line from the condenser outlet. Again, use two wrenches (one wrench should be a line or flare nut wrench-use this on fitting).

5. Cap the open lines immediately to prevent moisture from entering the system.

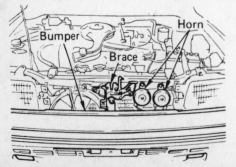

Condenser assembly removal

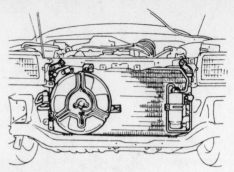

Condenser assembly removal

6. Remove the four bolts holding the condenser and remove the condenser. Take great care not to damage the fins on the condenser during removal.

7. When reinstalling, make sure the rubber cushions fit on the mounting flange correctly.

8. Install the four bolts holding the condenser.

9. Connect the liquid line to the condenser. Connect the flexible discharge hose and tighten it. Always replace the O-rings as necessary.

NOTE: *The lightweight fittings on the lines and hoses are easily damaged. Do not over tighten the threaded fittings.*

10. Install the front grille (install bumper assembly as necessary) and hood lock brace. Install all necessary components that were removed during removal procedures.

11. If a different condenser was installed, add 1.4-1.7 oz. of compressor oil to the compressor. Evacuate and recharge the system.

Water Pump

REMOVAL AND INSTALLATION

Rear Wheel Drive/4A-C Engine

1. Drain the radiator.

CAUTION: *When draining the coolant, keep in mind that cats and dogs are attracted by the ethylene glycol antifreeze, and are quite likely to drink any that is left in an uncovered container or in puddles on the ground. This will prove fatal in sufficient quantity. Always drain the coolant into a sealable container. Coolant should be reused unless it is contaminated or several years old.*

2. Remove the fan shroud.

3. Remove the fluid coupling, water pump pulley and the drive belt.

4. Remove the water outlet housing and bypass pipe.

5. Remove the water inlet housing and thermostat.

6. Remove the heater outlet pipe. Remove the oil level gauge guide and gauge.

7. Remove the lower front timing belt cover.

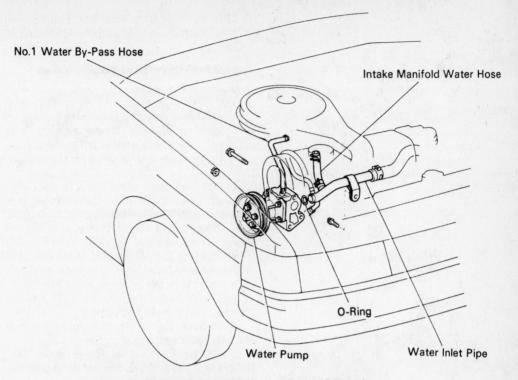

No.1 Water By-Pass Hose

Intake Manifold Water Hose

O-Ring

Water Pump

Water Inlet Pipe

Water pump installation — 3E and 3E-E engines

8. Remove the water pump.

9. Installation is in the reverse order of removal. Torque the water pump retaining bolts to 11 ft. lbs. Adjust the drive belt. Refill engine coolant. Start the engine and check for coolant leaks.

Front Wheel Drive/3A and 3A-C Engines

1. Drain the radiator.

CAUTION: *When draining the coolant, keep in mind that cats and dogs are attracted by the ethylene glycol antifreeze, and are quite likely to drink any that is left in an uncovered container or in puddles on the ground. This will prove fatal in sufficient quantity. Always drain the coolant into a sealable container. Coolant should be reused unless it is contaminated or several years old.*

2. Remove the water pump pulley and the drive belt.

3. Remove the water outlet housing and bypass pipe.

4. Remove the water inlet housing and thermostat.

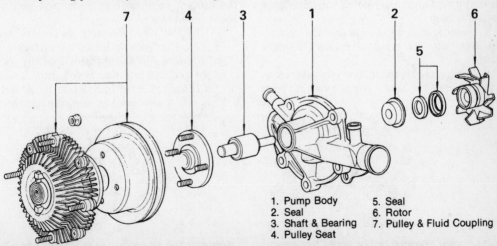

1. Pump Body
2. Seal
3. Shaft & Bearing
4. Pulley Seat
5. Seal
6. Rotor
7. Pulley & Fluid Coupling

Water pump components — RWD 4A-C engine

Remove these two hoses before removing the
water inlet pipe

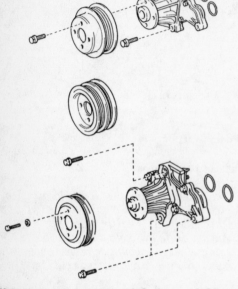

Water pump components 4A-C above, 4A-GE and
4A-FE below — other engines similar

5. Remove the upper front timing belt
cover.

6. Disconnect the heater outlet hose from
the outlet pipe and then remove the outlet pipe
mounting bolt.

7. Remove the oil level gauge guide (remove
retaining bolt) and gauge. Remove the water
pump.

8. Installation is in the reverse order of removal. Torque the water pump retaining bolts

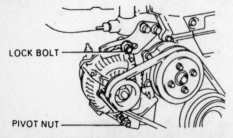

The alternator adjusting bolts must be loosened to
remove the water pump belt

to 11 ft. lbs. Adjust the drive belt. Refill engine
coolant. Start the engine and check for coolant
leaks.

Front Wheel Drive/3E and 3E-E Engines

1. Drain the radiator.

CAUTION: *When draining the coolant, keep
in mind that cats and dogs are attracted by
the ethylene glycol antifreeze, and are quite
likely to drink any that is left in an uncovered container or in puddles on the ground.
This will prove fatal in sufficient quantity.
Always drain the coolant into a sealable container. Coolant should be reused unless it is
contaminated or several years old.*

2. Remove the engine undercover. On 3E
engine remove the HAC valve from the bracket.

3. Remove the oil dipstick, drive belt and
intake manifold stay/bracket (remove any necessary component or hose to stay or bracket.

4. On 3E engine disconnect the No. 1 water
by-pass hose from the carburetor.

5. Remove the oil dipstick guide. Remove
the alternator and adjusting bar.

6. On the 3E engine disconnect intake manifold water hose from the intake manifold.
Remove the water pump pulley.

7. Remove the water inlet pipe mounting
bolt from the cylinder block.

8. Remove the water pump retaining bolts
and nuts. Remove the water pump.

9. Installation is in the reverse order of removal. Torque the water pump retaining bolts
to 13 ft. lbs. Adjust the drive belt. Refill engine
coolant. Start the engine and check for coolant
leaks.

Front Wheel Drive/4A-C and 4A-GE Engines
Rear Wheel Drive/4A-GE and 4A-GZE Engines

1. Drain the engine coolant by opening the
radiator and engine block drain cocks. Collect
the coolant in clean containers and save for
reuse if necessary.

CAUTION: *When draining the coolant, keep
in mind that cats and dogs are attracted by
the ethylene glycol antifreeze, and are quite
likely to drink any that is left in an uncovered container or in puddles on the ground.
This will prove fatal in sufficient quantity.*

Removing the oil dipstick tube. Always use a new
seal (O-ring) on the tube when reinstalling

Always drain the coolant into a sealable container. Coolant should be reused unless it is contaminated or several years old.

2. On the 4A-GE engine, remove the power steering drive belt.

3. Loosen the water pump pulley bolts.

4. Loosen the alternator locking bolt and the pivot nut.

5. Move the alternator to its loosest position and remove the belt.

6. On the 4A-C engine, remove the power steering drive belt.

7. Remove the four bolts on the water pump pulley and remove the pulley.

8. Disconnect the water inlet and the water bypass hoses from the water inlet pipe.

9. Disconnect and remove the water inlet pipe by removing the two clamp bolts and the two nuts at the back of the pump. Remove the O-ring from the back of the pump.

10. Remove the mounting bolt for the dipstick tube; remove the tube and dipstick. Immediately plug the hole in block to prevent fluid from polluting the oil.

NOTE: *During the following steps, if coolant should get by the plug in the dipstick hole and run into the motor, the engine oil MUST be changed before starting the motor.*

11. On 4A-C engines, remove the No.1 (upper) timing belt cover. On 4A-GE engines, both the No. 2 (lower) and No. 3 (middle) timing belt covers must be removed.

12. Remove the water pump bolts and the water pump.

13. To reinstall, place the water pump gasket (O-ring) on the block and install the pump. Tighten the mounting bolts to 11 ft. lbs.

14. Install the timing belt cover(s), making sure they are properly seated and not rubbing on the belt or other moving parts.

15. Install a new seal (O-ring) on the dipstick tube and lightly coat it with engine oil. Remove the plug and install the dipstick tube and dipstick; secure the mounting bolt.

16. Using a new O-ring, install the inlet pipe to the water pump.

17. Attach the clamps and bolts to hold the pipe in place.

18. Connect the water inlet and water bypass hoses to the inlet pipe.

19. Install the water pump pulley and tighten the four pulley bolts finger tight.

20. For 4A-C engines, install the power steering drive belt.

21. Install the drive belts on all the pulleys and adjust all of them to the correct tension.

22. With the belts in place and adjusted, the water pump pulley will now resist turning. Tighten the pulley bolts to 16–18 ft. lbs.

23. For the 4A-GE engine, install the power steering belt and adjust to the proper tension.

24. Confirm that the drain cocks are closed on the engine block and radiator. Refill the engine coolant. Start the engine and check for leaks.

Front Wheel Drive 4A-F and 4A-FE Engine

1. Remove the radiator cap. Drain the engine coolant by opening the radiator and engine block drain cocks. Collect the coolant in clean containers and save for reuse if necessary.

CAUTION: *When draining the coolant, keep in mind that cats and dogs are attracted by the ethylene glycol antifreeze, and are quite likely to drink any that is left in an uncovered container or in puddles on the ground. This will prove fatal in sufficient quantity. Always drain the coolant into a sealable container. Coolant should be reused unless it is contaminated or several years old.*

2. Raise and safely support the vehicle on jackstands.

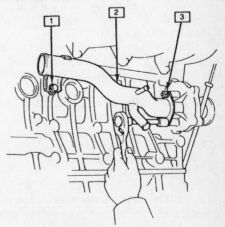

1. Pipe retaining brace
2. Water inlet pipe
3. Pipe retaining nuts

Removing the water inlet pipe — 4A-F and 4A-FE engines

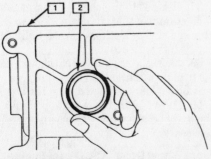

1. Cylinder block
2. Water pump o-ring

Always use a new gasket (O-ring) when installing a new water pump

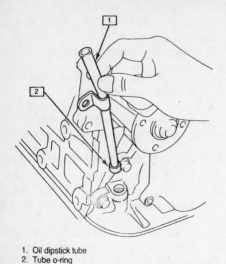

1. Oil dipstick tube
2. Tube o-ring

Removing the oil dipstick tube on the engine. Always plug the hole in the engine block when the tube is removed

3. Remove the two nuts for the rear motor mount.

4. Lower the vehicle to the ground.

5. Remove the windshield washer fluid container.

6. If so equipped, remove the cruise control bracket with the control module.

7. Remove the through bolt for the right motor mount.

8. Place a jack under the engine. Use a piece of wood between the engine and the jack.

9. Raise the engine slowly and carefully. Keep a close watch on lines and cables. The engine need only be raised enough to gain access to various nuts and bolts.

10. Loosen the water pump pulley bolts, but leave them in place.

11. Loosen the alternator lock bolt and pivot nut; swing the alternator towards the engine and remove the drive belt.

12. Loosen the pivot bolts and the lock bolt for the power steering pump and move it towards the engine; remove the power steering belt.

13. With the belts removed, the water pump pulley may be removed from the pump.

14. Lower the jack, allowing the engine to return to place.

15. Remove the water inlet and water bypass hoses from the water inlet pipe.

16. Remove the clamp holding the water inlet pipe to the engine. Loosen and remove the two nuts holding the inlet pipe to the water pump. Remove the pipe and its O-ring.

17. Remove the mounting bolt for the dipstick tube; remove the tube and dipstick. Immediately plug the hole in block to prevent fluid from polluting the oil.

NOTE: *During the following steps, if coolant should get by the plug in the dipstick hole and run into the motor, the engine oil MUST be changed before starting the motor.*

18. Remove the upper timing belt cover.

NOTE: *The timing belt is exposed with the cover(s) removed. Do not allow oil or coolant to contact the belt.*

19. Remove the three water pump bolts and remove the water pump.

20. When reinstalling, position a new O-ring on the engine and fit the water pump. Tighten the three bolts to 11 ft. lbs.

21. Install the upper timing belt cover.

22. Install a new O-ring on the dipstick tube.

23. Remove the plug in the engine and install the tube. Tighten the mounting bolt.

24. Using a new O-ring, install the water inlet pipe at the back of the water pump. Tighten the two nuts to 14 ft. lbs.

25. Connect the water inlet and water bypass hoses to the water inlet pipe.

26. Following the same jacking procedure as before, elevate the motor with the floor jack.

27. Install the water pump pulley and tighten the bolts finger tight. It will be easier to do the final tightening when the belts are installed.

28. Install the power steering belt and adjust its tension.

29. Install the alternator drive belt and adjust its tension.

30. Tighten the water pump pulley bolts to 17 ft. lbs.

31. Lower the jack, allowing the engine to return to its normal place.

32. Install the through bolt for the right motor mount. Tighten it to 64 ft. lbs.

33. Reinstall the cruise control module and the bracket, if so equipped.

34. Raise and safely support the vehicle on jackstands.

35. Install the two nuts for the rear mount and tighten them to 38 ft. lbs.

36. Lower the vehicle to the ground.

37. Replace the washer fluid container.

38. Confirm that the drain cocks on the radiator and engine block are closed. Refill the cooling system with coolant.

39. Start the engine and check for leaks. Pay particular attention to any hose or fitting which was disassembled during the repair.

40. After the engine is shut off, double check the drive belts for proper tension and adjust as necessary.

Front Wheel Drive 1C-L Diesel Engine

1. Drain the radiator.

CAUTION: *When draining the coolant, keep in mind that cats and dogs are attracted by the ethylene glycol antifreeze, and are quite likely to drink any that is left in an uncovered container or in puddles on the ground. This will prove fatal in sufficient quantity. Always drain the coolant into a sealable container. Coolant should be reused unless it is contaminated or several years old.*

2. Remove the injection pump pulley as detailed in Chapter 5.

3. Remove the water pump.

4. Installation is in the reverse order of removal. Torque the water pump retaining bolts to 13 ft. lbs. Make all necessary adjustments. Refill engine coolant. Start the engine and check for coolant leaks.

Cylinder Head

REMOVAL AND INSTALLATION

3A, 3A-C and 4A-C Engines

NOTE: *This Removal and Installation procedure is for all engines modify service steps as necessary. All wires and hoses should be labeled at the time of removal. Review the complete service procedure and refer to the Torque Specification Chart before starting this repair. Always change oil and oil filter after this repair is finished.*

1. Disconnect the negative battery cable.

2. Drain the cooling system.

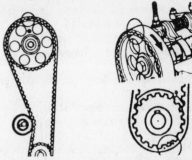

Mark the timing belt rotation before removal

CAUTION: *When draining the coolant, keep in mind that cats and dogs are attracted by the ethylene glycol antifreeze, and are quite likely to drink any that is left in an uncovered container or in puddles on the ground. This will prove fatal in sufficient quantity. Always drain the coolant into a sealable container. Coolant should be reused unless it is contaminated or several years old.*

3. Remove the air cleaner assembly.

4. Elevate and safely support the vehicle on jackstands.

5. Drain the engine oil.

CAUTION: *Used motor oil may cause skin cancer if repeatedly left in contact with the skin for prolonged periods. Although this is unlikely unless you handle oil on a daily basis, it is wise to thoroughly wash your*

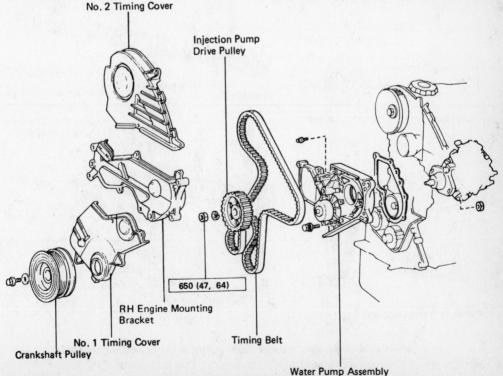

No. 2 Timing Cover

Injection Pump
Drive Pulley

650 (47, 64)

RH Engine Mounting
Bracket

No. 1 Timing Cover

Timing Belt

Crankshaft Pulley

Water Pump Assembly

Diesel engine water pump removal and installation

hands with soap and water immediately after handling used motor oil.

6. Disconnect the exhaust pipe from the exhaust manifold and the exhaust bracket from the engine.

7. Disconnect the hose at the converter pipe.

8. If equipped with power steering, loosen the pivot bolt at the power steering pump.

9. Lower the vehicle to the ground.

10. Disconnect the accelerator and throttle control cables at the carburetor and bracket.

11. Label and remove the wiring at the cowl, the oxygen sensor and the distributor.

12. Label and disconnect all vacuum hoses.

13. Disconnect the fuel hoses at the fuel pump.

14. Remove the upper radiator hose from the engine.

15. Remove the water outlet assembly from the head. Remove the heater hose.

16. If equipped with power steering, remove the adjusting bracket.

17. Label and disconnect the vacuum hoses and spark plug wires at the distributor. Remove the distributor.

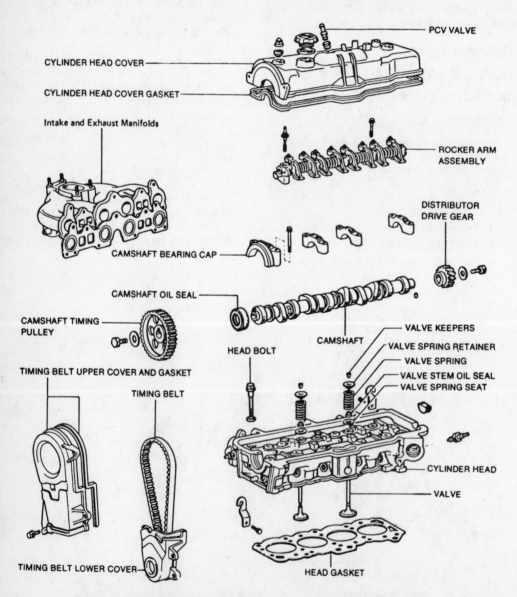

Exploded view of the 4A-C cylinder head — other A series engines similar

18. Remove the PCV from the valve cover.

19. Reposition or disconnect the wiring harness running along the head.

20. Remove the upper timing belt cover bolts.

21. Remove the valve cover and its gasket.

22. Remove the water pump pulley bolts and the pulley.

23. Remove the alternator belt.

24. Matchmark the camshaft pulley and the cylinder head so that the marks can be realigned during reinstallation. With chalk or crayon, mark the timing belt with an arrow showing the direction of rotation and mark the belt-to-pulley alignment as well.

25. Loosen the bolt holding the timing belt idler pulley; move the idler to release tension on the belt and snug the bolt to hold the idler in the loosened position.

26. Carefully pull or slide the timing belt off the cam pulley. Do not crimp the belt and do not force it off the pulley with tools.

27. Loosen and remove the head bolts gradually, in three passes and in the order shown in the illustration.

NOTE: *Head warpage or cracking can occur if the correct removal procedure is not followed.*

28. Remove the cylinder head with the manifolds and carburetor attached. If the head is difficult to lift off, gently pry it up with a suitable tool placed between the head and the projection on the block. If prying is needed, be careful not to score or gouge the mating surfaces of the head and/or the block.

29. Keeping the head upright, place it on wooden blocks on the workbench. If the head is to receive further work, the various external components will need to be removed. If the head is not to be worked on, the mating surface must be cleaned of all gasket and sealant material before reinstallation.

30. Clean the engine block mating surface of all gasket and sealant material. Use plastic or wooden scrapers so as not gouge the metal. Remove all traces of liquids from the surface and clean out the bolt holes.

31. Install the new head gasket on the block with the sealer facing upwards.

32. Place the head in position and make sure

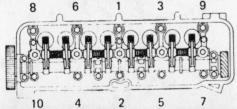

Cylinder head torque sequence — 3A, 3A-C and 4A-C (A series) engines

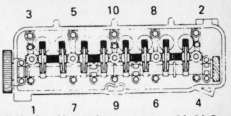

Cylinder head loosening sequence — 3A, 3A-C and 4A-C (A series) engines

it is properly seated and aligned.

33. Install and tighten the cylinder head bolts. Tighten then gradually, evenly, and in three passes in the order shown. On the first pass, tighten all the bolts to 14 ft. lbs. On the second pass the bolts are tightened to 30 ft. lbs. and on the last pass the bolts are tightened to their final setting of 43 ft. lbs.

WARNING: *Failure to follow this procedure exactly may cause either premature gasket failure or head damage.*

34. Align the camshaft pulley mark(s) made during disassembly with the marks on the head and or block.

35. Install the timing belt onto the cam pulley, being careful not to allow the belt to become mispositioned on the lower (crank) pulley. Handle the belt carefully and avoid getting fluids or lubricants on the belt.

36. Loosen the holding bolt for the timing belt idler pulley and allow it to tension the belt.

37. Turn the crankshaft clockwise through at least two full revolutions; finish the rotation by aligning the timing marks at TDC. Double check that the small triangular mark on the cam pulley is at the top and pointing up.

38. Tighten the bolt for the timing belt idler pulley to 27 ft. lbs.

39. Using a belt tension gauge, check the timing belt tension. Correct tension is 0.6mm at 4.4 lbs.

40. If the head was disassembled during the repair, adjust the valves at this time. If the head was not disassembled, the valves need not be adjusted.

41. Install the valve cover and the upper timing cover.

42. Install the water pump pulley and bolts; install the alternator belt and adjust it to the correct tension.

43. Correctly position or reconnect the wiring harness running along the head.

44. Install the PCV valve in the valve cover.

45. Correctly install the distributor and connect the wiring, vacuum lines and spark plug wires.

46. Install the power steering adjusting bracket if so equipped.

47. Install the heater hose, the water outlet

at the head and connect the upper radiator hose to the engine.

48. Connect the fuel lines to the fuel pump.

49. Observing the labels made earlier, connect the vacuum hoses to their ports. Make sure the hoses fit securely on the fittings and are not crimped or twisted.

50. Connect the wiring at the cowl, the oxygen sensor and the distributor.

51. Connect the accelerator and throttle control cables at the bracket and at the carburetor.

52. Safely raise and support the vehicle on jackstands.

53. If equipped with power steering, tighten the pivot bolt for the pump.

54. Connect the hose at the converter pipe.

55. Connect the exhaust bracket to the engine and connect the exhaust pipe to the manifold.

56. Lower the vehicle to the ground.

57. Install the air cleaner assembly.

58. Add the correct amount of engine oil.

59. Confirm that the radiator and engine drain cocks are closed and fill the cooling system with the correct amount of coolant. Install the radiator cap.

60. Double check all installation items, paying particular attention to loose hoses or hanging wires, untightened nuts, poor routing of hoses and wires (too tight or rubbing) and tools left in the engine area.

61. Connect the negative battery cable.

63. Start the engine; during the warm up period, check carefully for any signs of fluid leaks or engine overheating.

64. When the engine has reached normal operating temperature, check the ignition timing and adjust the idle speed as necessary. Roadtest the vehicle for proper operation.

3E and 3E-E Engines

NOTE: *This Removal and Installation procedure is for both engines modify service steps using exploded view illustration as necessary. All wires and hoses should be labeled or marked at the time of removal. Review the complete service procedure and refer to the Torque Specifications Chart before starting this repair. Always change oil and oil filter after this repair is finished.*

1. Disconnect the negative battery cable. Remove the right side under engine splash shield. Relieve the fuel pressure on the 3E-E engine.

2. Drain the engine coolant from the radiator.

CAUTION: *When draining the coolant, keep in mind that cats and dogs are attracted by the ethylene glycol antifreeze, and are quite likely to drink any that is left in an uncov-*

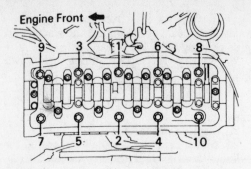

Cylinder head bolt torque sequence — 3E and 3E-E engines

ered container or in puddles on the ground. This will prove fatal in sufficient quantity. Always drain the coolant into a sealable container. Coolant should be reused unless it is contaminated or several years old.

3. Remove the power steering pump and bracket (if equipped).

4. If equipped with A/C, but not power steering, remove the idler pulley/bracket.

5. Disconnect the radiator hoses. Disconnect the accelerator and throttle valve cable linkage from the carburetor. On the 3E-E engine disconnect the accelerator and throttle cables.

6. Remove the timing belt and camshaft timing pulley.

7. Disconnect the heater inlet hose. Discon-

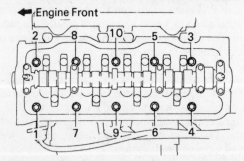

Cylinder head bolt removal sequence — 3E and 3E-E engines

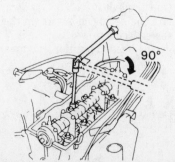

Cylinder head bolt torque procedure — 3E and 3E-E engines

nect and plug the fuel lines. On the 3E-E engine remove the pulsation damper and disconnect the fuel inlet and return hoses.

8. Disconnect the power brake booster vacuum line from the intake manifold.

9. Disconnect the water inlet hose. Disconnect the intake manifold water hose from the intake manifold.

10. Tag (for identification) all vacuum lines, hoses and wires or harnesses to the intake manifold and cylinder head and disconnect them.

11. Remove the evaporative valve and cold en-

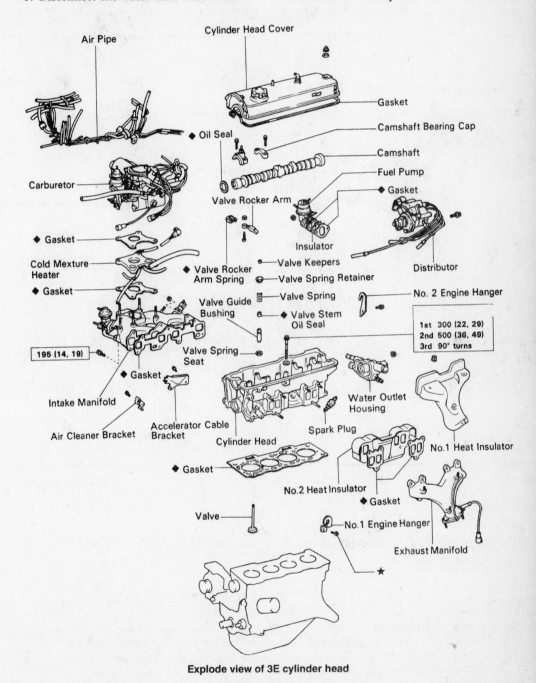

Explode view of 3E cylinder head

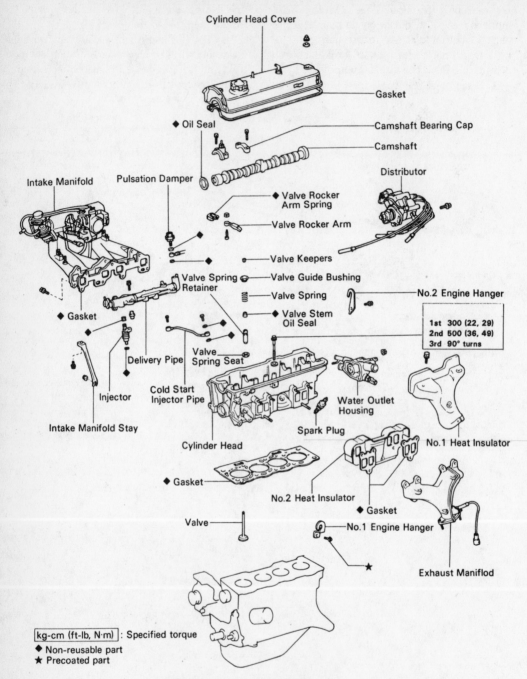

Cylinder Head Cover

Gasket

Oil Seal

Camshaft Bearing Cap

Camshaft

Pulsation Damper

Distributor

Intake Manifold

Valve Rocker Arm Spring

Valve Rocker Arm

Valve Keepers

Valve Guide Bushing

Valve Spring Retainer

Valve Spring

No.2 Engine Hanger

Gasket

Valve Stem Oil Seal

1st	300 (22, 29)
2nd	500 (36, 49)
3rd	90° turns

Delivery Pipe

Valve Spring Seat

Injector

Cold Start Injector Pipe

Water Outlet Housing

No.1 Heat Insulator

Intake Manifold Stay

Cylinder Head

Spark Plug

Gasket

No.2 Heat Insulator

Gasket

Valve

No.1 Engine Hanger

Exhaust Maniflod

kg-cm (ft-lb, N·m) : Specified torque
◆ Non-reusable part
★ Precoated part

Explode view of 3E-E cylinder head

richment valve if so equipped.

12. Disconnect the water by-pass hoses from the carburetor if so equipped.

13. Disconnect the exhaust pipe from the exhaust manifold.

14. Remove the intake manifold stay bracket and ground strap. Remove the engine wire harness bracket clamp from the intake manifold.

15. Remove the cylinder head cover.

16. Loosen and remove the head mounting bolts gradually in three passes working from the ends of the cylinder head inward.

17. Lift the head straight up from the engine block.

18. Clean all gasket surfaces.

19. Service as necessary. Install in the reverse order of removal. Install a new cylinder head gasket. Torque the cylinder head mount-

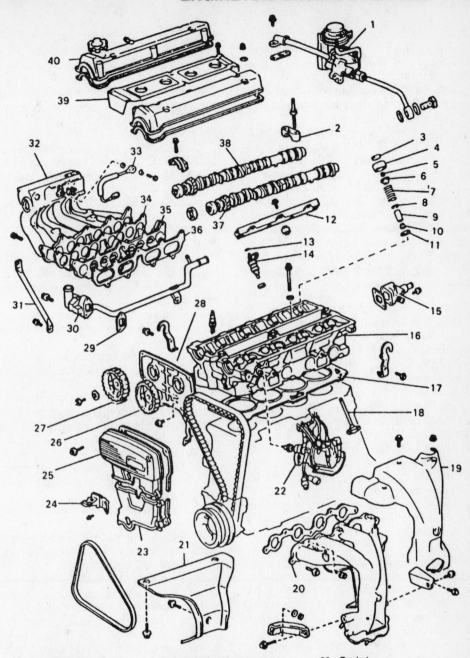

1. EGR valve	15. Cylinder head rear cover	29. Gasket
2. Camshaft bearing cap	16. Cylinder head	30. Water outlet
3. Adjusting shim	17. Cyllinder head gasket	31. Intake manifold stay
4. Valve lifter	18. Valve	32. Intake manifold
5. Valve keepers	19. Upper exhaust manifold insulator	33. Cold start injection pipe
6. Valve spring retainer	20. Exhaust manifold	34. Gasket
7. Valve spring	21. Lower exhaust manifold insulator	35. Air control valve
8. Snap ring	22. Distributor	36. Gasket
9. Valve guide bushing	23. No. 2 timing belt cover	37. Exhaust valve camshaft
10. Valve stem oil seal	24. Engine mounting bracket	38. Intake valve camshaft
11. Valve spring seal	25. No. 3 timing belt cover	39. Cylinder head center cover
12. Delivery pipe	26. Exhaust camshaft timing pulley	40. Cylinder head cover
13. O-ring	27. Intake camshaft timing pulley	
14. Injector	28. No. 4 timing belt cover	

Exploded view of the 4A-GE cylinder head 4A-GZE engine similar

ing bolts in three progressive steps. Torque to 22 ft. lbs. in the first pass. 36 ft. lbs. in the second pass, and finally for the third pass, tighten the head bolts an additional 90° from the second pass. Tighten the bolts in sequence from the center of the head outwards (refer to the torque sequence illustration).

20. Adjust the valves by turning the crankshaft pulley until the groove in the pulley is aligned with the 0 mark on the timing belt cover. Check that No. 1 cylinder rocker arms are loose and No. 4 rocker arms are tight. If not, turn the engine one complete revolution and align the marks again. Adjust the valves to correct specifications. Turn one complete revolution and adjust the remaining valves. Complete installation, start the engine and check ignition timing and carburetor adjustments. Roadtest for proper operation.

4A-GE and 4A-GZE Engines

NOTE: *This Removal and Installation procedure is for both engines modify service steps using exploded view illustration as necessary. All wires and hoses should be labeled or marked at the time of removal. Review the complete service procedure and refer to the Torque Specifications Chart before starting this repair. Always change oil and oil filter after this repair is finished.*

1. Disconnect the negative battery cable. Remove the right side under engine splash shield. Relieve the fuel pressure. On the 4A-GZE engine mark and remove the hood.

2. Open the drain cocks on the engine and radiator. Collect the coolant. On the 4A-GZE engine remove the intercooler assembly and battery.

CAUTION: *When draining the coolant, keep in mind that cats and dogs are attracted by the ethylene glycol antifreeze, and are quite likely to drink any that is left in an uncovered container or in puddles on the ground. This will prove fatal in sufficient quantity. Always drain the coolant into a sealable container. Coolant should be reused unless it is contaminated or several years old.*

3. Remove the air cleaner assembly. On the 4A-GZE engine remove the air flow meter.

4. Disconnect the cruise control cable if so equipped.

5. Disconnect the throttle cable from the throttle linkage.

6. Remove the heater hose from the cylinder head rear cover.

7. Label and remove the vacuum hoses from the throttle body.

8. If equipped with cruise control, remove the actuator and bracket assembly.

9. Remove the ignition coil.

10. Remove the upper radiator hose from the cylinder head and the radiator.

11. Remove the brake booster vacuum hose.

12. Remove the PCV hose.

13. Unbolt and remove as a unit the fuel pressure regulator.

14. Unbolt and remove the EGR valve with the lines attached.

15. Remove the cold start injector hose.

CAUTION: *The fuel system is under pressure. Release pressure slowly and contain spillage. Observe no smoking/no open flame precautions. Have a Class B-C (dry powder) fire extinguisher within arm's reach at all times.*

16. Remove the No. 1 fuel line.

17. Remove the first and second water bypass hoses from the auxiliary air valve.

18. Remove the vacuum pipe and the cylinder head rear cover.

19. Remove, disconnect or reposition the wiring harness(es) around the head as necessary.

20. Remove the distributor.

21. Remove the exhaust manifold and its gaskets.

22. Remove the fuel delivery pipe and the injectors. DO NOT drop the injectors.

23. Remove the intake manifold support bracket; remove the intake manifold and the intake air control valve.

24. Remove the power steering drive belt. On the 4A-GZE engine remove the supercharger assembly.

25. Remove the upper timing belt cover and the valve covers.

26. Remove the water outlet fitting with the bypass pipe and the belt adjusting bar.

27. Remove the spark plugs.

28. Turn the crankshaft clockwise, stopping so that the groove in the crank pulley aligns with the idler pulley bolt. Additionally, check that the valve lifters on No. 1 cylinder are loose (the cam lobes are NOT depressing the lifters). If the valves are under tension, rotate the crank one full revolution and check again. The engine is now on TDC/compression.

29. Remove the right motor mount.

30. Remove the water pump pulley.

31. Remove the lower and middle (Nos. 2 and 3) timing belt covers.

NOTE: *The bolts are different lengths. Label or diagram the correct location of each bolt as it is removed. Improper placement during reassembly can cause engine damage.*

32. Place matchmarks on the timing belt and the belt pulleys. Make sure that you mark each pulley and the belt clearly. Additionally, mark an arrow on the belt showing the direction of rotation.

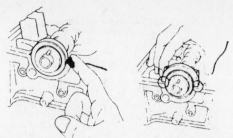

Sealant must be applied to the head before reinstalling the valve cover

33. Carefully slide the timing belt off the camshaft pulleys. Do not pry on the belt with tools. Keep the belt under light upward tension so that the bottom (crankshaft) end doesn't shift position on its pulley.

34. Remove the camshaft pulleys. Use an adjustable wrench to counterhold the cams during removal. Look for the flats on the cam and fit the wrench to them.

35. With the pulleys removed, the end plate (otherwise called No. 4 timing cover) may be removed.

36. Loosen the head bolts in the order shown in the diagram. Make three complete passes, loosening them slowly, evenly and in order.

37. Remove the cylinder head. If it is difficult to remove, it may be pried up gently with a suitable tool. Be very careful not to scratch or gouge the mating surfaces when prying the head up.

38. Keeping the head upright, place it on wooden blocks on the workbench. If the head is to receive further work, the various components will need to be removed. If the head is not to be worked on, the mating surface must be cleaned of all gasket and sealant material before reinstallation.

39. Clean the engine block mating surface of all gasket and sealant material. Use plastic or wooden scrapers so as not gouge the metal. Remove all traces of liquids from the surface and clean out the bolt holes.

40. Install the new head gasket on the block. Make sure it is properly placed and that all the holes and passages in the block line up with the holes in the gasket.

41. Place the head in position and make sure it is properly seated and aligned.

42. Apply a light coat of oil to the threads of the cylinder head bolts.

43. Install the ten cylinder head bolts.

NOTE: *The bolts for the exhaust side are 108mm long; the bolts for the intake side are 87.5mm long.*

44. Tighten the cylinder head bolts in three passes and in sequence. The first pass should tighten them to 8–10 ft. lbs., the second pass to 16. ft. lbs. and the third pass to 22 ft. lbs.

45. Mark the front (towards the front of the car) of each bolt with a dot of paint.

46. In the specified order, tighten each bolt through exactly 90° of rotation.

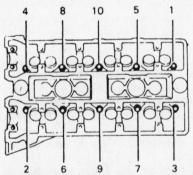

Cylinder head bolt removal sequence — 4A-GE and 4A-GZE engines

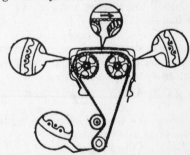

Examples of matchmarks on timing belt and pulleys. Don't forget arrow showing the direction of rotation.

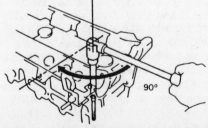

Apply a dot of paint to the front of each head bolt. Apply 90° of rotation in the correct sequence. After all are set, repeat the pattern, tighten each bolt an additional 90°

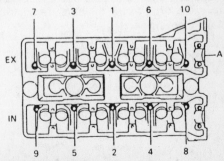

Cylinder head bolt torque sequence — 4A-GE and 4A-GZE engines

47. Repeat the procedure, tightening each bolt an additional 90°. Check that the paint marks on each bolt are now facing rearward.

48. Apply RTV sealer or similar to the cylinder head. Install new cam end seals and coat them lightly with multi-purpose grease.

49. Install the end plate or No.4 timing cover.

50. Install the right side engine mount bracket and tighten its bolts to 18 ft. lbs.

51. Install the camshaft pulleys. Be sure to align the camshaft knock pin and the camshaft pulley. Tighten the pulley bolts to 34 ft. lbs. Install timing belt in the correct position.

52. Install the lower and middle (No. 2 and 3) timing belt covers. Remember that the bolts are different lengths; make certain the correct bolt is in the correct location.

53. Install the water pump pulley.

54. Install the right engine mount. Tighten the through bolt to 58 ft. lbs.

55. Install the spark plugs.

56. Reinstall the water outlet with the bypass pipe and the belt adjusting bar.

57. Install the valve covers.

58. Install the alternator and power steering drive belts. Adjust the belts to the correct tension. On the 4A-GZE engine install the supercharger assembly.

59. Install the intake manifold and intake air control valve. Tighten the bolts to specifications.

60. Install the bracket and support for the intake manifold.

61. Install the fuel delivery pipe and the injectors. Make sure the insulators and spacers have been placed properly. Make sure the injectors rotate smoothly in their seats.

62. Tighten the delivery pipe retaining bolts to 13. ft. lbs.

63. Install the exhaust manifold tighten its nuts and bolts to specifications.

64. Reinstall the distributor.

65. Attach, reposition or connect the wiring harness(es) around the head. Make sure that all retaining clips are used and are secure. Double check the wiring to eliminate any contact with moving parts.

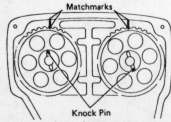

Align the camshaft knockpin with the camshaft timing pulley — 4A-GE and 4A-GZE engines

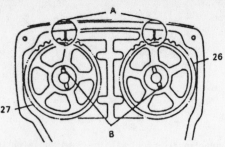

A MATCHMARK
B KNOCK PIN
26 EXHAUST CAMSHAFT TIMING PULLEY
27 INTAKE CAMSHAFT TIMING PULLEY

Align the cam pulleys before installing the timing belt — 4A-GE and 4A-GZE engines

66. Install the vacuum pipe and the cylinder head rear cover with a new gasket.

67. Connect the first and second bypass hoses to the auxiliary air valve.

68. Connect the No.1 fuel line.

69. Use new gaskets and connect the cold start injector line. Tighten the bolts to 13 ft. lbs.

70. Install the EGR valve and use a new gasket.

71. Use a new O-ring and attach the fuel pressure regulator. Tighten the regulator bolts to 6.8 ft. lbs (82 INCH lbs.)

72. Install the PCV hose and the brake vacuum hose.

73. Install the radiator hose at the radiator and the cylinder head.

74. Install the ignition coil.

75. Install the cruise control actuator and bracket assembly if so equipped.

76. Observing the labels made earlier, connect the vacuum hose to the throttle body.

77. Attach the heater hose to the cylinder head rear cover.

78. Connect the throttle valve and accelerator cables.

79. Connect the cruise control cable, if so equipped.

80. Install the air cleaner assembly. On the 4A-GZE engine install the air flow meter.

81. On the 4A-GZE engine install the intercooler assembly and battery. Confirm that the drain cocks on the radiator and engine block are closed. Fill the cooling system with coolant.

82. Double check all installation items, paying particular attention to loose hoses or hanging wires, untightened nuts, poor routing of hoses and wires (too tight or rubbing) and tools left in the engine area.

83. Connect the negative battery cable. On the 4A-GZE engine install the hood in the correct location.

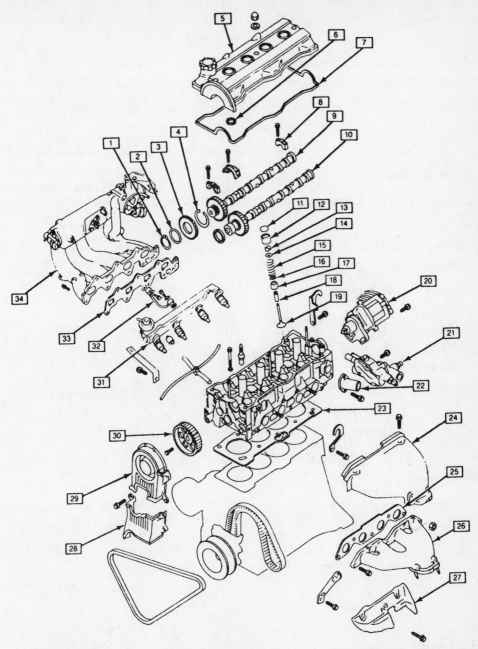

1. Camshaft snapring	13. Valve keepers	25. Exhaust manifold gasket
2. Wave washer	14. Valve spring retainer	26. Exhaust manifold
3. Camshaft sub-gear	15. Valve spring	27. Exhaust manifold lower
4. Camshaft gear spring	16. Valve spring seat	insulator (heat shield)
5. Valve cover (cylinder	17. Valve stem oil seal	28. Center timing belt cover
head cover)	18. Valve guide bushing	29. Upper timing belt cover
6. Spark plug tube gasket	19. Valve	30. Camshaft timing gear
7. Valve cover gasket	20. Distributor	31. Fuel rail
8. Camshaft bearing cap	21. Water inlet housing	32. Cold-start injector pipe
9. Instake camshaft	22. Water outlet housing	33. Intake manifold gasket
10. Exhaust camshaft	23. Head gasket	34. Intake manifold
11. Adjusting shim	24. Exhaust manifold upper	
12. Valve lifter	insulator (heat shield)	

Exploded view of the 4A-FE cylinder head assembly

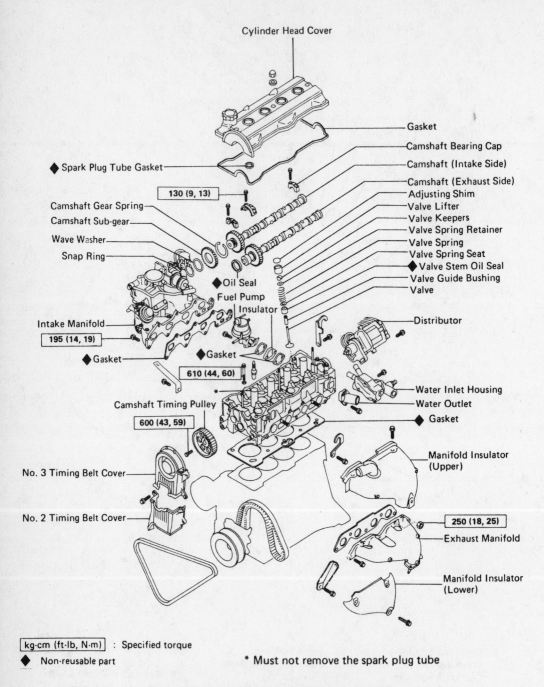

Cylinder Head Cover

Gasket

Camshaft Bearing Cap

Camshaft (Intake Side)

Camshaft (Exhaust Side)

Adjusting Shim

Valve Lifter

Valve Keepers

Valve Spring Retainer

Valve Spring

Valve Spring Seat

◆ Valve Stem Oil Seal

Valve Guide Bushing

Valve

◆ Spark Plug Tube Gasket

130 (9, 13)

Camshaft Gear Spring

Camshaft Sub-gear

Wave Washer

Snap Ring

◆ Oil Seal

Fuel Pump
Insulator

Intake Manifold

195 (14, 19)

◆ Gasket

◆ Gasket

610 (44, 60)

Distributor

Water Inlet Housing

Water Outlet

◆ Gasket

Camshaft Timing Pulley

600 (43, 59)

No. 3 Timing Belt Cover

No. 2 Timing Belt Cover

Manifold Insulator
(Upper)

250 (18, 25)

Exhaust Manifold

Manifold Insulator
(Lower)

kg-cm (ft-lb, N·m) : Specified torque

◆ Non-reusable part

* Must not remove the spark plug tube

Exploded view of the 4A-F cylinder head assembly

84. Start the engine. During the warm up period, check for any sign of leakage or over-heating. Check engine timing and adjust the idle speed if necessary.

85. After the engine is shut off, check the drive belts and adjust the tension if necessary. Roadtest for proper operation.

4A-F and 4A-FE Engines

NOTE: *This Removal and Installation procedure is for both engines modify service steps using exploded view illustration as necessary. All wires and hoses should be labeled or marked at the time of removal. Review the complete service procedure and refer to the Torque Specifications Chart before starting this repair. Always change oil and oil filter after this repair is finished.*

1. Disconnect the negative battery cable. Relieve the fuel pressure.

2. Open the drain cocks on the engine and radiator. Collect the coolant in clean containers.

CAUTION: *When draining the coolant, keep in mind that cats and dogs are attracted by the ethylene glycol antifreeze, and are quite likely to drink any that is left in an uncovered container or in puddles on the ground. This will prove fatal in sufficient quantity. Always drain the coolant into a sealable container. Coolant should be reused unless it is contaminated or several years old.*

3. Raise the vehicle and safely support it on jackstands.

4. Remove the lower right splash (stone) shield.

5. Remove the two covers for the rear engine mount nuts and studs.

6. Remove the two rear transaxle mount-to-main crossmember mounting nuts.

7. Remove the two center mount-to-center crossmember nuts.

8. Lower the vehicle to the ground.

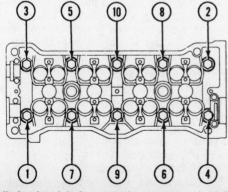

Cylinder head bolt removal sequence — 4A-FE engine

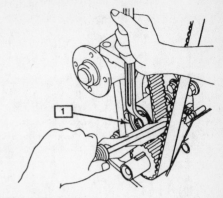

1 IDLER PULLEY

Loosen the idler pulley and move it to its loosest position

9. Remove the air cleaner assembly.

10. Disconnect or remove throttle cable, the transmission kick-down cable (automatic) and, if equipped, the cruise control actuator cable.

11. Label and disconnect the vacuum lines. Loosen, disconnect or reposition the wiring harnesses running to the head.

12. Disconnect the fuel inlet line.

CAUTION: *The fuel system is under pressure. Release pressure slowly and contain spillage. Observe no smoking/no open flame precautions. Have a Class B-C (dry powder) fire extinguisher within arm's reach at all times.*

13. Remove the cold start injector line.

14. Remove the coolant hoses by disconnecting their junctions at the head.

15. Disconnect the heater hoses.

16. Remove the water outlet housing and the water inlet housing.

17. Label and remove the spark plug wires.

18. Remove the PCV valve.

19. Loosen the air conditioning compressor, power steering pump and alternator brackets as necessary; remove the valve cover.

20. Remove the drive belts.

21. Remove the air conditioning idler pulley.

22. Disconnect the wiring at the cruise control actuator (if so equipped); remove the actuator and its bracket.

23. Remove the windshield washer reservoir.

24. Support the engine with a support fixture or a chain hoist. Alternatively, a floor jack may be placed below the engine; use a piece of wood on the jack to distribute the load.

25. Remove the right engine mount through bolt.

26. Raise the engine enough to gain access to the water pump pulley bolts.

27. Remove the water pump pulley.

28. Lower the engine back to its normal po-

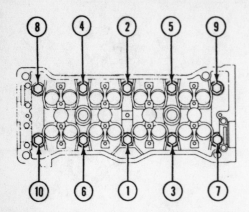

Cylinder head bolt torque sequence — 4A-FE engine

sition. Remove the wiring harness from the upper timing belt cover.

29. Raise the vehicle and safely support it on jackstands.

30. Remove the cylinder head-to-cylinder block bracket.

31. Remove the exhaust pipe support bracket and disconnect the exhaust pipe from the exhaust manifold.

32. Remove the upper timing belt cover and then the center timing belt cover.

NOTE: *The timing belt is exposed with the cover removed. Do not allow the belt to become contaminated with fluids or lubricants.*

33. Remove the right engine mount bracket.

34. By turning the crankshaft clockwise, set the engine to TDC/compression. Align the timing mark at zero (on the crank) and check that the valve lifters for No. 1 cylinder are NOT under compression from the camshafts; the cam lobes should be pointed up. The small hole in the exhaust camshaft pulley should be aligned with the mark on the camshaft cap.

35. Remove the distributor.

36. Remove the plug from the lower timing belt cover.

37. Matchmark the timing belt and pulleys at the crankshaft and both camshafts. Mark an arrow on the belt showing the direction of rotation.

38. Loosen the idler pulley bolt and push the pulley into its loosest position. Tighten the bolt to hold the idler in this loosened position.

39. Holding the timing belt with a clean cloth, slide the belt off the camshaft pulleys. Keep light upward tension on the belt so that it does not change its position on the lower (crankshaft) pulley.

NOTE: *Do not pry on the belt with tools. Do not crease or crimp the belt. Be careful not to drop anything into the lower belt cover. Keep*

the timing belt clean and free of fluids and lubricants.

40. Using a 10mm, 12-point deep socket wrench, loosen the cylinder head bolts in the proper sequence. It is recommended that the tension be released in two or even three passes.

WARNING: *Head warping or cracking can result from improper removal procedures.*

41. Remove the cylinder head with the manifolds attached. If the head is difficult to lift off, carefully pry with a suitable tool between the head and a projection on the block. Be careful not to scratch or gouge the mating surfaces of the head or block.

42. Place the head on wooden blocks on the workbench. If the head is to be disassembled, the external parts will need to be removed. If the head is to be reused intact, the mating surface must be cleaned of all gasket and sealant material. Clean the mating surface on the block of all traces of gasket material and fluids. Clean the bolt holes, removing all fluid and solid material.

43. When reassembling, place the new head gasket in position on the block. Make sure it is placed correctly and that all the holes line up.

44. Carefully install the cylinder head in position on the block. Make sure the head is seated over the guide dowels.

45. Apply a light coat of engine oil to the threads of the head bolts and under the caps of the bolts. Place the bolts in their holes.

46. Tighten the bolts in the proper sequence. Repeat the pattern three times, tightening the first pass to 14 ft. lbs., the second pass to 28 ft. lbs. and the third pass to the final setting of 44 ft. lbs.

47. If the camshafts have not been turned while the head was removed, double check their placement against the marks on the head. If the cams were moved, they must be turned into the TDC/compression position.

48. Double check that the crankshaft is still in its TDC position. Carefully reinstall the timing belt over the cam pulleys, making sure the matchmarks align exactly. The slightest error in placement can greatly reduce engine performance and possibly damage the engine.

With the belt correctly installed, loosen the bolt holding the idler pulley in the loosened position. The pulley will spring against the belt, providing tension on it. Turn the crankshaft pulley clockwise two full revolutions (from TDC to TDC) and double check that all the components are properly aligned. Tighten the idler pulley bolt to 27 ft. lbs.

49. Reinstall the distributor.

50. Attach the right side engine mount bracket.

51. Install the air conditioning idler pulley.

52. Install the center timing belt cover and the upper timing belt cover.

53. Raise the vehicle and safely support it on jackstands.

54. Using new gaskets and bolts, connect the exhaust pipe to the exhaust manifold. Install the exhaust manifold support bracket.

55. Install the cylinder head-to-cylinder block bracket.

56. Lower the vehicle to the ground. Connect or reinstall the wiring harness to the upper timing belt cover.

57. Raise the engine enough to gain access to the water pump. Install the water pump pulley and lower the engine into its normal position.

58. Install the right engine mount through bolt and tighten it to 64 ft. lbs. When this bolt is secured, the engine lifting apparatus may be removed from the car.

59. Install the windshield washer reservoir.

60. If equipped with cruise control, reinstall the actuator and its bracket and connect the wiring to the actuator.

61. Install the drive belts and adjust them to the proper tension.

62. Place sealant on the valve cover in the proper locations and install the valve cover. Tighten the retaining nuts to 15 ft. lbs.

63. Install the PCV valve.

64. Install the spark plugs, and connect the water inlet housing and the water outlet housing.

65. Reinstall the heater hoses and the coolant hoses.

66. Install the fuel rail and injectors.

67. Connect the cold start injector pipe.

68. Connect the fuel inlet line.

69. Observing the labels made earlier, carefully connect the vacuum lines and electrical leads. Make sure the vacuum hoses are properly seated on their ports and are not kinked or twisted. Electrical connectors must be clean and firmly attached at all points. Double check the routing of lines and wires to avoid any contact with moving parts.

70. Depending on equipment, connect the transaxle kick-down cable (automatic), the cruise control actuator cable and/or the accelerator cable.

71. Install the air cleaner assembly.

72. Raise the vehicle and safely support it on jackstands. Attach the two rear mount-to-main crossmember nuts and tighten them to 45 ft. lbs. Install the two center mount-to-center crossmember nuts and tighten them to 45 ft. lbs. Install the covers on the nuts and studs.

73. Install the lower right splash shield.

74. Lower the vehicle to the ground.

75. Confirm that the radiator and engine block drain cocks are closed and refill the cooling system.

76. Double check all installation items, paying particular attention to loose hoses or hanging wires, untightened nuts, poor routing of hoses and wires (too tight or rubbing) and tools left in the engine area.

77. Connect the negative battery cable.

78. Start the engine. During the warm up period, check for any sign of leakage or overheating. Check engine timing and adjust the idle speed if necessary.

79. After the engine is shut off, check the drive belts and adjust the tension if necessary. Roadtest the vehicle for proper operation.

1C-L Diesel Engine

NOTE: *All wires and hoses should be labeled or marked at the time of removal. Review the complete service procedure and refer to the Torque Specifications Chart before starting this repair. Always change oil and oil filter after this repair is finished.*

1. Disconnect the negative battery cable.
2. Drain the coolant.

CAUTION: *When draining the coolant, keep in mind that cats and dogs are attracted by the ethylene glycol antifreeze, and are quite likely to drink any that is left in an uncovered container or in puddles on the ground. This will prove fatal in sufficient quantity. Always drain the coolant into a sealable con-*

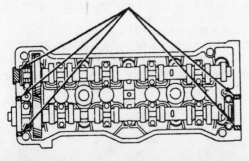

Apply sealant to these points before reinstalling valve cover

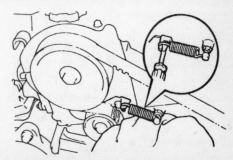

Use a small tool to remove the tension spring

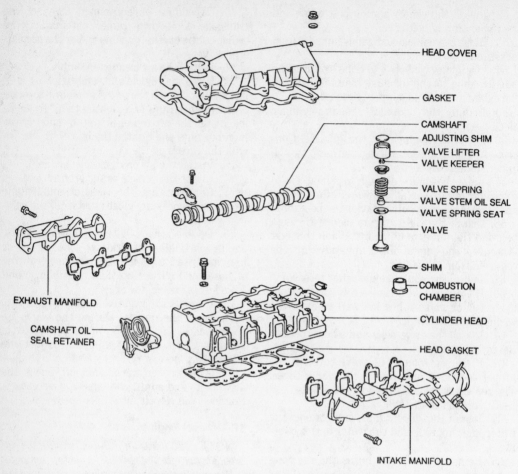

HEAD COVER

GASKET

CAMSHAFT
ADJUSTING SHIM
VALVE LIFTER
VALVE KEEPER

VALVE SPRING
VALVE STEM OIL SEAL
VALVE SPRING SEAT
VALVE

SHIM
COMBUSTION CHAMBER

CYLINDER HEAD

HEAD GASKET

EXHAUST MANIFOLD

CAMSHAFT OIL SEAL RETAINER

INTAKE MANIFOLD

Exploded view of the cylinder head — 1C-L diesel engine

tainer. Coolant should be reused unless it is contaminated or several years old.

3. Remove the engine undercover and then drain the oil.

CAUTION: *The EPA warns that prolonged contact with used engine oil may cause a number of skin disorders, including cancer! You should make every effort to minimize your exposure to used engine oil. Protective gloves should be worn when changing the oil.*

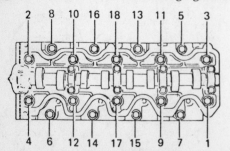

Cylinder head bolt removal sequence — 1C-L diesel engine

Wash your hands and any other exposed skin areas as soon as possible after exposure to used engine oil. Soap and water, or waterless hand cleaner should be used.

4. Disconnect the exhaust pipe from the manifold.

5. Disconnect the air inlet hose.

6. On models equipped with an automatic transmission, disconnect the accelerator and throttle cables from the injection pump.

7. Disconnect the water inlet hose and then remove the inlet pipe.

8. Disconnect the two heater hoses.

9. Remove the EGR valve and its pipe.

10. Tag and disconnect all wires and cables which might interfere with cylinder head removal.

11. Disconnect the water bypass hose from the cylinder head union.

12. Disconnect the fuel hoses from the fuel pipe.

13. Remove the clamp and then disconnect the injection pipe.

14. Disconnect the fuel return hose at the in-

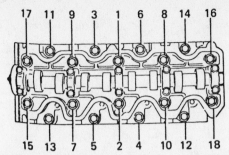

Cylinder head bolt torque sequence — 1C-L diesel engine

jection pump. Remove the four locknuts and then remove the return pipe.

15. Remove the current sensor and then remove the glow plugs.

16. Use special tool Toyota No. 09268064010 to remove the injectors. Don't lose the injection seats and gaskets.

NOTE: *Arrange the injector in holders in the proper order.*

17. Remove the No. 2 timing belt cover and its gasket.

18. Turn the crankshaft clockwise and set the No. 1 cylinder at TDC of the compression stroke. Place matchmarks on the camshaft timing pulley, the injection pump pulley and the timing belt.

19. Remove the tension spring. Loosen the No. 1 idler pulley mounting bolt and push it aside. Remove the timing belt from the gear.

NOTE: *DO NOT pinch the tension spring with pliers.*

20. Loosen the mounting bolt and remove the camshaft gear.

21. Support the timing belt so it doesn't slip a tooth.

NOTE: *Be very careful not to drop anything into the timing cover. Make sure that the timing belt does not touch oil or water.*

22. Remove the cylinder head cover and the oil level gauge guide clamp.

23. Loosen the remove the cylinder head bolts in two or three stages, in the order shown in the illustration.

24. The cylinder head is positioned by means of dowels — lift it straight upward when removing it. Never attempt to slide it off the block.

25. Installation is in the reverse order of removal procedure. Tighten the cylinder head bolts in two or three stages, in the sequence illustrated. Refer to the Timing Belt Removal and Installation procedure when installing the belt.

NOTE: *When replacing the cylinder head, ALWAYS USE A NEW GASKET. It's also a good idea to replace the camshaft oil seal, making sure to grease the lip before installation.*

26. Note the following tightening torques: Cylinder head bolts: 64 ft. lbs. Cylinder head cover nuts: 65 inch lbs. Camshaft gear bolt: 22 ft. lbs. Idler pulley set bolt: 27 ft. lbs. Injectors: 47 ft. lbs. Glow plugs: 9 ft. lbs.

27. Double check all installation items, paying particular attention to loose hoses or hanging wires, untightened nuts, poor routing of hoses and wires (too tight or rubbing) and tools left in the engine area.

28. Connect the negative battery cable.

29. Start the engine. During the warm up period, check for any sign of leakage or overheating. Check engine timing and adjust the idle speed if necessary.

30. After the engine is shut off, check the drive belts and adjust the tension if necessary. Roadtest for proper operation.

CLEANING AND INSPECTION

3A, 3A-C and 4A-C Engine

NOTE: *For the 3E and 3E-E engines use these service procedures as a guide. Refer to exploded view of cylinder head as necessary.*

1. With the head removed from the car, remove the carburetor, the fuel pump and the intake and exhaust or combination manifolds.

2. Remove the rocker arm assembly (keep all parts in order), following procedures outlined earlier in this Chapter.

3. Use a dial indicator to measure the camshaft end play (axial end play or thrust clearance). Standard play is 0.08–0.18mm. Maximum allowable free play is 0.25mm. Free play at or beyond the maximum requires replacement of the head. Refer to the Camshaft Specification Chart as necessary.

4. Remove the camshaft, following procedures outlined later in this Chapter.

5. Remove the valves, following procedures outlined later in this Chapter.

6. Using a wire brush chucked into an electric drill, remove all the carbon from the combustion chambers in the head. Be careful not to scratch the head.

7. Use a gasket scraper and remove all ma-

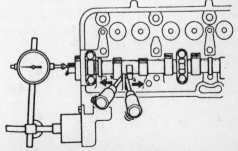

Checking the camshaft endplay on the 4A-C engine. Use of a dial indicator is required.

Maximum head surface warpage:
          0.05 mm (0.0020 in.)
Maximum manifold surface warpage:
          0.1 mm (0.004 in.)
Maximum reface: 0.1 mm (0.004 in.)

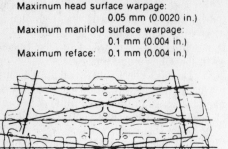

Cylinder head warpage clearances

terial from the manifold and head surfaces, again being careful not to scratch the surface.

8. Use a valve guide brush or a fine-bristled rifle bore brush with solvent to clean the valve guides.

9. Use a clean cloth and a stiff bristle brush with solvent to thoroughly clean the head assembly. Make sure that no material is washed into the bolt holes or passages. If possible, dry the head with compressed air to remove fluid and solid matter from all the passages.

NOTE: *Do not clean the head in a hot tank or chemical bath.*

10. With the head clean and dry, use a precision straight-edge and a feeler gauge to measure the head for warpage. Also measure the manifold faces. Any warpage in excess of the maximum requires replacement of the head.

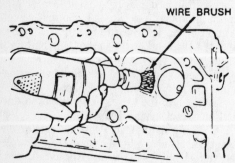

Removing combustion chamber carbon — make sure it is removed and not merely burnished

Checking the cylinder head for warpage

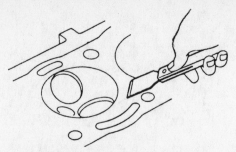

Do not scratch the head mating surface when removing old gasket material

11. If all is well with the head to this point, it is highly recommended that it be taken to a professional facility such as a machine shop for sophisticated crack testing. The various procedures are much more reliable than simple examination by eye. The cost is reasonable and the peace of mind is well worth the cost. If any cracks are found, the head must be replaced.

12. While the head is being checked, carefully scrape the carbon from the tops of the pistons. Don't scratch the metal of the piston tops and don't damage the cylinder walls. Remove all the carbon and fluid from the cylinder.

13. If repairs are needed to the valves, camshaft or other components, follow the appropriate procedures outlined in this Chapter.

4A-GE and 4A-GZE Engines

1. With the head removed from the car, remove the camshafts following procedures outlined later in this Chapter.

2. Remove the valve lifters and the adjusting shims (keep all parts in order) following procedures outlined later in this Chapter.

3. Remove any external fittings, brackets, cables, etc.

4. Remove the valves following procedures outlined later in this Chapter.

5. Carefully scrape the carbon from the tops of the pistons. Don't scratch the metal of the piston tops and don't damage the cylinder walls. Remove all the carbon and fluid from the cylinder.

6. Clean all the gasket material from the block, manifold and head surfaces. If possible, use compressed air to blow the carbon and oil from the bolt holes and passages.

7. Using a wire brush chucked into an electric drill, remove all the carbon from the combustion chambers in the head. Be careful not to scratch the head surface.

8. Use a valve guide brush or a fine-bristled rifle bore brush with solvent to clean the valve guides.

9. Use a clean cloth and a stiff bristle brush with solvent to thoroughly clean the head assembly. Make sure that no material is washed

into the bolt holes or passages. If possible, dry the head with compressed air to remove fluid and solid matter from all the passages.

NOTE: *Do not clean the head in a hot tank or chemical bath.*

10. With the head clean and dry, use a precision straight-edge and a feeler gauge to measure the head for warpage. Also measure the manifold faces. Any warpage in excess of the maximum requires replacement of the head.

Maximum allowable warpage:
- Cylinder block face: 0.05mm
- Intake manifold face: 0.05mm
- Exhaust manifold face: 0.10mm

11. If all is well with the head to this point, it is highly recommended that it be taken to a professional facility such as a machine shop for sophisticated crack testing. The various procedures are much more reliable than simple examination by eye. The cost is reasonable and the peace of mind is well worth the cost. If any cracks are found, the head must be replaced.

4A-FE Engine

NOTE: *For the 4A-F use these service procedures as a guide. Refer to exploded view of cylinder head as necessary.*

1. With the head removed from the engine, remove the intake and exhaust manifolds, following procedures outline earlier in this Chapter (remove the carburetor and fuel pump and any other external parts on the 4A-F engine).

2. Remove the camshafts, following procedures outlined later in this Chapter.

3. Remove the valve lifters and the adjusting shims.

4. Remove the spark plug tubes.

5. Remove the engine hoist hooks.

6. Remove the valves, using procedures outlined later in this chapter.

7. Remove the half-circle plug at the end of the head.

8. Using a wire brush chucked into an electric drill, remove all the carbon from the combustion chambers in the head. Be careful not to scratch the head surface.

9. Use a valve guide brush or a fine-bristled rifle bore brush with solvent to clean the valve guides.

10. Use a clean cloth and a stiff bristle brush with solvent to thoroughly clean the head assembly. Make sure that no material is washed into the bolt holes or passages. If possible, dry the head with compressed air to remove fluid and solid matter from all the passages.

NOTE: *Do not clean the head in a hot tank or chemical bath.*

11. With the head clean and dry, use a precision straight-edge and a feeler gauge to measure the head for warpage. Also measure the

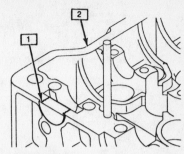

1. Half circle plug
2. Cylinder head

Half circle plug or seal in cylinder head assembly

manifold faces. Any warpage in excess of the maximum requires replacement of the head.

Maximum allowable warpage:
- Cylinder block face: 0.05mm
- Intake manifold face: 0.10mm
- Exhaust manifold face: 0.10mm

12. If all is well with the head to this point, it is highly recommended that it be taken to a professional facility such as a machine shop for sophisticated crack testing. The various procedures are much more reliable than simple examination by eye. The cost is reasonable and the peace of mind is well worth the cost. If any cracks are found, the head must be replaced.

CYLINDER HEAD RESURFACING

The Toyota cylinder heads for all engines may be resurfaced by a reputable machine shop. Resurfacing is recommended if the engine suffered a massive overheating, such as from a failed head gasket.

The heads are manufactured to be as light as possible; consequently, there is not much excess metal on the face. Any machining must be minimal. If too much metal is removed, the head becomes unusable. A head which exceeds the maximum warpage specification CANNOT be resurfaced. The machine shop will have a list of minimum head thicknesses; at no time may this minimum be exceeded.

Valve Springs and Valves

REMOVAL AND INSTALLATION

NOTE: *This procedure requires the use of a valve stem compressor. This common tool is available at most auto supply stores. It may also be possible to rent one from supplier. It is absolutely essential that all components be kept in order after removal. Old ice trays make excellent holders for small parts. The containers should be labeled so that the parts may be reinstalled in their original location. Keep the valves in numbered order in a holder such as an egg carton or an inverted box with holes punched in it. Label the con-*

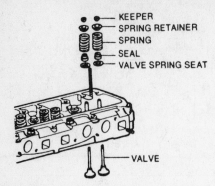

KEEPER
SPRING RETAINER
SPRING
SEAL
VALVE SPRING SEAT

VALVE

Valve and related components

Lapping a valve in by hand procedure

tainer so that each valve may be replaced in its exact position. (Example: Exhaust #1, #2 etc.)

3A, 3A-C and 4A-C Engine

NOTE: *For the 3E and 3E-E engines use these service procedures as a guide. Refer to exploded view of cylinder head as necessary.*

1. Remove the head from the engine and remove the rocker arm and cam shafts, following procedures outlined in this Chapter.

2. Using a valve spring compressor, com-

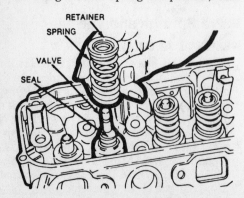

RETAINER
SPRING
VALVE
SEAL

Installing the valve

press the valve spring and remove the keeper at the top of the valve shaft.

3. Slowly release the tension on the compressor and remove it. Remove the spring retainer (upper cap), the valve spring, the valve stem oil seal and the lower spring seat.

4. The valve is then removed from the bottom of the head.

5. Repeat Steps 2–5 for each valve in the head, keeping them labeled and in order.

6. Thoroughly clean and decarbon each valve. Inspect each valve and spring as outlined later in this Chapter.

7. Lubricate the valve stem and guide with engine oil. Install the valve in the cylinder head and position the lower spring seat.

8. Coat the valve face and seat with a light coat of valve grinding compound. Attach the suction cup end of the valve grinding tool to the head of the valve (it helps to moisten it first).

9. Rotate the tool between the palms, changing position and lifting the tool often to prevent grooving. Lap in the until a smooth, evenly polished surface is evident on both the seat and face.

10. Remove the valve from the head. Wipe away all traces of grinding compound from the surfaces. Clean out the valve guide with a solvent-soaked rag. Make sure there are NO traces of compound in or on the head.

11. Proceed through the remaining valves, lapping them one at a time to their seats. Clean the area after each valve is done.

12. When all the valves have been lapped, thoroughly clean or wash the head with solvent. There must be NO trace of grinding compound present.

13. Lubricate the new valve stem seal with engine oil and install it onto the valve stem over the lower seat.

14. Install the valve spring and the upper seat, compress the spring and install the two keepers. Relax tension on the compressor and make sure everything is properly placed. Tap on the installed valve stem with a plastic mallet to ensure proper locking of the retainers.

15. Install the half-circle plug at the end of the head. Coat it with a silicone sealer before installation.

16. Complete the reassembly of the head by installing the camshafts and the manifolds.

4A-GE, 4A-GZE and 4A-FE Engines

NOTE: *For the 4A-F use these service procedures as a guide. Refer to exploded view of cylinder head as necessary.*

1. Remove the head following procedures outlined earlier in this Chapter.

2. On 4A-FE motors, remove the intake

and exhaust manifolds (remove the carburetor assembly on 4A-F engine).

3. Remove the camshafts following procedures outlined later in this Chapter. Label the shafts and their retainers.

4. Remove the valve lifters and the adjusting shims.

5. On the 4A-GE and 4A-GZE engines, remove the bond cable and the right engine hoist hook. Remove the temperature sensor bracket and the left engine hoist hook. On the 4A-FE and 4A-F engines, simply remove the hoist hooks.

6. Remove the spark plug tubes from the head.

7. Attach the spring compressor. Make sure the spring compressor tool is compatible with the cylinder head that you are working on.

8. Compress the valve spring and remove the keepers at the top of the valve shaft.

9. Slowly release the tension on the compressor and remove it. Remove the spring retainer (upper cap), the valve spring, the valve stem oil seal and the lower spring seat. The valve is then removed from the bottom of the head.

10. Repeat steps for each valve in the head, keeping them labeled and in order. Remove the half-circle plug at the end of the head.

11. Thoroughly clean and decarbon each valve. Inspect each valve and spring as outlined later in this chapter.

12. Lubricate the valve stem and guide with engine oil. Install the valve in the cylinder head.

13. Coat the valve face and seat with a light coat of valve grinding compound. Attach the suction cup end of the valve grinding tool to the head of the valve (it helps to moisten it first).

14. Rotate the tool between the palms, changing position and lifting the tool often to prevent grooving. Lap in the until a smooth, evenly polished surface is evident on both the seat and face.

15. Remove the valve from the head. Wipe away all traces of grinding compound from the surfaces. Clean out the valve guide with a solvent-soaked rag. Make sure there are NO traces of compound in or on the head.

16. Proceed through the remaining valves, lapping them one at a time to their seats. Clean the area after each valve is done.

17. When all the valves have been lapped, thoroughly clean or wash the head with solvent. There must be NO trace of grinding compound present. Lubricate the new valve stem seal with engine oil and install it onto the valve stem over the lower seat.

18. Install the valve spring and the upper seat, compress the spring and install the two keepers. Relax tension on the compressor and

make sure everything is properly placed. Tap on the installed valve stem with a plastic mallet to ensure proper locking of the retainers.

19. On the 4A-GE and 4A-GZE engines, install the spark plug tubes, the engine hangers, the temperature sensor bracket and the bond cable.

For the 4A-FE and 4A-F engines, install the tubes and the hangers.

20. Install the valve lifters and the adjusting shims. Don't attempt to adjust the valves until after the head is bolted onto the engine.

21. Coat the half-circle plug with silicone sealant and install it in position.

22. Complete the reassembly of the head by installing the camshafts and the manifolds following the necessary service in this Chapter.

INSPECTION AND MEASUREMENT

NOTE: *Accurate measuring equipment capable of reading to 0.0001 (ten thousandths)*

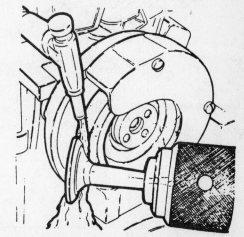

Valve refacing should be handled by a reputable machine shop

inch is necessary for this work. A micrometer and a hole (bore) gauge will be needed.

Inspect the valve faces and seats for pits, burned spots, and other evidence of poor seating. If the valve face is in such poor shape that the head of the valve must be cut to true the contact face, discard the valve.

The correct angle for the valve face is given in the Valve Specifications Chart at the beginning of this Chapter. It is recommended that any reaming or refacing be done by a reputable machine shop.

Check the valve stem for scoring and/or burned spots. If the stem and head are in acceptable condition, clean the valve thoroughly with solvent to remove all gum and varnish.

Use the micrometer to measure the diameter

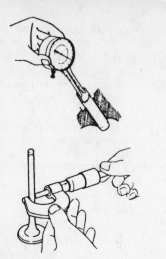

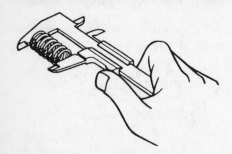

Measure the diameter of the valve guide and the valve stem. The difference is the stem clearance

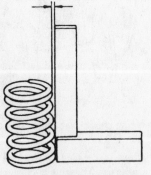

Checking the spring free height

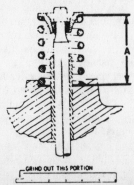

Checking the valve spring for squareness

Measure the valve spring installed height (A) with a modify steel ruler

of the valve stem. Use the hole gauge to measure the inside diameter of the valve guide for that valve. Subtract the stem diameter from the guide diameter and compare the difference to the chart. If not within specifications, determine the cause (worn valve or worn guide) and replace the worn part(s).

Using a steel square, check the valve spring for correct height and squareness. If the squareness is not within 2mm, replace the spring. If the free height of the spring is not within specification, replace the spring. The installed height of the spring must be measured with the spring under tension in the head. Assemble the valve and spring with the retainers and clips into the head; modify a small steel ruler to fit and record the distance from the bottom spring seat to the upper retainer. If not within specification, shim washers (one or more) any be added between the lower spring seat and the spring.

NOTE: *Use only washers designed for this purpose.*

Valve Seats

The valve seats for all Toyota engines are not replaceable. A failed seat (which cannot be recut) requires replacement of the head. Seat recutting is a precise art and is best performed by a machine shop. Seat concentricity should also be checked by a professional facility.

Valve Guides

INSPECTION

Valve guides should be cleaned as outlined earlier and checked when the stem-to-guide clearance is measured. As a general rule, if the engine admits oil through the guides (and the oil seals are in good condition), the guides are worn.

Valve guides which are not excessively worn or distorted may, in some cases, be knurled rather than replaced. Knurling is a process in which metal inside the valve guide is displaced and raised by a cutter, making a very fine cross-hatched pattern. This raised pattern reduces the clearance to the valve stem and provides excellent oil control. The possibility of knurling rather than replacing the valve guides should be discussed with a machinist.

REMOVAL AND INSTALLATION

NOTE: *Replacing the valve guides requires heating the head to high temperatures and the use of special tools. Do not attempt this repair if you are not equipped with the proper heating and handling equipment. Do not attempt this repair unless equipped with the correct valve guide tools and a reamer. This repair requires a high level of mechanical skill and machine shop procedures.*

3A, 3A-C and 4A-C Engines

For the 3E and 3E-E engines use these service procedures as a guide. Refer to exploded view of cylinder head as necessary.

1. Heat the cylinder head evenly to 194°F (90°C).

2. Carefully remove the head from the heat source and support it upright on the workbench.

3. Using valve guide tool and a hammer, drive the guide out of the head.

4. Reheat the head to 194°F (90°C) and support it on the workbench.

5. Use the guide tool and a hammer to drive in the new guide until it projects to specifications.

6. Allow the head and guide to air cool. Do not attempt to quick-cool the metal with any water or fluid.

7. Measure the inner diameter of the guide. Compare this to the stem diameter of the new valve. If the stem to guide clearance is insufficient, ream the new guide with a sharp reamer until the correct clearance is obtained.

4A-GE and 4A-GZE Engines

1. Break off the upper part of the old bushing. Wrap an old valve stem in tape to prevent the stem from dropping too far into the guide. Pad the surrounding area with rags. Insert the old valve into the guide and strike the valve with a hammer.

NOTE: *Be careful not to damage the surrounding area in which the lifter sits.*

2. Heat the cylinder head gradually, in water, to 212°F (100°C).

3. Carefully remove the head from the water. Use a correct tool and a hammer to drive out the guide.

4. With the guide removed, measure the bore (in the head) into which the guide fits. Refer to bore specifications as a new oversized guide or head assembly must be used.

5. Reheat the head in water to 212°F

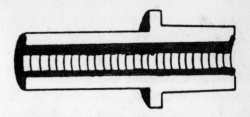

Cross-section of a knurled valve guide

(100°C), then carefully remove it from the water.

6. Using the removal tool, drive in the new guide until the snap ring makes contact with the cylinder head.

7. Measure the inner diameter of the guide. Compare this to the stem diameter of the new valve. If the stem to guide clearance is insufficient, ream the new guide with a sharp reamer until the correct clearance is obtained.

4A-FE Engine

NOTE: *For the 4A-F use these service procedures as a guide. Refer to exploded view of cylinder head as necessary.*

1. Gradually heat the cylinder head to 212°F (100°C).

2. Carefully remove the head from the heat source.

3. Using tool and a hammer to drive out the guide.

4. With the guide removed, measure the bore (in the head) into which the guide fits. Refer to bore specifications as a new oversized guide or head assembly must be used.

5. Reheat the head to 212°F (100°C) and then remove it from the heat.

6. Using the correct tools drive in the new guide until it projects to the correct specification above the head.

7. Measure the inner diameter of the guide. Compare this to the stem diameter of the new valve. If the stem to guide clearance is insuffi-

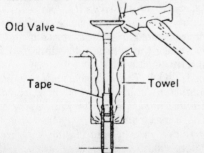

A quick and handy method for breaking off the tops of 4A-GE valve guides before removal

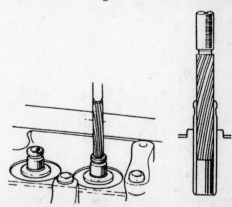

Use a precision reamer to enlarge new valve guides if necessary

cient, ream the new guide with a sharp reamer until the correct clearance is obtained.

Oil Pan

REMOVAL AND INSTALLATION

Corolla-Rear Wheel Drive

1. Disconnect the negative battery cable. Drain the oil.

CAUTION: *The EPA warns that prolonged contact with used engine oil may cause a number of skin disorders, including cancer! You should make every effort to minimize your exposure to used engine oil. Protective gloves should be worn when changing the oil. Wash your hands and any other exposed skin areas as soon as possible after exposure to used engine oil. Soap and water, or waterless hand cleaner should be used.*

2. Raise the vehicle and safely support.

3. Remove the fan shroud assembly.

4. Remove the engine stiffening plates as necessary.

5. Remove the splash shields from underneath the engine.

6. Support the front of the engine with a jack and remove the front engine mount attaching bolts.

7. Raise the front of the engine slightly with the jack. Be sure that the hood is open before raising the front of the engine.

8. If necessary remove any steering linkage (steering relay rod, tie rods, idler arm, etc.) to gain access to oil pan removal.

9. Unbolt and withdraw the oil pan. Installation is performed in the reverse order of removal. Always replace the oil pan gasket and torque retaining bolts to 5 ft. lbs. (working from the center to ends of oil pan) Refill with engine oil. Start engine check for leaks.

Corolla-Front Wheel Drive

NOTE: *On the Corolla diesel engine use this service procedure as guide-modify the service steps as necessary.*

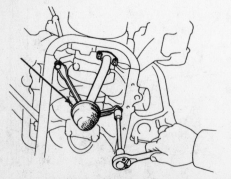

Arrow indicates the oil strainer and pick-up assembly on the 4A-FE engine

1. Disconnect the negative battery cable. Raise and support the vehicle safely. Drain the oil.

CAUTION: *The EPA warns that prolonged contact with used engine oil may cause a number of skin disorders, including cancer! You should make every effort to minimize your exposure to used engine oil. Protective gloves should be worn when changing the oil. Wash your hands and any other exposed skin areas as soon as possible after exposure to used engine oil. Soap and water, or waterless hand cleaner should be used.*

2. Remove the splash shield from underneath the engine.

3. Place a jack under the transaxle to support it.

4. Remove the bolts which secure the engine rear supporting crossmember to the chassis. On the 4A-GE, remove the center mounting and stiffener plate.

5. Raise the jack under the transaxle, slightly. Remove the front exhaust pipe.

6. Remove the oil pan retaining bolts. Remove the oil pan from the vehicle. If the oil pan does not come out easily, it may be necessary to unbolt the rear engine mounts from the crossmember. On some engines it may be necessary to remove the oil strainer and pick-up assembly to gain clearance for oil pan removal (drop oil strainer assembly right in the oil pan).

7. Installation is the reverse of the removal procedure. Tighten the oil pan bolts to 5 ft. lbs. (working from the center to the ends) Always replace the oil pan gasket and refill with engine oil. Start engine check for leaks.

Tercel-Front Wheel Drive and 4-Wheel Drive/3A-C Engine

1. Disconnect the negative battery cable. Drain the cooling system. Remove the radiator.

CAUTION: *When draining the coolant, keep in mind that cats and dogs are attracted by the ethylene glycol antifreeze, and are quite likely to drink any that is left in an uncovered container or in puddles on the ground. This will prove fatal in sufficient quantity. Always drain the coolant into a sealable container. Coolant should be reused unless it is contaminated or several years old.*

2. Raise the vehicle and support it safely. Drain the engine oil.

CAUTION: *The EPA warns that prolonged contact with used engine oil may cause a number of skin disorders, including cancer! You should make every effort to minimize your exposure to used engine oil. Protective gloves should be worn when changing the oil. Wash your hands and any other exposed skin areas as soon as possible after exposure to* used engine oil. Soap and water, or waterless hand cleaner should be used.

3. Remove the engine under cover. Remove the stabilizer bracket bolts and lower the stabilizer assembly. Remove the right and left stiffener plates.

4. Remove the oil pan retaining bolts. Remove the oil pan from the vehicle.

5. Installation is the reverse of the removal procedure. Tighten the oil pan bolts to 5 ft. lbs. (working from the center to the ends) Always replace the oil pan gasket and refill with engine oil. Start engine check for leaks.

Tercel-Front Wheel Drive/3E and 3E-E Engines

1. Disconnect the negative battery terminal. Raise the vehicle and support it safely. Drain the oil.

CAUTION: *The EPA warns that prolonged contact with used engine oil may cause a number of skin disorders, including cancer! You should make every effort to minimize your exposure to used engine oil. Protective gloves should be worn when changing the oil. Wash your hands and any other exposed skin areas as soon as possible after exposure to used engine oil. Soap and water, or waterless hand cleaner should be used.*

2. Remove the right hand engine under cover. Remove the sway bar and any other necessary steering linkage parts.

3. Disconnect the exhaust pipe from the manifold. Raise the engine enough to take the weight off of it.

4. Remove the timing belt. Refer to the necessary service procedure in this Chapter.

5. Continue to raise the engine enough to remove the oil pan. Remove the oil pan retaining bolts. Remove the oil pan.

6. Installation is the reverse of the removal procedure. Tighten the oil pan bolts to 6 ft. lbs. (working from the center to the ends) Always replace the oil pan gasket and refill with engine oil. Start engine check for leaks.

MR2-Rear Wheel Drive

1. Disconnect the negative battery cable. Raise and support the vehicle safely. Drain the engine oil.

CAUTION: *The EPA warns that prolonged contact with used engine oil may cause a number of skin disorders, including cancer! You should make every effort to minimize your exposure to used engine oil. Protective gloves should be worn when changing the oil. Wash your hands and any other exposed skin areas as soon as possible after exposure to used engine oil. Soap and water, or waterless hand cleaner should be used.*

NOTE: *Refer to the necessary service procedures in this Chapter. Review the service procedures before starting this repair.*

2. Remove the exhaust manifold pipe. Remove the timing belt. Remove the crankshaft timing pulley.

3. Support the weight of the engine with a floor jack and then remove the right side engine mount.

4. Remove the oil pan retaining bolts. Remove the oil pan..

5. Installation is in the reverse order of removal. Apply a 5mm bead of RTV gasket material to the groove around the pan flange. Apply the oil pan within 3 minutes of application and tighten the mounting bolts and nuts to 5 ft. lbs. Tighten the oil pan bolts working from the center to the ends. Always replace the oil pan gasket and refill with engine oil. Start engine check for leaks.

Oil Pump
REMOVAL AND INSTALLATION
3A, 3A-C, 4A-C Rear Wheel Drive Engines

1. Remove the fan shroud and then raise the front of the vehicle and support it on safety stands.

2. Drain the engine oil. On the Tercel, drain the coolant and then remove the radiator.

CAUTION: *The EPA warns that prolonged contact with used engine oil may cause a number of skin disorders, including cancer! You should make every effort to minimize your exposure to used engine oil. Protective gloves should be worn when changing the oil. Wash your hands and any other exposed skin areas as soon as possible after exposure to used engine oil. Soap and water, or waterless hand cleaner should be used.*

When draining the coolant, keep in mind that cats and dogs are attracted by the ethylene glycol antifreeze, and are quite likely to drink any that is left in an uncovered container or in puddles on the ground. This will prove fatal in sufficient quantity. Always drain the coolant into a sealable container. Coolant should be reused unless it is contaminated or several years old.

3. Remove the oil pan and the oil strainer.
4. Remove the crankshaft pulley and the timing belt as detailed in this Chapter.
5. Remove the oil level gauge guide and then the gauge.
6. Remove the mounting bolts and then use a rubber mallet to carefully tap the oil pump body from the cylinder block.
7. Position a new gasket on the cylinder block.
8. Position the oil pump on the block so

that the teeth on the pump drive gear are engaged with the teeth of the crankshaft gear.

9. Installation of the remaining components is in the reverse order of removal procedure. Torque the oil pump retaining bolts to 13–18 ft. lbs. Refill with engine oil. Start the engine and check for leaks.

4A-C Front Wheel Drive Engine

1. Disconnect the negative battery cable.
2. Remove the oil pan as previously outlined.
3. Drain the cooling system

CAUTION: *When draining the coolant, keep in mind that cats and dogs are attracted by the ethylene glycol antifreeze, and are quite likely to drink any that is left in an uncovered container or in puddles on the ground. This will prove fatal in sufficient quantity. Always drain the coolant into a sealable container. Coolant should be reused unless it is contaminated or several years old.*

4. Loosen the water pump pulley bolts.
5. Remove the alternator bolts.
6. If equipped with power steering, remove the drive belt.
7. If equipped with air conditioning, loosen

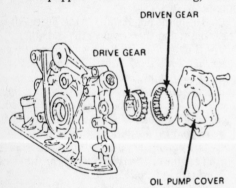

Exploded view of an oil pump

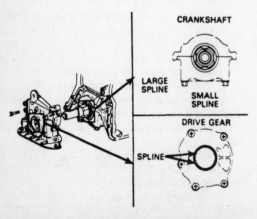

Aligning the oil pump drive gear with the crankshaft

the air conditioning idler pulley and the adjustor. Remove the drive belt and then remove the idler pulley and adjustor.

8. Remove the alternator bolts and remove the alternator; place it or suspend it out of the way.
9. Remove the water pump pulley.
10. Disconnect the upper radiator hose at the engine.
11. Label and disconnect the vacuum hoses running through the work area.
12. Remove the No.1 (upper) timing belt cover and its gasket.
13. Remove the No.3 (middle) timing belt cover and its gasket.
14. Rotate the crankshaft to the TDC/compression position.
15. Elevate and safely support the vehicle on jackstands. Double check the placement of the stands and the stability of the car on the stands.
16. Remove the right splash shield.
17. Remove the flywheel cover.
18. Remove the crankshaft pulley. Block the flywheel to prevent the crank from turning.
19. Remove the No.2 (lower) timing belt cover.
20. Mark the position of the camshaft and crankshaft timing pulleys on the timing belt and mark an arrow on the belt showing the direction of rotation.
21. Loosen the timing belt idler pulley bolt, move the pulley to release tension on the belt and tighten the bolt. This holds the pulley in the loosened position.
22. Slip the timing belt off the crankshaft timing pulley.
23. Remove the crankshaft timing pulley.
24. Remove the dipstick tube.
24. Remove the timing belt idler pulley.
25. Remove the bolts in the oil pump case and carefully remove the oil pump. It may require gentle tapping to loosen it; use only a plastic or rubber mallet.
26. When reinstalling, place the new gasket against the block and install the oil pump to the crankshaft with the spline teeth of the drive gear engaged with the large teeth of the crankshaft. Tighten the bolts to 18 ft. lbs.
27. Install the timing belt idler pulley.
28. Install the dipstick tube.
29. Install the crankshaft timing pulley.
30. Install the timing belt. Refer to Timing Belt Removal and Installation later in this Chapter.
31. Install the lower belt cover.
32. Install the crankshaft pulley and tighten it to specifications.
33. Install the flywheel cover.
34. Install the right splash guard and lower

the vehicle to the ground.

35. Install the middle and upper timing belt covers with their gaskets.

36. Reconnect the vacuum hoses.

37. Attach the water pump pulley; leave the bolts finger tight.

38. Position and secure the alternator.

39. If so equipped, install the air conditioning adjusting bolt, idler pulley and belt. Install the belt and adjust it to the proper tension.

40. Install the power steering belt and adjust it if so equipped.

41. Tighten the water pump bolts.

42. With a new gasket, install the oil pick-up and strainer assembly. Tighten the nuts and bolts to 7 ft. lbs.

43. Refill the cooling system.

44. Install the oil pan following procedures outlined previously.

45. Start the engine and check for leaks. Allow the engine to warm up fully and check the work area carefully under warm and cold conditions.

4A-GE Front Wheel Drive and 4A-GZE MR2 Engines

1. Disconnect the negative battery cable.

2. Remove the oil pan as previously outlined.

3. Remove the oil pick-up and strainer.

4. Remove the oil pan baffle plate.

5. Drain the cooling system.

CAUTION: *When draining the coolant, keep in mind that cats and dogs are attracted by the ethylene glycol antifreeze, and are quite likely to drink any that is left in an uncovered container or in puddles on the ground. This will prove fatal in sufficient quantity. Always drain the coolant into a sealable container. Coolant should be reused unless it is contaminated or several years old.*

6. Disconnect the accelerator cable or linkage.

7. Remove the cruise control actuator if so equipped.

8. Remove the washer tank.

9. Remove the upper radiator hose at the engine block.

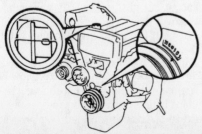

Aligning the 4A-GE engine at TDC/compression for No. 1 cylinder

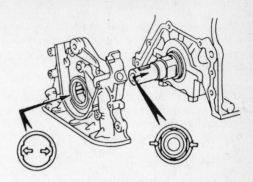

Correct position for installation of the oil pump on the 4A-GE and 4A-FE engines

10. Remove the power steering and/or the air conditioning drive belt(s).

11. Loosen the bolts to the water pump pulley and then remove the alternator drive belt.

12. Remove the spark plugs.

13. Rotate the crankshaft and position the engine at TDC/compression. The crankshaft mark aligns at zero and the camshaft, when viewed through the oil filler cap, has a small cavity pointing upward.

14. Use a floor jack and a piece of wood to slightly elevate the engine. Remove the right engine mount; then remove the three bolts and remove the right reinforcing plate for the engine mount.

15. Remove the water pump pulley.

16. Remove the crankshaft pulley.

NOTE: *Counterhold the crankshaft or block the flywheel to prevent the crank from turning.*

17. Remove the timing belt covers.

NOTE: *The timing belt cover bolts are different lengths and MUST be returned to the proper hole at reassembly. During removal, diagram or label each bolt and its correct position.*

18. Remove the timing belt guide.

19. Loosen the idler pulley bolt, push it all the way to the left and tighten the bolt. This removes tension from the belt.

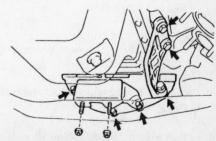

Arrows indicate the nuts and bolts holding the right engine mount and reinforcing plate on a 4A-GE engine

20. Matchmark the belt and all the pulleys so that the belt may be reinstalled exactly as it was before. Mark an arrow on the belt showing direction of rotation.

21. Remove the timing belt from the lower pulley (crankshaft timing pulley). If you are careful, the belt may remain undisturbed on the camshaft pulleys.

22. Remove the idler pulley and spring.

23. Remove the crankshaft timing pulley.

24. Remove the PCV hose.

25. Remove the dipstick and tube.

26. Remove the seven bolts in the oil pump and carefully remove the pump. If it is difficult to remove, tap it lightly with a plastic or rubber mallet. Do not pry it off or strike it with a metal hammer.

27. When reinstalling, place a new gasket on the block. Install the oil pump to the crankshaft with the spline teeth to the drive gear engaged with the large teeth of the crankshaft.

28. Install the seven retaining bolts and tighten them to 16 ft. lbs.

29. Install the dipstick tube and dipstick.

30. Install the crankshaft timing pulley.

31. Install the timing belt idler pulley.

32. Install the timing belt. Refer to Timing Belt Removal and Installation procedures in this Chapter.

33. Install the timing belt guide. It should install with the cupped side facing outward.

34. Make sure the gaskets are properly seated in the timing belt covers and reinstall the covers. Make sure each bolt is in the correct hole.

35. Install the crankshaft pulley. Again using a counterholding device, tighten the bolt to specifications.

36. Install the water pump pulley and tighten the bolts finger tight. Install the valve covers.

37. Install the right side engine mount. Tighten the nut to 38 ft. lbs. and the through bolt to 64 ft. lbs.

38. Install the reinforcement for the right motor mount and tighten the bolts to 31 ft. lbs.

39. Install the spark plugs.

40. Install the alternator drive belt and tighten the water pump pulley bolts.

41. Install and adjust the power steering and/or the air conditioner drive belts.

42. Connect the upper radiator hose.

43. Install the windshield washer reservoir.

44. If equipped with cruise control, reinstall the cruise control actuator.

45. Connect the accelerator cable or linkage.

46. Install the oil pan baffle plate. Clean the contact surfaces thoroughly, apply a bead of sealer to the baffle plate and press the baffle plate into position. Be very careful not to get any sealant into the oil passages.

47. Install the oil pick-up and strainer assembly. Install the PCV hose.

48. Install the oil pan, following procedures discussed in this Chapter.

49. Using new gaskets, reconnect the exhaust pipe. Tighten the bolts to the catalytic converter and the bolts to the exhaust manifold.

50. Install the flywheel cover.

51. Install the stiffener plate and the center engine mount.

52. Refill the engine with oil.

53. Refill the coolant system.

54. Start the engine and check for leaks. Allow the engine to warm up to normal operating temperature and check the work area carefully for signs of seepage.

55. With the engine shut off, check the tension of the drive belts and adjust if necessary. Reinstall the splash guards under the car.

4A-F and 4A-FE Engines

1. Disconnect the negative battery cable and elevate the vehicle. Safely support it on jackstands. Remove the splash shield(s).

2. Remove the protectors from the two center engine mount nuts and studs.

3. Remove the two center transaxle mount-to-center crossmember nuts.

4. Remove the two rear transaxle mount-to-main crossmember nuts.

5. Drain the engine oil

CAUTION: *Used motor oil may cause skin cancer if repeatedly left in contact with the skin for prolonged periods. Although this is unlikely unless you handle oil on a daily basis, it is wise to thoroughly wash your hands with soap and water immediately after handling used motor oil.*

6. Remove the oil pan. Remove the oil pick-up and strainer assembly.

7. Lower the vehicle to the ground.

8. Depending on equipment, loosen the air conditioning compressor bracket, the power steering pump bracket and the alternator bracket as applicable. Remove the drive belts.

9. Remove the alternator from its mounts and place it out of the way. The wiring may be left attached.

10. Lift out the windshield washer fluid reservoir.

11. Support the engine. This may be done from above with a chain hoist or from below with a floor jack. Be very careful of the jack placement (the oil pan is removed); use a piece of wood to distribute the load and protect the engine.

12. Remove the through bolt in the right engine mount.

13. Remove the water pump pulley.

14. Lower the engine to its normal position.

15. Remove the crankshaft pulley.

16. Remove the timing belt covers.

17. Remove the timing belt guide from the crank pulley.

18. Loosen the idler pulley bolt, push it all the way to the left and tighten the bolt. This removes tension from the belt.

19. Matchmark the belt and all the pulleys so that the belt may be reinstalled exactly as it was before. Mark an arrow on the belt showing direction of rotation.

20. Remove the timing belt from the lower pulley (crankshaft timing pulley). If you are careful, the belt may remain undisturbed on the camshaft pulleys.

21. Remove the idler pulley and spring.

22. Remove the dipstick and dipstick tube.

23. Remove the crankshaft timing pulley.

24. Raise the vehicle and safely support it on jackstands.

25. Remove the seven bolts holding the oil pump.

26. Remove the seven bolts in the oil pump and carefully remove the pump. If it is difficult to remove, tap it lightly with a plastic or rubber mallet. Do not pry it off or strike it with a metal hammer.

27. When reinstalling, place a new gasket on the block. Install the oil pump to the crankshaft with the spline teeth to the drive gear engaged with the large teeth of the crankshaft.

28. Install the seven retaining bolts and tighten them to 16 ft. lbs.

29. Lower the vehicle to the ground.

30. Install the timing belt idler pulley.

31. Install the dipstick tube and dipstick.

32. Install the timing belt. Refer to Timing Belt Removal and Installation procedures in this Chapter.

33. Install the timing belt guide. It should install with the cupped side facing outward.

34. Make sure the gaskets are properly seated in the timing belt covers and reinstall the covers. Make sure each bolt is in the correct hole.

35. Install the crankshaft pulley. Tighten the bolt to specifications.

36. Elevate the motor to gain access to the water pump.

37. Install the water pump pulley.

38. Install the right engine mount through bolt. Tighten the through bolt to 64 ft. lbs.

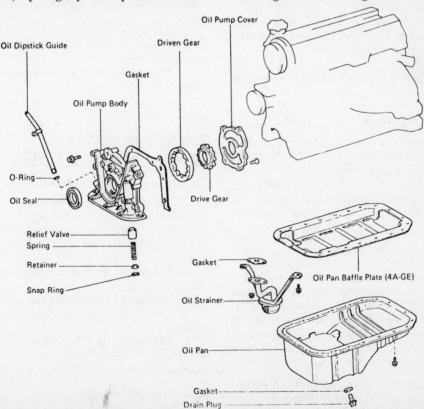

Detail of the oil pump system on the 4A-GE engine. The 4A-FE engine is similar without the baffle plate. Any gasket shown should be replaced before reassembly

When the bolt is secure, the engine lifting apparatus may be removed.

39. Position and install the alternator.

40. Reinstall the drive belts for the alternator, power steering and air conditioning as applicable. Adjust the belts to the correct tension.

41. Raise the vehicle and safely support it on jackstands.

42. Install the oil pick-up and strainer assembly.

43. Apply a continuous bead of sealer to both sides of the new pan gasket.

44. Place the gasket on the pan and install the pan to the block. Tighten the bolts and nuts to 5 ft. lbs.

45. Install the two rear transaxle mount-to-main crossmember nuts and tighten them to 45 ft. lbs. Install the two center transaxle mount-to-center crossmember nuts and tighten them to 45 ft. lbs.

46. Install the protectors over the nuts and studs for the mounts.

47. Lower the vehicle to the ground.

48. Install the windshield washer fluid reservoir.

49. Refill the engine with the correct amount of oil.

50. Connect the negative battery cable.

51. Start the engine and check for leaks. Allow the engine to warm up to normal operating temperature and check the work area carefully for signs of seepage.

52. With the engine shut off, check the tension of the drive belts and adjust if necessary. Reinstall the splash guard(s) under the car.

3E and 3E-E Engines

1. Remove the right hand engine splash shield. Disconnect the exhaust pipe from the manifold. Remove the timing belt.

2. Drain the engine oil. Remove the oil pan, the oil strainer and the dipstick. Refer to the necessary service procedures in this Chapter.

CAUTION: *The EPA warns that prolonged contact with used engine oil may cause a number of skin disorders, including cancer! You should make every effort to minimize your exposure to used engine oil. Protective gloves should be worn when changing the oil. Wash your hands and any other exposed skin areas as soon as possible after exposure to used engine oil. Soap and water, or waterless hand cleaner should be used.*

3. Remove the oil pump mounting bolts and the tensioner spring bracket. Remove the oil pump. Service as necessary and install in the reverse order of removal procedure. Refill with engine oil. Start the engine and check for leaks.

1C-L Diesel Engine

1. Remove the engine cover under the car and then drain the oil.

CAUTION: *The EPA warns that prolonged contact with used engine oil may cause a number of skin disorders, including cancer! You should make every effort to minimize your exposure to used engine oil. Protective gloves should be worn when changing the oil. Wash your hands and any other exposed skin areas as soon as possible after exposure to used engine oil. Soap and water, or waterless hand cleaner should be used.*

2. Remove the hood.

3. Disconnect the center engine mount.

4. Remove the oil pan and oil strainer.

5. Attach an engine hoist to the two engine lifting brackets and suspend the engine.

6. Remove all drive belts; remove the water pump pulley. A/C idler pulley and the crankshaft pulley.

7. Remove the timing belt.

8. Remove the oil level gauge guide and then the gauge.

9. Remove the mounting bolts and then use a rubber mallet to carefully tap the oil pump body from the cylinder block.

10. Position a new gasket on the cylinder block.

11. Position the oil pump on the block so that the teeth on the pump drive gear are engaged with the teeth of the crankshaft gear.

12. Installation of the remaining components is in the reverse order of removal procedure. Refill with engine oil. Start the engine and check for leaks.

Timing Belt Covers
REMOVAL AND INSTALLATION
3A, 3A-C and 4A-C Rear Wheel Drive

1. Disconnect the negative battery cable.

2. Remove all the drive belts.

3. Bring the engine to the top dead center timing position. See the cylinder head removal section.

4. Remove the crankshaft pulley with a suitable pulley.

5. Remove the water pump pulley.

6. Remove the upper and lower timing case covers.

7. Installation is the reverse of removal. Tighten the timing belt cover to 9 ft. lbs. Torque the crankshaft pulley to specifications.

4A-C Front Wheel Drive

1. Disconnect the negative battery cable.

2. Remove the right side splash shield under the engine.

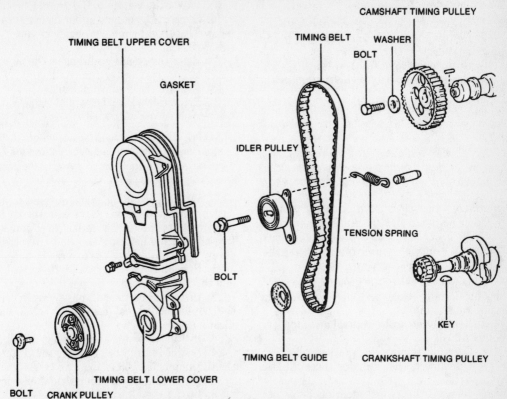

Timing belt cover — 3A, 3A-C and 4A-C RWD engines

3. Loosen the water pump pulley bolts and remove the alternator belt. Remove the power steering drive belt if so equipped.

4. Remove the bolts and remove the water pump pulley.

5. Loosen the air conditioning idler pulley mounting bolt. Loosen the adjusting nut and then remove the air conditioning drive belt if so equipped. Remove the idler pulley.

6. Rotate the crankshaft clockwise and set the engine to TDC/compression on No. 1 cylinder. Loosen the crankshaft pulley mounting bolt and remove the crank pulley.

NOTE: *Before removing the pulley, check that the rockers on the No. 1 cylinder are loose and that the timing marks on the crankshaft align at the zero setting. If the rockers are not loose, rotate the crankshaft one full revolution, stopping again at the zero point.*

7. Remove the mounting bolts and the No. 1 (upper) cover.

8. Remove the four bolts and remove the center engine mount.

9. Place a block of wood on a floor jack and position it under the motor. Raise the engine slightly, remove two bolts and then remove the right engine mount.

10. Lower the engine and then remove the No. 2 (lower) and the No. 3 (center) covers with their gaskets.

11. When reinstalling, make certain that the gaskets and their mating surfaces are clean and free from dirt and oil. The gasket itself must be free of cuts and deformations and must fit securely in the grooves of the covers.

12. Install the No. 3 cover with its gasket, then install the No. 2 cover and its gasket. Before tightening the bolts fully, check that the gaskets have not fallen out of place.

13. Raise the engine slightly and install the right engine mount.

14. Lower the engine into place and install the center engine mount. Tighten the bolts to 29 ft. lbs.

15. Install the upper timing belt cover.

16. Install the crankshaft pulley; tighten the bolt to 87 ft. lbs.

17. Install the water pump pulley and tighten the bolts finger tight.

18. Reinstall the idler pulley for the air conditioning belt. Install the belt and adjust it by turning the adjustor into position.

19. Tighten the water pump pulley bolts.

20. Install the power steering drive belt if so equipped.

21. Install the splash shield.

22. Connect the negative battery cable.

4A-GE and 4A-GZE Engines

1. Disconnect the negative battery cable.
2. Elevate the vehicle and safely support it on jackstands.
3. Remove the right front wheel.
4. Remove the splash shield from under the car.
5. Drain the coolant into clean containers. Close the drain cocks when the system is empty.

CAUTION: *When draining the coolant, keep in mind that cats and dogs are attracted by the ethylene glycol antifreeze, and are quite likely to drink any that is left in an uncovered container or in puddles on the ground. This will prove fatal in sufficient quantity. Always drain the coolant into a sealable container. Coolant should be reused unless it is contaminated or several years old.*

6. Lower the car to the ground. Disconnect the accelerator cable and, if equipped, the cruise control cable.
7. Remove the cruise control actuator if so equipped.
8. Carefully remove the ignition coil.
9. Disconnect the radiator hose at the water outlet.
10. Remove the power steering drive belt and the alternator drive belt.
11. Remove the spark plugs.
12. Rotate the crankshaft clockwise and set the engine to TDC/compression on No.1 cylinder. Align the crankshaft marks at zero; look through the oil filler hole and make sure the small hole in the end of the camshaft can be seen.
13. Raise and safely support the vehicle. Disconnect the center engine mount.

14. Lower the vehicle to the ground.
15. Support the engine either from above or below. Disconnect the right engine mount from the engine.
16. Raise the engine and remove the mount.
17. Remove the water pump pulley.
18. Remove the crankshaft pulley.
19. Remove the ten bolts and remove the timing belt covers with their gaskets.

NOTE: *The bolts are different lengths; they must be returned to their correct location at reassembly. Label or diagram the bolts during removal.*

20. When reinstalling, make certain that the gaskets and their mating surfaces are clean and free from dirt and oil. The gasket itself must be free of cuts and deformations and must fit securely in the grooves of the covers.
21. Reinstall the covers and their gaskets and the 10 bolts in their proper positions.
22. Install the crankshaft pulley, again using the counterholding tool. Tighten the bolt to specifications.
23. Install the water pump pulley.
24. Install the right engine mount. Tighten the through bolt to 58 ft. lbs.
25. Reinstall the spark plugs and their wires.
26. Install the alternator drive belt and the power steering drive belt. Adjust the belts to the correct tension.
27. Connect the radiator hose to the water outlet port.
28. Install the ignition coil.
29. Install the cruise control actuator and the cruise control cable if so equipped.
30. Connect the accelerator cable.
31. Refill the cooling system with the correct amount of anti-freeze and water.

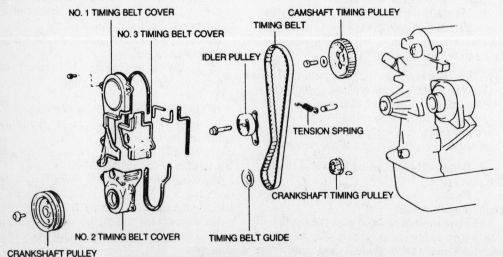

Timing belt and related components 4A-C FWD engine

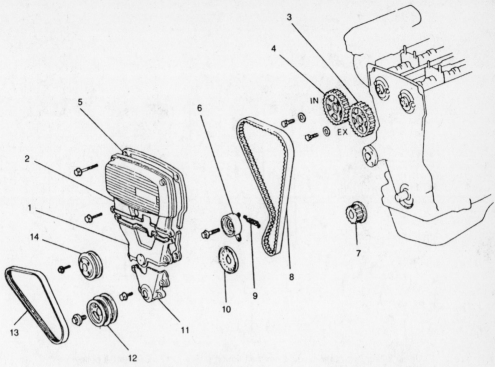

1.	No.2 Timing belt cover	5.	Gasket	10. Timing belt guide
2.	No.3 timing belt cover	6.	Idler pulley	11. No.1 timing belt cover
3.	Exhaust camshaft timing pulley	7.	Crankshaft timing pulley	12. Crankshaft pulley
4.	Intake camshaft pulley	8.	Timing belt	13. Drive belt
		9.	Tension spring	14. Water pump pulley

Timing belt, cover and related components 4A-GE engine

32. Connect the negative battery cable.

33. Start the engine and check for leaks. Allow the engine to warm up and check the work areas carefully for seepage.

34. Install the splash shield under the car. Install the right front wheel.

4A-F and 4A-FE Engines

1. Disconnect the negative battery cable.

2. Elevate the vehicle and safely support it on jackstands.

3. Remove the right splash shield under the car.

4. Lower the vehicle. Remove the wiring harness from the upper timing belt cover.

5. Depending on equipment, loosen the air conditioner compressor, the power steering pump and the alternator on their adjusting bolts. Remove the drive belts.

6. Remove the crankshaft pulley.

7. Remove the valve cover.

8. Remove the windshield washer reservoir.

9. Elevate and safely support the vehicle.

10. Support the engine either from above (chain hoist) or below (floor jack and wood

block) and remove the through bolt at the right engine mount.

11. Remove the protectors on the mount nuts and studs for the center and rear transaxle mounts.

12. Remove the two rear transaxle mount-to-main crossmember nuts. Remove the two center transaxle mount-to-center crossmember nuts.

13. Carefully elevate the engine enough to gain access to the water pump pulley.

14. Remove the water pump pulley. Lower

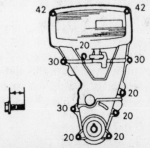

Timing cover bolts must be installed in the correct locations for 4A-GE series engines. Bolt lengths shown are in millimeters (mm)

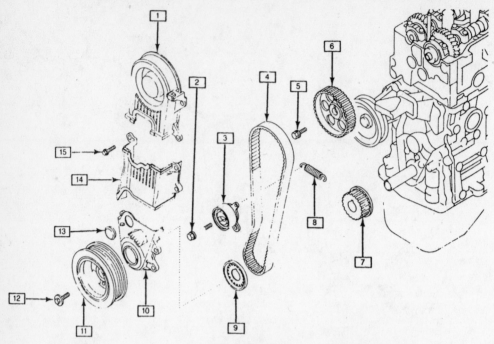

1. Upper timing belt cover
2. Bolt
3. Idler pulley
4. timing belt
5. . Bolt
6. Camshaft timing pulley
7. Crankshaft timing gear
8. Tension spring
9. Timing belt guide
10. Lower timing belt cover
11. Crankshaft pulley
12. Bolt
13. Inspection plug
14. Center timing belt cover
15. Bolt

Timing belt, cover and related components 4A-FE engine

the engine to its normal position.

15. Remove the four bolts and the lower timing cover. Remove the center timing cover and its bolt, then the upper cover with its four bolts.

16. If further work is to be done, the car may be lowered to the ground but the engine must remain supported until the mount(s) are reinstalled.

17. When reinstalling, make certain that the gaskets and their mating surfaces are clean and free from dirt and oil. The gasket itself must be free of cuts and deformations and must fit securely in the grooves of the covers.

18. Install the covers and the bolts; tighten the bolts to 4 ft. lbs.

19. Elevate the engine and install the water pump pulley.

20. Lower the engine to its normal position. Install the through bolt in the right engine mount and tighten it to 64 ft. lbs. with the bolt secure, the engine lifting apparatus may be removed.

21. Install the valve cover.

22. Install the crankshaft pulley and tighten it to specifications.

23. Reinstall the air conditioning compressor, the power steering pump and the alterna-

tor. Install their belts and adjust them to the correct tension.

24. Reconnect the wiring harness to the upper timing belt cover.

25. Raise the vehicle and safely support it on jackstands.

26. Install the two nuts on the center transaxle mount and the rear transaxle mount. Tighten all the nuts to 45 ft. lbs.

27. Install the protectors on the nuts and studs.

28. Install the splash shield under the car.

29. Lower the vehicle to the ground.

30. Install the windshield washer reservoir and connect the negative battery cable.

1C-L Diesel Engine

1. Disconnect the negative battery terminal.

2. Remove the cover under the engine.

3. Remove the power steering pump drive belt and pulley.

4. Remove the mounting bolts and then remove the power steering pump.

5. Remove the three clips and five bolts and then remove the No. 2 (upper) timing belt cover along with its gasket.

6. Remove the alternator drive belt.

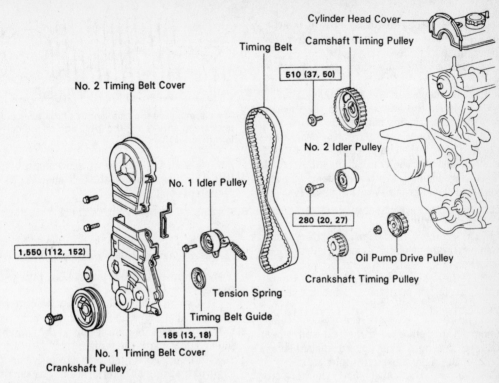

No. 2 Timing Belt Cover

Cylinder Head Cover

Camshaft Timing Pulley

Timing Belt

510 (37, 50)

No. 1 Idler Pulley

No. 2 Idler Pulley

1,550 (112, 152)

280 (20, 27)

Oil Pump Drive Pulley

Tension Spring

Crankshaft Timing Pulley

Timing Belt Guide

185 (13, 18)

No. 1 Timing Belt Cover

Crankshaft Pulley

kg-cm (ft-lb, N·m) : Specified torque

Timing belt, cover and related components 3E and 3E-E engines

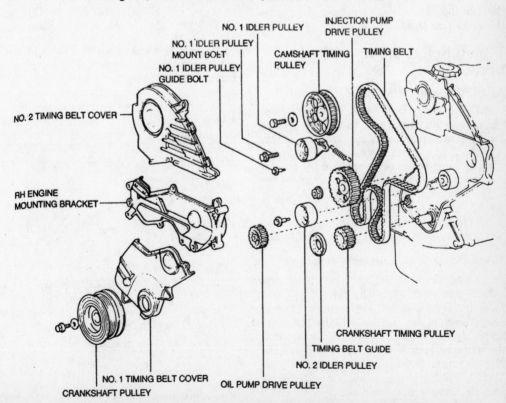

NO. 1 IDLER PULLEY

INJECTION PUMP
DRIVE PULLEY

NO. 1 IDLER PULLEY
MOUNT BOLT

CAMSHAFT TIMING
PULLEY

TIMING BELT

NO. 1 IDLER PULLEY
GUIDE BOLT

NO. 2 TIMING BELT COVER

RH ENGINE
MOUNTING BRACKET

CRANKSHAFT TIMING PULLEY

TIMING BELT GUIDE

NO. 2 IDLER PULLEY

NO. 1 TIMING BELT COVER

OIL PUMP DRIVE PULLEY

CRANKSHAFT PULLEY

Timing belt, cover and related components 1C-L diesel engine

7. Set the No. 1 piston to TDC of the compression stroke. Loosen the set bolt and remove the crankshaft pulley.

8. Remove the mounting bolts and then remove the No. 1 (lower) timing belt cover along with the gasket and belt guide.

9. Remove the four bolts and then disconnect the center engine mount.

10. Installation is in the reverse order of removal. Tighten the center engine mount bolts to 29 ft. lbs. and the crankshaft pulley bolt to 72 ft. lbs. Tighten the power steering pump bolts and the idler pulley nut to 29 ft. lbs.

3E and 3E-E Engines

1. Disconnect the negative battery cable. Remove the air cleaner assembly. Remove all drive belts.

2. If the vehicle is equipped with cruise control, remove the actuator and bracket assembly.

3. Raise and support the vehicle safely. Remove the right side front tire and wheel. Remove the right side engine splash shield. Remove the right side mount insulator.

4. Remove the valve cover. Remove the crankshaft pulley and remove the timing cover mounting bolts and cover.

5. Install in the reverse order procedure. Refer to the Timing Belt removal and installation section as necessary.

Timing Belt and Camshaft Sprocket

REMOVAL AND INSTALLATION

NOTE: *Timing belts must always be handled carefully and kept completely free of dirt, grease, fluids and lubricants. This includes any accidental contact from spillage. These same precautions apply to the pulleys and contact surfaces on which the belt rides. The belt must never be crimped, twisted or bent. Never use tools to pry or wedge the belt into place. Such actions will damage the structure of the belt and possibly cause breakage.*

3A, 3A-C and 4A-C (A Series) Engine

1. Remove the timing belt covers using procedures described in this Chapter.

2. If not done as part of the cover removal, rotate the crankshaft clockwise to the TDC/compression position for No. 1 cylinder. Insure that the crankshaft marks align at zero and that the rocker arms on No. 1 cylinder are loose.

3. Loosen the timing belt idler pulley to relieve the tension on the belt.

4. Make matchmarks on the belt and both

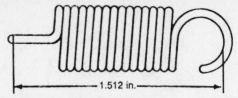

Always measure the free length of the idler pulley tensioning spring. For the 4A-C engine the correct length is 1.512 in.

pulleys showing the exact placement of the belt. Mark an arrow on the belt showing its direction of rotation.

5. Carefully slip the timing belt off the pulleys.

NOTE: *Do not disturb the position of the camshaft or the crankshaft during removal.*

6. Remove the idler pulley bolt, pulley and return spring.

7. Use an adjustable wrench mounted on the flats of the camshaft to hold the cam from moving. Loosen the center bolt in the camshaft pulley and remove the pulley.

8. Check the timing belt carefully for any signs of cracking or deterioration. Pay particular attention to the area where each tooth or cog attaches to the backing of the belt. If the belt shows signs of damage, check the contact faces of the pulleys for possible burrs or scratches.

9. Check the idler pulley by holding it in your hand and spinning it. It should rotate freely and quietly. Any sign of grinding or abnormal noise indicates replacement of the pulley.

10. Check the free length of the tension spring. Correct length is 38.5mm measured at the inside faces of the hooks for the 4A-C engine (some engines spring size may be different). A spring which has stretched during use

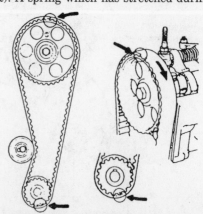

Always matchmark the belt and both pulleys before removing the timing belt. Mark an arrow on the belt showing direction of rotation

will not apply the correct tension to the pulley; replace the spring.

11. If you can test the tension of the spring, look for 8.4 lbs. of tension at 50mm of length. If in doubt, replace the spring.

12. Reinstall the camshaft timing belt pulley, making sure the pulley fits properly on the shaft and that the timing marks align correctly. Tighten the center bolt to 34 ft. lbs.

13. Before reinstalling the belt, double check that the crank and camshafts are exactly in their correct positions. The alignment mark on the end of the camshaft bearing cap should show through the small hole in the camshaft pulley and the small mark on the crankshaft timing belt pulley should align with the mark on the oil pump.

14. Reinstall the timing belt idler pulley and the tension spring. Pry the pulley to the left as far as it will go and temporarily tighten the retaining bolt. This will hold the pulley in its loosest position.

15. Install the timing belt, observing the matchmarks made earlier. Make sure the belt is fully and squarely seated on the upper and lower pulleys.

16. Using the equipment installed during the removal of the timing covers, elevate the engine enough to gain access to the work area.

17. Loosen the retaining bolt for the timing belt idler pulley and allow it to tension the belt.

18. Temporarily install the crankshaft pulley bolt and turn the crank clockwise two full revolutions from TDC to TDC. Insure that each timing mark realigns exactly.

19. Tighten the timing belt idler pulley retaining bolt to 27 ft. lbs.

20. Measure the timing belt deflection, looking for 6–7mm of deflection at 4.4 pounds of pressure. If the deflection is not correct, readjust the idler pulley by repeating Steps 15 through 18.

21. Remove the bolt from the end of the crankshaft.

22. Lower the engine into position and install the right engine mount.

23. Install the timing belt guide onto the crankshaft and install the lower timing belt cover.

24. Continue reassembly of the timing belt covers as outlined previously in this Chapter.

4A-GE and 4A-GZE Engines

1. Remove the timing belt covers following procedures explained previously in this chapter.

2. Remove the timing belt guide from the crankshaft pulley.

3. Loosen the timing belt idler pulley, move

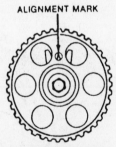

ALIGNMENT MARK

Make sure the camshaft alignment mark shows through the small hole in the pulley

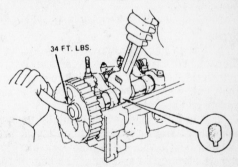

34 FT. LBS.

Make sure the cam is firmly held when removing the timing belt sprocket

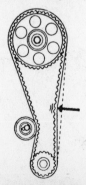

After the timing belt is reinstalled, always check for the correct tension. See text for correct procedure

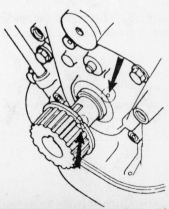

The crankshaft and oil pump marks must be aligned before reinstalling the timing belt

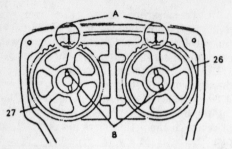

A   MATCHMARK
B   KNOCK PIN
26 EXHAUST CAMSHAFT TIMING PULLEY
27 INTAKE CAMSHAFT TIMING
    PULLEY

Align the cam pulleys before installing the timing belt

it to the left (to take tension off the belt) and tighten its bolt.

4. Make matchmarks on the belt and all pulleys showing the exact placement of the belt. Mark an arrow on the belt showing its direction of rotation.

5. Carefully slip the timing belt off the pulleys.

NOTE: *Do not disturb the position of the camshafts or the crankshaft during removal.*

6. Remove the idler pulley bolt, pulley and return spring.

7. Remove the PCV hose and the valve covers.

8. Use an adjustable wrench to counterhold the camshaft. Be careful not to damage the cylinder head. Loosen the center bolt in each camshaft pulley and remove the pulley. Label the pulleys and keep them clean.

9. Check the timing belt carefully for any signs of cracking or deterioration. Pay particular attention to the area where each tooth or cog attaches to the backing of the belt. If the belt shows signs of damage, check the contact faces of the pulleys for possible burrs or scratches.

10. Check the idler pulley by holding it in your hand and spinning it. It should rotate

freely and quietly. Any sign of grinding or abnormal noise indicates replacement of the pulley.

11. Check the free length of the tension spring. Correct length is 43.5mm measured at the inside faces of the hooks. A spring which has stretched during use will not apply the correct tension to the pulley; replace the spring.

12. If you can test the tension of the spring, look for 22 lbs. of tension at 50mm of length. If in doubt, replace the spring.

13. Align the camshaft knock pin and the pulley. Reinstall the camshaft timing belt pulleys, making sure the pulley fits properly on the shaft and that the timing marks align correctly. Tighten the center bolt on each pulley to 34 ft. lbs. Be careful not to damage the cylinder head during installation.

14. Before reinstalling the belt, double check that the crank and camshafts are exactly in their correct positions. The alignment marks on the pulleys should align with the cast marks on the head and oil pump.

15. Reinstall the valve covers and the PCV hose.

16. Install the timing belt idler pulley and its tensioning spring. Move the idler to the left and temporarily tighten its bolt.

17. Carefully observing the matchmarks made earlier, install the timing belt onto the pulleys.

18. Slowly release tension on the idler pulley

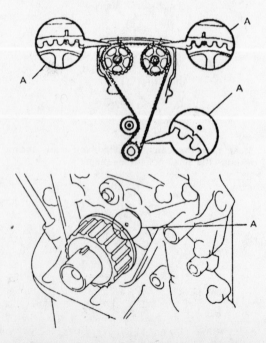

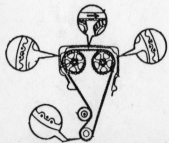

Examples of matchmarks on the timing belt and pulleys. Don't forget an arrow showing the direction of rotation

for the 4A-GE series engines, make certain all timing marks (A) are aligned before timing belt is installed

bolt and allow the idler to take up tension on the timing belt. DO NOT allow the idler to slam into the belt; the belt may become damaged.

19. Temporarily install the crankshaft pulley bolt. Turn the engine clockwise through two complete revolutions, stopping at TDC. Check that each pulley aligns with its marks.

20. Using a special tool, check the tension of the timing belt at a point halfway between the two camshaft sprockets. The correct deflection is 4mm at 4.4 lbs. pressure. If the belt tension is incorrect, readjust it by repeating steps 19 and 20. If the tension is correct, tighten the idler pulley bolt to 27 ft. lbs.

21. Remove the crankshaft pulley bolt.

22. Install the timing belt guide onto the crankshaft timing pulley.

23. Reinstall the timing belt covers, following procedures outlined previously in this Chapter.

4A-F and 4A-FE Engines

1. Remove the timing belt covers using procedures described earlier in this Chapter.

2. If not done as part of the cover removal, rotate the crankshaft clockwise to the TDC/compression position for No. 1 cylinder.

3. Loosen the timing belt idler pulley to relieve the tension on the belt, move the pulley away from the belt and temporarily tighten the bolt to hold it in the loose position.

4. Make matchmarks on the belt and both pulleys showing the exact placement of the belt. Mark an arrow on the belt showing its direction of rotation.

5. Carefully slip the timing belt off the pulleys.

NOTE: *Do not disturb the position of the camshafts or the crankshaft during removal.*

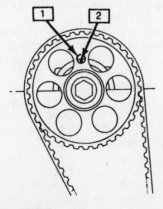

1. Camshaft gear hole
2. Exhaust camshaft cap mark

Correct alignment of the 4A-FE camshaft before reinstallation of the timing belt

6. Remove the idler pulley bolt, pulley and return spring.

7. Use an adjustable wrench mounted on the flats of the camshaft to hold the cam from moving. Loosen the center bolt in the camshaft timing pulley and remove the pulley.

8. Check the timing belt carefully for any signs of cracking or deterioration. Pay particular attention to the area where each tooth or cog attaches to the backing of the belt. If the belt shows signs of damage, check the contact faces of the pulleys for possible burrs or scratches.

9. Check the idler pulley by holding it in your hand and spinning it. It should rotate freely and quietly. Any sign of grinding or abnormal noise indicates replacement of the pulley.

10. Check the free length of the tension spring. Correct length is 38.5mm measured at the inside faces of the hooks. A spring which has stretched during use will not apply the correct tension to the pulley; replace the spring.

11. If you can test the tension of the spring, look for 8.4 lbs. of tension at 50mm of length. If in doubt, replace the spring.

12. Reinstall the camshaft timing belt pulley, making sure the pulley fits properly on the shaft and that the timing marks align correctly. Tighten the center bolt to 43 ft. lbs.

13. Before reinstalling the belt, double check that the crank and camshafts are exactly in their correct positions. The alignment mark on the end of the camshaft bearing cap should show through the small hole in the camshaft pulley and the small mark on the crankshaft timing belt pulley should align with the mark on the oil pump.

14. Reinstall the timing belt idler pulley and the tension spring. Pry the pulley to the left as far as it will go and temporarily tighten the retaining bolt. This will hold the pulley in its loosest position.

15. Install the timing belt, observing the matchmarks made earlier. Make sure the belt is fully and squarely seated on the upper and lower pulleys.

16. Loosen the retaining bolt for the timing belt idler pulley and allow it to tension the belt.

17. Temporarily install the crankshaft pulley bolt and turn the crank clockwise two full revolutions from TDC to TDC. Insure that each timing mark realigns exactly.

18. Tighten the timing belt idler pulley retaining bolt to 27 ft. lbs.

19. Measure the timing belt deflection using a special tool, looking for 5–6mm of deflection at 4.4 pounds of pressure. If the deflection is not correct, readjust the idler pulley by repeating steps 15 through 18.

20. Remove the bolt from the end of the crankshaft.

21. Install the timing belt guide onto the crankshaft and install the lower timing belt cover.

22. Continue reassembly of the timing belt covers as outlined previously in this Chapter.

3E and 3E-E Engines

1. Disconnect the negative battery cable. Remove the right side engine under cover. On 3E-E engines, disconnect the accelerator and throttle cables.

2. Remove the drive belts, alternator and alternator bracket. Remove the air cleaner and air intake collector assemblies and spark plugs on the 3E-E engine.

3. Raise the engine and remove the right side engine mounting insulator assembly.

4. Remove the cylinder head cover. Set the engine to TDC on the compression stroke. Remove the crankshaft pulley using the proper removal tool.

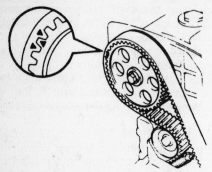

Timing belt alignment 3E and 3E-E engines

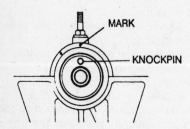

Camshaft alignment 3E and 3E-E engines

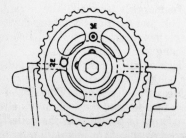

Timing sprocket installation 3E and 3E-E engines

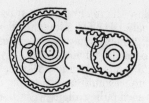

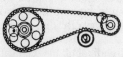

When checking the valve timing, turn the crankshaft two (2) complete revolutions clockwise from TDC to TDC and make sure that each pulley aligns with the marks shown

5. Remove both timing belt covers. Remove the timing belt guide. Remove the timing belt and the No. 1 idler pulley. If using the old belt matchmark it in the direction of engine rotation. Matchmark the pulleys.

6. Remove the tension spring. Remove the No. 2 idler pulley. Remove the crankshaft pulley, camshaft pulley and oil pump pulley using the proper tools.

7. Inspect the belt for defects. Replace as required. Inspect the idler pulleys and springs. Replace defective components as required.

8. Align and install the oil pump pulley. Torque the retaining bolt to 20 ft. lbs.

9. To install the camshaft timing pulley, align the camshaft knock pin with the No. 1 bearing cap mark. Align the knock pin hole on the 3E mark side with the camshaft knock pin hole. Torque the retaining bolt to 37 ft. lbs.

10. Install the crankshaft timing pulley and align the TDC marks on the oil pump body and the crankshaft timing pulley. Install the No. 1 idler pulley. Pry the idler pulley toward the left as far as it will go and temporarily tighten the retaining bolt.

11. Install the No. 2 idler pulley and torque the retaining bolt to 20 ft. lbs. Install the timing belt. If reusing the old belt align it with the marks made during the removal procedure.

12. Inspect the valve timing and the belt tension by loosening the No. 1 idler pulley set bolt. Temporarily install the crankshaft pulley bolt and turn the crankshaft 2 complete revolutions in the clockwise direction.

13. Check that each pulley aligns with the proper markings. Torque the No. 1 idler pulley bolt to 13 ft. lbs. Check for proper belt tension. The belt should deflect 6mm ($1/4$ inch) at $4^1/2$ lbs. pressure. Install the belt guide.

14. Install the timing belt covers. Align and install the crankshaft pulley. Torque the retaining bolt to specifications.

15. Installation of the remaining components is the reverse of the removal procedure.

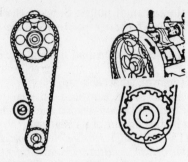

Mark the timing belt before removal

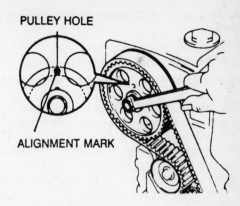

Timing sprocket alignment 3E and 3E-E engines

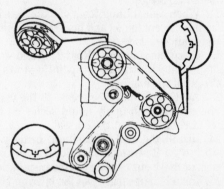

If the timing belt is to be reused, mark it as shown
1C-L diesel engine

Service components as required. Make all necessary engine adjustments and roadtest for
proper operation.

1C-L Diesel Engines

1. Remove the front covers as previously detailed.

2. Raise the engine slightly with a jack and
a block of wood. Disconnect the right engine
mount from its bracket.

3. Lower the engine and then remove the
right engine mount.

4. If the timing belt is to be reused, mark
an arrow in the direction of engine rotation on
its surface. Matchmark the belt to the pulleys
as shown in the illustration.

5. Use a screwdriver and remove the idler
pulley tension spring.

6. Loosen the idler pulley bolt, push it to
the left as far as it will go and then temporarily
tighten it.

7. Remove the timing belt.

NOTE: *Do not bend, twist or turn the belt
inside out. Do not allow grease or water to
come in contact with it.*

8. Inspect the belt for cracks, missing teeth
or overall wear. Replace as necessary.

9. Install the idler pulley and then install
the timing belt. Make sure that the belt is
aligned at all positions (as illustrated) if new, or

at all previously marked points are being
reused.

NOTE: *Be sure that the timing belt is securely meshed with the gear teeth.*

10. Install the tension spring and then turn
the engine two complete revolutions (from
TDC to TDC). Always turn the engine clockwise, using the crankshaft pulley bolt. All alignment marks should still be in alignment; if not,
remove the belt and try again.

11. Further installation is in the reverse
order of removal. Service components as required. Make all necessary engine adjustments
and roadtest for proper operation.

Camshaft and Bearings

REMOVAL AND INSTALLATION

NOTE: *Camshaft end play (thrust clearance) must be checked before the cam is removed. Please refer to the "Inspection" section for details of this check.*

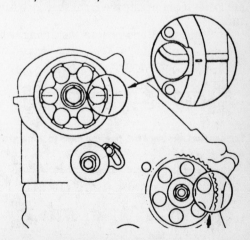

When installing a new timing belt, align it as shown
1C-L diesel engine

3A, 3A-C and 4A-C Engines 3E and 3E-E Engines

1. Remove the valve cover.
2. Drain the cooling system.

CAUTION: *When draining the coolant, keep in mind that cats and dogs are attracted by the ethylene glycol antifreeze, and are quite likely to drink any that is left in an uncovered container or in puddles on the ground. This will prove fatal in sufficient quantity. Always drain the coolant into a sealable container. Coolant should be reused unless it is contaminated or several years old.*

3. Loosen the water pump pulley bolts.
4. Remove the alternator belt.
5. Raise the vehicle and safely support it on jackstands.
6. Remove the power steering pivot bolt, if so equipped.
7. Remove the bolt which goes through both the upper and lower timing belt covers.
8. Lower the vehicle to the ground. Remove the power steering pump belt if so equipped.
9. Remove the water pump pulley.
10. Disconnect the upper radiator hose at the engine water outlet.
11. Label and disconnect vacuum hoses.
12. Remove the upper timing belt cover and its gasket.
13. At the distributor, label and disconnect the spark plug wires, the vacuum hoses and the electrical connections. Remove the distributor.
14. Disconnect the hoses at the fuel pump and remove the fuel pump.
15. Remove the distributor gear bolt.
16. Remove the rocker arm assembly.
17. Rotate the crankshaft clockwise and set the engine to TDC/compression on No. 1 cylinder. Make sure the rockers for cylinder No.1 are loose. If not, rotate the crankshaft one full turn.
18. Matchmark and remove the timing belt

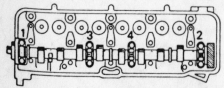

Loosen and remove 4A-C bearing caps in this order

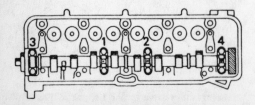

Tighten the bearing caps in this order

from the camshaft pulley. Support the belt so that it doesn't change position on the crankshaft pulley.
19. Loosen the camshaft bearing cap bolts a little at a time and in the correct sequence. After removal, label each cap.
20. Remove the camshaft oil seal (at the pulley end) and then remove the camshaft by lifting it straight out of its bearings.

NOTE: *Although reasonable in weight, the cam is brittle in nature. Handle it gently and do not allow it to fall or hit objects. It may break into pieces.*

21. When reinstalling, coat all the bearing journals with engine oil and place the camshaft in the cylinder head.
22. Place bearing caps Nos. 2, 3 and 4 on each journal with the arrows pointing towards the front of the engine.
23. Apply multi-purpose grease to the inside of the oil seal. and apply liquid sealer on the outer circumference of the oil seal.
24. Install the seal in position, being very careful to get it straight. Do not allow the seal to cock or move out of place during installation.
25. Install the bearing cap for bearing No.1 and apply silicone sealant to the lower ends of the of the seal.
26. Tighten each bearing cap little at a time and in the correct sequence. Tighten the bolts to 9 ft. lbs.
27. Hold the camshaft with an adjustable wrench and tighten the drive gear to 22 ft. lbs.
28. Install the timing belt as previously outlined.
29. Install the rocker arm assembly.
30. Install the fuel pump with a new gasket and connect the hoses.
31. Replace the distributor and connect its vacuum hoses, electrical connections and the spark plug wires.
32. Install the upper timing belt cover but don't install the bolt which holds both the upper and the lower covers yet.
33. Connect the vacuum hoses.
34. Connect the upper radiator hose to the water outlet.
35. Install the water pump pulley and tighten the bolts finger tight.
36. Install the power steering drive belt if so equipped.
37. Elevate the vehicle and safely support it on jackstands.
38. Install the bolt which connects the upper and lower timing belt covers.
39. Install the power steering pump pivot bolt and the belt; adjust the belt tension.
40. Lower the vehicle. Install the alternator belt and adjust it to the correct tension.
41. Tighten the water pump pulley bolts.

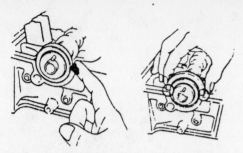

Apply sealant to these points before reinstalling the 4A-C (A series) valve cover

42. Refill the cooling system.
43. Install the valve cover with a new gasket.

4A-GE and 4A-GZE Engines

1. Remove the valve covers and the timing belt cover following procedures outlined previously in this chapter.

2. Make certain the engine is set to TDC/compression on No.1 cylinder. Remove the timing belt following procedures outlined earlier in this chapter.

3. Remove the crankshaft pulley if so desired.

4. Remove the camshaft timing belt pulleys.

5. Loosen and remove the camshaft bearing caps in the proper sequence. It it recommended that the bolts be loosened in two or three passes.

6. With the bearing caps removed, the camshaft(s) may be lifted clear of the head. If both cams are to be removed, label them clearly--they are not interchangeable.

NOTE: *Although reasonable in weight, the cam is brittle in nature. Handle it gently and do not allow it to fall or hit objects. It may break into pieces.*

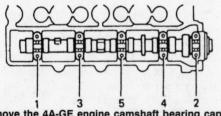

Remove the 4A-GE engine camshaft bearing caps in this order

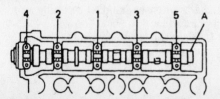

Tighten the 4A-GE bearing caps (intake and exhaust) in this order

7. When reinstalling, place the camshaft(s) in position on the head. The exhaust cam has the distributor drive gear on it. Observe the markings on the bearing caps and place them according to their numbered positions. The arrow should point to the front of the engine.

8. Tighten the bearing cap bolts in the correct sequence and in three passes to a final tightness of 9 ft. lbs.

9. Position the camshafts so that the guide pins (knock pins) are in the proper position. This step is critical to the correct valve timing of the engine.

10. Install the camshaft timing pulleys and tighten the bolts to 34 ft. lbs. Double check the positioning of the camshaft pulleys and the guide pin.

11. Double check the positioning of the camshaft pulleys and the guide pin.

12. Install the crankshaft pulley if it was removed. Tighten its bolt to 101 ft. lbs. and double check its position to be on TDC.

13. Install the timing belt and tensioner. Adjust the belt according to procedures outlined previously in this chapter.

14. Install the timing belt covers.

15. Install the valve covers.

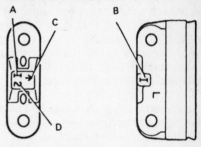

A   I = INTAKE   E = EXHAUST
B   I = INTAKE   E = EXHAUST
C   FRONT MARK
D   I.D. FOR BEARING NO. 2 THRU NO. 5

Examples of marking on camshaft bearing caps. Note that the bearing on the right is for position NO. 1 only. 4A-GE caps shown, other engines similar

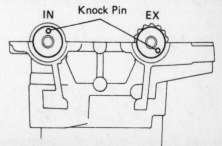

Correct position of guide pins — the exhaust camshaft has distributor drive gear 4A-GE engine

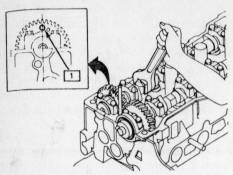

1 | SERVICE BOLT HOLE (INTAKE CAMSHAFT)

Correct position of the service bolt hole before removal of the 4A-FE intake camshaft

4A-F and 4A-FE Engines

1. Remove the valve cover.
2. Remove the timing belt covers.
3. Remove the timing belt and idler pulley following procedures outlined previously in this Chapter.
4. Hold the exhaust camshaft with an adjustable wrench and remove the camshaft timing belt gear. Be careful not to damage the head or the camshaft during this work.
5. Gently turn the camshafts with an adjustable wrench until the service bolt hole in the intake camshaft end gear is straight up or in the "12 o'clock" position.
6. Alternately loosen the bearing cap bolts in the number one (closest to the pulleys) intake and exhaust bearing caps.
7. Attach the intake camshaft end gear to the sub gear with a service bolt. The service bolt should match the following specifications:
   • Thread diameter: 6.0mm
   • Thread pitch: 1.0mm
   • Bolt length: 16–20mm
8. Uniformly loosen each intake camshaft bearing cap bolt a little at a time and in the correct sequence.

WARNING: *The camshaft must be held level while it is being removed. If the camshaft is not kept level, the portion of the cylinder head receiving the thrust may crack or*

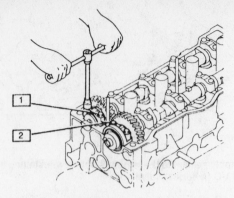

1. Intake bearing cap bolt
2. Exhaust bearing cap bolt

For the 4A-FE engine, alternately loosen the bolts for the NO. 1 bearing cap on both the intake and exhaust camshafts

become damaged. This in turn could cause the camshaft to bind or break.

Before removing the intake camshaft, make sure the rotational force has been removed from the sub gear; that is, the gear should be in a neutral or "unloaded" state.

9. Remove the bearing caps and remove the intake camshaft.

NOTE: *If the camshaft cannot be removed straight and level, retighten the No.3 bearing cap. Alternately loosen the bolts on the bearing cap a little at a time while pulling upwards on the camshaft gear. DO NOT attempt to pry or force the cam loose with tools.*

10. With the intake camshaft removed, turn the exhaust camshaft approximately 105°, so that the guide pin in the end is just past the "5 o'clock" position. This puts equal loadings on the camshaft, allowing easier and safer removal.
11. Loosen the exhaust camshaft bearing cap bolts a little at a time and in the correct sequence.
12. Remove the bearing caps and remove the exhaust camshaft.

NOTE: *If the camshaft cannot be removed straight and level, retighten the No.3 bearing cap. Alternately loosen the bolts on the bearing cap a little at a time while pulling upwards on the camshaft gear. DO NOT attempt to pry or force the cam loose with tools.*

13. When reinstalling, remember that the camshafts must be handled carefully and kept straight and level to avoid damage.
14. Place the exhaust camshaft on the cylinder head so that the cam lobes press evenly on the lifters for cylinders Nos. 1 and 3. This will put the guide pin in the "just past 5 o'clock" position.
15. Place the bearing caps in position according to the number cast into the cap. The arrow

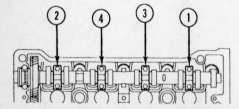

On the 4A-FE engine, remove the camshaft bearing caps in this order. Intake cam shown, exhaust cam uses identical order

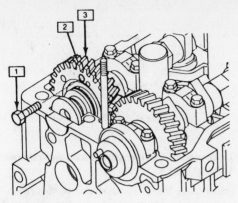

1. Service bolt
2. Sub-gear
3. Main gear

Always install a service bolt to lock the intake cam gears together

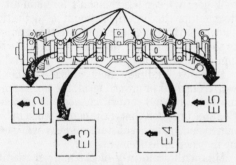

Examples of bearing cap markings and position. 4A-FE engine exhaust cam shown

should point towards the pulley end of the motor.

16. Tighten the bearing cap bolts gradually and in the proper sequence to 9.5 ft. lbs. (115 INCH lbs.)

17. Apply multi-purpose grease, to a new exhaust camshaft oil seal.

18. Install the exhaust camshaft oil seal using a special tool or similar. Be very careful not to install the seal on a slant or allow it to tilt during installation.

19. Turn the exhaust cam until the cam lobes of No.4 cylinder press down on their lifters.

20. Hold the intake camshaft next to the exhaust camshaft and engage the gears by matching the alignment marks on each gear.

21. Keeping the gears engaged, roll the intake camshaft down and into its bearing journals.

22. Place the bearing caps for Nos. 2,3,4 and 5 in position. Observe the numbers on each cap and make certain the arrows point to the pulley end of the motor.

23. Gradually tighten each bearing cap bolt

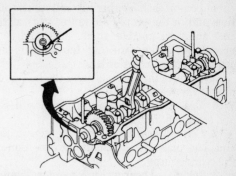

Setting the 4A-FE engine exhaust cam guide pin to the just past 5 o'clock position

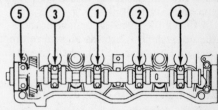

Tighten the 4A-FE engine camshaft bearing cap bolts in this order. Exhaust cam shown, intake uses identical order

in the same order as the exhaust camshaft bolts. Tighten each bolt to 9.5 ft. lbs.

24. Remove any retaining pins or bolts in the intake camshaft gears.

25. Install the number one bearing cap for the intake camshaft.

NOTE: *If the No.1 bearing cap does not fit properly, gently push the cam gear towards the rear of the engine by levering between the gear and the head.*

26. Turn the exhaust camshaft one full revolution from TDC/compression on No.1 cylinder to the same position. Check that the mark on the exhaust camshaft gear matches exactly with the mark on the intake camshaft gear.

27. Counterhold the exhaust camshaft and install the timing belt pulley. Tighten the bolt to 43 ft. lbs.

28. Double check both the crankshaft and camshaft positions, insuring that they are both set to TDC/compression for No.1 cylinder.

29. Install the timing belt following procedures outlined previously in this Chapter.

30. Install the timing belt covers and the valve cover.

1C-L Diesel Engine

NOTE: *Refer to the Camshaft and Bearing Removal and Installation service procedure for 3A, 3A-C and 4A-C Engines-use torque sequence as a guide-modify as necessary.*

1. Remove the cylinder head as outlined.
2. Remove the exhaust manifold.
3. Remove the camshaft oil seal retainer.

4. Loosen each bearing cap bolt a little at a time and in the proper sequence; start at the ends and work in (refer to 3A, 3A-C and 4A-C procedure). Make sure that the bearing caps are kept in the proper order.

5. Remove the camshaft and the half-circle plug at the rear of the head.

6. Coat the half-circle plug with adhesive and position it in the cylinder head.

7. Coat all bearing journals lightly with oil and then place the camshaft into position on the cylinder head.

8. Install the bearing caps in order. Tighten the cap bolts in two or three stages until they reach a final torque (refer to 3A, 3A-C and 4A-C procedure) of 13 ft. lbs.

9. Check the thrust and oil clearances.

10. Apply adhesive to the oil seal retainer as shown and then install it onto the cylinder head.

11. Installation of the remaining components is in the reverse order of removal.

INSPECTION AND MEASUREMENT

The end play or thrust clearance of the camshaft(s) must be measured with the camshaft installed in the head. It may be checked before removal or after reinstallation. To check the end play, mount a dial indicator accurate to ten one-thousandths (four decimal places) on the

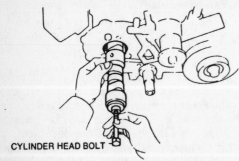

CYLINDER HEAD BOLT

Use a long service bolt to remove and install the camshaft

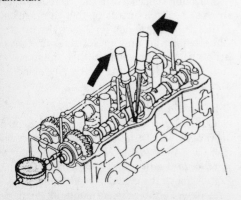

Checking camshaft endplay

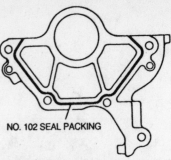

NO. 102 SEAL PACKING

Use sealant when installing the oil seal retainer 1C-L diesel engine

end of the block, so that the tip bears on the end of the camshaft. (The timing belt must be removed. On some motors, it will be necessary to remove the pulleys for unobstructed access to the camshaft.) Set the scale on the dial indicator to zero. Using a screwdriver or similar tool, gently lever the camshaft fore-and-aft in its mounts. Record the amount of deflection shown on the gauge and compare this number to the Camshaft Specifications Chart at the beginning of this Chapter.

Excessive end-play may indicate either a worn camshaft or a worn head; the worn cam is most likely and much cheaper to replace. Chances are good that if the cam is worn in this dimension (axial), substantial wear will show up in other measurements.

Mount the cam in V-blocks and set the dial indicator up on the round center journal. Zero the dial and rotate the camshaft. The circular runout should not exceed 0.06mm on the 4A-C or 0.04mm on the 4A-GE and 4A-FE motors (use these specifications as a replacement guide for all other engines). Excess runout means the cam must be replaced.

Using a micrometer or Vernier caliper, measure the diameter of all the journals and the height of all the lobes. Record the readings and compare them to the Camshaft Specifications Chart in the beginning of this Chapter. Any measurement beyond the stated limits indicates wear and the camshaft must be replaced.

Lobe wear is generally accompanied by scoring or visible metal damage on the lobes. Overhead camshaft engines are very sensitive to proper lubrication with clean, fresh oil. A worn cam may be your report card for poor maintenance intervals and late oil changes.

If a new cam is required on single cam engine, order new rockers to accompany it so that there are two new surfaces in contact. On the twin-cam motors, a new cam will require readjusting the valves, so new shims are in order. If, by coincidence, one valve measures out the same as before, replace the present shim with a new one to get two new surfaces in contact.

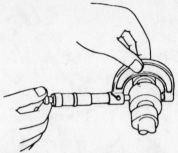

Use a micrometer to check the camshaft journal diameter

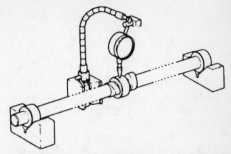

Use a dial indicator to check the run-out (eccentricity) of the center camshaft bearing

The clearance between the camshaft and its journals (bearings) must also be measured. Clean the camshaft, the journals and the bearing caps of any remaining oil and place the camshaft in position on the head. Lay a piece of compressible gauging material (Plastigage® or similar) on top of each journal on the cam.

Install the bearing caps in their correct order with the arrows pointing towards the front (pulley end) of the motor. Install the bearing cap bolts and tighten them in three passes to the correct tightness of 9 ft. lbs. (most engines).

NOTE: *Do not turn the camshaft with the gauging material installed.*

Remove the bearing caps (in the correct order) and measure the gauging material at its widest point by comparing it to the scale provided with the package. Compare these measurements to the Camshaft Specifications Chart at the beginning of this Chapter. Any measurement beyond specifications indicates wear. If you have already measured the cam (or replaced it) and determined it to be usable, excess bearing clearance indicates the need for a new head due to wear of the journals.

Remove the camshaft from the head and remove all traces of the gauging material. Check carefully for any small pieces clinging to contact faces.

Pistons and Connecting Rods

REMOVAL AND INSTALLATION

All Engines

NOTE: *These procedures may be performed with the engine in the car. If additional overhaul work is to be performed, it will be easier if the engine is removed and mounted on an engine stand. Most stands allow the block to be rotated, giving easy access to both the top and bottom. These procedures require certain hand tools which may not be in your tool box. A cylinder ridge reamer, a numbered punch set, piston ring expander, snap-ring tools and piston installation tool (ring compressor) are all necessary for correct piston and rod repair. These tools are commonly avail-*

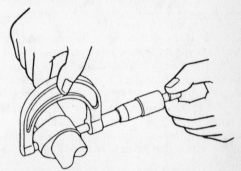

Measure the height of each camshaft lobe. Wear may be caused by infrequent oil changes

able from retail tool suppliers; you may be able to rent them from larger automotive supply houses.

1. Remove the cylinder head.
2. Elevate and safely support the vehicle on jackstands.
3. Drain the engine oil

CAUTION: *Used motor oil may cause skin cancer if repeatedly left in contact with the skin for prolonged periods. Although this is unlikely unless you handle oil on a daily*

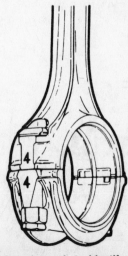

Use a numbered punch to identify both parts of each connecting rod with its cylinder number

basis, it is wise to thoroughly wash your hands with soap and water immediately after handling used motor oil.

4. Remove any splash shield or rock guards which are in the way and remove the oil pan.

5. Using a numbered punch set, mark the cylinder number on each piston rod and bearing cap. Do this BEFORE loosening any bolts.

6. Loosen and remove the rod cap nuts and the rod caps. It will probably be necessary to tap the caps loose; do so with a small plastic mallet or other soft-faced tool. Keep the bearing insert with the cap when it is removed.

7. Use short pieces of hose to cover the bolt threads; this protects the bolt, the crankshaft and the cylinder walls during removal.

8. One piston will be at the lowest point in its cylinder. Cover the top of this piston with a rag. Examine the top area of the cylinder with your fingers, looking for a noticeable ridge around the cylinder. If any ridge is felt, it must be carefully removed by using the ridge reamer. Work with extreme care to avoid cutting too deeply.

When the ridge is removed, carefully remove the rag and ALL the shavings from the cylinder. No metal cuttings may remain in the cylinder or the wall will be damaged when the piston is removed. A small magnet can be helpful in removing the fine shavings.

9. After the cylinder is de-ridged, squirt a liberal coating of engine oil onto the cylinder

RIDGE CAUSED BY CYLINDER WEAR

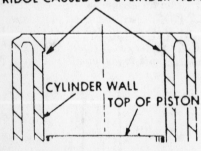

Push the piston out with a hammer handle

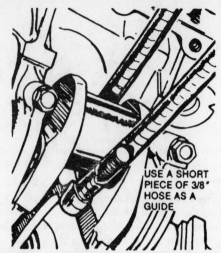

USE A SHORT PIECE OF 3/8" HOSE AS A GUIDE

Use lengths of vacuum hose or rubbing tubing to protect the crankshaft journals and cylinder walls during piston installation

walls until evenly coated. Carefully push the piston and rod assembly upwards from the bottom by using a wooden hammer handle on the bottom of the connecting rod.

10. The next lowest piston should be gently pushed downwards from above. This will cause the crankshaft to turn and relocate the other pistons as well. When the piston is in its lowest position, repeat Steps 8 and 9. Repeat the procedure for each of the remaining pistons.

11. When all the pistons are removed, clean the block and cylinder walls thoroughly with solvent.

12. When ready for reassembly, remember that all the pistons, rods and caps must be reinstalled in the correct cylinder. Make certain that all labels and stamped numbers are present and legible. Double check the piston rings; make certain that the ring gaps DO NOT line up, but are evenly spaced around the piston at about 120° intervals. Double check the bearing insert at the bottom of the rod for proper mounting. Reinstall the protective rubber hose pieces on the bolts.

13. Liberally coat the cylinder walls and the crankshaft journals with clean, fresh engine oil. Also apply oil to the bearing surfaces on the connecting rod and the cap.

14. Identify the "Front" mark on each piston and rod and position the piston loosely in its cylinder with the marks facing the front (pulley end) of the motor.

WARNING: *Failure to observe the "Front" marking and its correct placement can lead to sudden engine failure.*

15. Install the ring compressor (piston installation tool) around one piston and tighten it gently until the rings are compressed almost completely.

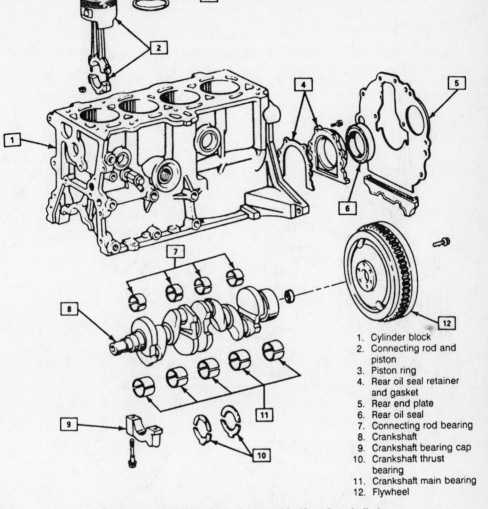

1. Cylinder block
2. Connecting rod and piston
3. Piston ring
4. Rear oil seal retainer and gasket
5. Rear end plate
6. Rear oil seal
7. Connecting rod bearing
8. Crankshaft
9. Crankshaft bearing cap
10. Crankshaft thrust bearing
11. Crankshaft main bearing
12. Flywheel

Component detail 4A-C block assembly (A series similar)

16. Gently push down on the piston top with a wooden hammer handle or similar soft-faced tool and drive the piston into the cylinder bore. Once all three rings are within the bore, the piston will move with some ease.

NOTE: *If any resistance or binding is encountered during the installation, DO NOT apply force. Tighten or adjust the ring compressor and/or reposition the piston. Brute force will break the ring(s) or damage the piston.*

17. From underneath, pull the connecting rod into place on the crankshaft. Remove the rubber hoses from the bolts. Check the rod cap to confirm that the bearing is present and correctly mounted, then install the rod cap (observing the correct number and position) and its nuts. Leaving the nuts finger tight will make installation of the remaining pistons and rods easier.

18. Assemble the remaining pistons in the same fashion, repeating Steps 15, 16 and 17.

19. With all the pistons installed and the bearing caps secured finger tight, the retaining nuts may be tightened to their final setting. For each pair of nuts, make three passes alternating between the two nuts on any given rod cap. The intent is to draw each cap up to the crank straight and under even pressure at the nuts.

20. Turn the crankshaft through several clockwise rotations, making sure everything moves smoothly and there is no binding. With the piston rods connected, the crank may be stiff to turn--try to turn it in a smooth continuous motion so that any binding or stiff spots may be felt.

21. Reinstall the oil pan. Even if the engine is to remain apart for other repairs, install the oil pan to protect the bottom end and tighten the bolts to the correct specification-this elimi-

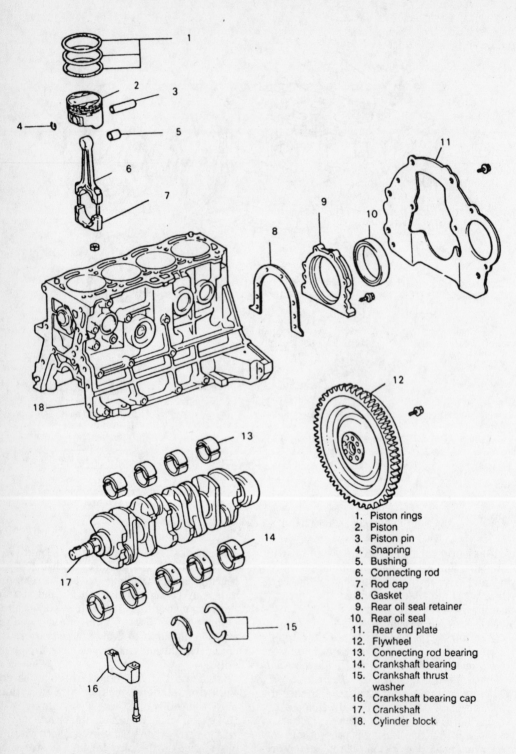

1. Piston rings
2. Piston
3. Piston pin
4. Snapring
5. Bushing
6. Connecting rod
7. Rod cap
8. Gasket
9. Rear oil seal retainer
10. Rear oil seal
11. Rear end plate
12. Flywheel
13. Connecting rod bearing
14. Crankshaft bearing
15. Crankshaft thrust
    washer
16. Crankshaft bearing cap
17. Crankshaft
18. Cylinder block

Component detail 4A-GE and 4A-FE block assemblies (other engine similar)

nates one easily overlooked mistake during future reassembly.

22. If the engine is to remain apart for other repairs, pack the cylinders with crumpled newspaper or clean rags (to keep out dust and grit) and cover the top of the motor with a large rag. If the engine is on a stand, the whole block can be protected with a large plastic trash bag.

23. If no further work is to be performed, continue reassembly by installing the head, timing belt, etc.

24. When the engine is restarted after reassembly, the exhaust will be very smoky as the oil within the cylinders burns off. This is normal; the smoke should clear quickly during warm up. Depending on the condition of the spark plugs, it may be wise to check for any oil fouling after the engine is shut off.

CLEANING AND INSPECTION

Pistons

With the pistons removed from the engine, use a ring removing tool (ring expander) to remove the rings. Keep the rings labeled and stored by piston number. Clearly label the pistons by number so that they do not get interchanged.

Clean the carbon from the piston top and sides with a stiff bristle brush and cleaning solvent. Do not use a wire brush for cleaning.

CAUTION: *Wear goggles during this cleaning; the solvent is very strong and can cause eye damage.*

Clean the ring grooves (lands) either with a specially designed tool or with a piece of a broken piston ring. Remove all the carbon from the grooves and make sure that the groove

shape (profile) is square all the way around the piston. When all the lands have been cleaned, again bathe the piston in solvent and clean the lands with the bristle brush.

Before any measurements are begun, visually examine the piston (a magnifying glass can be handy) for any signs of cracks--particularly in the skirt area--or scratches in the metal. Anything other than light surface scoring disqualifies the piston from further use. The metal will become unevenly heated and the piston may break apart during use.

Hold the piston and rod upright and attempt to move the piston back and forth along the piston pin (wrist pin). There should be NO motion in this axis. If there is, replace the piston and wrist pin.

Accurately measure the cylinder bore diame-

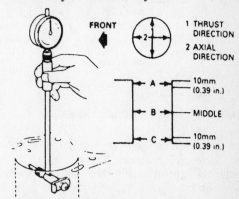

Checking the cylinder bore requires 6 measurements — 3 locations and 2 dimensions in each cylinder

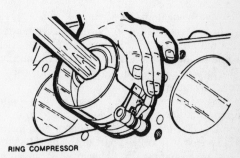

Install the piston using a ring compressor

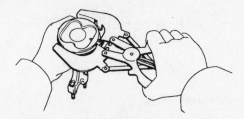

Removing the piston rings with a ring expander

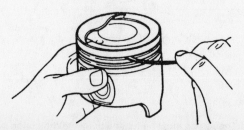

A piece of broken ring serves well to clean piston grooves

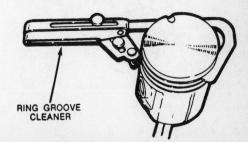

The ring grooves can be cleaned and de-carboned with a special tool

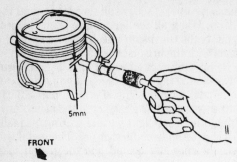

Measuring the 4A-C piston diameter

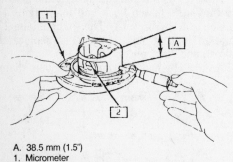

A. 38.5 mm (1.5")
1. Micrometer
2. Piston hole center line

Measuring the 4A-FE piston diameter

ter in two dimensions (thrust and axial, or if you prefer, left-right and fore-aft) and in three locations (upper, middle and bottom) within the cylinder. That's six measurements in each bore; record them in order. Normal measurements on most engines (use these service specifications as replacement guide) are:
• New: 81.0–81.03mm
• Max Wear limit: 81.23mm
Having recorded the bore measurements, now measure the piston diameter. Do this with a micrometer at right angles to the piston pin. The location at which the piston is measured varies by engine type:
• 3A, 3A-C and 4A-C: Measure at a point 5mm from lower edge of the oil ring groove.
• 4A-GE and 4A-GZE: Measure at a point 42mm from the longest part of the piston skirt.
• 4A-FE and 4A-F: Measure at a point 38.5mm from the longest part of the piston

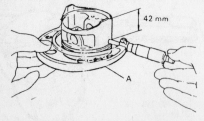

A MICROMETER

Measuring the 4A-GE piston diameter. 42mm = 1.65 in.

skirt. Record each measurement for each piston. Use these specifications as a guide for internal engine component replacement.

The piston-to-cylinder wall clearance (sometimes called oil clearance) is determined by subtracting the piston diameter from the measured diameter of its respective cylinder. The difference will be in thousandths or ten-thousandths of an inch. Compare this number to the Piston and Ring Specifications Chart at the beginning of this Chapter. Excess clearance may indicate the need for either new pistons or block reboring.

Connecting rods

The connecting rods must be free from wear, cracking and bending. Visually examine the rod, particularly at its upper and lower ends. Look for any sign of metal stretching or wear. The piston pin should fit cleanly and tightly through the upper end, allowing no side play or wobble. The bottom end should also be an exact $1/2$ circle, with no deformity of shape. The bolts must be firmly mounted and parallel.

The rods may be taken to a machine shop for exact measurement of twist or bend. This is generally easier and cheaper than purchasing a seldom used rod-alignment tool.

PISTON PIN (WRIST PIN) REPLACEMENT

NOTE: *The piston and pin are a matched set and must be kept together. Label everything and store parts in identified containers.*

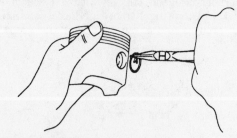

Remove the circlip

The piston must be heated to install the piston pin. At 176°F, the pin should push in with thumb pressure

1. Remove the pistons from the engine and remove the rings from the pistons.

2. Remove the snapring at the ends of the piston pin. This may be done with either snapring pliers or needle-nosed pliers; don't try to lever it out with a screwdriver.

3. Support the piston and rod on its side in a press. Make certain the piston is square to the motion of the press and that the rod is completely supported with blocks. Leave open space below the piston for the pin to emerge.

4. Line up the press and insert a brass rod of the same or slightly smaller diameter as the piston pin. It is important that the rod press evenly on the entire face of the pin, but not on the piston itself.

5. Using smooth and controlled motion, press the pin free of the piston. Do not use sudden or jerky motions; the piston may crack.

6. When reassembling, identify the front of the piston by its small dot or cavity on the top. Identify the front of the piston rod by the small mark cast into one face of the rod. Make sure the marks on the piston and rod are both facing the same direction. Also insure that the correct piston pin is to be reinstalled--they are not interchangeable.

7. On some model engines, install one snapring in the piston and insert the piston under the press with the snap-ring down. Position the rod and support it. Coat the piston pin with clean oil and press it into place, using the same press set-up as removal. The piston pin will bottom onto the snap-ring; don't force it beyond the stopping point. Install the other snapring to lock the pin in place.

8. On some model engines, install one snapring. Place the piston in water and gradually heat the water to the boiling point. DO NOT drop the piston into already hot water.

The minimum required temperature is 176° (80°C); a little hotter makes it a little easier. This will expand the piston so that the pin will fit smoothly. While the water is heating, apply a coat of clean oil to the piston pin and have the pin at hand when the piston is removed from the water.

CAUTION: *You are dealing with hot metal and boiling water. Tongs, thick heat-resistant gloves and towels are required.*

Remove the piston from the boiling water (carefully) and hold it with gloves or several towels. Making sure the front marks align on the piston and connecting rod, hold the rod in position and press the piston pin into place with your thumb. The pin will bottom against the snapring. Allow the piston to air cool and when it is cool to the touch, install the other snapring. Check that the piston rocks freely on its pin without binding.

PISTON RING REPLACEMENT

NOTE: *Although a piston ring can be reused if in good condition and carefully removed, it is recommended that the rings be replaced with new ones any time they are removed from the pistons.*

A piston ring expander is necessary for removing piston rings without damaging them; any other method (screwdriver blades, pliers, etc.) usually results in the rings becoming bent, scratched or broken. When the rings are removed, clean the grooves thoroughly with a bristle brush and solvent. Make sure that all traces of carbon and varnish are removed.

WARNING: *Wear goggles during this cleaning; the solvent is very strong and can cause eye damage. Do not use a wire brush or a caustic solvent on the pistons.*

Check the piston condition and diameter following procedures outlined earlier in this Chapter. Piston ring end gap should be checked when the rings are removed from the pistons.

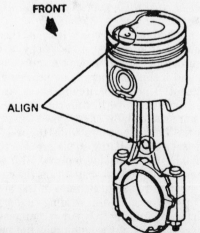

Align the piston and connecting rod "front" marks before reassembly

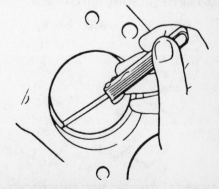

Checking the piston ring end gap

Incorrect end gap indicates that the wrong size rings are being used; ring breakage could occur.

Squirt some clean oil into the cylinder so that the top 50–75mm (2–3 in.) of the wall is covered. Gently compress one of the rings to be used and insert it into the cylinder. Use and upside-down piston and push the ring down about 25mm (1 in.) below the top of the cylinder. Using the piston to push the ring keeps the ring square in the cylinder; if it gets crooked, the next measurement may be inaccurate.

Using a feeler gauge, measure the end gap in the ring and compare it to the Piston and Ring Specifications chart at the beginning of this Chapter. If the gap is excessive, either the ring is incorrect or the cylinder walls are worn beyond acceptable limits. If the measurement is too tight, the ends of the ring may be filed to enlarge the gap after the ring is removed form the cylinder. If filing is needed, make certain that the ends are kept square and that a fine file is used.

Check the pistons to see that the ring grooves and oil return holes have been properly cleaned. Slide each piston ring into its groove and check the side clearance with a feeler gauge. Make sure you insert the feeler gauge between the ring and its lower edge; any wear that develops forms a step at the inner portion of the lower land. If the piston grooves have worn to the extent that fairly high steps exist on the lower land, the piston must be replaced.

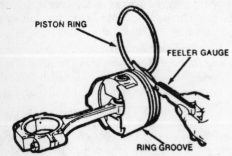

Checking the piston ring side clearance

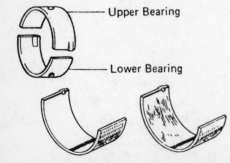

Examples of upper and lower bearing shells. Note the position of the oil hole

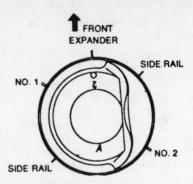

Piston ring positioning

Rings are not sold in oversize thicknesses to compensate for ring groove wear.

Using the ring expander, install the rings on the piston, *lowest ring first.* There is a high risk of ring breakage or piston damage if the rings are installed by hand or without the expander. The correct spacing of the ring end gaps is critical to oil control. No two gaps should align, they should be evenly spaced around the piston with the gap in the oil ring expander facing the front of the piston (aligned with the mark on the top of the piston). Once the rings are installed, the pistons must be handled carefully and protected from dirt and impact.

CONNECTING ROD BEARING REPLACEMENT

Connecting rod bearings on all engines consist of two halves or shells which are not interchangeable in the rod and cap. When the shells are in position, the ends extend slightly beyond the rod and cap surfaces so that when the bolts are tightened, the shells will be clamped tightly in place. This insures a positive seating and prevents turning. A small tang holds the shells in place within the cap and rod housings.

NOTE: *The ends of the bearing shells must never be filed flush with the mating surface of the rod or cap.*

If a rod becomes noisy or is worn so that its clearance on the crankshaft is sloppy, a new bearing of the correct undersize must be selected and installed. There is no provision for adjustment. Under no circumstances should the rod end or cap be filed to compensate for wear, nor should shims of any type be used.

Inspect the rod bearings while the rods are out of the engine. If the shells are scored or show flaking they should be replaced. ANY scoring or ridge on the crankshaft means the crankshaft must be replaced. Because of the metallurgy in the crankshaft, welding and/or regrinding the crankshaft is not recommended. The bearing faces of the crank may not be restored to their original condition causing premature bearing wear and possible failure.

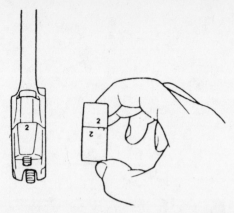

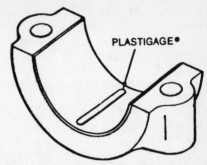

Plastic measuring material installed on the lower bearing shell

Look for the manufacturer's codes to identify standard bearing sizes. Don't confuse the number on the rod end caps with its position (cylinder) number

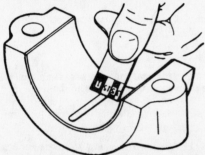

Measure the compressed plastic to determine the bearing clearance

Replacement bearings are available in three standard sizes marked either "1", "2" or "3" on the bearing shell and possibly on the rod cap. Do not confuse the mark on the bearing cap with the cylinder number. It is quite possible that No. 3 piston rod contains a number 1 size bearing. The rod cap may have a "1" marked on it. (You should have stamped a 3 or other identifying code on both halves of the rod before disassembly.)

Measuring the clearance between the connecting rod bearings and the crankshaft (oil clearance) is done with a plastic measuring material such as Plastigage® or similar product.

1. Remove the rod cap with the bearing shell. Completely clean the cap, bearing shells and the journal on the crankshaft. Blow any oil from the oil hole in the crank. The plastic measuring material is soluble in oil and will begin to dissolve if the area is not totally free of oil.

2. Place a piece of the measuring material lengthwise along the bottom center of the lower bearing shell. Install the cap and shell and tighten the bolts in three passes to specifications.

NOTE: *Do not turn the crankshaft with the measuring material installed.*

3. Remove the bearing cap with the shell. The flattened plastic material will be found sticking to either the bearing shell or the crank journal. DO NOT remove it yet.

4. Use the scale printed on the packaging for the measuring material to measure the flattened plastic at its widest point. The number within the scale which is closest to the width of the plastic indicates the bearing clearance in thousandths of an inch.

5. Check the specifications chart in the beginning of this Chapter for the proper clearance. If there is any measurement is approaching the maximum acceptable value, replace the bearing.

6. When the correct bearing is determined, clean off the gauging material, oil the bearing thoroughly on its working face and install it in the cap. Install the other half of the bearing into the rod end and attach the cap to the rod. Tighten the nuts evenly, in three passes to specifications.

7. With the proper bearing installed and the nuts properly tightened, it should be possible to move the connecting rod back and forth a bit on the crankshaft. If the rod cannot be moved, either the bearing is too small or the rod is misaligned.

Rear Main Seal

REMOVAL AND INSTALLATION

All Models and Engines

1. Remove the transmission/transaxle from the vehicle. Follow procedures outlined in Chapter 7.

2. If equipped with a manual transmission/transaxle, perform the following procedures:

  a. Matchmark the pressure plate and flywheel.

  b. Remove the pressure plate-to-flywheel bolts and the clutch assembly from the vehicle.

  c. Remove the flywheel-to-crankshaft bolts and the flywheel. The flywheel is a moderately heavy component. Handle it carefully and protect it on the workbench.

3. If equipped with an automatic transmission/transaxle, perform the following procedures:

    a. Matchmark the flywheel (flexplate or drive plate) and crankshaft.

    b. Remove the torque converter drive plate-to-crankshaft bolts and the torque converter drive plate.

4. Remove the bolts holding the rear end plate to the engine and the remove the rear end plate.

5. Remove the rear oil seal retainer-to-engine bolts, rear oil seal retainer to oil pan bolts and the rear oil seal retainer.

6. Using a small pry bar, pry the rear oil seal retainer from the mating surfaces.

7. Using a drive punch or a hammer and small screwdriver, drive the oil seal from the rear bearing retainer.

8. Using a putty knife, clean the gasket mounting surfaces. Make certain that the con-

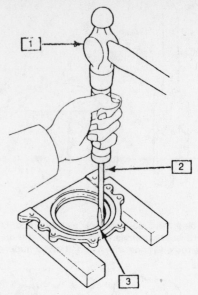

1. Hammer
2. Screwdriver
3. Rear main oil seal

Removing the rear main oil seal from the retainer. Note the supports under the housing

tact surfaces are completely free of oil and foreign matter.

NOTE: *When removing the rear oil seal, be careful not to damage the seal mounting surface.*

9. Clean the oil seal mounting surface.

10. Using multi-purpose grease, lubricate the new seal lips.

11. Using a seal installation tool or similar, tap the seal straight into the bore of the retainer.

12. Position a new gasket on the retainer and coat it lightly with gasket sealer. Fit the seal retainer into place on the motor; be careful when installing the oil seal over the crankshaft.

13. Install the six retaining bolts and tighten them to 7 ft. lbs.(84 INCH lbs.)

14. Install the rear end plate. Tighten its bolts to 7.5 ft. lbs. (90 INCH lbs.).

15. Reinstall either the flexplate (automatic) or the flywheel (manual), carefully observing the matchmarks made earlier. Tighten the flexplate bolts or the flywheel bolts specifications.

16. Install the torque converter (automatic) or the clutch disc and pressure plate (manual).

17. Reinstall the transmission/transaxle, following procedures outlined in Chapter 7.

Crankshaft and Main Bearings

REMOVAL AND INSTALLATION

1. Remove the engine assembly from the car, following procedures outlined earlier in

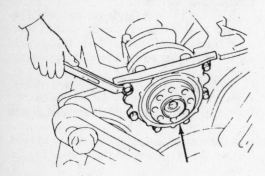

Removing the rear oil seal retainer

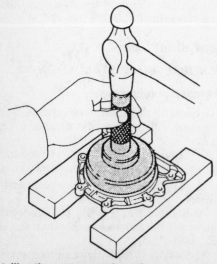

Installing the new rear main seal

this Chapter. Mount the engine securely on a stand which allows it to be rotated.

2. Remove the timing belt and tensioner assemblies.

3. Turn the engine upside down on the stand. Remove the oil pan and the oil strainer.

4. Remove the oil pump.

5. Remove either the clutch and pressure plate (manual transmission/transaxle).

6. Remove either the flywheel (manual) or the drive plate (automatic).

7. Remove the rear end plate.

8. Remove the rear oil seal retainer.

9. Using a numbered punch set, mark each connecting rod cap with its correct cylinder number. Remove the rod caps and their bearings; keep the bearings with their respective caps.

10. Measure the crankshaft endplay (thrust clearance) before removing the crank. Attach a dial indicator to the end of the block and set the tip to bear on the front end of the crankshaft. With a screw driver, gently move the crankshaft back and forth and record the reading shown on the dial.

- Standard Endplay, new: 0.02mm
- Acceptable Endplay
    4A-C: 0.020–0.185mm
    All others: 0.02–0.22mm
- Maximum allowable: 0.3mm

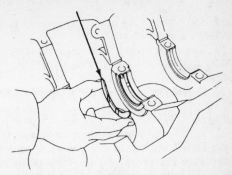

Correct position of the upper thrust washer when reinstalling

If the end play is excessive, the thrust washers will need to be replaced as a set.

11. Gradually loosen and remove the main bearing cap bolts in three passes and in the correct order. Remove just the bolts, leaving the caps in place.

12. When all the bolts are removed, use two bolts placed in the No. 3 bearing cap to wiggle the cap back and forth. This will loosen the cap and allow it and the thrust washers to be removed. Note and/or label the thrust washers as to their placement and position. If they are to be reused, they must be reinstalled exactly as they were.

13. Remove the remaining caps. Keep the caps in order and keep the bearing shell with its respective cap.

14. Lift the crankshaft out of the block. The crankshaft is a moderately heavy component.

15. Remove the upper bearing shells from the block and place them in order with the corresponding bearing caps.

16. Check and measure the crankshaft and bearings according to the procedures give in "Cleaning and Inspection" later in this section.

17. When reassembling, clean the bearing caps and journals in the block thoroughly. Coat the bearings with a liberal application of clean motor oil.

18. Fit the upper bearings halves into the

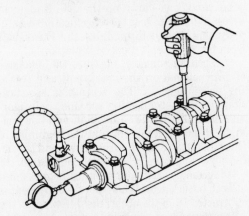

Use dial indicator to measure crankshaft endplay

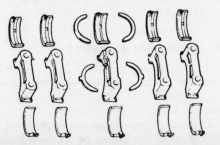

Keep all pieces in numbered order. Exact reassembly is required

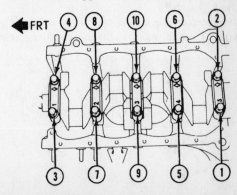

Remove the main bearing cap bolts in this order

block and position the lower bearing halves in the bearing caps.

19. Place the crankshaft into the engine block, making sure it fits exactly into its mounts.

20. Install the upper thrust washers on the center main bearing with the oil grooves facing outward.

21. Install the main bearing caps and the lower thrust washers in the proper sequence. Make sure the arrows on the caps point towards the front (pulley end) of the motor.

22. Tighten the cap bolts in three passes and in the correct sequence to specifications.

23. Double check the endplay of the crankshaft by repeating Step 10 of this procedure.

24. Turn the crankshaft through one or two full clockwise rotations, making sure that it turns smoothly and evenly with no binding.

25. Attach the piston rods, following procedures given earlier in this Chapter. Remember that the rod caps must be reinstalled in their original positions.

26. Install a new rear main oil seal into the retainer and install the retainer onto the block. Tighten the bolts to 7.0 ft. lbs. (84 INCH lbs.).

27. Install the rear end plate on the engine.

28. Install either the drive plate (automatic) or the flywheel (manual), observing the matchmarks made during removal.

29. If equipped with a manual transmission/transaxle, reinstall the clutch disc and pressure plate.

30. Install the oil pump.

31. Install the oil strainer and oil pan, using new gaskets.

32. Rotate the engine into its upright position and continue reassembly of the timing belt, idler pulley and covers.

33. Reinstall the engine in the car, following procedures outlined earlier in this Chapter.

CLEANING AND INSPECTION

With the crankshaft removed from the engine, clean the crank, bearings and block areas thoroughly. Visually inspect each crankshaft section for any sign of wear or damage, paying close attention to the main bearing jour-

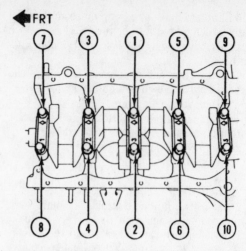

Install and tighten the main bearing cap bolts in this order

nals. ANY scoring or ridge on the crankshaft means the crankshaft must be replaced. Because of the metallurgy in the crankshaft, welding and/or regrinding the crankshaft is not recommended. The bearing faces of the crank may not be restored to their original condition causing premature bearing wear and possible failure.

Mount the crankshaft on V-blocks and set a dial indicator to bear on the center main journal. Slowly rotate the crank and record the circular runout as shown on the dial. Runout in excess of 0.06mm (use this specification as a replacement guide) disqualifies the crankshaft from further use. It must be replaced.

Using a micrometer, measure the diameter of each journal on the crankshaft and record the measurements. The acceptable specifications for both connecting rod and main journals are found in the Crankshaft and Connecting Rod specifications chart at the beginning of this Chapter. If ANY journal is beyond the acceptable range, the crank must be replaced.

Additionally, each journal must be measured at both outer edges. When one measurement is subtracted from the other, the difference is the measurement of journal taper. Any taper beyond 0.2mm is a sign of excess wear on the journal; the crankshaft must be replaced.

BEARING REPLACEMENT

1. With the engine out of the car and inverted on a stand, remove the main bearing caps in the correct sequence, following procedures given earlier in this section.

2. Once the bearing caps are removed, the lower bearing shell may be inspected. Check closely for scoring or abrasion of the bearing surface. If this lower bearing is worn or damaged,

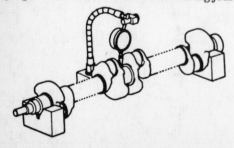

Measuring crankshaft run-out

both the upper and lower half should be replaced.

NOTE: *Always replace bearing shells in complete pairs.*

3. If the lower bearing half is in good condition, the upper shell may also be considered usable.

4. The bearing shells, the crank throws and the flat surface of the engine block (on the oil pan face) are stamped with numbers (1 through 5) indicating the standard bearing size. This size is determined during the initial manufacturing and assembly process; replacement bearings must be of the same code (thickness) if the correct clearances are to be maintained.

If the code on the bearing shell is unreadable, use the number on the block and the number on the crank throw to determine the bearing code. Refer to the proper selection chart to find the correct bearing for that position.

Cylinder Block

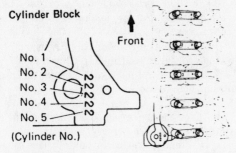

(Cylinder No.)

Crankshaft

Front

No. 1   No. 2   No. 3   No. 4   No. 5
(Cylinder No.)

Bearing

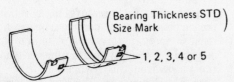

$\begin{pmatrix} \text{Bearing Thickness STD} \\ \text{Size Mark} \end{pmatrix}$

1, 2, 3, 4 or 5

Location of main bearing codes (most engines)

Crankshaft Block Mark	1	2	3	1	2	3	1	2	3
Crankshaft Mark	0	0	0	1	1	1	2	2	2
Bearing Mark	1	2	3	3	2	4	3	4	5

Main bearing selection table 4A-FE engine

Measure each journal at its outer points to determine taper

Cylinder Block No.	1	2	3	1	2	3	1	2	3
Crankshaft No.	0	0	0	1	1	1	2	2	2
Bearing No.	1	2	3	2	3	4	3	4	5

Example: Block mark "2", crankshaft mark "1" = bearing "3"

Main bearing selection table for 4A-C and 4A-GE engines

5. Lift the crankshaft from the engine block and remove the upper bearing shells. Clean the area thoroughly, allow the surfaces to air dry and coat all the journals with a liberal coating of clean engine oil.

6. Coat the new bearings to be installed with clean engine oil and install them in the block. Carefully place the crankshaft in position.

7. Do not oil the lower bearing shells or the caps at this time. Install the bearing shells into the clean, dry caps.

8. Place a piece of plastic gauging material (such as Plastigage® or similar) lengthwise (fore-and-aft) across the full width of each of the five crankshaft main bearing journals. Remember that the measuring material is dissolved by oil. Keep the exposed part of the crank clean and dry.

9. Install the bearing caps with their bearing shells in their correct location and with the arrows pointing towards the front of the motor.

10. Install the bearing cap bolts and tighten them in three passes and in the correct sequence to specifications.

NOTE: *Do not rotate the crankshaft with the measuring plastic installed.*

11. Observing the correct removal sequence, gradually loosen and remove the bearing cap bolts. Carefully remove the bearing caps; the measuring media will be stuck to either the inside of the bearing shell or the face of the crankshaft.

12. Using the scale provided with the package of the measuring media, measure the gauging material at its widest point. This measurement represents the main bearing oil clearance and should be checked against the Crankshaft and Connecting Rod Specifications chart at the beginning of this Chapter.

13. Remove every piece of the plastic gaug-

ing material from the crank and bearing caps. Coat the lower bearings (in the caps) with clean motor oil.

14. Install the main bearing caps and the lower thrust washers in the proper sequence. Make sure the arrows on the caps point towards the front (pulley end) of the motor.

15. Tighten the cap bolts in three passes and in the correct sequence to specifications.

16. Double check the endplay of the crankshaft. Turn the crankshaft through one or two full clockwise rotations, making sure that it turns smoothly and evenly with no binding.

Cylinder Block

Most inspection and service work on the cylinder block should be handled by a machinist or professional engine rebuilding shop. Included in this work are bearing alignment checks, line boring, deck resurfacing, hot-tanking and cylinder block boring. Any or all of this work requires that the block be completely stripped of all components and transported to the shop. A block that has been checked and properly serviced will last much longer than one whose owner cut corners during a repair.

Cylinder de-glazing (honing) can be performed by the owner/mechanic who is careful and takes time to be accurate. The cylinder bores become glazed during normal operation of the engine as the rings ride up and down constantly. This shiny glaze must be removed in order for a new set of piston rings to seat properly.

Cylinder hones are available at most auto tool stores and parts jobbers. With the piston and rod assemblies removed from the block, cover the crankshaft completely with a rag to keep grit from collecting on it. Install the hone into the chuck of a variable speed drill (preferred in place of a constant speed drill) and insert the hone into the cylinder.

NOTE: *Make sure the drill and hone are kept square to the cylinder bore during the entire honing procedure.*

Start the hone and move it up and down in the cylinder at a rate which will produce approximately a 60° crosshatch pattern. DO NOT extend the hone below the bottom of the cylinder bore. After the crosshatched pattern is established, remove the hone and check the piston fit.

Remove the piston and wash the cylinder with a solution of detergent and water to remove the honing and cylinder grit. Wipe the bores out several times with a clean rag soaked in fresh engine oil. Remove the cover from the crankshaft and check closely to see that NO grit has found its way onto the crankshaft.

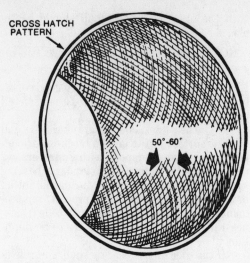

CROSS HATCH PATTERN

50°-60°

Cylinders should be honed to look like this

Flywheel and Ring Gear

REMOVAL AND INSTALLATION

NOTE: *This procedure may performed with the engine in the car, however, access will be cramped.*

1. Remove the transmission/transaxle, following procedures outlined in Chapter 7.

2. For cars equipped with automatic transmissions/transaxle:

   a. Matchmark the torque converter and the drive plate. Correct positioning will be required during reassembly.

   b. Remove the bolts holding the torque converter to the drive plate and remove the torque converter. DON'T drop it.

   c. Matchmark the drive plate and the crankshaft.

   d. Loosen the retaining bolts a little at a time and in a criss-cross pattern. Support the drive plate as the last bolts are removed and then lift the drive plate away from the engine.

3. For manual transmission/transaxle cars:

   a. Matchmark the pressure plate assembly and the flywheel.

   b. Loosen the pressure plate retaining bolts a little at a time and in a criss-cross pattern. Support the pressure plate and clutch assembly as the last bolt is removed and lift them away from the flywheel.

   c. Matchmark the flywheel and crankshaft. Loosen the retaining bolts evenly and in a criss-cross pattern. Support the flywheel during removal of the last bolts and remove the flywheel.

4. Carefully inspect the teeth on the flywheel or drive plate for any signs of wearing or chipping. If anything beyond minimal contact wear is found, replace the unit.

NOTE: *Since the flywheel is driven by the starter gear, you would be wise to inspect the starter drive if any wear is found on the flywheel teeth. A worn starter can cause damage to the flywheel.*

5. When reassembling, place the flywheel or drive plate in position on the crankshaft and make sure the matchmarks align. Install the retaining bolts finger tight.

6. Tighten the bolts in a diagonal pattern and in three passes. Tighten the flywheel bolts (manual transmission) or the drive plate bolts (automatic transmission) to specifications.

7. Install either the clutch and pressure plate assembly or the torque converter. Torque all mounting bolts to specifications.

NOTE: *If the clutch appears worn or cracked in any way, replace it with a new disc, pressure plate and release bearing. The slight extra cost of the parts will prevent having to remove the transmission/transaxle again later.*

8. Reinstall the transmission/transaxle assembly.

RING GEAR REPLACEMENT

If the ring gear teeth on the drive plate or flywheel are damaged, the unit must be replaced. The ring gear cannot be separated or reinstalled individually.

If a flywheel is replaced on a manual transmission car, the installation of a new clutch disc, pressure plate and release bearing is highly recommended.

EXHAUST SYSTEM

Safety Precautions

For a number of reasons, exhaust system work can be the most dangerous type of work you can do on your car. Always observe the following precautions:

• Support the car extra securely. Not only will you often be working directly under it, but you'll frequently be using a lot of force, say, heavy hammer blows, to dislodge rusted parts. This can cause a car that's improperly supported to shift and possibly fall.

• Wear goggles. Exhaust system parts are always rusty. Metal chips can be dislodged, even when you're only turning rusted bolts. Attempting to pry pipes apart with a chisel makes the chips fly even more frequently.

• If you're using a cutting torch, keep it a GREAT distance from either the fuel tank or lines. Stop what you're doing and feel the temperature of the fuel bearing pipes on the tank frequently. Even slight heat can expand and/or vaporize fuel, resulting in accumulated vapor, or even a liquid leak, near your torch.

• Watch where your hammer blows fall and make sure you hit squarely. You could easily tap a brake or fuel line when you hit an exhaust system part with a glancing blow. Inspect all lines and hoses in the area where you've been working.

CAUTION: *Be very careful when working on or near the catalytic converter. External temperatures can reach 1,500°F (816°C) and more, causing severe burns. Removal or installation should be performed only on a cold exhaust system.*

Special Tools

A number of special exhaust system tools can be rented from auto supply houses or local stores that rent special equipment. A common one is a tail pipe expander, designed to enable you to join pipes of identical diameter.

It may also be quite helpful to use solvents designed to loosen rusted bolts or flanges. Soaking rusted parts the night before you do the job can speed the work of freeing rusted parts considerably. Remember that these solvents are often flammable. Apply only to parts after they are cool.

The exhaust system of most engines consists of four pieces. At the front of the car, the first section of pipe connects the exhaust manifold to the catalytic converter. On some models, this pipe contains a section of flexible, braided pipe. The catalytic converter is a sealed, non-serviceable unit which can be easily unbolted from the system and replaced if necessary.

An intermediate or center pipe containing a built-in resonator (pre-muffler) runs from the catalytic converter to the muffler at the rear of the car. Should the resonator fail, the entire pipe must be replaced. The muffler and tailpipe at the rear should always be replaced as a unit.

The exhaust system is attached to the body by several welded hooks and flexible rubber hangers; these hangers absorb exhaust vibrations and isolate the system from the body of the car. A series of metal heat shields runs along the exhaust piping, protecting the underbody from excess heat.

When inspecting or replacing exhaust system parts, make sure there is adequate clearance from all points on the body to avoid possible overheating of the floor pan. Check the complete system for broken damaged, missing or poorly positioned parts. Rattles and vibrations in the exhaust system are usually caused by misalignment of parts. When aligning the system, leave all the nuts and bolts loose until everything is in its proper place, then tighten the hardware working from the front to the rear. Remember that what appears to be proper clearance during repair may change as the car moves down the road. The motion of the engine, body and suspension must be considered when replacing parts.

COMPONENT REMOVAL AND INSTALLATION

CAUTION: *DO NOT perform exhaust repairs with the engine or exhaust hot. Allow the system to cool completely before attempting any work.*
Also, exhaust systems are noted for sharp edges, flaking metal and rusted bolts. Gloves and eye protection are required.

NOTE: *ALWAYS use a new gasket at each pipe joint whenever the joint is disassembled. Use new nuts and bolts to hold the joint properly. These two low-cost items will serve to prevent future leaks as the system ages.*

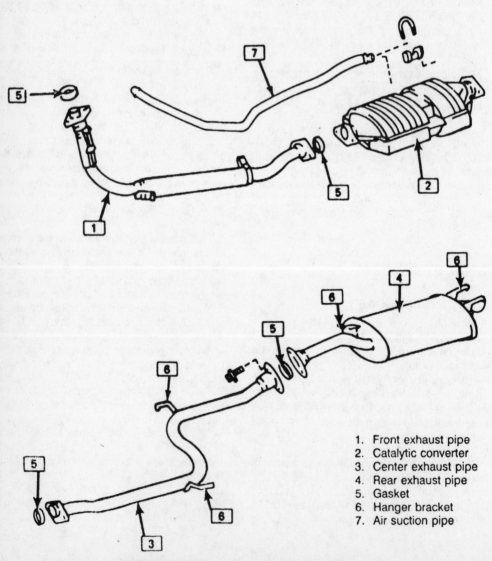

1. Front exhaust pipe
2. Catalytic converter
3. Center exhaust pipe
4. Rear exhaust pipe
5. Gasket
6. Hanger bracket
7. Air suction pipe

Exploded view of an early model exhaust system

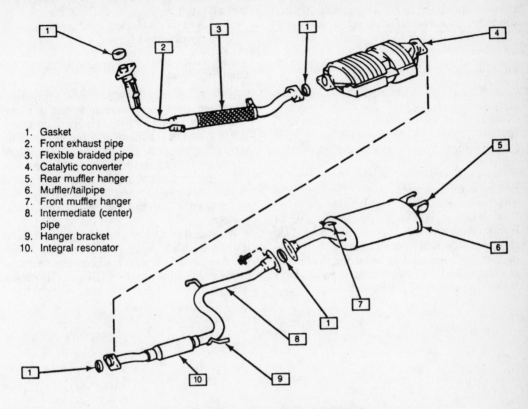

1. Gasket
2. Front exhaust pipe
3. Flexible braided pipe
4. Catalytic converter
5. Rear muffler hanger
6. Muffler/tailpipe
7. Front muffler hanger
8. Intermediate (center) pipe
9. Hanger bracket
10. Integral resonator

Exploded view of a late model exhaust system

Front Pipe

1. Elevate and safely support the vehicle on jackstands.

2. Disconnect the oxygen sensor.

3. Remove the two bolts holding the pipe to the exhaust manifold.

4. Remove the two bolts holding the pipe to the catalytic converter.

5. Remove the bolts from the crossmember bracket and remove the pipe from under the car.

6. Attach the new pipe to the crossmember bracket. Install the bolts at both the manifold and the catalyst ends, leaving them finger tight until the pipe is correctly positioned. Make certain the gaskets are in place and straight.

7. Tighten the pipe-to-manifold bolts to 46 ft. lbs.

8. Tighten the bolts at the converter to 32 ft. lbs.

9. Reconnect the oxygen sensor.

10. Lower the vehicle to the ground, start the system and check for leaks. Small exhaust leaks will be most easily heard when the system is cold.

Catalytic Converter

With the car safely supported on jackstands, the converter is removed simply by removing the two bolts at either end. Some models have an air suction pipe attached to the converter which must be disconnected (2 bolts) before removal. When reinstalling the converter, install it with new gaskets and tighten the end bolts to 32 ft. lbs. Reconnect the air suction pipe and lower the car to the ground.

Intermediate Pipe (Resonator Pipe)

1. Elevate and safely support the vehicle on jackstands.

2. Remove the two bolts holding the pipe to the catalytic converter.

3. Remove the bolts holding the intermediate pipe to the muffler inlet pipe.

4. Disconnect the rubber hangers and remove the pipe.

5. Install the new pipe by suspending it in place on the rubber hangers. Install the gaskets at each end and install the bolts finger tight.

6. Double check the placement of the pipe and insure proper clearance to all body and suspension components.

7. Tighten the bolts holding the pipe to the catalytic converter to 32 ft. lbs., then tighten the bolts to the muffler inlet pipe to 32 ft. lbs.

8. Lower the car to the ground. Start the engine and check for leaks.

Muffler and Tailpipe Assembly

1. Elevate and safely support the vehicle on jackstands.

2. Remove the two bolts holding the muffler inlet pipe to the intermediate pipe.

3. Disconnect the forward bracket on the muffler.

4. Disconnect the rear muffler bracket (three bolts) and remove the muffler from under the car.

5. When reinstalling, suspend the muffler from its front and rear hangers and check it for correct positioning under the body. If the old muffler had been rattling or hitting the body it is possible that the hangers and brackets have become bent from a light impact.

6. Attach the inlet pipe to the intermediate pipe and tighten the bolts to 32 ft. lbs.

7. Lower the vehicle to the ground, start the engine and check for leaks.

Complete System

If the entire exhaust system is to be replaced, it is much easier to remove the system as a unit than remove each individual piece. Disconnect the first pipe at the manifold joint and work towards the rear removing brackets and hangers as you go. Don't forget to disconnect the air suction pipe on the catalytic converter on some models. Remove the rear muffler bracket and slide the entire exhaust system out form under the car.

When installing the new assembly, suspend it from the flexible hangers first, then attach the fixed (solid) brackets. Check the clearance to the body and suspension and install the manifold joint bolts, tightening them to 46 ft. lbs.

Emission Controls

4

EMISSION CONTROLS

Component location and vacuum routing diagrams are located at the end of this chapter. Please refer to them before beginning any disassembly or testing.

There are three sources of automotive pollutants; crankcase fumes, exhaust gases, and gasoline evaporation. The pollutants formed from these substances fall into three categories: unburnt hydrocarbons (HC), carbon monoxide (CO), called emission control equipment.

Due to varying state, federal, and provincial regulations, specific emission control equipment may vary by area of sale. The U.S. emission equipment is divided into two categories: California and 49 State. In this section, the term "California" applies only to cars originally built to be sold in California. Some California emissions equipment is not shared with equipment installed on cars built to be sold in the other 49 states. Models built to be sold in Canada also have specific emissions equipment, although in many cases the 49 State and Canadian equipment is the same.

Both carbureted and fuel injected cars require an assortment of systems and devices to control emissions. Newer cars rely more heavily on computer (ECM) management of many of the engine controls. This eliminates the many of the vacuum hoses and linkages around the engine. In the lists that follow, remember that not every component is found on every car.

ECM CONTROLLED SYSTEMS
- Fuel Evaporative Control (EVAP)
- Carburetor Feedback System
- Deceleration Fuel Cutoff
- Three-Way Oxidation Catalyst (TWC-OC or TWC)
- Cold Mixture Heater (CMH)

NON-ECM CONTROLLED SYSTEMS
- Positive Crankcase Ventilation (PCV)
- Throttle Positioner (TP)
- Exhaust Gas Recirculation (EGR)
- Air Suction (AS)
- High Altitude Compensation (HAC)
- Automatic Hot Air Intake (HAI)
- Hot Idle Compensation (HIC)
- Automatic Choke
- Choke Breaker (CB)
- Choker Opener
- Auxiliary Accelerator Pump (AAP)
- Heat Control Valve

Positive Crankcase Ventilation (PCV) System

SYSTEM OPERATION

A closed positive crankcase ventilation system is used on all Toyota models. This system cycles incompletely burned fuel which works its way past the piston rings back into the intake manifold for reburning with the fuel/

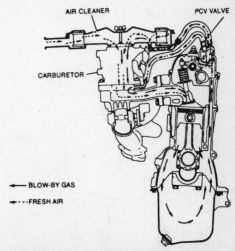

AIR CLEANER   PCV VALVE

CARBURETOR

← BLOW-BY GAS

◀---FRESH AIR

Typical positive crankcase ventilation system

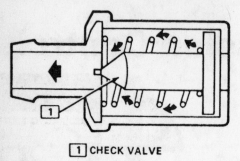

1 CHECK VALVE

Cross section of typical PCV valve. The valve should rattle when shaken

air mixture. The oil filler cap is sealed and the air is drawn from the top of the crankcase into the intake manifold through a valve with a variable orifice.

This valve (commonly known as the PCV valve) regulates the flow of air into the manifold according to the amount of manifold vacuum. When the throttle plates are open fairly wide, the valve fully. However, at idle speed, when the manifold vacuum is at maximum, the PCV valve reduces the flow in order not to unnecessarily affect the small volume of mixture passing into the engine.

During most driving conditions, manifold vacuum is high and all of the vapor from the crankcase, plus a small amount of excess air, is drawn into the manifold via the PCV valve. At full throttle, the increase in the volume of blow-by and the decrease in manifold vacuum make the flow via the PCV valve inadequate. Under these conditions, excess vapors are drawn into the air cleaner and pass into the engine along with the fresh air.

A plugged valve or hose may cause a rough idle, stalling or low idle speed, oil leaks in the engine and/or sludging and oil deposits within

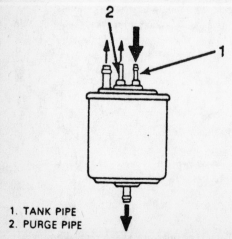

1. TANK PIPE
2. PURGE PIPE

Checking the charcoal canister

the engine and air cleaner. A leaking valve or hose could cause an erratic idle or stalling.

TESTING AND TROUBLESHOOTING

The PCV is easily checked with the engine running at normal idle speed (warmed up). Remove the PCV valve from the valve cover or intake manifold, but leave it connected to its hose. Place your thumb over the end of the valve to check for vacuum. If there is no vacuum, check for plugged hoses or ports. If these are open, the valve is faulty. With the engine off, remove the PCV valve completely. Shake it end to end, listening for the rattle of the needle inside the valve. If no rattle is heard, the needle is jammed (probably with oil sludge) and the valve should be replaced.

An engine which is operated without crankcase ventilation can be damaged very quickly. It is important to check and change the PCV valve (check PCV valve hose also) at regular maintenance intervals.

REMOVAL AND INSTALLATION

Remove the PCV valve from the cylinder head cover or intake manifold. Remove the hose from the valve. Take note of which end of the valve was in the manifold. This one-way valve must be reinstalled correctly or it will not function. While the valve is removed, the hoses should be checked for splits, kinks and blockages. Check the vacuum port (that the hoses connect to) for any clogging.

Remember that the correct function of the PCV system is based on a sealed engine--an air leak at the oil filler cap and/or around the oil pan can defeat the design of the system.

Evaporative Emission Control System (EVAP or EECS)

OPERATION

This system reduces hydrocarbon emissions by storing and routing evaporated fuel from the fuel tank and the carburetor's float chamber (carbureted engines only) through the charcoal canister to the intake manifold for combustion in the cylinders at the proper time.

When the ignition is OFF, hydrocarbons from the carburetor float chamber pass through the control valve into the canister. Fuel vapors from the fuel tank pass into the charcoal canister through a check valve located on the canister.

When the ignition is switch ON, but the engine is NOT running, the control valve is energized blocking the movement of fuel vapor from the carburetor's float chamber. Vapors from the fuel tank can still flow and be stored in the charcoal canister.

With the engine running above 1500 rpm, the fuel vapors are purged from the canister into the intake manifold. If deceleration occurs, the throttle position switch opens (disconnects) and the ECM detects the change. The control valve is de-energized and the purging of vapor is stopped. This eliminates the delivery of excess fuel vapor during periods of poor or reduced combustion.

When there is pressure in the fuel tank (such as from summer heat or long periods of driving) the canister valve opens, allowing vapor to enter the canister and be stored for future delivery to the engine.

TESTING AND CHECKING

Before embarking on component removal or extensive diagnosis, perform a complete visual check of the system. Every vacuum line and vapor line (including the lines running to the tank) should be inspected for cracking, loose clamps, kinks and obstructions. Additionally, check the tank for any signs of deformation or crushing. Each vacuum port on the engine or manifold should be checked for restriction by dirt or sludge.

The evaporative control system is generally not prone to component failure in normal circumstances; most problems can be tracked to the causes listed above.

Fuel Filler Cap

Check that the filler cap seals effectively. Remove the filler cap and pull the safety valve outward to check for smooth operation. Replace the filler cap if the seal is defective or if it is not operating properly.

Charcoal Canister

1. Label and disconnect the lines running to the canister. Remove the charcoal canister from the vehicle.

2. Visually check the charcoal canister for cracks or damage.

3. Check for a clogged filter and stuck check valve. Using low pressure compressed air, blow into the tank pipe and check that the air flows without resistance from the other pipes. If this does not test positive replace the canister.

4. Clean the filter in the canister by blowing no more than 43 psi of compressed air into the pipe to the outer vent control valve while holding the other upper canister pipes closed.

NOTE: *Do not attempt to wash the charcoal canister. Also be sure that no activated carbon comes out of the canister during the cleaning process.*

5. Replace or reinstall the canister as needed.

Cleaning the charcoal canister

Outer Vent Control Valve

1. Label and disconnect the hoses from the control valve but leave the wiring for the valve connected.

2. Check that the valve is open by blowing air through it when the ignition switch is in the OFF position.

3. Check that the valve is closed when the ignition switch is in the ON position.

4. Reconnect the hoses to the proper locations. If the valve doesn't operate correctly, double check the fuse and wiring before replacing the valve.

Thermo Switch

1. Drain the coolant from the radiator into a clean container.

CAUTION: *When draining the coolant, keep in mind that cats and dogs are attracted by the ethylene glycol antifreeze, and are quite likely to drink any that is left in an uncovered container or in puddles on the ground. This will prove fatal in sufficient quantity. Always drain the coolant into a sealable container. Coolant should be reused unless it is contaminated or several years old.*

2. Remove the thermoswitch from the intake manifold. The switch is located behind the TVSV (thermo vacuum switching valve).

3. Cool the thermo switch off until the tem-

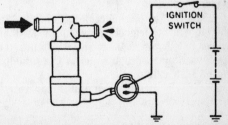

Check the outer vent control with the ignition OFF and ON. Note that there should be no flow with the ignition ON

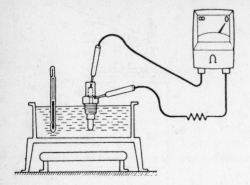

The thermo switch should have continuity if cooled below 109°F (43°C)

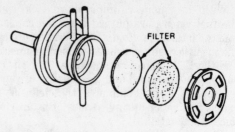

The EGR vacuum modulator filter

perature is below 109°F (43°C). Check that there is continuity through the switch by the use of an ohmmeter.

4. Using hot water, bring the temperature of the switch to above 131°F (55°C). Check that there is no continuity when the switch is in water above this temperature.

5. Apply sealer to the threads of the switch and reinstall it in the manifold.

6. Refill the radiator with coolant.

REMOVAL AND INSTALLATION

Removal and installation of the various evaporative emission control system components consists of labeling or marking and unfastening hoses, loosening retaining screws, and removing the part which is to be replaced from its mounting point.

NOTE: *When replacing any EVAP system hoses, always use hoses that are fuel-resistant or are marked EVAP. Use of hose which is not fuel-resistant will lead to premature hose failure.*

Exhaust Gas Recirculation (EGR) System

OPERATION

The EGR system reduces oxides of nitrogen. This is accomplished by recirculating some of the exhaust gases through the EGR valve to the intake manifold, lowering peak combustion temperatures.

Whenever the engine coolant is below 122°F (50°C), the thermostatic vacuum switching valve (TVSV) connects manifold vacuum to the EGR vacuum modulator and at the same time to the EGR valve.

The EGR vacuum modulator controls the EGR valve by modulating the vacuum signal with an atmospheric bleed. This bleed is controlled by the amount of exhaust pressure acting on the bottom of the EGR vacuum modulator (diaphragm).

Since recirculation of exhaust gas is undesirable at low rpm or idle, the system limits itself by sensing the exhaust flow. Under low load conditions, such as low speed driving, the exhaust pressure is low. In this state, the diaphragm in the modulator is pushed down by spring force and the modulator valve opens to allow outside air into the vacuum passage. The vacuum in the line is reduced, the EGR valve does not open as far, and the amount of recirculation is reduced.

Under high load conditions or high rpm driving, the exhaust pressure is increased. This pushes the modulator diaphragm upwards and closes the bleed valve. A full vacuum signal is transmitted to the EGR valve; it opens completely and allows full recirculation. The slight reduction in combustion temperature (and therefore power) is not noticed at highway speeds or under hard acceleration.

Some vehicles also control the EGR with a vacuum solenoid valve (VSV). This device allows the ECM to further control the EGR under certain conditions. The ECM will electrically close the VSV if the engine is not warmed up, the throttle valve is in the idle position or if the engine is under very hard acceleration. Aside from these conditions, this EGR system (late models) operates in accordance with the normal vacuum modulator function.

TESTING AND SERVICING

Carbureted Engine

EGR SYSTEM OPERATION

1. Check and clean the filter in the EGR vacuum modulator. Use compressed air (if possible) to blow the dirt out of the filters and check the filters for contamination or damage.

2. Using a tee (3-way connector), connect a vacuum gauge to the hose between the EGR valve and the vacuum pipe.

3. Check the seating of the EGR valve by starting the engine and seeing that it runs at a smooth idle. If the valve is not completely closed, the idle will be rough.

4. With the engine coolant temperature below 122°F (50°C), the vacuum gauge should

read zero at 2000 rpm. This indicates that the thermostatic vacuum control valve (TVCV) is functioning correctly at this temperature range.

5. Warm the engine to normal operating temperature. Check the vacuum gauge and confirm low vacuum at 2000 rpm. This indicates the TVSV and the EGR vacuum modulator are working correctly in this temperature range.

6. Disconnect the vacuum hose from the **R** port on the EGR vacuum modulator and, using another piece of hose, connect the **R** port directly to the intake manifold. Check that the vacuum gauge indicates high vacuum at 2,000 rpm.

NOTE: *As a large amount of exhaust gas enters, the engine will misfire slightly at this time.*

7. Disconnect the vacuum gauge and reconnect the vacuum hoses to their proper locations.

8. Check the EGR valve by applying vacuum directly to the valve with the engine at idle. (This may be accomplished wither by bridging vacuum directly from the intake manifold or by using a hand-held vacuum pump.) The engine should falter and die as the full load of recirculated gasses enters the engine.

9. If no problem is found with this inspec-

tion, the system is OK; otherwise inspect each part.

THERMOSTATIC VACUUM SWITCHING VALVE

1. Drain the cooling system.

CAUTION: *When draining the coolant, keep in mind that cats and dogs are attracted by the ethylene glycol antifreeze, and are quite likely to drink any that is left in an uncovered container or in puddles on the ground. This will prove fatal in sufficient quantity. Always drain the coolant into a sealable container. Coolant should be reused unless it is contaminated or several years old.*

2. Remove the thermostatic vacuum switching valve.

3. Cool the thermostatic vacuum switching valve to below 45°F (7°C).

4. Check that air flows from pipe **J** to pipes **M** and **L**, and flows from pipe **K** to pipe **N**.

5. Heat the thermostatic vacuum switching valve to 63–122°F (17–50°C) generally room temperature).

6. Check that air flows from pipe **K** to pipes **N** and **L** and flows from pipe **J** to pipe **M**.

7. Heat the TVSV to above 154°F (68°C).

8. Check that air flows from the pipe **K** to pipes **M** and **L**, and does **NOT** flow from pipe **J** to any other pipes.

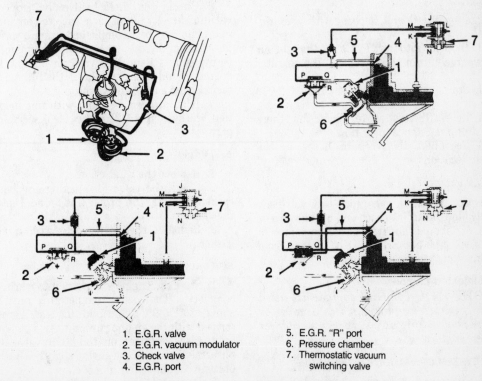

1. E.G.R. valve
2. E.G.R. vacuum modulator
3. Check valve
4. E.G.R. port
5. E.G.R. "R" port
6. Pressure chamber
7. Thermostatic vacuum switching valve

EGR system components-test port locations

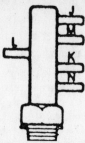

Port identification for testing the TVSV. Make sure you label each hose during disassembly

9. Apply liquid sealer to the threads of the TVSV and reinstall.

10. Refill the cooling system.

11. If a problem is found with any of the above procedures, replace the valve

EGR VALVE

1. Remove the EGR valve.

2. Check the valve for sticking and heavy carbon deposits. If a problem is found, replace the valve.

3. Reinstall the EGR valve with a new gasket.

EGR VACUUM MODULATOR

1. Label and disconnect the vacuum hoses from ports **P**, **Q**, and **R** of the EGR vacuum modulator.

2. Plug the **Q** and **R** ports with your fingers.

3. Blow air into port **P**. Check that the air passes freely through the sides of the air filter side.

4. Start the engine and maintain 2,000 rpm.

5. Repeat the test above. Check that there is a strong resistance to air flow.

6. Reconnect the vacuum hoses to the proper locations.

CHECK VALVE

Inspect the check valve (one-way valve) by gently blowing air into each end of the valve or hose. Air should flow from the orange pipe to the black pipe but SHOULD NOT flow from the black pipe to the orange pipe.

Fuel Injected Engines

NOTE: *For fuel injected engines not listed use these service procedures as a guide as emission control systems are very similar for these engines.*

EGR SYSTEM OPERATION 4A-GE ENGINE

1. Check and clean the filter in the EGR vacuum modulator. Use compressed air (if possible) to blow the dirt out of the filters and check the filters for contamination or damage.

2. Using a tee (3-way connector), connect a vacuum gauge to the hose between the EGR valve and the vacuum pipe.

3. Check the seating of the EGR valve by starting the engine and seeing that it runs at a smooth idle. If the valve is not completely closed, the idle will be rough.

4. With the engine coolant temperature below 95°F (35°C), the vacuum gauge should read 0 at 3500 rpm. This indicates that the bi-metal vacuum switching valve (BVSV) is functioning correctly at this temperature range.

5. Warm the engine to normal operating temperature. Check the vacuum gauge and confirm low vacuum at 3500 rpm. This indicates the BVSV and the EGR vacuum modulator are working correctly in this temperature range.

6. Disconnect the vacuum hose from the **R** port on the EGR vacuum modulator and, using another piece of hose, connect the **R** port directly to the intake manifold. Check that the vacuum gauge indicates high vacuum at 3500 rpm.

NOTE: *As a large amount of exhaust gas enters, the engine will misfire slightly at this time.*

7. Disconnect the vacuum gauge and reconnect the vacuum hoses to their proper locations.

8. Check the EGR valve by applying vacuum directly to the valve with the engine at idle. (This may be accomplished either by bridging vacuum directly from the intake manifold or by using a hand-held vacuum pump.) The engine should falter and die as the full load of recirculated gasses enters the engine.

9. If no problem is found with this inspection, the system is OK; otherwise inspect each part.

EGR VALVE

1. Remove the EGR valve.

2. Check the valve for sticking and heavy carbon deposits. If a problem is found, replace the valve.

3. Reinstall the EGR valve with a new gasket.

EGR VALVE 4A-FE ENGINE

1. Start the engine and allow it to warm up completely. The coolant temperature must be above 120°F (49°C). The following tests are performed with the engine running.

2. Place a finger on the EGR valve diaphragm. Accelerate the engine slightly; the diaphragm should be felt to move.

3. Disconnect a vacuum hose from the EGR valve and connect a hand held vacuum pump.

4. Apply 10 inches of vacuum to the valve. The diaphragm should move (check again with

your finger) and the engine may momentarily run rough or stall.

5. An EGR valve failing either of these quick tests should be replaced. The valves cannot be cleaned or adjusted.

EGR VACUUM MODULATOR 4A-GE ENGINE

1. Label and disconnect the vacuum hoses from ports **P**, **Q**, and **R** of the EGR vacuum modulator.

2. Plug the **P** and **R** ports with your fingers.

3. Blow air into port **Q**. Check that the air passes freely through the sides of the air filter.

4. Start the engine and maintain 3500 rpm.

5. Repeat the test above. Check that there is a strong resistance to air flow.

6. Reconnect the vacuum hoses to the proper locations.

Vacuum Switching Valve

1. The vacuum switching valve is located on the left strut tower. The vacuum switching circuit is checked by blowing air into the pipe under the following conditions:

a. Connect the vacuum switching valve terminals to the battery.

b. Blow into the tube and check that the VSV switch is open.

c. Disconnect the positive battery terminal.

d. Blow into the tube and check that the VSV switch is closed (no flow).

2. Check for a short circuit within the valve. Using an ohmmeter, check that there is no continuity between the positive terminal and the VSV body. If there is continuity, replace the VSV.

3. Check for an open circuit. Using an ohmmeter, measure the resistance (ohms) between the two terminals of the valve. The resistance should be 38–44Ω at 68°F (20°C). If the resistance is not within specifications, replace the VSV.

NOTE: *The resistance — in ohms — will vary slightly with temperature. It will de-crease in cooler temperatures and increase with heat. Use common sense; slight variations due to temperature range are not necessarily a sign of a failed valve.*

Bi-metal Vacuum Switching Valve (BVSV)

Fuel Injected Engines

Despite the impressive name, this valve does nothing more than allow vacuum to flow through the system depending on engine coolant temperature. The bi-metallic element within the switch reacts to temperature changes, opening or closing the valve at a predetermined level. To test the valve:

1. Drain the coolant from the radiator into a suitable container.

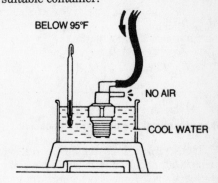

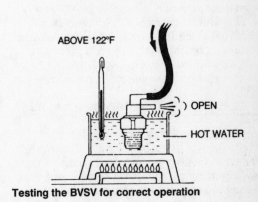

Testing the BVSV for correct operation

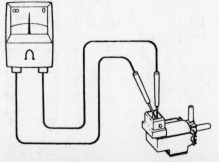

Checking the resistance on the vacuum suction valve

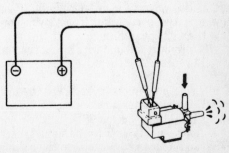

VACUUM SWITCHING VALVE

The vacuum switching valve allows air to pass when electricity is applied

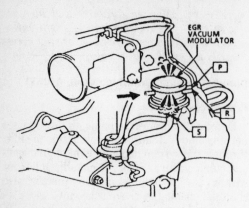

Port designations for EGR vacuum modulator

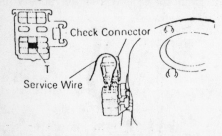

Location of terminal T in the check connector

CAUTION: *When draining the coolant, keep in mind that cats and dogs are attracted by the ethylene glycol antifreeze, and are quite likely to drink any that is left in an uncovered container or in puddles on the ground. This will prove fatal in sufficient quantity. Always drain the coolant into a sealable container. Coolant should be reused unless it is contaminated or several years old.*

2. Label and disconnect the hoses from the BVSV.

3. Remove the valve from the intake manifold.

4. Using cool water, cool the threaded part of the valve to below 95°F (35°C). Blow air into the upper (center) port; there should be NO air passage through the valve. It does not allow vacuum to pass until the engine warms up.

5. Using warm water, heat the threaded part of the valve to above 122°F (50°C) and blow into the port again. The valve should allow the air to pass through.

If a problem is found with either the "on" or "off" functions of the valve, replace it with a new one.

6. Using an ohmmeter, measure the resistance between the terminal on the VSV. Resistance should be 33–39Ω at 68°F (20°C).

7. Apply liquid sealer to the threads of the BVSV and reinstall it. Connect the vacuum lines.

8. Refill the radiator with coolant.

EGR VACUUM MODULATOR 4A-FE ENGINE

1. Label and remove the three hoses from the modulator.

2. Place your fingers over ports **P** and **R**; blow into port **Q**. Air should flow freely from the sides of the air filter on the modulator.

3. Connect a vacuum pump to port **S** (on the bottom of the unit) and plug tubes **P** and **R** with your fingers. Blow air into tube **Q** and attempt to draw a vacuum with the pump. You SHOULD NOT be able to develop a vacuum within the system.

4. If the modulator fails any of these tests, it must be replaced.

VACUUM SWITCHING VALVE (VSV) 4A-FE ENGINE

1. Label and disconnect the two hoses from the VSV.

2. With the ignition OFF, disconnect the connector at the VSV.

3. Check the resistance between the two terminals on the VSV. Look for 33–39Ω resistance. If the resistance is incorrect, replace the unit. If the resistance is proper, proceed with the next step.

4. Gently blow air into port **A**. Air should come out through the filter but SHOULD NOT come out through port **B**.

5. Reconnect the electrical connector.

6. Turn the ignition switch ON (but don't start the motor) and ground the Diagnosis Switch Terminal. This is found in the diagnostic connector near the air cleaner assembly and is labeled as terminal **T**. Use a jumper wire with clips to ground the terminal.

WARNING: *Be careful not to ground other terminals in the connector (even accidentally) — severe electrical damage may result!*

7. Blow air into port **A**; the air should exit through port **B**.

8. If the VSV fails either of the air flow tests, it should be replaced.

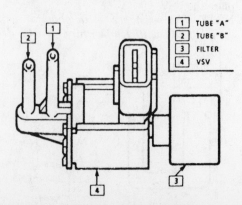

Vacuum switching valve testing locations

REMOVAL AND INSTALLATION OF COMPONENTS

Exhaust emission control equipment is generally simple to work on and easy to get to on the motor. The air cleaner assembly will need to be removed. Always label each vacuum hose before removing it — they must be replaced in the correct position.

Most of the valves and solenoids are made of plastic, particularly at the vacuum ports. Be very careful during removal not to break or crack the ports; you have NO chance of regluing a broken fitting. Remember that the plastic has been in a hostile environment (heat and vibration); the fittings become brittle and less resistant to abuse or accidental impact.

EGR valves are generally held in place by two bolts. The bolts can be difficult to remove due to corrosion. Once the EGR is off the engine, clean the bolts and the bolt holes of any rust or debris. Always replace the gasket any time the EGR valve is removed.

Oxygen Sensor

The oxygen (O_2) sensor is located on the exhaust manifold to detect the concentration of oxygen in the exhaust gas. Using highly refined metals (zirconia and platinum), the sensor uses changes in the oxygen content to generate an electrical signal which is transmitted to the ECM. The computer in turn reacts to the signal by adjusting the fuel metering at the injectors or at the carburetor. More or less fuel is delivered into the cylinders and the correct oxygen level is maintained.

4A-C ENGINE

NOTE: *For engines not listed use these service procedures as a guide as emission control systems are very similar for these engines.*

1. Warm up the engine to normal operating temperature.
2. Connect the voltmeter to the service connector. This round, green connector is located behind the right shock tower. Connect the positive probe to the OX terminal and the negative probe to the **E** terminal.
3. Run the engine at 2500 rpm for 90 seconds or more. This allows the sensor to achieve a stable temperature and the exhaust flow to stabilize.
4. Maintain the engine at 2500 rpm and check the meter. The meter needle should fluctuate at least 8 times in 10 seconds in the 0–6 volt range. This indicates that the sensor is working properly.
5. If the sensor fails the test, perform a careful inspection of all the wiring and connectors in the system. A loose connection can cause the sensor to fail this test. Repeat the voltage test after the inspection.

4A-GE ENGINE

NOTE: *For engines not listed use these service procedures as a guide as emission control systems are very similar for these engines.*

1. Warm up the engine to normal operating temperature.
2. Connect the voltmeter to the check connector. Hook the negative probe to terminal **VF** and the positive probe to terminal **E1**.
3. Run the engine at 2500 rpm for at least 90 seconds.
4. With the engine speed being maintained at 2500 rpm, use a jumper wire to connect terminals **T** and **E1** at the check connector.

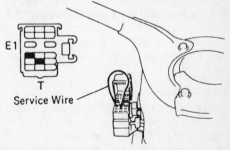

Location of terminal E$_1$ and T on check engine connector

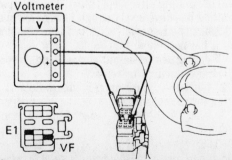

Testing hook-up for the 4A-GE oxygen sensor

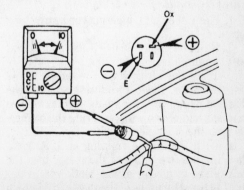

Testing hook-up for the 4A-C oxygen sensor

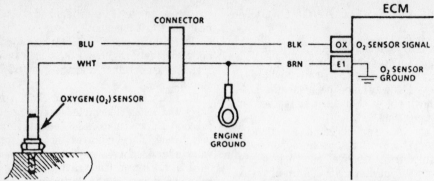

Wiring for oxygen sensor. Connect test probes at the back of the connector

5. Watch the voltmeter and note the number of times the needle fluctuates in 10 seconds. If it moves eight times or more, the sensor is working properly.

a. If the needle moves less than eight times but more than zero, disconnect the terminal **T-to-E1** jumper. Still maintaining 2500 rpm, measure the voltage between terminals **E1** and **VF**. If the voltage is above zero, replace the oxygen sensor. If the voltage is zero, read and record the diagnostic codes (refer to "Check Engine Light and Diagnostic Codes" later in this chapter) and repair the necessary items.

b. If the needle does not move at all (zero), read and record the trouble codes and repair the affected system.

NOTE: *Perform a careful inspection of all the wiring and connectors in the system. A loose connection can cause the sensor to fail these tests. Repeat the voltage test after the inspection. (Refer to "Check Engine Light and Diagnostic Codes" later in this chapter.).*

4A-FE ENGINE

NOTE: *Use only a 10MΩ digital voltmeter. Use of any other type of equipment may damage the ECM or other components. For engines not listed use these service procedures as a guide as emission control systems are very similar for these engines.*

1. Warm the car up to normal operating temperature.

2. Run the engine above 1200 rpm for at least two minutes.

3. Trace the wiring from the sensor to the first connector. Clean the wiring so that the blue and white wires are easily seen as well as the black and brown wires entering the connector from the other side.

4. With the engine running at 1200 rpm, place the positive probe of the meter into the back of the connector at the black wire. Connect the negative probe of the meter to a known good ground.

5. The meter should vary between 0 and 1 volt. If this is true, the sensor is working properly.

6. If the voltage does not vary from 0 to 1 volt, disconnect the oxygen sensor at the connector. Using a jumper wire, connect the black wire to ground. The voltmeter should display voltage less than 0.2v (200 mV) with the engine running. If the displayed voltage is at or less than 0.2v, either the sensor or the sensor connection has failed.

7. If the voltage is above 0.2v in the previous test, remove the jumper wire. Turn the engine off, then turn the ignition to the ON position without starting the motor. Recheck the voltage in the black wire:

a. Voltage of 0.3–0.6v shows that the ECM is faulty.

b. Voltage over 0.6 volts indicates a possibly faulty ECM, a bad connection or an open (break) in the brown wire.

c. Voltage less than 0.3 volts indicates a possibly faulty ECM, a bad connection or an open (break) in the black wire.

REMOVAL AND INSTALLATION

NOTE: *Care should be used during the removal of the oxygen sensor. Both the sensor and its wire can be easily damaged.*

1. The best condition in which to remove the sensor is with the engine in a "mid-warm" state. This is generally achieved after two to five minutes (depending on outside temperature) of running after a cold start. The exhaust manifold has developed enough heat to expand and make the removal easier but is not so hot that it has become untouchable.

Wearing heat resistant gloves is highly recommended during this repair.

2. With the ignition OFF, disconnect the wiring for the sensor.

3. Unscrew the oxygen sensor from the manifold.

NOTE: *Special wrenches, either socket or open-end, are available from reputable retail outlets for removing the oxygen sensor. These tools make the job much easier and often prevent unnecessary damage.*

4. During and after the removal, use great care to protect the tip of the sensor if it is to be reused. Do not allow it to come in contact with fluids or dirt. Do not attempt to clean it or wash it.

5. When re-installing, apply a coat of anti-seize compound to the threads but DO NOT allow any to get on the tip of the sensor. This includes any accidental or momentary contact from rags, etc.

Some replacement sensors come with the compound already on the threads. Do not remove it or try to clean it.

6. Install the sensor in the manifold. Tighten it to 30 ft. lbs.

7. Reconnect the electrical connector and insure a clean, tight connection.

3-Way and Oxidation Catalyst (TWC-OC) System

OPERATION

The catalytic converter is a muffler-like container built into the exhaust system to aid in the reduction of HC, CO and NOx emissions by changing them into nitrogen, carbon dioxide and water vapor through the action of the catalyst upon the exhaust gas.

The 3-way catalytic convertor is the best type to use since it can change all three types of emissions into non-polluting gases. In this type of converter nitrous oxides are chemically reduced by the catalyst and reformed into the molecules of oxygen and nitrogen. The oxygen formed by the reduction reaction is then used to oxidize carbon monoxide and the hydrocarbons, forming carbon dioxide and water vapor.

For the catalytic converter to work most effi-ciently, the following conditions must be met:
• Operating temperature must be over 500°F (260°C).
• Air/fuel ratio must be held closely at 14.7:1.

PRECAUTIONS

• Use only unleaded fuel.
• Avoid prolonged idling; the engine should run no longer than 20 minutes at curb idle, nor longer than 10 minutes at fast idle.
• Reduce the fast idle speed, by quickly depressing and releasing the accelerator pedal, as soon as the coolant temperature reaches 120°F (49°C).
• DO NOT disconnect any spark plug leads while the engine is running.
• Always make engine compression checks as quickly as possible. Excess fuel can be pumped through the motor and build up in the converter.
• DO NOT dispose of the catalyst in a place where anything coated with grease, gas, or oil is present; spontaneous combustion could result.
• Since the inside of the catalyst must reach 500°F (260°C) to work efficiently, the outside of the converter will also become very hot. Always be aware of what may be under the car when you park. Parking a hot exhaust system over dry grass, leaves or other flammable items may lead to a fire.

Feedback Carburetor System

OPERATION

The Carburetor Feedback system is designed to keep the air/fuel ratio at an optimum 14.7:1 during normal operation; excluding warm-up and acceleration.

This is a rather simple system. The carbure-

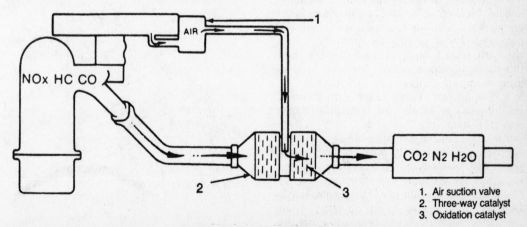

1. Air suction valve
2. Three-way catalyst
3. Oxidation catalyst

3-way oxidation catalyst system

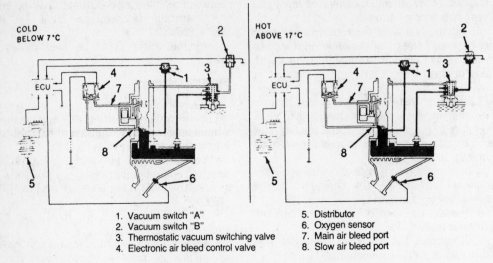

1. Vacuum switch "A"
2. Vacuum switch "B"
3. Thermostatic vacuum switching valve
4. Electronic air bleed control valve
5. Distributor
6. Oxygen sensor
7. Main air bleed port
8. Slow air bleed port

Feedback carburetor system operation

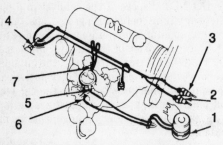

1. Electronic air bleed control valve (EBCV)
2. Vacuum switch "A"
3. Vacuum switch "B"
4. Thermostatic vacuum switching valve
5. Main air bleed port
6. Slow air bleed port
7. Throttle positioner port

Feedback carburetor component location

tor is designed to run richer than it normally should. This sets up a rich limit of system operation. When a leaner operation is desired, the computer (ECM) commands air to bleed into the carburetor's main metering system and into the carburetor's primary bore. A lean operating condition is therefore easy to obtain.

The computer (ECM) receives information from the oxygen sensor, two vacuum switches and the distributor.

The output of the computer is a signal to the electric air bleed control valve (EBCV). When the EBCV is energized, it bleeds air into the main air bleed circuit and into the slow air bleed port of the carburetor. This additional air leans the fuel mixture. When the EBCV is not energized, the air/fuel ratio moves towards the rich limit.

With the engine running and the coolant temperature below 45°F (7°C), the thermostatic

vacuum switch valve (TVSV) applies atmospheric pressure to vacuum switch **B** by connecting ports **J** to **L** (of the TVSV). With these conditions, vacuum switch **B** is de-energized, the electric bleed control valve (EBCV) is off (de-energized) and both air bleeds are off. The carburetor is therefore operating toward its rich limits, desirable on a cold motor. The computer will not be controlling or influencing air/fuel ratio while the engine is cold.

When the coolant temperature rises above 60°F (16°C), with the engine operating between 1500 and 4200 rpm, the thermostatic vacuum switching valve (TVSV) applies vacuum to vacuum switch **B** by connecting ports **K** to **L** of the TVSV.

Vacuum switch **B** closes, signaling the ECM. Vacuum switch **A** is closed (opens at high vacuum) also signaling the ECM. With these

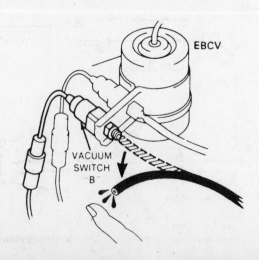

EBCV and vacuum switch

two switches closed, if the oxygen sensor senses a rich condition in the exhaust (high voltage-1.0v), the ECM commands the electric bleed control valve to be energized, bleeding air into the main metering system of the carburetor and the intake manifold. This action results in the air/fuel ratio becoming leaner.

Once the air/fuel ratio is detected as being too lean by the oxygen sensor (low voltage-0.1v), the ECM will de-energize the EBCV and close both bleed ports. By shutting off the air, the mixture begins moving back towards the rich limit. The system is operating in the "closed loop" mode, during which it will adjust itself and then react to the adjustments. It should be noted that to energize the electric bleed control valve (EBCV) the ECM completes its electrical circuit on its ground side.

TESTING

Checking the Carburetor Feedback System

1. Check the TVSV with the engine cold. The coolant temperature must be below 45°F (7°C).

2. Disconnect the vacuum hose from the vacuum switch **B**. Start the engine and check no vacuum is felt in the disconnected vacuum hose.

3. Reconnect the vacuum hose and check the EBCV with the engine warmed up to normal operating temperature.

4. Disconnect the EBCV connector. Maintain an engine speed of approximately 2,500 rpm.

5. Reconnect the connector and check that the engine speed drops by about 300 rpm momentarily.

6. With the engine at idle, repeat the disconnect/reconnect test on the EBCV connector. Check that the engine speed does NOT change.

7. Disconnect the hose from the vacuum switch **B**. Repeat steps 4 and 5 above. Check that the engine speed does not change.

8. If no problems are found with this inspection, the system is operating properly; otherwise inspect each component part.

Checking the Air Bleed Control Valve (EBCV)

1. Check for a short circuit. Using an ohmmeter, check that there is no continuity between the positive (+) terminal (the terminal closest to the lock tab) and the EBCV body. If there is continuity, replace the EBCV.

2. Check for an open circuit. Using an ohmmeter, measure the resistance between the positive (+) terminal and the other terminal. The resistance should be between 11–13Ω 68°F (20°C). If the resistance is not within specification, replace the EBCV. Remember that the resistance will vary slightly with temperature. Resistance (ohms) will decrease as the temperature drops. Use common sense here — a reading of 16Ω on a hot day does not necessarily indicate a failed valve.

Checking Vacuum Switch A

1. Using an ohmmeter, check that there is continuity between the switch terminal and the switch body.

2. Start the engine and run it until normal operating temperature is reached.

3. Using an ohmmeter, check that there is NO continuity between the switch terminal and the switch body.

4. If either test is failed, replace the switch.

By means of a signal from the Ox sensor, carburetor primary side main air bleed and slow air bleed volume are controlled to maintain optimum air-fuel mixture in accordance with existing driving conditions, thereby cleaning HC, CO and NOx. In addition, driveability and fuel economy are improved.

Coolant Temp.	TVSV	Condition	Engine rpm	Vacuum S/W A	Vacuum S/W B	Air Fuel Ratio in the Exhaust Manifold	Ox Sensor Signal	Computer	EBCV	Air Bleed
Below 7°C (45°F)	OPEN (J·L)	—	—	—	OFF	—	—	OFF	CLOSED	OFF
Above 17°C (63°F)	OPEN (K·L)	Idling	Below 1,300 rpm	—	—	—	—	OFF	CLOSED	OFF
		Cruising	Between 1,500 and 4,200	ON	ON	RICH	RICH	ON	OPEN	Feedback air bleed
						LEAN	LEAN	OFF	CLOSED	
			Above 4,400 rpm	—	—	—	—	OFF	CLOSED	OFF
		Heavy loads*		ON	OFF	—	—	OFF	CLOSED	OFF
		Deceleration	Above 1,500 rpm	OFF	ON	—	—	ON	OPEN	ON

Remark: *Intake vacuum: below 85 mmHg (3.35 in.Hg. 11.3 kPa)

Feedback carburetor system operation

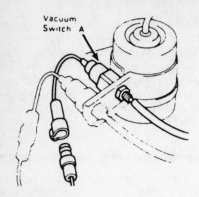

Vacuum switch A

Check Vacuum Switch B

1. Using an ohmmeter, check that there is NO continuity between the switch terminal and the switch body.

2. Start the engine and run until normal operating temperature is reached.

3. Using an ohmmeter, check that there is continuity between the switch terminal and the body.

4. If either test is failed, replace the switch.

Deceleration Fuel Cut-Off System

OPERATION

This system cuts off part of the fuel flow to the idle (or slow) circuit of the carburetor to prevent overheating and afterburning in the exhaust system. The first fuel cut solenoid is kept energized by the ECM whenever the engine is running. The only exception is if the vacuum signal is above 8.46 in.Hg with the rpm above 2290. (This combination will be sensed by the ECM when the vacuum switch A de-energizes with a vacuum signal above its calibrated value.) With the first fuel cut-off solenoid valve de-energized, the carburetor's slow (or idle) circuit fuel is cut off. This will occur whenever the vehicle is decelerated from an engine rpm higher than 2290.

CHECKING THE OPERATION OF THE FUEL CUT-OFF SYSTEM

NOTE: *Perform this test quickly to avoid overheating the catalytic converter.*

1. Connect a tachometer to the engine.
2. Start the engine.
3. Check that the engine runs normally.
4. Disconnect the vacuum switch **A** connector.

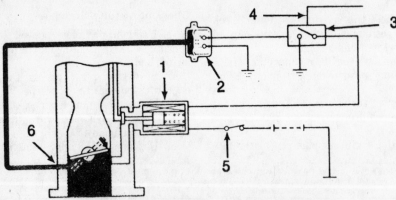

1. Primary fuel cut solenoid	4. Engine speed input
2. Vacuum switch "A"	5. Ignition switch
3. ECM	6. TP port

Deceleration fuel cut-off components

	This system cuts off part of the fuel in the slow circuit of the carburetor to prevent overheating and afterburning in the exhaust system.				
Engine RPM	**Vacuum in the Vacuum S/W**	**Vacuum S/W (A)**	**Computer**	**1st Fuel Cut Solenoid Valve**	**Slow Circuit in Carburetor**
Below 1,900 rpm	—	—	ON	ON	OPEN
Above 2,290 rpm	Below 180 mm Hg (7.09 in. Hg) (24.0 kPa)	ON	ON	ON	OPEN
	Above 215 mm Hg (8.46 in. Hg) (28.7 kPa)	OFF	OFF	OFF	CLOSED

Deceleration fuel cut-off system operation

To reduce cold engine emission and improve driveability, the intake manifold is heated during cold engine operation to accelerate vaporization of the liquid fuel.

IG S/W	Engine	Coolant Temp.	Thermo S/W	ECM	CMH Relay	CMH
OFF	Not running	—	—	—	OFF	OFF
ON	Not running	—	—	OFF	OFF	OFF
	Running	Below 43°C (109°F)	ON	ON	ON	ON (Heated)
		Above 55°C (131°F)	OFF	OFF	OFF	OFF

Cold mixture heater operation chart

5. Slowly increase the engine speed to 2,300 rpm, and check that the engine speed is fluctuating.

6. Reconnect the vacuum switch connector. Again slowly increase the engine speed to 2,300 rpm and check that the engine operation returns to normal.

7. If no problem is found with this test, the system is working properly. If any problem is found, inspect each component part.

CHECKING THE FIRST FUEL CUT-OFF SOLENOID VALVE

1. Remove the two-wire solenoid valve from the carburetor.

CAUTION: *Gasoline may run from the carburetor. Observe no smoking/no open flame precautions. Have a dry powder (Type B-C) fire extinguisher within reach at all times.*

2. Apply 12v to one of the solenoid wires while grounding the other.

3. You should be able to feel a distinct click within the solenoid as the circuit is completed and released. This shows that the solenoid is engaging and disengaging properly.

4. Check the O-ring for damage.

5. Reinstall the valve and connect the wiring connector.

Cold Mixture Heater (CMH)

OPERATION

The cold-mixture heater (CMH) system reduces cold engine emissions and improves driveability during engine warm-up. The intake manifold is heated during cold engine warm-up to accelerate vaporization of the liquid fuel.

The computer looks at alternator terminal **L** to determine if the engine is running and also watches the engine's coolant temperature. If the engine is running and the coolant temperature is below 109°F (43°C), the computer energizes the cold mixture heater relay, which in turn applies battery voltage to the cold mixture heater. The CMH is a multi-element heater ring that is mounted between the carburetor base and the intake manifold. Once the coolant temperature exceeds 131°F (55°C) the CMH

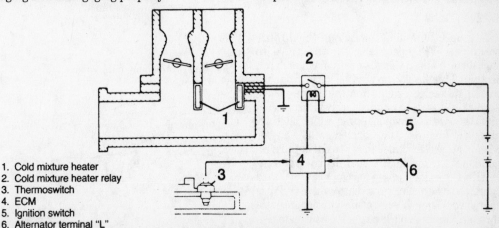

1. Cold mixture heater
2. Cold mixture heater relay
3. Thermoswitch
4. ECM
5. Ignition switch
6. Alternator terminal "L"

Cold mixture heater system

relay is de-energized and the heater elements turn off.

TESTING

Checking the Cold Mixture System Operation

1. Start the engine. The coolant temperature must be below 109°F (43°C).

2. Using a voltmeter, check that there is voltage between the positive (+) terminal (white/red wire) and the ground.

NOTE: *The voltmeter probe should be inserted from the rear side of the connector.*

3. Allow the engine to warm up and check the CHM with the engine warm. The coolant temperature should be above 131°F (55°C).

4. Using a voltmeter, check that there is NO voltage. If no problem is found with this inspection, the system is working properly.

Checking the Mixture Heater

1. Unplug the wiring connector.

2. Using an ohmmeter, check the resistance between the heater terminals. The resistance should be 0.5–2.0Ω. Readings outside this range require replacement of the heater element.

3. Replug the wiring connector.

Checking the Cold Mixture Heater Relay

1. Check that there is continuity between the No. 1 and 2 terminals. Check that there is NO continuity between the No. 3 and 4 terminals.

NOTE: *The relay is located under the air intake hose behind the battery.*

2. Apply battery voltage to terminal No. 1 and ground terminal No. 2. Use the ohmmeter to check for continuity between terminals 3 and 4.

Throttle Positioner System

OPERATION

To reduce HC and CO emissions, the throttle positioner (TP) opens the throttle valve to slightly more than the idle position when decelerating. This keeps the air/fuel ratio from becoming excessively rich when the throttle valve is quickly closed. In addition, the TP is used to increase idle rpm when power steering fluid pressure exceeds a calibrated value and/or when a large electrical load is placed on the electrical system (headlights, rear defogger etc).

With the engine idling and an electrical load energized, the vacuum switching valve (VSV) is energized. This directs atmospheric pressure through the VSV to the rear TP diaphragm (A). The action of the spring on the diaphragm is transmitted to the push rod. This causes the throttle valve to open slightly and increase

engine rpm. If all of the heavy electrical loads are off, the VSV is off, maintaining vacuum on the diaphragm and preventing the push rod from moving.

Vacuum from the **TP** port of the carburetor acts on a second diaphragm (B), closing the throttle valve. With the vehicle cruising, the vacuum signal in both chambers is low which maintains the **TP** in its high speed (open) position. However, when the vehicle is decelerated, vacuum on diaphragm A increases quickly which closes the throttle valve somewhat.

The delay action of the vacuum transmitting valve makes the vacuum increase on diaphragm **B** occur slowly which allows the throttle valve to close at a controlled rate. This slow closing prevents the radical change in emissions caused by the throttle valve slamming shut as the driver suddenly lifts completely off the accelerator, such as when going down a steep hill or preparing to use the brakes.

In the event that power steering pressure exceeds a calibrated value, (such as in a full-lock turn while parking) atmospheric pressure is pulled into chamber A causing diaphragm A to move, increasing rpm. This compensates for the power steering system dragging down the idle speed as it delivers needed fluid pressure.

TESTING

Checking the Throttle Positioner System Operation

1. Start the engine and warm up to normal

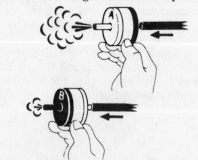

Checking the vacuum delay valve

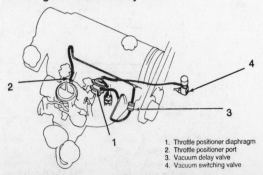

1. Throttle positioner diaphragm
2. Throttle positioner port
3. Vacuum delay valve
4. Vacuum switching valve

Throttle positioner component location

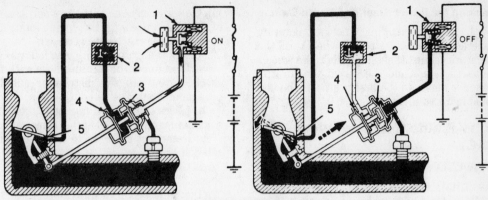

1. Vacuum switching valve
2. Vacuum delay valve
3. Diaphragm A
4. Diaphragm B
5. Throttle positioner port

Throttle positioner operation

To reduce HC and CO emissions, the throttle positioner opens the throttle valve slightly more than at idle when decelerating. This causes the air-fuel mixture to burn completely.

Condition	VSV for electrical load	TP Port Vacuum	Diaphragm A	Diaphragm B	Throttle Valve
Idling	ON	–	Pushed out by diaphragm spring	–	slightly opens (Idle up)
	OFF	Intake manifold vacuum	–	Pulled by intake manifold vacuum	Idle speed position
Cruising	–	Nearly atmospheric pressure	–	Pushed out by diaphragm spring	High speed position
Deceleration	–	Intake manifold vacuum	–	*Pulled by intake manifold vacuum	Slightly opens and *slowly closes to the idling position

Remarks: *This action is delayed by the VTV

Throttle positioner operation chart

operating temperature.

2. Check the idle speed and adjust if necessary.

3. Disconnect the hose from the TVSV **M** port and plug the **M** port. This will shut off the choke opener and EGR system.

4. Disconnect the vacuum hose from **TP** diaphragm **A**. Check that the **TP** is set at the first step (electrical load idle up). Throttle Positioner at the first setting speed:
• Manual Trans: 800 rpm
• Auto. Trans: 900 rpm

If not at the specified speed, adjust the speed with the adjusting screw.

NOTE: *The adjustment should be made with the cooling fan (at the radiator) OFF.*

5. Disconnect the vacuum hose from the throttle positioner diaphragm **B** and plug the end of the hose.

6. Check that the throttle positioner is set at the second step. The setting speed with the throttle positioner on the second step should be as follows:
• Manual Trans: 1,300 ± 200 rpm
• Auto. Trans: 1,400 ± 200 rpm

7. Reconnect the vacuum hose to the throttle positioner diaphragm **B** and check that the engine returns to the first step setting speed within 2–6 seconds.

8. Reconnect the vacuum hose to diaphragm **A**.

9. Reconnect the hose to the TVSV **M** port.

Checking the Vacuum Delay Valve

1. Check that air flows without resistance from **B** to **A**.

2. Check that air flows with difficulty from **A** to **B**.

3. If a problem is found, replace the vacuum delay valve.

NOTE: *When replacing the vacuum delay valve, side **A** should face the throttle positioner.*

Checking the Vacuum Switching Valve

With the engine at idling at normal operating temperature, turn on the high beam headlights. The throttle positioner should move to the first step positions and the idle should increase slightly.

Checking the Power Steering Idle-Up Switch

With the engine at idling at normal operating temperature, turn the steering wheel until the wheels are against their stops. Hold the wheels against the stops and check that the throttle positioner moves to the first position. The idle should increase slightly.

High Altitude Compensation (HAC)

OPERATION

As altitude increases, air density decreases so that the air/fuel mixture becomes richer. (The same amount of fuel is mixing with less air so the percentage of fuel is higher.) The high altitude compensation (HAC) system insures a proper air/fuel mixture by supplying additional air to the primary low and high speed circuits of the carburetor and advancing the ignition timing to improve driveability at altitudes above 3930 feet (1200 m). Above 3930 feet (1200 m), the bellows in the high altitude compensation valve is expanded which closes Port **A**.

With Port **A** closed, the manifold vacuum is allowed to act on the HAC diaphragm. The diaphragm opens Port **B** to the atmosphere (through the HAC valve), allowing air to enter the carburetor's primary low and high speed fuel circuits. This same vacuum signal acts on the distributor sub-diaphragm adding 8° of timing advance.

At altitudes below 2,570 feet (783 m), the HAC bellows are contracted opening Port **A**. This vacuum signal with air reduces the vacuum to the distributor's sub-diaphragm (no timing advance). With vacuum strength reduced, port **B** is closed allowing no air bleed into the carburetor's low and high speed circuits.

TESTING

Checking the High Altitude Compensation System Operation

NOTE: *Always refer to the underhood emission sticker for engine timing and idle speed specifications as some engines may be different.*

1. Check the HAC valve as follows:

a. Visually check and clean the air filter in the HAC valve.

b. At high altitude − above 3930 ft. (1200 m), blow into any one of the two ports on top of the HAC valve with the engine idling and check that the HAC valve is open to the atmosphere.

c. At low altitude − below 2570 ft. (783

m), blow into any one of the two ports on top of the HAC valve with the engine idling and check that the HAC valve is closed.

2. Check the ignition timing as follows:

a. Disconnect the vacuum hose with the check valve from the distributor sub-diaphragm and plug the end of the hose.

b. Check the ignition timing. It should be a maximum of 5° BTDC at 950 rpm.

c. Reconnect the hose to the distributor sub-diaphragm.

d. Check the ignition timing. It should be about 13° BTDC at 950 rpm.

3. Disconnect the vacuum hose from the check valve at the back side and plug the end of the hose. Check that the ignition timing remains stable for more than one minute.

4. Stop the engine and reconnect the hoses to their proper locations.

5. Disconnect the two hoses on the top of the HAC valve. Blow air into each hose and check that the air flows into the carburetor.

6. Reconnect the hoses to their proper locations.

7. Any component not opening or closing properly should be replaced.

Checking the Check Valve

1. Check the valve by blowing air into each pipe:

2. Check that air flows from the orange pipe to the black pipe.

3. Check that air does not flow from the black pipe to the orange pipe.

Checking the Distributor Vacuum Advance

Remove the distributor cap and rotor. Plug one port of the sub-diaphragm. Using a hand-held vacuum pump, apply vacuum to the diaphragm, checking that the vacuum advance

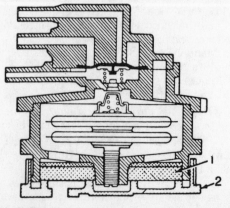

1. Air filter
2. Cover

High altitude compensation valve

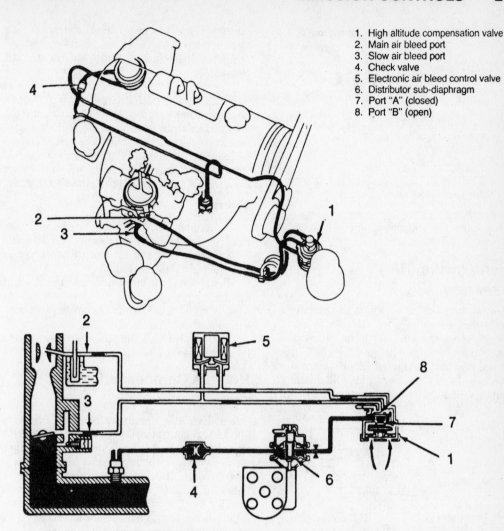

1. High altitude compensation valve
2. Main air bleed port
3. Slow air bleed port
4. Check valve
5. Electronic air bleed control valve
6. Distributor sub-diaphragm
7. Port "A" (closed)
8. Port "B" (open)

High altitude compensation system components

As altitude increases, the air-fuel mixture becomes richer. This system insures proper air-fuel mixture by supplying additional air to the primary low and high speed circuit of the carburetor and advances the ignition timing to improve driveability at high altitude above 1,198 m (3,930 ft.).

Altitude	Bellows in HAC Valve	Port A in HAC Valve	Port B in HAC Valve	Distributor Sub-diaphragm	Air from HAC Valve	Vacuum Ignition Timing
High Above 1,198 m (3,930 ft.)	Expanded	CLOSED	OPEN	Pulled (Always)	Led into primary low and high speed circuit	Advanced (+8°) (Always)
Low Below 783 m (2,570 ft)	Contracted	OPEN	CLOSED	*Not pulled	Stopped	*Not advanced

Remarks: * However, because of an orifice in the distributor sub-diaphragm pipe leading to the HAC valve, the sub-diaphragm is pulled only during high vacuum such as when idling.

High altitude compensation (HAC) system operation

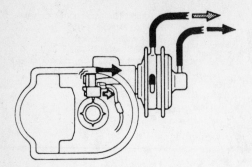

Distributor vacuum advance

moves when the vacuum is applied. Reinstall the rotor and distributor cap.

Hot Air Intake (HAI)

OPERATION

This system directs hot air to the carburetor in cold weather to improve driveability and to prevent carburetor icing. With the air temperature in the air cleaner below 72°F (22°C), the atmospheric port in the hot idle compensation valve is closed, sending the full manifold vacuum signal to the hot air intake (HAI) dia-

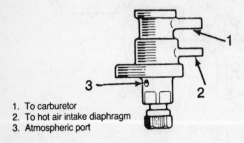

1. To carburetor
2. To hot air intake diaphragm
3. Atmospheric port

Hot air intake system components

phragm. The HAI diaphragm moves, opening the air control valve which directs the heated air (from the exhaust manifold) into the air cleaner.

Once the air cleaner temperature exceeds 84°F (29°C), the HIC atmospheric port is open allowing atmospheric pressure to act on the hot air intake diaphragm. This keeps the air control valve closed, allowing the intake air to come directly down the air cleaner's snorkel from outside the car. This air is always cooler than the air from around the exhaust manifold.

TESTING

1. Remove the air cleaner cover and cool the HIC valve by blowing compressed air on it.
2. Check that the air control valve closes the cool air passages at idle.
3. Reinstall the air cleaner cover and warm up the engine.
4. Check that the air control valve opens the cool air passage at idle.
5. Visually check the hoses and connections for cracks, leaks or damage.

Hot Idle Compensation (HIC)

OPERATION

The Hot Idle Compensation (HIC) System allows the air controlled by the HIC valve to enter the intake manifold, maintaining proper air/fuel mixture during idle at high temperatures. When the air cleaner temperature is below 72°F (22°C), the HIC valve's atmospheric port is closed. This allows supplies intake manifold vacuum to the hot air intake (HAI) valve, allowing heated air to enter the air cleaner.

As the temperature in the air cleaner rises, the HIC valve will increase its opening to the

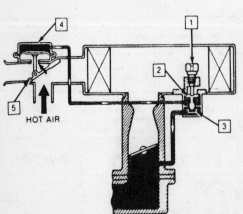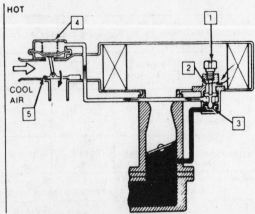

1. Hot idle compensator valve
2. Atmospheric port
3. Check valve
4. Hot air intake diaphragm
5. Air control valve

Hot air intake system components

atmosphere which, in turn, increases pressure on the diaphragm. As the pressure increases the HAC valve will close more, pulling cooler (more dense) air into the carburetor.

When air cleaner temperatures are between 84°F (29°C) and 126°F (52°C), the HIC valve's atmospheric port opens slightly. This begins to increase the pressure on the HAI diaphragm and its air control valve begins to close.

When intake air temperatures reach 138°F (59°C), both the atmospheric port and the vacuum port of the HIC valve open further. This action steadily increases the pressure on HAI diaphragm and continues to close the air control valve, pulling more cool air into the carburetor. At the same time, the opening of the

vacuum port allows outside air to bleed into the intake manifold to maintain the proper air/fuel mixture during high temperature at idle.

Finally at temperatures above 192°F (89°C), the HIC valve's atmospheric and vacuum ports open fully, applying maximum pressure to the HAI diaphragm and closing the air control valve completely. This allows the coolest possible air to enter the carburetor.

TESTING

1. Check that air flows from the HAI diaphragm side to the carburetor side while closing the atmospheric port.

2. Check that air does not flow from the carburetor side to the HAI diaphragm side.

This system leads a hot air supply to the carburetor in cold weather to improve driveability and to prevent the carburetor from icing in extremely cold weather.			
Temperature in Air Cleaner	HIC Valve	Air Control Valve	Intake Air
Cold Below 22°C (72°F)	Atmospheric port is CLOSED	Hot air passage OPEN	HOT
Hot Above 29°C (84°F)	Atmospheric port is OPEN	Cool air passage OPEN	COOL

Hot air intake system operation chart

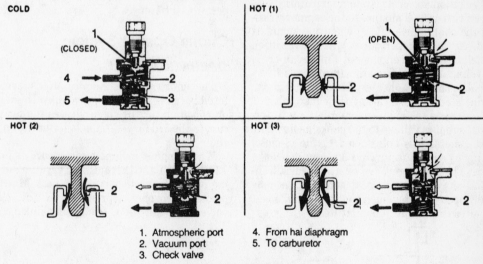

1. Atmospheric port
2. Vacuum port
3. Check valve
4. From hai diaphragm
5. To carburetor

HIC system operation

This system allows the air controlled by the HIC valve to enter the intake manifold to maintain proper air-fuel mixture during high temperatures at idle.			
Temperature in Air Cleaner	HIC Valve Atmospheric Port	HIC Valve Vacuum Port Opening	HIC System
HOT (1) Between 29°C (84°F) and 52°C (126°F)	OPEN	MINIMUM	OFF
HOT (2) Between 59°C (138°F) and 82°C (180°F)	OPEN	PARTIAL	ON Air volume is controlled by HIC valve
HOT (3) Above 89°C (192°F)	OPEN	MAXIMUM	ON

HIC system operation chart

This system temporarily supplies a rich mixture to the engine by closing the choke valve when the engine is cold.				
IG S/W	Engine	Current from L Terminal to Heater	Bimetal	Choke Valve
OFF	Not running	Not flowing	Expanded	CLOSED
ON	Not running	* Not flowing	Expanded	CLOSED
	Running	Flowing	Heated up and contracted	OPEN
Remarks:	* On alternators with IC regulator, slight voltage will occur when the ignition switch is turned ON, but not sufficient current to warm up the heater.			

Choke system operation chart

3. Below 72°F (22°C), check that air does NOT flow from the HAI diaphragm side to the atmosphere port while closing the intake manifold side.

4. Heat the HIC valve to above 84°F (29°C).

5. Check that air flows from the HAI diaphragm side to the atmospheric port while closing the carburetor side.

Automatic Choke

OPERATION

The automatic choke system temporarily supplies a rich air/fuel mixture to the engine by closing the choke valve (plate) when the engine is cold. At cold temperatures with the ignition switch ON but the engine not running, there is no voltage supplied from the alternator's **L** terminal at the choke heater. The bi-metal choke spring is contracted, closing the choke valve.

As soon as the engine is running, the **L** terminal supplies voltage to the choke heater. The heat generated is transferred to the bi-metal spring causing it to unwind-opening the choke valve. This helps provide a relatively quick transition between the rich (cold) setting to the normally open position when the engine no longer requires the rich air/fuel mixture.

TESTING

Checking the Automatic Choke

1. Allow the choke valve to close.
2. Start the engine.
3. Check that the choke valve begins to open and the choke housing is heated.

Checking the Heating Coil

1. Unplug the wire connector.
2. Measure the resistance with an ohmmeter. The resistance should read: 19–24Ω 68°F (20°C). Allow for slight variations due to temperature differences.

Choke Opener System

OPERATION

The choke opener system, after warm-up, forcibly holds the choke valve open to prevent an over-rich mixture and releases the fast idle cam to the 3rd (lowest) step to lower the engine rpm.

When engine coolant temperature is below 122°F (50°C), the thermostatic vacuum switching valve connects port **J** to port **M** which places atmospheric pressure on the choke valve. Through the choke opener linkage, the

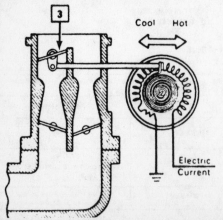

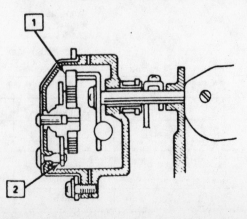

Choke system operation

fast idle cam is set at the first (high idle) or second step.

When the coolant temperature exceeds 154°F (68°C), the TVSV connects Port **K** to Port **M** which now applies manifold vacuum to the choke opener diaphragm. This action opens the choke valve further and releases the fast idle cam to the third step and idle speed decreases.

TESTING

Check the Choke Opener System Operation

1. Disconnect the vacuum hose from the choke opener diaphragm. With the coolant temperature below 122°F (50°C), step down on the accelerator pedal and release it.

2. Start the engine.

3. Reconnect the vacuum hose and check that the choke linkage does not move.

4. Warm the engine to normal operating temperature and shut it off.

5. Disconnect the vacuum hose from the choke opener diaphragm.

6. Set the fast idle cam. While holding the throttle slightly open, push the choke plate closed and hold it closed as you release the throttle.

7. Turn the key and start the motor but DO NOT touch the accelerator pedal.

8. Reconnect the vacuum hose. The choke linkage should move and the fast idle cam should release to the third step (lowest rpm).

Checking the TVSV

For testing procedures for the TVSV please refer to the EGR system testing procedures earlier in this chapter.

Checking the Diaphragm

Check that the choke linkage moves in accordance with the amount of vacuum applied. If a problem is found, replace the diaphragm.

Auxiliary Acceleration Pump (AAP)

OPERATION

When accelerating with a cold engine, the main acceleration pump's capacity is insufficient to provide enough fuel for good acceleration. The auxiliary acceleration pump system

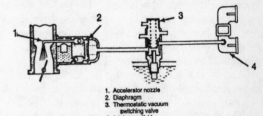

1. Accelerator nozzle
2. Diaphragm
3. Thermostatic vacuum switching valve
4. Intake manifold

Auxiliary acceleration pump system components

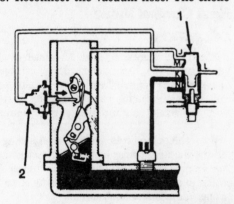 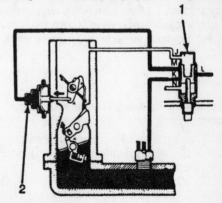

1. Thermostatic vacuum switching valve
2. Choke opener diaphram

Choke opener system operation

After warm up, this system forcibly holds the choke valve open to prevent an over-rich mixture and releases the fast idle to the 3rd step to lower engine rpm.					
Coolant Temp.	TVSV	Diaphragm	Choke Valve	Fast Idle Cam	Engine RPM
Below 50°C (122°F)	OPEN (J-M)	Released by spring tension	Closed by automatic choke	Set at 1st or 2nd step	HIGH
Above 68°C (154°F)	OPEN (K-M)	Pulled by manifold vacuum	OPEN	Released to 3rd step	LOW

Choke opener system operation chart

When accelerating with a cold engine, the main acceleration pump capacity is insufficient to provide good acceleration. The AAP system compensates for this by forcing more fuel into the acceleration nozzle to obtain better cold engine performance.

Coolant Temp.	TVSV	Engine	Intake Vacuum	Diaphragm in AAP	Fuel
Below 50°C (122°F)	OPEN (K-N)	Constant RPM	HIGH	Pulled by vacuum	Drawn into AAP chamber
		Acceleration	LOW	Returned by spring tension	Forced into acceleration nozzle
Above 68°C (154°F)	CLOSED (K-N)	—	—	No operation	—

Auxiliary acceleration pump system chart

compensates for this by forcing more fuel into the acceleration nozzle to obtain better cold engine performance.

When engine coolant temperature is below 122°F (50°C), the thermostatic vacuum switching valve connects port **K** to port **N** which connects manifold vacuum to the AAP diaphragm. When engine rpm is relatively steady, the diaphragm moves against its spring causing its fuel chamber to fill. Whenever the engine is accelerated, the vacuum signal to the AAP diaphragm diminishes quickly. The diaphragm is pushed by its spring, forcing its fuel into the main acceleration circuit and out its nozzle.

After coolant temperature exceeds 154°F (68°C), the TVSV blocks Port **K** and Port **N** stopping the operation of the auxiliary acceleration pump system. The additional fuel requirement for warm engine acceleration is adequately handled by the main acceleration pump (carburetor) circuit.

TESTING

Checking the Auxiliary Acceleration Pump System

1. Check that the coolant temperature is below 122°F (50°C). Remove the cover from the air cleaner and start the engine.
2. Pinch the AAP hose, and shut off the engine.
3. Release the hose. Check that gasoline spurts out from the accelerator nozzle in the carburetor. Don't perform this test too often — you may flood the motor.
3. Restart the engine and warm it to normal operating temperature. Repeat steps 2 and 3 above. Check that gasoline DOES NOT spurt out from the accelerator nozzle.
4. Reinstall the air cleaner cover.

Checking the Auxiliary Acceleration Pump Diaphragm

1. Start the engine.
2. Disconnect the hose from the AAP diaphragm.
3. Apply vacuum directly to the AAP diaphragm (at idle) with a hand held vacuum pump.
4. Check that the engine rpm changes as the vacuum is released from the system.
5. Reconnect the AAP hose.

Heat Control Valve

OPERATION

When the engine is cold, the heat control valve improves fuel vaporization for better driveability by quickly heating the intake manifold. Once the engine has warmed up, it helps keep the intake manifold at proper temperature.

With the engine cold, the bi-metal spring positions the heat control valve to direct some of the engine's hot exhaust gases under the intake manifold which quickly bring it to the proper operating temperature.

When the engine is hot, the bi-metal spring contracts, moving the position of the heat control valve to direct most of the exhaust under the valve and away from direct contact with the intake manifold.

When cold, this device improves fuel vaporization for better driveability by quickly heating the intake manifold. After warm-up, it keeps the intake manifold at the proper temperature.

Engine	Bimetal	Exhaust Gas Passage	Intake Manifold
COLD	EXPANDED	Above the heat control valve	Heated quickly
HOT	CONTRACTED	Under the heat control valve	Heated to a suitable temperature

Heat control valve operation chart

TESTING

The valve within the exhaust system has a counterweight on the outside of the pipe. This counterweight is viewed most easily from under the car. With the engine cold, check that the counterweight is in the upper position. After the engine has been warmed up, check that the weight has moved to the lower position.

Check Engine Light and Diagnostic Codes.

OPERATION

4A-GE Engine

NOTE: *For engines not listed use these service procedures as a guide as control systems are very similar for other engines.*

The *Check Engine* light is the device providing communication between the Electronic Control Module (ECM) and the driver. The ECM controls the electronic fuel injection, the electronic spark control, the diagnostic function and the fail-safe or default function.

The ECM receives signals from various sensors indicating changing engine operating conditions. These signals are utilized by the ECM to determine the injection duration (amount of time each injector stays open) to maintain the optimum air/fuel ratio under all conditions. The conditions affecting the injector duration are:

- Exhaust gas oxygen content
- Intake air mass
- Intake air temperature
- Coolant temperature
- Engine rpm
- Acceleration/deceleration
- Electrical load
- Air conditioning on/off

The ECM is programmed with data for optimum ignition timing under any and all operating conditions. Using data provide by the sensors, the ECM triggers the spark within each cylinder at precisely the right instant for the existing conditions.

The ECM detects any malfunctions or abnormalities in the sensor network and lights the *Check Engine* light on the dash panel. At the same time the trouble is identified by circuit and a diagnostic code is recorded within the ECM. This diagnostic code can be read by the number of blinks of the instrument light when both check engine terminals are shorted under the hood.

In the event of an internal computer malfunction, the ECM is programmed with back-up or default values. This allows the car to run on a fixed set of "rules" for engine operation. Driveability may suffer since the driving conditions cannot be dealt with by the faulty computer. This back-up programming allows the computer to fail with out stranding the car, hence the nickname fail-safe. No computer is safe from failure, but a back-up system helps make the best of the situation.

With the exception of the oxygen sensor (discussed earlier in this chapter) the testing and replacement of the various sensors is discussed in Chapter 5.

4A-FE Engine

NOTE: *For engines not listed use these service procedures as a guide as control systems are very similar for other engines.*

The ECM is a precision unit consisting of a one-chip micro computer, and analog/digital converter, an input/output unit, a read-only memory (ROM) and a random access memory (RAM). It is an essential part of the electronic control system, controlling many engine functions as well as possessing a self-diagnostic capability and a fail-safe or default memory.

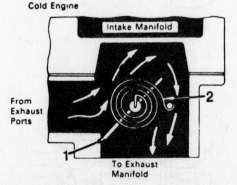

Cold Engine

Intake Manifold

From Exhaust Ports

2

1

To Exhaust Manifold

1. Heat control valve
2. Bi-metal

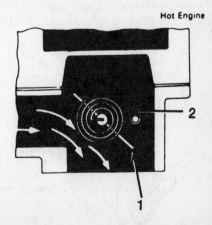

Hot Engine

2

1

Heat control valve operation

The ECM receives information from many sensors on the engine. Based on the constantly changing data, it controls the fuel delivery and spark timing. The sensors communicating with the ECM are:

- Oxygen sensor
- Coolant temperature sensor
- Throttle switch
- Manifold air temperature
- Manifold absolute pressure
- Ignition signal
- Crank angle sensor
- Vehicle speed sensor
- Exhaust gas recirculation system
- Central processing unit of the ECM

If the system is free of any faults after the engine starts, the warning light on the dashboard turns off. When the ECM detects a fault, the *Check Engine* light is illuminated to alert the driver. At the same time, the fault code is stored in the ECM for future reading. The code is stored in the memory even if the fault is momentary or self-corrects. The code is not erased from the memory until the power is removed from the ECM for 20 seconds or more.

Should the ECM detect a fault in any system for which it cannot compensate or develop its own internal fault, it will engage its back-up program. This program is a set of fixed values which allows the car to keep running under adverse circumstances. Because the fixed values in the memory may not correspond to the actual conditions, driveability may suffer when the system is in this default mode. The systems controlled by this back-up memory are:

- Oxygen sensor
- Coolant temperature sensor
- Throttle switch
- Vehicle speed sensor
- Manifold air temperature sensor
- Manifold absolute pressure sensor
- Central processing unit in the ECM

By maintaining the function of these critical sensors, the car is not disabled during the occurrence of an electrical fault in the main system.

With the exception of the oxygen sensor (discussed earlier in this chapter) the testing and replacement of the various sensors is discussed in Chapter 5.

FAULT CODES AND THEIR MEANING

4A-GE Engine

NOTE: *For engines not listed use these service procedures as a guide as control systems are very similar for other engines.*

To read the code(s) from the ECM:

1. The following initial conditions must be met or the code will not be transmitted from the ECM:

    a. Battery voltage above 11 volts

    b. Throttle plate fully closed — keep your foot off the accelerator

    c. Transmission selector in neutral

    d. All accessory switches off

2. Turn the ignition switch ON, but DO NOT start the engine.

3. Use a service (jumper) wire to short both terminals of the engine check connector, located under the hood near the wiper motor.

4. The diagnosis code(s) will be indicated by the number of flashes of the *Check Engine* light.

If the system is normal, the light will blink repeatedly every ½ second. This indication is

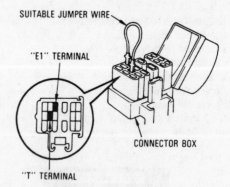

Typical engine check connector

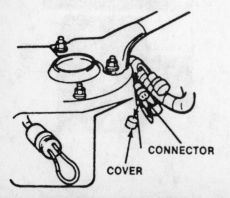

Location of check engine connector 4A-GE engine

displayed when no codes are stored in the ECM. It serves as a confirmation the ECM has nothing to tell you — all is well.

If a fault code is stored, its two digit code will be indicated in the pattern of the flashing. For example, code 21 would be indicated by two flashes, a pause, and one flash. There will be a $1^{1}/_{2}$ second pause between the first and second digit of a code. If more than one code is stored, the next will be transmitted after a $2^{1}/_{2}$ second pause. Once all the codes have been flashed, the system will wait $4^{1}/_{2}$ seconds and repeat the entire series. It will continue sending the fault codes as long as the initial conditions are met and the engine check connector is shorted across terminal **T** and **E1**.

NOTE: *If more than one code is stored, they will be delivered in numerical order from the lowest to the highest, regardless of which code occurred first. The order of the codes DOES NOT indicate the order of occurrence.*

5. After the code(s) have been read and recorded, turn the ignition switch to OFF and disconnect the jumper wire.

WARNING: *Disconnecting the wire with the ignition ON may cause severe damage to the ECM.*

4A-FE Engine

NOTE: *For engines not listed use these service procedures as a guide as control systems are very similar for other engines.*

To read the codes from the ECM:

1. With the ignition OFF, use a service (jumper) wire to ground the diagnostic switch in the connector under the hood.

2. Without touching the accelerator pedal, turn the ignition to ON but DO NOT start the motor.

3. The codes will be displayed through the flashing of the *Check Engine* light. Count the number of flashes to determine the numerical code.

If the system is normal and has no codes stored, the lamp will flash on and off several times rhythmically. If this signal is received, no

further codes will be transmitted from the ECM.

Stored fault codes will be displayed in numerical order from lowest to highest without regard to which code occurred first. All codes are two digit and will be displayed with a one second pause between digits. (Example: Code 21 will show two flashes, a one second pause and then one flash.) Each code will be displayed three times in a row with a three second pause between each code. After any one code has been flashed three times, the next stored code will be displayed three times and so on.

4. After the code(s) have been read and recorded, turn the ignition switch to OFF and disconnect the jumper wire.

WARNING: *Disconnecting the wire with the ignition ON may cause severe damage to the ECM.*

RESETTING THE CHECK ENGINE LIGHT

Once the codes have been read and recorded, the memory on the ECM may be cleared of any stored codes by removing the power to the ECM for at least 1 minute. This is most easily done by removing the STOP fuse from the fuse box for the necessary period of time.

WARNING: *The ignition MUST be OFF when the fuse is removed and reinstalled. Serious and disabling damage may occur if this precaution is not followed.*

Remember that the codes are there to indicate a problem area. Don't clear the code just to get the dashboard light off — find the problem and fix it for keeps. If you erase the code and ignore the problem, the code will reset (when the engine is restarted) if the problem is still present.

The necessary time to clear the computer increases as the temperature drops. To be safe, remove the fuse for a full minute under all conditions. The system can also be cleared by disconnecting the negative battery cable, but this will require resetting other memory devices such as the clock and/or radio. If for any reason the memory does not clear, any stored codes

CODE NO 13   CODE NO 21   CODE NO 13

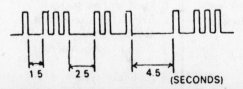

1 5   2 5   4.5
(SECONDS)

Examples of multiple code display of 4A-GE engine system

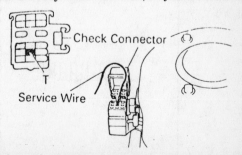

Ground the diagnostic switch terminal T to read trouble codes 4A-FE engine

Code No.	Number of CHECK ENGINE blinks	System	Trouble area
–		Normal	–
12	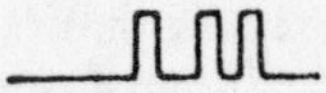	RPM signal	1. Distributor circuit 2. Distributor 3. Igniter circuit 4. Igniter 5. Starter signal circuit 6. ECM
13	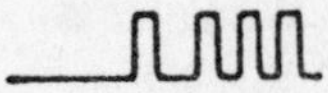	RPM signal	1. Distributor circuit 2. Distributor 3. ECM
14	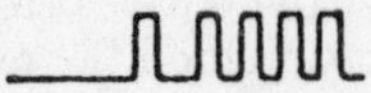	Ignition signal	1. Igniter and ignition coil circuit 2 Igniter and ignition coil 3. ECM
21	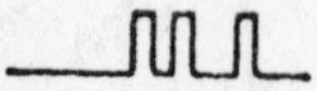	Exhaust oxygen sensor signal	1. Exhaust oxygen sensor circuit 2. Exhaust oxygen sensor 3. ECM
		Exhaust oxygen sensor heater	1. Exhaust oxygen sensor heater circuit 2. Exhaust oxygen sensor heater 3. ECM
22	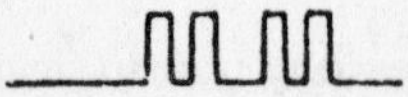	Coolant temp. sensor signal	1. Coolant temp. sensor circuit 2. Coolant temp. sensor 3. ECM
24	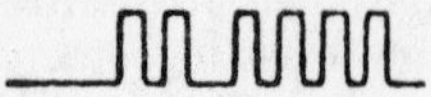	Manifold air temp. sensor signal	1. Manifold air temp. sensor circuit 2. Manifold air temp. sensor 3. ECM
25	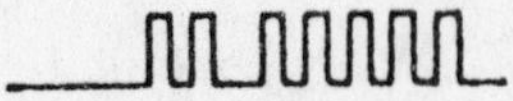	Air-fuel ratio lean malfunction	1. Injector circuit 2. Injector 3. Fuel line pressure 4. Ignition system 5. Mass air flow sensor 6. Exhaust oxygen sensor circuit 7. Exhaust oxygen sensor 8. ECM 9. Air intake system

Trouble codes for the 4A-GE engine

Code No.	Number of CHECK ENGINE blinks	System	Trouble area
26		Air-fuel ratio Rich malfunction	1. Injector circuit 2. Injector 3. Fuel line pressure 4. Cold start injector 5. Mass air flow sensor 6. ECM 7. Exhaust oxygen sensor circuit 8. Exhaust oxygen sensor
31		Mass air flow sensor signal	1. Mass air flow sensor circuit 2. Air flow meter 3. ECM
41		Throttle position sensor signal	1. Throttle position sensor circuit 2. Throttle position sensor 3. ECM
42		Vehicle speed sensor signal	1. Vehicle speed sensor circuit 2. Vehicle speed sensor 3. ECM
43		Starter signal	1. Starter relay circuit 2. IG switch, main relay circuit 3. ECM
51		Switch signal	1. A/C switch 2. Throttle position sensor circuit 3. Throttle position sensor 4. ECM 5. A/C switch circuit 6. A/C switch amplifier
* 71		EGR system malfunction	1. EGR system (EGR vale, EGR hose, etc.) 2. EGR gas temp. sensor circuit 3. EGR gas temp. sensor 4. VSV for EGR 5. VSV for EGR circuit 6. ECM

* For California

Trouble codes for the 4A-GE engine

Code No.	Number of check engine blinks	System	Diagnosis	Trouble area
—	(waveform) ON OFF	Normal	This appears when none of the other codes are identified.	—
12	(waveform)	RPM Signal	No signal to ECU within several seconds after engine is cranked (TAC).	• Ignition coil circuit • Ignition coil • Igniter circuit • Igniter • ECU
21	(waveform)	Oxygen Sensor Signal	During air-fuel ratio feedback correction, voltage output from the oxygen sensor does not exceed a set value on the lean side and the rich side continuously for a certain period.	• Oxygen sensor circuit • Oxygen sensor • ECU
22	(waveform)	Water Temp. Switch Signal	Open or short circuit in water temp. switch signal (TWS1, TWS2).	• No. 1 or No. 2 water temp. switch circuit • No. 1 or No. 2 water temp. switches • ECU
25	(waveform)	Lean Malfunction	• Open circuit in oxygen sensor signal (OX). • EBCV always open. • Short circuit in EBCV signal.	• Oxygen sensor circuit • Oxygen sensor • EBCV circuit • EBCV • Carburetor • ECU
26	(waveform)	Rich Malfunction	• EBCV always closed, or a clogged hose. • Open circuit in EBCV signal.	• EBCV circuit • EBCV hose • EBCV • Carburetor • ECU
31	(waveform)	Vacuum Switch Signal	Open or short circuit in vacuum switches signal (VSW1, VSW2).	• No. 1 or No. 2 vacuum switches signal • No. 1 or No. 2 vacuum switches • Vacuum hose • ECU
41	(waveform)	Throttle Switch Signal	Open or short circuit in throttle switch signal (THS).	• Throttle switch circuit • Throttle switch • ECU
71	(waveform)	EGR Malfunction	• EGR valve normally closed, or a clogged hose. • Open circuit in EGR gas temp. sensor signal (THG).	• EGR valve • EGR hose • EGR gas temp. sensor circuit • EGR gas temp. sensor • ECU
72	(waveform)	Fuel cut Solenoid Signal	Open circuit in fuel cut solenoid signal (FCS).	• Fuel cut solenoid circuit • Fuel cut solenoid • ECU

* If code 31 and 41 are both output, it is not possible to specify the trouble area.

Trouble codes for the 3E (California) engine

EXAMPLE: OXYGEN SENSOR SIGNAL (CODE 21)

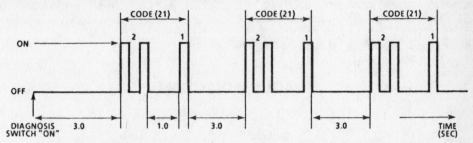

DIAGNOSTIC CODE		DIAGNOSTIC AREA
NO.	MODE	
--	(waveform) ON OFF	NORMAL
12	(waveform)	RPM SIGNAL
13	(waveform)	RPM SIGNAL
14	(waveform)	IGNITION SIGNAL
21	(waveform)	OXYGEN SENSOR
22	(waveform)	COOLANT TEMPERATURE SENSOR
24	(waveform)	MANIFOLD AIR TEMPERATURE SENSOR
25	(waveform)	LEAN AIR/FUEL RATIO
26	(waveform)	RICH AIR/FUEL RATIO
31	(waveform)	MANIFOLD ABSOLUTE PRESSURE SENSOR
41	(waveform)	THROTTLE POSITION SENSOR
42	(waveform)	VEHICLE SPEED SENSOR
43	(waveform)	STARTER SIGNAL
51	(waveform)	SWITCH SIGNAL
71	(waveform)	EGR MALFUNCTION

Code display and trouble codes for the 4A-FE engine

will be retained. Any time the ECM is cleared, the car should be driven and then re-checked to confirm a "normal" signal from the ECM.

NOTE: *In the event of any mechanical work requiring the disconnection of the negative battery cable, the ECM should be interro-* *gated for stored codes before removing the cable. Once the cable is removed, the codes will be lost almost immediately. Always check for stored codes before beginning any other diagnostic work.*

VACUUM DIAGRAMS

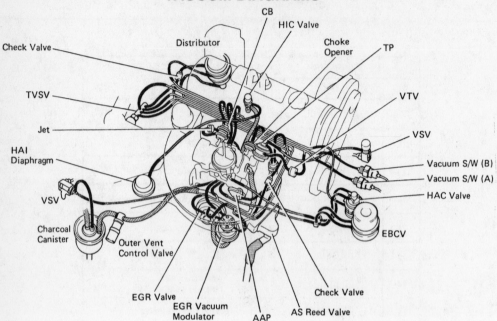

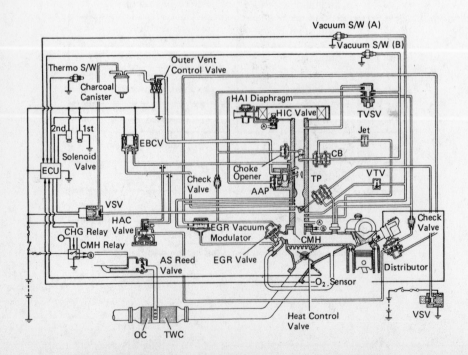

Component layout and schematic drawing 1984–85 Corolla FWD

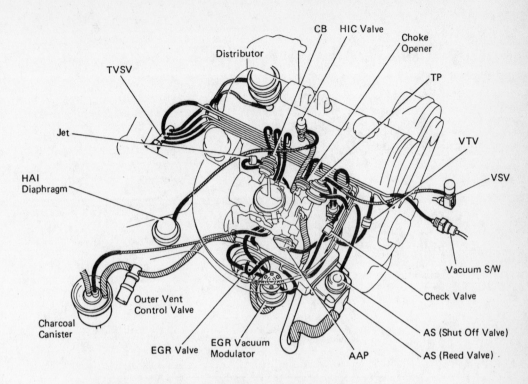

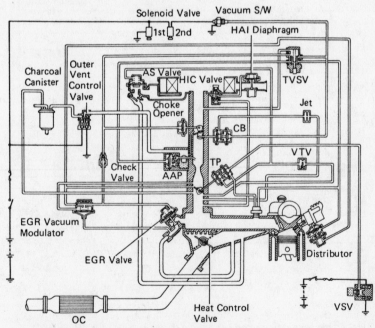

Component layout and schematic drawing 1984–85 Corolla FWD

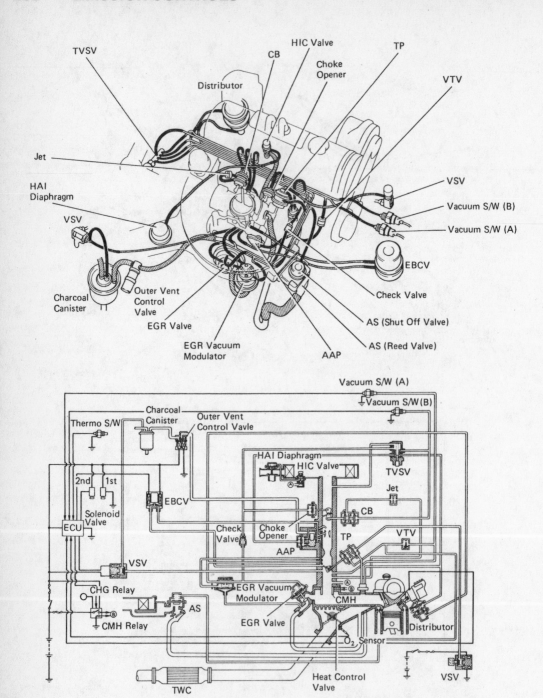

Component layout and schematic drawing 1984–85 Corolla FWD

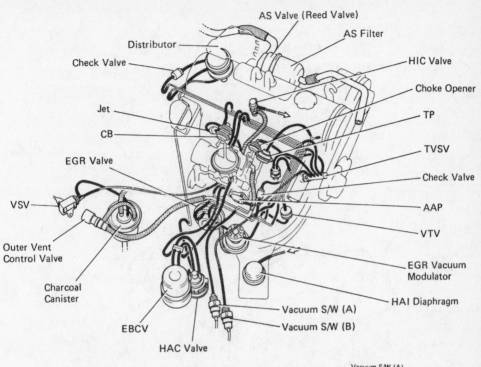

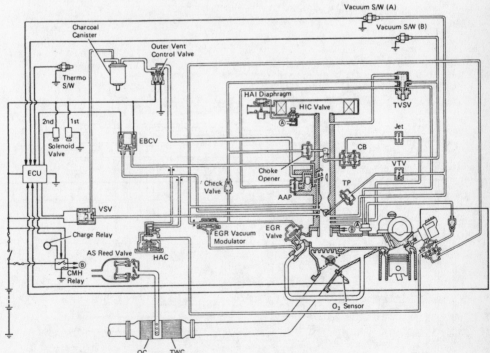

Component layout and schematic drawing 1984–85 Corolla RWD

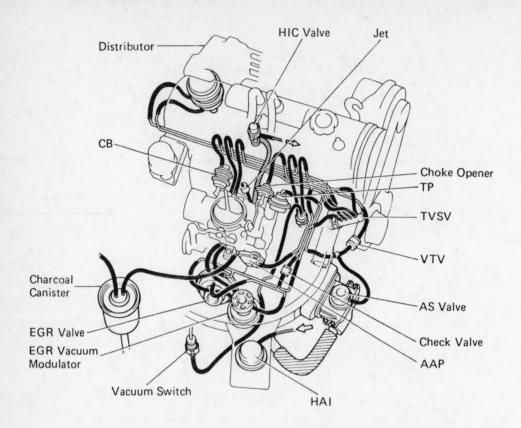

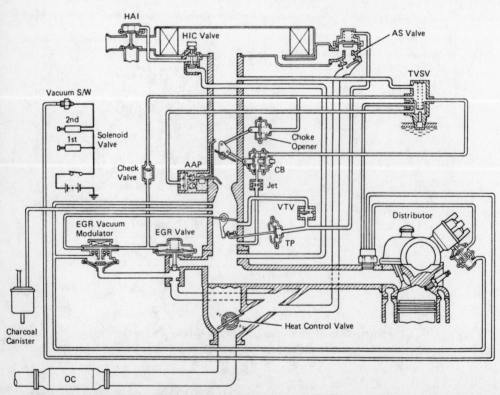

Component layout and schematic drawing 1984–85 Corolla RWD

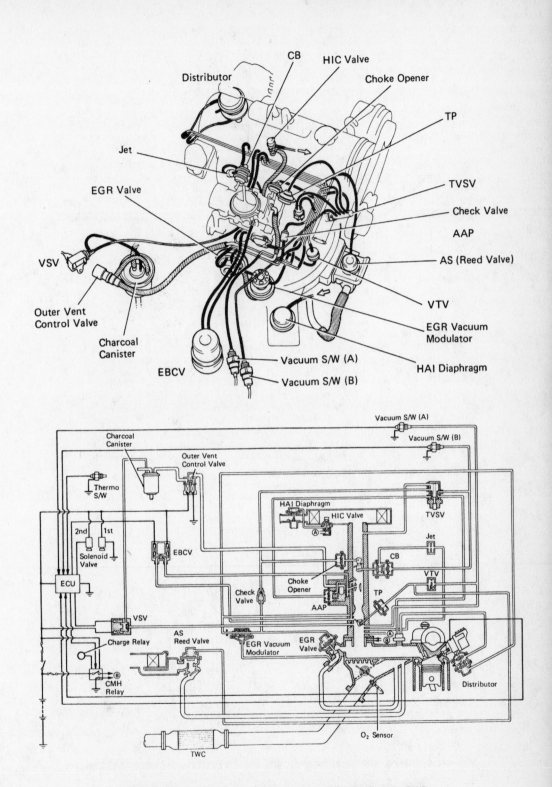

Component layout and schematic drawing 1984–85 Corolla RWD

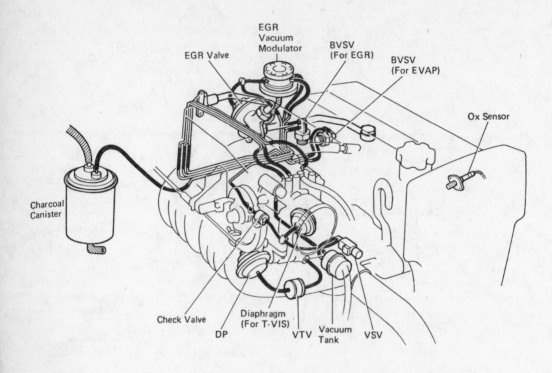

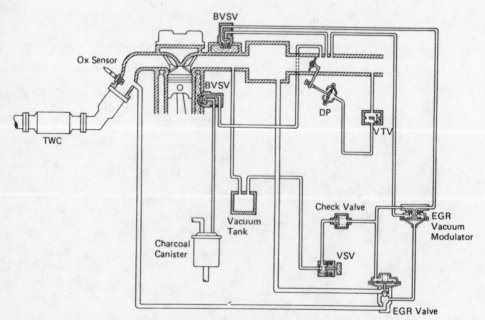

Component layout and schematic drawing 1985 Corolla RWD fuel injected 4A-GE engine

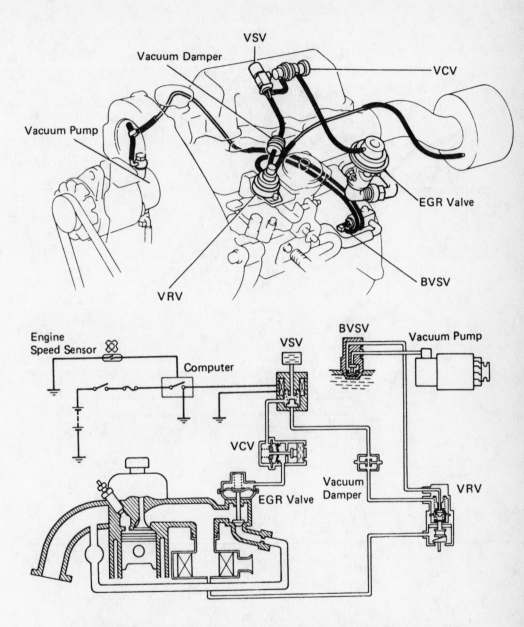

Component layout and schematic drawing 1984–85 Corolla FWD diesel engine 1C

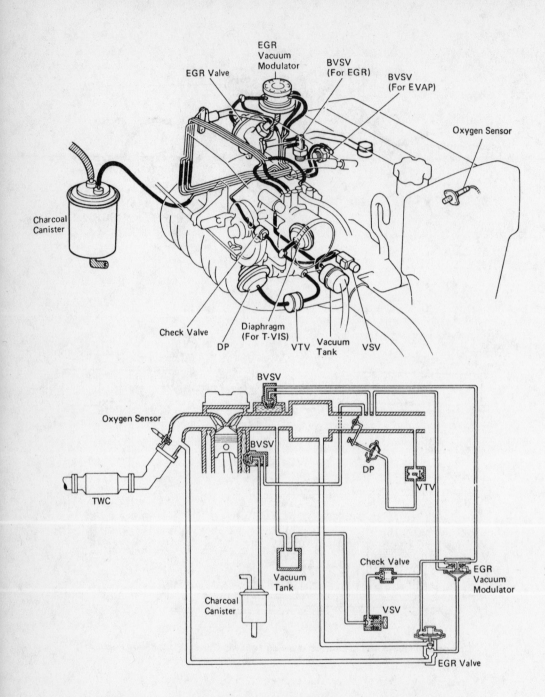

Component layout and schematic drawing 1986 Corolla RWD fuel injected 4A-GE engine

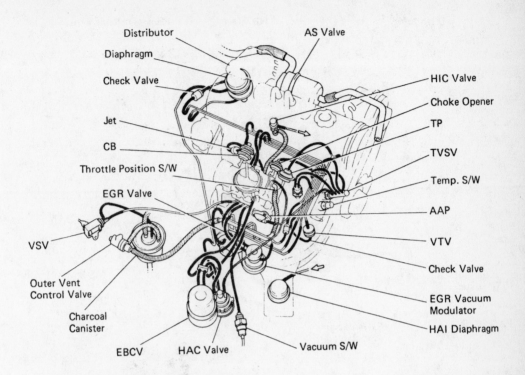

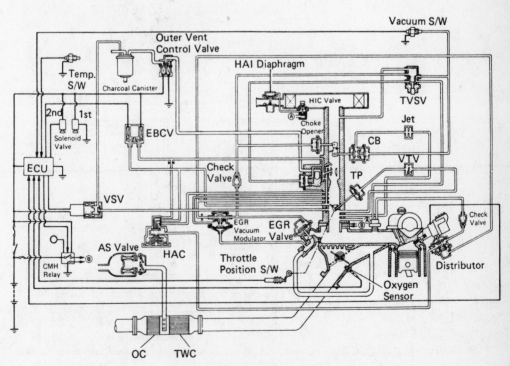

Component layout and schematic drawing 1986 Corolla RWD 4A-C engine

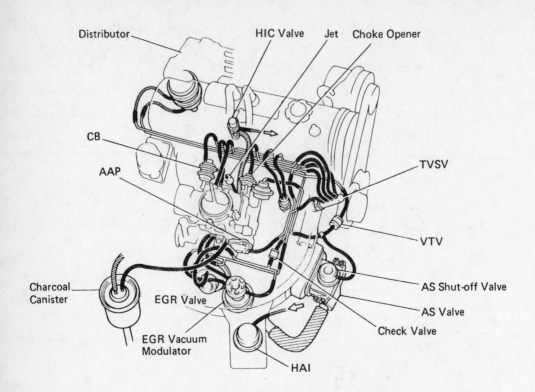

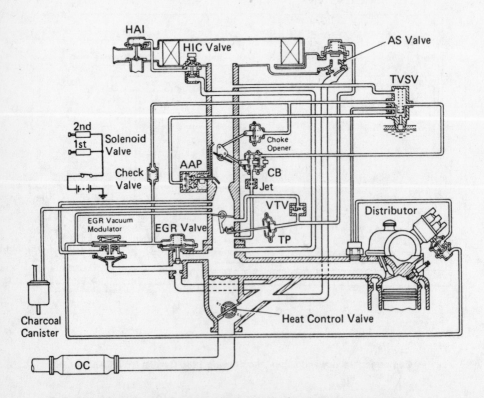

Component layout and schematic drawing 1986 Corolla RWD 4A-C engine

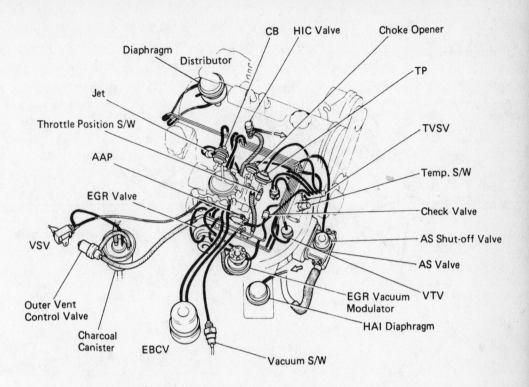

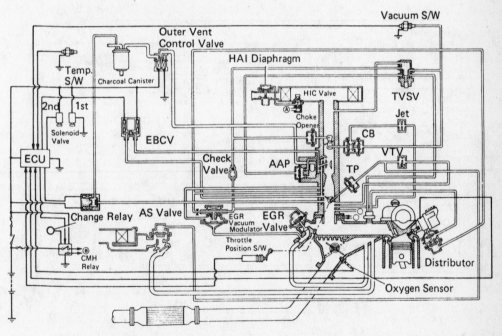

Component layout and schematic drawing 1986 Corolla RWD 4A-C engine

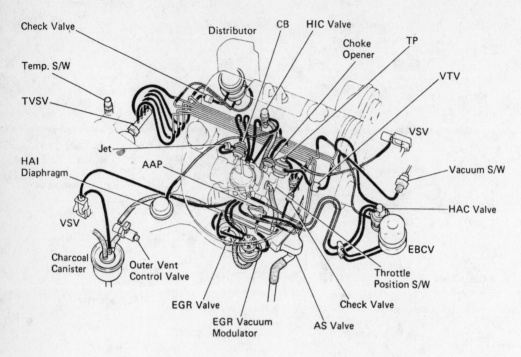

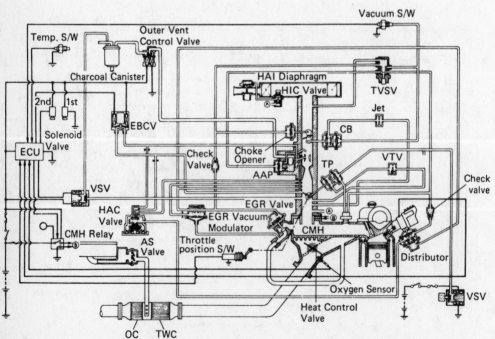

Component layout and schematic drawing 1986 Corolla FWD 4A-C engine

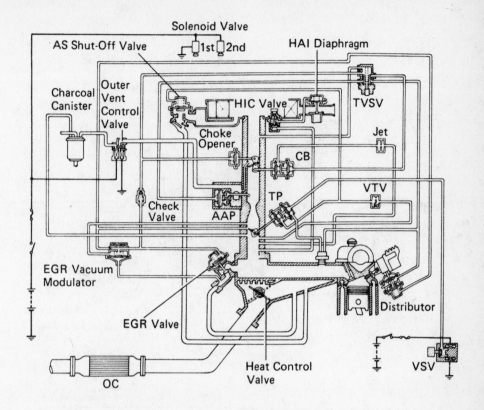

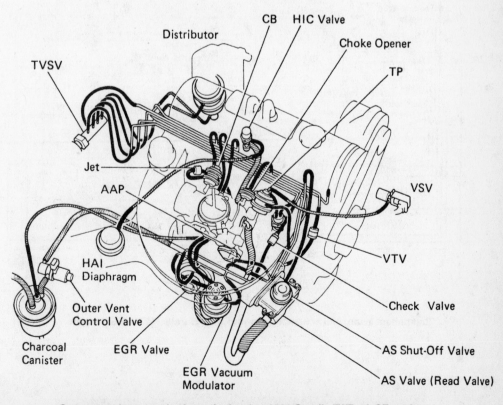

Component layout and schematic drawing 1986 Corolla FWD 4A-GE engine

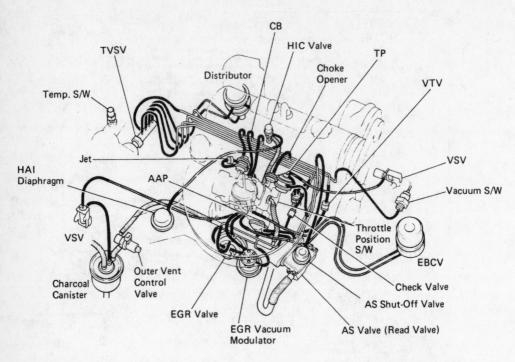

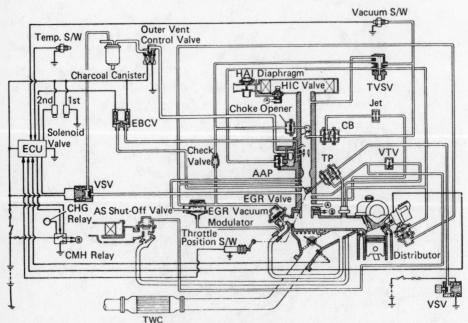

Component layout and schematic drawing 1986 Corolla FWD 4A-GE engine

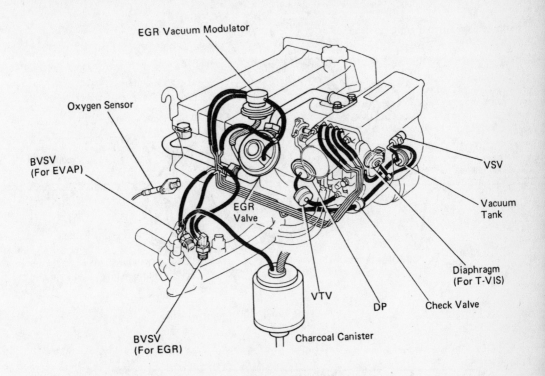

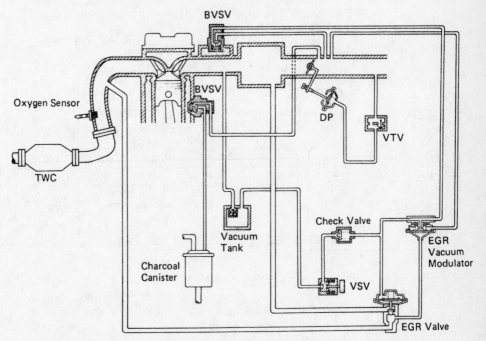

Component layout and schematic drawing 1987 Corolla FWD fuel injected 4A-GE engine

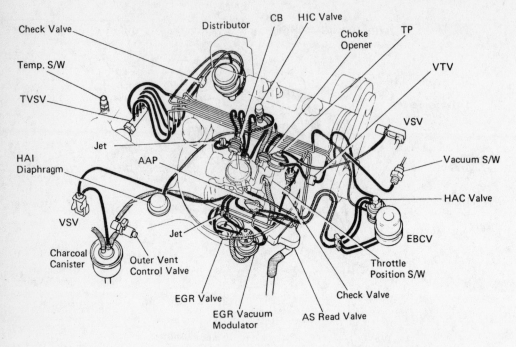

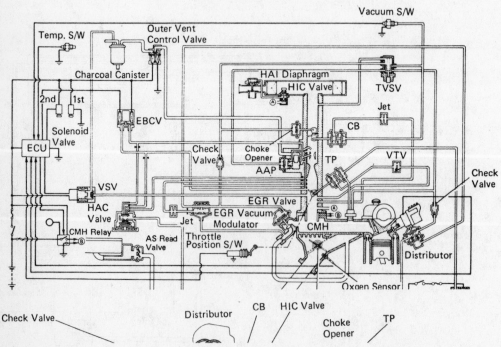

Component layout and schematic drawing 1987 Corolla FWD 4A-C engine

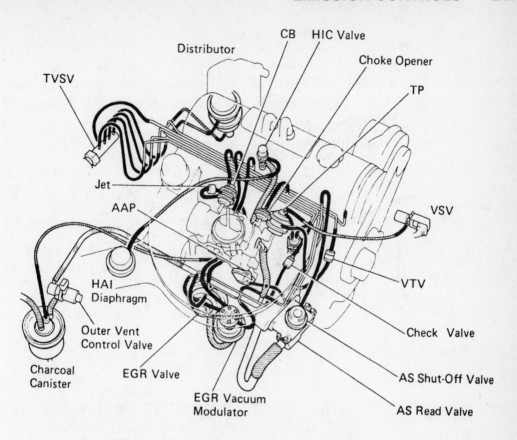

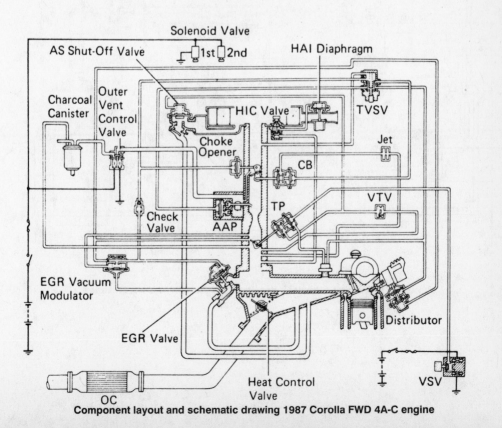

Component layout and schematic drawing 1987 Corolla FWD 4A-C engine

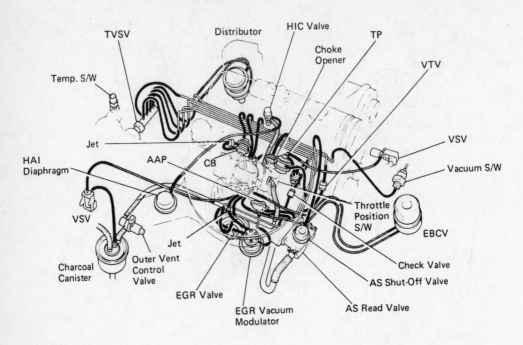

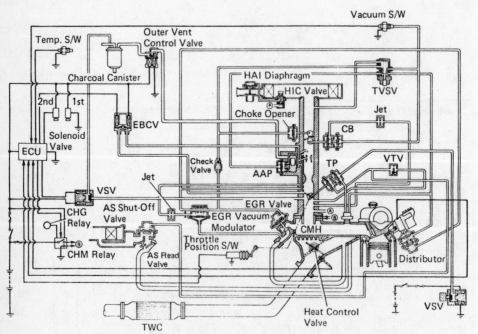

Component layout and schematic drawing 1987 Corolla FWD 4A-C engine

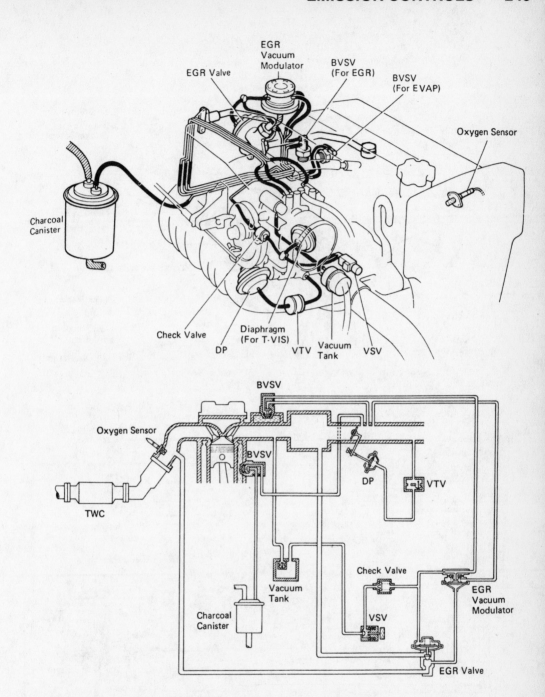

Component layout and schematic drawing 1987 Corolla RWD fuel injected 4A-GE engine

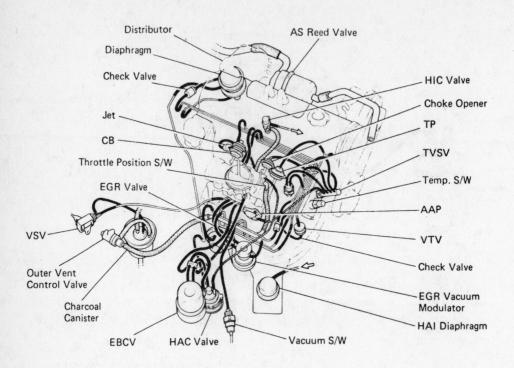

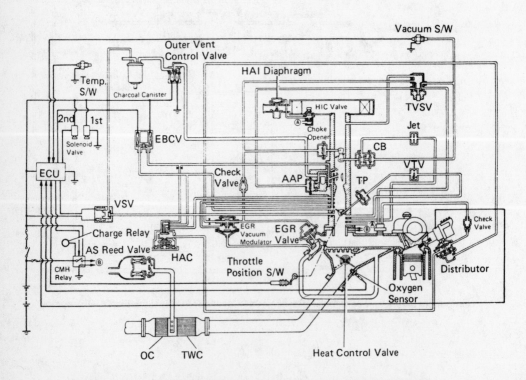

Component layout and schematic drawing 1987 Corolla RWD 4A-C engine

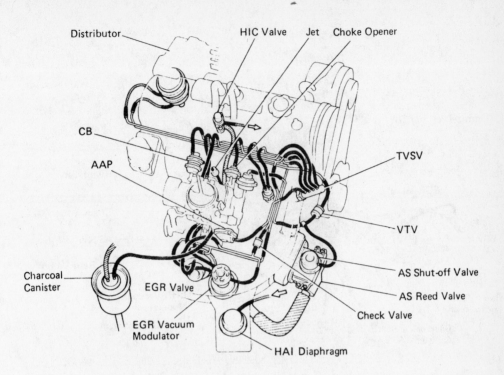

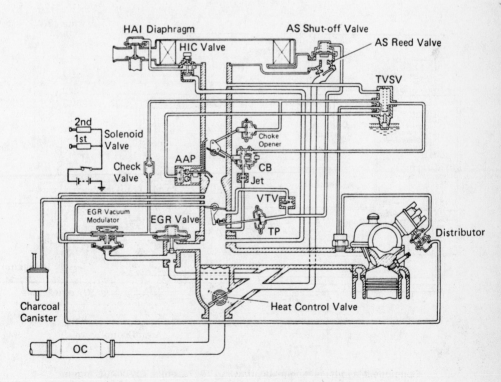

Component layout and schematic drawing 1987 Corolla RWD 4A-C engine

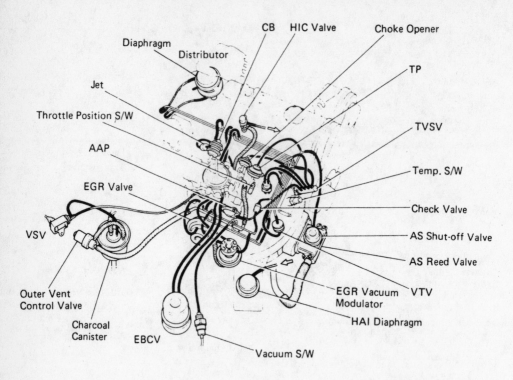

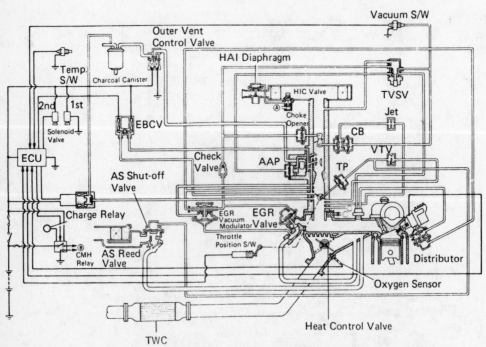

Component layout and schematic drawing 1987 Corolla RWD 4A-C engine

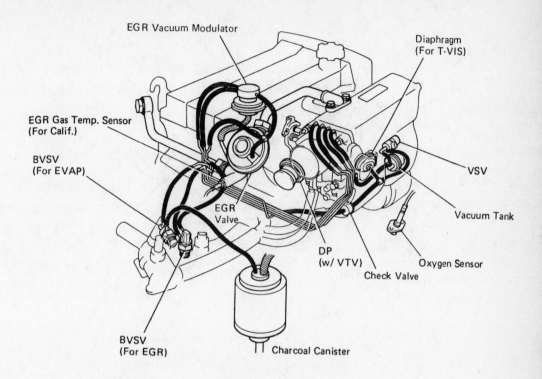

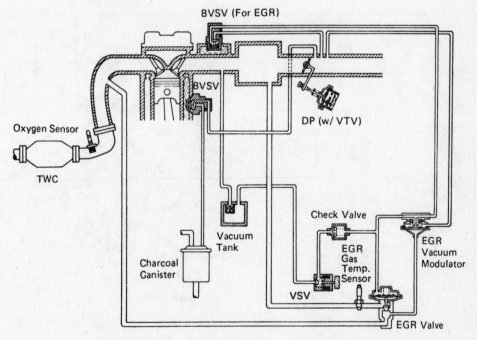

Component layout and schematic drawing 1988 Corolla fuel injected 4A-GE engine

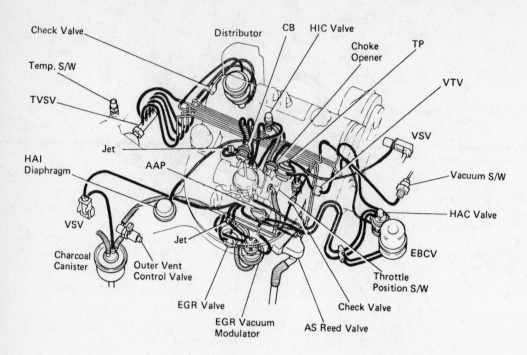

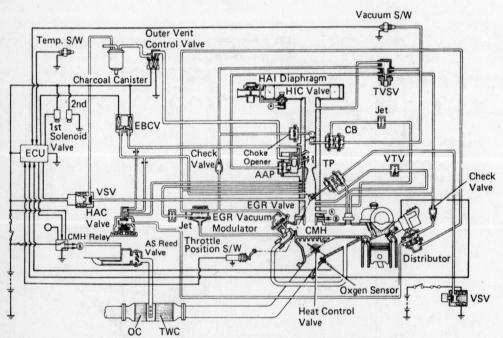

Component layout and schematic drawing 1988 Corolla 4A-C engine

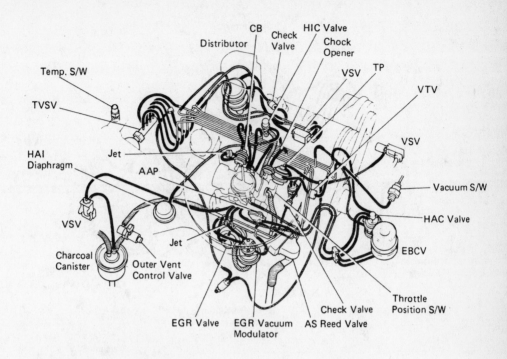

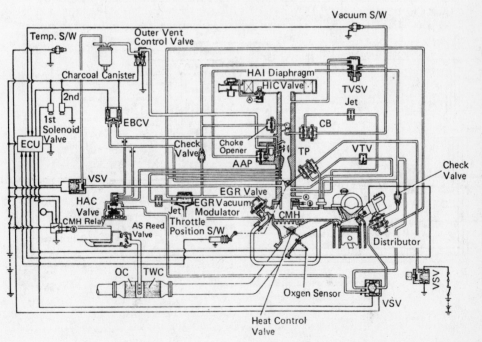

Component layout and schematic drawing 1988 Corolla 4A-C engine

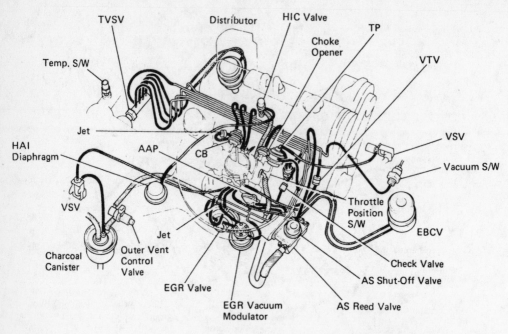

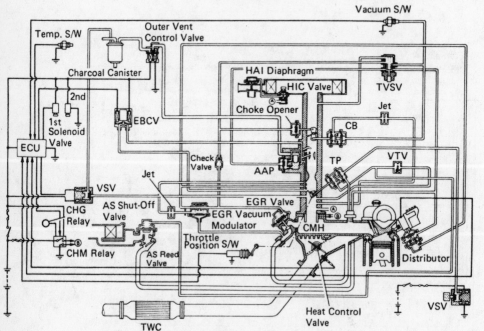

Component layout and schematic drawing 1988 Corolla 4A-C engine

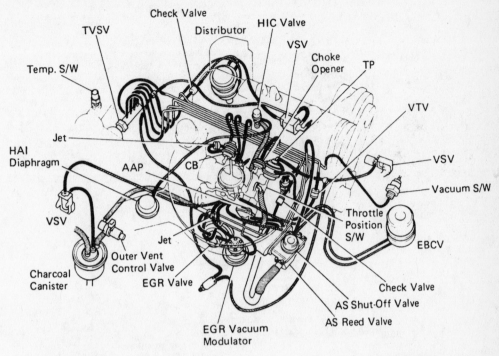

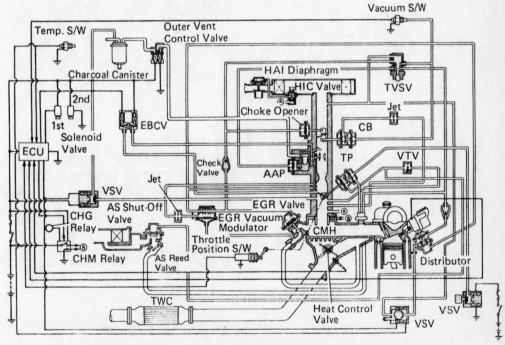

Component layout and schematic drawing 1988 Corolla 4A-C engine

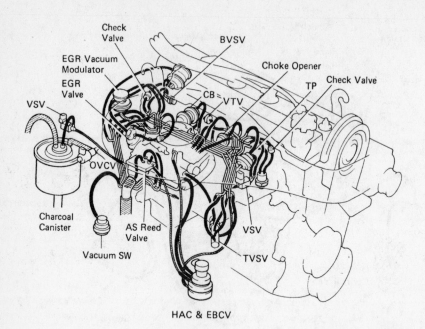

HAC & EBCV

Component layout and schematic drawing 1989 Corolla 4A-F engine

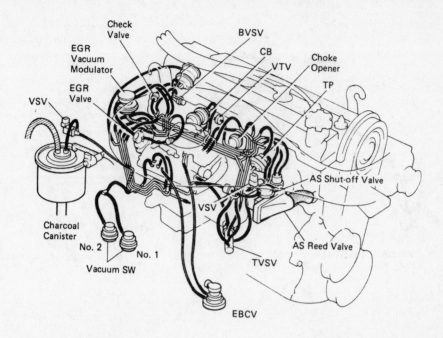

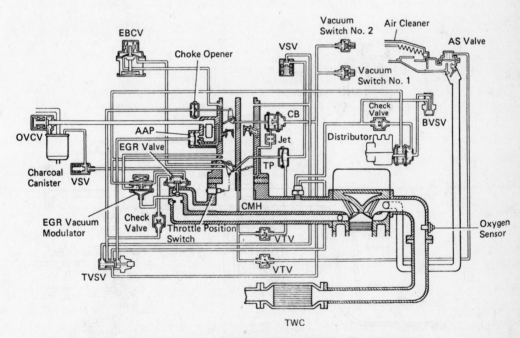

Component layout and schematic drawing 1989 Corolla 4A-F engine

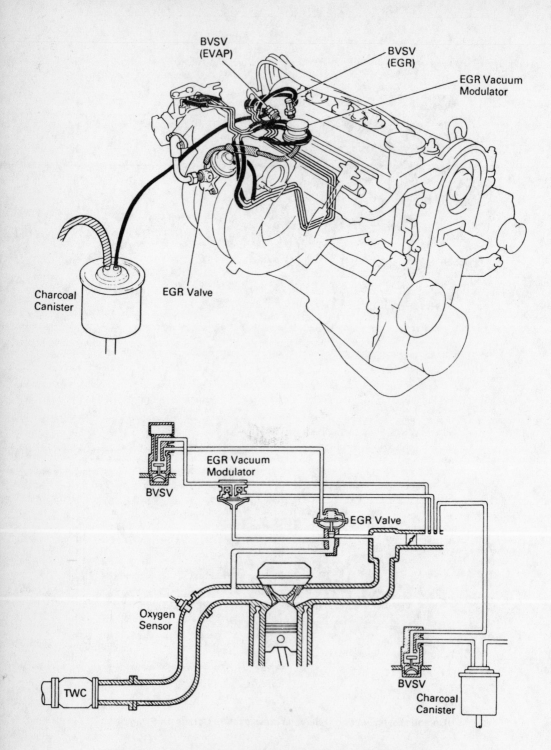

Component layout and schematic drawing 1989 Corolla 4A-FE enigne

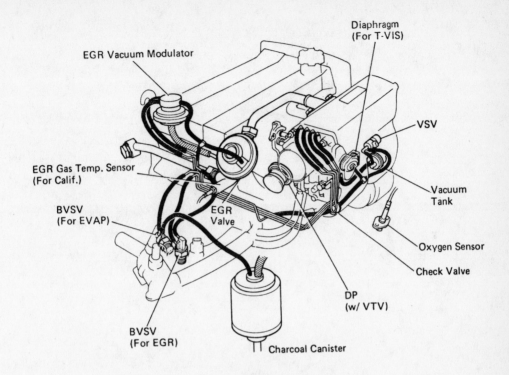

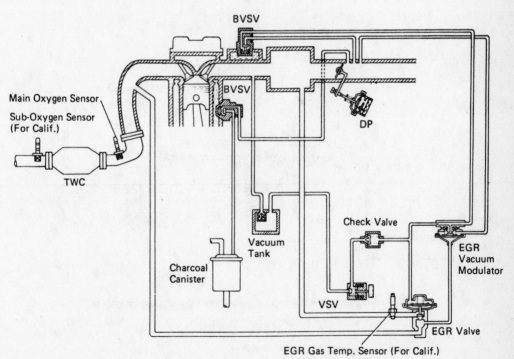

Component layout and schematic drawing 1989 Corolla 4A-GE engine

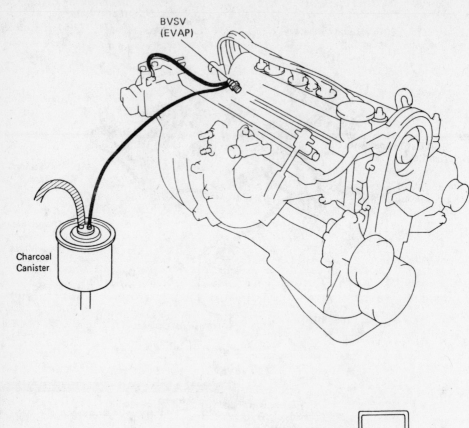

BVSV
(EVAP)

Charcoal
Canister

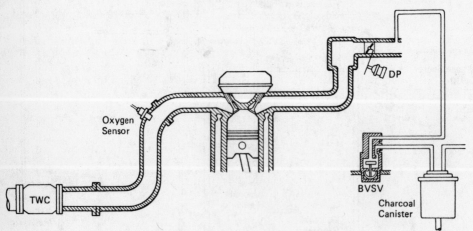

Oxygen
Sensor

DP

BVSV

Charcoal
Canister

TWC

Component layout and schematic drawing 1990 Corolla 4A-FE engine

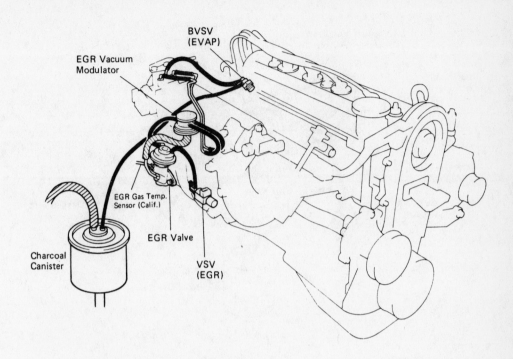

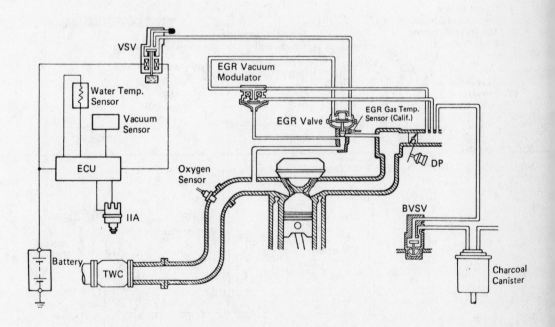

Component layout and schematic drawing 1990 Corolla 4A-FE engine

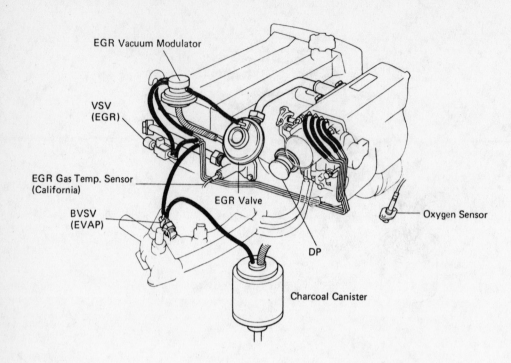

EGR Vacuum Modulator

VSV (EGR)

EGR Gas Temp. Sensor (California)

BVSV (EVAP)

EGR Valve

DP

Oxygen Sensor

Charcoal Canister

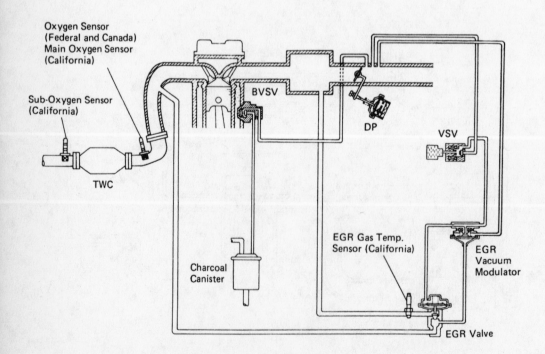

Oxygen Sensor (Federal and Canada) Main Oxygen Sensor (California)

Sub-Oxygen Sensor (California)

BVSV

DP

VSV

TWC

Charcoal Canister

EGR Gas Temp. Sensor (California)

EGR Vacuum Modulator

EGR Valve

Component layout and schematic drawing 1990 Corolla 4A-GE engine

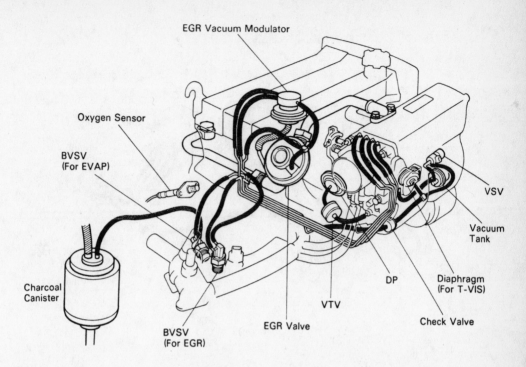

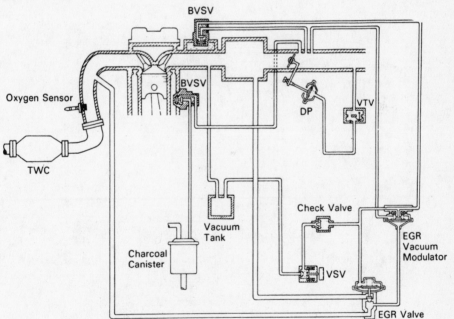

Component layout and schematic drawing 1985–87 MR2 4A-GE engine

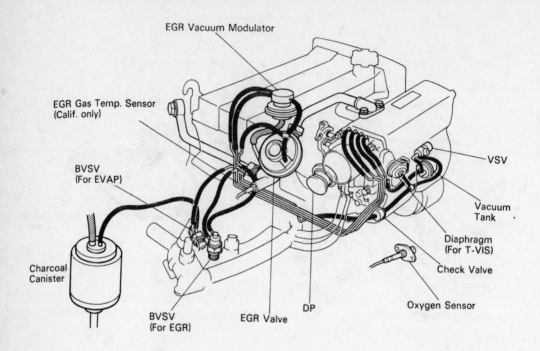

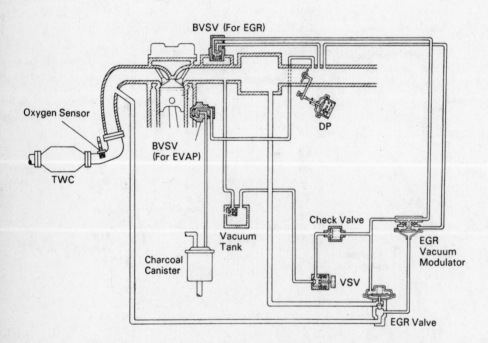

Component layout and schematic drawing 1988 MR2 4A-GE engine

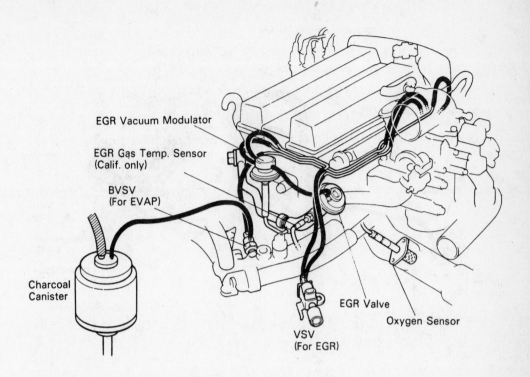

EGR Vacuum Modulator

EGR Gas Temp. Sensor
(Calif. only)

BVSV
(For EVAP)

Charcoal
Canister

EGR Valve

Oxygen Sensor

VSV
(For EGR)

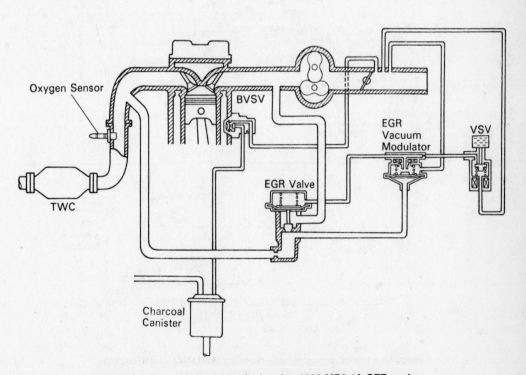

Oxygen Sensor

BVSV

EGR
Vacuum
Modulator

VSV

TWC

EGR Valve

Charcoal
Canister

Component layout and schematic drawing 1988 MR2 4A-GZE engine

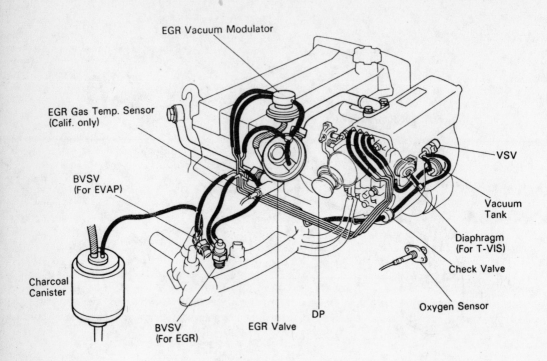

EGR Vacuum Modulator

EGR Gas Temp. Sensor
(Calif. only)

BVSV
(For EVAP)

Charcoal
Canister

VSV

Vacuum
Tank

Diaphragm
(For T-VIS)

Check Valve

Oxygen Sensor

BVSV
(For EGR)

EGR Valve

DP

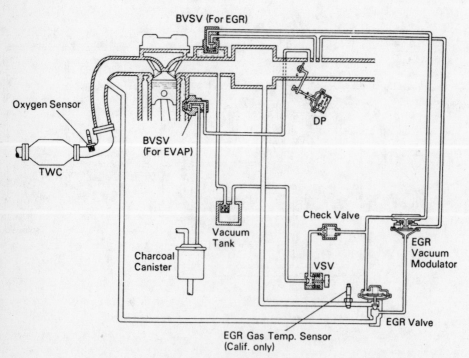

BVSV (For EGR)

Oxygen Sensor

DP

BVSV
(For EVAP)

TWC

Vacuum
Tank

Charcoal
Canister

Check Valve

VSV

EGR
Vacuum
Modulator

EGR Valve

EGR Gas Temp. Sensor
(Calif. only)

Component layout and schematic drawing 1989 MR2 4A-GE engine

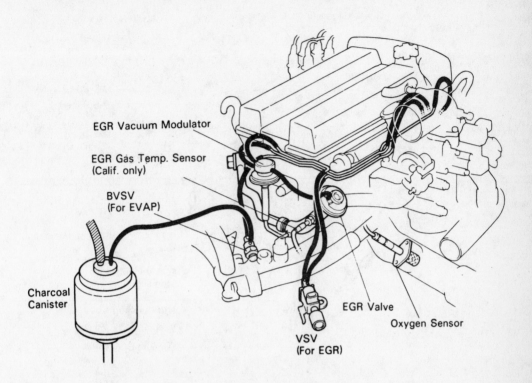

EGR Vacuum Modulator

EGR Gas Temp. Sensor
(Calif. only)

BVSV
(For EVAP)

Charcoal
Canister

EGR Valve

Oxygen Sensor

VSV
(For EGR)

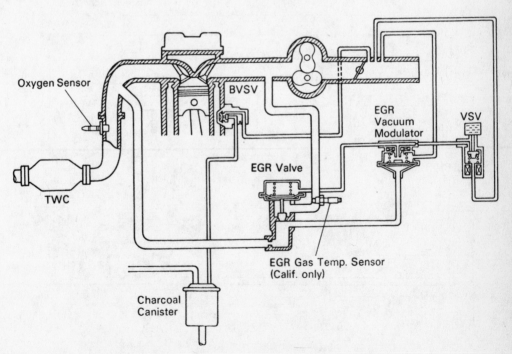

Oxygen Sensor

BVSV

EGR
Vacuum
Modulator

VSV

EGR Valve

TWC

EGR Gas Temp. Sensor
(Calif. only)

Charcoal
Canister

Component layout and schematic drawing 1989 MR2 4A-GZE engine

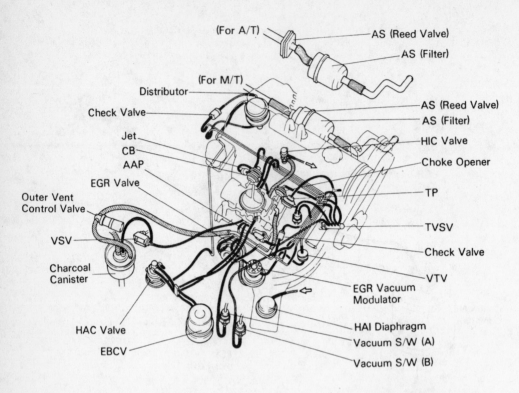

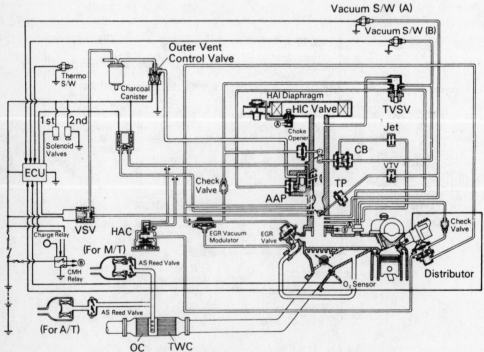

Component layout and schematic drawing 1984 Tercel

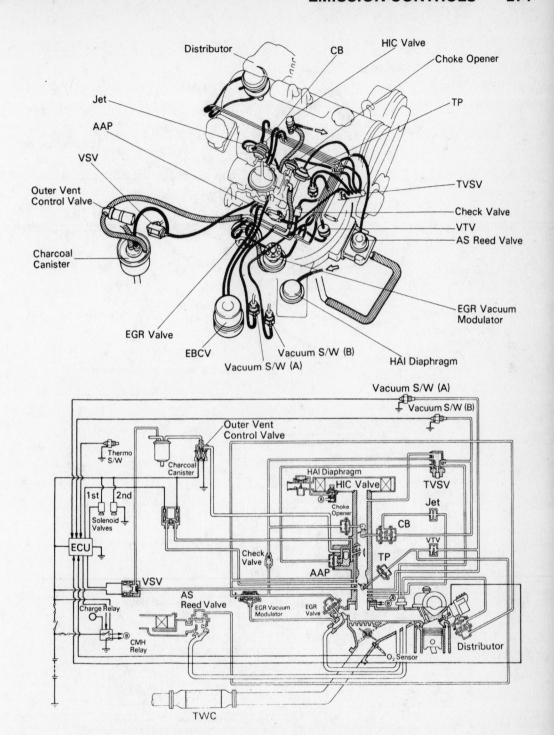

Component layout and schematic drawing 1984 Tercel

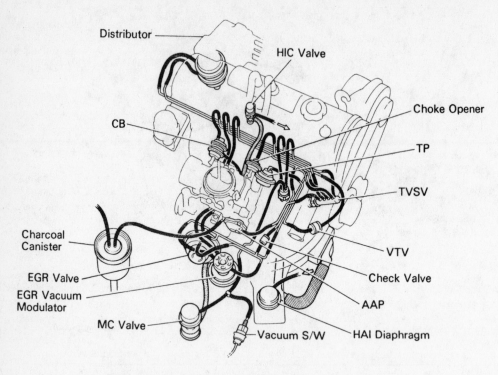

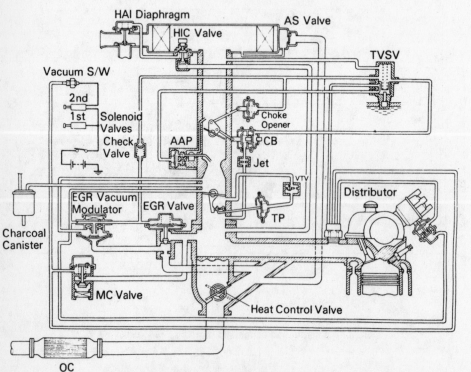

Component layout and schematic drawing 1984 Tercel

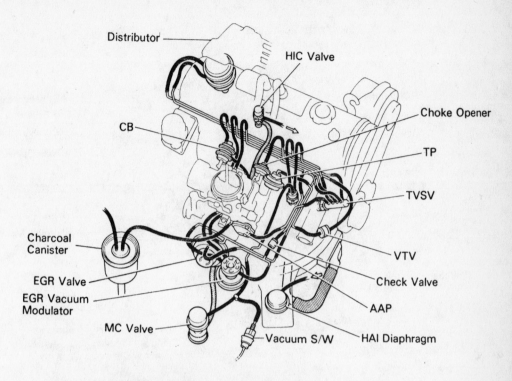

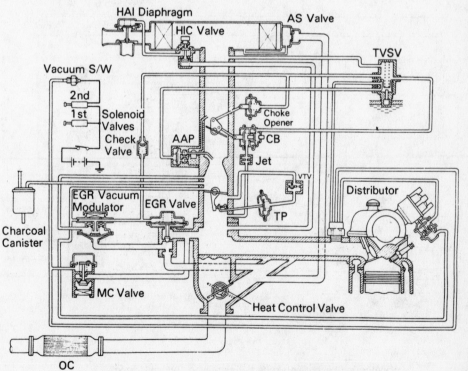

Component layout and schematic drawing 1984 Tercel

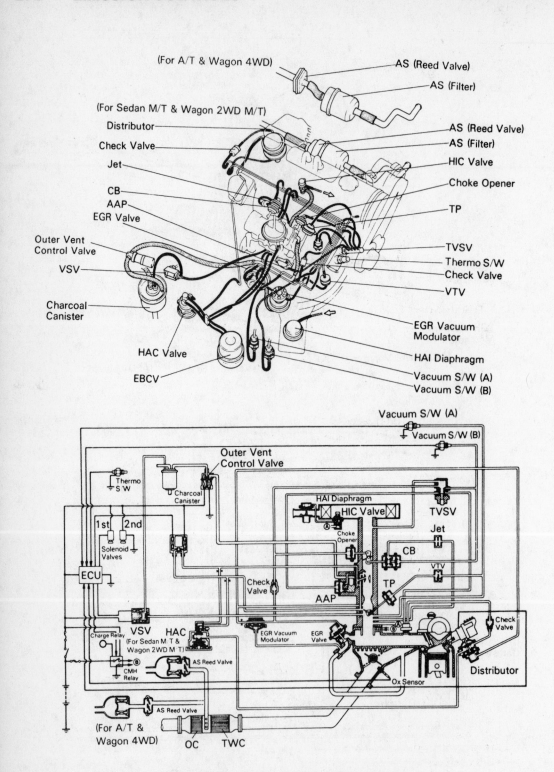

Component layout and schematic drawing 1985–86 Tercel

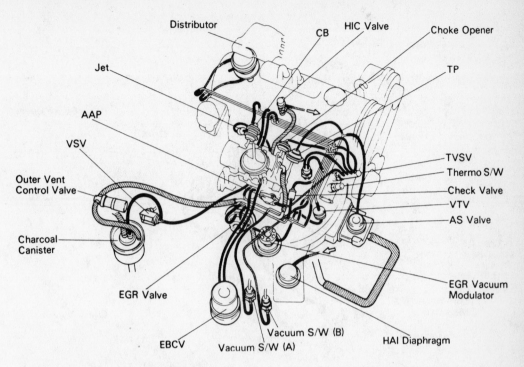

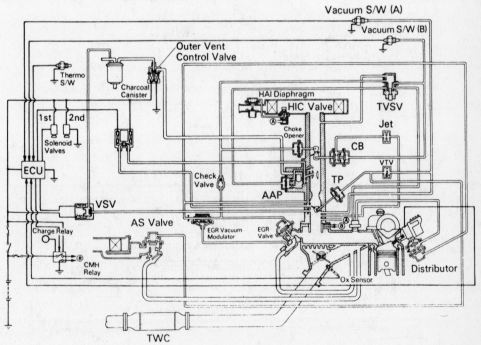

Component layout and schematic drawing 1985–86 Tercel

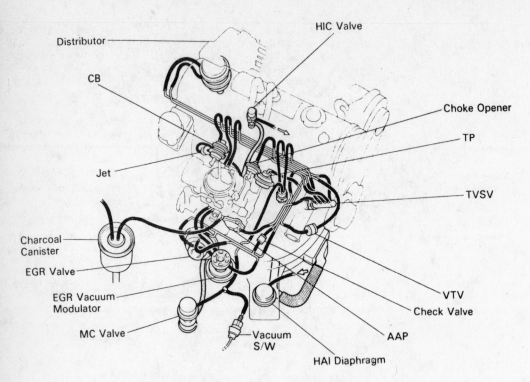

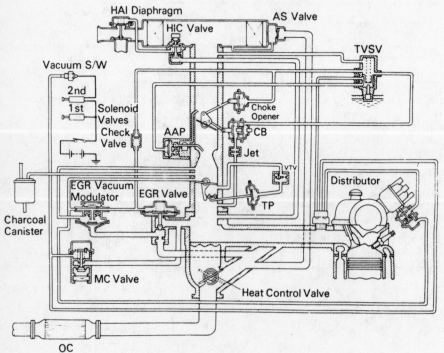

Component layout and schematic drawing 1985–86 Tercel

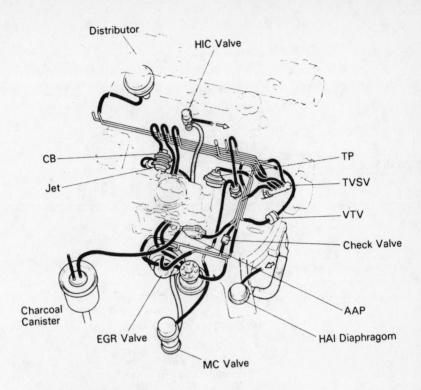

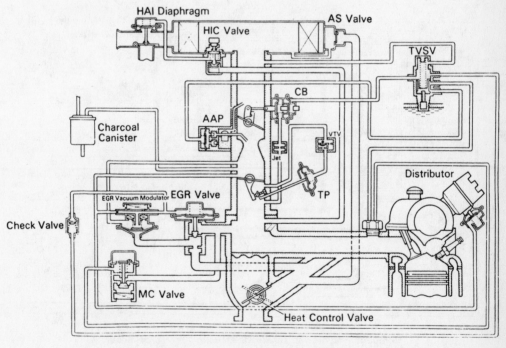

Component layout and schematic drawing 1985–86 Tercel

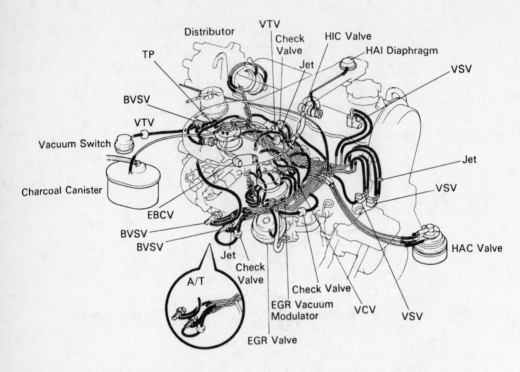

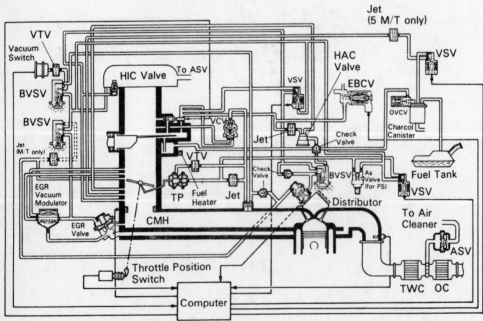

Component layout and schematic drawing 1987 Tercel sedan

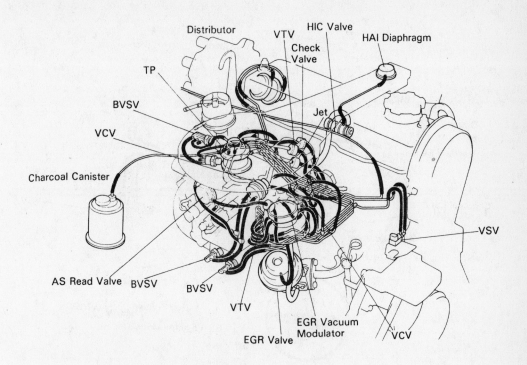

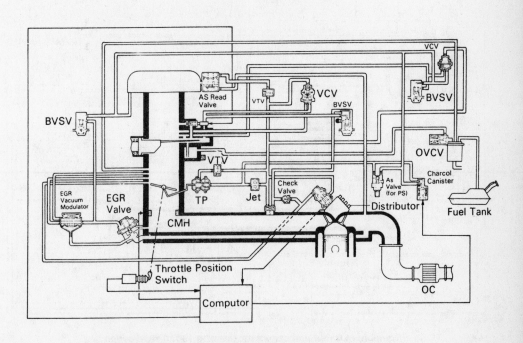

Component layout and schematic drawing 1987 Tercel sedan

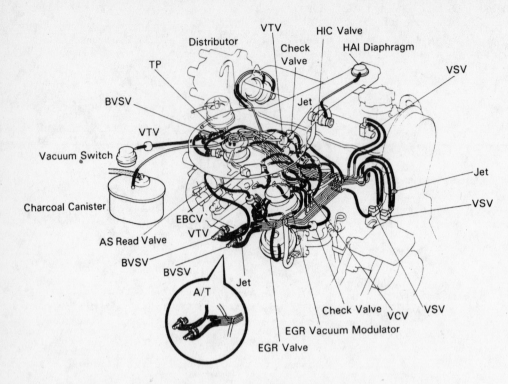

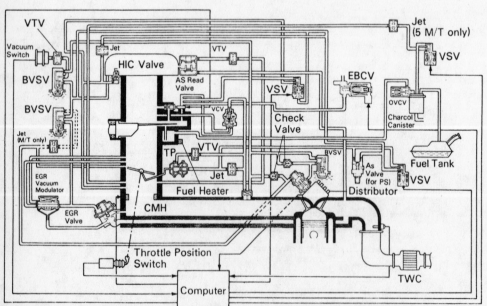

Component layout and schematic drawing 1987 Tercel sedan

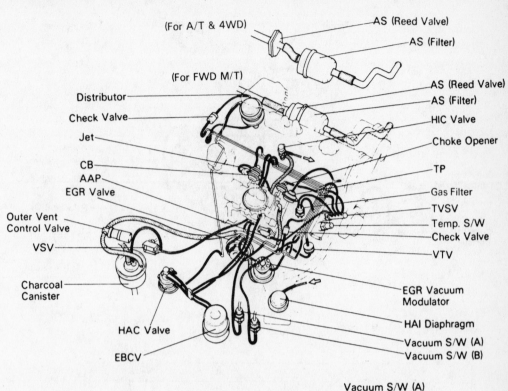

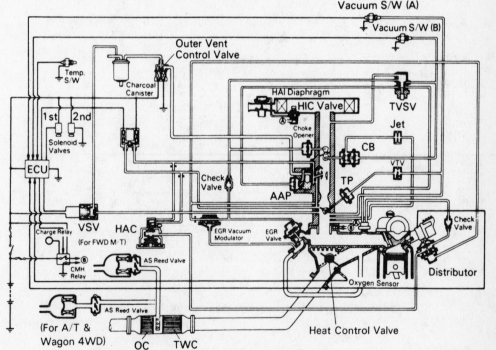

Component layout and schematic drawing 1987 Tercel wagon

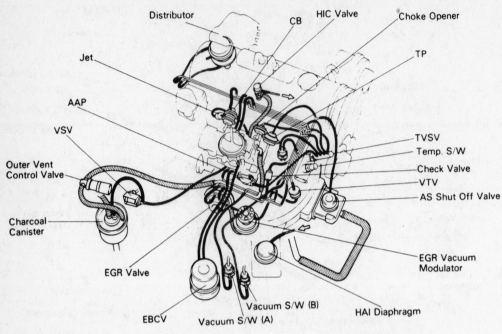

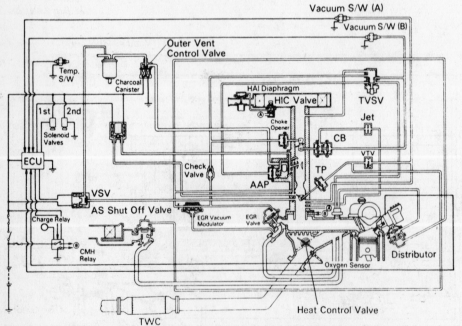

Component layout and schematic drawing 1987 Tercel wagon

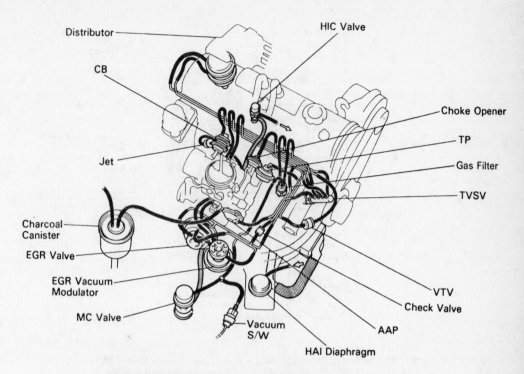

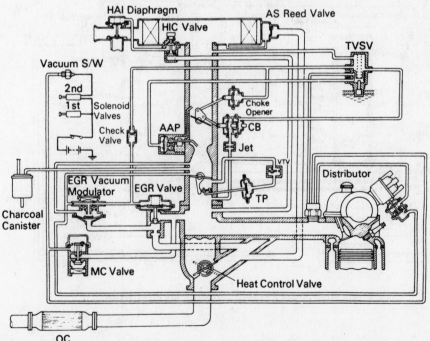

Component layout and schematic drawing 1987 Tercel wagon

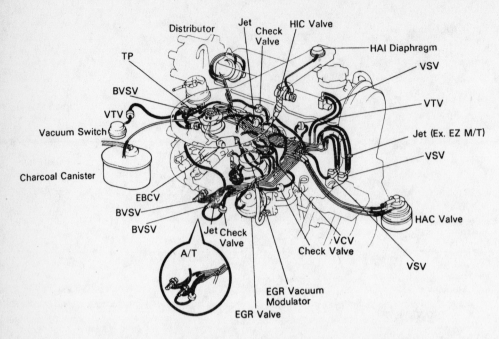

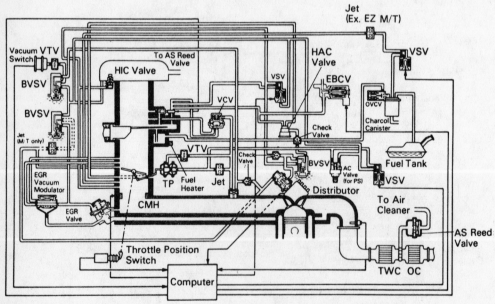

Component layout and schematic drawing 1988 Tercel sedan

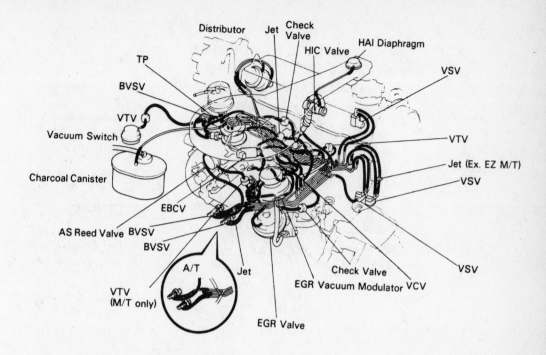

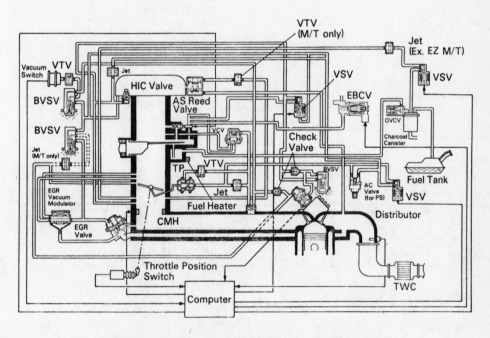

Component layout and schematic drawing 1988 Tercel sedan

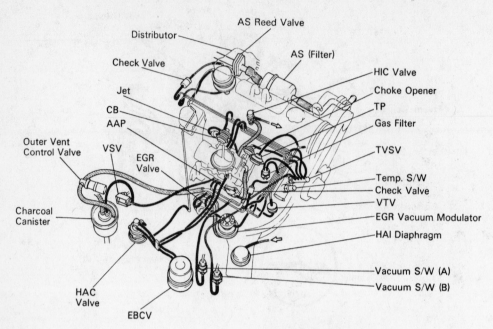

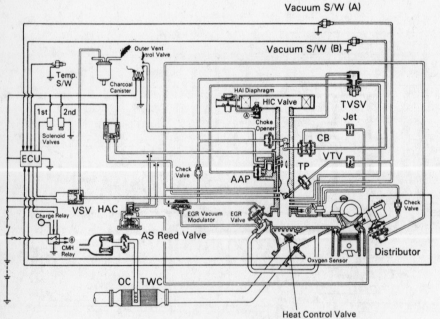

Component layout and schematic drawing 1988 Tercel wagon

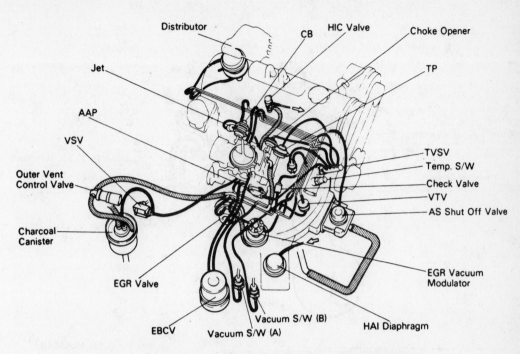

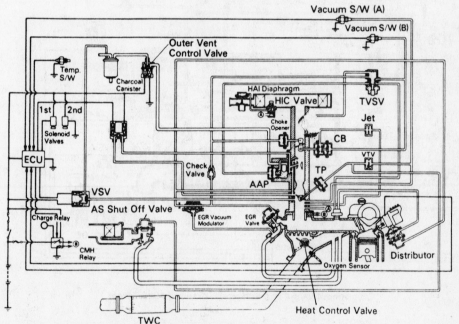

Component layout and schematic drawing 1988 Tercel wagon

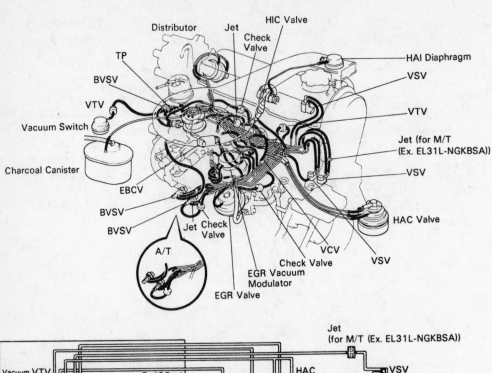

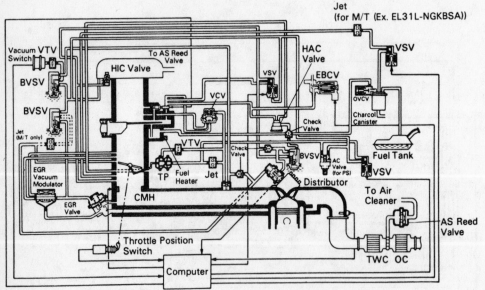

Component layout and schematic drawing 1989 Tercel

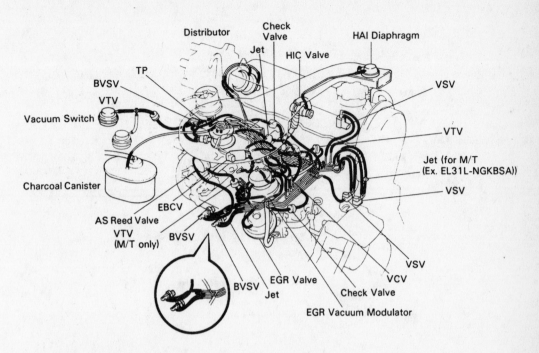

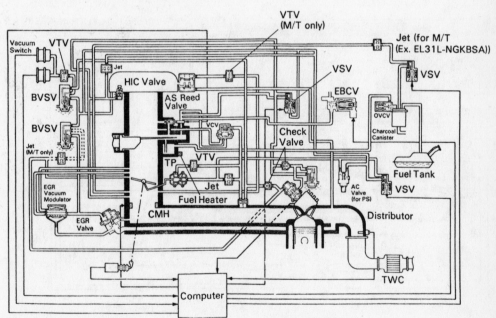

Component layout and schematic drawing 1989 Tercel

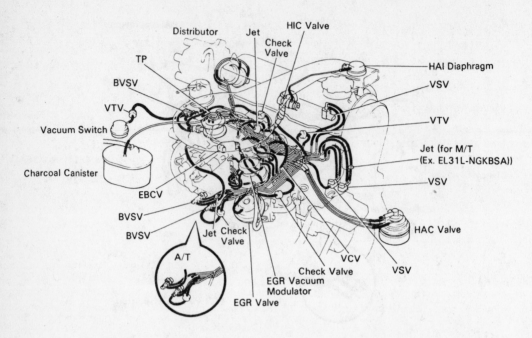

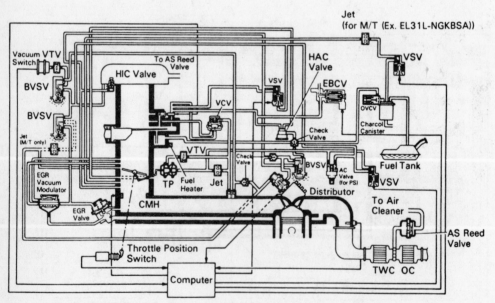

Component layout and schematic drawing 1990 Tercel 3E engine

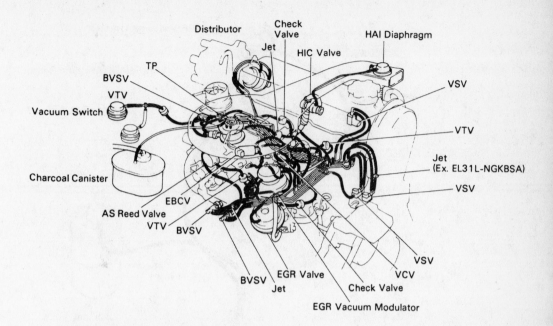

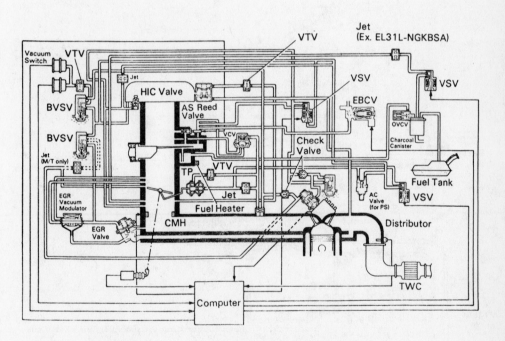

Component layout and schematic drawing 1990 Tercel 3E engine

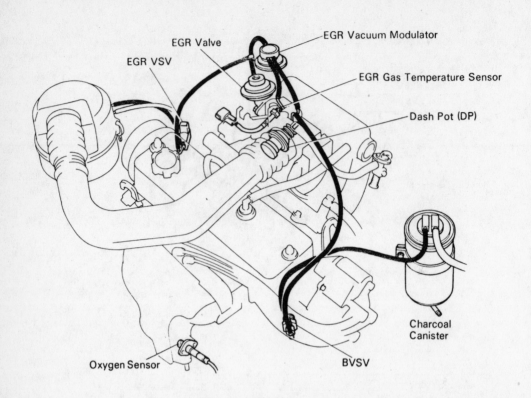

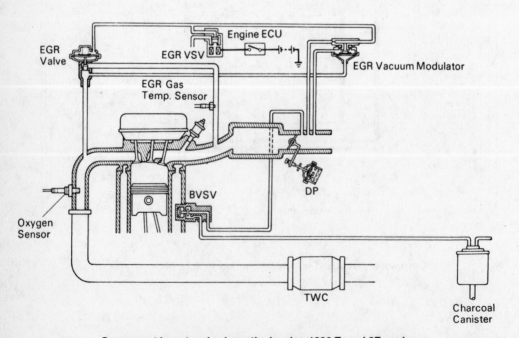

Component layout and schematic drawing 1990 Tercel 3E engine

Fuel System

5

Troubleshooting Basic Fuel System Problems

Problem	Cause	Solution
Engine cranks, but won't start (or is hard to start) when cold	• Empty fuel tank • Incorrect starting procedure • Defective fuel pump • No fuel in carburetor • Clogged fuel filter • Engine flooded • Defective choke	• Check for fuel in tank • Follow correct procedure • Check pump output • Check for fuel in the carburetor • Replace fuel filter • Wait 15 minutes; try again • Check choke plate
Engine cranks, but is hard to start (or does not start) when hot— (presence of fuel is assumed)	• Defective choke	• Check choke plate
Rough idle or engine runs rough	• Dirt or moisture in fuel • Clogged air filter • Faulty fuel pump	• Replace fuel filter • Replace air filter • Check fuel pump output
Engine stalls or hesitates on acceleration	• Dirt or moisture in the fuel • Dirty carburetor • Defective fuel pump • Incorrect float level, defective accelerator pump	• Replace fuel filter • Clean the carburetor • Check fuel pump output • Check carburetor
Poor gas mileage	• Clogged air filter • Dirty carburetor • Defective choke, faulty carburetor adjustment	• Replace air filter • Clean carburetor • Check carburetor
Engine is flooded (won't start accompanied by smell of raw fuel)	• Improperly adjusted choke or carburetor	• Wait 15 minutes and try again, without pumping gas pedal • If it won't start, check carburetor

CARBURETED FUEL SYSTEM

Mechanical Fuel Pump

REMOVAL AND INSTALLATION

Since the position of the fuel tank is lower than the carburetor, fuel cannot flow to the carburetor under its own power. The mechanical fuel pump is a diaphragm type with built in check valves in the pump chambers. These valves open only in the direction of fuel flow.

The pump is located at the side of the cylinder head intake manifold. To remove the fuel pump:

1. Disconnect the negative battery cable. With the engine cold and the key removed from the ignition, label and disconnect the fuel hoses from the fuel pump. Plug the lines as soon as they are removed.

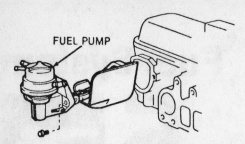

Location of mechanical fuel pump on the 4A-C engine — other engines similar

CAUTION: *The fuel system contains gasoline. Wear eye protection and contain spillage. Observe no smoking/no open flame precautions. Have a Class B-C (dry powder) fire extinguisher within arm's reach at all times.*

2. Remove the mounting bolts holding the pump.
3. Remove the fuel pump and the heat insulator assembly.
4. Cover the fuel pump mounting face on the cylinder head.
5. When reinstalling, always use a new gasket. Place the fuel pump and heat insulator in position and install the two bolts (tighten evenly).
6. Connect the hoses to the fuel pump.
7. Start the engine and check for leaks.

TESTING

Before performing any checks on the fuel pump, two conditions must be met. First, the pump must be internally "wet". Run a small amount of fuel into the pump so that the check valves will seal properly when tested. Dry valves may not seal and will yield false test results.

Hold the pump without blocking either pipe and operate the pump lever, noting the amount of force needed to move it. This is the reference point for all the tests. Do not apply more than this amount of force to the lever during the testing. Excessive force can damage an otherwise usable pump.

1. To check the inlet valve, block off the outlet and return pipes with your fingers. Op-

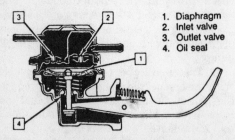

1. Diaphragm
2. Inlet valve
3. Outlet valve
4. Oil seal

Fuel pump components

erate the lever. There should be an increase in the free play and the arm should move freely.

2. Check the outlet valve by blocking the inlet port with your finger and operating the lever. The arm should lock when the normal amount of force is applied.

3. The diaphragm is checked by blocking the inlet and outlet pipes. When normal force is applied to the lever, the lever should lock and not move. Any lever motion indicates a ruptured diaphragm. This is a common cause of poor fuel mileage and poor acceleration since

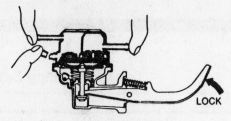

Checking the fuel pump diaphragm

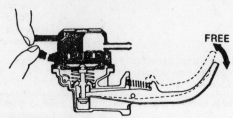

Checking the inlet valve

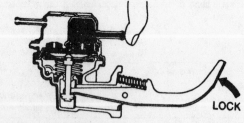

Checking the outlet valve

the correct amount of fuel is not being delivered to the carburetor.

NOTE: *The fuel pump must pass all three of these tests to be considered usable. If the pump fails one or more tests, it must be replaced.*

4. Check the oil seal within the pump. Block off the vent hole in the lower part of the pump housing. The lever arm should lock when normal force is applied.

Carburetor

The carburetor is the most complex part of the fuel system. Carburetors vary greatly in con-

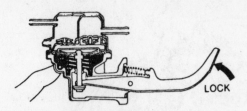

Checking the fuel pump oil seal

struction, but they all operate the same way; their job is to supply the correct mixture of fuel and air to the engine in response to varying conditions.

Despite their complexity, carburetors function on a simple physical principle known as the venturi principle. Air is drawn into the engine by the pumping action of the pistons. As the air enters the top of the carburetor, it passes through a venturi or restriction in the throttle bore. The air speeds up as it passes through the venturi, causing a slight drop in pressure. This pressure drop pulls fuel from the float bowl through a nozzle in the throttle bore. The air and fuel mix to form a fine mist, which is distributed to the cylinders through the intake manifold.

There are six different systems (fuel/air circuits) in a carburetor that make it work; the Float system, Main Metering system, Idle and Low Speed system, Accelerator Pump system, Power system, and the Choke System. The way

these systems are arranged in the carburetor determines the carburetor's size and shape.

It's important to remember that carburetors seldom give trouble during normal operation. Other than changing the fuel and air filters and making sure the idle speed and mixture are proper at every tune-up, there's not much maintenance you can perform on the average carburetor.

The carburetor used on Toyota models is a conventional 2-barrel, downdraft type similar to domestic carburetors. The main circuits are: primary, for normal operational requirements; secondary, to supply high speed fuel needs; float, to supply fuel to the primary and secondary circuits; accelerator, to supply fuel for quick and safe acceleration; choke, for reliable starting in cold weather; and power valve, for fuel economy.

ADJUSTMENTS

Before making any adjustments to the carburetor, ALL of the following conditions must be met:

- All accessories switched off
- Ignition timing correctly set
- Transmission in neutral, parking brake set, wheels blocked front and rear.
- Fuel level (float level) correctly set; view the fuel level in the small window on the right side of the carburetor.
- Tachometer correctly connected. Please

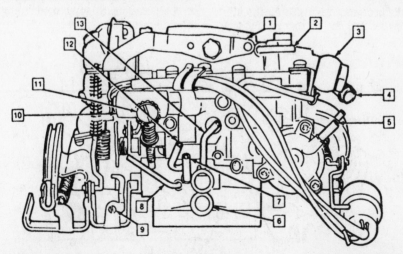

1. Main acceleration pump lever arm	6. Idle mixture adjustment screw plug	11. Idle speed adjustment screw
2. Main air bleed port to EBCV	7. EGR port to port P of EGR vacuum modulator	12. EGR R port to R port of EGR vacuum modulator
3. Fuel inlet union	8. Charcoal canister purge port from VSV	13. Slow air bleed port to EBCV
4. Bowl vent to charcoal canister	9. Fast idle adjusting screw	
5. Aux.accelerator pump-- vacuum from TVSV	10. No.1 slow cut fuel solenoid	

Rear view of the carburetor

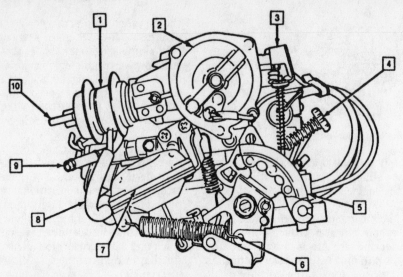

1. Choke breaker
2. Electric choke
3. Accelerator pump lever arm
4. Idle speed adjustment screw
5. Primary throttle lever
6. Throttle return spring
7. Secondary throttle vacuum actuator
8. Manifold vacuum
9. Fuel inlet line
10. From port L of TVSV

Left side view of the carburetor

refer to Chapter 2 for detailed instructions.

The many adjustments on a carburetor interrelate; if you change one setting you may affect other adjustments.

Curb Idle (Warm Idle)

The curb idle is adjusted by turning the idle adjusting screw located on the rear of the car-

buretor. The knob has a knurled plastic head to make grasping easier. Turn it clockwise to increase idle speed. Correct idle speed for the carbureted engine is 650 rpm w/manual transmission and 750 rpm w/automatic transmission. Always refer to the underhood emission sticker for specifications as some models/engines may differ slightly.

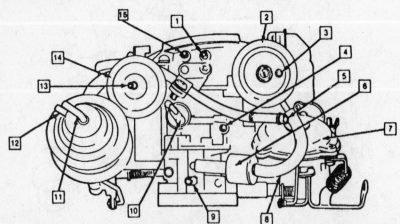

1. Atmosphere port to port J of TVSV
2. Choke breaker
3. To port L of TVSV
4. TP port to throttle positioner
5. Fuel inlet line
6. Vacuum delay valve
7. Secondary throttle vacuum actuator
8. Manifold vacuum to choke breaker
9. Manifold vacuum to HIC valve at the air cleaner
10. No. 2 secondary fuel cut relay
11. To VSV
12. Manifold vacuum (on intake manifold)
13. To M port of TVSV
14. Choke opener
15. Secondary air bleed port to high altitude compensator (HAC)

Front view of the carburetor

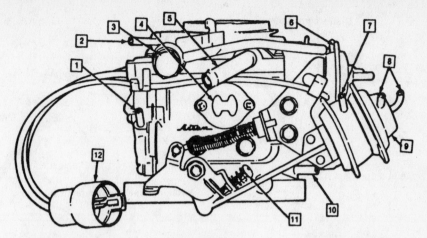

1. Vacuum signal from TVSV to aux. acceleration pump
2. Main air bleed from EBCV
3. Union--fuel line
4. Float bowl window
5. Bowl vent to charcoal canister
6. Choke opener
7. Ported vacuum signal from throttle port
8. Manifold vacuum to VSV
9. Throttle positioner diaphragm
10. Manifold vacuum to HIC valve at the air cleaner
11. Throttle positioner adjustment screw
12. Connector for electric choke and fuel cut solenoids 1 and 2

Right side view of the carburetor

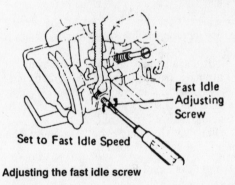

Fast Idle Adjusting Screw

Set to Fast Idle Speed

Adjusting the fast idle screw

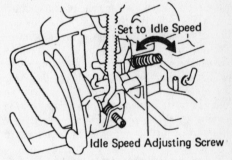

Set to Idle Speed

Idle Speed Adjusting Screw

Typical idle speed adjustment screw

Fast Idle

1. Stop the engine and remove the air cleaner housing.

2. Disconnect and plug the hot idle compensator hose to prevent rough idling.

3. Disconnect the hose from the Thermovacuum Switching Valve (TVSV) port M and plug

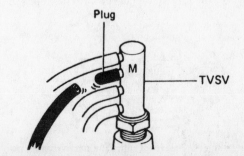

Plug

M

TVSV

M port on the TVSV valve

the port. This will shut off the choke opener and EGR systems.

4. Hold the throttle slightly open, (either move the linkage on the carburetor or pull lightly on the throttle cable.) push the choke plate closed and hold it closed as you release the throttle.

The carburetor is now "fooled" into thinking it is performing a cold start − the choke is set and the various external controls are not functioning. These conditions duplicate cold start conditions.

5. Start the engine but DO NOT touch the accelerator pedal or cable. (If you do, the choke will release and Step 4 will be needed again.)

CAUTION: *The engine will be running; be careful of moving parts and belts! Keep loose fitting clothes and long hair well away from the engine area!*

6. The correct fast idle speed is 3000 rpm. If adjustment is necessary, turn the fast idle ad-

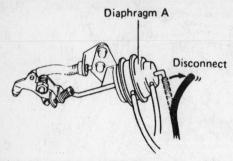

Vacuum hose at diaphragm A

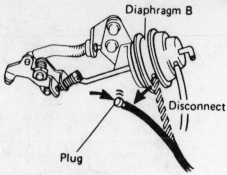

Vacuum hose at diaphragm B

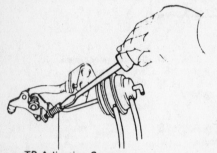

TP Adjusting Screw
Throttle positioner adjusting screw

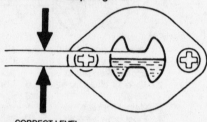

CORRECT LEVEL

No float level adjustment is necessary when the fuel level falls between the line on the carburetor sight glass

justing screw at the lower rear of the carburetor. Always refer to the underhood emission sticker for specifications as some models/engines may differ slightly.

WARNING: *Do not allow the engine to run on fast idle any longer than necessary. Once the correct fast idle is achieved, release the fast idle by depressing the accelerator and releasing it. Allow the engine to run at curb idle for about 30 seconds and switch the engine OFF.*

7. Remove the plug and reconnect the hose to the M port of the TVSV.

Throttle Positioner

1. Disconnect the hose from the Thermovacuum Switching Valve (TVSV) port **M** and plug the port. Disconnect the vacuum hose from throttle positioner (TP) diaphragm **A**.

2. Check that the TP is set at the first step; correct engine speed is:
• Manual transmission: 800 rpm
• Automatic transmission: 900 rpm If necessary, adjust the speed with the adjusting screw.
NOTE: *Make the adjustment with the cooling (radiator) fan OFF. Always refer to the underhood emission sticker for specifications as some models/engines may differ slightly — follow specifications on emission sticker if none appear follow the above.*

3. Reconnect the vacuum hose to diaphragm **A**.

4. Disconnect the hose from diaphragm **B** and plug the hose end.

5. Check that the TP is set at the second step. The correct engine speed in this position is:
• Manual transmission: 1400 ± 200 rpm
• Automatic transmission: 1500 ± 200 rpm

6. Reconnect the vacuum hose to diaphragm **B** and check that the engine returns to normal idle within 2–6 seconds.

7. Remove the plug and reconnect the vacuum hose to TVSV port **M**.

Float and Fuel Level

The float level is not externally adjustable. Removal of the air horn assembly or top of the carburetor is required. The engine should be cold during this procedure. All work is performed with the engine off.

The float in the carburetor controls the entry of fuel into the bowl of the carburetor. (The bowl is simply a reservoir which keeps fuel available at all times.) The function of the float is to react to the level of fuel in the bowl and open or

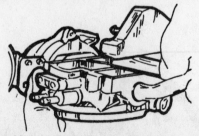

Checking the float level with the float in resting position on the needle valve

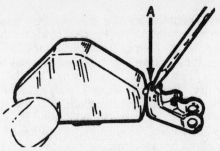

Float adjustment at point A while in the resting position

Measuring the float in the raised position

close a valve, thus maintaining the correct amount of fuel. The principle is identical to the float in a toilet tank; when the correct level is reached, the flow is shut off.

The position of the float (and therefore the amount of fuel available) is critical to the proper operation of the engine. If too little fuel is in the bowl, the engine may starve on sharp corners or on hills; too much fuel can literally lead to overflowing and flooding of the engine. To adjust the float level:

1. Remove the air cleaner assembly and disconnect the choke linkage.

2. Disconnect the accelerator pump connecting rod.

3. Remove the pump arm pivot screw and the pump arm.

4. Remove the fuel hose and union.

5. Remove the eight air horn screws. Be careful to identify and collect the external parts attached to the screws, such as wire clamps, brackets and the steel number plate.

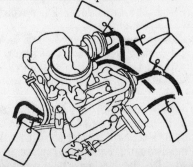

Tag and label every hose during removal procedure

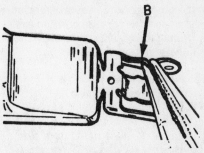

Tag and label every hose during removal procedure

6. Disconnect the choke link.

7. Lift the air horn with its gasket from the body of the carburetor.

8. Disconnect the wires at the connector.

9. Remove the gasket from the air horn assembly. Invert the air horn so that the float hangs down by its own weight. Check the clearance between the float tip and the air horn. The correct clearance is 7.0mm. If necessary, adjust the float lip by bending it gently into position.

10. Lift up the float and check the clearance between the needle valve plunger and the float lip. Correct clearance is 1.6–2.0mm. If necessary, adjust the clearance by bending the outer part of the float lip.

NOTE: *If the float has become misadjusted, it may be due to the float filling with gasoline (hole in float). Give the float a gentle shake and listen for any liquid within. If fuel is inside the float, replace the float and reset the levels.*

11. Install a new gasket onto the air horn.

12. Place the air horn in position on the carburetor body and install the choke link.

13. Install the eight screws. Make certain the brackets, clips and steel tag are reinstalled as well.

14. Connect the fuel hose and union.

15. Install the pump arm pivot screw and pump arm.

16. Connect the pump arm connecting rod.

17. Attach the choke linkage.

18. Install the air cleaner. Start the engine and check carefully for fuel and/or vacuum leaks. The engine may be difficult to start; once it is running smoothly, recheck the fuel level in the sight glass.

CARBURETOR REMOVAL AND INSTALLATION

NOTE: *Each fuel and vacuum line must be tagged or labeled individually during disassembly for correct installation. Never tilt the carburetor assembly during removal or installation.*

1. Remove the air cleaner assembly.

2. Disconnect the accelerator cable from the carburetor.

3. If equipped with automatic transmission, disconnect the throttle position cable.

4. Unplug the wiring connector.

5. Label and disconnect the:
   a. carburetor vacuum hoses
   b. fuel inlet hoses
   c. charcoal canister hose

CAUTION: *The carburetor contains gasoline. Wear eye protection and contain spillage. Observe no smoking/no open flame precautions. Have a Class B-C (dry powder) fire extinguisher within arm's reach at all times.*

6. Remove the carburetor mounting nuts.

7. Remove the cold mixture heater wire clamp and lift out the EGR vacuum modulator bracket.

8. Lift the carburetor off the engine and place it on a clean cloth on the workbench. If desired, the insulator (base gasket) may also be removed.

9. Cover the inlet area of the manifold with clean rags. This will prevent the entry of dust, dirt and loose parts.

10. When reinstalling, place the insulator on the manifold, making sure it is correctly positioned.

11. Install the carburetor onto the manifold.

12. Install the EGR vacuum modulator bracket. Clamp the cold mixture heater wire into place.

13. Tighten the carburetor mounting nuts (always torque the mounting bolts evenly in steps).

14. Reconnect the fuel inlet hose, the charcoal canister hose and the vacuum hoses.

15. Connect the wiring connector.

16. connect the accelerator cable; connect the throttle position cable if equipped with automatic transmission.

17. Reinstall the air cleaner.

CARBURETOR OVERHAUL

Efficient carburetion depends greatly on careful cleaning and inspection during overhaul since dirt, gum, water, or varnish in or on the carburetor parts are often responsible for poor performance.

Overhaul your carburetor in a clean, dust free area. Carefully disassemble the carburetor, referring often to the exploded views. Keep all similar and look-alike parts segregated during disassembly and cleaning to avoid accidental interchange during assembly. Make a note of all jet sizes.

When the carburetor is disassembled, wash all parts (except diaphragms, electric choke units, pump plunger, and any other plastic, leather, fiber, or rubber parts) in clean carburetor solvent. Do not leave parts in the solvent any longer than necessary to sufficiently loosen the deposits. Excessive cleaning may remove the special finish from the float bowl and check valve bodies leaving these parts unfit for service. Rinse all parts in clean solvent and blow them dry with compressed air or allow them to air dry. Wipe clean all cork, plastic, and fiber parts with clean, lint-free cloth.

Blow out all passages and jets with compressed air and be sure that there are no restrictions or blockages. Never use wire or similar tools to clean jets, fuel passages, or air bleeds. Clean all jets and valves separately to avoid accidental interchange.

Check all parts for wear or damage. If wear or damage is found, replace the defective parts. Pay special attention to the following areas:

1. Check the float needle and seat for wear. If wear is found, replace the complete assembly.

2. Check the float hinge pin for wear and the float(s) for dents or distortion. Replace the float (float assembly could have pin-hole it) if fuel has leaked into it.

3. Check the throttle and choke shaft bores for wear or an out-of-round condition. Damage or wear to the throttle arm, shaft or shaft bore will often require the replacement of the throttle body. These parts require a close tolerance of fit; wear may allow air leakage, which could affect starting and idling.

NOTE: *Throttle shafts and bushings are not included in overhaul kits. They may be available separately.*

4. Inspect the idle mixture adjusting needles for burrs or grooves. Any such condition requires replacement of the needle, since you will not be able to obtain a satisfactory idle.

NOTE: *If idle mixture screws plugs (for a complete overhaul) are going to be removed (drilled out) refer to Chapter 2 for the necessary service procedure after the carburetor assembly is removed from the vehicle.*

5. Test the accelerator pump check valves. They should pass air one way but not the other. Replace the valve if necessary. If the valve is satisfactory, wash the valve again to remove breath moisture.

6. Check the bowl cover for warped surfaces with a straightedge.

7. Closely inspect the valves and seats for wear and damage, replacing as necessary.

8. After the carburetor is assembled, check the choke valve (plate) for freedom of operation.

Carburetor overhaul kits are recommended for each overhaul. These kits contain all the gaskets and new parts to replace those that deteriorate most rapidly. Failure to replace all parts supplied with the kit (especially gaskets) can result in poor performance later.

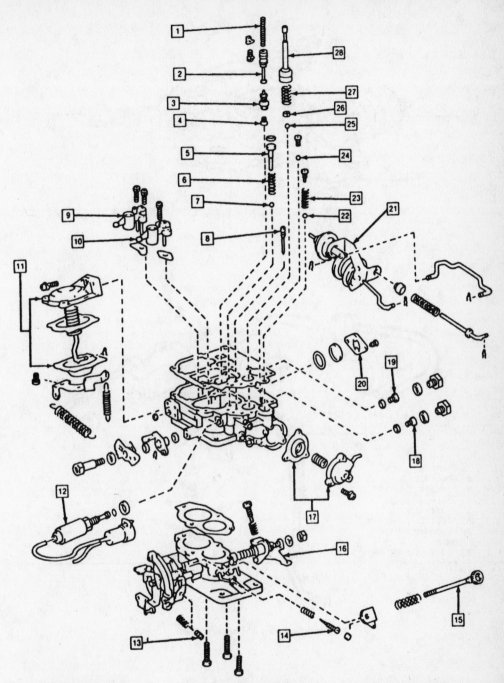

1. Power piston spring
2. Power piston
3. Power valve
4. Power jet
5. Pump discharge weight
6. Spring
7. Steel ball
8. Slow jet (idle jet)
9. Secondary small venturi
10. Primary small venturi
11. Secondary throttle valve actuator assembly
12. Primary solenoid valve
13. Fast idle adjusting screw
14. Idle mixture adjusting screw
15. Idle speed adjusting screw
16. Throttle positioner lever
17. Aux. accelerator pump
18. Primary main jet
19. Secondary main jet
20. Sight glass retainer
21. Choke breaker and throttle positioner diaphragm
22. Steel ball
23. Spring
24. Steel ball
25. Steel ball
26. Check ball retainer
27. Pump damping spring
28. Pump plunger

Exploded view of the carburetor

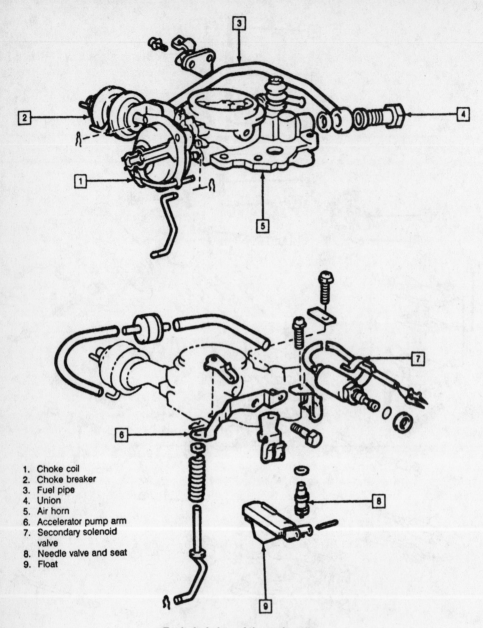

Exploded view of the carburetor

1. Choke coil
2. Choke breaker
3. Fuel pipe
4. Union
5. Air horn
6. Accelerator pump arm
7. Secondary solenoid valve
8. Needle valve and seat
9. Float

Some carburetor manufacturers supply overhaul kits of 3 basic types: minor repair; major repair; and gasket kits. Generally, they contain the following:

Minor Repair

• All gaskets
• Float needle valve
• Volume control screw
• All diaphragms
• Spring for the pump diaphragm
• All gaskets

Major Repair Kits:

• All jets and gaskets
• All diaphragms
• Float needle valve
• Volume control screw
• Pump ball valve
• Float(s)
• All gaskets

Gasket Kits:

• All gaskets

After cleaning and checking all components,

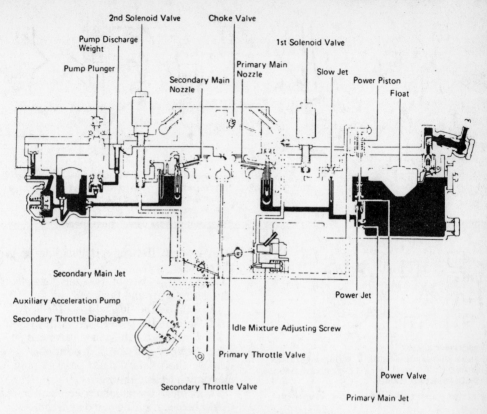

2nd Solenoid Valve

Pump Discharge
Weight

Pump Plunger

Choke Valve

1st Solenoid Valve

Primary Main
Nozzle

Slow Jet

Power Piston

Float

Secondary Main
Nozzle

Secondary Main Jet

Auxiliary Acceleration Pump

Secondary Throttle Diaphragm

Power Jet

Idle Mixture Adjusting Screw

Primary Throttle Valve

Secondary Throttle Valve

Power Valve

Primary Main Jet

Carburetor component location

reassemble the carburetor, using new parts and referring to the exploded view. When reassembling, make sure that all screws and jets are tight in their seats, but do not over tighten, as the tips will be distorted. Tighten all screws gradually, in rotation. Do not tighten the needle valve(s) into their seats; uneven jetting will result. Always use new gaskets. Be sure to adjust the float level when reassembling.

NOTE: *The following instructions are organized so that only one component group is being worked on at a time. This helps avoid confusion and interchange of parts. To make*

reassembly easier, always arrange disassembled parts in order on the workbench. Be very careful not to mix up or lose small pieces such as balls, clips or springs. Reassembly and adjustment of the carburetor requires accurate measuring equipment capable of checking clearances to the $^1/_{1000}$mm. These specialized carburetor clearance gauges are available at reputable tool retailers but may be difficult to find.

1. Remove the carburetor as outlined previously.

NOTE: *If idle mixture screws plugs are going to be drilled out refer to Chapter 2 for the necessary service procedure.*

2. To remove the AIR HORN assembly, disconnect the choke link and the pump connecting rod.

3. Remove the pump arm pivot screw and the pump arm.

4. Remove the fuel hose and union.

5. Remove the eight air horn screws. Be careful to identify and collect the external parts attached to the screws, such as wire clamps, brackets and the steel number plate.

6. Disconnect the choke link.

7. Lift the air horn with its gasket from the body of the carburetor.

8. Disconnect the wires at the connector.

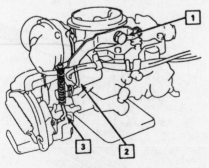

1. PUMP ARM PIVOT
2. CHOKE LINK
3. PUMP ROD

Carburetor pump linkage

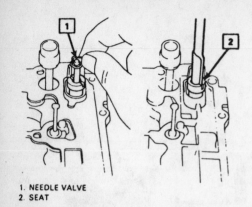

1. NEEDLE VALVE
2. SEAT

Needle valve removal

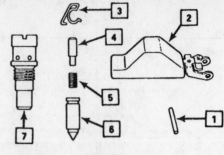

1. PIVOT PIN   5. SPRING
2. FLOAT   6. NEEDLE VALVE
3. PIN CLIP   7. STRAINER
4. PLUNGER

Float and needle valve components

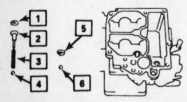

1. STOPPER GASKET
2. PUMP DISCHARGE WEIGHT   5. PLUNGER RETAINER
3. SPRING   6. CHECK BALL (SMALL)
4. DISCHARGE BALL (LARGE)

Accelerator pump check balls and components

9. Remove the first and second solenoids from the carburetor body.

10. Remove the float pivot pin, float and needle valve assembly.

11. Remove the air horn gasket.

12. Remove the needle valve seat and gasket.

13. Remove the power piston retainer, power piston and spring.

14. Pull out the pump plunger and remove the boot.

15. Begin disassembly of the BODY by removing the throttle positioner. Disconnect the link and remove the two bolts.

16. Remove the stopper gasket, the pump dis-

charge weight, the long spring and the large discharge ball.

17. Using a pair of tweezers, remove the plunger retainer and the small ball.

18. Remove the slow jet from the body.

19. Remove the power valve with the jet.

20. Disassemble the power valve and jet.

21. Remove the throttle positioner levers. Remove the primary main passage plug, primary main jet and the gasket.

22. Remove the auxiliary accelerator pump (AAP) housing, spring and diaphragm.

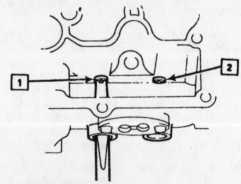

1. PRIMARY JET
2. SECONDARY JET

Removing the main jets

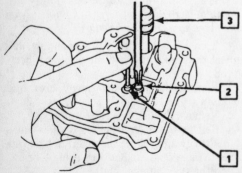

1. POWER PISTON
2. POWER PISTON RETAINER
3. PUMP PLUNGER

Removing the power piston

Removing the power valve

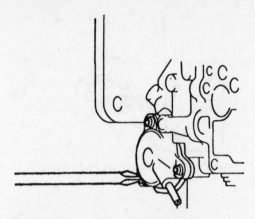

Removing the auxiliary accelerator pump

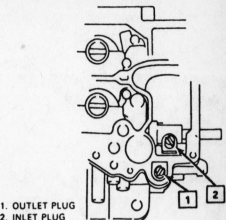

1. OUTLET PLUG
2. INLET PLUG

Removing the auxiliary accelerator pump check ball plugs

23. Remove the inlet plug and the small ball for the AAP.

24. Remove the outlet plug, short spring and the small ball.

25. Remove the primary and secondary venturies.

26. Remove the sight glass retainer, the glass and its O-ring.

27. Remove the throttle return spring and the throttle back spring.

28. Remove the nut and the throttle lever.

29. Remove the bolt and the fast idle cam.

30. Remove the secondary throttle valve diaphragm by disconnecting the linkage and removing the assembly with its gasket.

31. Remove the three bolts and the vacuum passage bolt. Separate the carburetor body from the carburetor flange.

32. Clean all the disassembled parts before inspecting them. Wash and clean the cast metal parts with a soft brush in carburetor cleaner. Clean off the carbon around the throttle plates. Wash the other parts thoroughly in cleaner.

Blow all dirt and other foreign matter from the jets, fuel passages and restrictions within the body.

33. Inspect the float and needle valve. Check the pivot pin for scratches and excessive wear. Inspect the float (make sure there is no fuel inside the float assembly. If so replace the float assembly) for breaks in the lip and wear in the pivot pin holes. Check the needle valve plunger for wear or damage and the spring for deformation. The strainer should be checked for rust or breaks.

34. Make certain the power piston moves smoothly within its bore.

35. Check the power valve for proper air flow. In its normal (expanded) condition, no air should pass through it. When compressed at one end, air should enter the end and exit through the side vent.

36. Inspect the fuel cut solenoids. Connect the solenoid leads to the battery terminals (the solenoid with only one lead requires a jumper between the case and the battery) and check that the solenoid clicks as the last connection is made. The solenoid should click each time the battery is connected or disconnected. If a solenoid is not operating correctly, replace it.

37. Install new O-rings on the solenoids.

38. Inspect the choke heater by using an ohmmeter to measure its resistance. Correct resis-

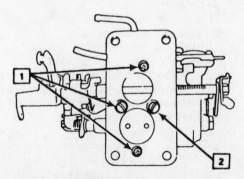

1. RETAINING SCREWS
2. SPECIAL PASSAGE SCREW

Body and flange retaining screws. Note that one screw contains a vacuum passage

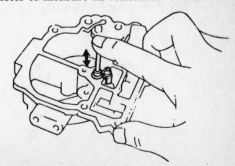

Inspecting the power piston

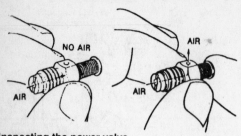

Inspecting the power valve

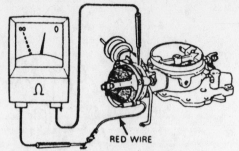

RED WIRE

Checking the resistance of the choke heater

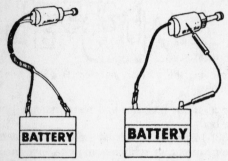

Testing the primary (left) and secondary fuel cut solenoids

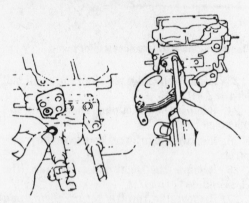

Installing the secondary throttle valve diaphragm

tance is 18Ω. If a problem is found, the air horn assembly must be replaced.

39. Reassembly begins by placing a new gasket and the carburetor body onto the flange.

40. Install the vacuum passage bolt, then install the three retaining bolts.

41. Assemble the secondary throttle diaphragm, position the gasket and install the assembly. Connect the linkage.

42. Install the fast idle cam with the bolt.

43. Install the throttle lever with its nut.

44. Install the throttle back spring and the throttle return spring.

45. Install the sight glass with its O-ring and retainer.

46. Install the primary and secondary small ventures over new gaskets. Install the O-ring on the primary small ventures.

47. Install the auxiliary accelerator pump by first installing the outer plug, the short spring and the small ball. Install the inlet plug and the small ball, followed by the AAP housing, spring and diaphragm.

Install the pin clip after the float is adjusted

48. Install the primary main jet and passage plug with a new gasket.

49. Install the secondary main jet and passage plug with a new gasket.

50. Install the throttle lever.

51. Install the slow jet.

52. Assemble the power valve and jet and install them in position.

53. Install the discharge large ball, the long spring, the pump discharge weight and the stopper gasket.

54. Use tweezers to insert the plunger small ball and the retainer.

55. Reinstall the throttle positioner and connect its linkage.

56. On the air horn, install the valve seat over the gasket into the fuel inlet.

57. Install the needle valve, spring, and plunger onto the seat.

58. Install the float and pivot pin.

59. Measure and adjust the float clearances (level) by following procedures and specifications outlined earlier in this Chapter.

60. After adjusting the float level, remove the float, plunger, spring and needle valve. Assemble the pin clip onto the needle valve.

61. Install the power piston spring and piston into its bore and install the retainer.

62. Install the acceleration pump plunger and its boot.

63. Place a new gasket onto the air horn.

MEASURING THE CLEARANCE

ADJUSTING

Adjusting the secondary throttle plate clearance

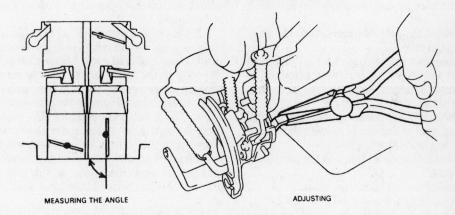

MEASURING THE ANGLE

ADJUSTING

Adjusting the primary throttle plate

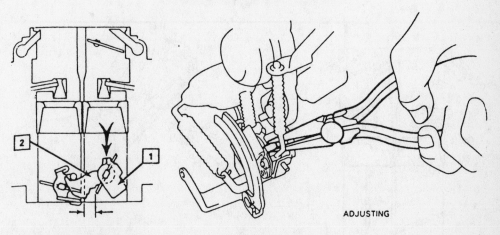

MEASURING THE CLEARANCE

ADJUSTING

1. PRIMARY KICK LEVER
2. SECONDARY KICK LEVER

Measuring and adjusting the secondary touch

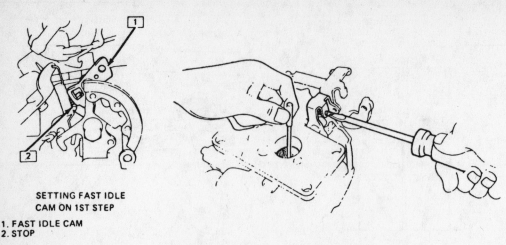

SETTING FAST IDLE
CAM ON 1ST STEP

1. FAST IDLE CAM
2. STOP

ADJUSTING
Adjusting the fast idle setting

64. Install the needle valve assembly, the float and the pivot pin. Insert the float lip between the plunger and the clip when installing the float.

65. Install the solenoid valves into the body of the carburetor.

66. Assemble the air horn and body. Install the eight screws, paying particular attention to the various brackets, wire clamps and steel number plate.

67. Install the accelerator pump arm. Install the pump arm to the air horn with the pump plunger hole and lever aligned.

68. Connect the choke link and the pump connecting link.

69. Install the fuel pipe and union.

70. With the carburetor still on the bench, move the various linkages by hand, checking for smooth operation.

71. Check the throttle plate for full opening. It should move 90° from horizontal. If needed, adjust its travel by bending the first throttle lever stopper.

72. Check the clearance of the secondary throttle plate. When wide open, the secondary throttle plate should have 13mm clearance to the body of the bore. Adjust this clearance by bending the secondary throttle lever stopper.

73. Check the clearance for the secondary touch. This is the point at which the secondary throttle begins to open under acceleration. Move the primary throttle plate open, watching for the point at which the first kick lever just touches the second kick lever. At this point, the primary throttle plate should have 6mm clearance.

74. Set the throttle lever to the first step of the fast idle cam. With the choke plate fully

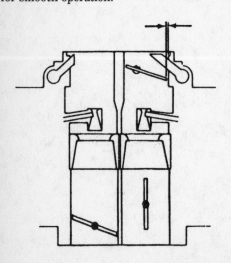

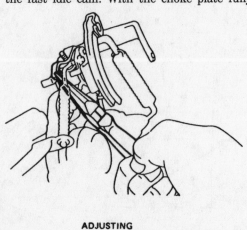

ADJUSTING

MEASURING THE CLEARANCE
Adjusting the choke unloader

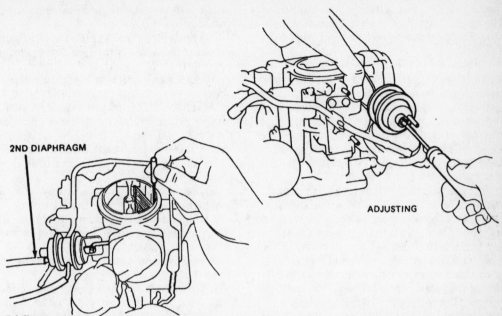

2ND DIAPHRAGM

ADJUSTING

Adjusting the choke breaker in two steps. Remember to apply vacuum to both diaphragms during the second step

closed, check the clearance of the primary throttle plate. The correct clearance is 1.15mm; the clearance may be adjusted by turning the fast idle adjusting screw.

75. The choke unloader is adjusted by bending the fast idle lever as necessary. Open the

primary throttle plate fully (with the choke plate closed, from the previous step) and check that the choke plate has 3mm of clearance.

76. Check the choke breaker. Hold the throttle slightly open, push the choke closed and hold it closed as your release the throttle. Apply

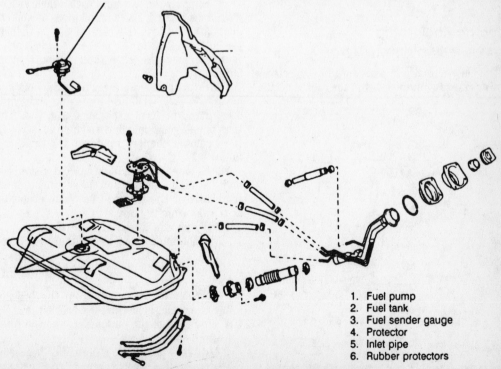

1. Fuel pump
2. Fuel tank
3. Fuel sender gauge
4. Protector
5. Inlet pipe
6. Rubber protectors

Exploded view fuel tank components 4A-GE engine

vacuum to the choke breaker 1st diaphragm. The choke plate should have 2.5mm of clearance. The clearance is adjusted by bending the relief lever.

77. Now apply vacuum to both the first and second diaphragms. Clearance at the choke plate should become 6mm. Adjustment is by turning the diaphragm adjustment screw.

78. Release the choke and throttle settings. With the choke plate fully open, measure the length of the pump stroke. Correct stroke is 2mm; it may be adjusted by bending the connecting link.

79. Reinstall the carburetor on the intake manifold, following directions outlined earlier.

80. Start the engine and allow it to warm up normally. During this time, pay careful attention to the high idle speed, the operation of the choke and its controls and the idle quality. If you worked carefully and accurately, and performed the bench set-up properly, the carburetor should need very little adjustment after reinstallation.

FUEL INJECTION SYSTEM

NOTE: *This book contains testing and service procedures for your car's fuel injection system. More comprehensive testing and diagnosis procedures may be found in CHILTON'S GUIDE TO FUEL INJECTION AND FEEDBACK CARBURETORS, available at your local retailer.*

Electric Fuel Pump

REMOVAL AND INSTALLATION

The electric fuel pump used on fuel injected Toyota cars is contained within the fuel tank. It

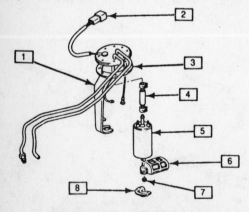

1. Fuel pump bracket	5. Pump
2. Electrical connector	6. Fuel pump filter
3. Gasket	7. Clip
4. Fuel hose	8. Rubber cushion

Fuel pump assembly 4A-FE engine 4A-GE engine similar

cannot be removed without removing the tank from the car.

NOTE: *Before removing fuel system parts, clean them with a spray-type engine cleaner. Follow the instructions on the cleaner. Do not soak fuel system parts in liquid cleaning solvent.*

CAUTION: *The fuel injection system is under pressure. Release pressure slowly and contain spillage. Observe no smoking/no open flame precautions. Have a Class B-C (dry powder) fire extinguisher within arm's reach at all times.*

1. Disconnect the negative battery cable. Relieve fuel pressure. Remove the filler cap.

2. Using a siphon or pump, drain the fuel from the tank and store it in a proper metal container with a tight cap.

3. Remove the rear seat cushion to gain access to the electrical wiring.

4. Disconnect the fuel pump and sending unit wiring at the connector.

5. Raise the vehicle and safely support it on jackstands.

6. Loosen the clamp and remove the filler neck and overflow pipe from the tank.

7. Remove the supply hose from the tank. Wrap a rag around the fitting to collect escaping fuel. Disconnect the breather hose from the tank, again using a rag to control spillage.

8. Cover or plug the end of each disconnected line to keep dirt out and fuel in.

9. Support the fuel tank with a floor jack or transmission jack. Use a broad piece of wood to distribute the load. Be careful not to deform the bottom of the tank.

10. Remove the fuel tank support strap bolts.

11. Swing the straps away from the tank and lower the jack. Balance the tank with your other hand or have a helper assist you. The tank is bulky and may have some fuel left in it. If its balance changes suddenly, the tank may fall.

12. Remove the fuel filler pipe extension, the breather pipe assembly and the sending unit assembly. Keep these items in a clean, protected area away from the car.

13. To remove the electric fuel pump:

  a. Disconnect the two pump-to-harness wires.

  b. Loosen the pump outlet hose clamp at the bracket pipe.

  c. Remove the pump from the bracket and the outlet hose from the bracket pipe.

  d. Separate the outlet hose and the filter from the pump.

14. While the tank is out and disassembled, inspect it for any signs of rust, leakage or metal damage. If any problem is found, re-

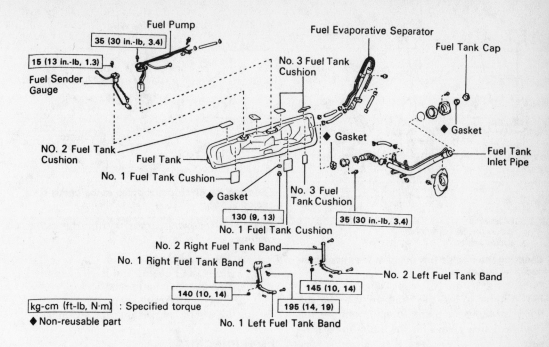

Fuel Pump

35 (30 in.-lb, 3.4)

15 (13 in.-lb, 1.3)

Fuel Sender
Gauge

Fuel Evaporative Separator

Fuel Tank Cap

No. 3 Fuel Tank
Cushion

◆ Gasket

◆ Gasket

Fuel Tank
Inlet Pipe

NO. 2 Fuel Tank
Cushion

Fuel Tank

No. 1 Fuel Tank Cushion

◆ Gasket

No. 3 Fuel
Tank Cushion

130 (9, 13)

No. 1 Fuel Tank Cushion

35 (30 in.-lb, 3.4)

No. 2 Right Fuel Tank Band

No. 1 Right Fuel Tank Band

No. 2 Left Fuel Tank Band

kg-cm (ft-lb, N·m) : Specified torque
◆ Non-reusable part

140 (10, 14)

145 (10, 14)

195 (14, 19)

No. 1 Left Fuel Tank Band

Exploded view fuel pump and fuel tank components — MR2

place the tank. Clean the inside of the tank with water and a light detergent and rinse the tank thoroughly several times.

15. Inspect all of the lines, hoses and fittings for any sign of corrosion, wear or damage to the surfaces. Check the pump outlet hose and the filter for restrictions.

16. When reassembling, ALWAYS replace the sealing gaskets with new ones. Also replace any rubber parts showing any sign of deterioration.

17. Assemble the outlet hose and filter onto the pump; then attach the pump to the bracket.

18. Connect the outlet hose clamp to the bracket pipe and connect the pump wiring to the harness wire.

19. Install the fuel pump and bracket assembly onto the tank.

20. Install the sending unit assembly.

21. Connect the breather pipe assembly and the filler pipe extension.
NOTE: *Tighten the breather pipe screw to 17 INCH lbs. and all other attaching screws to 30 INCH lbs.*

22. Place the fuel tank on the jack and elevate it into place within the car. Attach the straps and install the strap bolts, tightening them (in even steps) to 29 ft. lbs.

23. Connect the breather hose to the tank pipe, the return hose to the tank pipe and the supply hose to its tank pipe. tighten the supply hose fitting to 21 ft. lbs.

24. Connect the filler neck and overflow pipe to the tank. Make sure the clamps are properly seated and secure.

25. Lower the vehicle to the ground.

26. Connect the pump and sending unit electrical connectors to the harness.

27. Install the rear seat cushion.

28. Using a funnel, pour the fuel that was drained from its container into the fuel filler.

29. Install the fuel filler cap.

30. Start the engine and check carefully for any sign of leakage around the tank and lines. Road test the vehicle for proper operation.

TESTING

Since the fuel pump is concealed within the tank, it is difficult to test directly at the pump.

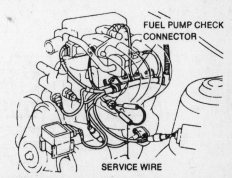

FUEL PUMP CHECK
CONNECTOR

SERVICE WIRE

Checking the electric fuel pump at the check connector — early models

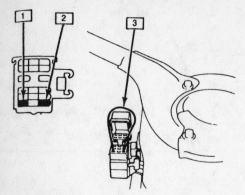

1. FP terminal
2. Battery positive (+) terminal
3. Jumper wire

Checking the electric fuel pump at the check connector — late models

It is possible to test the pump from under the hood, listening for pump function and feeling the fuel delivery lines for the build-up of pressure.

1. Turn the ignition switch ON, but do not start the motor.

2. Using a jumper wire, short both terminals of the fuel pump check connector. The check connector is located under the hood near the wiper motor. (On some early models refer to the illustrations of fuel pump check connector and service wire) Connect the terminals labeled **FP** and **+B**.

3. Check that there is pressure in the hose running to the delivery pipe. You should hear fuel pressure noise and possibly hear the pump at the rear of the car.

4. Remove the jumper wire.

5. Turn the ignition to OFF. If the fuel pump failed to function, it may indicate a faulty pump, but before removing the tank and pump,

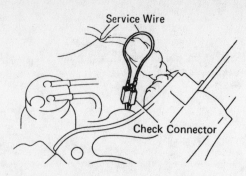

Checking the electric fuel pump at the check connector

check the following items within the pump system:

   a. the fusible link
   b. fuses (EFI/15amp and IGN/7.5amp)
   c. fuel injection main relay
   d. fuel pump circuit opening relay
   e. all wiring connections and grounds.

Fuel injectors

The injectors — electrically triggered valves — deliver a measured quantity of fuel into the intake manifold according to signals from the ECM. As driving conditions change, the computer signals each injector to stay open a longer or shorter period of time, thus controlling the amount of fuel introduced into the engine. An injector, being an electric component, is either on or off (open or closed); there is no variable control for an injector other than duration.

Cleanliness equals success when working on a fuel injected system. Every component must be treated with the greatest care and be protected from dust, grime and impact damage. The miniaturized and solid state circuitry is easily damaged by a jolt. Additionally, care must be used in dealing with electrical connectors. Look for and release any locking mecha-

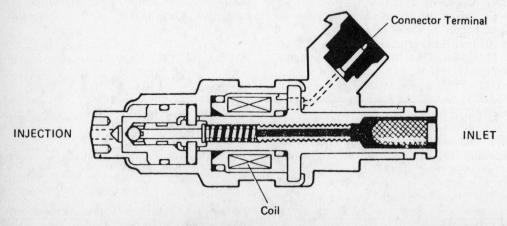

Cross section of a fuel injector

nisms on the connector before separating the connectors. When reattaching, make sure each pin is properly lined up and seated before pushing the connector closed.

REMOVAL AND INSTALLATION

4A-GE and 4A-GZE Engines

CAUTION: *The fuel system is under pressure. Release pressure slowly and contain spillage. Observe no smoking/no open flame precautions. Have a Class B-C (dry powder) fire extinguisher within arm's reach at all times.*

1. Disconnect the negative battery cable.

NOTE: *If you are diagnosing a driveability problem, check the ECM for any stored trouble codes BEFORE disconnecting the cable. The codes will be lost after the battery is disconnected.*

2. Disconnect the PCV hose from the valve cover.

3. Remove the vacuum sensing hose from the pressure regulator.

4. Disconnect the fuel return hose from the pressure regulator.

5. Place a towel or container under the cold start injector pipe. Loosen the two union bolts at the fuel line and remove the pipe with its gaskets.

6. Remove the fuel inlet pipe mounting bolt and disconnect the fuel inlet hose by removing the fuel union bolt, the two gaskets and the hose.

7. Disconnect the injector electrical connections.

8. At the fuel delivery pipe (rail), remove the three bolts. Lift the delivery pipe and the injectors free of the engine. DON'T drop the injectors.

9. Remove the four insulators and three collars from the cylinder head.

10. Pull the injectors free of the delivery pipe.

11. Before installing the injectors back into the fuel rail, install a NEW O-ring on each injector.

Removing fuel delivery pipe hose

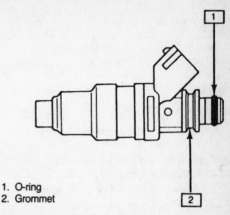

1. O-ring
2. Grommet

Injector with seals

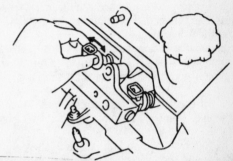

Make certain the injector can be rotated in place after installation

12. Coat each O-ring with a light coat of gasoline (NEVER use oil of any sort) and install the injectors into the delivery pipe. Make certain each injector can be smoothly rotated. If they do not rotate smoothly, the O-ring is not in its correct position.

13. Install the insulators into each injector hole. Place the three spacers on the delivery pipe mounting holes in the cylinder head.

14. Place the delivery pipe and injectors on the cylinder head and again check that the injectors rotate smoothly. Install the three bolts and tighten them to 13 ft. lbs.

15. Connect the electrical connectors to each injector.

16. Install two new gaskets and attach the inlet pipe and fuel union bolt. Tighten the bolt to 22 ft. lbs. Install the mounting bolt.

17. Install new gaskets and connect the cold start injector pipe to the delivery pipe and cold start injector. Install the fuel line union bolts and tighten them to 13 ft. lbs.

18. Connect the fuel return hose and the vacuum sensing hose to the pressure regulator. Attach the PCV hose to the valve cover.

19. Connect the battery cable to the negative battery terminal. Start the engine and check for leaks.

CAUTION: *If there is a leak at any fitting, the line will be under pressure and the fuel* may spray in a fine mist. This mist is extremely explosive. Shut the engine off immediately if any leakage is detected. Use rags to wrap the leaking fitting until the pressure diminishes and wipe up any fuel from the engine area.

4A-FE Engine

1. Disconnect the negative battery cable.
2. Disconnect the PCV hoses from the valve cover and the vacuum sensing hose from the fuel pressure regulator.
3. Disconnect the fuel return hose from the fuel pressure regulator.
4. Remove the wiring connectors from the injectors.
5. Remove the pressure regulator by loosening the two bolts and pulling the regulator from the delivery pipe.
6. Label and remove the four vacuum hoses running to the EGR vacuum modulator. Remove the nut and bracket with the modulator.
7. Disconnect the fuel union bolt at the inlet pipe. Remove the pipe and the two gaskets.
8. Remove the two bolts holding the delivery pipe and then remove the delivery pipe and the injectors. Don't drop the injectors!
9. Remove the two spacers and the four insulators from the cylinder head.
10. Pull the injectors free of the delivery pipe.
11. Before installing the injectors back into the fuel rail, install a NEW O-ring on each injector.
12. Coat each O-ring with a light coat of gasoline (NEVER use oil of any sort) and install the injectors into the delivery pipe. Make certain each injector can be smoothly rotated. If they do not rotate smoothly, the O-ring is not in its correct position.
13. Install the four insulators and two spacers in place.
14. Place the delivery pipe and injectors on the cylinder head and again check that the injectors rotate smoothly. Install the two bolts and tighten them to 11 ft. lbs.

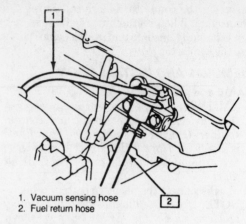

1. Vacuum sensing hose
2. Fuel return hose

Pressure regulator hoses

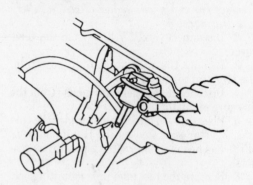

Removing the regulator mounting bolts

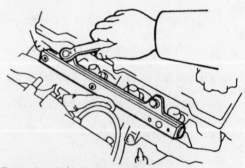

Removing the fuel delivery pipe

15. Install two new gaskets and attach the inlet pipe and fuel union bolt. Tighten the bolt to 22 ft. lbs.
16. Install the EGR vacuum modulator with its bracket and nut. Connect the four vacuum hoses to their proper ports.
17. Install new gaskets and connect the cold start injector pipe to the delivery pipe and cold start injector. Install the fuel line union bolts and tighten them to 13 ft. lbs.
18. Install a new O-ring on the pressure regulator. Push the regulator into the delivery pipe and install the two bolts. Tighten the bolts to 5.5 ft. lbs. (65 INCH lbs.)

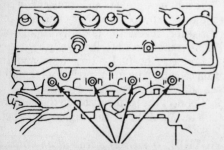

Placement of injectors insulators

19. Connect the injector wiring connectors.
20. Connect the fuel return hose and the vacuum sensing hose to the pressure regulator. Attach the PCV hoses to the valve cover.
21. Connect the battery cable to the negative battery terminal. Start the engine and check for leaks.

CAUTION: *If there is a leak at any fitting, the line will be under pressure and the fuel may spray in a fine mist. This mist is extremely explosive. Shut the engine off immediately if any leakage is detected. Use rags to wrap the leaking fitting until the pressure diminishes and wipe up any fuel from the engine area.*

3E-E Engine

CAUTION: *The fuel system is under pressure. Release pressure slowly and contain spillage. Observe no smoking/no open flame precautions. Have a Class B-C (dry powder)*

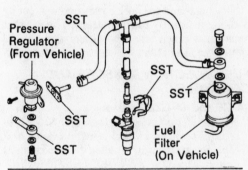

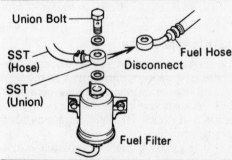

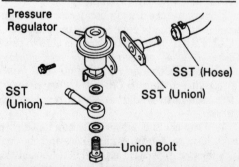

Typical fuel injector assembly

fire extinguisher within arm's reach at all times.

1. Disconnect the negative battery cable.

NOTE: *If you are diagnosing a driveability problem, check the ECM for any stored trouble codes BEFORE disconnecting the cable. The codes will be lost after the battery is disconnected.*

2. Disconnect the PCV hose from the valve cover.
3. Remove the air intake connector. Disconnect the accelerator cable and throttle cable.
4. Remove the vacuum sensing hose from the pressure regulator.
5. Remove the dash pot and link bracket.
6. Disconnect the fuel inlet and return hoses.
7. Place a towel or container under the cold start injector pipe. Loosen the two union bolts at the fuel line and remove the pipe with its gaskets.
8. Disconnect the injector electrical connections.
9. At the fuel delivery pipe (rail), remove the 2 bolts. Lift the delivery pipe and the injectors free of the engine. DON'T drop the injectors.
10. Remove the four insulators and 2 collars from the cylinder head.
11. Pull the injectors free of the delivery pipe.
12. Before installing the injectors back into the fuel rail, install a NEW O-ring on each injector.
13. Coat each O-ring with a light coat of gasoline (NEVER use oil of any sort) and install the injectors into the delivery pipe. Make certain each injector can be smoothly rotated. If they do not rotate smoothly, the O-ring is not in its correct position. REPLACE ALL FUEL INJECTOR AND FUEL LINE GASKETS refer to fuel injection assembly illustration.
14. Install the insulators into each injector hole. Place the 2 spacers on the delivery pipe mounting holes in the cylinder head.
15. Place the delivery pipe and injectors on the cylinder head and again check that the injectors rotate smoothly. Install the bolts and tighten them to 14 ft. lbs.
16. Connect the electrical connectors to each injector.
17. Install two new gaskets and attach the inlet pipe and fuel union bolt. Tighten the bolt to 22 ft. lbs. Install the mounting bolt.
18. Install new gaskets and connect the cold start injector pipe to the delivery pipe and cold start injector. Install the fuel line union bolts and tighten them to 13 ft. lbs.
19. Connect the fuel return hose and the

vacuum sensing hose to the pressure regulator. Attach the PCV hose to the valve cover.

20. Reconnect the accelerator cable, throttle cable and install the air intake connector. Install the dash pot and link bracket.

21. Connect the battery cable to the negative battery terminal. Start the engine and check for leaks.

CAUTION: *If there is a leak at any fitting, the line will be under pressure and the fuel may spray in a fine mist. This mist is extremely explosive. Shut the engine off immediately if any leakage is detected. Use rags to wrap the leaking fitting until the pressure diminishes and wipe up any fuel from the engine area.*

TESTING

The simplest way to test the injectors is simply to listen to them with the engine running. Use either a stethoscope-type tool or the blade of a long screw driver to touch each injector while the engine is idling. You should hear a distinct clicking as each injector opens and closes.

Additionally, the resistance of the injector can be easily checked. Disconnect the negative battery cable and remove the electrical connector from the injector to be tested. Use an ohmmeter to check the resistance across the terminals of the injector. Correct resistance is approximately 13.8Ω at 68°F (20°C); slight variations are acceptable due to temperature conditions.

Bench testing of the injectors can only be

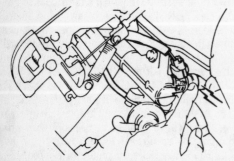

Checking fuel injector for operation

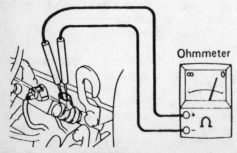

Ohmmeter

Testing injector resistance

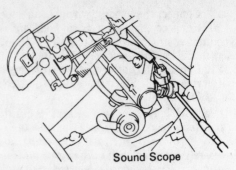

Sound Scope

Checking fuel injector for operation

done using expensive special equipment. Generally this equipment can be found at a dealership and sometimes at a well-equipped machine shop or performance shop. There is no provision for field testing the injectors by the owner/ mechanic. DO NOT attempt to test the injector by removing it from the engine and making it spray into a jar.

Never attempt to check a removed injector by hooking it directly to the battery. The injector runs on a much smaller voltage and the 12 volts from the battery will destroy it internally.

FUEL INJECTION SENSORS AND CONTROLS

4A-GE and 4A-GZE Engines

NOTE: *For all other engines refer to the procedures below as all fuel injector sensors and controls are similar — modify service steps as necessary. USE SERVICE TESTING PROCEDURES AS A GUIDE FOR REPLACEMENT OF COMPONENTS.*

COLD START INJECTOR

1. Test the resistance of the cold start injector before removing it. Disconnect its electrical lead and use an ohmmeter to measure resistance between the terminals. Correct resistance is $3–5\Omega$; allow for slight variations due to temperature.

2. If the injector must be replaced, disconnect the negative battery cable.

3. Remove the wiring connector at the injector if not already done for testing purposes.

CAUTION: *The fuel system is under pressure. Release pressure slowly and contain spillage. Observe no smoking/no open flame precautions. Have a Class B-C (dry powder) fire extinguisher within arm's reach at all times.*

4. Wrap the fuel pipe connection in a rag or towel. Remove the two union bolts and the cold start injector pipe with its gaskets. Loosen the union bolts at the other end as necessary.

5. Remove the two retaining bolts and remove the cold start injector with its gaskets.

CHILTON'S
FUEL ECONOMY
& TUNE-UP TIPS

55 WAYS TO IMPROVE FUEL ECONOMY

Tune-up • Spark Plug Diagnosis • Emission Controls

Fuel System • Cooling System • Tires and Wheels

General Maintenance

CHILTON'S FUEL ECONOMY & TUNE-UP TIPS

Fuel economy is important to everyone, no matter what kind of vehicle you drive. The maintenance-minded motorist can save both money and fuel using these tips and the periodic maintenance and tune-up procedures in this Repair and Tune-Up Guide.

There are more than 130,000,000 cars and trucks registered for private use in the United States. Each travels an average of 10-12,000 miles per year, and, and in total they consume close to 70 billion gallons of fuel each year. This represents nearly ⅔ of the oil imported by the United States each year. The Federal government's goal is to reduce consumption 10% by 1985. A variety of methods are either already in use or under serious consideration, and they all affect you driving and the cars you will drive. In addition to "down-sizing", the auto industry is using or investigating the use of electronic fuel delivery, electronic engine controls and alternative engines for use in smaller and lighter vehicles, among other alternatives to meet the federally mandated Corporate Average Fuel Economy (CAFE) of 27.5 mpg by 1985. The government, for its part, is considering rationing, mandatory driving curtailments and tax increases on motor vehicle fuel in an effort to reduce consumption. The government's goal of a 10% reduction could be realized — and further government regulation avoided — if every private vehicle could use just 1 less gallon of fuel per week.

How Much Can You Save?

Tests have proven that almost anyone can make at least a 10% reduction in fuel consumption through regular maintenance and tune-ups. When a major manufacturer of spark plugs sur-

TUNE-UP

1. Check the cylinder compression to be sure the engine will really benefit from a tune-up and that it is capable of producing good fuel economy. A tune-up will be wasted on an engine in poor mechanical condition.

2. Replace spark plugs regularly. New spark plugs alone can increase fuel economy 3%.

3. Be sure the spark plugs are the correct type (heat range) for your vehicle. See the Tune-Up Specifications.

Heat range refers to the spark plug's ability to conduct heat away from the firing end. It must conduct the heat away in an even pattern to avoid becoming a source of pre-ignition, yet it must also operate hot enough to burn off conductive deposits that could cause misfiring.

The heat range is usually indicated by a number on the spark plug, part of the manufacturer's designation for each individual spark plug. The numbers in bold-face indicate the heat range in each manufacturer's identification system.

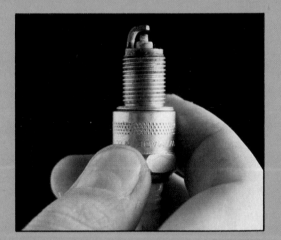

Periodically, check the spark plugs to be sure they are firing efficiently. They are excellent indicators of the internal condition of your engine.

On AC, Bosch (new), Champion, Fram/Autolite, Mopar, Motorcraft and Prestolite, a higher number indicates a hotter plug. On Bosch (old), NGK and Nippondenso, a higher number indicates a colder plug.

4. Make sure the spark plugs are properly gapped. See the Tune-Up Specifications in this book.

5. Be sure the spark plugs are firing efficiently. The illustrations on the next 2 pages show you how to "read" the firing end of the spark plug.

6. Check the ignition timing and set it to specifications. Tests show that almost all cars have incorrect ignition timing by more than 2°.

Manufacturer	Typical Designation
AC	R **45** TS
Bosch (old)	WA **145** T30
Bosch (new)	HR **8** Y
Champion	RBL **15** Y
Fram/Autolite	4**15**
Mopar	P-**62** PR
Motorcraft	BRF-**42**
NGK	BP **5** ES-15
Nippondenso	W **16** EP
Prestolite	14GR **5** 2A

veyed over 6,000 cars nationwide, they found that a tune-up, on cars that needed one, increased fuel economy over 11%. Replacing worn plugs alone, accounted for a 3% increase. The same test also revealed that 8 out of every 10 vehicles will have some maintenance deficiency that will directly affect fuel economy, emissions or performance. Most of this mileage-robbing neglect could be prevented with regular maintenance.

Modern engines require that all of the functioning systems operate properly for maximum efficiency. A malfunction anywhere wastes fuel. You can keep your vehicle running as efficiently and economically as possible, by being aware of your vehicle's operating and performance characteristics. If your vehicle suddenly develops performance or fuel economy problems it could be due to one or more of the following:

PROBLEM	POSSIBLE CAUSE
Engine Idles Rough	Ignition timing, idle mixture, vacuum leak or something amiss in the emission control system.
Hesitates on Acceleration	Dirty carburetor or fuel filter, improper accelerator pump setting, ignition timing or fouled spark plugs.
Starts Hard or Fails to Start	Worn spark plugs, improperly set automatic choke, ice (or water) in fuel system.
Stalls Frequently	Automatic choke improperly adjusted and possible dirty air filter or fuel filter.
Performs Sluggishly	Worn spark plugs, dirty fuel or air filter, ignition timing or automatic choke out of adjustment.

Check spark plug wires on conventional point type ignition for cracks by bending them in a loop around your finger.

Be sure that spark plug wires leading to adjacent cylinders do not run too close together. (Photo courtesy Champion Spark Plug Co.)

7. If your vehicle does not have electronic ignition, check the points, rotor and cap as specified.

8. Check the spark plug wires (used with conventional point-type ignitions) for cracks and burned or broken insulation by bending them in a loop around your finger. Cracked wires decrease fuel efficiency by failing to deliver full voltage to the spark plugs. One misfiring spark plug can cost you as much as 2 mpg.

9. Check the routing of the plug wires. Misfiring can be the result of spark plug leads to adjacent cylinders running parallel to each other and too close together. One wire tends to

pick up voltage from the other causing it to fire "out of time".

10. Check all electrical and ignition circuits for voltage drop and resistance.

11. Check the distributor mechanical and/or vacuum advance mechanisms for proper functioning. The vacuum advance can be checked by twisting the distributor plate in the opposite direction of rotation. It should spring back when released.

12. Check and adjust the valve clearance on engines with mechanical lifters. The clearance should be slightly loose rather than too tight.

SPARK PLUG DIAGNOSIS

Normal

APPEARANCE: This plug is typical of one operating normally. The insulator nose varies from a light tan to grayish color with slight electrode wear. The presence of slight deposits is normal on used plugs and will have no adverse effect on engine performance. The spark plug heat range is correct for the engine and the engine is running normally.

CAUSE: Properly running engine.

RECOMMENDATION: Before reinstalling this plug, the electrodes should be cleaned and filed square. Set the gap to specifications. If the plug has been in service for more than 10-12,000 miles, the entire set should probably be replaced with a fresh set of the same heat range.

Oil Deposits

APPEARANCE: The firing end of the plug is covered with a wet, oily coating.

CAUSE: The problem is poor oil control. On high mileage engines, oil is leaking past the rings or valve guides into the combustion chamber. A common cause is also a plugged PCV valve, and a ruptured fuel pump diaphragm can also cause this condition. Oil fouled plugs such as these are often found in new or recently overhauled engines, before normal oil control is achieved, and can be cleaned and reinstalled.

RECOMMENDATION: A hotter spark plug may temporarily relieve the problem, but the engine is probably in need of work.

Incorrect Heat Range

APPEARANCE: The effects of high temperature on a spark plug are indicated by clean white, often blistered insulator. This can also be accompanied by excessive wear of the electrode, and the absence of deposits.

CAUSE: Check for the correct spark plug heat range. A plug which is too hot for the engine can result in overheating. A car operated mostly at high speeds can require a colder plug. Also check ignition timing, cooling system level, fuel mixture and leaking intake manifold.

RECOMMENDATION: If all ignition and engine adjustments are known to be correct, and no other malfunction exists, install spark plugs one heat range colder.

Carbon Deposits

APPEARANCE: Carbon fouling is easily identified by the presence of dry, soft, black, sooty deposits.

CAUSE: Changing the heat range can often lead to carbon fouling, as can prolonged slow, stop-and-start driving. If the heat range is correct, carbon fouling can be attributed to a rich fuel mixture, sticking choke, clogged air cleaner, worn breaker points, retarded timing or low compression. If only one or two plugs are carbon fouled, check for corroded or cracked wires on the affected plugs. Also look for cracks in the distributor cap between the towers of affected cylinders.

RECOMMENDATION: After the problem is corrected, these plugs can be cleaned and reinstalled if not worn severely.

MMT Fouled

APPEARANCE: Spark plugs fouled by MMT (Methycyclopentadienyl Maganese Tricarbonyl) have reddish, rusty appearance on the insulator and side electrode.

CAUSE: MMT is an anti-knock additive in gasoline used to replace lead. During the combustion process, the MMT leaves a reddish deposit on the insulator and side electrode.

RECOMMENDATION: No engine malfunction is indicated and the deposits will not affect plug performance any more than lead deposits (see Ash Deposits). MMT fouled plugs can be cleaned, regapped and reinstalled.

High Speed Glazing

APPEARANCE: Glazing appears as shiny coating on the plug, either yellow or tan in color.

CAUSE: During hard, fast acceleration, plug temperatures rise suddenly. Deposits from normal combustion have no chance to fluff-off; instead, they melt on the insulator forming an electrically conductive coating which causes misfiring.

RECOMMENDATION: Glazed plugs are not easily cleaned. They should be replaced with a fresh set of plugs of the correct heat range. If the condition recurs, using plugs with a heat range one step colder may cure the problem.

Ash (Lead) Deposits

APPEARANCE: Ash deposits are characterized by light brown or white colored deposits crusted on the side or center electrodes. In some cases it may give the plug a rusty appearance.

CAUSE: Ash deposits are normally derived from oil or fuel additives burned during normal combustion. Normally they are harmless, though excessive amounts can cause misfiring. If deposits are excessive in short mileage, the valve guides may be worn.

RECOMMENDATION: Ash-fouled plugs can be cleaned, gapped and reinstalled.

Detonation

APPEARANCE: Detonation is usually characterized by a broken plug insulator.

CAUSE: A portion of the fuel charge will begin to burn spontaneously, from the increased heat following ignition. The explosion that results applies extreme pressure to engine components, frequently damaging spark plugs and pistons.

Detonation can result by over-advanced ignition timing, inferior gasoline (low octane) lean air/fuel mixture, poor carburetion, engine lugging or an increase in compression ratio due to combustion chamber deposits or engine modification.

RECOMMENDATION: Replace the plugs after correcting the problem.

Photos Courtesy Champion Spark Plug Co.

EMISSION CONTROLS

13. Be aware of the general condition of the emission control system. It contributes to reduced pollution and should be serviced regularly to maintain efficient engine operation.

14. Check all vacuum lines for dried, cracked or brittle conditions. Something as simple as a leaking vacuum hose can cause poor performance and loss of economy.

15. Avoid tampering with the emission control system. Attempting to improve fuel econ-

FUEL SYSTEM

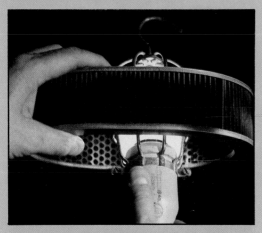

Check the air filter with a light behind it. If you can see light through the filter it can be reused.

Extremely clogged filters should be discarded and replaced with a new one.

18. Replace the air filter regularly. A dirty air filter richens the air/fuel mixture and can increase fuel consumption as much as 10%. Tests show that 1/3 of all vehicles have air filters in need of replacement.

19. Replace the fuel filter at least as often as recommended.

20. Set the idle speed and carburetor mixture to specifications.

21. Check the automatic choke. A sticking or malfunctioning choke wastes gas.

22. During the summer months, adjust the automatic choke for a leaner mixture which will produce faster engine warm-ups.

COOLING SYSTEM

29. Be sure all accessory drive belts are in good condition. Check for cracks or wear.

30. Adjust all accessory drive belts to proper tension.

31. Check all hoses for swollen areas, worn spots, or loose clamps.

32. Check coolant level in the radiator or ex-

pansion tank.

33. Be sure the thermostat is operating properly. A stuck thermostat delays engine warm-up and a cold engine uses nearly twice as much fuel as a warm engine.

34. Drain and replace the engine coolant at least as often as recommended. Rust and scale

TIRES & WHEELS

38. Check the tire pressure often with a pencil type gauge. Tests by a major tire manufacturer show that 90% of all vehicles have at least 1 tire improperly inflated. Better mileage can be achieved by over-inflating tires, but never exceed the maximum inflation pressure on the side of the tire.

39. If possible, install radial tires. Radial tires

deliver as much as 1/2 mpg more than bias belted tires.

40. Avoid installing super-wide tires. They only create extra rolling resistance and decrease fuel mileage. Stick to the manufacturer's recommendations.

41. Have the wheels properly balanced.

omy by tampering with emission controls is more likely to worsen fuel economy than improve it. Emission control changes on modern engines are not readily reversible.

16. Clean (or replace) the EGR valve and lines as recommended.

17. Be sure that all vacuum lines and hoses are reconnected properly after working under the hood. An unconnected or misrouted vacuum line can wreak havoc with engine performance.

---

23. Check for fuel leaks at the carburetor, fuel pump, fuel lines and fuel tank. Be sure all lines and connections are tight.

24. Periodically check the tightness of the carburetor and intake manifold attaching nuts and bolts. These are a common place for vacuum leaks to occur.

25. Clean the carburetor periodically and lubricate the linkage.

26. The condition of the tailpipe can be an excellent indicator of proper engine combustion. After a long drive at highway speeds, the inside of the tailpipe should be a light grey in color. Black or soot on the insides indicates an overly rich mixture.

27. Check the fuel pump pressure. The fuel pump may be supplying more fuel than the engine needs.

28. Use the proper grade of gasoline for your engine. Don't try to compensate for knocking or "pinging" by advancing the ignition timing. This practice will only increase plug temperature and the chances of detonation or pre-ignition with relatively little performance gain.

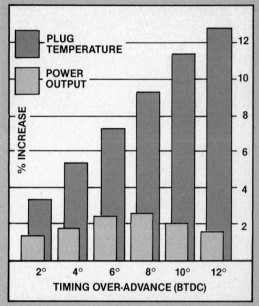

Increasing ignition timing past the specified setting results in a drastic increase in spark plug temperature with increased chance of detonation or preignition. Performance increase is considerably less. (Photo courtesy Champion Spark Plug Co.)

---

that form in the engine should be flushed out to allow the engine to operate at peak efficiency.

35. Clean the radiator of debris that can decrease cooling efficiency.

36. Install a flex-type or electric cooling fan, if you don't have a clutch type fan. Flex fans use curved plastic blades to push more air at low speeds when more cooling is needed; at high speeds the blades flatten out for less resistance. Electric fans only run when the engine temperature reaches a predetermined level.

37. Check the radiator cap for a worn or cracked gasket. If the cap does not seal properly, the cooling system will not function properly.

---

42. Be sure the front end is correctly aligned. A misaligned front end actually has wheels going in differed directions. The increased drag can reduce fuel economy by .3 mpg.

43. Correctly adjust the wheel bearings. Wheel bearings that are adjusted too tight increase rolling resistance.

Check tire pressures regularly with a reliable pocket type gauge. Be sure to check the pressure on a cold tire.

GENERAL MAINTENANCE

Check the fluid levels (particularly engine oil) on a regular basis. Be sure to check the oil for grit, water or other contamination.

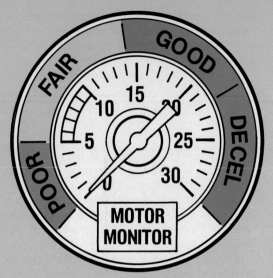

A vacuum gauge is another excellent indicator of internal engine condition and can also be installed in the dash as a mileage indicator.

44. Periodically check the fluid levels in the engine, power steering pump, master cylinder, automatic transmission and drive axle.

45. Change the oil at the recommended interval and change the filter at every oil change. Dirty oil is thick and causes extra friction between moving parts, cutting efficiency and increasing wear. A worn engine requires more frequent tune-ups and gets progressively worse fuel economy. In general, use the lightest viscosity oil for the driving conditions you will encounter.

46. Use the recommended viscosity fluids in the transmission and axle.

47. Be sure the battery is fully charged for fast starts. A slow starting engine wastes fuel.

48. Be sure battery terminals are clean and tight.

49. Check the battery electrolyte level and add distilled water if necessary.

50. Check the exhaust system for crushed pipes, blockages and leaks.

51. Adjust the brakes. Dragging brakes or brakes that are not releasing create increased drag on the engine.

52. Install a vacuum gauge or miles-per-gallon gauge. These gauges visually indicate engine vacuum in the intake manifold. High vacuum = good mileage and low vacuum = poorer mileage. The gauge can also be an excellent indicator of internal engine conditions.

53. Be sure the clutch is properly adjusted. A slipping clutch wastes fuel.

54. Check and periodically lubricate the heat control valve in the exhaust manifold. A sticking or inoperative valve prevents engine warm-up and wastes gas.

55. Keep accurate records to check fuel economy over a period of time. A sudden drop in fuel economy may signal a need for tune-up or other maintenance.

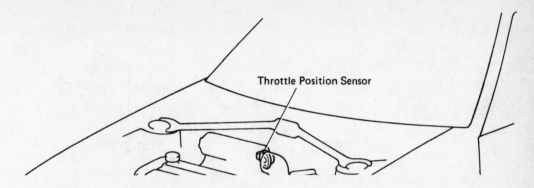

Typical location of electronic control parts 4A-GE engine

6. When reinstalling, always use a new gasket for the injector. Install it with the injector and tighten the two mounting bolts to 7 ft. lbs. (84 INCH lbs.).

7. Again using new gaskets, connect the cold start injector pipe to the delivery pipe (fuel rail) and to the cold start injector. Tighten the bolts to 13 ft. lbs.

8. Install the wiring to the cold start injector.

9. Connect the negative battery cable.

10. Start the engine and check for leaks.

FUEL PRESSURE REGULATOR

1. Remove the vacuum sensing hose from the fuel pressure regulator.

CAUTION: *The fuel system is under pressure. Release pressure slowly and contain spillage. Observe no smoking/no open flame precautions. Have a Class B-C (dry powder) fire extinguisher within arm's reach at all times.*

2. Remove the fuel hose from the regulator.

3. Remove the two retaining bolts and pull the regulator out of the fuel rail.

4. When reinstalling, the two retaining bolts are tightened to 5.5 ft. lbs. (65 INCH lbs) Connect the two hoses (fuel and vacuum).

5. Start the engine and check carefully for leaks.

MASS AIR FLOW SENSOR

The mass air flow sensor communicates with the ECM about the amount of air being taken into the engine. The intake air flow moves a trap door which is connected to a potentiometer. This variable load switch controls the amount of electricity sent to the ECM. Depending on the signal received, the ECM governs the fuel injectors to deliver the proportionally correct amount of fuel into the engine. The air box must be handled carefully during testing and/or replacement.

1. Unplug the wiring connector at the mass air flow sensor.

2. Using an ohmmeter and the chart, measure the resistance between the terminals as in-

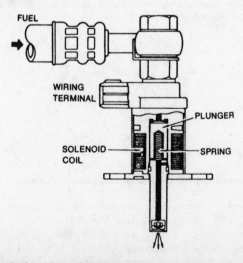

Typical cold start injector

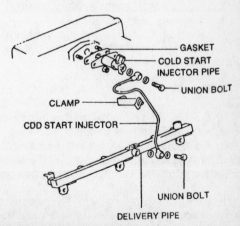

Removing the cold start injector

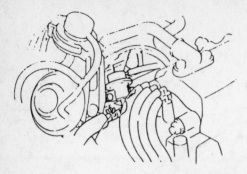

Location of fuel pressure regulator 4A-GE engine

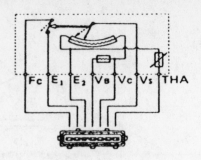

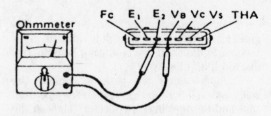

Mass air flow sensor schematic (above) and terminal identification 4A-GE engine

dicated. The sensor must pass ALL tests; if any one is failed, the air sensor must be replaced. Note that the temperature related reading is measured in "kΩ" or kilo-ohms. Don't forget to reset the meter to a higher scale. USE THIS SERVICE TESTING PROCEDURE AS A GUIDE FOR REPLACEMENT OF THIS COMPONENT.

3. If replacement is needed, label and disconnect the vacuum lines running to the sensor.

4. Remove the air cleaner hose.

5. Disconnect the wiring connector if not already done for testing purposes.

6. Remove the four nuts and the mass air flow sensor and its gasket.

7. When reinstalling, make absolutely sure that the air sensor and its gasket are correctly positioned. No air leaks are acceptable. Install and tighten the four nuts.

8. Install the wiring connector, the air cleaner hose and the vacuum hoses. Road test the vehicle for proper operation.

THROTTLE BODY

1. Either drain the coolant from the throttle body by disconnecting a coolant hose or open the engine drain cock.

2. Disconnect the throttle return spring.

3. Disconnect the throttle cable.

4. Label and disconnect the vacuum hoses.

5. Carefully remove the throttle position sensor wiring connector.

6. Remove the air cleaner hose.

7. Remove the water hoses from the air valve.

8. Remove the two bolts and two nuts and the throttle body with its gasket.

9. Wash and clean the cast metal parts with a soft brush and carburetor cleaner. Use compressed air to blow through all the passages and openings.

10. Check the throttle valve to see that there is NO clearance between the stop screw and the throttle lever when the throttle plate is fully closed.

Between terminals	Resistance	Temperature
Vs – E₂	20 – 3,000 Ω	–
Vc – E₂	100 – 300 Ω	–
VB – E₂	200 – 400 Ω	–
THA – E₂	10 – 20 kΩ	– 20°C (–4°F)
	4 – 7 kΩ	0°C (32°F)
	2 – 3 kΩ	20°C (68°F)
	0.9 – 1.3 kΩ	40°C (104°F)
	0.4 – 0.7 kΩ	60°C (204°F)
Fc – E₁	Infinity	–

Resistance chart for testing the mass air flow sensor 4A-GE engine

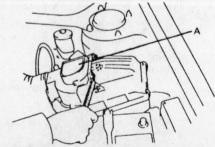

Removing the mass air flow sensor component (A)

11. Check the throttle position sensor (TPS). Insert a 0.47mm feeler gauge between the throttle stop screw and the lever. Connect an ohmmeter between terminal **IDL** and **E₂**. Loosen the two screws holding the TPS and gradually turn the TPS clockwise until the ohm-

meter deflects, but no more. Secure the TPS screws at this point. Double check the clearance at the lever and stop screw.

Additional resistance tests may be made on the TPS using the chart. USE THIS SERVICE

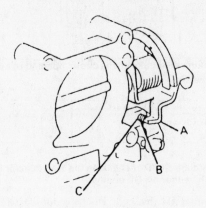

A THROTTLE LEVER
B NO CLEARANCE
C THROTTLE STOP SCREW

Checking the throttle valve

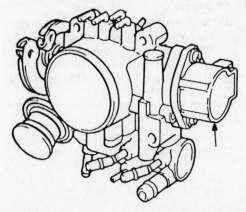

Throttle body assembly — arrow indicates throttle position sensor

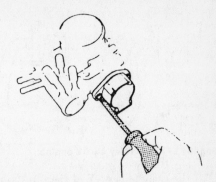

Adjusting the throttle position sensor

TESTING PROCEDURE AS A GUIDE FOR REPLACEMENT OF THIS COMPONENT.

12. To reinstall, place a new gasket in position and install the throttle body with its two nuts and two bolts. Make certain everything is properly positioned before securing the unit. Tighten the bolts to 16 ft. lbs.

13. Connect the water hoses to the air valve.

14. Install the air cleaner hose and the vacuum hoses.

15. Connect the wiring to the throttle position sensor.

16. Connect the accelerator cable and its return spring.

17. Refill the coolant to the proper level.

ELECTRONIC FUEL INJECTION (EFI) MAIN RELAY

1. The relay (refer to location of electronic control parts illustration) is located under the hood, behind the left headlight area. Turn the ignition ON without starting the engine and listen for a noise from the relay.

2. Turn the ignition off and remove the connector from the relay. Using the ohmmeter, check for continuity between terminals **1** and **3**.

3. Check that there is NO continuity between terminals **2** and **4**.

4. Check that there is NO continuity between terminals **3** and **4**.

Clearance between lever and stop screw	Between terminals	Resistance
0 mm (0 in.)	VTA -- E_2	0.2 – 0.8 kΩ
0.35 mm (0.0138 in.)	IDL – E_2	Less than 2.3 kΩ
0.59 mm (0.0232 in.)	IDL – E_2	Infinity
Throttle valve fully opened position	VTA – E_2	3.3 – 10 kΩ
—	Vcc – E_2	3 – 7 kΩ

Throttle position sensor resistance check 4A-GE engine

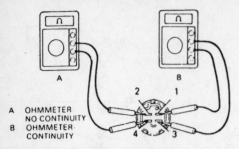

A OHMMETER NO CONTINUITY
B OHMMETER CONTINUITY

Testing the EFI main relay 4A-GE engine

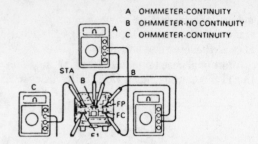

A OHMMETER-CONTINUITY
B OHMMETER-NO CONTINUITY
C OHMMETER-CONTINUITY

Checking continuity on the circuit opening relay 4A-GE engine

5. If the relay fails ANY of these tests, replace it. USE THIS SERVICE TESTING PROCEDURE AS A GUIDE FOR REPLACEMENT OF THIS COMPONENT.

CIRCUIT OPENING RELAY

1. The relay (refer to location of electronic components illustration) is located behind the lower center of the dashboard, adjacent to the ECM. With the ignition off, unplug the connector and use an ohmmeter to check for continuity between terminals **STA** and **E**.
2. Check that there is continuity between terminals **B** and **Fc**.
3. Check that there is NO continuity between terminals **B** and **Fp**.
4. If the relay fails any test, it must be replaced. USE THIS SERVICE TESTING PROCEDURE AS A GUIDE FOR REPLACEMENT OF THIS COMPONENT.

START INJECTOR TIME SWITCH

1. Remove the connector at the switch.
2. Use an ohmmeter to measure the resistance between terminals **STA** and **STJ**. Refer to the chart for the proper values. USE THIS SERVICE TESTING PROCEDURE AS A GUIDE FOR REPLACEMENT OF THIS COMPONENT.
3. If the time switch is to be replaced, drain the coolant from the system.
4. Remove the switch and its gasket.
5. Install the new switch with a new gasket and tighten it to 25 ft. lbs.
6. Refill the coolant and attach the wiring connector to the switch.

COOLANT TEMPERATURE SENSOR

1. Disconnect the wiring to the sensor.
2. Using an ohmmeter, measure the resistance across the terminals of the sensor. Refer to the chart for the correct resistance values. Note that the resistance will change as a function of the coolant temperature, not the air temperature. USE THIS SERVICE TESTING PROCEDURE AS A GUIDE FOR REPLACEMENT OF THIS COMPONENT.
3. If the sensor must be changed, the cool-

Between terminals	Resistance (Ω)	Coolant temp.
STA — STJ	20 — 40	Below 30°C (95°F)
	40 — 60	Above 40°C (95°F)
STA — Ground	20 — 80	—

Resistance chart for checking the start injector time switch sensor 4A-GE engine

ant must be drained. Do this only with the engine cold.
4. Using the correct size wrench, remove the sensor by unscrewing it. Install the new sensor and tighten it.
5. Refill the coolant to the proper level.
6. Connect the wiring to the sensor.

4A-FE Engine

NOTE: *For all other engines refer to the procedures below as all fuel injector sensors and controls are similar — modify service steps as necessary. USE SERVICE TESTING PROCEDURES AS A GUIDE FOR REPLACEMENT OF COMPONENTS.*

COLD START INJECTOR

1. Disconnect the negative battery cable.
2. Disconnect the wiring at the injector.

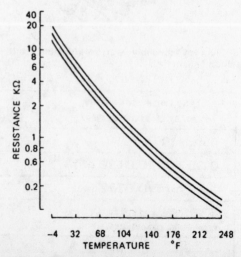

Resistance chart for testing the water temperature sensor 4A-GE engine

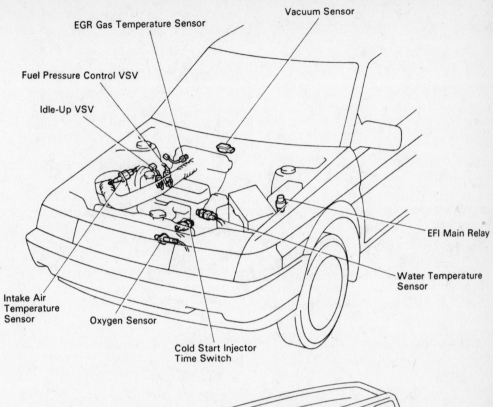

EGR Gas Temperature Sensor

Vacuum Sensor

Fuel Pressure Control VSV

Idle-Up VSV

EFI Main Relay

Water Temperature Sensor

Intake Air Temperature Sensor

Oxygen Sensor

Cold Start Injector Time Switch

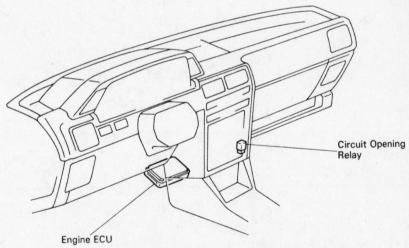

Circuit Opening Relay

Engine ECU

Location of electronic control parts 3E-E engine

3. Loosen and remove the fuel line at the injector.

CAUTION: *The fuel system is under pressure. Release pressure slowly and contain spillage. Observe no smoking/no open flame precautions. Have a Class B-C (dry powder) fire extinguisher within arm's reach at all times.*

4. Remove the two retaining bolts and remove the injector.

5. When reinstalling, position the new injector in the intake manifold, install the retaining bolts and tighten them to 7 ft. lbs. (84 INCH lbs.)

6. Connect the fuel line, then connect the wiring harness to the injector.

7. Connect the negative battery cable.

FUEL PRESSURE REGULATOR

1. Disconnect the negative battery cable.

2. Disconnect the vacuum hose from the regulator.

3. Disconnect the fuel return line from the regulator.

CAUTION: *The fuel system is under pressure. Release pressure slowly and contain spillage. Observe no smoking/no open flame precautions. Have a Class B-C (dry powder)*

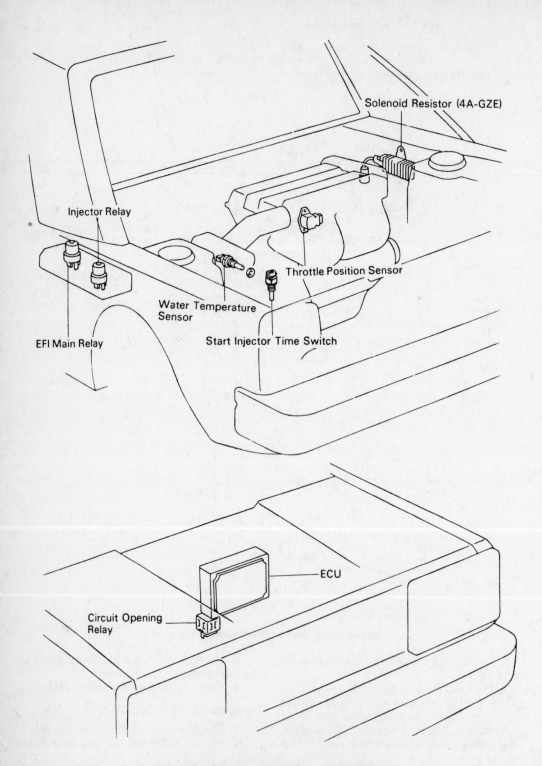

Solenoid Resistor (4A-GZE)

Injector Relay

Throttle Position Sensor

Water Temperature
Sensor

EFI Main Relay

Start Injector Time Switch

ECU

Circuit Opening
Relay

Location of electronic control parts — MR2 vehicle

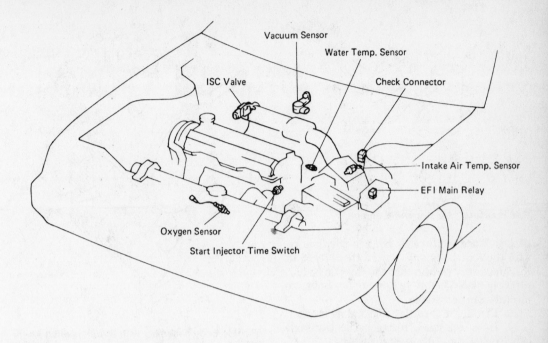

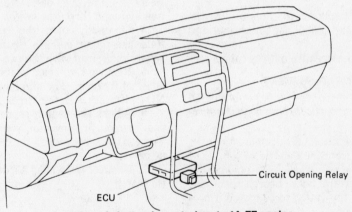

Location of electronic control parts 4A-FE engine

fire extinguisher within arm's reach at all times.

4. Remove the two retaining bolts and remove the fuel pressure regulator.

5. When reinstalling, place the new regulator on the fuel rail, install the bolts and tighten them to 7 ft. lbs. (84 INCH lbs.).

6. Connect the fuel return line, making sure the clamp is properly placed and secure.

7. Connect the vacuum hose, then connect the negative battery cable.

THROTTLE BODY

1. Disconnect the negative battery cable.
2. Remove the air cleaner and intake duct assembly.

3. Disconnect the electrical wiring from the throttle switch.

4. Remove the two bolts holding the throttle cable bracket.

5. If so equipped, remove the transaxle shift cable (automatic transmission) and/or the cruise control cable.

6. Label and remove the vacuum hoses to the throttle body.

7. Remove the vacuum hose to the air valve.

8. Remove the four bolts holding the throttle body and carefully remove the throttle body.

9. When reinstalling, always use a new gasket between the throttle body and the intake. Do not use sealants of any kind on the

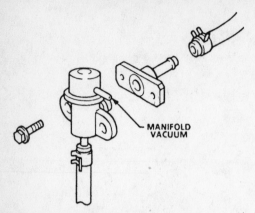

Fuel pressure regulator 4A-FE engine

gasket. Place the throttle body in position, install the four bolts and tighten them to 16 ft. lbs. Make very certain that the throttle body is properly placed before tightening the bolts; no air leaks are acceptable.

10. Install the throttle cable and its bracket.

11. If so equipped, reattach the transaxle cable and/or the cruise control cable.

12. Connect the vacuum hose to the air valve.

13. Connect the vacuum hoses to the throttle body.

14. Connect the electrical connector to the throttle switch and install the air cleaner and duct assembly.

15. Connect the negative battery cable.

THROTTLE SWITCH ADJUSTMENT

NOTE: *This procedure may be performed on the car; removal of the throttle body is not required.*

1. With the ignition OFF, remove the electrical connector from the throttle switch.

2. Loosen the two small bolts holding the switch to the throttle body. Loosen them just enough to allow the switch to be moved if necessary, but no more.

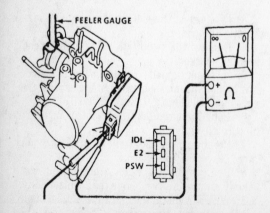

Adjusting the throttle switch 4A-FE engine

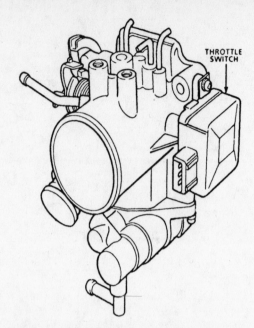

Throttle body assembly with throttle switch 4A-FE engine

3. Insert a 0.0276 in (0.70mm) feeler gauge between the throttle stop screw and the throttle lever. Connect an ohmmeter between terminals IDL and E2 on the switch.

4. Gradually turn the switch clockwise until the meter deflects, showing continuity; secure the sensor with the two screws.

5. Remove the feeler gauge and insert another of 0.80mm. The ohmmeter should show NO continuity with the larger gauge inserted.

6. Adjust the switch as necessary to gain the correct function for each feeler gauge. Tighten the screws when the correct position is achieved.

7. Connect the wiring harness to the throttle switch

MANIFOLD ABSOLUTE PRESSURE (MAP) SENSOR

This sensor advises the ECM of pressure changes in the intake manifold. It consists of a semi-conductor pressure converting element which converts a pressure change into an electrical signal. The ECM sends a 5 volt reference signal to the MAP sensor; the change in air pressure changes the resistance within the sensor. The ECM reads the change from its reference voltage and signals the injectors to react accordingly.

Replacing the MAP sensor simply requires disconnecting the vacuum hose and the electrical connector, and unbolting the sensor. Inspect the vacuum hose over its entire length for any signs of cracking or splitting. The slightest leak can cause false messages to be send to the ECM.

MANIFOLD AIR TEMPERATURE (MAT) SENSOR

The MAT sensor advises the ECM of changes in intake air temperature (and therefore air density). As air temperature of the intake varies, the ECM, by monitoring the voltage change, adjusts the amount of fuel injection according to the air temperature.

To replace the MAT sensor:

1. Remove the air cleaner cover.
2. With the ignition OFF, disconnect the electrical connector.
3. Push the MAT sensor out from inside the air cleaner housing.
4. Install the new sensor, making sure it is properly placed and secure.
5. Connect the wiring harness, and replace the air cleaner cover.

COOLANT TEMPERATURE SENSOR

The coolant temperature sensor is located (refer to location of electronic control parts illustration) under the air cleaner assembly and behind the distributor. Its function is to advise the ECM of changes in engine temperature by monitoring the changes in coolant temperature. The sensor must be handled carefully during removal. It can be damaged (thereby affecting engine performance) by impact.

The sensor may be tested following the procedures listed previously for the 4A-GE engine. USE THE SERVICE TESTING PROCEDURE AS A GUIDE FOR REPLACEMENT OF THIS COMPONENT. The temperature and resistance chart are the same. If the sensor must be replaced:

NOTE: *Perform this procedure only on a cold engine.*

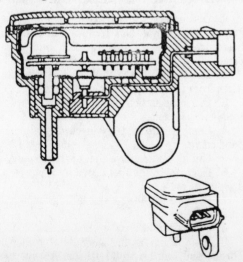

Cross section of MAP sensor

Coolant temperature sensor. Remember to coat the threads with sealant before installation

1. Drain the cooling system as necessary.
2. Remove the air cleaner assembly.
3. With the ignition OFF, disconnect the electrical connector to the coolant temperature sensor.
4. Using the proper sized wrench, carefully unscrew the sensor from the engine.
5. Before reinstalling, coat the threads of the sensor with a sealant. Install the sensor and tighten it to 18 ft. lbs.
6. Reconnect the electrical connector. Install the air cleaner assembly.
7. Refill the coolant to the proper level. Road test the vehicle for proper operation.

ELECTRONIC FUEL INJECTION (EFI) MAIN RELAY

1. The EFI relay is located (refer to location of electronic control parts illustration) on the fuse block (junction block) under the hood behind the left headlight. Test the function of the relay by turning the ignition ON and listening or feeling the relay. An operation noise should be heard (or felt) from the relay.
2. Turn the ignition OFF. Disconnect the connector from the relay and use an ohmmeter to check for continuity between relay terminals 3 and 4.
3. There should be NO continuity between terminals 1 and 2. If the relay fails either of these tests, replace it. USE THIS SERVICE TESTING PROCEDURE AS A GUIDE FOR REPLACEMENT OF THIS COMPONENT.
4. Using jumper wires, connect battery voltage across terminals 3 and 4 (Connect the battery positive (+) to terminal 4) and check terminals 1 and 2 for continuity. With 12 volts applied, continuity should be present.
5. Reinstall the relay in place.

CIRCUIT OPENING RELAY

1. Remove the ECM cover under the center console (refer to location of electronic control parts illustration). Remove the circuit opening relay and its wiring.
2. With the ignition OFF, disconnect the relay.
3. Using an ohmmeter, check that there is continuity between terminals STA and E1.
4. Check that there is continuity between terminals B and FC.

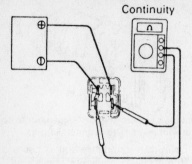

Function check EFI relay 4A-FE engine

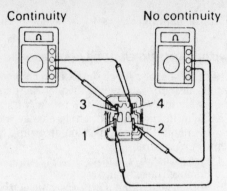

Continuity check EFI relay 4A-FE engine

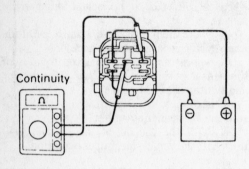

Checking the function of the circuit opening relay 4A-FE engine

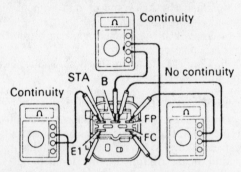

Checking continuity of circuit opening relay 4A-FE engine

SERVICE TESTING PROCEDURE AS A GUIDE FOR REPLACEMENT OF THIS COMPONENT.

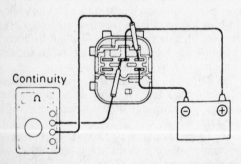

5. Check that there is NO continuity between terminals B and FP. If the relay fails any of these checks, it must be replaced. USE THIS SERVICE TESTING PROCEDURE AS A GUIDE FOR REPLACEMENT OF THIS COMPONENT.

6. Using jumper wires, connect the battery positive (+) terminal to terminal STA and the battery negative terminal to terminal E1. Use the ohmmeter to check that there is now continuity between terminals B and FP.

7. Change the jumper wires so that the positive terminal connects to terminal B and the negative connects to terminal FC. Check that there is now continuity between terminals B and FP.

8. If the relay fails either of these functional tests, it must be replace it. USE THIS

DIESEL ENGINE FUEL SYSTEM

Injection Line And Nozzle

REMOVAL AND INSTALLATION

1. Disconnect the negative battery cable. Loosen the clamps and remove the injection hoses from between the injection pump and pipe.

2. Disconnect both ends of the injection pipes from the pump and nozzle holders.

3. Disconnect the fuel cut off wire from the connector clamp.

4. Remove the nut, connector clamp and bond cable.

5. Unbolt and remove the injector pipes.

6. Disconnect the fuel hoses from the leakage pipes.

7. Remove the four nuts, leakage pipe and four washers.

8. Unscrew and remove the nozzles.

9. Installation is the reverse of removal. Torque the nozzles to 47 ft. lbs. Always use new nozzle seat gaskets and seats. Bleed the

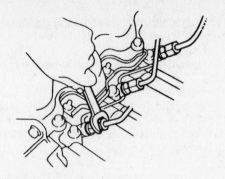

Removing the injector nozzle

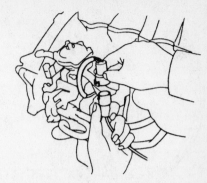

Disconnect the fuel cut off solenoid connector

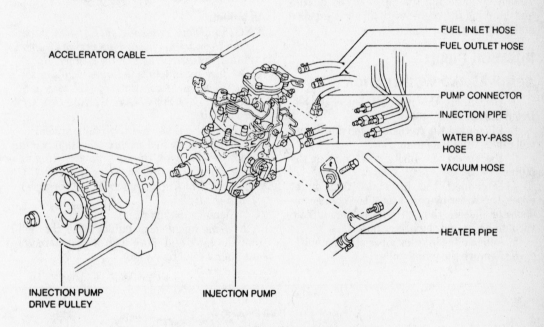

ACCELERATOR CABLE

FUEL INLET HOSE

FUEL OUTLET HOSE

PUMP CONNECTOR

INJECTION PIPE

WATER BY-PASS HOSE

VACUUM HOSE

HEATER PIPE

INJECTION PUMP DRIVE PULLEY

INJECTION PUMP

Exploded view of diesel injection pump

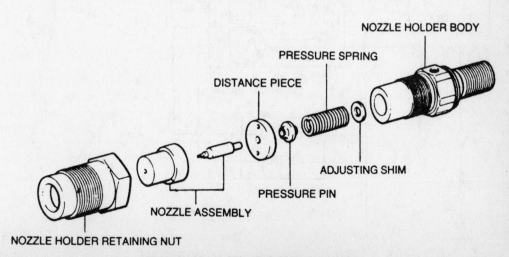

NOZZLE HOLDER BODY

PRESSURE SPRING

DISTANCE PIECE

ADJUSTING SHIM

PRESSURE PIN

NOZZLE ASSEMBLY

NOZZLE HOLDER RETAINING NUT

Exploded view of the diesel injector nozzle

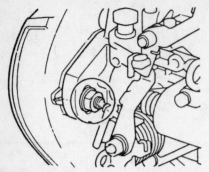

Matchmark the timing mark on the pump flange with the block diesel engine

system by loosening the pipes at the nozzles and cranking the engine until all air is expelled and fuel sprays.

Injection Pump

REMOVAL AND INSTALLATION

1. Disconnect the negative battery cable. Drain the cooling system.

2. Disconnect the accelerator and cruise control cables from the pump.

3. Disconnect the fuel cut off wire at the pump.

4. Disconnect the fuel inlet and outlet hoses, the water by-pass hoses, the boost compensator hoses, the A/C or heater idle-up vacuum hoses and the heater hose.

5. Remove the injector pipes at the pump.

6. Remove the pump pulley.

7. Matchmark the raised timing mark on the pump flange with the block. Unbolt and remove the pump.

8. Installation is the reverse of removal procedure. There must be no clearance between the pump bracket and stay.

9. Bleed the system by loosening the pipes at the nozzles and cranking the engine until all air is expelled and fuel sprays. Road test the vehicle for proper operation.

FUEL TANK

REMOVAL AND INSTALLATION

All Models

NOTE: *Before removing fuel system parts, clean them with a spray-type engine cleaner. Follow the instructions on the cleaner. Do not soak fuel system parts in liquid cleaning solvent. Refer to illustration of fuel tank and fuel pump assembly before starting this service repair.*

CAUTION: *The fuel injection system is under pressure. Release pressure slowly and contain spillage. Observe no smoking/no open flame precautions. Have a Class B-C (dry powder) fire extinguisher within arm's reach at all times.*

1. Remove the filler cap.

2. Using a siphon or pump, drain the fuel from the tank and store it in a proper metal container with a tight cap.

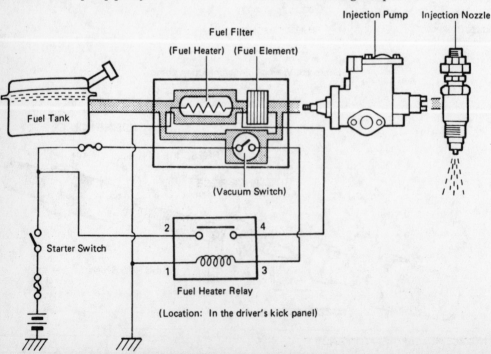

Diesel fuel system operation circuit

3. Remove the rear seat cushion to gain access to the electrical wiring.

4. Disconnect the fuel pump and sending unit wiring at the connector.

5. Raise the vehicle and safely support it on jackstands.

6. Loosen the clamp and remove the filler neck and overflow pipe from the tank.

7. Remove the supply hose from the tank. Wrap a rag around the fitting to collect escaping fuel. Disconnect the breather hose from the tank, again using a rag to control spillage.

8. Cover or plug the end of each disconnected line to keep dirt out and fuel in.

9. Support the fuel tank with a floor jack or transmission jack. Use a broad piece of wood to distribute the load. Be careful not to deform the bottom of the tank.

10. Remove the fuel tank support strap bolts.

11. Swing the straps away from the tank and lower the jack. Balance the tank with your other hand or have a helper assist you. The tank is bulky and may have some fuel left in it. If its balance changes suddenly, the tank may fall.

12. Remove the fuel filler pipe extension, the breather pipe assembly and the sending unit assembly. Keep these items in a clean, protected area away from the car.

13. While the tank is out and disassembled, inspect it for any signs of rust, leakage or metal damage. If any problem is found, replace the tank. Clean the inside of the tank with water and a light detergent and rinse the tank thoroughly several times.

14. Inspect all of the lines, hoses and fittings for any sign of corrosion, wear or damage to the surfaces. Check the pump outlet hose and the filter for restrictions.

15. When reassembling, ALWAYS replace the sealing gaskets with new ones. Also replace any rubber parts showing any sign of deterioration.

16. Connect the breather pipe assembly and the filler pipe extension.

NOTE: *Tighten the breather pipe screw to 17 INCH lbs. and all other attaching screws to 30 INCH lbs.*

17. Place the fuel tank on the jack and elevate it into place within the car. Attach the straps and install the strap bolts, tightening them to 29 ft. lbs.

18. Connect the breather hose to the tank pipe, the return hose to the tank pipe and the supply hose to its tank pipe. tighten the supply hose fitting to 21 ft. lbs.

19. Connect the filler neck and overflow pipe to the tank. Make sure the clamps are properly seated and secure.

20. Lower the vehicle to the ground.

21. Connect the pump and sending unit electrical connectors to the harness.

22. Install the rear seat cushion.

23. Using a funnel, pour the fuel that was drained from its container into the fuel filler.

24. Install the fuel filler cap.

25. Start the engine and check carefully for any sign of leakage around the tank and lines.

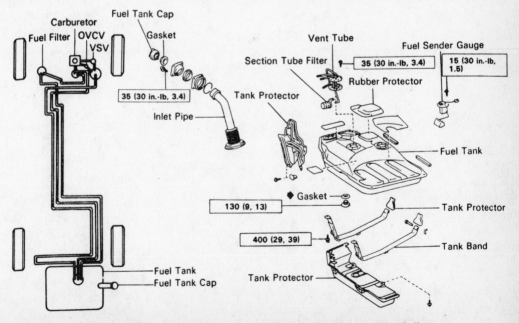

Fuel tank and fuel pump assembly — Tercel wagon other models similar

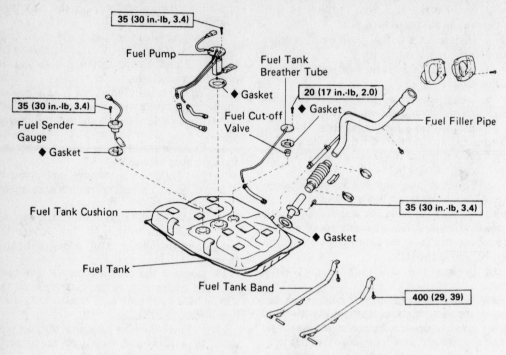

35 (30 in.-lb, 3.4)

Fuel Pump

Fuel Tank
Breather Tube

◆ Gasket

20 (17 in.-lb, 2.0)

35 (30 in.-lb, 3.4)

◆ Gasket

Fuel Sender
Gauge

Fuel Cut-off
Valve

Fuel Filler Pipe

◆ Gasket

Fuel Tank Cushion

35 (30 in.-lb, 3.4)

◆ Gasket

Fuel Tank

Fuel Tank Band

400 (29, 39)

Fuel tank and fuel pump assembly — Corolla other models similar

Chassis Electrical

6

UNDERSTANDING AND TROUBLESHOOTING ELECTRICAL SYSTEMS

At the rate which both import and domestic manufacturers are incorporating electronic control systems into their production lines, it won't be long before every new vehicle is equipped with one or more on-board computer. These electronic components (with no moving parts) should theoretically last the life of the vehicle, provided nothing external happens to damage the circuits or memory chips.

While it is true that electronic components should never wear out, in the real world malfunctions do occur. It is also true that any computer-based system is extremely sensitive to electrical voltages and cannot tolerate careless or haphazard testing or service procedures. An inexperienced individual can literally do major damage looking for a minor problem by using the wrong kind of test equipment or connecting test leads or connectors with the ignition switch ON. When selecting test equipment, make sure the manufacturers instructions state that the tester is compatible with whatever type of electronic control system is being serviced. Read all instructions carefully and double check all test points before installing probes or making any test connections.

The following section outlines basic diagnosis techniques for dealing with computerized automotive control systems. Along with a general explanation of the various types of test equipment available to aid in servicing modern electronic automotive systems, basic repair techniques for wiring harnesses and connectors is given. Read the basic information before attempting any repairs or testing on any computerized system, to provide the background of information necessary to avoid the most common and obvious mistakes that can cost both time and money. Although the replacement and testing procedures are simple in themselves, the systems are not, and unless one has a thorough understanding of all components and their function within a particular computerized control system, the logical test sequence that these systems demand cannot be followed. Minor malfunctions can make a big difference, so it is important to know how each component affect the operation of the overall electronic system to find the ultimate cause of a problem without replacing good components unnecessarily. It is not enough to use the correct test equipment; the test equipment must be used correctly.

Safety Precautions

CAUTION: *Whenever working on or around any computer based microprocessor control system, always observe these general precautions to prevent the possibility of personal injury or damage to electronic components.*

• Never install or remove battery cables with the key ON or the engine running. Jumper cables should be connected with the key OFF to avoid power surges that can damage electronic control units. Engines equipped with computer controlled systems should avoid both giving and getting jump starts due to the possibility of serious damage to components from arcing in the engine compartment when connections are made with the ignition ON.

• Always remove the battery cables before charging the battery. Never use a high output charger on an installed battery or attempt to use any type of "hot shot" (24 volt) starting aid.

• Exercise care when inserting test probes into connectors to insure good connections without damaging the connector or spreading the pins. Always probe connectors from the rear (wire) side, NOT the pin side, to avoid accidental shorting of terminals during test procedures.

• Never remove or attach wiring harness connectors with the ignition switch ON, especially to an electronic control unit.

• Do not drop any components during service procedures and never apply 12 volts directly to any component (like a solenoid or relay) unless instructed specifically to do so. Some component electrical windings are designed to safely handle only 4 or 5 volts and can be destroyed in seconds if 12 volts are applied directly to the connector.

• Remove the electronic control unit if the vehicle is to be placed in an environment where temperatures exceed approximately 176°F (80°C), such as a paint spray booth or when arc or gas welding near the control unit location in the car.

ORGANIZED TROUBLESHOOTING

When diagnosing a specific problem, organized troubleshooting is a must. The complexity of a modern automobile demands that you approach any problem in a logical, organized manner. There are certain troubleshooting techniques that are standard:

1. Establish when the problem occurs. Does the problem appear only under certain conditions? Were there any noises, odors, or other unusual symptoms?

2. Isolate the problem area. To do this, make some simple tests and observations; then eliminate the systems that are working properly. Check for obvious problems such as broken wires, dirty connections or split or disconnected vacuum hoses. Always check the obvious before assuming something complicated is the cause.

3. Test for problems systematically to determine the cause once the problem area is isolated. Are all the components functioning properly? Is there power going to electrical switches and motors? Is there vacuum at vacuum switches and/or actuators? Is there a mechanical problem such as bent linkage or loose mounting screws? Doing careful, systematic checks will often turn up most causes on the first inspection without wasting time checking components that have little or no relationship to the problem.

4. Test all repairs after the work is done to make sure that the problem is fixed. Some causes can be traced to more than one component, so a careful verification of repair work is important to pick up additional malfunctions that may cause a problem to reappear or a different problem to arise. A blown fuse, for example, is a simple problem that may require more than another fuse to repair. If you don't look

for a problem that caused a fuse to blow, for example, a shorted wire may go undetected.

Experience has shown that most problems tend to be the result of a fairly simple and obvious cause, such as loose or corroded connectors or air leaks in the intake system; making careful inspection of components during testing essential to quick and accurate troubleshooting. Special, hand held computerized testers designed specifically for diagnosing a system are available from a variety of aftermarket sources, as well as from the vehicle manufacturer, but care should be taken that any test equipment being used is designed to diagnose that particular computer controlled system accurately without damaging the control unit (ECU) or components being tested.

NOTE: *Pinpointing the exact cause of trouble in an electrical system can sometimes only be accomplished by the use of special test equipment. The following describes commonly used test equipment and explains how to put it to best use in diagnosis. In addition to the information covered below, the manufacturer's instructions booklet provided with the tester should be read and clearly understood before attempting any test procedures.*

TEST EQUIPMENT

Jumper Wires

Jumper wires are simple, yet extremely valuable, pieces of test equipment. Jumper wires are merely wires that are used to bypass sections of a circuit. The simplest type of jumper wire is merely a length of multi-strand wire with an alligator clip at each end. Jumper wires are usually fabricated from lengths of standard automotive wire and whatever type of connector (alligator clip, spade connector or pin connector) that is required for the particular vehicle being tested. The well equipped tool box will have several different styles of jumper wires in several different lengths. Some jumper wires are made with three or more terminals coming from a common splice for special purpose testing. In cramped, hard-to-reach areas it is advisable to have insulated boots over the jumper wire terminals in order to prevent accidental grounding, sparks, and possible fire, especially when testing fuel system components.

Jumper wires are used primarily to locate open electrical circuits, on either the ground (–) side of the circuit or on the hot (+) side. If an electrical component fails to operate, connect the jumper wire between the component and a good ground. If the component operates only with the jumper installed, the ground circuit is open. If the ground circuit is good, but the component does not operate, the circuit between the power feed and component is open. You can sometimes connect the jumper wire directly from the battery to the hot terminal of the component, but first make sure the component uses 12 volts in operation. Some electrical components, such as fuel injectors, are designed to operate on about 4 volts and running 12 volts directly to the injector terminals can burn out the wiring. By inserting an inline fuse holder between a set of test leads, a fused jumper wire can be used for bypassing open circuits. Use a 5 amp fuse to provide protection against voltage spikes. When in doubt, use a voltmeter to check the voltage input to the component and measure how much voltage is being applied normally. By moving the jumper wire successively back from the lamp toward the power source, you can isolate the area of the circuit where the open is located. When the component stops functioning, or the power is cut off, the open is in the segment of wire between the jumper and the point previously tested.

CAUTION: *Never use jumpers made from wire that is of lighter gauge than used in the circuit under test. If the jumper wire is of too small gauge, it may overheat and possibly melt. Never use jumpers to bypass high resistance loads (such as motors) in a circuit. Bypassing resistances, in effect, creates a short circuit which may, in turn, cause damage and fire. Never use a jumper for anything other than temporary bypassing of components in a circuit.*

12 Volt Test Light

The 12 volt test light is used to check circuits and components while electrical current is flowing through them. It is used for voltage and ground tests. Twelve volt test lights come in different styles but all have three main parts; a ground clip, a probe, and a light. The most commonly used 12 volt test lights have pick-type probes. To use a 12 volt test light, connect the ground clip to a good ground and probe wherever necessary with the pick. The pick should be sharp so that it can penetrate wire insulation to make contact with the wire, without making a large hole in the insulation. The wraparound light is handy in hard to reach areas or where it is difficult to support a wire to push a probe pick into it. To use the wrap around light, hook the wire to probed with the hook and pull the trigger. A small pick will be forced through the wire insulation into the wire core.

CAUTION: *Do not use a test light to probe electronic ignition spark plug or coil wires. Never use a pick-type test light to probe wiring on computer controlled systems unless specifically instructed to do so. Any wire insulation that is pierced by the test light probe should be taped and sealed with silicone after testing.*

Like the jumper wire, the 12 volt test light is used to isolate opens in circuits. But, whereas the jumper wire is used to bypass the open to operate the load, the 12 volt test light is used to locate the presence of voltage in a circuit. If the test light glows, you know that there is power up to that point; if the 12 volt test light does not glow when its probe is inserted into the wire or connector, you know that there is an open circuit (no power). Move the test light in successive steps back toward the power source until the light in the handle does glow. When it does glow, the open is between the probe and point previously probed.

NOTE: *The test light does not detect that 12 volts (or any particular amount of voltage) is present; it only detects that some voltage is present. It is advisable before using the test light to touch its terminals across the battery posts to make sure the light is operating properly.*

Self-Powered Test Light

The self-powered test light usually contains a 1.5 volt penlight battery. One type of self-powered test light is similar in design to the 12 volt test light. This type has both the battery and the light in the handle and pick-type probe tip. The second type has the light toward the open tip, so that the light illuminates the contact point. The self-powered test light is dual purpose piece of test equipment. It can be used to test for either open or short circuits when power is isolated from the circuit (continuity test). A powered test light should not be used on any computer controlled system or component unless specifically instructed to do so. Many engine sensors can be destroyed by even this small amount of voltage applied directly to the terminals.

Open Circuit Testing

To use the self-powered test light to check for open circuits, first isolate the circuit from the vehicle's 12 volt power source by disconnecting the battery or wiring harness connector. Connect the test light ground clip to a good ground and probe sections of the circuit sequentially with the test light. (start from either end of the circuit). If the light is out, the open is between the probe and the circuit ground. If the light is on, the open is between the probe and end of the circuit toward the power source.

Short Circuit Testing

By isolating the circuit both from power and from ground, and using a self-powered test light, you can check for shorts to ground in the circuit. Isolate the circuit from power and ground. Connect the test light ground clip to a good ground and probe any easy-to-reach test point in the circuit. If the light comes on, there is a short somewhere in the circuit. To isolate the short, probe a test point at either end of the isolated circuit (the light should be on). Leave the test light probe connected and open connectors, switches, remove parts, etc., sequentially, until the light goes out. When the light goes out, the short is between the last circuit component opened and the previous circuit opened.

NOTE: *The 1.5 volt battery in the test light does not provide much current. A weak battery may not provide enough power to illuminate the test light even when a complete circuit is made (especially if there are high resistances in the circuit). Always make sure that the test battery is strong. To check the battery, briefly touch the ground clip to the probe; if the light glows brightly the battery is strong enough for testing. Never use a self-powered test light to perform checks for opens or shorts when power is applied to the electrical system under test. The 12 volt vehicle power will quickly burn out the 1.5 volt light bulb in the test light.*

Voltmeter

A voltmeter is used to measure voltage at any point in a circuit, or to measure the voltage drop across any part of a circuit. It can also be used to check continuity in a wire or circuit by indicating current flow from one end to the other. Voltmeters usually have various scales on the meter dial and a selector switch to allow the selection of different voltages. The voltmeter has a positive and a negative lead. To avoid damage to the meter, always connect the negative lead to the negative (–) side of the circuit (to ground or nearest the ground side of the circuit) and connect the positive lead to the positive (+) side of the circuit (to the power source or the nearest power source). Note that the negative voltmeter lead will always be black and that the positive voltmeter will always be some color other than black (usually red). Depending on how the voltmeter is connected into the circuit, it has several uses.

A voltmeter can be connected either in parallel or in series with a circuit and it has a very high resistance to current flow. When connected in parallel, only a small amount of current will flow through the voltmeter current path; the rest will flow through the normal circuit current path and the circuit will work normally. When the voltmeter is connected in series with a circuit, only a small amount of current can flow through the circuit. The circuit

will not work properly, but the voltmeter reading will show if the circuit is complete or not.

Available Voltage Measurement

Set the voltmeter selector switch to the 20V position and connect the meter negative lead to the negative (–) post of the battery. Connect the positive meter lead to the positive (+) post of the battery and turn the ignition switch ON to provide a load. Read the voltage on the meter or digital display. A well charged battery should register over 12 volts. If the meter reads below 11.5 volts, the battery power may be insufficient to operate the electrical system properly. This test determines voltage available from the battery and should be the first step in any electrical trouble diagnosis procedure. Many electrical problems, especially on computer controlled systems, can be caused by a low state of charge in the battery. Excessive corrosion at the battery cable terminals can cause a poor contact that will prevent proper charging and full battery current flow.

Normal battery voltage is 12 volts when fully charged. When the battery is supplying current to one or more circuits it is said to be "under load". When everything is off the electrical system is under a "no-load" condition. A fully charged battery may show about 12.5 volts at no load; will drop to 12 volts under medium load; and will drop even lower under heavy load. If the battery is partially discharged the voltage decrease under heavy load may be excessive, even though the battery shows 12 volts or more at no load. When allowed to discharge further, the battery's available voltage under load will decrease more severely. For this reason, it is important that the battery be fully charged during all testing procedures to avoid errors in diagnosis and incorrect test results.

Voltage Drop

When current flows through a resistance, the voltage beyond the resistance is reduced (the larger the current, the greater the reduction in voltage). When no current is flowing, there is no voltage drop because there is no current flow. All points in the circuit which are connected to the power source are at the same voltage as the power source. The total voltage drop always equals the total source voltage. In a long circuit with many connectors, a series of small, unwanted voltage drops due to corrosion at the connectors can add up to a total loss of voltage which impairs the operation of the normal loads in the circuit.

INDIRECT COMPUTATION OF VOLTAGE DROPS

1. Set the voltmeter selector switch to the 20 volt position.

2. Connect the meter negative lead to a good ground.

3. Probe all resistances in the circuit with the positive meter lead.

4. Operate the circuit in all modes and observe the voltage readings.

DIRECT MEASUREMENT OF VOLTAGE DROPS

1. Set the voltmeter switch to the 20 volt position.

2. Connect the voltmeter negative lead to the ground side of the resistance load to be measured.

3. Connect the positive lead to the positive side of the resistance or load to be measured.

4. Read the voltage drop directly on the 20 volt scale.

Too high a voltage indicates too high a resistance. If, for example, a blower motor runs too slowly, you can determine if there is too high a resistance in the resistor pack. By taking voltage drop readings in all parts of the circuit, you can isolate the problem. Too low a voltage drop indicates too low a resistance. If, for example, a blower motor runs too fast in the MED and/or LOW position, the problem can be isolated in the resistor pack by taking voltage drop readings in all parts of the circuit to locate a possibly shorted resistor. The maximum allowable voltage drop under load is critical, especially if there is more than one high resistance problem in a circuit because all voltage drops are cumulative. A small drop is normal due to the resistance of the conductors.

HIGH RESISTANCE TESTING

1. Set the voltmeter selector switch to the 4 volt position.

2. Connect the voltmeter positive lead to the positive (+) post of the battery.

3. Turn on the headlights and heater blower to provide a load.

4. Probe various points in the circuit with the negative voltmeter lead.

5. Read the voltage drop on the 4 volt scale. Some average maximum allowable voltage drops are:

> FUSE PANEL – 7 volts
> IGNITION SWITCH – 5 volts
> HEADLIGHT SWITCH – 7 volts
> IGNITION COIL (+) – 5 volts
> ANY OTHER LOAD – 1.3 volts

NOTE: *Voltage drops are all measured while a load is operating; without current flow, there will be no voltage drop.*

Ohmmeter

The ohmmeter is designed to read resistance (ohms) in a circuit or component. Although there are several different styles of ohmmeters, all will usually have a selector switch which permits the measurement of different ranges of resistance (usually the selector switch allows the multiplication of the meter reading by 10, 100, 1000, and 10,000). A calibration knob allows the meter to be set at zero for accurate measurement. Since all ohmmeters are powered by an internal battery (usually 9 volts), the ohmmeter can be used as a self-powered test light. When the ohmmeter is connected, current from the ohmmeter flows through the circuit or component being tested. Since the ohmmeter's internal resistance and voltage are known values, the amount of current flow through the meter depends on the resistance of the circuit or component being tested.

The ohmmeter can be used to perform continuity test for opens or shorts (either by observation of the meter needle or as a self-powered test light), and to read actual resistance in a circuit. It should be noted that the ohmmeter is used to check the resistance of a component or wire while there is no voltage applied to the circuit. Current flow from an outside voltage source (such as the vehicle battery) can damage the ohmmeter, so the circuit or component should be isolated from the vehicle electrical system before any testing is done. Since the ohmmeter uses its own voltage source, either lead can be connected to any test point.

NOTE: *When checking diodes or other solid state components, the ohmmeter leads can only be connected one way in order to measure current flow in a single direction. Make sure the positive (+) and negative (–) terminal connections are as described in the test procedures to verify the one-way diode operation.*

In using the meter for making continuity checks, do not be concerned with the actual resistance readings. Zero resistance, or any resistance readings, indicate continuity in the circuit. Infinite resistance indicates an open in the circuit. A high resistance reading where there should be none indicates a problem in the circuit. Checks for short circuits are made in the same manner as checks for open circuits except that the circuit must be isolated from both power and normal ground. Infinite resistance indicates no continuity to ground, while zero resistance indicates a dead short to ground.

RESISTANCE MEASUREMENT

The batteries in an ohmmeter will weaken with age and temperature, so the ohmmeter must be calibrated or "zeroed" before taking measurements. To zero the meter, place the selector switch in its lowest range and touch the two ohmmeter leads together. Turn the calibration knob until the meter needle is exactly on zero.

NOTE: *All analog (needle) type ohmmeters must be zeroed before use, but some digital ohmmeter models are automatically calibrated when the switch is turned on. Self-calibrating digital ohmmeters do not have an adjusting knob, but its a good idea to check for a zero readout before use by touching the leads together. All computer controlled systems require the use of a digital ohmmeter with at least 10 megohms impedance for testing. Before any test procedures are attempted, make sure the ohmmeter used is compatible with the electrical system or damage to the on-board computer could result.*

To measure resistance, first isolate the circuit from the vehicle power source by disconnecting the battery cables or the harness connector. Make sure the key is OFF when disconnecting any components or the battery. Where necessary, also isolate at least one side of the circuit to be checked to avoid reading parallel resistances. Parallel circuit resistances will always give a lower reading than the actual resistance of either of the branches. When measuring the resistance of parallel circuits, the total resistance will always be lower than the smallest resistance in the circuit. Connect the meter leads to both sides of the circuit (wire or component) and read the actual measured ohms on the meter scale. Make sure the selector switch is set to the proper ohm scale for the circuit being tested to avoid misreading the ohmmeter test value.

CAUTION: *Never use an ohmmeter with power applied to the circuit. Like the self-powered test light, the ohmmeter is designed to operate on its own power supply. The normal 12 volt automotive electrical system current could damage the meter.*

Ammeters

An ammeter measures the amount of current flowing through a circuit in units called amperes or amps. Amperes are units of electron flow which indicate how fast the electrons are flowing through the circuit. Since Ohms Law dictates that current flow in a circuit is equal to the circuit voltage divided by the total circuit resistance, increasing voltage also increases the current level (amps). Likewise, any decrease in resistance will increase the amount of amps in a circuit. At normal operating voltage, most circuits have a characteristic amount of amperes, called "current draw" which can be measured using an ammeter. By referring to a specified current draw rating, measuring the amperes, and comparing the two values, one can determine what is happening within the circuit to

aid in diagnosis. An open circuit, for example, will not allow any current to flow so the ammeter reading will be zero. More current flows through a heavily loaded circuit or when the charging system is operating.

An ammeter is always connected in series with the circuit being tested. All of the current that normally flows through the circuit must also flow through the ammeter; if there is any other path for the current to follow, the ammeter reading will not be accurate. The ammeter itself has very little resistance to current flow and therefore will not affect the circuit, but it will measure current draw only when the circuit is closed and electricity is flowing. Excessive current draw can blow fuses and drain the battery, while a reduced current draw can cause motors to run slowly, lights to dim and other components to not operate properly. The ammeter can help diagnose these conditions by locating the cause of the high or low reading.

Multimeters

Different combinations of test meters can be built into a single unit designed for specific tests. Some of the more common combination test devices are known as Volt/Amp testers, Tach/Dwell meters, or Digital Multimeters. The Volt/Amp tester is used for charging system, starting system or battery tests and consists of a voltmeter, an ammeter and a variable resistance carbon pile. The voltmeter will usually have at least two ranges for use with 6, 12 and 24 volt systems. The ammeter also has more than one range for testing various levels of battery loads and starter current draw and the carbon pile can be adjusted to offer different amounts of resistance. The Volt/Amp tester has heavy leads to carry large amounts of current and many later models have an inductive ammeter pickup that clamps around the wire to simplify test connections. On some models, the ammeter also has a zero-center scale to allow testing of charging and starting systems without switching leads or polarity. A digital multimeter is a voltmeter, ammeter and ohmmeter combined in an instrument which gives a digital readout. These are often used when testing solid state circuits because of their high input impedance (usually 10 megohms or more).

The tach/dwell meter combines a tachometer and a dwell (cam angle) meter and is a specialized kind of voltmeter. The tachometer scale is marked to show engine speed in rpm and the dwell scale is marked to show degrees of distributor shaft rotation. In most electronic ignition systems, dwell is determined by the control unit, but the dwell meter can also be used to check the duty cycle (operation) of some electronic engine control systems. Some tach/dwell meters are powered by an internal battery, while others take their power from the car battery in use. The battery powered testers usually require calibration much like an ohmmeter before testing.

Special Test Equipment

A variety of diagnostic tools are available to help troubleshoot and repair computerized engine control systems. The most sophisticated of these devices are the console type engine analyzers that usually occupy a garage service bay, but there are several types of aftermarket electronic testers available that will allow quick circuit tests of the engine control system by plugging directly into a special connector located in the engine compartment or under the dashboard. Several tool and equipment manufacturers offer simple, hand held testers that measure various circuit voltage levels on command to check all system components for proper operation. Although these testers usually cost about $300–500, consider that the average computer control unit (or ECM) can cost just as much and the money saved by not replacing perfectly good sensors or components in an attempt to correct a problem could justify the purchase price of a special diagnostic tester the first time it's used.

These computerized testers can allow quick and easy test measurements while the engine is operating or while the car is being driven. In addition, the on-board computer memory can be read to access any stored trouble codes; in effect allowing the computer to tell you where it hurts and aid trouble diagnosis by pinpointing exactly which circuit or component is malfunctioning. In the same manner, repairs can be tested to make sure the problem has been corrected. The biggest advantage these special testers have is their relatively easy hookups that minimize or eliminate the chances of making the wrong connections and getting false voltage readings or damaging the computer accidentally.

NOTE: *It should be remembered that these testers check voltage levels in circuits; they don't detect mechanical problems or failed components if the circuit voltage falls within the preprogrammed limits stored in the tester PROM unit. Also, most of the hand held testes are designed to work only on one or two systems made by a specific manufacturer.*

A variety of aftermarket testers are available to help diagnose different computerized control systems. Owatonna Tool Company (OTC), for example, markets a device called the OTC Monitor which plugs directly into the assembly line diagnostic link (ALDL). The OTC tester makes diagnosis a simple matter of pressing the correct buttons and, by changing the internal PROM or inserting a different diagnosis cartridge, it will work on any model from full size to subcompact, over a wide range of years. An adapter is supplied with the tester to allow connection to all types of ALDL links, regardless of the number of pin terminals used. By inserting an updated PROM into the OTC tester, it can be easily updated to diagnose any new modifications of computerized control systems.

Wiring Harnesses

The average automobile contains about $1/2$ mile of wiring, with hundreds of individual connections. To protect the many wires from damage and to keep them from becoming a confusing tangle, they are organized into bundles, enclosed in plastic or taped together and called wire harnesses. Different wiring harnesses serve different parts of the vehicle. Individual wires are color coded to help trace them through a harness where sections are hidden from view.

A loose or corroded connection or a replacement wire that is too small for the circuit will add extra resistance and an additional voltage drop to the circuit. A ten percent voltage drop can result in slow or erratic motor operation, for example, even though the circuit is complete. Automotive wiring or circuit conductors can be in any one of three forms:

1. Single strand wire
2. Multi-strand wire
3. Printed circuitry

Single strand wire has a solid metal core and is usually used inside such components as alternators, motors, relays and other devices. Multi-strand wire has a core made of many small strands of wire twisted together into a single conductor. Most of the wiring in an automotive electrical system is made up of multi-strand wire, either as a single conductor or grouped together in a harness. All wiring is color coded on the insulator, either as a solid color or as a colored wire with an identification stripe. A printed circuit is a thin film of copper or other conductor that is printed on an insulator backing. Occasionally, a printed circuit is sandwiched between two sheets of plastic for more protection and flexibility. A complete printed circuit, consisting of conductors, insulating material and connectors for lamps or other components is called a printed circuit board. Printed circuitry is used in place of individual wires or harnesses in places where space is limited, such as behind instrument panels.

Wire Gauge

Since computer controlled automotive electrical systems are very sensitive to changes in resistance, the selection of properly sized wires is critical when systems are repaired. The wire gauge number is an expression of the cross section area of the conductor. The most common system for expressing wire size is the American Wire Gauge (AWG) system.

Wire cross section area is measured in circular mils. A mil is $\frac{1}{1000}$ in. (0.001 in.); a circular mil is the area of a circle one mil in diameter. For example, a conductor $\frac{1}{4}$ in. in diameter is 0.250 in. or 250 mils. The circular mil cross section area of the wire is 250 squared (250^2)or 62,500 circular mils. Imported car models usually use metric wire gauge designations, which is simply the cross section area of the conductor in square millimeters (mm^2).

Gauge numbers are assigned to conductors of various cross section areas. As gauge number increases, area decreases and the conductor becomes smaller. A 5 gauge conductor is smaller than a 1 gauge conductor and a 10 gauge is smaller than a 5 gauge. As the cross section area of a conductor decreases, resistance increases and so does the gauge number. A conductor with a higher gauge number will carry less current than a conductor with a lower gauge number.

NOTE: *Gauge wire size refers to the size of the conductor, not the size of the complete wire. It is possible to have two wires of the same gauge with different diameters because one may have thicker insulation than the other.*

12 volt automotive electrical systems generally use 10, 12, 14, 16 and 18 gauge wire. Main power distribution circuits and larger accessories usually use 10 and 12 gauge wire. Battery cables are usually 4 or 6 gauge, although 1 and 2 gauge wires are occasionally used. Wire length must also be considered when making repairs to a circuit. As conductor length increases, so does resistance. An 18 gauge wire, for example, can carry a 10 amp load for 10 feet without excessive voltage drop; however if a 15 foot wire is required for the same 10 amp load, it must be a 16 gauge wire.

An electrical schematic shows the electrical current paths when a circuit is operating properly. It is essential to understand how a circuit works before trying to figure out why it doesn't. Schematics break the entire electrical system down into individual circuits and show only one particular circuit. In a schematic, no attempt is made to represent wiring and components as they physically appear on the vehicle; switches and other components are shown as simply as possible. Face views of harness connectors show the cavity or terminal locations in all multi-pin connectors to help locate test points.

If you need to backprobe a connector while it is on the component, the order of the terminals must be mentally reversed. The wire color code can help in this situation, as well as a keyway, lock tab or other reference mark.

NOTE: *Wiring diagrams are not included in this book. As cars and trucks have become more complex and available with longer option lists, wiring diagrams have grown in size and complexity. It has become almost impossible to provide a readable reproduction of a wiring diagram in a book this size. Information on ordering wiring diagrams from the vehicle manufacturer can be found in the owner's manual.*

WIRING REPAIR

Soldering is a quick, efficient method of joining metals permanently. Everyone who has the occasion to make wiring repairs should know how to solder. Electrical connections that are soldered are far less likely to come apart and will conduct electricity much better than connections that are only "pig-tailed" together. The most popular (and preferred) method of soldering is with an electrical soldering gun. Soldering irons are available in many sizes and wattage ratings. Irons with higher wattage ratings deliver higher temperatures and recover lost heat faster. A small soldering iron rated for no more than 50 watts is recommended, especially on electrical systems where excess heat can damage the components being soldered.

There are three ingredients necessary for successful soldering; proper flux, good solder and sufficient heat. A soldering flux is necessary to clean the metal of tarnish, prepare it for soldering and to enable the solder to spread into tiny crevices. When soldering, always use a resin flux or resin core solder which is non-corrosive and will not attract moisture once the job is finished. Other types of flux (acid core) will leave a residue that will attract moisture and cause the wires to corrode. Tin is a unique metal with a low melting point. In a molten state, it dissolves and alloys easily with many metals. Solder is made by mixing tin with lead. The most common proportions are 40/60, 50/50 and 60/40, with the percentage of tin listed first. Low priced solders usually contain less tin, making them very difficult for a beginner to use because more heat is required to melt the solder. A common solder is 40/60 which is well suited for all-around general use, but 60/40 melts easier, has more tin for a better joint and is preferred for electrical work.

Soldering Techniques

Successful soldering requires that the metals to be joined be heated to a temperature that will melt the solder—usually 360–460°F (182–238°C). Contrary to popular belief, the purpose of the soldering iron is not to melt the solder itself, but to heat the parts being soldered to a temperature high enough to melt the solder when it is touched to the work. Melting flux-cored solder on the soldering iron will usually destroy the effectiveness of the flux.

NOTE: *Soldering tips are made of copper for good heat conductivity, but must be "tinned" regularly for quick transference of heat to the project and to prevent the solder from sticking to the iron. To "tin" the iron, simply heat it and touch the flux-cored solder to the tip; the solder will flow over the hot tip. Wipe the excess off with a clean rag, but be careful as the iron will be hot.*

After some use, the tip may become pitted. If so, simply dress the tip smooth with a smooth file and "tin" the tip again. An old saying holds that "metals well cleaned are half soldered." Flux-cored solder will remove oxides, but rust, bits of insulation and oil or grease must be removed with a wire brush or emery cloth. For maximum strength in soldered parts, the joint must start off clean and tight. Weak joints will result in gaps too wide for the solder to bridge.

If a separate soldering flux is used, it should be brushed or swabbed on only those areas that are to be soldered. Most solders contain a core of flux and separate fluxing is unnecessary. Hold the work to be soldered firmly. It is best to solder on a wooden board, because a metal vise will only rob the piece to be soldered of heat and make it difficult to melt the solder. Hold the soldering tip with the broadest face against the work to be soldered. Apply solder under the tip close to the work, using enough solder to give a heavy film between the iron and the piece being soldered, while moving slowly and making sure the solder melts properly. Keep the work level or the solder will run to the lowest part and favor the thicker parts, because these require more heat to melt the solder. If the soldering tip overheats (the solder coating on the face of the tip burns up), it should be retinned. Once the soldering is completed, let the soldered joint stand until cool. Tape and seal all soldered wire splices after the repair has cooled.

Wire Harness and Connectors

The on-board computer (ECM) wire harness electrically connects the control unit to the various solenoids, switches and sensors used by the control system. Most connectors in the engine compartment or otherwise exposed to the elements are protected against moisture and dirt which could create oxidation and deposits on the terminals. This protection is important because of the very low voltage and current levels used by the computer and sensors. All connectors have a lock which secures the male and female terminals together, with a secondary lock holding the seal and terminal into the connector. Both terminal locks must be released when disconnecting ECM connectors.

These special connectors are weather-proof and all repairs require the use of a special terminal and the tool required to service it. This tool is used to remove the pin and sleeve terminals. If removal is attempted with an ordinary pick, there is a good chance that the terminal will be bent or deformed. Unlike standard blade type terminals, these terminals cannot be straightened once they are bent. Make certain that the connectors are properly seated and all of the sealing rings in place when connecting leads. On some models, a hinge-type flap provides a backup or secondary locking feature for the terminals. Most secondary locks are used to improve the connector reliability by retaining the terminals if the small terminal lock tangs are not positioned properly.

Molded-on connectors require complete replacement of the connection. This means splicing a new connector assembly into the harness. All splices in on-board computer systems should be soldered to insure proper contact. Use care when probing the connections or replacing terminals in them as it is possible to short between opposite terminals. If this happens to the wrong terminal pair, it is possible to damage certain components. Always use jumper wires between connectors for circuit checking and never probe through weather-proof seals.

Open circuits are often difficult to locate by sight because corrosion or terminal misalignment are hidden by the connectors. Merely wiggling a connector on a sensor or in the wiring harness may correct the open circuit condition. This should always be considered when an open circuit or a failed sensor is indicated. Intermittent problems may also be caused by oxidized or loose connections. When using a circuit tester for diagnosis, always probe connections from the wire side. Be careful not to damage sealed connectors with test probes.

All wiring harnesses should be replaced with identical parts, using the same gauge wire and connectors. When signal wires are spliced into a harness, use wire with high temperature insulation only. With the low voltage and current levels found in the system, it is important that the best possible connection at all wire splices be made by soldering the splices together. It is seldom necessary to replace a complete harness. If replacement is necessary, pay close attention to insure proper harness routing. Secure the harness with suitable plastic wire clamps to prevent vibrations from causing the harness to wear in spots or contact any hot components.

NOTE: *Weatherproof connectors cannot be replaced with standard connectors. Instructions are provided with replacement connector and terminal packages. Some wire harnesses have mounting indicators (usually pieces of colored tape) to mark where the harness is to be secured.*

In making wiring repairs, it's important that you always replace damaged wires with wires that are the same gauge as the wire being replaced. The heavier the wire, the smaller the gauge number. Wires are color-coded to aid in identification and whenever possible the same color coded wire should be used for replacement. A wire stripping and crimping tool is necessary to install solderless terminal connectors. Test all crimps by pulling on the wires; it should not be possible to pull the wires out of a good crimp.

Wires which are open, exposed or otherwise damaged are repaired by simple splicing. Where possible, if the wiring harness is accessible and the damaged place in the wire can be located, it is best to open the harness and check for all possible damage. In an inaccessible harness, the wire must be bypassed with a new insert, usually taped to the outside of the old harness.

When replacing fusible links, be sure to use fusible link wire, NOT ordinary automotive wire. Make sure the fusible segment is of the same gauge and construction as the one being replaced and double the stripped end when crimping the terminal connector for a good contact. The melted (open) fusible link segment of the wiring harness should be cut off as close to the harness as possible, then a new segment spliced in as described. In the case of a damaged fusible link that feeds two harness wires, the harness connections should be replaced with two fusible link wires so that each circuit will have its own separate protection.

NOTE: *Most of the problems caused in the wiring harness are due to bad ground connections. Always check all vehicle ground connections for corrosion or looseness before performing any power feed checks to eliminate the chance of a bad ground affecting the circuit.*

Repairing Hard Shell Connectors

Unlike molded connectors, the terminal contacts in hard shell connectors can be replaced. Weatherproof hard-shell connectors with the leads molded into the shell have non-replaceable terminal ends. Replacement usually involves the use of a special terminal removal tool that depress the locking tangs (barbs) on the connector terminal and allow the connector to be removed from the rear of the shell. The connector shell should be replaced if it shows any evidence of burning, melting, cracks, or breaks. Replace individual terminals that are burnt, corroded, distorted or loose.

NOTE: *The insulation crimp must be tight to prevent the insulation from sliding back on the wire when the wire is pulled. The insulation must be visibly compressed under the crimp tabs, and the ends of the crimp should be turned in for a firm grip on the insulation.*

The wire crimp must be made with all wire strands inside the crimp. The terminal must be fully compressed on the wire strands with the ends of the crimp tabs turned in to make a firm grip on the wire. Check all connections with an ohmmeter to insure a good contact. There should be no measurable resistance between the wire and the terminal when connected.

Mechanical Test Equipment

Vacuum Gauge

Most gauges are graduated in inches of mercury (in.Hg), although a device called a manometer reads vacuum in inches of water (in. H_2O). The normal vacuum reading usually varies between 18 and 22 in.Hg at sea level. To test engine vacuum, the vacuum gauge must be connected to a source of manifold vacuum. Many engines have a plug in the intake manifold which can be removed and replaced with an adapter fitting. Connect the vacuum gauge to the fitting with a suitable rubber hose or, if no manifold plug is available, connect the vacuum gauge to any device using manifold vacuum, such as EGR valves, etc. The vacuum gauge can be used to determine if enough vacuum is reaching a component to allow its actuation.

Hand Vacuum Pump

Small, hand-held vacuum pumps come in a variety of designs. Most have a built-in vacuum gauge and allow the component to be tested without removing it from the vehicle. Operate the pump lever or plunger to apply the correct amount of vacuum required for the test specified in the diagnosis routines. The level of vacuum in inches of Mercury (in.Hg) is indicated on the pump gauge. For some testing, an additional vacuum gauge may be necessary.

Intake manifold vacuum is used to operate various systems and devices on late model vehicles. To correctly diagnose and solve problems in vacuum control systems, a vacuum source is necessary for testing. In some cases, vacuum can be taken from the intake manifold when the engine is running, but vacuum is normally provided by a hand vacuum pump. These hand vacuum pumps have a built-in vacuum gauge that allow testing while the device is still attached to the component. For some tests, an additional vacuum gauge may be necessary.

HEATING AND AIR CONDITIONING

Blower Motor

The blower motor is located under the dashboard on the far right side of the car. It is accessible (in most vehicles) from under the dashboard without removing the dash assembly. The blower motor turns the fan, which circulates the heated, cooled or fresh air within the car. Aside from common electrical problems, the blower motor may need to be removed to clean out leaves or debris which have been sucked into the casing.

NOTE: *On A/C equipped vehicles the air condition assembly is integral with the heater as-*

sembly (including the blower motor) and therefore the blower motor removal may differ from the procedures detailed below. In some case it may be necessary to remove the Air Conditioner/Heater Housing Assembly or Evaporator/Cooling Unit (listed later in this chapter) also refer to Chapter 1 for necessary A/C service procedures. On some models the package tray may have to be removed to gain access to the blower motor assembly. Due to the lack of information (no factory service procedure) available at the time of this publication, a general blower motor removal and installation procedure is outlined. The removal and installation steps can be altered as necessary.

REMOVAL AND INSTALLATION

Early Models

1. Disconnect the negative battery cable. Remove the three screws attaching the retainer.
2. Remove the glove box assembly.
3. Remove the air duct between the heater case and blower assembly.
4. Disconnect the blower motor wire connector at the motor case.
5. Disconnect the air source selector control cable at the blower assembly.

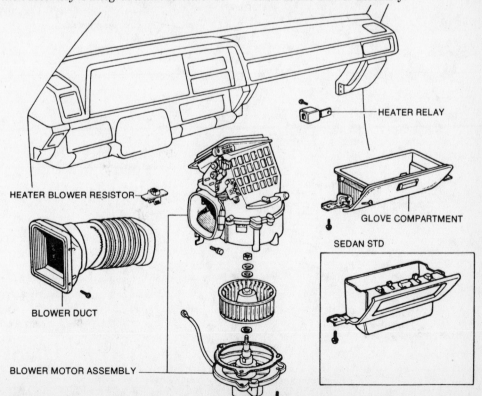

HEATER RELAY

HEATER BLOWER RESISTOR

GLOVE COMPARTMENT

SEDAN STD

BLOWER DUCT

BLOWER MOTOR ASSEMBLY

Typical early model heater blower assembly

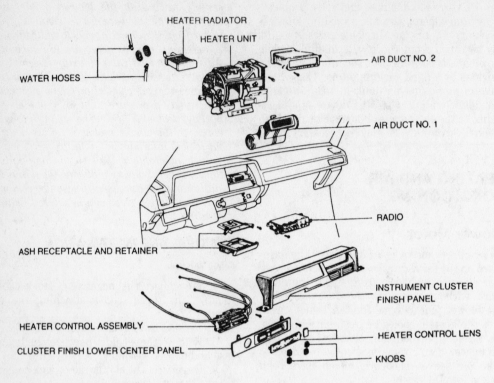

HEATER RADIATOR

HEATER UNIT

AIR DUCT NO. 2

WATER HOSES

AIR DUCT NO. 1

RADIO

ASH RECEPTACLE AND RETAINER

INSTRUMENT CLUSTER
FINISH PANEL

HEATER CONTROL ASSEMBLY

HEATER CONTROL LENS

CLUSTER FINISH LOWER CENTER PANEL

KNOBS

HARDTOP, COUPE AND LIFTBACK

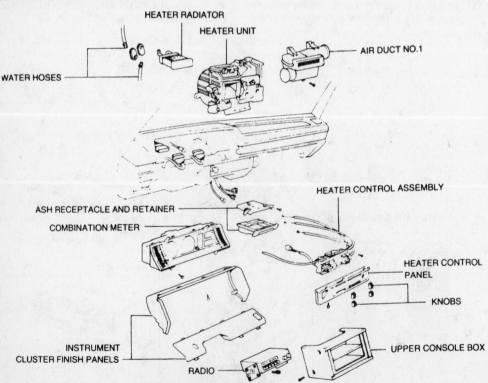

HEATER RADIATOR

HEATER UNIT

AIR DUCT NO.1

WATER HOSES

HEATER CONTROL ASSEMBLY

ASH RECEPTACLE AND RETAINER

COMBINATION METER

HEATER CONTROL
PANEL

KNOBS

INSTRUMENT
CLUSTER FINISH PANELS

RADIO

UPPER CONSOLE BOX

Heater unit assembly early model Corolla

6. Loosen the two nuts and the bolt attaching the blower assembly, then remove the blower.

7. With the blower removed, check the case for any debris or signs of fan contact. Inspect the fan for wear spots, cracked blades or hub, loose retaining nut or poor alignment.

8. To reinstall, place the blower in position, making sure it is properly aligned within the case. Install the two bolts and the nut and tighten them.

9. Connect the selector control cable at the blower assembly.

10. Connect the wire harness to the motor and install the ductwork between the heater case and the blower assembly.

11. Install the glove box assembly and install the retainer with its three screws. Reconnect battery and check operation of blower motor for all speeds and heater A/C system for proper operation.

Later Models

1. Disconnect the negative battery cable.
2. Remove the rubber duct running between the heater case and the blower.
3. Disconnect the wiring from the motor.
4. Remove the three screws holding the motor and remove the blower motor.
5. With the blower removed, check the case for any debris or signs of fan contact. Inspect the fan for wear spots, cracked blades or hub, loose retaining nut or poor alignment.
6. To reinstall, place the blower in position, making sure it is properly aligned within the case. Install the three screws and tighten them.
7. Connect the wiring to the motor.
8. Install the rubber air duct and connect the negative battery cable. Check operation of blower motor for all speeds and heater A/C system for proper operation.

Heater Core

The heater core is simply a small heat exchanger (radiator) within the heater housing assembly in the car. If the driver selects heat on the control panel, a water valve is opened allowing engine coolant to circulate through the heater core. The blower fan circulates air through the fins, picking up the heat from the engine coolant. The heated air is ducted into the car and the coolant is routed back to the engine. Moving the control to a cooler setting reduces the amount of hot water flowing into the core, thus reducing the amount of heat.

NOTE: *On A/C equipped vehicles the air condition assembly is integral with the heater housing assembly and therefore the heater housing assembly removal may differ from*

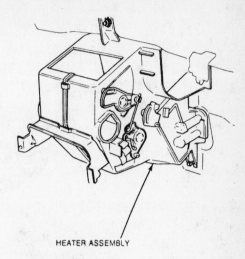

HEATER ASSEMBLY

Typical heater assembly

the procedures detailed below. In some case it may be necessary to remove the Air Conditioner/Heater Housing Assembly or Evaporator Unit (listed later in this chapter) refer to Chapter 1 for necessary A/C service procedures. Due to the lack of information (no factory service procedure) available at the time of this publication, a general heater housing assembly removal and installation procedure is outlined. The removal and installation steps can be altered as necessary.

REMOVAL AND INSTALLATION
Early Models

1. Disconnect the negative battery cable and then drain the cooling system.

CAUTION: *When draining the coolant, keep in mind that cats and dogs are attracted by the ethylene glycol antifreeze, and are quite likely to drink any that is left in an uncovered container or in puddles on the ground. This will prove fatal in sufficient quantity. Always drain the coolant into a sealable container. Coolant should be reused unless it is contaminated or several years old.*

2. Disconnect the heater hose from the core in the engine compartment. Note position and remove any control cables as necessary.
3. Remove the six clips from the lower part of the heater case, then remove the lower part of the case.
4. Carefully pry open the lower part of the heater case.
5. Remove the core assembly from the heater case. Handle the core carefully and do not allow the fins to be crushed or deformed.
6. When reinstalling, position the core properly and install the lower part of the case.

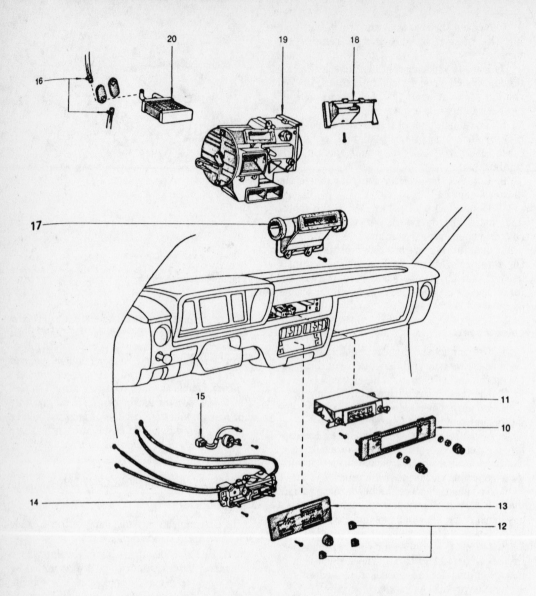

10.	Knob & Radio Tuner Finish Plate		16.	Heater Hose & Grommet
11.	Radio Tuner		17.	Air Duct
12.	Knob		18.	Air Duct
13.	Heater Control Panel		19.	Radiator Unit Assembly
14.	Heater Control Assembly		20.	Radiator Unit
15.	Heater Blower Switch & Heater Control Indicator Light			

Early model Tercel heater blower assembly

7. Install the six clips, making sure each is properly secured.

8. Connect the heater hoses. Check them for any signs of weakness or fraying and use new clamps if necessary. Install any control cable as required.

9. Refill the coolant to the proper level. Connect the negative battery cable. Start the engine and check heater system for proper operation.

Later Models

NOTE: *The heater case and core are located directly behind the center console. Access to the heater case requires removal of the entire console as well as most of the dashboard assembly. Please refer to the proper sub-topics* for removal procedures. *Instrument Cluster, Instrument Panel, Console and Radio Removal are explained later in this chapter. Steering Wheel Removal and Installation is discussed in Chapter 8.*

1. Disconnect the negative battery cable.
2. Remove the steering wheel.
3. Remove the trim bezel from the instrument cluster.
4. Remove the cup holder from the console.
5. Remove the radio.
6. Remove the instrument panel (dashboard) assembly and the instrument cluster. Label and carefully disconnect all of the dash wiring harnesses. Remember to release the locking mechanism on each connector first.
7. Remove the center console and all the console trim. Work carefully and don't break the plastic pieces.
8. Remove the lower dash trim and the side window air deflectors.
9. Drain the coolant from the cooling system.

CAUTION: *When draining the coolant, keep in mind that cats and dogs are attracted by the ethylene glycol antifreeze, and are quite likely to drink any that is left in an uncovered container or in puddles on the ground. This will prove fatal in sufficient quantity. Always drain the coolant into a sealable container. Coolant should be reused unless it is contaminated or several years old.*

10. Disconnect the control cables from the heater case. Don't lose any of the small clips.
11. Disconnect the ductwork from the heater case.
12. Disconnect the blower switch wiring harness and heater control assembly.
13. Remove the two center console support braces.
14. Loosen the clamps and remove the heater hoses from the case. Remove the grommet from the cowling.
15. Remove the mounting nuts and bolts holding the heater core and the air distribution case to the firewall.
16. Remove the heater case and air distribution case from the car as a unit.
17. Remove the screws and clips from the case halves and separate the case.
18. Remove the heater core from the case.
19. Install the heater core into the case, position the case halves and secure the retaining screws and clips.
20. Install the case assembly in the car and secure it with the mounting nuts and bolts.
21. Connect the heater hoses (use new clamps if necessary) and attach the grommet to the cowl.
22. Connect the air ducts to the case and connect the control cables.

1. BLOWER ASSEMBLY
2. DUCT
3. HEATER ASSEMBLY

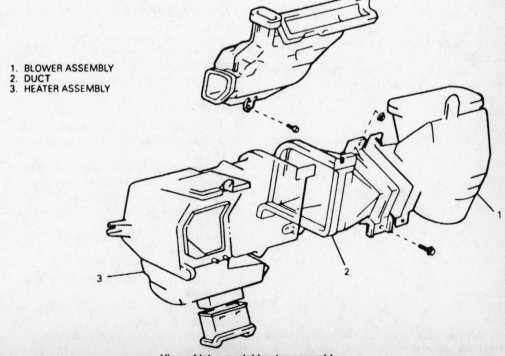

View of later model heater assembly

23. Install the two center console support braces.

24. Install the blower wiring harness and the heater control assembly.

25. Place the dashboard in position within the car. When it is loosely in place, connect the wiring harness connectors, making sure each is firmly seated and the wiring properly secured.

26. Install the center console and its trim pieces.

27. Install the radio.

28. Install the cup holder.

29. Install the trim bezel around the instrument cluster.

30. Install the steering wheel.

31. Refill the coolant to the proper level. Connect the negative battery cable. Start the engine and check heater system for proper operation.

Heater Control Panel (Control Head)

REMOVAL AND INSTALLATION

All Models

1. Disconnect the negative battery cable.

2. Remove the steering wheel.

3. Remove the two screws holding the hood release lever assembly.

4. Remove the four screws holding the left lower dashboard panel.

5. Remove the upper and lower steering column covers.

6. Use a small screwdriver or similar tool to gently pry the switches from the lower dash trim panel. Disconnect the wiring and remove the switches.

7. Remove the two screws under the panel and pull out the center cluster finish panel. It is also secured by spring clips behind the dash-pull straight out away from the dash so as not to break the plastic.

8. Remove the four screws holding the

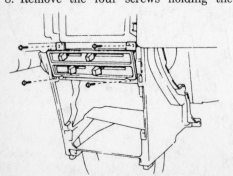

With the dash trim removed, the heater control panel bolts can be easily removed

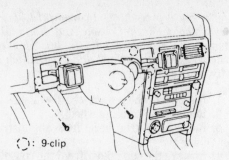

( ): 9-clip

Location of screws and clips holding the dashboard trim panel

heater control panel and slide the panel out of the dash.

9. When reinstalling, place the control panel in the dash, make sure it is straight and install the four retaining screws.

10. Place the finish panel in place and push it into the dash so that each spring clip engages. Install the two lower screws.

11. Connect the wiring to the switches and press the switches firmly into place.

12. Install the upper and lower steering wheel covers.

13. Install the lower left dash cover and its four screws.

14. Install the hood release lever assembly.

15. Install the steering wheel.

16. Connect the negative battery cable.

Evaporator (Cooling Unit)

REMOVAL AND INSTALLATION

CAUTION: *PLEASE RE-READ THE AIR CONDITIONING SECTION IN CHAPTER ONE SO THAT THE SYSTEM MAY BE DISCHARGED PROPERLY! ALWAYS WEAR EYE PROTECTION AND GLOVES WHEN DISCHARGING THE SYSTEM! OBSERVE NO SMOKING/NO OPEN FLAME RULES!*

Early Models

1. Disconnect the negative battery cable.

2. Safely discharge the air conditioning system.

3. Disconnect the suction tube from the evaporator assembly, then disconnect the liquid line from the assembly. Cap the open fittings immediately to prevent the entry of dirt and moisture.

4. Remove the grommets from the inlet and outlet fittings.

5. Remove the glove box.

6. Remove the lower cover from under the dashboard.

7. Disconnect the air conditioning switch connector.

8. Disconnect the vehicle wiring harness at the connector.

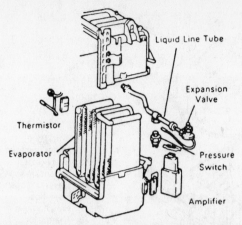

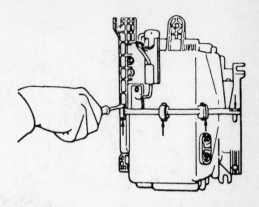

Separating the early model evaporator case halves

Exploded view of early models evaporator assembly

9. Remove the four nuts and three bolts securing the cooling assembly and remove the evaporator assembly from the car.

10. Remove the air conditioning amplifier.

11. Remove the air conditioning wiring harness from the case.

12. Remove the five clamps and two screws and remove the lower casing.

13. Remove the two screws holding the upper casing and remove the casing.

14. Remove the heat insulator and clamp from the outlet tube.

15. Disconnect the liquid line tube from the inlet fitting of the expansion valve.

16. Disconnect the expansion valve from the inlet fitting of the evaporator.

17. Remove the pressure switch if necessary.

18. Inspect the evaporator fins for blockage. Check all the fittings for cracks or scratches.

19. To reassemble, connect the expansion valve to the inlet fitting of the evaporator and tighten the nut to 17 ft. lbs.

20. Connect the liquid line tube to the inlet fitting of the expansion valve.

21. Install the pressure switch, if removed, and tighten it to 10 ft. lbs.

22. Install the clamp and heat insulator to the outlet tube.

23. Assemble the upper and lower cases onto the evaporator unit.

24. Reinstall the thermistor if it was removed.

25. Install the air conditioning wire harness onto the evaporator unit.

26. Install the air conditioning amplifier.

27. Place the assembled unit in place inside the car and install the retaining nuts and bolts.

WARNING: *Be careful not to pinch the wiring harness(es) during installation.*

28. Connect the air conditioning switch.

29. Connect the vehicle wiring harness to the connector.

30. Install the glove box and the under-dash cover.

31. Install the grommets on the inlet and outlet fittings.

32. Connect the liquid line to the evaporator inlet fitting and tighten it to 10 ft. lbs. Make sure the rubber washer (O-ring) is present inside the line and make certain the joint is correctly threaded before tightening it. Do not over tighten the joint.

33. Connect the suction tube to the evaporator unit outlet fitting and tighten it to 24 ft. lbs. Again, make sure the rubber washer (O-ring) is present inside the line and make certain the joint is correctly threaded before tightening it. Do not over tighten the joint.

34. If the evaporator was replaced with a NEW unit, add 1.5 oz. of compressor oil to the compressor. This replaces oil in the system removed with the old evaporator.

35. Connect the negative battery cable.

36. Evacuate and recharge the air conditioning system. Start the engine and check for proper operation of the A/C system in all cooling modes.

Later Models

1. Disconnect the negative battery cable.

2. Safely discharge the air conditioning system.

3. Disconnect the suction tube from the evaporator assembly, then disconnect the liquid line from the assembly. Cap the open fittings immediately to prevent the entry of dirt and moisture.

4. Remove the grommets from the inlet and outlet fittings.

5. Remove the glove box.

6. Disconnect the wiring harness connectors.

7. Remove the four nuts and four screws holding the evaporator unit. Remove the unit through the front of the instrument panel.

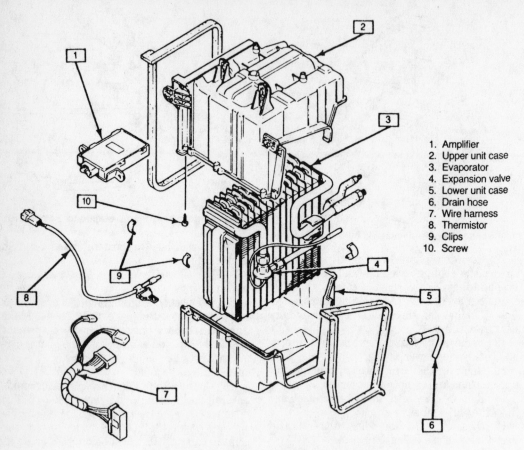

1. Amplifier
2. Upper unit case
3. Evaporator
4. Expansion valve
5. Lower unit case
6. Drain hose
7. Wire harness
8. Thermistor
9. Clips
10. Screw

Later model evaporator assembly components

8. Remove the connectors and the wiring harness from the case.

9. Remove the four clips and four screws; remove the upper casing and then the lower casing.

10. Disconnect the liquid tube from the inlet fitting of the expansion tube.

11. Remove the packing and the heat sens-

Removing the expansion valve. Note the use of two wrenches to hold the fittings — later models

ing tube from the suction tube of the evaporator.

NOTE: *Cap the open lines and fittings immediately to prevent the entry of dirt and moisture.*

12. Remove the expansion valve.

13. Inspect the evaporator fins for blockage. Check all the fittings for cracks or scratches. Never use water to clean the evaporator.

14. When reinstalling, assemble the expansion valve to the inlet fitting of the evaporator and tighten the nut to 17 ft. lbs.

15. Install the heat sensing tube and its packing to the suction tube of the evaporator.

16. Connect the liquid tube to the inlet fitting of the expansion valve and tighten it to 10 ft. lbs.

17. Assemble the lower casing and the upper casing and secure them with the four clips and the four screws.

18. Connect the wiring harness connectors.

19. Place the assembled unit in place within the car and secure its four mounting bolts and four nuts.

20. Install the wiring connectors onto the evaporator case.

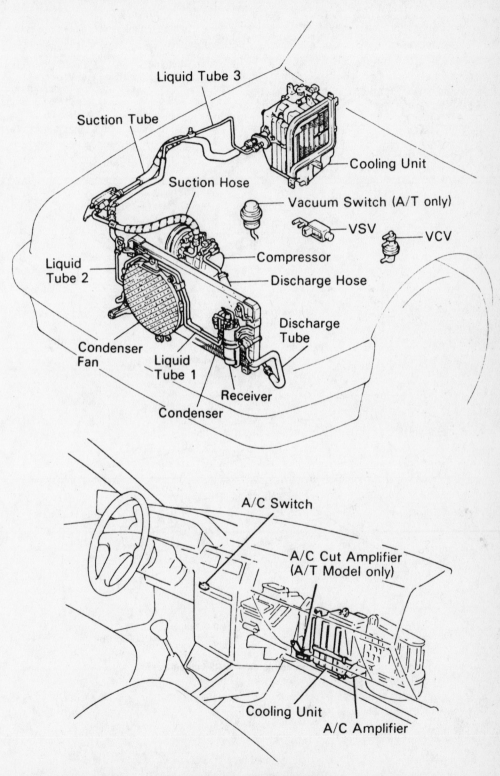

A/C components — late model Tercel

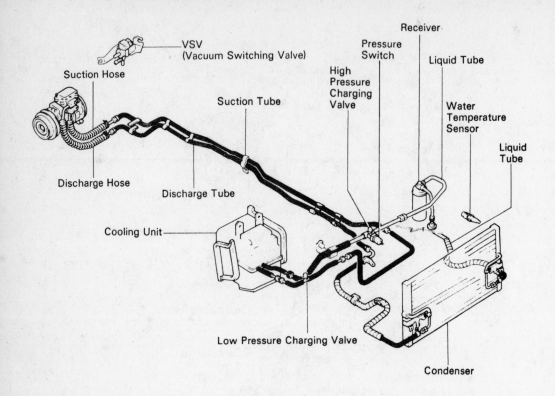

VSV
(Vacuum Switching Valve)

Suction Hose

Discharge Hose

Cooling Unit

Discharge Tube

Suction Tube

High
Pressure
Charging
Valve

Pressure
Switch

Receiver

Liquid Tube

Water
Temperature
Sensor

Liquid
Tube

Low Pressure Charging Valve

Condenser

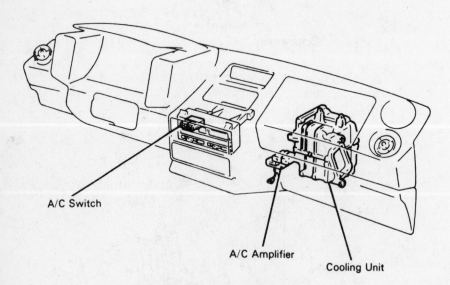

A/C Switch

A/C Amplifier

Cooling Unit

A/C components — MR2 vehicle

21. Install the glove box.

22. Install the grommets on inlet and outlet fittings.

23. Connect the liquid tube to the inlet fitting. Make sure the O-ring is in place and that the joint is correctly threaded. Tighten the joint to 10 ft. lbs. Do not over tighten.

24. Install the suction tube to the case inlet fitting. Make sure the O-ring is in place and that the joint is correctly threaded.

25. If the evaporator was replaced with a NEW unit, add 1.5 oz. of compressor oil to the compressor. This replaces oil in the A/C system removed with the old evaporator.

26. Connect the negative battery cable.

27. Evacuate and recharge the air conditioning system. Start the engine and check for proper operation of the A/C system in all cooling modes.

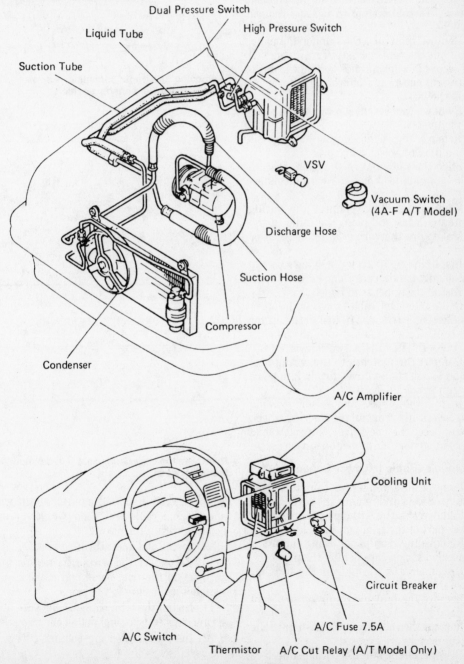

A/C components — late model Corolla

RADIO

REMOVAL AND INSTALLATION

Early Models (Radio In Upper Dash)

1. Disconnect the negative battery cable.
2. Remove (matchmark the location of steering wheel) the steering wheel and then the upper and lower steering column covers.
3. Use a small screwdriver or similar tool to gently pry the switches from the lower dash trim panel. Disconnect the wiring and remove the switches.
4. Remove the two screws under the panel and pull out the center cluster finish panel. It is also secured by spring clips behind the dash-pull straight out away from the dash so as not to break the plastic.
5. Remove the seven screws holding the upper trim panel.
6. Remove the eight screws holding the radio and its accessories trim cover.
7. Slide the radio out of the dash. Disconnect the antenna lead and the wiring connector.
8. When reinstalling, connect the wiring and antenna leads and place the radio in the dash. Make sure the wiring is not crushed or pinched.
9. Install the eight screws, making sure the radio is straight and in position.
10. Install the upper trim panel.
11. Route the switch cables through the openings in the center trim panel. Install the center cluster finish panel, making sure all the clips engage properly. Install the two screws.
12. Connect the switches to the wiring harnesses and push the switches firmly into place in the trim panel.
13. Install the upper and lower steering column covers and reinstall the steering wheel.
14. Connect the negative battery cable. Check radio system for proper operation.

Later Models (Radio In Lower Console)

1. Remove the seven screws from the steering column covers and remove the covers.
2. Remove the two attaching screws from the lower part of the trim panel.
3. Remove the trim panel, being careful of the concealed spring clips behind the panel.
4. Disconnect the wiring from the switches mounted in the trim panel.
5. Remove the four mounting screws from the radio.
6. Remove the radio from the dash until the wiring connectors are exposed.
7. Disconnect the two electrical connectors and the antenna cable from the body of the radio and remove the radio from the car.

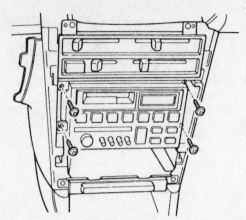

Removing the radio mounting screws — radio mounted in lower console position

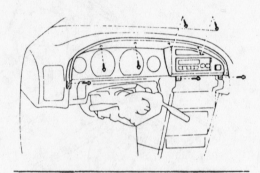

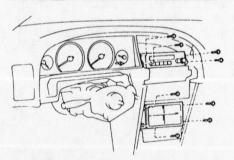

Removing the upper trim panel — radio mounted in the upper dash

8. When reinstalling, connect all the wiring and antenna cable first, then place the radio in position within the dash.
9. Install the four attaching screws.
10. Reconnect the wiring harnesses to the switches in the trim panel and make sure the switches are secure in the panel.
11. Install the trim panel (make sure all the spring clips engage) and install the two screws.
12. Install the steering column covers and the seven screws.
13. Install the steering wheel. Check radio system for proper operation.

WINDSHIELD WIPERS

Blade and Arm

REMOVAL AND INSTALLATION

1. To remove the wiper blades lift up on the spring release tab on the wiper blade-to-wiper arm connector.

2. Pull the blade assembly off the wiper arm.

3. Press the old wiper blade insert down, away from the blade assembly, to free it from the retaining clips on the blade ends. Slide the insert out of the blade. Slide the new insert into the blade assembly and bend the insert upward slightly to engage the retaining clips.

4. To replace a wiper arm, unscrew the acorn nut (on later models a cap covers this retaining nut at the bottom of the wiper arm) which secures it to the pivot and carefully pull the arm upward and off the pivot. Install the arm by placing it on the pivot and tightening the nut. Remember that the arm MUST BE reinstalled in its EXACT previous position or it will not cover the correct area during use.

NOTE: *If one wiper arm does not move when turned on or only moves a little bit, check the retaining nut at the bottom of the arm. The extra effort of moving wet snow or leaves off the glass can cause the nut to come loose--the pivot will turn without moving the arm.*

Windshield Wiper Motor

REMOVAL AND INSTALLATION

Front Wiper Assembly

1. Disconnect the negative battery terminal.

2. Disconnect the electrical connector from the wiper motor.

3. Remove the mounting bolts and remove the motor from the firewall.

4. Remove the wiper linkage from the wiper motor assembly.

5. Installation is the reverse of removal.

Rear Wiper Assembly

1. Remove the wiper arm from the pivot and remove the spacer and washer on the pivot.

2. Remove the cover (trim) panel on the inside of the hatch lid.

3. Remove the plastic cover on the wiper motor and disconnect the wiring connector from the motor.

4. Remove the mounting nuts and bolts and remove the wiper motor.

5. When reinstalling, position the motor and secure it in the hatch lid.

6. Connect the wiring harness and install the plastic cover.

7. Install the inner trim panel on the hatch lid.

8. Install the wiper arm with its washer and spacer, making sure the arm is correctly positioned before tightening the nut.

Front Wiper Linkage

REMOVAL AND INSTALLATION

1. Remove the windshield wiper motor as previously outlined.

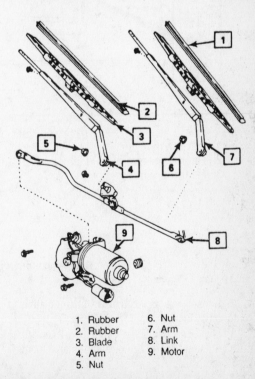

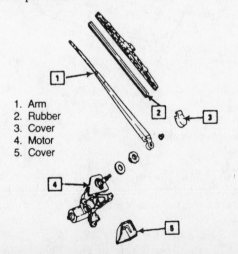

1. Arm
2. Rubber
3. Cover
4. Motor
5. Cover

Rear wiper components

1. Rubber
2. Rubber
3. Blade
4. Arm
5. Nut
6. Nut
7. Arm
8. Link
9. Motor

Typical wiper motor and linkage

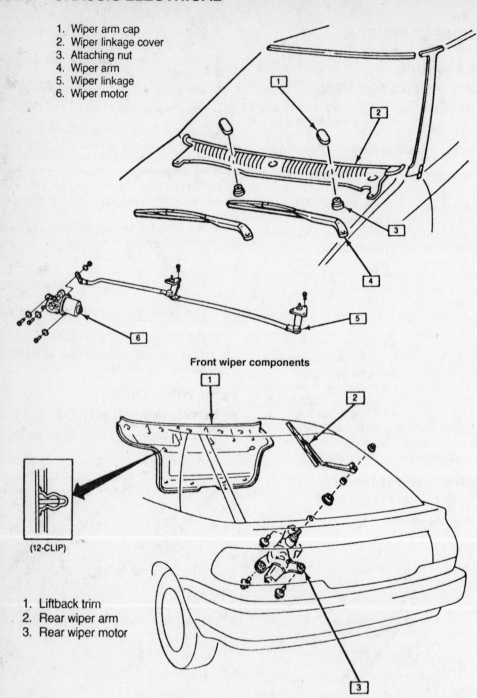

1. Wiper arm cap
2. Wiper linkage cover
3. Attaching nut
4. Wiper arm
5. Wiper linkage
6. Wiper motor

Front wiper components

(12-CLIP)

1. Liftback trim
2. Rear wiper arm
3. Rear wiper motor

Rear wiper components and installation

2. Loosen the wiper arm retaining nuts and remove the arms.

3. Unfasten the large wiper pivot retaining nuts and remove the linkage assembly through the access hole.

4. Place the linkage through the access hole and line up the pivots in their holes.

5. Install the two large pivot retaining nuts onto the pivots. Before the final tightening, make sure the linkage is aligned perfectly in all its holes.

6. Reinstall the wiper motor.

7. After installation of the wiper motor, check the wiper system for proper operation.

INSTRUMENTS AND SWITCHES

Instrument Cluster

REMOVAL AND INSTALLATION

Early Models

NOTE: *Always refer to the exploded view of dashboard components before starting this service procedure. Modify the service steps as necessary.*

1. Disconnect the negative battery cable.
2. Remove the steering wheel.
3. Remove the left side speaker grille. The grille may be attached with a clip (which must be pulled loose to remove the grille) or with a screw.
4. Remove the lower trim cover from the steering column.
5. Remove the hood release lever.
6. Remove the heater duct assembly.
7. Remove the instrument hood. Remove the air conditioner outlet register, then remove the four screws and remove the hood.
8. Remove the six screws from the instrument cluster, and disconnect the speedometer cable and the wiring connectors. Remove the meter assembly from the instrument panel.
9. To reinstall, connect the wiring harnesses and the speedometer cable to the cluster. Place the cluster in the dash and secure the six screws. Make certain the wiring is properly placed so as not to become pinched or crushed.

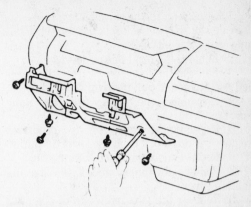

Removing the early model lower steering column cover

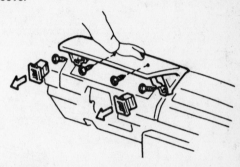

Removing the early model instrument hood

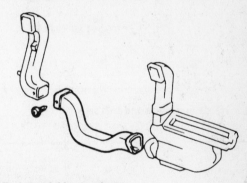

Early model heater ducts

10. Install the air conditioning outlet then install the hood and its screws.
11. Install the heater duct assembly.
12. Install the hood release lever and the lower steering column trim.
13. Reinstall the speaker grille.
14. Install the steering wheel and connect the negative battery cable. Road test the vehicle for proper operation.

Later Models

NOTE: *Always refer to the exploded view of dashboard components before starting this service procedure. Modify the service steps as necessary.*

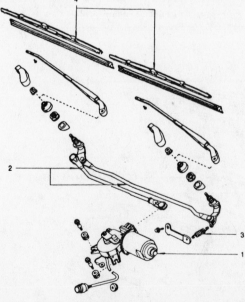

1. Wiper Motor
2. Wiper Link
3. Spring
4. Wiper Arm & Blade

Windshield wiper motor and linkage – Tercel

1. Disconnect the negative battery cable. Removing the steering wheel is not required, but may make the job easier.

2. Remove the hood release lever.

3. Remove the four screws from the lower left dash trim and pull the trim out.

4. Disconnect the wiring from the radio speaker.

5. If equipped with air conditioning, remove the ductwork from the lower air outlet.

6. Remove the trim panel from the car.

7. Remove the upper and lower steering column covers.

8. Remove the two screws from the trim panel (bezel).

9. Pull the panel out, releasing the spring clips behind the dash. With the panel loose, disconnect the wiring to the dash switches.

10. Remove the switches from the panel.

11. Remove the two electrical connectors and the cigarette lighter from the trim bezel and remove the bezel from the car.

12. Remove the four screws holding the instrument cluster trim.

13. Disconnect the wiring from the hazard (4-way) flasher and dimmer switches.

14. Remove the cluster trim panel.

15. Remove the four attaching screws holding the cluster, move it away from the dash and

Sedan and Wagon

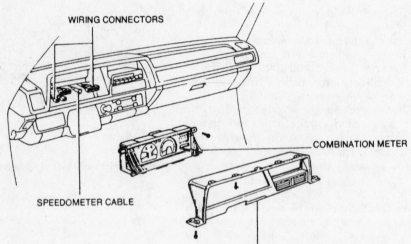

WIRING CONNECTORS

COMBINATION METER

SPEEDOMETER CABLE

INSTRUMENT CLUSTER FINISH PANEL

Hardtop, Coupe and Liftback

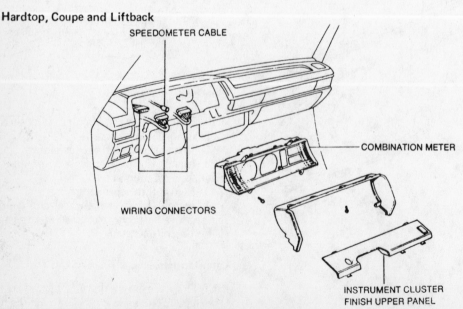

SPEEDOMETER CABLE

COMBINATION METER

WIRING CONNECTORS

INSTRUMENT CLUSTER FINISH UPPER PANEL

Instrument cluster — Corolla

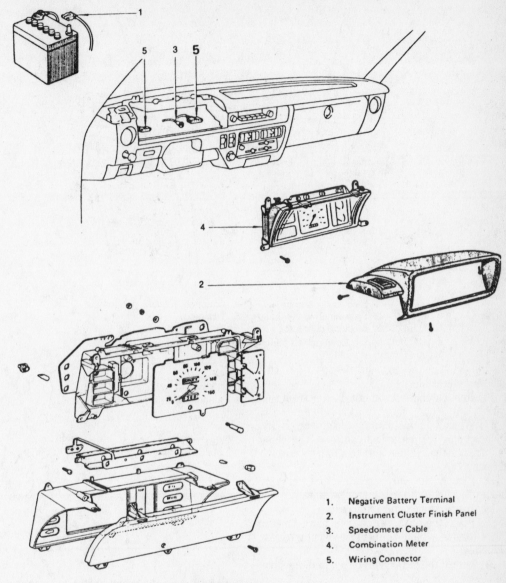

1.   Negative Battery Terminal
2.   Instrument Cluster Finish Panel
3.   Speedometer Cable
4.   Combination Meter
5.   Wiring Connector

Instrument cluster — Tercel

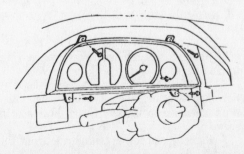

Removing the instrument cluster — late models

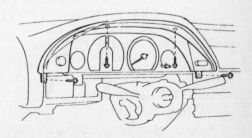

Instrument cluster trim panel — late models

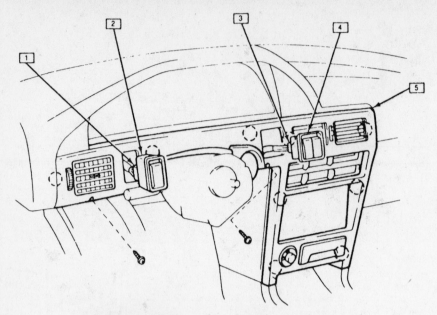

1. Electrical connector
2. Rear wiper-washer switch
3. Electrical connector
4. Cruise control/defogger switch
5. Trim bezel

Lower dash panel (bezel) — late models

disconnect the wiring harnesses and the speedometer cable.

16. Remove the instrument cluster from the car.

17. When reinstalling, connect the speedometer and electrical cables to the cluster. Install the cluster and the four retaining screws.

18. Attach the wiring connectors for the hazard flasher and the dimmer switches.

19. Install the cluster trim bezel.

20. Place the dash switches in place on the lower trim bezel and connect the wiring to the switches.

21. Install the lower trim bezel, making sure all the clips engage.

22. Install the steering column upper and lower covers.

23. Connect the air conditioning ductwork to the lower air outlet if so equipped.

24. Attach the wiring to the radio speaker.

25. Install the lower left dashboard trim panel and its four screws.

26. Install the hood release lever.

27. Connect the negative battery cable. Road test the vehicle for proper operation.

Instrument Dashboard (Safety Pad)

REMOVAL AND INSTALLATION

Early Models

NOTE: *Always refer to the exploded view of dashboard components before starting this*

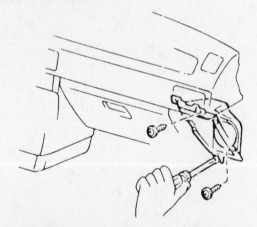

Removing the radio speaker and bracket assembly early models

service procedure. Using the exploded views as a guide to modify the service step procedures as necessary.

1. Disconnect the negative battery cable.

2. Remove (matchmark before removal) the steering wheel.

3. Remove the left side speaker grille. The grille may be attached with a clip (which must be pulled loose to remove the grille) or with screws.

4. Remove the lower trim cover from the steering column.

5. Remove the hood release lever.

6. Remove the heater duct assembly.

7. Remove the instrument hood. Remove

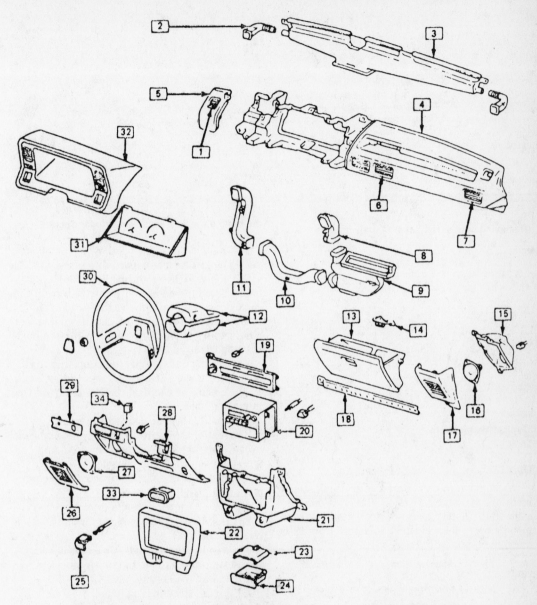

1. Side defroster nozzle
2. Side defroster duct
3. Defroster nozzle
4. Dashboard
5. End trim panel
6. Center register
7. Side register
8. No. 3 heater duct
9. Duct
10. No. 2 heater duct
11. No. 1 heater duct
12. Column covers

13. Glove compartment door
14. Door lock striker
15. Speaker bracket
16. Speaker
17. No. 2 speaker panel
18. Glove door reinforcement
19. Heater control panel
20. Radio
21. Lower center cluster finish panel
22. Center cluster finish panel
23. Retainer
24. Ash tray

25. Hood release lever
26. No. 1 speaker panel
27. Speaker
28. Lower finish panel
29. Finish panel
30. Steering wheel
31. Combination meter
32. Meter hood
33. Lower register
34. ECT indicator (A/T)

Typical early model dashboard components except MR2 vehicle

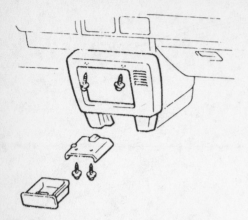

Removing center trim panel — early models

Removing the side window defroster ducts

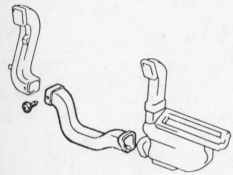

Typical heater ducts

the air conditioner outlet register, then remove the four screws and remove the hood.

8. Remove the six screws from the instrument cluster, and disconnect the speedometer cable and the wiring connectors. Remove the meter (instrument cluster) assembly from the instrument panel.

9. Disconnect the heating ducts to the dash vents.

10. Remove the finish panel on the end of the dash.

11. Remove the right side speaker grille.

12. Remove the right side speaker bracket with the speaker attached. Disconnect the wiring to the speaker.

13. Remove the glove compartment door with its reinforcement.

14. Remove the glove box door lock striker.

15. Remove the center trim panel over the console.

16. Remove the radio equipment and accessories.

17. Remove the lower center trim panel on the console.

18. Remove the heater control panel. Label and disconnect the electrical and vacuum connections to the panel.

19. Remove the side-window defroster nozzles. The grilles are snapped into place.

20. Remove the mounting bolts for the dashboard assembly and remove the dash from the car. Be careful of any wiring and/or hoses routed along the back of the dash. Do not damage any other components while the dash is being removed from the car.

21. When reinstalling, position the dashboard in the car. Attach any wiring harnesses to the inside of the dash before securing the mounting bolts.

22. Install the side defroster nozzles.

23. Install the heater control panel and connect its wiring and vacuum lines. Install the trim panel on the lower console.

24. Install the radio and accessory equipment and install its trim panel.

25. Install the glove box door lock striker.

26. Install the glove box door with the door reinforcement.

27. Install the right side speaker bracket and speaker. Connect the wiring to the speaker.

28. Install the speaker grille.

29. Install the end trim panel.

30. Install the heater ducts to the dash vents. Make sure they are properly connected and will not come loose.

31. Install the instrument assembly, connecting the speedometer cable and the wiring connectors.

32. Install the hood for the instrument cluster and then install the air outlet grilles.

33. Connect the air ductwork to the grilles.

34. Install the hood release lever.

35. Install the steering column trim covers.

36. Install the left side speaker grille.

37. Install the steering wheel. Connect the negative battery cable. Start engine roadtest the vehicle for proper operation and check operation of all instrument dashboard components.

Later Models

1. Disconnect the negative battery cable.
2. Remove the hood release lever.
3. Remove the four screws from the lower left dash trim and pull the trim out.
4. Disconnect the wiring from the radio speaker.
5. If equipped with air conditioning,

remove the ductwork from the lower air outlet and remove the trim panel from the car.

6. Remove the steering wheel.
7. Remove the upper and lower steering column covers.
8. Remove the two screws from the trim panel (bezel).
9. Pull the panel out, releasing the spring

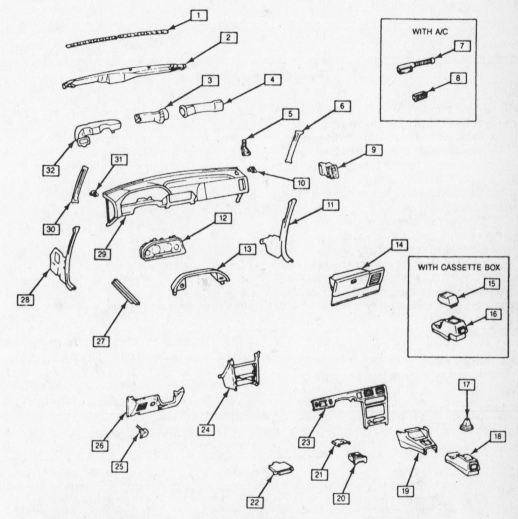

WITH A/C

WITH CASSETTE BOX

1. Defroster grille	12. Instrument cluster	23. Trim bezel
2. Defroster duct	13. Cluster bezel	24. Center console triim
3. Center ventilation duct	14. Gove box and trim assembly	25. Hood release lever
4. Right ventilation duct	15. Cassette box	26. Left lower dash trim
5. Brace	16. Rear console	27. Scuff plate
6. "A" pillar trim	17. Shift lever boot (M/T)	28. Cowl side trim
7. A/C duct	18. Rear console	29. Instrument panel
8. Lower A/C deflector	19. Front console	30. "A" pillar trim
9. Right ventilation deflector	20. Ashtray	31. Left window deflector
10. Right window deflector	21. Retainer	32. Left ventilation duct
11. Cowl side trim	22. Cup holder	

Typical late model dashboard components — except MR2 vehicles

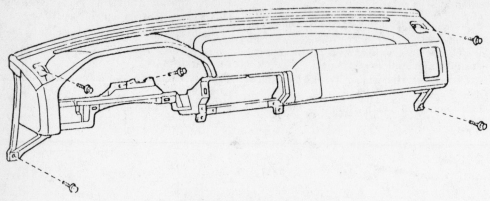

Dashboard retaining bolts

clips behind the dash. With the panel loose, disconnect the wiring to the dash switches.

10. Remove the switches from the panel.

11. Remove the two electrical connectors and the cigarette lighter from the trim bezel and remove the bezel from the car.

12. Remove the four screws holding the instrument cluster trim.

13. Disconnect the wiring from the hazard (4-way) flasher and dimmer switches.

14. Remove the cluster trim panel.

15. Remove the four attaching screws holding the cluster, move it away from the dash and disconnect the wiring harnesses and the speedometer cable. Remove the instrument cluster from the car.

16. Remove the cup holder.

17. Remove the radio. Disconnect the wiring and antenna cables.

18. Remove the glove box and trim assembly.

19. Remove the four screws holding the heater control panel and remove the panel.

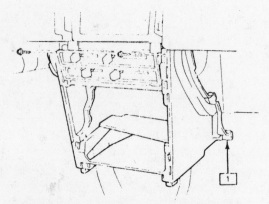

Removing the late model center dash trim panel

20. Remove the screws from the center console trim panel and remove the panel.

21. Carefully pry the left and right side-window defroster vents loose from the dash.

22. Remove the five attaching bolts from the instrument panel.

NOTE: Screw sizes are indicated by following the code use for removal and installation of the safety pad.

Code	Shape		Code	Shape		Code	Shape	
A		φ 6 L=16	F		φ 5 L=12	K		φ 5.22 L=20
B		φ 6	G		φ 5 L=8	L		φ 6 L=16
C		φ 5.22 L=12	H		φ 5 L=18	M		φ 5.22 L=14
D		φ 5.22 L=14	I		φ 5.22 L=14	N		φ 5.22 L=16
E		φ 5.22 L=12	J		φ 5.22 L=16	P		φ 6 L=14

Fastener size chart for dashboard components — MR2 vehicles

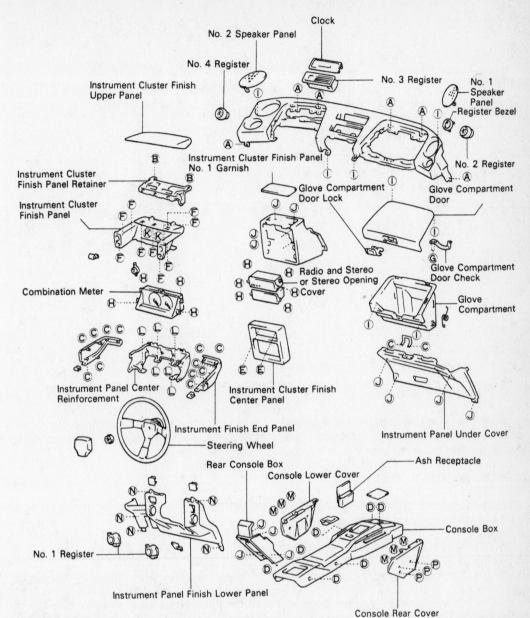

Dashboard components — MR2 vehicle — the letters on illustration indicate fastener size refer to size chart as necessary

23. Disconnect the three wiring connectors and the relay unit on the left side of the dash.

24. Disconnect the electrical connector on the right side of the dashboard.

25. Detach the defroster duct retainers behind the dash and remove the dashboard from the vehicle. Be careful of any wiring and/or hoses routed along the back of the dash. Do not damage any other components while the dash is being removed from the car.

26. When reinstalling, place the dash in position inside the car. Be careful to insert the defroster duct retainers into their bulkhead (firewall) clips.

27. Connect the three electrical connectors and the relay unit on the left side and the harness connector on the right side to their proper wire harnesses.

28. Install the dashboard mounting bolts.

29. Install the left and right side-window defroster outlets.

30. Install the center console trim panel.

31. Reinstall the heater control panel.

32. Install the glove box and trim assembly.

33. Install the radio and connect the electrical and antenna cables.

34. Install the cup holder and its attaching screws.

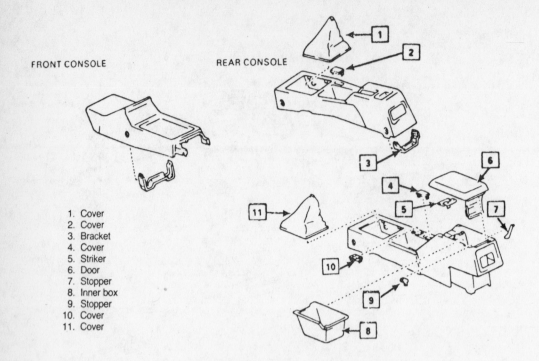

FRONT CONSOLE   REAR CONSOLE

1. Cover
2. Cover
3. Bracket
4. Cover
5. Striker
6. Door
7. Stopper
8. Inner box
9. Stopper
10. Cover
11. Cover

Typical console components

35. Connect the speedometer and electrical cables to the instrument cluster. Install the cluster and the four retaining screws.

36. Attach the wiring connectors for the hazard flasher and the dimmer switches.

37. Install the cluster trim bezel.

38. Place the dash switches in place on the lower trim bezel and connect the wiring to the switches.

39. Install the lower trim bezel, making sure all the clips engage.

40. Install the steering column upper and lower covers.

41. Connect the air conditioning ductwork to the lower air outlet if so equipped.

42. Attach the wiring to the radio speaker.

43. Install the lower left dashboard trim panel and its four screws.

44. Install the hood release lever. Install the steering wheel.

45. Connect the negative battery cable. Start

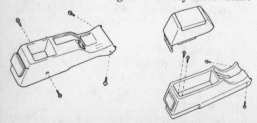

Console (left) and console with cassette box

engine roadtest the vehicle for proper operation and check operation of all instrument dashboard components.

Console

REMOVAL AND INSTALLATION

The consoles in most models are simply removed by detaching the mounting screws refer to the illustrations as a guide for this repair. On the MR2 vehicle refer to the Dashboard Component illustrations for view of the console assembly. On most models, many of these screws are concealed by plastic covers which may be popped off with a small screwdriver or similar tool. The consoles can be lifted over the shifter handle and removed from the car. Be very careful not to lose any small parts between the floor pan and carpet while the console is out.

Once the console is removed, take an extra moment to clean it thoroughly and apply a vinyl protectant. You can now get all the crevices that have been blocked by the seats and hidden by the carpet. When the console is reinstalled, make sure that any wires in the area are not pinched by the console or pierced by the mounting screws.

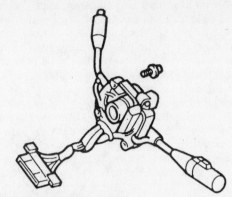

Typical combination switch

Combination Switch

REMOVAL AND INSTALLATION

All Models

1. Disconnect the negative battery cable. Remove the steering wheel.

2. Remove the lower left dashboard trim panel.

3. Disconnect the air duct from the vent in the lower panel.

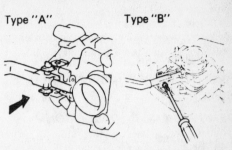

Combination switch handle (stalk) replacement

4. Remove the upper and lower steering column covers.

5. Disconnect the wiring from the combination switch to the dashboard wiring harness.

6. Remove the mounting bolts and remove the combination switch.

7. When reinstalling, position the switch carefully onto the column and secure the mounting screws.

8. Connect the wiring harness(es) from the switch to the dashboard harness.

9. Install the upper and lower column covers.

10. Install the air duct to the lower trim

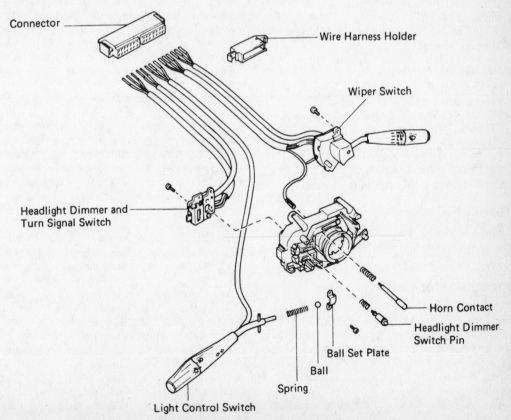

Exploded view of combination switch

panel and install the panel.

11. Install the steering wheel. Reconnect the negative battery cable. Check the combination switch for proper operation in all modes.

Rear Window Wiper/Washer Switch

REMOVAL AND INSTALLATION

1. Disconnect the negative battery cable.
2. Remove the hood release lever.
3. Remove the four screws from the lower left dash trim and pull the trim out.
4. Disconnect the wiring from the radio speaker.
5. If equipped with air conditioning, remove the ductwork from the lower air outlet and remove the trim panel from the car.
6. Remove the steering wheel.
7. Remove the upper and lower steering column covers.
8. Remove the two screws from the trim panel (bezel).
9. Pull the panel out, releasing the spring clips behind the dash. With the panel loose, disconnect the wiring to the dash switches.
10. Remove the switch from the panel.
11. To reinstall, press the switch into place in the lower trim bezel and connect the wiring to the switches.
12. Install the lower trim bezel, making sure all the clips engage.
13. Install the steering column upper and lower covers.
14. Connect the air conditioning ductwork to the lower air outlet if so equipped.
15. Attach the wiring to the radio speaker.
16. Install the lower left dashboard trim panel and its four screws.
17. Install the hood release lever.
18. Install the steering wheel.
19. Connect the negative battery cable.

Headlight Switch

Please refer to "Combination Switch" service procedures outlined earlier in this Chapter.

Speedometer Cable

The speedometer cable connects a rotating gear within the transmission/transaxle to the dashboard speedometer/odometer assembly. The dashboard unit interprets the number of turns the made by the cable and displays the information as miles per hour and total mileage.

Assuming that the transmission/transaxale contains the correct gear for the car, the accuracy of the speedometer depends primarily on tire condition and tire diameter. Badly worn tires (too small in diameter) or over inflation (too large in diameter) can affect the speedometer reading. Replacement tires of the incorrect overall diameter (such as oversize snow tires) can also affect the readings.

Generally, manufacturers state that speedometer/odometer error of ±10% is considered normal due to wear and other variables. Stated another way, if you drove the car over a measured 1 mile course and the odometer showed anything between 0.9 and 1.1 miles, the error is considered normal. If you plan to do any checking, always use a measured course such as mileposts on an Interstate highway or turnpike. Never use another car for comparison--the other car's inherent error may further cloud your readings.

The speedometer cable can become dry or develop a kink within its case. As it turns, the ticking or light knocking noise it makes can easily lead an owner to chase engine related problems in error. If such a noise is heard, carefully watch the speedometer needle during the speed range in which the noise is heard. Generally, the needle will jump or deflect each time the cable binds.

NOTE: *The slightest bind in the speedometer cable can cause unpredictable behavior in the cruise control system. If the cruise control exhibits intermittent surging or loss of set speed symptoms, check the speedometer cable first.*

To replace the speedometer cable and housing:

1. Follow the appropriate procedure given previously for removal of the instrument cluster. The cluster need not be fully removed, but only loosened to the point of being able to disconnect the speedometer cable.
2. Disconnect the speedometer cable and check that any retaining clamps or clips between the dash and the firewall are released.
3. Safely raise the car and support it on jackstands.

NOTE: *Depending on the length of your arm, you may be able to reach the cable connection at the transmission/transaxle without raising the car, but it's much easier with the car elevated.*

4. Disconnect the cable fitting at the transmission/transaxle and lift the cable and case away from the transmission/transaxle.
5. Follow the cable back to the firewall, releasing any clips or retainers.
6. From inside the car, work the speedometer cable through the grommet in the firewall into the engine compartment. It may be necessary to pop the grommet out of the firewall and transfer it to the new cable.

7. When reinstalling, track the new cable into position, remembering to attach the grommet to the firewall securely. Make absolutely certain that the cable is not kinked, or routed near hot or moving parts. All curves in the cable should be very gentle and not located near the ends. Note the speedometer cable inside the housing must be lubricated with the proper lubricant before installing it to the vehicle.

8. Attach any retaining clips, brackets or retainers, beginning from the middle of the cable and working towards each end.

9. Attach the cable to the transmission/transaxle. Remember that the cable has a formed, square end on it; this shaped end must fit into a matching hole in the transmission/transaxle mount. Don't try to force the cable collar (screw fitting) into place if the cable isn't seated properly.

10. Inside the car, hold the other end of the

cable with your fingers or a pair of tapered-nose pliers. Gently attempt to turn the cable; if it's properly seated at the other end, the cable will NOT turn more than about 1/4 turn. If the cable turns freely, the other end is not correctly seated.

11. Lower the car to the ground.

12. Attach the speedometer cable to the instrument cluster, again paying close attention to the fit of the square-cut end into the square hole. Don't force the cable retainer--you'll break the clips.

13. Reinstall the instrument cluster following procedures outlined previously. Road test the vehicle for proper operation.

LIGHTING

Headlights

REMOVAL AND INSTALLATION

Sealed Beam Type

1. Remove the headlight bezel (trim) and/or the radiator grille, as necessary.

2. The sealed beam is held in place by a retainer and either 2 or 4 small screws. Identify these screws before applying any tools.

NOTE: *DO NOT confuse the small retaining screws with the larger aiming screws! There will be two aiming screws or adjustors for each lamp. (One adjustor controls the up/down motion and the other controls the left/right motion.) Identify the adjustors and avoid them during removal. If they are not*

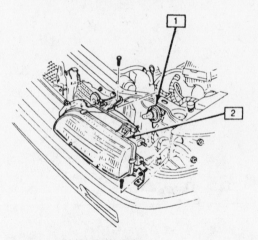

1. Headlamp bulb
2. Headlamp assembly

Replacing a headlight bulb semi-sealed beam or fixed lens type

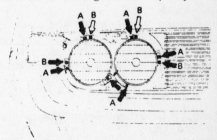

On early models to remove the headlights, remove the retaining screws "A" but do not loosen adjusting screws "B"

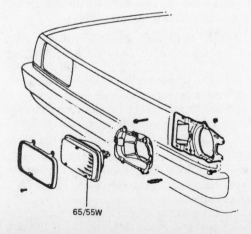

65/55W

Removing the headlight – late model Corolla

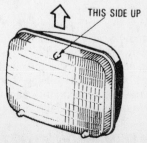

THIS SIDE UP

Correct installation of headlight

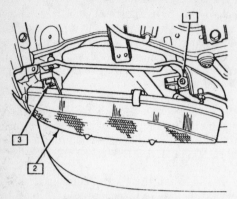

1. Right-left adjustment screw
2. Headlamp assembly
3. Up-down adjustment screw

Adjustor locations for replaceable bulb headlamp assembly

disturbed, the new headlamp will be in identical aim to the old one.

3. Using a small screwdriver (preferably magnetic) and a pair of taper-nose pliers if necessary, remove the small screws in the headlamp retainer. DON'T drop the screws.

4. Remove the retainer and the headlamp may be gently pulled free from its mounts. Detach the connector from the back of the sealed beam unit and remove the unit from the car.

CAUTION: *The retainers can have very sharp edges! Wear gloves.*

5. Place the new headlamp in position and connect the wiring harness. Remember to install the rubber boot on the back of the new lamp--its a water seal. Make sure the headlight is right-side up.

6. Turn on the headlights and check the new lamp for proper function, checking both high and low beams before final assembly.

7. Install the retainer and the small screws that hold it.

8. Reinstall the headlight bezel and/or grille

Replaceable Bulb (Semi-Sealed Beam) Fixed Lens Type

NOTE: *This type of light is replace from behind the unit. The lens is not removed or loosened.*

1. Open and support the hood.

2. Remove the wiring connector from the back the lamp. Be careful to release the locking tab completely before removal.

3. Grasp the base of the bulb holder and collar, twist it counterclockwise (as viewed from the engine compartment) and carefully remove the bulb holder and bulb from the housing.

4. Using gloves or a rag, hold the bulb and release the clip on the holder. Remove the bulb.

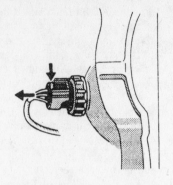

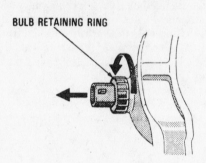

BULB RETAINING RING

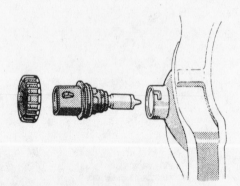

Replacing semi-sealed beam headlight bulb

5. Install the new bulb in the holder and make sure the clip engages firmly.

NOTE: *Hold the new bulb with a clean cloth or a piece of paper. DO NOT touch or grasp the bulb with your fingers. The oils from your skin will produce a hot spot on the glass envelope, shortening bulb life by up to 50%. If the bulb is touched accidentally, clean it with alcohol and a clean rag before installation.*

6. Install the holder and bulb into the housing. Note that the holder has guides which must align with the housing. When the holder is correctly seated, turn the collar clockwise to lock the holder in place.

7. Connect the wiring harness. Turn on the headlights and check the function of the new bulb on both high and low beam.

Manual operation knob on retractable headlight doors

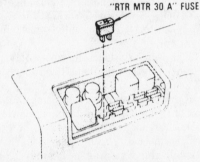

Remove the fuse before operating manual operation knob on retractable headlight doors

RETRACTABLE HEADLIGHTS – MANUAL OPERATION

The retractable headlights can be manually operated if their electrical mechanism fails. To raise or lower the lights, Turn the ignition and headlight switches OFF and pull out the "RTR MTR 30A" fuse. Unless the power is disconnected, there is a danger of the headlights suddenly retracting. Remove the rubber cover from the manual operation knob (under the hood next to the headlight unit) and turn the knob clockwise. Manual operation should only be used if the system has failed; be sure to check the electrical operation of the lights as soon as possible.

When the headlights are retracted, they should match the silhouette of the vehicle body.

Signal and Marker Lights

REMOVAL AND INSTALLATION

Front Turn Signals

NOTE: *This can be done with the car on the ground. Access is improved if the car is safely supported on jackstands.*

1. From behind the bumper, disconnect the electrical connector.
2. Remove the two nuts from the housing.
3. Remove the turn signal lamp housing.

NOTE: *If only the bulb is to be changed, the lens may be removed from the front.*

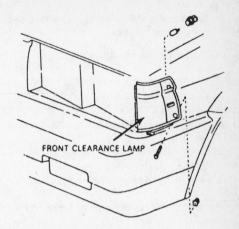

Typical front parking lamp assembly

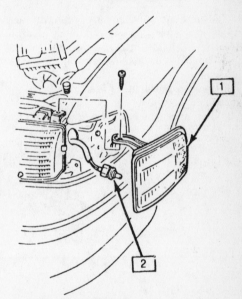

1. Front parking/sidemarker lamp housing
2. Front parking lamp

Typical front parking lamp assembly

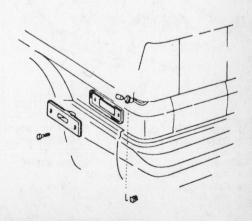

Typical rear side marker lamp

4. Reassemble the housing in reverse order of disassembly procedure.

Side Marker Lights (Parking Lights)

FRONT

1. Remove the retaining screws. On some models, the screws are visible at the rear corner of the lens. On other models, the screw is under the hood.

2. Gently remove the lighting assembly from the body of the car.

3. Disconnect the bulb and socket(s) from the housing.

4. Reassemble in reverse order of removal procedure.

REAR

1. Most early models have separate rear side marker lights. Some later models incorporates the sidelights into the taillight assemblies. Remove the two screws in the side marker lens.

2. Remove the lighting assembly from the body work.

3. Disconnect the bulb and socket from the lighting assembly.

4. Reassemble in reverse order of the removal procedure.

Rear Turn Signal, Brake and Parking Lights

1. Raise the trunk lid and remove or fold back the trunk carpeting.

2. Disconnect the wiring from the bulb holder(s).

3. If a bulb is to be changed, remove the bulb holder from the housing by pressing the tab and lifting out the holder. Replace the bulb and reinsert the housing.

4. Remove the nuts holding the taillight assembly in place. Some may be difficult to reach.

5. Remove the lens assembly from the outside of the car.

6. When reinstalling the lens assembly, pay close attention to the placement of the gasket. It must be correctly positioned and evenly positioned to prevent water from entering the lens or trunk area. Double check the holes through which the threaded studs pass; caulk them with sealer if needed.

7. Install the retaining nuts and tighten them evenly. Do not over tighten them or the lens may crack.

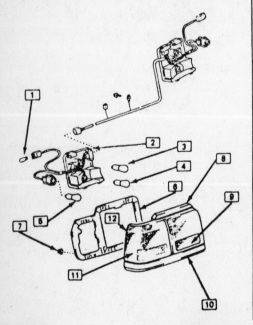

1. Bulb	8. (RH) lens assy
2. Socket & wire	(LH) lens assy
3. Bulb	9. Back up
4. Bulb	10. Stop and tail
5. Bulb	11. Turn
6. Gasket	12. Marker
7. Nuts (6)	

1. Bulb	8. (RH) lens assy.
2. Socket & wire	(LH) lens assy.
3. Bulb	9. Backup
4. Bulb	10. Stop and tail
5. Bulb	11. Moulding
6. Gasket	12. Turn
7. Nuts (6)	13. Marker

Tail light assemblies — Corolla (sedan, left; hatchback, right)

8. Install the electrical connectors. Operate the lights while you check the function at the rear of the car. Replace the trunk carpet.

TRAILER WIRING

Wiring the car for towing is fairly easy. There are a number of good wiring kits available and these should be used, rather than trying to design your own. All trailers will need brake lights and turn signals as well as tail lights and side marker lights. Most states require extra marker lights for overly wide trailers. Also, most states have recently required back-up lights for trailers, and most trailer manufacturers have been building trailers with back-up lights for several years.

Additionally, some trailers have electric brakes. Others can be fitted with them as an option, depending on the weight to be carried.

Add to this an accessories wire, to operate trailer internal equipment or to charge the trailer's battery, and you can have as many as seven wires in the harness.

Determine the equipment on your trailer and buy the wiring kit necessary. The kit will contain all the wires needed, plus a plug adapter set which includes the female plug, mounted on the bumper or hitch, and the male plug to be wired into the trailer harness.

When installing the kit, follow the manufacturer's instructions. The color coding of the wires is standard throughout the industry.

One point to note: some domestic vehicles, and most imported vehicles, have separate turn signals at the rear. On most domestic vehicles, the brake lights and rear turn signals operate with the same bulb. For those vehicles with separate turn signals, you can purchase an isolation unit so that the brake lights won't blink whenever the turn signals are operated.

You can also go to your local electronics supply house and buy four diodes to wire in series with the brake and turn signal bulbs. Diodes will isolate the brake and turn signals. The choice is yours. The isolation units are simple and quick to install, but far more expensive than the diodes. The diodes, however, require more work to install properly, since they require the cutting of each bulb's wire and soldering the diode into place.

The best wiring kits are those with a spring loaded cover on the vehicle mounted socket. This cover prevents dirt and moisture from corroding the terminals. Never let the vehicle socket hang loosely. Always mount it securely to the bumper or hitch. If you don't get a connector with a cover, at least put a piece of tape over the end of the connector when not in use. Most trailer lighting failures can be traced to corroded connectors and/or poor grounds.

CIRCUIT PROTECTION

Fuses

REPLACEMENT

Most models have fuses found in two locations. One fuse box is located within the cabin of the car, just under the extreme left side of the dashboard. This fuse box generally contains the fuses for body and cabin electrical circuits such as the wipers, rear defogger, ignition, cigarette lighter, etc. In addition, various relays and circuit breakers for cabin equipment are also mounted on or around this fuse box.

The second fuse block is found under the hood on the forward part of the left wheelhouse. Some models uses a combination fuse block and relay board while other models has an additional relay board next to the fuse box. The fuses and relays generally control the engine and major electrical systems on the car, such as headlights (separate fuses for left and right), air conditioning, horns, fuel injection, ECM, and fans.

Most models have an additional small panel below the right side dash board containing a fuse (air conditioner) and a relay and circuit breaker for the heater system.

Each fuse location is labeled on the fuse block identifying its primary circuit, but designations such as "Engine", "CDS Fan" or "ECU-B" may not tell you what you need to know. A fuse can control more than one circuit, so check related fuses. As an example, you'll find on the later model vehicles the cruise control drawing its power through the fuse labeled "ECM-IG". This sharing of fuses is necessary to conserve space and wiring.

The individual fuses are of the plastic or "slip-fuse" type. They connect into the fuse box with two small blades, similar to a household wall plug. Removing the fuse with the fingers can be difficult; there isn't a lot to grab

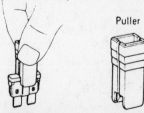

Puller

Use the fuse puller to remove a fuse — do not twist the fuse when removing

onto. For this reason, the fuse box contains a small plastic fuse remover which can be clipped over the back of the fuse and used as a handle to pull it free.

Once the fuse is out, view the fusible element through the clear plastic of the fuse case. An intact fuse will show a continuous horseshoe-shaped wire within the plastic. This element simply connects one blade with the other; if it's intact, power can pass. If the fuse is blown, the link inside the fuse will show a break, possibly accompanied by a small black mark. This shows that the link broke when the electrical current exceeded the wires ability to carry it.

It is possible for the link to become weakened (from age or vibration) without breaking. In this case, the fuse will look good but fail to pass the proper amount of current, causing some electrical item to not work.

Once removed, any fuse may be checked for continuity with an ohmmeter. A reliable general rule is to always replace a suspect fuse with a new one. So doing eliminates one variable in the diagnostic path and may cure the problem outright. Remember, however, that a blown fuse is rarely the cause of a problem; the fuse is opening to protect the circuit from some other malfunction either in the wiring or the component itself. Always replace a fuse or other electrical component with one of equal amperage rating; NEVER increase the ampere rating of the circuit. The number on the back of the fuse body (5, 7.5, 10, 15 ,etc.) indicates the rated amperage of the fuse.

Circuit Breakers

REPLACEMENT

The circuit breakers found on the fuse and relay boards mount to the boards with blades similar to the fuses. Before removing a breaker,

always disconnect the negative battery cable to prevent potentially damaging electrical "spikes" within the system. Simply remove the breaker by pulling straight out from the relay board. Do not twist the relay; damage may occur to the connectors inside the housing.

NOTE: *Some circuit breakers do not reset automatically. Once tripped, they must be reset by hand. Use a small screwdriver or similar tool; insert it in the hole in the back of the breaker and push gently. Once the breaker is reset, either check it for continuity with an ohmmeter or reinstall it and check the circuit for function.*

Reinstall the circuit breaker by pressing it straight in to its mount. Make certain the blades line up correctly and that the circuit breaker is fully seated. Reconnect the negative battery cable and check the circuit for function.

Turn Signal and Hazard Flasher

The combination turn signal and hazard flasher unit is located under the dash on the left side near the fuse box. The flasher unit is not the classic round "can" found on many domestic cars; instead, it is a small box-shaped unit easily mistaken for another relay. Depending on the year and model of your vehicle, the flasher may be plugged directly into the fuse and relay panel or it may be plugged into its own connector and mounted near the fuse panel. The flasher unit emits the familiar ticking sound when the signals are in use and may be identified by touching the case and feeling the "click" as the system functions.

The flasher unit simply unplugs from its connector and a replacement may be installed. Assuming that all the bulbs on the exterior of the

A blown fuse (left) compared with an intact fuse — the fuse cannot be inspected without removing it from the fusebox

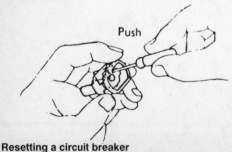

Resetting a circuit breaker

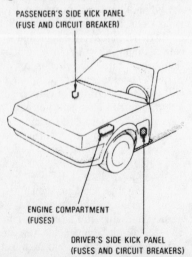

PASSENGER'S SIDE KICK PANEL (FUSE AND CIRCUIT BREAKER)

ENGINE COMPARTMENT (FUSES)

DRIVER'S SIDE KICK PANEL (FUSES AND CIRCUIT BREAKERS)

Typical fuse box location all models — except MR2 vehicle

car are working properly, the correct rate of flash for the turn signals or hazard lights is 60–75 flashes per minute. Very rapid flashing on one side only or no flashing on one side generally indicates a failed bulb rather than a failed flasher.

Communication and "Add-On" Electrical Equipment

The electrical system in your car is designed to perform under reasonable operating conditions without interference between compo-

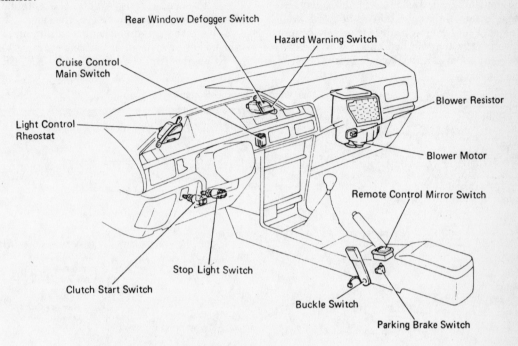

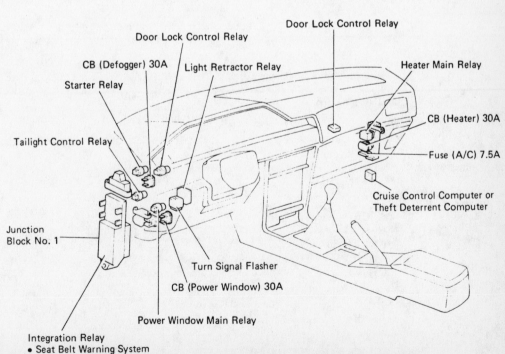

Switches and relays — 1989 Corolla other models and years similar

nents. Before any additional electrical equipment is installed, it is recommended that you consult your Toyota dealer or a reputable repair facility familiar with the vehicle and its systems.

If the vehicle is equipped with mobile radio equipment and or mobile telephone it may have an effect upon the operation of the ECM. Radio frequency interference (RFI) from the communications system can be picked up by the car's wiring harnesses and conducted into the ECM,

giving it the wrong messages at the wrong time. Although well shielded against RFI, the ECM should be further protected through the following steps:

1. Install the antenna as far as possible from the ECM. Since the ECM is located behind the center console area, the antenna should be mounted at the rear of the car.

2. Keep the antenna wiring a minimum of eight inches away from any wiring running to the ECM and from the ECM itself. NEVER

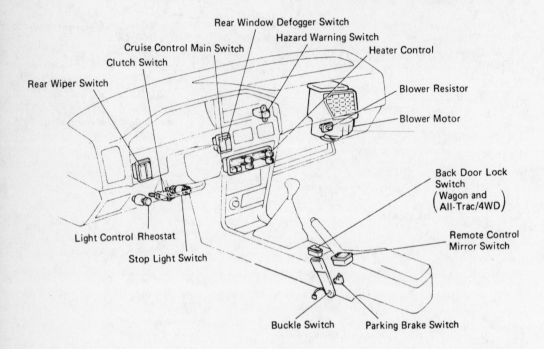

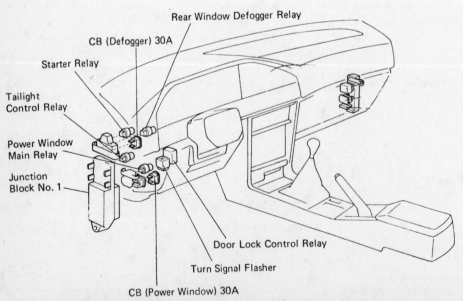

Switches and relays — 1989 Corolla other models and years similar

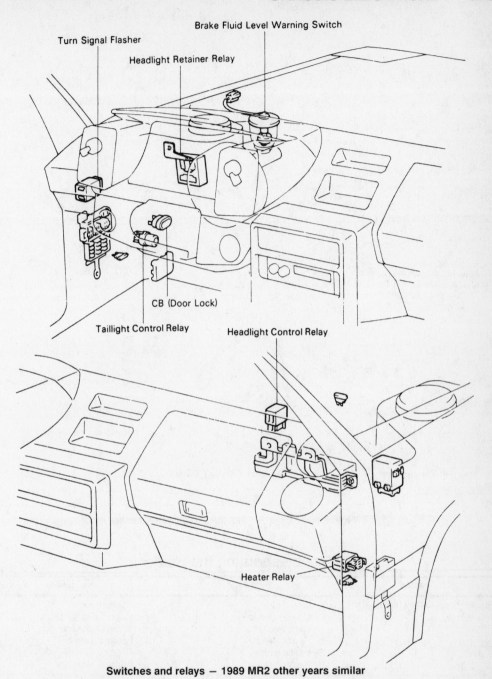

Switches and relays — 1989 MR2 other years similar

wind the antenna wire around any other wiring.

3. Mount the equipment as far from the ECM as possible. Be very careful during installation not to drill through any wires or short a wire harness with a mounting screw.

4. Insure that the feed wires to the equip-ment are properly and tightly connected. Loose connectors can cause interference.

5. Make certain that the equipment is prop-erly grounded to the car. Poor grounding can damage expensive equipment.

6. Make sure the antenna is "trimmed" or adjusted for optimum function.

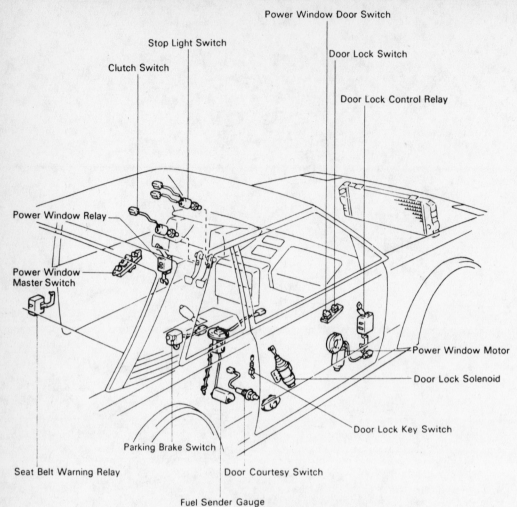

Power Window Door Switch

Stop Light Switch

Door Lock Switch

Clutch Switch

Door Lock Control Relay

Power Window Relay

Power Window Master Switch

Power Window Motor

Door Lock Solenoid

Door Lock Key Switch

Parking Brake Switch

Seat Belt Warning Relay

Door Courtesy Switch

Fuel Sender Gauge

Switches and relays — 1989 MR2 other years similar

Troubleshooting the Heater

Problem	Cause	Solution
Blower motor will not turn at any speed	• Blown fuse • Loose connection • Defective ground • Faulty switch • Faulty motor • Faulty resistor	• Replace fuse • Inspect and tighten • Clean and tighten • Replace switch • Replace motor • Replace resistor
Blower motor turns at one speed only	• Faulty switch • Faulty resistor	• Replace switch • Replace resistor
Blower motor turns but does not circulate air	• Intake blocked • Fan not secured to the motor shaft	• Clean intake • Tighten security
Heater will not heat	• Coolant does not reach proper temperature • Heater core blocked internally • Heater core air-bound • Blend-air door not in proper position	• Check and replace thermostat if necessary • Flush or replace core if necessary • Purge air from core • Adjust cable
Heater will not defrost	• Control cable adjustment incorrect • Defroster hose damaged	• Adjust control cable • Replace defroster hose

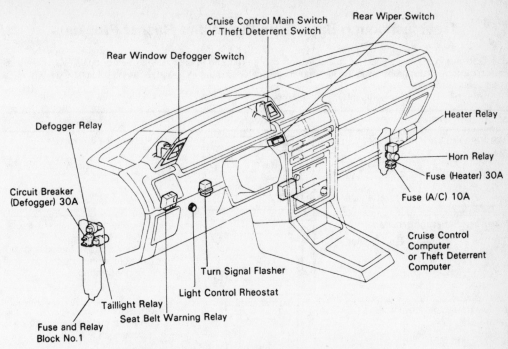

Cruise Control Main Switch
or Theft Deterrent Switch

Rear Wiper Switch

Rear Window Defogger Switch

Defogger Relay

Heater Relay

Horn Relay

Fuse (Heater) 30A

Fuse (A/C) 10A

Circuit Breaker
(Defogger) 30A

Cruise Control
Computer
or Theft Deterrent
Computer

Turn Signal Flasher

Light Control Rheostat

Taillight Relay

Seat Belt Warning Relay

Fuse and Relay
Block No.1

Switches and rewlays — 1989 Tercel other years similar

Troubleshooting Basic Windshield Wiper Problems

Problem	Cause	Solution
Electric Wipers		

Wipers do not operate—
Wiper motor heats up or hums
	• Internal motor defect
	• Bent or damaged linkage
	• Arms improperly installed on link-
	  ing pivots
		• Replace motor
		• Repair or replace linkage
		• Position linkage in park and rein-
		  stall wiper arms

Wipers do not operate— No current to motor	• Fuse or circuit breaker blown • Loose, open or broken wiring • Defective switch • Defective or corroded terminals • No ground circuit for motor or switch	• Replace fuse or circuit breaker • Repair wiring and connections • Replace switch • Replace or clean terminals • Repair ground circuits
Wipers do not operate— Motor runs	• Linkage disconnected or broken	• Connect wiper linkage or replace broken linkage
Vacuum Wipers		

Wipers do not operate	• Control switch or cable inoperative
	• Loss of engine vacuum to wiper
	  motor (broken hoses, low
	  engine vacuum, defective
	  vacuum/fuel pump)
	• Linkage broken or disconnected
	• Defective wiper motor
		• Repair or replace switch or cable
		• Check vacuum lines, engine
		  vacuum and fuel pump
		
		• Repair linkage
		• Replace wiper motor

Wipers stop on engine acceleration	• Leaking vacuum hoses • Dry windshield • Oversize wiper blades • Defective vacuum/fuel pump	• Repair or replace hoses • Wet windshield with washers • Replace with proper size wiper blades • Replace pump

Troubleshooting Basic Turn Signal and Flasher Problems

Most problems in the turn signals or flasher system can be reduced to defective flashers or bulbs, which are easily replaced. Occasionally, problems in the turn signals are traced to the switch in the steering column, which will require professional service.

F = Front   R = Rear   ● = Lights off   ○ = Lights on

Problem		Solution
Turn signals light, but do not flash		• Replace the flasher
No turn signals light on either side		• Check the fuse. Replace if defective. • Check the flasher by substitution • Check for open circuit, short circuit or poor ground
Both turn signals on one side don't work		• Check for bad bulbs • Check for bad ground in both housings
One turn signal light on one side doesn't work		• Check and/or replace bulb • Check for corrosion in socket. Clean contacts. • Check for poor ground at socket
Turn signal flashes too fast or too slow		• Check any bulb on the side flashing too fast. A heavy-duty bulb is probably installed in place of a regular bulb. • Check the bulb flashing too slow. A standard bulb was probably installed in place of a heavy-duty bulb. • Check for loose connections or corrosion at the bulb socket
Indicator lights don't work in either direction		• Check if the turn signals are working • Check the dash indicator lights • Check the flasher by substitution
One indicator light doesn't light		• On systems with 1 dash indicator: See if the lights work on the same side. Often the filaments have been reversed in systems combining stoplights with taillights and turn signals. Check the flasher by substitution • On systems with 2 indicators: Check the bulbs on the same side Check the indicator light bulb Check the flasher by substitution

Troubleshooting Basic Lighting Problems

Problem	Cause	Solution
Lights		
One or more lights don't work, but others do	• Defective bulb(s) • Blown fuse(s) • Dirty fuse clips or light sockets • Poor ground circuit	• Replace bulb(s) • Replace fuse(s) • Clean connections • Run ground wire from light socket housing to car frame
Lights burn out quickly	• Incorrect voltage regulator setting or defective regulator • Poor battery/alternator connections	• Replace voltage regulator • Check battery/alternator connections
Lights go dim	• Low/discharged battery • Alternator not charging • Corroded sockets or connections • Low voltage output	• Check battery • Check drive belt tension; repair or replace alternator • Clean bulb and socket contacts and connections • Replace voltage regulator
Lights flicker	• Loose connection • Poor ground • Circuit breaker operating (short circuit)	• Tighten all connections • Run ground wire from light housing to car frame • Check connections and look for bare wires
Lights "flare"—Some flare is normal on acceleration—if excessive, see "Lights Burn Out Quickly"	• High voltage setting	• Replace voltage regulator
Lights glare—approaching drivers are blinded	• Lights adjusted too high • Rear springs or shocks sagging • Rear tires soft	• Have headlights aimed • Check rear springs/shocks • Check/correct rear tire pressure
Turn Signals		
Turn signals don't work in either direction	• Blown fuse • Defective flasher • Loose connection	• Replace fuse • Replace flasher • Check/tighten all connections
Right (or left) turn signal only won't work	• Bulb burned out • Right (or left) indicator bulb burned out • Short circuit	• Replace bulb • Check/replace indicator bulb • Check/repair wiring
Flasher rate too slow or too fast	• Incorrect wattage bulb • Incorrect flasher	• Flasher bulb • Replace flasher (use a variable load flasher if you pull a trailer)
Indicator lights do not flash (burn steadily)	• Burned out bulb • Defective flasher	• Replace bulb • Replace flasher
Indicator lights do not light at all	• Burned out indicator bulb • Defective flasher	• Replace indicator bulb • Replace flasher

Troubleshooting Basic Dash Gauge Problems

Problem	Cause	Solution
Coolant Temperature Gauge		
Gauge reads erratically or not at all	• Loose or dirty connections • Defective sending unit	• Clean/tighten connections • Bi-metal gauge: remove the wire from the sending unit. Ground the wire for an instant. If the gauge registers, replace the sending unit.
	• Defective gauge	• Magnetic gauge: disconnect the wire at the sending unit. With ignition ON gauge should register COLD. Ground the wire; gauge should register HOT.
Ammeter Gauge—Turn Headlights ON (do not start engine). Note reaction		
Ammeter shows charge Ammeter shows discharge Ammeter does not move	• Connections reversed on gauge • Ammeter is OK • Loose connections or faulty wiring • Defective gauge	• Reinstall connections • Nothing • Check/correct wiring • Replace gauge
Oil Pressure Gauge		
Gauge does not register or is inaccurate	• On mechanical gauge, Bourdon tube may be bent or kinked	• Check tube for kinks or bends preventing oil from reaching the gauge
	• Low oil pressure	• Remove sending unit. Idle the engine briefly. If no oil flows from sending unit hole, problem is in engine.
	• Defective gauge	• Remove the wire from the sending unit and ground it for an instant with the ignition ON. A good gauge will go to the top of the scale.
	• Defective wiring	• Check the wiring to the gauge. If it's OK and the gauge doesn't register when grounded, replace the gauge.
	• Defective sending unit	• If the wiring is OK and the gauge functions when grounded, replace the sending unit
All Gauges		
All gauges do not operate	• Blown fuse • Defective instrument regulator	• Replace fuse • Replace instrument voltage regulator
All gauges read low or erratically	• Defective or dirty instrument voltage regulator	• Clean contacts or replace
All gauges pegged	• Loss of ground between instrument voltage regulator and car • Defective instrument regulator	• Check ground • Replace regulator
Warning Lights		
Light(s) do not come on when ignition is ON, but engine is not started	• Defective bulb • Defective wire	• Replace bulb • Check wire from light to sending unit
	• Defective sending unit	• Disconnect the wire from the sending unit and ground it. Replace the sending unit if the light comes on with the ignition ON.
Light comes on with engine running	• Problem in individual system • Defective sending unit	• Check system • Check sending unit (see above)

MANUAL TRANSMISSION

Identification

The transmission model identification number is located on the bottom of the Vehicle Identification Number (VIN) plate.

ADJUSTMENTS

On all Toyota models with manual transmission, no external adjustments are needed or possible.

Back-up Light Switch

REMOVAL AND INSTALLATION

1. Raise and safely support the vehicle.
2. Disconnect the electrical connector from the back-up light switch.

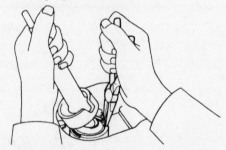

Removing shift lever — manual transmission

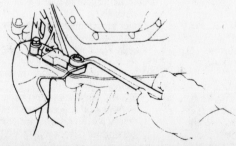

Removing stiffener plate — manual transmission

3. Loosen and remove the back-up light switch from the transmission case.
4. Remove the gasket. Discard the gasket and purchase a new one.
5. Install the new gasket onto the switch.
6. Screw the switch and gasket into the transmission case. Torque the switch to 27 ft. lbs.
7. Connect the electrical connector and lower the vehicle. Check the back-up light switch for proper operation.

Transmission

REMOVAL AND INSTALLATION

1984–87 Corolla RWD

1. Disconnect the negative battery cable.
2. Loosen the distributor bolt and rotate the distributor so it will not touch the cowl.
3. Remove the console and the shift control lever.
4. Raise and safely support the vehicle.
5. Remove the drain and filler plugs and drain the transmission.
6. Remove the front exhaust pipe by performing the following procedures:

    a. Remove the exhaust pipe-to-exhaust manifold nuts and separate the exhaust pipe from the manifold.

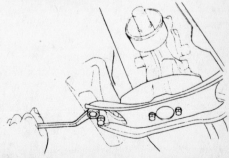

Removing the crossmember — manual transmission

Troubleshooting the Manual Transmission

Problem	Cause	Solution
Transmission shifts hard	• Clutch adjustment incorrect • Clutch linkage or cable binding • Shift rail binding	• Adjust clutch • Lubricate or repair as necessary • Check for mispositioned selector arm roll pin, loose cover bolts, worn shift rail bores, worn shift rail, distorted oil seal, or extension housing not aligned with case. Repair as necessary.
	• Internal bind in transmission caused by shift forks, selector plates, or synchronizer assemblies • Clutch housing misalignment • Incorrect lubricant • Block rings and/or cone seats worn	• Remove, dissemble and inspect transmission. Replace worn or damaged components as necessary. • Check runout at rear face of clutch housing • Drain and refill transmission • Blocking ring to gear clutch tooth face clearance must be 0.030 inch or greater. If clearance is correct it may still be necessary to inspect blocking rings and cone seats for excessive wear. Repair as necessary.
Gear clash when shifting from one gear to another	• Clutch adjustment incorrect • Clutch linkage or cable binding • Clutch housing misalignment • Lubricant level low or incorrect lubricant • Gearshift components, or synchronizer assemblies worn or damaged	• Adjust clutch • Lubricate or repair as necessary • Check runout at rear of clutch housing • Drain and refill transmission and check for lubricant leaks if level was low. Repair as necessary. • Remove, disassemble and inspect transmission. Replace worn or damaged components as necessary.
Transmission noisy	• Lubricant level low or incorrect lubricant • Clutch housing-to-engine, or transmission-to-clutch housing bolts loose • Dirt, chips, foreign material in transmission • Gearshift mechanism, transmission gears, or bearing components worn or damaged • Clutch housing misalignment	• Drain and refill transmission. If lubricant level was low, check for leaks and repair as necessary. • Check and correct bolt torque as necessary • Drain, flush, and refill transmission • Remove, disassemble and inspect transmission. Replace worn or damaged components as necessary. • Check runout at rear face of clutch housing
Jumps out of gear	• Clutch housing misalignment • Gearshift lever loose • Offset lever nylon insert worn or lever attaching nut loose • Gearshift mechanism, shift forks, selector plates, interlock plate, selector arm, shift rail, detent plugs, springs or shift cover worn or damaged • Clutch shaft or roller bearings worn or damaged	• Check runout at rear face of clutch housing • Check lever for worn fork. Tighten loose attaching bolts. • Remove gearshift lever and check for loose offset lever nut or worn insert. Repair or replace as necessary. • Remove, disassemble and inspect transmission cover assembly. Replace worn or damaged components as necessary. • Replace clutch shaft or roller bearings as necessary

Troubleshooting the Manual Transmission

Problem	Cause	Solution
Jumps out of gear (cont.)	• Gear teeth worn or tapered, synchronizer assemblies worn or damaged, excessive end play caused by worn thrust washers or output shaft gears • Pilot bushing worn	• Remove, disassemble, and inspect transmission. Replace worn or damaged components as necessary. • Replace pilot bushing
Will not shift into one gear	• Gearshift selector plates, interlock plate, or selector arm, worn, damaged, or incorrectly assembled • Shift rail detent plunger worn, spring broken, or plug loose • Gearshift lever worn or damaged • Synchronizer sleeves or hubs, damaged or worn	• Remove, disassemble, and inspect transmission cover assembly. Repair or replace components as necessary. • Tighten plug or replace worn or damaged components as necessary • Replace gearshift lever • Remove, disassemble and inspect transmission. Replace worn or damaged components.
Locked in one gear—cannot be shifted out	• Shift rail(s) worn or broken, shifter fork bent, setscrew loose, center detent plug missing or worn • Broken gear teeth on countershaft gear, clutch shaft, or reverse idler gear Gearshift lever broken or worn, shift mechanism in cover incorrectly assembled or broken, worn damaged gear train components	• Inspect and replace worn or damaged parts • Inspect and replace damaged part • Disassemble transmission. Replace damaged parts or assemble correctly.

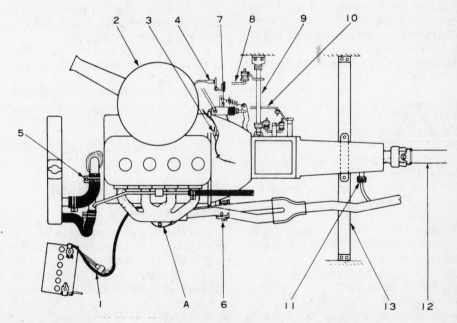

A. Exhaust pipe flange
1. Positive battery cable (+)
2. Air cleaner
3. Back-up lamp connector
4. Torque rod
5. Radiator hose
6. Exhaust pipe clamp
7. Master cylinder w/line support bracket
8. Accelerator linkage
9. Pivot—not applicable in USA
10. Bellcrank—not applicable in the USA
11. Speedometer cable
12. Driveshaft
13. Rear supporting crossmember

Early model transmission removal and installation

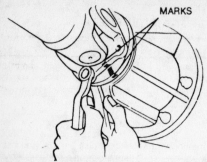

MARKS

Matchmark the driveshaft flange to the differential assembly before removal

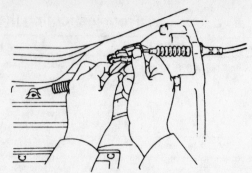

Disconnecting the clutch cable from the release fork

b. Remove the clamp from the front exhaust pipe.

c. Disconnect the front exhaust pipe from the catalytic converter.

d. Remove the brackets and the front pipe.

7. Remove the driveshaft by performing the following procedures:

a. Place matchmarks on the driveshaft-to-differential flanges.

b. Remove the driveshaft-to-differential flange nuts, washers and bolts.

c. Remove the center support bearing-to-chassis bolts.

d. Separate the driveshaft from the differential.

e. Lower the driveshaft and pull it from the extension housing.

8. Disconnect the speedometer cable and the back-up light switch connector.

9. Remove the clutch release cylinder-to-flywheel housing bolts and move the cylinder aside.

10. Disconnect the electrical connectors from the starter.

11. Remove the starter bolts and the starter from the vehicle.

12. Using a transmission jack, connect it to and support the transmission.

NOTE: *If may be necessary to position a floor jack and board under the engine to support its weight.*

13. Remove the crossmember-to-chassis bolts, the crossmember-to-transmission mount bolts and the crossmember.

14. Remove the stiffener plate-to-transmission bolts and the plate.

15. Remove the transmission-to-engine bolts, lower the transmission, move it rearward and remove it from the vehicle.

16. To install the transmission align the input shaft with the clutch disc, push the transmission upward and forward until it aligns with the engine. Torque the flywheel housing-to-engine bolts to 53 ft. lbs.

17. Raise the transmission.

18. Install the crossmember-to-transmission

bolts and the crossmember-to-chassis bolts and torque the bolts to 38 ft. lbs.

19. Install the stiffener plate-to-transmission bolts and torque to 27 ft. lbs.

20. Install the exhaust pipe bracket and torque the bolts to 27 ft. lbs.

21. Install the starter and torque the bolts to 27 ft. lbs.

22. Install the clutch release cylinder.

23. Reconnect the back-up light connector and the speedometer cable.

24. Install the driveshaft by performing the following procedures:

a. Insert the driveshaft yoke into the extension housing.

b. Align the driveshaft-to-differential flange matchmarks, install bolts, washers and nuts and torque to 31 ft. lbs.

c. Install the center support bearing-to-chassis bolts and torque to 30 ft. lbs.

25. Install the front exhaust pipe and torque the exhaust pipe-to-manifold nuts to 46 ft. lbs.

26. Refill the transmission if necessary.

27. Install the shift lever and the console box.

28. Adjust the ignition timing and road test the vehicle.

Transmission Overhaul

Before Disassembly

Cleanliness is an important factor in the overhaul of the manual transmission. Before opening up this unit, the entire outside of the transmission assembly should be cleaned, preferably with a high pressure washer such as a car wash spray unit. Dirt entering the transmission internal parts will negate all the time and effort spent on the overhaul. During inspection and reassembly all parts should be thoroughly cleaned with solvent then dried with compressed air. Wiping cloths and rags should not be used to dry parts.

Wheel bearing grease, long used to hold thrust washers and lube parts, should not be used. Lube seals with clean transmission oil

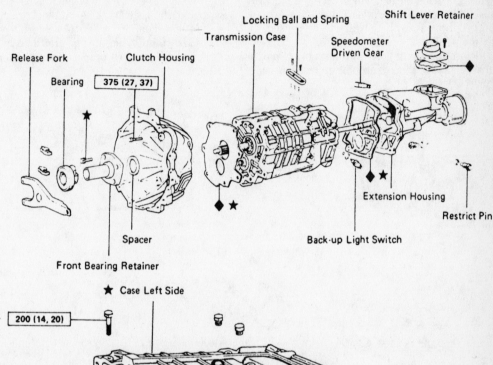

Locking Ball and Spring

Shift Lever Retainer

Transmission Case

Speedometer
Driven Gear

Release Fork

Clutch Housing

Bearing

375 (27, 37)

Extension Housing

Restrict Pin

Back-up Light Switch

Spacer

Front Bearing Retainer

★ Case Left Side

★ 200 (14, 20)

Output Shaft

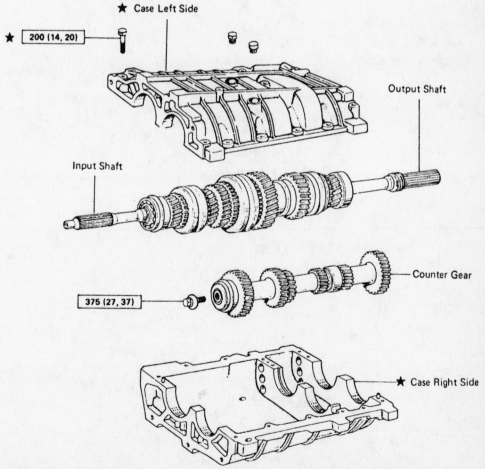

Input Shaft

Counter Gear

375 (27, 37)

★ Case Right Side

Exploded view of the transmission and components

and use ordinary unmedicated petroleum jelly to hold the thrust washers and to ease the assembly of seals, since it will not leave a harmful residue as grease often will. Do not use solvent on neoprene seals, if they are to be reused, or thrust washers.

Before installing bolts into aluminum parts, always dip the threads into clean transmission oil. Antiseize compound can also be used to prevent bolts from galling the aluminum and seizing. Always use a torque wrench to keep from stripping the threads. The internal snaprings should be expanded and the external rings should be compressed, if they are to be reused. This will help insure proper seating when installed.

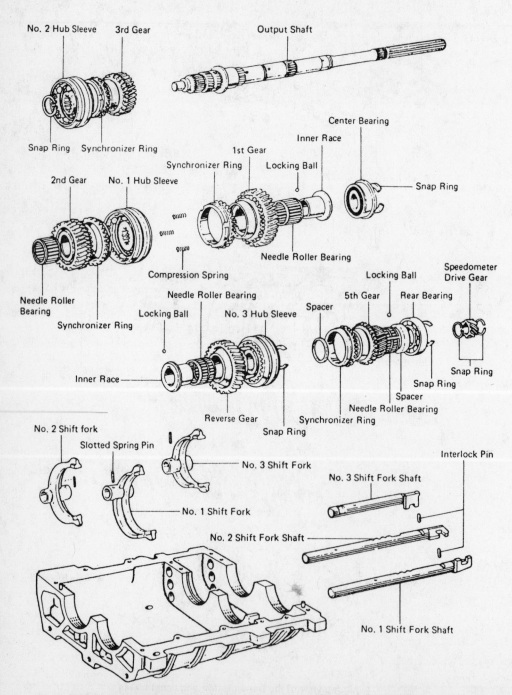

Exploded view of the output shaft assembly and shifting fork assemblies

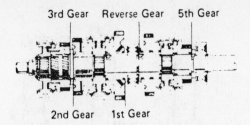

3rd Gear   Reverse Gear   5th Gear

2nd Gear   1st Gear

Location of the output shaft thrust clearances

TRANSMISSION DISASSEMBLY

1. Remove the back-up light switch, the speedometer driven gear, the shift lever retainer restrict pins, the clutch release bearing and the clutch fork.

2. Remove the front bearing retainer-to-clutch housing bolts, the retainer and the spacer.

3. Remove the clutch housing-to-transmission bolts and the clutch housing.

4. Remove the extension housing-to-transmission case bolts and the extension housing.

5. From the top the transmission, remove the locking ball plate cover-to-transmission bolts and the cover.

6. Using a magnetic finger, remove the locking balls and springs from the transmission.

7. Remove the transmission's left case-to-right case bolts and separate left case from the right case, using a plastic hammer.

8. From the right case, lift and remove the input, output and countershafts.

9. Remove the shift forks and shift shafts by performing the following procedures:

    a. Using a pin punch and a hammer, drive the spring pin from the No. 1 shift fork through the hole in the case.

    b. Using a pin punch and a hammer, drive the spring pin from the No. 2 and No. 3 shift forks.

    c. Move the shift fork shafts to the **N** position and pull them from the case.

10. Using a magnetic finger, remove the interlock pins from the shift shaft holes.

UNIT DISASSEMBLY AND ASSEMBLY

Output Shaft

DISASSEMBLY

1. Using a feeler gauge, measure the thrust clearance of each gear.

Output shaft thrust gear clearances:
- 1st — 0.150–0.275mm
- 2nd — 0.150–0.250mm
- 3rd — 0.150–0.300mm
- 5th — 0.100–0.930mm
- Reverse — 0.200–0.325mm

2. Using snapring pliers, remove the speedometer drive snapring, the speedometer drive and the other snapring.

3. Remove the 5th gear assembly by performing the following procedures:

    a. Using 2 pry bars and a hammer, tap the rear bearing snapring from the output shaft.

    b. Using a bearing remover tool, press the rear bearing from the output shaft.

    c. Remove the rear bearing spacer.

    d. Remove the 5th gear, the synchronizer ring and the needle roller bearing.

    e. Using a magnetic finger, remove the locking ball from the shaft.

    f. Remove the needle roller bearing spacer.

4. Remove the No. 3 hub assembly and reverse gear by performing the following procedures:

    a. Using 2 pry bars and a hammer, tap the No. 3 hub sleeve assembly snapring from the output shaft.

    b. Using a shop press, support the reverse gear, then, press the output shaft from the reverse gear and the hub assembly.

    c. Remove the bearing and inner race.

    d. Using a magnetic finger, remove the locking ball from the shaft.

    e. Using 2 pry bars and a hammer, tap the next snapring from the output shaft.

5. Remove the center bearing and 1st gear assembly by performing the following procedures:

    a. Using a shop press, support the 1st gear and the bearing, then, press the output shaft from the center bearing and the 1st gear.

    b. Remove the synchronizer ring.

    c. Remove the locking ball and the springs.

6. Using a shop press, support the 2nd gear, then, press the output shaft from the No. 1 hub sleeve assembly, the synchronizer ring and the 2nd gear. Remove the needle roller bearing.

7. Using snapring pliers, remove the snapring.

8. Using a shop press, support the 3rd gear, then, press the output shaft from the No. 2 hub sleeve assembly, the synchronizer ring and the 3rd gear.

INSPECTION

1. Inspect the output shaft and inner races by performing the following procedures:

    a. Using vernier calipers, measure the output shaft flange thickness; it should be greater than 0.157 in. (4.0mm).

    b. Using vernier calipers, measure th inner race flange thickness; it should l greater than 0.150 in. (3.8mm).

c. Using a micrometer, measure the outer diameter of the output shaft journals; they should be greater than:
- 2nd gear – 36.80mm
- 3rd gear – 37.80mm
- 5th gear – 27.30mm

d. Using a micrometer, measure the outer diameter of each inner race; it should be greater than 1.4508 in. (36.85mm).

e. Using a dial indicator, check the shaft runnout; it should be less than 0.0024 in. (0.06mm).

2. Using a dial indicator, measure the oil clearance between the 1st gear and the inner race, with the needle bearing installed. Standard clearance is 0.0004–0.0024 in. (0.009–0.060mm); maximum clearance is 0.0059 in. (0.15mm). If the clearance exceeds the limit, replace the gear, the inner race or the needle roller bearing.

3. Using a dial indicator, measure the oil clearance between the 2nd gear, the 5th gear and the output shaft, with the needle roller bearing installed. Standard clearance is 0.0004–0.0024 in. (0.009–0.060mm) for the 2nd gear or 0.0004–0.0020 in. (0.010–0.050mm) for the 5th gear; maximum clearance is 0.0059 in. (0.15mm). If the clearance exceeds the limit, replace the gear, the output shaft or the needle roller bearing.

4. Using a dial indicator, measure the oil clearance between the 3rd gear and the output shaft. Standard clearance is 0.0024–0.0040 in. (0.060–0.101mm); maximum clearance is 0.0079 in. (0.20mm). If the clearance exceeds the limit, replace the gear or the output shaft.

5. Inspect the synchronizer rings by performing the following procedures:

a. Assemble the synchronizer rings onto the gears and turn them to inspect the braking action.

b. Using a feeler gauge, measure the clearance between the synchronizer ring back and the gear splined end. Standard clearance is 0.039–0.079 in. (1.0–2.0mm); minimum clearance is 0.031 in. (0.8mm). If the clearance is less than the limit, replace the synchronizer ring.

6. Using a feeler gauge, assemble the shifting forks onto the hub sleeves and measure the clearance between the fork and the sleeve. Maximum clearance is 0.031 in. (0.8mm). If the clearance exceeds the limit, replace the shift fork of the hub sleeve.

ASSEMBLY

1. Assemble each clutch hub and shifting keys onto its hub sleeve; be careful not to install them backwards. Install the shifting key

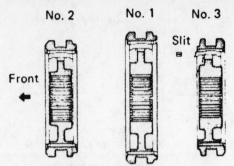

View of the clutch hubs to be installed on the output shaft

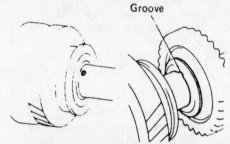

Positioning the reverse gear groove over the locking ball on the output shaft

springs under the keys; position the springs so the end gaps are not aligned.

2. Install the 2nd gear and No. 1 clutch hub by performing the following procedures:

a. Lubricate the output shaft with multipurpose grease.

b. Install the needle roller bearing.

c. Place the synchronizer ring on the gear and align the ring slots with the shifting keys.

d. Using a shop press, press the 2nd gear and No. 1 clutch hub onto the output shaft.

e. Install the 3 springs into the clutch hub holes.

3. Install the locking ball and 1st gear assembly by performing the following procedures:

a. Position the locking ball into the shaft.

b. Install the needle roller bearings.

c. Assemble the 1st gear, the synchronizer ring, the needle roller bearing and the bearing inner race.

d. Position the inner race securely over the locking ball.

e. Install the 1st gear assembly onto the output shaft with the synchronizer ring slots aligned with the shifting keys.

4. Using a shop press and a support tool, press the center bearing onto the output shaft. NOTE: *When installing center bearing, support the 1st gear and the inner race by hand. Be sure the flange is facing rearward.*

5. Using a snapring which will allow 0–0.004 in. (0–0.1mm) axial play, install it onto the output shaft.

6. Install the locking ball and the reverse gear by performing the following procedures:

   a. Install the locking ball onto the shaft.

   b. Position the inner race and roller bearing into the reverse gear.

   c. When installing the reverse gear onto the output shaft, fit the inner race groove securely over the locking ball.

7. Using a shop press, support the reverse gear by hand and press the No. 3 clutch hub assembly onto the output shaft.

8. Using a snapring which will allow 0–0.004 in. (0–0.1mm) axial play, install it onto the output shaft.

9. Install the 5th gear and spacer by performing the following procedures:

   a. Install the needle roller bearing spacer.

   b. Position the synchronizer ring and the roller bearing onto the gear.

   c. Install the 5th gear onto the shaft with the synchronizer ring slots aligned with the shifting keys.

   d. Install the locking ball onto the shaft.

   e. Install the spacer by securely positioning it over the locking ball.

10. Using a shop press and a support tool, support the rear bearing and press it onto the output shaft.

NOTE: *When installing the rear bearing, support the 5th gear and inner race by hand. Be sure the ball shield is positioned rearward.*

11. Using a snapring which will allow 0–0.004 in. (0–0.1mm) axial play, install it onto the output shaft.

12. Install the 3rd gear and No. 2 clutch hub by performing the following procedures:

   a. Lubricate the shaft with multi-purpose grease.

   b. Install the 3rd gear and synchronizer ring onto the shaft.

   c. Install the No. 2 clutch hub onto the shaft and align the ring slots with the keys.

   d. Using a shop press and a collar, press the No. 2 clutch hub onto the shaft.

13. Using a snapring which will allow 0–0.004 in. (0–0.1mm) axial play, install it onto the output shaft.

14. Using a feeler gauge, measure all of the gear thrust clearances on the output shaft.

Output shaft thrust gear clearances:
- 1st – 0.150–0.275mm
- 2nd – 0.150–0.250mm
- 3rd – 0.150–0.300mm
- 5th – 0.100–0.930mm
- Reverse – 0.200–0.325mm

15. Install the speedometer drive gear and snaprings onto the output shaft.

Input Shaft

DISASSEMBLY

1. Using snapring pliers, remove the snapring from the input shaft.

2. Using a shop press, press the bearing from the input shaft.

INSPECTION

1. Inspect the bearing for wear and/or damage.

2. Inspect the input shaft for wear, broken splines and/or damage.

3. If necessary, replace the damaged parts.

ASSEMBLY

1. Using a shop press, press the new bearing onto the input shaft until it seats.

2. Select a snapring which will allow minimum axial play and install it onto the input shaft.

Countershaft

DISASSEMBLY

1. Remove the countershaft's front bearing by performing the following procedures:

   a. Remove the lock plate bolt and the lock plate.

   b. Using snapring pliers, remove the snapring.

   c. Using a bearing removal tool, press the bearing from the countershaft.

2. Remove the countershaft's rear bearing, 5th gear, reverse gear and center bearing by performing the following procedures:

   a. Using snapring pliers, remove the snapring.

   b. Using a shop press and a 12mm socket, press the rear bearing and the 5th gear from the countershaft.

   c. Remove the reverse gear and the center bearing.

INSPECTION

1. Inspect the bearings for wear and/or damage.

2. Inspect the countershaft for wear, broken gear teeth and/or damage.

3. If necessary, replace the damaged parts.

ASSEMBLY

1. Assemble the countershaft's rear bearing, 5th gear, reverse gear and center bearing by performing the following procedures:

   a. Assemble the center bearing and the reverse gear onto the countershaft.

   b. Using a shop press and a bearing installation tool, press the rear bearing and the 5th gear onto the countershaft.

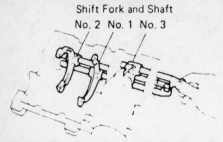

Positioning the shifting forks and shafts into the case

NOTE: *When installing the bearing and 5th gear, lift the reverse gear to the upper side before pressing.*

c. Select a snapring which will allow minimum axial play and install it onto the shaft.

2. Install the front bearing by performing the following procedures:

a. Using a shop press and socket, support the front bearing inner race and press the bearing onto the countershaft.

b. Install the snapring.

c. Install the lock plate and torque the bolt to 27 ft. lbs. (37 Nm).

TRANSMISSION ASSEMBLY

1. Install the reverse idler gear and shaft into the right transmission case and torque the bolt to 11 ft. lbs. (15 Nm); be sure to fit the projected part of the thrust washer into the case slot.

2. Grease the shift fork shaft interlock pins and install them into the case.

3. Install the shift forks and shafts by performing the following procedures:

a. Assemble the shafts with their locking ball grooves positioned toward the top of the case.

b. Insert each shaft through each fork and push them to their **N** positions.

c. Install the fork shafts and forks in the following orders:

• No. 2 fork shaft and the No. 2 shift fork
• No. 1 fork shaft and the No. 1 shift fork
• No. 3 fork shaft and the No. 3 shift fork

d. Move the No. 2 fork shaft into the 3rd speed position; do not move the No. 1 and No. 3 fork shafts.

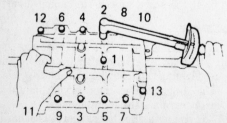

Torquing the transmission case bolts in numerical order

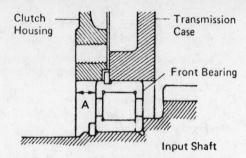

Measuring the front bearing retainer spacer

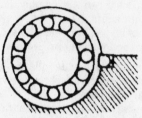

Installing the countershaft and lock pin into the case

e. Align the shafts with the fork pin holes and drive the slotted spring pins into the holes using a pin punch.

4. Install the input and output shafts by performing the following procedures:

a. Lubricate the needle roller bearing with multi-purpose grease.

b. Position the synchronizer ring onto the gear and align the ring slots with the shifting keys.

c. Move the shifting forks and hubs to the **N** position and assemble the input and output shafts into the case.

5. Install the countershaft into the case by meshing the gear teeth and fit the lock pin into the case groove.

6. Install the left case by performing the following procedures:

a. Clean the mating and bearing surfaces of the case.

b. Using sealant, apply it to the mating surfaces and assemble the cases.

c. Apply sealant to the bolt threads and torque, in numerical order, using 3–4 passes, to 14 ft. lbs. (20 Nm).

7. After assembling the case, turn the input shaft and output shafts to make sure they turn freely; make sure shifting can be made smoothly in all positions.

8. Install the extension housing by performing the following procedures:

a. Apply sealant to the mating surfaces.

b. Engage the end of the shift and select levers to the No. 2 fork shaft; be careful not to damage the oil seal in the extension housing.

TORQUE SPECIFICATIONS

Part	ft. lbs.	Nm
Transmission case RH-to-LH	14	20
Extension housing-to-transmission case	27	37
Restrict pin-to-extension housing	29	39
Shift lever retainer-to-extension housing	9	13
Front bearing retainer-to-clutch housing	13	18
Clutch housing-to-transmission case	27	37
Counter gear front bearing lock plate	27	37
Reverse idler shaft lock bolt	11	15
Back-up light switch	24	32

OUTPUT SHAFT SPECIFICATIONS

Item		in.	mm
2nd gear journal diameter	Limit	1.4488	36.80
3rd gear journal diameter	Limit	1.4882	37.80
5th gear journal diameter	Limit	1.0748	27.30
Flange thickness	Limit	0.157	4.0
Runout	Limit	0.0024	0.06

CLEARANCE SPECIFICATIONS

Part			in.	mm
Gear thrust	1st	STD	0.0059–0.0108	0.150–0.275
		Limit	0.020	0.5
	2nd	STD	0.0059–0.0098	0.150–0.250
		Limit	0.020	0.5
	3rd	STD	0.0059–0.0118	0.150–0.300
		Limit	0.024	0.6
	5th	STD	0.0039–0.0366	0.100–0.930
		Limit	0.039	1.0
	Reverse	STD	0.0079–0.0128	0.200–0.325
		Limit	0.024	0.6
	Reverse idle	STD	0.0020–0.0197	0.05–0.50
		Limit	0.039	1.0
Gear journal oil 1st, 2nd, 5th and Reverse		Limit	0.0059	0.150
3rd and Reverse idle		Limit	0.0079	0.200
Shift fork to hub sleeve		Limit	0.031	0.8
Synchronizer ring to gear		STD	0.030–0.079	1.0–2.0
		Limit	0.031	0.8

c. Torque the extension housing-to-transmission bolts to 27 ft. lbs. (37 Nm).

9. At the rear of the extension housing, install the restrict pins and torque to 29 ft. lbs. (39 Nm).

10. At the upper side of the transmission case, install the locking balls and springs into each hole. Using a new gasket, install the case cover.

11. Install the back-up light switch.

12. Install the shift lever retainer and torque the bolts to 9 ft. lbs. (13 Nm).

13. Install the speedometer driven gear.

14. Apply sealant to the clutch housing and torque the clutch housing-to-transmission bolts to 27 ft. lbs. (37 Nm).

15. Measure the distance **A**, between the input bearing tip and the clutch housing front bearing retainer surface, and select a front bearing spacer and install it.

NOTE: *Be sure the bearing snapring is securely depressed onto the transmission case before measuring.*

16. Install the spacer and front bearing retainer by performing the following procedures:

a. Install the spacer onto the input shaft bearing.

b. Lubricate the oil seal lip with grease.

c. Install the front bearing retainer; be careful not to damage the oil seal lip.

d. Apply sealant to the bolt threads and torque the bearing retainer-to-transmission bolts to 13 ft. lbs. (18 Nm).

17. Install the clutch release fork and bearing.

MANUAL TRANSAXLE

Identification

The transaxle model identification number is located on the bottom of the Vehicle Identification Number (VIN) plate.

Adjustments

NOTE: *On some model vehicles the service adjustments and procedures below may be used as a guide-modify the service steps as necessary.*

SHIFT LEVER FREE PLAY

C Series Type Manual Transaxle (Until 1988 Year)

1. Remove the console.

2. Disconnect the shift control cables from the control shift lever assembly.

3. Using a spring gauge, connect it to the top of the shift control lever, move the lever rearward and measure the pressure necessary to

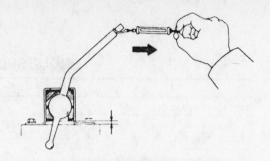

SHIM THICKNESS			
mm	in.	mm	in.
0.3	(0.012)	0.8	(0.031)
0.4	(0.016)	0.9	(0.035)
0.5	(0.020)	1.0	(0.039)
0.6	(0.024)	1.1	(0.043)
0.7	(0.028)	1.2	(0.047)

Checking shift lever free play — C series manual transaxle till 1988 year

move the lever; it should be 0.1–0.2 lbs. (0.5–1.0 N).

4. If necessary to adjust the free play, perform the following procedures:

a. Remove the shift lever cover.

b. Remove the shift lever cap-to-control shift lever retainer screws and the cap.

c. Remove the spacer, the upper seat, the shift lever, the lower seat and the adjusting shim.

d. Select the correct shift lever shim and reverse the removal procedures.

5. Recheck the shift lever movement.

C Series Type Manual Transaxle (1989–90 Year)

1. Remove the console.

2. Disconnect the shift control cables from the control shift lever assembly.

3. Using a dial indicator, measure the up and down movement of the shift lever; it should be 0.0059 in. (0.15mm).

4. If necessary to adjust the free play, perform the following procedures:

a. Remove the shift lever cover-to-housing screws and the cover.

b. Remove the snapring, the shift lever, the shift lever ball seat and the bushing.

d. Select the correct shift lever bushing and reverse the removal procedures.

5. Recheck the shift lever movement.

SHIFT CABLES

The shift control cables are precisely adjusted at the factory during assembly and cannot be accurately adjusted in the field. Should either of the cables become stretched and therefore out of adjustment, the individual cable must be replaced. Any attempt to adjust the shift cables can cause poor shifting and/or transaxle damage. If the shift cable(s) must be replaced, proceed as follows:

C Series Type Manual Transaxle (Until 1988 Year)

1. Disconnect the negative battery cable.
2. Disconnect the shift cable(s) and retaining clips at the transaxle.
3. Remove the center console and shifter boot.
4. Disconnect the shift cable(s) from the shifter assembly.
5. Remove the left front sill plate and lift or pull the carpet back to gain access to the cables.
6. Remove the retaining screws at the floor pan and remove the shift cable(s) from the car.
7. Position the new cable(s) and install the retaining screws.
8. Reposition the carpet and install the sill plate.
9. Route the cable(s) to the transaxle. This is easier if the car is elevated and safely supported. Lower the car after the cables are in position.

10. Position the cable(s) and install the retaining clips at the transaxle.
11. Connect the cable(s) to the shifter assembly.
12. Install the center console and shifter boot. Connect the negative battery cable. Roadtest the vehicle for correct shift operation.

C Series Type Manual Transaxle 1989–90 Year

1. Disconnect the negative battery cable.
2. Remove the shift lever knob and the shifter boot.
3. Remove the front and rear center console halves.
4. Remove the center air duct.
5. Remove the ECM mounting nuts and remove the ECM from under the dashboard.
6. Remove the cable hold-down brackets.
7. Remove the four shifter assembly mounting bolts.
8. Remove the shift cable retainer and end clips from the shifter assembly.
9. Remove the shifter control assembly.

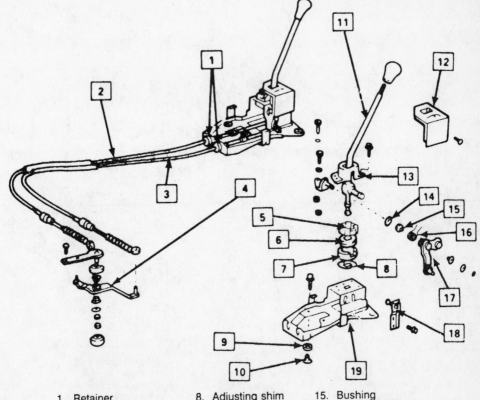

1. Retainer
2. Shift control cable
3. Select control cable
4. Selecting bellcrank
5. Spacer
6. Upper seat
7. Lower seat
8. Adjusting shim
9. Bushing No. 2
10. Bushing No. 1
11. Shift lever
12. Shift lever cover
13. Shift lever cap
14. Washer
15. Bushing
16. Torsion spring
17. Selecting bellcrank
18. Spring holder
19. Shift lever retainer

Shifter and cable assembly — C series manual transaxle till 1988 year

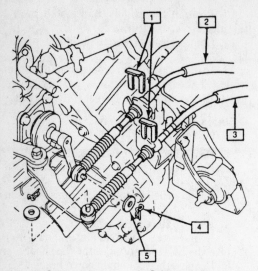

1. Cable retainer
2. Shift control cable
3. Shift select cable
4. Cable end clip
5. Cable end washer

Shift cables at transaxle

10. Disconnect the cable retainers at the transaxle.

11. Remove the shift cables by pulling them from the outside of the firewall.

12. Install the new cables by going through the firewall from the outside.

13. Position the cables in their brackets at the transaxle and install the retaining clips.

14. Connect the cables to their transaxle mounts and install the clips.

15. Connect the cables and install the clips at the shifter assembly.

16. Install the shifter assembly and its four bolts. Tighten the bolts to 15 ft. lbs.

17. Install the cable hold-down brackets.

18. Reinstall the ECM and the center air duct.

19. Install the front and rear halves of the console.

20. Install the shift lever boot and knob. Connect the negative battery cable. roadtest the vehicle for proper shifter operation.

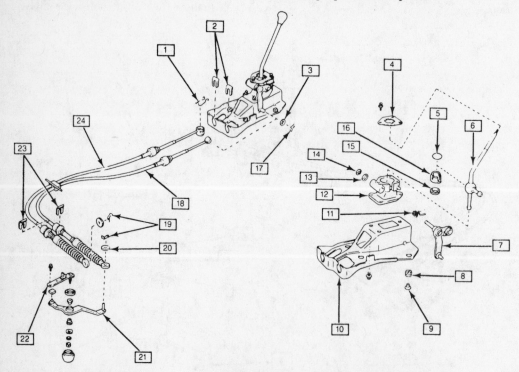

1. Cable end clips	10. Control shift lever retainer plate	18. Shift select cable
2. Retainer clips	11. Torsion spring	19. Clips
3. Plate washer	12. Shift lever housing	20. Plate washer
4. Shift lever cover	13. Plate washer	21. Selecting bellcrank
5. Snap ring	14. E-clip	22. Selecting bellcrank support
6. Shift lever	15. shift lever seat bushing	23. Retainer clips
7. Selecting bellcrank	16. Shift lever ball seat	24. Shift control cable
8. Bushing No. 2	17. Clip	
9. Bushing No.1		

Shifter and cable assembly − C series manual transaxle 1989–90 year

Back-up Light Switch

REMOVAL AND INSTALLATION

The reverse light switch is mounted on the side of the manual transaxle housing. Its removal and replacement is easily accomplished by disconnecting the wiring connector from the switch and unscrewing the switch from the case (always replace the mounting gasket below it). A specially sized socket or its equivalent is necessary for this service operation. Install the new switch and tighten it to 15 ft. lbs. for models up to 1988 and 30 ft. lbs. for 1989–90 vehicles. Reinstall the electrical connector. Turn key to the ON position, depress clutch pedal and place shifter in REVERSE position. Check operation of back-up lights.

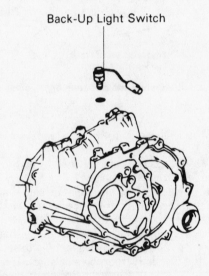

Back-Up Light Switch

Back-up light switch

Transaxle
REMOVAL AND INSTALLATION
C Series Type Manual Transaxle
1984–90 Corolla FWD
1986–89 MR2
1987–90 Tercel

NOTE: *Before performing Removal and Installation or Overhaul service procedures make sure to identify the manual transaxle type for your vehicle. On MR2 vehicles refer to E series "Removal and Installation" service procedures outlined in this section for ADDITIONAL INFORMATION-modify steps as necessary.*

1. Remove the negative battery cable.
2. Raise and safely support the vehicle. Drain the cooling system.

3. Remove the air cleaner with the air hose. Disconnect the back-up light switch connector.

4. Remove the speedometer cable. Remove the shift control cables-to-transaxle shift lever clips, washers and the cable ends.

5. Remove the water inlet-to-transaxle nut/bolt and the water inlet from the transaxle.

6. Remove the clutch slave cylinder-to-transaxle bolts, move the cylinder aside and suspend it on a wire.

7. Remove the engine undercover(s).

8. Using a block of wood and a floor jack, place it under the engine's oil pan and support it.

9. If equipped with a crossmember, remove the crossmember-to-chassis bolts and the crossmember.

10. Remove the center member-to-chassis bolts, the center member-to-engine mount bolts and the center member.

11. Disconnect the left halfshaft by performing the following procedures:

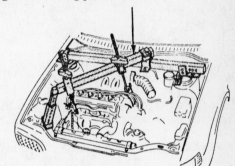

Engine support equipment

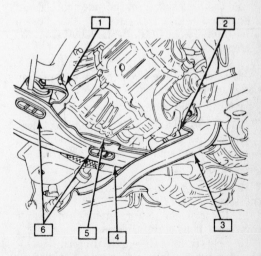

1. Front transaxle mount   4. Center crossmember
2. Rear transaxle mount   5. Center transaxle mount
3. Main crossmember   6. Mount bolt shields

Location of mounts and crossmembers

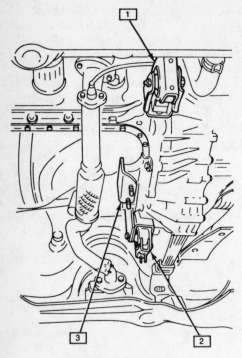

1. Front transaxle mount
2. Rear transaxle mount
3. Center transaxle mount

Location of transaxle mounts

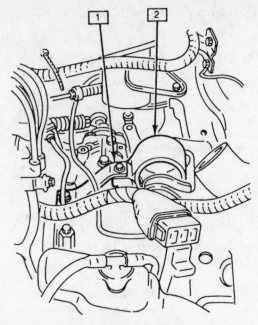

1. Transaxle mount brace
2. Left transaxle mount

Detail of left transaxle mount assembly — most vehicles

a. If equipped with a transaxle side shaft, remove the halfshaft-to-side shaft flange bolts.

b. Remove the lower control arm-to-ball joint (at the steering knuckle) bolts.

c. If equipped with a transaxle side shaft, pull the steering knuckle outward and separate the halfshaft from the side shaft. If not equipped with a transaxle side shaft, use a medium pry bar to pry the halfshaft from the transaxle.

d. Using a wire, support the halfshaft.

12. Disconnect the electrical connectors from the starter. Remove the starter-to-transaxle bolts and the starter.

NOTE: *On some vehicles, it may be necessary to remove the exhaust pipe-to-exhaust manifold bolts and separate the pipe from the manifold.*

13. Disconnect the ground strap from the transaxle.

14. Remove the lower engine-to-transaxle cover plate bolts and the plate.

15. Slightly, raise the engine/transaxle assembly. Remove the left engine mount-to-chassis through bolt, the left engine mount-to-transaxle bolts and the engine mount.

16. Using a floor jack, position it under the transaxle and support it's weight. Slightly,

lower the left side of the engine/transaxle assembly.

17. Disconnect the right halfshaft by performing the following procedures:

a. If equipped with a transaxle side shaft, remove the halfshaft-to-side shaft flange bolts.

b. If equipped with a transaxle side shaft, move the engine/transaxle assembly to separate the halfshaft from the side shaft. If not equipped with a transaxle side shaft, use a medium pry bar to pry the halfshaft from the transaxle.

c. Using a wire, support the halfshaft.

18. Remove the transaxle-to-engine bolts, move the transaxle rearward and remove it from the vehicle.

19. To install the transaxle align the input shaft splines with the clutch disc, install the transaxle to the engine and torque the engine-to-transaxle bolts to 47 ft. lbs. for 12mm bolts and 34 ft. lbs. for 10mm bolts.

NOTE: *When installing the transaxle, partially assembly the right halfshaft with transaxle.*

20. Install the left engine-to-transaxle mount bolts torque to 38 ft. lbs. Raise the engine and install the left engine mount-to-chassis through bolt.

21. Remove the floor jack from under the transaxle.

22. Install the lower engine-to-transaxle plate.

23. Connect the ground strap to the transaxle.

24. Install the starter-to-transaxle bolts and torque to 29 ft. lbs. Connect the electrical connectors to the starter.

25. Align the left halfshaft with the transaxle, install the lower control arm-to-ball joint bolts and torque the bolts to 47 ft. lbs.

26. If the halfshaft are equipped with flanges, torque the halfshaft flange-to-side shaft flange bolts to 27 ft. lbs. If the halfshafts are insertable type, tap the shaft into the transaxle until the snapring grips the shaft.

27. Install the center member-to-engine mount bolts to 29 ft. lbs. for 1984–88 transaxles or nuts to 45 ft. lbs. for 1989–90 transaxles and the center member-to-chassis bolts 29 ft. lbs. for 1984–88 transaxles or 45 ft. lbs. for 1989–90 transaxles.

28. If equipped with a crossmember, torque the upper crossmember-to-chassis bolts to 94 ft. lbs. and the lower crossmember-to-chassis nuts/bolts to 94 ft. lbs.

29. If the exhaust pipe was disconnected, use a new gasket and torque the exhaust pipe-to-manifold nuts.

30. Install the undercover(s).

31. Install the clutch slave cylinder-to-transaxle bolts to 18 ft. lbs.

32. Install the water inlet to the transaxle.

33. Install the shift control cables, the washers and clips.

34. Connect the back-up electrical connector and the air cleaner with air hose.

35. Connect the speedometer cable.

36. Connect the negative battery cable.

37. Refill the transaxle with clean 80W-90 gear oil and road test the vehicle.

Z Series Type Manual Transaxle
1984–88 Tercel and Tercel Wagon
2-Wheel Drive and 4-Wheel Drive

2-WHEEL DRIVE TRANSAXLE

NOTE: *Before performing Removal and Installation or Overhaul service procedures make sure to identify the manual transaxle type for your vehicle.*

1. Disconnect the negative battery cable. Raise and safely support the vehicle. Remove the drain plugs and drain the transaxle.

2. On the 1984 transaxles, drain the cooling system, remove the upper radiator hose from the engine and the air cleaner inlet duct.

3. Disconnect the clutch cable.

4. Remove the upper transaxle-to-engine bolts.

5. To remove the halfshafts, perform the following procedures:

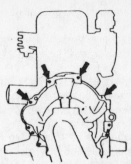

Remove the upper transaxle bolts — manual transaxle

a. From the halfshaft, remove the cotter pin and the locknut cap. Loosen the hub nut but do not remove it.

b. Raise and support the front of the vehicle. Remove the wheels.

c. Remove the hub nut. Remove the brake caliper-to-steering knuckle bolts and suspend the caliper on a wire.

d. Remove the brake disc.

e. Remove the tie rod end-to-steering knuckle cotter pin and nut. Using a ball joint removal tool, press the tie rod end from the steering knuckle.

f. On the lower shock absorber bracket, matchmark the camber adjusting bolt and the bracket.

g. Remove the shock absorber-to-steering knuckle bolts.

h. Using a wheel pressing tool, press the halfshaft from the steering knuckle and support it on a wire.

i. On the left side of the transaxle, remove the halfshaft-to-transaxle stiffener plate.

j. Using a halfshaft removal tool, attach it to the front of each halfshaft and tap the halfshafts from the transaxle.

6. If equipped, remove air inlet pipe from the converter.

7. Remove the exhaust pipe flange-to-exhaust manifold flange nuts and the stiffener plate, if equipped.

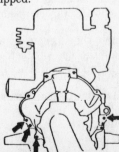

Remove the lower transaxle bolts — manual transaxle

8. Disconnect the gear shift rod and shift lever housing rod.

9. Disconnect the back-up light switch electrical connector and the speedometer cable.

10. Using a floor jack, position it under the transaxle, secure the transaxle to the jack and support the transaxle's weight.

11. If equipped, remove the lower bond cable.

12. Using a block of wood, position it between the engine and the cowl.

13. Remove the transaxle-to-crossmember bolts, the crossmember-to-chassis bolts and the crossmember.

14. Remove the lower transaxle-to-engine bolts and lower the transaxle from the vehicle.

15. To install the transaxle, use clutch grease apply it to the input shaft splines, input shaft tip and the front of the release bearing.

16. Align and move the transaxle into the installation position.

17. Install the lower transaxle-to-engine bolts. Torque the 14mm bolts to 29 ft. lbs. and the 17mm bolts to 43 ft. lbs.

18. Install the crossmember-to-chassis bolts and torque to 70 ft. lbs. Remove the floor jack and the wooden block.

19. Install the stiffener plate and torque the bolts to 29 ft. lbs.

20. Connect the speedometer cable and the back-up light switch connector.

21. Connect the shift lever housing rod and the gear shift rod.

22. Install the exhaust pipe-to-exhaust manifold nuts and torque to 46 ft. lbs.

23. If equipped with an air inlet pipe, connect it to the converter.

24. Connect the clutch cable.

25. Install the halfshafts by performing the following procedures:

a. Lubricate the oil seal lip.

b. Using a halfshaft installation and a hammer, tap the halfshaft into the transaxle until it snaps into the retaining ring.

c. On the left side, install the stiffener plate and torque the bolts to 29 ft. lbs.

d. Insert the halfshaft into the steering knuckle. Install the thrust washer and hub nut but do not torque.

e. Assemble the steering knuckle to the lower shock absorber bracket, insert the bolts, align the matchmarks and torque the bolts to 105 ft. lbs.

f. Install the brake disc and the brake caliper. Torque the brake caliper-to-steering knuckle bolts to 70 ft. lbs.

g. Install the tie rod end-to-steering knuckle nut to 36 ft. lbs. and install a new cotter pin. Install the wheels.

h. Lower the vehicle and torque the halfshaft nut to 137 ft. lbs. Install the locknut cap and a new cotter pin.

i. Check and/or adjust the front wheel alignment.

26. Install the upper transaxle-to-engine bolts. Torque the 14mm bolts to 29 ft. lbs. and the 17mm bolts to 43 ft. lbs.

27. On the 1984 transaxles, reconnect the upper radiator hose and the air cleaner inlet duct. Refill the cooling system, if necessary.

28. Reconnect the negative battery cable. Refill the transaxle and road test the vehicle.

4-WHEEL DRIVE TRANSAXLE

NOTE: *Before performing Removal and Installation or Overhaul service procedures make sure to identify the manual transaxle type for your vehicle.*

1. Disconnect the negative battery cable. Raise and safely support the vehicle. Remove the drain plugs and drain the transaxle.

2. On the 1984 transaxles, drain the cooling system, remove the upper radiator hose from the engine and the air cleaner inlet duct.

3. Disconnect the clutch cable.

4. Remove the upper transaxle-to-engine bolts.

5. Remove the console. Working inside the vehicle and using snapring pliers, remove the snapring from the shift lever and the shift lever.

6. To remove the halfshafts, perform the following procedures:

a. From the halfshaft, remove the cotter pin and the locknut cap. Loosen the hub nut but do not remove it.

b. Raise and support the front of the vehicle. Remove the wheels.

c. Remove the hub nut. Remove the brake caliper-to-steering knuckle bolts and suspend the caliper on a wire.

d. Remove the brake disc.

e. Remove the tie rod end-to-steering knuckle cotter pin and nut. Using a ball joint removal tool, press the tie rod end from the steering knuckle.

f. On the lower shock absorber bracket, matchmark the camber adjusting bolt and the bracket.

g. Remove the shock absorber-to-steering knuckle bolts.

h. Using a wheel pressing tool, press the halfshaft from the steering knuckle and support it on a wire.

i. On the left side of the transaxle, remove the halfshaft-to-transaxle stiffener plate.

j. Using a halfshaft removal tool, attach it to the front of each halfshaft and tap the halfshafts from the transaxle.

7. Remove the rear driveshaft and plug the transaxle opening.

8. If equipped, remove air inlet pipe from the converter.

9. Remove the exhaust pipe flange-to-exhaust manifold flange nuts and the stiffener plate, if equipped.

10. Disconnect the selecting rod from the rear drive shift link lever.

11. Disconnect the electrical connectors from the back-up light switch, the 4WD indicator switch and the extra low gear (EL) indicator, if equipped. Disconnect the speedometer cable.

12. Using a floor jack, position it under the transaxle, secure the transaxle to the jack and support the transaxle's weight.

13. If equipped, remove the lower bond cable.

14. Using a block of wood, position it between the engine and the cowl.

15. Remove the transaxle-to-crossmember bolts, the crossmember-to-chassis bolts and the crossmember.

16. Remove the lower transaxle-to-engine bolts and lower the transaxle from the vehicle.

17. To install transaxle use clutch grease, apply it to the input shaft splines, input shaft tip and the front of the release bearing.

18. Align and move the transaxle into the installation position.

19. Install the lower transaxle-to-engine bolts. Torque the 14mm bolts to 29 ft. lbs. and the 17mm bolts to 43 ft. lbs.

20. Install the crossmember-to-chassis bolts and torque to 70 ft. lbs. Remove the floor jack and the wooden block.

21. Install the stiffener plate and torque the bolts to 29 ft. lbs.

22. Connect the speedometer cable. Connect the electrical connectors to the back-up light switch, the 4WD indicator switch and the extra low gear (EL) indicator switch.

23. Connect the selecting rod to the rear driveshaft link lever.

24. Install the exhaust pipe-to-exhaust manifold nuts.

25. Install the rear driveshaft and torque the bolts to 31 ft. lbs.

26. If equipped with an air inlet pipe, connect it to the converter.

27. Connect the clutch cable.

28. Install the halfshafts by performing the following procedures:

   a. Lubricate the oil seal lip.

   b. Using a halfshaft installation and a hammer, tap the halfshaft into the transaxle until it snaps into the retaining ring.

   c. On the left side, install the stiffener plate and torque the bolts to 29 ft. lbs.

   d. Insert the halfshaft into the steering knuckle. Install the thrust washer and hub nut but do not torque.

   e. Assemble the steering knuckle to the lower shock absorber bracket, insert the bolts, align the matchmarks and torque the bolts to 105 ft. lbs.

   f. Install the brake disc and the brake caliper. Torque the brake caliper-to-steering knuckle bolts to 70 ft. lbs.

   g. Install the tie rod end-to-steering knuckle nut to 36 ft. lbs. and install a new cotter pin. Install the wheels.

   h. Lower the vehicle and torque the halfshaft nut to 137 ft. lbs. Install the locknut cap and a new cotter pin.

   i. Check and/or adjust the front wheel alignment.

29. Install the upper transaxle-to-engine bolts. Torque the 14mm bolts to 29 ft. lbs. and the 17mm bolts to 43 ft. lbs.

30. Install the shift lever and secure it with a snapring. Install the console.

31. On the 1984 transaxles, reconnect the upper radiator hose and the air cleaner inlet duct. Refill the cooling system, if necessary.

32. Reconnect the negative battery cable. Refill the transaxle and road test the vehicle.

E Series Type Manual Transaxle 1988–89 MR2

NOTE: *Before performing Removal and Installation or Overhaul service procedures make sure to identify the manual transaxle type for your vehicle. On non-supercharged engine applications modify this service procedure as necessary.*

1. Disconnect the negative battery cable.

2. Raise and safely support the vehicle. Drain the cooling system.

3. Remove the air cleaner with the air hose. Disconnect the back-up light switch connector.

4. Remove the hose clamps and the hoses from the intercooler. Remove the intercooler-to-chassis bolts and the intercooler.

5. Remove the speedometer cable. Remove the shift control cables-to-transaxle shift lever clips, washers and the cable ends.

6. Remove the water inlet-to-transaxle nut/bolt and the water inlet from the transaxle.

7. Remove the water hose clamp from the control cable bracket.

8. Remove the clutch release cylinder pipe bracket, the clamp, the clutch release cylinder-to-transaxle bolts, move the cylinder aside and suspend it on a wire.

9. Remove the engine undercover and the fuel tank protector.

10. Remove the exhaust pipe assembly by performing the following procedures:

a. Disconnect the exhaust pipe from the exhaust manifold.

b. Remove the exhaust pipe from the No. 1 front bracket.

c. Disconnect the electrical connector and remove the oxygen sensor from the exhaust pipe.

d. Remove the No. 2 front bracket from the body.

e. Remove the exhaust pipe assembly from the rear bracket.

11. Disconnect the halfshafts by performing the following procedures:

a. Firmly apply the brake pedal and remove the halfshaft-to-side shaft flange bolts.

b. On the left side, remove the lower arm-to-rear axle carrier bolts.

c. Remove the left suspension arm-to-rear axle carrier, cotter pin, nut and separate the arm from the rear axle carrier.

d. Pull the rear axle carrier outward and separate the halfshaft from the side shaft.

e. Remove the joint end cover gasket. Using a wire, support the halfshaft.

12. Disconnect the electrical connectors from the starter. Remove the starter-to-transaxle bolts and the starter.

13. Remove the lower engine-to-transaxle cover plate bolts and the plate.

14. Using a block of wood and a floor jack, place it under the engine's oil pan and support it.

15. If equipped with a crossmember, remove the crossmember-to-chassis bolts and the crossmember.

16. If equipped with a center member, remove the center member-to-chassis bolts, the center member-to-engine mount bolts and the center member.

17. Disconnect the ground strap from the transaxle.

18. Using a floor jack, position it under the transaxle and support it's weight. Slightly, lower the left side of the engine/transaxle assembly.

19. Slightly, raise the engine/transaxle assembly. Remove the front, rear and left engine mount-to-chassis bolts and the mounts.

20. Remove the transaxle-to-engine bolts, lower the engine's left side, move the transaxle rearward and remove it from the vehicle.

NOTE: *As the transaxle is being removed, separate the right halfshaft and support it on a wire.*

21. Remove the side gear shaft(s) by performing the following procedures:

a. Push the side shaft or center drive-shaft into the differential and measure the distance between the transaxle case and the side gear shaft.

b. Using a differential side gear shaft puller, attach it to the side gear shaft and pull the shaft(s) from the transaxle.

22. Using a brass bar and a hammer, drive the side gear shaft(s) into the transaxle until the snapring grips the shaft(s).

23. Align the input shaft splines with the clutch disc, install the transaxle to the engine and torque the engine-to-transaxle bolts to 47 ft. lbs. for 12mm bolts and 34 ft. lbs. for 10mm bolts.

NOTE: *When installing the transaxle, partially assembly the right halfshaft with side gear shaft.*

24. Install the left engine-to-transaxle mount bolts to 38 ft. lbs. raise the engine and install the left engine mount-to-chassis through bolt.

25. Install the rear engine mount and torque the bolts to 38 ft. lbs.

26. Install the front engine mount by performing the following procedures:

a. Install the rear engine mount and torque the bolts to 38 ft. lbs.

b. Loosen the insulator set bolt.

c. Bounce the engine to confirm the front mount insulator is mounted on the middle of the insulator mount bracket.

d. Torque the insulator set bolt to 38 ft. lbs.

27. Remove the floor jack from under the transaxle. Install the lower engine-to-transaxle plate.

28. Connect the ground strap to the transaxle.

29. Install the starter-to-transaxle bolts and torque to 29 ft. lbs. Connect the electrical connectors to the starter.

30. Align the left halfshaft with the side gear shaft. Install and torque the lower arm-to-rear axle carrier nuts to 83 ft. lbs. and the suspension arm-to-rear axle carrier nut to 36 ft. lbs.; be sure to install a new cotter pin.

31. Apply the brakes and torque the halfshaft flange-to-side gear shaft flange bolts to 27 ft. lbs. and 48 ft. lbs. on supercharged engine applications.

32. Install the transaxle protector and torque the bolts to 9 ft. lbs.

33. If equipped, install the center member-to-engine mount bolts to 29 ft. lbs. and the center member-to-chassis bolts to 29 ft. lbs.

34. If equipped with a crossmember, torque the crossmember-to-engine bolts to 29 ft. lbs. and the crossmember-to-chassis nuts and bolts to 153 ft. lbs.

35. Follow the torque specifications below as noted on each item:

• Exhaust pipe-to-rear bracket bolts − 15 ft. lbs.

• No. 2 front bracket-to-chassis bolts − 9 ft. lbs.

• Exhaust pipe-to-No. 1 front bracket bolts − 14 ft. lbs.

• Exhaust pipe-to-manifold nuts − 46 ft. lbs.

• Oxygen sensor-to-exhaust manifold − 14 ft. lbs.

36. Install the clutch release assembly by performing the following procedures:

    a. Install and torque the control cable bracket and the clutch release cylinder bolts to 47 ft. lbs. for transaxle side and 13 ft. lbs. for the clutch release side.

    b. Install and torque the No. 2 control cable brackets bolts to 14 ft. lbs.

    c. Install and torque the clutch release cylinder pipe bracket bolts to 13 ft. lbs.

37. Install the shift control cables, the washers and clips.

38. Install the fuel tank protector and the undercover(s).

39. Install the No. 2 engine rear plate.

40. Install the water inlet and torque the bolts to 14 ft. lbs.

41. Connect the speedometer cable.

42. Connect the back-up electrical connector.

43. Install the intercooler and torque the bolts to 13 ft. lbs. (17 Nm).

44. Connect the negative battery cable.

45. Refill the transaxle with clean 75W-90 or 80W-90 gear oil and road test the vehicle.

**All-Trac 4WD Type Manual Transaxle
1988–90 Corolla 4WD**

NOTE: *Before performing Removal and Installation or Overhaul service procedures make sure to identify the manual transaxle type for your vehicle.*

1. THE TRANSAXLE MUST BE REMOVED WITH THE ENGINE AS AN ASSEMBLY. Properly relieve the fuel system pressure − see Chapter 5. Disconnect the negative battery cable. Remove the hood.

2. Drain the cooling system and the transaxle. If equipped with an intercooler, drain it.

3. Disconnect the accelerator cable from the throttle body.

4. Remove the cooling system reservoir tank and the radiator.

5. If equipped with cruise control system with an anti-lock brake system, disconnect the actuator connector and remove the actuator and bracket.

6. If equipped with cruise control system without an anti-lock brake system, perform the following procedures:

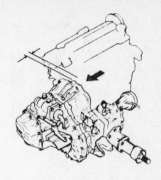

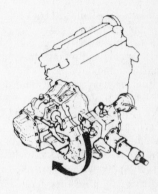

Removal of All-Trac transaxle

    a. Disconnect the ground strap connector.

    b. Remove the actuator cover.

    c. Disconnect the actuator vacuum hose and the connector.

    d. Remove the actuator and bracket.

7. Remove the upper suspension brace by performing the following procedures:

    a. If necessary, disconnect the ignition coil connector and the high tension cord from the ignition coil.

    b. Remove the upper suspension brace-to-chassis nuts, bolts and braces.

8. Remove the air cleaner and bracket.

9. Remove the igniter.

10. Disconnect the heater hoses, the fuel hoses and the intercooler hoses, if equipped.

11. Disconnect the speedometer cable and the transaxle control cables. If necessary, remove the alternator.

12. Remove the clutch release cylinder and tube bracket without disconnecting the tube.

13. If equipped with air conditioning, disconnect the electrical connectors, remove the compressor-to-bracket bolts and move the compressor aside.

14. Label and disconnect the necessary electrical connectors, wires and vacuum hoses.

15. Raise and safely support the vehicle. Remove the undercovers and drain the engine oil. Drain the transaxle fluid.

16. Remove the lower crossmember-to-chassis bolts and the crossmember.

17. Remove the halfshafts by performing the following procedures:

a. If equipped with a transaxle side shaft, apply the brakes and remove the halfshaft-to-side shaft flange bolts.

b. Remove the tie rod end-to-steering knuckle cotter pin and nut. Using a ball joint remover tool, separate the tie rod end from the steering knuckle.

c. Remove the lower control arm-to-ball joint (at the steering knuckle) bolts.

d. If equipped with a transaxle side shaft, pull the steering knuckle outward and separate the halfshaft from the side shaft. If not equipped with a transaxle side shaft, use a medium pry bar to pry the halfshaft from the transaxle.

e. Using a wire, support the halfshaft.

18. Remove the front section of the driveshaft by performing the following procedures:

a. Place matchmarks on the front and intermediate drive shaft flanges.

b. Remove the front-to-intermediate driveshaft nuts, washers and bolts.

c. Lower the front driveshaft and pull it from the transfer case.

19. Remove the deflector from the transfer extension housing.

20. Remove the power steering-to-bracket bolts and move it aside.

21. Remove the front exhaust pipe from the engine. If equipped with an oxygen sensor, disconnect the electrical.

22. Remove the center member-to-engine bolts, the center member-to-chassis bolts and the center member.

23. Remove the front and rear engine mounting insulators and bracket.

24. Lower the vehicle.

25. Remove the glove box, label and disconnect the necessary electrical connectors and pull the engine wiring harness from the cowl.

26. Remove the power steering pump reservoir bolts and move the reservoir aside.

27. Attach a vertical lift to the engine hangers and support the weight.

28. Remove the engine/transaxle assembly mounts and lift the assembly from the vehicle.

29. Remove the transaxle-to-engine bolts, pull the transaxle straight out until there is approximately 2–3 in. (60–80mm) clearance between the engine and the transaxle case, rotate it counterclockwise and remove it from the engine.

30. Assemble the transaxle to the engine and torque the engine-to-transaxle bolts to 47 ft. lbs. for 12mm bolts and 34 ft. lbs. for 10mm bolts.

31. Install the engine/transaxle assembly by performing the following procedures:

a. Lower the engine/transaxle assembly into the vehicle.

b. Attach the right mounting insulator to the mounting bracket and body, then, temporarily install the through bolt and nuts.

c. Install the left mounting bracket to the transaxle and torque the bolts to 38 ft. lbs.

d. Attach the left mounting insulator to the mounting bracket and body. Torque the mounting bolts to 38 ft. lbs. and the through bolt to 58 ft. lbs.

e. Torque the right mounting insulator bolts to 38 ft. lbs. and the through bolt to 58 ft. lbs.

f. Remove the engine hoist chain from the engine.

32. Install the power steering pump reservoir tank bolts.

33. Connect the engine wires by performing the following procedures:

a. Push the engine wire through the cowl panel.

b. Connect the 3 TCCS ECU connectors, the circuit opening relay connector, the cowl wire connector and the instrument panel wire connector.

c. Install the glove box.

34. Raise and safely support the vehicle.

35. Install the front mounting bracket-to-engine bolts and torque to 38 ft. lbs. Temporarily install the through bolts and nut.

36. Install the rear mounting bracket-to-engine bolts and torque to 38 ft. lbs. Temporarily install the through bolts and nut.

37. Install the center member-to-chassis bolts to 29 ft. lbs. and the center member-to-insulator bolts to 29 ft. lbs.

38. Torque the engine-to-rear mount through bolt to 58 ft. lbs.

39. Install all exhaust components using new gaskets as necessary.

40. If equipped with an oxygen sensor, connect the electrical connector.

41. Install the power steering pump and the deflector to transfer extension housing.

42. Install the front section of the driveshaft by performing the following procedures:

a. Install the front driveshaft into the transfer case.

b. Align the matchmarks on the front and intermediate drive shaft flanges.

c. Install the front-to-intermediate driveshaft nuts, washers and bolts; torque them to 27 ft. lbs.

43. Install the halfshafts by performing the following procedures:

a. If equipped with a side gear shaft, align the halfshaft with the side shaft and install the bolts.

b. If not equipped with a side gear shaft, lubricate the oil seal lip. Using a brass rod and a hammer, tap the halfshaft into the transaxle until it locks into the snapring.

c. Install the lower control arm-to-ball joint bolts and torque the bolts to 105 ft. lbs.

d. Install the tie rod end and torque the tie rod end-to-steering knuckle nut to 36 ft. lbs.; be sure to install a new cotter pin.

e. If equipped with side shafts, apply the brakes and torque the halfshaft-to-side shaft flange bolts to 48 ft. lbs.

44. Install the lower crossmember-to-chassis bolts and torque to 153 ft. lbs. and the crossmember-to-center member bolts to 29 ft. lbs.

45. Install the engine undercovers and lower the vehicle.

46. Connect the necessary electrical connectors and hoses.

47. If equipped with air conditioning, install the compressor and connect the electrical connectors.

48. Install the clutch release cylinder and tube bracket.

49. Connect the speedometer cable, the transaxle control cables and the alternator, if removed.

50. Install the igniter, the air cleaner and bracket.

51. Install the upper suspension brace by performing the following procedures:

a. Install the upper suspension brace-to-chassis nuts, bolts and braces.

b. If disconnected, connect the ignition coil connector and the high tension cord to the ignition coil.

52. If equipped with cruise control system without an anti-lock brake system, perform the following procedures:

a. Install the actuator and bracket.

b. Connect the actuator vacuum hose and the connector.

c. Install the actuator cover.

d. Connect the ground strap connector.

53. If equipped with cruise control system with an anti-lock brake system, install the actuator and bracket and connect the actuator connector.

54. Refill the cooling system reservoir tank and the radiator. Refill the transaxle.

55. Connect the accelerator cable to the throttle body. Connect the negative battery cable. Install the hood. Roadtest the vehicle for proper operation.

Transaxle Overhaul

Before Disassembly

Cleanliness is an important factor in the overhaul of the manual transaxle. Before opening up this unit, the entire outside of the transaxle assembly should be cleaned, preferable with a high pressure washer such as a car wash spray unit. Dirt entering the transaxle internal parts will negate all the time and effort spent on the overhaul. During inspection and reassembly all parts should be thoroughly cleaned with solvent then dried with compressed air. Wiping cloths and rags should not be used to dry parts.

Wheel bearing grease, long used to hold thrust washers and lube parts, should not be used. Lube seals with clean transaxle oil and use ordinary unmedicated petroleum jelly to hold the thrust washers and to ease the assembly of seals, since it will not leave a harmful residue as grease often will. Do not use solvent on neoprene seals, if they are to be reused, or thrust washers.

Before installing bolts into aluminum parts, always dip the threads into clean transaxle oil. Anti-seize compound can also be used to prevent bolts from galling the aluminum and seizing. Always use a torque wrench to keep from stripping the threads. The internal snaprings should be expanded and the external rings should be compressed, if they are to be reused. This will help insure proper seating when installed.

NOTE: *When overhauling the All-Trac and other series manual transaxles, use this service procedure as a guide. Modify the service procedure steps as required. Refer to exploded view of the manual transaxle assembly as necessary.*

TRANSAXLE DISASSEMBLY

C50, C51, C52 and C150

1. Remove the release fork, the bearing and the speedometer driven gear.

2. Using a back-up light switch socket, remove the back-up light switch from the transaxle.

3. Remove the front bearing retainer-to-transaxle bolts and the retainer.

4. Remove the transmission case cover bolts and the cover.

5. Using a dial indicator, measure the 5th

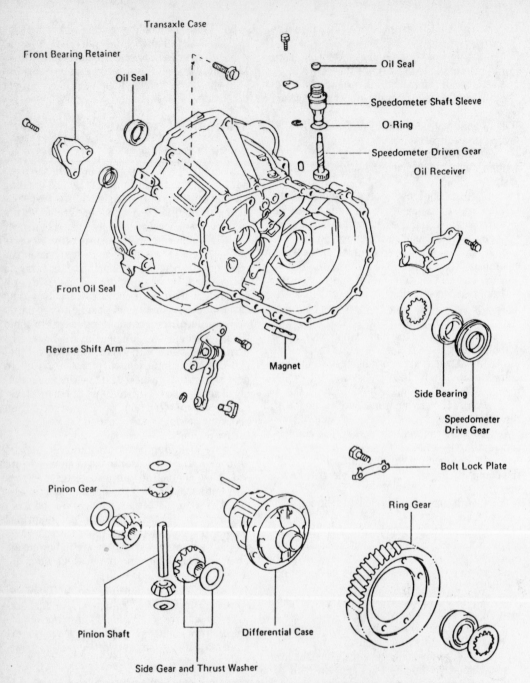

Exploded view of the transaxle case and components — C50, C51 and C52 transaxles

gear thrust clearance; it should be 0.004–0.022 in. (0.10–0.57mm).

6. Remove the selecting bellcrank and lock bolt.

7. Remove the shift/selector lever shaft assembly-to-transaxle bolts and the assembly.

8. Remove the 5th gear locknut by performing the following procedures:

a. From inside the transaxle, move the shift forks rearward to lock the transaxle into 2 gears, simultaneously.

b. Remove the locknut.

c. Move the shift forks to unlock the transaxle.

9. Remove the No. 3 hub sleeve assembly and No. 3 shift fork by performing the following procedures:

a. Using 2 pry bars and a hammer, tap out the snapring from the end of the input shaft.

b. From the No. 3 shift fork, remove the lock bolt.

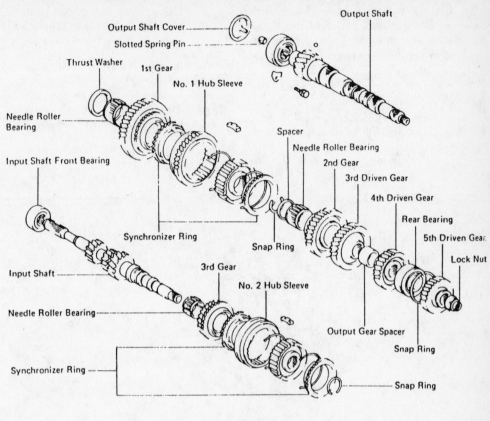

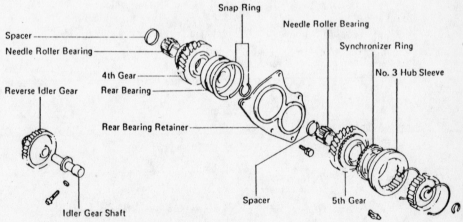

Exploded view of the gear and shaft components — C50, C51 and C52 transaxles

c. Remove the No. 3 hub sleeve and No. 3 shift fork.

d. Using a timing gear remover tool, press the 5th gear, with the No. 3 hub and the synchronizer ring, from the input shaft.

10. Remove the needle roller bearing and spacer.

11. Using a universal puller, press the 5th driven gear from the output shaft.

12. Remove the rear bearing retainer. Using

snapring pliers, remove both snaprings.

13. From the outside of the case, remove the reverse idler gear shaft lock bolt.

14. Using 2 small pry bars and a hammer, tap out the snapring from the No. 2 shift fork shaft.

15. Using a detent ball plug socket, remove the 3 plugs from the outside of the case. Using a magnetic finger, remove the 3 seats, springs and balls.

16. Remove the transmission case-to-transaxle case bolts; using a plastic hammer, tap the transmission case from the transaxle case.

17. Remove the reverse shift arm bracket-to-transaxle case bolts and the bracket.

18. Pull out the reverse idler shaft and remove the reverse idler gear.

19. Remove the shift forks and shift fork shafts by performing the following procedures:

a. Using 2 pry bars and a hammer, tap out the 3 snaprings from the shift shafts.

b. Remove the set bolts from the shift forks.

c. Remove the No. 2 fork shaft and the shift head.

d. Using a magnetic finger, remove both lock balls.

e. Remove the No. 3 fork shaft and the reverse shift fork.

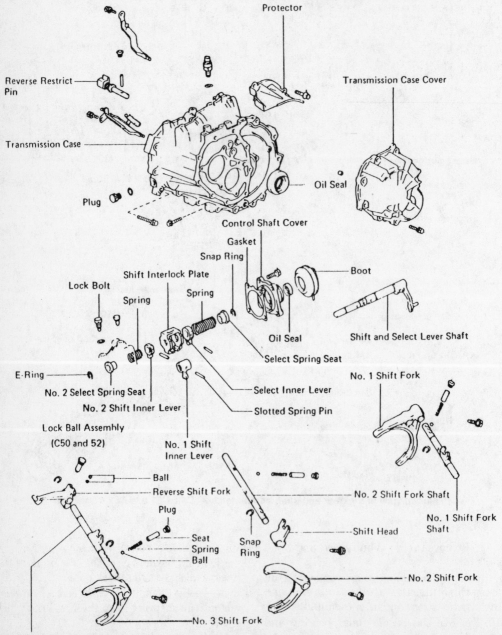

Protector
Reverse Restrict Pin
Transmission Case Cover
Transmission Case
Oil Seal
Plug
Control Shaft Cover
Gasket
Snap Ring
Lock Bolt
Shift Interlock Plate
Spring
Spring
Boot
Oil Seal
Shift and Select Lever Shaft
Select Spring Seat
E-Ring
No. 2 Select Spring Seat
Select Inner Lever
No. 1 Shift Fork
No. 2 Shift Inner Lever
Slotted Spring Pin
Lock Ball Assembly (C50 and 52)
No. 1 Shift Inner Lever
Ball
Reverse Shift Fork
No. 2 Shift Fork Shaft
Plug
No. 1 Shift Fork Shaft
Seat
Snap Ring
Shift Head
Spring
Ball
No. 2 Shift Fork
No. 3 Shift Fork
No. 3 Shift Fork Shaft

Exploded view of the transmission case and shifting components — C50, C51 and C52 transaxles

f. Pull out the No. 1 fork shaft and remove the No. 1 and No. 2 shift forks.

20. Remove both the input and output shaft, simultaneously, from the transaxle case.

21. Remove the differential assembly, the magnet and the oil receiver.

C140 and C141

1. Remove the release fork, the bearing and the speedometer driven gear.

2. Using a back-up light switch socket, remove the back-up light switch from the transaxle.

3. Remove the transmission case cover bolts and the cover.

4. Remove the shift selecting lever lock bolt.

5. Remove the shift/selector lever shaft assembly-to-transaxle bolts and the assembly.

6. Remove the 4th gear locknut by performing the following procedures:

a. From inside the transaxle, move the shift forks rearward to lock the transaxle into 2 gears, simultaneously.

b. Remove the locknut.

c. Move the shift forks to unlock the transaxle.

7. Remove the rear bearing retainer. Using snapring pliers, remove both snaprings.

8. From the outside of the case, remove the reverse idler gear shaft lock bolt.

9. Using 2 small pry bars and a hammer, tap out the snapring from the No. 2 shift fork shaft.

10. Using a detent ball plug socket, remove the 3 plugs and straight screw plug from the outside of the case. Using a magnetic finger, remove the 3 seats, springs and balls.

11. Remove the transmission case-to-transaxle case bolts; using a plastic hammer, tap the transmission case from the transaxle case.

12. Remove the reverse shift arm bracket-to-transaxle case bolts and the bracket.

13. Pull out the reverse idler shaft and remove the reverse idler gear.

14. Remove the shift forks and shift fork shafts by performing the following procedures:

a. Using 2 pry bars and a hammer, tap out both snaprings from the shift shafts.

b. Remove the set bolts from the shift forks.

c. Using a pin punch and a hammer, drive out the slotted spring pin from the reverse shift shaft.

d. Remove the No. 2 fork shaft and the shift head.

e. Remove the No. 3 fork shaft and the reverse shift fork.

f. Pull out the No. 1 fork shaft and remove the No. 1 and No. 2 shift forks.

15. Remove both the input and output shaft, simultaneously, from the transaxle case.

16. Remove the differential assembly, the magnet and the oil receiver.

UNIT DISASSEMBLY AND ASSEMBLY

Output Shaft

DISASSEMBLY

1. Using a feeler gauge, measure the thrust clearance of the 1st and 2nd gears; the thrust clearance should be 0.004–0.016 in. (0.10–0.40mm) for the 1st gear and 0.004–0.018 in. (0.10–0.45mm) for the 2nd gear.

2. Using a shop press and a bearing remover tool, press the 4th driven gear and radial roller bearing from the output shaft and remove the spacer.

3. Remove the 3rd driven gear and the 2nd gear by performing the following procedures:

a. Move the No. 1 hub sleeve into the 1st gear position.

b. Using a shop press and a bearing remover tool, press the 3rd driven gear and 2nd gear from the output shaft.

c. Remove the needle roller bearing, the spacer and the synchronizer.

4. Using 2 pry bars and a hammer, tap the snapring from the output shaft.

5. Using a shop press, press the No. 1 hub sleeve, the 1st gear and the synchronizer ring from the output shaft. Remove the needle roller bearing, the thrust washer and the locking ball.

INSPECTION

1. Using a micrometer, measure the output shaft journal outside diameter sections shown in the accompanying figure.

Minimum outside diameters:
- Section A – 32.0mm
- Section B – 38.0mm
- Section C – 32.0mm

2. Using a dial indicator, mount the output shaft on V-blocks and measure the runout. Maximum allowable runout is 0.0020 in. (0.050mm).

ASSEMBLY

1. If the output shaft was replaced, drive a slotted spring pin into the end of the shaft to a depth of 0.236 in. (6.0mm).

2. Assemble the No. 1 clutch hub with the shifting keys into the hub sleeve and install the shifting key springs under the keys; install the key springs so the end gaps do not align.

3. Install the 1st gear and No. 1 clutch hub sleeve assembly by performing the following procedures:

a. Position the locking ball onto the output shaft.

b. Install the thrust washer onto the output shaft; make sure the washer groove fits securely over the locking ball.

c. Apply multi-purpose grease to the needle roller bearing.

d. Position the synchronizer ring on the 1st gear and align the ring slots with the shifting keys.

e. Assemble the 1st gear and the No. 1 clutch hub assembly; the No. 1 clutch hub nose and the large sleeve flange must face rearward.

f. Using a shop press, press the output shaft into the 1st gear/No. 1 clutch hub assembly.

4. Select a snapring which will allow minimum axial play and install it onto the output shaft to secure the 1st gear/No. 1 clutch hub assembly.

5. Using a feeler gauge, measure the 1st gear thrust clearance; it should be 0.004–0.016 in. (0.10–0.40mm).

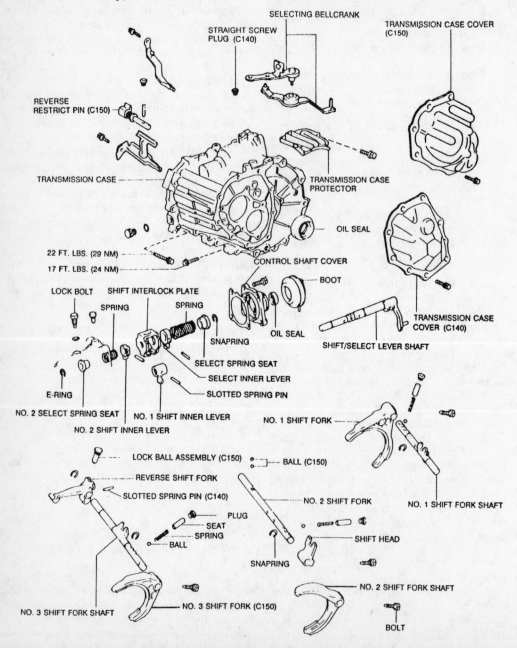

Exploded view of the transmission case and shifting components — C140, C141 and C150 transaxles

6. Install the 2nd gear and 3rd driven gear by performing the following procedures:

a. Install the spacer.

b. Position the synchronizer ring on the 2nd gear and align the ring slots with the shifting keys.

c. Apply multi-purpose grease to the needle roller bearing.

d. Install the 2nd gear onto the output shaft.

e. Using a shop press, press the output shaft assembly into the 3rd driven gear.

7. Using a feeler gauge, measure the 2nd gear thrust clearance; it should be 0.004–0.018 in. (0.10–0.45mm).

8. Install the spacer onto the output shaft. Using a shop press and a drive pinion rear bearing cone replacer tool, press output shaft assembly into the 4th driven gear and radial ball bearing.

Input Shaft

DISASSEMBLY

1. Using a feeler gauge, measure the thrust clearance of the 3rd and 4th gears; the thrust clearance should be 0.004–0.014 in. (0.10–

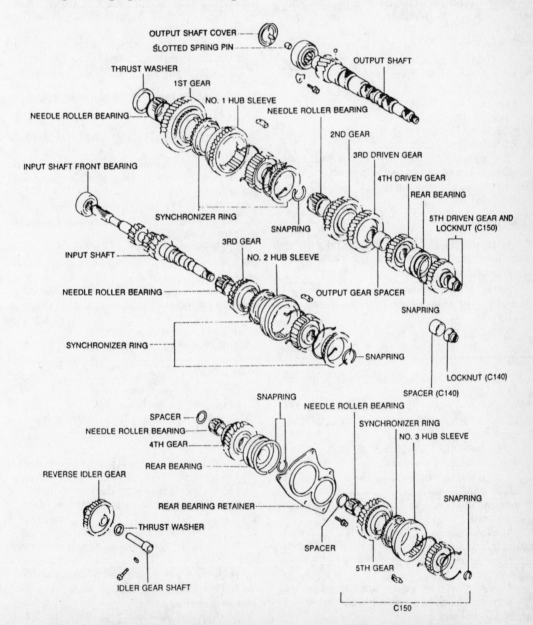

Exploded view of the gear and shaft components — C140, C141 and C150 transaxles

0.35mm) for the 3rd gear and 0.004–0.022 in. (0.10–0.55mm) for the 4th gear.

2. Using 2 pry bars and a hammer, tap the snapring from the input shaft.

3. Using a shop press and a bearing remover tool, press the radial ball bearing from the input shaft. Remove the 4th gear, the needle roller bearing and the synchronizer ring.

4. Using 2 pry bars and a hammer, tap the snapring from the input shaft.

5. Using a shop press and a bearing remover tool, press the No. 2 hub sleeve, the 3rd gear, the synchronizer ring and needle roller bearings from the input shaft as an assembly.

INSPECTION

1. Using a micrometer, measure the input shaft journal outside diameter sections.

Minimum outer diameters:
- Section A – 27.0mm
- Section B – 32.5mm
- Section C – 33.0mm
- Section D – 30.0mm

2. Using a dial indicator, mount the input shaft on V-blocks and measure the runout. Maximum allowable runout is 0.0020 in. (0.050mm).

ASSEMBLY

1. Install the No. 2 clutch hub and shifting keys into the hub sleeve and the shifting key springs under the keys.

NOTE: *When installing the key springs, make sure the spring end gaps are not aligned.*

2. Install the 3rd gear and No. 2 hub sleeve assembly by performing the following procedures:

a. Using multi-purpose grease, lubricate the needle roller bearings.

b. Position the synchronizer ring on the 3rd gear and align the ring slots with the shifting keys.

c. Assemble the 3rd gear assembly to the No. 2 hub sleeve assembly.

d. Using a shop press, press the input shaft into the 3rd gear/No. 2 hub sleeve assembly; the nose on the hub sleeve must face rearward.

3. Select a snapring which will allow minimum axial play and install it onto the input shaft to secure the 3rd gear/No. 2 hub sleeve assembly.

4. Using a feeler gauge, measure the 3rd gear thrust clearance; it should be 0.004–0.014 in. (0.10–0.35mm).

5. Install the 4th gear assembly by performing the following procedures:

a. Using multi-purpose grease, lubricate the needle roller bearing and install it onto the input shaft.

b. Position the synchronizer ring onto the No. 2 hub sleeve assembly and align the ring slots with the keys.

c. Position the 4th gear and the radial ball bearing onto the input shaft.

d. Using a shop press and a drive pinion rear bearing cone replacer tool, press the input shaft assembly into the radial ball bearing.

6. Select a snapring which will allow minimum axial play and install it onto the input shaft to secure the 4th gear/radial ball bearing assembly.

7. Using a feeler gauge, measure the 4th gear thrust clearance; it should be 0.004–0.022 in. (0.10–0.55mm).

Shift/Select Lever Shaft Assembly

DISASSEMBLY

1. Remove the E-ring and compression spring.

2. Using a pin punch and a hammer, drive the slotted spring pins from the No. 1 and No. 2 shift inner levers.

3. Remove the No. 2 shift inner lever.

4. Remove the No. 1 shift inner lever and shift interlock plate.

5. Using a pin punch and a hammer, drive the slotted spring pin from the select inner lever.

6. Remove the select inner lever, the compression spring and the spring seat.

7. Using 2 pry bars and a hammer, tap the snapring from the lever shaft.

8. Remove the lever shaft and boot.

INSPECTION

1. Clean the parts in solvent.

2. Inspect the parts for wear or damage.

3. replace the parts if necessary.

ASSEMBLY

1. Apply multi-purpose grease to the shaft.

2. Install the boot and shaft onto the control shaft cover; make sure the boot is installed in the correct direction with the air bleed facing downward.

3. Install the snapring and the spring seat.

4. Install the compression spring and select inner lever.

5. Using a pin punch and a hammer, drive the slotted spring pin through the select inner lever and shaft.

6. Align the interlock plate with the No. 1 shift inner lever and install it.

7. Install the No. 2 shift inner lever.

8. Using a pin punch and a hammer, drive the slotted spring pins into the shaft.

9. Install the compression spring, the seat and the E-ring.

TRANSAXLE ASSEMBLY

C50, C51, C52 and C150

1. Install the magnet into the transaxle case. Install the oil receiver-to-transaxle case and torque the bolts to 8 ft. lbs. (11 Nm).

2. Adjust the differential side bearing preload by performing the following procedures:

    a. Install the thinnest shim into the transmission case.

    b. Using the front hub and drive pinion bearing replacer set, drive the side bearing outer race into the transaxle case.

    c. Install the differential into the transaxle case.

    d. Install the transmission case and torque the transmission-to-transaxle case bolt to 22 ft. lbs. (29 Nm).

    e. Using a differential preload adaptor tool and a torque wrench, measure the bearing preload; it should be 6.9–13.9 inch lbs. (0.8–1.6 Nm) for new bearings or 4.3–8.7 inch lbs. (0.5–1.0 Nm) for used bearings.

    f. If the preload is not within specifications, remove the transmission case side bearing outer race, select another adjusting shim, reinstall the side bearing outer race and recheck the preload torque.

NOTE: *The preload will change about 2.6–3.5 inch lbs. (0.3–0.4 Nm) with each shim thickness.*

3. Remove the transmission case.

4. Align both the input and output shaft, mesh the gears and install the assemblies into the transaxle case.

5. Install the shift forks and shift fork shafts by performing the following procedures:

    a. Position both the No. 1 and No. 2 shift forks into the groove of the No. 1 and No. 2 hub sleeves, respectively.

    b. Install the No. 1 fork shaft into the No. 1 shift fork hole.

    c. Install both interlock balls into the reverse shift fork hole.

    d. Install the No. 3 fork shaft and the reverse shift fork.

    e. Install the No. 2 fork shaft and shift head.

    f. Install the shift head positioning bolts and torque to 12 ft. lbs. (16 Nm).

    g. Using a drift punch and a hammer, drive the snaprings onto the 3 shift shafts.

6. Position the reverse shift fork pivot into the reverse shift arm. Install the reverse shift arm into the transaxle case and torque the bolts to 13 ft. lbs. (17 Nm).

7. Install the reverse idler gear and shaft; be sure to align the matchmarks.

8. Install the transmission case by performing the following procedures:

    a. Clean the transmission case and transaxle case mounting surfaces.

    b. Using sealant, apply a 0.04 in. (1mm) bead on the transaxle case mounting surface; place the bead inside the bolt holes.

    c. Install the transmission case and torque the transmission case-to-transaxle bolts to 22 ft. lbs. (29 Nm).

9. Install the lock ball and screw plug assemblies by performing the following procedures:

    a. Insert the balls, the springs and the seats into the screw plug holes.

    b. Apply sealant to the screw plug threads.

    c. Using a detent ball plug socket, torque the screw plugs to 18 ft. lbs. (25 Nm) for the shift fork shafts or to 29 ft. lbs. (39 Nm) for the lock ball assemblies.

10. Install and torque the reverse idler gear shaft lock bolt to 17 ft. lbs. (24 Nm).

11. Install the large snapring to the rear bearing.

Mark	Thickness mm (in.)	Mark	Thickness mm (in.)
A	2.10 (0.0827)	L	2.60 (0.1024)
B	2.15 (0.0846)	M	2.65 (0.1043)
C	2.20 (0.0866)	N	2.70 (0.1063)
D	2.25 (0.0886)	P	2.75 (0.1083)
E	2.30 (0.0906)	Q	2.80 (0.1102)
F	2.35 (0.0925)	R	2.85 (0.1122)
G	2.40 (0.0945)	S	2.90 (0.1142)
H	2.45 (0.0965)	T	2.95 (0.1161)
J	2.50 (0.0984)	U	3.00 (0.1181)
K	2.55 (0.1004)		

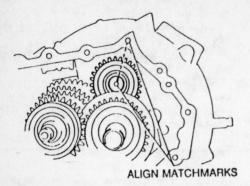

ALIGN MATCHMARKS

Aligning the matchmarks of the reverse idler shaft with the transaxle case

12. Install the rear bearing retainer-to-transmission case and torque the bolts to 14 ft. lbs. (19 Nm).

13. Position the 5th driven gear onto the output shaft. Using the 5th driven gear replacer tool, secure it to the output shaft and press the 5th driven gear onto the output shaft.

14. Install the 5th gear by performing the following procedures:

a. Install the spacer.

b. Apply multi-purpose grease to the needle roller bearing.

c. Install the 5th gear with the needle roller bearing and the synchronizer ring.

15. Assemble the No. 3 clutch hub with the shifting keys into the hub sleeve and install the shifting key springs under the shifting keys; install the key springs so the end gaps are not aligned.

16. Install the No. 3 hub sleeve assembly by performing the following procedures:

a. Using a spacer, support the tip of the input shaft to raise the transaxle assembly.

b. Position the No. 3 hub sleeve assembly, with the No. 3 shift fork, onto the input shaft and transmission case; be sure to align the ring slots of the synchronizer ring with the shifting keys.

NOTE: *When installing the No. 3 clutch hub/ sleeve assembly, make sure the recessed nose of the hub and the nose of the sleeve are facing forward.*

c. Using a tilt handle bearing replacer tool and a hammer, drive the No. 3 hub sleeve assembly onto the input shaft.

17. Using a dial micrometer, measure the 5th gear thrust clearance; it should be 0.004–0.022 in. (0.10–0.57mm).

18. Select a snapring with minimal axial play and install in onto the input shaft to secure the No. 3 hub/sleeve assembly.

19. Install the output shaft locknut by performing the following procedures:

a. Move the shift forks to lock the transaxle into 2 gears.

b. Install the locknut and torque it to 87 ft. lbs. (118 Nm).

c. Move the shift forks to unlock the transaxle.

d. Stake the locknut.

20. Install the No. 3 shift fork positioning bolt and torque it to 12 ft. lbs. (16 Nm).

21. Install the shift/select lever shaft assembly by performing the following procedures:

a. Using a new gasket position it onto the control shaft cover.

b. Install the shift/select lever shaft assembly into the transmission case and torque the bolts to 14 ft. lbs. (20 Nm).

c. Install the bellcrank to the transmission case.

22. Using sealant, apply a 0.04 in. (1mm) bead to the transmission case; be sure to place the sealant inside the bolt holes. Install the transmission case cover to the transmission case and torque the bolts to 13 ft. lbs. (18 Nm).

23. Install the front bearing retainer and torque the bolts to 8 ft. lbs. (11 Nm).

24. Using molybdenum disulphide lithium grease, lubricate the working surfaces of the release bearing hub inside groove, the input shaft spline and the release fork contact surface and install the parts.

25. Using a back-up light switch adapter, install the back-up light switch and torque it to 30 ft. lbs. (40 Nm).

26. Install the speedometer driven gear.

C140 and C141

1. Install the magnet into the transaxle case. Install the oil receiver-to-transaxle case and torque the bolts to 8 ft. lbs. (11 Nm).

2. Adjust the differential side bearing preload by performing the following procedures:

a. Install the thinnest shim into the transmission case.

b. Using the front hub and drive pinion bearing replacer set, drive the side bearing outer race into the transaxle case.

c. Install the differential into the transaxle case.

d. Install the transmission case and torque the transmission-to-transaxle case bolt to 22 ft. lbs. (29 Nm).

e. Using a differential preload adaptor tool and a torque wrench, measure the bearing preload; it should be 6.9–13.9 inch lbs. (0.8–1.6 Nm) for new bearings or 4.3–8.7 inch lbs. (0.5–1.0 Nm) for used bearings.

f. If the preload is not within specifications, remove the transmission case side bearing outer race, select another adjusting shim, reinstall the side bearing outer race and re-check the preload torque.

NOTE: *The preload will change about 2.6–3.5 inch lbs. (0.3–0.4 Nm) with each shim thickness.*

3. Remove the transmission case.

4. Align both the input and output shaft, mesh the gears and install the assemblies into the transaxle case.

5. Install the shift forks and shift fork shafts by performing the following procedures:

a. Position both the No. 1 and No. 2 shift forks into the groove of the No. 1 and No. 2 hub sleeves, respectively.

b. Install the No. 1 fork shaft into the No. 1 shift fork hole.

c. Install the No. 3 fork shaft and the reverse shift fork.

d. Install the No. 2 fork shaft and shift head.

e. Install the shift head positioning bolts and torque to 12 ft. lbs. (16 Nm).

f. Using a drift punch and a hammer, drive the snaprings onto both shift shafts.

g. Using a pin punch and a hammer, drive in the slotted spring pin into the reverse shift fork.

6. Position the reverse shift fork pivot into the reverse shift arm. Install the reverse shift arm into the transaxle case and torque the bolts to 13 ft. lbs. (17 Nm).

7. Install the reverse idler gear and shaft; be sure to align the matchmarks.

8. Install the transmission case by performing the following procedures:

a. Clean the transmission case and transaxle case mounting surfaces.

b. Using sealant, apply a 0.04 in. (1mm) bead on the transaxle case mounting surface; place the bead inside the bolt holes.

c. Install the transmission case and torque the transmission case-to-transaxle bolts to 22 ft. lbs. (29 Nm).

9. Install the lock ball and screw plug assemblies by performing the following procedures:

a. Insert the balls, the springs and the seats into the screw plug holes.

b. Apply sealant to the screw plug threads.

c. Using a detent ball plug socket, torque the screw plugs to 18 ft. lbs. (25 Nm) for the shift fork shafts or to 29 ft. lbs. (39 Nm) for the straight screw plug.

10. Install and torque the reverse idler gear shaft lock bolt to 17 ft. lbs. (24 Nm).

11. Install the large snaprings to the rear bearings.

12. Using a drift punch and a hammer, tap the snapring onto the No. 2 fork shaft.

13. Install the rear bearing retainer-to-transmission case and torque the bolts to 14 ft. lbs. (19 Nm).

TORQUE SPECIFICATIONS

Part	ft. lbs.	Nm.
Transmission case to transaxle case	22	29
Transmission case to case cover	13	18
Transmission case protector	9	13
Rear bearing retainer	14	19
Output shaft bearing lock plate	8	11
5th driven gear locknut	87	118
Reverse idler shaft lock bolt	17	24
Shift and select lever assembly	14	20
Reverse shift arm bracket	13	17
Shift fork to Set bolt	12	16
Reverse restrict pin holder	14	20
Filler plug	29	39
Drain plug	29	39
Back-up light switch	30	40
Front bearing retainer	8	11
Speedometer driven gear lock plate	8	11
Straight screw plug (shift fork shaft)	18	25
Lock ball assembly	29	39

VALVE STEM GUIDE REMOVER
AND REPLACER
09201-60011

INPUT SHAFT FRONT
BEARING REPLACER
09304-12012

DIFFERENTIAL SIDE
BEARING PULLER
09502-10012

OIL SEAL PULLER
09308-00010

CRANKSHAFT FRONT OIL SEAL
REPLACER
09223-46011

INPUT SHAFT FRONT
BEARING REPLACER
09304-30012

DIFFERENTIAL SIDE WASHER
REMOVER AND REPLACER
09504-22021

COUNTERSHAFT
BEARING PULLER
09310-36021

EXTENSION HOUSING
BUSHING REPLACER
09307-12010

INPUT SHAFT FRONT BEARING
REPLACER
09304-47010

DIFFERENTIAL DRIVE PINION
BEARING CONE REPLACER
09506-30011

DETENT BALL PLUG
09313-30021

OIL SEAL PULLER
09308-10010

DIFFERENTIAL DRIVE PINION
HOLDING TOOL
09556-16010

REAR AXLE SHAFT
BEARING REPLACER
09515-20010

TRANSAXLE OIL PLUG
09325-12010

STEERING RACK SHAFT
BUSHING PULLER
09612-10032

DIFFERENTIAL DRIVE PINION
HOLDING TOOL
09556-16020

REAR WHEEL
BEARING
REPLACER
09515-30010

BEARING REMOVER
09950-00020

TILT HANDLE BEARING
REPLACER
09612-22011

DRIVE PINION LOCK NUT
WRENCH
09564-16010

DRIVE PINION FRONT BEARING
REMOVER
09556-12010

UNIVERSAL PULLER
09995-20016

Special tools for manual transaxle overhaul

SHIFT LEVER SEAT SHIM THICKNESS

in.	mm
0.012	0.3
0.016	0.4
0.020	0.5
0.024	0.6
0.028	0.7
0.031	0.8
0.035	0.9
0.039	1.0
0.043	1.1
0.047	1.2

INPUT AND OUTPUT SHAFT JOURNAL DIAMETERS

Journals		in.	mm
Input shaft			
Roller bearing journal diameter	Limit	0.9831	24.970
3rd gear journal diameter	Limit	1.2193	30.970
4th gear journal diameter	Limit	1.0421	26.470
5th gear journal diameter	Limit	0.9791	24.870
Runout	Limit	0.0020	0.05
Output shaft			
Roller bearing journal diameter	Limit	1.2980	32.970
1st gear journal diameter	Limit	1.4949	37.970
2nd gear journal diameter	Limit	1.2587	31.970
Runout	Limit	0.0020	0.05

THRUST WASHER AND SHIM THICKNESS

Part	Mark	in.	mm
Side gear thrust washer thickness		0.0374	0.95
		0.0394	1.00
		0.0413	1.05
		0.0433	1.10
		0.0453	1.15
		0.0472	1.20
Side bearing adjusting shim thickness	A	0.0827	2.10
	B	0.0846	2.15
	C	0.0866	2.20
	D	0.0886	2.25
	E	0.0906	2.30
	F	0.0925	2.35
	G	0.0945	2.40
	H	0.0965	2.45
	J	0.0984	2.50
	K	0.1004	2.55
	L	0.1024	2.60
	M	0.1043	2.65
	N	0.1063	2.70
	P	0.1083	2.75
	Q	0.1102	2.80
	R	0.1122	2.85
	S	0.1142	2.90
	T	0.1161	2.95
	U	0.1181	3.00

GEAR THRUST CLEARANCES

Gear		in.	mm
1st	STD	0.0039–0.0157	0.10–0.40
	Limit	0.0177	0.45
2nd	STD	0.0039–0.0177	0.10–0.45
	Limit	0.0197	0.50
3rd	STD	0.0039–0.0138	0.10–0.35
	Limit	0.0157	0.40
4th	STD	0.0039–0.0217	0.10–0.55
	Limit	0.0236	0.60
5th	STD	0.0039–0.0224	0.10–0.57
	Limit	0.0256	0.65

SNAPRING THICKNESS SPECIFICATIONS

Part	Mark	in.	mm
Input shaft No. clutch hub			
	0	0.0906	2.30
	1	0.0929	2.36
	2	0.0953	2.42
	3	0.0976	2.48
	4	0.1000	2.54
	5	0.1024	2.60
Input rear bearing			
	A	0.0902	2.29
	B	0.0925	2.35
	C	0.0949	2.41
	D	0.0972	2.47
	E	0.0996	2.53
	F	0.1020	2.59
Output shaft No. 1 clutch hub			
	A	0.0984	2.50
	B	0.1008	2.56
	C	0.1031	2.62
	D	0.1055	2.68
	E	0.1079	2.74
	F	0.1102	2.80

CLEARANCE SPECIFICATIONS

Item		in.	mm
Gear oil clearance 1st, 2nd, 3rd, 4th and 5th	Standard	0.0006–0.0023	0.015–0.058
	Limit	0.0028	0.070
Reverse idler	Standard	0.0022–0.0036	0.056–0.092
	Limit	0.0047	0.120
Shift fork to hub sleeve clearance	Limit	0.039	1.0
Synchronizer ring to gear clearance	Limit	0.024	0.6

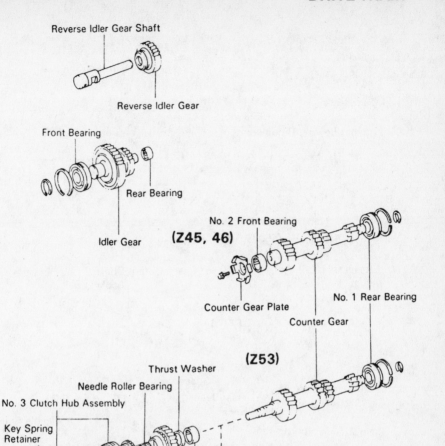

Exploded view of the reverse idler and countergear shaft assemblies — Z45, Z46, Z53 and Z54F transaxles

SNAPRING THICKNESS SPECIFICATIONS

Part	Mark	in.	mm
No. 3 clutch hub			
	A	0.0886	2.25
	B	0.0909	2.31
	C	0.0933	2.37
	D	0.0957	2.43
	E	0.0980	2.49
	F	0.1004	2.55
	G	0.1028	2.61

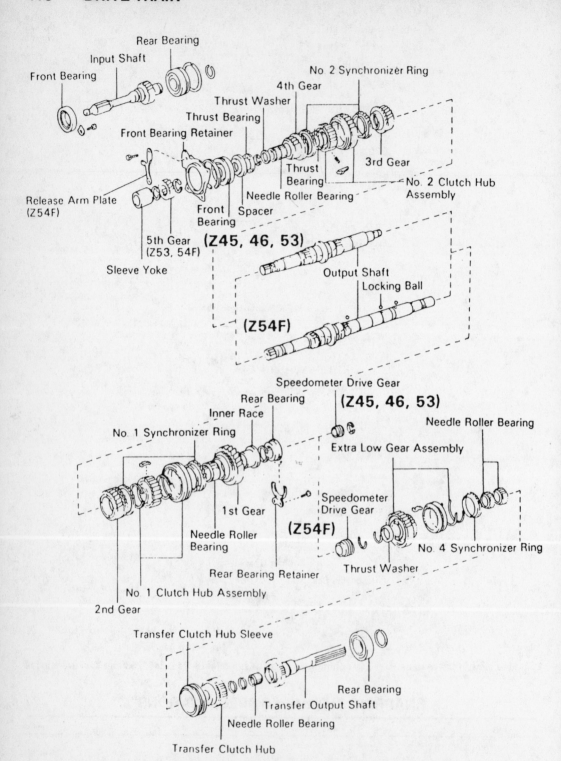

Exploded view of the input and output shaft assemblies — Z45, Z46, Z53 and Z54F transaxles

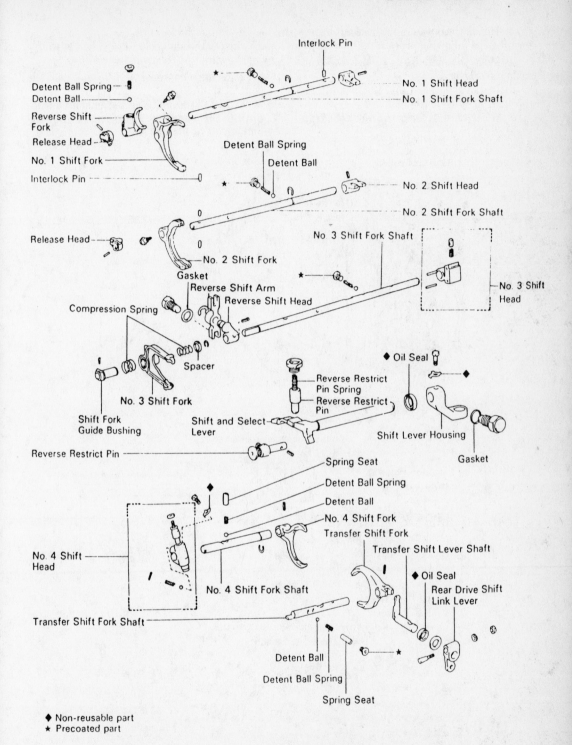

Interlock Pin

Detent Ball Spring
Detent Ball

No. 1 Shift Head
No. 1 Shift Fork Shaft

Reverse Shift
Fork

Release Head

Detent Ball Spring
Detent Ball

No. 1 Shift Fork

No. 2 Shift Head

Interlock Pin

No. 2 Shift Fork Shaft

Release Head

No 3 Shift Fork Shaft

No. 2 Shift Fork
Gasket

Reverse Shift Arm
Reverse Shift Head

No. 3 Shift
Head

Compression Spring

Spacer

Oil Seal

Reverse Restrict
Pin Spring
Reverse Restrict
Pin

No. 3 Shift Fork

Shift Fork
Guide Bushing

Shift and Select
Lever

Shift Lever Housing

Reverse Restrict Pin

Gasket

Spring Seat
Detent Ball Spring
Detent Ball
No. 4 Shift Fork
Transfer Shift Fork
Transfer Shift Lever Shaft

No. 4 Shift
Head

Oil Seal
Rear Drive Shift
Link Lever

No. 4 Shift Fork Shaft

Transfer Shift Fork Shaft

Detent Ball
Detent Ball Spring
Spring Seat

♦ Non-reusable part
★ Precoated part

Exploded view of the shifting fork, shafts and components — Z54F transaxle

14. Install the output shaft locknut by performing the following procedures:

a. Move the shift forks to lock the transaxle into 2 gears.

b. Install the spacer and the locknut and torque it to 87 ft. lbs. (118 Nm).

c. Move the shift forks to unlock the transaxle.

d. Stake the locknut.

15. Install the shift/select lever shaft assembly by performing the following procedures:

a. Using a new gasket position it onto the control shaft cover.

b. Install the shift/select lever shaft assembly into the transmission case and torque the bolts to 14 ft. lbs. (20 Nm).

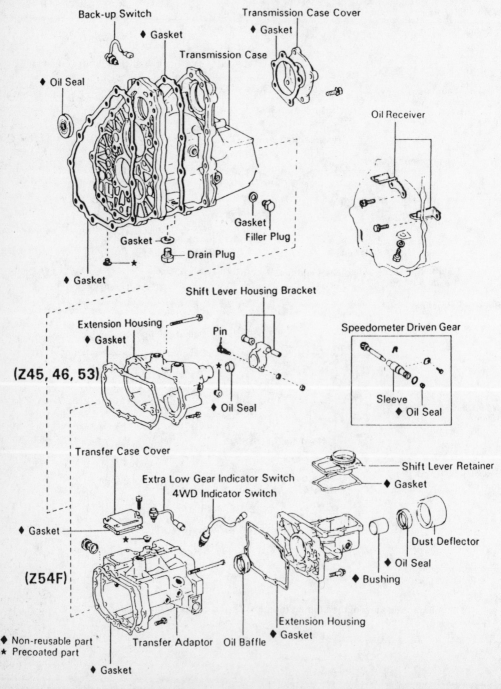

Exploded view of the transaxle case, the transfer adaptor and extension housing — Z45, Z46, Z53 and Z54F transaxles

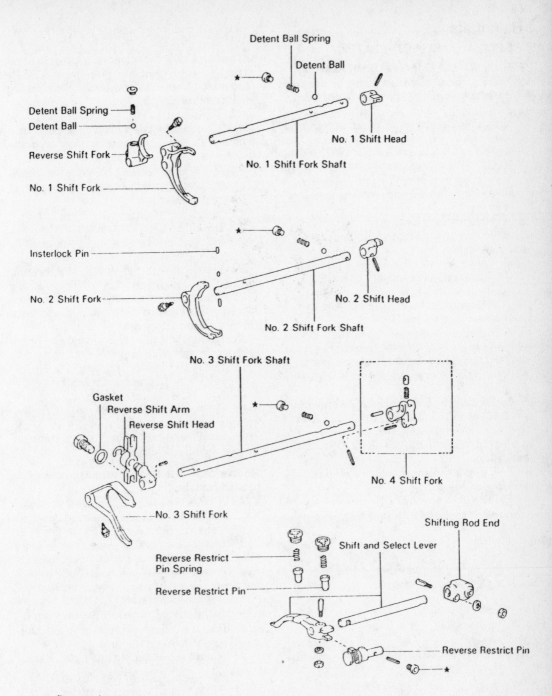

Detent Ball Spring

Detent Ball

Detent Ball Spring

Detent Ball

Reverse Shift Fork

No. 1 Shift Fork

No. 1 Shift Head

No. 1 Shift Fork Shaft

Insterlock Pin

No. 2 Shift Fork

No. 2 Shift Head

No. 2 Shift Fork Shaft

No. 3 Shift Fork Shaft

Gasket
Reverse Shift Arm
Reverse Shift Head

No. 4 Shift Fork

No. 3 Shift Fork

Shifting Rod End

Shift and Select Lever

Reverse Restrict Pin Spring

Reverse Restrict Pin

Reverse Restrict Pin

★ Precoated part

Exploded view of the shifting fork, shafts and components — Z45, Z46 and Z53 transaxles

16. Using sealant, apply a 0.04 in. (1mm) bead to the transmission case; be sure to place the sealant inside the bolt holes. Install the transmission case cover to the transmission case and torque the bolts to 13 ft. lbs. (18 Nm).

17. Using molybdenum disulphide lithium grease, lubricate the working surfaces of the release bearing hub inside groove, the input shaft spline and the release fork contact surface and install the parts.

18. Using a back-up light switch adapter, install the back-up light switch and torque it to 33 ft. lbs. (44 Nm).

19. Install the speedometer driven gear.

Halfshafts

REMOVAL AND INSTALLATION

Models Without Side Gear Shaft Assembly

NOTE: *The hub bearing could be damaged if it is subjected to the vehicle weight, such as when moving the vehicle with the halfshaft (driveshaft) removed. If it is necessary to place the vehicle weight on the hub bearing, support it with a special tool SST 09608–16041. Refer to the accompanying illustrations of this tool and halfshaft assembly. On MR2 vehicles modify the service procedure as necessary.*

1. Remove the wheel cover.
2. Remove the cotter pin, hub nut cap, hub nut and washer.
3. Loosen the wheel nuts.
4. Raise and safely support the car.
5. Remove the wheel.
6. Remove the lower control arm to ball joint attaching nuts and bolts.
7. Use a ball joint separator or equivalent to remove the tie rod ball joint from the knuckle. On MR2 vehicle disconnect the lower arm from the rear axle carrier. Disconnect the suspension arm.
8. Remove the bolts holding the brake caliper bracket to the steering knuckle. Use stiff wire to suspend the caliper out of the way; do not let the caliper hang by its hose. Remove the brake disc.
9. Using a puller or equivalent, push the axle from the hub.

NOTE: *On some models the axle can be separated from the hub using a brass or plastic*

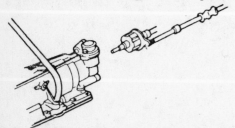

Using a tool to remove halfshaft from the transaxle

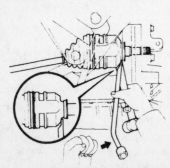

Removing the halfshaft

hammer some other models require the use of a puller.

10. Use a slide hammer and appropriate end fitting or equivalents to pull the driveshaft (halfshaft) from the transaxle. Remove the shaft from the car.
11. When reinstalling, install shaft into transaxle. If necessary, use a long brass drift and a hammer to drive the housing ribs onto the inner joint.

NOTE: *Before installing the halfshaft (driveshaft), position the snapring opening side facing downward.*

12. Install the shaft into the wheel hub.
13. Install the lower control arm to the lower ball joint. Tighten the nuts and bolts to 59 ft. lbs.
14. Install the tie rod end to the steering knuckle and tighten the nut to 36 ft. lbs. On MR2 vehicle connect the lower arm to the rear axle carrier torque to 83 ft. lbs. and reconnect the suspension arm torque to 36 ft. lbs.
15. Install the brake disc; install the brake caliper and tighten the bolts.
16. Install the wheel.
17. Install the hub nut and washer.
18. Lower the vehicle to the ground.
19. Tighten the wheel lugs to 76 ft. lbs. Tighten the hub nut to 137 ft. lbs.
20. Install the nut, cap, cotter pin and washer. Install the wheel cover.

Models With Side Gear Shaft Assembly (Bolted Halfshaft)

NOTE: *The hub bearing could be damaged if it is subjected to the vehicle weight, such as when moving the vehicle with the halfshaft (driveshaft) removed. If necessary to place the vehicle weight on the hub bearing, support it with a special tool SST 09608–16041. Refer to the necessary illustration of this tool and halfshaft assembly. On MR2 vehicles modify the service procedure as necessary.*

1. Raise the vehicle and support it with jackstands safely. Remove the tires.
2. Remove the cotter pin and locknut cap.

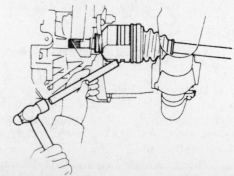

Removing the halfshaft

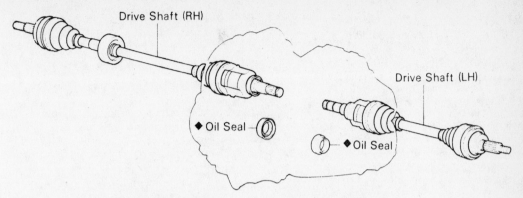

Halfshaft assembly — models without side gear shaft

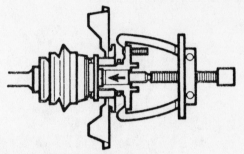

Using tool to remove axle from hub

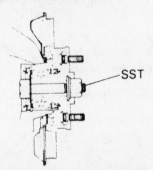

Toyota special tool number 09608–16041

3. Have an assistant step on the brake pedal and at the same time, loosen and remove the bearing locknut.

4. While the assistant is still depressing the brake pedal, loosen and remove the six nuts or bolts which connect the halfshaft to the differential side gear shaft. Place matchmarks on halfshaft (driveshaft) and side gear shaft.

5. Remove the brake caliper and position it out of the way. Remove the brake disc.

6. Remove the two retaining nuts and then disconnect the lower arm from the steering knuckle. On MR2 vehicle disconnect the lower arm from the rear axle carrier. Disconnect the suspension arm.

7. Use a two-armed puller or equivalent and remove the axle hub from the outer end of the halfshaft.

8. Remove the halfshaft (driveshaft).

9. To reinstall, place the outboard side of the shaft into the axle hub and then insert the inner end into the differential. Align the knock pins or matchmarks of the side gear shaft with the matchmarks or knock pins of the halfshaft. Finger tighten the six nuts.

NOTE: *Be careful not to damage the boots during installation.*

10. Install the lower arm to the steering knuckle and tighten the bolts to 47 ft. lbs. On MR2 vehicle connect the lower arm to the rear axle carrier torque to 83 ft. lbs. and reconnect the suspension arm torque to 36 ft. lbs.

11. Install the disc and reinstall the caliper and bracket.

12. While an assistant depresses the brake pedal, tighten the six nuts or bolts holding the axle to the side gear shaft to 27 ft. lbs. (nuts)

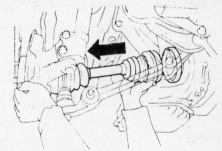

Removing halfshaft (bolted type)

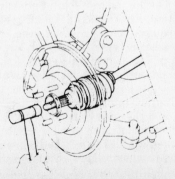

Disconnect halfshaft from the axle hub

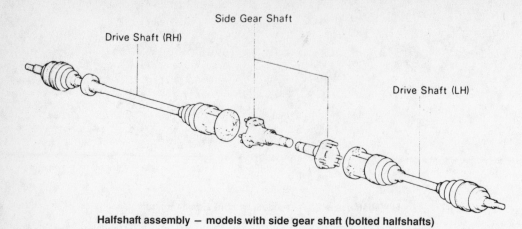

Halfshaft assembly — models with side gear shaft (bolted halfshafts)

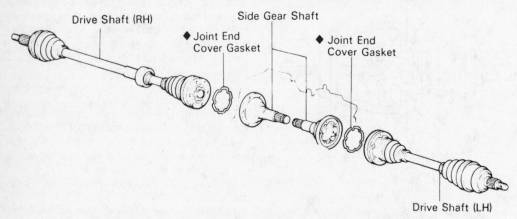

Halfshaft assembly — models with side gear shaft (bolted halfshafts)

and on MR2 vehicle supercharged applications to 48 ft. lbs. (bolts).

13. Install the hub nut and washer.

14. Install the wheel.

15. Lower the vehicle to the ground.

16. Tighten the wheel lugs to 76 ft. lbs. Tighten the hub nut to 137 ft. lbs.

17. Install the nut, cap, cotter pin and washer. Install the wheel cover.

OVERHAUL

The drive axle assembly is a flexible unit consisting of an inner and outer constant velocity (cv) joint joined by an axle shaft. Care must be taken not to over-extend the joint assembly during repairs or handling. When either end of the shaft is disconnected from the car, any over-extension could result in separation of the internal components and possible joint failure.

The CV joints are protected by rubber boots or seals, designed to keep the high-temperature grease in and the road grime and water out. The most common cause of joint failure is a ripped boot (tow hooks on halfshaft when car is being towed) which allows the lubricant to leave the joint, thus causing heavy wear. The boots are exposed to road hazards all the time

and should be inspected frequently. Any time a boot is found to be damaged or slit, it should be replaced immediately.

NOTE: *Whenever the driveshaft is held in a vise, use pieces of wood in the jaws to protect the components from damage or deformation. Refer to exploded view of halfshaft assembly components as a guide and modify the service procedures for overhaul.*

Models Without Side Gear Shaft Assembly Type

1. Remove the axle and mount in a vise so that the outer joint may be worked on.

2. Remove the boot retaining clamps. Slide the boot out of the way, exposing the joint.

3. Use snapring pliers to release the race retaining ring. Pull the shaft from the cage.

4. Using a brass drift, gently tap on the bottom of the cage until it tilts enough to all the first ball to be removed at the top.

5. Continue removing other balls is a similar fashion.

6. Rotate the cage and inner race 90° and remove the cage and inner race.

7. Clean and inspect all parts. The slightest imperfection on either the balls or the race will

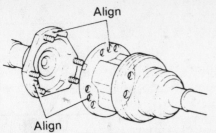

Align knock pins on halfshaft assembly (bolted type) installation

require replacement of the components. Look for any scratches, cracks or galling of the metal.

8. Position the driveshaft in the vise so that the inner joint may be worked on.

9. Remove the boot clamps. Slide the boot back, exposing the joint.

10. Remove the tri-pot housing from the axle shaft.

11. Remove the spacer ring with snapring pliers.

12. Use a brass drift and hammer to gently tap the joint assembly towards the center of the axle.

13. Remove the outer driveshaft snapring.

14. Remove the spider assembly from the axle by tapping it off with a brass punch and hammer. Apply force evenly around spider.

NOTE: *The spider assembly and axle should have factory alignment marks showing. Also note the marks on axle shaft and tri-pot housing. If no marks are present, make matchmarks before disassembly.*

15. Remove the boot.

16. Disassemble the spider assembly into its component parts of retainer, ball, needle bearing and spider.

17. Clean all parts thoroughly and inspect for wear, damage or corrosion. Replace any component which is not in virtually perfect condition.

18. Reassemble the spider assembly

19. Apply molybdenum grease liberally to tri-pot housing and spider.

20. Install the new boot onto the axle shaft and install a new small clamp.

21. Using the brass drift and hammer, install the spider assembly onto the shaft.

22. Install the outboard snapring, then tap the tri-pot assembly down over the snapring.

23. Install the spider assembly and drive axle assembly into the tri-pot housing.

24. Install the boot over the joint and secure the new large clamp.

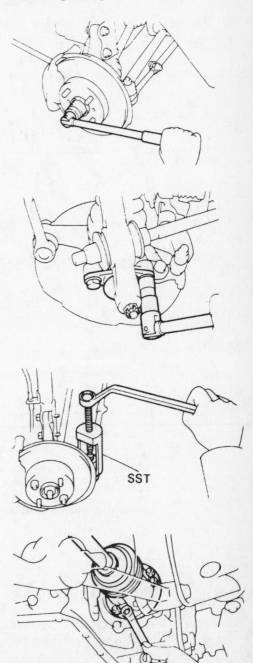

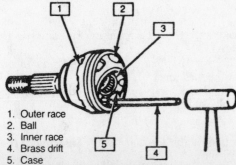

1. Outer race
2. Ball
3. Inner race
4. Brass drift
5. Case

Removing ball bearing assembly

Removing the halfshaft from the MR2 vehicle

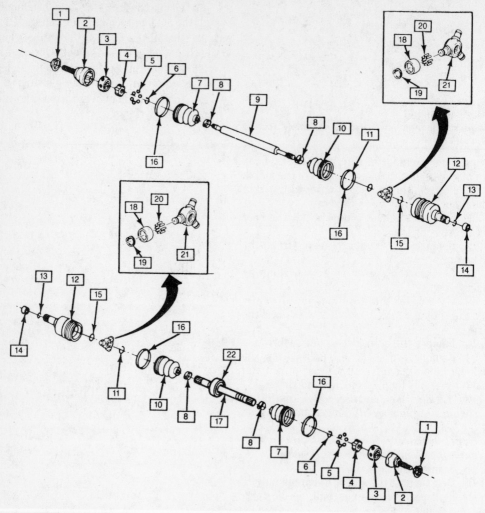

1. Deflector ring
2. CV joint outer race
3. Case
4. CV joint inner race
5. Balls
6. Axle shaft snap ring
7. Outboard boot
8. Small boot clamp
9. Right side drive shaft
10. Tri-pot (inboard) boot
11. Axle shaft retaining ring
12. Tri-pot joint housing
13. Axle shaft retaining pins
14. Drive axle dust cover
15. Axle shaft snapring
16. Large boot clamps
17. Left side drive shaft
18. Tri-pot joint ball
19. Joint ball and bearing retainer
20. Needle bearings
21. Joint spider
22. Drive axle damper

Halfshaft components — without side gear shaft assembly type

25. Position the axle shaft so that the outer joint may be worked on.

26. Install the cage into the race with the retaining ring side of the inner race facing the transaxle side of the shaft.

27. Pack the joint liberally with molybdenum grease and install the cage and inner race at 90° into the outer race.

28. Tip the race and install the six balls.

29. Install a new boot onto the shaft.

30. Install the race retaining ring on the shaft.

31. Insert the shaft into the inner race and make sure that the retaining ring is properly seated.

32. Fit the boot over the joint and install new boot clamps.

33. Check both joints for freedom of motion and lack of binding.

Models With Side Gear Shaft Assembly Type

1. Remove the boot retaining clamps.

2. Using paint or a scribing tool, place

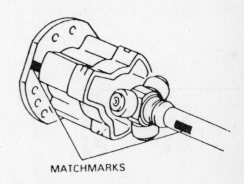

SHAFT RETAINING RING
REMOVE FROM AXLE SHAFT
THEN SLIDE SPIDER
ASSEMBLY OFF AXLE   SPIDER ASSEMBLY

SNAP RING
PLIERS

SPACER
RING

SPACER RING
SLIDE RING BACK ON
AXLE SHAFT

NOTICE: BE SURE
SPACER RING IS SEATED IN
GROOVE AT REASSEMBLY

Removing the spider assembly from the shaft

matchmarks on the tri-pod housing and drive-shaft. Do not punch the marks into the metal.

3. Remove the tri-pot housing from the driveshaft.

4. Use snapring pliers to remove the shaft retaining ring.

5. Use a punch and hammer to matchmark the driveshaft and spider.

6. Remove the spider assembly from the drive shaft with a brass punch and hammer.

7. Remove the boot from the inner joint.

8. If working on the right axle, remove the driveshaft damper.

9. If working on the right axle, remove the outer joint boot.

10. Check the inside and outside of the seals for damage.

11. Clean all parts thoroughly and inspect for wear, damage or corrosion. Replace any component which is not in virtually perfect condition.

12. Reassemble the spider assembly.

13. If working on the right axle, temporarily install a new boot and new clamp to the outer joint.

14. If working on the right axle, install the drive shaft damper with a new clamp. Place the clamp in line with the groove of the driveshaft.

15. Temporarily install a new inner joint boot and new clamp to the driveshaft.

NOTE: *The boot and clamp for the inner joint are larger than those for the outer joint.*

16. Position the beveled side of the spider splines toward the outer CV-joint. Align the matchmarks made earlier and tap the spider onto the driveshaft with a brass punch and hammer.

17. Install a NEW shaft retaining ring.

18. If working on the right axle, pack the outer joint boot with molybdenum grease. (Capacity is 0.25–0.30 lbs).

19. Install the boot over the joint.

20. Pack the tri-pot joint and boot with molybdenum grease. Correct capacities are: Manual transmission, 158.75–181.5 g (0.35–0.40 lbs.) and Automatic transmission, 181.5–227 g (0.40–0.50 lbs.).

21. Align the matchmarks made earlier and install the tri-pot housing onto the drive shaft.

22. Install the boot over the joint.

23. Be sure each boot in on the shaft groove. Bend each boot clamp into place and secure it.

24. Check both joints for freedom of motion and lack of binding.

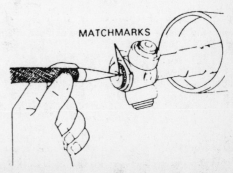

MATCHMARKS

PIVOT CAGE AND INNER RACE AT 90°
TO CENTER LINE OF OUTER RACE
WITH CAGE WINDOWS ALIGNED
WITH LANDS OF OUTER RACE,
LIFT OUT CAGE AND INNER RACE

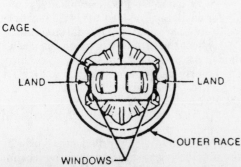

CAGE

LAND — LAND

OUTER RACE

WINDOWS

Removing the cage and inner race

MATCHMARKS

Correct placement of matchmarks before disassembly

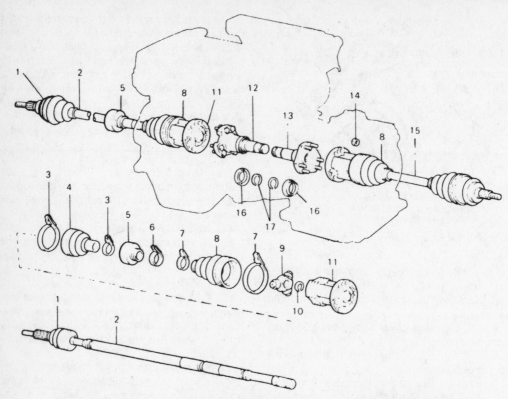

1. Joint, outer CV
2. Shaft, drive (RH)
3. Clamp, outer CV joint seal ret.
4. Seal, outer CV joint
5. Damper, drive shaft
6. Clamp, damper ret.
7. Clamp, tri-pot joint seal ret.
8. Seal, tri-pot joint
9. Spider tri pot joint
10. Ring, shaft ret.
11. Housing, tri pot
12. Shaft, side gear (RH)
13. Shaft, side gear (LH)
14. Nut, axle to side gear shaft
15. Shaft, drive (LH)
16. Seal, side gear shaft oil
17. Ring, oil seal ret

Halfshaft components — with side gear shaft assembly type

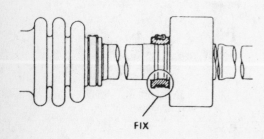

FIX

Right side axle — make certain the damper retaining ring is in the groove

25. Check that the boots are not stretched or compressed when the axle is in a normal or "at rest" position.

CLUTCH

CAUTION: *The clutch driven disc contains asbestos which has been determined to be a cancer causing agent. Never clean clutch sur-* faces *with compressed air. Avoid inhaling any dust from any clutch area! When cleaning clutch surfaces, use commercially available brake cleaning fluids.*

Adjustments

PEDAL HEIGHT AND FREE PLAY

Refer to the "Clutch Pedal Height and Pedal Free Play Chart" for specifications and procedure for adjustment. Adjust the pedal height to specification, by rotating the pedal stop (nut).

1. Adjust the clearance between the master cylinder piston and the pushrod to specification. Loosen the pushrod locknut and rotate the pushrod while depressing the clutch pedal lightly with your finger.

2. Tighten the locknut when finished with the adjustment.

3. Adjust the release cylinder free-play by loosening the release cylinder pushrod locknut and rotating the pushrod until the specification is obtained.

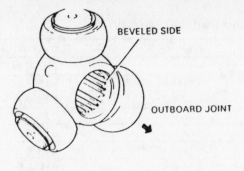

BEVELED SIDE

OUTBOARD JOINT

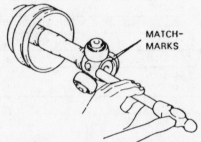

MATCH-
MARKS

Observe the matchmarks when installing the spider onto the shaft

4. Measure the clutch pedal free-play after performing the above adjustments. If it is not within specifications, repeat Steps 1–3 until it is.

Disc and Pressure Plate

REMOVAL AND INSTALLATION

NOTE: *Do not allow grease or oil to get on any of the disc, pressure plate, or flywheel surfaces.*

1. Remove the transmission/transaxle from the car as previously detailed.
2. Remove the clutch cover and disc from the bell housing.
3. Unfasten the release fork bearing clips. Withdraw the release bearing hub, complete with the release bearing.
4. Remove the tension spring from the clutch linkage.
5. Remove the release fork and support.
6. Punch matchmarks on the clutch cover (pressure plate) and flywheel so that the pres-

Troubleshooting Basic Clutch Problems

Problem	Cause
Excessive clutch noise	Throwout bearing noises are more audible at the lower end of pedal travel. The usual causes are: • Riding the clutch • Too little pedal free-play • Lack of bearing lubrication A bad clutch shaft pilot bearing will make a high pitched squeal, when the clutch is disengaged and the transmission is in gear or within the first 2″ of pedal travel. The bearing must be replaced. Noise from the clutch linkage is a clicking or snapping that can be heard or felt as the pedal is moved completely up or down. This usually requires lubrication. Transmitted engine noises are amplified by the clutch housing and heard in the passenger compartment. They are usually the result of insufficient pedal free-play and can be changed by manipulating the clutch pedal.
Clutch slips (the car does not move as it should when the clutch is engaged)	This is usually most noticeable when pulling away from a standing start. A severe test is to start the engine, apply the brakes, shift into high gear and SLOWLY release the clutch pedal. A healthy clutch will stall the engine. If it slips it may be due to: • A worn pressure plate or clutch plate • Oil soaked clutch plate • Insufficient pedal free-play
Clutch drags or fails to release	The clutch disc and some transmission gears spin briefly after clutch disengagement. Under normal conditions in average temperatures, 3 seconds is maximum spin-time. Failure to release properly can be caused by: • Too light transmission lubricant or low lubricant level • Improperly adjusted clutch linkage
Low clutch life	Low clutch life is usually a result of poor driving habits or heavy duty use. Riding the clutch, pulling heavy loads, holding the car on a grade with the clutch instead of the brakes and rapid clutch engagement all contribute to low clutch life.

Clutch Pedal Height and Pedal Free Play

Year	Model	Pedal Height	Pedal Freeplay
1984–85	Corolla (RWD)	6.34–6.73	0.51–0.91
	Corolla (FWD)	5.65–6.04	0.51–0.91 ①
1986–87	Corolla (RWD)	6.44–6.83	0.51–0.91 ②
	Corolla (FWD)	5.82–6.22	0.28–0.67
1988	Corolla (FWD)	5.82–6.22	0.20–0.59
1989–90	Corolla (FWD)	5.71–6.10	0.20–0.59
1986–87	MR2	6.03–6.41	0.20–0.59
1988–89	MR2	6.18–6.57	0.20–0.59
1984	Tercel	7.24–7.64	0.08–1.10 ③
1985	Tercel	6.97–7.36	0.08–1.10 ③
1986	Tercel	7.13–7.44	0.08–0.98 ③
1987–90	Tercel Sedan	6.38–6.77 6.14–6.54	0.20–0.59
1987–88	Tercel Wagon	6.93–7.24	0.08–1.10 ③

① 0.20–0.59 Diesel engine
② 0.20–0.59 4A-6 engine
③ Check release sector and pawl—6 notches should be remaining on the sector—if not service system

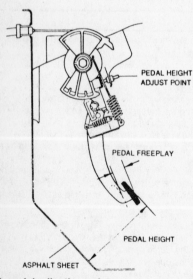

Clutch pedal adjusting points

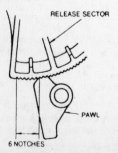

Minimum pawl and sector position for used clutch — Tercel

sure plate can be returned to its original position during installation.

7. Slowly unfasten the screws which attach the retracting springs. Loosen each screw one turn at a time until the tension is released.

CAUTION: *If the screws are released too quickly, the clutch assembly will fly apart, causing possible injury!*

8. Separate the pressure plate from the clutch cover/spring assembly.

9. Inspect the parts for wear or deterioration. It is strongly recommended that all three components of the clutch system–disc, pressure plate and bearing–be replaced as a unit if any part is worn. The slight additional cost of the parts is more than offset by not having to disassemble it again later on to replace another component.

10. Inspect the flywheel for any signs of cracking, bluing in the steel (a sign of extreme heat) or scoring. Any bluing or cracks which are found require replacement of the flywheel. The flywheel should be free of all but the slightest ridges and valleys or scores. Any gouging deep enough to catch your fingernail during inspection requires replacement. A scored flywheel will immediately attack a new clutch disc, causing slippage and vibration.

If the flywheel must be replaced, please refer to Chapter 3 for further directions.

11. When reassembling, apply a thin coating of multipurpose grease to the release bearing hub and release fork contact points. Also, pack

PUSH ROD PLAY AND FREEPLAY ADJUST POINT

PEDAL HEIGHT ADJUST POINT

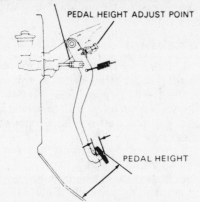

PEDAL HEIGHT

Clutch pedal height and freeplay adjustment

PEDAL FREEPLAY

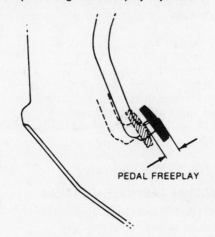

Clutch pedal freeplay

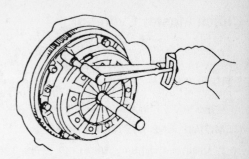

Use a pilot tool when installing the clutch assembly

the groove inside the clutch hub with multipurpose grease and lubricate the pivot points of the release fork.

12. Align the matchmarks on the clutch cover and flywheel which were made during disassembly. Install the clutch and pressure plate assembly and tighten the retaining bolts just finger tight.

13. Center the clutch disc by using a clutch pilot tool or an old input shaft. (Pilot tools are available at most automotive parts stores.) Insert the pilot into the end of the input shaft front bearing, wiggle it gently to align the clutch disc and pressure plate and tighten the retaining bolts. The bolts should be tightened in two or three steps, gradually and evenly. Final bolt torque is 14 ft. lbs.

14. Install the release bearing, fork and boot.

15. Reinstall the transmission/transaxle as outlined. Roadtest the vehicle for proper operation.

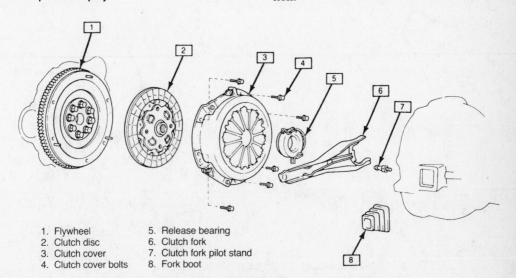

1. Flywheel
2. Clutch disc
3. Clutch cover
4. Clutch cover bolts
5. Release bearing
6. Clutch fork
7. Clutch fork pilot stand
8. Fork boot

Clutch components

Clutch Master Cylinder

NOTE: *When inspecting the clutch hydraulic system for leakage or impaired function, check the inside of the firewall (under the carpet) below the clutch master cylinder. A master cylinder leak may not show up under the cylinder on the engine side of the firewall.*

REMOVAL AND INSTALLATION

1. Drain or siphon the fluid from the master cylinder.
2. Disconnect the hydraulic line to the clutch from the master cylinder.

NOTE: *Do not spill brake fluid on the painted surfaced of the vehicle.*

3. Inside the car, remove the under dash panel and the air duct.
4. Remove the pedal return spring.
5. Remove the spring clip and clevis pin.
6. Unfasten the bolts which secure the master cylinder to the firewall. Withdraw the assembly from the firewall side.
7. Install the master cylinder with its retaining nuts to the firewall.
8. Connect the line from the clutch to the master cylinder.
9. Connect the clevis and install the clevis pin and spring clip.
10. Install the pedal return spring.
11. Fill the reservoir with clean, fresh brake fluid and bleed the system.
12. Check the cylinder and the hose connection for leaks.
13. Adjust the clutch pedal.
14. Reinstall the air duct and under dash cover panel.

OVERHAUL

1. Refer to the exploded view of clutch master cylinder components use this as a guide for the overhaul procedure. Clamp the master cylinder body in a vise with protected jaws.
2. Separate the reservoir assembly from the master cylinder.
3. Remove the snapring and remove the pushrod/piston assembly.
4. Inspect the master cylinder bore for scoring, grooving or corrosion. If any of these conditions are observed, replace the cylinder. Inspect piston, spring, push rod and boot for damage or wear replace any parts which are worn or defective.
5. Before reassembly, coat all parts with clean brake fluid.
6. Install the piston assembly in the cylinder bore.
7. Fit the pushrod over the washer and secure them with the snapring.
8. Install the reservoir and tighten the nut to 18 ft. lbs.

Clutch Slave Cylinder

REMOVAL AND INSTALLATION

NOTE: *Do not spill brake fluid on the painted surface of the vehicle.*

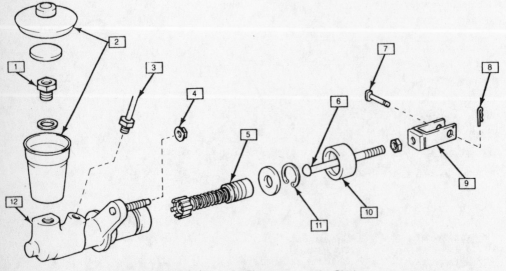

1. Reservoir tank bolt	5. Piston
2. Reservoir tank	6. Pushrod
3. Clutch line	7. Clevis pin
4. Mounting nut	8. Spring clip

9. Clevis	
10. Boot	
11. Snap ring	
12. Master cylinder	

Exploded view clutch master cylinder

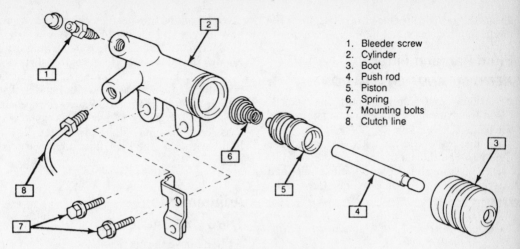

1. Bleeder screw
2. Cylinder
3. Boot
4. Push rod
5. Piston
6. Spring
7. Mounting bolts
8. Clutch line

Exploded view clutch slave (actuator) cylinder

1. Raise the vehicle and safely support it with jackstands or equivalent.

2. If necessary, remove the splash shield to gain access to the release cylinder.

3. Remove the clutch fork return spring.

4. Unfasten the hydraulic line from the release cylinder by removing its retaining nut.

5. Remove the release cylinder retaining nuts and remove the cylinder.

6. Reinstall the cylinder to the clutch housing and tighten the bolts to 9 ft. lbs.

7. Connect the hydraulic line and tighten it to 11 ft. lbs.

8. Install the clutch release spring.

9. Bleed the system and remember to top up the fluid in the master cylinder when finished.

10. Install the splash shield as necessary. Lower the car to the ground.

OVERHAUL

1. Refer to the exploded view of clutch slave (actuator) cylinder components use this as a guide for the overhaul procedure. Remove the pushrod assembly and the rubber boot.

2. Withdraw the piston, complete with its cup; don't remove the cup unless it is being replaced.

3. Wash all the parts in brake fluid.

4. Replace any worn or damaged parts. Inspect the cylinder bore carefully for any sign of damage, wear or corrosion.

5. Before reassembly, coat all the parts in clean brake fluid. Insert the spring and piston into the cylinder.

6. Install the boot and insert the pushrod.

BLEEDING

1. Fill the master cylinder reservoir with brake fluid.

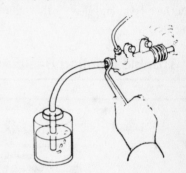

Slave cylinder bleeding

NOTE: *Do not spill brake fluid on the painted surface of the vehicle!*

2. Fit a tube over the bleeder plug and place the other end into a clean jar half-filled with brake fluid.

3. Depress the clutch pedal, loosen the bleeder plug with a wrench, and allow the fluid to flow into the jar.

4. Tighten the plug and then release the clutch pedal.

5. Repeat these steps until no air bubbles are visible in the bleeder tube.

6. When there are no more air bubbles, tighten the plug while keeping the clutch pedal fully depressed.

7. Top off the fluid in the master cylinder reservoir.

8. Check the system for leaks.

AUTOMATIC TRANSMISSION

Identification

On some models an identification tag is attached to the side of the transmission case above the oil pan. Included on the tag is the model number and serial number of the unit.

Fluid Pan and Filter

REMOVAL AND INSTALLATION

1. Raise and safely support the vehicle. Clean the exterior of the transmission around the pan.

2. Remove the drain plug and drain the fluid into a suitable container.

3. Unscrew all the pan retaining bolts and carefully remove the pan assembly. Discard the gasket.

NOTE: *There will still be some fluid in the oil pan. Be careful not to damage the filler tube or the O-ring.*

4. Remove the small magnet from the bottom of the oil pan and clean it thoroughly if so equipped.

5. Clean the transmission oil pan with a suitable solvent and allow it to air dry.

6. Remove the retaining bolts and then remove the oil strainer (filter) and gaskets.

7. Installation is the reverse of the removal procedures. Always use a new filter and gasket. Torque the oil strainer (filter) retaining bolts 48 in. lbs. Torque the oil pan retaining bolts in (criss-cross manner) steps to about 4 ft. lbs. Refill with the specified fluid to the correct level.

Adjustments

THROTTLE CABLE

1. Remove the air cleaner.

2. Confirm that the accelerator linkage opens the throttle fully. Adjust the linkage as necessary.

Troubleshooting Basic Automatic Transmission Problems

Problem	Cause	Solution
Fluid leakage	• Defective pan gasket	• Replace gasket or tighten pan bolts
	• Loose filler tube	• Tighten tube nut
	• Loose extension housing to transmission case	• Tighten bolts
	• Converter housing area leakage	• Have transmission checked professionally
Fluid flows out the oil filler tube	• High fluid level	• Check and correct fluid level
	• Breather vent clogged	• Open breather vent
	• Clogged oil filter or screen	• Replace filter or clean screen (change fluid also)
	• Internal fluid leakage	• Have transmission checked professionally
Transmission overheats (this is usually accompanied by a strong burned odor to the fluid)	• Low fluid level	• Check and correct fluid level
	• Fluid cooler lines clogged	• Drain and refill transmission. If this doesn't cure the problem, have cooler lines cleared or replaced.
	• Heavy pulling or hauling with insufficient cooling	• Install a transmission oil cooler
	• Faulty oil pump, internal slippage	• Have transmission checked professionally
Buzzing or whining noise	• Low fluid level	• Check and correct fluid level
	• Defective torque converter, scored gears	• Have transmission checked professionally
No forward or reverse gears or slippage in one or more gears	• Low fluid level	• Check and correct fluid level
	• Defective vacuum or linkage controls, internal clutch or band failure	• Have unit checked professionally
Delayed or erratic shift	• Low fluid level	• Check and correct fluid level
	• Broken vacuum lines	• Repair or replace lines
	• Internal malfunction	• Have transmission checked professionally

Lockup Torque Converter Service Diagnosis

Problem	Cause	Solution

No lockup	· Faulty oil pump
	· Sticking governor valve
	· Valve body malfunction
	   (a) Stuck switch valve
	   (b) Stuck lockup valve
	   (c) Stuck fail-safe valve
	· Failed locking clutch
	· Leaking turbine hub seal
	· Faulty input shaft or seal ring
		· Replace oil pump
		· Repair or replace as necessary
		· Repair or replace valve body or its internal components as necessary
		
		· Replace torque converter
		· Replace torque converter
		· Repair or replace as necessary

Will not unlock	· Sticking governor valve
	· Valve body malfunction
	   (a) Stuck switch valve
	   (b) Stuck lockup valve
	   (c) Stuck fail-safe valve
		· Repair or replace as necessary
		· Repair or replace valve body or its internal components as necessary

Stays locked up at too low a speed in direct	· Sticking governor valve
	· Valve body malfunction
	   (a) Stuck switch valve
	   (b) Stuck lockup valve
	   (c) Stuck fail-safe valve
		· Repair or replace as necessary
		· Repair or replace valve body or its internal components as necessary

Locks up or drags in low or second	· Faulty oil pump
	· Valve body malfunction
	   (a) Stuck switch valve
	   (b) Stuck fail-safe valve
		· Replace oil pump
		· Repair or replace valve body or its internal components as necessary

Sluggish or stalls in reverse	· Faulty oil pump
	· Plugged cooler, cooler lines or fittings
	· Valve body malfunction
	   (a) Stuck switch valve
	   (b) Faulty input shaft or seal ring
		· Replace oil pump as necessary
		· Flush or replace cooler and flush lines and fittings
		· Repair or replace valve body or its internal components as necessary

Loud chatter during lockup engagement (cold)	· Faulty torque converter · Failed locking clutch · Leaking turbine hub seal	· Replace torque converter · Replace torque converter · Replace torque converter
Vibration or shudder during lockup engagement	· Faulty oil pump · Valve body malfunction · Faulty torque converter · Engine needs tune-up	· Repair or replace oil pump as necessary · Repair or replace valve body or its internal components as necessary · Replace torque converter · Tune engine
Vibration after lockup engagement	· Faulty torque converter · Exhaust system strikes underbody · Engine needs tune-up · Throttle linkage misadjusted	· Replace torque converter · Align exhaust system · Tune engine · Adjust throttle linkage
Vibration when revved in neutral Overheating: oil blows out of dip stick tube or pump seal	· Torque converter out of balance · Plugged cooler, cooler lines or fittings · Stuck switch valve	· Replace torque converter · Flush or replace cooler and flush lines and fittings · Repair switch valve in valve body or replace valve body
Shudder after lockup engagement	· Faulty oil pump · Plugged cooler, cooler lines or fittings · Valve body malfunction · Faulty torque converter · Fail locking clutch · Exhaust system strikes underbody · Engine needs tune-up · Throttle linkage misadjusted	· Replace oil pump · Flush or replace cooler and flush lines and fittings · Repair or replace valve body or its internal components as necessary · Replace torque converter · Replace torque converter · Align exhaust system · Tune engine · Adjust throttle linkage

Transmission Fluid Indications

The appearance and odor of the transmission fluid can give valuable clues to the overall condition of the transmission. Always note the appearance of the fluid when you check the fluid level or change the fluid. Rub a small amount of fluid between your fingers to feel for grit and smell the fluid on the dipstick.

If the fluid appears:	It indicates:
Clear and red colored	• Normal operation
Discolored (extremely dark red or brownish) or smells burned	• Band or clutch pack failure, usually caused by an overheated transmission. Hauling very heavy loads with insufficient power or failure to change the fluid, often result in overheating. Do not confuse this appearance with newer fluids that have a darker red color and a strong odor (though not a burned odor).
Foamy or aerated (light in color and full of bubbles)	• The level is too high (gear train is churning oil) • An internal air leak (air is mixing with the fluid). Have the transmission checked professionally.
Solid residue in the fluid	• Defective bands, clutch pack or bearings. Bits of band material or metal abrasives are clinging to the dipstick. Have the transmission checked professionally.
Varnish coating on the dipstick	• The transmission fluid is overheating

3. Peel the rubber dust boot back from the throttle cable.

4. Loosen the adjustment nuts on the throttle cable bracket just enough to allow cable housing movement.

5. Have an assistant depress the accelerator pedal fully.

6. Adjust the cable housing so that the distance between its end and the cable stop collar is 0.04 in. (1mm).

7. Tighten the adjustment nuts. Make sure that the adjustment hasn't changed. Install the dust boot and the air cleaner.

SHIFT LINKAGE

1. Raise and safely support the vehicle. Loosen the adjusting nut on the shift lever.

2. Push the control shaft lever fully rearward.

3. Bring the lever (control shaft) back 2 notches to N (Neutral) position. Set the shifter lever to the N (neutral) position. Tighten the shifter lever nut.

4. Road test the vehicle for proper operation.

Neutral Safety Switch

NOTE: *On the Corolla RWD vehicle the back-up light switch is incorporated in the neutral safety switch assembly.*

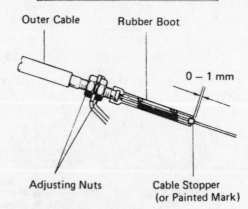

WHEN THROTTLE VALVE IS FULLY OPENED

Outer Cable   Rubber Boot

0 – 1 mm

Adjusting Nuts   Cable Stopper (or Painted Mark)

Throttle linkage adjustment

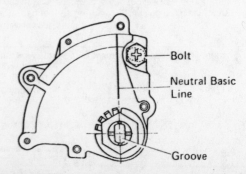

Bolt

Neutral Basic Line

Groove

Neutral safety switch adjustment

Automatic transmission filter replacement

REMOVAL AND INSTALLATION

1. Raise and safely support the vehicle.
2. Place vehicle in the N (neutral position). Remove the control shaft lever nut. Remove the neutral safety switch adjusting bolt.
3. Disconnect the electrical connections to the switch. Remove the switch assembly.
4. Installation is the reverse of the removal procedures. Torque the switch adjusting bolt to 48 in. lbs. and control shaft nut (install the grommet facing the groove toward the switch body) to 61 in. lbs. Adjust the neutral safety switch as necessary. The vehicle should start ONLY in N or P position.

ADJUSTMENT

NOTE: *If the engine will start with the selector in any range other than "N" or "P", the neutral safety switch will require adjustment.*

1. Locate the neutral safety switch on the right side of the transmission and loosen the switch bolt.
2. Move the gear selector to the N position.
3. Align the groove on the safety switch shaft with the basic line which is scribed on the housing.
4. With the groove and the line aligned (hold position), tighten the switch bolt to 48 in. lbs. Check switch for proper operation.

Back-Up Light Switch

REMOVAL AND INSTALLATION

Corolla RWD

For back-up light removal and installation service procedure refer to the "Neutral Safety Switch".

Transmission

REMOVAL AND INSTALLATION

Corolla RWD

1. Disconnect the negative battery cable.
2. Remove the air cleaner assembly. Disconnect the transmission throttle cable. Disconnect the starter assembly electrical connections.
3. Raise the vehicle and support it safely. Drain the transmission fluid. Remove the (matchmark flange for correct installation) driveshaft.
4. Remove the exhaust pipe clamp. Disconnect the exhaust pipe from the exhaust manifold.
5. Disconnect the manual shift linkage. Disconnect the oil cooler lines. Remove the starter.
6. Support the engine and transmission using the proper equipment. Remove the rear crossmember.
7. Disconnect the speedometer cable. Disconnect all necessary electrical wiring from the transmission.
8. Remove the torque converter cover. Remove the torque converter-to-engine retaining bolts.
NOTE: *Install a guide pin in one of the torque converter bolt holes. A guide pin can be made by cutting off the head of a bolt. Pry on the end of the guide pin to begin moving the transmission with the converter to the rear of the vehicle. The guide pin helps keep the converter with the transmission assembly.*
9. Remove the bolts retaining the transmission to the engine. Carefully lower and remove the transmission from the vehicle.
10. Installation is the reverse of the removal procedure. To check torque converter installa-

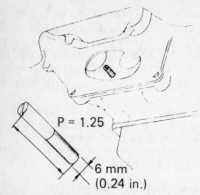

P = 1.25

6 mm
(0.24 in.)

Guide pin — automatic transmission removal

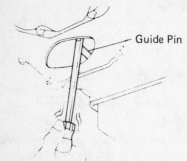

Guide Pin

Removing converter assembly

tion measure from the installed surface to the front surface of the transmission housing the correct distance should be 1.02 inch or more. Torque transmission housing mounting bolts to 47 ft. lbs. and torque converter bolts evenly to 20 ft. lbs. Fill transmission to the correct level, make all necessary adjustments. Perform roadtest check for abnormal noise, shock slippage, correct shift points and smooth operation.

AUTOMATIC TRANSAXLE

Identification

On most models the transaxle identification tag is located at the top front of the transaxle case.

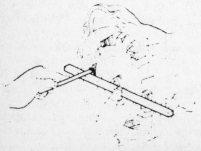

Install torque converter — automatic transmission installation

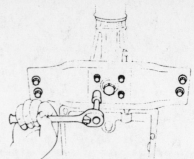

Removing crossmember — automatic transmission removal

Fluid Pan and Filter

REMOVAL AND INSTALLATION

1. Raise and safely support the vehicle.
2. Drain the transmission fluid.
3. Carefully loosen and remove the bolts holding the oil pan. Tap around the pan lightly with a plastic mallet, breaking the gasket tension by vibration. Do not pry the pan down with a screwdriver or similar tool; the pan is lightweight metal and will deform, causing leaks.
4. Remove all traces of gasket material from the pan and the transaxle mating faces. Clean then carefully with a plastic or wooden scraper. Do not gouge the metal.
5. Clean the pan thoroughly of all oil and sediment.
6. Remove the bolts holding the screen (filter) and remove it from the car. Note that the bolts holding the filter may be different lengths; they must be replaced in the correct positions at reassembly.
7. Install the filter and tighten the bolts to 7 ft. lbs. (84 INCH lbs.).
8. Install a new gasket on the pan and bolt the pan into place. Snug the bolts in a crisscross pattern, working from the center out. Tighten the pan bolts to about 5 ft. lbs.

NOTE: *If the mating surfaces of the oil pan and transaxle are clean and straight, there is no need for gasket sealer during reassembly.*

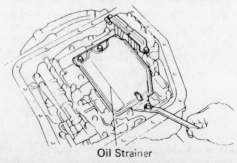

Oil Strainer

Removing automatic transaxle oil filter (strainer)

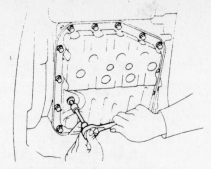

Removing automatic transaxle oil pan

The use of sealer is generally not recommended on these transmissions.

9. Lower the vehicle to the ground and refill the automatic transmission fluid.

Adjustments

THROTTLE VALVE (TV) CABLE

1. With the ignition **OFF**, depress the accelerator pedal all the way. On carbureted vehicles, check that the throttle plates are fully open. If they are not, adjust the throttle linkage.
2. Peel the rubber dust boot back from the throttle valve cable.
3. Loosen the adjustment nuts on the throttle cable bracket (rocker cover) just enough to allow cable housing movement.
4. Have an assistant depress the accelerator pedal fully.
5. Adjust the cable housing so that the distance between its end and the cable stop collar is 0–1.0mm.
6. Tighten the adjustment nuts. Make sure that the adjustment hasn't changed. Install the dust boot.

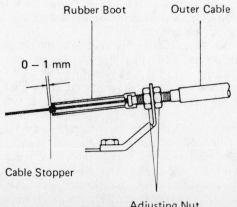

Throttle linkage adjustment

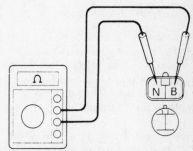

Connect an ohmmeter between terminals 2 and 3—Tercel (A-55)

Connect an ohmmeter between terminals N and B—1984 Corolla RWD (A-42DL)

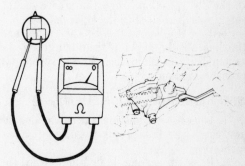

Connect an ohmmeter between the terminals as shown—Corolla FWD (A-130L, A-131L)

NEUTRAL SAFETY SWITCH

1. Locate the neutral safety switch on the side of the transaxle and loosen the switch retaining bolts.
2. Move the gear selector to the **NEUTRAL** position.
3. Disconnect the neutral safety switch connector and connect an ohmmeter between the two adjacent terminals on the switch lead.
4. Adjust the switch to the point where

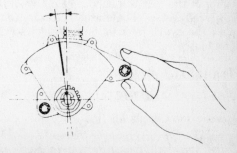

Neutral safety switch adjustment

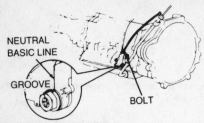

Neutral safety switch adjustment

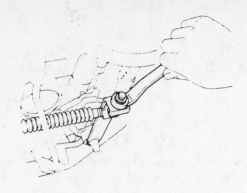

Adjust shift linkage

there is continuity between the two terminals. Tighten the retaining bolts.

5. Move the shift selector to **PARK** and check that continuity is present. Move the selector to any of the other positions and check that there is no continuity when the car is in gear.

6. Reconnect the wiring to the switch.

An alternate method to adjust the neutral safety switch is locate the neutral safety and loosen the switch bolt. Move the gear selector to the "N" position. Align the groove on the safety switch shaft with the basic line which is scribed on the housing. With the groove and the line aligned (hold position), tighten the switch bolt to 48 in. lbs. Check switch for proper operation.

SHIFT LINKAGE ADJUSTMENT

1. Loosen the adjusting nut on the linkage and check the linkage for freedom of movement.

2. Push the manual lever fully toward the right side of the car as far as it will go.

3. Return the lever two notches to the **NEUTRAL** position.

4. Set the gear selector to **NEUTRAL**. While holding the selector slightly to the right, have someone tighten the adjusting nut on the manual lever.

Back-up Light Switch

REMOVAL AND INSTALLATION

The reverse light or back-up lights function is controlled by the neutral safety switch. When the switch is properly adjusted, the white lamps at the rear will only come on when the car is in reverse. Should it be necessary to replace the switch refer to the necessary service procedure.

Transaxle

REMOVAL AND INSTALLATION

Corolla and Corolla All-Trac

NOTE: *On All-Trac type transaxle vehicles, the automatic transaxle unit must be removed with the engine as an assembly. Use* *this service procedure as a guide. The procedure can be modified as required.*

1. Disconnect the negative battery cable. Remove the air cleaner.

2. Disconnect the neutral start switch. Disconnect the speedometer cable.

3. Disconnect the shift control cable and throttle linkage.

4. Disconnect the oil cooler hose. Plug the end of the hose to prevent leakage.

5. Drain the radiator and remove the water inlet pipe.

6. Raise and support the vehicle safely. Drain the transaxle fluid. As required remove the exhaust front pipe.

7. Remove the engine undercover. Remove the front and rear transaxle mounts.

8. Support the engine and transaxle using the proper equipment. Remove the engine center support member.

9. Remove the halfshafts. Remove the starter assembly. Remove the steering knuckles, as required.

10. Remove the flywheel cover plate. Remove the torque converter bolts.

11. Remove the left engine mount. Remove the transaxle-to-engine bolts. Slowly back the transaxle away from the engine. Lower the assembly to the floor.

12. Installation is the reverse of the removal procedure. When installing the A241H vehicle transaxle on 4WD All-Trac vehicles, be sure the mode selector lever is positioned in the **FREE** mode and attach the lock bolt. To check torque converter installation measure from the installed surface to the front surface of the transaxle housing the correct distance should be 0.91 inch or more. Torque the 12mm bolts to 47 ft. lbs. and 10mm bolts to 34 ft. lbs. Torque the converter bolts (coat threads with Loctite or equivalent) evenly to 20 ft. lbs. Fill transaxle to the correct level, roadtest the vehicle, check fluid level.

Tercel 2-Wheel Drive
Tercel Wagon 4-Wheel Drive

1. Disconnect the negative battery cable. Drain the radiator and remove the upper radiator hose, as required. Remove the air cleaner assembly.

2. Raise the vehicle and support it safely. Remove both halfshafts. Drain the fluid from the transaxle and differential, if equipped.

3. Remove the torque converter cover. Remove the bolts that retain the torque converter to the crankshaft. Remove the exhaust pipe. Remove the shift lever rod.

4. Remove the speedometer cable aback-up light connector. If equipped with 4WD, remove the electrical solenoid connector. Disconnect and remove all throttle linkage.

5. Remove the fluid lines from the transaxle. Remove the starter assembly, as re-

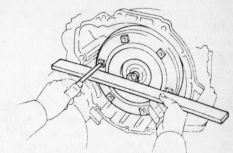

Checking torque converter installation

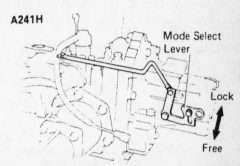

Inspect mode select lever position — Corolla All-Trac

quired. On 4WD vehicles, remove the rear driveshaft.

6. Support the engine and transaxle using a suitable jack or equivalent. Remove the rear crossmember.

7. Remove the transaxle-to-engine retaining bolts. Separate the transaxle from the engine and carefully remove it from the vehicle.

8. Installation is the reverse of the removal procedure. To check torque converter installation measure from the installed surface to the front surface of the transaxle housing the correct distance should 0.528 inch or more. Tighten the transmission-to-engine bolts to 47 ft. lbs. Tighten the left engine mount bracket bolts to 32 ft. lbs. Tighten the rear engine mount bracket bolts to 43 ft. lbs. Tighten the torque converter mounting bolts UNIFORMLY to 13 ft. lbs. (18 Nm). Fill differential assembly with gear oil (most models 1 qt.) and fill automatic transaxle (most models 4.4 qts. drain and refill) with transmission fluid. Check front end alignment as necessary. Perform roadtest and check transaxle fluid level.

MR2

1. Disconnect the negative battery cable. Remove the air flow meter and the air cleaner hose.

2. Remove the intercooler on the 4A-GZE.

3. Remove the water inlet set bolts. Disconnect the ground strap. Remove the transaxle mounting set bolt.

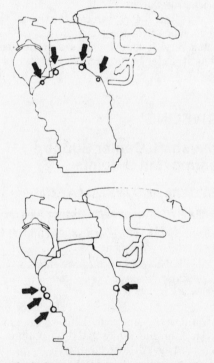

Remove the bolts marked for automatic transaxle removal — Tercel 2WD and 4WD

Using a tool to support the engine — transaxle removal and installation

4. Disconnect the speedometer cable or speed sensor connector at the transaxle. Disconnect the throttle cable from the throttle linkage and the bracket.

5. Raise and support the vehicle safely. Drain the transaxle fluid. Remove the left tire.

6. Remove the transaxle gravel shield.

7. Disconnect the oil cooler lines at the transaxle. Remove the transaxle control cable clip and retainer and then disconnect the cable from the bracket. Remove the bracket.

8. Remove the starter assembly. Disconnect the exhaust pipe at the manifold. Remove the pipe.

9. Remove the stiffener plate. Remove the rear engine end plate. Remove the torque converter cover. Remove the torque converter retaining bolts.

10. Disconnect both the right and left halfshafts from their side gear shafts. Depress and hold the brake pedal while removing the halfshaft retaining nuts. Properly position the halfshaft out of the way. Refer to the necessary service procedures as outlined to remove the halfshaft assemblies.

11. Support the engine and transaxle assembly, using the proper equipment. Remove the

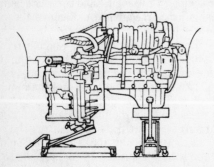

Removal of automatic transaxle — MR2 vehicle

transaxle-to-engine retaining bolts. Disconnect the front and rear transaxle mount bolts.

12. Carefully lower the transaxle assembly to the floor.

13. Installation is the reverse of the removal procedure. To check torque converter for correct installation measure from the installed surface to the front surface of the transaxle housing the correct distance should 0.906 inch or more. Tighten the transmission-to-engine bolts to 47 ft. lbs. and transaxle mounting set bolts 83 ft. lbs. Torque the torque converter bolts to 20 ft. lbs. and 30 ft. lbs. on A241E automatic transaxle type. Fill all fluid levels perform roadtest and check transaxle fluid level.

Halfshafts

REMOVAL AND INSTALLATION

Refer to the "Manual Transaxle Halfshaft Removal and Installation" section in this Chapter for the necessary service procedures.

OVERHAUL

Refer to the "Manual Transaxle Halfshaft Overhaul" section in this Chapter for the necessary service procedures.

TRANSFER CASE

The transfer case assembly used on the Corolla All-Trac vehicles is a component of the transaxle. No normal service adjustments are preformed on this unit. Refer to the necessary service procedures.

On the Tercel 4WD vehicles the transfer case is a component of the transaxle assembly. No normal service adjustments are preformed on this unit. Refer to the necessary service procedures.

DRIVELINE

Driveshaft, Center Support Bearing and U-Joints

REMOVAL AND INSTALLATION

Corolla RWD Tercel 4WD, Except All-Trac

1. Raise the vehicle and safely support with jackstands or equivalent.

CAUTION: *Be sure that the car is securely supported. Remember, you will be working underneath it.*

2. Unfasten the bolts which attach the driveshaft universal joint yoke flange to the mounting flange on the differential drive pinion.

NOTE: *Be sure to matchmark the yoke flange to the mounting flange on the drive pinion.*

3. Remove (2 retaining bolts) the center support bearing and heat insulator from the body.

4. Remove the propeller shaft with intermediate shaft.

5. Install an old U-joint yoke in the transmission or, if none is available, use a plastic bag secured with a rubber band over the hole to keep the transmission oil from running out. Withdraw the driveshaft assembly from beneath the vehicle.

6. Installation is performed in the following order: Apply multipurpose grease on the sec-

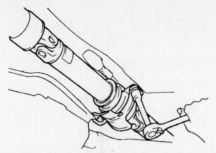

Removing the center support bearing mounting bolts

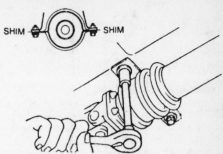

Installing the center support bearing to the body of the car

tion of the U-joint sleeve which is to be inserted into the transmission.

7. Insert the driveshaft sleeve (remove tool form transmission to stop oil from dripping out) into the transmission.

8. Secure the U-joint flange (align matchmarks) to the differential flange with the mounting bolts. Torque the retaining bolts to 27–31 ft. lbs. Be sure that the bolts are of the same type as those removed.

9. Connect the center support bearing assembly to the body. Place a height spacer (shim) if so equipped, between the body and the center support bearing and install the two mounting bolts finger tight.

10. Check that the bearing bracket is at right angles to the propeller shaft. Adjust if necessary.

11. Check that the center line of the bearing

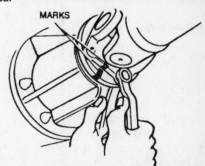

Matchmark yoke flange to mounting flange on rear axle

is set to the center line of the bracket when the car is in the no-load condition. Adjust if necessary.

12. Tighten the center support bearing mounting bolts to 27 ft. lbs. lower the vehicle.

Troubleshooting Basic Driveshaft and Rear Axle Problems

When abnormal vibrations or noises are detected in the driveshaft area, this chart can be used to help diagnose possible causes. Remember that other components such as wheels, tires, rear axle and suspension can also produce similar conditions.

BASIC DRIVESHAFT PROBLEMS

Problem	Cause	Solution
Shudder as car accelerates from stop or low speed	• Loose U-joint • Defective center bearing	• Replace U-joint • Replace center bearing
Loud clunk in driveshaft when shifting gears	• Worn U-joints	• Replace U-joints
Roughness or vibration at any speed	• Out-of-balance, bent or dented driveshaft • Worn U-joints • U-joint clamp bolts loose	• Balance or replace driveshaft • Replace U-joints • Tighten U-joint clamp bolts
Squeaking noise at low speeds	• Lack of U-joint lubrication	• Lubricate U-joint; if problem persists, replace U-joint
Knock or clicking noise	• U-joint or driveshaft hitting frame tunnel • Worn CV joint	• Correct overloaded condition • Replace CV joint

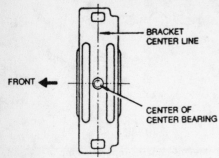

Positioning of the center support bearing

Corolla All-Trac

1. Matchmark the front driveshaft flange and the front center bearing flange. Remove the 4 bolts, washers and nuts and disconnect the rear end of the front driveshaft from the front center bearing flange. Pull the shaft out of the transfer assembly and remove it. Plug the transfer assembly to prevent leakage.

2. With an assistant depressing the brake pedal, loosen the cross groove set bolts $1/2$ turn. These bolts are at the front edge of the rear driveshaft (rear edge of the rear center bearing).

3. Matchmark the rear flange of the rear driveshaft to the differential pinion flange and then disconnect them.

4. Remove the 2 mounting bolts from the front and rear center bearings and then remove the 2 center bearings, intermediate shaft and rear driveshaft as an assembly.

5. Matchmark the universal joint and the rear center bearing flange, remove the bolts and separate the intermediate shaft and rear propeller shaft.

7. Temporarily install the assembly. Align the matchmarks and connect the rear driveshaft to the differential. Tighten the bolts to 27 ft. lbs.

8. Install the front driveshaft yoke into the transfer assembly, align the matchmarks at the rear of the shaft with those on the front center bearing flange and tighten the bolts to 27 ft. lbs.

9. With the driveshaft in position, depress the brake pedal and tighten the cross groove joint set bolts to 20 ft. lbs.

10. With the car in an unladen condition, adjust the distance between the rear edge of the boot cover and the rear driveshaft to 2.579–2.776 in. (62.5–70.5mm).

11. With the car in an unladen condition, adjust the distance between the rear side of the center bearing housing and the rear side of the cushion to 0.45–0.53 in. (11.5–13.5mm).

12. Tighten the center bearing mounting bolts to 27 ft. lbs. Make sure that the center

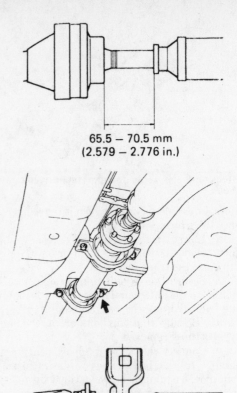

65.5 – 70.5 mm
(2.579 – 2.776 in.)

11.5—13.5 mm (0.453—0.531 in.)

Installing Corolla All-Trac driveshaft assembly

line of the bracket is at right angles to the shaft axial direction.

OVERHAUL

Corolla RWD Tercel 4WD, Except All-Trac

NOTE: *As the U-joints on the Tercel 4WD and Corolla RWD are non-serviceable, the intermediate shaft and/or propeller shaft must be replaced in the event of U-joint problems. Refer to the exploded view of driveshaft assembly before starting this repair.*

1. Separate the propeller shaft and intermediate shaft by making alignment marks across the two flanges of the propeller shaft.

2. Remove the 4 bolts and remove the propeller shaft form the intermediate (front) shaft.

3. Put alignment marks on the flange (attached to the center support bearing) and the intermediate shaft and then unscrew (loosen staked part of nut) the retaining nut using tool to hold flange.

4. Slide (tap off with brass punch) the

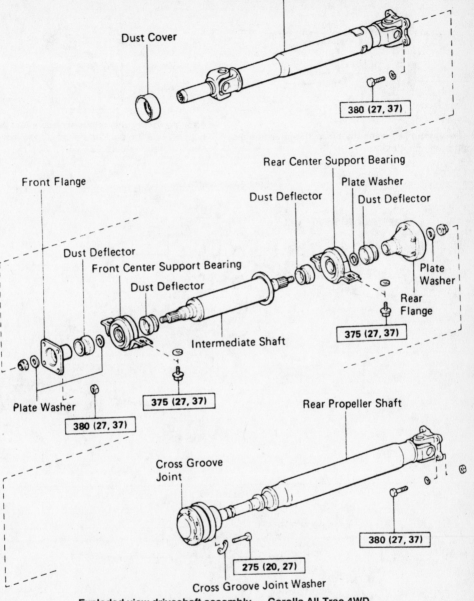

Front Propeller Shaft

Dust Cover

380 (27, 37)

Rear Center Support Bearing

Plate Washer

Dust Deflector

Dust Deflector

Front Flange

Dust Deflector

Front Center Support Bearing

Dust Deflector

Plate Washer

Rear Flange

375 (27, 37)

Intermediate Shaft

375 (27, 37)

Plate Washer

380 (27, 37)

Rear Propeller Shaft

Cross Groove Joint

380 (27, 37)

275 (20, 27)

Cross Groove Joint Washer

Exploded view driveshaft assembly — Corolla All-Trac 4WD

flange and the center support bearing off the intermediate shaft.

5. Slide the center support bearing and the flange onto the shaft and align the marks (cutout on the rear side).

6. Place the flange (align matchmark) in a soft jawed vise and install a new nut to press the bearing into position. Tighten the nut to 134 ft. lbs. Loosen the nut and then tighten it again, this time to 51 ft. lbs.

7. Using a hammer and a punch, stake the nut.

8. Align the marks on the bearing flange

and the propeller shaft flange and insert the bolts. Tighten the bolts to 27 ft. lbs.

Corolla All-Trac

NOTE: *When preforming this service operation always replace all necessary parts (snaprings, clamps, boots etc.) Always matchmark all flanges, yokes and shafts for correct installation. Refer to the exploded view of the driveshaft assembly before starting this repair.*

1. Loosen the staked part of the locking nut located on the rear center support bearing front flange.

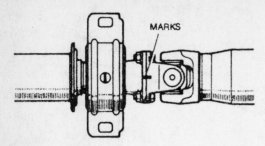

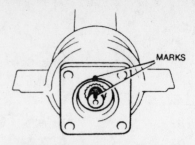

Removing the propeller shaft from the intermediate shaft note matchmarks

After removing the retaining nut, slide the center support bearing and the flange off the intermediate shaft (noted matchmarks)

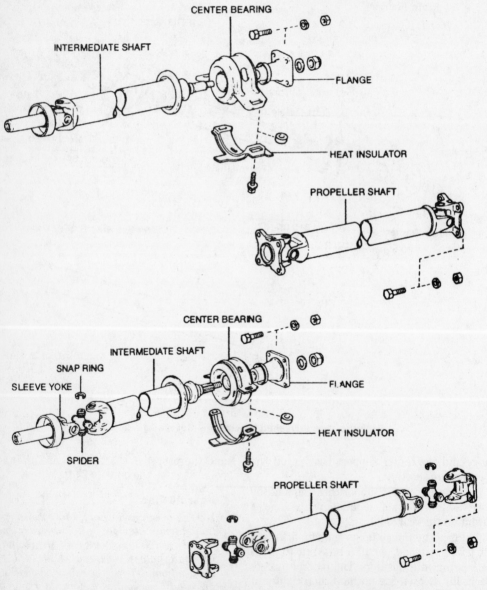

Exploded view driveshaft assembly — Corolla and Tercel 4WD

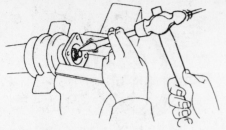

Use a hammer and punch to stake the center support bearing retaining nut

2. Using a suitable tool hold the front flange and remove the nut and plate washer.

3. Matchmark the rear flange and the front shaft. Using a suitable tool remove the rear flange.

4. Remove the rear center support bearing and plate washer. Repeat Steps 1–4 remove the front center support bearing.

5. Turn the center support bearing by hand while applying force in the direction of rotation. Check the bearing for smooth operation. Inspect both support seals for cracks and damage.

6. Set the front center support bearing onto the intermediate shaft. Install the plate washer and install flange (matchmarks in the correct position).

7. Using a suitable tool hold the flange, press the bearing into position by tightening down a NEW nut and washer to 134 ft. lbs. Loosen the nut. Torque the nut again to 51 ft. lbs. Stake the nut with hammer and chisel.

8. Set the rear center support bearing onto the intermediate shaft. Install the plate washer and install flange (matchmarks in the correct position).

9. Using a suitable tool hold the flange, press the bearing into position by tightening down a NEW nut and washer to 134 ft. lbs. Loosen the nut. Torque the nut again to 51 ft. lbs. Stake the nut with hammer and chisel.

10. Reconnect the intermediate shaft with the rear driveshaft (tighten 6 bolts temporarily-refer to removal and installation service procedures).

REAR AXLE

Axle Ratio

The drive axle of a car is said to have a certain axle ratio. This number (usually a whole number and a decimal fraction) is actually a comparison of the number of gear teeth on the ring gear and the pinion gear. For example, a 4.11 rear means that theoretically, there are 4.11 teeth on the ring gear and one tooth on the pinion gear or, put another way, the driveshaft must turn 4.11 times to turn the wheels once. Actually, on a 4.11 rear, there might be 37 teeth on the ring gear and 9 teeth on the pinion gear. By dividing the number of teeth on the pinion gear into the number of teeth on the ring gear, the numerical axle ratio (4.11) is obtained. This also provides a good method of ascertaining exactly which axle ratio one is dealing with.

Another method of determining gear ratio is to jack up and support the car so that both rear wheels are off the ground. Make a chalk mark on the rear wheel and the drive shaft. Put the transmission in neutral. Turn the rear wheel one complete turn and count the number of turns that the driveshaft makes. The number of turns that the driveshaft makes in one complete revolution of the rear wheel is an approximation of the rear axle ratio.

Axle Shaft, Bearing and Seal

REMOVAL AND INSTALLATION

Corolla RWD
Tercel 4WD
Corolla All-Trac

NOTE: *This service procedures requires use of special tools-machine shop press and oil bath or equivalent-it is best to remove axle shaft and send it out to a machine shop to replace the axle bearing assembly. Refer to exploded view of rear axle shaft.*

1. Raise and safely support the vehicle.

CAUTION: *Be sure that the vehicle is securely supported. Remember, you will be working underneath it.*

2. Remove the wheel cover, unfasten the lug nuts, and remove the wheel.

3. Punch matchmarks on the brake drum and the axle shaft to maintain rotational balance.

4. Remove the brake drum or disc brake caliper, disc rotor and related components.

5. Remove the backing plate attachment nuts through the access holes in the rear axle shaft flange.

6. Use a slide hammer with a suitable adaptor to withdraw the axle shaft from its housing. Use care not to damage the oil seal when removing the axle shaft.

7. Disconnect the brake line, remove the backing plate and remove the end gasket from the axle housing.

8. To replace the axle bearing, cut the axle bearing retainer and press the bearing off the axle shaft.

9. Position bearing outer retainer and new bearing on shaft using a press install it to the correct location.

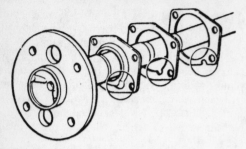

Align notches of gaskets and bearing outer retainer

Drum Brake Type

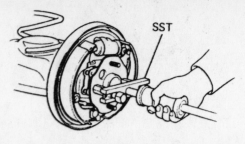

SST

Removing axle shaft from the axle housing using a tool

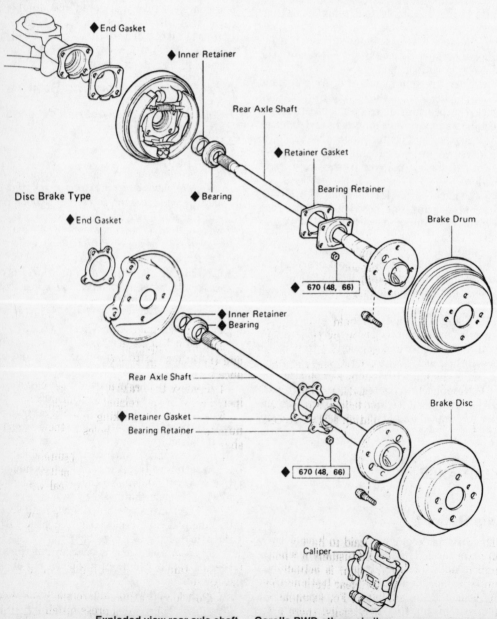

◆ End Gasket

◆ Inner Retainer

Rear Axle Shaft

◆ Retainer Gasket

Disc Brake Type

◆ Bearing

Bearing Retainer

Brake Drum

◆ End Gasket

670 (48, 66)

◆ Inner Retainer
◆ Bearing

Rear Axle Shaft

Brake Disc

◆ Retainer Gasket
Bearing Retainer

◆ 670 (48, 66)

Caliper

Exploded view rear axle shaft — Corolla RWD others similar

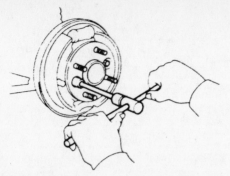

Removing axle shaft retaining bolts through access holes

10. Heat the inner bearing retainer to about 150°C in an oil bath-press the inner retainer on the axle shaft. Face the non-beveled side of the inner retainer toward the bearing.

11. Remove the oil seal from the axle housing.

NOTE: *The oil seal can be removed from the axle housing by using the end of the rear axle shaft for a puller by placing the outmost lip of the axle shaft against the oil seal inner lip and prying it downward.*

12. Install the oil seal in the axle housing Drive the oil seal into the axle housing to a depth of 5.7–6.1mm for drum brakes and 1.5–2.5mm for disc brakes on Corolla RWD vehicles. On Tercel 4WD and Corolla All-Trac drive the oil seal into the axle housing to a depth of 5.6mm using the proper tools.

13. Clean flange of the axle housing and backing plate. Apply sealer to the end gasket and retainer gasket as necessary.

14. Place end gasket onto end of axle housing with the notch of gasket facing downward. Align the notches of the 2 gaskets and bearing outer retainer with the oil hole of the backing plate.

15. Install the backing plate to the axle housing and all necessary components.

16. Install the retainer gasket on the axle shaft. Install the rear axle shaft with 4 NEW SELF-LOCKING NUTS torque to 48 ft. lbs.

17. Install all other necessary parts in reverse order of removal.

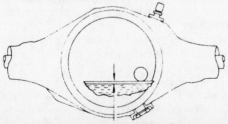

0 – 5 mm (0 – 0.20 in.)

Fill rear axle assembly to this level with the correct fluid

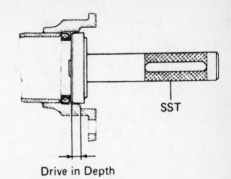

Drive in Depth

Installing oil seal into rear axle housing

18. Bleed brake system, install wheel and roadtest for proper operation.

Differential Carrier

REMOVAL AND INSTALLATION

Corolla RWD
Tercel 4WD
Corolla All-Trac

1. Raise and safely support the vehicle. Remove drain plug and drain differential oil.

2. Remove the rear axle shafts as outlined in this Chapter.

3. Disconnect the propeller shaft or driveshaft (matchmark flange for correct installation) form the differential assembly.

4. Remove the differential carrier assembly retaining bolts. Remove the carrier assembly.

5. Installation is the reverse of the removal procedures. Torque the differential carrier retaining bolts to 23 ft. lbs. the driveshaft flange bolts 27–31 ft. lbs. Install drain plug and refill the unit with 1–1.5 qts. as necessary of API GL-5 gear oil.

Pinion Seal

REMOVAL AND INSTALLATION

Corolla RWD
Tercel 4WD
Corolla All-Trac

In order to replace the pinion seal the drive pinion assembly must be disassembled, in-

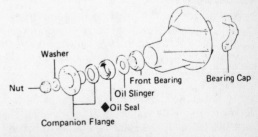

Washer — Nut — Front Bearing — Bearing Cap — Oil Slinger — ◆Oil Seal — Companion Flange

Differential carrier assembly

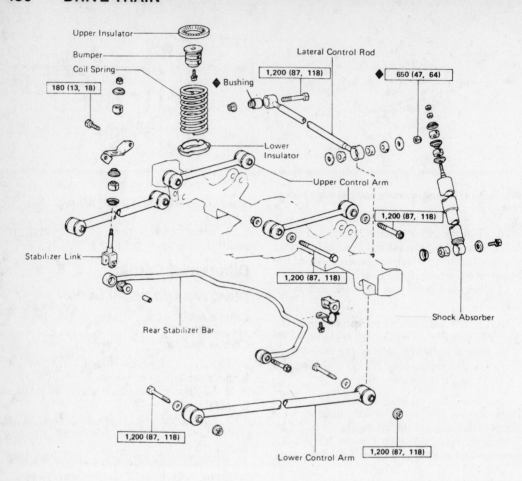

Upper Insulator

Bumper

Coil Spring

Lateral Control Rod

180 (13, 18)

1,200 (87, 118)

650 (47, 64)

◆ Bushing

Lower Insulator

Upper Control Arm

1,200 (87, 118)

Stabilizer Link

1,200 (87, 118)

Rear Stabilizer Bar

Shock Absorber

1,200 (87, 118)

Lower Control Arm

1,200 (87, 118)

kg·cm (ft-lb, N·m) : Specified torque

◆ Non-reusable part

Exploded view of the rear axle housing assembly

spected, assembled and adjusted. See the OVER-HAUL procedures, earlier in this Chapter.

Axle Housing

REMOVAL AND INSTALLATION

Corolla RWD
Tercel 4WD
Corolla All-Trac

NOTE: *Due to the range of optional equipment, a general procedure is outlined. The removal and installation steps can be modified as necessary. Refer to the exploded view of axle housing and see Chapter 8 as a guide for this repair.*

1. Raise and safely support the vehicle. Remove drain plug and drain differential oil.

2. Remove the rear axle shafts as outlined in this Chapter. Disconnect and reposition all lines or vacuum hoses that are necessary to remove the axle housing assembly from the vehicle.

3. Disconnect the propeller shaft or driveshaft (matchmark flange for correct installation) form the differential assembly.

4. Support the rear axle assembly with proper equipment. Disconnect the rear shock absorbers, upper and lower control arms, rear stabilizer bar.

5. Slowly lower the rear axle assembly, remove the rear coil springs. Remove the axle assembly from the vehicle.

6. Installation is the reverse of the removal procedure. Refer to the exploded view of axle housing as a guide for torque all necessary rear suspension components. Install drain plug and refill the unit (refill to the proper level) with 1–1.5 qts. as necessary of API GL-5 gear oil.

Suspension and Steering

8

FRONT SUSPENSION

The front suspension system is MacPherson strut design on all models. The struts used on either side are a combination spring and shock absorber with the outer casing of the shock actually supporting the bottom of the spring. This arrangement saves space, weight and allows the spring and shock absorber to work on the same axis of compression.

The wheel hub is attached to the bottom of the strut. A strut mounting bearing at the top and a ball joint at the bottom allow the entire strut to rotate during cornering. The strut assembly, steering arm and steering knuckle are all combined in one assembly; there is no upper control arm. A rubber-bushed transverse link (control arm) connects the lower portion of the strut to the front crossmember via the ball joint; the link thus allows for vertical movement of the suspension. Some models have a front stabilizer bar (sway bar) connected between the control arms; this bar serves to reduce body roll during cornering.

The strut assembly provides rigidity and actually positions the wheel and driveshaft relative to the car, thus affecting alignment. If any component of the suspension is found to be bent or damaged, it must be replaced with an identical part. Do not substitute parts of lesser quality or different design. Torque values must be observed during reassembly to assure proper retention of the parts.

CAUTION: *Exercise great caution when working with the front suspension. Coil springs and other suspension components are under extreme tension and result in severe injury if released improperly. Never remove the nut on the top of the shock absorber piston without using the proper spring compressor tool.*

Spring And Shock Absorbers/ MacPherson Strut

TESTING

Shock Absorbers

The purpose of the shock absorber is simply to limit the motion of the spring during compression (bump) and rebound cycles. If the car were not equipped with these motion dampers, the up and down motion of the springs would multiply until the vehicle was alternately trying to leap off the ground and to pound itself into the pavement.

Worn shock absorbers can affect handling; if the front of the car is rising or falling excessively, the tires changes on the pavement and steering response is affected. The simplest test of the shock absorbers is simply to push down on one corner of the unladen car and release it.

Observe the motion of the body as it is released. In most cases, it will come up beyond its original rest position, dip back below it and settle quickly to rest. This shows that the damper is slowing and controlling the spring action. Any tendency to excessive pitch (up-and-down) motion or failure to return to rest within 2–3 cycles is a sign of poor function.

While each shock absorber can be replaced individually, it is recommended that they be changed as a pair (both front or both rear) to maintain equal response on both sides of the car.

NOTE: *On MacPherson strut shock absorbers if oil is leaking from the cylinder portion of the assembly the shock absorber must be replaced. ALWAYS REFER TO THE NECESSARY EXPLODED VIEW OF THE SUSPENSION COMPONENT AS GUIDE FOR THE REPAIR OR OVERHAUL.*

MacPherson Struts

The struts are precise parts and retain the springs under tremendous pressure even when removed from the car. For this reason, several special tools and substantial specialized knowledge are required to safely and effectively work on these components. If spring and shock absorber work is required, it may not be a bad idea to remove the strut involved yourself and then consider taking it to a repair facility which is fully equipped and familiar with the car.

REMOVAL AND INSTALLATION

Corolla RWD

NOTE: *To overhaul the Corolla RWD vehicle strut assembly follow the service procedure outlined below modify steps as necessary.*

1. Remove the hubcap and loosen the lug nuts.
2. Raise the front of the car and support it on the chassis jacking plates provided with jack stands. Do not support the weight of the car on the suspension arm.

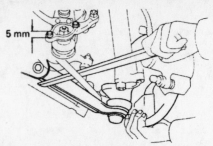

Make sure you clear the knuckle collars when prying down on the control arm

3. Unfasten the lug nuts and remove the wheel.
4. Detach the front brake line from its retaining clamp.
5. Remove the caliper and wire it out of the way if necessary.
6. Remove the 3 nuts which secure the upper shock absorber mounting plate to the top of the wheel arch.
7. Remove the 2 bolts which attach the shock absorber lower end to the steering knuckle low arm.

Troubleshooting Basic Steering and Suspension Problems

Problem	Cause	Solution
Hard steering (steering wheel is hard to turn)	• Low or uneven tire pressure	• Inflate tires to correct pressure
	• Loose power steering pump drive belt	• Adjust belt
	• Low or incorrect power steering fluid	• Add fluid as necessary
	• Incorrect front end alignment	• Have front end alignment checked/adjusted
	• Defective power steering pump	• Check pump
	• Bent or poorly lubricated front end parts	• Lubricate and/or replace defective parts
Loose steering (too much play in the steering wheel)	• Loose wheel bearings	• Adjust wheel bearings
	• Loose or worn steering linkage	• Replace worn parts
	• Faulty shocks	• Replace shocks
	• Worn ball joints	• Replace ball joints
Car veers or wanders (car pulls to one side with hands off the steering wheel)	• Incorrect tire pressure	• Inflate tires to correct pressure
	• Improper front end alignment	• Have front end alignment checked/adjusted
	• Loose wheel bearings	• Adjust wheel bearings
	• Loose or bent front end components	• Replace worn components
	• Faulty shocks	• Replace shocks
Wheel oscillation or vibration transmitted through steering wheel	• Improper tire pressures	• Inflate tires to correct pressure
	• Tires out of balance	• Have tires balanced
	• Loose wheel bearings	• Adjust wheel bearings
	• Improper front end alignment	• Have front end alignment checked/adjusted
	• Worn or bent front end components	• Replace worn parts
Uneven tire wear	• Incorrect tire pressure	• Inflate tires to correct pressure
	• Front end out of alignment	• Have front end alignment checked/adjusted
	• Tires out of balance	• Have tires balanced

NOTE: *Press down on the suspension lower arm, in order to remove the strut assembly (front axle hub and disc brake assembly--all as one unit). This must be done to clear the collars on the steering knuckle arm bolt holes when removing the shock/spring assembly. The steering knuckle bolt holes have collars that extend about 0.20 in.. Be careful to clear them when separating the steering knuckle from the strut assembly.*

8. Installation is performed in the reverse order of removal procedure. Torque the steering knuckle arm to shock absorber bolts to 58 ft. lbs.

9. Install the 3 nuts holding top of the shock absorber to 13 ft. lbs.

10. Bleed brake system. Check front end alignment.

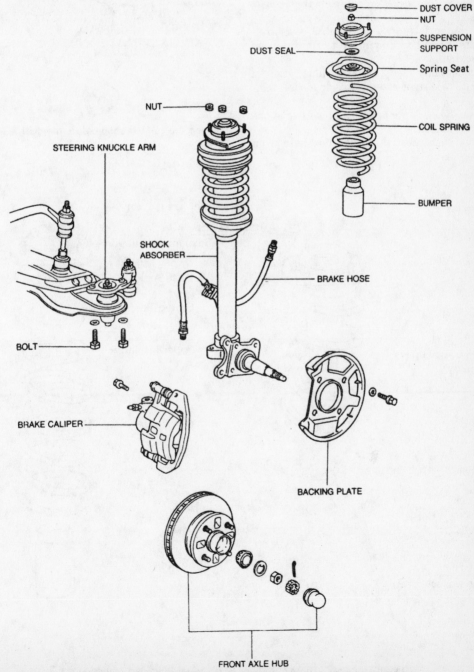

Components of the the MacPherson strut assembly — Corolla RWD

REMOVAL

Corolla FWD, Tercel 2WD/4WD and MR2

1. Under the hood, remove the 3 or 4 nuts holding the top of the strut to the shock tower. DO NOT loosen the larger center nut.

2. Loosen the wheel lug nuts at the appropriate wheel.

3. Raise the vehicle and safely support it. It need not be any higher than the distance necessary to separate the tire from the ground. Do not place the jackstands under the control arms.

4. Remove the wheel. Install a cover over the driveshaft boot to protect it from fluid and impact damage.

5. On early model (refer to illustration of typical FWD strut assembly-early model) vehicles:

 a. Remove the brake flex hose clip at the strut bracket.

 b. Disconnect the brake flex hose from the brake pipe at the strut. Remove the brake hose clips. Use a small pan to catch any leakage.

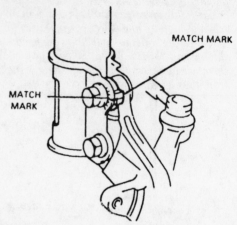

Marking the camber shim before removal — early model

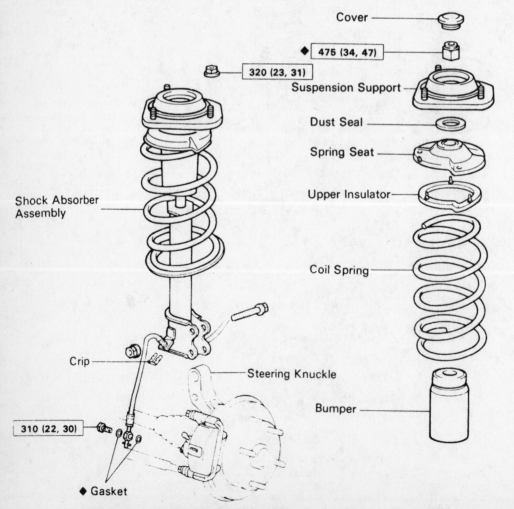

FWD strut assembly — note difference of the lower mounting — late model

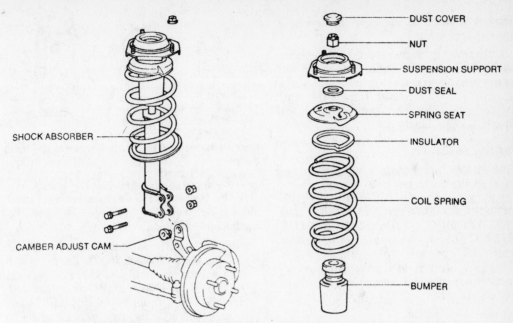

SHOCK ABSORBER

CAMBER ADJUST CAM

DUST COVER

NUT

SUSPENSION SUPPORT

DUST SEAL

SPRING SEAT

INSULATOR

COIL SPRING

BUMPER

FWD strut assembly — note difference of the lower mounting — early model

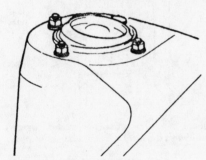

Strut assembly upper mounting

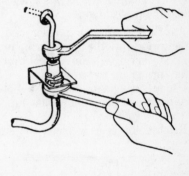

c. Pull the brake hose back through the opening in the strut bracket. Plug the lines to prevent any dirt form entering.

d. Remove the 2 brake caliper mounting bolts and remove the caliper. Hang it out of the way with a piece of wire. Do not allow it to hang by the flex hose and do not disconnect the hose from the caliper.

e. Mark the position of the adjusting cam for reassembly.

6. On all other model (refer to illustration of typical FWD strut assembly-late model) vehicles:

a. Disconnect the brake hose from the brake caliper and drain the fluid into a small pan.

b. Remove the clip from the brake hose and remove the hose from the bracket.

c. Use a sharp instrument or scribing tool to make matchmarks in all three dimensions on the steering knuckle. The strut must be reinstalled in its exact previous position.

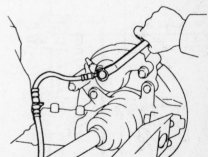

Use care in disconnecting the brake lines

7. Remove the 2 bolts which attach the shock absorber to the steering knuckle. The steering knuckle bolt holes have collars that extend about 5mm. Be careful to clear them when separating the steering knuckle from the strut assembly.

NOTE: *Press down on the lower suspension arm in order to remove the strut assembly. This must be done to clear the collars on the steering knuckle bolt holes when removing the strut assembly.*

8. Remove the strut assembly. Remember that the spring is still under tension. It will stay in place as long as the top nut on the shock piston shaft is not loosened. Handle the strut carefully and do not allow the coating on the spring to become damaged.

DISASSEMBLY

CAUTION: *This procedure requires the use of a spring compressor; it cannot be performed without one. IF YOU DO NOT HAVE ACCESS TO THIS SPECIAL TOOL, DO NOT ATTEMPT TO DISASSEMBLE THE STRUT! The coil springs are retained under considerable pressure. They can exert enough force to cause serious injury. Exercise extreme caution when disassembling the strut.*

1. Place the strut assembly in a pipe vise or strut vise or equivalent.

NOTE: *Do not attempt to clamp the strut assembly in a flat jaw vise as this will result in damage to the strut tube.*

2. Attach a spring compressor and compress the spring until the upper spring retainer is free of any spring tension. Do not over-compress the spring.

3. Use a spring seat holder to hold the upper support and then remove the nut on the end of the shock piston rod.

4. Remove the bearing plate, the support

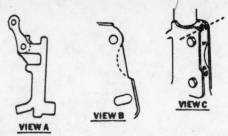

Marking the steering knuckle before removal — late model

and the upper spring retainer. Slowly and CAUTIOUSLY unscrew the spring compressor until all spring tension is relieved. Remove the spring and the dust cover.

NOTE: *Do not allow the piston rod to retract into the shock absorber. If it falls, screw a nut onto the rod and pull the rod out by the nut. Do not use pliers to grip the rod as they will damage its surface, resulting in leaks, uneven operation or seal damage. Be extremely careful not to stress or hit the rod.*

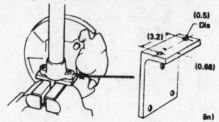

Fabricate a shock absorber stand (arrow) and mount it with the shock in the vise as shown

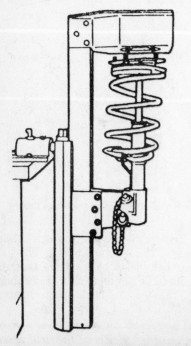

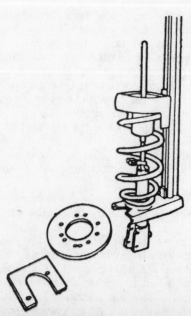

MacPherson strut service tools — FWD vehicles

INSPECTION

Check the shock absorber by moving the piston shaft through its full range of travel. It should move smoothly and evenly throughout its entire travel without any trace of binding or notching. Use a small straightedge to check the piston shaft for any bending or deformation. If a shock absorber is replaced, the old one should be drilled at the bottom to vent the internal gas. Wear safety goggles and drill a small hole (2–3mm) into the base of the shock absorber. The gas within the strut is colorless, odorless and non-toxic, but should be vented to make the unit safe for disposal.

Inspect the spring for any sign of deterioration or cracking. The waterproof coating on the coils should be intact to prevent rusting.

Check the upper strut mount assembly for any abnormal noise, binding or restricted motion. Lubricate the upper bearing with multi-purpose grease before reinstallation.

ASSEMBLY AND INSTALLATION

NOTE: *Never reuse a self-locking nut. Always replace self-locking nuts.*

1. Loosely assemble all components onto the strut assembly. Make sure the mark on the upper spring seat is facing the outside of the vehicle.
2. Compress the spring, carefully aligning the shaft guide rod with the hole in the upper mount. Align the lower spring seat. Do not over-compress the spring; compress it just enough to allow installation of the shaft nut.
3. Install the shaft nut and tighten it until the strut shaft begins to rotate.
4. Double check that the spring is correctly seated in the upper and lower mounts and re-position it as needed. Slowly release the tension on the spring compressor and remove it from the strut assembly.
5. Tighten the NEW shaft nut to 34–36 ft. lbs.
6. Install (early model vehicles), the camber adjusting cam into the knuckle if so equipped, observing the matchmarks made during disassembly.
7. Place the strut assembly in position and install the strut to knuckle attaching bolts. Tighten the bolts to the correct torque (FWD vehicles only):
   • 1984–85 Corolla with gasoline engine — 105 ft. lbs.
   • 1984-85 Corolla with diesel engine — 152 ft. lbs.
   • 1986–87 Corolla — 105 ft. lbs.
   • 1987–88 Corolla — 194 ft. lbs.
   • 1990 Corolla — 203 ft. lbs.
   • 1984–87 Tercel, exc. Wagon — 105 ft. lbs.
   • 1988–90 Tercel, exc. Wagon — 166 ft. lbs.
   • 1987–88 Tercel Wagon — 105 ft. lbs.
   • 1985–88 MR2 — 105 ft. lbs.
   • 1989–90 MR2 — 119 ft. lbs.
8. Using a floor jack and a piece of wood, gently elevate the control arm to the point that the upper mount can be aligned with the holes in the shock tower. Insert the bolts into the upper holes and install the nuts. Tighten the nuts to 23–29 ft. lbs.
9. Pack the shaft nut area with grease and install the dust cover.
10. On some model vehicles, install the brake caliper and tighten the bolts. Pull the brake hose through the strut bracket opening and connect the fitting. Tighten the fitting and install the flex hose clip at the strut bracket.
11. On other vehicles, install the brake hose

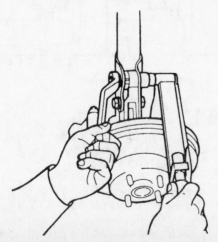

The strut to knuckle bolts must be torqued to the the correct specification

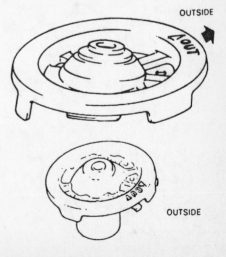

Make sure the upper strut seat marks face to the outside of the vehicle during reassembly

in the bracket and install the clip. Connect the hose to the caliper and tighten the fitting.

12. Install the wheel and install the lug nuts snugly. Lower the vehicle to the ground. Tighten the wheel lug nuts.

14. Bleed the brake system and top up the brake fluid level. Inspect the front end alignment.

Upper Ball Joint

INSPECTION

All vehicles cover in this repair manual do not use a upper ball assembly as a front suspension component.

REMOVAL AND INSTALLATION

All vehicles cover in this repair manual do not use a upper ball assembly as a front suspension component.

Lower Ball Joint

INSPECTION

Raise the front of the vehicle and safely support it on stands. Do not place stands under the control arms; the arms must hang free. Grasp the tire at the top and bottom and move the top of the tire through an in-and-out motion. Look for any horizontal motion in the steering knuckle relative to the control arm. Such motion is an indication of looseness within the ball joint. If the joint is checked while discon-

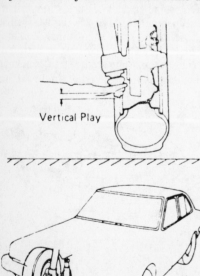

Vertical Play

Checking lower ball joint

nected from the knuckle, it should have minimal or no free play and should not twist in its socket under finger pressure. Replace any joint showing looseness or free play.

NOTE: *The maximum ball joint vertical play on Corolla RWD models is 0.098 in. (2.5mm). The maximum ball joint vertical play on ALL OTHER models is 0.0 in. (0.0mm).*

REMOVAL AND INSTALLATION

NOTE: *The use of the correct tools is REQUIRED for this procedure. A ball joint separator is a commonly available tool which prevents damage to the joint and knuckle. Do not attempt to separate the joint with hammers, pry bars or similar tools.*

Corolla RWD

To replace the lower ball joint on these models the lower control (suspension arm) assembly must be removed and replaced as an assembly. Refer to the "Lower Control Arm" removal and installation service procedures.

Corolla FWD, Tercel and MR2

NOTE: *The service procedure below is a general service procedure (modify service steps as necessary) for removing lower ball joint assembly with the lower control arm attached to the vehicle. IF NECESSARY remove the Lower Control arm assembly then remove the lower ball joint from the lower control arm. Refer to the "Lower Control Arm Assembly Removal and Installation" outlined in this Chapter.*

1. Raise and safely support the front of the vehicle. Do not place the stands under the con-

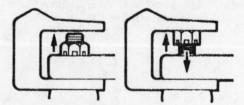

Using a ball joint tool separator

trol arms; they must hang free.

NOTE: *Do not allow the driveshaft joints to over-extend. The CV-joints can become disconnected under extreme extension.*

2. Install a protective cover over the CV boot.

3. Remove the wheel.

4. Remove the cotter pin from the ball joint nut.

5. Loosen the castle nut but do not remove it. Unscrew it just to the top of the threads and install the ball joint separator. Use the nut to

bear on the tool; this protects the threaded shaft from damage during removal.

6. Use the separator to loosen the ball joint from the steering knuckle.

7. Remove the nuts and bolt holding the ball joint to the control arm.

8. Remove the ball joint from the control arm and steering knuckle.

9. When reinstalling, attach the ball joint to the control arm and tighten the bolts/nuts to 105 ft. lbs. (Late model Corolla) and 59 ft. lbs. on most other models.

10. Carefully install the ball joint to the steering knuckle. Use a NEW CASTLE NUT and tighten it to 72–76 ft. lbs. on most models or 58 ft. lbs. MR2 and some Tercel models.

11. Install a NEW COTTER PIN through the castle nut and stud.

12. Remove the protector from the CV boot.

13. Install the wheel.

14. Lower the vehicle to the ground. Check wheel Alignment as necessary.

Stabilizer Bar, Sway Bar and Bushings

REMOVAL AND INSTALLATION

1. Disconnect the sway bar links from the lower control arms. Disconnect stabilizer link from stabilizer bar as necessary. Refer to exploded view of front suspension components as necessary.

2. Disconnect the sway bar brackets from the body.

NOTE: *Check the bushings inside the brackets for wear or deformation. A worn bushing can cause a distinct noise as the bar twists during cornering operation.*

3. Disconnect the exhaust system or driveshaft assembly as necessary.

4. Remove the sway bar from the car. Examine the insulators (bushings) carefully for any sign of wear and replace them if necessary.

5. To reinstall, place the bar in position and reconnect the exhaust system using new nuts. Install the driveshaft assembly as necessary.

6. Install both stabilizer bar brackets and

tighten the bolts to 14 ft. lbs. and 29 ft. lbs. Corolla All-Trac

7. Connect the sway bar links to the control arms with the bolts, insulators (in the correct order) and new nuts. Tighten the nuts to 13 ft. lbs. Reconnect stabilizer link (inspect link for wear) to stabilizer bar (47 ft. lbs.) as necessary.

Strut Bar

REMOVAL AND INSTALLATION

Corolla RWD

1. Remove the nut, washer, retainer, spacer and cushion from the strut bar where it attaches to the chassis. Do not remove the staked nut.

2. Raise the lower control arm with a floor jack and then disconnect the strut bar assembly.

3. To install check that the distance between the staked nut and the center of the bolt hole on the bar is 372mm (14.642 in.) for Corolla RWD. Adjust the staked nut as necessary. Never adjust the staked nut unless required.

4. Raise the lower arm and connect the strut bar. Tighten to 34 ft. lbs.

5. Reconnect the bar and all the hardware to the chassis bracket. Tighten the bolt to 67 ft. lbs. Check front end alignment.

MR2

1. To remove the strut bar measure the length as illustrated. Raise and safely support the front of the vehicle.

2. Remove the front retainer assembly to strut bar. Disconnect the strut bar from the lower arm. Refer to exploded view of front suspension components. Remove the strut bar.

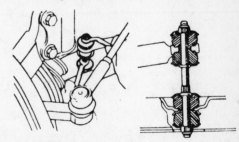

Front stabilizer bar link and bushings

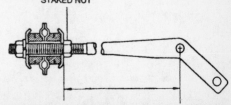

When installing the strut bar, the distance between the staked nut and the center of the bolt hole must be measured — Corolla RWD

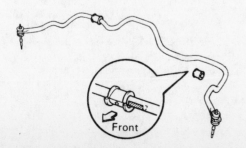

Installing stabilizer bar cushion

3. Installation is the reverse of the removal procedure. Install strut bar, cushion, retainer and nut to the vehicle. Torque the lower arm to the strut bar to 83 ft. lbs. Adjust strut bar to position measured before starting this repair. Rock vehicle up and down to stabilize the suspension before final torque to 83 ft. lbs. Check front end alignment.

Lower Control Arm

REMOVAL AND INSTALLATION

Most Models

1. Raise and safely support the vehicle. Do not place the stands under the control arms. Refer to exploded view of front suspension components as necessary.
2. Remove the nuts and bolts holding lower control arm to steering knuckle (ball joint MR2 vehicles).
3. Remove the nut holding the sway bar link (strut bar-MR2 vehicle) to the control arm and disconnect the link and bar from the control arm as necessary.
4. Remove the nuts and bolts holding the control arm to the body.
5. Remove the control arm from the car and check it carefully for cracks, bends or crimps in the metal or corrosion damage. Check the rubber bushing and replace it if any sign of damage or deformation is found.
6. On some models, install or replace the

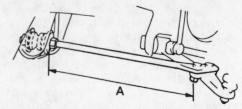
Measure length "A" strut bar removal — MR2

bushing and tighten its retaining nut to 76 ft. lbs. as necessary.

NOTE: *Never reuse a self-locking nut. Always replace cotter pins. Rock vehicle up and down to settle the suspension before final torque.*

7. Position the control arm to the body and install the nuts and bolts. The front nut and bolt should be tightened to 105 ft. lbs. and the rear to 72 ft. lbs.
8. Connect the lower arm to steering knuckle. Torque retaining bolts to 47–59 ft. lbs (ball joint 58 ft. lbs. MR2 vehicle).
9. Reinstall the sway bar and link; tighten the nut to 13 ft. lbs. As necessary install strut bar to lower arm on MR2 vehicle.
10. Check front wheel alignment.

Corolla 1989–90 With Automatic Transmission Left side
NOTE: *Both lower control arms and the suspension crossmember must be removed as a unit.*

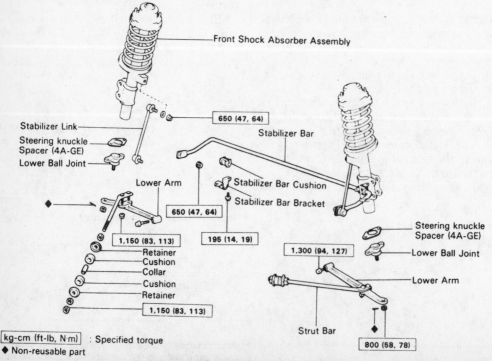

Front suspension components — MR2

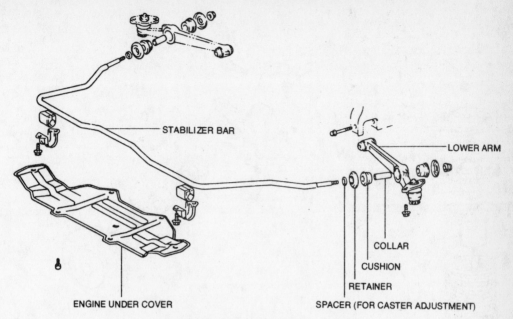

STABILIZER BAR

LOWER ARM

COLLAR

CUSHION

RETAINER

SPACER (FOR CASTER ADJUSTMENT)

ENGINE UNDER COVER

Front suspension components — Tercel

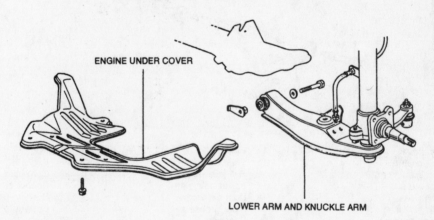

ENGINE UNDER COVER

LOWER ARM AND KNUCKLE ARM

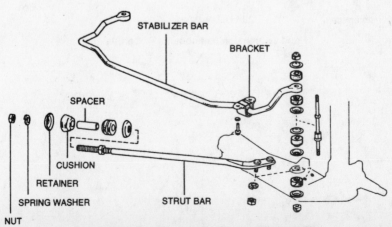

STABILIZER BAR

BRACKET

SPACER

CUSHION

RETAINER

SPRING WASHER

STRUT BAR

NUT

Front suspension components — Corolla RWD

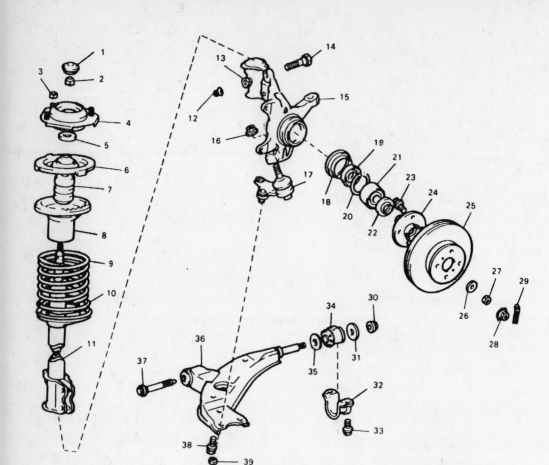

1. Dust cover
2. Strut shaft nut
3. Strut support nut
4. Strut support
5. Spring seal
6. Spring seat
7. Spring bumper
8. Upper insulator
9. Coil spring
10. Lower insulator
11. Shock absorber/strut
12. Nut
13. Camber adjustment cam

14. Bolt
15. Steering knuckle
16. Ball joint nut
17. Lower ball joint
18. Dust deflector
19. Inner grease seal
20. Snapring
21. Front axle hub bearing
22. Outer grease seal
23. Wheel stud
24. Front axle hub
25. Brake disc
26. Hub washer

27. Nut
28. Cap
29. Cotter pin
30. Control arm nut
31. Bushing retainer
32. Bushing bracket
33. Bolt
34. Bushing
35. Bushing retainer
36. Lower control arm
37. Bolt
38. Bolt
39. Nut

Front suspension components — Corolla

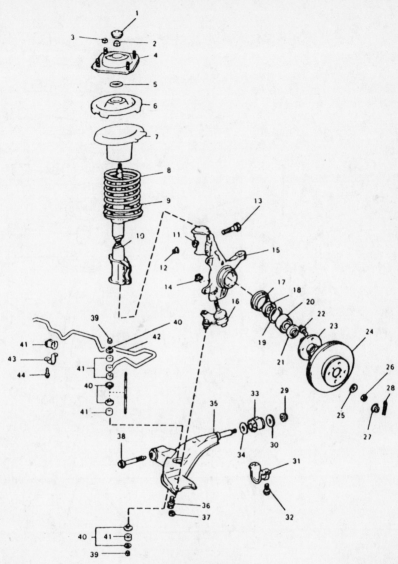

1. Dust cover
2. Strut shaft nut
3. Strut support nut
4. Strut support
5. Support seal
6. Spring seat
7. Upper insulator
8. Coil spring
9. Lower insulator
10. Shock absorber/strut
11. Camber adjustment cam
12. Nut
13. Bolt
14. Nut
15. Steering knuckle

16. Lower ball joint
17. Dust deflector
18. Inner grease seal
19. Snapring
20. Front axle hub bearing
21. Outer hub seal
22. Wheel stud
23. Front axle hub
24. Brake disc
25. Hub washer
26. Nut
27. Cap
28. Cotter pin
29. Nut
30. Bushing retainer

31. Bushing bracket
32. Bolt
33. Control arm bushing
34. Bushing retainer
35. Lower control arm
36. Bolt
37. Nut
38. Bolt
39. Nut
40. Stabilizer bar retainer
41. Insulator
42. Stabilizer bar
43. Bracket
44. Bolt

Front suspension components — Corolla

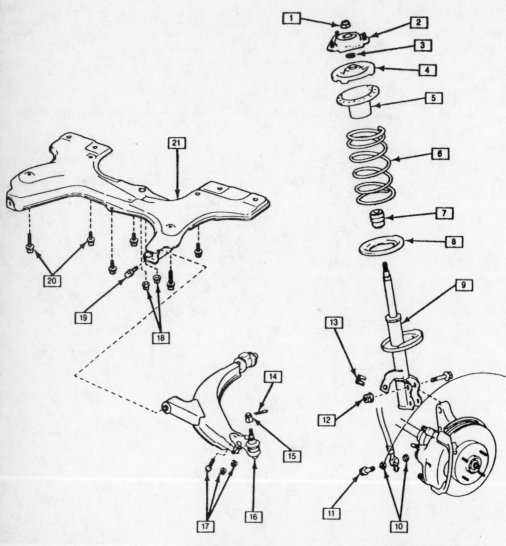

1. Strut rod piston nut
2. Suspension support
3. Dust seal
4. Spring seat
5. Upper insulator
6. Coil spring
7. Spring bumper
8. Lower insulator
9. Shock absorber
10. Brake line gaskets
11. Brake line to caliper bolt
12. Nut and bolt
13. Brake hose clip
14. Cotter pin
15. Ball joint castle nut
16. Ball joint
17. Nuts and bolt
18. Crossmember mounting nuts
19. Bolt
20. Crossmember mounting bolts
21. Suspension crossmember

Front suspension components — Corolla

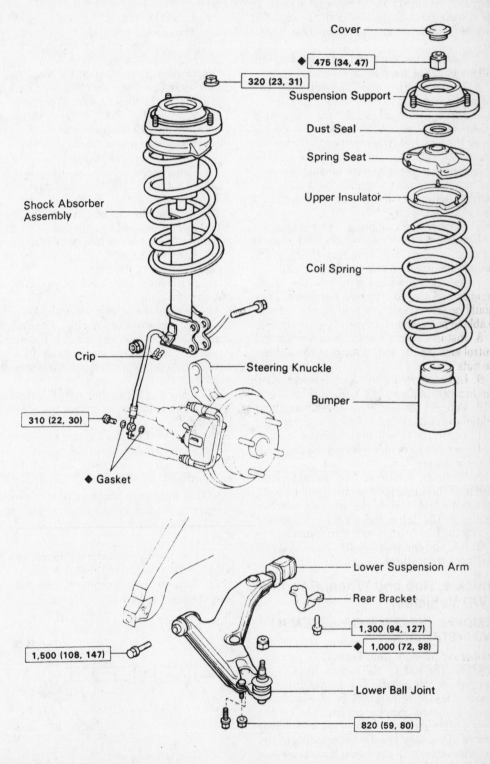

Cover

◆ 475 (34, 47)

320 (23, 31)

Suspension Support

Dust Seal

Spring Seat

Upper Insulator

Coil Spring

Shock Absorber Assembly

Crip

Steering Knuckle

Bumper

310 (22, 30)

◆ Gasket

Lower Suspension Arm

Rear Bracket

1,300 (94, 127)

◆ 1,000 (72, 98)

1,500 (108, 147)

Lower Ball Joint

820 (59, 80)

kg-cm (ft-lb, N·m) : Specified torque

◆ Non-reusable part

Front suspension components — Tercel

1. Raise and safely support the vehicle. Do not place the stands under the control arms or the suspension crossmember. Refer to exploded view of front suspension components as necessary.

2. Remove the nuts and bolts holding the ball joints to the lower control arms.

3. Remove the nut and bolt holding the control arm rear brackets to the crossmember.

4. Place a floor jack under the suspension crossmember. Use a broad piece of wood between the jack and crossmember to evenly distribute the loading.

5. Remove the bolts/nuts holding the suspension crossmember. Carefully lower the crossmember (with the control arms attached) and remove from the car.

6. Remove the mounting bolt holding the control arm to the crossmember and remove the arm. Inspect the arm and bushing for damage, deformation or corrosion damage.

7. Install the control arm(s) to the crossmember and partially tighten the bolts. They should be tight enough to hold firmly, yet still be able to pivot when moderate force is applied.

8. Install the suspension crossmember and control arms to the body of the car and tighten the nuts.

9. Install the bolts holding the rear control arm brackets and partially tighten them.

10. Connect the ball joints to each arm and tighten the bolts to 105 ft. lbs.

11. Lower the vehicle to the ground. Bounce the front end up and down several times to stabilize the suspension.

12. With the vehicle on the ground (don't raise it or the suspension position will be lost), tighten the bolt holding the arm to the crossmember to 152 ft. lbs. Tighten the nut and bolt holding the rear bracket to the crossmember to 14 ft. lbs. and the rear bracket bolts to 94 ft. lbs. Check front wheel alignment.

Knuckle, Hub and Wheel Bearing (FWD Vehicles)

REMOVAL, DISASSEMBLY ASSEMBLY AND INSTALLATION

Camber Adjustment Cam Type

NOTE: *The use of the correct tools is required for this repair. These procedures require the use of assorted joint separators, slide hammers, bearing pullers, seal extractors/drivers and snapring pliers which may not be in your tool box. Do not attempt repairs or disassembly if the correct tools are not available; damage and/or injury may result. Refer to exploded view "Front Axle Hub and Bearing Assembly" for a guide to overhaul both type assemblies.*

1. Loosen the wheel nuts and the center axle nut.

2. Raise the vehicle and safely support it.

3. Remove the wheel.

4. Remove the brake hose retaining clip at the strut.

5. Disconnect the brake flex hose from the metal brake line. Use a small pan to collect spillage and plug the lines as soon as possible.

6. Remove the bolts holding the brake caliper to the knuckle; support the caliper with a piece of stiff wire out of the way.

7. Remove the brake disc.

8. Remove the drive axle nut. Use a SPECIAL PULLER TYPE TOOL to push out the drive axle.

9. Remove the cotter pin and the tie rod (steering rod) nut at the knuckle. Use a tie rod separator or equivalent to separate the joint.

10. Remove the nuts and bolt holding the ball joint to the control arm.

11. Matchmark the camber adjusting cam and the strut.

12. Remove the bolts holding the knuckle to the strut. Remove the knuckle. The ball joint may be removed from the knuckle if desired.

13. Mount the knuckle securely in a vise. Use a screwdriver to remove the outer dust cover.

14. Using a slide hammer and puller or equivalent, remove the inner grease seal from the knuckle.

15. Remove the inner bearing snapring.

16. Remove the brake splash shield.

17. Remove the hub using an extractor tool or equivalent.

NOTE: *Whenever the hub is removed, the inner and outer grease seals MUST be replaced with new seals. The seals are not reusable.*

18. Use the same extractor to remove the outer bearing race from the hub.

19. Remove the outer grease seal with the slide hammer and puller.

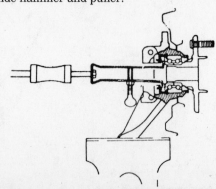

Removing the inner grease seal

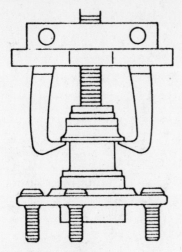

Removing the outer bearing race

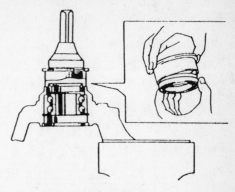

Installing the outer grease seal

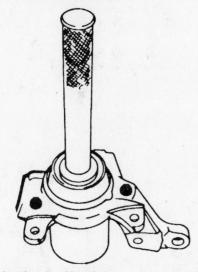

Removing the wheel bearing

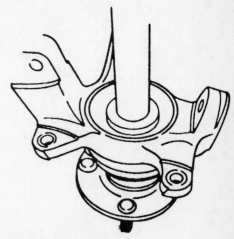

Installation of the hub

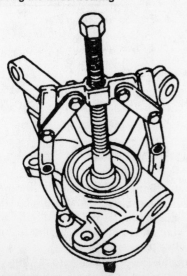

Removing the hub

20. Using a bearing driver of the correct size tools remove the bearing assembly.

21. Clean and inspect all parts but do not wash or clean the wheel bearing; it cannot be repacked. If the bearing is damaged or noisy, it must be replaced.

22. Using a bearing driver of the correct size or equivalent, install the bearing into the hub.

23. Use a seal driver to install a new outer grease seal.

24. Apply sealer to the brake splash shield and install it to the knuckle.

25. Apply a layer of multi-purpose grease to the seal lip, seal and bearing. Install the hub.

26. Install the snapring.

27. Install a new inner grease seal using the correct size driver.

28. Install the outer dust cover (open end down) with tool or equivalent.

29. Install the lower ball joint to the control arm and tighten the nuts and bolt to 47–59 ft. lbs.

30. If the ball joint was removed from the knuckle, reinstall it. Install a new nut and temporarily tighten it to 14 ft. lbs. Back off the nut

Stabilizer Link

Stabilizer Bar

Camber Adjusting Cam

Tie Rod

650 (47, 64)

1,650 (119, 162)

500 (36, 49)

Cotter Pin

Disc Rotor

Steering Knuckle
with Axle Hub

Lower Arm

820 (59, 80)

Strut Bar

Steering Knuckle Spacer (4A-GE)

900 (65, 88)

Disc Brake Caliper

Hub Grease Cap

1,250 (90, 123)

Hole Snap Ring

Steering Knuckle

Bearing Inner
Race (Outside)

Hub Bolt

1,050 (76, 103)

O-ring

Bearing Inner
Race (Inside)

Hub Bearing

Disc Brake
Dust Cover

Outer Oil Seal

Axle Hub

kg-cm (ft-lb, N·m) : Specified torque

◆ Non-reusable part

Exploded view front axle hub and bearing assembly — MR2

until clear of the knuckle and then retighten it to 82 ft. lbs. (58 ft. lbs. MR2 vehicle).

31. Install the camber adjusting cam into the knuckle. Connect the knuckle to the strut lower bracket.

32. Insert the bolts from rear to front and align the matchmarks of the camber adjusting cam and the strut. Tighten the nuts to 105 ft.

lbs. (4A-C engine Corolla), 166 ft. lbs. (4A-GE engines Corolla) 119 ft. lbs. (MR2 vehicle).

33. Connect the tie rod to the knuckle. Install the nut and tighten to 36 ft. lbs. Install the NEW cotter pin.

34. Install the driveshaft into the hub.

35. Double check the nuts and bolt holding the ball joint to the lower control arm.

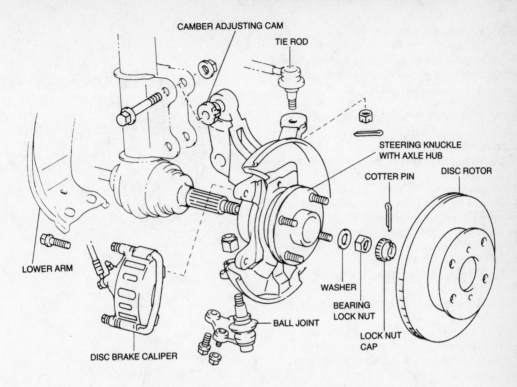

CAMBER ADJUSTING CAM

TIE ROD

STEERING KNUCKLE
WITH AXLE HUB

COTTER PIN

DISC ROTOR

LOWER ARM

DISC BRAKE CALIPER

BALL JOINT

WASHER

BEARING
LOCK NUT

LOCK NUT
CAP

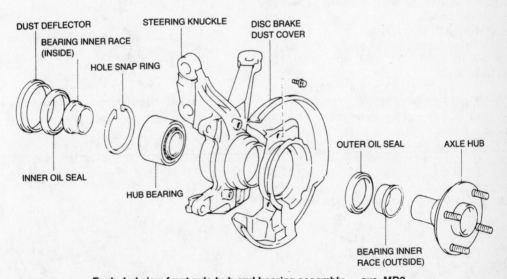

DUST DEFLECTOR

BEARING INNER RACE
(INSIDE)

HOLE SNAP RING

STEERING KNUCKLE

DISC BRAKE
DUST COVER

INNER OIL SEAL

HUB BEARING

OUTER OIL SEAL

AXLE HUB

BEARING INNER
RACE (OUTSIDE)

Exploded view front axle hub and bearing assembly — exc. MR2

36. Install the brake disc.

37. Reinstall the brake caliper. Tighten the bolts. Connect the brake flex hose to the metal brake line. Correct tightness is 11 ft. lbs. Do not over-tighten this connection.

38. Install the wheel

39. Lower the car to the ground.

40. Tighten the wheel nuts. Install the washer and nut onto the driveshaft end.

Tighten the bolt to 137 ft. lbs. and install the cap and cotter pin.

41. Bleed the brake system, following directions in Chapter 9. Check front end alignment.

Non-Camber Adjustment Cam Type

1. Loosen the wheel nuts and the center axle nut.

2. Raise the vehicle and safely support it.

3. Remove the wheel.

4. Remove the center axle nut.

5. Remove the brake caliper and hang it out of the way on a piece of stiff wire. Do not disconnect the brake line; do not allow the caliper to hang by the hose.

6. Remove the brake disc.

7. Remove the cotter pin and nut from the tie rod end.

8. Remove the tie rod end from the knuckle using a joint separator or equivalent.

9. Remove the bolt and 2 nuts holding the bottom of the ball joint to the control arm and remove the arm from the knuckle.

10. Remove the 2 nuts from the steering knuckle. Place a protective cover or shield over the CV boot on the driveshaft.

11. Using a plastic mallet, tap the driveshaft free of the hub assembly.

12. Remove the bolts and remove the axle hub assembly.

13. Clamp the knuckle in a vise with protected jaws.

14. Remove the dust deflector. Loosen the nut holding the ball joint to the knuckle. Use a ball joint separator tool or equivalent) to loosen and remove the joint

15. Use a slide hammer/extractor to remove the outer oil seal.

16. Remove the snapring.

17. Using a hub puller and pilot tools or equivalents, pull the axle hub from the knuckle.

18. Remove the brake splash shield (3 bolts).

19. Use a split plate bearing remover, puller pilot and a shop press, remove the inner bearing race from the hub.

20. Remove the inner oil seal with the same tools used to remove the outer seal.

21. Place the inner race in the bearing. Support the knuckle and use an axle hub remover with a plastic mallet to drive out the bearing.

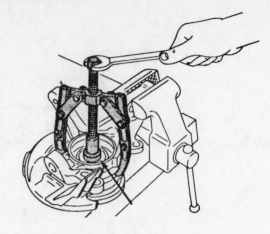

Axle hub removal

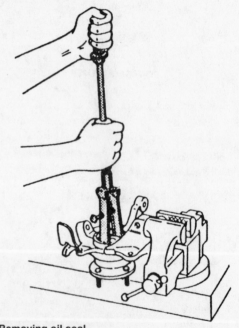

Removing oil seal

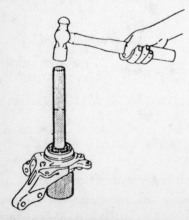

Removing inner bearing race

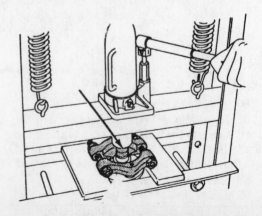

Using a split plate tool to remove outer bearing race

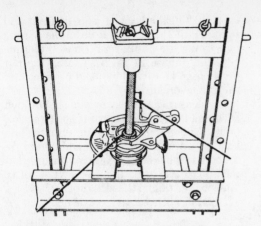

Installing axle hub into steering knuckle

22. Clean and inspect all parts but do not wash or clean the wheel bearing; it cannot be repacked. If the bearing is damaged or noisy, it must be replaced.

23. Press a new bearing race into the steering knuckle using a bearing driver of the correct size.

24. Place a new bearing inner race on the hub bearing.

25. Insert the side lip of a new oil seal into the seal installer and drive the oil seal into the steering knuckle.

26. Apply multi-purpose grease to the oil seal lip.

27. Apply sealer to the brake splash shield and install the shield.

28. Use a hub installer to press the hub into the steering knuckle.

29. Install a new snapring into the hub.

30. Using a seal installer of the correct size, install a new outer oil seal into the steering knuckle.

31. Apply multi-purpose grease to the seal surfaces which will contact the driveshaft.

32. Support the knuckle and drive in a new dust deflector.

33. Install the ball joint into the knuckle and tighten the nut to 72–76 ft. lbs.

34. Temporarily install the hub assembly to the lower control arm and fit the drive axle into the hub.

35. Install the knuckle to strut bolts, then install the tie rod end to the knuckle.

36. Tighten the strut bracket nuts to (166 ft. lbs. Tercel) 194 ft. lbs. and tighten the tie rod end nut to 36 ft. lbs. Install the NEW cotter pin.

37. Remove the old nut from the lower ball joint and install a new castle nut. Tighten the nut to 72–76 ft. lbs. and install a new cotter pin. (The old nut was used to draw the joint into the knuckle; the new nut assures retention.)

38. Connect the ball joint to the lower control arm and tighten the nuts to 105 ft. lbs (59 ft. lbs. Tercel).

39. Install the brake disc.

40. Install the brake caliper and tighten the bolts.

41. Install the center nut and washer on the drive axle.

42. Install the wheel

43. Lower the car to the ground.

44. Tighten the wheel nuts and the axle bolt to 137 ft. lbs. Install the cap and cotter pin.

45. Remove the protective cover from the CV boot. Check front end alignment.

Front Axle Hub and Wheel Bearing (RWD Corolla Vehicle)

REMOVAL, REPACKING AND INSTALLATION

1. Raise the front of the vehicle and support it with jackstands. Remove the wheel.

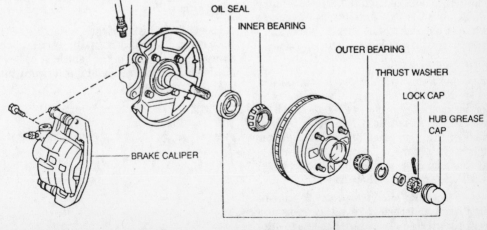

Front axle hub and wheel bearing — Corolla RWD

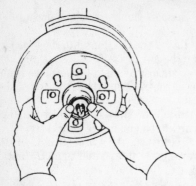

Slide the axle hub and disc off the wheel spindle Corolla RWD

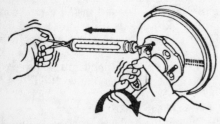

Use a spring scale to measure the wheel bearing preload — Corolla RWD

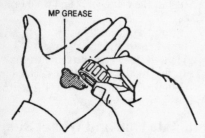

MP GREASE

Packing the wheel bearing with grease

2. Remove the front disc brake caliper mounting bolts and position it safely out of the way.

3. Pry off the bearing cap and then remove the cotter pin, lock cap and the adjusting nut.

4. Remove the axle hub and disc together with the outer bearing and thrust washer.

NOTE: *Be careful not to drop the outer bearing during removal.*

5. Using a small prybar, pry out the oil seal from the back of the hub and then remove the inner bearing. Remove races (note depth of race for correct installation) if necessary by driving out of axle hub assembly with a hammer and brass drift pin.

6. Installation is in the reverse order of removal. Please note the following:

a. Place some axle grease into the palm of your hand and then take the bearing and work the grease into it until it begins to ooze out the other side. Coat the inside of the axle hub and bearing cap with the same grease.

b. Install the bearing adjusting nut and tighten it to 21 ft. lbs. Snug down the bearing by turning the hub several times. Retorque adjusting nut to 21 ft. lbs. Loosen the nut until it can be turned by hand confirm that there is no brake drag.

c. Measure and make note of the rotation frictional force of oil seal using spring scale.

d. Tighten the adjusting nut until the preload measures 0.0–2.3 lbs. in addition to rotation frictional force of oil seal. Insure that the hub rotates smoothly. Use a NEW cotter pin when installing the lock cap.

7. Install all necessary components as required.

Front End Alignment

Alignment of the front wheels is essential if your car is to go, stop and turn as designed. Alignment can be altered by collision, overloading, poor repair or bent components.

If you are diagnosing bizarre handling and/or poor road manners, the first place to look is the tires. Although the tires may wear as a result of an alignment problem, worn or poorly inflated tires can make you chase alignment problems which don't exist.

Once you have eliminated all other causes (always check and repair front end parts BEFORE wheel alignment), unload everything from the trunk except the spare tire, set the tire pressures to the correct level and take the car to a reputable alignment facility. Since the alignment settings are measured in very small increments, it is almost impossible for the home mechanic to accurately determine the settings. The explanations that follow will help you understand the three dimensions of alignment: caster, camber and toe.

CASTER

Caster is the tilting of the steering axis either forward or backward from the vertical, when viewed from the side of the vehicle. A backward tilt is said to be positive and a forward tilt is said to be negative.

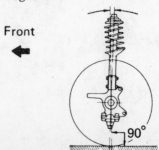

Front

90°

Caster angle affects the tracking of the steering

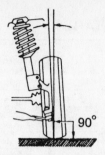

Camber is the inward or outward tilt of the wheel on the road

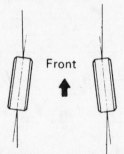

Toe in (out) can affect tire wear and fuel economy

CAMBER

Camber is the tilting of the wheels from the vertical (leaning in or out) when viewed from the front of the vehicle. When the wheels tilt outward at the top, the camber is said to be positive. When the wheels tilt inward at the top the camber is said to be negative. The amount of tilt is measured in degrees from the vertical. This measurement is called camber angle.

TOE

Toe is the turning in or out (parallelism) of the wheels. The actual amount of toe setting is normally only a fraction of an inch. The purpose of toe-in (or out) specification is to ensure parallel rolling of the wheels. Toe-in also serves to offset the small deflections of the steering support system which occur when the vehicle is rolling forward or under braking.

Changing the toe setting will radically affect the overall "feel" of the steering, the behavior of the car under braking, tire wear and even fuel economy. Excessive toe (in or out) causes excessive drag or scrubbing on the tires.

REAR SUSPENSION

NOTE: *Refer to exploded views of "Rear Suspension Components" to identify the suspension component.*

Coil Springs

REMOVAL AND INSTALLATION

1. Remove the hubcap and loosen the lug nuts.
2. Jack up the rear axle housing and support the frame (not rear axle housing) with jackstands. Leave the jack in place under the rear axle housing.

CAUTION: *Support the car securely. Remember; you will be working underneath it.*

3. Remove the lug nuts and wheel.
4. Unfasten the lower shock absorber end.
5. If equipped with a stabilizer bar; remove the bracket bolts.
6. If equipped with a lateral control rod disconnect the rod from the rear axle housing.
7. Slowly lower the jack under the rear axle housing until the axle is at the bottom of its travel.
8. Withdraw the coil spring, complete with its insulator.
9. Inspect the coil spring and insulator for wear and cracks, or weakness; replace either or both as necessary.
10. Installation is performed in the reverse order of removal procedure (install the lower in-

REAR WHEEL ALIGNMENT CHART

Year	Model	Caster Range (deg.)	Caster Preferred Setting (deg.)	Camber Range (deg.)	Camber Preferred Setting (deg.)	Toe (in.)
1984–85	Corolla (FWD)	—	—	1N–0	1/2N	9/64
1986–87	Corolla (FWD)	—	—	1N–0	1/2N	9/64
1988–90	Corolla (FWD)	—	—	1⁷/₁₆N–¹/₁₆P	1¹/₁₆N	5/32
1984	Tercel (Sedan)	—	—	³/₁₆N–¹³/₁₆P	5/16P	0
1985–86	Tercel (Sedan)	—	—	⁹/₁₆N–⁷/₁₆P	1/16N	0
1985–86	MR2	—	—	1¹/₄N–¹/₄N	3/4N	13/64
1987–89	MR2	—	—	1⁷/₁₆N–⁷/₁₆N	15/16N	13/64

FRONT WHEEL ALIGNMENT CHART

Year	Model	Caster Range (deg.)	Caster Preferred Setting (deg.)	Camber Range (deg.)	Camber Preferred Setting (deg.)	Toe-in (in.)
1984–87	Corolla (RWD) w/manual steering	$2^{1/4}P$–$3^{1/4}P$	$2^{3/4}P$	$^{1/4}N$–$^{3/4}P$	$^{1/4}P$	$^{3/64}$
	w/power steering	$3^{3/16}P$–$4^{3/16}P$	$3^{11/16}P$	$^{1/4}N$–$^{3/4}P$	$^{1/4}P$	$^{3/64}$
1984–85	Corolla (FWD)	$^{3/8}P$–$1^{9/16}P$	$^{7/8}P$	$1N$–0	$^{1/2}N$	0
1986–87	Corolla (FWD)	$^{1/8}P$–$1^{3/8}P$	$^{7/8}P$	$^{3/4}N$–$^{1/4}P$	$^{1/4}N$	$^{3/64}$
1988–90	Corolla (FWD)	$^{9/16}P$–$2^{1/16}P$	$1^{5/16}P$	$1N$–$^{1/2}P$	$^{1/4}N$	$^{3/64}$
1989–90	Corolla (4WD)	$^{3/4}P$–$1^{3/4}P$	$1^{1/4}P$	$^{5/16}N$–$1^{1/16}P$	$^{3/16}P$	$^{3/64}$
1984	Tercel (4WD)	$1^{15/16}P$–$2^{15/16}P$	$2^{7/16}P$	$^{5/16}P$–$1^{5/16}P$	$1^{3/16}P$	0
1985–88	Tercel (4WD)	$1^{15/16}P$–$2^{15/16}P$	$2^{7/16}P$	$^{1/16}P$–$1^{1/16}P$	$^{9/16}P$	$^{3/64}$ (out)
1984	Tercel (Sedan) w/manual steering	$1^{1/16}P$–$1^{11/16}P$	$1^{3/16}P$	$^{3/16}N$–$1^{3/16}P$	$^{5/16}P$	0
	w/power steering	$2^{3/16}P$–$3^{3/16}P$	$2^{11/16}P$	$^{3/16}N$–$1^{3/16}P$	$^{5/16}P$	0
1985–86	Tercel (Sedan) w/manual steering	$1^{1/16}P$–$1^{11/16}P$	$1^{3/16}P$	$^{5/16}N$–$1^{1/16}P$	$^{1/16}P$	$^{3/64}$ (out)
	w/power steering	$2^{3/16}P$–$3^{3/16}P$	$2^{11/16}P$	$^{5/16}N$–$1^{1/16}P$	$^{1/16}P$	$^{3/64}$ (out)
1987–90	Tercel (Sedan) w/manual steering	$^{1/4}P$–$1^{3/4}P$	$1P$	$^{3/4}N$–$^{3/4}P$	0	0
	w/power steering	$1^{3/4}P$–$3^{1/4}P$	$2^{1/2}P$	$^{3/4}N$–$^{3/4}P$	0	0
1985–86	MR2	$4^{13/16}P$–$5^{13/16}P$	$5^{5/16}P$	$^{1/4}N$–$^{3/4}P$	$^{1/4}P$	$^{3/64}$
1987–89	MR2	$4^{9/16}P$–$5^{9/16}P$	$5^{1/16}P$	$^{1/4}N$–$^{3/4}P$	$^{1/4}P$	$^{3/64}$

sulator or spring seat in the correct position-see illustration). When reconnecting the lateral control rod, tighten the bolt finger tight. When the car is lowered, bounce it a few times to stabilize the rear suspension. Raise the rear axle housing until the body is free and then tighten the nut to 47 ft. lbs.

Lateral Control Rod

REMOVAL AND INSTALLATION

1. Raise the rear of the vehicle and support the axle housing with jackstands.
2. Disconnect the lateral rod from the rear axle housing.
3. Disconnect the lateral rod from the body and remove the rod.

4. Install the arm-to-body nut and finger tighten it.
5. Position the arm on the axle housing and install a washer, bushing, spacer, the arm, bushing, washer and then the nut. Finger tighten the nut.
6. Lower the vehicle and bounce it a few times to stabilize the suspension.
7. Raise the rear of the vehicle again then tighten the control rod-to-body nut to 83 ft. lbs. and the control rod-to-axle housing nut to 47 ft. lbs.

NOTE: *Refer to exploded views of "Rear Suspension Components" to identify the suspension component.*

Make sure that the spring is installed correctly in the lower insulator (spring seat)

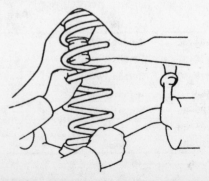

Removing the coil spring

Rear Stabilizer Bar
REMOVAL AND INSTALLATION

1. Remove all necessary components to gain access for removal and installation of stabilizer bar. Remove the stabilizer bar brackets.

2. Remove the nuts, cushions and links holding both sides of the stabilizer bar from the suspension arms. Remove the stabilizer bar.

3. To install assemble the stabilizer link sub-assembly and install the link to the arm.

4. Install the stabilizer bar to the link.

5. Install the stabilizer bar bracket to the differential support member.

6. Install all necessary components that were removed for removal access of stabilizer bar.

Shock Absorbers
TESTING

Shock absorbers require replacement if the car fails to recover quickly after hitting a large bump or if it sways excessively following a directional change.

A good way to test the shock absorbers is to intermittently apply downward pressure to the side of the car until it is moving up and down for almost its full suspension travel. Release it and observe its recovery. If the car bounces once or twice after having been released and then comes to a rest, the shocks are all right. If the car continues to bounce, the shocks will probably require replacement.

NOTE: *On MacPherson strut shock absorbers and conventional rear shock absorbers if oil is leaking from the cylinder portion of the assembly the shock absorber must be replaced.*

REMOVAL AND INSTALLATION

Conventional Rear Shock Absorber

1. Raise the rear of the car and support the rear axle with jackstands.

2. Unfasten the upper shock absorber retaining nuts. Use a tool to keep the shaft from spinning.

NOTE: *On some models, upper retaining nut removal will require removing the rear seat. Always remove and install the shock absorbers one at a time. Do not allow the rear axle to hang.*

3. Remove the lower shock retaining nut where it attaches to the rear axle housing.

4. Remove the shock absorber.

5. Inspect the shock for wear, leaks or other signs of damage.

6. Installation is in the reverse order of removal procedure. Make sure when you are installing the rear shock absorbers that rubber

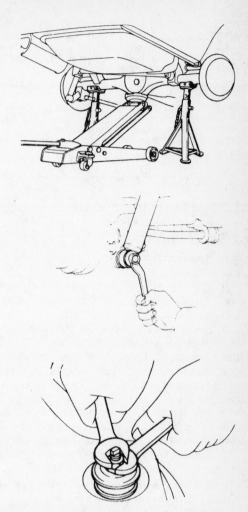

Removing conventional rear shock absorber

bushings (cushions) and washers (retainers) are installed in the correct position. Tighten the upper shock mounting retaining nut to 16–24 ft. lbs. Tighten the lower shock mounting retaining nut to 22–32 ft. lbs.

MacPherson Struts
REMOVAL

NOTE: *On some Tercel FWD models the rear strut assembly is mount to the axle beam. Refer to the exploded view illustration of the rear suspension components as a guide-modify the service steps as necessary.*

1. Working inside the car, remove the shock absorber cover and rear window shelf. On some models it is necessary to remove the quarter window trim panel and the rear shelf to gain access to the shock/strut mounts. Remove the speakers and/or speaker grilles as needed. On later model Corolla remove the seat back side cushion (sedan) or the rear sill side panel (hatchback) to gain access to the upper strut mount.

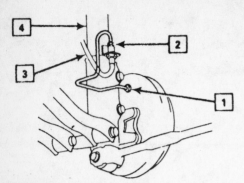

1. BRAKE LINE FITTING AT WHEEL CYLINDER
2. FITTING AT FLEXIBLE HOSE
3. FLEXIBLE HOSE
4. STRUT ASSEMBLY

Brake lines and strut bracket

2. Raise the rear of the vehicle and support it with jackstands (do not place stands under suspension arms). Remove the wheel.

3. Disconnect the brake line from the flexible hose at the mounting bracket on the strut tube. Disconnect the flexible hose from the strut. Reconnect the 2 brake lines to each other but not to the strut. This will prevent excessive leakage.

4. Disconnect the sway bar link from the strut assembly as necessary. Remove the 2 lower bolts holding the strut to the axle carrier.

5. Remove the 3 upper strut mounting nuts and carefully remove the strut assembly.

WARNING: *Do not loosen the center nut on the top of the shock absorber piston.*

DISASSEMBLY

CAUTION: *THIS PROCEDURE REQUIRES THE USE OF A SPRING COMPRESSOR; IT CANNOT BE PERFORMED WITHOUT ONE! IF YOU DO NOT HAVE ACCESS TO THIS SPECIAL TOOL, DO NOT ATTEMPT TO DISASSEMBLE THE STRUT. THE COIL SPRINGS ARE RETAINED UNDER CONSIDERABLE PRESSURE. THEY CAN EXERT ENOUGH FORCE TO CAUSE SERIOUS INJURY! EXERCISE EXTREME CAUTION WHEN DISASSEMBLING THE STRUT.*

1. Place the strut assembly in a pipe vise or strut vise.

NOTE: *Do not attempt to clamp the strut assembly in a flat jaw vise as this will result in damage to the strut tube.*

2. Attach a spring compressor and compress the spring until the upper suspension support is free of any spring tension. Do not overcompress the spring.

3. Hold the upper support and then remove the nut on the end of the shock piston rod.

4. Remove the support, coil spring, insulator and bumper.

INSPECTION

Check the shock absorber by moving the piston shaft through its full range of travel. It should move smoothly and evenly throughout its entire travel without any trace of binding or notching. Use a small straightedge to check the piston shaft for any bending or deformation. If a shock absorber is replaced, the old one should be drilled at the bottom to vent the internal gas. Wear safety goggles and drill a small hole (2–3mm) into the base of the shock absorber. The gas within the strut is colorless, odorless and non-toxic, but should be vented to make the unit safe for disposal.

Inspect the spring for any sign of deterioration or cracking. The waterproof coating on the coils should be intact to prevent rusting.

NOTE: *Do not turn the piston rod within the cylinder if the piston rod is fully extended.*

ASSEMBLY AND INSTALLATION

NOTE: *Never reuse a self-locking nut. Always replace self-locking nuts and cotter pins as applicable.*

1. Loosely assemble all components onto the strut assembly. Make sure the spring end aligns with the hollow in the lower seat.

2. Align the upper suspension support with the piston rod and install the support.

3. Align the suspension support with the strut lower bracket. This assures the spring will be properly seated top and bottom.

4. Compress the spring slightly by pushing on the suspension support with one hand to expose the strut piston rod threads.

5. Install a new strut piston nut and tighten it to 36 ft. lbs. (54 ft. lbs. MR2 vehicle).

6. Place the complete strut assembly into

1. SUSPENSION SUPPORT
2. STRUT LOWER BRACKET

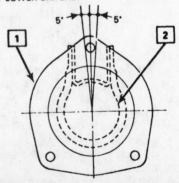

Correct position of upper and lower mounts when reassembling rear strut

the lower mount and mount it in position with the bolts.

7. Use a floor jack to gently raise the suspension and guide the upper strut mount into position.

CAUTION: *The car is on jackstands. Elevate the floor jack only enough to swing the strut into position; do not raise the car.*

8. Disconnect the flexible brake line and the metal pipe. Connect the flexible hose to the strut, then reconnect the metal brake line to the flexible hose.

9. Tighten the lower strut retaining nuts and bolts to 105 ft. lbs. (166 ft. lbs. MR2 vehicle).

10. Tighten the 3 upper retaining bolts to 29–36 ft. lbs. (17 ft. lbs. early model Tercel FWD).

11. Reconnect the sway bar link to the strut assembly as necessary. Install the wheel.

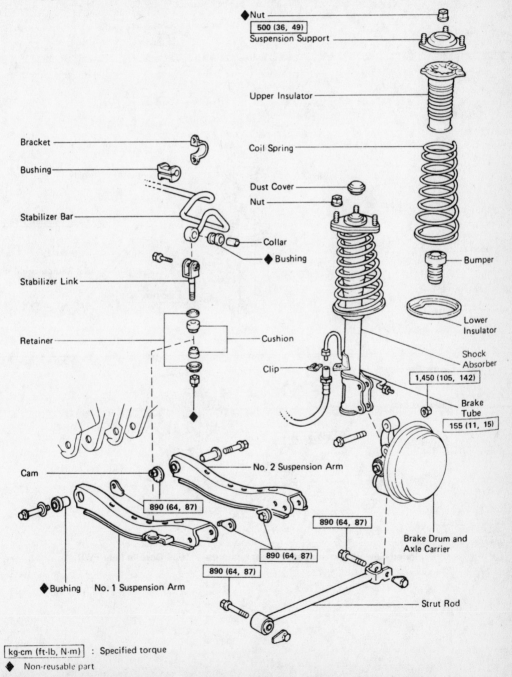

Exploded view of rear suspension components — 1986 Corolla (early FWD)

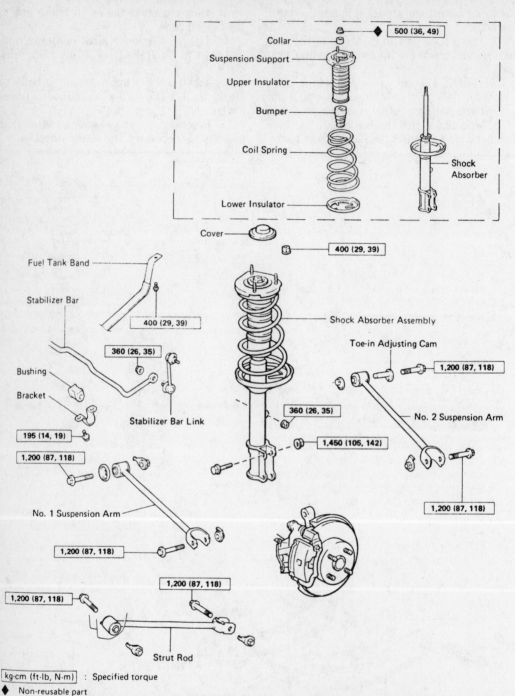

Collar

Suspension Support

Upper Insulator

Bumper

Coil Spring

Shock Absorber

Lower Insulator

500 (36, 49)

Cover

400 (29, 39)

Fuel Tank Band

Stabilizer Bar

400 (29, 39)

360 (26, 35)

Bushing

Bracket

Stabilizer Bar Link

195 (14, 19)

1,200 (87, 118)

No. 1 Suspension Arm

1,200 (87, 118)

Shock Absorber Assembly

Toe-in Adjusting Cam

1,200 (87, 118)

No. 2 Suspension Arm

360 (26, 35)

1,450 (105, 142)

1,200 (87, 118)

1,200 (87, 118)

1,200 (87, 118)

Strut Rod

kg-cm (ft-lb, N·m) : Specified torque

◆ Non-reusable part

Exploded view of rear suspension components — 1989 Corolla (late FWD)

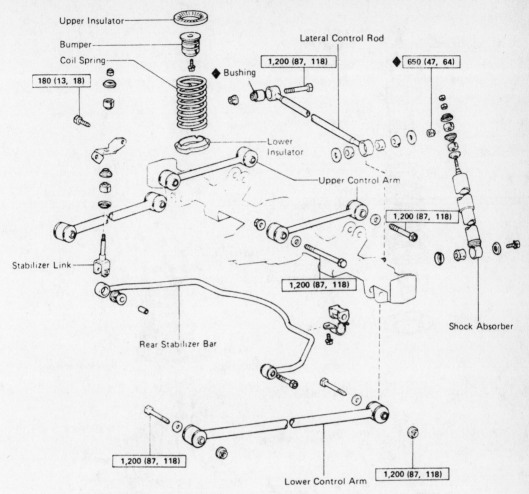

Upper Insulator

Bumper

Coil Spring

180 (13, 18)

Lateral Control Rod

1,200 (87, 118)

◆ 650 (47, 64)

◆ Bushing

Lower Insulator

Upper Control Arm

1,200 (87, 118)

Stabilizer Link

1,200 (87, 118)

Shock Absorber

Rear Stabilizer Bar

1,200 (87, 118)

1,200 (87, 118)

Lower Control Arm

Exploded view of rear suspension components — 1987 Corolla (RWD)

12. Lower the vehicle to the ground.

13. Reinstall the interior components as necessary.

14. Bleed the brake system. Please refer to Chapter 9 for complete directions. Check rear wheel alignment.

Upper and Lower Control Arms

REMOVAL AND INSTALLATION

Corolla RWD, Corolla 4WD and Tercel 4WD

1. Raise the rear of the vehicle and support the body with jackstands. Support the rear axle housing with a jack.

2. Remove the bolt holding the upper control arm to the body.

3. Remove the bolt holding the upper control arm to the axle housing and then remove the upper control arm.

4. Disconnect the parking brake cable assembly from the control arm if necessary.

5. Remove the bolt holding the lower control arm to the body.

6. Remove the bolt holding the lower control arm to the rear axle housing and then remove the lower control arm.

7. Position the upper control arm and install the arm-to-body and arm-to-axle housing bolts. Do not tighten the nuts.

8. Position the lower control arm and install the arm-to-body and arm-to-axle housing bolts. Do not tighten the nuts.

9. Reconnect the parking brake cable clamp to the axle housing if necessary.

10. Lower the vehicle and bounce it a few times to stabilize the suspension.

11. Raise and support the vehicle once again. Raise the rear axle housing until the body is just free from the jackstands.

12. Tighten the upper arm-to-body nut to 87 ft. lbs. Do the same for the upper arm-to-axle housing nuts.

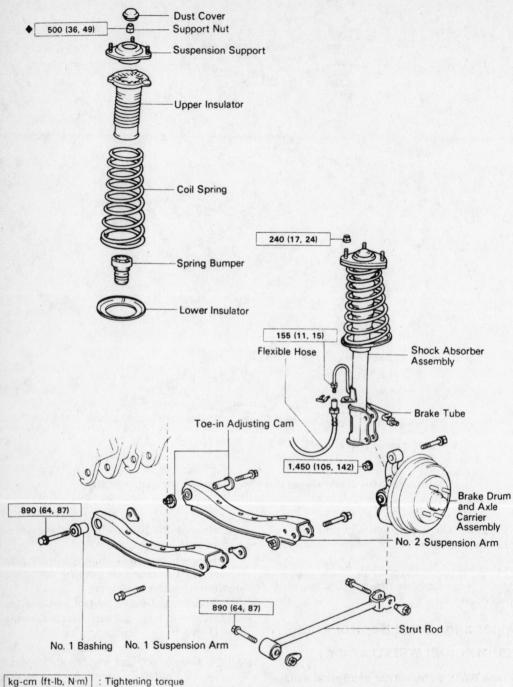

Dust Cover
◆ 500 (36, 49)
Support Nut
Suspension Support

Upper Insulator

Coil Spring

240 (17, 24)

Spring Bumper

Lower Insulator

155 (11, 15)
Flexible Hose

Shock Absorber
Assembly

Brake Tube

Toe-in Adjusting Cam

1,450 (105, 142)

Brake Drum
and Axle
Carrier
Assembly

890 (64, 87)

No. 2 Suspension Arm

890 (64, 87)

Strut Rod

No. 1 Bashing   No. 1 Suspension Arm

kg-cm (ft-lb, N·m) : Tightening torque

◆ : Non-reusable part

Exploded view of rear suspension components — 1985 Tercel (early FWD)

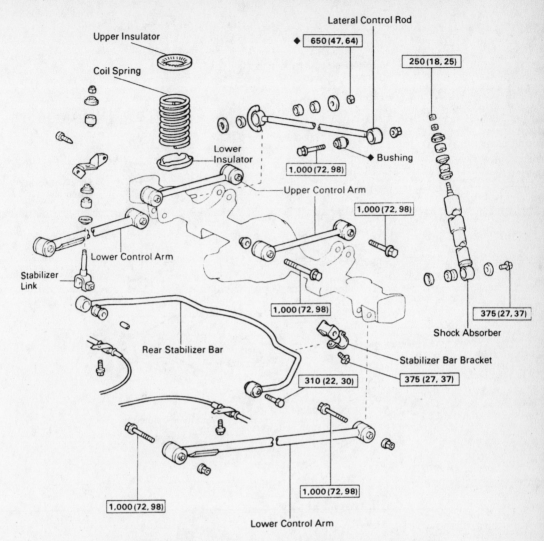

Upper Insulator

Coil Spring

Lower Insulator

Lateral Control Rod

◆ 650 (47, 64)

250 (18, 25)

◆ Bushing

1,000 (72, 98)

Upper Control Arm

1,000 (72, 98)

Lower Control Arm

Stabilizer Link

Rear Stabilizer Bar

1,000 (72, 98)

Stabilizer Bar Bracket

375 (27, 37)

Shock Absorber

375 (27, 37)

310 (22, 30)

1,000 (72, 98)

1,000 (72, 98)

Lower Control Arm

Exploded view of rear suspension components — 1989 Corolla (4WD)

13. Tighten the lower arm-to-body nuts to 87 ft. lbs. Do the same for the lower arm-to-axle housing nuts.

Control Arms

REMOVAL

Corolla FWD and Tercel FWD

These vehicles use two control arms on each rear wheel. To avoid the obvious confusion they are referred to as No. 1 and No. 2, with arm No.1 being the closest to the front of the car. Refer to the exploded view of "Rear Suspension Components".

No. 1 Arm

1. Raise and safely support the vehicle.
2. Disconnect the sway bar link if so equipped.

3. Remove the bolt holding the arm to the body.
4. Remove the bolt holding the arm to the suspension knuckle.
5. Remove the arm.

No. 2 Arm

1. Raise and safely support the vehicle.
2. Observe and matchmark the position of the adjusting cam at the body mount.
3. Disconnect the bolt holding the arm to the suspension knuckle.
4. Disconnect the bolt holding the arm to the body.
5. Remove the arm.
6. Inspect the arms for any bending or cracking. If the arm is not true in all dimensions, it must be replaced. Any attempt to straighten a bent arm will damage it. Also check the bush-

Retainer ⸺ ◆ 550 (40, 54)

Suspension Support

Coil Spring

320 (23, 31)

Spring Bumper

Shock Absorber
Assembly

Axle Beam

Washer

Bushing

650 (47, 64)

1,450 (105, 142)

Lateral Control Rod

◆ Bushing

1,150 (83, 113)

650 (47, 64)

710 (51, 70)

kg-cm (ft-lb, N·m) : Specified torque
◆ Non-reusable part

Exploded view of rear suspension components — 1988 Tercel (late FWD)

ings within the ends of the arms and replace any which are deformed or too spongy. If a bushing must be replaced, do not grease it before installation.

INSTALLATION

1. Place the arm in position, install the arm to body bolts and partially tighten them. If installing arm No. 2, make sure the matchmarks for the adjusting cam are aligned.

2. Install the arm to the knuckle and partially tighten the bolts.

3. Reconnect the sway bar link if it was removed. Use a new nut and tighten it to 11 ft. lbs.

4. Install the wheel.

5. Lower the car to the ground. Bounce the car rear and front several times to position the suspension.

6. Tighten the retaining bolts at the body

and the knuckle: early (flat) type, 64 ft. lbs. and later (cylindrical) type, 87 ft. lbs.

7. Check rear wheel alignment.

Lower Arm

REMOVAL AND INSTALLATION

MR2

1. Raise and safely support the vehicle.
2. Disconnect the lower arm from ball joint (remove cotter pin and nut).

3. Remove the strut rod nut and retainer from the lower arm.

4. Remove the lower arm.

5. Installation is the reverse of removal procedure. Torque the lower arm to ball joint to 67 ft. lbs. (install new cotter pin-if the cotter pin hole does not line up tighten the nut by the smallest amount possible).

6. Lower the car to the ground. Bounce the car rear and front several times to position the suspension.

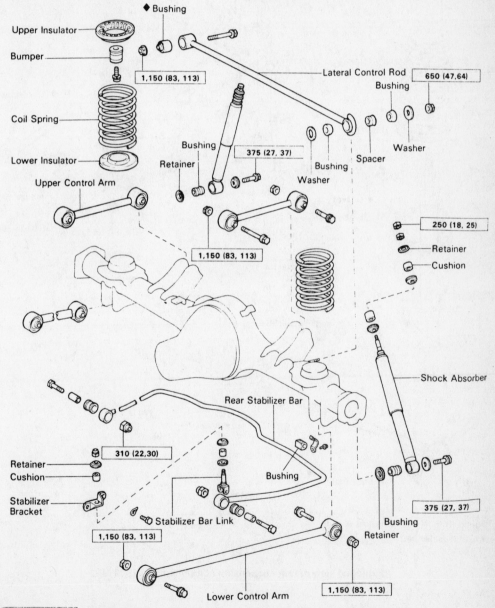

kg-cm (ft-lb, N·m) : Specified torque
◆ Non-reusable part

Exploded view of rear suspension components — 1988 Tercel (4WD)

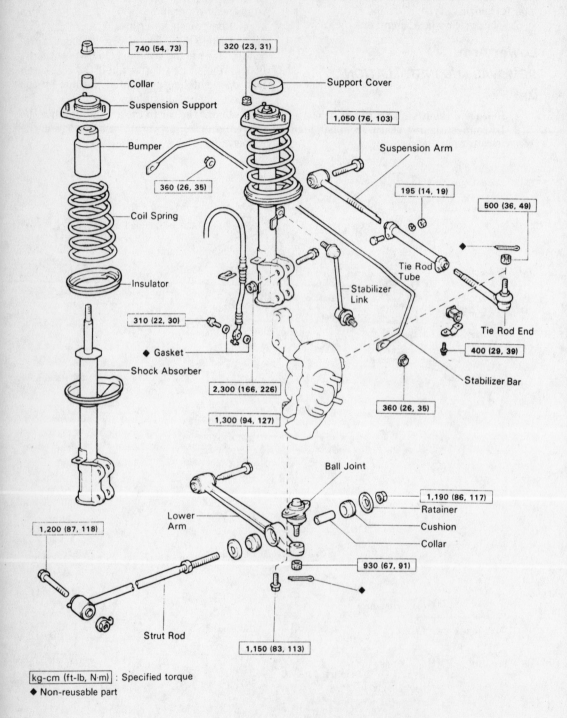

740 (54, 73)

Collar

Suspension Support

Bumper

360 (26, 35)

Coil Spring

Insulator

310 (22, 30)

◆ Gasket

Shock Absorber

1,200 (87, 118)

Strut Rod

320 (23, 31)

Support Cover

1,050 (76, 103)

Suspension Arm

195 (14, 19)

500 (36, 49)

Tie Rod Tube

Stabilizer Link

Tie Rod End

400 (29, 39)

Stabilizer Bar

2,300 (166, 226)

1,300 (94, 127)

360 (26, 35)

Ball Joint

1,190 (86, 117)

Rataıner

Cushion

Collar

Lower Arm

930 (67, 91)

1,150 (83, 113)

kg-cm (ft-lb, N·m) : Specified torque
◆ Non-reusable part

Exploded view of rear suspension components — 1989 MR2

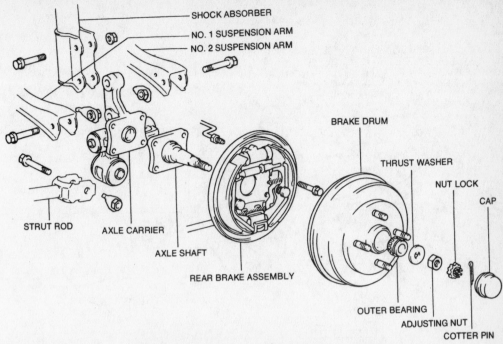

SHOCK ABSORBER
NO. 1 SUSPENSION ARM
NO. 2 SUSPENSION ARM
BRAKE DRUM
THRUST WASHER
NUT LOCK
CAP
STRUT ROD
AXLE CARRIER
AXLE SHAFT
REAR BRAKE ASSEMBLY
OUTER BEARING
ADJUSTING NUT
COTTER PIN

Exploded view of rear axle, hub and carrier — Tercel

7. Torque the strut rod nut to 86 ft. lbs. and the lower arm retaining bolt to 94 ft. lbs.

8. Check rear wheel alignment.

Rear Axle Hub, Carrier And Bearing

REMOVAL AND INSTALLATION

Corolla FWD

1. Raise and safely support the vehicle.

2. Remove the brake drum or disc rotor. Disconnect the hydraulic brake line.

3. Remove the 4 axle hub and carrier mounting bolts. Remove the axle hub and brake assembly.

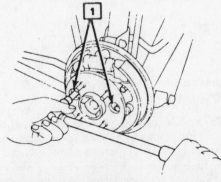

1. AXLE HUB BOLT ACCESS HOLES

Removing the axle hub from the brake packing plate

NOTE: *The bearing assembly can be replaced by removing staked nut, bearing races, seal and pressing bearing in and out. Torque the bearing assembly retaining nut to 90 ft. lbs. then stake nut.*

4. At this point of the service remove the rear axle carrier by following this procedure:

a. Remove the strut rod mounting bolt from the axle carrier.

b. Remove all rear suspension arm mounting bolts from the axle carrier.

c. Remove the 2 axle carrier mounting bolts from the shock absorber. Remove the rear axle carrier assembly from vehicle.

5. Installation is the reverse of the removal procedure. Install new O-ring in axle carrier. Torque the rear axle carrier to shock absorber to 105 ft. lbs. and the 4 axle hub retaining bolts to 59 ft. lbs. Torque strut rod to 64 ft. lbs. (87 ft. lbs. later model Corolla) and suspension arm to 64 ft. lbs. (87 ft. lbs. later model Corolla) with vehicle weight on suspension (bounce the vehicle a few times to stabilize the suspension). Check rear wheel alignment as necessary.

MR2

1. Raise the rear of the vehicle and support it with jackstands.

2. Remove the rear wheel. Remove the cotter pin, bearing lock nut cap and bearing lock nut. Remove the disc brake caliper from the rear axle carrier and suspend it with wire. Remove the rotor disc.

3. Disconnect the parking brake cable.

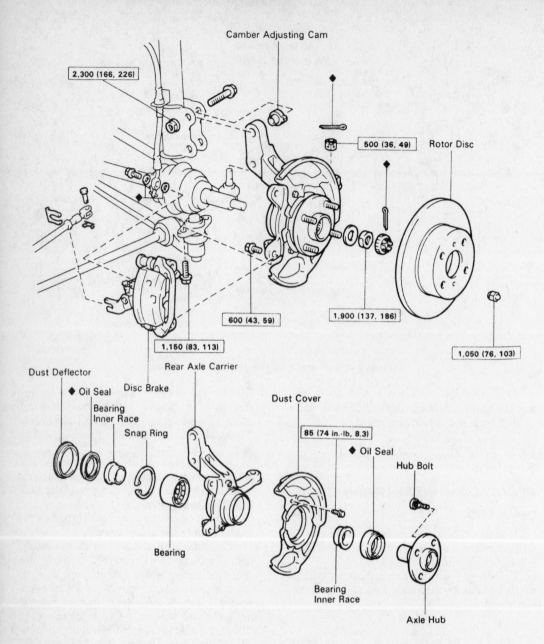

Camber Adjusting Cam

2,300 (166, 226)

500 (36, 49)

Rotor Disc

600 (43, 59)

1,900 (137, 186)

1,150 (83, 113)

1,050 (76, 103)

Dust Deflector

◆ Oil Seal

Disc Brake

Rear Axle Carrier

Bearing Inner Race

Snap Ring

Dust Cover

85 (74 in.-lb, 8.3)

◆ Oil Seal

Hub Bolt

Bearing

Bearing Inner Race

Axle Hub

kg-cm (ft-lb, N·m) : Specified torque
◆ Non-reusable part

Exploded view of rear axle, hub and carrier — MR2

4. Disconnect the rear axle carrier from the lower arm.

5. Disconnect the suspension lower arm.

6. Remove the 2 axle carrier set nuts and the 2 bolts and then remove the camber adjusting cam (matchmark camber adjusting cam to lower strut bracket for correct installation).

7. Remove the axle carrier and hub.

NOTE: *The bearing assembly can be replaced by removing bearing races, seals and snaprings and pressing bearing in and out.*

8. Installation is in the reverse order of removal. Please observe the following notes:

a. Tighten the axle carrier-to-shock bolts to (align matchmarks) 166 ft. lbs.

b. Tighten the brake caliper mounting bolts to 43 ft. lbs.

c. Torque suspension arm to 36 ft. lbs. and rear axle carrier to lower arm to 83 ft. lbs.

d. Tighten the bearing locknut to 137 ft. lbs. (use new cotter pin). Check the rear wheel alignment as necessary.

Tercel

1. Raise the rear of the vehicle and support it with jackstands. Remove the wheel.

2. Remove the cap, cotter pin, nut lock and nut. Remove the axle hub together with the outer bearing, thrust washer and brake drum.

3. Disconnect the brake line from the rear wheel cylinder. Disconnect the parking brake cable.

4. Remove the four bolts attaching the axle shaft to the carrier and then remove the axle shaft and the brake backing plate.

5. Installation is in the reverse order of removal. Tighten the axle shaft-to-carrier nuts to 59 ft. lbs. Torque the axle carrier retaining bolts (in the correct position) to 105 ft. lbs. and suspension arm bolts to 64 ft. lbs. with weight on the suspension. Adjust Wheel bearing preload (outlined below) Bleed the brakes.

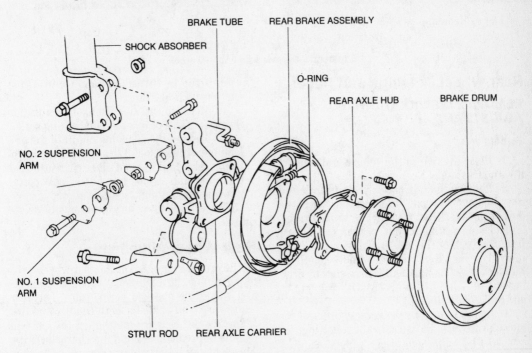

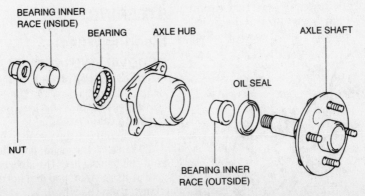

Exploded view of rear axle, hub and carrier — Corolla FWD

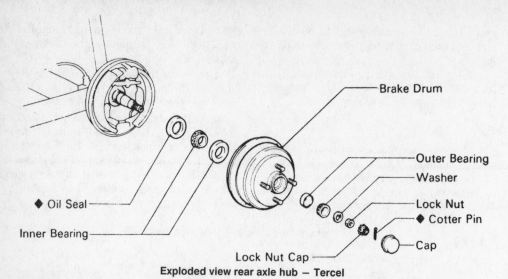

Exploded view rear axle hub — Tercel

Rear Wheel Bearings and Races

REMOVAL, INSTALLATION AND ADJUSTMENT

Tercel FWD

1. Raise the rear of the vehicle and support it with jackstands. Remove the wheel.

2. Remove the cap, cotter pin, nut lock and nut. Remove the axle hub together with the outer bearing, thrust washer and brake drum.

3. Using a small prybar, pry out the oil seal from the back of the hub and then remove the inner bearing. Remove races (note depth of race for correct installation) if necessary by driving out of axle hub assembly with a hammer and brass drift pin.

4. Installation is in the reverse order of removal procedure. Please note the following:

a. Place some axle grease into the palm of your hand and then take the bearing and work the grease into it until it begins to ooze out the other side. Coat the inside of the axle hub and bearing cap with the same grease.

b. Install the bearing adjusting nut and tighten it to 22 ft. lbs. Snug down the bearing by turning the hub several times. Retorque adjusting nut to 22 ft. lbs. Loosen the nut

until it can be turned by hand confirm that there is no brake drag.

c. Measure and make note of the rotation frictional force of oil seal using spring scale.

d. Tighten the adjusting nut until the preload measures 0.9–2.2 lbs. in addition to rotation frictional force of oil seal. Insure that the hub rotates smoothly. Use a NEW cotter pin when installing the lock cap.

5. Install all necessary components as required.

Rear Wheel Alignment

The proper alignment of the rear wheels is as important as the alignment of the front wheels and should be checked periodically. The rear wheels are adjustable for both camber and toe. If the rear wheels are misaligned the car will exhibit unpredictable handling characteristics. This behavior is particularly hazardous on slick surfaces; the back wheels of the car may attempt to go in directions unrelated to the front during braking or turning maneuvers.

STEERING

Steering Wheel

REMOVAL AND INSTALLATION

NOTE: *Do not attempt to remove or install the steering wheel by hammering on it. Damage to the energy-absorbing steering column could result.*

1. Disconnect the negative battery cable.

2. Loosen the trim pad retaining screws from the back side of the steering wheel.

3. Lift the trim pad and horn button assembly(ies) from the wheel.

4. Remove the steering wheel hub retaining nut and washer.

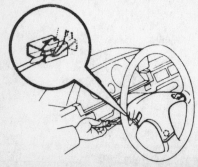

Removing trim pad — some models

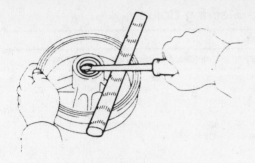

Using a steering wheel puller to remove the steering wheel

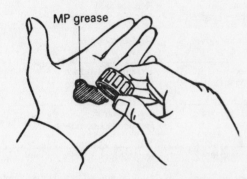

MP grease

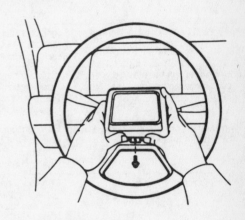

Removing the steering wheel pad

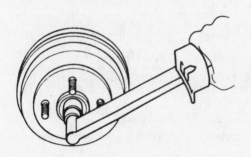

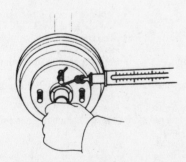

Rear wheel bearing service procedures

5. Scratch matchmarks on the hub and shaft to aid in correct installation.

6. Use a steering wheel puller to remove the steering wheel.

7. Installation is performed in the reverse order of removal. Tighten the wheel retaining nut to 25 ft. lbs.

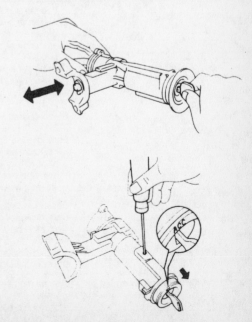

Removing key cylinder from the assembly

Troubleshooting the Steering Column

Problem	Cause	Solution
Will not lock	• Lockbolt spring broken or defective	• Replace lock bolt spring
High effort (required to turn ignition key and lock cylinder)	• Lock cylinder defective	• Replace lock cylinder
	• Ignition switch defective	• Replace ignition switch
	• Rack preload spring broken or deformed	• Replace preload spring
	• Burr on lock sector, lock rack, housing, support or remote rod coupling	• Remove burr
	• Bent sector shaft	• Replace shaft
	• Defective lock rack	• Replace lock rack
	• Remote rod bent, deformed	• Replace rod
	• Ignition switch mounting bracket bent	• Straighten or replace
	• Distorted coupling slot in lock rack (tilt column)	• Replace lock rack
Will stick in "start"	• Remote rod deformed	• Straighten or replace
	• Ignition switch mounting bracket bent	• Straighten or replace
Key cannot be removed in "off-lock"	• Ignition switch is not adjusted correctly	• Adjust switch
	• Defective lock cylinder	• Replace lock cylinder
Lock cylinder can be removed without depressing retainer	• Lock cylinder with defective retainer	• Replace lock cylinder
	• Burr over retainer slot in housing cover or on cylinder retainer	• Remove burr
High effort on lock cylinder between "off" and "off-lock"	• Distorted lock rack	• Replace lock rack
	• Burr on tang of shift gate (automatic column)	• Remove burr
	• Gearshift linkage not adjusted	• Adjust linkage
Noise in column	• One click when in "off-lock" position and the steering wheel is moved (all except automatic column)	• Normal—lock bolt is seating
	• Coupling bolts not tightened	• Tighten pinch bolts
	• Lack of grease on bearings or bearing surfaces	• Lubricate with chassis grease
	• Upper shaft bearing worn or broken	• Replace bearing assembly
	• Lower shaft bearing worn or broken	• Replace bearing. Check shaft and replace if scored.
	• Column not correctly aligned	• Align column
	• Coupling pulled apart	• Replace coupling
	• Broken coupling lower joint	• Repair or replace joint and align column
	• Steering shaft snap ring not seated	• Replace ring. Check for proper seating in groove.
	• Shroud loose on shift bowl. Housing loose on jacket—will be noticed with ignition in "off-lock" and when torque is applied to steering wheel.	• Position shroud over lugs on shift bowl. Tighten mounting screws.
High steering shaft effort	• Column misaligned	• Align column
	• Defective upper or lower bearing	• Replace as required
	• Tight steering shaft universal joint	• Repair or replace
	• Flash on I.D. of shift tube at plastic joint (tilt column only)	• Replace shift tube
	• Upper or lower bearing seized	• Replace bearings
Lash in mounted column assembly	• Column mounting bracket bolts loose	• Tighten bolts
	• Broken weld nuts on column jacket	• Replace column jacket
	• Column capsule bracket sheared	• Replace bracket assembly

Troubleshooting the Steering Column (cont.)

Problem	Cause	Solution
Lash in mounted column assembly (cont.)	• Column bracket to column jacket mounting bolts loose	• Tighten to specified torque
	• Loose lock shoes in housing (tilt column only)	• Replace shoes
	• Loose pivot pins (tilt column only)	• Replace pivot pins and support
	• Loose lock shoe pin (tilt column only)	• Replace pin and housing
	• Loose support screws (tilt column only)	• Tighten screws
Housing loose (tilt column only)	• Excessive clearance between holes in support or housing and pivot pin diameters	• Replace pivot pins and support
	• Housing support-screws loose	• Tighten screws
Steering wheel loose—every other tilt position (tilt column only)	• Loose fit between lock shoe and lock shoe pivot pin	• Replace lock shoes and pivot pin
Steering column not locking in any tilt position (tilt column only)	• Lock shoe seized on pivot pin	• Replace lock shoes and pin
	• Lock shoe grooves have burrs or are filled with foreign material	• Clean or replace lock shoes
	• Lock shoe springs weak or broken	• Replace springs
Noise when tilting column (tilt column only)	• Upper tilt bumpers worn	• Replace tilt bumper
	• Tilt spring rubbing in housing	• Lubricate with chassis grease
One click when in "off-lock" position and the steering wheel is moved	• Seating of lock bolt	• None. Click is normal characteristic sound produced by lock bolt as it seats.
High shift effort (automatic and tilt column only)	• Column not correctly aligned	• Align column
	• Lower bearing not aligned correctly	• Assemble correctly
	• Lack of grease on seal or lower bearing areas	• Lubricate with chassis grease
Improper transmission shifting—automatic and tilt column only	• Sheared shift tube joint	• Replace shift tube
	• Improper transmission gearshift linkage adjustment	• Adjust linkage
	• Loose lower shift lever	• Replace shift tube

Combination Switch

REMOVAL AND INSTALLATION

1. Disconnect the negative battery cable.
2. Remove the lower dash cover and the air duct.
3. On some vehicles, remove the upper and lower steering column covers. On other vehi-

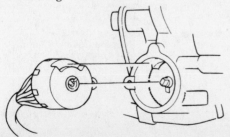

Align the switch before installation

cles, remove the lower column cover; the upper cover will come off with the switch.
4. Remove the steering wheel. Refer to the necessary service procedure.
5. Disconnect the wiring at the connector.
6. Unscrew the mounting screws and remove the switch. On some models the switch will come off with the upper column cover.
7. When reinstalling, place the switch in position and tighten the bolts.
8. Connect the wiring harness and reinstall the steering wheel.
9. Reinstall the column cover(s).
10. Install the lower dash trim panel.
11. Connect the negative battery cable.

Ignition Switch/Ignition Lock

REMOVAL AND INSTALLATION

1. Disconnect the negative battery cable.
2. Unscrew the retaining screws and

Troubleshooting the Ignition Switch

Problem	Cause	Solution
Ignition switch electrically inoperative	• Loose or defective switch connector • Feed wire open (fusible link) • Defective ignition switch	• Tighten or replace connector • Repair or replace • Replace ignition switch
Engine will not crank	• Ignition switch not adjusted properly	• Adjust switch
Ignition switch wil not actuate mechanically	• Defective ignition switch • Defective lock sector • Defective remote rod	• Replace switch • Replace lock sector • Replace remote rod
Ignition switch cannot be adjusted correctly	• Remote rod deformed	• Repair, straighten or replace

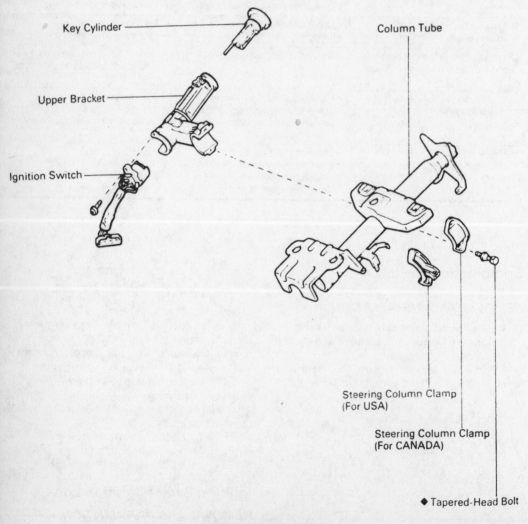

Key Cylinder

Column Tube

Upper Bracket

Ignition Switch

Steering Column Clamp
(For USA)

Steering Column Clamp
(For CANADA)

◆ Tapered-Head Bolt

Ignition switch assembly

Troubleshooting the Turn Signal Switch

Problem	Cause	Solution
Turn signal will not cancel	• Loose switch mounting screws • Switch or anchor bosses broken • Broken, missing or out of position detent, or cancelling spring	• Tighten screws • Replace switch • Reposition springs or replace switch as required
Turn signal difficult to operate	• Turn signal lever loose • Switch yoke broken or distorted • Loose or misplaced springs • Foreign parts and/or materials in switch • Switch mounted loosely	• Tighten mounting screws • Replace switch • Reposition springs or replace switch • Remove foreign parts and/or material • Tighten mounting screws
Turn signal will not indicate lane change	• Broken lane change pressure pad or spring hanger • Broken, missing or misplaced lane change spring • Jammed wires	• Replace switch • Replace or reposition as required • Loosen mounting screws, reposition wires and retighten screws
Turn signal will not stay in turn position	• Foreign material or loose parts impeding movement of switch yoke • Defective switch	• Remove material and/or parts • Replace switch
Hazard switch cannot be pulled out	• Foreign material between hazard support cancelling leg and yoke	• Remove foreign material. No foreign material impeding function of hazard switch—replace turn signal switch.
No turn signal lights	• Inoperative turn signal flasher • Defective or blown fuse • Loose chassis to column harness connector • Disconnect column to chassis connector. Connect new switch to chassis and operate switch by hand. If vehicle lights now operate normally, signal switch is inoperative • If vehicle lights do not operate, check chassis wiring for opens, grounds, etc.	• Replace turn signal flasher • Replace fuse • Connect securely • Replace signal switch • Repair chassis wiring as required
Instrument panel turn indicator lights on but not flashing	• Burned out or damaged front or rear turn signal bulb • If vehicle lights do not operate, check light sockets for high resistance connections, the chassis wiring for opens, grounds, etc. • Inoperative flasher • Loose chassis to column harness connection • Inoperative turn signal switch • To determine if turn signal switch is defective, substitute new switch into circuit and operate switch by hand. If the vehicle's lights operate normally, signal switch is inoperative.	• Replace bulb • Repair chassis wiring as required • Replace flasher • Connect securely • Replace turn signal switch • Replace turn signal switch
Stop light not on when turn indicated	• Loose column to chassis connection • Disconnect column to chassis connector. Connect new switch into system without removing old.	• Connect securely • Replace signal switch

Troubleshooting the Turn Signal Switch (cont.)

Problem	Cause	Solution
Stop light not on when turn indicated (cont.)	Operate switch by hand. If brake lights work with switch in the turn position, signal switch is defective.	
	• If brake lights do not work, check connector to stop light sockets for grounds, opens, etc.	• Repair connector to stop light circuits using service manual as guide
Turn indicator panel lights not flashing	• Burned out bulbs • High resistance to ground at bulb socket	• Replace bulbs • Replace socket
	• Opens, ground in wiring harness from front turn signal bulb socket to indicator lights	• Locate and repair as required
Turn signal lights flash very slowly	• High resistance ground at light sockets	• Repair high resistance grounds at light sockets
	• Incorrect capacity turn signal flasher or bulb	• Replace turn signal flasher or bulb
	• If flashing rate is still extremely slow, check chassis wiring harness from the connector to light sockets for high resistance	• Locate and repair as required
	• Loose chassis to column harness connection	• Connect securely
	• Disconnect column to chassis connector. Connect new switch into system without removing old. Operate switch by hand. If flashing occurs at normal rate, the signal switch is defective.	• Replace turn signal switch
Hazard signal lights will not flash— turn signal functions normally	• Blow fuse • Inoperative hazard warning flasher	• Replace fuse • Replace hazard warning flasher in fuse panel
	• Loose chassis-to-column harness connection	• Conect securely
	• Disconnect column to chassis connector. Connect new switch into system without removing old. Depress the hazard warning lights. If they now work normally, turn signal switch is defective.	• Replace turn signal switch
	• If lights do not flash, check wiring harness "K" lead for open between hazard flasher and connector. If open, fuse block is defective	• Repair or replace brown wire or connector as required

remove the upper and lower steering column covers.

3. Remove the 2 retaining screws and remove the steering column trim.

4. Turn the ignition key to the **ACC** position.

5. Push the lock cylinder stop in with a small, round object (cotter pin, punch, etc.) and pull out the ignition key and the lock cylinder.

NOTE: *You may find that removing the steering wheel and the combination switch makes the job easier.*

6. Loosen the mounting screw and withdraw the ignition switch from the lock housing.

7. When reinstalling, position the switch so that the recess and the bracket tab are properly aligned. Install the retaining screw.

8. Make sure that both the lock cylinder and the column lock are in the ACC position. Slide the cylinder into the lock housing until the stop tab engages the hole in the lock.

9. Make certain the stop tab is firmly seated in the slot. Turn the key to each switch position, checking for smoothness of motions and a

Troubleshooting the Manual Steering Gear

Problem	Cause	Solution
Hard or erratic steering	• Incorrect tire pressure	• Inflate tires to recommended pressures
	• Insufficient or incorrect lubrication	• Lubricate as required (refer to Maintenance Section)
	• Suspension, or steering linkage parts damaged or misaligned	• Repair or replace parts as necessary
	• Improper front wheel alignment	• Adjust incorrect wheel alignment angles
	• Incorrect steering gear adjustment	• Adjust steering gear
	• Sagging springs	• Replace springs
Play or looseness in steering	• Steering wheel loose	• Inspect shaft spines and repair as necessary. Tighten attaching nut and stake in place.
	• Steering linkage or attaching parts loose or worn	• Tighten, adjust, or replace faulty components
	• Pitman arm loose	• Inspect shaft splines and repair as necessary. Tighten attaching nut and stake in place
	• Steering gear attaching bolts loose	• Tighten bolts
	• Loose or worn wheel bearings	• Adjust or replace bearings
	• Steering gear adjustment incorrect or parts badly worn	• Adjust gear or replace defective parts
Wheel shimmy or tramp	• Improper tire pressure	• Inflate tires to recommended pressures
	• Wheels, tires, or brake rotors out-of-balance or out-of-round	• Inspect and replace or balance parts
	• Inoperative, worn, or loose shock absorbers or mounting parts	• Repair or replace shocks or mountings
	• Loose or worn steering or suspension parts	• Tighten or replace as necessary
	• Loose or worn wheel bearings	• Adjust or replace bearings
	• Incorrect steering gear adjustments	• Adjust steering gear
	• Incorrect front wheel alignment	• Correct front wheel alignment
Tire wear	• Improper tire pressure	• Inflate tires to recommended pressures
	• Failure to rotate tires	• Rotate tires
	• Brakes grabbing	• Adjust or repair brakes
	• Incorrect front wheel alignment	• Align incorrect angles
	• Broken or damaged steering and suspension parts	• Repair or replace defective parts
	• Wheel runout	• Replace faulty wheel
	• Excessive speed on turns	• Make driver aware of conditions
Vehicle leads to one side	• Improper tire pressures	• Inflate tires to recommended pressures
	• Front tires with uneven tread depth, wear pattern, or different cord design (i.e., one bias ply and one belted or radial tire on front wheels)	• Install tires of same cord construction and reasonably even tread depth, design, and wear pattern
	• Incorrect front wheel alignment	• Align incorrect angles
	• Brakes dragging	• Adjust or repair brakes
	• Pulling due to uneven tire construction	• Replace faulty tire

Troubleshooting the Power Steering Gear

Problem	Cause	Solution
Hissing noise in steering gear	• There is some noise in all power steering systems. One of the most common is a hissing sound most evident at standstill parking. There is no relationship between this noise and performance of the steering. Hiss may be expected when steering wheel is at end of travel or when slowly turning at standstill.	• Slight hiss is normal and in no way affects steering. Do not replace valve unless hiss is extremely objectionable. A replacement valve will also exhibit slight noise and is not always a cure. Investigate clearance around flexible coupling rivets. Be sure steering shaft and gear are aligned so flexible coupling rotates in a flat plane and is not distorted as shaft rotates. Any metal-to-metal contacts through flexible coupling will transmit valve hiss into passenger compartment through the steering column.
Rattle or chuckle noise in steering gear	• Gear loose on frame	• Check gear-to-frame mounting screws. Tighten screws to 88 N·m (65 foot pounds) torque.
	• Steering linkage looseness	• Check linkage pivot points for wear. Replace if necessary.
	• Pressure hose touching other parts of car	• Adjust hose position. Do not bend tubing by hand.
	• Loose pitman shaft over center adjustment	• Adjust to specifications
	NOTE: A slight rattle may occur on turns because of increased clearance off the "high point." This is normal and clearance must not be reduced below specified limits to eliminate this slight rattle.	
	• Loose pitman arm	• Tighten pitman arm nut to specifications
Squawk noise in steering gear when turning or recovering from a turn	• Damper O-ring on valve spool cut	• Replace damper O-ring
Poor return of steering wheel to center	• Tires not properly inflated	• Inflate to specified pressure
	• Lack of lubrication in linkage and ball joints	• Lube linkage and ball joints
	• Lower coupling flange rubbing against steering gear adjuster plug	• Loosen pinch bolt and assemble properly
	• Steering gear to column misalignment	• Align steering column
	• Improper front wheel alignment	• Check and adjust as necessary
	• Steering linkage binding	• Replace pivots
	• Ball joints binding	• Replace ball joints
	• Steering wheel rubbing against housing	• Align housing
	• Tight or frozen steering shaft bearings	• Replace bearings
	• Sticking or plugged valve spool	• Remove and clean or replace valve
	• Steering gear adjustments over specifications	• Check adjustment with gear out of car. Adjust as required.
	• Kink in return hose	• Replace hose
Car leads to one side or the other (keep in mind road condition and wind. Test car in both directions on flat road)	• Front end misaligned	• Adjust to specifications
	• Unbalanced steering gear valve	• Replace valve
	NOTE: If this is cause, steering effort will be very light in direction of lead and normal or heavier in opposite direction	

Troubleshooting the Power Steering Gear (cont.)

Problem	Cause	Solution
Momentary increase in effort when turning wheel fast to right or left	• Low oil level • Pump belt slipping • High internal leakage	• Add power steering fluid as required • Tighten or replace belt • Check pump pressure. (See pressure test)
Steering wheel surges or jerks when turning with engine running especially during parking	• Low oil level • Loose pump belt • Steering linkage hitting engine oil pan at full turn • Insufficient pump pressure • Pump flow control valve sticking	• Fill as required • Adjust tension to specification • Correct clearance • Check pump pressure. (See pressure test). Replace relief valve if defective. • Inspect for varnish or damage, replace if necessary
Excessive wheel kickback or loose steering	• Air in system • Steering gear loose on frame • Steering linkage joints worn enough to be loose • Worn poppet valve • Loose thrust bearing preload adjustment • Excessive overcenter lash	• Add oil to pump reservoir and bleed by operating steering. Check hose connectors for proper torque and adjust as required. • Tighten attaching screws to specified torque • Replace loose pivots • Replace poppet valve • Adjust to specification with gear out of vehicle • Adjust to specification with gear out of car
Hard steering or lack of assist	• Loose pump belt • Low oil level **NOTE:** Low oil level will also result in excessive pump noise • Steering gear to column misalignment • Lower coupling flange rubbing against steering gear adjuster plug • Tires not properly inflated	• Adjust belt tension to specification • Fill to proper level. If excessively low, check all lines and joints for evidence of external leakage. Tighten loose connectors. • Align steering column • Loosen pinch bolt and assemble properly • Inflate to recommended pressure
Foamy milky power steering fluid, low fluid level and possible low pressure	• Air in the fluid, and loss of fluid due to internal pump leakage causing overflow	• Check for leak and correct. Bleed system. Extremely cold temperatures will cause system aeriation should the oil level be low. If oil level is correct and pump still foams, remove pump from vehicle and separate reservoir from housing. Check welsh plug and housing for cracks. If plug is loose or housing is cracked, replace housing.
Low pressure due to steering pump	• Flow control valve stuck or inoperative • Pressure plate not flat against cam ring	• Remove burrs or dirt or replace. Flush system. • Correct
Low pressure due to steering gear	• Pressure loss in cylinder due to worn piston ring or badly worn housing bore • Leakage at valve rings, valve body-to-worm seal	• Remove gear from car for disassembly and inspection of ring and housing bore • Remove gear from car for disassembly and replace seals

Troubleshooting the Power Steering Pump

Problem	Cause	Solution
Chirp noise in steering pump	• Loose belt	• Adjust belt tension to specification
Belt squeal (particularly noticeable at full wheel travel and stand still parking)	• Loose belt	• Adjust belt tension to specification
Growl noise in steering pump	• Excessive back pressure in hoses or steering gear caused by restriction	• Locate restriction and correct. Replace part if necessary.
Growl noise in steering pump (particularly noticeable at stand still parking)	• Scored pressure plates, thrust plate or rotor • Extreme wear of cam ring	• Replace parts and flush system • Replace parts
Groan noise in steering pump	• Low oil level • Air in the oil. Poor pressure hose connection.	• Fill reservoir to proper level • Tighten connector to specified torque. Bleed system by operating steering from right to left—full turn.
Rattle noise in steering pump	• Vanes not installed properly • Vanes sticking in rotor slots	• Install properly • Free up by removing burrs, varnish, or dirt
Swish noise in steering pump	• Defective flow control valve	• Replace part
Whine noise in steering pump	• Pump shaft bearing scored	• Replace housing and shaft. Flush system.
Hard steering or lack of assist	• Loose pump belt • Low oil level in reservoir **NOTE:** Low oil level will also result in excessive pump noise • Steering gear to column misalignment • Lower coupling flange rubbing against steering gear adjuster plug • Tires not properly inflated	• Adjust belt tension to specification • Fill to proper level. If excessively low, check all lines and joints for evidence of external leakage. Tighten loose connectors. • Align steering column • Loosen pinch bolt and assemble properly • Inflate to recommended pressure
Foaming milky power steering fluid, low fluid level and possible low pressure	• Air in the fluid, and loss of fluid due to internal pump leakage causing overflow	• Check for leaks and correct. Bleed system. Extremely cold temperatures will cause system aeration should the oil level be low. If oil level is correct and pump still foams, remove pump from vehicle and separate reservoir from body. Check welsh plug and body for cracks. If plug is loose or body is cracked, replace body.
Low pump pressure	• Flow control valve stuck or inoperative • Pressure plate not flat against cam ring	• Remove burrs or dirt or replace. Flush system. • Correct
Momentary increase in effort when turning wheel fast to right or left	• Low oil level in pump • Pump belt slipping • High internal leakage	• Add power steering fluid as required • Tighten or replace belt • Check pump pressure. (See pressure test)
Steering wheel surges or jerks when turning with engine running especially during parking	• Low oil level • Loose pump belt • Steering linkage hitting engine oil pan at full turn • Insufficient pump pressure	• Fill as required • Adjust tension to specification • Correct clearance • Check pump pressure. (See pressure test). Replace flow control valve if defective.

Troubleshooting the Power Steering Pump (cont.)

Problem	Cause	Solution
Steering wheel surges or jerks when turning with engine running especially during parking (cont.)	• Sticking flow control valve	• Inspect for varnish or damage, replace if necessary
Excessive wheel kickback or loose steering	• Air in system	• Add oil to pump reservoir and bleed by operating steering. Check hose connectors for proper torque and adjust as required
Low pump pressure	• Extreme wear of cam ring • Scored pressure plate, thrust plate, or rotor • Vanes not installed properly • Vanes sticking in rotor slots • Cracked or broken thrust or pressure plate	• Replace parts. Flush system. • Replace parts. Flush system. • Install properly • Freeup by removing burrs, varnish, or dirt • Replace part

positive feel. Remove and insert the key a few times, each time turning the key to each switch position.

10. Reinstall the combination switch and the steering wheel if they were removed.

11. Install the steering column trim and the upper and lower column covers.

12. Connect the negative battery cable.

Steering Column
REMOVAL AND INSTALLATION

NOTE: *On some models this service procedure (some steps are not necessary) may have to be modified. Use this service procedure and exploded views of "Steering Column" as a guide.*

1. Disconnect the negative battery cable. Remove the steering wheel.

2. On some models remove the left side dash trim panel as necessary. Remove the combination switch and all electrical connections.

3. Loosen the hole cover clamp screw.

4. Remove the air filter assembly if necessary. Remove the pinch bolt from the yoke.

5. Remove the yoke from the steering gear.

6. Remove the bolts holding the lower column mounting brackets.

7. Remove the bolts holding the upper column to the instrument panel.

8. Remove the column from the car.

9. When reinstalling, place the column assembly into position and install the upper and lower bracket nuts and bolts finger tight.

10. Position the column assembly so the end of the lower support holes touch the mounting bolts.

11. Tighten the upper and lower support nuts and bolts to 19 ft. lbs.

12. Install the yoke and tighten the pinch

bolt to 26 ft. lbs. Install the air filter as necessary.

13. Install the hole cover clamp.

14. Install the combination switch and all electrical connections.

15. Install the steering wheel. Install side dash trim panel as necessary.

Tie Rod Ends
REMOVAL AND INSTALLATION

1. Raise the front of the vehicle and support it safely. Remove the wheel.

2. Remove the cotter pin and nut holding the tie rod to the steering knuckle.

3. Using a tie rod separator, press the tie rod out of the knuckle.

NOTE: *Use only the correct tool to separate the tie rod joint. Replace the joint if the rubber boot is cracked or ripped.*

4. Matchmark the inner end of the tie rod to the end of the steering rack.

5. Loosen the locknut and remove the tie rod from the steering rack.

6. Install the tie rod ends onto the rack ends and align the matchmarks made earlier.

7. Tighten the locknuts to 35 ft. lbs.

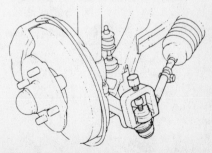

Removing the tie-rod end from the steering rack

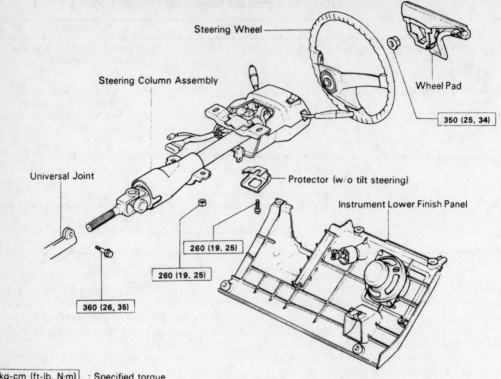

Steering Wheel

Steering Column Assembly

Wheel Pad

350 (25, 34)

Universal Joint

Protector (w/o tilt steering)

Instrument Lower Finish Panel

260 (19, 25)

260 (19, 25)

360 (26, 35)

kg-cm (ft-lb, N·m) : Specified torque

Exploded view of steering column assembly — Tercel

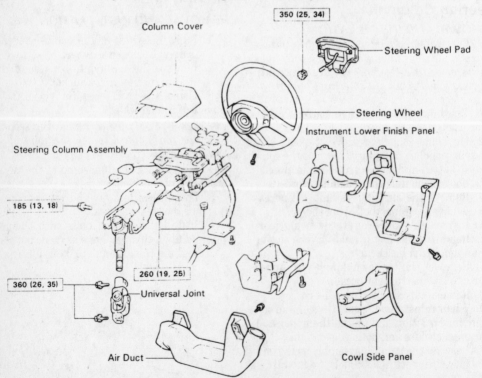

Column Cover

350 (25, 34)

Steering Wheel Pad

Steering Wheel

Instrument Lower Finish Panel

Steering Column Assembly

185 (13, 18)

260 (19, 25)

360 (26, 35)

Universal Joint

Air Duct

Cowl Side Panel

kg-cm (ft-lb, N·m) : Specified torque

Exploded view of steering column assembly — MR2

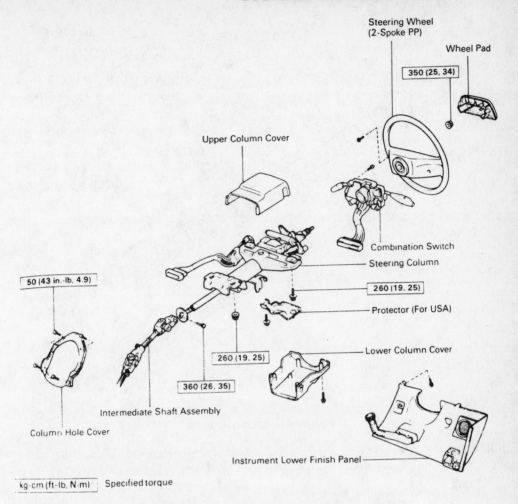

Steering Wheel
(2-Spoke PP)

Wheel Pad

350 (25, 34)

Upper Column Cover

Combination Switch

Steering Column

50 (43 in.-lb, 4.9)

260 (19, 25)

Protector (For USA)

Lower Column Cover

260 (19, 25)

360 (26, 35)

Intermediate Shaft Assembly

Column Hole Cover

Instrument Lower Finish Panel

kg-cm (ft-lb, N·m)   Specified torque

Exploded view of steering column assembly — Corolla

8. Connect the tie rod joint to the knuckle. Tighten the nut to 36 ft. lbs. and install a new cotter pin.

9. Install the wheel and lower the vehicle to the ground. Have the alignment checked at a reputable repair facility. The toe adjustment may have to be reset.

Manual Steering Gear Rack And Pinion

Adjustments

Adjustments to the manual steering gear/rack and pinion are not necessary during normal service. Adjustments are preformed only as part of overhaul.

REMOVAL AND INSTALLATION

All Models Except Corolla 4WD

1. Remove the cover from the intermediate shaft.

2. Loosen the upper pinch bolt. Remove the lower pinch bolt at the pinion shaft.

3. Loosen the wheel lug nuts.

4. Elevate and safely support the vehicle.

5. Remove both front wheels.

6. Remove the cotter pins from both tie rod joints and remove the nuts.

7. Using a tie rod separator, remove both tie rod joints from the knuckles.

8. Remove the nuts and bolts attaching the steering rack to the body.

9. Remove any necessary component to gain working access (if possible slide assembly

Removing the rack and pinion assembly from the vehicle

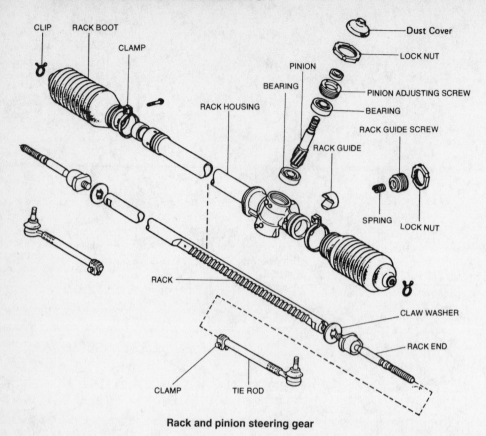

Rack and pinion steering gear

out the wheel well opening) to remove the rack and pinion assembly from the vehicle. Remove the rack assembly.

10. Install the rack assembly. Secure it with the retaining bolts and nuts and tighten them to 43 ft. lbs.

11. Connect the tie rods to each knuckle. Tighten the nuts to 36 ft. lbs. and install new cotter pins.

12. Install the front wheels.

13. Lower the car to the ground.

14. Install the lower pinch bolt at the pinion shaft. Tighten the upper and lower bolts to 26 ft. lbs.

15. Install the cover on the intermediate shaft. Check front end alignment.

Corolla 4WD
With Crossmember/Lower Arm
Removal and Installation
Service Procedure

1. Remove the cover from the intermediate shaft.

2. Loosen the upper pinch bolt. Remove the lower pinch bolt at the pinion shaft.

3. Loosen the wheel lug nuts.

4. Elevate and safely support the vehicle.

5. Remove both front wheels and engine under covers as necessary.

6. Install an engine support and tension it to support the engine without raising it.

CAUTION: *The engine hoist is in place and under tension. Use care when repositioning the vehicle and make necessary adjustments to the engine support.*

7. Remove the bolts holding the center crossmember to the radiator support.

8. Remove the covers from the front and center mount bolts.

9. Remove the front mount bolts, then the center mount bolts.

10. Support the crossmember (disconnect the stabilizer bar as necessary) and remove the rear mount bolts.

11. Remove the bolts holding the center crossmember to the main crossmember.

12. Use a floor jack and a wide piece of wood to support the main crossmember.

13. Remove the bolts holding the main crossmember to the body.

14. Remove the bolts holding the lower control arm brackets to the body.

CAUTION: *The crossmembers are loose and free to fall. Make sure they are properly supported.*

15. Slowly lower the main crossmember while holding onto the center crossmember.

16. Remove the cotter pins from both tie rod joints and remove the nuts.

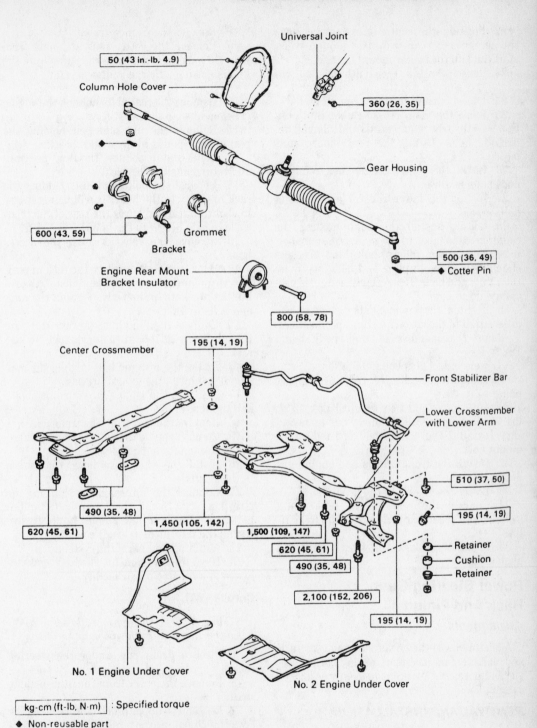

50 (43 in.-lb, 4.9)

Universal Joint

Column Hole Cover

360 (26, 35)

Gear Housing

600 (43, 59)

Grommet

Bracket

Engine Rear Mount
Bracket Insulator

500 (36, 49)

◆ Cotter Pin

800 (58, 78)

Center Crossmember

195 (14, 19)

Front Stabilizer Bar

Lower Crossmember
with Lower Arm

510 (37, 50)

195 (14, 19)

490 (35, 48)

620 (45, 61)

1,450 (105, 142)

1,500 (109, 147)

620 (45, 61)

490 (35, 48)

Retainer

Cushion

Retainer

2,100 (152, 206)

195 (14, 19)

No. 1 Engine Under Cover

No. 2 Engine Under Cover

kg-cm (ft-lb, N·m) : Specified torque

◆ Non-reusable part

Manual steering gear/rack and pinion — Corolla 4WD

17. Using a tie rod separator, remove both tie rod joints from the knuckles.

18. Remove the nuts and bolts attaching the steering rack to the body.

19. Remove the rack through the right side wheel well.

20. To reinstall the rack, place it in position through the right wheel well and tighten the bracket bolts to 45 ft. lbs.

21. Attach the tie rods to the knuckles. Tighten the nuts to 36 ft. lbs. and install new cotter pins.

22. Position the center crossmember over the center and rear transaxle mount studs; start nuts on the center mount.

23. Loosely install the bolts holding the center crossmember to the radiator support.

24. Loosely install the front mount bolts.

25. Raise the main crossmember into position over the rear mount studs and align all underbody bolts. Install the rear mount nuts loosely.

26. Install the main crossmember to underbody bolts loosely.

27. Install the lower control arm bracket bolts loosely.

28. Loosely install the bolts holding the center crossmember to the main crossmember.

29. The crossmembers, bolts and brackets should now all be in place and held loosely by their nuts and bolts. If any repositioning is necessary, do so now.

30. Tighten the components below in the order listed to the correct torque specification:
• Main crossmember to underbody bolts: 152 ft. lbs.
• Lower control arm bolts: 94 ft. lbs.
• Center crossmember to radiator support bolts: 45 ft. lbs.
• Front, center and rear mount bolts: 45 ft. lbs. 31. Reconnect the stabilizer bar as necessary. Install the covers on the front and center mount bolts.

32. Install the front wheels and engine undercovers as necessary.

33. Lower the vehicle to the ground.

34. Connect the yoke to the pinion and tighten both the upper and lower bolts to 26 ft. lbs.

35. Install the yoke cover. Check front end alignment.

Power Steering Gear
Rack And Pinion

Adjustments

Adjustments to the power steering gear/rack and pinion are not necessary during normal service. Adjustments are preformed only as part of overhaul.

REMOVAL AND INSTALLATION

All Models Except Corolla 4WD

1. Remove the intermediate shaft cover.

2. Loosen the upper pinch bolt and remove the lower pinch bolt.

3. Place a drain pan below the power steering rack assembly. Clean the area around the line fittings on the rack.

4. Loosen the front wheel lug nuts.

5. Safely elevate and support the vehicle.

6. Remove the front wheels.

7. Remove the cotter pins and nuts from both tie rod joints. Separate the joints from the knuckle using a tie rod joint separator.

8. Support the transaxle with a jack.

9. Remove the rear bolts holding the engine crossmember to the body.

10. Remove the nut and bolt holding the rear engine mount to the mount bracket.

11. Label and disconnect the fluid pressure and return lines at the rack.

12. Remove the bolts and nuts holding the rack brackets to the body. It will be necessary to slightly raise and lower the rear of the transaxle to gain access to the bolts.

13. Remove the rack through the access hole.

14. When reinstalling, place the rack in position through the access hole and install the retaining brackets to the body. Tighten the nuts and bolts to 43 ft. lbs.

15. Connect the fluid lines (always start the threads by hand before using a tool) to the rack.

16. Install the nut and bolt holding the rear engine mount to the mount bracket.

17. Reinstall the engine crossmember bolts and tighten.

18. Remove the jack from the transaxle.

19. Connect the tie rod ends to the knuckles. Tighten the nuts to 36 ft. lbs.

20. Install the wheels and lower the vehicle to the ground.

21. Connect the intermediate shaft to the steering rack. Install the lower bolt; tighten both the upper and lower bolts to 26. ft. lbs. Install the intermediate shaft cover.

22. Add fluid and bleed the system.

23. Have the alignment checked and adjusted at a reliable repair facility.

Corolla 4WD

NOTE: *Refer to the appropriate service procedures outlined in this book as necessary.*

1. Place a drain pan under the steering rack.

2. Remove the cover from the intermediate shaft.

3. Loosen the upper pinch bolt. Remove the lower pinch bolt at the pinion shaft.

4. Loosen the wheel lug nuts.

5. Elevate and safely support the vehicle.

6. Remove both front wheels and engine undercovers.

7. Install an engine support and tension it to support the engine without raising it.

CAUTION: *The engine hoist is now in place and under tension. Use care when repositioning the vehicle and make necessary adjust-*

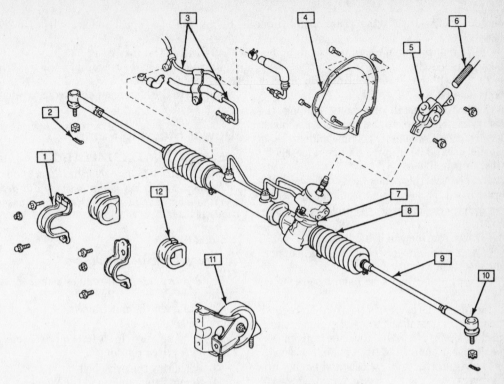

1. Mounting bracket
2. Cotter pin
3. Pressure and return lines
4. Column hole cover
5. Universal joint (yoke)
6. Intermediate shaft
7. Steering gear housing
8. Boot
9. Tie rod
10. Tie rod end
11. Engine mount
12. Grommet

Power steering gear/rack and pinion

ing the vehicle and make necessary adjustments to the engine support.

8. Disconnect and (position out of the way) front exhaust pipe. Matchmark and remove the propeller shaft assembly. Disconnect the front stabilizer bar.

9. Remove the bolts holding the center crossmember to the radiator support. Remove the covers from the front and center mount bolts.

10. Remove the front mount bolts, then the center mount bolts and then the rear mount bolts.

11. Remove the bolts holding the center crossmember to the main crossmember.

12. Use a floor jack and a wide piece of wood to support the main crossmember.

13. Remove the bolts holding the main crossmember to the body.

14. Remove the bolts holding the lower control arm brackets to the body.

CAUTION: *The crossmembers are loose and free to fall. Make sure they are properly supported.*

15. Slowly lower the main crossmember while holding onto the center crossmember.

16. Remove the cotter pins from both tie rod ball joints and remove the nuts.

17. Using a tie rod separator, remove both tie rod joints from the knuckles.

18. Label and disconnect the fluid pressure and return lines from the rack.

19. Remove the nuts and bolts attaching the steering rack to the body.

20. Remove the rack through the right side wheel well.

21. To reinstall the rack, place it in position through the right wheel well and tighten the bracket bolts to 43 ft. lbs.

22. Connect the fluid lines to the rack. Make certain the fittings are correctly threaded before tightening them.

23. Attach the tie rods to the knuckles. Tighten the nuts to 36 ft. lbs. and install new cotter pins.

24. Position the center crossmember over the center and rear transaxle mount studs; start nuts on the center mount.

25. Loosely install the bolts holding the center crossmember to the radiator support.

26. Loosely install the front mount bolts.

27. Raise the main crossmember into position over the rear mount studs and align all un-

derbody bolts. Install the rear mount nuts loosely.

28. Install the main crossmember to underbody bolts loosely.

29. Install the lower control arm bracket bolts loosely.

30. Loosely install the bolts holding the center crossmember to the main crossmember.

31. The crossmembers, bolts and brackets should now all be in place and held loosely by their nuts and bolts.

32. Tighten the components below in the order listed to the correct torque specification:
• Main crossmember to underbody bolts: 152 ft. lbs.
• Lower control arm bolts: 94 ft. lbs.
• Center crossmember to radiator support bolts: 45 ft. lbs.
• Front, center and rear mount bolts: 45 ft. lbs.

33. Install the covers on the front and center mount bolts. Install the propeller (align matchmarks) shaft assembly. Reconnect front exhaust pipe. Connect the front stabilizer bar.

34. Install the front wheels and engine undercovers.

35. Lower the vehicle to the ground.

36. Connect the yoke to the pinion and tighten both the upper and lower bolts to 26 ft. lbs.

37. Install the yoke cover.

38. Add power steering fluid to the reservoir and bleed the system.

39. Have the alignment checked at a reliable repair facility.

Power Steering Pump

REMOVAL AND INSTALLATION

NOTE: *Refer to the exploded illustrations of the power steering pump assembly to determine what type power steering pump assembly is used.*

Corolla RWD

ALL ENGINES/BOTH TYPE PUMPS

1. Remove the fan shroud as required with A/C system.

2. Unfasten the nut from the center of the pump pulley.

NOTE: *Use the drive belt as a brake to keep the pulley from rotating.*

3. Withdraw the drive belt.

4. Remove the pulley and the Woodruff key from the pump shaft.

5. Detach the intake and outlet hoses from

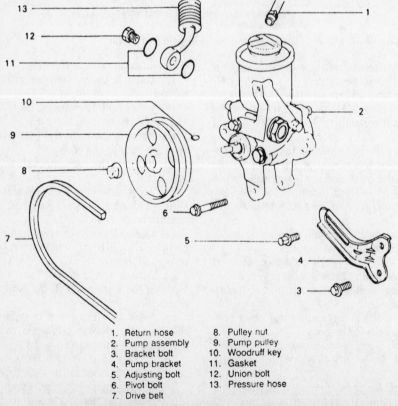

1. Return hose	8. Pulley nut
2. Pump assembly	9. Pump pulley
3. Bracket bolt	10. Woodruff key
4. Pump bracket	11. Gasket
5. Adjusting bolt	12. Union bolt
6. Pivot bolt	13. Pressure hose
7. Drive belt	

Power steering pump components — Corolla 4A-C engine

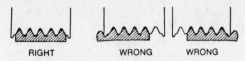

RIGHT   WRONG   WRONG

Correct installation of drive belt

the pump reservoir. Tie the hose ends up high, so that the fluid cannot flow out of them.

6. Remove the bolt from the rear mounting brace.

7. Remove the front bracket bolts and withdraw the pump.

8. Installation is performed in the reverse order of removal. Tighten the pump pulley mounting bolt to 25–39 ft. lbs. Adjust the pump drive belt tension. Fill the reservoir with power steering fluid. Bleed the air from the system. Check for fluid leaks.

Corolla FWD All Engines Except 4A-GE Engine

REGULAR PUMP BRACKET TYPE ADJUSTMENT

1. Place a drain pan below the pump.
2. Remove the air cleaner assembly
3. Remove the clamp from the fluid return hose. Disconnect the pressure and return hoses at the pump. Plug the hoses and suspend them with the ends upward to prevent leakage.
4. Loosen the pump pulley nut. Push down on the belt to keep the pulley from turning.
5. Remove the adjusting bolt.
6. Remove the pivot bolt and remove the drive belt.
7. Remove the pump assembly.
8. Remove the pump bracket.
9. Remove the pulley. Be careful not to lose the small woodruff key between the pulley and the shaft.
10. To reinstall, place the pump in position and temporarily install the 2 mounting bolts.

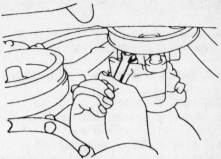

Removing the upper pump mounting bolt — Corolla 4A-GE engine

11. Install the pump bracket and tighten the bolts to 29 ft. lbs.

12. Install the pump pulley and the woodruff key. Tighten the pulley nut to 32 ft. lbs.

13. Install the drive belt, making certain that all the grooves of the belt are engaged on the pulley. Adjust the belt to the proper tension.

14. Connect the pressure and return lines to the pump. Tighten the fittings to 33 ft. lbs. Install the clamp on the return hose.

15. Install the air cleaner assembly.

16. Fill the reservoir to the proper level with power steering fluid and bleed the system.

17. After the car has been driven for about an hour, double check the belt adjustment.

Corolla FWD 4A-GE Engine

IDLER PULLEY ASSEMBLY TYPE ADJUSTMENT

1. Place a drain pan below the pump.
2. Remove the air cleaner assembly.
3. Disconnect the return hose from the pump, then disconnect the pressure hose. Plug the lines immediately to prevent fluid loss and contamination.

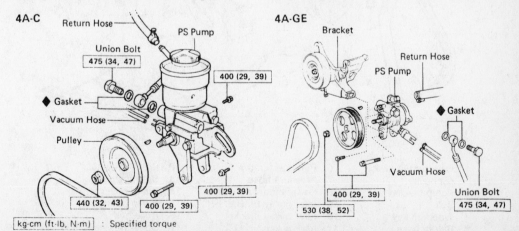

4A-C

Return Hose — PS Pump
Union Bolt
475 (34, 47)
400 (29, 39)
♦ Gasket
Vacuum Hose
Pulley
440 (32, 43)   400 (29, 39)   400 (29, 39)

4A-GE

Bracket
Return Hose
PS Pump
♦ Gasket
Vacuum Hose
Union Bolt
475 (34, 47)
400 (29, 39)
530 (38, 52)

kg-cm (ft-lb, N·m) : Specified torque
♦ Non-reusable part

Exploded view of power steering pump assembly — both engines/both types — Corolla RWD

4. Remove the splash shield under the engine.

5. Remove the pulley nut. Push down on the drive belt to prevent the pulley from turning.

6. Loosen the idler pulley nut and loosen the adjusting bolt.

7. Remove the drive belt.

8. Loosen the pump pulley and woodruff key. Don't lose the woodruff key.

9. Remove the upper mounting bolt.

10. Loosen the lower mounting bolt and pivot the pump downward.

11. Disconnect the oil pressure switch connector.

12. Remove the pump bracket mounting bolts; remove the pump from the engine with the bracket attached.

13. Remove the pulley from the pump and the pump from the bracket.

14. Remove the idler pulley bracket.

15. When reinstalling, mount the pump on the bracket and loosely install the lower mounting bolt.

16. Temporarily insert the pulley onto the pump shaft without the woodruff key. The pulley cannot be installed after the pump is installed on the engine.

17. Install the pump and bracket onto the engine. Tighten the upper mounting bolts to 29 ft. lbs.

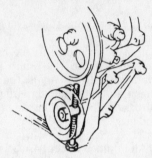

Idler pulley and adjusting bolt – Corolla 4A-GE engine

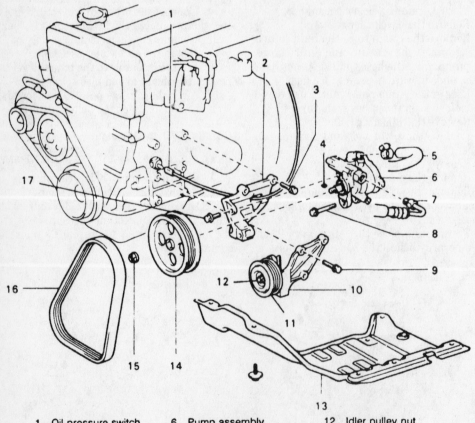

1. Oil pressure switch connector
2. Pump bracket
3. Bolt
4. Woodruff key
5. Return hose
6. Pump assembly
7. Pressure hose
8. Lower mounting bolt
9. Idler pulley bracket bolt
10. Idler pulley bracket
11. Idler pulley
12. Idler pulley nut
13. Splash shield
14. Pump pulley
15. Pump pulley nut
16. Drive belt
17. Upper mounting bolt

Power steering pump components – Corolla 4A-GE engine

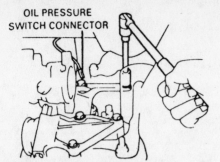

OIL PRESSURE
SWITCH CONNECTOR

Location oil pressure switch connector — Corolla 4A-GE engine

18. Connect the oil pressure switch connector.

19. Install the idler pulley bracket; tighten the 3 mounting bolts to 29 ft. lbs.

20. Tighten the lower mounting bolts to 29 ft. lbs.

21. Install the woodruff key into the pulley and install the drive belt. Make certain the ribs of the belt are properly placed on all the pulleys.

22. Tighten the pulley nuts on the pump and idler to 28 ft. lbs.

23. Connect the pressure hose and tighten its fitting to 33 ft. lbs.

24. Connect the return hose.

25. Install the air cleaner and install the lower splash shield.

26. Adjust the belt to the proper tension.

27. Fill the reservoir to the proper level with power steering fluid and bleed the system.

28. After the car has been driven for about an hour, double check the belt adjustment.

Corolla FWD 1989–90 (Late Model)

NOTE: *Refer to the necessary service procedure according to what type power steering pump that is used on the vehicle.*

1. Place a drain pan below the pump.

2. Elevate and safely support the vehicle.

3. Remove the right front wheel.

4. Place a floor jack under the engine block and support it. Use a broad piece of wood to spread the load evenly and prevent damage.

5. Remove the bolt from the right side engine mount and lower the engine about 50mm to gain access to the lower power steering pump through-bolt.

6. Working through the right wheel well, remove the lower pump through-bolt.

7. Disconnect the fluid lines from the pump and plug them immediately.

8. Remove the upper mounting bolt from the pump and remove the pump.

9. When reinstalling, place the pump in position and install the mounting bolts. Tighten them to 29 ft. lbs.

10. Raise the engine to its normal position and install the engine mount bolt, tightening it to 69 ft. lbs.

11. Connect the fluid lines to the pump and tighten the pressure hose fitting to 34 ft. lbs.

12. Install the belt and adjust it to the proper tension.

13. Install the right front wheel.

14. Remove the jack and drain pan from under the engine.

15. Lower the vehicle to the ground.

16. Fill the reservoir to the proper level with power steering fluid and bleed the system.

17. After the car has been driven for about an hour, double check the belt adjustment.

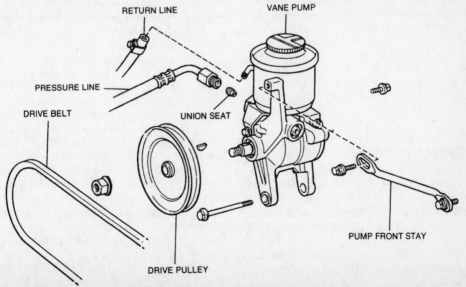

Power steering pump assembly components — Tercel (reservoir mounted/top of pump type)

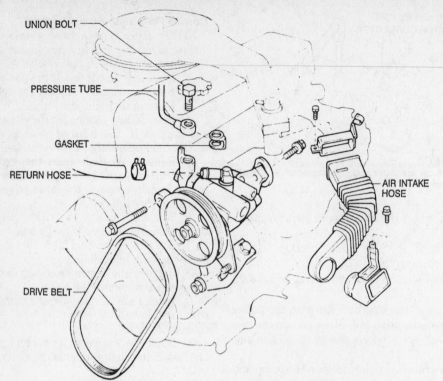

UNION BOLT

PRESSURE TUBE

GASKET

RETURN HOSE

AIR INTAKE HOSE

DRIVE BELT

Power steering pump assembly components — Tercel

Tercel

RESERVOIR MOUNTED/TOP OF PUMP

1. Remove the power steering fluid from the reservoir. Disconnect pressure line and return hose.

2. Raise and safely support the vehicle.

3. Remove the engine under cover.

4. Loosen the pump pulley nut. Push down on the belt to keep the pulley from turning.

5. Remove the front stay (mount bracket), drive belt and retaining bolts. Remove the power steering pump assembly from the vehicle.

6. Installation is the reverse of the removal procedure. Tighten pulley nut to 32 ft. lbs. and stay and retaining bolts to 27 ft. lbs. Adjust drive belt tension, bleed power steering and check for leaks.

Tercel

NO RESERVOIR ON PUMP

1. Remove the power steering fluid from the reservoir. Disconnect pressure line and return hose.

2. Raise and safely support the vehicle.

3. Remove the engine under cover as necessary.

4. Remove the drive belt and retaining bolts. Remove the power steering pump assembly from the vehicle.

5. Installation is the reverse of the removal procedure. Tighten the retaining bolts to 32 ft. lbs. Adjust drive belt tension, bleed power steering and check for leaks.

BLEEDING THE POWER STEERING SYSTEM

Any time the power steering system has been opened or disassembled, the system must be bled to remove any air which may be trapped in the lines. Air will prevent the system from providing the correct pressures to the rack. The correct fluid level reading will not be obtained if the system is not bled.

1. With the engine running, turn the wheel all the way to the left and shut off the engine.

2. Add power steering fluid to the **COLD** mark on the indicator.

3. Start the engine and run at fast idle for about 15 seconds. Stop the engine and recheck the fluid level. Add to the **COLD** mark as needed.

4. Start the engine and bleed the system by turning the wheels from left to right 3 or 4 times.

5. Stop the engine and check the fluid level and condition. Fluid with air in it is a light tan color. This air must be eliminated from the system before normal operation can be obtained. Repeat Steps 3 and 4 until the correct fluid color and fluid level is obtained.

BRAKE SYSTEM

Understanding the Brakes

HYDRAULIC SYSTEM

Hydraulic systems are used to actuate the brakes of all modern automobiles. A hydraulic system rather than a mechanical system is used for two reasons. First, fluid under pressure can be carried to all parts of an automobile by small hoses—some of which are flexible—without taking up a significant amount of room or posing routing problems. Second, a great mechanical advantage can be given to the brake pedal, and the foot pressure required to actuate the brakes can be reduced by making the surface area of the master cylinder pistons smaller than that of any of the pistons in the wheel cylinders or calipers.

The master cylinder consists of a fluid reservoir and a single or double cylinder and piston assembly. Double type master cylinders are designed to separate the front and rear braking systems hydraulically in case of a leak. The master cylinder coverts mechanical motion from the pedal into hydraulic pressure within the lines. This pressure is translated back into mechanical motion at the wheels by either the wheel cylinder (drum brakes) or the caliper (disc brakes). Since these components receive the pressure from the master cylinder, they are generically classed as slave cylinders in the system.

Steel lines carry the brake fluid to a point on the vehicle's frame near each of the vehicle's wheels. The fluid is then carried to the slave cylinders by flexible tubes in order to allow for suspension and steering movements.

Each wheel cylinder contains two pistons, one at either end, which push outward in opposite directions and force the brake shoe into contact with the drum. In disc brake systems, the slave cylinders are part of the calipers. One or four cylinders are used to force the brake pads against the disc, but all cylinders contain one piston only. All slave cylinder pistons employ some type of seal, usually made of rubber, to minimize the leakage of fluid around the piston. A rubber dust boot seals the outer end of the cylinder against dust and dirt. The boot fits around the outer end of either the piston or the brake actuating rod.

When at rest the entire hydraulic system, from the piston(s) in the master cylinder to those in the wheel cylinders or calipers, is full of brake fluid. Upon application of the brake pedal, fluid trapped in front of the master cylinder piston(s) is forced through the lines to the slave cylinders. Here it forces the pistons outward, in the case of drum brakes, and inward toward the disc in the case of disc brakes. The motion of the pistons is opposed by return springs mounted outside the cylinders in drum brakes, and by internal springs or spring seals, in disc brakes.

Upon release of the brake pedal, a spring located inside the master cylinder immediately returns the master cylinder piston(s) to the normal position. The pistons contain check valves and the master cylinder has compensating ports drilled within it. These are uncovered as the pistons reach their normal position. The piston check valves allow fluid to flow toward the wheel cylinders or calipers as the pistons withdraw. Then, as the return springs force the brake pads or shoes into the released position, the excess fluid in the lines is allowed to reenter the reservoir through the compensating ports.

Dual circuit master cylinders employ two pistons, located one behind the other, in the same cylinder. The primary piston is actuated directly by mechanical linkage from the brake pedal. The secondary piston is actuated by fluid

Troubleshooting the Brake System

Problem	Cause	Solution
Low brake pedal (excessive pedal travel required for braking action.)	• Excessive clearance between rear linings and drums caused by inoperative automatic adjusters	• Make 10 to 15 alternate forward and reverse brake stops to adjust brakes. If brake pedal does not come up, repair or replace adjuster parts as necessary.
	• Worn rear brakelining	• Inspect and replace lining if worn beyond minimum thickness specification
	• Bent, distorted brakeshoes, front or rear	• Replace brakeshoes in axle sets
	• Air in hydraulic system	• Remove air from system. Refer to Brake Bleeding.
Low brake pedal (pedal may go to floor with steady pressure applied.)	• Fluid leak in hydraulic system	• Fill master cylinder to fill line; have helper apply brakes and check calipers, wheel cylinders, differential valve tubes, hoses and fittings for leaks. Repair or replace as necessary.
	• Air in hydraulic system	• Remove air from system. Refer to Brake Bleeding.
	• Incorrect or non-recommended brake fluid (fluid evaporates at below normal temp).	• Flush hydraulic system with clean brake fluid. Refill with correct-type fluid.
	• Master cylinder piston seals worn, or master cylinder bore is scored, worn or corroded	• Repair or replace master cylinder
Low brake pedal (pedal goes to floor on first application—o.k. on subsequent applications.)	• Disc brake pads sticking on abutment surfaces of anchor plate. Caused by a build-up of dirt, rust, or corrosion on abutment surfaces	• Clean abutment surfaces
Fading brake pedal (pedal height decreases with steady pressure applied.)	• Fluid leak in hydraulic system	• Fill master cylinder reservoirs to fill mark, have helper apply brakes, check calipers, wheel cylinders, differential valve, tubes, hoses, and fittings for fluid leaks. Repair or replace parts as necessary.
	• Master cylinder piston seals worn, or master cylinder bore is scored, worn or corroded	• Repair or replace master cylinder
Decreasing brake pedal travel (pedal travel required for braking action decreases and may be accompanied by a hard pedal.)	• Caliper or wheel cylinder pistons sticking or seized	• Repair or replace the calipers, or wheel cylinders
	• Master cylinder compensator ports blocked (preventing fluid return to reservoirs) or pistons sticking or seized in master cylinder bore	• Repair or replace the master cylinder
	• Power brake unit binding internally	• Test unit according to the following procedure: (a) Shift transmission into neutral and start engine (b) Increase engine speed to 1500 rpm, close throttle and fully depress brake pedal (c) Slow release brake pedal and stop engine (d) Have helper remove vacuum check valve and hose from power unit. Observe for backward movement of brake pedal. (e) If the pedal moves backward, the power unit has an internal bind—replace power unit

Troubleshooting the Brake System (cont.)

Problem	Cause	Solution
Spongy brake pedal (pedal has abnormally soft, springy, spongy feel when depressed.)	• Air in hydraulic system	• Remove air from system. Refer to Brake Bleeding.
	• Brakeshoes bent or distorted	• Replace brakeshoes
	• Brakelining not yet seated with drums and rotors	• Burnish brakes
	• Rear drum brakes not properly adjusted	• Adjust brakes
Hard brake pedal (excessive pedal pressure required to stop vehicle. May be accompanied by brake fade.)	• Loose or leaking power brake unit vacuum hose	• Tighten connections or replace leaking hose
	• Incorrect or poor quality brakelining	• Replace with lining in axle sets
	• Bent, broken, distorted brakeshoes	• Replace brakeshoes
	• Calipers binding or dragging on mounting pins. Rear brakeshoes dragging on support plate.	• Replace mounting pins and bushings. Clean rust or burrs from rear brake support plate ledges and lubricate ledges with molydisulfide grease. **NOTE:** If ledges are deeply grooved or scored, do not attempt to sand or grind them smooth—replace support plate.
	• Caliper, wheel cylinder, or master cylinder pistons sticking or seized	• Repair or replace parts as necessary
	• Power brake unit vacuum check valve malfunction	• Test valve according to the following procedure: (a) Start engine, increase engine speed to 1500 rpm, close throttle and immediately stop engine (b) Wait at least 90 seconds then depress brake pedal (c) If brakes are not vacuum assisted for 2 or more applications, check valve is faulty
	• Power brake unit has internal bind	• Test unit according to the following procedure: (a) With engine stopped, apply brakes several times to exhaust all vacuum in system (b) Shift transmission into neutral, depress brake pedal and start engine (c) If pedal height decreases with foot pressure and less pressure is required to hold pedal in applied position, power unit vacuum system is operating normally. Test power unit. If power unit exhibits a bind condition, replace the power unit.
	• Master cylinder compensator ports (at bottom of reservoirs) blocked by dirt, scale, rust, or have small burrs (blocked ports prevent fluid return to reservoirs).	• Repair or replace master cylinder **CAUTION:** Do not attempt to clean blocked ports with wire, pencils, or similar implements. Use compressed air only.
	• Brake hoses, tubes, fittings clogged or restricted	• Use compressed air to check or unclog parts. Replace any damaged parts.
	• Brake fluid contaminated with improper fluids (motor oil, transmission fluid, causing rubber components to swell and stick in bores	• Replace all rubber components, combination valve and hoses. Flush entire brake system with DOT 3 brake fluid or equivalent.
	• Low engine vacuum	• Adjust or repair engine

Troubleshooting the Brake System (cont.)

Problem	Cause	Solution
Grabbing brakes (severe reaction to brake pedal pressure.)	• Brakelining(s) contaminated by grease or brake fluid	• Determine and correct cause of contamination and replace brakeshoes in axle sets
	• Parking brake cables incorrectly adjusted or seized	• Adjust cables. Replace seized cables.
	• Incorrect brakelining or lining loose on brakeshoes	• Replace brakeshoes in axle sets
	• Caliper anchor plate bolts loose	• Tighten bolts
	• Rear brakeshoes binding on support plate ledges	• Clean and lubricate ledges. Replace support plate(s) if ledges are deeply grooved. Do not attempt to smooth ledges by grinding.
	• Incorrect or missing power brake reaction disc	• Install correct disc
	• Rear brake support plates loose	• Tighten mounting bolts
Dragging brakes (slow or incomplete release of brakes)	• Brake pedal binding at pivot	• Loosen and lubricate
	• Power brake unit has internal bind	• Inspect for internal bind. Replace unit if internal bind exists.
	• Parking brake cables incorrrectly adjusted or seized	• Adjust cables. Replace seized cables.
	• Rear brakeshoe return springs weak or broken	• Replace return springs. Replace brakeshoe if necessary in axle sets.
	• Automatic adjusters malfunctioning	• Repair or replace adjuster parts as required
	• Caliper, wheel cylinder or master cylinder pistons sticking or seized	• Repair or replace parts as necessary
	• Master cylinder compensating ports blocked (fluid does not return to reservoirs).	• Use compressed air to clear ports. Do not use wire, pencils, or similar objects to open blocked ports.
Vehicle moves to one side when brakes are applied	• Incorrect front tire pressure	• Inflate to recommended cold (reduced load) inflation pressure
	• Worn or damaged wheel bearings	• Replace worn or damaged bearings
	• Brakelining on one side contaminated	• Determine and correct cause of contamination and replace brakelining in axle sets
	• Brakeshoes on one side bent, distorted, or lining loose on shoe	• Replace brakeshoes in axle sets
	• Support plate bent or loose on one side	• Tighten or replace support plate
	• Brakelining not yet seated with drums or rotors	• Burnish brakelining
	• Caliper anchor plate loose on one side	• Tighten anchor plate bolts
	• Caliper piston sticking or seized	• Repair or replace caliper
	• Brakelinings water soaked	• Drive vehicle with brakes lightly applied to dry linings
	• Loose suspension component attaching or mounting bolts	• Tighten suspension bolts. Replace worn suspension components.
	• Brake combination valve failure	• Replace combination valve
Chatter or shudder when brakes are applied (pedal pulsation and roughness may also occur.)	• Brakeshoes distorted, bent, contaminated, or worn	• Replace brakeshoes in axle sets
	• Caliper anchor plate or support plate loose	• Tighten mounting bolts
	• Excessive thickness variation of rotor(s)	• Refinish or replace rotors in axle sets
Noisy brakes (squealing, clicking, scraping sound when brakes are applied.)	• Bent, broken, distorted brakeshoes	• Replace brakeshoes in axle sets
	• Excessive rust on outer edge of rotor braking surface	• Remove rust

Troubleshooting the Brake System (cont.)

Problem	Cause	Solution
Noisy brakes (squealing, clicking, scraping sound when brakes are applied.) (cont.)	• Brakelining worn out—shoes contacting drum of rotor	• Replace brakeshoes and lining in axle sets. Refinish or replace drums or rotors.
	• Broken or loose holddown or return springs	• Replace parts as necessary
	• Rough or dry drum brake support plate ledges	• Lubricate support plate ledges
	• Cracked, grooved, or scored rotor(s) or drum(s)	• Replace rotor(s) or drum(s). Replace brakeshoes and lining in axle sets if necessary.
	• Incorrect brakelining and/or shoes (front or rear).	• Install specified shoe and lining assemblies
Pulsating brake pedal	• Out of round drums or excessive lateral runout in disc brake rotor(s)	• Refinish or replace drums, re-index rotors or replace

trapped between the two pistons. If a leak develops in front of the secondary pistons, it moves forward until it bottoms against the front of the master cylinder, and the fluid trapped between the pistons will operate the rear brakes. If the rear brakes develop a leak, the primary piston will move forward until direct contact with the secondary piston takes place, and it will force the secondary piston to actuate the front brakes. In either case, the brake pedal moves farther when the brakes are applied and less braking power is available.

All dual-circuit systems incorporate switch which senses either line pressure or fluid level. This system will warn the driver when only half of the brake system is operational.

In some disc brake systems, this valve body also contains a metering valve and, in some cases, a proportioning valve. The metering valve keeps pressure from traveling to the disc brakes on the front wheels until the brake shoes on the rear wheels have contacted the drum, insuring that the front brakes will never be used alone. The proportioning valve controls the pressure to the rear brakes avoiding rear wheel lock-up during very hard braking.

DISC BRAKES

CAUTION: *Brake pads contain asbestos, which has been determined to be a cancer causing agent. never clean the brake surfaces with compressed air! Avoid inhaling any dust from any brake surface! When cleaning brake surfaces, use a commercially available brake cleaning fluid.*

Instead of the traditional expanding brakes that press outward against a circular drum, disc brake systems utilize a cast iron disc with brake pads positioned on either side of it. An easily seen analogy is the hand brake arrangement on a bicycle. The pads squeeze onto the rim of the bike wheel, slowing its motion. Automobile disc brakes use the identical principal but apply the braking effort to a separate disc instead of the wheel.

The disc or rotor is a one-piece casting mounted just inside the wheel. Some discs are one solid piece while others have cooling fins between the two braking surfaces. These vented rotors enable air to circulate between the braking surfaces cooling them quicker and making them less sensitive to heat buildup and fade. Disc brakes are only slightly affected by dirt and water since contaminants are thrown off by the centrifugal action of the rotor or scraped off by the pads. Also, the equal clamping action of the two brake pads tend to ensure uniform, straight-line stops, although unequal application of the pads between the left and right wheels can cause a vicious pull under braking. All disc brakes are inherently self-adjusting.

There are three general types of disc brakes: The fixed caliper design uses two pistons mounted on either side of the rotor (in each side of the caliper). The caliper is mounted rigidly and does not move. This is a very efficient brake system but the size of the caliper and its mounts adds weight and bulk to the car.

The sliding and floating designs are quite similar. In fact, these two types are often lumped together. In both designs, one is moved into contact with the rotor by hydraulic force. The caliper, which is not held in a fixed position, moves slightly, bringing the other pad into contact with the rotor. There are various methods of attaching floating calipers. Some pivot at the bottom or top, and some slide on mounting bolts. Many uneven brake wear problems can be caused by dirty or seized slides or pivots.

DRUM BRAKES

CAUTION: *Brake shoes contain asbestos, which has been determined to be a cancer causing agent. never clean the brake surfaces with Compressed air! Avoid inhaling any dust from any brake surface! When cleaning brake surfaces, use a commercially available brake cleaning fluid.*

Drum brakes employ two brake shoes mounted on a stationary backing plate. These shoes are positioned inside a circular cast iron drum which rotates with the wheel. The shoes are held in place by springs; this allows them to slide toward the drum (when they are applied) while keeping the linings and drums in alignment. The shoes are actuated by a wheel cylinder which is mounted at the top of the backing plate. When the brakes are applied, hydraulic pressure forces the wheel cylinder's two actuating links outward. Since these links bear directly against the top of the brake shoes, the tops of the shoes are then forced outward against the inside of the drum. This action forces the bottoms of the two shoes to contact the brake drum by rotating the entire assembly

slightly (known as servo action). When the pressure within the wheel cylinder is relaxed, return springs pull the shoes away from the drum.

Most modern drum brakes are designed to self-adjust during application when the vehicle is moving in reverse. This motion caused both shoes to rotate very slightly with the drum, rocking an adjusting lever, thereby causing rotation of the adjusting screw by means of a star wheel. This on-board adjustment system reduces the need for maintenance adjustments but most drivers don't back up enough to keep the brakes properly set.

POWER BRAKE BOOSTER

Virtually all cars today use a vacuum assisted power brake system to multiply the braking force and reduce pedal effort. Since vacuum is always available when the engine is operating, the system is simple and efficient. A vacuum diaphragm is located on the front of the master cylinder and assists the driver in applying the brakes, reducing both the effort and travel he must put into moving the brake pedal.

The vacuum diaphragm housing is connected to the intake manifold by a vacuum hose. A check valve is placed at the point where the hose enters the diaphragm housing, so that

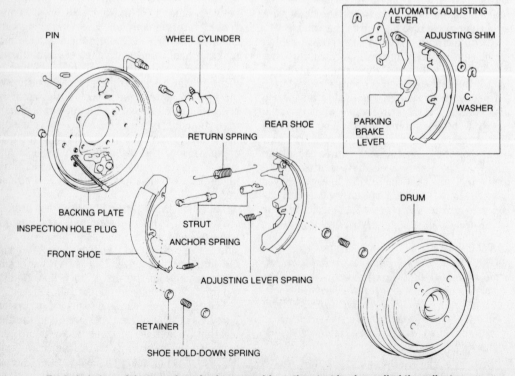

Exploded view of the rear drum brake assembly — the strut is also called the adjuster

during periods of low manifold vacuum brakes assist will not be lost.

Depressing the brake pedal closes off the vacuum source and allows atmospheric pressure to enter on one side of the diaphragm. This causes the master cylinder pistons to move and apply the brakes. When the brake pedal is released, vacuum is applied to both sides of the diaphragm and springs return the diaphragm and master cylinder pistons to the released position.

If the vacuum supply fails, the brake pedal rod will contact the end of the master cylinder actuator rod and the system will apply the brakes without any power assistance. The driver will notice that much higher pedal effort is needed to stop the car and that the pedal feels "harder" than usual.

Adjustments

DRUM BRAKES

The rear drum brakes are equipped with automatic adjusters actuated by the brake mechanism. No periodic adjustment of the drum brakes is necessary if this mechanism is working properly. If the pedal travel is greater than normal, it may be due to a lack of adjustment at the rear. In a safe location, drive the car backwards at low speed. While backing, pump the brake pedal slowly several times. (Neither the speed of the car or the speed of pumping the pedal has any effect on the adjustment. The idea is to apply the brakes several times while backing.) Drive forward and check the pedal feel by braking from moderate speed. It may take 2 or 3 passes in reverse to bring the pedal to the correct travel; each brake application moves the adjuster very little. It will take several applications to take up excess clearance.

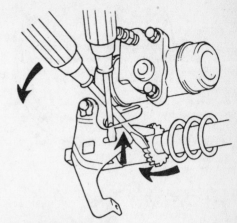

Backing off the adjustors

If brake shoe-to-drum clearance is incorrect and applying and releasing the brakes in reverse does not adjust it properly, the parts will have to be disassembled for repair.

An alternate method of adjustment can be used when the brakes have been disassembled or when the reversing method does not work.

1. Elevate and safely support the vehicle. If only the rear wheels are elevated, block the front wheels with chocks. Once the vehicle is firmly on stands, release the parking brake.

2. Remove the rear wheels.

3. Remove the brake drum. It will not come off if the parking brake is applied.

CAUTION: *Brake pads and shoes contain asbestos, which has been determined to be a cancer causing agent. Never clean the brake surfaces with compressed air! Avoid inhaling any dust from brake surfaces! When cleaning brakes, use commercially available brake cleaning fluids.*

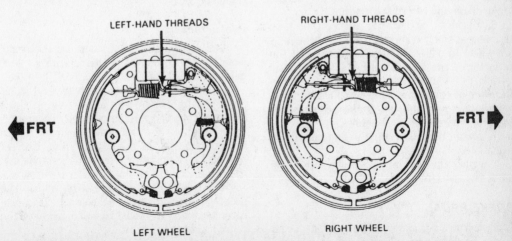

Rear drum brake assemblies — note that the adjustors are threaded differently on each side

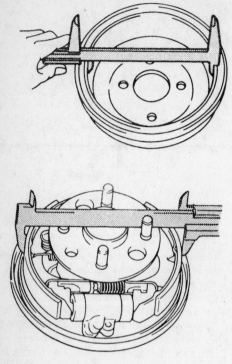

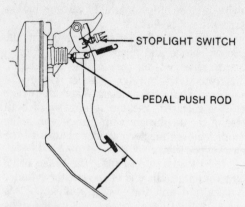

STOPLIGHT SWITCH

PEDAL PUSH ROD

Measuring the diameters of the drum and shoe assemblies

4. If the brake drum cannot be removed easily:

a. Insert a screwdriver through the hole in the backing plate and hold the adjusting lever away from the star wheel.

b. Using another screw driver or a brake adjusting tool, turn the wheel to reduce the tension (increase the clearance) on the brake shoes.

5. Use a brake drum measuring tool with both inside diameter and outside diameter capability. Measure the inside diameter of the brake drum and record the reading.

6. Measure the diameter of the brake shoe assemble at the friction surface. Use the adjusting wheel to adjust the brake shoes until the diameter of the shoes is either 0.60mm (new models) or 0.33mm (older models) less than the diameter of the drum. This small clearance is important; over-adjusted brakes cause drag and premature wear on the shoes.

7. Install the brake drum(s) and install the rear wheel(s).

8. Apply the parking brake and lower the car to the ground.

BRAKE PEDAL

The correct adjustment of the brake pedal height, free play and reserve distance is critical to the correct operation of the brake system.

Pedal height

These three measurements inter-relate and should be performed in sequence.

Pedal Height

1. Measure the pedal height from the top of the pedal pad to the floor. Correct distances are: Corolla RWD 161–171mm, early model Corolla 147–157mm, late model Corolla 134–149mm, Tercel FWD 147–157mm, Tercel 4WD 184–194mm and MR2 vehicle 154–164mm. Always use the above specifications as a guide for this adjustment.

2. If it is necessary to adjust the pedal height, loosen the brake light switch and back it off so that some clearance exists between it and the pedal arm.

NOTE: *On some models, it may be necessary to remove the lower dash trim panel and air duct for access.*

3. Adjust the pedal height by loosening the locknut and turning the pedal pushrod.

4. Return the brake light switch to a position in which it lightly contacts the stopper on the pedal arm.

Pedal Freeplay

5. With the engine off, depress the brake pedal several times until there is no vacuum held in the booster.

6. The free play distance is between the "at rest" pedal position and the position at which beginning of pedal resistance is felt. This represents the distance the pedal pushrod moves before actuating the booster air valve. Correct free play is 3–6mm for all years and models in this book.

7. If adjustment is necessary, adjust the pedal pushrod to give the correct clearance. After adjusting the pedal free play, recheck the pedal height.

8. Double check the adjustment of the brake light switch.

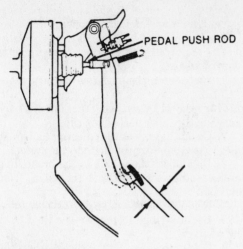

Pedal freeplay

Pedal Reserve Distance

9. With the transmission/transaxle in **PARK** or **NEUTRAL** and the parking brake fully released, start the engine and apply normal braking effort to the pedal. Depress the pedal fully, but don't try to put it through the floor.

10. While the pedal is depressed, have a helper measure the distance from the top of the pedal pad to the floor. This distance is the extra travel available to the pushrod if it must work without vacuum assist or if the brakes are worn or severely out of adjustment. If the pedal height and pedal free play are correctly adjusted, the pedal reserve distance must be at least to specifications. The reserve distance can be greater than specified but must not be less. If the reserve distance is less than specification,

the brake system must be diagnosed for leaks or component failure.

11. The reserve distance specification is Corolla RWD 75mm, Corolla FWD 60mm, Corolla 4WD 65mm, Tercel FWD 56mm, Tercel 4WD 90mm and MR2 vehicle 82mm. Always use the above specifications as a guide for this adjustment.

Brake Light Switch

The brake light switch is located at the top of the pedal arm. It is the switch which turns the brake lights on when the brakes are applied. The plunger type switch is held in the off position by the normal position of the brake pedal; when the pedal moves during brake application, the switch plunger moves forward and the brake lights are brought on.

The switch is almost always the first place to look for the cause of the brake lights flickering over bumps or staying on without use of the brakes. If the brake lights fail to work with the brakes applied, check the fuse first and then check the switch.

REMOVAL AND INSTALLATION

1. Remove the wiring from the switch terminals. Put a piece of tape over each exposed wiring connector; one wire terminal may be HOT even though the ignition is OFF. If it accidentally touches metal, a fuse will blow.

NOTE: *On some models, it may be necessary to remove the lower dash trim panel and air duct for access.*

2. Loosen the locknut closest to the brake pedal arm. Unscrew the switch from the nut and remove it from the bracket.

3. Install the new switch and tighten the retaining nuts finger tight when the switch

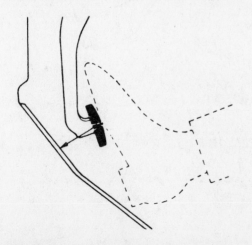

Pedal reserve

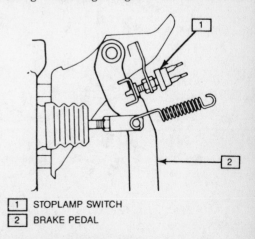

| 1 | STOPLAMP SWITCH |
| 2 | BRAKE PEDAL |

Location of brake lamp switch

plunger is lightly compressed against the stopper on the pedal.

4. Connect an ohmmeter across the terminals of the switch. Move the brake pedal and check the on–off behavior of the switch. Adjust the switch so that the switch comes on at the bottom of the pedal free play. This brings the brake lights on just as the brakes apply but no sooner.

5. Tighten the locknuts to hold the switch in position.

6. Remove the tape and connect the wiring to the switch.

Master Cylinder

REMOVAL AND INSTALLATION

NOTE: *Be careful not to spill brake fluid on the painted surfaces of the vehicle; it will* *damage the paint. If spillage occurs, rinse the area immediately with water.*
Handle the steel brake lines very carefully. Once they are bent or kinked, they cannot be straightened.

1. Disconnect the negative battery cable. On MR2 vehicle, remove the luggage compartment trim cover by removing the clips after disengaging the inner part of the clip.

2. Clean the area at the reservoir and brake lines to prevent entry of dirt into the system.

3. Disconnect the wiring to the brake fluid level warning switch. Release the wiring from any clips.

4. Remove the air intake duct as necessary.

5. Use a syringe to remove the fluid from the reservoir.

6. Disconnect the brake lines from the master cylinder. Plug or tape the lines immedi-

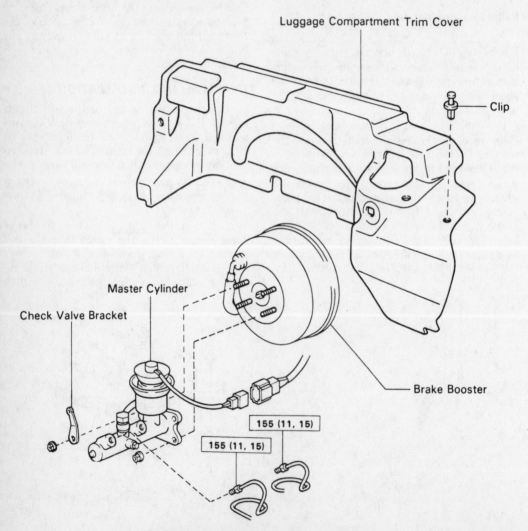

Removing the master cylinder — MR2

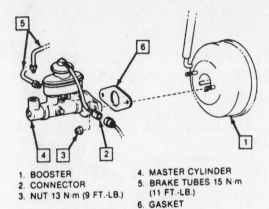

1. BOOSTER
2. CONNECTOR
3. NUT 13 N·m (9 FT.-LB.)
4. MASTER CYLINDER
5. BRAKE TUBES 15 N·m (11 FT.-LB.)
6. GASKET

Removing the brake master cylinder

ately to keep dirt and moisture out of the system.

7. Remove the retaining nuts holding the master cylinder to the brake booster.

8. Remove the three-way union from the booster stud.

9. Remove the master cylinder from the studs.

10. Remove the seal or gasket from the booster.

11. When reinstalling, always use a new gasket or seal and install the master cylinder to the booster. On some models, confirm that the "UP" mark on the master cylinder boot is in the correct position.

12. Install the three-way union bracket over the stud and install the retaining nuts finger tight.

13. Connect the brake lines to the master cylinder. Make certain each fitting is correctly threaded and tighten each fitting. The job is made easier by having a small amount of movement available at the master cylinder mounting studs.

14. Tighten the master cylinder retaining nuts to 10 ft. lbs.

15. Tighten the brake line fittings. Do not over tighten these fittings.

16. Install the air intake duct as necessary.

17. Connect the wiring to the brake fluid sensing switch and attach any wiring clips.

18. Fill the master cylinder reservoir WITH NEW BRAKE FLUID. Install the luggage compartment trim cover on the MR2 vehicles.

19. Connect the negative battery cable. Bleed the brake system.

NOTE: *When replacing the master cylinder it is best to BENCH BLEED the master cylinder before installing it to the vehicle. Mount the master cylinder into a vise or suitable equivalent (do not damage the cylinder). Fill the cylinder to the correct level with the speci-*

fied fluid. Block off all the outer brake line holes but one—then using a long tool such as rod, position it in the cylinder to actuate the brake master cylinder. Pump (push tool in and out) the brake master cylinder 3 or 4 times till brake fluid is release out and no air is in the brake fluid. Repeat this procedure until all brake fluid is released out of every hole and no air is expelled.

OVERHAUL

NOTE: *Use this service procedure and exploded view diagrams as a guide for overhaul of the master cylinder assembly. If in doubt about overhaul condition or service procedure REPLACE the complete assembly with a new master cylinder assembly.*

1. Remove master cylinder from the car. Remove the cap and strainer from the reservoir.

2. Remove the set screw and remove the reservoir.

3. Mount the cylinder (protect the cylinder from damage) in a vise.

4. Remove the two grommets from the cylinder.

5. Using a screwdriver or similar tool, push

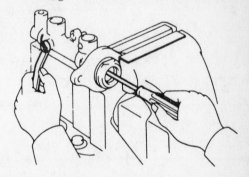

Removing the stopper bolt

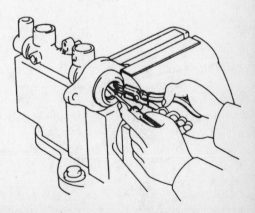

To remove the snapring, the piston must be pushed into the bore

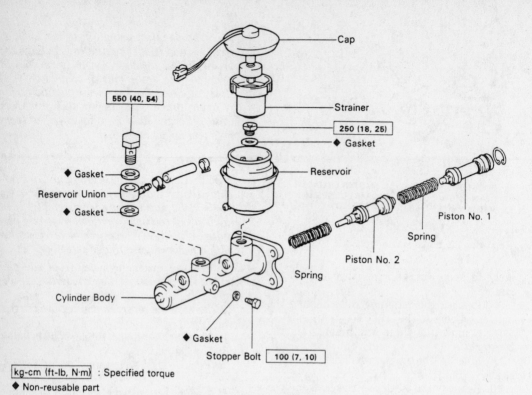

550 (40, 54)

◆ Gasket

Reservoir Union

◆ Gasket

Cap

Strainer

250 (18, 25)

◆ Gasket

Reservoir

Piston No. 1

Spring

Spring

Piston No. 2

Spring

Cylinder Body

◆ Gasket

Stopper Bolt   100 (7, 10)

kg-cm (ft-lb, N·m) : Specified torque

◆ Non-reusable part

Master cylinder components

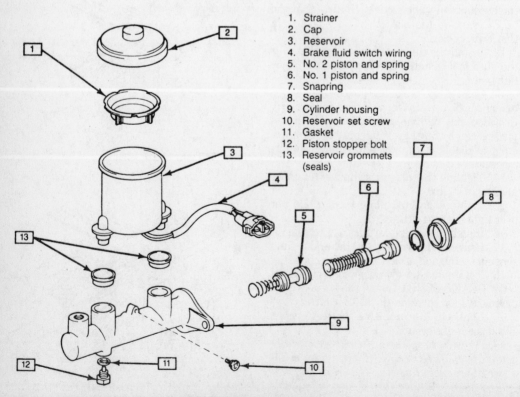

1. Strainer
2. Cap
3. Reservoir
4. Brake fluid switch wiring
5. No. 2 piston and spring
6. No. 1 piston and spring
7. Snapring
8. Seal
9. Cylinder housing
10. Reservoir set screw
11. Gasket
12. Piston stopper bolt
13. Reservoir grommets (seals)

Master cylinder components

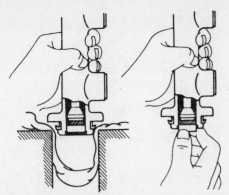

Lightly tapping the flanges on protected blocks will release the pistons

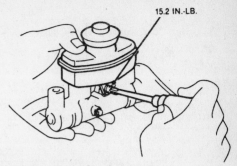

Tightening the reservoir set screw

the pistons all the way into the bore and remove the piston stopper bolt with its gasket.

6. Hold the piston into the bore and remove the snapring with snapring pliers.

7. Place a rag on two wooden blocks. Remove the master cylinder from the vise and tap the cylinder flange between the blocks until the piston tip protrudes.

8. Remove the piston by pulling it straight out.

NOTE: *If the piston is removed at an angle, the cylinder bore may become damaged.*

9. Inspect all parts of the pistons, grommets and bore for any sign of wear, cuts, corrosion or scoring. Check the inlet port and return port for obstructions. Use compressed air to clear any dirt or foreign matter from the area.

10. Apply clean brake fluid to the rubber parts of the pistons.

11. Insert the 2 springs and pistons straight into the bore. Do not angle them during installation.

NOTE: *Be careful not to damage the rubber lips on the pistons.*

12. Install the snapring while pushing in the piston.

13. Push the pistons all the way in and in-stall the piston stopper bolt and gasket. Tighten it to 7 ft. lbs.

14. Install the 2 grommets.

15. Install the cap and strainer onto the reservoir, then press the reservoir into position on the cylinder.

16. Install the set screw while pushing on the reservoir. Tighten the screw to 15 INCH lbs.

NOTE: *There may be a slight bit of play in the reservoir after the set screw is installed. This is normal and no washers or spacers should be installed.*

17. Reinstall the master cylinder and follow all necessary service procedures.

Power Brake Booster/Vacuum Booster

REMOVAL AND INSTALLATION

1. Disconnect the negative battery cable.

2. On some vehicles, remove the top of the air cleaner and the intake duct to gain working access. Remove the charcoal canister mounting nuts.

3. Remove the brake master cylinder from the booster. Refer to the necessary service procedures.

4. Remove the vacuum hose from the booster.

5. Inside the car, disconnect the pedal

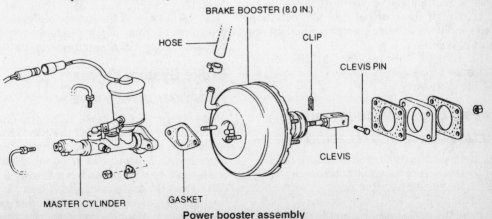

Power booster assembly

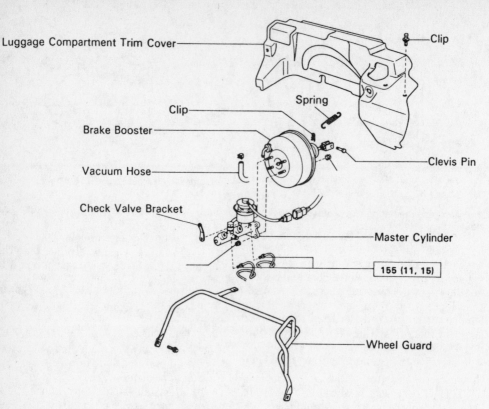

Brake booster assembly — MR2 vehicle

return spring. Disconnect the clip and the clevis pin.

6. Remove the brake booster retaining nuts. It will be helpful to have a helper support the booster while the nuts are loosened.

7. Remove the booster from the engine compartment.

8. When reinstalling, have a helper hold the booster in position while you install the retaining nuts. Tighten the nuts to 10 ft. lbs.

9. Install the clevis pin and clip, then install the pedal return spring.

10. Connect the vacuum hose to the booster.

11. Install the master cylinder onto the booster and tighten the nuts to 10 ft. lbs.

12. Install the charcoal canister mounting bolts and install the air cleaner top and intake duct as necessary.

13. Connect the negative battery cable. Bleed the brake system. Refer to the necessary service procedure.

Diesel Engine Vacuum Pump

REMOVAL AND INSTALLATION

1. Disconnect the negative battery cable.
2. Disconnect the vacuum hose.
3. Disconnect oil outlet hose.
4. Remove the pump retaining bolts. Remove the pump assembly and O-ring.

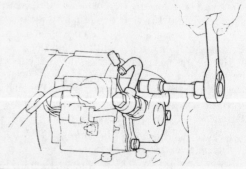

Removing vacuum pump assembly — Corolla diesel engine

5. Installation is the reverse of the removal procedure. Torque pump assembly retaining bolts to 7 ft. lbs. Check pump operation.

Brake System Valves

PROPORTIONING VALVE

The proportioning valve is located on the center of the firewall under the hood. Except for leakage or impact damage, it rarely needs replacement. If it must be removed, all brake lines must be labeled and removed and the valve removed from its mount. Clean the fittings before removal to prevent dirt from entering the ports. After the lines are reconnected

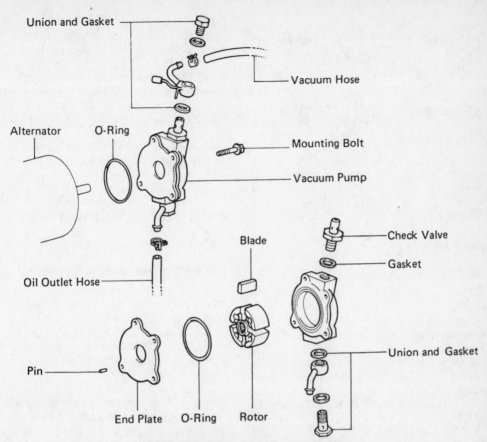

Union and Gasket

Vacuum Hose

Alternator   O-Ring

Mounting Bolt

Vacuum Pump

Blade

Check Valve

Gasket

Oil Outlet Hose

Pin

Union and Gasket

End Plate   O-Ring   Rotor

Exploded view diesel engine vacuum pump

and carefully (use a line wrench) tightened to 11 ft. lbs., the entire brake system must be bled.

VACUUM CHECK VALVE

The brake vacuum check valve allows vacuum to flow out of the brake booster but will not allow back-flow. This maintains a supply of vacuum within the booster during periods of low engine vacuum. The valve can be removed from the hose by hand. Once removed, the valve can be tested by gently blowing through it. It should allow airflow in one direction but not the other. When installing a new valve, make sure it is positioned so that the air can flow from the booster to the engine. Most

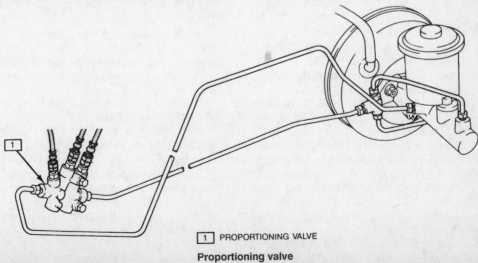

1 PROPORTIONING VALVE

Proportioning valve

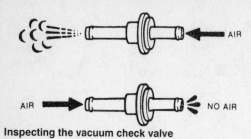

Inspecting the vacuum check valve

replacement valves have an arrow showing the direction of airflow. IF IN DOUBT ABOUT CONDITION OF THIS VALVE-REPLACE THE VALVE.

Brake Hoses

INSPECTION

1. Inspect the lines and hoses in a well lighted area. Use a small mirror to allow you to see concealed parts of the hose or line. Check the entire length and circumference of each line or hose.

2. Look for any sign of wear, deformation, corrosion, cracking, bends, swelling or thread damage.

3. The slightest sign of leakage requires IMMEDIATE ATTENTION.

4. Check all clamps for tightness and check that all lines and hoses have sufficient clearance from moving parts and heat sources.

5. Check that any lines passing through grommets pass through the center of the grommet and are not forced against the side of the hole. Relieve any excess tension.

6. Some metal lines may contain spring-like coils. These coils absorb vibration and prevent the line from cracking under strain. Do not attempt to straighten the coils or change their diameter.

REMOVAL AND INSTALLATION

1. Elevate and safely support the vehicle.
2. Remove the wheel.
3. Clean all dirt from the hose junctions.
4. Place a catch pan under the hose area.
5. Using 2 (one should be line or flare wrench) wrenches, disconnect the flexible hose from the steel brake line at the strut assembly.
6. If equipped with disc brakes, disconnect the brake hose union bolt at the brake caliper. If equipped with drum brakes, disconnect the hose from the steel pipe running to the wheel cylinder.
7. Remove the hose retaining clips and remove the hose from the vehicle.
8. If the system is to remain disconnected for more than the time it takes to swap hoses,

tape or plug the line and caliper to prevent dirt and moisture from entering.

9. Install the new brake hose into the retaining clips.

10. Connect the hose to the caliper (disc brakes) and tighten the union bolt to 22 ft. lbs. or connect the hose to the short line running into the wheel cylinder and tighten the fitting to 11 ft. lbs.

11. Connect the steel brake line to the hose at the strut. Start the threads by hand and make sure the joint is properly threaded before tightening. Tighten the fitting to 11 ft. lbs.

12. Install the wheel. Bleed the brake system. Refer to the necessary service procedures.

13. Lower the car to the ground.

Bleeding the Brake System

It is necessary to bleed the hydraulic system any time system has been opened or has trapped air within the fluid lines. It may be necessary to bleed the system at all four brakes if air has been introduced through a low fluid level or by disconnecting brake pipes at the master cylinder.

If a line is disconnected at one wheel only, generally only that brake needs bleeding. If lines are disconnected at any fitting between the master cylinder and the brake, the system served by the disconnected pipe must be bled.

NOTE: *Do not allow brake fluid to splash or spill onto painted surfaces; the paint will be damaged. If spillage occurs, flush the area immediately with clean water.*

1. Fill the master cylinder reservoir to the "MAX" line with brake fluid and keep it full throughout the bleeding procedure.

2. If the master cylinder has been removed or disconnected, it must be bled before any brake unit is bled. To bleed the master cylinder:

a. Disconnect the front brake line from the master cylinder and allow fluid to flow from the front connector port.

b. Reconnect the line to the master cylinder and tighten it until it is fluid tight.

c. Have a helper press the brake pedal down one time and hold it down.

d. Loosen the front brake line connection at the master cylinder. This will allow trapped air to escape, along with some fluid.

e. Again tighten the line, release the pedal slowly and repeat the sequence (steps c–d–e) until only fluid runs from the port. No air bubbles should be present in the fluid.

f. Final tighten the line fitting at the master cylinder to 11 ft. lbs.

g. After all the air has been bled from the

Brake bleeding

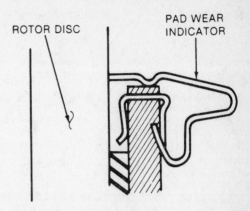

ROTOR DISC

PAD WEAR INDICATOR

Disc brake pad wear indicator

front connection, bleed the master cylinder at the rear connection by repeating steps a–e.

3. Place the correct size box-end or line wrench over the bleeder valve and attach a tight-fitting transparent hose over the bleeder. Allow the tube to hang submerged in a transparent container of clean brake fluid. The fluid must remain above the end of the hose at all times, otherwise the system will ingest air instead of fluid.

4. Have an assistant pump the brake pedal several times slowly and hold it down.

5. Slowly unscrew the bleeder valve ($^1/_4$–$^1/_2$ turn is usually enough). After the initial rush of air and fluid, have the assistant slowly release the brake pedal. When the pedal is released, tighten the bleeder.

6. Repeat Steps 4 and 5 until no air bubbles are seen in the hose or container. If air is constantly appearing after repeated bleeding, the system must be examined for the source of the leak or loose fitting.

7. If the entire system must be bled, begin with the right rear, then the left front, left rear and right front brake in that order. After each brake is bled, check and top off the fluid level in the reservoir.

NOTE: *Do not reuse brake fluid which has been bled from the brake system.*

8. After bleeding, check the pedal for sponginess feel. Repeat the bleeding procedure as necessary to correct.

FRONT DISC BRAKES

CAUTION: *Brake pads and shoes contain asbestos, which has been determined to be a cancer causing agent. Never clean the brake surfaces with compressed air! Avoid inhaling any dust from brake surfaces! When cleaning brakes, use commercially available brake cleaning fluids.*

Brake Pads

WEAR INDICATORS

The front disc brake pads are equipped with a metal tab which will come into contact with the disc after the friction surface material has

worn near its usable minimum. The wear indicators make a constant, distinct metallic sound that should be easily heard. (The sound has been described as similar to either fingernails on a blackboard or a field full of crickets.) The key to recognizing that it is the wear indicators and not some other brake noise is that the sound is heard when the car is being driven WITHOUT the brakes applied. It may or may not be present under braking is heard during normal driving.

It should also be noted that any disc brake system, by its design, cannot be made to work silently under all conditions. Each system includes various shims, plates, cushions and brackets to suppress brake noise but no system can completely silence all noises. Some brake noise–either high or low frequency–can be considered normal under some conditions. Such noises can be controlled and perhaps lessened, but cannot be totally eliminated.

INSPECTION

The front brake pads may be inspected without removal. With the front end elevated and supported, remove the wheel(s). Unlock the steering column lock and turn the wheel so that the brake caliper is out from under the fender.

View the pads–inner and outer–through the cut-out in the center of the caliper. Remember to look at the thickness of the pad friction material (the part that actually presses on the disc) rather than the thickness of the backing plate which does not change with wear.

Remember that you are looking at the profile of the pad, not the whole thing. Brake pads can wear on a taper which may not be visible through the window. It is also not possible to check the contact surface for cracking or scoring from this position. THIS QUICK CHECK CAN BE HELPFUL ONLY AS A REFER-

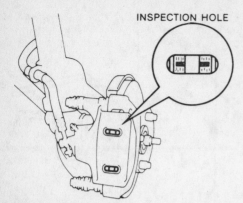

INSPECTION HOLE

Disc brake pad inspection

ENCE; DETAILED INSPECTION RE-
QUIRES PAD REMOVAL.

REMOVAL AND INSTALLATION

1. Raise and safely support the front of the vehicle on jackstands. Set the parking brake and block the rear wheels.

2. Siphon a sufficient quantity of brake fluid from the master cylinder reservoir to prevent the brake fluid from overflowing the master cylinder when removing or installing the brake pads. This is necessary as the piston must be forced into the cylinder bore to provide sufficient clearance to install the pads.

3. Remove the wheel, then reinstall 2 lug nuts finger tight to hold the disc in place.

NOTE: *Disassemble brakes one wheel at a time. This will prevent parts confusion and also prevent the opposite caliper piston from popping out during pad installation.*

4. Remove the two caliper mounting bolts and then remove the caliper from the mounting bracket. Position the caliper out of the way and support it with wire so it doesn't hang by the brake line.

NOTE: *It may be necessary to rock the caliper back and forth a bit in order to reposition the piston so it will clear the brake pads.*

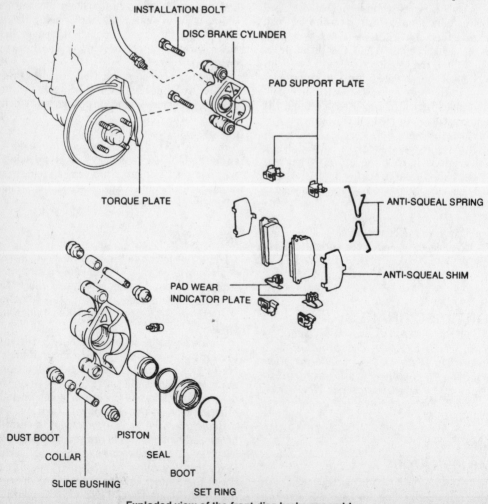

INSTALLATION BOLT

DISC BRAKE CYLINDER

PAD SUPPORT PLATE

TORQUE PLATE

ANTI-SQUEAL SPRING

ANTI-SQUEAL SHIM

PAD WEAR
INDICATOR PLATE

DUST BOOT   PISTON

COLLAR   SEAL

BOOT

SLIDE BUSHING

SET RING

Exploded view of the front disc brake assembly

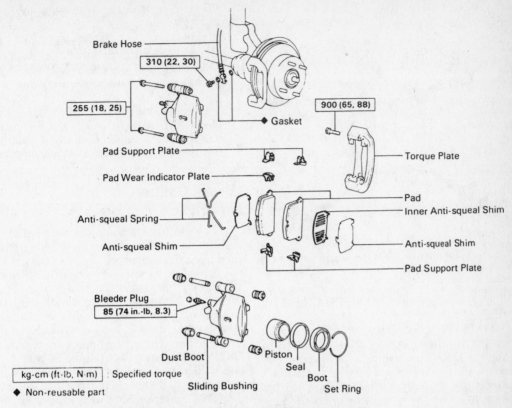

Brake Hose

310 (22, 30)

255 (18, 25)

♦ Gasket

900 (65, 88)

Pad Support Plate

Pad Wear Indicator Plate

Torque Plate

Anti-squeal Spring

Pad

Inner Anti-squeal Shim

Anti-squeal Shim

Anti-squeal Shim

Pad Support Plate

Bleeder Plug
85 (74 in.-lb, 8.3)

Dust Boot

Piston

Seal

Boot

Sliding Bushing

Set Ring

kg·cm (ft-lb, N·m) : Specified torque

♦ Non-reusable part

Exploded view of the front disc brake assembly

5. Remove the 2 brake pads, the 2 wear indicators, the 2 anti-squeal shims, the 4 support plates and the 2 anti squeal springs. Disassemble slowly and take note (refer to exploded view of components) of how the parts fit together. This will save much time during reassembly.

6. Inspect the brake disc (both sides) for scoring or gouging. Measure the disc for both thickness and run-out. Complete inspection procedures are given later in this section.

7. Inspect the pads for remaining thickness and condition. Any sign of uneven wear, cracking, heat checking or spotting is cause for replacement. Compare the wear of the inner pad to the outer pad. While they will not wear at exactly the same rate, the remaining thickness should be about the same on both pads. If one is heavily worn and the other is not, suspect either a binding caliper piston or dirty slides in the caliper mount.

8. Examine the two caliper retaining bolts and the slide bushings in which they run. Everything should be clean and dry. If cleaning is needed, use spray solvents and a clean cloth. Do not wire brush or sand the bolts–this will cause grooves in the metal which will trap more dirt. Check the condition of the rubber dust boots and replace them if damaged.

9. Install the pad support plates onto the mounting bracket.

10. Install new pad wear indicators onto each pad, making sure the arrow on the tab points in the direction of disc rotation.

11. Install new anti-squeal pads to the back of the pads.

12. Install the pads into the mounting bracket and install the anti-squeal springs.

13. Use a caliper compressor, a C-clamp or large pair of pliers to slowly press the caliper piston back into the caliper. If the piston is

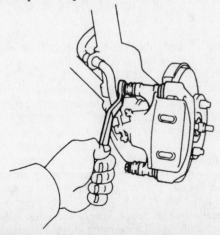

Removing the front caliper mounting bolts

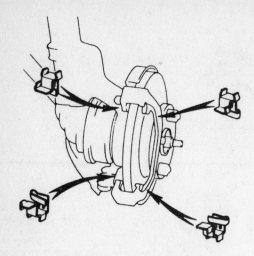

Correct placement of the brake support plates

frozen, or if the caliper is leaking hydraulic fluid, the caliper must be OVERHAULED OR REPLACED.

14. Install the caliper assembly to the mounting plate. Before installing the retaining bolts, apply a thin, even coating of anti-seize compound to the threads and slide surfaces. Don't use grease or spray lubricants; they will not hold up under the extreme temperatures generated by the brakes. Tighten the bolts to 18 ft. lbs.

15. Remove the 2 lugs holding the disc in place and install the wheel.

16. Lower the vehicle to the ground. Check the level of the brake fluid in the master cylinder reservoir; it should be at least to the middle of the reservoir.

17. Depress the brake pedal several times and make sure that the movement feels normal. The first brake pedal application may result in a very "long" pedal due to the pistons being retracted. Always make several brake applications before starting the vehicle. Bleeding is not usually necessary after pad replacement.

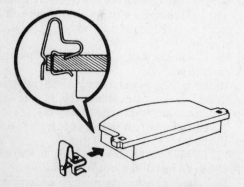

Make certain the brake wear indicators are correctly installed

18. Recheck the fluid level and add to the "MAX" line if necessary.

NOTE: *Braking should be moderate for the first 5 miles or so until the new pads seat correctly. The new pads will bed best if put through several moderate heating and cooling cycles. Avoid hard braking until the brakes have experienced several long, slow stops with time to cool in between. Taking the time to properly bed the brakes will yield quieter operation, more efficient stopping and contribute to extended brake life.*

Brake Caliper

REMOVAL

1. Raise and safely support the front of the vehicle on jackstands. Set the parking brake and block the rear wheels.

2. Siphon a sufficient quantity of brake fluid from the master cylinder reservoir to prevent the brake fluid from overflowing the master cylinder when removing or installing the calipers. This is necessary as the piston must be forced into the cylinder bore to provide sufficient clearance to install the caliper.

3. Remove the wheel, then reinstall 2 lug nuts finger tight to hold the disc in place.

NOTE: *Disassemble brakes one wheel at a time. This will prevent parts confusion and also prevent the opposite caliper piston from popping out during installation.*

4. Disconnect the hose union at the caliper. Use a pan to catch any spilled fluid and immediately plug the disconnected hose.

5. Remove the two caliper mounting bolts and then remove the caliper from the mounting bracket.

OVERHAUL

6. Drain the remaining fluid from the caliper.

7. Carefully remove the dust boot from around the piston.

8. Pad the inside arms of the caliper with rags. Apply compressed air into the brake line port; this will force the piston out.

CAUTION: *Do not place fingers in front of the piston in an attempt to catch it or protect it when applying compressed air. Injury can result. Use just enough air pressure to ease the piston out of the bore.*

9. Remove the seal from the inside of the caliper bore. Check all the parts for wear, scoring, deterioration, cracking or other abnormal conditions. Corrosion — generally caused by water in the system — will appear as white deposits on the metal, similar to what may be found on an old aluminum storm door on your house. Pay close attention to the condition of

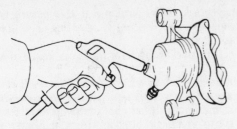

Use just enough air to ease the piston out of the caliper — keep fingers out of the way of the piston

the inside of the caliper bore and the outside of the piston. Any sign of corrosion or scoring requires new parts; do not attempt to clean or resurface either face.

10. The caliper overhaul kit will, at minimum, contain new seals and dust boots. A good kit will contain a new piston as well, but you may have to buy the piston separately. Any time the caliper is disassembled, a new piston is highly recommended in addition to the new seals.

11. Clean all the components to be reused with an aerosol brake solvent and dry them thoroughly. Take any steps necessary to eliminate moisture or water vapor from the parts.

12. Coat all the caliper components with fresh brake fluid from a new can.

NOTE: *Some repair kits come with special assembly lubricant for the piston and seal. Use this lubricant according to directions with the kit.*

13. Install the piston seal and piston into the caliper bore. This is an exacting job; the clearances are very small. Make sure that the seal is seated in its groove and that the piston is not cocked when inserted into the bore.

14. Install the dust boot and its clip or ring.

15. Install the slide bushings and rubber boots onto the caliper if they were removed during disassembly.

INSTALLATION

16. Use a caliper compressor, a C-clamp or large pair of pliers to slowly press the caliper piston back into the caliper.

17. Install the caliper assembly to the mounting plate. Before installing the retaining bolts, apply a thin, even coating of anti-seize compound to the threads and slide surfaces. Don't use grease or spray lubricants; they will not hold up under the extreme temperatures generated by the brakes. Tighten the bolts to 18 ft. lbs.

18. Install the brake hose to the caliper. Always use a new gasket and tighten the union to 17 ft. lbs.

19. Bleed the brake system.

20. Remove the 2 lugs holding the disc in place and install the wheel.

21. Lower the vehicle to the ground. Check the level of the brake fluid in the master cylinder reservoir; it should be at least to the middle of the reservoir.

Brake Disc (Rotor)

REMOVAL AND INSTALLATION

NOTE: *Refer to the necessary wheel bearing service procedures in Chapter 8.*

1. Elevate and safely support the car. If only the front end is supported, set the parking brake and block the rear wheels.

2. Remove the wheel.

3. Remove the brake caliper from its mount and suspend it out of the way. Don't disconnect the hose and don't let the caliper hang by the hose. Remove the brake pads with all the clips, shims, etc.

4. Install all the lug nuts to hold the rotor in place. If the nuts are open at both ends, it is helpful to install them backwards (tapered end out) to secure the disc. Tighten the nuts a bit tighter than finger tight, but make sure all are at approximately the same tightness.

5. Perform the run-out and thickness measurements explained in "Inspection". Run-out must be measured with the rotor mounted on the car. Thickness measurements can be made either on or off the car.

6. Remove the two bolts holding the caliper mounting bracket to the steering knuckle. These bolts will be tight. Remove the 4 lug nuts holding the rotor.

7. Remove the bracket from the knuckle. Before removing the rotor, make a mark on the rotor indexing one wheel stud to one hole in the rotor. This assures the rotor will be re-installed in its original position, serving to eliminate minor vibrations in the brake system.

8. When reinstalling, make certain the rotor is clean and free of any particles of rust or metal from resurfacing. Observe the index mark made earlier and fit the rotor over the wheel lugs. Install 2 lug nuts to hold it in place.

9. Install the caliper mounting bracket in position and tighten its bolts to 65 ft. lbs.

10. Install the brake pads and the hardware.

11. Install the caliper. Tighten the mounting bolts to 18 ft. lbs.

12. Install the wheel and lower the car to the ground.

INSPECTION

Run-out

NOTE: *Before measuring the run-out on the front discs, confirm that the front wheel bearing play is within specification.*

1. Elevate and safely support the car. If only the front end is supported, set the parking brake and block the rear wheels.

2. Remove the wheel.

3. Remove the brake caliper from its mount and suspend it out of the way. Don't disconnect the hose and don't let the caliper hang by the hose. Remove the brake pads with all the clips, shims, etc.

4. Install all the lug nuts to hold the rotor in place. If the nuts are open at both ends, it is helpful to install them backwards (tapered end out) to secure the disc. Tighten the nuts a bit tighter than finger tight, but make sure all are at approximately the same tightness.

5. Mount a dial indicator with a magnetic or universal base on the strut so that the tip of the indicator contacts the rotor about $1/2$ in. from the outer edge.

6. Zero the dial indicator. Turn the rotor one complete revolution and observe the total indicated run-out.

7. If the run-out exceeds 0.15mm (older models) or 0.09mm (newer models), clean the wheel hub and rotor mating surfaces and re-measure. If the run-out still exceeds maximum, remove the rotor and remount it so that the wheel studs now run through different holes. If this re-indexing does not provide correct run-out measurements, the rotor should be considered warped beyond use and either resurfaced or replaced.

Thickness

The thickness of the rotor partially determines its ability to withstand heat and provide adequate stopping force. Every rotor has a minimum thickness established by the manufacturer. This minimum measurement MUST NOT be exceeded. A rotor which is too thin may crack under braking; if this occurs the wheel can lock instantly, resulting in sudden loss of control.

If any part of the rotor measures below minimum thickness, the disc must be replaced. Additionally, a rotor which needs to be resurfaced may not allow sufficient cutting before reaching minimum. Since the allowable wear from new to minimum is about 1mm, it is wise to replace the rotor rather than resurface it.

Thickness and thickness variation can be measured with a micrometer capable of reading to one ten-thousandth inch. All measurements must be made at the same distance in from the edge of the rotor. Measure at four equally spaced points around the disc and record the measurements. Compare each measurement to the minimum thickness specifications in the chart at the end of this chapter.

Compare the four measurements to each

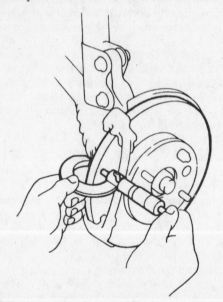

Never reuse a rotor which is below minimum thickness

other and find the difference between each pair. A rotor varying by more than 0.013mm can cause pedal vibration and/or front end vibration during stops. A rotor which does not meet these specifications should be resurfaced or replaced.

Condition

A new rotor will have a smooth even surface which rapidly changes during use. It is not uncommon for a rotor to develop very fine concentric scoring (like the grooves on a record) due to dust and grit being trapped by the brake pad. This slight irregularity is normal, but as the grooves deepen, wear and noise increase and

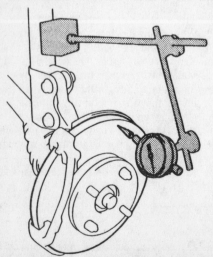

Measuring rotor run-out

stopping may be affected. As a general rule, any groove deep enough to snag a fingernail during inspection is cause for action or replacement.

Any sign of blue spots, discoloration, heavy rusting or outright gouges require replacement of the rotor. If you are checking the disc on the car (such as during pad replacement or tire rotation) remember to turn the disc and check both the inner and outer faces completely. If anything looks questionable or requires consideration, choose the safer option and replace the rotor. The front brakes are a critical system and must be maintained at 100% reliability.

Any time a rotor is replaced, the pads should also be replaced so that the surfaces mate properly. Since brake pads should be replaced in axle sets (both front or rear wheels), consider replacing both rotors instead of just one. The restored feel and accurate stopping make the extra investment worthwhile.

REAR DRUM BRAKES

CAUTION: *Brake pads and shoes contain asbestos, which has been determined to be a cancer causing agent. Never clean the brake surfaces with compressed air! Avoid inhaling any dust from brake surfaces! When cleaning brakes, use commercially available brake cleaning fluids.*

Brake Drums

REMOVAL AND INSTALLATION

1. Elevate and safely support the vehicle. If only the rear wheels are elevated, block the front wheels with chocks. Once the vehicle is firmly on stands, release the parking brake.

2. Remove the rear wheel.

3. Make an index mark showing the relationship between one wheel lug and one hole in the drum. This will allow the drum to be reinstalled in its original position.

4. Tap the drum with a rubber mallet or wooden hammer handle. Remove the brake drum. It will not come off if the parking brake is applied. If the brake drum cannot be removed easily:

    a. Insert a screwdriver through the hole in the backing plate and hold the adjusting lever away from the star wheel.

    b. Using another screw driver or a brake adjusting tool, turn the star wheel to reduce the tension (increase the clearance) on the brake shoes.

WARNING: *Do not apply the brake pedal while the drum is removed.*

5. Before reinstalling the drum, perform the measurements and adjustments explained in the "Adjustments" section earlier in this chapter.

6. Reinstall the drum, observing the matchmarks made earlier. Keep the drum straight while installing it; if it goes on crooked it can damage the brake shoes.

7. Install the wheel.

8. Lower the car to the ground.

9. Test drive the car at safe speeds and in a safe location to check the pedal feel and brake function. Adjust as necessary.

INSPECTION

1. Clean the drum.

2. Inspect the drum for scoring, cracks, grooves and out-of-roundness. Measure it to determine maximum diameter. A cracked drum must be replaced; do not attempt to weld a drum.

3. Light scoring may be removed by dressing the drum with fine emery cloth. If brake linings are replaced, always resurface a grooved drum.

4. Heavy scoring will require the use of a brake drum lathe to turn the drum.

NOTE: *During manufacture, weights are used to balance brake drums. These weights must not be removed. After a drum is refinished or if there are vibration problems not traceable to wheel balance, the brake drums should be checked for balance. This can be done on most off-vehicle balancers; a bubble balancer is particularly handy for this check. If the drum is out of balance, it must be replaced.*

Brake Shoes

INSPECTION

An inspection hole is provided in the backing plate of each rear wheel which allows the brakes to be checked without removing the drum. Remove the hole plug and check the lining thickness through the hole. If below minimum, the shoes will need replacement. Always replace the plug after checking and make certain it is properly seated and tight.

It should be obvious that this method doesn't provide a lot of information about how the brakes are wearing since it only shows one part of one shoe, but is a quick and easy first check. The only way to see the friction faces of the shoes is to remove the brake drums. No generalities can be drawn between the left and right side shoes, so both drums must be removed to perform a proper inspection.

With the drums removed:

1. Liberally spray the entire brake assembly with aerosol brake cleaner. Do not use other solvents, compressed air or a dry brush.

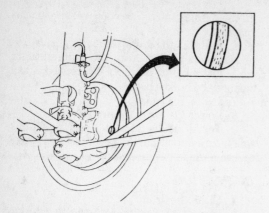

One brake shoe on each rear wheel can be checked through the inspection hole — but a complete inspection requires removing the brake drums

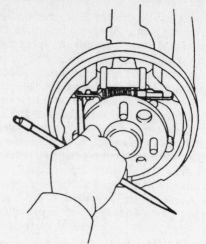

Removing the return spring with a brake spring tool

2. Measure the thickness of the friction surface on each shoe at several different locations. If any measurement is below the minimum thickness, replace all the shoes as a set.

3. Check the contact surfaces closely for any signs of scoring, cracking, uneven or tapered wear, discoloration or separation from the backing plate. Anything that looks unusual requires replacement.

4. If the shoes are in otherwise good condition except for glazing (a shiny, hard surface), the glaze may be removed by light sanding with emery cloth. Also lightly sand the inside of the drum to de-glaze its surface. Do not attempt to rub out grooves or ridges; this is best done with a resurfacing lathe. After sanding the components wash them thoroughly with aerosol brake cleaner to remove any grit.

REMOVAL AND INSTALLATION

NOTE: *The brake shoes can be removed and replaced using everyday hand tools, but the use of brake spring tools and assorted specialty tools makes the job much easier. These common brake tools are available at low cost and can greatly reduce working time.*

Record the location of all brake hardware (spring etc.) before starting this service procedure. Do one side at a time, so that the other side may be used as guide.

1. Elevate and safely support the vehicle. If only the rear wheels are elevated, block the front wheels with chocks. Once the vehicle is firmly on stands, release the parking brake.

2. Remove the rear wheel.

3. Make an index mark showing the relationship between one wheel lug and one hole in the drum. This will allow the drum to be reinstalled in its original position.

4. Tap the drum with a rubber mallet or wooden hammer handle. Remove the brake drum. It will not come off if the parking brake is applied. If the brake drum cannot be removed easily:

a. Insert a screwdriver through the hole in the backing plate and hold the adjusting lever away from the star wheel.

b. Using another screw driver or a brake adjusting tool, turn the star wheel to reduce the tension (increase the clearance) on the brake shoes.

WARNING: *Do not apply the brake pedal while the drum is removed.*

5. Remove the return spring.

6. Disconnect and remove the retainers, hold down springs and pins.

7. Remove the anchor spring.

8. Use a pair of pliers to disconnect the parking brake cable from the parking brake lever.

9. Remove the adjusting lever spring.

10. Remove the shoes and adjuster as a unit.

11. Disassemble the adjustor, the parking brake lever and the automatic adjuster lever. The "C" washer holding the shoe to the adjuster may need to be spread a little before removal.

12. Clean all the parts with aerosol brake solvent. Do not use other solvents.

13. Closely inspect all the parts. Any part of doubtful strength or quality must be replaced.

14. Before reinstallation, apply high-temperature grease to the points at which the brake shoes contact the backing plate and to both the contact and pivot points on the adjuster strut.

15. Install the parking brake lever and automatic adjusting lever to the rear (trailing) shoe.

16. Install a new C-washer and use pliers to close it. Do not bend it more than necessary to hold in place.

17. Install the adjuster (strut) and return spring in place on the rear shoe and install the adjusting lever spring.

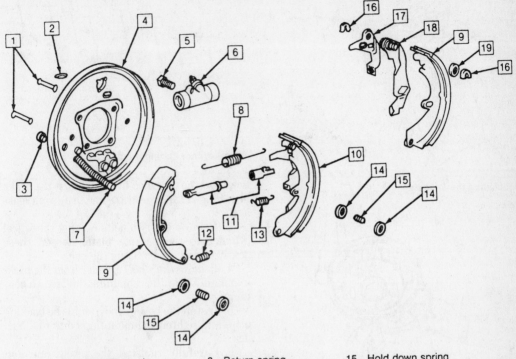

1. Holddown pin
2. Plug
3. Inspection hole plug
4. Backing plate
5. Bolt
6. Wheel cylinder
7. Parking brake cable
8. Return spring
9. Front (leading) shoe
10. Rear (trailing) shoe
11. Strut (adjuster)
12. Anchor spring
13. Adjusting lever spring
14. Retainer
15. Hold down spring
16. "C" washer
17. Adjusting lever
18. Parking brake lever
19. Shim

Rear brake components

NOTE: *Do not allow oil or grease to get on the lining surface.*

18. Using pliers, connect the parking brake cable to the lever.

19. Pass the parking brake cable through the notch in the anchor plate.

20. Set the rear shoe in place with the end of the shoe inserted in the wheel cylinder and the adjuster in place.

21. Install the hold-down spring, retainers and pin.

22. Install the anchor spring between the front (leading) and rear shoe.

23. Position the front shoe with the end of the shoe inserted in the wheel cylinder and the adjuster in place.

24. Install the hold-down spring, retainers and pin.

25. Connect the return spring.

26. Measure both the brake diameter and the drum diameter as explained in "Adjustments" and adjust the brake shoes to the proper clearance.

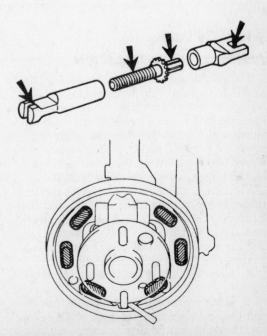

Areas to be lubricated during reassembly

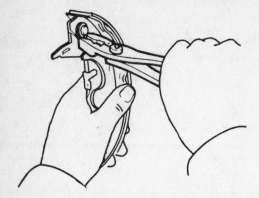

Installing the C-washer

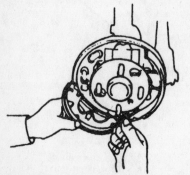

Instal the front shoe by engaging the spring when swinging the shoe into position

27. Install the drum. Install the wheel.

28. Lower the car to the ground.

29. While not absolutely required, bleeding the brakes is recommended after replacing shoes.

Wheel Cylinders

REMOVAL AND INSTALLATION

If wheel cylinders are leaking or seized, they should be replaced. The units are inexpensive enough to make replacement a better choice than repair. Even if the pistons and seals can be replaced, the internal bore can rarely be restored to perfect condition. A faulty repair can reduce braking effort on the wheel or cause a leak which soaks the brake shoes in fluid.

When inspecting the cylinders on the car, the rubber boots must be lifted carefully and the inner area checked for leaks. A very slight moistness—usually coated with dust—is normal, but any accumulation of fluid is evidence of a leak and must be dealt with immediately.

1. Remove the rear brake shoes and hardware.

2. Using a line wrench if possible, disconnect the brake line from the back of the cylinder. This joint may be dirty or corroded. Clean it off and apply penetrating oil if necessary. Do

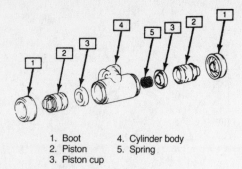

1. Boot
2. Piston
3. Piston cup
4. Cylinder body
5. Spring

Wheel cylinder components

not allow the threaded fitting to twist the brake line. Plug or tape the brake line to prevent leakage.

3. Remove the two bolts holding the wheel cylinder to the backing plate. Loosen these gently to prevent breaking the bolts.

4. Remove the wheel cylinder from the backing plate. Drain the remaining fluid into a container.

5. Install the new cylinder onto the backing plate and tighten the mounting bolts to 7.5 ft. lbs.

6. Carefully reinstall the brake line and tighten it to 11 ft. lbs.

7. Reinstall the shoes and hardware.

8. Install the brake drum and wheel.

9. Bleed the brake system. Repeated bleedings may be needed to eliminate all the air within the line and cylinder. Refer to the necessary service procedures in this chapter.

REAR DISC BRAKES

CAUTION: *Brake pads and shoes contain asbestos, which has been determined to be a cancer causing agent. Never clean the brake surfaces with compressed air! Avoid inhaling any dust from brake surfaces! When cleaning brakes, use commercially available brake cleaning fluids.*

Brake Pads

INSPECTION

The rear brake pads may be inspected without removal. With the rear end elevated and supported, remove the wheel(s).

View the pads—inner and outer—through the cut-out in the center of the caliper. Remember to look at the thickness of the pad friction material (the part that actually presses on the disc) rather than the thickness of the backing plate which does not change with wear.

Remember that you are looking at the profile of the pad, not the whole thing. Brake pads can wear on a taper which may not be visible through the window. It is also not possible to check the contact surface for cracking or scoring from this position. This quick check can be helpful only as a reference; detailed inspection requires pad removal.

REMOVAL AND INSTALLATION

1. Raise and safely support the rear of the vehicle on jackstands. Block the front wheels.

2. Siphon a sufficient quantity of brake fluid from the master cylinder reservoir to prevent the brake fluid from overflowing the master cylinder when removing or installing the brake pads. This is necessary as the piston must be forced into the cylinder bore to provide sufficient clearance to install the pads.

3. Remove the wheel, then reinstall 2 lug nuts finger tight to hold the disc in place.

NOTE: *Disassemble brakes one wheel at a time. This will prevent parts confusion and also prevent the opposite caliper piston from popping out during pad installation.*

4. Remove the mounting (lower) bolt from the mounting bracket. Do not remove the caliper from the main (upper) pin.

5. Lift the caliper from the bottom so that it hinges upward on the upper pin. Use a piece of wire to hold the caliper up. Do not allow the brake hose to become twisted or kinked during this operation.

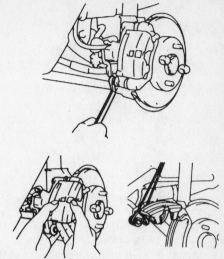

Correct method of raising the rear caliper for access to the brake pads

6. Remove the brake pads with their shims, springs and support plates.

7. Check the rotor thickness and run-out following the procedures explained under Front Disc Brakes in this chapter. Refer to the Specifications Chart at the end of this chapter for the correct measurements.

8. Install new pad support plates to the lower sides of the mounting bracket.

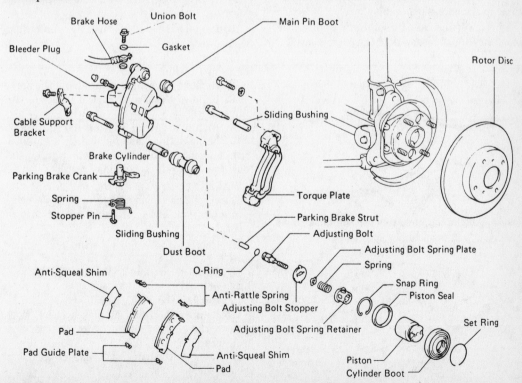

Rear disc brake components

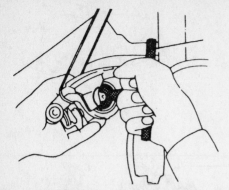

Using a special tool to retract the rear caliper piston

9. Install new anti-rattle springs to the upper side of the mounting bracket.

10. Install a new anti-squeal shim to the back of each pad and install the pads onto the mounting bracket. Install the pads so that the wear indicator is at the top side.

11. Using a special tool or its equivalent to slowly turn the caliper piston clockwise while pressing it into the bore until it locks.

12. Lower the caliper so that the pad protrusion fits into the piston stopper groove.

13. Install the mounting bolt and tighten it to 14 ft. lbs.

14. Install the rear wheel.

15. Depress the brake pedal once or twice to take up the excess piston play.

16. Lower the car to the ground and fill the master cylinder reservoir to the correct level.

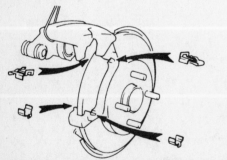

Installing brake support plates and anti-rattle shims

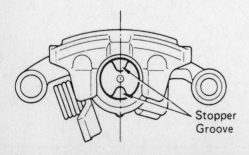

Align the stopper groove with the pad protrusion

Brake Caliper

REMOVAL

1. Raise and safely support the rear of the vehicle on jackstands. Block the front wheels. Remove the rear wheel and install two lug nuts hand tight to hold the rotor in place.

2. Siphon a sufficient quantity of brake fluid from the master cylinder reservoir to prevent the brake fluid from overflowing when replacing pads. This is necessary as the piston must be forced into the cylinder bore to provide sufficient clearance to install the pads.

3. Place a container under the caliper assembly to catch spillage. Disconnect the union bolt holding the brake hose to the caliper. Plug or tape the hose immediately.

4. Remove the clip from the parking brake cable and remove the cable.

5. Remove the caliper mounting bolt.

6. Lift the caliper up and remove the parking brake pin clip.

7. Push on the parking brake crank (arm) to relieve the tension and remove the pin.

8. Slide the caliper off the upper pin.

9. Remove the brake pads, springs and clips.

OVERHAUL

NOTE: *The use of the correct special tools or their equivalent is REQUIRED for this procedure.*

10. Remove the slide bushings and dust boots.

11. Remove the set ring and dust boot from the caliper piston.

12. Remove the caliper piston from the bore.

13. Remove the seal from the inside of the caliper bore.

14. Install a special tool or its equivalent onto the adjusting bolt and lightly tighten it with a 14mm socket. Do not over tighten the tool; damage to the spring may result.

WARNING: *Always use this tool during disassembly. The spring may fly out, causing personal injury and/or damage to the caliper bore!*

15. Remove the snapring from the caliper bore.

16. Carefully remove the adjusting bolt and disassemble it.

17. Remove the parking brake strut.

18. Remove the cable support bracket, then remove the torsion spring from the parking brake crank.

19. Remove the parking brake crank from the caliper.

20. Remove the parking brake crank boot by tapping it lightly on the metal portion of the

boot. Do not remove the boot unless it is to be replaced.

21. Use a pin punch to tap out the stopper pin.

22. Check all the parts for wear, scoring, deterioration, cracking or other abnormal conditions. Corrosion — generally caused by water in the system — will appear as white deposits on the metal. Pay close attention to the condition of the inside of the caliper bore and the outside of the piston. Any sign of corrosion or scoring requires new parts; do not attempt to clean or resurface either face.

23. The caliper overhaul kit will, at minimum, contain new seals and dust boots. A good kit will contain a new piston as well, but you may have to buy the piston separately. Any time the caliper is disassembled, a new piston is highly recommended in addition to the new seals.

24. Clean all the components to be reused with an aerosol brake solvent and dry them thoroughly. Take any steps necessary to eliminate moisture or water vapor from the parts.

25. Coat all the caliper components with fresh brake fluid from a new can.

NOTE: *Some repair kits come with special assembly lubricant for the piston and seal. Use this lubricant according to directions with the kit.*

26. Install the stopper pin into the caliper until the pin extends 25mm.

27. Install the parking brake crank boot. Use a 24mm socket to tap the boot to the caliper.

28. Install the parking brake crank onto the caliper. Make certain the crank boot is securely matched to the groove of the crank seal.

29. Install the cable support bracket. Press the surface of the bracket flush against the wall of the caliper and tighten the bolt to 34 ft. lbs.

30. Check that the clearance between the parking brake crank and the cable support is 6mm.

31. Install the torsion spring.

32. Inspect the crank sub-assembly, making sure it touches the stopper pin.

33. Install the parking brake strut. Before adjusting the strut, adjust the rollers of the needle roller bearing so they do not catch on the caliper bore.

34. Install a new O-ring on the adjusting bolt.

35. Install the stopper, plate, spring, and spring retainer onto the adjusting bolt. Using a special tool or equivalent hand tighten the assembly. Make certain the inscribed portion of the stopper faces upward. Align the notches of the spring retainer with the notches of the stopper.

36. Install the adjusting bolt assembly into the cylinder.

37. Install snapring into the bore. Make cer-

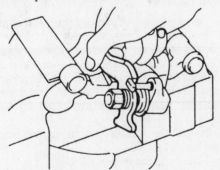

Removing the parking brake crank

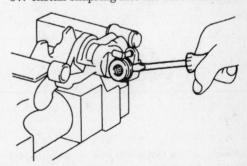

Removing the parking brake crank boot

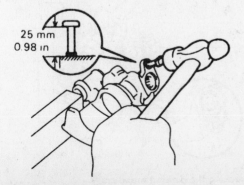

Installing the stopper pin

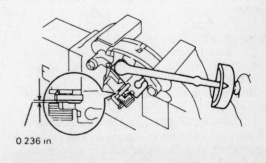

Installing the cable support bracket

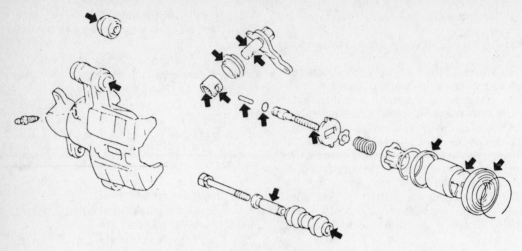

Exploded view of the rear disc brake — parking brake adjuster assembly

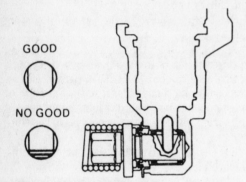

GOOD

NO GOOD

Installation of parking brake strut

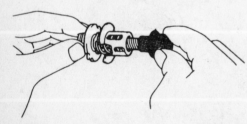

Assembly of the adjusting bolt — special tool shown

tain the gap in the ring faces toward the bleeder side.

38. Pull up on the adjusting bolt by hand to make certain it does not move.

39. Move the parking brake crank by hand and make certain adjusting bolt moves smoothly.

40. Install a new piston seal in the caliper bore.

41. Install the piston into the caliper bore. Using a special tool or its equivalent, slowly screw the piston clockwise until it will not descend any further.

42. Align the center of the piston stopper groove with the positioning marks of the caliper bore.

43. Install the piston dust boot and its set ring.

44. Install a new boot on the main (upper) caliper pin. Use a 21mm socket to press in the new boot.

45. Install the slide bushings and boots onto the caliper.

INSTALLATION

46. Install the brake pads, springs and clips.

47. Install the caliper assembly to the main pin. Before installing the retaining bolts, apply a thin, even coating of anti-seize compound to the threads and slide surfaces. Don't use grease or spray lubricants; they will not hold up under the extreme temperatures generated by the brakes.

48. Install the caliper mounting bolt and tighten it to 14 ft. lbs.

49. Install the parking brake clip.

50. Install the brake hose to the caliper.

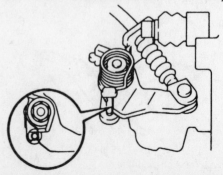

Checking the parking brake crank

Always use new gaskets and tighten the union to 22 ft. lbs.

51. Bleed the brake system.

52. To automatically adjust the parking brake, pull up on the lever several times, then release the lever and step on the brake pedal.

53. Double check that the parking brake crank touches the stopper.

54. Install the rear wheel and lower the car to the ground.

Brake Rotor

REMOVAL

1. Raise and safely support the rear of the vehicle on jackstands. Block the front wheels.

2. Siphon a sufficient quantity of brake fluid from the master cylinder reservoir to prevent the brake fluid from overflowing when removing or installing the brake pads. This is necessary as the piston must be forced into the cylinder bore to provide sufficient clearance to install the pads.

3. Remove the wheel.

NOTE: *Disassemble brakes one wheel at a time. This will prevent parts confusion and also prevent the opposite caliper piston from popping out during pad installation.*

4. Remove the mounting (lower) bolt from the mounting bracket.

5. Lift the caliper from the bottom so that it hinges upward on the upper pin and slide the caliper off the pin. Use a piece of wire to hold the caliper out of the way. Do not disconnect the brake hose and do not allow the brake hose to become twisted or kinked during this operation.

6. Remove the brake pads with their shims, springs and support plates.

7. If the rotor is to be measured, install all the lug nuts to hold the rotor in place. If the nuts are open at both ends, it is helpful to install them backwards (tapered end out) to secure the disc. Tighten the nuts a bit tighter than finger tight, but make sure all are at approximately the same tightness. Follow the measurement and inspection procedures listed under "INSPECTION".

8. Remove the mounting bolts holding the mounting bracket to the rear axle carrier.

9. Remove the lug nuts and remove the rotor.

INSPECTION

Run-out

1. Mount a dial indicator with a magnetic or universal base on the strut so that the tip of the indicator contacts the rotor about 1/2 in. from the outer edge.

2. Zero the dial indicator. Turn the rotor one complete revolution and observe the total indicated run-out.

3. If the run-out exceeds 0.15mm, clean the wheel hub and rotor mating surfaces and re-measure. If the run-out still exceeds maximum, remove the rotor and remount it so that the wheel studs now run through different holes. If this re-indexing does not provide correct run-out measurements, the rotor should be considered warped beyond use and either resurfaced or replaced.

Thickness

The thickness of the rotor partially determines its ability to withstand heat and provide adequate stopping force. Every rotor has a minimum thickness established by the manufacturer. This minimum measurement must not be exceeded. A rotor which is too thin may crack under braking; if this occurs the wheel can lock instantly, resulting in sudden loss of control.

If any part of the rotor measures below minimum thickness, the disc must be replaced. Additionally, a rotor which needs to be resurfaced may not allow sufficient cutting before reaching minimum. Since the allowable wear from new to minimum is about 1mm, it is wise to replace the rotor rather than resurface it.

Thickness and thickness variation can be measured with a micrometer capable of reading to one ten-thousandth inch. All measurements must be made at the same distance in from the edge of the rotor. Measure at four equally spaced points around the disc and record the measurements. Compare each measurement to the minimum thickness specifications in the chart at the end of this chapter.

Compare the four measurements to each other and find the difference between each pair. A rotor varying by more than 0.013mm can cause pedal vibration and/or front end vibration during stops. A rotor which does not meet these specifications should be resurfaced or replaced.

Condition

A new rotor will have a smooth, even surface which rapidly changes during use. It is not uncommon for a rotor to develop very fine concentric scoring (like the grooves on a record) due to dust and grit being trapped by the brake pad. This slight irregularity is normal, but as the grooves deepen, wear and noise increase and stopping may be affected. As a general rule, any groove deep enough to snag a fingernail during inspection is cause for action or replacement.

Any sign of blue spots, discoloration, heavy rusting or outright gouges require replacement of the rotor. If you are checking the disc on the car (such as during pad replacement or tire rotation) remember to turn the disc and check both the inner and outer faces completely. If anything looks questionable or requires consideration, choose the safer option and replace the rotor. The brakes are a critical system and must be maintained at 100% reliability.

Any time a rotor is replaced, the pads should also be replaced so that the surfaces mate properly. Since brake pads should be replaced in axle sets (both front or rear wheels), consider replacing both rotors instead of just one. The restored feel and accurate stopping make the extra investment worthwhile.

INSTALLATION

1. Place the rotor in position over the studs and install two lug nuts finger tight to hold it in place.

2. Install the mounting plate to the rear axle carrier and tighten the mounting bolts to 34 ft. lbs.

3. Install the brake pads, springs and clips.

4. Carefully mount the caliper onto the upper slide pin.

5. Using a special tool or its equivalent to slowly turn the caliper piston clockwise while pressing it into the bore until it locks.

6. Lower the caliper so that the pad protrusion fits into the piston stopper groove.

7. Install the mounting bolt and tighten it to 14 ft. lbs.

8. Remove the lug nuts holding the disc, install the rear wheel and install all the lug nuts.

9. Depress the brake pedal once or twice to take up the excess piston play.

10. Lower the car to the ground and fill the master cylinder reservoir to the correct level. Final tighten the lug nuts.

PARKING BRAKE

Cables

REMOVAL AND INSTALLATION

NOTE: *This procedure is general service procedure (no factory service procedure given). On all models modify the service steps as required.*

1. Elevate and safely support the car. If only the rear wheels are elevated, block the front wheels. Release the parking brake after the car is supported.

2. Remove the rear wheel(s).

3. If equipped with drum brakes, remove the brake drum and remove the brake shoes.

4. If equipped with disc brakes, remove the clip from the parking brake cable and remove the cable from the caliper assembly.

5. If equipped with drum brakes, remove the parking brake retaining bolts at the backing plate.

6. Remove any exhaust heat shields which interfere with the removal of the cable.

7. Remove the 2 cable clamps.

8. Disconnect the cable retainer.

9. Remove the cable from the equalizer (yoke).

10. When reinstalling, fit the end of the new cable into the equalizer and make certain it is properly seated.

11. Install the cable retainer, and, working along the length of the cable, install the clamps.

12. Feed the cable through the backing plate and install the retaining bolts.

13. If equipped with disc brakes, connect the cable to the arm and install the clip.

14. If equipped with drum brakes, re-install the shoes. The cable will be connected to the shoes during the installation process.

15. Reinstall the wheel(s) and lower the car to the ground.

ADJUSTMENT

All models except MR2

Pull the parking brake lever all the way up and count the number of clicks. The correct range is 4–7 clicks rear drum brake type and 5–8 clicks rear disc brake type for all Corolla models before full application. Also the correct range is 6–9 clicks for all Tercel models before full application. A system which is too tight or too loose requires adjustment.

NOTE: *BEFORE ADJUSTING THE PARKING BRAKE CABLE, MAKE CERTAIN THAT THE REAR BRAKE SHOE TO DRUM CLEARANCE IS CORRECT.*

1. Remove the center console box.

2. At the rear of the hand brake lever, loosen the locknut on the brake cable.

3. Turn the adjusting nut until the parking brake travel is correct.

4. Tighten the locknut.

5. Reinstall the console.

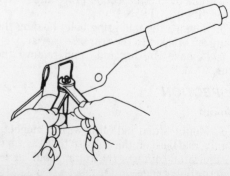

Parking brake adjustment

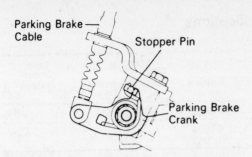

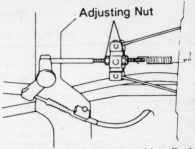

Checking parking brake crank — touches stopper pin — MR2

Adjusting nut parking brake assembly adjustment — MR2

MR2

Depress the brake pedal several times. Pull the parking brake lever all the way up and count the number of clicks. The correct range is 5–8 clicks before full application. A system which is too tight or too loose requires adjustment.

1. Raise and safely support the vehicle.
2. Remove the fuel tank protector.

3. Loosen the adjusting nut and brake cable. Check that the parking brake crank touches stopper pin.

4. Stretch the brake cable by turning the adjusting nut before the parking brake crank begin moving. Tighten the adjusting nuts to 12 ft. lbs. (equalizer should be horizontal to the ground).

5. Install the fuel tank protector.

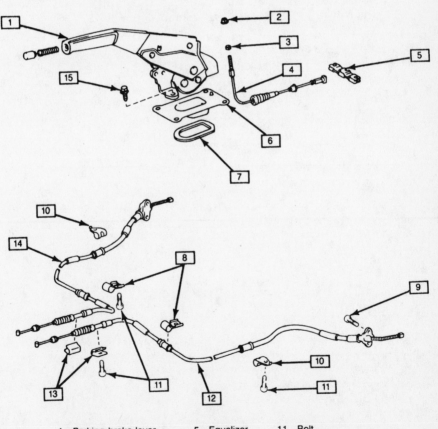

1. Parking brake lever assembly	5. Equalizer	11. Bolt
2. Lock nut	6. Lever boot	12. Left cable
3. Parking brake adjuster nut	7. Shield	13. Retainer clamp
	8. Clamp	14. Right cable
4. Front cable	9. Bolt	15. Lever retaining bolt
	10. Clamp	

Exploded view of parking brake cable assembly

Brake Specifications
All measurements given are inches unless noted

Years	Models	Original Thickness	Brake Disc Minimum Thickness	Maximum Run-out	Brake Drum Max. Inside Dia.	Wear Limit	Lining Minimum Thickness Front	Rear
1985–88	Corolla	0.551	0.492	0.0059	7.874	7.913	0.039	0.039
1988	Corolla	F 0.354 R 0.354	0.315 0.315	0.0059 0.0059	—	—	0.039	0.309
1989–90	Corolla	0.709	0.669	0.0035	7.874	7.913	0.039	0.039
1985–86	MR2	—	F 0.670 R 0.354	0.006 0.006	—	—	0.039	0.039
1987–89	MR2	—	F 0.827 R 0.354	0.005 0.005	—	—	0.039	0.039
1984	Tercel (4 × 2)	—	0.394	0.006	7.087	7.126	0.040	0.040
	Tercel (4 × 4)	—	0.394	0.006	7.874	7.913	0.040	0.040
1985–90	Tercel (Sedan)	—	0.394	0.006	7.087	7.126	0.040	0.040
	Tercel (Wagon)	—	0.394	0.006	7.874	7.913	0.040	0.040

NOTE: Minimum lining thickness is as recommended by the manufacturer. Because of variations in state inspection regulations, the minimum allowable thickness may be different than recommended by the manufacturer. Always use these specifications as a guide—refer to a local machine shop for drum and disc resurfacing limits.

EXTERIOR

Doors

REMOVAL AND INSTALLATION

1. Pull the door stopper pin upward while pushing in on the claw. Leave the claw raised after removing the pin.

2. Place a wooden block or equivalent under the door for protection and support it with a floor jack.

3. Remove the door mounting bolts (special box wrenches are available to remove the door hinge mounting bolts) and remove the door.

4. Installation is the reverse of removal. Adjust the door as necessary.

ADJUSTMENT

NOTE: *Since the centering bolt is used as the door hinge set bolt, the door can not be adjusted with it on. Replace the bolt with washer for the centering bolt refer to the necessary illustration.*

1. To adjust the door in the forward/rearward and vertical directions, loosen the body side hinge bolts and move the door to the desired position.

2. To adjust the door in the left/right and vertical direction, loosen the door side hinge bolts and move the door to the desired position.

3. Adjust the door lock striker as necessary

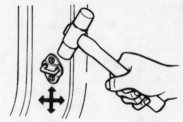

Front door lock striker adjustment

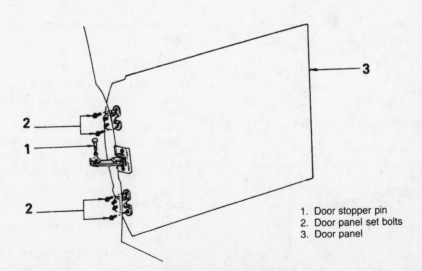

1. Door stopper pin
2. Door panel set bolts
3. Door panel

Front door hinge assemblies

by slightly loosening the striker mounting screws, and hitting the striker lightly with a hammer or equivalent. Tighten the striker mounting screws.

Hood

REMOVAL AND INSTALLATION

1. Protect the painted areas such as the fenders with a protective cover or equivalent.
2. Matchmark the hood hinges to the vehicle body. Loosen the hinge to vehicle body retaining bolts.
3. With the aid of an assistant remove the retaining bolts and lift the hood (with hood hinge assemblies attached to hood) away from the car. Remove the hood hinges (matchmark hinges to the hood for correct installation) if necessary.
4. Installation is the reverse of removal. Align the hood to the proper position.

Alignment

NOTE: *Since the centering bolt is used as the hood hinge set bolt, the hood can not be adjusted with it on. Replace the bolt with washer for the centering bolt refer to the necessary illustration.*

1. For forward/rearward and left/right adjustments, loosen the body side hinge bolts and move the hood the desired position.
2. For vertical adjustment of the hoods front edge, turn the cushion.
3. For vertical adjustment of the rear end of the hood, increase or decrease the number of washers or shims.

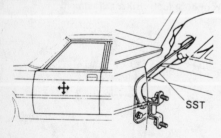

Front door forward/rearward adjustment

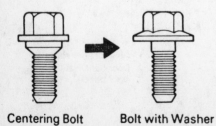

Centering Bolt   **Bolt with Washer**

Adjustment bolt

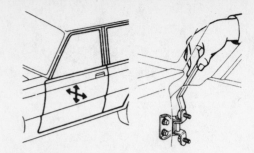

Front door up and down adjustment

4. Adjust the hood lock if necessary by loosening the bolts.

Luggage Compartment Lid

REMOVAL AND INSTALLATION

Coupe/Sedan

1. Remove the hinge mounting bolts.
2. It may be necessary to remove the torsion bar.
3. Installation is the reverse of removal. Adjust as necessary.

Liftback

1. Disconnect the lift cylinder from the body.
2. Remove the hinge bolts and remove the lid.
3. Installation is the reverse of removal. Adjust as necessary.

ADJUSTMENT

1. For forward/rearward and left/right adjustments, loosen the bolts and move the hood the desired position.
2. For vertical adjustment of the front end of the lid, increase or decrease the number of washers.

Lift Cylinder

REMOVAL AND INSTALLATION

NOTE: *Do not disassemble the cylinder because it is filled with pressurized gas. If the damper cylinder is to be replaced, drill a 2mm hole in the bottom of the REMOVED damper cylinder to completely release the high pressure gas before disposing of the assembly.*

Coupe/Sedan

1. Remove the lift cylinder upper end from the lid.
2. Remove the lift cylinder lower end from hinge.
3. Install lift cylinder lower end to hinge.
4. Install lift cylinder upper end to lid. Adjust the lid as necessary.

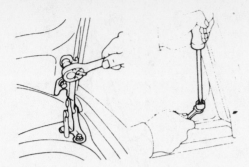

Adjust hood hinge (all directions)

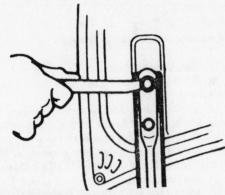

Adjust the luggage compartment lid Coupe/sedan

Liftback

1. Remove the roof side inner garnish as necessary.
2. Remove the lift cylinder lower end from the body.
3. Remove the lift cylinder upper end from the back door.
4. Installation is the reverse of the removal procedures. Adjust the liftback as necessary.

Bumpers

REMOVAL AND INSTALLATION

NOTE: *This is a general procedure for front and rear bumpers assemblies-modify service steps as necessary.*
1. Raise and safely support the vehicle as necessary.
2. Disconnect all electrical connections at the bumper assembly.
3. Remove the bumper mounting bolts and bumper assembly. Remove the shock absorbers from the bumper as necessary.
NOTE: *The shock absorber is filled with a high pressure gas and should not be disassembled.*
4. Install shock absorber and bumper assemble in the reverse order of the removal. Align the bumper assemblies for the correct fit as necessary.

Outside Mirror
REMOVAL AND INSTALLATION
Manual And Electric

1. On manual mirrors, remove the setting screw and knob. Tape the end of a thin screwdriver or equivalent and pry retainer loose to remove the cover.
2. Remove the 3 retaining screws and remove the mirror assembly.
3. On electric mirrors (follow service procedure as outlined-remove cover and mounting screws) disconnect electrical connector to mirror then remove the mirror assembly.
4. Installation is the reverse of the removal procedure. Cycle the mirror several times to make sure that it works properly.

Antenna

NOTE: *On most applications the mast and cable are one piece. If the mast is damaged or broken, the entire antenna assembly including the cable must be replaced.*

REMOVAL AND INSTALLATION

1. Remove the console side panel, to the right of the accelerator pedal as necessary.
2. Disconnect the antenna cable from the radio by reaching through the back of the console and disconnecting the cable from its socket. If you can't quite reach or release the cable, the radio will have to be loosened in the dash and disconnected from the front.
3. Remove the two screws holding the hood release lever and move the lever out of the way.

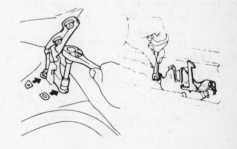

Adjust hood (vertical direction) and hood lock

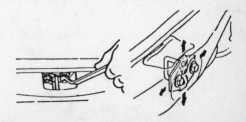

Adjust the luggage compartment lock and striker — Coupe/sedan

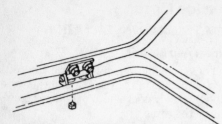

Adjust the luggage compartment lid — liftback

4. Remove the lower left dashboard trim and disconnect the speaker wiring.

5. Remove the left side kick panel.

6. Remove the retaining screw and remove the left side cowl trim.

7. Attach a long piece of mechanic's wire or heavy string to the end of the antenna wire. This will track up through the pillar as you remove the old antenna and be available to pull the new line into place.

8. Remove the two attaching screws at the antenna mast. Remove the antenna and carefully pull the cable up the pillar. Use a helper to insure the end inside the car does not snag or pull other wires.

9. Remove the mechanic's wire or twine from the old cable and attach it to the new cable. Make sure it is tied so that the plug will stay straight during installation.

10. With your helper, feed the new cable into the pillar while pulling gently on the guide wire or string. Route the antenna cable properly under the dash, making sure it will not foul on the steering column or pedal linkages. Route the cable high enough that there is no chance of it hanging around the driver's feet. Use tape or cable ties to secure it.

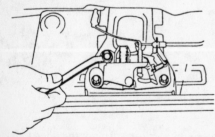

Adjust the luggage compartment lock and striker — liftback

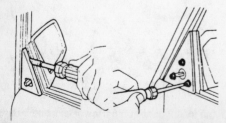

Removal of the outside mirror

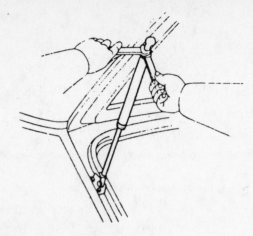

Removal of damper stay — liftback

11. Remove the guide line from the antenna cable. Route the antenna into the radio and install the connector.

12. Install the attaching screws holding the mast to the pillar. Make sure the screws are properly threaded and that both the screws and their holes are free of dirt or corrosion. A poor connection at these screws can affect antenna and radio performance.

13. Install the left side cowl trim and the left side kick panel.

14. Connect the speaker wiring and install the lower left dashboard trim.

15. Install the hood release lever.

16. Install the console side panel.

Windshield Rear Window Glass (Coupe/Sedan) Back Door Glass (Liftback)

REMOVAL AND INSTALLATION

The windshield and rear glass assemblies are installed with a urethane bonding agent and installation has to conform to Federal Motor Vehicle Safety Standards. Special tools and service procedures are necessary to perform this kind of repair. Therefore all glass replacement work should be performed by a qualified technician at a professional glass shop.

INTERIOR

Door Panels

REMOVAL AND INSTALLATION

1. Remove the door inside handle (pull handle) and arm rest, if so equipped.

2. Remove the regulator handle snap ring with a tool or pull off the snap ring with a cloth.

3. Remove the door lock lever bezel, inside

Removing the door regulator handle with a soft cloth

handle bezel and door courtesy light, if so equipped.

4. Remove the door trim retaining screws.

5. Loosen the door trim by prying between the retainers (tape the screwdriver before use) and the door trim then disconnect the power window switch, if so equipped.

6. Installation is the reverse of removal procedure. Handle the door trim panel with care after removal.

Door Locks

REMOVAL AND INSTALLATION

1. Remove the inside door trim panel and access cover.

2. Disconnect the links from the outside handle and door lock cylinder.

3. On models with power door locks it will be necessary to disconnect the connectors from the door lock solenoid and key unlock switch.

4. Remove the door lock retaining bolts or screws and remove the door lock.

5. Installation is the reverse of removal procedure.

Door Lock Cylinders

REMOVAL AND INSTALLATION

1. Remove the door trim panel.

2. Carefully remove the water deflector shield from inside the door. Take your time and don't rip it.

3. Disconnect the link rod running between the lock cylinder and the lock/latch mechanism.

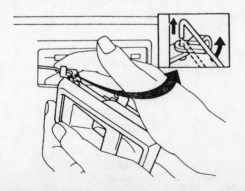

Disconnecting door handle

4. The lock is held to the door by a horseshoe shaped retaining clip. Slide the clip free of the lock and remove the cylinder from the outside of the door.

5. Install the new cylinder and install the clip. The retaining clip has a slight bend in it and will install under tension. Do not attempt to straighten the clip.

6. Connect the link rod.

7. Install the water deflector shield, making sure that it is intact and firmly attached all the way around.

8. Reinstall the door trim panel.

Door Glass and Regulator

REMOVAL AND INSTALLATION

Early Model Front Glass

NOTE: *Refer to exploded view of door assembly components as a guide for this repair-for all models modify this service procedure as necessary.*

1. Remove the door trim panel.

2. Carefully remove the water deflector shield and lower the window glass fully.

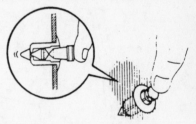

Locking the trim panel with locking clip

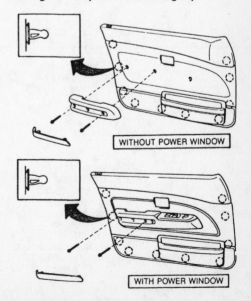

Removing the front door panels — rear door panels are similar

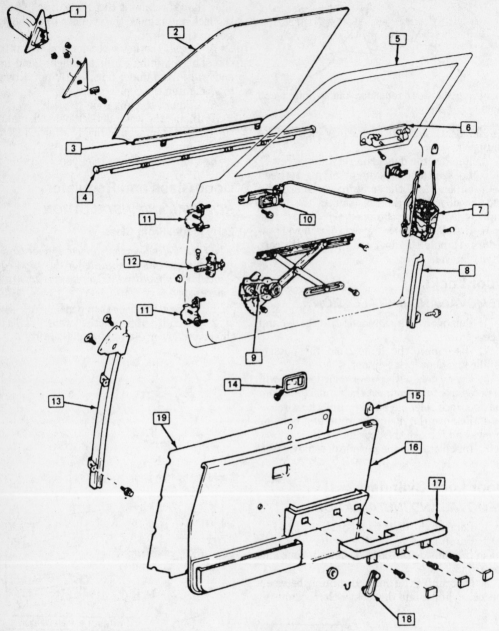

1. Mirror assembly
2. Window glass
3. Sash channel
4. Door belt molding
5. Door assembly
6. Outer handle
7. Door latch/lock assembly
8. Rear run channel guide
9. Window regulator
10. Inner handle
11. Hinge
12. Door check
13. Front run channel guide
14. Inner handle bezel
15. Lock knob
16. Door trim panel
17. Armrest
18. Window winder handle
19. Water deflector shield

Front door assembly components — early model

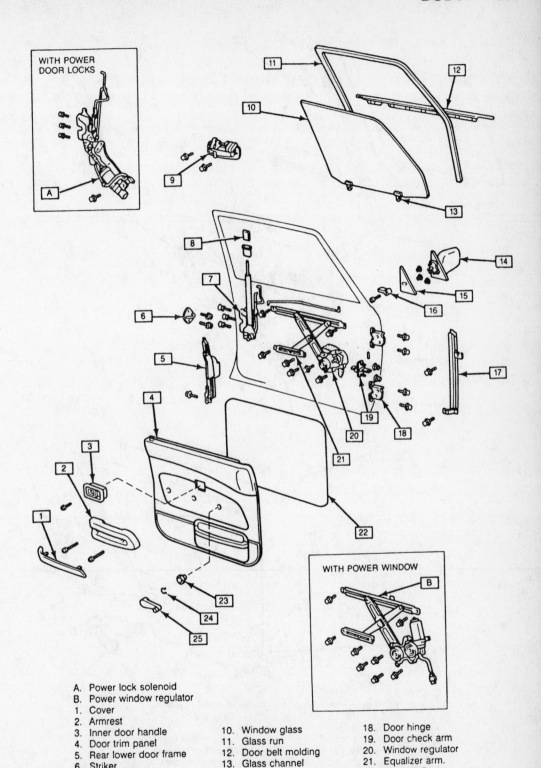

WITH POWER DOOR LOCKS

WITH POWER WINDOW

A. Power lock solenoid
B. Power window regulator
1. Cover
2. Armrest
3. Inner door handle
4. Door trim panel
5. Rear lower door frame
6. Striker
7. Door latch/lock
8. Lock knob
9. Outer handle and lock
   cylinder

10. Window glass
11. Glass run
12. Door belt molding
13. Glass channel
14. Side mirror
15. Cover
16. Adjustment knob
17. Front lower door frame

18. Door hinge
19. Door check arm
20. Window regulator
21. Equalizer arm.
22. Water deflector
23. Plate
24. Spring clip
25. Window winder handle

Front door assembly components — late model

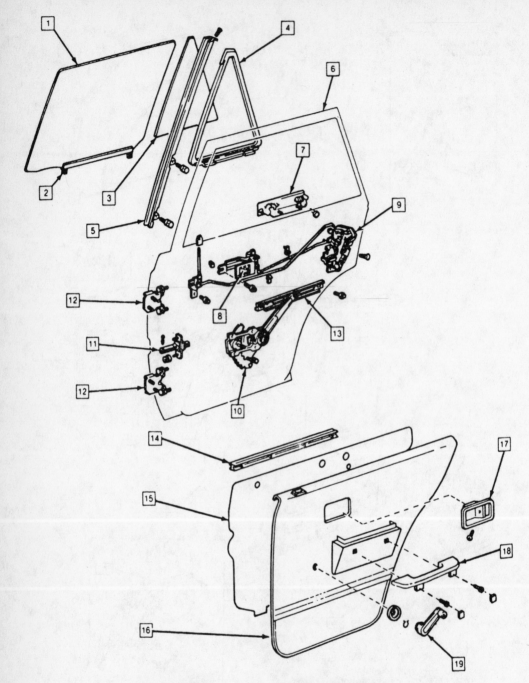

1. Window glass
2. Sash channel
3. Stationary window
4. Weather strip
5. Run channel guide
6. Door assembly
7. Outer handle
8. Inner handle
9. Door latch/lock assembly
10. Window regulator
11. Door check
12. Hinge
13. Lift arm bracket
14. Door belt molding
15. Water deflector
16. Trim panel
17. Inner handle bezel
18. Armrest
19. Window winder handle

Rear door assembly components — early model

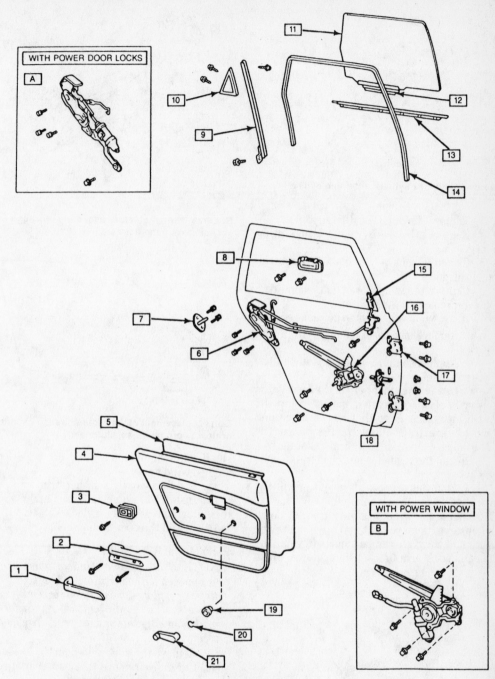

WITH POWER DOOR LOCKS

A

WITH POWER WINDOW

B

A.	Door lock solenoid	7.	Striker	15.	Lock knob
B.	Power window regulator	8.	Outer handle	16.	window regulator
1.	Cover	9.	Rear lower frame	17.	Hinge
2.	Armrest	10.	Rear guide seal	18.	Door check arm
3.	Inner handle	11.	Window glass	19.	Plate
4.	Trim panel	12.	Glass channel	20.	Spring clip
5.	Water deflector	13.	Belt molding	21.	Regulator arms
6.	Door latch/lock	14.	Glass run		

Rear door assembly components — late model

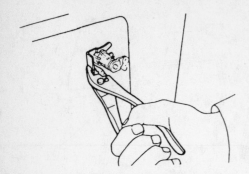

Removing the lock cylinder retaining clip

3. Remove the outer weatherstrip.
4. Remove the sash channel mounting bolts.
5. Carefully remove the glass through the top of the door.
6. Remove the window regulator mounting bolts and remove the regulator
7. If the window glass is to be replaced:
   a. Remove the sash channel from the glass.
   b. Apply a solution of soapy water to the sash channel.
   c. Install the channel to the new glass using a plastic or leather mallet to tap the sash into place. Note that the sash channel must be exactly positioned on the glass or the bolt holes will not align at reinstallation.
8. Install the regulator and tighten the bolts evenly.
9. Install the window glass and install the sash channel mounting bolts.
10. Wind the window slowly up and down and observe its movement and alignment. The position of the glass can be adjusted by moving the equalizing arm bracket up or down. Make

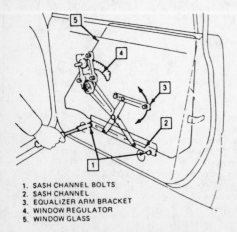

1. SASH CHANNEL BOLTS
2. SASH CHANNEL
3. EQUALIZER ARM BRACKET
4. WINDOW REGULATOR
5. WINDOW GLASS

Removing the sash channel mounting bolts

Remove the regulator assembly through the access hole in the door

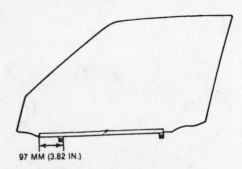

97 MM (3.82 IN.)

Correct placement of the regulator sash channel is critical to proper glass alignment

small adjustments and work for a perfectly aligned window.
11. Install the outer weatherstrip.
12. Install the water deflector, making sure it is intact and properly sealed.
13. Install the door trim panel.

Early Model Rear Glass

NOTE: *The movable window glass cannot be removed without removing the fixed glass. Refer to exploded view of door assembly components as a guide for this repair-for all models modify this service procedure as necessary.*

1. Remove the door trim panel.
2. Carefully remove the water deflector shield and lower the window glass fully.
3. Remove the outer weatherstrip.
4. Partially remove the door weatherstrip to remove the run channel guide upper retaining screw.
5. Remove the rubber or felt run channel.
6. Remove the 2 lower run channel guide bolts and remove the guide.
7. Pull the fixed glass forward and remove it. Place it in a safe and protected location, away from the work area.
8. Remove the sash channel bolts.

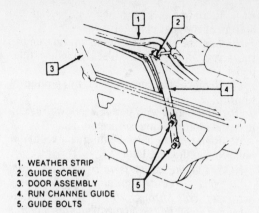

1. WEATHER STRIP
2. GUIDE SCREW
3. DOOR ASSEMBLY
4. RUN CHANNEL GUIDE
5. GUIDE BOLTS

Removing rear door run channel guide

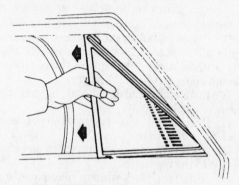

Removing fixed rear glass

9. Carefully remove the glass through the top of the door.

10. Remove the window regulator mounting bolts and remove the regulator.

11. If the window glass is to be replaced:

   a. Remove the sash channel from the glass.

   b. Apply a solution of soapy water to the sash channel.

   c. Install the channel to the new glass using a plastic or leather mallet to tap the sash into place. Note that the sash channel must be exactly positioned on the glass or the bolt holes will not align at reinstallation.

12. Install the regulator and tighten the bolts evenly.

13. Install the window glass and install the sash channel mounting bolts.

14. Reinstall the fixed glass and make certain it is correctly positioned.

15. Install the run channel guide and install the two lower retaining bolts.

16. Install the felt or rubber run channel. Make certain there are no twists or kinks in the channel.

17. Install the top screw in the channel guide and secure the door weatherstrip.

18. Wind the window slowly up and down

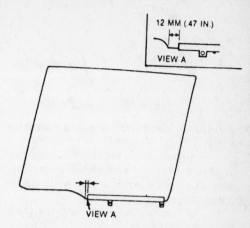

Correct placement of sash channel on rear glass

and observe its movement and alignment. The position of the glass can be adjusted by moving the equalizing arm bracket up or down. Make small adjustments and work for a perfectly aligned window.

19. Install the outer weatherstrip.

20. Install the water deflector, making sure it is intact and properly sealed.

21. Install the door trim panel.

Late Model Front Glass

NOTE: *Refer to exploded view of door assembly components as a guide for this repair-for all models modify this service procedure as necessary.*

1. Remove the door trim panel.

2. Carefully remove the water deflector shield and lower the window glass fully.

3. Remove the glass channel mounting bolts.

4. Remove the window glass by lifting it through the top of the door.

5. Disconnect the window regulator as follows:

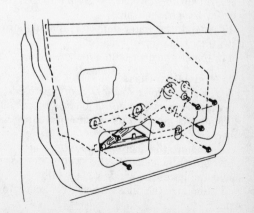

Front door window regulator

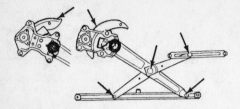

Points to be lubricated before installing front or rear regulator — do not lubricate the spiral spring

a. For power windows, disconnect the electrical connector and remove the 4 mounting bolts. The regulator will be removed with the motor attached.

b. For manual windows, remove the 3 mounting bolts.

6. Remove the two mounting bolts holding the equalizer arm bracket.

7. Remove the window regulator.

NOTE: *If the motor is to be removed from the power window regulator, install a large stopper bolt through the regulator frame before removing the motor. When the motor is removed, the spring loaded gear will be disengaged, causing the gear to rotate until the spring is unwound. Install the stopper bolt to prevent possible injury by the spinning gear.*

8. Before installing the regulator assembly, apply a light coat of lithium grease to the sliding surfaces and pivot points of the regulator. Do not apply grease to the spring.

9. Install the regulator:

a. With power windows, install the 4 mounting bolts and connect the motor wiring.

b. With manual windows, install the 3 mounting bolts.

10. Install the bolts holding the equalizer arm bracket.

11. Place the glass into the door and install the glass channel retaining bolts.

12. Adjust the door glass by moving the equalizer arm up or down as necessary to get the window level in the frame.

13. Install the water deflector, making sure it is intact and properly sealed.

14. Install the door trim panel.

Late Model Rear Glass

NOTE: *Refer to exploded view of door assembly components as a guide for this repair-for all models modify this service procedure as necessary.*

1. Remove the door trim panel.

2. Carefully remove the water deflector shield and lower the window glass fully.

3. Remove the glass from the regulator arm.

4. Loosen the window weatherstrip at the rear edge of the glass run channel.

5. Remove the screws holding the top and bottom of the rear channel guide.

6. Lift the door weatherstrip and remove the screws holding the (black) window filler panel.

7. Remove the door glass by pulling it upward.

8. If equipped with power windows, disconnect the motor wiring connector.

9. Remove the bolts holding the regulator and remove the regulator.

NOTE: *If the motor is to be removed from the power window regulator, install a large stopper bolt through the regulator frame before removing the motor. When the motor is removed, the spring loaded gear will be disengaged, causing the gear to rotate until the spring is unwound. Install the stopper bolt to prevent possible injury by the spinning gear.*

10. Before installing the regulator assembly, apply a light coat of lithium grease to the sliding surfaces and pivot points of the regulator. Do not apply grease to the spring.

11. Install the regulator and tighten the mounting bolts evenly.

12. If equipped with power windows, connect the wiring to the motor.

13. Install the glass into the door and connect it to the regulator.

14. Install the black window filler panel and its 2 screws.

15. Install the rear glass guide channel.

16. Install the window weatherstrip.

17. Install the water deflector, making sure it is intact and properly sealed.

18. Install the door trim panel.

Inside Mirror

REMOVAL AND INSTALLATION

The inside mirror is removed by carefully prying off the plastic cover and removing the retaining bolts. The inside mirror is designed to break loose from the roof mount if it receives moderate impact. If the mirror has come off

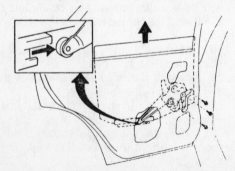

Rear door glass regulator

CHILTON'S
AUTO BODY REPAIR TIPS

Tools and Materials • Step-by-Step Illustrated Procedures
How To Repair Dents, Scratches and Rust Holes
Spray Painting and Refinishing Tips

With a little practice, basic body repair procedures can be mastered by any do-it-yourself mechanic. The step-by-step repairs shown here can be applied to almost any type of auto body repair.

TOOLS & MATERIALS

You may already have basic tools, such as hammers and electric drills. Other tools unique to body repair — body hammers, grinding attachments, sanding blocks, dent puller, half-round plastic file and plastic spreaders — are relatively inexpensive and can be obtained wherever auto parts or auto body repair parts are sold. Portable air compressors and paint spray guns can be purchased or rented.

Auto Body Repair Kits

The best and most often used products are available to the do-it-yourselfer in kit form, from major manufacturers of auto body repair products. The same manufacturers also merchandise the individual products for use by pros.

Kits are available to make a wide variety of repairs, including holes, dents and scratches and fiberglass, and offer the advantage of buying the materials you'll need for the job. There is little waste or chance of materials going bad from not being used. Many kits may also contain basic body-working tools such as body files, sanding blocks and spreaders. Check the contents of the kit before buying your tools.

BODY REPAIR TIPS

Safety

Many of the products associated with auto body repair and refinishing contain toxic chemicals. Read all labels before opening containers and store them in a safe place and manner.

• Wear eye protection (safety goggles) when using power tools or when performing any operation that involves the removal of any type of material.

• Wear lung protection (disposable mask or respirator) when grinding, sanding or painting.

Sanding

1 Sand off paint before using a dent puller. When using a non-adhesive sanding disc, cover the back of the disc with an overlapping layer or two of masking tape and trim the edges. The disc will last considerably longer.

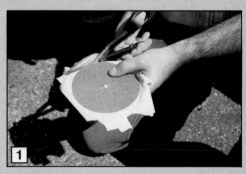

2 Use the circular motion of the sanding disc to grind *into* the edge of the repair. Grinding or sanding away from the jagged edge will only tear the sandpaper.

3 Use the palm of your hand flat on the panel to detect high and low spots. Do not use your fingertips. Slide your hand slowly back and forth.

WORKING WITH BODY FILLER

Mixing The Filler

Cleanliness and proper mixing and application are extremely important. Use a clean piece of plastic or glass or a disposable artist's palette to mix body filler.

1 Allow plenty of time and follow directions. No useful purpose will be served by adding more hardener to make it cure (set-up) faster. Less hardener means more curing time, but the mixture dries harder; more hardener means less curing time but a softer mixture.

2 Both the hardener and the filler should be thoroughly kneaded or stirred before mixing. Hardener should be a solid paste and dispense like thin toothpaste. Body filler should be smooth, and free of lumps or thick spots.

Getting the proper amount of hardener in the filler is the trickiest part of preparing the filler. Use the same amount of hardener in cold or warm weather. For contour filler (thick coats), a bead of hardener twice the diameter of the filler is about right. There's about a 15% margin on either side, but, if in doubt use less hardener.

3 Mix the body filler and hardener by wiping across the mixing surface, picking the mixture up and wiping it again. Colder weather requires longer mixing times. Do not mix in a circular motion; this will trap air bubbles which will become holes in the cured filler.

Applying The Filler

1 For best results, filler should not be applied over 1/4" thick.

Apply the filler in several coats. Build it up to above the level of the repair surface so that it can be sanded or grated down.

The first coat of filler must be pressed on with a firm wiping motion.

Apply the filler in one direction only. Working the filler back and forth will either pull it off the metal or trap air bubbles.

REPAIRING DENTS

Before you start, take a few minutes to study the damaged area. Try to visualize the shape of the panel before it was damaged. If the damage is on the left fender, look at the right fender and use it as a guide. If there is access to the panel from behind, you can reshape it with a body hammer. If not, you'll have to use a dent puller. Go slowly and work the metal a little at a time. Get the panel as straight as possible before applying filler.

1 This dent is typical of one that can be pulled out or hammered out from behind. Remove the headlight cover, headlight assembly and turn signal housing.

2 Drill a series of holes ½ the size of the end of the dent puller along the stress line. Make some trial pulls and assess the results. If necessary, drill more holes and try again. Do not hurry.

3 If possible, use a body hammer and block to shape the metal back to its original contours. Get the metal back as close to its original shape as possible. Don't depend on body filler to fill dents.

4 Using an 80-grit grinding disc on an electric drill, grind the paint from the surrounding area down to bare metal. Use a new grinding pad to prevent heat buildup that will warp metal.

5 The area should look like this when you're finished grinding. Knock the drill holes in and tape over small openings to keep plastic filler out.

6 Mix the body filler (see Body Repair Tips). Spread the body filler evenly over the entire area (see Body Repair Tips). Be sure to cover the area completely.

7 Let the body filler dry until the surface can just be scratched with your fingernail. Knock the high spots from the body filler with a body file ("Cheesegrater"). Check frequently with the palm of your hand for high and low spots.

8 Check to be sure that trim pieces that will be installed later will fit exactly. Sand the area with 40-grit paper.

9 If you wind up with low spots, you may have to apply another layer of filler.

10 Knock the high spots off with 40-grit paper. When you are satisfied with the contours of the repair, apply a thin coat of filler to cover pin holes and scratches.

11 Block sand the area with 40-grit paper to a smooth finish. Pay particular attention to body lines and ridges that must be well-defined.

12 Sand the area with 400 paper and then finish with a scuff pad. The finished repair is ready for priming and painting (see Painting Tips).

Materials and photos courtesy of Ritt Jones Auto Body, Prospect Park, PA.

REPAIRING RUST HOLES

There are many ways to repair rust holes. The fiberglass cloth kit shown here is one of the most cost efficient for the owner because it provides a strong repair that resists cracking and moisture and is relatively easy to use. It can be used on large and small holes (with or without backing) and can be applied over contoured areas. Remember, however, that short of replacing an entire panel, no repair is a guarantee that the rust will not return.

1 Remove any trim that will be in the way. Clean away all loose debris. Cut away all the rusted metal. But be sure to leave enough metal to retain the contour or body shape.

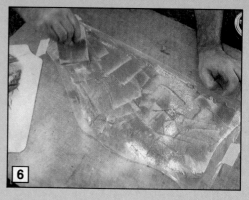

2 Grind away all traces of rust with a 24-grit grinding disc. Be sure to grind back 3-4 inches from the edge of the hole down to bare metal and be sure all traces of paint, primer and rust are removed.

6 Lay the release sheet on a flat surface and spread an even layer of filler, large enough to cover the repair. Lay the smaller piece of fiberglass cloth in the center of the sheet and spread another layer of filler over the fiberglass cloth. Repeat the operation for the larger piece of cloth.

3 Block sand the area with 80 or 100 grit sandpaper to get a clear, shiny surface and feathered paint edge. Tap the edges of the hole inward with a ball peen hammer.

4 If you are going to use release film, cut a piece about 2-3″ larger than the area you have sanded. Place the film over the repair and mark the sanded area on the film. Avoid any unnecessary wrinkling of the film.

7 Place the repair material over the repair area, with the release film facing outward. Use a spreader and work from the center outward to smooth the material, following the body contours. Be sure to remove all air bubbles.

5 Cut 2 pieces of fiberglass matte to match the shape of the repair. One piece should be about 1″ smaller than the sanded area and the second piece should be 1″ smaller than the first. Mix enough filler and hardener to saturate the fiberglass material (see Body Repair Tips).

8 Wait until the repair has dried tack-free and peel off the release sheet. The ideal working temperature is 60°-90° F. Cooler or warmer temperatures or high humidity may require additional curing time. Wait longer, if in doubt.

9 Sand and feather-edge the entire area. The initial sanding can be done with a sanding disc on an electric drill if care is used. Finish the sanding with a block sander. Low spots can be filled with body filler; this may require several applications.

10 When the filler can just be scratched with a fingernail, knock the high spots down with a body file and smooth the entire area with 80-grit. Feather the filled areas into the surrounding areas.

11 When the area is sanded smooth, mix some topcoat and hardener and apply it directly with a spreader. This will give a smooth finish and prevent the glass matte from showing through the paint.

12 Block sand the topcoat smooth with finishing sandpaper (200 grit), and 400 grit. The repair is ready for masking, priming and painting (see Painting Tips).

Materials and photos courtesy Marson Corporation, Chelsea, Massachusetts

PAINTING TIPS

Preparation

1 SANDING — Use a 400 or 600 grit wet or dry sandpaper. Wet-sand the area with a ¼ sheet of sandpaper soaked in clean water. Keep the paper wet while sanding. Sand the area until the repaired area tapers into the original finish.

2 CLEANING — Wash the area to be painted thoroughly with water and a clean rag. Rinse it thoroughly and wipe the surface dry until you're sure it's completely free of dirt, dust, fingerprints, wax, detergent or other foreign matter.

3 MASKING — Protect any areas you don't want to overspray by covering them with masking tape and newspaper. Be careful not get fingerprints on the area to be painted.

4 PRIMING — All exposed metal should be primed before painting. Primer protects the metal and provides an excellent surface for paint adhesion. When the primer is dry, wet-sand the area again with 600 grit wet-sandpaper. Clean the area again after sanding.

Painting Techniques

P aint applied from either a spray gun or a spray can (for small areas) will provide good results. Experiment on an old piece of metal to get the right combination before you begin painting.

SPRAYING VISCOSITY (SPRAY GUN ONLY) — Paint should be thinned to spraying viscosity according to the directions on the can. Use only the recommended thinner or reducer and the same amount of reduction regardless of temperature.

AIR PRESSURE (SPRAY GUN ONLY) — This is extremely important. Be sure you are using the proper recommended pressure.

TEMPERATURE — The surface to be painted should be approximately the same temperature as the surrounding air. Applying warm paint to a cold surface, or vice versa, will completely upset the paint characteristics.

THICKNESS — Spray with smooth strokes. In general, the thicker the coat of paint, the longer the drying time. Apply several thin coats about 30 seconds apart. The paint should remain wet long enough to flow out and no longer; heavier coats will only produce sags or wrinkles. Spray a light (fog) coat, followed by heavier color coats.

DISTANCE — The ideal spraying distance is 8"-12" from the gun or can to the surface. Shorter distances will produce ripples, while greater distances will result in orange peel, dry film and poor color match and loss of material due to overspray.

OVERLAPPING — The gun or can should be kept at right angles to the surface at all times. Work to a wet edge at an even speed, using a 50% overlap and direct the center of the spray at the lower or nearest edge of the previous stroke.

RUBBING OUT (BLENDING) FRESH PAINT — Let the paint dry thoroughly. Runs or imperfections can be sanded out, primed and repainted.

Don't be in too big a hurry to remove the masking. This only produces paint ridges. When the finish has dried for at least a week, apply a small amount of fine grade rubbing compound with a clean, wet cloth. Use lots of water and blend the new paint with the surrounding area.

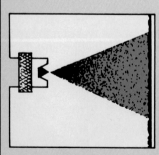

WRONG

Thin coat. Stroke too fast, not enough overlap, gun too far away.

CORRECT

Medium coat. Proper distance, good stroke, proper overlap.

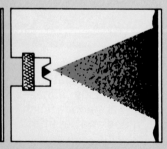

WRONG

Heavy coat. Stroke too slow, too much overlap, gun too close.

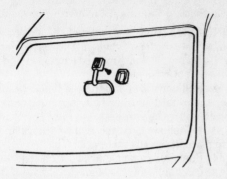

Inside mirror

due to impact, it can usually be remounted by installing a new mirror base rather than an entire new mirror. If the glass is cracked, the mirror must be replaced.

Seats

REMOVAL AND INSTALLATION

Front Seats

The front seats are removed by disconnecting the 4 mounting bolts holding the seat to the floor rails. The bolts may be under plastic covers which can be popped off with a small

tool. The seat assembly will come out of the car complete with the tracks and adjuster. When reinstalling the seat, make certain that the bolts are properly threaded and tightened to 27 ft. lbs. SEAT MOUNTING AND RETENTION IS A CRITICAL SAFETY ITEM. NEVER ATTEMPT TO ALTER THE MOUNTS OR THE SEAT TRACKS.

Rear Bench Seat Cushion

1. Pull forward on the seat cushion releases. These are small levers on the lower front of the cushion.
2. Pull upward on the front of the seat cushion and rotate it free. It is not retained or bolted under the seat back.
3. To reinstall, fit the rear of the cushion into place under the seat back.
4. Push inward and downward on the front of the cushion until the releases lock into place. Make sure the seat is locked into place and the releases are secure.

Rear Bench Seat Back

NOTE: *The seat bottom cushion need not be removed for this procedure, but access is improved with the cushion removed.*

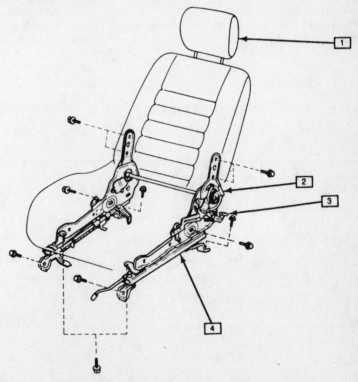

1. Head restraint
2. Recliner mechanism
3. Recliner actuator handle
4. Seat adjuster

Front seat components

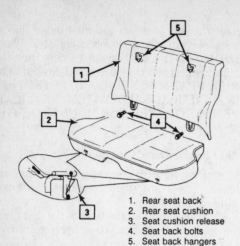

1. Rear seat back
2. Rear seat cushion
3. Seat cushion release
4. Seat back bolts
5. Seat back hangers

Rear bench seat components

1. Remove the two lower bolts holding the seat back to the body.

2. Pull outward and push upward on the bottom edge of the seat back. This will release the seat back from the L–shaped hangers holding it.

3. Remove the seat back from the car.

4. When reinstalling, carefully fit the seat back onto the hangers.

5. Swing the back down and into place.

6. Install the lower retaining bolts and tighten them to 5 ft. lbs.

Split/Folding Rear Seat Cushion

1. At the front lower edge of the seat cushion, remove the 2 bolts holding the seat cushion to the body. The bolts may be concealed under carpeting or trim pieces.

2. Pull upward on the front of the seat cushion and rotate it free. It is not retained or bolted under the seat back.

3. To reinstall, fit the rear of the cushion into place under the seat back.

4. Push inward and downward on the front of the cushion until it is aligned.

5. Install the retaining bolts and tighten them.

Split/Folding Rear Seat Back

1. Push the seat back forward into a folded position.

2. Remove the carpeting from the rear of the seat back.

3. At the side hinge, remove the bolt holding the seat back to the hinge.

4. At the center hinge, remove the 2 bolts holding the seat back to the hinge.

5. Remove the seat back from the car.

6. Reinstall the seat back and install the bolts finger tight.

7. Tighten the side hinge bolt to 13 ft. lbs.

8. Tighten the center hinge bolts to 6 ft. lbs.

9. Install the carpeting and trim on the rear of the seat back.

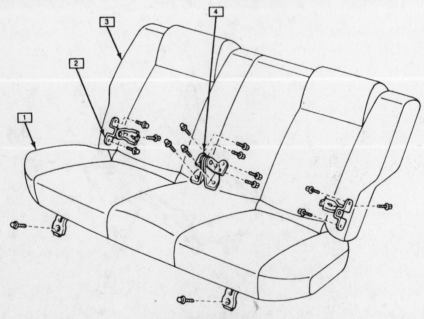

1. Rear seat cushion
2. Side hinge
3. Seat back
4. Center hinge

Split/folding rear seat components

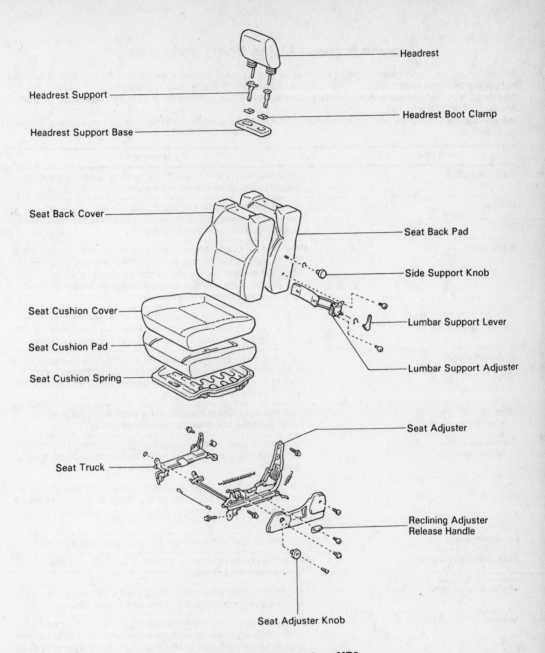

Headrest

Headrest Support

Headrest Boot Clamp

Headrest Support Base

Seat Back Cover

Seat Back Pad

Side Support Knob

Seat Cushion Cover

Lumbar Support Lever

Seat Cushion Pad

Seat Cushion Spring

Lumbar Support Adjuster

Seat Adjuster

Seat Truck

Reclining Adjuster
Release Handle

Seat Adjuster Knob

Front seat components — MR2

How to Remove Stains from Fabric Interior

For best results, spots and stains should be removed as soon as possible. Never use gasoline, lacquer thinner, acetone, nail polish remover or bleach. Use a 3' x 3" piece of cheesecloth. Squeeze most of the liquid from the fabric and wipe the stained fabric from the outside of the stain toward the center with a lifting motion. Turn the cheesecloth as soon as one side becomes soiled. When using water to remove a stain, be sure to wash the entire section after the spot has been removed to avoid water stains. Encrusted spots can be broken up with a dull knife and vacuumed before removing the stain.

Type of Stain	How to Remove It
Surface spots	Brush the spots out with a small hand brush or use a commercial preparation such as K2R to lift the stain.
Mildew	Clean around the mildew with warm suds. Rinse in cold water and soak the mildew area in a solution of 1 part table salt and 2 parts water. Wash with upholstery cleaner.
Water stains	Water stains in fabric materials can be removed with a solution made from 1 cup of table salt dissolved in 1 quart of water. Vigorously scrub the solution into the stain and rinse with clear water. Water stains in nylon or other synthetic fabrics should be removed with a commercial type spot remover.
Chewing gum, tar, crayons, shoe polish (greasy stains)	Do not use a cleaner that will soften gum or tar. Harden the deposit with an ice cube and scrape away as much as possible with a dull knife. Moisten the remainder with cleaning fluid and scrub clean.
Ice cream, candy	Most candy has a sugar base and can be removed with a cloth wrung out in warm water. Oily candy, after cleaning with warm water, should be cleaned with upholstery cleaner. Rinse with warm water and clean the remainder with cleaning fluid.
Wine, alcohol, egg, milk, soft drink (non-greasy stains)	Do not use soap. Scrub the stain with a cloth wrung out in warm water. Remove the remainder with cleaning fluid.
Grease, oil, lipstick, butter and related stains	Use a spot remover to avoid leaving a ring. Work from the outisde of the stain to the center and dry with a clean cloth when the spot is gone.
Headliners (cloth)	Mix a solution of warm water and foam upholstery cleaner to give thick suds. Use only foam—liquid may streak or spot. Clean the entire headliner in one operation using a circular motion with a natural sponge.
Headliner (vinyl)	Use a vinyl cleaner with a sponge and wipe clean with a dry cloth.
Seats and door panels	Mix 1 pint upholstery cleaner in 1 gallon of water. Do not soak the fabric around the buttons.
Leather or vinyl fabric	Use a multi-purpose cleaner full strength and a stiff brush. Let stand 2 minutes and scrub thoroughly. Wipe with a clean, soft rag.
Nylon or synthetic fabrics	For normal stains, use the same procedures you would for washing cloth upholstery. If the fabric is extremely dirty, use a multi-purpose cleaner full strength with a stiff scrub brush. Scrub thoroughly in all directions and wipe with a cotton towel or soft rag.

Mechanic's Data

11

1":254mm
TAX
10.16mm
Liter
Parts
Overhaul

General Conversion Table

Multiply By	To Convert	To	
		LENGTH	
2.54	Inches	Centimeters	.3937
25.4	Inches	Millimeters	.03937
30.48	Feet	Centimeters	.0328
.304	Feet	Meters	3.28
.914	Yards	Meters	1.094
1.609	Miles	Kilometers	.621
		VOLUME	
.473	Pints	Liters	2.11
.946	Quarts	Liters	1.06
3.785	Gallons	Liters	.264
.164	Cubic inches	Liters	61.02
16.39	Cubic inches	Cubic cms.	.061
28.32	Cubic feet	Liters	.0353
		MASS (Weight)	
28.35	Ounces	Grams	.035
.4536	Pounds	Kilograms	2.20
—	To obtain	From	Multiply by

Multiply By	To Convert	To	
		AREA	
6.45	Square inches	Square cms.	.155
.836	Square yds.	Square meters	1.196
		FORCE	
4.448	Pounds	Newtons	.225
.138	Ft. lbs.	Kilogram/meters	7.23
1.356	Ft. lbs.	Newton-meters	.737
.113	In. lbs.	Newton-meters	8.844
		PRESSURE	
.068	Psi	Atmospheres	14.7
6.89	Psi	Kilopascals	.145
		OTHER	
1.104	Horsepower (DIN)	Horsepower (SAE)	.9861
.746	Horsepower (SAE)	Kilowatts (KW)	1.34
1.609	Mph	Km/h	.621
.425	Mpg	Km/L	2.35
—	To obtain	From	Multiply by

Tap Drill Sizes

National Coarse or U.S.S.

Screw & Tap Size	Threads Per Inch	Use Drill Number
No. 5	40	39
No. 6	32	36
No. 8	32	29
No. 10	24	25
No. 12	24	17
1/4	20	8
5/16	18	F
3/8	16	5/16
7/16	14	U
1/2	13	27/64
9/16	12	31/64
5/8	11	17/32
3/4	10	21/32
7/8	9	49/64

National Coarse or U.S.S.

Screw & Tap Size	Threads Per Inch	Use Drill Number
1	8	7/8
1 1/8	7	63/64
1 1/4	7	1 7/64
1 1/2	6	1 11/32

National Fine or S.A.E.

Screw & Tap Size	Threads Per Inch	Use Drill Number
No. 5	44	37
No. 6	40	33
No. 8	36	29
No. 10	32	21

National Fine or S.A.E.

Screw & Tap Size	Threads Per Inch	Use Drill Number
No. 12	28	15
1/4	28	3
6/16	24	1
3/8	28	Q
7/16	20	W
1/2	20	29/64
9/16	18	33/64
5/8	18	37/64
3/4	16	11/16
7/8	14	13/16
1 1/8	12	1 3/64
1 1/4	12	1 11/64
1 1/2	12	1 27/64

Drill Sizes In Decimal Equivalents

Inch	Decimal	Wire	mm	Inch	Decimal	Wire	mm	Inch	Decimal	Wire & Letter	mm	Inch	Decimal	Letter	mm	Inch	Decimal	mm
1/64	.0156		.39		.0730	49			.1614		4.1		.2717		6.9		.4331	11.0
	.0157		.4		.0748		1.9		.1654		4.2		.2720	I		7/16	.4375	11.11
	.0160	78			.0760	48			.1660	19			.2756		7.0		.4528	11.5
	.0165		.42		.0768		1.95		.1673		4.25		.2770	J		29/64	.4531	11.51
	.0173		.44	5/64	.0781		1.98		.1693		4.3		.2795		7.1	15/32	.4688	11.90
	.0177		.45		.0785	47			.1695	18			.2810	K			.4724	12.0
	.0180	77			.0787		2.0	11/64	.1719		4.36	9/32	.2812		7.14	31/64	.4844	12.30
	.0181		.46		.0807		2.05		.1730	17			.2835		7.2		.4921	12.5
	.0189		.48		.0810	46			.1732		4.4		.2854		7.25	1/2	.5000	12.70
	.0197		.5		.0820	45			.1770	16			.2874		7.3		.5118	13.0
	.0200	76			.0827		2.1		.1772		4.5		.2900	L		33/64	.5156	13.09
	.0210	75			.0846		2.15		.1800	15			.2913		7.4	17/32	.5312	13.49
	.0217		.55		.0860	44			.1811		4.6		.2950	M			.5315	13.5
	.0225	74			.0866		2.2		.1820	14			.2953		7.5	35/64	.5469	13.89
	.0236		.6		.0886		2.25		.1850	13		19/64	.2969		7.54		.5512	14.0
	.0240	73			.0890	43			.1850		4.7		.2992		7.6	9/16	.5625	14.28
	.0250	72			.0906		2.3		.1870		4.75		.3020	N			.5709	14.5
	.0256		.65		.0925		2.35	3/16	.1875		4.76		.3031		7.7	37/64	.5781	14.68
	.0260	71			.0935	42			.1890		4.8		.3051		7.75		.5906	15.0
	.0276		.7	3/32	.0938		2.38		.1890	12			.3071		7.8	19/32	.5938	15.08
	.0280	70			.0945		2.4		.1910	11			.3110		7.9	39/64	.6094	15.47
	.0292	69			.0960	41			.1929		4.9	5/16	.3125		7.93		.6102	15.5
	.0295		.75		.0965		2.45		.1935	10			.3150		8.0	5/8	.6250	15.87
	.0310	68			.0980	40			.1960	9			.3160	O			.6299	16.0
1/32	.0312		.79		.0981		2.5		.1969		5.0		.3189		8.1	41/64	.6406	16.27
	.0315		.8		.0995	39			.1990	8			.3228		8.2		.6496	16.5
	.0320	67			.1015	38			.2008		5.1		.3230	P		21/32	.6562	16.66
	.0330	66			.1024		2.6		.2010	7			.3248		8.25		.6693	17.0
	.0335		.85		.1040	37		13/64	.2031		5.16		.3268		8.3	43/64	.6719	17.06
	.0350	65			.1063		2.7		.2040	6		21/64	.3281		8.33	11/16	.6875	17.46
	.0354		.9		.1065	36			.2047		5.2		.3307		8.4		.6890	17.5
	.0360	64			.1083		2.75		.2055	5			.3320	Q		45/64	.7031	17.85
	.0370	63		7/64	.1094		2.77		.2067		5.25		.3346		8.5		.7087	18.0
	.0374		.95		.1100	35			.2087		5.3		.3386		8.6	23/32	.7188	18.25
	.0380	62			.1102		2.8		.2090	4			.3390	R			.7283	18.5
	.0390	61			.1110	34			.2126		5.4		.3425		8.7	47/64	.7344	18.65
	.0394		1.0		.1130	33			.2130	3		11/32	.3438		8.73		.7480	19.0
	.0400	60			.1142		2.9		.2165		5.5		.3445		8.75	3/4	.7500	19.05
	.0410	59			.1160	32		7/32	.2188		5.55		.3465		8.8	49/64	.7656	19.44
	.0413		1.05		.1181		3.0		.2205		5.6		.3480	S			.7677	19.5
	.0420	58			.1200	31			.2210	2			.3504		8.9	25/32	.7812	19.84
	.0430	57			.1220		3.1		.2244		5.7		.3543		9.0		.7874	20.0
	.0433		1.1	1/8	.1250		3.17		.2264		5.75		.3580	T		51/64	.7969	20.24
	.0453		1.15		.1260		3.2		.2280	1			.3583		9.1		.8071	20.5
3/64	.0465	56			.1280		3.25		.2283		5.8	23/64	.3594		9.12	13/16	.8125	20.63
	.0469		1.19		.1285	30			.2323		5.9		.3622		9.2		.8268	21.0
	.0472		1.2		.1299		3.3		.2340	A			.3642		9.25	53/64	.8281	21.03
	.0492		1.25		.1339		3.4	15/64	.2344		5.95		.3661		9.3	27/32	.8438	21.43
	.0512		1.3		.1360	29			.2362		6.0		.3680	U			.8465	21.5
	.0520	55			.1378		3.5		.2380	B			.3701		9.4	55/64	.8594	21.82
	.0531		1.35		.1405	28			.2402		6.1		.3740		9.5		.8661	22.0
	.0550	54		9/64	.1406		3.57		.2420	C		3/8	.3750		9.52	7/8	.8750	22.22
	.0551		1.4		.1417		3.6		.2441		6.2		.3770	V			.8858	22.5
	.0571		1.45		.1440	27			.2460	D			.3780		9.6	57/64	.8906	22.62
	.0591		1.5		.1457		3.7		.2461		6.25		.3819		9.7		.9055	23.0
	.0595	53			.1470	26			.2480		6.3		.3839		9.75	29/32	.9062	23.01
	.0610		1.55		.1476		3.75	1/4	.2500	E	6.35		.3858		9.8	59/64	.9219	23.41
1/16	.0625		1.59		.1495	25			.2520		6.		.3860	W			.9252	23.5
	.0630		1.6		.1496		3.8		.2559		6.5		.3898		9.9	15/16	.9375	23.81
	.0635	52			.1520	24			.2570	F		25/64	.3906		9.92		.9449	24.0
	.0650		1.65		.1535		3.9		.2598		6.6		.3937		10.0	61/64	.9531	24.2
	.0669		1.7		.1540	23			.2610	G			.3970	X			.9646	24.5
	.0670	51		5/32	.1562		3.96		.2638		6.7		.4040	Y		31/32	.9688	24.6
	.0689		1.75		.1570	22		17/64	.2656		6.74	13/32	.4062		10.31		.9843	25.0
	.0700	50			.1575		4.0		.2657		6.75		.4130	Z		63/64	.9844	25.0
	.0709		1.8		.1590	21			.2660	H			.4134		10.5	1	1.0000	25.4
	.0728		1.85		.1610	20			.2677		6.8	27/64	.4219		10.71			

AIR/FUEL RATIO: The ratio of air to gasoline by weight in the fuel mixture drawn into the engine.

AIR INJECTION: One method of reducing harmful exhaust emissions by injecting air into each of the exhaust ports of an engine. The fresh air entering the hot exhaust manifold causes any remaining fuel to be burned before it can exit the tailpipe.

ALTERNATOR: A device used for converting mechanical energy into electrical energy.

AMMETER: An instrument, calibrated in amperes, used to measure the flow of an electrical current in a circuit. Ammeters are always connected in series with the circuit being tested.

AMPERE: The rate of flow of electrical current present when one volt of electrical pressure is applied against one ohm of electrical resistance.

ANALOG COMPUTER: Any microprocessor that uses similar (analogous) electrical signals to make its calculations.

ARMATURE: A laminated, soft iron core wrapped by a wire that converts electrical energy to mechanical energy as in a motor or relay. When rotated in a magnetic field, it changes mechanical energy into electrical energy as in a generator.

ATMOSPHERIC PRESSURE: The pressure on the Earth's surface caused by the weight of the air in the atmosphere. At sea level, this pressure is 14.7 psi at 32°F (101 kPa at 0°C).

ATOMIZATION: The breaking down of a liquid into a fine mist that can be suspended in air.

AXIAL PLAY: Movement parallel to a shaft or bearing bore.

BACKFIRE: The sudden combustion of gases in the intake or exhaust system that results in a loud explosion.

BACKLASH: The clearance or play between two parts, such as meshed gears.

BACKPRESSURE: Restrictions in the exhaust system that slow the exit of exhaust gases from the combustion chamber.

BAKELITE: A heat resistant, plastic insulator material commonly used in printed circuit boards and transistorized components.

BALL BEARING: A bearing made up of hardened inner and outer races between which hardened steel balls roll.

BALLAST RESISTOR: A resistor in the primary ignition circuit that lowers voltage after the engine is started to reduce wear on ignition components.

BEARING: A friction reducing, supportive device usually located between a stationary part and a moving part.

BIMETAL TEMPERATURE SENSOR: Any sensor or switch made of two dissimilar types of metal that bend when heated or cooled due to the different expansion rates of the alloys. These types of sensors usually function as an on/off switch.

BLOWBY: Combustion gases, composed of water vapor and unburned fuel, that leak past the piston rings into the crankcase during normal engine operation. These gases are removed by the PCV system to prevent the buildup of harmful acids in the crankcase.

BRAKE PAD: A brake shoe and lining assembly used with disc brakes.

BRAKE SHOE: The backing for the brake lining. The term is, however, usually applied to the assembly of the brake backing and lining.

BUSHING: A liner, usually removable, for a bearing; an anti-friction liner used in place of a bearing.

BYPASS: System used to bypass ballast resistor during engine cranking to increase voltage supplied to the coil.

CALIPER: A hydraulically activated device in a disc brake system, which is mounted straddling the brake rotor (disc). The caliper contains at least one piston and two brake pads. Hydraulic pressure on the piston(s) forces the pads against the rotor.

CAMSHAFT: A shaft in the engine on which are the lobes (cams) which operate the valves. The camshaft is driven by the crankshaft, via a belt, chain or gears, at one half the crankshaft speed.

CAPACITOR: A device which stores an electrical charge.

CARBON MONOXIDE (CO): A colorless, odorless gas given off as a normal byproduct of combustion. It is poisonous and extremely dangerous in confined areas, building up slowly to toxic levels without warning if adequate ventilation is not available.

CARBURETOR: A device, usually mounted on the intake manifold of an engine, which mixes the air and fuel in the proper proportion to allow even combustion.

CATALYTIC CONVERTER: A device installed in the exhaust system, like a muffler, that converts harmful byproducts of combustion into carbon dioxide and water vapor by means of a heat-producing chemical reaction.

CENTRIFUGAL ADVANCE: A mechanical method of advancing the spark timing by using fly weights in the distributor that react to centrifugal force generated by the distributor shaft rotation.

CHECK VALVE: Any one-way valve installed to permit the flow of air, fuel or vacuum in one direction only.

CHOKE: A device, usually a movable valve, placed in the intake path of a carburetor to restrict the flow of air.

CIRCUIT: Any unbroken path through which an electrical current can flow. Also used to describe fuel flow in some instances.

CIRCUIT BREAKER: A switch which protects an electrical circuit from overload by opening the circuit when the current flow exceeds a predetermined level. Some circuit breakers must be reset manually, while most reset automatically

COIL (IGNITION): A transformer in the ignition circuit which steps up the voltage provided to the spark plugs.

COMBINATION MANIFOLD: An assembly which includes both the intake and exhaust manifolds in one casting.

COMBINATION VALVE: A device used in some fuel systems that routes fuel vapors to a charcoal storage canister instead of venting

them into the atmosphere. The valve relieves fuel tank pressure and allows fresh air into the tank as the fuel level drops to prevent a vapor lock situation.

COMPRESSION RATIO: The comparison of the total volume of the cylinder and combustion chamber with the piston at BDC and the piston at TDC.

CONDENSER: 1. An electrical device which acts to store an electrical charge, preventing voltage surges.
2. A radiator-like device in the air conditioning system in which refrigerant gas condenses into a liquid, giving off heat.

CONDUCTOR: Any material through which an electrical current can be transmitted easily.

CONTINUITY: Continuous or complete circuit. Can be checked with an ohmmeter.

COUNTERSHAFT: An intermediate shaft which is rotated by a mainshaft and transmits, in turn, that rotation to a working part.

CRANKCASE: The lower part of an engine in which the crankshaft and related parts operate.

CRANKSHAFT: The main driving shaft of an engine which receives reciprocating motion from the pistons and converts it to rotary motion.

CYLINDER: In an engine, the round hole in the engine block in which the piston(s) ride.

CYLINDER BLOCK: The main structural member of an engine in which is found the cylinders, crankshaft and other principal parts.

CYLINDER HEAD: The detachable portion of the engine, fastened, usually, to the top of the cylinder block, containing all or most of the combustion chambers. On overhead valve engines, it contains the valves and their operating parts. On overhead cam engines, it contains the camshaft as well.

DEAD CENTER: The extreme top or bottom of the piston stroke.

DETONATION: An unwanted explosion of the air/fuel mixture in the combustion chamber caused by excess heat and compression, advanced timing, or an overly lean mixture. Also referred to as "ping".

DIAPHRAGM: A thin, flexible wall separating two cavities, such as in a vacuum advance unit.

DIESELING: A condition in which hot spots in the combustion chamber cause the engine to run on after the key is turned off.

DIFFERENTIAL: A geared assembly which allows the transmission of motion between drive axles, giving one axle the ability to turn faster than the other.

DIODE: An electrical device that will allow current to flow in one direction only.

DISC BRAKE: A hydraulic braking assembly consisting of a brake disc, or rotor, mounted on an axle, and a caliper assembly containing, usually two brake pads which are activated by hydraulic pressure. The pads are forced against the sides of the disc, creating friction which slows the vehicle.

DISTRIBUTOR: A mechanically driven device on an engine which is responsible for electrically firing the spark plug at a predetermined point of the piston stroke.

DOWEL PIN: A pin, inserted in mating holes in two different parts allowing those parts to maintain a fixed relationship.

DRUM BRAKE: A braking system which consists of two brake shoes and one or two wheel cylinders, mounted on a fixed backing plate, and a brake drum, mounted on an axle, which revolves around the assembly. Hydraulic action applied to the wheel cylinders forces the shoes outward against the drum, creating friction, slowing the vehicle.

DWELL: The rate, measured in degrees of shaft rotation, at which an electrical circuit cycles on and off.

ELECTRONIC CONTROL UNIT (ECU): Ignition module, amplifier or igniter. See Module for definition.

ELECTRONIC IGNITION: A system in which the timing and firing of the spark plugs is controlled by an electronic control unit, usually called a module. These systems have no points or condenser.

ENDPLAY: The measured amount of axial movement in a shaft.

ENGINE: A device that converts heat into mechanical energy.

EXHAUST MANIFOLD: A set of cast passages or pipes which conduct exhaust gases from the engine.

FEELER GAUGE: A blade, usually metal, of precisely predetermined thickness, used to measure the clearance between two parts. These blades usually are available in sets of assorted thicknesses.

F-HEAD: An engine configuration in which the intake valves are in the cylinder head, while the camshaft and exhaust valves are located in the cylinder block. The camshaft operates the intake valves via lifters and pushrods, while it operates the exhaust valves directly.

FIRING ORDER: The order in which combustion occurs in the cylinders of an engine. Also the order in which spark is distributed to the plugs by the distributor.

FLATHEAD: An engine configuration in which the camshaft and all the valves are located in the cylinder block.

FLOODING: The presence of too much fuel in the intake manifold and combustion chamber which prevents the air/fuel mixture from firing, thereby causing a no-start situation.

FLYWHEEL: A disc shaped part bolted to the rear end of the crankshaft. Around the outer perimeter is affixed the ring gear. The starter drive engages the ring gear, turning the flywheel, which rotates the crankshaft, imparting the initial starting motion to the engine.

FOOT POUND (ft.lb. or sometimes, ft. lbs.): The amount of energy or work needed to raise an item weighing one pound, a distance of one foot.

FUSE: A protective device in a circuit which prevents circuit overload by breaking the circuit when a specific amperage is present. The device is constructed around a strip or wire of a lower amperage rating than the circuit it is designed to protect. When an amperage higher than that stamped on the fuse is present in the circuit, the strip or wire melts, opening the circuit.

GEAR RATIO: The ratio between the number of teeth on meshing gears.

GENERATOR: A device which converts mechanical energy into electrical energy.

HEAT RANGE: The measure of a spark plug's ability to dissipate heat from its firing end. The higher the heat range, the hotter the plug fires. **HUB:** The center part of a wheel or gear.

HYDROCARBON (HC): Any chemical compound made up of hydrogen and carbon. A major pollutant formed by the engine as a byproduct of combustion.

HYDROMETER: An instrument used to measure the specific gravity of a solution.

INCH POUND (in.lb. or sometimes, in. lbs.): One twelfth of a foot pound.

INDUCTION: A means of transferring electrical energy in the form of a magnetic field. Principle used in the ignition coil to increase voltage.

INJECTION PUMP: A device, usually mechanically operated, which meters and delivers fuel under pressure to the fuel injector.

INJECTOR: A device which receives metered fuel under relatively low pressure and is activated to inject the fuel into the engine under relatively high pressure at a predetermined time.

INPUT SHAFT: The shaft to which torque is applied, usually carrying the driving gear or gears.

INTAKE MANIFOLD: A casting of passages or pipes used to conduct air or a fuel/air mixture to the cylinders.

JOURNAL: The bearing surface within which a shaft operates.

KEY: A small block usually fitted in a notch between a shaft and a hub to prevent slippage of the two parts.

MANIFOLD: A casting of passages or set of pipes which connect the cylinders to an inlet or outlet source.

MANIFOLD VACUUM: Low pressure in an engine intake manifold formed just below the throttle plates. Manifold vacuum is highest at idle and drops under acceleration.

MASTER CYLINDER: The primary fluid pressurizing device in a hydraulic system. In automotive use, it is found in brake and hydraulic clutch systems and is pedal activated, either directly or, in a power brake system, through the power booster.

MODULE: Electronic control unit, amplifier or igniter of solid state or integrated design which controls the current flow in the ignition primary circuit based on input from the pickup coil. When the module opens the primary circuit, the high secondary voltage is induced in the coil.

NEEDLE BEARING: A bearing which consists of a number (usually a large number) of long, thin rollers.

OHM:(Ω) The unit used to measure the resistance of conductor to electrical flow. One ohm is the amount of resistance that limits current flow to one ampere in a circuit with one volt of pressure.

OHMMETER: An instrument used for measuring the resistance, in ohms, in an electrical circuit.

OUTPUT SHAFT: The shaft which transmits torque from a device, such as a transmission.

OVERDRIVE: A gear assembly which produces more shaft revolutions than that transmitted to it.

OVERHEAD CAMSHAFT (OHC): An engine configuration in which the camshaft is mounted on top of the cylinder head and operates the valves either directly or by means of rocker arms.

OVERHEAD VALVE (OHV): An engine configuration in which all of the valves are located in the cylinder head and the camshaft is located in the cylinder block. The camshaft operates the valves via lifters and pushrods.

OXIDES OF NITROGEN (NOx): Chemical compounds of nitrogen produced as a byproduct of combustion. They combine with hydrocarbons to produce smog.

OXYGEN SENSOR: Used with the feedback system to sense the presence of oxygen in the exhaust gas and signal the computer which can reference the voltage signal to an air/fuel ratio.

PINION: The smaller of two meshing gears.

PISTON RING: An open ended ring which fits into a groove on the outer diameter of the piston. Its chief function is to form a seal between the piston and cylinder wall. Most automotive pistons have three rings: two for compression sealing; one for oil sealing.

PRELOAD: A predetermined load placed on a bearing during assembly or by adjustment.

PRIMARY CIRCUIT: Is the low voltage side of the ignition system which consists of the ignition switch, ballast resistor or resistance wire, bypass, coil, electronic control unit and pick-up coil as well as the connecting wires and harnesses.

PRESS FIT: The mating of two parts under pressure, due to the inner diameter of one being smaller than the outer diameter of the other, or vice versa; an interference fit.

RACE: The surface on the inner or outer ring of a bearing on which the balls, needles or rollers move.

REGULATOR: A device which maintains the amperage and/or voltage levels of a circuit at predetermined values.

RELAY: A switch which automatically opens and/or closes a circuit.

RESISTANCE: The opposition to the flow of current through a circuit or electrical device, and is measured in ohms. Resistance is equal to the voltage divided by the amperage.

RESISTOR: A device, usually made of wire, which offers a preset amount of resistance in an electrical circuit.

RING GEAR: The name given to a ring-shaped gear attached to a differential case, or affixed to a flywheel or as part a planetary gear set.

ROLLER BEARING: A bearing made up of hardened inner and outer races between which hardened steel rollers move.

ROTOR: 1. The disc-shaped part of a disc brake assembly, upon which the brake pads bear; also called, brake disc.
2. The device mounted atop the distributor shaft, which passes current to the distributor cap tower contacts.

SECONDARY CIRCUIT: The high voltage side of the ignition system, usually above 20,000 volts. The secondary includes the ignition coil, coil wire, distributor cap and rotor, spark plug wires and spark plugs.

SENDING UNIT: A mechanical, electrical, hydraulic or electromagnetic device which transmits information to a gauge.

SENSOR: Any device designed to measure engine operating conditions or ambient pressures and temperatures. Usually electronic in nature and designed to send a voltage signal to an on-board computer, some sensors may operate as a simple on/off switch or they may provide a variable voltage signal (like a potentiometer) as conditions or measured parameters change.

SHIM: Spacers of precise, predetermined thickness used between parts to establish a proper working relationship.

SLAVE CYLINDER: In automotive use, a device in the hydraulic clutch system which is activated by hydraulic force, disengaging the clutch.

SOLENOID: A coil used to produce a magnetic field, the effect of which is to produce work.

SPARK PLUG: A device screwed into the combustion chamber of a spark ignition engine. The basic construction is a conductive core inside of a ceramic insulator, mounted in an outer conductive base. An electrical charge from the spark plug wire travels along the conductive core and jumps a preset air gap to a grounding point or points at the end of the conductive base. The resultant spark ignites the fuel/air mixture in the combustion chamber.

SPLINES: Ridges machined or cast onto the outer diameter of a shaft or inner diameter of a bore to enable parts to mate without rotation.

TACHOMETER: A device used to measure the rotary speed of an engine, shaft, gear, etc., usually in rotations per minute.

THERMOSTAT: A valve, located in the cooling system of an engine, which is closed when cold and opens gradually in response to engine heating, controlling the temperature of the coolant and rate of coolant flow.

TOP DEAD CENTER (TDC): The point at which the piston reaches the top of its travel on the compression stroke.

TORQUE: The twisting force applied to an object.

TORQUE CONVERTER: A turbine used to transmit power from a driving member to a driven member via hydraulic action, providing changes in drive ratio and torque. In automotive use, it links the driveplate at the rear of the engine to the automatic transmission.

TRANSDUCER: A device used to change a force into an electrical signal.

TRANSISTOR: A semi-conductor component which can be actuated by a small voltage to perform an electrical switching function.

TUNE-UP: A regular maintenance function, usually associated with the replacement and adjustment of parts and components in the electrical and fuel systems of a vehicle for the purpose of attaining optimum performance.

TURBOCHARGER: An exhaust driven pump which compresses intake air and forces it into the combustion chambers at higher than atmospheric pressures. The increased air pressure allows more fuel to be burned and results in increased horsepower being produced.

VACUUM ADVANCE: A device which advances the ignition timing in response to increased engine vacuum.

VACUUM GAUGE: An instrument used to measure the presence of vacuum in a chamber.

VALVE: A device which control the pressure, direction of flow or rate of flow of a liquid or gas.

VALVE CLEARANCE: The measured gap between the end of the valve stem and the rocker arm, cam lobe or follower that activates the valve.

VISCOSITY: The rating of a liquid's internal resistance to flow.

VOLTMETER: An instrument used for measuring electrical force in units called volts. Voltmeters are always connected parallel with the circuit being tested.

WHEEL CYLINDER: Found in the automotive drum brake assembly, it is a device, actuated by hydraulic pressure, which, through internal pistons, pushes the brake shoes outward against the drums.

A: Ampere

AC: Alternating current

A/C: Air conditioning

A–h: Amper hour

AT: Automatic transmission

ATDC: After top dead center

μA: Microampere

bbl: Barrel

BDC: Bottom dead center

bhp: Brake horsepower

BTDC: Before top dead center

BTU: British thermal unit

C: Celsius (Centigrade)

CCA: Cold cranking amps

cd: Candela

cm^2: Square centimeter

cm^3, cc: Cubic centimeter

CO: Carbon monoxide

CO_2: Carbon dioxide

cu.in., in^3: Cubic inch

CV: Constant velocity

Cyl.: Cylinder

DC: Direct current

ECM: Electronic control module

EFE: Early fuel evaporation

EFI: Electronic fuel injection

EGR: Exhaust gas recirculation

Exh.: Exhaust

F: Farenheit

F: Farad

pF: Picofarad

μF: Microfarad

FI: Fuel injection

ft.lb., ft. lb., ft. lbs.: foot pound(s)

gal: Gallon

g: Gram

HC: Hydrocarbon

HEI: High energy ignition

HO: High output

hp: Horsepower

Hyd: Hydraulic

Hz: Hertz

ID: Inside diameter

in.lb; in. lbs.; in. lbs.: inch pound(s)

Int: Intake

K: Kelvin

kg: Kilogram

kHz: Kilohertz

km: Kilometer

km/h: Kilometers per hour

kΩ: Kilohm

kPa: Kilopascal

kV: Kilovolt

kW: Kilowatt

l: Liter

l/s: Liters per second

m: Meter

mA: Milliampere

mg: Milligram

mHz: Megahertz

mm: Millimeter

mm^2: Square millimeter

m^3: Cubic meter

MΩ: Megohm

m/s: Meters per second

MT: Manual transmission

mV: Millivolt

μm: Micrometer

N: Newton

N–m: Newton meter

NOx: Nitrous oxide

OD: Outside diameter

OHC: Over head camshaft

OHV: Over head valve

Ω: Ohm

PCV: Positive crankcase ventilation

psi: Pounds per square inch

pts: Pints

qts: Quarts

rpm: Rotations per minute

rps: Rotations per second

R–12: refrigerant gas (Freon)

SAE: Society of Automotive Engineers

SO$_2$: Sulfur dioxide

T: Ton

t: Megagram

TBI: Throttle Body Injection

TPS: Throttle Position Sensor

V: 1. Volt; 2. Venturi

μV: Microvolt

W: Watt

∞: Infinity

$<$: Less than

$>$: Greater than

A

Abbreviations and Symbols 569
Air cleaner 6
Air conditioning
  Blower 341
  Charging 22
  Compressor 126
  Condenser 130
  Control panel 346
  Discharging 20
  Evacuating 20
  Evaporator 346
  Expansion valve 348
  Gauge sets 20
  General service 18
  Inspection 18
  Leak testing 19
  Preventive maintenance 18
  Receiver-drier 349
  Safety precautions 18
  Sight glass check 19
  System tests 18
  Troubleshooting 21
Alternator
  Alternator precautions 88
  Removal and installation 89
  Specifications 93
  Troubleshooting 92
Alignment, wheel 472, 488
  Camber 473
  Caster 472
  Toe 473
Antenna 547
Antifreeze 38
Automatic Transaxle 433
  Back up light switch 440
  Filter change 438
  Fluid change 438
  Linkage adjustments 439
  Neutral safety switch 439
  Removal and installation 440
Automatic transmission 433
  Adjustments 434
  Back-up light switch 437
  Filter change 36, 434
  Fluid change 36, 434
  Linkage adjustments 436
  Neutral safety switch 436
  Pan removal 434
  Removal and installation 437
  Troubleshooting 434
Axle
  Rear 447

B

Back-up light switch
  Automatic transmission 437, 440
  Manual transmission 381, 395
Ball joints
  Inspection 458
  Removal and installation 458
Battery 11
  Fluid level and maintenance 11
  Jump starting 49
  Removal and installation 13, 91
Bearings
  Axle 466
  Differential 447
  Driveline 442
  Engine 188
  Wheel 471
Belts 13
Body lubrication 41
Boot (CV Joint)
  Replacement 424
Brakes
  Bleeding 526
  Brake light switch 519
  Disc brakes (Front)
  Caliper 530
  Operating principles 515
  Pads 527
  Rotor (Disc) 531
  Disc brakes (Rear)
  Caliper 538
  Operating principals 536
  Pads 536
  Rotor (Disc) 541
  Drum brakes (Rear)
  Adjustment 517
  Drum 533
  Operating principals 516
  Shoes 533
  Wheel cylinder 536
  Fluid level 40
  Hoses and lines 526
  Master cylinder 520
  Parking brake 542
  Adjustment 542
  Removal and installation 542
  Power booster 523
  Operating principals 516
  Removal and installation 523
  Proportioning valve 524
  Specifications 544
  Troubleshooting 512
  Vacuum pump 524

Bulbs 367
Bumpers 547

C

Calipers
   Overhaul 530, 538
   Removal and installation 528, 538
Camber 473
Camshaft and bearings 175
   Service 180
   Specifications 102
   Camshaft sprocket 170
Capacities Chart 56
Carburetor
   Adjustments 295
   Overhaul 300
   Removal and Installation 299
Caster 472
Catalytic converter 197
Center bearing 447
Charging system
Chassis electrical system 331
   Circuit protection 371
   Heater and air conditioning 341
   Instrument panel 355
   Lighting 367
   Troubleshooting 331
   Windshield wipers 353
   Wiring diagrams 230–292
Chassis lubrication 41
Circuit breakers 372
Circuit protection 371
Clutch
   Adjustment 428
   Hydraulic system bleeding 433
   Master cylinder 432
   Pedal 428
   Removal and installation 432
   Slave cylinder 432
   Troubleshooting 429
Coil (ignition) 84
Combination manifold 120
Combination switch 365, 491
Compression testing 100
Compressor
   Removal and installation 126
Condenser
   Air conditioning 130
Connecting rods and bearings
   Service 188
   Specifications 103
Console 364
Constant velocity (CV) joints 422, 442
Control arm
   Lower 460
Cooling system 38
   Cooling unit 346

Crankcase ventilation valve 199
Crankshaft
   Service 190
   Specifications 103
Cylinder block 194
Cylinder head 135
Cylinders
   Inspection 194
   Reboring 194
   Refinishing 194

D

Diagnostic codes 223
Diesel fuel system
Disc brakes 515, 536
Distributor
   Removal and installation 86
Door glass 548
Door locks 549
Doors
   Glass 549
   Hinges 545
   Locks 549
   Removal and installation 545
   Striker plate 545
Door trim panel 548
Drive axle (front)
   Axle shaft, bearing and seal 466
   Front hub and wheel bearings 466
   Removal and installation 466
Drive axle (rear)
   Axle shaft 447
   Axle shaft bearing 447
   Fluid recommendations 38
   Identification 447
   Lubricant level 38
   Pinion oil seal 449
   Ratios 447
   Removal and installation 447
   Troubleshooting 443
Driveshaft 442
   Rear 442
Drive Train 381
Drum brakes 516

E

EGR valve 202
Electrical
   Chassis 331
   Battery 11
   Bulbs 367
   Circuit breakers 372
   Fuses 371
   Heater and air conditioning 341

Jump starting 49
Spark plug wires 60
Engine 81
Alternator 88
Coil 84
Distributor 86
Electronic engine controls 223
Ignition module 87
Scematics 230–292
Starter 92
Electronic engine controls 223
Electronic Ignition 61
Emission controls 199
Catalytic Converter 209
Cold mixtue heater 213
Evaporative canister 200
Exhaust Gas Recirculation
(EGR) system 202
Feedback system 209
Fuel Return system 209
Fuel Tank Vapor Control system 200
Oxygen (O$_2$) sensor 207
PCV valve 199
Throttle position system 214
Troubleshooting 199
Engine
Application chart 104
Camshaft 175
Combination manifold 120
Compression testing 100
Connecting rods and bearings 181, 188
Crankshaft 190
Cylinder head 135
Cylinders 194
Electronic controls 223
Exhaust manifold 124
Fluids and lubricants 28
Flywheel 194
Front (timing) cover 164
Identification 7
Intake manifold 121
Main bearings 190
Oil pan 158
Oil pump 159
Overhaul 98
Piston pin 186
Pistons 181
Rear main seal 189
Removal and installation 101
Rings 187
Rocker cover 117
Rocker shafts 118
Spark plug wires 60
Specifications 101–104
Supercharger 126
Thermostat 119
Timing belt covers 164
Timing belt 170

Tools 98
Torque specifications 101
Valve guides 156
Valves 153
Valve seats 156
Valve springs 153
Water pump 130
Evaporative canister 10
Evaporator 346
Exhaust Manifold 124
Exhaust pipe 196
Exhaust system 195

F

Filters
Air 6
Fuel 8
Oil 32
Firing orders 61
Flashers 372
Flex plate 195
Fluids and lubricants 28
Automatic transmission 35
Battery 12
Chassis greasing 41
Coolant 38
Drive axle 38
Engine oil 28
Fuel 31
Manual transmission 34
Master cylinder 40
Brake 40
Clutch 40
Power steering pump 40
Flywheel and ring gear 195
Front bumper 547
Front drive axle
Axle shaft, bearing and seal 466
Front hub and wheel bearings 466
Removal and installation 466
Front brakes 515
Front hubs 466
Front suspension 451
Ball joints 458
Description 451
Knuckles 466
Lower control arm 460
Shock absorbers 451
Spindles 471
Springs 451
Stabilizer bar 459
Struts 452
Track bar 459
Troubleshooting 452
Wheel alignment 472

Front wheel bearings 466, 471
Fuel injection
  Cold start injector 316
  Fuel pressure regulator 317, 321
  Fuel pump 310
  Injectors 312
  Manifold absolute pressure
  sensor 324
  Mass air flow sensor 317
  Throttle body 318, 323
  Throttle position sensor 318
Fuel filter 8
Fuel pump
  Electric 310
  Mechanical 293
Fuel system
  Carbureted 293
  Diesel 326
  Gasoline Fuel injection 310
  Troubleshooting 293
Fuel tank 328
Fuses and circuit breakers 371

G
Gauges 355
Gearshift linkage
  Automatic 436, 440
  Manual 381, 392
Glass
  Door 549
  Liftgate 548
  Side window 548
  Windshield 548
Glossary 563

H
Halfshaft 422, 442
Hazard flasher 372
Headlights 367
Heater
  Blower 341
  Control panel 346
  Core 343
Hinges 545
Hoisting 50
Hood 546
Hoses
  Brake 526
  Coolant 16
How to Use This Book 1
Hubs 466

I
Identification
  Engine 6, 7
  Model 6
  Serial number 6
  Transmission 6, 381
  Automatic 6
  Manual 6, 381
  Vehicle 6
Idle speed and mixture
adjustment 76
Ignition
  Coil 64, 84
  Electronic 61
  Lock cylinder 491
  Module 87
  Switch 491
  Timing 65, 86
Injection pump 328
Injectors, fuel 312
Instrument cluster 355
Instrument panel
  Cluster 355
  Console 364
  Panel removal 358
  Radio 352
  Speedometer cable 366
Intake manifold 121

J
Jacking points 50
Jump starting 49

K
Knuckles 466
Knuckle oil seal 466

L
Lighting
  Headlights 367
  Signal and marker lights 369
Liftgate 546
Liftgate glass 548
Liftgate lock 546
Lower ball joint 458
Lubrication
  Automatic transmission 35

Body   41
Chassis   41
Differential   38
Engine   28
Manual transmission   34
Luggage compartment lid   546

M

MacPherson struts   452
Main bearings   190
Maintenance intervals   52
Manifolds
  Combination   120
  Intake   121
  Exhaust   124
Manual steering gear   501
  Adjustments   501
  Removal and installation   501
  Troubleshooting   495
Manual transaxle
  Adjustment   329
  Removal and installation   395
  Overhaul   403
Manual transmission
  Adjustment   381
  Overhaul   384
  Removal and installation   381
  Troubleshooting   382
Marker lights   369
Master cylinder
  Brake   520
  Clutch   432
Mechanic's data   561
Mirrors   547, 556
Model identification   6
Module (ignition)   87
Muffler   198
Multi-function switch   365, 491

N

Neutral safety switch   436

O

Oil and fuel recommendations   28
Oil and filter change (engine)   32
Oil level check
  Differential   38
  Engine   32
Transmission
  Automatic   34
  Manual   35

Oil pan   158
Oil pump   159
Outside vehicle maintenance
  Lock cylinders   41
  Door hinges   41
  Tailgate   41
  Body drain holes   41
Oxygen (O_2) sensor   207

P

Parking brake   542
Pilot bearing   429
Piston pin   186
Pistons   181
PCV valve   10, 199
Power brake booster   523
Power seat motor   557
Power steering gear   504
  Adjustments   504
  Removal and installation   504
  Troubleshooting   496
Power steering pump
  Fluid level   40
  Removal and installation   504
  Troubleshooting   498
Preventive Maintenance Charts   52
Pushing   47

R

Radiator   129
Radio   352
Rear axle   447
  Axle housing   450
  Axle shaft   447
  Axle shaft bearing   447
  Fluid recommendations   38
  Lubricant level   38
  Pinion oil seal   449
  Ratios   447
  Removal and installation   447
Rear brakes   533
Rear bumper   547
Rear main oil seal   189
Rear suspension   473
  Control arms   479
  Shock absorbers   475
  Springs   473
  Sway bar   475
  Track bar   474
  Troubleshooting   496
Rear wheel bearings   485
Regulator
  Removal and installation   90
  Resetting engine light   225

Rings   187
Rocker arms or shaft   118
Rotor (Brake disc)   531
Routine maintenance   6

S

Safety pad   358
Safety notice   4
Schematics   230–292
Seats   557
Serial number location   6
Shock absorbers   451
Slave cylinder   432
Solenoid   92
Spark plugs   57
Spark plug wires   60
Special tools   2
Specifications Charts
    Alternator and regulator   93
    Brakes   544
    Camshaft   102
    Capacities   56
    Crankshaft and connecting rod   103
    General engine   104
    Piston and ring   102
    Preventive Maintenance   52
    Starter   94
    Torque   101
    Tune-up   58
    Valves   103
    Wheel alignment   473, 474
Speedometer   366
Speedometer cable   366
Spindles   471
Springs   451
Sprocket   170
Stabilizer bar   459
Stain removal   560
Starter
    Drive replacement   92
    Overhaul   92
    Removal and installation   92
    Solenoid or relay replacement   92
    Specifications   94
    Troubleshooting   97
Steering column   499
Steering gear
    Manual   561
    Power   564
Steering knuckles   466
Steering knuckle oil seal   466
Steering linkage
    Tie rod ends   499
Steering lock   491
Steering wheel   488
Striker plate   545
Stripped threads   98

Supercharger   126
Switches
    Back-up light   381, 395, 437, 440
    Brakelight switch   519
    Headlight   366
    Ignition switch   491
    Multi-function switch   365, 491
    Rear window wiper   360
    Windshield wiper   366

T

Tailpipe   198
Thermostat   119
Throttle body   318, 323
Tie rod ends   499
Timing (ignition)
    Electronic systems   65, 80
Timing belt cover   164
Timing belt   170
Tires
    Description   24
    Rotation   24
    Troubleshooting   26
    Wear problems   26
Toe-in   473
Tools   2
Torque specifications   101
Towing   47, 48
Trailer towing   45
Trailer wiring   371
Transfer Case   442
Transmission
    Automatic   433
    Manual   381
    Overhaul   384
Trouble codes   223
Troubleshooting Charts
    Air conditioning   21
    Automatic transmission   434
    Brakes   512
    Charging system   92
    Clutch   429
    Driveshaft   443
    Gauges   380
    Heater   376
    Ignition switch   492
    Lights   379
    Lockup torque converter   435
    Manual steering gear   495
    Manual transmission   382
    Power steering gear   496
    Power steering pump   498
    Rear axle   443
    Starting system   97
    Steering and suspension   452
    Steering column   490
    Tires   27

Transmission fluid indications   436
Turn signals and flashers   378
Turn signal switch   493
Wheels   26
Windshield wipers   377
Tune-up
  Distributor   86
  Idle speed   76
  Ignition timing   65
  Procedures   57
  Spark plugs and wires   57, 60
  Specifications   58
  Troubleshooting   58
Turn signal flasher   372
Turn signal switch   372

U

U-joints   442
  Overhaul   444
  Replacement   442
Upper ball joint   458

V

Vacuum diagrams   230–292
Valve cover   117
Valve guides   156
Valve lash adjustment   68

Valve seats   156
Valve service   153
Valve specifications   103
Valve springs   153
Vehicle identification   7

W

Water pump   130
Wheel alignment
  Specifications   473, 474
Wheel bearings
  Front drive axle   466, 471
  Front wheel   41, 466
  Rear wheel   44, 471
Wheels   26
Window glass   549
Window regulator   549
Windshield wipers
  Arm   353
  Blade   353
  Linkage   353
  Motor   353
  Windshield wiper switch   366
Wiring
  Spark plug   60
  Trailer   371
Wiring Diagrams   230–292
Wiring harnesses   337
Wiring repair   338

CHILTON'S REPAIR MANUAL MODEL INDEX

Car and truck model names are listed in alphabetical and numerical order

Part No.	Model	Repair Manual Title
6980	Accord	Honda 1973-88
7747	Aerostar	Ford Aerostar 1986-90
7165	Alliance	Renault 1975-85
7199	AMX	AMC 1975-86
7163	Aries	Chrysler Front Wheel Drive 1981-88
7041	Arrow	Champ/Arrow/Sapporo 1978-83
7032	Arrow Pick-Ups	D-50/Arrow Pick-Up 1979-81
6637	Aspen	Aspen/Volare 1976-80
6935	Astre	GM Subcompact 1971-80
7750	Astro	Chevrolet Astro/GMC Safari 1985-90
6934	A100, 200, 300	Dodge/Plymouth Vans 1967-88
5807	Barracuda	Barracuda/Challenger 1965-72
6844	Bavaria	BMW 1970-88
5796	Beetle	Volkswagen 1949-71
6837	Beetle	Volkswagen 1970-81
7135	Bel Air	Chevrolet 1968-88
5821	Belvedere	Roadrunner/Satellite/Belvedere/GTX 1968-73
7849	Beretta	Chevrolet Corsica and Beretta 1988
7317	Berlinetta	Camaro 1982-88
7135	Biscayne	Chevrolet 1968-88
6931	Blazer	Blazer/Jimmy 1969-82
7383	Blazer	Chevy S-10 Blazer/GMC S-15 Jimmy 1982-87
7027	Bobcat	Pinto/Bobcat 1971-80
7308	Bonneville	Buick/Olds/Pontiac 1975-87
6982	BRAT	Subaru 1970-88
7042	Brava	Fiat 1969-81
7140	Bronco	Ford Bronco 1966-86
7829	Bronco	Ford Pick-Ups and Bronco 1987-88
7408	Bronco II	Ford Ranger/Bronco II 1983-88
7135	Brookwood	Chevrolet 1968-88
6326	Brougham 1975-75	Valiant/Duster 1968-76
6934	B100, 150, 200, 250, 300, 350	Dodge/Plymouth Vans 1967-88
7197	B210	Datsun 1200/210/Nissan Sentra 1973-88
7659	B1600, 1800, 2000, 2200, 2600	Mazda Trucks 1971-89
6840	Caballero	Chevrolet Mid-Size 1964-88
7657	Calais	Calais, Grand Am, Skylark, Somerset 1985-86
6735	Camaro	Camaro 1967-81
7317	Camaro	Camaro 1982-88
7740	Camry	Toyota Camry 1983-88
6695	Capri, Capri II	Capri 1970-77
6963	Capri	Mustang/Capri/Merkur 1979-88
7135	Caprice	Chevrolet 1968-88
7482	Caravan	Dodge Caravan/Plymouth Voyager 1984-89
7163	Caravelle	Chrysler Front Wheel Drive 1981-88
7036	Carina	Toyota Corolla/Carina/Tercel/Starlet 1970-87
7308	Catalina	Buick/Olds/Pontiac 1975-90
7059	Cavalier	Cavalier, Skyhawk, Cimarron, 2000 1982-88
7309	Celebrity	Celebrity, Century, Ciera, 6000 1982-88
7043	Celica	Toyota Celica/Supra 1971-87
8058	Celica	Toyota Celica/Supra 1986-90
7309	Century FWD	Celebrity, Century, Ciera, 6000 1982-88
7307	Century RWD	Century/Regal 1975-87
5807	Challenger 1965-72	Barracuda/Challenger 1965-72
7037	Challenger 1977-83	Colt/Challenger/Vista/Conquest 1971-88
7041	Champ	Champ/Arrow/Sapporo 1978-83
6486	Charger	Dodge Charger 1967-70
6845	Charger 2.2	Omni/Horizon/Rampage 1978-88

Part No.	Model	Repair Manual Title
6739	Cherokee 1974-83	Jeep Wagoneer, Commando, Cherokee, Truck 1957-86
7939	Cherokee 1984-89	Jeep Wagoneer, Comanche, Cherokee 1984-89
6840	Chevelle	Chevrolet Mid-Size 1964-88
6836	Chevette	Chevette/T-1000 1976-88
6841	Chevy II	Chevy II/Nova 1962-79
7309	Ciera	Celebrity, Century, Ciera, 6000 1982-88
7059	Cimarron	Cavalier, Skyhawk, Cimarron, 2000 1982-88
7049	Citation	GM X-Body 1980-85
6980	Civic	Honda 1973-88
6817	CJ-2A, 3A, 3B, 5, 6, 7	Jeep 1945-87
8034	CJ-5, 6, 7	Jeep 1971-90
6842	Colony Park	Ford/Mercury/Lincoln 1968-88
7037	Colt	Colt/Challenger/Vista/Conquest 1971-88
6634	Comet	Maverick/Comet 1971-77
7939	Comanche	Jeep Wagoneer, Comanche, Cherokee 1984-89
6739	Commando	Jeep Wagoneer, Commando, Cherokee, Truck 1957-86
6842	Commuter	Ford/Mercury/Lincoln 1968-88
7199	Concord	AMC 1975-86
7037	Conquest	Colt/Challenger/Vista/Conquest 1971-88
6696	Continental 1982-85	Ford/Mercury/Lincoln Mid-Size 1971-85
7814	Continental 1982-87	Thunderbird, Cougar, Continental 1980-87
7830	Continental 1988-89	Taurus/Sable/Continental 1986-89
7583	Cordia	Mitsubishi 1983-89
5795	Corolla 1968-70	Toyota 1966-70
7036	Corolla	Toyota Corolla/Carina/Tercel/Starlet 1970-87
5795	Corona	Toyota 1966-70
7004	Corona	Toyota Corona/Crown/Cressida/Mk.II/Van 1970-87
6962	Corrado	VW Front Wheel Drive 1974-90
7849	Corsica	Chevrolet Corsica and Beretta 1988
6576	Corvette	Corvette 1953-62
6843	Corvette	Corvette 1963-86
6542	Cougar	Mustang/Cougar 1965-73
6696	Cougar	Ford/Mercury/Lincoln Mid-Size 1971-85
7814	Cougar	Thunderbird, Cougar, Continental 1980-87
6842	Country Sedan	Ford/Mercury/Lincoln 1968-88
6842	Country Squire	Ford/Mercury/Lincoln 1968-88
6983	Courier	Ford Courier 1972-82
7004	Cressida	Toyota Corona/Crown/Cressida/Mk.II/Van 1970-87
5795	Crown	Toyota 1966-70
7004	Crown	Toyota Corona/Crown/Cressida/Mk.II/Van 1970-87
6842	Crown Victoria	Ford/Mercury/Lincoln 1968-88
6980	CRX	Honda 1973-88
6842	Custom	Ford/Mercury/Lincoln 1968-88
6326	Custom	Valiant/Duster 1968-76
6842	Custom 500	Ford/Mercury/Lincoln 1968-88
7950	Cutlass FWD	Lumina/Grand Prix/Cutlass/Regal 1988-90
6933	Cutlass RWD	Cutlass 1970-87
7309	Cutlass Ciera	Celebrity, Century, Ciera, 6000 1982-88
6936	C-10, 20, 30	Chevrolet/GMC Pick-Ups & Suburban 1970-87

CHILTON'S REPAIR MANUAL MODEL INDEX

Car and truck model names are listed in alphabetical and numerical order

Part No.	Model	Repair Manual Title
8055	C-15, 25, 35	Chevrolet/GMC Pick-Ups & Suburban 1988-90
6324	Dart	Dart/Demon 1968-76
6962	Dasher	VW Front Wheel Drive 1974-90
5790	Datsun Pickups	Datsun 1961-72
6816	Datsun Pickups	Datsun Pick-Ups and Pathfinder 1970-89
7163	Daytona	Chrysler Front Wheel Drive 1981-88
6486	Daytona Charger	Dodge Charger 1967-70
6324	Demon	Dart/Demon 1968-76
7462	deVille	Cadillac 1967-89
7587	deVille	GM C-Body 1985
6817	DJ-3B	Jeep 1945-87
7040	DL	Volvo 1970-88
6326	Duster	Valiant/Duster 1968-76
7032	D-50	D-50/Arrow Pick-Ups 1979-81
7459	D100, 150, 200, 250, 300, 350	Dodge/Plymouth Trucks 1967-88
7199	Eagle	AMC 1975-86
7163	E-Class	Chrysler Front Wheel Drive 1981-88
6840	El Camino	Chevrolet Mid-Size 1964-88
7462	Eldorado	Cadillac 1967-89
7308	Electra	Buick/Olds/Pontiac 1975-90
7587	Electra	GM C-Body 1985
6696	Elite	Ford/Mercury/Lincoln Mid-Size 1971-85
7165	Encore	Renault 1975-85
7055	Escort	Ford/Mercury Front Wheel Drive 1981-87
7059	Eurosport	Cavalier, Skyhawk, Cimarron, 2000 1982-88
7760	Excel	Hyundai 1986-90
7163	Executive Sedan	Chrysler Front Wheel Drive 1981-88
7055	EXP	Ford/Mercury Front Wheel Drive 1981-87
6849	E-100, 150, 200, 250, 300, 350	Ford Vans 1961-88
6320	Fairlane	Fairlane/Torino 1962-75
6965	Fairmont	Fairmont/Zephyr 1978-83
5796	Fastback	Volkswagen 1949-71
6837	Fastback	Volkswagen 1970-81
6739	FC-150, 170	Jeep Wagoneer, Commando, Cherokee, Truck 1957-86
6982	FF-1	Subaru 1970-88
7571	Fiero	Pontiac Fiero 1984-88
6846	Fiesta	Fiesta 1978-80
5996	Firebird	Firebird 1967-81
7345	Firebird	Firebird 1982-90
7059	Firenza	Cavalier, Skyhawk, Cimarron, 2000 1982-88
7462	Fleetwood	Cadillac 1967-89
7587	Fleetwood	GM C-Body 1985
7829	F-Super Duty	Ford Pick-Ups and Bronco 1987-88
7165	Fuego	Renault 1975-85
6552	Fury	Plymouth 1968-76
7196	F-10	Datsun/Nissan F-10, 310, Stanza, Pulsar 1976-88
6933	F-85	Cutlass 1970-87
6913	F-100, 150, 200, 250, 300, 350	Ford Pick-Ups 1965-86
7829	F-150, 250, 350	Ford Pick-Ups and Bronco 1987-88
7583	Galant	Mitsubishi 1983-89
6842	Galaxie	Ford/Mercury/Lincoln 1968-88
7040	GL	Volvo 1970-88
6739	Gladiator	Jeep Wagoneer, Commando, Cherokee, Truck 1962-86
6981	GLC	Mazda 1978-89
7040	GLE	Volvo 1970-88
7040	GLT	Volvo 1970-88
7593	Golf	VW Front Wheel Drive 1974-90
7165	Gordini	Renault 1975-85
6937	Granada	Granada/Monarch 1975-82
6552	Gran Coupe	Plymouth 1968-76
6552	Gran Fury	Plymouth 1968-76
6842	Gran Marquis	Ford/Mercury/Lincoln 1968-88
6552	Gran Sedan	Plymouth 1968-76
6696	Gran Torino	Ford/Mercury/Lincoln Mid-Size 1971-85
7346	Grand Am	Pontiac Mid-Size 1974-83
7657	Grand Am	Calais, Grand Am, Skylark, Somerset 1985-86
7346	Grand LeMans	Pontiac Mid-Size 1974-83
7346	Grand Prix	Pontiac Mid-Size 1974-83
7950	Grand Prix FWD	Lumina/Grand Prix/Cutlass/Regal 1988-90
7308	Grand Safari	Buick/Olds/Pontiac 1975-87
7308	Grand Ville	Buick/Olds/Pontiac 1975-87
6739	Grand Wagoneer	Jeep Wagoneer, Commando, Cherokee, Truck 1957-86
7199	Gremlin	AMC 1975-86
6575	GT	Opel 1971-75
7593	GTI	VW Front Wheel Drive 1974-90
5905	GTO 1968-73	Tempest/GTO/LeMans 1968-73
7346	GTO 1974	Pontiac Mid-Size 1974-83
5821	GTX	Roadrunner/Satellite/Belvedere/GTX 1968-73
5910	GT6	Triumph 1969-73
6542	G.T.350, 500	Mustang/Cougar 1965-73
6930	G-10, 20, 30	Chevy/GMC Vans 1967-86
6930	G-1500, 2500, 3500	Chevy/GMC Vans 1967-86
8040	G-10, 20, 30	Chevy/GMC Vans 1987-90
8040	G-1500, 2500, 3500	Chevy/GMC Vans 1987-90
5795	Hi-Lux	Toyota 1966-70
6845	Horizon	Omni/Horizon/Rampage 1978-88
7199	Hornet	AMC 1975-86
7135	Impala	Chevrolet 1968-88
7317	IROC-Z	Camaro 1982-88
6739	Jeepster	Jeep Wagoneer, Commando, Cherokee, Truck 1957-86
7593	Jetta	VW Front Wheel Drive 1974-90
6931	Jimmy	Blazer/Jimmy 1969-82
7383	Jimmy	Chevy S-10 Blazer/GMC S-15 Jimmy 1982-87
6739	J-10, 20	Jeep Wagoneer, Commando, Cherokee, Truck 1957-86
6739	J-100, 200, 300	Jeep Wagoneer, Commando, Cherokee, Truck 1957-86
6575	Kadett	Opel 1971-75
7199	Kammback	AMC 1975-86
5796	Karmann Ghia	Volkswagen 1949-71
6837	Karmann Ghia	Volkswagen 1970-81
7135	Kingswood	Chevrolet 1968-88
6931	K-5	Blazer/Jimmy 1969-82
6936	K-10, 20, 30	Chevy/GMC Pick-Ups & Suburban 1970-87
6936	K-1500, 2500, 3500	Chevy/GMC Pick-Ups & Suburban 1970-87
8055	K-10, 20, 30	Chevy/GMC Pick-Ups & Suburban 1988-90
8055	K-1500, 2500, 3500	Chevy/GMC Pick-Ups & Suburban 1988-90
6840	Laguna	Chevrolet Mid-Size 1964-88
7041	Lancer	Champ/Arrow/Sapporo 1977-83
5795	Land Cruiser	Toyota 1966-70
7035	Land Cruiser	Toyota Trucks 1970-88
7163	Laser	Chrysler Front Wheel Drive 1981-88
7163	LeBaron	Chrysler Front Wheel Drive 1981-88
7165	LeCar	Renault 1975-85

Chilton's Repair Manuals are available at your local retailer or by mailing a check or money order for **$14.95** per book plus **$3.50** for 1st book and **$.50** for each additional book to cover postage and handling to:

Chilton Book Company
Dept. DM
Radnor, PA 19089

NOTE: When ordering be sure to include your name & address, book part No. & title.

CHILTON'S REPAIR MANUAL MODEL INDEX

Car and truck model names are listed in alphabetical and numerical order

Part No.	Model	Repair Manual Title
5905	LeMans	Tempest/GTO/LeMans 1968-73
7346	LeMans	Pontiac Mid-Size 1974-83
7308	LeSabre	Buick/Olds/Pontiac 1975-87
6842	Lincoln	Ford/Mercury/Lincoln 1968-88
7055	LN-7	Ford/Mercury Front Wheel Drive 1981-87
6842	LTD	Ford/Mercury/Lincoln 1968-88
6696	LTD II	Ford/Mercury/Lincoln Mid-Size 1971-85
7950	Lumina	Lumina/Grand Prix/Cutlass/Regal 1988-90
6815	LUV	Chevrolet LUV 1972-81
6575	Luxus	Opel 1971-75
7055	Lynx	Ford/Mercury Front Wheel Drive 1981-87
6844	L6	BMW 1970-88
6844	L7	BMW 1970-88
6542	Mach I	Mustang/Cougar 1965-73
6812	Mach I Ghia	Mustang II 1974-78
6840	Malibu	Chevrolet Mid-Size 1964-88
6575	Manta	Opel 1971-75
6696	Mark IV, V, VI, VII	Ford/Mercury/Lincoln Mid-Size 1971-85
7814	Mark VII	Thunderbird, Cougar, Continental 1980-87
6842	Marquis	Ford/Mercury/Lincoln 1968-88
6696	Marquis	Ford/Mercury/Lincoln Mid-Size 1971-85
7199	Matador	AMC 1975-86
6634	Maverick	Maverick/Comet 1970-77
6817	Maverick	Jeep 1945-87
7170	Maxima	Nissan 200SX, 240SX, 510, 610, 710, 810, Maxima 1973-88
6842	Mercury	Ford/Mercury/Lincoln 1968-88
6963	Merkur	Mustang/Capri/Merkur 1979-88
6780	MGB, MGB-GT, MGC-GT	MG 1961-81
6780	Midget	MG 1961-81
7583	Mighty Max	Mitsubishi 1983-89
7583	Mirage	Mitsubishi 1983-89
5795	Mk.II 1969-70	Toyota 1966-70
7004	Mk.II 1970-76	Toyota Corona/Crown/Cressida/Mk.II/Van 1970-87
6554	Monaco	Dodge 1968-77
6937	Monarch	Granada/Monarch 1975-82
6840	Monte Carlo	Chevrolet Mid-Size 1964-88
6696	Montego	Ford/Mercury/Lincoln Mid-Size 1971-85
6842	Monterey	Ford/Mercury/Lincoln 1968-88
7583	Montero	Mitsubishi 1983-89
6935	Monza 1975-80	GM Subcompact 1971-80
6981	MPV	Mazda 1978-89
6542	Mustang	Mustang/Cougar 1965-73
6963	Mustang	Mustang/Capri/Merkur 1979-88
6812	Mustang II	Mustang II 1974-78
6981	MX6	Mazda 1978-89
6844	M3, M6	BMW 1970-88
7163	New Yorker	Chrysler Front Wheel Drive 1981-88
6841	Nova	Chevy II/Nova 1962-79
7658	Nova	Chevrolet Nova/GEO Prizm 1985-89
7049	Omega	GM X-Body 1980-85
6845	Omni	Omni/Horizon/Rampage 1978-88
6575	Opel	Opel 1971-75
7199	Pacer	AMC 1975-86
7587	Park Avenue	GM C-Body 1985
6842	Park Lane	Ford/Mercury/Lincoln 1968-88
6962	Passat	VW Front Wheel Drive 1974-90
6816	Pathfinder	Datsun/Nissan Pick-Ups and Pathfinder 1970-89
5790	Patrol	Datsun 1961-72
6934	PB100, 150, 200, 250, 300, 350	Dodge/Plymouth Vans 1967-88
5982	Peugeot	Peugeot 1970-74
7049	Phoenix	GM X-Body 1980-85
7027	Pinto	Pinto/Bobcat 1971-80
6554	Polara	Dodge 1968-77
7583	Precis	Mitsubishi 1983-89
6980	Prelude	Honda 1973-88
7658	Prizm	Chevrolet Nova/GEO Prizm 1985-89
8012	Probe	Ford Probe 1989
7660	Pulsar	Datsun/Nissan F-10, 310, Stanza, Pulsar 1976-88
6529	PV-444	Volvo 1956-69
6529	PV-544	Volvo 1956-69
6529	P-1800	Volvo 1956-69
7593	Quantum	VW Front Wheel Drive 1974-87
7593	Rabbit	VW Front Wheel Drive 1974-87
7593	Rabbit Pickup	VW Front Wheel Drive 1974-87
6575	Rallye	Opel 1971-75
7459	Ramcharger	Dodge/Plymouth Trucks 1967-88
6845	Rampage	Omni/Horizon/Rampage 1978-88
6320	Ranchero	Fairlane/Torino 1962-70
6696	Ranchero	Ford/Mercury/Lincoln Mid-Size 1971-85
6842	Ranch Wagon	Ford/Mercury/Lincoln 1968-88
7338	Ranger Pickup	Ford Ranger/Bronco II 1983-88
7307	Regal RWD	Century/Regal 1975-87
7950	Regal FWD 1988-90	Lumina/Grand Prix/Cutlass/Regal 1988-90
7163	Reliant	Chrysler Front Wheel Drive 1981-88
5821	Roadrunner	Roadrunner/Satellite/Belvedere/GTX 1968-73
7659	Rotary Pick-Up	Mazda Trucks 1971-89
6981	RX-7	Mazda 1978-89
7165	R-12, 15, 17, 18, 18i	Renault 1975-85
7830	Sable	Taurus/Sable/Continental 1986-89
7750	Safari	Chevrolet Astro/GMC Safari 1985-90
7041	Sapporo	Champ/Arrow/Sapporo 1978-83
5821	Satellite	Roadrunner/Satellite/Belvedere/GTX 1968-73
6326	Scamp	Valiant/Duster 1968-76
6845	Scamp	Omni/Horizon/Rampage 1978-88
6962	Scirocco	VW Front Wheel Drive 1974-90
6936	Scottsdale	Chevrolet/GMC Pick-Ups & Suburban 1970-87
8055	Scottsdale	Chevrolet/GMC Pick-Ups & Suburban 1988-90
5912	Scout	International Scout 1967-73
8034	Scrambler	Jeep 1971-90
7197	Sentra	Datsun 1200, 210, Nissan Sentra 1973-88
7462	Seville	Cadillac 1967-89
7163	Shadow	Chrysler Front Wheel Drive 1981-88
6936	Siera	Chevrolet/GMC Pick-Ups & Suburban 1970-87
8055	Siera	Chevrolet/GMC Pick-Ups & Suburban 1988-90
7583	Sigma	Mitsubishi 1983-89
6326	Signet	Valiant/Duster 1968-76
6936	Silverado	Chevrolet/GMC Pick-Ups & Suburban 1970-87
8055	Silverado	Chevrolet/GMC Pick-Ups & Suburban 1988-90
6935	Skyhawk	GM Subcompact 1971-80
7059	Skyhawk	Cavalier, Skyhawk, Cimarron, 2000 1982-88
7049	Skylark	GM X-Body 1980-85

Chilton's Repair Manuals are available at your local retailer or by mailing a check or money order for **$14.95** per book plus **$3.50** for 1st book and **$.50** for each additional book to cover postage and handling to:

Chilton Book Company
Dept. DM
Radnor, PA 19089

NOTE: When ordering be sure to include your name & address, book part No. & title.

CHILTON'S REPAIR MANUAL MODEL INDEX
Car and truck model names are listed in alphabetical and numerical order

Part No.	Model	Repair Manual Title	Part No.	Model	Repair Manual Title
7675	Skylark	Calais, Grand Am, Skylark, Somerset 1985-86	7040	Turbo	Volvo 1970-88
7657	Somerset	Calais, Grand Am, Skylark, Somerset 1985-86	5796	Type 1 Sedan 1949-71	Volkswagen 1949-71
7042	Spider 2000	Fiat 1969-81	6837	Type 1 Sedan 1970-80	Volkswagen 1970-81
7199	Spirit	AMC 1975-86	5796	Type 1 Karmann Ghia 1960-71	Volkswagen 1949-71
6552	Sport Fury	Plymouth 1968–76			
7165	Sport Wagon	Renault 1975-85	6837	Type 1 Karmann Ghia 1970-74	Volkswagen 1970-81
5796	Squareback	Volkswagen 1949-71			
6837	Squareback	Volkswagen 1970-81	5796	Type 1 Convertible 1964-71	Volkswagen 1949-71
7196	Stanza	Datsun/Nissan F-10, 310, Stanza, Pulsar 1976-88	6837	Type 1 Convertible 1970-80	Volkswagen 1970-81
6935	Starfire	GM Subcompact 1971-80	5796	Type 1 Super Beetle 1971	Volkswagen 1949-71
7583	Starion	Mitsubishi 1983-89			
7036	Starlet	Toyota Corolla/Carina/Tercel/Starlet 1970-87	6837	Type 1 Super Beetle 1971-75	Volkswagen 1970-81
7059	STE	Cavalier, Skyhawk, Cimarron, 2000 1982-88	5796	Type 2 Bus 1953-71	Volkswagen 1949-71
			6837	Type 2 Bus 1970-80	Volkswagen 1970-81
5795	Stout	Toyota 1966-70	5796	Type 2 Kombi 1954-71	Volkswagen 1949-71
7042	Strada	Fiat 1969-81			
6552	Suburban	Plymouth 1968-76	6837	Type 2 Kombi 1970-73	Volkswagen 1970-81
6936	Suburban	Chevy/GMC Pick-Ups & Suburban 1970-87			
8055	Suburban	Chevy/GMC Pick-Ups & Suburban 1988-90	6837	Type 2 Vanagon 1981	Volkswagen 1970-81
6935	Sunbird	GM Subcompact 1971-80	5796	Type 3 Fastback & Squareback 1961-71	Volkswagen 1949-71
7059	Sunbird	Cavalier, Skyhawk, Cimarron, 2000, 1982-88	7081	Type 3 Fastback & Squareback 1970-73	Volkswagen 1970-70
7163	Sundance	Chrysler Front Wheel Drive 1981-88	5796	Type 4 411 1971	Volkswagen 1949-71
7043	Supra	Toyota Celica/Supra 1971-87	6837	Type 4 411 1971-72	Volkswagen 1970-81
8058	Supra	Toyota Celica/Supra 1986-90	5796	Type 4 412 1971	Volkswagen 1949-71
6837	Super Beetle	Volkswagen 1970-81	6845	Turismo	Omni/Horizon/Rampage 1978-88
7199	SX-4	AMC 1975-86	5905	T-37	Tempest/GTO/LeMans 1968-73
7383	S-10 Blazer	Chevy S-10 Blazer/GMC S-15 Jimmy 1982-87	6836	T-1000	Chevette/T-1000 1976-88
7310	S-10 Pick-Up	Chevy S-10/GMC S-15 Pick-Ups 1982-87	6935	Vega	GM Subcompact 1971-80
			7346	Ventura	Pontiac Mid-Size 1974-83
7383	S-15 Jimmy	Chevy S-10 Blazer/GMC S-15 Jimmy 1982-87	6696	Versailles	Ford/Mercury/Lincoln Mid-Size 1971-85
7310	S-15 Pick-Up	Chevy S-10/GMC S-15 Pick-Ups 1982-87	6552	VIP	Plymouth 1968-76
7830	Taurus	Taurus/Sable/Continental 1986-89	7037	Vista	Colt/Challenger/Vista/Conquest 1971-88
6845	TC-3	Omni/Horizon/Rampage 1978-88	6933	Vista Cruiser	Cutlass 1970-87
5905	Tempest	Tempest/GTO/LeMans 1968-73	6637	Volare	Aspen/Volare 1976-80
7055	Tempo	Ford/Mercury Front Wheel Drive 1981-87	7482	Voyager	Dodge Caravan/Plymouth Voyager 1984-88
7036	Tercel	Toyota Corolla/Carina/Tercel/Starlet 1970-87	6326	V-100	Valiant/Duster 1968-76
7081	Thing	Volkswagen 1970-81	6739	Wagoneer 1962-83	Jeep Wagoneer, Commando, Cherokee, Truck 1957-86
6696	Thunderbird	Ford/Mercury/Lincoln Mid-Size 1971-85	7939	Wagoneer 1984-89	Jeep Wagoneer, Comanche, Cherokee 1984-89
7814	Thunderbird	Thunderbird, Cougar, Continental 1980-87	8034	Wrangler	Jeep 1971-90
7055	Topaz	Ford/Mercury Front Wheel Drive 1981-87	7459	W100, 150, 200, 250, 300, 350	Dodge/Plymouth Trucks 1967-88
6320	Torino	Fairlane/Torino 1962-75	7459	WM300	Dodge/Plymouth Trucks 1967-88
6696	Torino	Ford/Mercury/Lincoln Mid-Size 1971-85	6842	XL	Ford/Mercury/Lincoln 1968-88
7163	Town & Country	Chrysler Front Wheel Drive 1981-88	6963	XR4Ti	Mustang/Capri/Merkur 1979-88
6842	Town Car	Ford/Mercury/Lincoln 1968-88	6696	XR-7	Ford/Mercury/Lincoln Mid-Size 1971-85
7135	Townsman	Chevrolet 1968-88			
5795	Toyota Pickups	Toyota 1966-70	6982	XT Coupe	Subaru 1970-88
7035	Toyota Pickups	Toyota Trucks 1970-88	7042	X1/9	Fiat 1969-81
7004	Toyota Van	Toyota Corona/Crown/Cressida/Mk.II/Van 1970-87	6965	Zephyr	Fairmont/Zephyr 1978-83
7459	Trail Duster	Dodge/Plymouth Trucks 1967-88	7059	Z-24	Cavalier, Skyhawk, Cimarron, 2000 1982-88
7046	Trans Am	Firebird 1967-81	6735	Z-28	Camaro 1967-81
7345	Trans Am	Firebird 1982-90	7318	Z-28	Camaro 1982-88
7583	Tredia	Mitsubishi 1983-89	6845	024	Omni/Horizon/Rampage 1978-88
			6844	3.0S, 3.0Si, 3.0CS	BMW 1970-88
			6817	4-63	Jeep 1981-87

Chilton's Repair Manuals are available at your local retailer or by mailing a check or money order for **$14.95** per book plus **$3.50** for 1st book and **$.50** for each additional book to cover postage and handling to:

Chilton Book Company
Dept. DM
Radnor, PA 19089

NOTE: When ordering be sure to include your name & address, book part No. & title.

CHILTON'S REPAIR MANUAL MODEL INDEX
Car and truck model names are listed in alphabetical and numerical order

Part No.	Model	Repair Manual Title	Part No.	Model	Repair Manual Title
6817	4×4-63	Jeep 1981-87	6932	300ZX	Datsun Z & ZX 1970-87
6817	4-73	Jeep 1981-87	5982	304	Peugeot 1970-74
6817	4×4-73	Jeep 1981-87	5790	310	Datsun 1961-72
6817	4-75	Jeep 1981-87	7196	310	Datsun/Nissan F-10, 310, Stanza,
7035	4Runner	Toyota Trucks 1970-88			Pulsar 1977-88
6982	4wd Wagon	Subaru 1970-88	5790	311	Datsun 1961-72
6982	4wd Coupe	Subaru 1970-88	6844	318i, 320i	BMW 1970-88
6933	4-4-2 1970-80	Cutlass 1970-87	6981	323	Mazda 1978-89
6817	6-63	Jeep 1981-87	6844	325E, 325ES, 325i,	BMW 1970-88
6809	6.9	Mercedes-Benz 1974-84		325iS, 325iX	
7308	88	Buick/Olds/Pontiac 1975-90	6809	380SEC, 380SEL,	Mercedes-Benz 1974-84
7308	98	Buick/Olds/Pontiac 1975-90		380SL, 380SLC	
7587	98 Regency	GM C-Body 1985	5907	350SL	Mercedes-Benz 1968-73
5902	100LS, 100GL	Audi 1970-73	7163	400	Chrysler Front Wheel Drive 1981-88
6529	122, 122S	Volvo 1956-69	5790	410	Datsun 1961-72
7042	124	Fiat 1969-81	5790	411	Datsun 1961-72
7042	128	Fiat 1969-81	7081	411, 412	Volkswagen 1970-81
7042	131	Fiat 1969-81	6809	450SE, 450SEL, 450	Mercedes-Benz 1974-84
6529	142	Volvo 1956-69		SEL 6.9	
7040	142	Volvo 1970-88	6809	450SL, 450SLC	Mercedes-Benz 1974-84
6529	144	Volvo 1956-69	5907	450SLC	Mercedes-Benz 1968-73
7040	144	Volvo 1970-88	6809	500SEC, 500SEL	Mercedes-Benz 1974-84
6529	145	Volvo 1956-69	5982	504	Peugeot 1970-74
7040	145	Volvo 1970-88	5790	510	Datsun 1961-72
6529	164	Volvo 1956-69	7170	510	Nissan 200SX, 240SX, 510, 610,
7040	164	Volvo 1970-88			710, 810, Maxima 1973-88
6065	190C	Mercedes-Benz 1959-70	6816	520	Datsun/Nissan Pick-Ups and Path-
6809	190D	Mercedes-Benz 1974-84			finder 1970-89
6065	190DC	Mercedes-Benz 1959-70	6844	524TD	BMW 1970-88
6809	190E	Mercedes-Benz 1974-84	6844	525i	BMW 1970-88
6065	200, 200D	Mercedes-Benz 1959-70	6844	528e	BMW 1970-88
7170	200SX	Nissan 200SX, 240SX, 510, 610,	6844	528i	BMW 1970-88
		710, 810, Maxima 1973-88	6844	530i	BMW 1970-88
7197	210	Datsun 1200, 210, Nissan Sentra	6844	533i	BMW 1970-88
		1971-88	6844	535i, 535iS	BMW 1970-88
6065	220B, 220D, 220Sb,	Mercedes-Benz 1959-70	6980	600	Honda 1973-88
	220SEb		7163	600	Chrysler Front Wheel Drive 1981-88
5907	220/8 1968-73	Mercedes-Benz 1968-73	7170	610	Nissan 200SX, 240SX, 510, 610,
6809	230 1974-78	Mercedes-Benz 1974-84			710, 810, Maxima 1973-88
6065	230S, 230SL	Mercedes-Benz 1959-70	6816	620	Datsun/Nissan Pick-Ups and Path-
5907	230/8	Mercedes-Benz 1968-73			finder 1970-89
6809	240D	Mercedes-Benz 1974-84	6981	626	Mazda 1978-89
7170	240SX	Nissan 200SX, 240SX, 510, 610,	6844	630 CSi	BMW 1970-88
		710, 810, Maxima 1973-88	6844	633 CSi	BMW 1970-88
6932	240Z	Datsun Z & ZX 1970-87	6844	635CSi	BMW 1970-88
7040	242, 244, 245	Volvo 1970-88	7170	710	Nissan 200SX, 240SX, 510, 610,
5907	250C	Mercedes-Benz 1968-73			710, 810, Maxima 1973-88
6065	250S, 250SE,	Mercedes-Benz 1959-70	6816	720	Datsun/Nissan Pick-Ups and Path-
	250SL				finder 1970-89
5907	250/8	Mercedes-Benz 1968-73	6844	733i	BMW 1970-88
6932	260Z	Datsun Z & ZX 1970-87	6844	735i	BMW 1970-88
7040	262, 264, 265	Volvo 1970-88	7040	760, 760GLE	Volvo 1970-88
5907	280	Mercedes-Benz 1968-73	7040	780	Volvo 1970-88
6809	280	Mercedes-Benz 1974-84	6981	808	Mazda 1978-89
5907	280C	Mercedes-Benz 1968-73	7170	810	Nissan 200SX, 240SX, 510, 610,
6809	280C, 280CE, 280E	Mercedes-Benz 1974-84			710, 810, Maxima 1973-88
6065	280S, 280SE	Mercedes-Benz 1959-70	7042	850	Fiat 1969-81
5907	280SE, 280S/8,	Mercedes-Benz 1968-73	7572	900, 900 Turbo	SAAB 900 1976-85
	280SE/8		7048	924	Porsche 924/928 1976-81
6809	280SEL, 280SEL/8,	Mercedes-Benz 1974-84	7048	928	Porsche 924/928 1976-81
	280SL		6981	929	Mazda 1978-89
6932	280Z, 280ZX	Datsun Z & ZX 1970-87	6836	1000	Chevette/1000 1976-88
6065	300CD, 300D,	Mercedes-Benz 1959-70	6780	1100	MG 1961-81
	300SD, 300SE		5790	1200	Datsun 1961-72
5907	300SEL 3.5,	Mercedes-Benz 1968-73	7197	1200	Datsun 1200, 210, Nissan Sentra
	300SEL 4.5				1973-88
5907	300SEL 6.3,	Mercedes-Benz 1968-73	6982	1400GL, 1400DL,	Subaru 1970-88
	300SEL/8			1400GF	
6809	300TD	Mercedes-Benz 1974-84	5790	1500	Datsun 1961-72

Chilton's Repair Manuals are available at your local retailer or by mailing a check or money order for **$14.95** per book plus **$3.50** for 1st book and **$.50** for each additional book to cover postage and handling to:

**Chilton Book Company
Dept. DM
Radnor, PA 19089**

NOTE: When ordering be sure to include your name & address, book part No. & title.

CHILTON'S REPAIR MANUAL MODEL INDEX
Car and truck model names are listed in alphabetical and numerical order

Part No.	Model	Repair Manual Title	Part No.	Model	Repair Manual Title
6844	1500	DMW 1970-88	6844	2000	BMW 1970-88
6936	1500	Chevy/GMC Pick-Ups & Suburban 1970-87	6844	2002, 2002Ti, 2002Tii	BMW 1970-88
8055	1500	Chevy/GMC Pick-Ups & Suburban 1988-90	6936	2500	Chevy/GMC Pick-Ups & Suburban 1970-87
6844	1600	BMW 1970-88	8055	2500	Chevy/GMC Pick-Ups & Suburban 1988-90
5790	1600	Datsun 1961-72			
6982	1600DL, 1600GL, 1600GLF	Subaru 1970-88	6844	2500	BMW 1970-88
			6844	2800	BMW 1970-88
6844	1600-2	BMW 1970-88	6936	3500	Chevy/GMC Pick-Ups & Suburban 1970-87
6844	1800	BMW 1970-88			
6982	1800DL, 1800GL, 1800GLF	Subaru 1970-88	8055	3500	Chevy/GMC Pick-Ups & Suburban 1988-90
6529	1800, 1800S	Volvo 1956-69	7028	4000	Audi 4000/5000 1978-81
7040	1800E, 1800ES	Volvo 1970-88	7028	5000	Audi 4000/5000 1978-81
5790	2000	Datsun 1961-72	7309	6000	Celebrity, Century, Ciera, 6000 1982-88
7059	2000	Cavalier, Skyhawk, Cimarron, 2000 1982-88			

Chilton's Repair Manuals are available at your local retailer or by mailing a check or money order for **$14.95** per book plus **$3.50** for 1st book and **$.50** for each additional book to cover postage and handling to:

Chilton Book Company
Dept. DM
Radnor, PA 19089

NOTE: When ordering be sure to include your name & address, book part No. & title.